I0819996

H G Wells Science Fiction Omnibus

By

H G Wells

Cover Photograph: NASA Goddard Photo and Video

ISBN: 978-1-78139-296-6

Contents

THE TIME MACHINE

THE WAR OF THE WORLDS

BOOK ONE - THE COMING OF THE MARTIANS

BOOK TWO - THE EARTH UNDER THE MARTIANS

THE SHAPE OF THINGS TO COME

BOOK THE FIRST - TODAY AND TOMORROW: THE AGE OF FRUSTRATION DAWNS

BOOK THE SECOND - THE DAYS AFTER TOMORROW: THE AGE OF FRUSTRATION

BOOK THE THIRD - THE WORLD RENASCENCE: THE BIRTH OF THE MODERN STATE

BOOK THE FOURTH - THE MODERN STATE MILITANT

BOOK THE FIFTH - THE MODERN STATE IN CONTROL OF LIFE

THE INVISIBLE MAN A GROTESQUE ROMANCE

THE ISLAND OF DOCTOR MOREAU

THE STORY WRITTEN BY EDWARD PRENDICK

THE FIRST MEN IN THE MOON

THE FOOD OF THE GODS AND HOW IT CAME TO EARTH

BOOK I - THE DAWN OF THE FOOD

IN THE DAYS OF THE COMET

BOOK THE THIRD - THE NEW WORLD

THE TIME MACHINE

Serialized in this form in *The New Review*, January-May 1895
First book edition: William Heinemann, London, May 1895

H.G. Wells began work on what would eventually evolve into *The Time Machine* nearly eight years before its publication as a novel. The original story was serialized in 1888 as "The Chronic Argonauts" in *The Science Schools Journal* (which Wells founded and edited) at The Royal College of Science. After two further drafts, now lost, it was published as a series of loosely connected articles under the title "The Time Traveller's Story" in *The National Observer*, then edited by William Ernest Henley. Seven installments were published beginning in March 1894, and the final installment in June. The magazine never published the conclusion, owing to Henley accepting a position as editor of *The New Review*. Henley arranged to have the story published again under the title "The Time Machine" in five installments in the New Review from January to May of 1895.

I

The Time Traveller (for so it will be convenient to speak of him) was expounding a recondite matter to us. His grey eyes shone and twinkled, and his usually pale face was flushed and animated. The fire burned brightly, and the soft radiance of the incandescent lights in the lilies of silver caught the bubbles that flashed and passed in our glasses. Our chairs, being his patents, embraced and caressed us rather than submitted to be sat upon, and there was that luxurious after-dinner atmosphere when thought roams gracefully free of the trammels of precision. And he put it to us in this way—marking the points with a lean forefinger—as we sat and lazily admired his earnestness over this new paradox (as we thought it) and his fecundity.

'You must follow me carefully. I shall have to controvert one or two ideas that are almost universally accepted. The geometry, for instance, they taught you at school is founded on a misconception.'

'Is not that rather a large thing to expect us to begin upon?' said Filby, an argumentative person with red hair.

'I do not mean to ask you to accept anything without reasonable ground for it. You will soon admit as much as I need from you. You know of course that a mathematical line, a line of thickness *nil*, has no real existence. They taught you that? Neither has a mathematical plane. These things are mere abstractions.'

'That is all right,' said the Psychologist.

'Nor, having only length, breadth, and thickness, can a cube have a real existence.'

'There I object,' said Filby. 'Of course a solid body may exist. All real things—'

'So most people think. But wait a moment. Can an *instantaneous* cube exist?'

'Don't follow you,' said Filby.

'Can a cube that does not last for any time at all, have a real existence?'

Filby became pensive. 'Clearly,' the Time Traveller proceeded, 'any real body must have extension in *four* directions: it must have Length, Breadth, Thickness, and—Duration. But through a natural infirmity of the flesh, which I will explain to you in a moment, we incline to overlook this fact. There are really four dimensions, three which we call the three planes of Space, and a fourth, Time. There is, however, a tendency to draw an unreal distinction between the former three dimensions and the latter, because it happens that our consciousness moves intermittently in one direction along the latter from the beginning to the end of our lives.'

'That,' said a very young man, making spasmodic efforts to relight his cigar over the lamp; 'that ... very clear indeed.'

'Now, it is very remarkable that this is so extensively overlooked,' continued the Time Traveller, with a slight accession of cheerfulness. 'Really this is what is meant by the Fourth Dimension, though some people who talk about the Fourth Dimension do not know they mean it. It is only another way of looking at Time. *There is no difference between Time and any of the three dimensions of Space except that our consciousness moves along it.* But some foolish people have got hold of the wrong side of that idea. You have all heard what they have to say about this Fourth Dimension?'

'*I* have not,' said the Provincial Mayor.

'It is simply this. That Space, as our mathematicians have it, is spoken of as having three dimensions, which one may call Length, Breadth, and Thickness, and is always definable by reference to three planes, each at right angles to the others. But some philosophical people have been asking why *three* dimensions particularly—why not another direction at right angles to the other three?—and have even tried to construct a Four- Dimension geometry. Professor Simon Newcomb was expounding this to the New York Mathematical Society only a month or so ago. You know how on a flat surface, which has only two dimensions, we can represent a figure of a three-dimensional solid, and similarly they think that by models of three dimensions they could represent one of four—if they could master the perspective of the thing. See?'

'I think so,' murmured the Provincial Mayor; and, knitting his brows, he lapsed into an introspective state, his lips moving as one who repeats mystic words. 'Yes, I think I see it now,' he said after some time, brightening in a quite transitory manner.

'Well, I do not mind telling you I have been at work upon this geometry of Four Dimensions for some time. Some of my results are curious. For instance, here is a portrait of a man at eight years old, another at fifteen, another at seventeen, another at twenty-three, and so on. All these are evidently sections, as it were, Three-Dimensional representations of his Four-Dimensioned being, which is a fixed and unalterable thing.

'Scientific people,' proceeded the Time Traveller, after the pause required for the proper assimilation of this, 'know very well that Time is only a kind of Space. Here is a popular scientific diagram, a weather record. This line I trace with my finger shows the movement of the barometer. Yesterday it was so high, yesterday night it fell, then this morning it rose again, and so gently upward to here. Surely the mercury did not trace this line in any of the dimensions of Space generally recognized? But certainly it traced such a line, and that line, therefore, we must conclude was along the Time-Dimension.'

'But,' said the Medical Man, staring hard at a coal in the fire, 'if Time is really only a fourth dimension of Space, why is it, and why has it always been, regarded as something different? And why cannot we move in Time as we move about in the other dimensions of Space?'

The Time Traveller smiled. 'Are you sure we can move freely in Space? Right and left we can go, backward and forward freely enough, and men always have done so. I admit we move freely in two dimensions. But how about up and down? Gravitation limits us there.'

'Not exactly,' said the Medical Man. 'There are balloons.'

'But before the balloons, save for spasmodic jumping and the inequalities of the surface, man had no freedom of vertical movement.'

'Still they could move a little up and down,' said the Medical Man.

'Easier, far easier down than up.'

'And you cannot move at all in Time, you cannot get away from the present moment.'

'My dear sir, that is just where you are wrong. That is just where the whole world has gone wrong. We are always getting away from the present moment. Our mental existences, which are immaterial and have no dimensions, are passing along the Time-Dimension with a uniform velocity from the cradle to the grave. Just as we should travel *down* if we began our existence fifty miles above the earth's surface.'

'But the great difficulty is this,' interrupted the Psychologist. 'You *can* move about in all directions of Space, but you cannot move about in Time.'

'That is the germ of my great discovery. But you are wrong to say that we cannot move about in Time. For instance, if I am recalling an incident very vividly I go back to the instant of its occurrence: I become absent-minded, as you say. I jump back for a moment. Of course we have no means of staying back for any length of Time, any more than a savage or an animal has of staying six feet above the ground. But a civilized man is better off than the savage in this respect. He can go up against gravitation in a balloon, and why should he not hope that ultimately he may be able to stop or accelerate his drift along the Time-Dimension, or even turn about and travel the other way?'

'Oh, *this*,' began Filby, 'is all—'

'Why not?' said the Time Traveller.

'It's against reason,' said Filby.

'What reason?' said the Time Traveller.

'You can show black is white by argument,' said Filby, 'but you will never convince me.'

'Possibly not,' said the Time Traveller. 'But now you begin to see the object of my investigations into the geometry of Four Dimensions. Long ago I had a vague inkling of a machine—'

'To travel through Time!' exclaimed the Very Young Man.

'That shall travel indifferently in any direction of Space and Time, as the driver determines.'

Filby contented himself with laughter.

'But I have experimental verification,' said the Time Traveller.

'It would be remarkably convenient for the historian,' the Psychologist suggested. 'One might travel back and verify the accepted account of the Battle of Hastings, for instance!'

'Don't you think you would attract attention?' said the Medical Man. 'Our ancestors had no great tolerance for anachronisms.'

'One might get one's Greek from the very lips of Homer and Plato,' the Very Young Man thought.

'In which case they would certainly plough you for the Little-go. The German scholars have improved Greek so much.'

'Then there is the future,' said the Very Young Man. 'Just think! One might invest all one's money, leave it to accumulate at interest, and hurry on ahead!'

'To discover a society,' said I, 'erected on a strictly communistic basis.'

'Of all the wild extravagant theories!' began the Psychologist.

'Yes, so it seemed to me, and so I never talked of it until—'

'Experimental verification!' cried I. 'You are going to verify *that*?'

'The experiment!' cried Filby, who was getting brain-weary.

'Let's see your experiment anyhow,' said the Psychologist, 'though it's all humbug, you know.'

The Time Traveller smiled round at us. Then, still smiling faintly, and with his hands deep in his trousers pockets, he walked slowly out of the room, and we heard his slippers shuffling down the long passage to his laboratory.

The Psychologist looked at us. 'I wonder what he's got?'

'Some sleight-of-hand trick or other,' said the Medical Man, and Filby tried to tell us about a conjurer he had seen at Burslem; but before he had finished his preface the Time Traveller came back, and Filby's anecdote collapsed.

The thing the Time Traveller held in his hand was a glittering metallic framework, scarcely larger than a small clock, and very delicately made. There was ivory in it, and some transparent crystalline substance. And now I must be explicit, for this that follows—unless his explanation is to be accepted—is an absolutely unaccountable thing. He took one of the small octagonal tables that were scattered about the room, and set it in front of the fire, with two legs on the hearthrug. On this table he placed the mechanism. Then he drew up a chair, and sat down. The only other object on the table was a small shaded lamp, the bright light of which fell upon the model. There were also perhaps a dozen candles about, two in brass candlesticks upon the mantel and several in sconces, so that the room was brilliantly illuminated. I sat in a low arm-chair nearest the fire, and I drew this forward so as to be almost between the Time Traveller and the fireplace. Filby sat behind him, looking over his shoulder. The Medical Man and the Provincial Mayor watched him in profile from the right, the Psychologist from the left. The Very Young Man stood behind the Psychologist. We were all on the alert. It appears incredible to me that any kind of trick, however subtly conceived and however adroitly done, could have been played upon us under these conditions.

The Time Traveller looked at us, and then at the mechanism. 'Well?' said the Psychologist.

'This little affair,' said the Time Traveller, resting his elbows upon the table and pressing his hands together above the apparatus, 'is only a model. It is my plan for a machine to travel through time. You will notice that it looks singularly askew, and that there is an odd twinkling appearance about this bar, as though it was in some way unreal.' He pointed to the part with his finger. 'Also, here is one little white lever, and here is another.'

The Medical Man got up out of his chair and peered into the thing. 'It's beautifully made,' he said.

'It took two years to make,' retorted the Time Traveller. Then, when we had all imitated the action of the Medical Man, he said: 'Now I want you clearly to understand that this lever, being pressed over, sends the machine gliding into the future, and this other reverses the motion. This saddle represents the seat of a time traveller. Presently I am going to press the lever, and off the machine will go. It will vanish, pass into future Time, and disappear. Have a good look at the thing. Look at the table too, and satisfy yourselves there is no trickery. I don't want to waste this model, and then be told I'm a quack.'

There was a minute's pause perhaps. The Psychologist seemed about to speak to me, but changed his mind. Then the Time Traveller put forth his finger towards the lever. 'No,' he said suddenly. 'Lend me your hand.' And turning to the Psychologist, he took that individual's hand in his own and told him to put out his forefinger. So that it was the Psychologist himself who sent forth the model Time Machine on its interminable voyage. We all saw the lever turn. I am absolutely certain there was no trickery. There was a breath of wind, and the lamp flame jumped. One of the candles on the mantel was blown out, and the little machine suddenly swung round, became indistinct, was seen as a ghost for a second perhaps, as an eddy of faintly glittering brass and ivory; and it was gone—vanished! Save for the lamp the table was bare.

Everyone was silent for a minute. Then Filby said he was damned.

The Psychologist recovered from his stupor, and suddenly looked under the table. At that the Time Traveller laughed cheerfully. 'Well?' he said, with a reminiscence of the Psychologist. Then, getting up, he went to the tobacco jar on the mantel, and with his back to us began to fill his pipe.

We stared at each other. 'Look here,' said the Medical Man, 'are you in earnest about this? Do you seriously believe that that machine has travelled into time?'

'Certainly,' said the Time Traveller, stooping to light a spill at the fire. Then he turned, lighting his pipe, to look at the Psychologist's face. (The Psychologist, to show that he was not unhinged, helped himself to a cigar and tried to light it uncut.) 'What is more, I have a big machine nearly finished in there'—he indicated the laboratory—'and when that is put together I mean to have a journey on my own account.'

'You mean to say that that machine has travelled into the future?' said Filby.

'Into the future or the past—I don't, for certain, know which.'

After an interval the Psychologist had an inspiration. 'It must have gone into the past if it has gone anywhere,' he said.

'Why?' said the Time Traveller.

'Because I presume that it has not moved in space, and if it travelled into the future it would still be here all this time, since it must have travelled through this time.'

'But,' I said, 'If it travelled into the past it would have been visible when we came first into this room; and last Thursday when we were here; and the Thursday before that; and so forth!'

'Serious objections,' remarked the Provincial Mayor, with an air of impartiality, turning towards the Time Traveller.

'Not a bit,' said the Time Traveller, and, to the Psychologist: 'You think. You can explain that. It's presentation below the threshold, you know, diluted presentation.'

'Of course,' said the Psychologist, and reassured us. 'That's a simple point of psychology. I should have thought of it. It's plain enough, and helps the paradox delightfully. We cannot see it, nor can we appreciate this machine, any more than we can the spoke of a wheel spinning, or a bullet flying through the air. If it is travelling through time fifty times or a hundred times faster than we are, if it gets through a minute while we get through a second, the impression it creates will of course be only one-fiftieth or one-hundredth of what it would make if it were not travelling in time. That's plain enough.' He passed his hand through the space in which the machine had been. 'You see?' he said, laughing.

We sat and stared at the vacant table for a minute or so. Then the Time Traveller asked us what we thought of it all.

'It sounds plausible enough to-night,' said the Medical Man; 'but wait until to-morrow. Wait for the common sense of the morning.'

'Would you like to see the Time Machine itself?' asked the Time Traveller. And therewith, taking the lamp in his hand, he led the way down the long, draughty corridor to his laboratory. I remember vividly the flickering light, his queer, broad head in silhouette, the dance of the shadows, how we all followed him, puzzled but incredulous, and how there in the laboratory we beheld a larger edition of the little mechanism which we had seen vanish from before our eyes. Parts were of nickel, parts of ivory, parts had certainly been filed or sawn out of rock crystal. The thing was generally complete, but the twisted crystalline bars lay unfinished upon the bench beside some sheets of drawings, and I took one up for a better look at it. Quartz it seemed to be.

'Look here,' said the Medical Man, 'are you perfectly serious? Or is this a trick—like that ghost you showed us last Christmas?'

'Upon that machine,' said the Time Traveller, holding the lamp aloft, 'I intend to explore time. Is that plain? I was never more serious in my life.'

None of us quite knew how to take it.

I caught Filby's eye over the shoulder of the Medical Man, and he winked at me solemnly.

II

I think that at that time none of us quite believed in the Time Machine. The fact is, the Time Traveller was one of those men who are too clever to be believed: you never felt that you saw all round him; you always suspected some subtle reserve, some ingenuity in ambush, behind his lucid frankness. Had Filby shown the model and explained the matter in the Time Traveller's words, we should have shown *him* far less scepticism. For we should have perceived his motives; a pork butcher could understand Filby. But the Time Traveller had more than a touch of whim among his elements, and we distrusted him. Things that would have made the frame of a less clever man seemed tricks in his hands. It is a mistake to do things too easily. The serious people who took him seriously never felt quite sure of his deportment; they were somehow aware that trusting their reputations for judgment with him was like furnishing a nursery with egg-shell china. So I don't think any of us said very much about time travelling in the interval between that Thursday and the next, though its odd potentialities ran, no doubt, in most of our minds: its plausibility, that is, its practical incredibleness, the curious possibilities of anachronism and of utter confusion it suggested. For my own part, I was particularly preoccupied with the trick of the model. That I remember discussing with the Medical Man, whom I met on Friday at the Linnaean. He said he had seen a similar thing at Tubingen, and laid considerable stress on the blowing out of the candle. But how the trick was done he could not explain.

The next Thursday I went again to Richmond—I suppose I was one of the Time Traveller's most constant guests—and, arriving late, found four or five men already assembled in his drawing-room. The Medical Man was standing before the fire with a sheet of paper in one hand and his watch in the other. I looked round for the Time Traveller, and—'It's half-past seven now,' said the Medical Man. 'I suppose we'd better have dinner?'

'Where's—?' said I, naming our host.

'You've just come? It's rather odd. He's unavoidably detained. He asks me in this note to lead off with dinner at seven if he's not back. Says he'll explain when he comes.'

'It seems a pity to let the dinner spoil,' said the Editor of a well- known daily paper; and thereupon the Doctor rang the bell.

The Psychologist was the only person besides the Doctor and myself who had attended the previous dinner. The other men were Blank, the Editor aforemen-

tioned, a certain journalist, and another—a quiet, shy man with a beard—whom I didn't know, and who, as far as my observation went, never opened his mouth all the evening. There was some speculation at the dinner-table about the Time Traveller's absence, and I suggested time travelling, in a half-jocular spirit. The Editor wanted that explained to him, and the Psychologist volunteered a wooden account of the 'ingenious paradox and trick' we had witnessed that day week. He was in the midst of his exposition when the door from the corridor opened slowly and without noise. I was facing the door, and saw it first. 'Hallo!' I said. 'At last!' And the door opened wider, and the Time Traveller stood before us. I gave a cry of surprise. 'Good heavens! man, what's the matter?' cried the Medical Man, who saw him next. And the whole tableful turned towards the door.

He was in an amazing plight. His coat was dusty and dirty, and smeared with green down the sleeves; his hair disordered, and as it seemed to me greyer — either with dust and dirt or because its colour had actually faded. His face was ghastly pale; his chin had a brown cut on it—a cut half healed; his expression was haggard and drawn, as by intense suffering. For a moment he hesitated in the doorway, as if he had been dazzled by the light. Then he came into the room. He walked with just such a limp as I have seen in footsore tramps. We stared at him in silence, expecting him to speak.

He said not a word, but came painfully to the table, and made a motion towards the wine. The Editor filled a glass of champagne, and pushed it towards him. He drained it, and it seemed to do him good: for he looked round the table, and the ghost of his old smile flickered across his face. 'What on earth have you been up to, man?' said the Doctor. The Time Traveller did not seem to hear. 'Don't let me disturb you,' he said, with a certain faltering articulation. 'I'm all right.' He stopped, held out his glass for more, and took it off at a draught. 'That's good,' he said. His eyes grew brighter, and a faint colour came into his cheeks. His glance flickered over our faces with a certain dull approval, and then went round the warm and comfortable room. Then he spoke again, still as it were feeling his way among his words. 'I'm going to wash and dress, and then I'll come down and explain things ... Save me some of that mutton. I'm starving for a bit of meat.'

He looked across at the Editor, who was a rare visitor, and hoped he was all right. The Editor began a question. 'Tell you presently,' said the Time Traveller. 'I'm—funny! Be all right in a minute.'

He put down his glass, and walked towards the staircase door. Again I remarked his lameness and the soft padding sound of his footfall, and standing up in my place, I saw his feet as he went out. He had nothing on them but a pair of tattered, blood-stained socks. Then the door closed upon him. I had half a mind to follow, till I remembered how he detested any fuss about himself. For a minute, perhaps, my mind was wool-gathering. Then, 'Remarkable Behaviour of an Eminent Scientist,' I heard the Editor say, thinking (after his wont) in headlines. And this brought my attention back to the bright dinner- table.

'What's the game?' said the Journalist. 'Has he been doing the Amateur Cadger? I don't follow.' I met the eye of the Psychologist, and read my own

interpretation in his face. I thought of the Time Traveller limping painfully upstairs. I don't think any one else had noticed his lameness.

The first to recover completely from this surprise was the Medical Man, who rang the bell—the Time Traveller hated to have servants waiting at dinner—for a hot plate. At that the Editor turned to his knife and fork with a grunt, and the Silent Man followed suit. The dinner was resumed. Conversation was exclamatory for a little while, with gaps of wonderment; and then the Editor got fervent in his curiosity. 'Does our friend eke out his modest income with a crossing? or has he his Nebuchadnezzar phases?' he inquired. 'I feel assured it's this business of the Time Machine,' I said, and took up the Psychologist's account of our previous meeting. The new guests were frankly incredulous. The Editor raised objections. 'What *was* this time travelling? A man couldn't cover himself with dust by rolling in a paradox, could he?' And then, as the idea came home to him, he resorted to caricature. Hadn't they any clothes-brushes in the Future? The Journalist too, would not believe at any price, and joined the Editor in the easy work of heaping ridicule on the whole thing. They were both the new kind of journalist—very joyous, irreverent young men. 'Our Special Correspondent in the Day after Tomorrow reports,' the Journalist was saying—or rather shouting —when the Time Traveller came back. He was dressed in ordinary evening clothes, and nothing save his haggard look remained of the change that had startled me.

'I say,' said the Editor hilariously, 'these chaps here say you have been travelling into the middle of next week! Tell us all about little Rosebery, will you? What will you take for the lot?'

The Time Traveller came to the place reserved for him without a word. He smiled quietly, in his old way. 'Where's my mutton?' he said. 'What a treat it is to stick a fork into meat again!'

'Story!' cried the Editor.

'Story be damned!' said the Time Traveller. 'I want something to eat. I won't say a word until I get some peptone into my arteries. Thanks. And the salt.'

'One word,' said I. 'Have you been time travelling?'

'Yes,' said the Time Traveller, with his mouth full, nodding his head.

'I'd give a shilling a line for a verbatim note,' said the Editor. The Time Traveller pushed his glass towards the Silent Man and rang it with his fingernail; at which the Silent Man, who had been staring at his face, started convulsively, and poured him wine. The rest of the dinner was uncomfortable. For my own part, sudden questions kept on rising to my lips, and I dare say it was the same with the others. The Journalist tried to relieve the tension by telling anecdotes of Hettie Potter. The Time Traveller devoted his attention to his dinner, and displayed the appetite of a tramp. The Medical Man smoked a cigarette, and watched the Time Traveller through his eyelashes. The Silent Man seemed even more clumsy than usual, and drank champagne with regularity and determination out of sheer nervousness. At last the Time Traveller pushed his plate away, and looked round us. 'I suppose I must apologize,' he said. 'I was simply starving. I've had a most amazing time.' He reached out his hand for a cigar, and cut the end. 'But come into the

smoking-room. It's too long a story to tell over greasy plates.' And ringing the bell in passing, he led the way into the adjoining room.

'You have told Blank, and Dash, and Chose about the machine?' he said to me, leaning back in his easy-chair and naming the three new guests.

'But the thing's a mere paradox,' said the Editor.

'I can't argue to-night. I don't mind telling you the story, but I can't argue. I will,' he went on, 'tell you the story of what has happened to me, if you like, but you must refrain from interruptions. I want to tell it. Badly. Most of it will sound like lying. So be it! It's true—every word of it, all the same. I was in my laboratory at four o'clock, and since then ... I've lived eight days ... such days as no human being ever lived before! I'm nearly worn out, but I shan't sleep till I've told this thing over to you. Then I shall go to bed. But no interruptions! Is it agreed?'

'Agreed,' said the Editor, and the rest of us echoed 'Agreed.' And with that the Time Traveller began his story as I have set it forth. He sat back in his chair at first, and spoke like a weary man. Afterwards he got more animated. In writing it down I feel with only too much keenness the inadequacy of pen and ink—and, above all, my own inadequacy—to express its quality. You read, I will suppose, attentively enough; but you cannot see the speaker's white, sincere face in the bright circle of the little lamp, nor hear the intonation of his voice. You cannot know how his expression followed the turns of his story! Most of us hearers were in shadow, for the candles in the smoking-room had not been lighted, and only the face of the Journalist and the legs of the Silent Man from the knees downward were illuminated. At first we glanced now and again at each other. After a time we ceased to do that, and looked only at the Time Traveller's face.

III

'I told some of you last Thursday of the principles of the Time Machine, and showed you the actual thing itself, incomplete in the workshop. There it is now, a little travel-worn, truly; and one of the ivory bars is cracked, and a brass rail bent; but the rest of it's sound enough. I expected to finish it on Friday, but on Friday, when the putting together was nearly done, I found that one of the nickel bars was exactly one inch too short, and this I had to get remade; so that the thing was not complete until this morning. It was at ten o'clock to-day that the first of all Time Machines began its career. I gave it a last tap, tried all the screws again, put one more drop of oil on the quartz rod, and sat myself in the saddle. I suppose a suicide who holds a pistol to his skull feels much the same wonder at what will come next as I felt then. I took the starting lever in one hand and the stopping one in the other, pressed the first, and almost immediately the second. I seemed to reel; I felt a nightmare sensation of falling; and, looking round, I saw the laboratory exactly as before. Had anything happened? For a moment I suspected that my intellect had tricked me. Then I noted the clock. A moment before, as it seemed, it had stood at a minute or so past ten; now it was nearly half-past three!

'I drew a breath, set my teeth, gripped the starting lever with both hands, and went off with a thud. The laboratory got hazy and went dark. Mrs. Watchett came in and walked, apparently without seeing me, towards the garden door. I suppose it took her a minute or so to traverse the place, but to me she seemed to shoot across the room like a rocket. I pressed the lever over to its extreme position. The night came like the turning out of a lamp, and in another moment came tomorrow. The laboratory grew faint and hazy, then fainter and ever fainter. Tomorrow night came black, then day again, night again, day again, faster and faster still. An eddying murmur filled my ears, and a strange, dumb confusedness descended on my mind.

'I am afraid I cannot convey the peculiar sensations of time travelling. They are excessively unpleasant. There is a feeling exactly like that one has upon a switchback—of a helpless headlong motion! I felt the same horrible anticipation, too, of an imminent smash. As I put on pace, night followed day like the flapping of a black wing. The dim suggestion of the laboratory seemed presently to fall away from me, and I saw the sun hopping swiftly across the sky, leaping it every minute, and every minute marking a day. I supposed the laboratory had been destroyed and I had come into the open air. I had a dim impression of scaffolding, but I was already going too fast to be conscious of any moving things. The slow-

est snail that ever crawled dashed by too fast for me. The twinkling succession of darkness and light was excessively painful to the eye. Then, in the intermittent darknesses, I saw the moon spinning swiftly through her quarters from new to full, and had a faint glimpse of the circling stars. Presently, as I went on, still gaining velocity, the palpitation of night and day merged into one continuous greyness; the sky took on a wonderful deepness of blue, a splendid luminous color like that of early twilight; the jerking sun became a streak of fire, a brilliant arch, in space; the moon a fainter fluctuating band; and I could see nothing of the stars, save now and then a brighter circle flickering in the blue.

'The landscape was misty and vague. I was still on the hill-side upon which this house now stands, and the shoulder rose above me grey and dim. I saw trees growing and changing like puffs of vapour, now brown, now green; they grew, spread, shivered, and passed away. I saw huge buildings rise up faint and fair, and pass like dreams. The whole surface of the earth seemed changed —melting and flowing under my eyes. The little hands upon the dials that registered my speed raced round faster and faster. Presently I noted that the sun belt swayed up and down, from solstice to solstice, in a minute or less, and that consequently my pace was over a year a minute; and minute by minute the white snow flashed across the world, and vanished, and was followed by the bright, brief green of spring.

'The unpleasant sensations of the start were less poignant now. They merged at last into a kind of hysterical exhilaration. I remarked indeed a clumsy swaying of the machine, for which I was unable to account. But my mind was too confused to attend to it, so with a kind of madness growing upon me, I flung myself into futurity. At first I scarce thought of stopping, scarce thought of anything but these new sensations. But presently a fresh series of impressions grew up in my mind—a certain curiosity and therewith a certain dread—until at last they took complete possession of me. What strange developments of humanity, what wonderful advances upon our rudimentary civilization, I thought, might not appear when I came to look nearly into the dim elusive world that raced and fluctuated before my eyes! I saw great and splendid architecture rising about me, more massive than any buildings of our own time, and yet, as it seemed, built of glimmer and mist. I saw a richer green flow up the hill-side, and remain there, without any wintry intermission. Even through the veil of my confusion the earth seemed very fair. And so my mind came round to the business of stopping.

'The peculiar risk lay in the possibility of my finding some substance in the space which I, or the machine, occupied. So long as I travelled at a high velocity through time, this scarcely mattered; I was, so to speak, attenuated —was slipping like a vapour through the interstices of intervening substances! But to come to a stop involved the jamming of myself, molecule by molecule, into whatever lay in my way; meant bringing my atoms into such intimate contact with those of the obstacle that a profound chemical reaction —possibly a far-reaching explosion—would result, and blow myself and my apparatus out of all possible dimensions—into the Unknown. This possibility had occurred to me again and again while I was making the machine; but then I had cheerfully accepted it as an unavoidable

risk—one of the risks a man has got to take! Now the risk was inevitable, I no longer saw it in the same cheerful light. The fact is that, insensibly, the absolute strangeness of everything, the sickly jarring and swaying of the machine, above all, the feeling of prolonged falling, had absolutely upset my nerve. I told myself that I could never stop, and with a gust of petulance I resolved to stop forthwith. Like an impatient fool, I lugged over the lever, and incontinently the thing went reeling over, and I was flung headlong through the air.

'There was the sound of a clap of thunder in my ears. I may have been stunned for a moment. A pitiless hail was hissing round me, and I was sitting on soft turf in front of the overset machine. Everything still seemed grey, but presently I remarked that the confusion in my ears was gone. I looked round me. I was on what seemed to be a little lawn in a garden, surrounded by rhododendron bushes, and I noticed that their mauve and purple blossoms were dropping in a shower under the beating of the hail-stones. The rebounding, dancing hail hung in a cloud over the machine, and drove along the ground like smoke. In a moment I was wet to the skin. "Fine hospitality," said I, "to a man who has travelled innumerable years to see you."

'Presently I thought what a fool I was to get wet. I stood up and looked round me. A colossal figure, carved apparently in some white stone, loomed indistinctly beyond the rhododendrons through the hazy downpour. But all else of the world was invisible.

'My sensations would be hard to describe. As the columns of hail grew thinner, I saw the white figure more distinctly. It was very large, for a silver birch-tree touched its shoulder. It was of white marble, in shape something like a winged sphinx, but the wings, instead of being carried vertically at the sides, were spread so that it seemed to hover. The pedestal, it appeared to me, was of bronze, and was thick with verdigris. It chanced that the face was towards me; the sightless eyes seemed to watch me; there was the faint shadow of a smile on the lips. It was greatly weather-worn, and that imparted an unpleasant suggestion of disease. I stood looking at it for a little space—half a minute, perhaps, or half an hour. It seemed to advance and to recede as the hail drove before it denser or thinner. At last I tore my eyes from it for a moment and saw that the hail curtain had worn threadbare, and that the sky was lightening with the promise of the sun.

'I looked up again at the crouching white shape, and the full temerity of my voyage came suddenly upon me. What might appear when that hazy curtain was altogether withdrawn? What might not have happened to men? What if cruelty had grown into a common passion? What if in this interval the race had lost its manliness and had developed into something inhuman, unsympathetic, and overwhelmingly powerful? I might seem some old-world savage animal, only the more dreadful and disgusting for our common likeness—a foul creature to be incontinently slain.

'Already I saw other vast shapes—huge buildings with intricate parapets and tall columns, with a wooded hill-side dimly creeping in upon me through the lessening storm. I was seized with a panic fear. I turned frantically to the Time

Machine, and strove hard to readjust it. As I did so the shafts of the sun smote through the thunderstorm. The grey downpour was swept aside and vanished like the trailing garments of a ghost. Above me, in the intense blue of the summer sky, some faint brown shreds of cloud whirled into nothingness. The great buildings about me stood out clear and distinct, shining with the wet of the thunderstorm, and picked out in white by the unmelted hailstones piled along their courses. I felt naked in a strange world. I felt as perhaps a bird may feel in the clear air, knowing the hawk wings above and will swoop. My fear grew to frenzy. I took a breathing space, set my teeth, and again grappled fiercely, wrist and knee, with the machine. It gave under my desperate onset and turned over. It struck my chin violently. One hand on the saddle, the other on the lever, I stood panting heavily in attitude to mount again.

'But with this recovery of a prompt retreat my courage recovered. I looked more curiously and less fearfully at this world of the remote future. In a circular opening, high up in the wall of the nearer house, I saw a group of figures clad in rich soft robes. They had seen me, and their faces were directed towards me.

'Then I heard voices approaching me. Coming through the bushes by the White Sphinx were the heads and shoulders of men running. One of these emerged in a pathway leading straight to the little lawn upon which I stood with my machine. He was a slight creature—perhaps four feet high—clad in a purple tunic, girdled at the waist with a leather belt. Sandals or buskins —I could not clearly distinguish which—were on his feet; his legs were bare to the knees, and his head was bare. Noticing that, I noticed for the first time how warm the air was.

'He struck me as being a very beautiful and graceful creature, but indescribably frail. His flushed face reminded me of the more beautiful kind of consumptive—that hectic beauty of which we used to hear so much. At the sight of him I suddenly regained confidence. I took my hands from the machine.

IV

'In another moment we were standing face to face, I and this fragile thing out of futurity. He came straight up to me and laughed into my eyes. The absence from his bearing of any sign of fear struck me at once. Then he turned to the two others who were following him and spoke to them in a strange and very sweet and liquid tongue.

'There were others coming, and presently a little group of perhaps eight or ten of these exquisite creatures were about me. One of them addressed me. It came into my head, oddly enough, that my voice was too harsh and deep for them. So I shook my head, and, pointing to my ears, shook it again. He came a step forward, hesitated, and then touched my hand. Then I felt other soft little tentacles upon my back and shoulders. They wanted to make sure I was real. There was nothing in this at all alarming. Indeed, there was something in these pretty little people that inspired confidence—a graceful gentleness, a certain childlike ease. And besides, they looked so frail that I could fancy myself flinging the whole dozen of them about like nine-pins. But I made a sudden motion to warn them when I saw their little pink hands feeling at the Time Machine. Happily then, when it was not too late, I thought of a danger I had hitherto forgotten, and reaching over the bars of the machine I unscrewed the little levers that would set it in motion, and put these in my pocket. Then I turned again to see what I could do in the way of communication.

'And then, looking more nearly into their features, I saw some further peculiarities in their Dresden-china type of prettiness. Their hair, which was uniformly curly, came to a sharp end at the neck and cheek; there was not the faintest suggestion of it on the face, and their ears were singularly minute. The mouths were small, with bright red, rather thin lips, and the little chins ran to a point. The eyes were large and mild; and—this may seem egotism on my part—I fancied even that there was a certain lack of the interest I might have expected in them.

'As they made no effort to communicate with me, but simply stood round me smiling and speaking in soft cooing notes to each other, I began the conversation. I pointed to the Time Machine and to myself. Then hesitating for a moment how to express time, I pointed to the sun. At once a quaintly pretty little figure in chequered purple and white followed my gesture, and then astonished me by imitating the sound of thunder.

'For a moment I was staggered, though the import of his gesture was plain enough. The question had come into my mind abruptly: were these creatures

fools? You may hardly understand how it took me. You see I had always anticipated that the people of the year Eight Hundred and Two Thousand odd would be incredibly in front of us in knowledge, art, everything. Then one of them suddenly asked me a question that showed him to be on the intellectual level of one of our five-year-old children—asked me, in fact, if I had come from the sun in a thunderstorm! It let loose the judgment I had suspended upon their clothes, their frail light limbs, and fragile features. A flow of disappointment rushed across my mind. For a moment I felt that I had built the Time Machine in vain.

'I nodded, pointed to the sun, and gave them such a vivid rendering of a thunderclap as startled them. They all withdrew a pace or so and bowed. Then came one laughing towards me, carrying a chain of beautiful flowers altogether new to me, and put it about my neck. The idea was received with melodious applause; and presently they were all running to and fro for flowers, and laughingly flinging them upon me until I was almost smothered with blossom. You who have never seen the like can scarcely imagine what delicate and wonderful flowers countless years of culture had created. Then someone suggested that their plaything should be exhibited in the nearest building, and so I was led past the sphinx of white marble, which had seemed to watch me all the while with a smile at my astonishment, towards a vast grey edifice of fretted stone. As I went with them the memory of my confident anticipations of a profoundly grave and intellectual posterity came, with irresistible merriment, to my mind.

'The building had a huge entry, and was altogether of colossal dimensions. I was naturally most occupied with the growing crowd of little people, and with the big open portals that yawned before me shadowy and mysterious. My general impression of the world I saw over their heads was a tangled waste of beautiful bushes and flowers, a long neglected and yet weedless garden. I saw a number of tall spikes of strange white flowers, measuring a foot perhaps across the spread of the waxen petals. They grew scattered, as if wild, among the variegated shrubs, but, as I say, I did not examine them closely at this time. The Time Machine was left deserted on the turf among the rhododendrons.

'The arch of the doorway was richly carved, but naturally I did not observe the carving very narrowly, though I fancied I saw suggestions of old Phoenician decorations as I passed through, and it struck me that they were very badly broken and weather-worn. Several more brightly clad people met me in the doorway, and so we entered, I, dressed in dingy nineteenth-century garments, looking grotesque enough, garlanded with flowers, and surrounded by an eddying mass of bright, soft-colored robes and shining white limbs, in a melodious whirl of laughter and laughing speech.

'The big doorway opened into a proportionately great hall hung with brown. The roof was in shadow, and the windows, partially glazed with coloured glass and partially unglazed, admitted a tempered light. The floor was made up of huge blocks of some very hard white metal, not plates nor slabs—blocks, and it was so much worn, as I judged by the going to and fro of past generations, as to be deeply channelled along the more frequented ways. Transverse to the length were

innumerable tables made of slabs of polished stone, raised perhaps a foot from the floor, and upon these were heaps of fruits. Some I recognized as a kind of hypertrophied raspberry and orange, but for the most part they were strange.

'Between the tables was scattered a great number of cushions. Upon these my conductors seated themselves, signing for me to do likewise. With a pretty absence of ceremony they began to eat the fruit with their hands, flinging peel and stalks, and so forth, into the round openings in the sides of the tables. I was not loath to follow their example, for I felt thirsty and hungry. As I did so I surveyed the hall at my leisure.

'And perhaps the thing that struck me most was its dilapidated look. The stained-glass windows, which displayed only a geometrical pattern, were broken in many places, and the curtains that hung across the lower end were thick with dust. And it caught my eye that the corner of the marble table near me was fractured. Nevertheless, the general effect was extremely rich and picturesque. There were, perhaps, a couple of hundred people dining in the hall, and most of them, seated as near to me as they could come, were watching me with interest, their little eyes shining over the fruit they were eating. All were clad in the same soft and yet strong, silky material.

'Fruit, by the by, was all their diet. These people of the remote future were strict vegetarians, and while I was with them, in spite of some carnal cravings, I had to be frugivorous also. Indeed, I found afterwards that horses, cattle, sheep, dogs, had followed the Ichthyosaurus into extinction. But the fruits were very delightful; one, in particular, that seemed to be in season all the time I was there—a floury thing in a three-sided husk—was especially good, and I made it my staple. At first I was puzzled by all these strange fruits, and by the strange flowers I saw, but later I began to perceive their import.

'However, I am telling you of my fruit dinner in the distant future now. So soon as my appetite was a little checked, I determined to make a resolute attempt to learn the speech of these new men of mine. Clearly that was the next thing to do. The fruits seemed a convenient thing to begin upon, and holding one of these up I began a series of interrogative sounds and gestures. I had some considerable difficulty in conveying my meaning. At first my efforts met with a stare of surprise or inextinguishable laughter, but presently a fair- haired little creature seemed to grasp my intention and repeated a name. They had to chatter and explain the business at great length to each other, and my first attempts to make the exquisite little sounds of their language caused an immense amount of amusement. However, I felt like a schoolmaster amidst children, and persisted, and presently I had a score of noun substantives at least at my command; and then I got to demonstrative pronouns, and even the verb "to eat." But it was slow work, and the little people soon tired and wanted to get away from my interrogations, so I determined, rather of necessity, to let them give their lessons in little doses when they felt inclined. And very little doses I found they were before long, for I never met people more indolent or more easily fatigued.

'A queer thing I soon discovered about my little hosts, and that was their lack of interest. They would come to me with eager cries of astonishment, like children, but like children they would soon stop examining me and wander away after some other toy. The dinner and my conversational beginnings ended, I noted for the first time that almost all those who had surrounded me at first were gone. It is odd, too, how speedily I came to disregard these little people. I went out through the portal into the sunlit world again as soon as my hunger was satisfied. I was continually meeting more of these men of the future, who would follow me a little distance, chatter and laugh about me, and, having smiled and gesticulated in a friendly way, leave me again to my own devices.

'The calm of evening was upon the world as I emerged from the great hall, and the scene was lit by the warm glow of the setting sun. At first things were very confusing. Everything was so entirely different from the world I had known — even the flowers. The big building I had left was situated on the slope of a broad river valley, but the Thames had shifted perhaps a mile from its present position. I resolved to mount to the summit of a crest, perhaps a mile and a half away, from which I could get a wider view of this our planet in the year Eight Hundred and Two Thousand Seven Hundred and One A.D. For that, I should explain, was the date the little dials of my machine recorded.

'As I walked I was watching for every impression that could possibly help to explain the condition of ruinous splendour in which I found the world —for ruinous it was. A little way up the hill, for instance, was a great heap of granite, bound together by masses of aluminium, a vast labyrinth of precipitous walls and crumpled heaps, amidst which were thick heaps of very beautiful pagoda-like plants—nettles possibly—but wonderfully tinted with brown about the leaves, and incapable of stinging. It was evidently the derelict remains of some vast structure, to what end built I could not determine. It was here that I was destined, at a later date, to have a very strange experience—the first intimation of a still stranger discovery —but of that I will speak in its proper place.

'Looking round with a sudden thought, from a terrace on which I rested for a while, I realized that there were no small houses to be seen. Apparently the single house, and possibly even the household, had vanished. Here and there among the greenery were palace-like buildings, but the house and the cottage, which form such characteristic features of our own English landscape, had disappeared.

'"Communism," said I to myself.

'And on the heels of that came another thought. I looked at the half- dozen little figures that were following me. Then, in a flash, I perceived that all had the same form of costume, the same soft hairless visage, and the same girlish rotundity of limb. It may seem strange, perhaps, that I had not noticed this before. But everything was so strange. Now, I saw the fact plainly enough. In costume, and in all the differences of texture and bearing that now mark off the sexes from each other, these people of the future were alike. And the children seemed to my eyes to be but the miniatures of their parents. I judged, then, that the children of that

time were extremely precocious, physically at least, and I found afterwards abundant verification of my opinion.

'Seeing the ease and security in which these people were living, I felt that this close resemblance of the sexes was after all what one would expect; for the strength of a man and the softness of a woman, the institution of the family, and the differentiation of occupations are mere militant necessities of an age of physical force; where population is balanced and abundant, much childbearing becomes an evil rather than a blessing to the State; where violence comes but rarely and off-spring are secure, there is less necessity —indeed there is no necessity—for an efficient family, and the specialization of the sexes with reference to their children's needs disappears. We see some beginnings of this even in our own time, and in this future age it was complete. This, I must remind you, was my speculation at the time. Later, I was to appreciate how far it fell short of the reality.

'While I was musing upon these things, my attention was attracted by a pretty little structure, like a well under a cupola. I thought in a transitory way of the oddness of wells still existing, and then resumed the thread of my speculations. There were no large buildings towards the top of the hill, and as my walking powers were evidently miraculous, I was presently left alone for the first time. With a strange sense of freedom and adventure I pushed on up to the crest.

'There I found a seat of some yellow metal that I did not recognize, corroded in places with a kind of pinkish rust and half smothered in soft moss, the arm-rests cast and filed into the resemblance of griffins' heads. I sat down on it, and I surveyed the broad view of our old world under the sunset of that long day. It was as sweet and fair a view as I have ever seen. The sun had already gone below the horizon and the west was flaming gold, touched with some horizontal bars of purple and crimson. Below was the valley of the Thames, in which the river lay like a band of burnished steel. I have already spoken of the great palaces dotted about among the variegated greenery, some in ruins and some still occupied. Here and there rose a white or silvery figure in the waste garden of the earth, here and there came the sharp vertical line of some cupola or obelisk. There were no hedges, no signs of proprietary rights, no evidences of agriculture; the whole earth had become a garden.

'So watching, I began to put my interpretation upon the things I had seen, and as it shaped itself to me that evening, my interpretation was something in this way. (Afterwards I found I had got only a half- truth—or only a glimpse of one facet of the truth.)

'It seemed to me that I had happened upon humanity upon the wane. The ruddy sunset set me thinking of the sunset of mankind. For the first time I began to realize an odd consequence of the social effort in which we are at present engaged. And yet, come to think, it is a logical consequence enough. Strength is the outcome of need; security sets a premium on feebleness. The work of ameliorating the conditions of life—the true civilizing process that makes life more and more secure—had gone steadily on to a climax. One triumph of a united humanity over

Nature had followed another. Things that are now mere dreams had become projects deliberately put in hand and carried forward. And the harvest was what I saw!

'After all, the sanitation and the agriculture of to-day are still in the rudimentary stage. The science of our time has attacked but a little department of the field of human disease, but even so, it spreads its operations very steadily and persistently. Our agriculture and horticulture destroy a weed just here and there and cultivate perhaps a score or so of wholesome plants, leaving the greater number to fight out a balance as they can. We improve our favourite plants and animals—and how few they are—gradually by selective breeding; now a new and better peach, now a seedless grape, now a sweeter and larger flower, now a more convenient breed of cattle. We improve them gradually, because our ideals are vague and tentative, and our knowledge is very limited; because Nature, too, is shy and slow in our clumsy hands. Some day all this will be better organized, and still better. That is the drift of the current in spite of the eddies. The whole world will be intelligent, educated, and co-operating; things will move faster and faster towards the subjugation of Nature. In the end, wisely and carefully we shall readjust the balance of animal and vegetable life to suit our human needs.

'This adjustment, I say, must have been done, and done well; done indeed for all Time, in the space of Time across which my machine had leaped. The air was free from gnats, the earth from weeds or fungi; everywhere were fruits and sweet and delightful flowers; brilliant butterflies flew hither and thither. The ideal of preventive medicine was attained. Diseases had been stamped out. I saw no evidence of any contagious diseases during all my stay. And I shall have to tell you later that even the processes of putrefaction and decay had been profoundly affected by these changes.

'Social triumphs, too, had been effected. I saw mankind housed in splendid shelters, gloriously clothed, and as yet I had found them engaged in no toil. There were no signs of struggle, neither social nor economical struggle. The shop, the advertisement, traffic, all that commerce which constitutes the body of our world, was gone. It was natural on that golden evening that I should jump at the idea of a social paradise. The difficulty of increasing population had been met, I guessed, and population had ceased to increase.

'But with this change in condition comes inevitably adaptations to the change. What, unless biological science is a mass of errors, is the cause of human intelligence and vigour? Hardship and freedom: conditions under which the active, strong, and subtle survive and the weaker go to the wall; conditions that put a premium upon the loyal alliance of capable men, upon self-restraint, patience, and decision. And the institution of the family, and the emotions that arise therein, the fierce jealousy, the tenderness for offspring, parental self-devotion, all found their justification and support in the imminent dangers of the young. *Now*, where are these imminent dangers? There is a sentiment arising, and it will grow, against connubial jealousy, against fierce maternity, against passion of all sorts; unneces-

sary things now, and things that make us uncomfortable, savage survivals, discords in a refined and pleasant life.

'I thought of the physical slightness of the people, their lack of intelligence, and those big abundant ruins, and it strengthened my belief in a perfect conquest of Nature. For after the battle comes Quiet. Humanity had been strong, energetic, and intelligent, and had used all its abundant vitality to alter the conditions under which it lived. And now came the reaction of the altered conditions.

'Under the new conditions of perfect comfort and security, that restless energy, that with us is strength, would become weakness. Even in our own time certain tendencies and desires, once necessary to survival, are a constant source of failure. Physical courage and the love of battle, for instance, are no great help—may even be hindrances—to a civilized man. And in a state of physical balance and security, power, intellectual as well as physical, would be out of place. For countless years I judged there had been no danger of war or solitary violence, no danger from wild beasts, no wasting disease to require strength of constitution, no need of toil. For such a life, what we should call the weak are as well equipped as the strong, are indeed no longer weak. Better equipped indeed they are, for the strong would be fretted by an energy for which there was no outlet. No doubt the exquisite beauty of the buildings I saw was the outcome of the last surgings of the now purposeless energy of mankind before it settled down into perfect harmony with the conditions under which it lived—the flourish of that triumph which began the last great peace. This has ever been the fate of energy in security; it takes to art and to eroticism, and then come languor and decay.

'Even this artistic impetus would at last die away—had almost died in the Time I saw. To adorn themselves with flowers, to dance, to sing in the sunlight: so much was left of the artistic spirit, and no more. Even that would fade in the end into a contented inactivity. We are kept keen on the grindstone of pain and necessity, and, it seemed to me, that here was that hateful grindstone broken at last!

'As I stood there in the gathering dark I thought that in this simple explanation I had mastered the problem of the world—mastered the whole secret of these delicious people. Possibly the checks they had devised for the increase of population had succeeded too well, and their numbers had rather diminished than kept stationary. That would account for the abandoned ruins. Very simple was my explanation, and plausible enough—as most wrong theories are!

V

'As I stood there musing over this too perfect triumph of man, the full moon, yellow and gibbous, came up out of an overflow of silver light in the north-east. The bright little figures ceased to move about below, a noiseless owl flitted by, and I shivered with the chill of the night. I determined to descend and find where I could sleep.

'I looked for the building I knew. Then my eye travelled along to the figure of the White Sphinx upon the pedestal of bronze, growing distinct as the light of the rising moon grew brighter. I could see the silver birch against it. There was the tangle of rhododendron bushes, black in the pale light, and there was the little lawn. I looked at the lawn again. A queer doubt chilled my complacency. "No," said I stoutly to myself, "that was not the lawn."

'But it *was* the lawn. For the white leprous face of the sphinx was towards it. Can you imagine what I felt as this conviction came home to me? But you cannot. The Time Machine was gone!

'At once, like a lash across the face, came the possibility of losing my own age, of being left helpless in this strange new world. The bare thought of it was an actual physical sensation. I could feel it grip me at the throat and stop my breathing. In another moment I was in a passion of fear and running with great leaping strides down the slope. Once I fell headlong and cut my face; I lost no time in stanching the blood, but jumped up and ran on, with a warm trickle down my cheek and chin. All the time I ran I was saying to myself: "They have moved it a little, pushed it under the bushes out of the way." Nevertheless, I ran with all my might. All the time, with the certainty that sometimes comes with excessive dread, I knew that such assurance was folly, knew instinctively that the machine was removed out of my reach. My breath came with pain. I suppose I covered the whole distance from the hill crest to the little lawn, two miles perhaps, in ten minutes. And I am not a young man. I cursed aloud, as I ran, at my confident folly in leaving the machine, wasting good breath thereby. I cried aloud, and none answered. Not a creature seemed to be stirring in that moonlit world.

'When I reached the lawn my worst fears were realized. Not a trace of the thing was to be seen. I felt faint and cold when I faced the empty space among the black tangle of bushes. I ran round it furiously, as if the thing might be hidden in a corner, and then stopped abruptly, with my hands clutching my hair. Above me towered the sphinx, upon the bronze pedestal, white, shining, leprous, in the light of the rising moon. It seemed to smile in mockery of my dismay.

'I might have consoled myself by imagining the little people had put the mechanism in some shelter for me, had I not felt assured of their physical and intellectual inadequacy. That is what dismayed me: the sense of some hitherto unsuspected power, through whose intervention my invention had vanished. Yet, for one thing I felt assured: unless some other age had produced its exact duplicate, the machine could not have moved in time. The attachment of the levers—I will show you the method later—prevented any one from tampering with it in that way when they were removed. It had moved, and was hid, only in space. But then, where could it be?

'I think I must have had a kind of frenzy. I remember running violently in and out among the moonlit bushes all round the sphinx, and startling some white animal that, in the dim light, I took for a small deer. I remember, too, late that night, beating the bushes with my clenched fist until my knuckles were gashed and bleeding from the broken twigs. Then, sobbing and raving in my anguish of mind, I went down to the great building of stone. The big hall was dark, silent, and deserted. I slipped on the uneven floor, and fell over one of the malachite tables, almost breaking my shin. I lit a match and went on past the dusty curtains, of which I have told you.

'There I found a second great hall covered with cushions, upon which, perhaps, a score or so of the little people were sleeping. I have no doubt they found my second appearance strange enough, coming suddenly out of the quiet darkness with inarticulate noises and the splutter and flare of a match. For they had forgotten about matches. "Where is my Time Machine?" I began, bawling like an angry child, laying hands upon them and shaking them up together. It must have been very queer to them. Some laughed, most of them looked sorely frightened. When I saw them standing round me, it came into my head that I was doing as foolish a thing as it was possible for me to do under the circumstances, in trying to revive the sensation of fear. For, reasoning from their daylight behaviour, I thought that fear must be forgotten.

'Abruptly, I dashed down the match, and, knocking one of the people over in my course, went blundering across the big dining-hall again, out under the moonlight. I heard cries of terror and their little feet running and stumbling this way and that. I do not remember all I did as the moon crept up the sky. I suppose it was the unexpected nature of my loss that maddened me. I felt hopelessly cut off from my own kind—a strange animal in an unknown world. I must have raved to and fro, screaming and crying upon God and Fate. I have a memory of horrible fatigue, as the long night of despair wore away; of looking in this impossible place and that; of groping among moon-lit ruins and touching strange creatures in the black shadows; at last, of lying on the ground near the sphinx and weeping with absolute wretchedness. I had nothing left but misery. Then I slept, and when I woke again it was full day, and a couple of sparrows were hopping round me on the turf within reach of my arm.

'I sat up in the freshness of the morning, trying to remember how I had got there, and why I had such a profound sense of desertion and despair. Then things

came clear in my mind. With the plain, reasonable daylight, I could look my circumstances fairly in the face. I saw the wild folly of my frenzy overnight, and I could reason with myself. "Suppose the worst?" I said. "Suppose the machine altogether lost—perhaps destroyed? It behoves me to be calm and patient, to learn the way of the people, to get a clear idea of the method of my loss, and the means of getting materials and tools; so that in the end, perhaps, I may make another." That would be my only hope, perhaps, but better than despair. And, after all, it was a beautiful and curious world.

'But probably, the machine had only been taken away. Still, I must be calm and patient, find its hiding-place, and recover it by force or cunning. And with that I scrambled to my feet and looked about me, wondering where I could bathe. I felt weary, stiff, and travel-soiled. The freshness of the morning made me desire an equal freshness. I had exhausted my emotion. Indeed, as I went about my business, I found myself wondering at my intense excitement overnight. I made a careful examination of the ground about the little lawn. I wasted some time in futile questionings, conveyed, as well as I was able, to such of the little people as came by. They all failed to understand my gestures; some were simply stolid, some thought it was a jest and laughed at me. I had the hardest task in the world to keep my hands off their pretty laughing faces. It was a foolish impulse, but the devil begotten of fear and blind anger was ill curbed and still eager to take advantage of my perplexity. The turf gave better counsel. I found a groove ripped in it, about midway between the pedestal of the sphinx and the marks of my feet where, on arrival, I had struggled with the overturned machine. There were other signs of removal about, with queer narrow footprints like those I could imagine made by a sloth. This directed my closer attention to the pedestal. It was, as I think I have said, of bronze. It was not a mere block, but highly decorated with deep framed panels on either side. I went and rapped at these. The pedestal was hollow. Examining the panels with care I found them discontinuous with the frames. There were no handles or keyholes, but possibly the panels, if they were doors, as I supposed, opened from within. One thing was clear enough to my mind. It took no very great mental effort to infer that my Time Machine was inside that pedestal. But how it got there was a different problem.

'I saw the heads of two orange-clad people coming through the bushes and under some blossom-covered apple-trees towards me. I turned smiling to them and beckoned them to me. They came, and then, pointing to the bronze pedestal, I tried to intimate my wish to open it. But at my first gesture towards this they behaved very oddly. I don't know how to convey their expression to you. Suppose you were to use a grossly improper gesture to a delicate-minded woman—it is how she would look. They went off as if they had received the last possible insult. I tried a sweet-looking little chap in white next, with exactly the same result. Somehow, his manner made me feel ashamed of myself. But, as you know, I wanted the Time Machine, and I tried him once more. As he turned off, like the others, my temper got the better of me. In three strides I was after him, had him by the loose part of his robe round the neck, and began dragging him towards the

sphinx. Then I saw the horror and repugnance of his face, and all of a sudden I let him go.

'But I was not beaten yet. I banged with my fist at the bronze panels. I thought I heard something stir inside—to be explicit, I thought I heard a sound like a chuckle—but I must have been mistaken. Then I got a big pebble from the river, and came and hammered till I had flattened a coil in the decorations, and the verdigris came off in powdery flakes. The delicate little people must have heard me hammering in gusty outbreaks a mile away on either hand, but nothing came of it. I saw a crowd of them upon the slopes, looking furtively at me. At last, hot and tired, I sat down to watch the place. But I was too restless to watch long; I am too Occidental for a long vigil. I could work at a problem for years, but to wait inactive for twenty-four hours—that is another matter.

'I got up after a time, and began walking aimlessly through the bushes towards the hill again. "Patience," said I to myself. "If you want your machine again you must leave that sphinx alone. If they mean to take your machine away, it's little good your wrecking their bronze panels, and if they don't, you will get it back as soon as you can ask for it. To sit among all those unknown things before a puzzle like that is hopeless. That way lies monomania. Face this world. Learn its ways, watch it, be careful of too hasty guesses at its meaning. In the end you will find clues to it all." Then suddenly the humour of the situation came into my mind: the thought of the years I had spent in study and toil to get into the future age, and now my passion of anxiety to get out of it. I had made myself the most complicated and the most hopeless trap that ever a man devised. Although it was at my own expense, I could not help myself. I laughed aloud.

'Going through the big palace, it seemed to me that the little people avoided me. It may have been my fancy, or it may have had something to do with my hammering at the gates of bronze. Yet I felt tolerably sure of the avoidance. I was careful, however, to show no concern and to abstain from any pursuit of them, and in the course of a day or two things got back to the old footing. I made what progress I could in the language, and in addition I pushed my explorations here and there. Either I missed some subtle point or their language was excessively simple—almost exclusively composed of concrete substantives and verbs. There seemed to be few, if any, abstract terms, or little use of figurative language. Their sentences were usually simple and of two words, and I failed to convey or understand any but the simplest propositions. I determined to put the thought of my Time Machine and the mystery of the bronze doors under the sphinx as much as possible in a corner of memory, until my growing knowledge would lead me back to them in a natural way. Yet a certain feeling, you may understand, tethered me in a circle of a few miles round the point of my arrival.

'So far as I could see, all the world displayed the same exuberant richness as the Thames valley. From every hill I climbed I saw the same abundance of splendid buildings, endlessly varied in material and style, the same clustering thickets of evergreens, the same blossom-laden trees and tree- ferns. Here and there water shone like silver, and beyond, the land rose into blue undulating hills, and so fad-

ed into the serenity of the sky. A peculiar feature, which presently attracted my attention, was the presence of certain circular wells, several, as it seemed to me, of a very great depth. One lay by the path up the hill, which I had followed during my first walk. Like the others, it was rimmed with bronze, curiously wrought, and protected by a little cupola from the rain. Sitting by the side of these wells, and peering down into the shafted darkness, I could see no gleam of water, nor could I start any reflection with a lighted match. But in all of them I heard a certain sound: a thud—thud—thud, like the beating of some big engine; and I discovered, from the flaring of my matches, that a steady current of air set down the shafts. Further, I threw a scrap of paper into the throat of one, and, instead of fluttering slowly down, it was at once sucked swiftly out of sight.

'After a time, too, I came to connect these wells with tall towers standing here and there upon the slopes; for above them there was often just such a flicker in the air as one sees on a hot day above a sun-scorched beach. Putting things together, I reached a strong suggestion of an extensive system of subterranean ventilation, whose true import it was difficult to imagine. I was at first inclined to associate it with the sanitary apparatus of these people. It was an obvious conclusion, but it was absolutely wrong.

'And here I must admit that I learned very little of drains and bells and modes of conveyance, and the like conveniences, during my time in this real future. In some of these visions of Utopias and coming times which I have read, there is a vast amount of detail about building, and social arrangements, and so forth. But while such details are easy enough to obtain when the whole world is contained in one's imagination, they are altogether inaccessible to a real traveller amid such realities as I found here. Conceive the tale of London which a negro, fresh from Central Africa, would take back to his tribe! What would he know of railway companies, of social movements, of telephone and telegraph wires, of the Parcels Delivery Company, and postal orders and the like? Yet we, at least, should be willing enough to explain these things to him! And even of what he knew, how much could he make his untravelled friend either apprehend or believe? Then, think how narrow the gap between a negro and a white man of our own times, and how wide the interval between myself and these of the Golden Age! I was sensible of much which was unseen, and which contributed to my comfort; but save for a general impression of automatic organization, I fear I can convey very little of the difference to your mind.

'In the matter of sepulture, for instance, I could see no signs of crematoria nor anything suggestive of tombs. But it occurred to me that, possibly, there might be cemeteries (or crematoria) somewhere beyond the range of my explorings. This, again, was a question I deliberately put to myself, and my curiosity was at first entirely defeated upon the point. The thing puzzled me, and I was led to make a further remark, which puzzled me still more: that aged and infirm among this people there were none.

'I must confess that my satisfaction with my first theories of an automatic civilization and a decadent humanity did not long endure. Yet I could think of no

other. Let me put my difficulties. The several big palaces I had explored were mere living places, great dining-halls and sleeping apartments. I could find no machinery, no appliances of any kind. Yet these people were clothed in pleasant fabrics that must at times need renewal, and their sandals, though undecorated, were fairly complex specimens of metalwork. Somehow such things must be made. And the little people displayed no vestige of a creative tendency. There were no shops, no workshops, no sign of importations among them. They spent all their time in playing gently, in bathing in the river, in making love in a half-playful fashion, in eating fruit and sleeping. I could not see how things were kept going.

'Then, again, about the Time Machine: something, I knew not what, had taken it into the hollow pedestal of the White Sphinx. Why? For the life of me I could not imagine. Those waterless wells, too, those flickering pillars. I felt I lacked a clue. I felt—how shall I put it? Suppose you found an inscription, with sentences here and there in excellent plain English, and interpolated therewith, others made up of words, of letters even, absolutely unknown to you? Well, on the third day of my visit, that was how the world of Eight Hundred and Two Thousand Seven Hundred and One presented itself to me!

'That day, too, I made a friend—of a sort. It happened that, as I was watching some of the little people bathing in a shallow, one of them was seized with cramp and began drifting downstream. The main current ran rather swiftly, but not too strongly for even a moderate swimmer. It will give you an idea, therefore, of the strange deficiency in these creatures, when I tell you that none made the slightest attempt to rescue the weakly crying little thing which was drowning before their eyes. When I realized this, I hurriedly slipped off my clothes, and, wading in at a point lower down, I caught the poor mite and drew her safe to land. A little rubbing of the limbs soon brought her round, and I had the satisfaction of seeing she was all right before I left her. I had got to such a low estimate of her kind that I did not expect any gratitude from her. In that, however, I was wrong.

'This happened in the morning. In the afternoon I met my little woman, as I believe it was, as I was returning towards my centre from an exploration, and she received me with cries of delight and presented me with a big garland of flowers—evidently made for me and me alone. The thing took my imagination. Very possibly I had been feeling desolate. At any rate I did my best to display my appreciation of the gift. We were soon seated together in a little stone arbour, engaged in conversation, chiefly of smiles. The creature's friendliness affected me exactly as a child's might have done. We passed each other flowers, and she kissed my hands. I did the same to hers. Then I tried talk, and found that her name was Weena, which, though I don't know what it meant, somehow seemed appropriate enough. That was the beginning of a queer friendship which lasted a week, and ended—as I will tell you!

'She was exactly like a child. She wanted to be with me always. She tried to follow me everywhere, and on my next journey out and about it went to my heart to tire her down, and leave her at last, exhausted and calling after me rather plain-

tively. But the problems of the world had to be mastered. I had not, I said to myself, come into the future to carry on a miniature flirtation. Yet her distress when I left her was very great, her expostulations at the parting were sometimes frantic, and I think, altogether, I had as much trouble as comfort from her devotion. Nevertheless she was, somehow, a very great comfort. I thought it was mere childish affection that made her cling to me. Until it was too late, I did not clearly know what I had inflicted upon her when I left her. Nor until it was too late did I clearly understand what she was to me. For, by merely seeming fond of me, and showing in her weak, futile way that she cared for me, the little doll of a creature presently gave my return to the neighbourhood of the White Sphinx almost the feeling of coming home; and I would watch for her tiny figure of white and gold so soon as I came over the hill.

'It was from her, too, that I learned that fear had not yet left the world. She was fearless enough in the daylight, and she had the oddest confidence in me; for once, in a foolish moment, I made threatening grimaces at her, and she simply laughed at them. But she dreaded the dark, dreaded shadows, dreaded black things. Darkness to her was the one thing dreadful. It was a singularly passionate emotion, and it set me thinking and observing. I discovered then, among other things, that these little people gathered into the great houses after dark, and slept in droves. To enter upon them without a light was to put them into a tumult of apprehension. I never found one out of doors, or one sleeping alone within doors, after dark. Yet I was still such a blockhead that I missed the lesson of that fear, and in spite of Weena's distress I insisted upon sleeping away from these slumbering multitudes.

'It troubled her greatly, but in the end her odd affection for me triumphed, and for five of the nights of our acquaintance, including the last night of all, she slept with her head pillowed on my arm. But my story slips away from me as I speak of her. It must have been the night before her rescue that I was awakened about dawn. I had been restless, dreaming most disagreeably that I was drowned, and that sea anemones were feeling over my face with their soft palps. I woke with a start, and with an odd fancy that some greyish animal had just rushed out of the chamber. I tried to get to sleep again, but I felt restless and uncomfortable. It was that dim grey hour when things are just creeping out of darkness, when everything is colourless and clear cut, and yet unreal. I got up, and went down into the great hall, and so out upon the flagstones in front of the palace. I thought I would make a virtue of necessity, and see the sunrise.

'The moon was setting, and the dying moonlight and the first pallor of dawn were mingled in a ghastly half-light. The bushes were inky black, the ground a sombre grey, the sky colourless and cheerless. And up the hill I thought I could see ghosts. There several times, as I scanned the slope, I saw white figures. Twice I fancied I saw a solitary white, ape-like creature running rather quickly up the hill, and once near the ruins I saw a leash of them carrying some dark body. They moved hastily. I did not see what became of them. It seemed that they vanished among the bushes. The dawn was still indistinct, you must understand. I was feel-

ing that chill, uncertain, early- morning feeling you may have known. I doubted my eyes.

'As the eastern sky grew brighter, and the light of the day came on and its vivid colouring returned upon the world once more, I scanned the view keenly. But I saw no vestige of my white figures. They were mere creatures of the half light. "They must have been ghosts," I said; "I wonder whence they dated." For a queer notion of Grant Allen's came into my head, and amused me. If each generation die and leave ghosts, he argued, the world at last will get overcrowded with them. On that theory they would have grown innumerable some Eight Hundred Thousand Years hence, and it was no great wonder to see four at once. But the jest was unsatisfying, and I was thinking of these figures all the morning, until Weena's rescue drove them out of my head. I associated them in some indefinite way with the white animal I had startled in my first passionate search for the Time Machine. But Weena was a pleasant substitute. Yet all the same, they were soon destined to take far deadlier possession of my mind.

'I think I have said how much hotter than our own was the weather of this Golden Age. I cannot account for it. It may be that the sun was hotter, or the earth nearer the sun. It is usual to assume that the sun will go on cooling steadily in the future. But people, unfamiliar with such speculations as those of the younger Darwin, forget that the planets must ultimately fall back one by one into the parent body. As these catastrophes occur, the sun will blaze with renewed energy; and it may be that some inner planet had suffered this fate. Whatever the reason, the fact remains that the sun was very much hotter than we know it.

'Well, one very hot morning—my fourth, I think—as I was seeking shelter from the heat and glare in a colossal ruin near the great house where I slept and fed, there happened this strange thing: Clambering among these heaps of masonry, I found a narrow gallery, whose end and side windows were blocked by fallen masses of stone. By contrast with the brilliancy outside, it seemed at first impenetrably dark to me. I entered it groping, for the change from light to blackness made spots of colour swim before me. Suddenly I halted spellbound. A pair of eyes, luminous by reflection against the daylight without, was watching me out of the darkness.

'The old instinctive dread of wild beasts came upon me. I clenched my hands and steadfastly looked into the glaring eyeballs. I was afraid to turn. Then the thought of the absolute security in which humanity appeared to be living came to my mind. And then I remembered that strange terror of the dark. Overcoming my fear to some extent, I advanced a step and spoke. I will admit that my voice was harsh and ill-controlled. I put out my hand and touched something soft. At once the eyes darted sideways, and something white ran past me. I turned with my heart in my mouth, and saw a queer little ape-like figure, its head held down in a peculiar manner, running across the sunlit space behind me. It blundered against a block of granite, staggered aside, and in a moment was hidden in a black shadow beneath another pile of ruined masonry.

'My impression of it is, of course, imperfect; but I know it was a dull white, and had strange large greyish-red eyes; also that there was flaxen hair on its head and down its back. But, as I say, it went too fast for me to see distinctly. I cannot even say whether it ran on all-fours, or only with its forearms held very low. After an instant's pause I followed it into the second heap of ruins. I could not find it at first; but, after a time in the profound obscurity, I came upon one of those round well-like openings of which I have told you, half closed by a fallen pillar. A sudden thought came to me. Could this Thing have vanished down the shaft? I lit a match, and, looking down, I saw a small, white, moving creature, with large bright eyes which regarded me steadfastly as it retreated. It made me shudder. It was so like a human spider! It was clambering down the wall, and now I saw for the first time a number of metal foot and hand rests forming a kind of ladder down the shaft. Then the light burned my fingers and fell out of my hand, going out as it dropped, and when I had lit another the little monster had disappeared.

'I do not know how long I sat peering down that well. It was not for some time that I could succeed in persuading myself that the thing I had seen was human. But, gradually, the truth dawned on me: that Man had not remained one species, but had differentiated into two distinct animals: that my graceful children of the Upper-world were not the sole descendants of our generation, but that this bleached, obscene, nocturnal Thing, which had flashed before me, was also heir to all the ages.

'I thought of the flickering pillars and of my theory of an underground ventilation. I began to suspect their true import. And what, I wondered, was this Lemur doing in my scheme of a perfectly balanced organization? How was it related to the indolent serenity of the beautiful Upper-worlders? And what was hidden down there, at the foot of that shaft? I sat upon the edge of the well telling myself that, at any rate, there was nothing to fear, and that there I must descend for the solution of my difficulties. And withal I was absolutely afraid to go! As I hesitated, two of the beautiful Upper-world people came running in their amorous sport across the daylight in the shadow. The male pursued the female, flinging flowers at her as he ran.

'They seemed distressed to find me, my arm against the overturned pillar, peering down the well. Apparently it was considered bad form to remark these apertures; for when I pointed to this one, and tried to frame a question about it in their tongue, they were still more visibly distressed and turned away. But they were interested by my matches, and I struck some to amuse them. I tried them again about the well, and again I failed. So presently I left them, meaning to go back to Weena, and see what I could get from her. But my mind was already in revolution; my guesses and impressions were slipping and sliding to a new adjustment. I had now a clue to the import of these wells, to the ventilating towers, to the mystery of the ghosts; to say nothing of a hint at the meaning of the bronze gates and the fate of the Time Machine! And very vaguely there came a suggestion towards the solution of the economic problem that had puzzled me.

'Here was the new view. Plainly, this second species of Man was subterranean. There were three circumstances in particular which made me think that its rare emergence above ground was the outcome of a long-continued underground habit. In the first place, there was the bleached look common in most animals that live largely in the dark—the white fish of the Kentucky caves, for instance. Then, those large eyes, with that capacity for reflecting light, are common features of nocturnal things—witness the owl and the cat. And last of all, that evident confusion in the sunshine, that hasty yet fumbling awkward flight towards dark shadow, and that peculiar carriage of the head while in the light—all reinforced the theory of an extreme sensitiveness of the retina.

'Beneath my feet, then, the earth must be tunnelled enormously, and these tunnellings were the habitat of the new race. The presence of ventilating shafts and wells along the hill slopes—everywhere, in fact, except along the river valley—showed how universal were its ramifications. What so natural, then, as to assume that it was in this artificial Underworld that such work as was necessary to the comfort of the daylight race was done? The notion was so plausible that I at once accepted it, and went on to assume the *how* of this splitting of the human species. I dare say you will anticipate the shape of my theory; though, for myself, I very soon felt that it fell far short of the truth.

'At first, proceeding from the problems of our own age, it seemed clear as daylight to me that the gradual widening of the present merely temporary and social difference between the Capitalist and the Labourer, was the key to the whole position. No doubt it will seem grotesque enough to you—and wildly incredible!—and yet even now there are existing circumstances to point that way. There is a tendency to utilize underground space for the less ornamental purposes of civilization; there is the Metropolitan Railway in London, for instance, there are new electric railways, there are subways, there are underground workrooms and restaurants, and they increase and multiply. Evidently, I thought, this tendency had increased till Industry had gradually lost its birthright in the sky. I mean that it had gone deeper and deeper into larger and ever larger underground factories, spending a still-increasing amount of its time therein, till, in the end—! Even now, does not an East-end worker live in such artificial conditions as practically to be cut off from the natural surface of the earth?

'Again, the exclusive tendency of richer people—due, no doubt, to the increasing refinement of their education, and the widening gulf between them and the rude violence of the poor—is already leading to the closing, in their interest, of considerable portions of the surface of the land. About London, for instance, perhaps half the prettier country is shut in against intrusion. And this same widening gulf—which is due to the length and expense of the higher educational process and the increased facilities for and temptations towards refined habits on the part of the rich —will make that exchange between class and class, that promotion by intermarriage which at present retards the splitting of our species along lines of social stratification, less and less frequent. So, in the end, above ground you must have the Haves, pursuing pleasure and comfort and beauty, and below ground the

Have-nots, the Workers getting continually adapted to the conditions of their labour. Once they were there, they would no doubt have to pay rent, and not a little of it, for the ventilation of their caverns; and if they refused, they would starve or be suffocated for arrears. Such of them as were so constituted as to be miserable and rebellious would die; and, in the end, the balance being permanent, the survivors would become as well adapted to the conditions of underground life, and as happy in their way, as the Upper-world people were to theirs. As it seemed to me, the refined beauty and the etiolated pallor followed naturally enough.

'The great triumph of Humanity I had dreamed of took a different shape in my mind. It had been no such triumph of moral education and general co- operation as I had imagined. Instead, I saw a real aristocracy, armed with a perfected science and working to a logical conclusion the industrial system of to-day. Its triumph had not been simply a triumph over Nature, but a triumph over Nature and the fellow-man. This, I must warn you, was my theory at the time. I had no convenient cicerone in the pattern of the Utopian books. My explanation may be absolutely wrong. I still think it is the most plausible one. But even on this supposition the balanced civilization that was at last attained must have long since passed its zenith, and was now far fallen into decay. The too-perfect security of the Upper-worlders had led them to a slow movement of degeneration, to a general dwindling in size, strength, and intelligence. That I could see clearly enough already. What had happened to the Under-grounders I did not yet suspect; but from what I had seen of the Morlocks —that, by the by, was the name by which these creatures were called —I could imagine that the modification of the human type was even far more profound than among the "Eloi," the beautiful race that I already knew.

'Then came troublesome doubts. Why had the Morlocks taken my Time Machine? For I felt sure it was they who had taken it. Why, too, if the Eloi were masters, could they not restore the machine to me? And why were they so terribly afraid of the dark? I proceeded, as I have said, to question Weena about this Under-world, but here again I was disappointed. At first she would not understand my questions, and presently she refused to answer them. She shivered as though the topic was unendurable. And when I pressed her, perhaps a little harshly, she burst into tears. They were the only tears, except my own, I ever saw in that Golden Age. When I saw them I ceased abruptly to trouble about the Morlocks, and was only concerned in banishing these signs of the human inheritance from Weena's eyes. And very soon she was smiling and clapping her hands, while I solemnly burned a match.

VI

'It may seem odd to you, but it was two days before I could follow up the new-found clue in what was manifestly the proper way. I felt a peculiar shrinking from those pallid bodies. They were just the half-bleached colour of the worms and things one sees preserved in spirit in a zoological museum. And they were filthily cold to the touch. Probably my shrinking was largely due to the sympathetic influence of the Eloi, whose disgust of the Morlocks I now began to appreciate.

'The next night I did not sleep well. Probably my health was a little disordered. I was oppressed with perplexity and doubt. Once or twice I had a feeling of intense fear for which I could perceive no definite reason. I remember creeping noiselessly into the great hall where the little people were sleeping in the moonlight—that night Weena was among them—and feeling reassured by their presence. It occurred to me even then, that in the course of a few days the moon must pass through its last quarter, and the nights grow dark, when the appearances of these unpleasant creatures from below, these whitened Lemurs, this new vermin that had replaced the old, might be more abundant. And on both these days I had the restless feeling of one who shirks an inevitable duty. I felt assured that the Time Machine was only to be recovered by boldly penetrating these underground mysteries. Yet I could not face the mystery. If only I had had a companion it would have been different. But I was so horribly alone, and even to clamber down into the darkness of the well appalled me. I don't know if you will understand my feeling, but I never felt quite safe at my back.

'It was this restlessness, this insecurity, perhaps, that drove me further and further afield in my exploring expeditions. Going to the south- westward towards the rising country that is now called Combe Wood, I observed far off, in the direction of nineteenth-century Banstead, a vast green structure, different in character from any I had hitherto seen. It was larger than the largest of the palaces or ruins I knew, and the facade had an Oriental look: the face of it having the lustre, as well as the pale-green tint, a kind of bluish-green, of a certain type of Chinese porcelain. This difference in aspect suggested a difference in use, and I was minded to push on and explore. But the day was growing late, and I had come upon the sight of the place after a long and tiring circuit; so I resolved to hold over the adventure for the following day, and I returned to the welcome and the caresses of little Weena. But next morning I perceived clearly enough that my curiosity regarding the Palace of Green Porcelain was a piece of self-deception, to enable me to shirk, by another day, an experience I dreaded. I resolved I would make the descent

without further waste of time, and started out in the early morning towards a well near the ruins of granite and aluminium.

'Little Weena ran with me. She danced beside me to the well, but when she saw me lean over the mouth and look downward, she seemed strangely disconcerted. "Good-bye, little Weena," I said, kissing her; and then putting her down, I began to feel over the parapet for the climbing hooks. Rather hastily, I may as well confess, for I feared my courage might leak away! At first she watched me in amazement. Then she gave a most piteous cry, and running to me, she began to pull at me with her little hands. I think her opposition nerved me rather to proceed. I shook her off, perhaps a little roughly, and in another moment I was in the throat of the well. I saw her agonized face over the parapet, and smiled to reassure her. Then I had to look down at the unstable hooks to which I clung.

'I had to clamber down a shaft of perhaps two hundred yards. The descent was effected by means of metallic bars projecting from the sides of the well, and these being adapted to the needs of a creature much smaller and lighter than myself, I was speedily cramped and fatigued by the descent. And not simply fatigued! One of the bars bent suddenly under my weight, and almost swung me off into the blackness beneath. For a moment I hung by one hand, and after that experience I did not dare to rest again. Though my arms and back were presently acutely painful, I went on clambering down the sheer descent with as quick a motion as possible. Glancing upward, I saw the aperture, a small blue disk, in which a star was visible, while little Weena's head showed as a round black projection. The thudding sound of a machine below grew louder and more oppressive. Everything save that little disk above was profoundly dark, and when I looked up again Weena had disappeared.

'I was in an agony of discomfort. I had some thought of trying to go up the shaft again, and leave the Under-world alone. But even while I turned this over in my mind I continued to descend. At last, with intense relief, I saw dimly coming up, a foot to the right of me, a slender loophole in the wall. Swinging myself in, I found it was the aperture of a narrow horizontal tunnel in which I could lie down and rest. It was not too soon. My arms ached, my back was cramped, and I was trembling with the prolonged terror of a fall. Besides this, the unbroken darkness had had a distressing effect upon my eyes. The air was full of the throb and hum of machinery pumping air down the shaft.

'I do not know how long I lay. I was roused by a soft hand touching my face. Starting up in the darkness I snatched at my matches and, hastily striking one, I saw three stooping white creatures similar to the one I had seen above ground in the ruin, hastily retreating before the light. Living, as they did, in what appeared to me impenetrable darkness, their eyes were abnormally large and sensitive, just as are the pupils of the abysmal fishes, and they reflected the light in the same way. I have no doubt they could see me in that rayless obscurity, and they did not seem to have any fear of me apart from the light. But, so soon as I struck a match in order to see them, they fled incontinently, vanishing into dark gutters and tunnels, from which their eyes glared at me in the strangest fashion.

'I tried to call to them, but the language they had was apparently different from that of the Over-world people; so that I was needs left to my own unaided efforts, and the thought of flight before exploration was even then in my mind. But I said to myself, "You are in for it now," and, feeling my way along the tunnel, I found the noise of machinery grow louder. Presently the walls fell away from me, and I came to a large open space, and striking another match, saw that I had entered a vast arched cavern, which stretched into utter darkness beyond the range of my light. The view I had of it was as much as one could see in the burning of a match.

'Necessarily my memory is vague. Great shapes like big machines rose out of the dimness, and cast grotesque black shadows, in which dim spectral Morlocks sheltered from the glare. The place, by the by, was very stuffy and oppressive, and the faint halitus of freshly shed blood was in the air. Some way down the central vista was a little table of white metal, laid with what seemed a meal. The Morlocks at any rate were carnivorous! Even at the time, I remember wondering what large animal could have survived to furnish the red joint I saw. It was all very indistinct: the heavy smell, the big unmeaning shapes, the obscene figures lurking in the shadows, and only waiting for the darkness to come at me again! Then the match burned down, and stung my fingers, and fell, a wriggling red spot in the blackness.

'I have thought since how particularly ill-equipped I was for such an experience. When I had started with the Time Machine, I had started with the absurd assumption that the men of the Future would certainly be infinitely ahead of ourselves in all their appliances. I had come without arms, without medicine, without anything to smoke—at times I missed tobacco frightfully—even without enough matches. If only I had thought of a Kodak! I could have flashed that glimpse of the Underworld in a second, and examined it at leisure. But, as it was, I stood there with only the weapons and the powers that Nature had endowed me with—hands, feet, and teeth; these, and four safety-matches that still remained to me.

'I was afraid to push my way in among all this machinery in the dark, and it was only with my last glimpse of light I discovered that my store of matches had run low. It had never occurred to me until that moment that there was any need to economize them, and I had wasted almost half the box in astonishing the Upper-worlders, to whom fire was a novelty. Now, as I say, I had four left, and while I stood in the dark, a hand touched mine, lank fingers came feeling over my face, and I was sensible of a peculiar unpleasant odour. I fancied I heard the breathing of a crowd of those dreadful little beings about me. I felt the box of matches in my hand being gently disengaged, and other hands behind me plucking at my clothing. The sense of these unseen creatures examining me was indescribably unpleasant. The sudden realization of my ignorance of their ways of thinking and doing came home to me very vividly in the darkness. I shouted at them as loudly as I could. They started away, and then I could feel them approaching me again. They clutched at me more boldly, whispering odd sounds to each other. I shivered violently, and shouted again—rather discordantly. This time they were not so seriously alarmed, and they made a queer laughing noise as they came back at me. I

will confess I was horribly frightened. I determined to strike another match and escape under the protection of its glare. I did so, and eking out the flicker with a scrap of paper from my pocket, I made good my retreat to the narrow tunnel. But I had scarce entered this when my light was blown out and in the blackness I could hear the Morlocks rustling like wind among leaves, and pattering like the rain, as they hurried after me.

'In a moment I was clutched by several hands, and there was no mistaking that they were trying to haul me back. I struck another light, and waved it in their dazzled faces. You can scarce imagine how nauseatingly inhuman they looked—those pale, chinless faces and great, lidless, pinkish-grey eyes!—as they stared in their blindness and bewilderment. But I did not stay to look, I promise you: I retreated again, and when my second match had ended, I struck my third. It had almost burned through when I reached the opening into the shaft. I lay down on the edge, for the throb of the great pump below made me giddy. Then I felt sideways for the projecting hooks, and, as I did so, my feet were grasped from behind, and I was violently tugged backward. I lit my last match ... and it incontinently went out. But I had my hand on the climbing bars now, and, kicking violently, I disengaged myself from the clutches of the Morlocks and was speedily clambering up the shaft, while they stayed peering and blinking up at me: all but one little wretch who followed me for some way, and well-nigh secured my boot as a trophy.

'That climb seemed interminable to me. With the last twenty or thirty feet of it a deadly nausea came upon me. I had the greatest difficulty in keeping my hold. The last few yards was a frightful struggle against this faintness. Several times my head swam, and I felt all the sensations of falling. At last, however, I got over the well-mouth somehow, and staggered out of the ruin into the blinding sunlight. I fell upon my face. Even the soil smelt sweet and clean. Then I remember Weena kissing my hands and ears, and the voices of others among the Eloi. Then, for a time, I was insensible.

VII

'Now, indeed, I seemed in a worse case than before. Hitherto, except during my night's anguish at the loss of the Time Machine, I had felt a sustaining hope of ultimate escape, but that hope was staggered by these new discoveries. Hitherto I had merely thought myself impeded by the childish simplicity of the little people, and by some unknown forces which I had only to understand to overcome; but there was an altogether new element in the sickening quality of the Morlocks—a something inhuman and malign. Instinctively I loathed them. Before, I had felt as a man might feel who had fallen into a pit: my concern was with the pit and how to get out of it. Now I felt like a beast in a trap, whose enemy would come upon him soon.

'The enemy I dreaded may surprise you. It was the darkness of the new moon. Weena had put this into my head by some at first incomprehensible remarks about the Dark Nights. It was not now such a very difficult problem to guess what the coming Dark Nights might mean. The moon was on the wane: each night there was a longer interval of darkness. And I now understood to some slight degree at least the reason of the fear of the little Upper-world people for the dark. I wondered vaguely what foul villainy it might be that the Morlocks did under the new moon. I felt pretty sure now that my second hypothesis was all wrong. The Upper-world people might once have been the favoured aristocracy, and the Morlocks their mechanical servants: but that had long since passed away. The two species that had resulted from the evolution of man were sliding down towards, or had already arrived at, an altogether new relationship. The Eloi, like the Carolingian kings, had decayed to a mere beautiful futility. They still possessed the earth on sufferance: since the Morlocks, subterranean for innumerable generations, had come at last to find the daylit surface intolerable. And the Morlocks made their garments, I inferred, and maintained them in their habitual needs, perhaps through the survival of an old habit of service. They did it as a standing horse paws with his foot, or as a man enjoys killing animals in sport: because ancient and departed necessities had impressed it on the organism. But, clearly, the old order was already in part reversed. The Nemesis of the delicate ones was creeping on apace. Ages ago, thousands of generations ago, man had thrust his brother man out of the ease and the sunshine. And now that brother was coming back changed! Already the Eloi had begun to learn one old lesson anew. They were becoming reacquainted with Fear. And suddenly there came into my head the memory of the meat I had seen in the Under-world. It seemed odd how it floated into my mind: not

stirred up as it were by the current of my meditations, but coming in almost like a question from outside. I tried to recall the form of it. I had a vague sense of something familiar, but I could not tell what it was at the time.

'Still, however helpless the little people in the presence of their mysterious Fear, I was differently constituted. I came out of this age of ours, this ripe prime of the human race, when Fear does not paralyse and mystery has lost its terrors. I at least would defend myself. Without further delay I determined to make myself arms and a fastness where I might sleep. With that refuge as a base, I could face this strange world with some of that confidence I had lost in realizing to what creatures night by night I lay exposed. I felt I could never sleep again until my bed was secure from them. I shuddered with horror to think how they must already have examined me.

'I wandered during the afternoon along the valley of the Thames, but found nothing that commended itself to my mind as inaccessible. All the buildings and trees seemed easily practicable to such dexterous climbers as the Morlocks, to judge by their wells, must be. Then the tall pinnacles of the Palace of Green Porcelain and the polished gleam of its walls came back to my memory; and in the evening, taking Weena like a child upon my shoulder, I went up the hills towards the south-west. The distance, I had reckoned, was seven or eight miles, but it must have been nearer eighteen. I had first seen the place on a moist afternoon when distances are deceptively diminished. In addition, the heel of one of my shoes was loose, and a nail was working through the sole —they were comfortable old shoes I wore about indoors—so that I was lame. And it was already long past sunset when I came in sight of the palace, silhouetted black against the pale yellow of the sky.

'Weena had been hugely delighted when I began to carry her, but after a while she desired me to let her down, and ran along by the side of me, occasionally darting off on either hand to pick flowers to stick in my pockets. My pockets had always puzzled Weena, but at the last she had concluded that they were an eccentric kind of vase for floral decoration. At least she utilized them for that purpose. And that reminds me! In changing my jacket I found...'

The Time Traveller paused, put his hand into his pocket, and silently placed two withered flowers, not unlike very large white mallows, upon the little table. Then he resumed his narrative.

'As the hush of evening crept over the world and we proceeded over the hill crest towards Wimbledon, Weena grew tired and wanted to return to the house of grey stone. But I pointed out the distant pinnacles of the Palace of Green Porcelain to her, and contrived to make her understand that we were seeking a refuge there from her Fear. You know that great pause that comes upon things before the dusk? Even the breeze stops in the trees. To me there is always an air of expectation about that evening stillness. The sky was clear, remote, and empty save for a few horizontal bars far down in the sunset. Well, that night the expectation took the colour of my fears. In that darkling calm my senses seemed preternaturally sharpened. I fancied I could even feel the hollowness of the ground beneath my

feet: could, indeed, almost see through it the Morlocks on their ant-hill going hither and thither and waiting for the dark. In my excitement I fancied that they would receive my invasion of their burrows as a declaration of war. And why had they taken my Time Machine?

'So we went on in the quiet, and the twilight deepened into night. The clear blue of the distance faded, and one star after another came out. The ground grew dim and the trees black. Weena's fears and her fatigue grew upon her. I took her in my arms and talked to her and caressed her. Then, as the darkness grew deeper, she put her arms round my neck, and, closing her eyes, tightly pressed her face against my shoulder. So we went down a long slope into a valley, and there in the dimness I almost walked into a little river. This I waded, and went up the opposite side of the valley, past a number of sleeping houses, and by a statue—a Faun, or some such figure, *minus* the head. Here too were acacias. So far I had seen nothing of the Morlocks, but it was yet early in the night, and the darker hours before the old moon rose were still to come.

'From the brow of the next hill I saw a thick wood spreading wide and black before me. I hesitated at this. I could see no end to it, either to the right or the left. Feeling tired—my feet, in particular, were very sore —I carefully lowered Weena from my shoulder as I halted, and sat down upon the turf. I could no longer see the Palace of Green Porcelain, and I was in doubt of my direction. I looked into the thickness of the wood and thought of what it might hide. Under that dense tangle of branches one would be out of sight of the stars. Even were there no other lurking danger—a danger I did not care to let my imagination loose upon—there would still be all the roots to stumble over and the tree-boles to strike against.

'I was very tired, too, after the excitements of the day; so I decided that I would not face it, but would pass the night upon the open hill.

'Weena, I was glad to find, was fast asleep. I carefully wrapped her in my jacket, and sat down beside her to wait for the moonrise. The hill-side was quiet and deserted, but from the black of the wood there came now and then a stir of living things. Above me shone the stars, for the night was very clear. I felt a certain sense of friendly comfort in their twinkling. All the old constellations had gone from the sky, however: that slow movement which is imperceptible in a hundred human lifetimes, had long since rearranged them in unfamiliar groupings. But the Milky Way, it seemed to me, was still the same tattered streamer of star-dust as of yore. Southward (as I judged it) was a very bright red star that was new to me; it was even more splendid than our own green Sirius. And amid all these scintillating points of light one bright planet shone kindly and steadily like the face of an old friend.

'Looking at these stars suddenly dwarfed my own troubles and all the gravities of terrestrial life. I thought of their unfathomable distance, and the slow inevitable drift of their movements out of the unknown past into the unknown future. I thought of the great precessional cycle that the pole of the earth describes. Only forty times had that silent revolution occurred during all the years that I had traversed. And during these few revolutions all the activity, all the traditions, the

complex organizations, the nations, languages, literatures, aspirations, even the mere memory of Man as I knew him, had been swept out of existence. Instead were these frail creatures who had forgotten their high ancestry, and the white Things of which I went in terror. Then I thought of the Great Fear that was between the two species, and for the first time, with a sudden shiver, came the clear knowledge of what the meat I had seen might be. Yet it was too horrible! I looked at little Weena sleeping beside me, her face white and starlike under the stars, and forthwith dismissed the thought.

'Through that long night I held my mind off the Morlocks as well as I could, and whiled away the time by trying to fancy I could find signs of the old constellations in the new confusion. The sky kept very clear, except for a hazy cloud or so. No doubt I dozed at times. Then, as my vigil wore on, came a faintness in the eastward sky, like the reflection of some colourless fire, and the old moon rose, thin and peaked and white. And close behind, and overtaking it, and overflowing it, the dawn came, pale at first, and then growing pink and warm. No Morlocks had approached us. Indeed, I had seen none upon the hill that night. And in the confidence of renewed day it almost seemed to me that my fear had been unreasonable. I stood up and found my foot with the loose heel swollen at the ankle and painful under the heel; so I sat down again, took off my shoes, and flung them away.

'I awakened Weena, and we went down into the wood, now green and pleasant instead of black and forbidding. We found some fruit wherewith to break our fast. We soon met others of the dainty ones, laughing and dancing in the sunlight as though there was no such thing in nature as the night. And then I thought once more of the meat that I had seen. I felt assured now of what it was, and from the bottom of my heart I pitied this last feeble rill from the great flood of humanity. Clearly, at some time in the Long-Ago of human decay the Morlocks' food had run short. Possibly they had lived on rats and such-like vermin. Even now man is far less discriminating and exclusive in his food than he was—far less than any monkey. His prejudice against human flesh is no deep-seated instinct. And so these inhuman sons of men—! I tried to look at the thing in a scientific spirit. After all, they were less human and more remote than our cannibal ancestors of three or four thousand years ago. And the intelligence that would have made this state of things a torment had gone. Why should I trouble myself? These Eloi were mere fatted cattle, which the ant-like Morlocks preserved and preyed upon—probably saw to the breeding of. And there was Weena dancing at my side!

'Then I tried to preserve myself from the horror that was coming upon me, by regarding it as a rigorous punishment of human selfishness. Man had been content to live in ease and delight upon the labours of his fellow-man, had taken Necessity as his watchword and excuse, and in the fullness of time Necessity had come home to him. I even tried a Carlyle-like scorn of this wretched aristocracy in decay. But this attitude of mind was impossible. However great their intellectual degradation, the Eloi had kept too much of the human form not to claim my sympathy, and to make me perforce a sharer in their degradation and their Fear.

'I had at that time very vague ideas as to the course I should pursue. My first was to secure some safe place of refuge, and to make myself such arms of metal or stone as I could contrive. That necessity was immediate. In the next place, I hoped to procure some means of fire, so that I should have the weapon of a torch at hand, for nothing, I knew, would be more efficient against these Morlocks. Then I wanted to arrange some contrivance to break open the doors of bronze under the White Sphinx. I had in mind a battering ram. I had a persuasion that if I could enter those doors and carry a blaze of light before me I should discover the Time Machine and escape. I could not imagine the Morlocks were strong enough to move it far away. Weena I had resolved to bring with me to our own time. And turning such schemes over in my mind I pursued our way towards the building which my fancy had chosen as our dwelling.

VIII

'I found the Palace of Green Porcelain, when we approached it about noon, deserted and falling into ruin. Only ragged vestiges of glass remained in its windows, and great sheets of the green facing had fallen away from the corroded metallic framework. It lay very high upon a turfy down, and looking north- eastward before I entered it, I was surprised to see a large estuary, or even creek, where I judged Wandsworth and Battersea must once have been. I thought then—though I never followed up the thought—of what might have happened, or might be happening, to the living things in the sea.

'The material of the Palace proved on examination to be indeed porcelain, and along the face of it I saw an inscription in some unknown character. I thought, rather foolishly, that Weena might help me to interpret this, but I only learned that the bare idea of writing had never entered her head. She always seemed to me, I fancy, more human than she was, perhaps because her affection was so human.

'Within the big valves of the door—which were open and broken —we found, instead of the customary hall, a long gallery lit by many side windows. At the first glance I was reminded of a museum. The tiled floor was thick with dust, and a remarkable array of miscellaneous objects was shrouded in the same grey covering. Then I perceived, standing strange and gaunt in the centre of the hall, what was clearly the lower part of a huge skeleton. I recognized by the oblique feet that it was some extinct creature after the fashion of the Megatherium. The skull and the upper bones lay beside it in the thick dust, and in one place, where rain-water had dropped through a leak in the roof, the thing itself had been worn away. Further in the gallery was the huge skeleton barrel of a Brontosaurus. My museum hypothesis was confirmed. Going towards the side I found what appeared to be sloping shelves, and clearing away the thick dust, I found the old familiar glass cases of our own time. But they must have been air-tight to judge from the fair preservation of some of their contents.

'Clearly we stood among the ruins of some latter-day South Kensington! Here, apparently, was the Palaeontological Section, and a very splendid array of fossils it must have been, though the inevitable process of decay that had been staved off for a time, and had, through the extinction of bacteria and fungi, lost ninety-nine hundredths of its force, was nevertheless, with extreme sureness if with extreme slowness at work again upon all its treasures. Here and there I found traces of the little people in the shape of rare fossils broken to pieces or threaded in strings upon reeds. And the cases had in some instances been bodily removed—by the

Morlocks as I judged. The place was very silent. The thick dust deadened our footsteps. Weena, who had been rolling a sea urchin down the sloping glass of a case, presently came, as I stared about me, and very quietly took my hand and stood beside me.

'And at first I was so much surprised by this ancient monument of an intellectual age, that I gave no thought to the possibilities it presented. Even my preoccupation about the Time Machine receded a little from my mind.

'To judge from the size of the place, this Palace of Green Porcelain had a great deal more in it than a Gallery of Palaeontology; possibly historical galleries; it might be, even a library! To me, at least in my present circumstances, these would be vastly more interesting than this spectacle of oldtime geology in decay. Exploring, I found another short gallery running transversely to the first. This appeared to be devoted to minerals, and the sight of a block of sulphur set my mind running on gunpowder. But I could find no saltpeter; indeed, no nitrates of any kind. Doubtless they had deliquesced ages ago. Yet the sulphur hung in my mind, and set up a train of thinking. As for the rest of the contents of that gallery, though on the whole they were the best preserved of all I saw, I had little interest. I am no specialist in mineralogy, and I went on down a very ruinous aisle running parallel to the first hall I had entered. Apparently this section had been devoted to natural history, but everything had long since passed out of recognition. A few shrivelled and blackened vestiges of what had once been stuffed animals, desiccated mummies in jars that had once held spirit, a brown dust of departed plants: that was all! I was sorry for that, because I should have been glad to trace the patent readjustments by which the conquest of animated nature had been attained. Then we came to a gallery of simply colossal proportions, but singularly ill-lit, the floor of it running downward at a slight angle from the end at which I entered. At intervals white globes hung from the ceiling—many of them cracked and smashed—which suggested that originally the place had been artificially lit. Here I was more in my element, for rising on either side of me were the huge bulks of big machines, all greatly corroded and many broken down, but some still fairly complete. You know I have a certain weakness for mechanism, and I was inclined to linger among these; the more so as for the most part they had the interest of puzzles, and I could make only the vaguest guesses at what they were for. I fancied that if I could solve their puzzles I should find myself in possession of powers that might be of use against the Morlocks.

'Suddenly Weena came very close to my side. So suddenly that she startled me. Had it not been for her I do not think I should have noticed that the floor of the gallery sloped at all[1]. The end I had come in at was quite above ground, and was lit by rare slit- like windows. As you went down the length, the ground came up against these windows, until at last there was a pit like the "area" of a London house before each, and only a narrow line of daylight at the top. I went slowly

[1] It may be, of course, that the floor did not slope, but that the museum was built into the side of a hill.—ED.

along, puzzling about the machines, and had been too intent upon them to notice the gradual diminution of the light, until Weena's increasing apprehensions drew my attention. Then I saw that the gallery ran down at last into a thick darkness. I hesitated, and then, as I looked round me, I saw that the dust was less abundant and its surface less even. Further away towards the dimness, it appeared to be broken by a number of small narrow footprints. My sense of the immediate presence of the Morlocks revived at that. I felt that I was wasting my time in the academic examination of machinery. I called to mind that it was already far advanced in the afternoon, and that I had still no weapon, no refuge, and no means of making a fire. And then down in the remote blackness of the gallery I heard a peculiar pattering, and the same odd noises I had heard down the well.

'I took Weena's hand. Then, struck with a sudden idea, I left her and turned to a machine from which projected a lever not unlike those in a signal- box. Clambering upon the stand, and grasping this lever in my hands, I put all my weight upon it sideways. Suddenly Weena, deserted in the central aisle, began to whimper. I had judged the strength of the lever pretty correctly, for it snapped after a minute's strain, and I rejoined her with a mace in my hand more than sufficient, I judged, for any Morlock skull I might encounter. And I longed very much to kill a Morlock or so. Very inhuman, you may think, to want to go killing one's own descendants! But it was impossible, somehow, to feel any humanity in the things. Only my disinclination to leave Weena, and a persuasion that if I began to slake my thirst for murder my Time Machine might suffer, restrained me from going straight down the gallery and killing the brutes I heard.

'Well, mace in one hand and Weena in the other, I went out of that gallery and into another and still larger one, which at the first glance reminded me of a military chapel hung with tattered flags. The brown and charred rags that hung from the sides of it, I presently recognized as the decaying vestiges of books. They had long since dropped to pieces, and every semblance of print had left them. But here and there were warped boards and cracked metallic clasps that told the tale well enough. Had I been a literary man I might, perhaps, have moralized upon the futility of all ambition. But as it was, the thing that struck me with keenest force was the enormous waste of labour to which this sombre wilderness of rotting paper testified. At the time I will confess that I thought chiefly of the *Philosophical Transactions* and my own seventeen papers upon physical optics.

'Then, going up a broad staircase, we came to what may once have been a gallery of technical chemistry. And here I had not a little hope of useful discoveries. Except at one end where the roof had collapsed, this gallery was well preserved. I went eagerly to every unbroken case. And at last, in one of the really air-tight cases, I found a box of matches. Very eagerly I tried them. They were perfectly good. They were not even damp. I turned to Weena. "Dance," I cried to her in her own tongue. For now I had a weapon indeed against the horrible creatures we feared. And so, in that derelict museum, upon the thick soft carpeting of dust, to Weena's huge delight, I solemnly performed a kind of composite dance, whistling *The Land of the Leal* as cheerfully as I could. In part it was a modest *cancan*, in part a

step dance, in part a skirt-dance (so far as my tail-coat permitted), and in part original. For I am naturally inventive, as you know.

'Now, I still think that for this box of matches to have escaped the wear of time for immemorial years was a most strange, as for me it was a most fortunate thing. Yet, oddly enough, I found a far unlikelier substance, and that was camphor. I found it in a sealed jar, that by chance, I suppose, had been really hermetically sealed. I fancied at first that it was paraffin wax, and smashed the glass accordingly. But the odour of camphor was unmistakable. In the universal decay this volatile substance had chanced to survive, perhaps through many thousands of centuries. It reminded me of a sepia painting I had once seen done from the ink of a fossil Belemnite that must have perished and become fossilized millions of years ago. I was about to throw it away, but I remembered that it was inflammable and burned with a good bright flame—was, in fact, an excellent candle—and I put it in my pocket. I found no explosives, however, nor any means of breaking down the bronze doors. As yet my iron crowbar was the most helpful thing I had chanced upon. Nevertheless I left that gallery greatly elated.

'I cannot tell you all the story of that long afternoon. It would require a great effort of memory to recall my explorations in at all the proper order. I remember a long gallery of rusting stands of arms, and how I hesitated between my crowbar and a hatchet or a sword. I could not carry both, however, and my bar of iron promised best against the bronze gates. There were numbers of guns, pistols, and rifles. The most were masses of rust, but many were of some new metal, and still fairly sound. But any cartridges or powder there may once have been had rotted into dust. One corner I saw was charred and shattered; perhaps, I thought, by an explosion among the specimens. In another place was a vast array of idols—Polynesian, Mexican, Grecian, Phoenician, every country on earth I should think. And here, yielding to an irresistible impulse, I wrote my name upon the nose of a steatite monster from South America that particularly took my fancy.

'As the evening drew on, my interest waned. I went through gallery after gallery, dusty, silent, often ruinous, the exhibits sometimes mere heaps of rust and lignite, sometimes fresher. In one place I suddenly found myself near the model of a tin-mine, and then by the merest accident I discovered, in an air-tight case, two dynamite cartridges! I shouted "Eureka!" and smashed the case with joy. Then came a doubt. I hesitated. Then, selecting a little side gallery, I made my essay. I never felt such a disappointment as I did in waiting five, ten, fifteen minutes for an explosion that never came. Of course the things were dummies, as I might have guessed from their presence. I really believe that had they not been so, I should have rushed off incontinently and blown Sphinx, bronze doors, and (as it proved) my chances of finding the Time Machine, all together into non-existence.

'It was after that, I think, that we came to a little open court within the palace. It was turfed, and had three fruit-trees. So we rested and refreshed ourselves. Towards sunset I began to consider our position. Night was creeping upon us, and my inaccessible hiding-place had still to be found. But that troubled me very little

now. I had in my possession a thing that was, perhaps, the best of all defences against the Morlocks—I had matches! I had the camphor in my pocket, too, if a blaze were needed. It seemed to me that the best thing we could do would be to pass the night in the open, protected by a fire. In the morning there was the getting of the Time Machine. Towards that, as yet, I had only my iron mace. But now, with my growing knowledge, I felt very differently towards those bronze doors. Up to this, I had refrained from forcing them, largely because of the mystery on the other side. They had never impressed me as being very strong, and I hoped to find my bar of iron not altogether inadequate for the work.

IX

'We emerged from the palace while the sun was still in part above the horizon. I was determined to reach the White Sphinx early the next morning, and ere the dusk I purposed pushing through the woods that had stopped me on the previous journey. My plan was to go as far as possible that night, and then, building a fire, to sleep in the protection of its glare. Accordingly, as we went along I gathered any sticks or dried grass I saw, and presently had my arms full of such litter. Thus loaded, our progress was slower than I had anticipated, and besides Weena was tired. And I began to suffer from sleepiness too; so that it was full night before we reached the wood. Upon the shrubby hill of its edge Weena would have stopped, fearing the darkness before us; but a singular sense of impending calamity, that should indeed have served me as a warning, drove me onward. I had been without sleep for a night and two days, and I was feverish and irritable. I felt sleep coming upon me, and the Morlocks with it.

'While we hesitated, among the black bushes behind us, and dim against their blackness, I saw three crouching figures. There was scrub and long grass all about us, and I did not feel safe from their insidious approach. The forest, I calculated, was rather less than a mile across. If we could get through it to the bare hill-side, there, as it seemed to me, was an altogether safer resting-place; I thought that with my matches and my camphor I could contrive to keep my path illuminated through the woods. Yet it was evident that if I was to flourish matches with my hands I should have to abandon my firewood; so, rather reluctantly, I put it down. And then it came into my head that I would amaze our friends behind by lighting it. I was to discover the atrocious folly of this proceeding, but it came to my mind as an ingenious move for covering our retreat.

'I don't know if you have ever thought what a rare thing flame must be in the absence of man and in a temperate climate. The sun's heat is rarely strong enough to burn, even when it is focused by dewdrops, as is sometimes the case in more tropical districts. Lightning may blast and blacken, but it rarely gives rise to wide-spread fire. Decaying vegetation may occasionally smoulder with the heat of its fermentation, but this rarely results in flame. In this decadence, too, the art of fire-making had been forgotten on the earth. The red tongues that went licking up my heap of wood were an altogether new and strange thing to Weena.

'She wanted to run to it and play with it. I believe she would have cast herself into it had I not restrained her. But I caught her up, and in spite of her struggles, plunged boldly before me into the wood. For a little way the glare of my fire lit

the path. Looking back presently, I could see, through the crowded stems, that from my heap of sticks the blaze had spread to some bushes adjacent, and a curved line of fire was creeping up the grass of the hill. I laughed at that, and turned again to the dark trees before me. It was very black, and Weena clung to me convulsively, but there was still, as my eyes grew accustomed to the darkness, sufficient light for me to avoid the stems. Overhead it was simply black, except where a gap of remote blue sky shone down upon us here and there. I struck none of my matches because I had no hand free. Upon my left arm I carried my little one, in my right hand I had my iron bar.

'For some way I heard nothing but the crackling twigs under my feet, the faint rustle of the breeze above, and my own breathing and the throb of the blood-vessels in my ears. Then I seemed to know of a pattering about me. I pushed on grimly. The pattering grew more distinct, and then I caught the same queer sound and voices I had heard in the Under-world. There were evidently several of the Morlocks, and they were closing in upon me. Indeed, in another minute I felt a tug at my coat, then something at my arm. And Weena shivered violently, and became quite still.

'It was time for a match. But to get one I must put her down. I did so, and, as I fumbled with my pocket, a struggle began in the darkness about my knees, perfectly silent on her part and with the same peculiar cooing sounds from the Morlocks. Soft little hands, too, were creeping over my coat and back, touching even my neck. Then the match scratched and fizzed. I held it flaring, and saw the white backs of the Morlocks in flight amid the trees. I hastily took a lump of camphor from my pocket, and prepared to light it as soon as the match should wane. Then I looked at Weena. She was lying clutching my feet and quite motionless, with her face to the ground. With a sudden fright I stooped to her. She seemed scarcely to breathe. I lit the block of camphor and flung it to the ground, and as it split and flared up and drove back the Morlocks and the shadows, I knelt down and lifted her. The wood behind seemed full of the stir and murmur of a great company!

'She seemed to have fainted. I put her carefully upon my shoulder and rose to push on, and then there came a horrible realization. In manoeuvring with my matches and Weena, I had turned myself about several times, and now I had not the faintest idea in what direction lay my path. For all I knew, I might be facing back towards the Palace of Green Porcelain. I found myself in a cold sweat. I had to think rapidly what to do. I determined to build a fire and encamp where we were. I put Weena, still motionless, down upon a turfy bole, and very hastily, as my first lump of camphor waned, I began collecting sticks and leaves. Here and there out of the darkness round me the Morlocks' eyes shone like carbuncles.

'The camphor flickered and went out. I lit a match, and as I did so, two white forms that had been approaching Weena dashed hastily away. One was so blinded by the light that he came straight for me, and I felt his bones grind under the blow of my fist. He gave a whoop of dismay, staggered a little way, and fell down. I lit another piece of camphor, and went on gathering my bonfire. Presently I noticed

how dry was some of the foliage above me, for since my arrival on the Time Machine, a matter of a week, no rain had fallen. So, instead of casting about among the trees for fallen twigs, I began leaping up and dragging down branches. Very soon I had a choking smoky fire of green wood and dry sticks, and could economize my camphor. Then I turned to where Weena lay beside my iron mace. I tried what I could to revive her, but she lay like one dead. I could not even satisfy myself whether or not she breathed.

'Now, the smoke of the fire beat over towards me, and it must have made me heavy of a sudden. Moreover, the vapour of camphor was in the air. My fire would not need replenishing for an hour or so. I felt very weary after my exertion, and sat down. The wood, too, was full of a slumbrous murmur that I did not understand. I seemed just to nod and open my eyes. But all was dark, and the Morlocks had their hands upon me. Flinging off their clinging fingers I hastily felt in my pocket for the match-box, and—it had gone! Then they gripped and closed with me again. In a moment I knew what had happened. I had slept, and my fire had gone out, and the bitterness of death came over my soul. The forest seemed full of the smell of burning wood. I was caught by the neck, by the hair, by the arms, and pulled down. It was indescribably horrible in the darkness to feel all these soft creatures heaped upon me. I felt as if I was in a monstrous spider's web. I was overpowered, and went down. I felt little teeth nipping at my neck. I rolled over, and as I did so my hand came against my iron lever. It gave me strength. I struggled up, shaking the human rats from me, and, holding the bar short, I thrust where I judged their faces might be. I could feel the succulent giving of flesh and bone under my blows, and for a moment I was free.

'The strange exultation that so often seems to accompany hard fighting came upon me. I knew that both I and Weena were lost, but I determined to make the Morlocks pay for their meat. I stood with my back to a tree, swinging the iron bar before me. The whole wood was full of the stir and cries of them. A minute passed. Their voices seemed to rise to a higher pitch of excitement, and their movements grew faster. Yet none came within reach. I stood glaring at the blackness. Then suddenly came hope. What if the Morlocks were afraid? And close on the heels of that came a strange thing. The darkness seemed to grow luminous. Very dimly I began to see the Morlocks about me—three battered at my feet—and then I recognized, with incredulous surprise, that the others were running, in an incessant stream, as it seemed, from behind me, and away through the wood in front. And their backs seemed no longer white, but reddish. As I stood agape, I saw a little red spark go drifting across a gap of starlight between the branches, and vanish. And at that I understood the smell of burning wood, the slumbrous murmur that was growing now into a gusty roar, the red glow, and the Morlocks' flight.

'Stepping out from behind my tree and looking back, I saw, through the black pillars of the nearer trees, the flames of the burning forest. It was my first fire coming after me. With that I looked for Weena, but she was gone. The hissing and crackling behind me, the explosive thud as each fresh tree burst into flame,

left little time for reflection. My iron bar still gripped, I followed in the Morlocks' path. It was a close race. Once the flames crept forward so swiftly on my right as I ran that I was outflanked and had to strike off to the left. But at last I emerged upon a small open space, and as I did so, a Morlock came blundering towards me, and past me, and went on straight into the fire!

'And now I was to see the most weird and horrible thing, I think, of all that I beheld in that future age. This whole space was as bright as day with the reflection of the fire. In the centre was a hillock or tumulus, surmounted by a scorched hawthorn. Beyond this was another arm of the burning forest, with yellow tongues already writhing from it, completely encircling the space with a fence of fire. Upon the hill-side were some thirty or forty Morlocks, dazzled by the light and heat, and blundering hither and thither against each other in their bewilderment. At first I did not realize their blindness, and struck furiously at them with my bar, in a frenzy of fear, as they approached me, killing one and crippling several more. But when I had watched the gestures of one of them groping under the hawthorn against the red sky, and heard their moans, I was assured of their absolute helplessness and misery in the glare, and I struck no more of them.

'Yet every now and then one would come straight towards me, setting loose a quivering horror that made me quick to elude him. At one time the flames died down somewhat, and I feared the foul creatures would presently be able to see me. I was thinking of beginning the fight by killing some of them before this should happen; but the fire burst out again brightly, and I stayed my hand. I walked about the hill among them and avoided them, looking for some trace of Weena. But Weena was gone.

'At last I sat down on the summit of the hillock, and watched this strange incredible company of blind things groping to and fro, and making uncanny noises to each other, as the glare of the fire beat on them. The coiling uprush of smoke streamed across the sky, and through the rare tatters of that red canopy, remote as though they belonged to another universe, shone the little stars. Two or three Morlocks came blundering into me, and I drove them off with blows of my fists, trembling as I did so.

'For the most part of that night I was persuaded it was a nightmare. I bit myself and screamed in a passionate desire to awake. I beat the ground with my hands, and got up and sat down again, and wandered here and there, and again sat down. Then I would fall to rubbing my eyes and calling upon God to let me awake. Thrice I saw Morlocks put their heads down in a kind of agony and rush into the flames. But, at last, above the subsiding red of the fire, above the streaming masses of black smoke and the whitening and blackening tree stumps, and the diminishing numbers of these dim creatures, came the white light of the day.

'I searched again for traces of Weena, but there were none. It was plain that they had left her poor little body in the forest. I cannot describe how it relieved me to think that it had escaped the awful fate to which it seemed destined. As I thought of that, I was almost moved to begin a massacre of the helpless abominations about me, but I contained myself. The hillock, as I have said, was a kind of

island in the forest. From its summit I could now make out through a haze of smoke the Palace of Green Porcelain, and from that I could get my bearings for the White Sphinx. And so, leaving the remnant of these damned souls still going hither and thither and moaning, as the day grew clearer, I tied some grass about my feet and limped on across smoking ashes and among black stems, that still pulsated internally with fire, towards the hiding- place of the Time Machine. I walked slowly, for I was almost exhausted, as well as lame, and I felt the intensest wretchedness for the horrible death of little Weena. It seemed an overwhelming calamity. Now, in this old familiar room, it is more like the sorrow of a dream than an actual loss. But that morning it left me absolutely lonely again—terribly alone. I began to think of this house of mine, of this fireside, of some of you, and with such thoughts came a longing that was pain.

'But as I walked over the smoking ashes under the bright morning sky, I made a discovery. In my trouser pocket were still some loose matches. The box must have leaked before it was lost.

X

'About eight or nine in the morning I came to the same seat of yellow metal from which I had viewed the world upon the evening of my arrival. I thought of my hasty conclusions upon that evening and could not refrain from laughing bitterly at my confidence. Here was the same beautiful scene, the same abundant foliage, the same splendid palaces and magnificent ruins, the same silver river running between its fertile banks. The gay robes of the beautiful people moved hither and thither among the trees. Some were bathing in exactly the place where I had saved Weena, and that suddenly gave me a keen stab of pain. And like blots upon the landscape rose the cupolas above the ways to the Under-world. I understood now what all the beauty of the Over-world people covered. Very pleasant was their day, as pleasant as the day of the cattle in the field. Like the cattle, they knew of no enemies and provided against no needs. And their end was the same.

'I grieved to think how brief the dream of the human intellect had been. It had committed suicide. It had set itself steadfastly towards comfort and ease, a balanced society with security and permanency as its watchword, it had attained its hopes—to come to this at last. Once, life and property must have reached almost absolute safety. The rich had been assured of his wealth and comfort, the toiler assured of his life and work. No doubt in that perfect world there had been no unemployed problem, no social question left unsolved. And a great quiet had followed.

'It is a law of nature we overlook, that intellectual versatility is the compensation for change, danger, and trouble. An animal perfectly in harmony with its environment is a perfect mechanism. Nature never appeals to intelligence until habit and instinct are useless. There is no intelligence where there is no change and no need of change. Only those animals partake of intelligence that have to meet a huge variety of needs and dangers.

'So, as I see it, the Upper-world man had drifted towards his feeble prettiness, and the Under-world to mere mechanical industry. But that perfect state had lacked one thing even for mechanical perfection—absolute permanency. Apparently as time went on, the feeding of the Under-world, however it was effected, had become disjointed. Mother Necessity, who had been staved off for a few thousand years, came back again, and she began below. The Under- world being in contact with machinery, which, however perfect, still needs some little thought outside habit, had probably retained perforce rather more initiative, if less of every other human character, than the Upper. And when other meat failed them, they

turned to what old habit had hitherto forbidden. So I say I saw it in my last view of the world of Eight Hundred and Two Thousand Seven Hundred and One. It may be as wrong an explanation as mortal wit could invent. It is how the thing shaped itself to me, and as that I give it to you.

'After the fatigues, excitements, and terrors of the past days, and in spite of my grief, this seat and the tranquil view and the warm sunlight were very pleasant. I was very tired and sleepy, and soon my theorizing passed into dozing. Catching myself at that, I took my own hint, and spreading myself out upon the turf I had a long and refreshing sleep.

'I awoke a little before sunsetting. I now felt safe against being caught napping by the Morlocks, and, stretching myself, I came on down the hill towards the White Sphinx. I had my crowbar in one hand, and the other hand played with the matches in my pocket.

'And now came a most unexpected thing. As I approached the pedestal of the sphinx I found the bronze valves were open. They had slid down into grooves.

'At that I stopped short before them, hesitating to enter.

'Within was a small apartment, and on a raised place in the corner of this was the Time Machine. I had the small levers in my pocket. So here, after all my elaborate preparations for the siege of the White Sphinx, was a meek surrender. I threw my iron bar away, almost sorry not to use it.

'A sudden thought came into my head as I stooped towards the portal. For once, at least, I grasped the mental operations of the Morlocks. Suppressing a strong inclination to laugh, I stepped through the bronze frame and up to the Time Machine. I was surprised to find it had been carefully oiled and cleaned. I have suspected since that the Morlocks had even partially taken it to pieces while trying in their dim way to grasp its purpose.

'Now as I stood and examined it, finding a pleasure in the mere touch of the contrivance, the thing I had expected happened. The bronze panels suddenly slid up and struck the frame with a clang. I was in the dark—trapped. So the Morlocks thought. At that I chuckled gleefully.

'I could already hear their murmuring laughter as they came towards me. Very calmly I tried to strike the match. I had only to fix on the levers and depart then like a ghost. But I had overlooked one little thing. The matches were of that abominable kind that light only on the box.

'You may imagine how all my calm vanished. The little brutes were close upon me. One touched me. I made a sweeping blow in the dark at them with the levers, and began to scramble into the saddle of the machine. Then came one hand upon me and then another. Then I had simply to fight against their persistent fingers for my levers, and at the same time feel for the studs over which these fitted. One, indeed, they almost got away from me. As it slipped from my hand, I had to butt in the dark with my head—I could hear the Morlock's skull ring—to recover it. It was a nearer thing than the fight in the forest, I think, this last scramble.

'But at last the lever was fitted and pulled over. The clinging hands slipped from me. The darkness presently fell from my eyes. I found myself in the same grey light and tumult I have already described.

XI

'I have already told you of the sickness and confusion that comes with time travelling. And this time I was not seated properly in the saddle, but sideways and in an unstable fashion. For an indefinite time I clung to the machine as it swayed and vibrated, quite unheeding how I went, and when I brought myself to look at the dials again I was amazed to find where I had arrived. One dial records days, and another thousands of days, another millions of days, and another thousands of millions. Now, instead of reversing the levers, I had pulled them over so as to go forward with them, and when I came to look at these indicators I found that the thousands hand was sweeping round as fast as the seconds hand of a watch—into futurity.

'As I drove on, a peculiar change crept over the appearance of things. The palpitating greyness grew darker; then—though I was still travelling with prodigious velocity—the blinking succession of day and night, which was usually indicative of a slower pace, returned, and grew more and more marked. This puzzled me very much at first. The alternations of night and day grew slower and slower, and so did the passage of the sun across the sky, until they seemed to stretch through centuries. At last a steady twilight brooded over the earth, a twilight only broken now and then when a comet glared across the darkling sky. The band of light that had indicated the sun had long since disappeared; for the sun had ceased to set—it simply rose and fell in the west, and grew ever broader and more red. All trace of the moon had vanished. The circling of the stars, growing slower and slower, had given place to creeping points of light. At last, some time before I stopped, the sun, red and very large, halted motionless upon the horizon, a vast dome glowing with a dull heat, and now and then suffering a momentary extinction. At one time it had for a little while glowed more brilliantly again, but it speedily reverted to its sullen red heat. I perceived by this slowing down of its rising and setting that the work of the tidal drag was done. The earth had come to rest with one face to the sun, even as in our own time the moon faces the earth. Very cautiously, for I remembered my former headlong fall, I began to reverse my motion. Slower and slower went the circling hands until the thousands one seemed motionless and the daily one was no longer a mere mist upon its scale. Still slower, until the dim outlines of a desolate beach grew visible.

'I stopped very gently and sat upon the Time Machine, looking round. The sky was no longer blue. North-eastward it was inky black, and out of the blackness shone brightly and steadily the pale white stars. Overhead it was a deep Indian red

and starless, and south-eastward it grew brighter to a glowing scarlet where, cut by the horizon, lay the huge hull of the sun, red and motionless. The rocks about me were of a harsh reddish colour, and all the trace of life that I could see at first was the intensely green vegetation that covered every projecting point on their south-eastern face. It was the same rich green that one sees on forest moss or on the lichen in caves: plants which like these grow in a perpetual twilight.

'The machine was standing on a sloping beach. The sea stretched away to the south-west, to rise into a sharp bright horizon against the wan sky. There were no breakers and no waves, for not a breath of wind was stirring. Only a slight oily swell rose and fell like a gentle breathing, and showed that the eternal sea was still moving and living. And along the margin where the water sometimes broke was a thick incrustation of salt—pink under the lurid sky. There was a sense of oppression in my head, and I noticed that I was breathing very fast. The sensation reminded me of my only experience of mountaineering, and from that I judged the air to be more rarefied than it is now.

'Far away up the desolate slope I heard a harsh scream, and saw a thing like a huge white butterfly go slanting and fluttering up into the sky and, circling, disappear over some low hillocks beyond. The sound of its voice was so dismal that I shivered and seated myself more firmly upon the machine. Looking round me again, I saw that, quite near, what I had taken to be a reddish mass of rock was moving slowly towards me. Then I saw the thing was really a monstrous crab-like creature. Can you imagine a crab as large as yonder table, with its many legs moving slowly and uncertainly, its big claws swaying, its long antennae, like carters' whips, waving and feeling, and its stalked eyes gleaming at you on either side of its metallic front? Its back was corrugated and ornamented with ungainly bosses, and a greenish incrustation blotched it here and there. I could see the many palps of its complicated mouth flickering and feeling as it moved.

'As I stared at this sinister apparition crawling towards me, I felt a tickling on my cheek as though a fly had lighted there. I tried to brush it away with my hand, but in a moment it returned, and almost immediately came another by my ear. I struck at this, and caught something threadlike. It was drawn swiftly out of my hand. With a frightful qualm, I turned, and I saw that I had grasped the antenna of another monster crab that stood just behind me. Its evil eyes were wriggling on their stalks, its mouth was all alive with appetite, and its vast ungainly claws, smeared with an algal slime, were descending upon me. In a moment my hand was on the lever, and I had placed a month between myself and these monsters. But I was still on the same beach, and I saw them distinctly now as soon as I stopped. Dozens of them seemed to be crawling here and there, in the sombre light, among the foliated sheets of intense green.

'I cannot convey the sense of abominable desolation that hung over the world. The red eastern sky, the northward blackness, the salt Dead Sea, the stony beach crawling with these foul, slow-stirring monsters, the uniform poisonous-looking green of the lichenous plants, the thin air that hurts one's lungs: all contributed to an appalling effect. I moved on a hundred years, and there was the same red

sun—a little larger, a little duller—the same dying sea, the same chill air, and the same crowd of earthy crustacea creeping in and out among the green weed and the red rocks. And in the westward sky, I saw a curved pale line like a vast new moon.

'So I travelled, stopping ever and again, in great strides of a thousand years or more, drawn on by the mystery of the earth's fate, watching with a strange fascination the sun grow larger and duller in the westward sky, and the life of the old earth ebb away. At last, more than thirty million years hence, the huge red-hot dome of the sun had come to obscure nearly a tenth part of the darkling heavens. Then I stopped once more, for the crawling multitude of crabs had disappeared, and the red beach, save for its livid green liverworts and lichens, seemed lifeless. And now it was flecked with white. A bitter cold assailed me. Rare white flakes ever and again came eddying down. To the north- eastward, the glare of snow lay under the starlight of the sable sky and I could see an undulating crest of hillocks pinkish white. There were fringes of ice along the sea margin, with drifting masses further out; but the main expanse of that salt ocean, all bloody under the eternal sunset, was still unfrozen.

'I looked about me to see if any traces of animal life remained. A certain indefinable apprehension still kept me in the saddle of the machine. But I saw nothing moving, in earth or sky or sea. The green slime on the rocks alone testified that life was not extinct. A shallow sandbank had appeared in the sea and the water had receded from the beach. I fancied I saw some black object flopping about upon this bank, but it became motionless as I looked at it, and I judged that my eye had been deceived, and that the black object was merely a rock. The stars in the sky were intensely bright and seemed to me to twinkle very little.

'Suddenly I noticed that the circular westward outline of the sun had changed; that a concavity, a bay, had appeared in the curve. I saw this grow larger. For a minute perhaps I stared aghast at this blackness that was creeping over the day, and then I realized that an eclipse was beginning. Either the moon or the planet Mercury was passing across the sun's disk. Naturally, at first I took it to be the moon, but there is much to incline me to believe that what I really saw was the transit of an inner planet passing very near to the earth.

'The darkness grew apace; a cold wind began to blow in freshening gusts from the east, and the showering white flakes in the air increased in number. From the edge of the sea came a ripple and whisper. Beyond these lifeless sounds the world was silent. Silent? It would be hard to convey the stillness of it. All the sounds of man, the bleating of sheep, the cries of birds, the hum of insects, the stir that makes the background of our lives—all that was over. As the darkness thickened, the eddying flakes grew more abundant, dancing before my eyes; and the cold of the air more intense. At last, one by one, swiftly, one after the other, the white peaks of the distant hills vanished into blackness. The breeze rose to a moaning wind. I saw the black central shadow of the eclipse sweeping towards me. In another moment the pale stars alone were visible. All else was rayless obscurity. The sky was absolutely black.

'A horror of this great darkness came on me. The cold, that smote to my marrow, and the pain I felt in breathing, overcame me. I shivered, and a deadly nausea seized me. Then like a red-hot bow in the sky appeared the edge of the sun. I got off the machine to recover myself. I felt giddy and incapable of facing the return journey. As I stood sick and confused I saw again the moving thing upon the shoal—there was no mistake now that it was a moving thing—against the red water of the sea. It was a round thing, the size of a football perhaps, or, it may be, bigger, and tentacles trailed down from it; it seemed black against the weltering blood-red water, and it was hopping fitfully about. Then I felt I was fainting. But a terrible dread of lying helpless in that remote and awful twilight sustained me while I clambered upon the saddle.

XII

'So I came back. For a long time I must have been insensible upon the machine. The blinking succession of the days and nights was resumed, the sun got golden again, the sky blue. I breathed with greater freedom. The fluctuating contours of the land ebbed and flowed. The hands spun backward upon the dials. At last I saw again the dim shadows of houses, the evidences of decadent humanity. These, too, changed and passed, and others came. Presently, when the million dial was at zero, I slackened speed. I began to recognize our own petty and familiar architecture, the thousands hand ran back to the starting-point, the night and day flapped slower and slower. Then the old walls of the laboratory came round me. Very gently, now, I slowed the mechanism down.

'I saw one little thing that seemed odd to me. I think I have told you that when I set out, before my velocity became very high, Mrs. Watchett had walked across the room, travelling, as it seemed to me, like a rocket. As I returned, I passed again across that minute when she traversed the laboratory. But now her every motion appeared to be the exact inversion of her previous ones. The door at the lower end opened, and she glided quietly up the laboratory, back foremost, and disappeared behind the door by which she had previously entered. Just before that I seemed to see Hillyer for a moment; but he passed like a flash.

'Then I stopped the machine, and saw about me again the old familiar laboratory, my tools, my appliances just as I had left them. I got off the thing very shakily, and sat down upon my bench. For several minutes I trembled violently. Then I became calmer. Around me was my old workshop again, exactly as it had been. I might have slept there, and the whole thing have been a dream.

'And yet, not exactly! The thing had started from the south-east corner of the laboratory. It had come to rest again in the north-west, against the wall where you saw it. That gives you the exact distance from my little lawn to the pedestal of the White Sphinx, into which the Morlocks had carried my machine.

'For a time my brain went stagnant. Presently I got up and came through the passage here, limping, because my heel was still painful, and feeling sorely begrimed. I saw the *Pall Mall Gazette* on the table by the door. I found the date was indeed to-day, and looking at the timepiece, saw the hour was almost eight o'clock. I heard your voices and the clatter of plates. I hesitated—I felt so sick and weak. Then I sniffed good wholesome meat, and opened the door on you. You know the rest. I washed, and dined, and now I am telling you the story.

'I know,' he said, after a pause, 'that all this will be absolutely incredible to you. To me the one incredible thing is that I am here to-night in this old familiar room looking into your friendly faces and telling you these strange adventures.'

He looked at the Medical Man. 'No. I cannot expect you to believe it. Take it as a lie—or a prophecy. Say I dreamed it in the workshop. Consider I have been speculating upon the destinies of our race until I have hatched this fiction. Treat my assertion of its truth as a mere stroke of art to enhance its interest. And taking it as a story, what do you think of it?'

He took up his pipe, and began, in his old accustomed manner, to tap with it nervously upon the bars of the grate. There was a momentary stillness. Then chairs began to creak and shoes to scrape upon the carpet. I took my eyes off the Time Traveller's face, and looked round at his audience. They were in the dark, and little spots of colour swam before them. The Medical Man seemed absorbed in the contemplation of our host. The Editor was looking hard at the end of his cigar—the sixth. The Journalist fumbled for his watch. The others, as far as I remember, were motionless.

The Editor stood up with a sigh. 'What a pity it is you're not a writer of stories!' he said, putting his hand on the Time Traveller's shoulder.

'You don't believe it?'

'Well—'

'I thought not.'

The Time Traveller turned to us. 'Where are the matches?' he said. He lit one and spoke over his pipe, puffing. 'To tell you the truth ... I hardly believe it myself... And yet...'

His eye fell with a mute inquiry upon the withered white flowers upon the little table. Then he turned over the hand holding his pipe, and I saw he was looking at some half-healed scars on his knuckles.

The Medical Man rose, came to the lamp, and examined the flowers. 'The gynaeceum's odd,' he said. The Psychologist leant forward to see, holding out his hand for a specimen.

'I'm hanged if it isn't a quarter to one,' said the Journalist. 'How shall we get home?'

'Plenty of cabs at the station,' said the Psychologist.

'It's a curious thing,' said the Medical Man; 'but I certainly don't know the natural order of these flowers. May I have them?'

The Time Traveller hesitated. Then suddenly: 'Certainly not.'

'Where did you really get them?' said the Medical Man.

The Time Traveller put his hand to his head. He spoke like one who was trying to keep hold of an idea that eluded him. 'They were put into my pocket by Weena, when I travelled into Time.' He stared round the room. 'I'm damned if it isn't all going. This room and you and the atmosphere of every day is too much for my memory. Did I ever make a Time Machine, or a model of a Time Machine? Or is it all only a dream? They say life is a dream, a precious poor dream at times—but

I can't stand another that won't fit. It's madness. And where did the dream come from? ... I must look at that machine. If there is one!'

He caught up the lamp swiftly, and carried it, flaring red, through the door into the corridor. We followed him. There in the flickering light of the lamp was the machine sure enough, squat, ugly, and askew; a thing of brass, ebony, ivory, and translucent glimmering quartz. Solid to the touch—for I put out my hand and felt the rail of it—and with brown spots and smears upon the ivory, and bits of grass and moss upon the lower parts, and one rail bent awry.

The Time Traveller put the lamp down on the bench, and ran his hand along the damaged rail. 'It's all right now,' he said. 'The story I told you was true. I'm sorry to have brought you out here in the cold.' He took up the lamp, and, in an absolute silence, we returned to the smoking-room.

He came into the hall with us and helped the Editor on with his coat. The Medical Man looked into his face and, with a certain hesitation, told him he was suffering from overwork, at which he laughed hugely. I remember him standing in the open doorway, bawling good night.

I shared a cab with the Editor. He thought the tale a 'gaudy lie.' For my own part I was unable to come to a conclusion. The story was so fantastic and incredible, the telling so credible and sober. I lay awake most of the night thinking about it. I determined to go next day and see the Time Traveller again. I was told he was in the laboratory, and being on easy terms in the house, I went up to him. The laboratory, however, was empty. I stared for a minute at the Time Machine and put out my hand and touched the lever. At that the squat substantial-looking mass swayed like a bough shaken by the wind. Its instability startled me extremely, and I had a queer reminiscence of the childish days when I used to be forbidden to meddle. I came back through the corridor. The Time Traveller met me in the smoking-room. He was coming from the house. He had a small camera under one arm and a knapsack under the other. He laughed when he saw me, and gave me an elbow to shake. 'I'm frightfully busy,' said he, 'with that thing in there.'

'But is it not some hoax?' I said. 'Do you really travel through time?'

'Really and truly I do.' And he looked frankly into my eyes. He hesitated. His eye wandered about the room. 'I only want half an hour,' he said. 'I know why you came, and it's awfully good of you. There's some magazines here. If you'll stop to lunch I'll prove you this time travelling up to the hilt, specimen and all. If you'll forgive my leaving you now?'

I consented, hardly comprehending then the full import of his words, and he nodded and went on down the corridor. I heard the door of the laboratory slam, seated myself in a chair, and took up a daily paper. What was he going to do before lunch-time? Then suddenly I was reminded by an advertisement that I had promised to meet Richardson, the publisher, at two. I looked at my watch, and saw that I could barely save that engagement. I got up and went down the passage to tell the Time Traveller.

As I took hold of the handle of the door I heard an exclamation, oddly truncated at the end, and a click and a thud. A gust of air whirled round me as I opened

the door, and from within came the sound of broken glass falling on the floor. The Time Traveller was not there. I seemed to see a ghostly, indistinct figure sitting in a whirling mass of black and brass for a moment —a figure so transparent that the bench behind with its sheets of drawings was absolutely distinct; but this phantasm vanished as I rubbed my eyes. The Time Machine had gone. Save for a subsiding stir of dust, the further end of the laboratory was empty. A pane of the skylight had, apparently, just been blown in.

I felt an unreasonable amazement. I knew that something strange had happened, and for the moment could not distinguish what the strange thing might be. As I stood staring, the door into the garden opened, and the man-servant appeared.

We looked at each other. Then ideas began to come. 'Has Mr.—gone out that way?' said I.

'No, sir. No one has come out this way. I was expecting to find him here.'

At that I understood. At the risk of disappointing Richardson I stayed on, waiting for the Time Traveller; waiting for the second, perhaps still stranger story, and the specimens and photographs he would bring with him. But I am beginning now to fear that I must wait a lifetime. The Time Traveller vanished three years ago. And, as everybody knows now, he has never returned.

EPILOGUE

One cannot choose but wonder. Will he ever return? It may be that he swept back into the past, and fell among the blood-drinking, hairy savages of the Age of Unpolished Stone; into the abysses of the Cretaceous Sea; or among the grotesque saurians, the huge reptilian brutes of the Jurassic times. He may even now—if I may use the phrase—be wandering on some plesiosaurus-haunted Oolitic coral reef, or beside the lonely saline lakes of the Triassic Age. Or did he go forward, into one of the nearer ages, in which men are still men, but with the riddles of our own time answered and its wearisome problems solved? Into the manhood of the race: for I, for my own part, cannot think that these latter days of weak experiment, fragmentary theory, and mutual discord are indeed man's culminating time! I say, for my own part. He, I know—for the question had been discussed among us long before the Time Machine was made—thought but cheerlessly of the Advancement of Mankind, and saw in the growing pile of civilization only a foolish heaping that must inevitably fall back upon and destroy its makers in the end. If that is so, it remains for us to live as though it were not so. But to me the future is still black and blank—is a vast ignorance, lit at a few casual places by the memory of his story. And I have by me, for my comfort, two strange white flowers—shrivelled now, and brown and flat and brittle—to witness that even when mind and strength had gone, gratitude and a mutual tenderness still lived on in the heart of man.

THE WAR OF THE WORLDS

Serialised in Pearson's Magazine, Apr-Dec 1897, with illustrations by Warwick Goble
First UK book edition: William Heinemann, London, 1898
First US book edition: Harper & Brothers, New York, 1898

But who shall dwell in these worlds if they be inhabited?
... Are we or they Lords of the World?
... And how are all things made for man?
—KEPLER (quoted in *The Anatomy of Melancholy*)

BOOK ONE - THE COMING OF THE MARTIANS

CHAPTER ONE - THE EVE OF THE WAR

No one would have believed in the last years of the nineteenth century that this world was being watched keenly and closely by intelligences greater than man's and yet as mortal as his own; that as men busied themselves about their various concerns they were scrutinised and studied, perhaps almost as narrowly as a man with a microscope might scrutinise the transient creatures that swarm and multiply in a drop of water. With infinite complacency men went to and fro over this globe about their little affairs, serene in their assurance of their empire over matter. It is possible that the infusoria under the microscope do the same. No one gave a thought to the older worlds of space as sources of human danger, or thought of them only to dismiss the idea of life upon them as impossible or improbable. It is curious to recall some of the mental habits of those departed days. At most terrestrial men fancied there might be other men upon Mars, perhaps inferior to themselves and ready to welcome a missionary enterprise. Yet across the gulf of space, minds that are to our minds as ours are to those of the beasts that perish, intellects vast and cool and unsympathetic, regarded this earth with envious eyes, and slowly and surely drew their plans against us. And early in the twentieth century came the great disillusionment.

The planet Mars, I scarcely need remind the reader, revolves about the sun at a mean distance of 140,000,000 miles, and the light and heat it receives from the sun is barely half of that received by this world. It must be, if the nebular hypothesis has any truth, older than our world; and long before this earth ceased to be molten, life upon its surface must have begun its course. The fact that it is scarcely one seventh of the volume of the earth must have accelerated its cooling to the temperature at which life could begin. It has air and water and all that is necessary for the support of animated existence.

Yet so vain is man, and so blinded by his vanity, that no writer, up to the very end of the nineteenth century, expressed any idea that intelligent life might have developed there far, or indeed at all, beyond its earthly level. Nor was it generally understood that since Mars is older than our earth, with scarcely a quarter of the

superficial area and remoter from the sun, it necessarily follows that it is not only more distant from time's beginning but nearer its end.

The secular cooling that must someday overtake our planet has already gone far indeed with our neighbour. Its physical condition is still largely a mystery, but we know now that even in its equatorial region the midday temperature barely approaches that of our coldest winter. Its air is much more attenuated than ours, its oceans have shrunk until they cover but a third of its surface, and as its slow seasons change huge snowcaps gather and melt about either pole and periodically inundate its temperate zones. That last stage of exhaustion, which to us is still incredibly remote, has become a present-day problem for the inhabitants of Mars. The immediate pressure of necessity has brightened their intellects, enlarged their powers, and hardened their hearts. And looking across space with instruments, and intelligences such as we have scarcely dreamed of, they see, at its nearest distance only 35,000,000 of miles sunward of them, a morning star of hope, our own warmer planet, green with vegetation and grey with water, with a cloudy atmosphere eloquent of fertility, with glimpses through its drifting cloud wisps of broad stretches of populous country and narrow, navy-crowded seas.

And we men, the creatures who inhabit this earth, must be to them at least as alien and lowly as are the monkeys and lemurs to us. The intellectual side of man already admits that life is an incessant struggle for existence, and it would seem that this too is the belief of the minds upon Mars. Their world is far gone in its cooling and this world is still crowded with life, but crowded only with what they regard as inferior animals. To carry warfare sunward is, indeed, their only escape from the destruction that, generation after generation, creeps upon them.

And before we judge of them too harshly we must remember what ruthless and utter destruction our own species has wrought, not only upon animals, such as the vanished bison and the dodo, but upon its inferior races. The Tasmanians, in spite of their human likeness, were entirely swept out of existence in a war of extermination waged by European immigrants, in the space of fifty years. Are we such apostles of mercy as to complain if the Martians warred in the same spirit?

The Martians seem to have calculated their descent with amazing subtlety — their mathematical learning is evidently far in excess of ours—and to have carried out their preparations with a well-nigh perfect unanimity. Had our instruments permitted it, we might have seen the gathering trouble far back in the nineteenth century. Men like Schiaparelli watched the red planet—it is odd, by-the-bye, that for countless centuries Mars has been the star of war—but failed to interpret the fluctuating appearances of the markings they mapped so well. All that time the Martians must have been getting ready.

During the opposition of 1894 a great light was seen on the illuminated part of the disk, first at the Lick Observatory, then by Perrotin of Nice, and then by other observers. English readers heard of it first in the issue of *Nature* dated August 2. I am inclined to think that this blaze may have been the casting of the huge gun, in the vast pit sunk into their planet, from which their shots were fired at us. Peculiar

markings, as yet unexplained, were seen near the site of that outbreak during the next two oppositions.

The storm burst upon us six years ago now. As Mars approached opposition, Lavelle of Java set the wires of the astronomical exchange palpitating with the amazing intelligence of a huge outbreak of incandescent gas upon the planet. It had occurred towards midnight of the twelfth; and the spectroscope, to which he had at once resorted, indicated a mass of flaming gas, chiefly hydrogen, moving with an enormous velocity towards this earth. This jet of fire had become invisible about a quarter past twelve. He compared it to a colossal puff of flame suddenly and violently squirted out of the planet, "as flaming gases rushed out of a gun."

A singularly appropriate phrase it proved. Yet the next day there was nothing of this in the papers except a little note in the *Daily Telegraph*, and the world went in ignorance of one of the gravest dangers that ever threatened the human race. I might not have heard of the eruption at all had I not met Ogilvy, the well-known astronomer, at Ottershaw. He was immensely excited at the news, and in the excess of his feelings invited me up to take a turn with him that night in a scrutiny of the red planet.

In spite of all that has happened since, I still remember that vigil very distinctly: the black and silent observatory, the shadowed lantern throwing a feeble glow upon the floor in the corner, the steady ticking of the clockwork of the telescope, the little slit in the roof—an oblong profundity with the stardust streaked across it. Ogilvy moved about, invisible but audible. Looking through the telescope, one saw a circle of deep blue and the little round planet swimming in the field. It seemed such a little thing, so bright and small and still, faintly marked with transverse stripes, and slightly flattened from the perfect round. But so little it was, so silvery warm—a pin's-head of light! It was as if it quivered, but really this was the telescope vibrating with the activity of the clockwork that kept the planet in view.

As I watched, the planet seemed to grow larger and smaller and to advance and recede, but that was simply that my eye was tired. Forty millions of miles it was from us—more than forty millions of miles of void. Few people realise the immensity of vacancy in which the dust of the material universe swims.

Near it in the field, I remember, were three faint points of light, three telescopic stars infinitely remote, and all around it was the unfathomable darkness of empty space. You know how that blackness looks on a frosty starlight night. In a telescope it seems far profounder. And invisible to me because it was so remote and small, flying swiftly and steadily towards me across that incredible distance, drawing nearer every minute by so many thousands of miles, came the Thing they were sending us, the Thing that was to bring so much struggle and calamity and death to the earth. I never dreamed of it then as I watched; no one on earth dreamed of that unerring missile.

That night, too, there was another jetting out of gas from the distant planet. I saw it. A reddish flash at the edge, the slightest projection of the outline just as the chronometer struck midnight; and at that I told Ogilvy and he took my place.

The night was warm and I was thirsty, and I went stretching my legs clumsily and feeling my way in the darkness, to the little table where the siphon stood, while Ogilvy exclaimed at the streamer of gas that came out towards us.

That night another invisible missile started on its way to the earth from Mars, just a second or so under twenty-four hours after the first one. I remember how I sat on the table there in the blackness, with patches of green and crimson swimming before my eyes. I wished I had a light to smoke by, little suspecting the meaning of the minute gleam I had seen and all that it would presently bring me. Ogilvy watched till one, and then gave it up; and we lit the lantern and walked over to his house. Down below in the darkness were Ottershaw and Chertsey and all their hundreds of people, sleeping in peace.

He was full of speculation that night about the condition of Mars, and scoffed at the vulgar idea of its having inhabitants who were signalling us. His idea was that meteorites might be falling in a heavy shower upon the planet, or that a huge volcanic explosion was in progress. He pointed out to me how unlikely it was that organic evolution had taken the same direction in the two adjacent planets.

"The chances against anything manlike on Mars are a million to one," he said.

Hundreds of observers saw the flame that night and the night after about midnight, and again the night after; and so for ten nights, a flame each night. Why the shots ceased after the tenth no one on earth has attempted to explain. It may be the gases of the firing caused the Martians inconvenience. Dense clouds of smoke or dust, visible through a powerful telescope on earth as little grey, fluctuating patches, spread through the clearness of the planet's atmosphere and obscured its more familiar features.

Even the daily papers woke up to the disturbances at last, and popular notes appeared here, there, and everywhere concerning the volcanoes upon Mars. The seriocomic periodical *Punch*, I remember, made a happy use of it in the political cartoon. And, all unsuspected, those missiles the Martians had fired at us drew earthward, rushing now at a pace of many miles a second through the empty gulf of space, hour by hour and day by day, nearer and nearer. It seems to me now almost incredibly wonderful that, with that swift fate hanging over us, men could go about their petty concerns as they did. I remember how jubilant Markham was at securing a new photograph of the planet for the illustrated paper he edited in those days. People in these latter times scarcely realise the abundance and enterprise of our nineteenth-century papers. For my own part, I was much occupied in learning to ride the bicycle, and busy upon a series of papers discussing the probable developments of moral ideas as civilisation progressed.

One night (the first missile then could scarcely have been 10,000,000 miles away) I went for a walk with my wife. It was starlight and I explained the Signs of the Zodiac to her, and pointed out Mars, a bright dot of light creeping zenithward, towards which so many telescopes were pointed. It was a warm night. Coming home, a party of excursionists from Chertsey or Isleworth passed us singing and playing music. There were lights in the upper windows of the houses as the people went to bed. From the railway station in the distance came the sound of

shunting trains, ringing and rumbling, softened almost into melody by the distance. My wife pointed out to me the brightness of the red, green, and yellow signal lights hanging in a framework against the sky. It seemed so safe and tranquil.

CHAPTER TWO - THE FALLING STAR

Then came the night of the first falling star. It was seen early in the morning, rushing over Winchester eastward, a line of flame high in the atmosphere. Hundreds must have seen it, and taken it for an ordinary falling star. Albin described it as leaving a greenish streak behind it that glowed for some seconds. Denning, our greatest authority on meteorites, stated that the height of its first appearance was about ninety or one hundred miles. It seemed to him that it fell to earth about one hundred miles east of him.

I was at home at that hour and writing in my study; and although my French windows face towards Ottershaw and the blind was up (for I loved in those days to look up at the night sky), I saw nothing of it. Yet this strangest of all things that ever came to earth from outer space must have fallen while I was sitting there, visible to me had I only looked up as it passed. Some of those who saw its flight say it travelled with a hissing sound. I myself heard nothing of that. Many people in Berkshire, Surrey, and Middlesex must have seen the fall of it, and, at most, have thought that another meteorite had descended. No one seems to have troubled to look for the fallen mass that night.

But very early in the morning poor Ogilvy, who had seen the shooting star and who was persuaded that a meteorite lay somewhere on the common between Horsell, Ottershaw, and Woking, rose early with the idea of finding it. Find it he did, soon after dawn, and not far from the sand pits. An enormous hole had been made by the impact of the projectile, and the sand and gravel had been flung violently in every direction over the heath, forming heaps visible a mile and a half away. The heather was on fire eastward, and a thin blue smoke rose against the dawn.

The Thing itself lay almost entirely buried in sand, amidst the scattered splinters of a fir tree it had shivered to fragments in its descent. The uncovered part had the appearance of a huge cylinder, caked over and its outline softened by a thick scaly dun-coloured incrustation. It had a diameter of about thirty yards. He approached the mass, surprised at the size and more so at the shape, since most meteorites are rounded more or less completely. It was, however, still so hot from its flight through the air as to forbid his near approach. A stirring noise within its cylinder he ascribed to the unequal cooling of its surface; for at that time it had not occurred to him that it might be hollow.

He remained standing at the edge of the pit that the Thing had made for itself, staring at its strange appearance, astonished chiefly at its unusual shape and col-

our, and dimly perceiving even then some evidence of design in its arrival. The early morning was wonderfully still, and the sun, just clearing the pine trees towards Weybridge, was already warm. He did not remember hearing any birds that morning, there was certainly no breeze stirring, and the only sounds were the faint movements from within the cindery cylinder. He was all alone on the common.

Then suddenly he noticed with a start that some of the grey clinker, the ashy incrustation that covered the meteorite, was falling off the circular edge of the end. It was dropping off in flakes and raining down upon the sand. A large piece suddenly came off and fell with a sharp noise that brought his heart into his mouth.

For a minute he scarcely realised what this meant, and, although the heat was excessive, he clambered down into the pit close to the bulk to see the Thing more clearly. He fancied even then that the cooling of the body might account for this, but what disturbed that idea was the fact that the ash was falling only from the end of the cylinder.

And then he perceived that, very slowly, the circular top of the cylinder was rotating on its body. It was such a gradual movement that he discovered it only through noticing that a black mark that had been near him five minutes ago was now at the other side of the circumference. Even then he scarcely understood what this indicated, until he heard a muffled grating sound and saw the black mark jerk forward an inch or so. Then the thing came upon him in a flash. The cylinder was artificial—hollow—with an end that screwed out! Something within the cylinder was unscrewing the top!

"Good heavens!" said Ogilvy. "There's a man in it—men in it! Half roasted to death! Trying to escape!"

At once, with a quick mental leap, he linked the Thing with the flash upon Mars.

The thought of the confined creature was so dreadful to him that he forgot the heat and went forward to the cylinder to help turn. But luckily the dull radiation arrested him before he could burn his hands on the still-glowing metal. At that he stood irresolute for a moment, then turned, scrambled out of the pit, and set off running wildly into Woking. The time then must have been somewhere about six o'clock. He met a waggoner and tried to make him understand, but the tale he told and his appearance were so wild—his hat had fallen off in the pit—that the man simply drove on. He was equally unsuccessful with the potman who was just unlocking the doors of the public-house by Horsell Bridge. The fellow thought he was a lunatic at large and made an unsuccessful attempt to shut him into the taproom. That sobered him a little; and when he saw Henderson, the London journalist, in his garden, he called over the palings and made himself understood.

"Henderson," he called, "you saw that shooting star last night?"

"Well?" said Henderson.

"It's out on Horsell Common now."

"Good Lord!" said Henderson. "Fallen meteorite! That's good."

"But it's something more than a meteorite. It's a cylinder—an artificial cylinder, man! And there's something inside."

Henderson stood up with his spade in his hand.

"What's that?" he said. He was deaf in one ear.

Ogilvy told him all that he had seen. Henderson was a minute or so taking it in. Then he dropped his spade, snatched up his jacket, and came out into the road. The two men hurried back at once to the common, and found the cylinder still lying in the same position. But now the sounds inside had ceased, and a thin circle of bright metal showed between the top and the body of the cylinder. Air was either entering or escaping at the rim with a thin, sizzling sound.

They listened, rapped on the scaly burnt metal with a stick, and, meeting with no response, they both concluded the man or men inside must be insensible or dead.

Of course the two were quite unable to do anything. They shouted consolation and promises, and went off back to the town again to get help. One can imagine them, covered with sand, excited and disordered, running up the little street in the bright sunlight just as the shop folks were taking down their shutters and people were opening their bedroom windows. Henderson went into the railway station at once, in order to telegraph the news to London. The newspaper articles had prepared men's minds for the reception of the idea.

By eight o'clock a number of boys and unemployed men had already started for the common to see the "dead men from Mars." That was the form the story took. I heard of it first from my newspaper boy about a quarter to nine when I went out to get my *Daily Chronicle*. I was naturally startled, and lost no time in going out and across the Ottershaw bridge to the sand pits.

CHAPTER THREE - ON HORSELL COMMON

I found a little crowd of perhaps twenty people surrounding the huge hole in which the cylinder lay. I have already described the appearance of that colossal bulk, embedded in the ground. The turf and gravel about it seemed charred as if by a sudden explosion. No doubt its impact had caused a flash of fire. Henderson and Ogilvy were not there. I think they perceived that nothing was to be done for the present, and had gone away to breakfast at Henderson's house.

There were four or five boys sitting on the edge of the Pit, with their feet dangling, and amusing themselves—until I stopped them—by throwing stones at the giant mass. After I had spoken to them about it, they began playing at "touch" in and out of the group of bystanders.

Among these were a couple of cyclists, a jobbing gardener I employed sometimes, a girl carrying a baby, Gregg the butcher and his little boy, and two or three loafers and golf caddies who were accustomed to hang about the railway station. There was very little talking. Few of the common people in England had anything but the vaguest astronomical ideas in those days. Most of them were staring quietly at the big table like end of the cylinder, which was still as Ogilvy and Henderson had left it. I fancy the popular expectation of a heap of charred corpses was disappointed at this inanimate bulk. Some went away while I was there, and other people came. I clambered into the pit and fancied I heard a faint movement under my feet. The top had certainly ceased to rotate.

It was only when I got thus close to it that the strangeness of this object was at all evident to me. At the first glance it was really no more exciting than an overturned carriage or a tree blown across the road. Not so much so, indeed. It looked like a rusty gas float. It required a certain amount of scientific education to perceive that the grey scale of the Thing was no common oxide, that the yellowish-white metal that gleamed in the crack between the lid and the cylinder had an unfamiliar hue. "Extra-terrestrial" had no meaning for most of the onlookers.

At that time it was quite clear in my own mind that the Thing had come from the planet Mars, but I judged it improbable that it contained any living creature. I thought the unscrewing might be automatic. In spite of Ogilvy, I still believed that there were men in Mars. My mind ran fancifully on the possibilities of its containing manuscript, on the difficulties in translation that might arise, whether we should find coins and models in it, and so forth. Yet it was a little too large for assurance on this idea. I felt an impatience to see it opened. About eleven, as

nothing seemed happening, I walked back, full of such thought, to my home in Maybury. But I found it difficult to get to work upon my abstract investigations.

In the afternoon the appearance of the common had altered very much. The early editions of the evening papers had startled London with enormous headlines:

"A MESSAGE RECEIVED FROM MARS."
"REMARKABLE STORY FROM WOKING,"

and so forth. In addition, Ogilvy's wire to the Astronomical Exchange had roused every observatory in the three kingdoms.

There were half a dozen flies or more from the Woking station standing in the road by the sand pits, a basket-chaise from Chobham, and a rather lordly carriage. Besides that, there was quite a heap of bicycles. In addition, a large number of people must have walked, in spite of the heat of the day, from Woking and Chertsey, so that there was altogether quite a considerable crowd—one or two gaily dressed ladies among the others.

It was glaringly hot, not a cloud in the sky nor a breath of wind, and the only shadow was that of the few scattered pine trees. The burning heather had been extinguished, but the level ground towards Ottershaw was blackened as far as one could see, and still giving off vertical streamers of smoke. An enterprising sweetstuff dealer in the Chobham Road had sent up his son with a barrow-load of green apples and ginger beer.

Going to the edge of the pit, I found it occupied by a group of about half a dozen men—Henderson, Ogilvy, and a tall, fair-haired man that I afterwards learned was Stent, the Astronomer Royal, with several workmen wielding spades and pickaxes. Stent was giving directions in a clear, high- pitched voice. He was standing on the cylinder, which was now evidently much cooler; his face was crimson and streaming with perspiration, and something seemed to have irritated him.

A large portion of the cylinder had been uncovered, though its lower end was still embedded. As soon as Ogilvy saw me among the staring crowd on the edge of the pit he called to me to come down, and asked me if I would mind going over to see Lord Hilton, the lord of the manor.

The growing crowd, he said, was becoming a serious impediment to their excavations, especially the boys. They wanted a light railing put up, and help to keep the people back. He told me that a faint stirring was occasionally still audible within the case, but that the workmen had failed to unscrew the top, as it afforded no grip to them. The case appeared to be enormously thick, and it was possible that the faint sounds we heard represented a noisy tumult in the interior.

I was very glad to do as he asked, and so become one of the privileged spectators within the contemplated enclosure. I failed to find Lord Hilton at his house, but I was told he was expected from London by the six o'clock train from Waterloo; and as it was then about a quarter past five, I went home, had some tea, and walked up to the station to waylay him.

CHAPTER FOUR - THE CYLINDER OPENS

When I returned to the common the sun was setting. Scattered groups were hurrying from the direction of Woking, and one or two persons were returning. The crowd about the pit had increased, and stood out black against the lemon yellow of the sky—a couple of hundred people, perhaps. There were raised voices, and some sort of struggle appeared to be going on about the pit. Strange imaginings passed through my mind. As I drew nearer I heard Stent's voice:

"Keep back! Keep back!"

A boy came running towards me.

"It's a-movin'," he said to me as he passed; "a-screwin' and a-screwin' out. I don't like it. I'm a-goin' 'ome, I am."

I went on to the crowd. There were really, I should think, two or three hundred people elbowing and jostling one another, the one or two ladies there being by no means the least active.

"He's fallen in the pit!" cried some one.

"Keep back!" said several.

The crowd swayed a little, and I elbowed my way through. Every one seemed greatly excited. I heard a peculiar humming sound from the pit.

"I say!" said Ogilvy; "help keep these idiots back. We don't know what's in the confounded thing, you know!"

I saw a young man, a shop assistant in Woking I believe he was, standing on the cylinder and trying to scramble out of the hole again. The crowd had pushed him in.

The end of the cylinder was being screwed out from within. Nearly two feet of shining screw projected. Somebody blundered against me, and I narrowly missed being pitched onto the top of the screw. I turned, and as I did so the screw must have come out, for the lid of the cylinder fell upon the gravel with a ringing concussion. I stuck my elbow into the person behind me, and turned my head towards the Thing again. For a moment that circular cavity seemed perfectly black. I had the sunset in my eyes.

I think everyone expected to see a man emerge—possibly something a little unlike us terrestrial men, but in all essentials a man. I know I did. But, looking, I presently saw something stirring within the shadow: greyish billowy movements, one above another, and then two luminous disks—like eyes. Then something resembling a little grey snake, about the thickness of a walking stick, coiled up out of the writhing middle, and wriggled in the air towards me—and then another.

A sudden chill came over me. There was a loud shriek from a woman behind. I half turned, keeping my eyes fixed upon the cylinder still, from which other tentacles were now projecting, and began pushing my way back from the edge of the pit. I saw astonishment giving place to horror on the faces of the people about me. I heard inarticulate exclamations on all sides. There was a general movement backwards. I saw the shopman struggling still on the edge of the pit. I found myself alone, and saw the people on the other side of the pit running off, Stent among them. I looked again at the cylinder, and ungovernable terror gripped me. I stood petrified and staring.

A big greyish rounded bulk, the size, perhaps, of a bear, was rising slowly and painfully out of the cylinder. As it bulged up and caught the light, it glistened like wet leather.

Two large dark-coloured eyes were regarding me steadfastly. The mass that framed them, the head of the thing, was rounded, and had, one might say, a face. There was a mouth under the eyes, the lipless brim of which quivered and panted, and dropped saliva. The whole creature heaved and pulsated convulsively. A lank tentacular appendage gripped the edge of the cylinder, another swayed in the air.

Those who have never seen a living Martian can scarcely imagine the strange horror of its appearance. The peculiar V-shaped mouth with its pointed upper lip, the absence of brow ridges, the absence of a chin beneath the wedgelike lower lip, the incessant quivering of this mouth, the Gorgon groups of tentacles, the tumultuous breathing of the lungs in a strange atmosphere, the evident heaviness and painfulness of movement due to the greater gravitational energy of the earth—above all, the extraordinary intensity of the immense eyes—were at once vital, intense, inhuman, crippled and monstrous. There was something fungoid in the oily brown skin, something in the clumsy deliberation of the tedious movements unspeakably nasty. Even at this first encounter, this first glimpse, I was overcome with disgust and dread.

Suddenly the monster vanished. It had toppled over the brim of the cylinder and fallen into the pit, with a thud like the fall of a great mass of leather. I heard it give a peculiar thick cry, and forthwith another of these creatures appeared darkly in the deep shadow of the aperture.

I turned and, running madly, made for the first group of trees, perhaps a hundred yards away; but I ran slantingly and stumbling, for I could not avert my face from these things.

There, among some young pine trees and furze bushes, I stopped, panting, and waited further developments. The common round the sand pits was dotted with people, standing like myself in a half-fascinated terror, staring at these creatures, or rather at the heaped gravel at the edge of the pit in which they lay. And then, with a renewed horror, I saw a round, black object bobbing up and down on the edge of the pit. It was the head of the shopman who had fallen in, but showing as a little black object against the hot western sun. Now he got his shoulder and knee up, and again he seemed to slip back until only his head was visible. Suddenly he

vanished, and I could have fancied a faint shriek had reached me. I had a momentary impulse to go back and help him that my fears overruled.

Everything was then quite invisible, hidden by the deep pit and the heap of sand that the fall of the cylinder had made. Anyone coming along the road from Chobham or Woking would have been amazed at the sight—a dwindling multitude of perhaps a hundred people or more standing in a great irregular circle, in ditches, behind bushes, behind gates and hedges, saying little to one another and that in short, excited shouts, and staring, staring hard at a few heaps of sand. The barrow of ginger beer stood, a queer derelict, black against the burning sky, and in the sand pits was a row of deserted vehicles with their horses feeding out of nosebags or pawing the ground.

CHAPTER FIVE - THE HEAT-RAY

After the glimpse I had had of the Martians emerging from the cylinder in which they had come to the earth from their planet, a kind of fascination paralysed my actions. I remained standing knee-deep in the heather, staring at the mound that hid them. I was a battleground of fear and curiosity.

I did not dare to go back towards the pit, but I felt a passionate longing to peer into it. I began walking, therefore, in a big curve, seeking some point of vantage and continually looking at the sand heaps that hid these new-comers to our earth. Once a leash of thin black whips, like the arms of an octopus, flashed across the sunset and was immediately withdrawn, and afterwards a thin rod rose up, joint by joint, bearing at its apex a circular disk that spun with a wobbling motion. What could be going on there?

Most of the spectators had gathered in one or two groups—one a little crowd towards Woking, the other a knot of people in the direction of Chobham. Evidently they shared my mental conflict. There were few near me. One man I approached—he was, I perceived, a neighbour of mine, though I did not know his name—and accosted. But it was scarcely a time for articulate conversation.

"What ugly *brutes*!" he said. "Good God! What ugly brutes!" He repeated this over and over again.

"Did you see a man in the pit?" I said; but he made no answer to that. We became silent, and stood watching for a time side by side, deriving, I fancy, a certain comfort in one another's company. Then I shifted my position to a little knoll that gave me the advantage of a yard or more of elevation and when I looked for him presently he was walking towards Woking.

The sunset faded to twilight before anything further happened. The crowd far away on the left, towards Woking, seemed to grow, and I heard now a faint murmur from it. The little knot of people towards Chobham dispersed. There was scarcely an intimation of movement from the pit.

It was this, as much as anything, that gave people courage, and I suppose the new arrivals from Woking also helped to restore confidence. At any rate, as the dusk came on a slow, intermittent movement upon the sand pits began, a movement that seemed to gather force as the stillness of the evening about the cylinder remained unbroken. Vertical black figures in twos and threes would advance, stop, watch, and advance again, spreading out as they did so in a thin irregular crescent that promised to enclose the pit in its attenuated horns. I, too, on my side began to move towards the pit.

Then I saw some cabmen and others had walked boldly into the sand pits, and heard the clatter of hoofs and the gride of wheels. I saw a lad trundling off the barrow of apples. And then, within thirty yards of the pit, advancing from the direction of Horsell, I noted a little black knot of men, the foremost of whom was waving a white flag.

This was the Deputation. There had been a hasty consultation, and since the Martians were evidently, in spite of their repulsive forms, intelligent creatures, it had been resolved to show them, by approaching them with signals, that we too were intelligent.

Flutter, flutter, went the flag, first to the right, then to the left. It was too far for me to recognise anyone there, but afterwards I learned that Ogilvy, Stent, and Henderson were with others in this attempt at communication. This little group had in its advance dragged inward, so to speak, the circumference of the now almost complete circle of people, and a number of dim black figures followed it at discreet distances.

Suddenly there was a flash of light, and a quantity of luminous greenish smoke came out of the pit in three distinct puffs, which drove up, one after the other, straight into the still air.

This smoke (or flame, perhaps, would be the better word for it) was so bright that the deep blue sky overhead and the hazy stretches of brown common towards Chertsey, set with black pine trees, seemed to darken abruptly as these puffs arose, and to remain the darker after their dispersal. At the same time a faint hissing sound became audible.

Beyond the pit stood the little wedge of people with the white flag at its apex, arrested by these phenomena, a little knot of small vertical black shapes upon the black ground. As the green smoke arose, their faces flashed out pallid green, and faded again as it vanished. Then slowly the hissing passed into a humming, into a long, loud, droning noise. Slowly a humped shape rose out of the pit, and the ghost of a beam of light seemed to flicker out from it.

Forthwith flashes of actual flame, a bright glare leaping from one to another, sprang from the scattered group of men. It was as if some invisible jet impinged upon them and flashed into white flame. It was as if each man were suddenly and momentarily turned to fire.

Then, by the light of their own destruction, I saw them staggering and falling, and their supporters turning to run.

I stood staring, not as yet realising that this was death leaping from man to man in that little distant crowd. All I felt was that it was something very strange. An almost noiseless and blinding flash of light, and a man fell headlong and lay still; and as the unseen shaft of heat passed over them, pine trees burst into fire, and every dry furze bush became with one dull thud a mass of flames. And far away towards Knaphill I saw the flashes of trees and hedges and wooden buildings suddenly set alight.

It was sweeping round swiftly and steadily, this flaming death, this invisible, inevitable sword of heat. I perceived it coming towards me by the flashing bushes

it touched, and was too astounded and stupefied to stir. I heard the crackle of fire in the sand pits and the sudden squeal of a horse that was as suddenly stilled. Then it was as if an invisible yet intensely heated finger were drawn through the heather between me and the Martians, and all along a curving line beyond the sand pits the dark ground smoked and crackled. Something fell with a crash far away to the left where the road from Woking station opens out on the common. Forthwith the hissing and humming ceased, and the black, dome-like object sank slowly out of sight into the pit.

All this had happened with such swiftness that I had stood motionless, dumbfounded and dazzled by the flashes of light. Had that death swept through a full circle, it must inevitably have slain me in my surprise. But it passed and spared me, and left the night about me suddenly dark and unfamiliar.

The undulating common seemed now dark almost to blackness, except where its roadways lay grey and pale under the deep blue sky of the early night. It was dark, and suddenly void of men. Overhead the stars were mustering, and in the west the sky was still a pale, bright, almost greenish blue. The tops of the pine trees and the roofs of Horsell came out sharp and black against the western afterglow. The Martians and their appliances were altogether invisible, save for that thin mast upon which their restless mirror wobbled. Patches of bush and isolated trees here and there smoked and glowed still, and the houses towards Woking station were sending up spires of flame into the stillness of the evening air.

Nothing was changed save for that and a terrible astonishment. The little group of black specks with the flag of white had been swept out of existence, and the stillness of the evening, so it seemed to me, had scarcely been broken.

It came to me that I was upon this dark common, helpless, unprotected, and alone. Suddenly, like a thing falling upon me from without, came—fear.

With an effort I turned and began a stumbling run through the heather.

The fear I felt was no rational fear, but a panic terror not only of the Martians, but of the dusk and stillness all about me. Such an extraordinary effect in unmanning me it had that I ran weeping silently as a child might do. Once I had turned, I did not dare to look back.

I remember I felt an extraordinary persuasion that I was being played with, that presently, when I was upon the very verge of safety, this mysterious death—as swift as the passage of light—would leap after me from the pit about the cylinder and strike me down.

CHAPTER SIX - THE HEAT-RAY IN THE CHOBHAM ROAD

It is still a matter of wonder how the Martians are able to slay men so swiftly and so silently. Many think that in some way they are able to generate an intense heat in a chamber of practically absolute non-conductivity. This intense heat they project in a parallel beam against any object they choose, by means of a polished parabolic mirror of unknown composition, much as the parabolic mirror of a lighthouse projects a beam of light. But no one has absolutely proved these details. However it is done, it is certain that a beam of heat is the essence of the matter. Heat, and invisible, instead of visible, light. Whatever is combustible flashes into flame at its touch, lead runs like water, it softens iron, cracks and melts glass, and when it falls upon water, incontinently that explodes into steam.

That night nearly forty people lay under the starlight about the pit, charred and distorted beyond recognition, and all night long the common from Horsell to Maybury was deserted and brightly ablaze.

The news of the massacre probably reached Chobham, Woking, and Ottershaw about the same time. In Woking the shops had closed when the tragedy happened, and a number of people, shop people and so forth, attracted by the stories they had heard, were walking over the Horsell Bridge and along the road between the hedges that runs out at last upon the common. You may imagine the young people brushed up after the labours of the day, and making this novelty, as they would make any novelty, the excuse for walking together and enjoying a trivial flirtation. You may figure to yourself the hum of voices along the road in the gloaming...

As yet, of course, few people in Woking even knew that the cylinder had opened, though poor Henderson had sent a messenger on a bicycle to the post office with a special wire to an evening paper.

As these folks came out by twos and threes upon the open, they found little knots of people talking excitedly and peering at the spinning mirror over the sand pits, and the newcomers were, no doubt, soon infected by the excitement of the occasion.

By half past eight, when the Deputation was destroyed, there may have been a crowd of three hundred people or more at this place, besides those who had left the road to approach the Martians nearer. There were three policemen too, one of whom was mounted, doing their best, under instructions from Stent, to keep the people back and deter them from approaching the cylinder. There was some boo-

ing from those more thoughtless and excitable souls to whom a crowd is always an occasion for noise and horse-play.

Stent and Ogilvy, anticipating some possibilities of a collision, had telegraphed from Horsell to the barracks as soon as the Martians emerged, for the help of a company of soldiers to protect these strange creatures from violence. After that they returned to lead that ill-fated advance. The description of their death, as it was seen by the crowd, tallies very closely with my own impressions: the three puffs of green smoke, the deep humming note, and the flashes of flame.

But that crowd of people had a far narrower escape than mine. Only the fact that a hummock of heathery sand intercepted the lower part of the Heat-Ray saved them. Had the elevation of the parabolic mirror been a few yards higher, none could have lived to tell the tale. They saw the flashes and the men falling and an invisible hand, as it were, lit the bushes as it hurried towards them through the twilight. Then, with a whistling note that rose above the droning of the pit, the beam swung close over their heads, lighting the tops of the beech trees that line the road, and splitting the bricks, smashing the windows, firing the window frames, and bringing down in crumbling ruin a portion of the gable of the house nearest the corner.

In the sudden thud, hiss, and glare of the igniting trees, the panic- stricken crowd seems to have swayed hesitatingly for some moments. Sparks and burning twigs began to fall into the road, and single leaves like puffs of flame. Hats and dresses caught fire. Then came a crying from the common. There were shrieks and shouts, and suddenly a mounted policeman came galloping through the confusion with his hands clasped over his head, screaming.

"They're coming!" a woman shrieked, and incontinently everyone was turning and pushing at those behind, in order to clear their way to Woking again. They must have bolted as blindly as a flock of sheep. Where the road grows narrow and black between the high banks the crowd jammed, and a desperate struggle occurred. All that crowd did not escape; three persons at least, two women and a little boy, were crushed and trampled there, and left to die amid the terror and the darkness.

CHAPTER SEVEN - HOW I REACHED HOME

For my own part, I remember nothing of my flight except the stress of blundering against trees and stumbling through the heather. All about me gathered the invisible terrors of the Martians; that pitiless sword of heat seemed whirling to and fro, flourishing overhead before it descended and smote me out of life. I came into the road between the crossroads and Horsell, and ran along this to the crossroads.

At last I could go no further; I was exhausted with the violence of my emotion and of my flight, and I staggered and fell by the wayside. That was near the bridge that crosses the canal by the gasworks. I fell and lay still.

I must have remained there some time.

I sat up, strangely perplexed. For a moment, perhaps, I could not clearly understand how I came there. My terror had fallen from me like a garment. My hat had gone, and my collar had burst away from its fastener. A few minutes before, there had only been three real things before me—the immensity of the night and space and nature, my own feebleness and anguish, and the near approach of death. Now it was as if something turned over, and the point of view altered abruptly. There was no sensible transition from one state of mind to the other. I was immediately the self of every day again—a decent, ordinary citizen. The silent common, the impulse of my flight, the starting flames, were as if they had been in a dream. I asked myself had these latter things indeed happened? I could not credit it.

I rose and walked unsteadily up the steep incline of the bridge. My mind was blank wonder. My muscles and nerves seemed drained of their strength. I dare say I staggered drunkenly. A head rose over the arch, and the figure of a workman carrying a basket appeared. Beside him ran a little boy. He passed me, wishing me good night. I was minded to speak to him, but did not. I answered his greeting with a meaningless mumble and went on over the bridge.

Over the Maybury arch a train, a billowing tumult of white, firelit smoke, and a long caterpillar of lighted windows, went flying south—clatter, clatter, clap, rap, and it had gone. A dim group of people talked in the gate of one of the houses in the pretty little row of gables that was called Oriental Terrace. It was all so real and so familiar. And that behind me! It was frantic, fantastic! Such things, I told myself, could not be.

Perhaps I am a man of exceptional moods. I do not know how far my experience is common. At times I suffer from the strangest sense of detachment from

myself and the world about me; I seem to watch it all from the outside, from somewhere inconceivably remote, out of time, out of space, out of the stress and tragedy of it all. This feeling was very strong upon me that night. Here was another side to my dream.

But the trouble was the blank incongruity of this serenity and the swift death flying yonder, not two miles away. There was a noise of business from the gasworks, and the electric lamps were all alight. I stopped at the group of people.

"What news from the common?" said I.

There were two men and a woman at the gate.

"Eh?" said one of the men, turning.

"What news from the common?" I said.

"'Ain't yer just *been* there?" asked the men.

"People seem fair silly about the common," said the woman over the gate. "What's it all abart?"

"Haven't you heard of the men from Mars?" said I; "the creatures from Mars?"

"Quite enough," said the woman over the gate. "Thenks"; and all three of them laughed.

I felt foolish and angry. I tried and found I could not tell them what I had seen. They laughed again at my broken sentences.

"You'll hear more yet," I said, and went on to my home.

I startled my wife at the doorway, so haggard was I. I went into the dining room, sat down, drank some wine, and so soon as I could collect myself sufficiently I told her the things I had seen. The dinner, which was a cold one, had already been served, and remained neglected on the table while I told my story.

"There is one thing," I said, to allay the fears I had aroused; "they are the most sluggish things I ever saw crawl. They may keep the pit and kill people who come near them, but they cannot get out of it... But the horror of them!"

"Don't, dear!" said my wife, knitting her brows and putting her hand on mine.

"Poor Ogilvy!" I said. "To think he may be lying dead there!"

My wife at least did not find my experience incredible. When I saw how deadly white her face was, I ceased abruptly.

"They may come here," she said again and again.

I pressed her to take wine, and tried to reassure her.

"They can scarcely move," I said.

I began to comfort her and myself by repeating all that Ogilvy had told me of the impossibility of the Martians establishing themselves on the earth. In particular I laid stress on the gravitational difficulty. On the surface of the earth the force of gravity is three times what it is on the surface of Mars. A Martian, therefore, would weigh three times more than on Mars, albeit his muscular strength would be the same. His own body would be a cope of lead to him. That, indeed, was the general opinion. Both *The Times* and the *Daily Telegraph*, for instance, insisted on it the next morning, and both overlooked, just as I did, two obvious modifying influences.

The atmosphere of the earth, we now know, contains far more oxygen or far less argon (whichever way one likes to put it) than does Mars. The invigorating influences of this excess of oxygen upon the Martians indisputably did much to counterbalance the increased weight of their bodies. And, in the second place, we all overlooked the fact that such mechanical intelligence as the Martian possessed was quite able to dispense with muscular exertion at a pinch.

But I did not consider these points at the time, and so my reasoning was dead against the chances of the invaders. With wine and food, the confidence of my own table, and the necessity of reassuring my wife, I grew by insensible degrees courageous and secure.

"They have done a foolish thing," said I, fingering my wineglass. "They are dangerous because, no doubt, they are mad with terror. Perhaps they expected to find no living things—certainly no intelligent living things."

"A shell in the pit" said I, "if the worst comes to the worst will kill them all."

The intense excitement of the events had no doubt left my perceptive powers in a state of erethism. I remember that dinner table with extraordinary vividness even now. My dear wife's sweet anxious face peering at me from under the pink lamp shade, the white cloth with its silver and glass table furniture—for in those days even philosophical writers had many little luxuries—the crimson-purple wine in my glass, are photographically distinct. At the end of it I sat, tempering nuts with a cigarette, regretting Ogilvy's rashness, and denouncing the shortsighted timidity of the Martians.

So some respectable dodo in the Mauritius might have lorded it in his nest, and discussed the arrival of that shipful of pitiless sailors in want of animal food. "We will peck them to death tomorrow, my dear."

I did not know it, but that was the last civilised dinner I was to eat for very many strange and terrible days.

CHAPTER EIGHT - FRIDAY NIGHT

The most extraordinary thing to my mind, of all the strange and wonderful things that happened upon that Friday, was the dovetailing of the commonplace habits of our social order with the first beginnings of the series of events that was to topple that social order headlong. If on Friday night you had taken a pair of compasses and drawn a circle with a radius of five miles round the Woking sand pits, I doubt if you would have had one human being outside it, unless it were some relation of Stent or of the three or four cyclists or London people lying dead on the common, whose emotions or habits were at all affected by the new-comers. Many people had heard of the cylinder, of course, and talked about it in their leisure, but it certainly did not make the sensation that an ultimatum to Germany would have done.

In London that night poor Henderson's telegram describing the gradual unscrewing of the shot was judged to be a canard, and his evening paper, after wiring for authentication from him and receiving no reply—the man was killed—decided not to print a special edition.

Even within the five-mile circle the great majority of people were inert. I have already described the behaviour of the men and women to whom I spoke. All over the district people were dining and supping; working men were gardening after the labours of the day, children were being put to bed, young people were wandering through the lanes love-making, students sat over their books.

Maybe there was a murmur in the village streets, a novel and dominant topic in the public-houses, and here and there a messenger, or even an eye- witness of the later occurrences, caused a whirl of excitement, a shouting, and a running to and fro; but for the most part the daily routine of working, eating, drinking, sleeping, went on as it had done for countless years—as though no planet Mars existed in the sky. Even at Woking station and Horsell and Chobham that was the case.

In Woking junction, until a late hour, trains were stopping and going on, others were shunting on the sidings, passengers were alighting and waiting, and everything was proceeding in the most ordinary way. A boy from the town, trenching on Smith's monopoly, was selling papers with the afternoon's news. The ringing impact of trucks, the sharp whistle of the engines from the junction, mingled with their shouts of "Men from Mars!" Excited men came into the station about nine o'clock with incredible tidings, and caused no more disturbance than drunkards might have done. People rattling Londonwards peered into the darkness outside the carriage windows, and saw only a rare, flickering, vanishing spark dance up

from the direction of Horsell, a red glow and a thin veil of smoke driving across the stars, and thought that nothing more serious than a heath fire was happening. It was only round the edge of the common that any disturbance was perceptible. There were half a dozen villas burning on the Woking border. There were lights in all the houses on the common side of the three villages, and the people there kept awake till dawn.

A curious crowd lingered restlessly, people coming and going but the crowd remaining, both on the Chobham and Horsell bridges. One or two adventurous souls, it was afterwards found, went into the darkness and crawled quite near the Martians; but they never returned, for now and again a light- ray, like the beam of a warship's searchlight swept the common, and the Heat- Ray was ready to follow. Save for such, that big area of common was silent and desolate, and the charred bodies lay about on it all night under the stars, and all the next day. A noise of hammering from the pit was heard by many people.

So you have the state of things on Friday night. In the centre, sticking into the skin of our old planet Earth like a poisoned dart, was this cylinder. But the poison was scarcely working yet. Around it was a patch of silent common, smouldering in places, and with a few dark, dimly seen objects lying in contorted attitudes here and there. Here and there was a burning bush or tree. Beyond was a fringe of excitement, and farther than that fringe the inflammation had not crept as yet. In the rest of the world the stream of life still flowed as it had flowed for immemorial years. The fever of war that would presently clog vein and artery, deaden nerve and destroy brain, had still to develop.

All night long the Martians were hammering and stirring, sleepless, indefatigable, at work upon the machines they were making ready, and ever and again a puff of greenish-white smoke whirled up to the starlit sky.

About eleven a company of soldiers came through Horsell, and deployed along the edge of the common to form a cordon. Later a second company marched through Chobham to deploy on the north side of the common. Several officers from the Inkerman barracks had been on the common earlier in the day, and one, Major Eden, was reported to be missing. The colonel of the regiment came to the Chobham bridge and was busy questioning the crowd at midnight. The military authorities were certainly alive to the seriousness of the business. About eleven, the next morning's papers were able to say, a squadron of hussars, two Maxims, and about four hundred men of the Cardigan regiment started from Aldershot.

A few seconds after midnight the crowd in the Chertsey road, Woking, saw a star fall from heaven into the pine woods to the northwest. It had a greenish colour, and caused a silent brightness like summer lightning. This was the second cylinder.

CHAPTER NINE - THE FIGHTING BEGINS

Saturday lives in my memory as a day of suspense. It was a day of lassitude too, hot and close, with, I am told, a rapidly fluctuating barometer. I had slept but little, though my wife had succeeded in sleeping, and I rose early. I went into my garden before breakfast and stood listening, but towards the common there was nothing stirring but a lark.

The milkman came as usual. I heard the rattle of his chariot and I went round to the side gate to ask the latest news. He told me that during the night the Martians had been surrounded by troops, and that guns were expected. Then—a familiar, reassuring note—I heard a train running towards Woking.

"They aren't to be killed," said the milkman, "if that can possibly be avoided."

I saw my neighbour gardening, chatted with him for a time, and then strolled in to breakfast. It was a most unexceptional morning. My neighbour was of opinion that the troops would be able to capture or to destroy the Martians during the day.

"It's a pity they make themselves so unapproachable," he said. "It would be curious to know how they live on another planet; we might learn a thing or two."

He came up to the fence and extended a handful of strawberries, for his gardening was as generous as it was enthusiastic. At the same time he told me of the burning of the pine woods about the Byfleet Golf Links.

"They say," said he, "that there's another of those blessed things fallen there—number two. But one's enough, surely. This lot'll cost the insurance people a pretty penny before everything's settled." He laughed with an air of the greatest good humour as he said this. The woods, he said, were still burning, and pointed out a haze of smoke to me. "They will be hot under foot for days, on account of the thick soil of pine needles and turf," he said, and then grew serious over "poor Ogilvy."

After breakfast, instead of working, I decided to walk down towards the common. Under the railway bridge I found a group of soldiers—sappers, I think, men in small round caps, dirty red jackets unbuttoned, and showing their blue shirts, dark trousers, and boots coming to the calf. They told me no one was allowed over the canal, and, looking along the road towards the bridge, I saw one of the Cardigan men standing sentinel there. I talked with these soldiers for a time; I told them of my sight of the Martians on the previous evening. None of them had seen the Martians, and they had but the vaguest ideas of them, so that they plied me with questions. They said that they did not know who had authorised the move-

ments of the troops; their idea was that a dispute had arisen at the Horse Guards. The ordinary sapper is a great deal better educated than the common soldier, and they discussed the peculiar conditions of the possible fight with some acuteness. I described the Heat-Ray to them, and they began to argue among themselves.

"Crawl up under cover and rush 'em, say I," said one.

"Get aht!" said another. "What's cover against this 'ere 'eat? Sticks to cook yer! What we got to do is to go as near as the ground'll let us, and then drive a trench."

"Blow yer trenches! You always want trenches; you ought to ha' been born a rabbit Snippy."

"Ain't they got any necks, then?" said a third, abruptly—a little, contemplative, dark man, smoking a pipe.

I repeated my description.

"Octopuses," said he, "that's what I calls 'em. Talk about fishers of men — fighters of fish it is this time!"

"It ain't no murder killing beasts like that," said the first speaker.

"Why not shell the darned things strite off and finish 'em?" said the little dark man. "You carn tell what they might do."

"Where's your shells?" said the first speaker. "There ain't no time. Do it in a rush, that's my tip, and do it at once."

So they discussed it. After a while I left them, and went on to the railway station to get as many morning papers as I could.

But I will not weary the reader with a description of that long morning and of the longer afternoon. I did not succeed in getting a glimpse of the common, for even Horsell and Chobham church towers were in the hands of the military authorities. The soldiers I addressed didn't know anything; the officers were mysterious as well as busy. I found people in the town quite secure again in the presence of the military, and I heard for the first time from Marshall, the tobacconist, that his son was among the dead on the common. The soldiers had made the people on the outskirts of Horsell lock up and leave their houses.

I got back to lunch about two, very tired for, as I have said, the day was extremely hot and dull; and in order to refresh myself I took a cold bath in the afternoon. About half past four I went up to the railway station to get an evening paper, for the morning papers had contained only a very inaccurate description of the killing of Stent, Henderson, Ogilvy, and the others. But there was little I didn't know. The Martians did not show an inch of themselves. They seemed busy in their pit, and there was a sound of hammering and an almost continuous streamer of smoke. Apparently they were busy getting ready for a struggle. "Fresh attempts have been made to signal, but without success," was the stereotyped formula of the papers. A sapper told me it was done by a man in a ditch with a flag on a long pole. The Martians took as much notice of such advances as we should of the lowing of a cow.

I must confess the sight of all this armament, all this preparation, greatly excited me. My imagination became belligerent, and defeated the invaders in a dozen striking ways; something of my schoolboy dreams of battle and heroism came

back. It hardly seemed a fair fight to me at that time. They seemed very helpless in that pit of theirs.

About three o'clock there began the thud of a gun at measured intervals from Chertsey or Addlestone. I learned that the smouldering pine wood into which the second cylinder had fallen was being shelled, in the hope of destroying that object before it opened. It was only about five, however, that a field gun reached Chobham for use against the first body of Martians.

About six in the evening, as I sat at tea with my wife in the summerhouse talking vigorously about the battle that was lowering upon us, I heard a muffled detonation from the common, and immediately after a gust of firing. Close on the heels of that came a violent rattling crash, quite close to us, that shook the ground; and, starting out upon the lawn, I saw the tops of the trees about the Oriental College burst into smoky red flame, and the tower of the little church beside it slide down into ruin. The pinnacle of the mosque had vanished, and the roof line of the college itself looked as if a hundred- ton gun had been at work upon it. One of our chimneys cracked as if a shot had hit it, flew, and a piece of it came clattering down the tiles and made a heap of broken red fragments upon the flower bed by my study window.

I and my wife stood amazed. Then I realised that the crest of Maybury Hill must be within range of the Martians' Heat-Ray now that the college was cleared out of the way.

At that I gripped my wife's arm, and without ceremony ran her out into the road. Then I fetched out the servant, telling her I would go upstairs myself for the box she was clamouring for.

"We can't possibly stay here," I said; and as I spoke the firing reopened for a moment upon the common.

"But where are we to go?" said my wife in terror.

I thought perplexed. Then I remembered her cousins at Leatherhead.

"Leatherhead!" I shouted above the sudden noise.

She looked away from me downhill. The people were coming out of their houses, astonished.

"How are we to get to Leatherhead?" she said.

Down the hill I saw a bevy of hussars ride under the railway bridge; three galloped through the open gates of the Oriental College; two others dismounted, and began running from house to house. The sun, shining through the smoke that drove up from the tops of the trees, seemed blood red, and threw an unfamiliar lurid light upon everything.

"Stop here," said I; "you are safe here"; and I started off at once for the Spotted Dog, for I knew the landlord had a horse and dog cart. I ran, for I perceived that in a moment everyone upon this side of the hill would be moving. I found him in his bar, quite unaware of what was going on behind his house. A man stood with his back to me, talking to him.

"I must have a pound," said the landlord, "and I've no one to drive it."

"I'll give you two," said I, over the stranger's shoulder.

"What for?"

"And I'll bring it back by midnight," I said.

"Lord!" said the landlord; "what's the hurry? I'm selling my bit of a pig. Two pounds, and you bring it back? What's going on now?"

I explained hastily that I had to leave my home, and so secured the dog cart. At the time it did not seem to me nearly so urgent that the landlord should leave his. I took care to have the cart there and then, drove it off down the road, and, leaving it in charge of my wife and servant, rushed into my house and packed a few valuables, such plate as we had, and so forth. The beech trees below the house were burning while I did this, and the palings up the road glowed red. While I was occupied in this way, one of the dismounted hussars came running up. He was going from house to house, warning people to leave. He was going on as I came out of my front door, lugging my treasures, done up in a tablecloth. I shouted after him:

"What news?"

He turned, stared, bawled something about "crawling out in a thing like a dish cover," and ran on to the gate of the house at the crest. A sudden whirl of black smoke driving across the road hid him for a moment. I ran to my neighbour's door and rapped to satisfy myself of what I already knew, that his wife had gone to London with him and had locked up their house. I went in again, according to my promise, to get my servant's box, lugged it out, clapped it beside her on the tail of the dog cart, and then caught the reins and jumped up into the driver's seat beside my wife. In another moment we were clear of the smoke and noise, and spanking down the opposite slope of Maybury Hill towards Old Woking.

In front was a quiet sunny landscape, a wheat field ahead on either side of the road, and the Maybury Inn with its swinging sign. I saw the doctor's cart ahead of me. At the bottom of the hill I turned my head to look at the hillside I was leaving. Thick streamers of black smoke shot with threads of red fire were driving up into the still air, and throwing dark shadows upon the green treetops eastward. The smoke already extended far away to the east and west—to the Byfleet pine woods eastward, and to Woking on the west. The road was dotted with people running towards us. And very faint now, but very distinct through the hot, quiet air, one heard the whirr of a machine-gun that was presently stilled, and an intermittent cracking of rifles. Apparently the Martians were setting fire to everything within range of their Heat-Ray.

I am not an expert driver, and I had immediately to turn my attention to the horse. When I looked back again the second hill had hidden the black smoke. I slashed the horse with the whip, and gave him a loose rein until Woking and Send lay between us and that quivering tumult. I overtook and passed the doctor between Woking and Send.

CHAPTER TEN - IN THE STORM

Leatherhead is about twelve miles from Maybury Hill. The scent of hay was in the air through the lush meadows beyond Pyrford, and the hedges on either side were sweet and gay with multitudes of dog-roses. The heavy firing that had broken out while we were driving down Maybury Hill ceased as abruptly as it began, leaving the evening very peaceful and still. We got to Leatherhead without misadventure about nine o'clock, and the horse had an hour's rest while I took supper with my cousins and commended my wife to their care.

My wife was curiously silent throughout the drive, and seemed oppressed with forebodings of evil. I talked to her reassuringly, pointing out that the Martians were tied to the Pit by sheer heaviness, and at the utmost could but crawl a little out of it; but she answered only in monosyllables. Had it not been for my promise to the innkeeper, she would, I think, have urged me to stay in Leatherhead that night. Would that I had! Her face, I remember, was very white as we parted.

For my own part, I had been feverishly excited all day. Something very like the war fever that occasionally runs through a civilised community had got into my blood, and in my heart I was not so very sorry that I had to return to Maybury that night. I was even afraid that that last fusillade I had heard might mean the extermination of our invaders from Mars. I can best express my state of mind by saying that I wanted to be in at the death.

It was nearly eleven when I started to return. The night was unexpectedly dark; to me, walking out of the lighted passage of my cousins' house, it seemed indeed black, and it was as hot and close as the day. Overhead the clouds were driving fast, albeit not a breath stirred the shrubs about us. My cousins' man lit both lamps. Happily, I knew the road intimately. My wife stood in the light of the doorway, and watched me until I jumped up into the dog cart. Then abruptly she turned and went in, leaving my cousins side by side wishing me good hap.

I was a little depressed at first with the contagion of my wife's fears, but very soon my thoughts reverted to the Martians. At that time I was absolutely in the dark as to the course of the evening's fighting. I did not know even the circumstances that had precipitated the conflict. As I came through Ockham (for that was the way I returned, and not through Send and Old Woking) I saw along the western horizon a blood-red glow, which as I drew nearer, crept slowly up the sky. The driving clouds of the gathering thunderstorm mingled there with masses of black and red smoke.

Ripley Street was deserted, and except for a lighted window or so the village showed not a sign of life; but I narrowly escaped an accident at the corner of the road to Pyrford, where a knot of people stood with their backs to me. They said nothing to me as I passed. I do not know what they knew of the things happening beyond the hill, nor do I know if the silent houses I passed on my way were sleeping securely, or deserted and empty, or harassed and watching against the terror of the night.

From Ripley until I came through Pyrford I was in the valley of the Wey, and the red glare was hidden from me. As I ascended the little hill beyond Pyrford Church the glare came into view again, and the trees about me shivered with the first intimation of the storm that was upon me. Then I heard midnight pealing out from Pyrford Church behind me, and then came the silhouette of Maybury Hill, with its tree-tops and roofs black and sharp against the red.

Even as I beheld this a lurid green glare lit the road about me and showed the distant woods towards Addlestone. I felt a tug at the reins. I saw that the driving clouds had been pierced as it were by a thread of green fire, suddenly lighting their confusion and falling into the field to my left. It was the third falling star!

Close on its apparition, and blindingly violet by contrast, danced out the first lightning of the gathering storm, and the thunder burst like a rocket overhead. The horse took the bit between his teeth and bolted.

A moderate incline runs towards the foot of Maybury Hill, and down this we clattered. Once the lightning had begun, it went on in as rapid a succession of flashes as I have ever seen. The thunderclaps, treading one on the heels of another and with a strange crackling accompaniment, sounded more like the working of a gigantic electric machine than the usual detonating reverberations. The flickering light was blinding and confusing, and a thin hail smote gustily at my face as I drove down the slope.

At first I regarded little but the road before me, and then abruptly my attention was arrested by something that was moving rapidly down the opposite slope of Maybury Hill. At first I took it for the wet roof of a house, but one flash following another showed it to be in swift rolling movement. It was an elusive vision—a moment of bewildering darkness, and then, in a flash like daylight, the red masses of the Orphanage near the crest of the hill, the green tops of the pine trees, and this problematical object came out clear and sharp and bright.

And this Thing I saw! How can I describe it? A monstrous tripod, higher than many houses, striding over the young pine trees, and smashing them aside in its career; a walking engine of glittering metal, striding now across the heather; articulate ropes of steel dangling from it, and the clattering tumult of its passage mingling with the riot of the thunder. A flash, and it came out vividly, heeling over one way with two feet in the air, to vanish and reappear almost instantly as it seemed, with the next flash, a hundred yards nearer. Can you imagine a milking stool tilted and bowled violently along the ground? That was the impression those instant flashes gave. But instead of a milking stool imagine it a great body of machinery on a tripod stand.

Then suddenly the trees in the pine wood ahead of me were parted, as brittle reeds are parted by a man thrusting through them; they were snapped off and driven headlong, and a second huge tripod appeared, rushing, as it seemed, headlong towards me. And I was galloping hard to meet it! At the sight of the second monster my nerve went altogether. Not stopping to look again, I wrenched the horse's head hard round to the right and in another moment the dog cart had heeled over upon the horse; the shafts smashed noisily, and I was flung sideways and fell heavily into a shallow pool of water.

I crawled out almost immediately, and crouched, my feet still in the water, under a clump of furze. The horse lay motionless (his neck was broken, poor brute!) and by the lightning flashes I saw the black bulk of the overturned dog cart and the silhouette of the wheel still spinning slowly. In another moment the colossal mechanism went striding by me, and passed uphill towards Pyrford.

Seen nearer, the Thing was incredibly strange, for it was no mere insensate machine driving on its way. Machine it was, with a ringing metallic pace, and long, flexible, glittering tentacles (one of which gripped a young pine tree) swinging and rattling about its strange body. It picked its road as it went striding along, and the brazen hood that surmounted it moved to and fro with the inevitable suggestion of a head looking about. Behind the main body was a huge mass of white metal like a gigantic fisherman's basket, and puffs of green smoke squirted out from the joints of the limbs as the monster swept by me. And in an instant it was gone.

So much I saw then, all vaguely for the flickering of the lightning, in blinding highlights and dense black shadows.

As it passed it set up an exultant deafening howl that drowned the thunder—"Aloo! Aloo!"—and in another minute it was with its companion, half a mile away, stooping over something in the field. I have no doubt this Thing in the field was the third of the ten cylinders they had fired at us from Mars.

For some minutes I lay there in the rain and darkness watching, by the intermittent light, these monstrous beings of metal moving about in the distance over the hedge tops. A thin hail was now beginning, and as it came and went their figures grew misty and then flashed into clearness again. Now and then came a gap in the lightning, and the night swallowed them up.

I was soaked with hail above and puddle water below. It was some time before my blank astonishment would let me struggle up the bank to a drier position, or think at all of my imminent peril.

Not far from me was a little one-roomed squatter's hut of wood, surrounded by a patch of potato garden. I struggled to my feet at last, and, crouching and making use of every chance of cover, I made a run for this. I hammered at the door, but I could not make the people hear (if there were any people inside), and after a time I desisted, and, availing myself of a ditch for the greater part of the way, succeeded in crawling, unobserved by these monstrous machines, into the pine woods towards Maybury.

Under cover of this I pushed on, wet and shivering now, towards my own house. I walked among the trees trying to find the footpath. It was very dark indeed in the wood, for the lightning was now becoming infrequent, and the hail, which was pouring down in a torrent, fell in columns through the gaps in the heavy foliage.

If I had fully realised the meaning of all the things I had seen I should have immediately worked my way round through Byfleet to Street Cobham, and so gone back to rejoin my wife at Leatherhead. But that night the strangeness of things about me, and my physical wretchedness, prevented me, for I was bruised, weary, wet to the skin, deafened and blinded by the storm.

I had a vague idea of going on to my own house, and that was as much motive as I had. I staggered through the trees, fell into a ditch and bruised my knees against a plank, and finally splashed out into the lane that ran down from the College Arms. I say splashed, for the storm water was sweeping the sand down the hill in a muddy torrent. There in the darkness a man blundered into me and sent me reeling back.

He gave a cry of terror, sprang sideways, and rushed on before I could gather my wits sufficiently to speak to him. So heavy was the stress of the storm just at this place that I had the hardest task to win my way up the hill. I went close up to the fence on the left and worked my way along its palings.

Near the top I stumbled upon something soft, and, by a flash of lightning, saw between my feet a heap of black broadcloth and a pair of boots. Before I could distinguish clearly how the man lay, the flicker of light had passed. I stood over him waiting for the next flash. When it came, I saw that he was a sturdy man, cheaply but not shabbily dressed; his head was bent under his body, and he lay crumpled up close to the fence, as though he had been flung violently against it.

Overcoming the repugnance natural to one who had never before touched a dead body, I stooped and turned him over to feel for his heart. He was quite dead. Apparently his neck had been broken. The lightning flashed for a third time, and his face leaped upon me. I sprang to my feet. It was the landlord of the Spotted Dog, whose conveyance I had taken.

I stepped over him gingerly and pushed on up the hill. I made my way by the police station and the College Arms towards my own house. Nothing was burning on the hillside, though from the common there still came a red glare and a rolling tumult of ruddy smoke beating up against the drenching hail. So far as I could see by the flashes, the houses about me were mostly uninjured. By the College Arms a dark heap lay in the road.

Down the road towards Maybury Bridge there were voices and the sound of feet, but I had not the courage to shout or to go to them. I let myself in with my latchkey, closed, locked and bolted the door, staggered to the foot of the staircase, and sat down. My imagination was full of those striding metallic monsters, and of the dead body smashed against the fence.

I crouched at the foot of the staircase with my back to the wall, shivering violently.

CHAPTER ELEVEN - AT THE WINDOW

I have already said that my storms of emotion have a trick of exhausting themselves. After a time I discovered that I was cold and wet, and with little pools of water about me on the stair carpet. I got up almost mechanically, went into the dining room and drank some whiskey, and then I was moved to change my clothes.

After I had done that I went upstairs to my study, but why I did so I do not know. The window of my study looks over the trees and the railway towards Horsell Common. In the hurry of our departure this window had been left open. The passage was dark, and, by contrast with the picture the window frame enclosed, the side of the room seemed impenetrably dark. I stopped short in the doorway.

The thunderstorm had passed. The towers of the Oriental College and the pine trees about it had gone, and very far away, lit by a vivid red glare, the common about the sand pits was visible. Across the light huge black shapes, grotesque and strange, moved busily to and fro.

It seemed indeed as if the whole country in that direction was on fire —a broad hillside set with minute tongues of flame, swaying and writhing with the gusts of the dying storm, and throwing a red reflection upon the cloud- scud above. Every now and then a haze of smoke from some nearer conflagration drove across the window and hid the Martian shapes. I could not see what they were doing, nor the clear form of them, nor recognise the black objects they were busied upon. Neither could I see the nearer fire, though the reflections of it danced on the wall and ceiling of the study. A sharp, resinous tang of burning was in the air.

I closed the door noiselessly and crept towards the window. As I did so, the view opened out until, on the one hand, it reached to the houses about Woking station, and on the other to the charred and blackened pine woods of Byfleet. There was a light down below the hill, on the railway, near the arch, and several of the houses along the Maybury road and the streets near the station were glowing ruins. The light upon the railway puzzled me at first; there were a black heap and a vivid glare, and to the right of that a row of yellow oblongs. Then I perceived this was a wrecked train, the fore part smashed and on fire, the hinder carriages still upon the rails.

Between these three main centres of light—the houses, the train, and the burning county towards Chobham—stretched irregular patches of dark country, broken here and there by intervals of dimly glowing and smoking ground. It was

the strangest spectacle, that black expanse set with fire. It reminded me, more than anything else, of the Potteries at night. At first I could distinguish no people at all, though I peered intently for them. Later I saw against the light of Woking station a number of black figures hurrying one after the other across the line.

And this was the little world in which I had been living securely for years, this fiery chaos! What had happened in the last seven hours I still did not know; nor did I know, though I was beginning to guess, the relation between these mechanical colossi and the sluggish lumps I had seen disgorged from the cylinder. With a queer feeling of impersonal interest I turned my desk chair to the window, sat down, and stared at the blackened country, and particularly at the three gigantic black things that were going to and fro in the glare about the sand pits.

They seemed amazingly busy. I began to ask myself what they could be. Were they intelligent mechanisms? Such a thing I felt was impossible. Or did a Martian sit within each, ruling, directing, using, much as a man's brain sits and rules in his body? I began to compare the things to human machines, to ask myself for the first time in my life how an ironclad or a steam engine would seem to an intelligent lower animal.

The storm had left the sky clear, and over the smoke of the burning land the little fading pinpoint of Mars was dropping into the west, when a soldier came into my garden. I heard a slight scraping at the fence, and rousing myself from the lethargy that had fallen upon me, I looked down and saw him dimly, clambering over the palings. At the sight of another human being my torpor passed, and I leaned out of the window eagerly.

"Hist!" said I, in a whisper.

He stopped astride of the fence in doubt. Then he came over and across the lawn to the corner of the house. He bent down and stepped softly.

"Who's there?" he said, also whispering, standing under the window and peering up.

"Where are you going?" I asked.

"God knows."

"Are you trying to hide?"

"That's it."

"Come into the house," I said.

I went down, unfastened the door, and let him in, and locked the door again. I could not see his face. He was hatless, and his coat was unbuttoned.

"My God!" he said, as I drew him in.

"What has happened?" I asked.

"What hasn't?" In the obscurity I could see he made a gesture of despair. "They wiped us out—simply wiped us out," he repeated again and again.

He followed me, almost mechanically, into the dining room.

"Take some whiskey," I said, pouring out a stiff dose.

He drank it. Then abruptly he sat down before the table, put his head on his arms, and began to sob and weep like a little boy, in a perfect passion of emotion,

while I, with a curious forgetfulness of my own recent despair, stood beside him, wondering.

It was a long time before he could steady his nerves to answer my questions, and then he answered perplexingly and brokenly. He was a driver in the artillery, and had only come into action about seven. At that time firing was going on across the common, and it was said the first party of Martians were crawling slowly towards their second cylinder under cover of a metal shield.

Later this shield staggered up on tripod legs and became the first of the fighting-machines I had seen. The gun he drove had been unlimbered near Horsell, in order to command the sand pits, and its arrival it was that had precipitated the action. As the limber gunners went to the rear, his horse trod in a rabbit hole and came down, throwing him into a depression of the ground. At the same moment the gun exploded behind him, the ammunition blew up, there was fire all about him, and he found himself lying under a heap of charred dead men and dead horses.

"I lay still," he said, "scared out of my wits, with the fore quarter of a horse atop of me. We'd been wiped out. And the smell—good God! Like burnt meat! I was hurt across the back by the fall of the horse, and there I had to lie until I felt better. Just like parade it had been a minute before —then stumble, bang, swish!"

"Wiped out!" he said.

He had hid under the dead horse for a long time, peeping out furtively across the common. The Cardigan men had tried a rush, in skirmishing order, at the pit, simply to be swept out of existence. Then the monster had risen to its feet and had begun to walk leisurely to and fro across the common among the few fugitives, with its headlike hood turning about exactly like the head of a cowled human being. A kind of arm carried a complicated metallic case, about which green flashes scintillated, and out of the funnel of this there smoked the Heat-Ray.

In a few minutes there was, so far as the soldier could see, not a living thing left upon the common, and every bush and tree upon it that was not already a blackened skeleton was burning. The hussars had been on the road beyond the curvature of the ground, and he saw nothing of them. He heard the Martians rattle for a time and then become still. The giant saved Woking station and its cluster of houses until the last; then in a moment the Heat-Ray was brought to bear, and the town became a heap of fiery ruins. Then the Thing shut off the Heat-Ray, and turning its back upon the artilleryman, began to waddle away towards the smouldering pine woods that sheltered the second cylinder. As it did so a second glittering Titan built itself up out of the pit.

The second monster followed the first, and at that the artilleryman began to crawl very cautiously across the hot heather ash towards Horsell. He managed to get alive into the ditch by the side of the road, and so escaped to Woking. There his story became ejaculatory. The place was impassable. It seems there were a few people alive there, frantic for the most part and many burned and scalded. He was turned aside by the fire, and hid among some almost scorching heaps of broken wall as one of the Martian giants returned. He saw this one pursue a man,

catch him up in one of its steely tentacles, and knock his head against the trunk of a pine tree. At last, after nightfall, the artilleryman made a rush for it and got over the railway embankment.

Since then he had been skulking along towards Maybury, in the hope of getting out of danger Londonward. People were hiding in trenches and cellars, and many of the survivors had made off towards Woking village and Send. He had been consumed with thirst until he found one of the water mains near the railway arch smashed, and the water bubbling out like a spring upon the road.

That was the story I got from him, bit by bit. He grew calmer telling me and trying to make me see the things he had seen. He had eaten no food since midday, he told me early in his narrative, and I found some mutton and bread in the pantry and brought it into the room. We lit no lamp for fear of attracting the Martians, and ever and again our hands would touch upon bread or meat. As he talked, things about us came darkly out of the darkness, and the trampled bushes and broken rose trees outside the window grew distinct. It would seem that a number of men or animals had rushed across the lawn. I began to see his face, blackened and haggard, as no doubt mine was also.

When we had finished eating we went softly upstairs to my study, and I looked again out of the open window. In one night the valley had become a valley of ashes. The fires had dwindled now. Where flames had been there were now streamers of smoke; but the countless ruins of shattered and gutted houses and blasted and blackened trees that the night had hidden stood out now gaunt and terrible in the pitiless light of dawn. Yet here and there some object had had the luck to escape—a white railway signal here, the end of a greenhouse there, white and fresh amid the wreckage. Never before in the history of warfare had destruction been so indiscriminate and so universal. And shining with the growing light of the east, three of the metallic giants stood about the pit, their cowls rotating as though they were surveying the desolation they had made.

It seemed to me that the pit had been enlarged, and ever and again puffs of vivid green vapour streamed up and out of it towards the brightening dawn — streamed up, whirled, broke, and vanished.

Beyond were the pillars of fire about Chobham. They became pillars of bloodshot smoke at the first touch of day.

CHAPTER TWELVE - WHAT I SAW OF THE DESTRUCTION OF WEYBRIDGE AND SHEPPERTON

As the dawn grew brighter we withdrew from the window from which we had watched the Martians, and went very quietly downstairs.

The artilleryman agreed with me that the house was no place to stay in. He proposed, he said, to make his way Londonward, and thence rejoin his battery — No. 12, of the Horse Artillery. My plan was to return at once to Leatherhead; and so greatly had the strength of the Martians impressed me that I had determined to take my wife to Newhaven, and go with her out of the country forthwith. For I already perceived clearly that the country about London must inevitably be the scene of a disastrous struggle before such creatures as these could be destroyed.

Between us and Leatherhead, however, lay the third cylinder, with its guarding giants. Had I been alone, I think I should have taken my chance and struck across country. But the artilleryman dissuaded me: "It's no kindness to the right sort of wife," he said, "to make her a widow"; and in the end I agreed to go with him, under cover of the woods, northward as far as Street Cobham before I parted with him. Thence I would make a big detour by Epsom to reach Leatherhead.

I should have started at once, but my companion had been in active service and he knew better than that. He made me ransack the house for a flask, which he filled with whiskey; and we lined every available pocket with packets of biscuits and slices of meat. Then we crept out of the house, and ran as quickly as we could down the ill-made road by which I had come overnight. The houses seemed deserted. In the road lay a group of three charred bodies close together, struck dead by the Heat-Ray; and here and there were things that people had dropped—a clock, a slipper, a silver spoon, and the like poor valuables. At the corner turning up towards the post office a little cart, filled with boxes and furniture, and horseless, heeled over on a broken wheel. A cash box had been hastily smashed open and thrown under the debris.

Except the lodge at the Orphanage, which was still on fire, none of the houses had suffered very greatly here. The Heat-Ray had shaved the chimney tops and passed. Yet, save ourselves, there did not seem to be a living soul on Maybury Hill. The majority of the inhabitants had escaped, I suppose, by way of the Old Woking road—the road I had taken when I drove to Leatherhead—or they had hidden.

We went down the lane, by the body of the man in black, sodden now from the overnight hail, and broke into the woods at the foot of the hill. We pushed through

these towards the railway without meeting a soul. The woods across the line were but the scarred and blackened ruins of woods; for the most part the trees had fallen, but a certain proportion still stood, dismal grey stems, with dark brown foliage instead of green.

On our side the fire had done no more than scorch the nearer trees; it had failed to secure its footing. In one place the woodmen had been at work on Saturday; trees, felled and freshly trimmed, lay in a clearing, with heaps of sawdust by the sawing-machine and its engine. Hard by was a temporary hut, deserted. There was not a breath of wind this morning, and everything was strangely still. Even the birds were hushed, and as we hurried along I and the artilleryman talked in whispers and looked now and again over our shoulders. Once or twice we stopped to listen.

After a time we drew near the road, and as we did so we heard the clatter of hoofs and saw through the tree stems three cavalry soldiers riding slowly towards Woking. We hailed them, and they halted while we hurried towards them. It was a lieutenant and a couple of privates of the 8th Hussars, with a stand like a theodolite, which the artilleryman told me was a heliograph.

"You are the first men I've seen coming this way this morning," said the lieutenant. "What's brewing?"

His voice and face were eager. The men behind him stared curiously. The artilleryman jumped down the bank into the road and saluted.

"Gun destroyed last night, sir. Have been hiding. Trying to rejoin battery, sir. You'll come in sight of the Martians, I expect, about half a mile along this road."

"What the dickens are they like?" asked the lieutenant.

"Giants in armour, sir. Hundred feet high. Three legs and a body like 'luminium, with a mighty great head in a hood, sir."

"Get out!" said the lieutenant. "What confounded nonsense!"

"You'll see, sir. They carry a kind of box, sir, that shoots fire and strikes you dead."

"What d'ye mean—a gun?"

"No, sir," and the artilleryman began a vivid account of the Heat-Ray. Halfway through, the lieutenant interrupted him and looked up at me. I was still standing on the bank by the side of the road.

"It's perfectly true," I said.

"Well," said the lieutenant, "I suppose it's my business to see it too. Look here"—to the artilleryman—"we're detailed here clearing people out of their houses. You'd better go along and report yourself to Brigadier-General Marvin, and tell him all you know. He's at Weybridge. Know the way?"

"I do," I said; and he turned his horse southward again.

"Half a mile, you say?" said he.

"At most," I answered, and pointed over the treetops southward. He thanked me and rode on, and we saw them no more.

Farther along we came upon a group of three women and two children in the road, busy clearing out a labourer's cottage. They had got hold of a little hand

truck, and were piling it up with unclean-looking bundles and shabby furniture. They were all too assiduously engaged to talk to us as we passed.

By Byfleet station we emerged from the pine trees, and found the country calm and peaceful under the morning sunlight. We were far beyond the range of the Heat-Ray there, and had it not been for the silent desertion of some of the houses, the stirring movement of packing in others, and the knot of soldiers standing on the bridge over the railway and staring down the line towards Woking, the day would have seemed very like any other Sunday.

Several farm waggons and carts were moving creakily along the road to Addlestone, and suddenly through the gate of a field we saw, across a stretch of flat meadow, six twelve-pounders standing neatly at equal distances pointing towards Woking. The gunners stood by the guns waiting, and the ammunition waggons were at a business-like distance. The men stood almost as if under inspection.

"That's good!" said I. "They will get one fair shot, at any rate."

The artilleryman hesitated at the gate.

"I shall go on," he said.

Farther on towards Weybridge, just over the bridge, there were a number of men in white fatigue jackets throwing up a long rampart, and more guns behind.

"It's bows and arrows against the lightning, anyhow," said the artilleryman. "They 'aven't seen that fire-beam yet."

The officers who were not actively engaged stood and stared over the treetops southwestward, and the men digging would stop every now and again to stare in the same direction.

Byfleet was in a tumult; people packing, and a score of hussars, some of them dismounted, some on horseback, were hunting them about. Three or four black government waggons, with crosses in white circles, and an old omnibus, among other vehicles, were being loaded in the village street. There were scores of people, most of them sufficiently sabbatical to have assumed their best clothes. The soldiers were having the greatest difficulty in making them realise the gravity of their position. We saw one shrivelled old fellow with a huge box and a score or more of flower pots containing orchids, angrily expostulating with the corporal who would leave them behind. I stopped and gripped his arm.

"Do you know what's over there?" I said, pointing at the pine tops that hid the Martians.

"Eh?" said he, turning. "I was explainin' these is vallyble."

"Death!" I shouted. "Death is coming! Death!" and leaving him to digest that if he could, I hurried on after the artillery-man. At the corner I looked back. The soldier had left him, and he was still standing by his box, with the pots of orchids on the lid of it, and staring vaguely over the trees.

No one in Weybridge could tell us where the headquarters were established; the whole place was in such confusion as I had never seen in any town before. Carts, carriages everywhere, the most astonishing miscellany of conveyances and horseflesh. The respectable inhabitants of the place, men in golf and boating costumes, wives prettily dressed, were packing, river-side loafers energetically

helping, children excited, and, for the most part, highly delighted at this astonishing variation of their Sunday experiences. In the midst of it all the worthy vicar was very pluckily holding an early celebration, and his bell was jangling out above the excitement.

I and the artilleryman, seated on the step of the drinking fountain, made a very passable meal upon what we had brought with us. Patrols of soldiers —here no longer hussars, but grenadiers in white—were warning people to move now or to take refuge in their cellars as soon as the firing began. We saw as we crossed the railway bridge that a growing crowd of people had assembled in and about the railway station, and the swarming platform was piled with boxes and packages. The ordinary traffic had been stopped, I believe, in order to allow of the passage of troops and guns to Chertsey, and I have heard since that a savage struggle occurred for places in the special trains that were put on at a later hour.

We remained at Weybridge until midday, and at that hour we found ourselves at the place near Shepperton Lock where the Wey and Thames join. Part of the time we spent helping two old women to pack a little cart. The Wey has a treble mouth, and at this point boats are to be hired, and there was a ferry across the river. On the Shepperton side was an inn with a lawn, and beyond that the tower of Shepperton Church—it has been replaced by a spire —rose above the trees.

Here we found an excited and noisy crowd of fugitives. As yet the flight had not grown to a panic, but there were already far more people than all the boats going to and fro could enable to cross. People came panting along under heavy burdens; one husband and wife were even carrying a small outhouse door between them, with some of their household goods piled thereon. One man told us he meant to try to get away from Shepperton station.

There was a lot of shouting, and one man was even jesting. The idea people seemed to have here was that the Martians were simply formidable human beings, who might attack and sack the town, to be certainly destroyed in the end. Every now and then people would glance nervously across the Wey, at the meadows towards Chertsey, but everything over there was still.

Across the Thames, except just where the boats landed, everything was quiet, in vivid contrast with the Surrey side. The people who landed there from the boats went tramping off down the lane. The big ferryboat had just made a journey. Three or four soldiers stood on the lawn of the inn, staring and jesting at the fugitives, without offering to help. The inn was closed, as it was now within prohibited hours.

"What's that?" cried a boatman, and "Shut up, you fool!" said a man near me to a yelping dog. Then the sound came again, this time from the direction of Chertsey, a muffled thud—the sound of a gun.

The fighting was beginning. Almost immediately unseen batteries across the river to our right, unseen because of the trees, took up the chorus, firing heavily one after the other. A woman screamed. Everyone stood arrested by the sudden stir of battle, near us and yet invisible to us. Nothing was to be seen save flat

meadows, cows feeding unconcernedly for the most part, and silvery pollard willows motionless in the warm sunlight.

"The sojers'll stop 'em," said a woman beside me, doubtfully. A haziness rose over the treetops.

Then suddenly we saw a rush of smoke far away up the river, a puff of smoke that jerked up into the air and hung; and forthwith the ground heaved under foot and a heavy explosion shook the air, smashing two or three windows in the houses near, and leaving us astonished.

"Here they are!" shouted a man in a blue jersey. "Yonder! D'yer see them? Yonder!"

Quickly, one after the other, one, two, three, four of the armoured Martians appeared, far away over the little trees, across the flat meadows that stretched towards Chertsey, and striding hurriedly towards the river. Little cowled figures they seemed at first, going with a rolling motion and as fast as flying birds.

Then, advancing obliquely towards us, came a fifth. Their armoured bodies glittered in the sun as they swept swiftly forward upon the guns, growing rapidly larger as they drew nearer. One on the extreme left, the remotest that is, flourished a huge case high in the air, and the ghostly, terrible Heat-Ray I had already seen on Friday night smote towards Chertsey, and struck the town.

At sight of these strange, swift, and terrible creatures the crowd near the water's edge seemed to me to be for a moment horror-struck. There was no screaming or shouting, but a silence. Then a hoarse murmur and a movement of feet—a splashing from the water. A man, too frightened to drop the portmanteau he carried on his shoulder, swung round and sent me staggering with a blow from the corner of his burden. A woman thrust at me with her hand and rushed past me. I turned with the rush of the people, but I was not too terrified for thought. The terrible Heat-Ray was in my mind. To get under water! That was it!

"Get under water!" I shouted, unheeded.

I faced about again, and rushed towards the approaching Martian, rushed right down the gravelly beach and headlong into the water. Others did the same. A boatload of people putting back came leaping out as I rushed past. The stones under my feet were muddy and slippery, and the river was so low that I ran perhaps twenty feet scarcely waist-deep. Then, as the Martian towered overhead scarcely a couple of hundred yards away, I flung myself forward under the surface. The splashes of the people in the boats leaping into the river sounded like thunderclaps in my ears. People were landing hastily on both sides of the river. But the Martian machine took no more notice for the moment of the people running this way and that than a man would of the confusion of ants in a nest against which his foot has kicked. When, half suffocated, I raised my head above water, the Martian's hood pointed at the batteries that were still firing across the river, and as it advanced it swung loose what must have been the generator of the Heat-Ray.

In another moment it was on the bank, and in a stride wading halfway across. The knees of its foremost legs bent at the farther bank, and in another moment it had raised itself to its full height again, close to the village of Shepperton. Forth-

with the six guns which, unknown to anyone on the right bank, had been hidden behind the outskirts of that village, fired simultaneously. The sudden near concussion, the last close upon the first, made my heart jump. The monster was already raising the case generating the Heat-Ray as the first shell burst six yards above the hood.

I gave a cry of astonishment. I saw and thought nothing of the other four Martian monsters; my attention was riveted upon the nearer incident. Simultaneously two other shells burst in the air near the body as the hood twisted round in time to receive, but not in time to dodge, the fourth shell.

The shell burst clean in the face of the Thing. The hood bulged, flashed, was whirled off in a dozen tattered fragments of red flesh and glittering metal.

"Hit!" shouted I, with something between a scream and a cheer.

I heard answering shouts from the people in the water about me. I could have leaped out of the water with that momentary exultation.

The decapitated colossus reeled like a drunken giant; but it did not fall over. It recovered its balance by a miracle, and, no longer heeding its steps and with the camera that fired the Heat-Ray now rigidly upheld, it reeled swiftly upon Shepperton. The living intelligence, the Martian within the hood, was slain and splashed to the four winds of heaven, and the Thing was now but a mere intricate device of metal whirling to destruction. It drove along in a straight line, incapable of guidance. It struck the tower of Shepperton Church, smashing it down as the impact of a battering ram might have done, swerved aside, blundered on and collapsed with tremendous force into the river out of my sight.

A violent explosion shook the air, and a spout of water, steam, mud, and shattered metal shot far up into the sky. As the camera of the Heat-Ray hit the water, the latter had immediately flashed into steam. In another moment a huge wave, like a muddy tidal bore but almost scaldingly hot, came sweeping round the bend upstream. I saw people struggling shorewards, and heard their screaming and shouting faintly above the seething and roar of the Martian's collapse.

For a moment I heeded nothing of the heat, forgot the patent need of self-preservation. I splashed through the tumultuous water, pushing aside a man in black to do so, until I could see round the bend. Half a dozen deserted boats pitched aimlessly upon the confusion of the waves. The fallen Martian came into sight downstream, lying across the river, and for the most part submerged.

Thick clouds of steam were pouring off the wreckage, and through the tumultuously whirling wisps I could see, intermittently and vaguely, the gigantic limbs churning the water and flinging a splash and spray of mud and froth into the air. The tentacles swayed and struck like living arms, and, save for the helpless purposelessness of these movements, it was as if some wounded thing were struggling for its life amid the waves. Enormous quantities of a ruddy-brown fluid were spurting up in noisy jets out of the machine.

My attention was diverted from this death flurry by a furious yelling, like that of the thing called a siren in our manufacturing towns. A man, knee- deep near the towing path, shouted inaudibly to me and pointed. Looking back, I saw the other

Martians advancing with gigantic strides down the riverbank from the direction of Chertsey. The Shepperton guns spoke this time unavailingly.

At that I ducked at once under water, and, holding my breath until movement was an agony, blundered painfully ahead under the surface as long as I could. The water was in a tumult about me, and rapidly growing hotter.

When for a moment I raised my head to take breath and throw the hair and water from my eyes, the steam was rising in a whirling white fog that at first hid the Martians altogether. The noise was deafening. Then I saw them dimly, colossal figures of grey, magnified by the mist. They had passed by me, and two were stooping over the frothing, tumultuous ruins of their comrade.

The third and fourth stood beside him in the water, one perhaps two hundred yards from me, the other towards Laleham. The generators of the Heat- Rays waved high, and the hissing beams smote down this way and that.

The air was full of sound, a deafening and confusing conflict of noises —the clangorous din of the Martians, the crash of falling houses, the thud of trees, fences, sheds flashing into flame, and the crackling and roaring of fire. Dense black smoke was leaping up to mingle with the steam from the river, and as the Heat-Ray went to and fro over Weybridge its impact was marked by flashes of incandescent white, that gave place at once to a smoky dance of lurid flames. The nearer houses still stood intact, awaiting their fate, shadowy, faint and pallid in the steam, with the fire behind them going to and fro.

For a moment perhaps I stood there, breast-high in the almost boiling water, dumbfounded at my position, hopeless of escape. Through the reek I could see the people who had been with me in the river scrambling out of the water through the reeds, like little frogs hurrying through grass from the advance of a man, or running to and fro in utter dismay on the towing path.

Then suddenly the white flashes of the Heat-Ray came leaping towards me. The houses caved in as they dissolved at its touch, and darted out flames; the trees changed to fire with a roar. The Ray flickered up and down the towing path, licking off the people who ran this way and that, and came down to the water's edge not fifty yards from where I stood. It swept across the river to Shepperton, and the water in its track rose in a boiling weal crested with steam. I turned shoreward.

In another moment the huge wave, well-nigh at the boiling-point had rushed upon me. I screamed aloud, and scalded, half blinded, agonised, I staggered through the leaping, hissing water towards the shore. Had my foot stumbled, it would have been the end. I fell helplessly, in full sight of the Martians, upon the broad, bare gravelly spit that runs down to mark the angle of the Wey and Thames. I expected nothing but death.

I have a dim memory of the foot of a Martian coming down within a score of yards of my head, driving straight into the loose gravel, whirling it this way and that and lifting again; of a long suspense, and then of the four carrying the debris of their comrade between them, now clear and then presently faint through a veil of smoke, receding interminably, as it seemed to me, across a vast space of river and meadow. And then, very slowly, I realised that by a miracle I had escaped.

CHAPTER THIRTEEN - HOW I FELL IN WITH THE CURATE

After getting this sudden lesson in the power of terrestrial weapons, the Martians retreated to their original position upon Horsell Common; and in their haste, and encumbered with the debris of their smashed companion, they no doubt overlooked many such a stray and negligible victim as myself. Had they left their comrade and pushed on forthwith, there was nothing at that time between them and London but batteries of twelve-pounder guns, and they would certainly have reached the capital in advance of the tidings of their approach; as sudden, dreadful, and destructive their advent would have been as the earthquake that destroyed Lisbon a century ago.

But they were in no hurry. Cylinder followed cylinder on its interplanetary flight; every twenty-four hours brought them reinforcement. And meanwhile the military and naval authorities, now fully alive to the tremendous power of their antagonists, worked with furious energy. Every minute a fresh gun came into position until, before twilight, every copse, every row of suburban villas on the hilly slopes about Kingston and Richmond, masked an expectant black muzzle. And through the charred and desolated area—perhaps twenty square miles altogether—that encircled the Martian encampment on Horsell Common, through charred and ruined villages among the green trees, through the blackened and smoking arcades that had been but a day ago pine spinneys, crawled the devoted scouts with the heliographs that were presently to warn the gunners of the Martian approach. But the Martians now understood our command of artillery and the danger of human proximity, and not a man ventured within a mile of either cylinder, save at the price of his life.

It would seem that these giants spent the earlier part of the afternoon in going to and fro, transferring everything from the second and third cylinders—the second in Addlestone Golf Links and the third at Pyrford —to their original pit on Horsell Common. Over that, above the blackened heather and ruined buildings that stretched far and wide, stood one as sentinel, while the rest abandoned their vast fighting-machines and descended into the pit. They were hard at work there far into the night, and the towering pillar of dense green smoke that rose therefrom could be seen from the hills about Merrow, and even, it is said, from Banstead and Epsom Downs.

And while the Martians behind me were thus preparing for their next sally, and in front of me Humanity gathered for the battle, I made my way with infinite pains and labour from the fire and smoke of burning Weybridge towards London.

I saw an abandoned boat, very small and remote, drifting down-stream; and throwing off the most of my sodden clothes, I went after it, gained it, and so escaped out of that destruction. There were no oars in the boat, but I contrived to paddle, as well as my parboiled hands would allow, down the river towards Halliford and Walton, going very tediously and continually looking behind me, as you may well understand. I followed the river, because I considered that the water gave me my best chance of escape should these giants return.

The hot water from the Martian's overthrow drifted downstream with me, so that for the best part of a mile I could see little of either bank. Once, however, I made out a string of black figures hurrying across the meadows from the direction of Weybridge. Halliford, it seemed, was deserted, and several of the houses facing the river were on fire. It was strange to see the place quite tranquil, quite desolate under the hot blue sky, with the smoke and little threads of flame going straight up into the heat of the afternoon. Never before had I seen houses burning without the accompaniment of an obstructive crowd. A little farther on the dry reeds up the bank were smoking and glowing, and a line of fire inland was marching steadily across a late field of hay.

For a long time I drifted, so painful and weary was I after the violence I had been through, and so intense the heat upon the water. Then my fears got the better of me again, and I resumed my paddling. The sun scorched my bare back. At last, as the bridge at Walton was coming into sight round the bend, my fever and faintness overcame my fears, and I landed on the Middlesex bank and lay down, deadly sick, amid the long grass. I suppose the time was then about four or five o'clock. I got up presently, walked perhaps half a mile without meeting a soul, and then lay down again in the shadow of a hedge. I seem to remember talking, wanderingly, to myself during that last spurt. I was also very thirsty, and bitterly regretful I had drunk no more water. It is a curious thing that I felt angry with my wife; I cannot account for it, but my impotent desire to reach Leatherhead worried me excessively.

I do not clearly remember the arrival of the curate, so that probably I dozed. I became aware of him as a seated figure in soot-smudged shirt sleeves, and with his upturned, clean-shaven face staring at a faint flickering that danced over the sky. The sky was what is called a mackerel sky—rows and rows of faint down-plumes of cloud, just tinted with the midsummer sunset.

I sat up, and at the rustle of my motion he looked at me quickly.

"Have you any water?" I asked abruptly.

He shook his head.

"You have been asking for water for the last hour," he said.

For a moment we were silent, taking stock of each other. I dare say he found me a strange enough figure, naked, save for my water-soaked trousers and socks, scalded, and my face and shoulders blackened by the smoke. His face was a fair

weakness, his chin retreated, and his hair lay in crisp, almost flaxen curls on his low forehead; his eyes were rather large, pale blue, and blankly staring. He spoke abruptly, looking vacantly away from me.

"What does it mean?" he said. "What do these things mean?"

I stared at him and made no answer.

He extended a thin white hand and spoke in almost a complaining tone.

"Why are these things permitted? What sins have we done? The morning service was over, I was walking through the roads to clear my brain for the afternoon, and then—fire, earthquake, death! As if it were Sodom and Gomorrah! All our work undone, all the work—What are these Martians?"

"What are we?" I answered, clearing my throat.

He gripped his knees and turned to look at me again. For half a minute, perhaps, he stared silently.

"I was walking through the roads to clear my brain," he said. "And suddenly—fire, earthquake, death!"

He relapsed into silence, with his chin now sunken almost to his knees.

Presently he began waving his hand.

"All the work—all the Sunday schools—What have we done —what has Weybridge done? Everything gone—everything destroyed. The church! We rebuilt it only three years ago. Gone! Swept out of existence! Why?"

Another pause, and he broke out again like one demented.

"The smoke of her burning goeth up for ever and ever!" he shouted.

His eyes flamed, and he pointed a lean finger in the direction of Weybridge.

By this time I was beginning to take his measure. The tremendous tragedy in which he had been involved—it was evident he was a fugitive from Weybridge—had driven him to the very verge of his reason.

"Are we far from Sunbury?" I said, in a matter-of-fact tone.

"What are we to do?" he asked. "Are these creatures everywhere? Has the earth been given over to them?"

"Are we far from Sunbury?"

"Only this morning I officiated at early celebration—"

"Things have changed," I said, quietly. "You must keep your head. There is still hope."

"Hope!"

"Yes. Plentiful hope—for all this destruction!"

I began to explain my view of our position. He listened at first, but as I went on the interest dawning in his eyes gave place to their former stare, and his regard wandered from me.

"This must be the beginning of the end," he said, interrupting me. "The end! The great and terrible day of the Lord! When men shall call upon the mountains and the rocks to fall upon them and hide them—hide them from the face of Him that sitteth upon the throne!"

I began to understand the position. I ceased my laboured reasoning, struggled to my feet, and, standing over him, laid my hand on his shoulder.

"Be a man!" said I. "You are scared out of your wits! What good is religion if it collapses under calamity? Think of what earthquakes and floods, wars and volcanoes, have done before to men! Did you think God had exempted Weybridge? He is not an insurance agent."

For a time he sat in blank silence.

"But how can we escape?" he asked, suddenly. "They are invulnerable, they are pitiless."

"Neither the one nor, perhaps, the other," I answered. "And the mightier they are the more sane and wary should we be. One of them was killed yonder not three hours ago."

"Killed!" he said, staring about him. "How can God's ministers be killed?"

"I saw it happen." I proceeded to tell him. "We have chanced to come in for the thick of it," said I, "and that is all."

"What is that flicker in the sky?" he asked abruptly.

I told him it was the heliograph signalling—that it was the sign of human help and effort in the sky.

"We are in the midst of it," I said, "quiet as it is. That flicker in the sky tells of the gathering storm. Yonder, I take it are the Martians, and Londonward, where those hills rise about Richmond and Kingston and the trees give cover, earthworks are being thrown up and guns are being placed. Presently the Martians will be coming this way again."

And even as I spoke he sprang to his feet and stopped me by a gesture.

"Listen!" he said.

From beyond the low hills across the water came the dull resonance of distant guns and a remote weird crying. Then everything was still. A cockchafer came droning over the hedge and past us. High in the west the crescent moon hung faint and pale above the smoke of Weybridge and Shepperton and the hot, still splendour of the sunset.

"We had better follow this path," I said, "northward."

CHAPTER FOURTEEN - IN LONDON

My younger brother was in London when the Martians fell at Woking. He was a medical student working for an imminent examination, and he heard nothing of the arrival until Saturday morning. The morning papers on Saturday contained, in addition to lengthy special articles on the planet Mars, on life in the planets, and so forth, a brief and vaguely worded telegram, all the more striking for its brevity.

The Martians, alarmed by the approach of a crowd, had killed a number of people with a quick-firing gun, so the story ran. The telegram concluded with the words: "Formidable as they seem to be, the Martians have not moved from the pit into which they have fallen, and, indeed, seem incapable of doing so. Probably this is due to the relative strength of the earth's gravitational energy." On that last text their leader-writer expanded very comfortingly.

Of course all the students in the crammer's biology class, to which my brother went that day, were intensely interested, but there were no signs of any unusual excitement in the streets. The afternoon papers puffed scraps of news under big headlines. They had nothing to tell beyond the movements of troops about the common, and the burning of the pine woods between Woking and Weybridge, until eight. Then the *St. James's Gazette*, in an extra- special edition, announced the bare fact of the interruption of telegraphic communication. This was thought to be due to the falling of burning pine trees across the line. Nothing more of the fighting was known that night, the night of my drive to Leatherhead and back.

My brother felt no anxiety about us, as he knew from the description in the papers that the cylinder was a good two miles from my house. He made up his mind to run down that night to me, in order, as he says, to see the Things before they were killed. He dispatched a telegram, which never reached me, about four o'clock, and spent the evening at a music hall.

In London, also, on Saturday night there was a thunderstorm, and my brother reached Waterloo in a cab. On the platform from which the midnight train usually starts he learned, after some waiting, that an accident prevented trains from reaching Woking that night. The nature of the accident he could not ascertain; indeed, the railway authorities did not clearly know at that time. There was very little excitement in the station, as the officials, failing to realise that anything further than a breakdown between Byfleet and Woking junction had occurred, were running the theatre trains which usually passed through Woking round by Virginia Water or Guildford. They were busy making the necessary arrangements to alter the route of the Southampton and Portsmouth Sunday League excursions. A nocturnal

newspaper reporter, mistaking my brother for the traffic manager, to whom he bears a slight resemblance, waylaid and tried to interview him. Few people, excepting the railway officials, connected the breakdown with the Martians.

I have read, in another account of these events, that on Sunday morning "all London was electrified by the news from Woking." As a matter of fact, there was nothing to justify that very extravagant phrase. Plenty of Londoners did not hear of the Martians until the panic of Monday morning. Those who did took some time to realise all that the hastily worded telegrams in the Sunday papers conveyed. The majority of people in London do not read Sunday papers.

The habit of personal security, moreover, is so deeply fixed in the Londoner's mind, and startling intelligence so much a matter of course in the papers, that they could read without any personal tremors: "About seven o'clock last night the Martians came out of the cylinder, and, moving about under an armour of metallic shields, have completely wrecked Woking station with the adjacent houses, and massacred an entire battalion of the Cardigan Regiment. No details are known. Maxims have been absolutely useless against their armour; the field guns have been disabled by them. Flying hussars have been galloping into Chertsey. The Martians appear to be moving slowly towards Chertsey or Windsor. Great anxiety prevails in West Surrey, and earthworks are being thrown up to check the advance Londonward." That was how the Sunday *Sun* put it, and a clever and remarkably prompt "handbook" article in the *Referee* compared the affair to a menagerie suddenly let loose in a village.

No one in London knew positively of the nature of the armoured Martians, and there was still a fixed idea that these monsters must be sluggish: "crawling," "creeping painfully"—such expressions occurred in almost all the earlier reports. None of the telegrams could have been written by an eyewitness of their advance. The Sunday papers printed separate editions as further news came to hand, some even in default of it. But there was practically nothing more to tell people until late in the afternoon, when the authorities gave the press agencies the news in their possession. It was stated that the people of Walton and Weybridge, and all the district were pouring along the roads Londonward, and that was all.

My brother went to church at the Foundling Hospital in the morning, still in ignorance of what had happened on the previous night. There he heard allusions made to the invasion, and a special prayer for peace. Coming out, he bought a *Referee*. He became alarmed at the news in this, and went again to Waterloo station to find out if communication were restored. The omnibuses, carriages, cyclists, and innumerable people walking in their best clothes seemed scarcely affected by the strange intelligence that the news venders were disseminating. People were interested, or, if alarmed, alarmed only on account of the local residents. At the station he heard for the first time that the Windsor and Chertsey lines were now interrupted. The porters told him that several remarkable telegrams had been received in the morning from Byfleet and Chertsey stations, but that these had abruptly ceased. My brother could get very little precise detail out of them.

"There's fighting going on about Weybridge" was the extent of their information.

The train service was now very much disorganised. Quite a number of people who had been expecting friends from places on the South-Western network were standing about the station. One grey-headed old gentleman came and abused the South-Western Company bitterly to my brother. "It wants showing up," he said.

One or two trains came in from Richmond, Putney, and Kingston, containing people who had gone out for a day's boating and found the locks closed and a feeling of panic in the air. A man in a blue and white blazer addressed my brother, full of strange tidings.

"There's hosts of people driving into Kingston in traps and carts and things, with boxes of valuables and all that," he said. "They come from Molesey and Weybridge and Walton, and they say there's been guns heard at Chertsey, heavy firing, and that mounted soldiers have told them to get off at once because the Martians are coming. We heard guns firing at Hampton Court station, but we thought it was thunder. What the dickens does it all mean? The Martians can't get out of their pit, can they?"

My brother could not tell him.

Afterwards he found that the vague feeling of alarm had spread to the clients of the underground railway, and that the Sunday excursionists began to return from all over the South-Western "lung"—Barnes, Wimbledon, Richmond Park, Kew, and so forth—at unnaturally early hours; but not a soul had anything more than vague hearsay to tell of. Everyone connected with the terminus seemed ill-tempered.

About five o'clock the gathering crowd in the station was immensely excited by the opening of the line of communication, which is almost invariably closed, between the South-Eastern and the South-Western stations, and the passage of carriage trucks bearing huge guns and carriages crammed with soldiers. These were the guns that were brought up from Woolwich and Chatham to cover Kingston. There was an exchange of pleasantries: "You'll get eaten!" "We're the beast-tamers!" and so forth. A little while after that a squad of police came into the station and began to clear the public off the platforms, and my brother went out into the street again.

The church bells were ringing for evensong, and a squad of Salvation Army lassies came singing down Waterloo Road. On the bridge a number of loafers were watching a curious brown scum that came drifting down the stream in patches. The sun was just setting, and the Clock Tower and the Houses of Parliament rose against one of the most peaceful skies it is possible to imagine, a sky of gold, barred with long transverse stripes of reddish-purple cloud. There was talk of a floating body. One of the men there, a reservist he said he was, told my brother he had seen the heliograph flickering in the west.

In Wellington Street my brother met a couple of sturdy roughs who had just been rushed out of Fleet Street with still-wet newspapers and staring placards. "Dreadful catastrophe!" they bawled one to the other down Wellington Street.

"Fighting at Weybridge! Full description! Repulse of the Martians! London in Danger!" He had to give threepence for a copy of that paper.

Then it was, and then only, that he realised something of the full power and terror of these monsters. He learned that they were not merely a handful of small sluggish creatures, but that they were minds swaying vast mechanical bodies; and that they could move swiftly and smite with such power that even the mightiest guns could not stand against them.

They were described as "vast spiderlike machines, nearly a hundred feet high, capable of the speed of an express train, and able to shoot out a beam of intense heat." Masked batteries, chiefly of field guns, had been planted in the country about Horsell Common, and especially between the Woking district and London. Five of the machines had been seen moving towards the Thames, and one, by a happy chance, had been destroyed. In the other cases the shells had missed, and the batteries had been at once annihilated by the Heat-Rays. Heavy losses of soldiers were mentioned, but the tone of the dispatch was optimistic.

The Martians had been repulsed; they were not invulnerable. They had retreated to their triangle of cylinders again, in the circle about Woking. Signallers with heliographs were pushing forward upon them from all sides. Guns were in rapid transit from Windsor, Portsmouth, Aldershot, Woolwich—even from the north; among others, long wire-guns of ninety-five tons from Woolwich. Altogether one hundred and sixteen were in position or being hastily placed, chiefly covering London. Never before in England had there been such a vast or rapid concentration of military material.

Any further cylinders that fell, it was hoped, could be destroyed at once by high explosives, which were being rapidly manufactured and distributed. No doubt, ran the report, the situation was of the strangest and gravest description, but the public was exhorted to avoid and discourage panic. No doubt the Martians were strange and terrible in the extreme, but at the outside there could not be more than twenty of them against our millions.

The authorities had reason to suppose, from the size of the cylinders, that at the outside there could not be more than five in each cylinder—fifteen altogether. And one at least was disposed of—perhaps more. The public would be fairly warned of the approach of danger, and elaborate measures were being taken for the protection of the people in the threatened southwestern suburbs. And so, with reiterated assurances of the safety of London and the ability of the authorities to cope with the difficulty, this quasi-proclamation closed.

This was printed in enormous type on paper so fresh that it was still wet, and there had been no time to add a word of comment. It was curious, my brother said, to see how ruthlessly the usual contents of the paper had been hacked and taken out to give this place.

All down Wellington Street people could be seen fluttering out the pink sheets and reading, and the Strand was suddenly noisy with the voices of an army of hawkers following these pioneers. Men came scrambling off buses to secure copies. Certainly this news excited people intensely, whatever their previous apathy.

The shutters of a map shop in the Strand were being taken down, my brother said, and a man in his Sunday raiment, lemon-yellow gloves even, was visible inside the window hastily fastening maps of Surrey to the glass.

Going on along the Strand to Trafalgar Square, the paper in his hand, my brother saw some of the fugitives from West Surrey. There was a man with his wife and two boys and some articles of furniture in a cart such as greengrocers use. He was driving from the direction of Westminster Bridge; and close behind him came a hay waggon with five or six respectable-looking people in it, and some boxes and bundles. The faces of these people were haggard, and their entire appearance contrasted conspicuously with the Sabbath-best appearance of the people on the omnibuses. People in fashionable clothing peeped at them out of cabs. They stopped at the Square as if undecided which way to take, and finally turned eastward along the Strand. Some way behind these came a man in workday clothes, riding one of those old-fashioned tricycles with a small front wheel. He was dirty and white in the face.

My brother turned down towards Victoria, and met a number of such people. He had a vague idea that he might see something of me. He noticed an unusual number of police regulating the traffic. Some of the refugees were exchanging news with the people on the omnibuses. One was professing to have seen the Martians. "Boilers on stilts, I tell you, striding along like men." Most of them were excited and animated by their strange experience.

Beyond Victoria the public-houses were doing a lively trade with these arrivals. At all the street corners groups of people were reading papers, talking excitedly, or staring at these unusual Sunday visitors. They seemed to increase as night drew on, until at last the roads, my brother said, were like Epsom High Street on a Derby Day. My brother addressed several of these fugitives and got unsatisfactory answers from most.

None of them could tell him any news of Woking except one man, who assured him that Woking had been entirely destroyed on the previous night.

"I come from Byfleet," he said; "man on a bicycle came through the place in the early morning, and ran from door to door warning us to come away. Then came soldiers. We went out to look, and there were clouds of smoke to the south—nothing but smoke, and not a soul coming that way. Then we heard the guns at Chertsey, and folks coming from Weybridge. So I've locked up my house and come on."

At the time there was a strong feeling in the streets that the authorities were to blame for their incapacity to dispose of the invaders without all this inconvenience.

About eight o'clock a noise of heavy firing was distinctly audible all over the south of London. My brother could not hear it for the traffic in the main thoroughfares, but by striking through the quiet back streets to the river he was able to distinguish it quite plainly.

He walked from Westminster to his apartments near Regent's Park, about two. He was now very anxious on my account, and disturbed at the evident magnitude

of the trouble. His mind was inclined to run, even as mine had run on Saturday, on military details. He thought of all those silent, expectant guns, of the suddenly nomadic countryside; he tried to imagine "boilers on stilts" a hundred feet high.

There were one or two cartloads of refugees passing along Oxford Street, and several in the Marylebone Road, but so slowly was the news spreading that Regent Street and Portland Place were full of their usual Sunday-night promenaders, albeit they talked in groups, and along the edge of Regent's Park there were as many silent couples "walking out" together under the scattered gas lamps as ever there had been. The night was warm and still, and a little oppressive; the sound of guns continued intermittently, and after midnight there seemed to be sheet lightning in the south.

He read and re-read the paper, fearing the worst had happened to me. He was restless, and after supper prowled out again aimlessly. He returned and tried in vain to divert his attention to his examination notes. He went to bed a little after midnight, and was awakened from lurid dreams in the small hours of Monday by the sound of door knockers, feet running in the street, distant drumming, and a clamour of bells. Red reflections danced on the ceiling. For a moment he lay astonished, wondering whether day had come or the world gone mad. Then he jumped out of bed and ran to the window.

His room was an attic and as he thrust his head out, up and down the street there were a dozen echoes to the noise of his window sash, and heads in every kind of night disarray appeared. Enquiries were being shouted. "They are coming!" bawled a policeman, hammering at the door; "the Martians are coming!" and hurried to the next door.

The sound of drumming and trumpeting came from the Albany Street Barracks, and every church within earshot was hard at work killing sleep with a vehement disorderly tocsin. There was a noise of doors opening, and window after window in the houses opposite flashed from darkness into yellow illumination.

Up the street came galloping a closed carriage, bursting abruptly into noise at the corner, rising to a clattering climax under the window, and dying away slowly in the distance. Close on the rear of this came a couple of cabs, the forerunners of a long procession of flying vehicles, going for the most part to Chalk Farm station, where the North-Western special trains were loading up, instead of coming down the gradient into Euston.

For a long time my brother stared out of the window in blank astonishment, watching the policemen hammering at door after door, and delivering their incomprehensible message. Then the door behind him opened, and the man who lodged across the landing came in, dressed only in shirt, trousers, and slippers, his braces loose about his waist, his hair disordered from his pillow.

"What the devil is it?" he asked. "A fire? What a devil of a row!"

They both craned their heads out of the window, straining to hear what the policemen were shouting. People were coming out of the side streets, and standing in groups at the corners talking.

"What the devil is it all about?" said my brother's fellow lodger.

My brother answered him vaguely and began to dress, running with each garment to the window in order to miss nothing of the growing excitement. And presently men selling unnaturally early newspapers came bawling into the street:

"London in danger of suffocation! The Kingston and Richmond defences forced! Fearful massacres in the Thames Valley!"

And all about him—in the rooms below, in the houses on each side and across the road, and behind in the Park Terraces and in the hundred other streets of that part of Marylebone, and the Westbourne Park district and St. Pancras, and westward and northward in Kilburn and St. John's Wood and Hampstead, and eastward in Shoreditch and Highbury and Haggerston and Hoxton, and, indeed, through all the vastness of London from Ealing to East Ham—people were rubbing their eyes, and opening windows to stare out and ask aimless questions, dressing hastily as the first breath of the coming storm of Fear blew through the streets. It was the dawn of the great panic. London, which had gone to bed on Sunday night oblivious and inert, was awakened, in the small hours of Monday morning, to a vivid sense of danger.

Unable from his window to learn what was happening, my brother went down and out into the street, just as the sky between the parapets of the houses grew pink with the early dawn. The flying people on foot and in vehicles grew more numerous every moment. "Black Smoke!" he heard people crying, and again "Black Smoke!" The contagion of such a unanimous fear was inevitable. As my brother hesitated on the door-step, he saw another news vender approaching, and got a paper forthwith. The man was running away with the rest, and selling his papers for a shilling each as he ran—a grotesque mingling of profit and panic.

And from this paper my brother read that catastrophic dispatch of the Commander-in-Chief:

"The Martians are able to discharge enormous clouds of a black and poisonous vapour by means of rockets. They have smothered our batteries, destroyed Richmond, Kingston, and Wimbledon, and are advancing slowly towards London, destroying everything on the way. It is impossible to stop them. There is no safety from the Black Smoke but in instant flight."

That was all, but it was enough. The whole population of the great six- million city was stirring, slipping, running; presently it would be pouring *en masse* northward.

"Black Smoke!" the voices cried. "Fire!"

The bells of the neighbouring church made a jangling tumult, a cart carelessly driven smashed, amid shrieks and curses, against the water trough up the street. Sickly yellow lights went to and fro in the houses, and some of the passing cabs flaunted unextinguished lamps. And overhead the dawn was growing brighter, clear and steady and calm.

He heard footsteps running to and fro in the rooms, and up and down stairs behind him. His landlady came to the door, loosely wrapped in dressing gown and shawl; her husband followed ejaculating.

As my brother began to realise the import of all these things, he turned hastily to his own room, put all his available money—some ten pounds altogether—into his pockets, and went out again into the streets.

CHAPTER FIFTEEN - WHAT HAD HAPPENED IN SURREY

It was while the curate had sat and talked so wildly to me under the hedge in the flat meadows near Halliford, and while my brother was watching the fugitives stream over Westminster Bridge, that the Martians had resumed the offensive. So far as one can ascertain from the conflicting accounts that have been put forth, the majority of them remained busied with preparations in the Horsell pit until nine that night, hurrying on some operation that disengaged huge volumes of green smoke.

But three certainly came out about eight o'clock and, advancing slowly and cautiously, made their way through Byfleet and Pyrford towards Ripley and Weybridge, and so came in sight of the expectant batteries against the setting sun. These Martians did not advance in a body, but in a line, each perhaps a mile and a half from his nearest fellow. They communicated with one another by means of sirenlike howls, running up and down the scale from one note to another.

It was this howling and firing of the guns at Ripley and St. George's Hill that we had heard at Upper Halliford. The Ripley gunners, unseasoned artillery volunteers who ought never to have been placed in such a position, fired one wild, premature, ineffectual volley, and bolted on horse and foot through the deserted village, while the Martian, without using his Heat-Ray, walked serenely over their guns, stepped gingerly among them, passed in front of them, and so came unexpectedly upon the guns in Painshill Park, which he destroyed.

The St. George's Hill men, however, were better led or of a better mettle. Hidden by a pine wood as they were, they seem to have been quite unsuspected by the Martian nearest to them. They laid their guns as deliberately as if they had been on parade, and fired at about a thousand yards' range.

The shells flashed all round him, and he was seen to advance a few paces, stagger, and go down. Everybody yelled together, and the guns were reloaded in frantic haste. The overthrown Martian set up a prolonged ululation, and immediately a second glittering giant, answering him, appeared over the trees to the south. It would seem that a leg of the tripod had been smashed by one of the shells. The whole of the second volley flew wide of the Martian on the ground, and, simultaneously, both his companions brought their Heat-Rays to bear on the battery. The ammunition blew up, the pine trees all about the guns flashed into fire, and only one or two of the men who were already running over the crest of the hill escaped.

After this it would seem that the three took counsel together and halted, and the scouts who were watching them report that they remained absolutely stationary for the next half hour. The Martian who had been overthrown crawled tediously out of his hood, a small brown figure, oddly suggestive from that distance of a speck of blight, and apparently engaged in the repair of his support. About nine he had finished, for his cowl was then seen above the trees again.

It was a few minutes past nine that night when these three sentinels were joined by four other Martians, each carrying a thick black tube. A similar tube was handed to each of the three, and the seven proceeded to distribute themselves at equal distances along a curved line between St. George's Hill, Weybridge, and the village of Send, southwest of Ripley.

A dozen rockets sprang out of the hills before them so soon as they began to move, and warned the waiting batteries about Ditton and Esher. At the same time four of their fighting machines, similarly armed with tubes, crossed the river, and two of them, black against the western sky, came into sight of myself and the curate as we hurried wearily and painfully along the road that runs northward out of Halliford. They moved, as it seemed to us, upon a cloud, for a milky mist covered the fields and rose to a third of their height.

At this sight the curate cried faintly in his throat, and began running; but I knew it was no good running from a Martian, and I turned aside and crawled through dewy nettles and brambles into the broad ditch by the side of the road. He looked back, saw what I was doing, and turned to join me.

The two halted, the nearer to us standing and facing Sunbury, the remoter being a grey indistinctness towards the evening star, away towards Staines.

The occasional howling of the Martians had ceased; they took up their positions in the huge crescent about their cylinders in absolute silence. It was a crescent with twelve miles between its horns. Never since the devising of gunpowder was the beginning of a battle so still. To us and to an observer about Ripley it would have had precisely the same effect—the Martians seemed in solitary possession of the darkling night, lit only as it was by the slender moon, the stars, the afterglow of the daylight, and the ruddy glare from St. George's Hill and the woods of Painshill.

But facing that crescent everywhere—at Staines, Hounslow, Ditton, Esher, Ockham, behind hills and woods south of the river, and across the flat grass meadows to the north of it, wherever a cluster of trees or village houses gave sufficient cover—the guns were waiting. The signal rockets burst and rained their sparks through the night and vanished, and the spirit of all those watching batteries rose to a tense expectation. The Martians had but to advance into the line of fire, and instantly those motionless black forms of men, those guns glittering so darkly in the early night, would explode into a thunderous fury of battle.

No doubt the thought that was uppermost in a thousand of those vigilant minds, even as it was uppermost in mine, was the riddle—how much they understood of us. Did they grasp that we in our millions were organized, disciplined, working together? Or did they interpret our spurts of fire, the sudden stinging of

our shells, our steady investment of their encampment, as we should the furious unanimity of onslaught in a disturbed hive of bees? Did they dream they might exterminate us? (At that time no one knew what food they needed.) A hundred such questions struggled together in my mind as I watched that vast sentinel shape. And in the back of my mind was the sense of all the huge unknown and hidden forces Londonward. Had they prepared pitfalls? Were the powder mills at Hounslow ready as a snare? Would the Londoners have the heart and courage to make a greater Moscow of their mighty province of houses?

Then, after an interminable time, as it seemed to us, crouching and peering through the hedge, came a sound like the distant concussion of a gun. Another nearer, and then another. And then the Martian beside us raised his tube on high and discharged it, gunwise, with a heavy report that made the ground heave. The one towards Staines answered him. There was no flash, no smoke, simply that loaded detonation.

I was so excited by these heavy minute-guns following one another that I so far forgot my personal safety and my scalded hands as to clamber up into the hedge and stare towards Sunbury. As I did so a second report followed, and a big projectile hurtled overhead towards Hounslow. I expected at least to see smoke or fire, or some such evidence of its work. But all I saw was the deep blue sky above, with one solitary star, and the white mist spreading wide and low beneath. And there had been no crash, no answering explosion. The silence was restored; the minute lengthened to three.

"What has happened?" said the curate, standing up beside me.

"Heaven knows!" said I.

A bat flickered by and vanished. A distant tumult of shouting began and ceased. I looked again at the Martian, and saw he was now moving eastward along the riverbank, with a swift, rolling motion.

Every moment I expected the fire of some hidden battery to spring upon him; but the evening calm was unbroken. The figure of the Martian grew smaller as he receded, and presently the mist and the gathering night had swallowed him up. By a common impulse we clambered higher. Towards Sunbury was a dark appearance, as though a conical hill had suddenly come into being there, hiding our view of the farther country; and then, remoter across the river, over Walton, we saw another such summit. These hill-like forms grew lower and broader even as we stared.

Moved by a sudden thought, I looked northward, and there I perceived a third of these cloudy black kopjes had risen.

Everything had suddenly become very still. Far away to the southeast, marking the quiet, we heard the Martians hooting to one another, and then the air quivered again with the distant thud of their guns. But the earthly artillery made no reply.

Now at the time we could not understand these things, but later I was to learn the meaning of these ominous kopjes that gathered in the twilight. Each of the Martians, standing in the great crescent I have described, had discharged, by means of the gunlike tube he carried, a huge canister over whatever hill, copse,

cluster[1] of houses, or other possible cover for guns, chanced to be in front of him. Some fired only one of these, some two—as in the case of the one we had seen; the one at Ripley is said to have discharged no fewer than five at that time. These canisters smashed on striking the ground—they did not explode—and incontinently disengaged an enormous volume of heavy, inky vapour, coiling and pouring upward in a huge and ebony cumulus cloud, a gaseous hill that sank and spread itself slowly over the surrounding country. And the touch of that vapour, the inhaling of its pungent wisps, was death to all that breathes.

It was heavy, this vapour, heavier than the densest smoke, so that, after the first tumultuous uprush and outflow of its impact, it sank down through the air and poured over the ground in a manner rather liquid than gaseous, abandoning the hills, and streaming into the valleys and ditches and watercourses even as I have heard the carbonic-acid gas that pours from volcanic clefts is wont to do. And where it came upon water some chemical action occurred, and the surface would be instantly covered with a powdery scum that sank slowly and made way for more. The scum was absolutely insoluble, and it is a strange thing, seeing the instant effect of the gas, that one could drink without hurt the water from which it had been strained. The vapour did not diffuse as a true gas would do. It hung together in banks, flowing sluggishly down the slope of the land and driving reluctantly before the wind, and very slowly it combined with the mist and moisture of the air, and sank to the earth in the form of dust. Save that an unknown element giving a group of four lines in the blue of the spectrum is concerned, we are still entirely ignorant of the nature of this substance.

Once the tumultuous upheaval of its dispersion was over, the black smoke clung so closely to the ground, even before its precipitation, that fifty feet up in the air, on the roofs and upper stories of high houses and on great trees, there was a chance of escaping its poison altogether, as was proved even that night at Street Cobham and Ditton.

The man who escaped at the former place tells a wonderful story of the strangeness of its coiling flow, and how he looked down from the church spire and saw the houses of the village rising like ghosts out of its inky nothingness. For a day and a half he remained there, weary, starving and sun- scorched, the earth under the blue sky and against the prospect of the distant hills a velvet-black expanse, with red roofs, green trees, and, later, black- veiled shrubs and gates, barns, outhouses, and walls, rising here and there into the sunlight.

But that was at Street Cobham, where the black vapour was allowed to remain until it sank of its own accord into the ground. As a rule the Martians, when it had served its purpose, cleared the air of it again by wading into it and directing a jet of steam upon it.

This they did with the vapour banks near us, as we saw in the starlight from the window of a deserted house at Upper Halliford, whither we had returned. From there we could see the searchlights on Richmond Hill and Kingston Hill going to and fro, and about eleven the windows rattled, and we heard the sound of the huge siege guns that had been put in position there. These continued intermit-

tently for the space of a quarter of an hour, sending chance shots at the invisible Martians at Hampton and Ditton, and then the pale beams of the electric light vanished, and were replaced by a bright red glow.

Then the fourth cylinder fell—a brilliant green meteor—as I learned afterwards, in Bushey Park. Before the guns on the Richmond and Kingston line of hills began, there was a fitful cannonade far away in the southwest, due, I believe, to guns being fired haphazard before the black vapour could overwhelm the gunners.

So, setting about it as methodically as men might smoke out a wasps' nest, the Martians spread this strange stifling vapour over the Londonward country. The horns of the crescent slowly moved apart, until at last they formed a line from Hanwell to Coombe and Malden. All night through their destructive tubes advanced. Never once, after the Martian at St. George's Hill was brought down, did they give the artillery the ghost of a chance against them. Wherever there was a possibility of guns being laid for them unseen, a fresh canister of the black vapour was discharged, and where the guns were openly displayed the Heat-Ray was brought to bear.

By midnight the blazing trees along the slopes of Richmond Park and the glare of Kingston Hill threw their light upon a network of black smoke, blotting out the whole valley of the Thames and extending as far as the eye could reach. And through this two Martians slowly waded, and turned their hissing steam jets this way and that.

They were sparing of the Heat-Ray that night, either because they had but a limited supply of material for its production or because they did not wish to destroy the country but only to crush and overawe the opposition they had aroused. In the latter aim they certainly succeeded. Sunday night was the end of the organised opposition to their movements. After that no body of men would stand against them, so hopeless was the enterprise. Even the crews of the torpedo-boats and destroyers that had brought their quick-firers up the Thames refused to stop, mutinied, and went down again. The only offensive operation men ventured upon after that night was the preparation of mines and pitfalls, and even in that their energies were frantic and spasmodic.

One has to imagine, as well as one may, the fate of those batteries towards Esher, waiting so tensely in the twilight. Survivors there were none. One may picture the orderly expectation, the officers alert and watchful, the gunners ready, the ammunition piled to hand, the limber gunners with their horses and waggons, the groups of civilian spectators standing as near as they were permitted, the evening stillness, the ambulances and hospital tents with the burned and wounded from Weybridge; then the dull resonance of the shots the Martians fired, and the clumsy projectile whirling over the trees and houses and smashing amid the neighbouring fields.

One may picture, too, the sudden shifting of the attention, the swiftly spreading coils and bellyings of that blackness advancing headlong, towering heavenward, turning the twilight to a palpable darkness, a strange and horrible

antagonist of vapour striding upon its victims, men and horses near it seen dimly, running, shrieking, falling headlong, shouts of dismay, the guns suddenly abandoned, men choking and writhing on the ground, and the swift broadening-out of the opaque cone of smoke. And then night and extinction—nothing but a silent mass of impenetrable vapour hiding its dead.

Before dawn the black vapour was pouring through the streets of Richmond, and the disintegrating organism of government was, with a last expiring effort, rousing the population of London to the necessity of flight.

CHAPTER SIXTEEN - THE EXODUS FROM LONDON

So you understand the roaring wave of fear that swept through the greatest city in the world just as Monday was dawning—the stream of flight rising swiftly to a torrent, lashing in a foaming tumult round the railway stations, banked up into a horrible struggle about the shipping in the Thames, and hurrying by every available channel northward and eastward. By ten o'clock the police organisation, and by midday even the railway organisations, were losing coherency, losing shape and efficiency, guttering, softening, running at last in that swift liquefaction of the social body.

All the railway lines north of the Thames and the South-Eastern people at Cannon Street had been warned by midnight on Sunday, and trains were being filled. People were fighting savagely for standing-room in the carriages even at two o'clock. By three, people were being trampled and crushed even in Bishopsgate Street, a couple of hundred yards or more from Liverpool Street station; revolvers were fired, people stabbed, and the policemen who had been sent to direct the traffic, exhausted and infuriated, were breaking the heads of the people they were called out to protect.

And as the day advanced and the engine drivers and stokers refused to return to London, the pressure of the flight drove the people in an ever- thickening multitude away from the stations and along the northward-running roads. By midday a Martian had been seen at Barnes, and a cloud of slowly sinking black vapour drove along the Thames and across the flats of Lambeth, cutting off all escape over the bridges in its sluggish advance. Another bank drove over Ealing, and surrounded a little island of survivors on Castle Hill, alive, but unable to escape.

After a fruitless struggle to get aboard a North-Western train at Chalk Farm—the engines of the trains that had loaded in the goods yard there *ploughed* through shrieking people, and a dozen stalwart men fought to keep the crowd from crushing the driver against his furnace—my brother emerged upon the Chalk Farm road, dodged across through a hurrying swarm of vehicles, and had the luck to be foremost in the sack of a cycle shop. The front tire of the machine he got was punctured in dragging it through the window, but he got up and off, notwithstanding, with no further injury than a cut wrist. The steep foot of Haverstock Hill was impassable owing to several overturned horses, and my brother struck into Belsize Road.

So he got out of the fury of the panic, and, skirting the Edgware Road, reached Edgware about seven, fasting and wearied, but well ahead of the crowd. Along

the road people were standing in the roadway, curious, wondering. He was passed by a number of cyclists, some horsemen, and two motor cars. A mile from Edgware the rim of the wheel broke, and the machine became unridable. He left it by the roadside and trudged through the village. There were shops half opened in the main street of the place, and people crowded on the pavement and in the doorways and windows, staring astonished at this extraordinary procession of fugitives that was beginning. He succeeded in getting some food at an inn.

For a time he remained in Edgware not knowing what next to do. The flying people increased in number. Many of them, like my brother, seemed inclined to loiter in the place. There was no fresh news of the invaders from Mars.

At that time the road was crowded, but as yet far from congested. Most of the fugitives at that hour were mounted on cycles, but there were soon motor cars, hansom cabs, and carriages hurrying along, and the dust hung in heavy clouds along the road to St. Albans.

It was perhaps a vague idea of making his way to Chelmsford, where some friends of his lived, that at last induced my brother to strike into a quiet lane running eastward. Presently he came upon a stile, and, crossing it, followed a footpath northeastward. He passed near several farmhouses and some little places whose names he did not learn. He saw few fugitives until, in a grass lane towards High Barnet, he happened upon two ladies who became his fellow travellers. He came upon them just in time to save them.

He heard their screams, and, hurrying round the corner, saw a couple of men struggling to drag them out of the little pony-chaise in which they had been driving, while a third with difficulty held the frightened pony's head. One of the ladies, a short woman dressed in white, was simply screaming; the other, a dark, slender figure, slashed at the man who gripped her arm with a whip she held in her disengaged hand.

My brother immediately grasped the situation, shouted, and hurried towards the struggle. One of the men desisted and turned towards him, and my brother, realising from his antagonist's face that a fight was unavoidable, and being an expert boxer, went into him forthwith and sent him down against the wheel of the chaise.

It was no time for pugilistic chivalry and my brother laid him quiet with a kick, and gripped the collar of the man who pulled at the slender lady's arm. He heard the clatter of hoofs, the whip stung across his face, a third antagonist struck him between the eyes, and the man he held wrenched himself free and made off down the lane in the direction from which he had come.

Partly stunned, he found himself facing the man who had held the horse's head, and became aware of the chaise receding from him down the lane, swaying from side to side, and with the women in it looking back. The man before him, a burly rough, tried to close, and he stopped him with a blow in the face. Then, realising that he was deserted, he dodged round and made off down the lane after the chaise, with the sturdy man close behind him, and the fugitive, who had turned now, following remotely.

Suddenly he stumbled and fell; his immediate pursuer went headlong, and he rose to his feet to find himself with a couple of antagonists again. He would have had little chance against them had not the slender lady very pluckily pulled up and returned to his help. It seems she had had a revolver all this time, but it had been under the seat when she and her companion were attacked. She fired at six yards' distance, narrowly missing my brother. The less courageous of the robbers made off, and his companion followed him, cursing his cowardice. They both stopped in sight down the lane, where the third man lay insensible.

"Take this!" said the slender lady, and she gave my brother her revolver.

"Go back to the chaise," said my brother, wiping the blood from his split lip.

She turned without a word—they were both panting—and they went back to where the lady in white struggled to hold back the frightened pony.

The robbers had evidently had enough of it. When my brother looked again they were retreating.

"I'll sit here," said my brother, "if I may"; and he got upon the empty front seat. The lady looked over her shoulder.

"Give me the reins," she said, and laid the whip along the pony's side. In another moment a bend in the road hid the three men from my brother's eyes.

So, quite unexpectedly, my brother found himself, panting, with a cut mouth, a bruised jaw, and bloodstained knuckles, driving along an unknown lane with these two women.

He learned they were the wife and the younger sister of a surgeon living at Stanmore, who had come in the small hours from a dangerous case at Pinner, and heard at some railway station on his way of the Martian advance. He had hurried home, roused the women—their servant had left them two days before—packed some provisions, put his revolver under the seat—luckily for my brother—and told them to drive on to Edgware, with the idea of getting a train there. He stopped behind to tell the neighbours. He would overtake them, he said, at about half past four in the morning, and now it was nearly nine and they had seen nothing of him. They could not stop in Edgware because of the growing traffic through the place, and so they had come into this side lane.

That was the story they told my brother in fragments when presently they stopped again, nearer to New Barnet. He promised to stay with them, at least until they could determine what to do, or until the missing man arrived, and professed to be an expert shot with the revolver—a weapon strange to him—in order to give them confidence.

They made a sort of encampment by the wayside, and the pony became happy in the hedge. He told them of his own escape out of London, and all that he knew of these Martians and their ways. The sun crept higher in the sky, and after a time their talk died out and gave place to an uneasy state of anticipation. Several wayfarers came along the lane, and of these my brother gathered such news as he could. Every broken answer he had deepened his impression of the great disaster that had come on humanity, deepened his persuasion of the immediate necessity for prosecuting this flight. He urged the matter upon them.

"We have money," said the slender woman, and hesitated.

Her eyes met my brother's, and her hesitation ended.

"So have I," said my brother.

She explained that they had as much as thirty pounds in gold, besides a five-pound note, and suggested that with that they might get upon a train at St. Albans or New Barnet. My brother thought that was hopeless, seeing the fury of the Londoners to crowd upon the trains, and broached his own idea of striking across Essex towards Harwich and thence escaping from the country altogether.

Mrs. Elphinstone—that was the name of the woman in white—would listen to no reasoning, and kept calling upon "George"; but her sister-in- law was astonishingly quiet and deliberate, and at last agreed to my brother's suggestion. So, designing to cross the Great North Road, they went on towards Barnet, my brother leading the pony to save it as much as possible. As the sun crept up the sky the day became excessively hot, and under foot a thick, whitish sand grew burning and blinding, so that they travelled only very slowly. The hedges were grey with dust. And as they advanced towards Barnet a tumultuous murmuring grew stronger.

They began to meet more people. For the most part these were staring before them, murmuring indistinct questions, jaded, haggard, unclean. One man in evening dress passed them on foot, his eyes on the ground. They heard his voice, and, looking back at him, saw one hand clutched in his hair and the other beating invisible things. His paroxysm of rage over, he went on his way without once looking back.

As my brother's party went on towards the crossroads to the south of Barnet they saw a woman approaching the road across some fields on their left, carrying a child and with two other children; and then passed a man in dirty black, with a thick stick in one hand and a small portmanteau in the other. Then round the corner of the lane, from between the villas that guarded it at its confluence with the high road, came a little cart drawn by a sweating black pony and driven by a sallow youth in a bowler hat, grey with dust. There were three girls, East End factory girls, and a couple of little children crowded in the cart.

"This'll tike us rahnd Edgware?" asked the driver, wild-eyed, white- faced; and when my brother told him it would if he turned to the left, he whipped up at once without the formality of thanks.

My brother noticed a pale grey smoke or haze rising among the houses in front of them, and veiling the white facade of a terrace beyond the road that appeared between the backs of the villas. Mrs. Elphinstone suddenly cried out at a number of tongues of smoky red flame leaping up above the houses in front of them against the hot, blue sky. The tumultuous noise resolved itself now into the disorderly mingling of many voices, the gride of many wheels, the creaking of waggons, and the staccato of hoofs. The lane came round sharply not fifty yards from the crossroads.

"Good heavens!" cried Mrs. Elphinstone. "What is this you are driving us into?"

My brother stopped.

For the main road was a boiling stream of people, a torrent of human beings rushing northward, one pressing on another. A great bank of dust, white and luminous in the blaze of the sun, made everything within twenty feet of the ground grey and indistinct and was perpetually renewed by the hurrying feet of a dense crowd of horses and of men and women on foot, and by the wheels of vehicles of every description.

"Way!" my brother heard voices crying. "Make way!"

It was like riding into the smoke of a fire to approach the meeting point of the lane and road; the crowd roared like a fire, and the dust was hot and pungent. And, indeed, a little way up the road a villa was burning and sending rolling masses of black smoke across the road to add to the confusion.

Two men came past them. Then a dirty woman, carrying a heavy bundle and weeping. A lost retriever dog, with hanging tongue, circled dubiously round them, scared and wretched, and fled at my brother's threat.

So much as they could see of the road Londonward between the houses to the right was a tumultuous stream of dirty, hurrying people, pent in between the villas on either side; the black heads, the crowded forms, grew into distinctness as they rushed towards the corner, hurried past, and merged their individuality again in a receding multitude that was swallowed up at last in a cloud of dust.

"Go on! Go on!" cried the voices. "Way! Way!"

One man's hands pressed on the back of another. My brother stood at the pony's head. Irresistibly attracted, he advanced slowly, pace by pace, down the lane.

Edgware had been a scene of confusion, Chalk Farm a riotous tumult, but this was a whole population in movement. It is hard to imagine that host. It had no character of its own. The figures poured out past the corner, and receded with their backs to the group in the lane. Along the margin came those who were on foot threatened by the wheels, stumbling in the ditches, blundering into one another.

The carts and carriages crowded close upon one another, making little way for those swifter and more impatient vehicles that darted forward every now and then when an opportunity showed itself of doing so, sending the people scattering against the fences and gates of the villas.

"Push on!" was the cry. "Push on! They are coming!"

In one cart stood a blind man in the uniform of the Salvation Army, gesticulating with his crooked fingers and bawling, "Eternity! Eternity!" His voice was hoarse and very loud so that my brother could hear him long after he was lost to sight in the dust. Some of the people who crowded in the carts whipped stupidly at their horses and quarrelled with other drivers; some sat motionless, staring at nothing with miserable eyes; some gnawed their hands with thirst, or lay prostrate in the bottoms of their conveyances. The horses' bits were covered with foam, their eyes bloodshot.

There were cabs, carriages, shop cars, waggons, beyond counting; a mail cart, a road-cleaner's cart marked "Vestry of St. Pancras," a huge timber waggon

crowded with roughs. A brewer's dray rumbled by with its two near wheels splashed with fresh blood.

"Clear the way!" cried the voices. "Clear the way!"

"Eter-nity! Eter-nity!" came echoing down the road.

There were sad, haggard women tramping by, well dressed, with children that cried and stumbled, their dainty clothes smothered in dust, their weary faces smeared with tears. With many of these came men, sometimes helpful, sometimes lowering and savage. Fighting side by side with them pushed some weary street outcast in faded black rags, wide-eyed, loud-voiced, and foul- mouthed. There were sturdy workmen thrusting their way along, wretched, unkempt men, clothed like clerks or shopmen, struggling spasmodically; a wounded soldier my brother noticed, men dressed in the clothes of railway porters, one wretched creature in a nightshirt with a coat thrown over it.

But varied as its composition was, certain things all that host had in common. There were fear and pain on their faces, and fear behind them. A tumult up the road, a quarrel for a place in a waggon, sent the whole host of them quickening their pace; even a man so scared and broken that his knees bent under him was galvanised for a moment into renewed activity. The heat and dust had already been at work upon this multitude. Their skins were dry, their lips black and cracked. They were all thirsty, weary, and footsore. And amid the various cries one heard disputes, reproaches, groans of weariness and fatigue; the voices of most of them were hoarse and weak. Through it all ran a refrain:

"Way! Way! The Martians are coming!"

Few stopped and came aside from that flood. The lane opened slantingly into the main road with a narrow opening, and had a delusive appearance of coming from the direction of London. Yet a kind of eddy of people drove into its mouth; weaklings elbowed out of the stream, who for the most part rested but a moment before plunging into it again. A little way down the lane, with two friends bending over him, lay a man with a bare leg, wrapped about with bloody rags. He was a lucky man to have friends.

A little old man, with a grey military moustache and a filthy black frock coat, limped out and sat down beside the trap, removed his boot—his sock was blood-stained—shook out a pebble, and hobbled on again; and then a little girl of eight or nine, all alone, threw herself under the hedge close by my brother, weeping.

"I can't go on! I can't go on!"

My brother woke from his torpor of astonishment and lifted her up, speaking gently to her, and carried her to Miss Elphinstone. So soon as my brother touched her she became quite still, as if frightened.

"Ellen!" shrieked a woman in the crowd, with tears in her voice—"Ellen!" And the child suddenly darted away from my brother, crying "Mother!"

"They are coming," said a man on horseback, riding past along the lane.

"Out of the way, there!" bawled a coachman, towering high; and my brother saw a closed carriage turning into the lane.

The people crushed back on one another to avoid the horse. My brother pushed the pony and chaise back into the hedge, and the man drove by and stopped at the turn of the way. It was a carriage, with a pole for a pair of horses, but only one was in the traces. My brother saw dimly through the dust that two men lifted out something on a white stretcher and put it gently on the grass beneath the privet hedge.

One of the men came running to my brother.

"Where is there any water?" he said. "He is dying fast, and very thirsty. It is Lord Garrick."

"Lord Garrick!" said my brother; "the Chief Justice?"

"The water?" he said.

"There may be a tap," said my brother, "in some of the houses. We have no water. I dare not leave my people."

The man pushed against the crowd towards the gate of the corner house.

"Go on!" said the people, thrusting at him. "They are coming! Go on!"

Then my brother's attention was distracted by a bearded, eagle-faced man lugging a small handbag, which split even as my brother's eyes rested on it and disgorged a mass of sovereigns that seemed to break up into separate coins as it struck the ground. They rolled hither and thither among the struggling feet of men and horses. The man stopped and looked stupidly at the heap, and the shaft of a cab struck his shoulder and sent him reeling. He gave a shriek and dodged back, and a cartwheel shaved him narrowly.

"Way!" cried the men all about him. "Make way!"

So soon as the cab had passed, he flung himself, with both hands open, upon the heap of coins, and began thrusting handfuls in his pocket. A horse rose close upon him, and in another moment, half rising, he had been borne down under the horse's hoofs.

"Stop!" screamed my brother, and pushing a woman out of his way, tried to clutch the bit of the horse.

Before he could get to it, he heard a scream under the wheels, and saw through the dust the rim passing over the poor wretch's back. The driver of the cart slashed his whip at my brother, who ran round behind the cart. The multitudinous shouting confused his ears. The man was writhing in the dust among his scattered money, unable to rise, for the wheel had broken his back, and his lower limbs lay limp and dead. My brother stood up and yelled at the next driver, and a man on a black horse came to his assistance.

"Get him out of the road," said he; and, clutching the man's collar with his free hand, my brother lugged him sideways. But he still clutched after his money, and regarded my brother fiercely, hammering at his arm with a handful of gold. "Go on! Go on!" shouted angry voices behind.

"Way! Way!"

There was a smash as the pole of a carriage crashed into the cart that the man on horseback stopped. My brother looked up, and the man with the gold twisted his head round and bit the wrist that held his collar. There was a concussion, and

the black horse came staggering sideways, and the carthorse pushed beside it. A hoof missed my brother's foot by a hair's breadth. He released his grip on the fallen man and jumped back. He saw anger change to terror on the face of the poor wretch on the ground, and in a moment he was hidden and my brother was borne backward and carried past the entrance of the lane, and had to fight hard in the torrent to recover it.

He saw Miss Elphinstone covering her eyes, and a little child, with all a child's want of sympathetic imagination, staring with dilated eyes at a dusty something that lay black and still, ground and crushed under the rolling wheels. "Let us go back!" he shouted, and began turning the pony round. "We cannot cross this—hell," he said and they went back a hundred yards the way they had come, until the fighting crowd was hidden. As they passed the bend in the lane my brother saw the face of the dying man in the ditch under the privet, deadly white and drawn, and shining with perspiration. The two women sat silent, crouching in their seat and shivering.

Then beyond the bend my brother stopped again. Miss Elphinstone was white and pale, and her sister-in-law sat weeping, too wretched even to call upon "George." My brother was horrified and perplexed. So soon as they had retreated he realised how urgent and unavoidable it was to attempt this crossing. He turned to Miss Elphinstone, suddenly resolute.

"We must go that way," he said, and led the pony round again.

For the second time that day this girl proved her quality. To force their way into the torrent of people, my brother plunged into the traffic and held back a cab horse, while she drove the pony across its head. A waggon locked wheels for a moment and ripped a long splinter from the chaise. In another moment they were caught and swept forward by the stream. My brother, with the cabman's whip marks red across his face and hands, scrambled into the chaise and took the reins from her.

"Point the revolver at the man behind," he said, giving it to her, "if he presses us too hard. No!—point it at his horse."

Then he began to look out for a chance of edging to the right across the road. But once in the stream he seemed to lose volition, to become a part of that dusty rout. They swept through Chipping Barnet with the torrent; they were nearly a mile beyond the centre of the town before they had fought across to the opposite side of the way. It was din and confusion indescribable; but in and beyond the town the road forks repeatedly, and this to some extent relieved the stress.

They struck eastward through Hadley, and there on either side of the road, and at another place farther on they came upon a great multitude of people drinking at the stream, some fighting to come at the water. And farther on, from a lull near East Barnet, they saw two trains running slowly one after the other without signal or order—trains swarming with people, with men even among the coals behind the engines—going northward along the Great Northern Railway. My brother supposes they must have filled outside London, for at that time the furious terror of the people had rendered the central termini impossible.

Near this place they halted for the rest of the afternoon, for the violence of the day had already utterly exhausted all three of them. They began to suffer the beginnings of hunger; the night was cold, and none of them dared to sleep. And in the evening many people came hurrying along the road nearby their stopping place, fleeing from unknown dangers before them, and going in the direction from which my brother had come.

CHAPTER SEVENTEEN - THE "THUNDER CHILD"

Had the Martians aimed only at destruction, they might on Monday have annihilated the entire population of London, as it spread itself slowly through the home counties. Not only along the road through Barnet, but also through Edgware and Waltham Abbey, and along the roads eastward to Southend and Shoeburyness, and south of the Thames to Deal and Broadstairs, poured the same frantic rout. If one could have hung that June morning in a balloon in the blazing blue above London every northward and eastward road running out of the tangled maze of streets would have seemed stippled black with the streaming fugitives, each dot a human agony of terror and physical distress. I have set forth at length in the last chapter my brother's account of the road through Chipping Barnet, in order that my readers may realise how that swarming of black dots appeared to one of those concerned. Never before in the history of the world had such a mass of human beings moved and suffered together. The legendary hosts of Goths and Huns, the hugest armies Asia has ever seen, would have been but a drop in that current. And this was no disciplined march; it was a stampede—a stampede gigantic and terrible—without order and without a goal, six million people unarmed and unprovisioned, driving headlong. It was the beginning of the rout of civilisation, of the massacre of mankind.

Directly below him the balloonist would have seen the network of streets far and wide, houses, churches, squares, crescents, gardens—already derelict—spread out like a huge map, and in the southward *blotted*. Over Ealing, Richmond, Wimbledon, it would have seemed as if some monstrous pen had flung ink upon the chart. Steadily, incessantly, each black splash grew and spread, shooting out ramifications this way and that, now banking itself against rising ground, now pouring swiftly over a crest into a new-found valley, exactly as a gout of ink would spread itself upon blotting paper.

And beyond, over the blue hills that rise southward of the river, the glittering Martians went to and fro, calmly and methodically spreading their poison cloud over this patch of country and then over that, laying it again with their steam jets when it had served its purpose, and taking possession of the conquered country. They do not seem to have aimed at extermination so much as at complete demoralisation and the destruction of any opposition. They exploded any stores of powder they came upon, cut every telegraph, and wrecked the railways here and there. They were hamstringing mankind. They seemed in no hurry to extend the field of their operations, and did not come beyond the central part of London all

that day. It is possible that a very considerable number of people in London stuck to their houses through Monday morning. Certain it is that many died at home suffocated by the Black Smoke.

Until about midday the Pool of London was an astonishing scene. Steamboats and shipping of all sorts lay there, tempted by the enormous sums of money offered by fugitives, and it is said that many who swam out to these vessels were thrust off with boathooks and drowned. About one o'clock in the afternoon the thinning remnant of a cloud of the black vapour appeared between the arches of Blackfriars Bridge. At that the Pool became a scene of mad confusion, fighting, and collision, and for some time a multitude of boats and barges jammed in the northern arch of the Tower Bridge, and the sailors and lightermen had to fight savagely against the people who swarmed upon them from the riverfront. People were actually clambering down the piers of the bridge from above.

When, an hour later, a Martian appeared beyond the Clock Tower and waded down the river, nothing but wreckage floated above Limehouse.

Of the falling of the fifth cylinder I have presently to tell. The sixth star fell at Wimbledon. My brother, keeping watch beside the women in the chaise in a meadow, saw the green flash of it far beyond the hills. On Tuesday the little party, still set upon getting across the sea, made its way through the swarming country towards Colchester. The news that the Martians were now in possession of the whole of London was confirmed. They had been seen at Highgate, and even, it was said, at Neasden. But they did not come into my brother's view until the morrow.

That day the scattered multitudes began to realise the urgent need of provisions. As they grew hungry the rights of property ceased to be regarded. Farmers were out to defend their cattle-sheds, granaries, and ripening root crops with arms in their hands. A number of people now, like my brother, had their faces eastward, and there were some desperate souls even going back towards London to get food. These were chiefly people from the northern suburbs, whose knowledge of the Black Smoke came by hearsay. He heard that about half the members of the government had gathered at Birmingham, and that enormous quantities of high explosives were being prepared to be used in automatic mines across the Midland counties.

He was also told that the Midland Railway Company had replaced the desertions of the first day's panic, had resumed traffic, and was running northward trains from St. Albans to relieve the congestion of the home counties. There was also a placard in Chipping Ongar announcing that large stores of flour were available in the northern towns and that within twenty- four hours bread would be distributed among the starving people in the neighbourhood. But this intelligence did not deter him from the plan of escape he had formed, and the three pressed eastward all day, and heard no more of the bread distribution than this promise. Nor, as a matter of fact, did anyone else hear more of it. That night fell the seventh star, falling upon Primrose Hill. It fell while Miss Elphinstone was watching, for she took that duty alternately with my brother. She saw it.

On Wednesday the three fugitives—they had passed the night in a field of unripe wheat—reached Chelmsford, and there a body of the inhabitants, calling itself the Committee of Public Supply, seized the pony as provisions, and would give nothing in exchange for it but the promise of a share in it the next day. Here there were rumours of Martians at Epping, and news of the destruction of Waltham Abbey Powder Mills in a vain attempt to blow up one of the invaders.

People were watching for Martians here from the church towers. My brother, very luckily for him as it chanced, preferred to push on at once to the coast rather than wait for food, although all three of them were very hungry. By midday they passed through Tillingham, which, strangely enough, seemed to be quite silent and deserted, save for a few furtive plunderers hunting for food. Near Tillingham they suddenly came in sight of the sea, and the most amazing crowd of shipping of all sorts that it is possible to imagine.

For after the sailors could no longer come up the Thames, they came on to the Essex coast, to Harwich and Walton and Clacton, and afterwards to Foulness and Shoebury, to bring off the people. They lay in a huge sickle-shaped curve that vanished into mist at last towards the Naze. Close inshore was a multitude of fishing smacks—English, Scotch, French, Dutch, and Swedish; steam launches from the Thames, yachts, electric boats; and beyond were ships of large burden, a multitude of filthy colliers, trim merchantmen, cattle ships, passenger boats, petroleum tanks, ocean tramps, an old white transport even, neat white and grey liners from Southampton and Hamburg; and along the blue coast across the Blackwater my brother could make out dimly a dense swarm of boats chaffering with the people on the beach, a swarm which also extended up the Blackwater almost to Maldon.

About a couple of miles out lay an ironclad, very low in the water, almost, to my brother's perception, like a water-logged ship. This was the ram *Thunder Child.* It was the only warship in sight, but far away to the right over the smooth surface of the sea—for that day there was a dead calm—lay a serpent of black smoke to mark the next ironclads of the Channel Fleet, which hovered in an extended line, steam up and ready for action, across the Thames estuary during the course of the Martian conquest, vigilant and yet powerless to prevent it.

At the sight of the sea, Mrs. Elphinstone, in spite of the assurances of her sister-in-law, gave way to panic. She had never been out of England before, she would rather die than trust herself friendless in a foreign country, and so forth. She seemed, poor woman, to imagine that the French and the Martians might prove very similar. She had been growing increasingly hysterical, fearful, and depressed during the two days' journeyings. Her great idea was to return to Stanmore. Things had been always well and safe at Stanmore. They would find George at Stanmore.

It was with the greatest difficulty they could get her down to the beach, where presently my brother succeeded in attracting the attention of some men on a paddle steamer from the Thames. They sent a boat and drove a bargain for thirty-six pounds for the three. The steamer was going, these men said, to Ostend.

It was about two o'clock when my brother, having paid their fares at the gangway, found himself safely aboard the steamboat with his charges. There was food aboard, albeit at exorbitant prices, and the three of them contrived to eat a meal on one of the seats forward.

There were already a couple of score of passengers aboard, some of whom had expended their last money in securing a passage, but the captain lay off the Blackwater until five in the afternoon, picking up passengers until the seated decks were even dangerously crowded. He would probably have remained longer had it not been for the sound of guns that began about that hour in the south. As if in answer, the ironclad seaward fired a small gun and hoisted a string of flags. A jet of smoke sprang out of her funnels.

Some of the passengers were of opinion that this firing came from Shoeburyness, until it was noticed that it was growing louder. At the same time, far away in the southeast the masts and upperworks of three ironclads rose one after the other out of the sea, beneath clouds of black smoke. But my brother's attention speedily reverted to the distant firing in the south. He fancied he saw a column of smoke rising out of the distant grey haze.

The little steamer was already flapping her way eastward of the big crescent of shipping, and the low Essex coast was growing blue and hazy, when a Martian appeared, small and faint in the remote distance, advancing along the muddy coast from the direction of Foulness. At that the captain on the bridge swore at the top of his voice with fear and anger at his own delay, and the paddles seemed infected with his terror. Every soul aboard stood at the bulwarks or on the seats of the steamer and stared at that distant shape, higher than the trees or church towers inland, and advancing with a leisurely parody of a human stride.

It was the first Martian my brother had seen, and he stood, more amazed than terrified, watching this Titan advancing deliberately towards the shipping, wading farther and farther into the water as the coast fell away. Then, far away beyond the Crouch, came another, striding over some stunted trees, and then yet another, still farther off, wading deeply through a shiny mudflat that seemed to hang halfway up between sea and sky. They were all stalking seaward, as if to intercept the escape of the multitudinous vessels that were crowded between Foulness and the Naze. In spite of the throbbing exertions of the engines of the little paddle-boat, and the pouring foam that her wheels flung behind her, she receded with terrifying slowness from this ominous advance.

Glancing northwestward, my brother saw the large crescent of shipping already writhing with the approaching terror; one ship passing behind another, another coming round from broadside to end on, steamships whistling and giving off volumes of steam, sails being let out, launches rushing hither and thither. He was so fascinated by this and by the creeping danger away to the left that he had no eyes for anything seaward. And then a swift movement of the steamboat (she had suddenly come round to avoid being run down) flung him headlong from the seat upon which he was standing. There was a shouting all about him, a trampling

of feet, and a cheer that seemed to be answered faintly. The steamboat lurched and rolled him over upon his hands.

He sprang to his feet and saw to starboard, and not a hundred yards from their heeling, pitching boat, a vast iron bulk like the blade of a plough tearing through the water, tossing it on either side in huge waves of foam that leaped towards the steamer, flinging her paddles helplessly in the air, and then sucking her deck down almost to the waterline.

A douche of spray blinded my brother for a moment. When his eyes were clear again he saw the monster had passed and was rushing landward. Big iron upper-works rose out of this headlong structure, and from that twin funnels projected and spat a smoking blast shot with fire. It was the torpedo ram, *Thunder Child*, steaming headlong, coming to the rescue of the threatened shipping.

Keeping his footing on the heaving deck by clutching the bulwarks, my brother looked past this charging leviathan at the Martians again, and he saw the three of them now close together, and standing so far out to sea that their tripod supports were almost entirely submerged. Thus sunken, and seen in remote perspective, they appeared far less formidable than the huge iron bulk in whose wake the steamer was pitching so helplessly. It would seem they were regarding this new antagonist with astonishment. To their intelligence, it may be, the giant was even such another as themselves. The *Thunder Child* fired no gun, but simply drove full speed towards them. It was probably her not firing that enabled her to get so near the enemy as she did. They did not know what to make of her. One shell, and they would have sent her to the bottom forthwith with the Heat-Ray.

She was steaming at such a pace that in a minute she seemed halfway between the steamboat and the Martians—a diminishing black bulk against the receding horizontal expanse of the Essex coast.

Suddenly the foremost Martian lowered his tube and discharged a canister of the black gas at the ironclad. It hit her larboard side and glanced off in an inky jet that rolled away to seaward, an unfolding torrent of Black Smoke, from which the ironclad drove clear. To the watchers from the steamer, low in the water and with the sun in their eyes, it seemed as though she were already among the Martians.

They saw the gaunt figures separating and rising out of the water as they retreated shoreward, and one of them raised the camera-like generator of the Heat-Ray. He held it pointing obliquely downward, and a bank of steam sprang from the water at its touch. It must have driven through the iron of the ship's side like a white-hot iron rod through paper.

A flicker of flame went up through the rising steam, and then the Martian reeled and staggered. In another moment he was cut down, and a great body of water and steam shot high in the air. The guns of the *Thunder Child* sounded through the reek, going off one after the other, and one shot splashed the water high close by the steamer, ricocheted towards the other flying ships to the north, and smashed a smack to matchwood.

But no one heeded that very much. At the sight of the Martian's collapse the captain on the bridge yelled inarticulately, and all the crowding passengers on the

steamer's stern shouted together. And then they yelled again. For, surging out beyond the white tumult, drove something long and black, the flames streaming from its middle parts, its ventilators and funnels spouting fire.

She was alive still; the steering gear, it seems, was intact and her engines working. She headed straight for a second Martian, and was within a hundred yards of him when the Heat-Ray came to bear. Then with a violent thud, a blinding flash, her decks, her funnels, leaped upward. The Martian staggered with the violence of her explosion, and in another moment the flaming wreckage, still driving forward with the impetus of its pace, had struck him and crumpled him up like a thing of cardboard. My brother shouted involuntarily. A boiling tumult of steam hid everything again.

"Two!" yelled the captain.

Everyone was shouting. The whole steamer from end to end rang with frantic cheering that was taken up first by one and then by all in the crowding multitude of ships and boats that was driving out to sea.

The steam hung upon the water for many minutes, hiding the third Martian and the coast altogether. And all this time the boat was paddling steadily out to sea and away from the fight; and when at last the confusion cleared, the drifting bank of black vapour intervened, and nothing of the *Thunder Child* could be made out, nor could the third Martian be seen. But the ironclads to seaward were now quite close and standing in towards shore past the steamboat.

The little vessel continued to beat its way seaward, and the ironclads receded slowly towards the coast, which was hidden still by a marbled bank of vapour, part steam, part black gas, eddying and combining in the strangest way. The fleet of refugees was scattering to the northeast; several smacks were sailing between the ironclads and the steamboat. After a time, and before they reached the sinking cloud bank, the warships turned northward, and then abruptly went about and passed into the thickening haze of evening southward. The coast grew faint, and at last indistinguishable amid the low banks of clouds that were gathering about the sinking sun.

Then suddenly out of the golden haze of the sunset came the vibration of guns, and a form of black shadows moving. Everyone struggled to the rail of the steamer and peered into the blinding furnace of the west, but nothing was to be distinguished clearly. A mass of smoke rose slanting and barred the face of the sun. The steamboat throbbed on its way through an interminable suspense.

The sun sank into grey clouds, the sky flushed and darkened, the evening star trembled into sight. It was deep twilight when the captain cried out and pointed. My brother strained his eyes. Something rushed up into the sky out of the greyness—rushed slantingly upward and very swiftly into the luminous clearness above the clouds in the western sky; something flat and broad, and very large, that swept round in a vast curve, grew smaller, sank slowly, and vanished again into the grey mystery of the night. And as it flew it rained down darkness upon the land.

BOOK TWO - THE EARTH UNDER THE MARTIANS

CHAPTER ONE - UNDER FOOT

In the first book I have wandered so much from my own adventures to tell of the experiences of my brother that all through the last two chapters I and the curate have been lurking in the empty house at Halliford whither we fled to escape the Black Smoke. There I will resume. We stopped there all Sunday night and all the next day—the day of the panic—in a little island of daylight, cut off by the Black Smoke from the rest of the world. We could do nothing but wait in aching inactivity during those two weary days.

My mind was occupied by anxiety for my wife. I figured her at Leatherhead, terrified, in danger, mourning me already as a dead man. I paced the rooms and cried aloud when I thought of how I was cut off from her, of all that might happen to her in my absence. My cousin I knew was brave enough for any emergency, but he was not the sort of man to realise danger quickly, to rise promptly. What was needed now was not bravery, but circumspection. My only consolation was to believe that the Martians were moving London-ward and away from her. Such vague anxieties keep the mind sensitive and painful. I grew very weary and irritable with the curate's perpetual ejaculations; I tired of the sight of his selfish despair. After some ineffectual remonstrance I kept away from him, staying in a room—evidently a children's schoolroom—containing globes, forms, and copy-books. When he followed me thither, I went to a box room at the top of the house and, in order to be alone with my aching miseries, locked myself in.

We were hopelessly hemmed in by the Black Smoke all that day and the morning of the next. There were signs of people in the next house on Sunday evening—a face at a window and moving lights, and later the slamming of a door. But I do not know who these people were, nor what became of them. We saw nothing of them next day. The Black Smoke drifted slowly riverward all through Monday morning, creeping nearer and nearer to us, driving at last along the roadway outside the house that hid us.

A Martian came across the fields about midday, laying the stuff with a jet of superheated steam that hissed against the walls, smashed all the windows it

touched, and scalded the curate's hand as he fled out of the front room. When at last we crept across the sodden rooms and looked out again, the country northward was as though a black snowstorm had passed over it. Looking towards the river, we were astonished to see an unaccountable redness mingling with the black of the scorched meadows.

For a time we did not see how this change affected our position, save that we were relieved of our fear of the Black Smoke. But later I perceived that we were no longer hemmed in, that now we might get away. So soon as I realised that the way of escape was open, my dream of action returned. But the curate was lethargic, unreasonable.

"We are safe here," he repeated; "safe here."

I resolved to leave him—would that I had! Wiser now for the artilleryman's teaching, I sought out food and drink. I had found oil and rags for my burns, and I also took a hat and a flannel shirt that I found in one of the bedrooms. When it was clear to him that I meant to go alone—had reconciled myself to going alone—he suddenly roused himself to come. And all being quiet throughout the afternoon, we started about five o'clock, as I should judge, along the blackened road to Sunbury.

In Sunbury, and at intervals along the road, were dead bodies lying in contorted attitudes, horses as well as men, overturned carts and luggage, all covered thickly with black dust. That pall of cindery powder made me think of what I had read of the destruction of Pompeii. We got to Hampton Court without misadventure, our minds full of strange and unfamiliar appearances, and at Hampton Court our eyes were relieved to find a patch of green that had escaped the suffocating drift. We went through Bushey Park, with its deer going to and fro under the chestnuts, and some men and women hurrying in the distance towards Hampton, and so we came to Twickenham. These were the first people we saw.

Away across the road the woods beyond Ham and Petersham were still afire. Twickenham was uninjured by either Heat-Ray or Black Smoke, and there were more people about here, though none could give us news. For the most part they were like ourselves, taking advantage of a lull to shift their quarters. I have an impression that many of the houses here were still occupied by scared inhabitants, too frightened even for flight. Here too the evidence of a hasty rout was abundant along the road. I remember most vividly three smashed bicycles in a heap, pounded into the road by the wheels of subsequent carts. We crossed Richmond Bridge about half past eight. We hurried across the exposed bridge, of course, but I noticed floating down the stream a number of red masses, some many feet across. I did not know what these were—there was no time for scrutiny—and I put a more horrible interpretation on them than they deserved. Here again on the Surrey side were black dust that had once been smoke, and dead bodies—a heap near the approach to the station; but we had no glimpse of the Martians until we were some way towards Barnes.

We saw in the blackened distance a group of three people running down a side street towards the river, but otherwise it seemed deserted. Up the hill Richmond

town was burning briskly; outside the town of Richmond there was no trace of the Black Smoke.

Then suddenly, as we approached Kew, came a number of people running, and the upperworks of a Martian fighting-machine loomed in sight over the house-tops, not a hundred yards away from us. We stood aghast at our danger, and had the Martian looked down we must immediately have perished. We were so terrified that we dared not go on, but turned aside and hid in a shed in a garden. There the curate crouched, weeping silently, and refusing to stir again.

But my fixed idea of reaching Leatherhead would not let me rest, and in the twilight I ventured out again. I went through a shrubbery, and along a passage beside a big house standing in its own grounds, and so emerged upon the road towards Kew. The curate I left in the shed, but he came hurrying after me.

That second start was the most foolhardy thing I ever did. For it was manifest the Martians were about us. No sooner had the curate overtaken me than we saw either the fighting-machine we had seen before or another, far away across the meadows in the direction of Kew Lodge. Four or five little black figures hurried before it across the green-grey of the field, and in a moment it was evident this Martian pursued them. In three strides he was among them, and they ran radiating from his feet in all directions. He used no Heat-Ray to destroy them, but picked them up one by one. Apparently he tossed them into the great metallic carrier which projected behind him, much as a workman's basket hangs over his shoulder.

It was the first time I realised that the Martians might have any other purpose than destruction with defeated humanity. We stood for a moment petrified, then turned and fled through a gate behind us into a walled garden, fell into, rather than found, a fortunate ditch, and lay there, scarce daring to whisper to each other until the stars were out.

I suppose it was nearly eleven o'clock before we gathered courage to start again, no longer venturing into the road, but sneaking along hedgerows and through plantations, and watching keenly through the darkness, he on the right and I on the left, for the Martians, who seemed to be all about us. In one place we blundered upon a scorched and blackened area, now cooling and ashen, and a number of scattered dead bodies of men, burned horribly about the heads and trunks but with their legs and boots mostly intact; and of dead horses, fifty feet, perhaps, behind a line of four ripped guns and smashed gun carriages.

Sheen, it seemed, had escaped destruction, but the place was silent and deserted. Here we happened on no dead, though the night was too dark for us to see into the side roads of the place. In Sheen my companion suddenly complained of faintness and thirst, and we decided to try one of the houses.

The first house we entered, after a little difficulty with the window, was a small semi-detached villa, and I found nothing eatable left in the place but some mouldy cheese. There was, however, water to drink; and I took a hatchet, which promised to be useful in our next house-breaking.

We then crossed to a place where the road turns towards Mortlake. Here there stood a white house within a walled garden, and in the pantry of this domicile we found a store of food—two loaves of bread in a pan, an uncooked steak, and the half of a ham. I give this catalogue so precisely because, as it happened, we were destined to subsist upon this store for the next fortnight. Bottled beer stood under a shelf, and there were two bags of haricot beans and some limp lettuces. This pantry opened into a kind of wash-up kitchen, and in this was firewood; there was also a cupboard, in which we found nearly a dozen of burgundy, tinned soups and salmon, and two tins of biscuits.

We sat in the adjacent kitchen in the dark—for we dared not strike a light—and ate bread and ham, and drank beer out of the same bottle. The curate, who was still timorous and restless, was now, oddly enough, for pushing on, and I was urging him to keep up his strength by eating when the thing happened that was to imprison us.

"It can't be midnight yet," I said, and then came a blinding glare of vivid green light. Everything in the kitchen leaped out, clearly visible in green and black, and vanished again. And then followed such a concussion as I have never heard before or since. So close on the heels of this as to seem instantaneous came a thud behind me, a clash of glass, a crash and rattle of falling masonry all about us, and the plaster of the ceiling came down upon us, smashing into a multitude of fragments upon our heads. I was knocked headlong across the floor against the oven handle and stunned. I was insensible for a long time, the curate told me, and when I came to we were in darkness again, and he, with a face wet, as I found afterwards, with blood from a cut forehead, was dabbing water over me.

For some time I could not recollect what had happened. Then things came to me slowly. A bruise on my temple asserted itself.

"Are you better?" asked the curate in a whisper.

At last I answered him. I sat up.

"Don't move," he said. "The floor is covered with smashed crockery from the dresser. You can't possibly move without making a noise, and I fancy *they* are outside."

We both sat quite silent, so that we could scarcely hear each other breathing. Everything seemed deadly still, but once something near us, some plaster or broken brickwork, slid down with a rumbling sound. Outside and very near was an intermittent, metallic rattle.

"That!" said the curate, when presently it happened again.

"Yes," I said. "But what is it?"

"A Martian!" said the curate.

I listened again.

"It was not like the Heat-Ray," I said, and for a time I was inclined to think one of the great fighting-machines had stumbled against the house, as I had seen one stumble against the tower of Shepperton Church.

Our situation was so strange and incomprehensible that for three or four hours, until the dawn came, we scarcely moved. And then the light filtered in, not

through the window, which remained black, but through a triangular aperture between a beam and a heap of broken bricks in the wall behind us. The interior of the kitchen we now saw greyly for the first time.

The window had been burst in by a mass of garden mould, which flowed over the table upon which we had been sitting and lay about our feet. Outside, the soil was banked high against the house. At the top of the window frame we could see an uprooted drainpipe. The floor was littered with smashed hardware; the end of the kitchen towards the house was broken into, and since the daylight shone in there, it was evident the greater part of the house had collapsed. Contrasting vividly with this ruin was the neat dresser, stained in the fashion, pale green, and with a number of copper and tin vessels below it, the wallpaper imitating blue and white tiles, and a couple of coloured supplements fluttering from the walls above the kitchen range.

As the dawn grew clearer, we saw through the gap in the wall the body of a Martian, standing sentinel, I suppose, over the still glowing cylinder. At the sight of that we crawled as circumspectly as possible out of the twilight of the kitchen into the darkness of the scullery.

Abruptly the right interpretation dawned upon my mind.

"The fifth cylinder," I whispered, "the fifth shot from Mars, has struck this house and buried us under the ruins!"

For a time the curate was silent, and then he whispered:

"God have mercy upon us!"

I heard him presently whimpering to himself.

Save for that sound we lay quite still in the scullery; I for my part scarce dared breathe, and sat with my eyes fixed on the faint light of the kitchen door. I could just see the curate's face, a dim, oval shape, and his collar and cuffs. Outside there began a metallic hammering, then a violent hooting, and then again, after a quiet interval, a hissing like the hissing of an engine. These noises, for the most part problematical, continued intermittently, and seemed if anything to increase in number as time wore on. Presently a measured thudding and a vibration that made everything about us quiver and the vessels in the pantry ring and shift, began and continued. Once the light was eclipsed, and the ghostly kitchen doorway became absolutely dark. For many hours we must have crouched there, silent and shivering, until our tired attention failed...

At last I found myself awake and very hungry. I am inclined to believe we must have spent the greater portion of a day before that awakening. My hunger was at a stride so insistent that it moved me to action. I told the curate I was going to seek food, and felt my way towards the pantry. He made me no answer, but so soon as I began eating the faint noise I made stirred him up and I heard him crawling after me.

CHAPTER TWO - WHAT WE SAW FROM THE RUINED HOUSE

After eating we crept back to the scullery, and there I must have dozed again, for when presently I looked round I was alone. The thudding vibration continued with wearisome persistence. I whispered for the curate several times, and at last felt my way to the door of the kitchen. It was still daylight, and I perceived him across the room, lying against the triangular hole that looked out upon the Martians. His shoulders were hunched, so that his head was hidden from me.

I could hear a number of noises almost like those in an engine shed; and the place rocked with that beating thud. Through the aperture in the wall I could see the top of a tree touched with gold and the warm blue of a tranquil evening sky. For a minute or so I remained watching the curate, and then I advanced, crouching and stepping with extreme care amid the broken crockery that littered the floor.

I touched the curate's leg, and he started so violently that a mass of plaster went sliding down outside and fell with a loud impact. I gripped his arm, fearing he might cry out, and for a long time we crouched motionless. Then I turned to see how much of our rampart remained. The detachment of the plaster had left a vertical slit open in the debris, and by raising myself cautiously across a beam I was able to see out of this gap into what had been overnight a quiet suburban roadway. Vast, indeed, was the change that we beheld.

The fifth cylinder must have fallen right into the midst of the house we had first visited. The building had vanished, completely smashed, pulverised, and dispersed by the blow. The cylinder lay now far beneath the original foundations—deep in a hole, already vastly larger than the pit I had looked into at Woking. The earth all round it had splashed under that tremendous impact—"splashed" is the only word—and lay in heaped piles that hid the masses of the adjacent houses. It had behaved exactly like mud under the violent blow of a hammer. Our house had collapsed backward; the front portion, even on the ground floor, had been destroyed completely; by a chance the kitchen and scullery had escaped, and stood buried now under soil and ruins, closed in by tons of earth on every side save towards the cylinder. Over that aspect we hung now on the very edge of the great circular pit the Martians were engaged in making. The heavy beating sound was evidently just behind us, and ever and again a bright green vapour drove up like a veil across our peephole.

The cylinder was already opened in the centre of the pit, and on the farther edge of the pit, amid the smashed and gravel-heaped shrubbery, one of the great fighting-machines, deserted by its occupant, stood stiff and tall against the evening sky. At first I scarcely noticed the pit and the cylinder, although it has been convenient to describe them first, on account of the extraordinary glittering mechanism I saw busy in the excavation, and on account of the strange creatures that were crawling slowly and painfully across the heaped mould near it.

The mechanism it certainly was that held my attention first. It was one of those complicated fabrics that have since been called handling-machines, and the study of which has already given such an enormous impetus to terrestrial invention. As it dawned upon me first, it presented a sort of metallic spider with five jointed, agile legs, and with an extraordinary number of jointed levers, bars, and reaching and clutching tentacles about its body. Most of its arms were retracted, but with three long tentacles it was fishing out a number of rods, plates, and bars which lined the covering and apparently strengthened the walls of the cylinder. These, as it extracted them, were lifted out and deposited upon a level surface of earth behind it.

Its motion was so swift, complex, and perfect that at first I did not see it as a machine, in spite of its metallic glitter. The fighting-machines were coordinated and animated to an extraordinary pitch, but nothing to compare with this. People who have never seen these structures, and have only the ill- imagined efforts of artists or the imperfect descriptions of such eye-witnesses as myself to go upon, scarcely realise that living quality.

I recall particularly the illustration of one of the first pamphlets to give a consecutive account of the war. The artist had evidently made a hasty study of one of the fighting-machines, and there his knowledge ended. He presented them as tilted, stiff tripods, without either flexibility or subtlety, and with an altogether misleading monotony of effect. The pamphlet containing these renderings had a considerable vogue, and I mention them here simply to warn the reader against the impression they may have created. They were no more like the Martians I saw in action than a Dutch doll is like a human being. To my mind, the pamphlet would have been much better without them.

At first, I say, the handling-machine did not impress me as a machine, but as a crablike creature with a glittering integument, the controlling Martian whose delicate tentacles actuated its movements seeming to be simply the equivalent of the crab's cerebral portion. But then I perceived the resemblance of its grey-brown, shiny, leathery integument to that of the other sprawling bodies beyond, and the true nature of this dexterous workman dawned upon me. With that realisation my interest shifted to those other creatures, the real Martians. Already I had had a transient impression of these, and the first nausea no longer obscured my observation. Moreover, I was concealed and motionless, and under no urgency of action.

They were, I now saw, the most unearthly creatures it is possible to conceive. They were huge round bodies—or, rather, heads—about four feet in diameter, each body having in front of it a face. This face had no nostrils—indeed, the Mar-

tians do not seem to have had any sense of smell, but it had a pair of very large dark-coloured eyes, and just beneath this a kind of fleshy beak. In the back of this head or body—I scarcely know how to speak of it—was the single tight tympanic surface, since known to be anatomically an ear, though it must have been almost useless in our dense air. In a group round the mouth were sixteen slender, almost whiplike tentacles, arranged in two bunches of eight each. These bunches have since been named rather aptly, by that distinguished anatomist, Professor Howes, the *hands*. Even as I saw these Martians for the first time they seemed to be endeavouring to raise themselves on these hands, but of course, with the increased weight of terrestrial conditions, this was impossible. There is reason to suppose that on Mars they may have progressed upon them with some facility.

The internal anatomy, I may remark here, as dissection has since shown, was almost equally simple. The greater part of the structure was the brain, sending enormous nerves to the eyes, ear, and tactile tentacles. Besides this were the bulky lungs, into which the mouth opened, and the heart and its vessels. The pulmonary distress caused by the denser atmosphere and greater gravitational attraction was only too evident in the convulsive movements of the outer skin.

And this was the sum of the Martian organs. Strange as it may seem to a human being, all the complex apparatus of digestion, which makes up the bulk of our bodies, did not exist in the Martians. They were heads—merely heads. Entrails they had none. They did not eat, much less digest. Instead, they took the fresh, living blood of other creatures, and *injected* it into their own veins. I have myself seen this being done, as I shall mention in its place. But, squeamish as I may seem, I cannot bring myself to describe what I could not endure even to continue watching. Let it suffice to say, blood obtained from a still living animal, in most cases from a human being, was run directly by means of a little pipette into the recipient canal...

The bare idea of this is no doubt horribly repulsive to us, but at the same time I think that we should remember how repulsive our carnivorous habits would seem to an intelligent rabbit.

The physiological advantages of the practice of injection are undeniable, if one thinks of the tremendous waste of human time and energy occasioned by eating and the digestive process. Our bodies are half made up of glands and tubes and organs, occupied in turning heterogeneous food into blood. The digestive processes and their reaction upon the nervous system sap our strength and colour our minds. Men go happy or miserable as they have healthy or unhealthy livers, or sound gastric glands. But the Martians were lifted above all these organic fluctuations of mood and emotion.

Their undeniable preference for men as their source of nourishment is partly explained by the nature of the remains of the victims they had brought with them as provisions from Mars. These creatures, to judge from the shrivelled remains that have fallen into human hands, were bipeds with flimsy, silicious skeletons (almost like those of the silicious sponges) and feeble musculature, standing about six feet high and having round, erect heads, and large eyes in flinty sockets. Two

or three of these seem to have been brought in each cylinder, and all were killed before earth was reached. It was just as well for them, for the mere attempt to stand upright upon our planet would have broken every bone in their bodies.

And while I am engaged in this description, I may add in this place certain further details which, although they were not all evident to us at the time, will enable the reader who is unacquainted with them to form a clearer picture of these offensive creatures.

In three other points their physiology differed strangely from ours. Their organisms did not sleep, any more than the heart of man sleeps. Since they had no extensive muscular mechanism to recuperate, that periodical extinction was unknown to them. They had little or no sense of fatigue, it would seem. On earth they could never have moved without effort, yet even to the last they kept in action. In twenty-four hours they did twenty-four hours of work, as even on earth is perhaps the case with the ants.

In the next place, wonderful as it seems in a sexual world, the Martians were absolutely without sex, and therefore without any of the tumultuous emotions that arise from that difference among men. A young Martian, there can now be no dispute, was really born upon earth during the war, and it was found attached to its parent, partially *budded* off, just as young lilybulbs bud off, or like the young animals in the fresh-water polyp.

In man, in all the higher terrestrial animals, such a method of increase has disappeared; but even on this earth it was certainly the primitive method. Among the lower animals, up even to those first cousins of the vertebrated animals, the Tunicates, the two processes occur side by side, but finally the sexual method superseded its competitor altogether. On Mars, however, just the reverse has apparently been the case.

It is worthy of remark that a certain speculative writer of quasi- scientific repute, writing long before the Martian invasion, did forecast for man a final structure not unlike the actual Martian condition. His prophecy, I remember, appeared in November or December, 1893, in a long-defunct publication, the *Pall Mall Budget*, and I recall a caricature of it in a pre-Martian periodical called *Punch*. He pointed out—writing in a foolish, facetious tone—that the perfection of mechanical appliances must ultimately supersede limbs; the perfection of chemical devices, digestion; that such organs as hair, external nose, teeth, ears, and chin were no longer essential parts of the human being, and that the tendency of natural selection would lie in the direction of their steady diminution through the coming ages. The brain alone remained a cardinal necessity. Only one other part of the body had a strong case for survival, and that was the hand, "teacher and agent of the brain." While the rest of the body dwindled, the hands would grow larger.

There is many a true word written in jest, and here in the Martians we have beyond dispute the actual accomplishment of such a suppression of the animal side of the organism by the intelligence. To me it is quite credible that the Martians may be descended from beings not unlike ourselves, by a gradual

development of brain and hands (the latter giving rise to the two bunches of delicate tentacles at last) at the expense of the rest of the body. Without the body the brain would, of course, become a mere selfish intelligence, without any of the emotional substratum of the human being.

The last salient point in which the systems of these creatures differed from ours was in what one might have thought a very trivial particular. Micro- organisms, which cause so much disease and pain on earth, have either never appeared upon Mars or Martian sanitary science eliminated them ages ago. A hundred diseases, all the fevers and contagions of human life, consumption, cancers, tumours and such morbidities, never enter the scheme of their life. And speaking of the differences between the life on Mars and terrestrial life, I may allude here to the curious suggestions of the red weed.

Apparently the vegetable kingdom in Mars, instead of having green for a dominant colour, is of a vivid blood-red tint. At any rate, the seeds which the Martians (intentionally or accidentally) brought with them gave rise in all cases to red-coloured growths. Only that known popularly as the red weed, however, gained any footing in competition with terrestrial forms. The red creeper was quite a transitory growth, and few people have seen it growing. For a time, however, the red weed grew with astonishing vigour and luxuriance. It spread up the sides of the pit by the third or fourth day of our imprisonment, and its cactus-like branches formed a carmine fringe to the edges of our triangular window. And afterwards I found it broadcast throughout the country, and especially wherever there was a stream of water.

The Martians had what appears to have been an auditory organ, a single round drum at the back of the head-body, and eyes with a visual range not very different from ours except that, according to Philips, blue and violet were as black to them. It is commonly supposed that they communicated by sounds and tentacular gesticulations; this is asserted, for instance, in the able but hastily compiled pamphlet (written evidently by someone not an eye-witness of Martian actions) to which I have already alluded, and which, so far, has been the chief source of information concerning them. Now no surviving human being saw so much of the Martians in action as I did. I take no credit to myself for an accident, but the fact is so. And I assert that I watched them closely time after time, and that I have seen four, five, and (once) six of them sluggishly performing the most elaborately complicated operations together without either sound or gesture. Their peculiar hooting invariably preceded feeding; it had no modulation, and was, I believe, in no sense a signal, but merely the expiration of air preparatory to the suctional operation. I have a certain claim to at least an elementary knowledge of psychology, and in this matter I am convinced—as firmly as I am convinced of anything—that the Martians interchanged thoughts without any physical intermediation. And I have been convinced of this in spite of strong preconceptions. Before the Martian invasion, as an occasional reader here or there may remember, I had written with some little vehemence against the telepathic theory.

The Martians wore no clothing. Their conceptions of ornament and decorum were necessarily different from ours; and not only were they evidently much less sensible of changes of temperature than we are, but changes of pressure do not seem to have affected their health at all seriously. Yet though they wore no clothing, it was in the other artificial additions to their bodily resources that their great superiority over man lay. We men, with our bicycles and road- skates, our Lilienthal soaring-machines, our guns and sticks and so forth, are just in the beginning of the evolution that the Martians have worked out. They have become practically mere brains, wearing different bodies according to their needs just as men wear suits of clothes and take a bicycle in a hurry or an umbrella in the wet. And of their appliances, perhaps nothing is more wonderful to a man than the curious fact that what is the dominant feature of almost all human devices in mechanism is absent—the *wheel* is absent; among all the things they brought to earth there is no trace or suggestion of their use of wheels. One would have at least expected it in locomotion. And in this connection it is curious to remark that even on this earth Nature has never hit upon the wheel, or has preferred other expedients to its development. And not only did the Martians either not know of (which is incredible), or abstain from, the wheel, but in their apparatus singularly little use is made of the fixed pivot or relatively fixed pivot, with circular motions thereabout confined to one plane. Almost all the joints of the machinery present a complicated system of sliding parts moving over small but beautifully curved friction bearings. And while upon this matter of detail, it is remarkable that the long leverages of their machines are in most cases actuated by a sort of sham musculature of the disks in an elastic sheath; these disks become polarised and drawn closely and powerfully together when traversed by a current of electricity. In this way the curious parallelism to animal motions, which was so striking and disturbing to the human beholder, was attained. Such quasi-muscles abounded in the crablike handling-machine which, on my first peeping out of the slit, I watched unpacking the cylinder. It seemed infinitely more alive than the actual Martians lying beyond it in the sunset light, panting, stirring ineffectual tentacles, and moving feebly after their vast journey across space.

While I was still watching their sluggish motions in the sunlight, and noting each strange detail of their form, the curate reminded me of his presence by pulling violently at my arm. I turned to a scowling face, and silent, eloquent lips. He wanted the slit, which permitted only one of us to peep through; and so I had to forego watching them for a time while he enjoyed that privilege.

When I looked again, the busy handling-machine had already put together several of the pieces of apparatus it had taken out of the cylinder into a shape having an unmistakable likeness to its own; and down on the left a busy little digging mechanism had come into view, emitting jets of green vapour and working its way round the pit, excavating and embanking in a methodical and discriminating manner. This it was which had caused the regular beating noise, and the rhythmic shocks that had kept our ruinous refuge quivering. It piped and whistled as it worked. So far as I could see, the thing was without a directing Martian at all.

CHAPTER THREE - THE DAYS OF IMPRISONMENT

The arrival of a second fighting-machine drove us from our peephole into the scullery, for we feared that from his elevation the Martian might see down upon us behind our barrier. At a later date we began to feel less in danger of their eyes, for to an eye in the dazzle of the sunlight outside our refuge must have been blank blackness, but at first the slightest suggestion of approach drove us into the scullery in heart-throbbing retreat. Yet terrible as was the danger we incurred, the attraction of peeping was for both of us irresistible. And I recall now with a sort of wonder that, in spite of the infinite danger in which we were between starvation and a still more terrible death, we could yet struggle bitterly for that horrible privilege of sight. We would race across the kitchen in a grotesque way between eagerness and the dread of making a noise, and strike each other, and thrust and kick, within a few inches of exposure.

The fact is that we had absolutely incompatible dispositions and habits of thought and action, and our danger and isolation only accentuated the incompatibility. At Halliford I had already come to hate the curate's trick of helpless exclamation, his stupid rigidity of mind. His endless muttering monologue vitiated every effort I made to think out a line of action, and drove me at times, thus pent up and intensified, almost to the verge of craziness. He was as lacking in restraiht as a silly woman. He would weep for hours together, and I verily believe that to the very end this spoiled child of life thought his weak tears in some way efficacious. And I would sit in the darkness unable to keep my mind off him by reason of his importunities. He ate more than I did, and it was in vain I pointed out that our only chance of life was to stop in the house until the Martians had done with their pit, that in that long patience a time might presently come when we should need food. He ate and drank impulsively in heavy meals at long intervals. He slept little.

As the days wore on, his utter carelessness of any consideration so intensified our distress and danger that I had, much as I loathed doing it, to resort to threats, and at last to blows. That brought him to reason for a time. But he was one of those weak creatures, void of pride, timorous, anaemic, hateful souls, full of shifty cunning, who face neither God nor man, who face not even themselves.

It is disagreeable for me to recall and write these things, but I set them down that my story may lack nothing. Those who have escaped the dark and terrible aspects of life will find my brutality, my flash of rage in our final tragedy, easy enough to blame; for they know what is wrong as well as any, but not what is

possible to tortured men. But those who have been under the shadow, who have gone down at last to elemental things, will have a wider charity.

And while within we fought out our dark, dim contest of whispers, snatched food and drink, and gripping hands and blows, without, in the pitiless sunlight of that terrible June, was the strange wonder, the unfamiliar routine of the Martians in the pit. Let me return to those first new experiences of mine. After a long time I ventured back to the peephole, to find that the new- comers had been reinforced by the occupants of no fewer than three of the fighting-machines. These last had brought with them certain fresh appliances that stood in an orderly manner about the cylinder. The second handling-machine was now completed, and was busied in serving one of the novel contrivances the big machine had brought. This was a body resembling a milk can in its general form, above which oscillated a pear-shaped receptacle, and from which a stream of white powder flowed into a circular basin below.

The oscillatory motion was imparted to this by one tentacle of the handling-machine. With two spatulate hands the handling-machine was digging out and flinging masses of clay into the pear-shaped receptacle above, while with another arm it periodically opened a door and removed rusty and blackened clinkers from the middle part of the machine. Another steely tentacle directed the powder from the basin along a ribbed channel towards some receiver that was hidden from me by the mound of bluish dust. From this unseen receiver a little thread of green smoke rose vertically into the quiet air. As I looked, the handling-machine, with a faint and musical clinking, extended, telescopic fashion, a tentacle that had been a moment before a mere blunt projection, until its end was hidden behind the mound of clay. In another second it had lifted a bar of white aluminium into sight, untarnished as yet, and shining dazzlingly, and deposited it in a growing stack of bars that stood at the side of the pit. Between sunset and starlight this dexterous machine must have made more than a hundred such bars out of the crude clay, and the mound of bluish dust rose steadily until it topped the side of the pit.

The contrast between the swift and complex movements of these contrivances and the inert panting clumsiness of their masters was acute, and for days I had to tell myself repeatedly that these latter were indeed the living of the two things.

The curate had possession of the slit when the first men were brought to the pit. I was sitting below, huddled up, listening with all my ears. He made a sudden movement backward, and I, fearful that we were observed, crouched in a spasm of terror. He came sliding down the rubbish and crept beside me in the darkness, inarticulate, gesticulating, and for a moment I shared his panic. His gesture suggested a resignation of the slit, and after a little while my curiosity gave me courage, and I rose up, stepped across him, and clambered up to it. At first I could see no reason for his frantic behaviour. The twilight had now come, the stars were little and faint, but the pit was illuminated by the flickering green fire that came from the aluminium-making. The whole picture was a flickering scheme of green gleams and shifting rusty black shadows, strangely trying to the eyes. Over and through it all went the bats, heeding it not at all. The sprawling Martians were no

longer to be seen, the mound of blue-green powder had risen to cover them from sight, and a fighting- machine, with its legs contracted, crumpled, and abbreviated, stood across the corner of the pit. And then, amid the clangour of the machinery, came a drifting suspicion of human voices, that I entertained at first only to dismiss.

I crouched, watching this fighting-machine closely, satisfying myself now for the first time that the hood did indeed contain a Martian. As the green flames lifted I could see the oily gleam of his integument and the brightness of his eyes. And suddenly I heard a yell, and saw a long tentacle reaching over the shoulder of the machine to the little cage that hunched upon its back. Then something—something struggling violently—was lifted high against the sky, a black, vague enigma against the starlight; and as this black object came down again, I saw by the green brightness that it was a man. For an instant he was clearly visible. He was a stout, ruddy, middle-aged man, well dressed; three days before, he must have been walking the world, a man of considerable consequence. I could see his staring eyes and gleams of light on his studs and watch chain. He vanished behind the mound, and for a moment there was silence. And then began a shrieking and a sustained and cheerful hooting from the Martians.

I slid down the rubbish, struggled to my feet, clapped my hands over my ears, and bolted into the scullery. The curate, who had been crouching silently with his arms over his head, looked up as I passed, cried out quite loudly at my desertion of him, and came running after me.

That night, as we lurked in the scullery, balanced between our horror and the terrible fascination this peeping had, although I felt an urgent need of action I tried in vain to conceive some plan of escape; but afterwards, during the second day, I was able to consider our position with great clearness. The curate, I found, was quite incapable of discussion; this new and culminating atrocity had robbed him of all vestiges of reason or forethought. Practically he had already sunk to the level of an animal. But as the saying goes, I gripped myself with both hands. It grew upon my mind, once I could face the facts, that terrible as our position was, there was as yet no justification for absolute despair. Our chief chance lay in the possibility of the Martians making the pit nothing more than a temporary encampment. Or even if they kept it permanently, they might not consider it necessary to guard it, and a chance of escape might be afforded us. I also weighed very carefully the possibility of our digging a way out in a direction away from the pit, but the chances of our emerging within sight of some sentinel fighting-machine seemed at first too great. And I should have had to do all the digging myself. The curate would certainly have failed me.

It was on the third day, if my memory serves me right, that I saw the lad killed. It was the only occasion on which I actually saw the Martians feed. After that experience I avoided the hole in the wall for the better part of a day. I went into the scullery, removed the door, and spent some hours digging with my hatchet as silently as possible; but when I had made a hole about a couple of feet deep the loose earth collapsed noisily, and I did not dare continue. I lost heart, and lay

down on the scullery floor for a long time, having no spirit even to move. And after that I abandoned altogether the idea of escaping by excavation.

It says much for the impression the Martians had made upon me that at first I entertained little or no hope of our escape being brought about by their overthrow through any human effort. But on the fourth or fifth night I heard a sound like heavy guns.

It was very late in the night, and the moon was shining brightly. The Martians had taken away the excavating-machine, and, save for a fighting- machine that stood in the remoter bank of the pit and a handling-machine that was buried out of my sight in a corner of the pit immediately beneath my peephole, the place was deserted by them. Except for the pale glow from the handling-machine and the bars and patches of white moonlight the pit was in darkness, and, except for the clinking of the handling-machine, quite still. That night was a beautiful serenity; save for one planet, the moon seemed to have the sky to herself. I heard a dog howling, and that familiar sound it was that made me listen. Then I heard quite distinctly a booming exactly like the sound of great guns. Six distinct reports I counted, and after a long interval six again. And that was all.

CHAPTER FOUR - THE DEATH OF THE CURATE

It was on the sixth day of our imprisonment that I peeped for the last time, and presently found myself alone. Instead of keeping close to me and trying to oust me from the slit, the curate had gone back into the scullery. I was struck by a sudden thought. I went back quickly and quietly into the scullery. In the darkness I heard the curate drinking. I snatched in the darkness, and my fingers caught a bottle of burgundy.

For a few minutes there was a tussle. The bottle struck the floor and broke, and I desisted and rose. We stood panting and threatening each other. In the end I planted myself between him and the food, and told him of my determination to begin a discipline. I divided the food in the pantry, into rations to last us ten days. I would not let him eat any more that day. In the afternoon he made a feeble effort to get at the food. I had been dozing, but in an instant I was awake. All day and all night we sat face to face, I weary but resolute, and he weeping and complaining of his immediate hunger. It was, I know, a night and a day, but to me it seemed—it seems now—an interminable length of time.

And so our widened incompatibility ended at last in open conflict. For two vast days we struggled in undertones and wrestling contests. There were times when I beat and kicked him madly, times when I cajoled and persuaded him, and once I tried to bribe him with the last bottle of burgundy, for there was a rain-water pump from which I could get water. But neither force nor kindness availed; he was indeed beyond reason. He would neither desist from his attacks on the food nor from his noisy babbling to himself. The rudimentary precautions to keep our imprisonment endurable he would not observe. Slowly I began to realise the complete overthrow of his intelligence, to perceive that my sole companion in this close and sickly darkness was a man insane.

From certain vague memories I am inclined to think my own mind wandered at times. I had strange and hideous dreams whenever I slept. It sounds paradoxical, but I am inclined to think that the weakness and insanity of the curate warned me, braced me, and kept me a sane man.

On the eighth day he began to talk aloud instead of whispering, and nothing I could do would moderate his speech.

"It is just, O God!" he would say, over and over again. "It is just. On me and mine be the punishment laid. We have sinned, we have fallen short. There was poverty, sorrow; the poor were trodden in the dust, and I held my peace. I preached acceptable folly—my God, what folly!—when I should have stood up,

though I died for it, and called upon them to repent-repent! ... Oppressors of the poor and needy ...! The wine press of God!"

Then he would suddenly revert to the matter of the food I withheld from him, praying, begging, weeping, at last threatening. He began to raise his voice—I prayed him not to. He perceived a hold on me—he threatened he would shout and bring the Martians upon us. For a time that scared me; but any concession would have shortened our chance of escape beyond estimating. I defied him, although I felt no assurance that he might not do this thing. But that day, at any rate, he did not. He talked with his voice rising slowly, through the greater part of the eighth and ninth days—threats, entreaties, mingled with a torrent of half-sane and always frothy repentance for his vacant sham of God's service, such as made me pity him. Then he slept awhile, and began again with renewed strength, so loudly that I must needs make him desist.

"Be still!" I implored.

He rose to his knees, for he had been sitting in the darkness near the copper.

"I have been still too long," he said, in a tone that must have reached the pit, "and now I must bear my witness. Woe unto this unfaithful city! Woe! Woe! Woe! Woe! Woe! To the inhabitants of the earth by reason of the other voices of the trumpet—"

"Shut up!" I said, rising to my feet, and in a terror lest the Martians should hear us. "For God's sake—"

"Nay," shouted the curate, at the top of his voice, standing likewise and extending his arms. "Speak! The word of the Lord is upon me!"

In three strides he was at the door leading into the kitchen.

"I must bear my witness! I go! It has already been too long delayed."

I put out my hand and felt the meat chopper hanging to the wall. In a flash I was after him. I was fierce with fear. Before he was halfway across the kitchen I had overtaken him. With one last touch of humanity I turned the blade back and struck him with the butt. He went headlong forward and lay stretched on the ground. I stumbled over him and stood panting. He lay still.

Suddenly I heard a noise without, the run and smash of slipping plaster, and the triangular aperture in the wall was darkened. I looked up and saw the lower surface of a handling-machine coming slowly across the hole. One of its gripping limbs curled amid the debris; another limb appeared, feeling its way over the fallen beams. I stood petrified, staring. Then I saw through a sort of glass plate near the edge of the body the face, as we may call it, and the large dark eyes of a Martian, peering, and then a long metallic snake of tentacle came feeling slowly through the hole.

I turned by an effort, stumbled over the curate, and stopped at the scullery door. The tentacle was now some way, two yards or more, in the room, and twisting and turning, with queer sudden movements, this way and that. For a while I stood fascinated by that slow, fitful advance. Then, with a faint, hoarse cry, I forced myself across the scullery. I trembled violently; I could scarcely stand upright. I opened the door of the coal cellar, and stood there in the darkness staring

at the faintly lit doorway into the kitchen, and listening. Had the Martian seen me? What was it doing now?

Something was moving to and fro there, very quietly; every now and then it tapped against the wall, or started on its movements with a faint metallic ringing, like the movements of keys on a split-ring. Then a heavy body—I knew too well what—was dragged across the floor of the kitchen towards the opening. Irresistibly attracted, I crept to the door and peeped into the kitchen. In the triangle of bright outer sunlight I saw the Martian, in its Briareus of a handling-machine, scrutinizing the curate's head. I thought at once that it would infer my presence from the mark of the blow I had given him.

I crept back to the coal cellar, shut the door, and began to cover myself up as much as I could, and as noiselessly as possible in the darkness, among the firewood and coal therein. Every now and then I paused, rigid, to hear if the Martian had thrust its tentacles through the opening again.

Then the faint metallic jingle returned. I traced it slowly feeling over the kitchen. Presently I heard it nearer—in the scullery, as I judged. I thought that its length might be insufficient to reach me. I prayed copiously. It passed, scraping faintly across the cellar door. An age of almost intolerable suspense intervened; then I heard it fumbling at the latch! It had found the door! The Martians understood doors!

It worried at the catch for a minute, perhaps, and then the door opened.

In the darkness I could just see the thing—like an elephant's trunk more than anything else—waving towards me and touching and examining the wall, coals, wood and ceiling. It was like a black worm swaying its blind head to and fro.

Once, even, it touched the heel of my boot. I was on the verge of screaming; I bit my hand. For a time the tentacle was silent. I could have fancied it had been withdrawn. Presently, with an abrupt click, it gripped something—I thought it had me!—and seemed to go out of the cellar again. For a minute I was not sure. Apparently it had taken a lump of coal to examine.

I seized the opportunity of slightly shifting my position, which had become cramped, and then listened. I whispered passionate prayers for safety.

Then I heard the slow, deliberate sound creeping towards me again. Slowly, slowly it drew near, scratching against the walls and tapping the furniture.

While I was still doubtful, it rapped smartly against the cellar door and closed it. I heard it go into the pantry, and the biscuit-tins rattled and a bottle smashed, and then came a heavy bump against the cellar door. Then silence that passed into an infinity of suspense.

Had it gone?

At last I decided that it had.

It came into the scullery no more; but I lay all the tenth day in the close darkness, buried among coals and firewood, not daring even to crawl out for the drink for which I craved. It was the eleventh day before I ventured so far from my security.

CHAPTER FIVE - THE STILLNESS

My first act before I went into the pantry was to fasten the door between the kitchen and the scullery. But the pantry was empty; every scrap of food had gone. Apparently, the Martian had taken it all on the previous day. At that discovery I despaired for the first time. I took no food, or no drink either, on the eleventh or the twelfth day.

At first my mouth and throat were parched, and my strength ebbed sensibly. I sat about in the darkness of the scullery, in a state of despondent wretchedness. My mind ran on eating. I thought I had become deaf, for the noises of movement I had been accustomed to hear from the pit had ceased absolutely. I did not feel strong enough to crawl noiselessly to the peephole, or I would have gone there.

On the twelfth day my throat was so painful that, taking the chance of alarming the Martians, I attacked the creaking rain-water pump that stood by the sink, and got a couple of glassfuls of blackened and tainted rain water. I was greatly refreshed by this, and emboldened by the fact that no enquiring tentacle followed the noise of my pumping.

During these days, in a rambling, inconclusive way, I thought much of the curate and of the manner of his death.

On the thirteenth day I drank some more water, and dozed and thought disjointedly of eating and of vague impossible plans of escape. Whenever I dozed I dreamt of horrible phantasms, of the death of the curate, or of sumptuous dinners; but, asleep or awake, I felt a keen pain that urged me to drink again and again. The light that came into the scullery was no longer grey, but red. To my disordered imagination it seemed the colour of blood.

On the fourteenth day I went into the kitchen, and I was surprised to find that the fronds of the red weed had grown right across the hole in the wall, turning the half-light of the place into a crimson-coloured obscurity.

It was early on the fifteenth day that I heard a curious, familiar sequence of sounds in the kitchen, and, listening, identified it as the snuffing and scratching of a dog. Going into the kitchen, I saw a dog's nose peering in through a break among the ruddy fronds. This greatly surprised me. At the scent of me he barked shortly.

I thought if I could induce him to come into the place quietly I should be able, perhaps, to kill and eat him; and in any case, it would be advisable to kill him, lest his actions attracted the attention of the Martians.

I crept forward, saying "Good dog!" very softly; but he suddenly withdrew his head and disappeared.

I listened—I was not deaf—but certainly the pit was still. I heard a sound like the flutter of a bird's wings, and a hoarse croaking, but that was all.

For a long while I lay close to the peephole, but not daring to move aside the red plants that obscured it. Once or twice I heard a faint pitter- patter like the feet of the dog going hither and thither on the sand far below me, and there were more birdlike sounds, but that was all. At length, encouraged by the silence, I looked out.

Except in the corner, where a multitude of crows hopped and fought over the skeletons of the dead the Martians had consumed, there was not a living thing in the pit.

I stared about me, scarcely believing my eyes. All the machinery had gone. Save for the big mound of greyish-blue powder in one corner, certain bars of aluminium in another, the black birds, and the skeletons of the killed, the place was merely an empty circular pit in the sand.

Slowly I thrust myself out through the red weed, and stood upon the mound of rubble. I could see in any direction save behind me, to the north, and neither Martians nor sign of Martians were to be seen. The pit dropped sheerly from my feet, but a little way along the rubbish afforded a practicable slope to the summit of the ruins. My chance of escape had come. I began to tremble.

I hesitated for some time, and then, in a gust of desperate resolution, and with a heart that throbbed violently, I scrambled to the top of the mound in which I had been buried so long.

I looked about again. To the northward, too, no Martian was visible.

When I had last seen this part of Sheen in the daylight it had been a straggling street of comfortable white and red houses, interspersed with abundant shady trees. Now I stood on a mound of smashed brickwork, clay, and gravel, over which spread a multitude of red cactus-shaped plants, knee-high, without a solitary terrestrial growth to dispute their footing. The trees near me were dead and brown, but further a network of red thread scaled the still living stems.

The neighbouring houses had all been wrecked, but none had been burned; their walls stood, sometimes to the second story, with smashed windows and shattered doors. The red weed grew tumultuously in their roofless rooms. Below me was the great pit, with the crows struggling for its refuse. A number of other birds hopped about among the ruins. Far away I saw a gaunt cat slink crouchingly along a wall, but traces of men there were none.

The day seemed, by contrast with my recent confinement, dazzlingly bright, the sky a glowing blue. A gentle breeze kept the red weed that covered every scrap of unoccupied ground gently swaying. And oh! the sweetness of the air!

CHAPTER SIX - THE WORK OF FIFTEEN DAYS

For some time I stood tottering on the mound regardless of my safety. Within that noisome den from which I had emerged I had thought with a narrow intensity only of our immediate security. I had not realised what had been happening to the world, had not anticipated this startling vision of unfamiliar things. I had expected to see Sheen in ruins—I found about me the landscape, weird and lurid, of another planet.

For that moment I touched an emotion beyond the common range of men, yet one that the poor brutes we dominate know only too well. I felt as a rabbit might feel returning to his burrow and suddenly confronted by the work of a dozen busy navvies digging the foundations of a house. I felt the first inkling of a thing that presently grew quite clear in my mind, that oppressed me for many days, a sense of dethronement, a persuasion that I was no longer a master, but an animal among the animals, under the Martian heel. With us it would be as with them, to lurk and watch, to run and hide; the fear and empire of man had passed away.

But so soon as this strangeness had been realised it passed, and my dominant motive became the hunger of my long and dismal fast. In the direction away from the pit I saw, beyond a red-covered wall, a patch of garden ground unburied. This gave me a hint, and I went knee-deep, and sometimes neck-deep, in the red weed. The density of the weed gave me a reassuring sense of hiding. The wall was some six feet high, and when I attempted to clamber it I found I could not lift my feet to the crest. So I went along by the side of it, and came to a corner and a rockwork that enabled me to get to the top, and tumble into the garden I coveted. Here I found some young onions, a couple of gladiolus bulbs, and a quantity of immature carrots, all of which I secured, and, scrambling over a ruined wall, went on my way through scarlet and crimson trees towards Kew—it was like walking through an avenue of gigantic blood drops—possessed with two ideas: to get more food, and to limp, as soon and as far as my strength permitted, out of this accursed unearthly region of the pit.

Some way farther, in a grassy place, was a group of mushrooms which also I devoured, and then I came upon a brown sheet of flowing shallow water, where meadows used to be. These fragments of nourishment served only to whet my hunger. At first I was surprised at this flood in a hot, dry summer, but afterwards I discovered that it was caused by the tropical exuberance of the red weed. Directly this extraordinary growth encountered water it straightway became gigantic and of unparalleled fecundity. Its seeds were simply poured down into the water of the

Wey and Thames, and its swiftly growing and Titanic water fronds speedily choked both those rivers.

At Putney, as I afterwards saw, the bridge was almost lost in a tangle of this weed, and at Richmond, too, the Thames water poured in a broad and shallow stream across the meadows of Hampton and Twickenham. As the water spread the weed followed them, until the ruined villas of the Thames valley were for a time lost in this red swamp, whose margin I explored, and much of the desolation the Martians had caused was concealed.

In the end the red weed succumbed almost as quickly as it had spread. A cankering disease, due, it is believed, to the action of certain bacteria, presently seized upon it. Now by the action of natural selection, all terrestrial plants have acquired a resisting power against bacterial diseases —they never succumb without a severe struggle, but the red weed rotted like a thing already dead. The fronds became bleached, and then shrivelled and brittle. They broke off at the least touch, and the waters that had stimulated their early growth carried their last vestiges out to sea.

My first act on coming to this water was, of course, to slake my thirst. I drank a great deal of it and, moved by an impulse, gnawed some fronds of red weed; but they were watery, and had a sickly, metallic taste. I found the water was sufficiently shallow for me to wade securely, although the red weed impeded my feet a little; but the flood evidently got deeper towards the river, and I turned back to Mortlake. I managed to make out the road by means of occasional ruins of its villas and fences and lamps, and so presently I got out of this spate and made my way to the hill going up towards Roehampton and came out on Putney Common.

Here the scenery changed from the strange and unfamiliar to the wreckage of the familiar: patches of ground exhibited the devastation of a cyclone, and in a few score yards I would come upon perfectly undisturbed spaces, houses with their blinds trimly drawn and doors closed, as if they had been left for a day by the owners, or as if their inhabitants slept within. The red weed was less abundant; the tall trees along the lane were free from the red creeper. I hunted for food among the trees, finding nothing, and I also raided a couple of silent houses, but they had already been broken into and ransacked. I rested for the remainder of the daylight in a shrubbery, being, in my enfeebled condition, too fatigued to push on.

All this time I saw no human beings, and no signs of the Martians. I encountered a couple of hungry-looking dogs, but both hurried circuitously away from the advances I made them. Near Roehampton I had seen two human skeletons—not bodies, but skeletons, picked clean—and in the wood by me I found the crushed and scattered bones of several cats and rabbits and the skull of a sheep. But though I gnawed parts of these in my mouth, there was nothing to be got from them.

After sunset I struggled on along the road towards Putney, where I think the Heat-Ray must have been used for some reason. And in the garden beyond Roehampton I got a quantity of immature potatoes, sufficient to stay my hunger. From this garden one looked down upon Putney and the river. The aspect of the place in

the dusk was singularly desolate: blackened trees, blackened, desolate ruins, and down the hill the sheets of the flooded river, red-tinged with the weed. And over all—silence. It filled me with indescribable terror to think how swiftly that desolating change had come.

For a time I believed that mankind had been swept out of existence, and that I stood there alone, the last man left alive. Hard by the top of Putney Hill I came upon another skeleton, with the arms dislocated and removed several yards from the rest of the body. As I proceeded I became more and more convinced that the extermination of mankind was, save for such stragglers as myself, already accomplished in this part of the world. The Martians, I thought, had gone on and left the country desolated, seeking food elsewhere. Perhaps even now they were destroying Berlin or Paris, or it might be they had gone northward.

CHAPTER SEVEN - THE MAN ON PUTNEY HILL

I spent that night in the inn that stands at the top of Putney Hill, sleeping in a made bed for the first time since my flight to Leatherhead. I will not tell the needless trouble I had breaking into that house—afterwards I found the front door was on the latch—nor how I ransacked every room for food, until just on the verge of despair, in what seemed to me to be a servant's bedroom, I found a rat-gnawed crust and two tins of pineapple. The place had been already searched and emptied. In the bar I afterwards found some biscuits and sandwiches that had been overlooked. The latter I could not eat, they were too rotten, but the former not only stayed my hunger, but filled my pockets. I lit no lamps, fearing some Martian might come beating that part of London for food in the night. Before I went to bed I had an interval of restlessness, and prowled from window to window, peering out for some sign of these monsters. I slept little. As I lay in bed I found myself thinking consecutively—a thing I do not remember to have done since my last argument with the curate. During all the intervening time my mental condition had been a hurrying succession of vague emotional states or a sort of stupid receptivity. But in the night my brain, reinforced, I suppose, by the food I had eaten, grew clear again, and I thought.

Three things struggled for possession of my mind: the killing of the curate, the whereabouts of the Martians, and the possible fate of my wife. The former gave me no sensation of horror or remorse to recall; I saw it simply as a thing done, a memory infinitely disagreeable but quite without the quality of remorse. I saw myself then as I see myself now, driven step by step towards that hasty blow, the creature of a sequence of accidents leading inevitably to that. I felt no condemnation; yet the memory, static, unprogressive, haunted me. In the silence of the night, with that sense of the nearness of God that sometimes comes into the stillness and the darkness, I stood my trial, my only trial, for that moment of wrath and fear. I retraced every step of our conversation from the moment when I had found him crouching beside me, heedless of my thirst, and pointing to the fire and smoke that streamed up from the ruins of Weybridge. We had been incapable of co-operation—grim chance had taken no heed of that. Had I foreseen, I should have left him at Halliford. But I did not foresee; and crime is to foresee and do. And I set this down as I have set all this story down, as it was. There were no witnesses—all these things I might have concealed. But I set it down, and the reader must form his judgment as he will.

And when, by an effort, I had set aside that picture of a prostrate body, I faced the problem of the Martians and the fate of my wife. For the former I had no data; I could imagine a hundred things, and so, unhappily, I could for the latter. And suddenly that night became terrible. I found myself sitting up in bed, staring at the dark. I found myself praying that the Heat-Ray might have suddenly and painlessly struck her out of being. Since the night of my return from Leatherhead I had not prayed. I had uttered prayers, fetish prayers, had prayed as heathens mutter charms when I was in extremity; but now I prayed indeed, pleading steadfastly and sanely, face to face with the darkness of God. Strange night! Strangest in this, that so soon as dawn had come, I, who had talked with God, crept out of the house like a rat leaving its hiding place—a creature scarcely larger, an inferior animal, a thing that for any passing whim of our masters might be hunted and killed. Perhaps they also prayed confidently to God. Surely, if we have learned nothing else, this war has taught us pity—pity for those witless souls that suffer our dominion.

The morning was bright and fine, and the eastern sky glowed pink, and was fretted with little golden clouds. In the road that runs from the top of Putney Hill to Wimbledon was a number of poor vestiges of the panic torrent that must have poured Londonward on the Sunday night after the fighting began. There was a little two-wheeled cart inscribed with the name of Thomas Lobb, Greengrocer, New Malden, with a smashed wheel and an abandoned tin trunk; there was a straw hat trampled into the now hardened mud, and at the top of West Hill a lot of blood-stained glass about the overturned water trough. My movements were languid, my plans of the vaguest. I had an idea of going to Leatherhead, though I knew that there I had the poorest chance of finding my wife. Certainly, unless death had overtaken them suddenly, my cousins and she would have fled thence; but it seemed to me I might find or learn there whither the Surrey people had fled. I knew I wanted to find my wife, that my heart ached for her and the world of men, but I had no clear idea how the finding might be done. I was also sharply aware now of my intense loneliness. From the corner I went, under cover of a thicket of trees and bushes, to the edge of Wimbledon Common, stretching wide and far.

That dark expanse was lit in patches by yellow gorse and broom; there was no red weed to be seen, and as I prowled, hesitating, on the verge of the open, the sun rose, flooding it all with light and vitality. I came upon a busy swarm of little frogs in a swampy place among the trees. I stopped to look at them, drawing a lesson from their stout resolve to live. And presently, turning suddenly, with an odd feeling of being watched, I beheld something crouching amid a clump of bushes. I stood regarding this. I made a step towards it, and it rose up and became a man armed with a cutlass. I approached him slowly. He stood silent and motionless, regarding me.

As I drew nearer I perceived he was dressed in clothes as dusty and filthy as my own; he looked, indeed, as though he had been dragged through a culvert. Nearer, I distinguished the green slime of ditches mixing with the pale drab of

dried clay and shiny, coaly patches. His black hair fell over his eyes, and his face was dark and dirty and sunken, so that at first I did not recognise him. There was a red cut across the lower part of his face.

"Stop!" he cried, when I was within ten yards of him, and I stopped. His voice was hoarse. "Where do you come from?" he said.

I thought, surveying him.

"I come from Mortlake," I said. "I was buried near the pit the Martians made about their cylinder. I have worked my way out and escaped."

"There is no food about here," he said. "This is my country. All this hill down to the river, and back to Clapham, and up to the edge of the common. There is only food for one. Which way are you going?"

I answered slowly.

"I don't know," I said. "I have been buried in the ruins of a house thirteen or fourteen days. I don't know what has happened."

He looked at me doubtfully, then started, and looked with a changed expression.

"I've no wish to stop about here," said I. "I think I shall go to Leatherhead, for my wife was there."

He shot out a pointing finger.

"It is you," said he; "the man from Woking. And you weren't killed at Weybridge?"

I recognised him at the same moment.

"You are the artilleryman who came into my garden."

"Good luck!" he said. "We are lucky ones! Fancy *you*!" He put out a hand, and I took it. "I crawled up a drain," he said. "But they didn't kill everyone. And after they went away I got off towards Walton across the fields. But—It's not sixteen days altogether—and your hair is grey." He looked over his shoulder suddenly. "Only a rook," he said. "One gets to know that birds have shadows these days. This is a bit open. Let us crawl under those bushes and talk."

"Have you seen any Martians?" I said. "Since I crawled out—"

"They've gone away across London," he said. "I guess they've got a bigger camp there. Of a night, all over there, Hampstead way, the sky is alive with their lights. It's like a great city, and in the glare you can just see them moving. By daylight you can't. But nearer—I haven't seen them—" (he counted on his fingers) "five days. Then I saw a couple across Hammersmith way carrying something big. And the night before last"—he stopped and spoke impressively—"it was just a matter of lights, but it was something up in the air. I believe they've built a flying-machine, and are learning to fly."

I stopped, on hands and knees, for we had come to the bushes.

"Fly!"

"Yes," he said, "fly."

I went on into a little bower, and sat down.

"It is all over with humanity," I said. "If they can do that they will simply go round the world."

He nodded.

"They will. But—It will relieve things over here a bit. And besides—" He looked at me. "Aren't you satisfied it *is* up with humanity? I am. We're down; we're beat."

I stared. Strange as it may seem, I had not arrived at this fact—a fact perfectly obvious so soon as he spoke. I had still held a vague hope; rather, I had kept a lifelong habit of mind. He repeated his words, "We're beat." They carried absolute conviction.

"It's all over," he said. "They've lost *one*—just *one*. And they've made their footing good and crippled the greatest power in the world. They've walked over us. The death of that one at Weybridge was an accident. And these are only pioneers. They kept on coming. These green stars —I've seen none these five or six days, but I've no doubt they're falling somewhere every night. Nothing's to be done. We're under! We're beat!"

I made him no answer. I sat staring before me, trying in vain to devise some countervailing thought.

"This isn't a war," said the artilleryman. "It never was a war, any more than there's war between man and ants."

Suddenly I recalled the night in the observatory.

"After the tenth shot they fired no more—at least, until the first cylinder came."

"How do you know?" said the artilleryman. I explained. He thought. "Something wrong with the gun," he said. "But what if there is? They'll get it right again. And even if there's a delay, how can it alter the end? It's just men and ants. There's the ants builds their cities, live their lives, have wars, revolutions, until the men want them out of the way, and then they go out of the way. That's what we are now—just ants. Only—"

"Yes," I said.

"We're eatable ants."

We sat looking at each other.

"And what will they do with us?" I said.

"That's what I've been thinking," he said; "that's what I've been thinking. After Weybridge I went south—thinking. I saw what was up. Most of the people were hard at it squealing and exciting themselves. But I'm not so fond of squealing. I've been in sight of death once or twice; I'm not an ornamental soldier, and at the best and worst, death—it's just death. And it's the man that keeps on thinking comes through. I saw everyone tracking away south. Says I, 'Food won't last this way,' and I turned right back. I went for the Martians like a sparrow goes for man. All round"—he waved a hand to the horizon—"they're starving in heaps, bolting, treading on each other...."

He saw my face, and halted awkwardly.

"No doubt lots who had money have gone away to France," he said. He seemed to hesitate whether to apologise, met my eyes, and went on: "There's food all about here. Canned things in shops; wines, spirits, mineral waters; and the wa-

ter mains and drains are empty. Well, I was telling you what I was thinking. 'Here's intelligent things,' I said, 'and it seems they want us for food. First, they'll smash us up—ships, machines, guns, cities, all the order and organisation. All that will go. If we were the size of ants we might pull through. But we're not. It's all too bulky to stop. That's the first certainty.' Eh?"

I assented.

"It is; I've thought it out. Very well, then—next; at present we're caught as we're wanted. A Martian has only to go a few miles to get a crowd on the run. And I saw one, one day, out by Wandsworth, picking houses to pieces and routing among the wreckage. But they won't keep on doing that. So soon as they've settled all our guns and ships, and smashed our railways, and done all the things they are doing over there, they will begin catching us systematic, picking the best and storing us in cages and things. That's what they will start doing in a bit. Lord! They haven't begun on us yet. Don't you see that?"

"Not begun!" I exclaimed.

"Not begun. All that's happened so far is through our not having the sense to keep quiet—worrying them with guns and such foolery. And losing our heads, and rushing off in crowds to where there wasn't any more safety than where we were. They don't want to bother us yet. They're making their things—making all the things they couldn't bring with them, getting things ready for the rest of their people. Very likely that's why the cylinders have stopped for a bit, for fear of hitting those who are here. And instead of our rushing about blind, on the howl, or getting dynamite on the chance of busting them up, we've got to fix ourselves up according to the new state of affairs. That's how I figure it out. It isn't quite according to what a man wants for his species, but it's about what the facts point to. And that's the principle I acted upon. Cities, nations, civilisation, progress—it's all over. That game's up. We're beat."

"But if that is so, what is there to live for?"

The artilleryman looked at me for a moment.

"There won't be any more blessed concerts for a million years or so; there won't be any Royal Academy of Arts, and no nice little feeds at restaurants. If it's amusement you're after, I reckon the game is up. If you've got any drawing-room manners or a dislike to eating peas with a knife or dropping aitches, you'd better chuck 'em away. They ain't no further use."

"You mean—"

"I mean that men like me are going on living—for the sake of the breed. I tell you, I'm grim set on living. And if I'm not mistaken, you'll show what insides *you've* got, too, before long. We aren't going to be exterminated. And I don't mean to be caught either, and tamed and fattened and bred like a thundering ox. Ugh! Fancy those brown creepers!"

"You don't mean to say—"

"I do. I'm going on, under their feet. I've got it planned; I've thought it out. We men are beat. We don't know enough. We've got to learn before we've got a

chance. And we've got to live and keep independent while we learn. See! That's what has to be done."

I stared, astonished, and stirred profoundly by the man's resolution.

"Great God!" cried I. "But you are a man indeed!" And suddenly I gripped his hand.

"Eh!" he said, with his eyes shining. "I've thought it out, eh?"

"Go on," I said.

"Well, those who mean to escape their catching must get ready. I'm getting ready. Mind you, it isn't all of us that are made for wild beasts; and that's what it's got to be. That's why I watched you. I had my doubts. You're slender. I didn't know that it was you, you see, or just how you'd been buried. All these—the sort of people that lived in these houses, and all those damn little clerks that used to live down that way—they'd be no good. They haven't any spirit in them—no proud dreams and no proud lusts; and a man who hasn't one or the other—Lord! What is he but funk and precautions? They just used to skedaddle off to work—I've seen hundreds of 'em, bit of breakfast in hand, running wild and shining to catch their little season-ticket train, for fear they'd get dismissed if they didn't; working at businesses they were afraid to take the trouble to understand; skedaddling back for fear they wouldn't be in time for dinner; keeping indoors after dinner for fear of the back streets, and sleeping with the wives they married, not because they wanted them, but because they had a bit of money that would make for safety in their one little miserable skedaddle through the world. Lives insured and a bit invested for fear of accidents. And on Sundays—fear of the hereafter. As if hell was built for rabbits! Well, the Martians will just be a godsend to these. Nice roomy cages, fattening food, careful breeding, no worry. After a week or so chasing about the fields and lands on empty stomachs, they'll come and be caught cheerful. They'll be quite glad after a bit. They'll wonder what people did before there were Martians to take care of them. And the bar loafers, and mashers, and singers—I can imagine them. I can imagine them," he said, with a sort of sombre gratification. "There'll be any amount of sentiment and religion loose among them. There's hundreds of things I saw with my eyes that I've only begun to see clearly these last few days. There's lots will take things as they are—fat and stupid; and lots will be worried by a sort of feeling that it's all wrong, and that they ought to be doing something. Now whenever things are so that a lot of people feel they ought to be doing something, the weak, and those who go weak with a lot of complicated thinking, always make for a sort of do- nothing religion, very pious and superior, and submit to persecution and the will of the Lord. Very likely you've seen the same thing. It's energy in a gale of funk, and turned clean inside out. These cages will be full of psalms and hymns and piety. And those of a less simple sort will work in a bit of—what is it?—eroticism."

He paused.

"Very likely these Martians will make pets of some of them; train them to do tricks—who knows?—get sentimental over the pet boy who grew up and had to be killed. And some, maybe, they will train to hunt us."

"No," I cried, "that's impossible! No human being—"

"What's the good of going on with such lies?" said the artilleryman. "There's men who'd do it cheerful. What nonsense to pretend there isn't!"

And I succumbed to his conviction.

"If they come after me," he said; "Lord, if they come after me!" and subsided into a grim meditation.

I sat contemplating these things. I could find nothing to bring against this man's reasoning. In the days before the invasion no one would have questioned my intellectual superiority to his—I, a professed and recognised writer on philosophical themes, and he, a common soldier; and yet he had already formulated a situation that I had scarcely realised.

"What are you doing?" I said presently. "What plans have you made?"

He hesitated.

"Well, it's like this," he said. "What have we to do? We have to invent a sort of life where men can live and breed, and be sufficiently secure to bring the children up. Yes—wait a bit, and I'll make it clearer what I think ought to be done. The tame ones will go like all tame beasts; in a few generations they'll be big, beautiful, rich-blooded, stupid—rubbish! The risk is that we who keep wild will go savage—degenerate into a sort of big, savage rat... You see, how I mean to live is underground. I've been thinking about the drains. Of course those who don't know drains think horrible things; but under this London are miles and miles—hundreds of miles—and a few days rain and London empty will leave them sweet and clean. The main drains are big enough and airy enough for anyone. Then there's cellars, vaults, stores, from which bolting passages may be made to the drains. And the railway tunnels and subways. Eh? You begin to see? And we form a band—able-bodied, clean-minded men. We're not going to pick up any rubbish that drifts in. Weaklings go out again."

"As you meant me to go?"

"Well—I parleyed, didn't I?"

"We won't quarrel about that. Go on."

"Those who stop obey orders. Able-bodied, clean-minded women we want also —mothers and teachers. No lackadaisical ladies—no blasted rolling eyes. We can't have any weak or silly. Life is real again, and the useless and cumbersome and mischievous have to die. They ought to die. They ought to be willing to die. It's a sort of disloyalty, after all, to live and taint the race. And they can't be happy. Moreover, dying's none so dreadful; it's the funking makes it bad. And in all those places we shall gather. Our district will be London. And we may even be able to keep a watch, and run about in the open when the Martians keep away. Play cricket, perhaps. That's how we shall save the race. Eh? It's a possible thing? But saving the race is nothing in itself. As I say, that's only being rats. It's saving our knowledge and adding to it is the thing. There men like you come in. There's books, there's models. We must make great safe places down deep, and get all the books we can; not novels and poetry swipes, but ideas, science books. That's where men like you come in. We must go to the British Museum and pick all

those books through. Especially we must keep up our science—learn more. We must watch these Martians. Some of us must go as spies. When it's all working, perhaps I will. Get caught, I mean. And the great thing is, we must leave the Martians alone. We mustn't even steal. If we get in their way, we clear out. We must show them we mean no harm. Yes, I know. But they're intelligent things, and they won't hunt us down if they have all they want, and think we're just harmless vermin."

The artilleryman paused and laid a brown hand upon my arm.

"After all, it may not be so much we may have to learn before—Just imagine this: four or five of their fighting machines suddenly starting off—Heat-Rays right and left, and not a Martian in 'em. Not a Martian in 'em, but men—men who have learned the way how. It may be in my time, even—those men. Fancy having one of them lovely things, with its Heat- Ray wide and free! Fancy having it in control! What would it matter if you smashed to smithereens at the end of the run, after a bust like that? I reckon the Martians'll open their beautiful eyes! Can't you see them, man? Can't you see them hurrying, hurrying—puffing and blowing and hooting to their other mechanical affairs? Something out of gear in every case. And swish, bang, rattle, swish! Just as they are fumbling over it, *swish* comes the Heat- Ray, and, behold! man has come back to his own."

For a while the imaginative daring of the artilleryman, and the tone of assurance and courage he assumed, completely dominated my mind. I believed unhesitatingly both in his forecast of human destiny and in the practicability of his astonishing scheme, and the reader who thinks me susceptible and foolish must contrast his position, reading steadily with all his thoughts about his subject, and mine, crouching fearfully in the bushes and listening, distracted by apprehension. We talked in this manner through the early morning time, and later crept out of the bushes, and, after scanning the sky for Martians, hurried precipitately to the house on Putney Hill where he had made his lair. It was the coal cellar of the place, and when I saw the work he had spent a week upon—it was a burrow scarcely ten yards long, which he designed to reach to the main drain on Putney Hill—I had my first inkling of the gulf between his dreams and his powers. Such a hole I could have dug in a day. But I believed in him sufficiently to work with him all that morning until past midday at his digging. We had a garden barrow and shot the earth we removed against the kitchen range. We refreshed ourselves with a tin of mock-turtle soup and wine from the neighbouring pantry. I found a curious relief from the aching strangeness of the world in this steady labour. As we worked, I turned his project over in my mind, and presently objections and doubts began to arise; but I worked there all the morning, so glad was I to find myself with a purpose again. After working an hour I began to speculate on the distance one had to go before the cloaca was reached, the chances we had of missing it altogether. My immediate trouble was why we should dig this long tunnel, when it was possible to get into the drain at once down one of the manholes, and work back to the house. It seemed to me, too, that the house was inconveniently

chosen, and required a needless length of tunnel. And just as I was beginning to face these things, the artilleryman stopped digging, and looked at me.

"We're working well," he said. He put down his spade. "Let us knock off a bit" he said. "I think it's time we reconnoitred from the roof of the house."

I was for going on, and after a little hesitation he resumed his spade; and then suddenly I was struck by a thought. I stopped, and so did he at once.

"Why were you walking about the common," I said, "instead of being here?"

"Taking the air," he said. "I was coming back. It's safer by night."

"But the work?"

"Oh, one can't always work," he said, and in a flash I saw the man plain. He hesitated, holding his spade. "We ought to reconnoitre now," he said, "because if any come near they may hear the spades and drop upon us unawares."

I was no longer disposed to object. We went together to the roof and stood on a ladder peeping out of the roof door. No Martians were to be seen, and we ventured out on the tiles, and slipped down under shelter of the parapet.

From this position a shrubbery hid the greater portion of Putney, but we could see the river below, a bubbly mass of red weed, and the low parts of Lambeth flooded and red. The red creeper swarmed up the trees about the old palace, and their branches stretched gaunt and dead, and set with shrivelled leaves, from amid its clusters. It was strange how entirely dependent both these things were upon flowing water for their propagation. About us neither had gained a footing; laburnums, pink mays, snowballs, and trees of arbor- vitae, rose out of laurels and hydrangeas, green and brilliant into the sunlight. Beyond Kensington dense smoke was rising, and that and a blue haze hid the northward hills.

The artilleryman began to tell me of the sort of people who still remained in London.

"One night last week," he said, "some fools got the electric light in order, and there was all Regent Street and the Circus ablaze, crowded with painted and ragged drunkards, men and women, dancing and shouting till dawn. A man who was there told me. And as the day came they became aware of a fighting- machine standing near by the Langham and looking down at them. Heaven knows how long he had been there. It must have given some of them a nasty turn. He came down the road towards them, and picked up nearly a hundred too drunk or frightened to run away."

Grotesque gleam of a time no history will ever fully describe!

From that, in answer to my questions, he came round to his grandiose plans again. He grew enthusiastic. He talked so eloquently of the possibility of capturing a fighting-machine that I more than half believed in him again. But now that I was beginning to understand something of his quality, I could divine the stress he laid on doing nothing precipitately. And I noted that now there was no question that he personally was to capture and fight the great machine.

After a time we went down to the cellar. Neither of us seemed disposed to resume digging, and when he suggested a meal, I was nothing loath. He became suddenly very generous, and when we had eaten he went away and returned with

some excellent cigars. We lit these, and his optimism glowed. He was inclined to regard my coming as a great occasion.

"There's some champagne in the cellar," he said.

"We can dig better on this Thames-side burgundy," said I.

"No," said he; "I am host today. Champagne! Great God! We've a heavy enough task before us! Let us take a rest and gather strength while we may. Look at these blistered hands!"

And pursuant to this idea of a holiday, he insisted upon playing cards after we had eaten. He taught me euchre, and after dividing London between us, I taking the northern side and he the southern, we played for parish points. Grotesque and foolish as this will seem to the sober reader, it is absolutely true, and what is more remarkable, I found the card game and several others we played extremely interesting.

Strange mind of man! that, with our species upon the edge of extermination or appalling degradation, with no clear prospect before us but the chance of a horrible death, we could sit following the chance of this painted pasteboard, and playing the "joker" with vivid delight. Afterwards he taught me poker, and I beat him at three tough chess games. When dark came we decided to take the risk, and lit a lamp.

After an interminable string of games, we supped, and the artilleryman finished the champagne. We went on smoking the cigars. He was no longer the energetic regenerator of his species I had encountered in the morning. He was still optimistic, but it was a less kinetic, a more thoughtful optimism. I remember he wound up with my health, proposed in a speech of small variety and considerable intermittence. I took a cigar, and went upstairs to look at the lights of which he had spoken that blazed so greenly along the Highgate hills.

At first I stared unintelligently across the London valley. The northern hills were shrouded in darkness; the fires near Kensington glowed redly, and now and then an orange-red tongue of flame flashed up and vanished in the deep blue night. All the rest of London was black. Then, nearer, I perceived a strange light, a pale, violet-purple fluorescent glow, quivering under the night breeze. For a space I could not understand it, and then I knew that it must be the red weed from which this faint irradiation proceeded. With that realisation my dormant sense of wonder, my sense of the proportion of things, awoke again. I glanced from that to Mars, red and clear, glowing high in the west, and then gazed long and earnestly at the darkness of Hampstead and Highgate.

I remained a very long time upon the roof, wondering at the grotesque changes of the day. I recalled my mental states from the midnight prayer to the foolish card-playing. I had a violent revulsion of feeling. I remember I flung away the cigar with a certain wasteful symbolism. My folly came to me with glaring exaggeration. I seemed a traitor to my wife and to my kind; I was filled with remorse. I resolved to leave this strange undisciplined dreamer of great things to his drink and gluttony, and to go on into London. There, it seemed to me, I had the best

chance of learning what the Martians and my fellowmen were doing. I was still upon the roof when the late moon rose.

CHAPTER EIGHT - DEAD LONDON

After I had parted from the artilleryman, I went down the hill, and by the High Street across the bridge to Fulham. The red weed was tumultuous at that time, and nearly choked the bridge roadway; but its fronds were already whitened in patches by the spreading disease that presently removed it so swiftly.

At the corner of the lane that runs to Putney Bridge station I found a man lying. He was as black as a sweep with the black dust, alive, but helplessly and speechlessly drunk. I could get nothing from him but curses and furious lunges at my head. I think I should have stayed by him but for the brutal expression of his face.

There was black dust along the roadway from the bridge onwards, and it grew thicker in Fulham. The streets were horribly quiet. I got food—sour, hard, and mouldy, but quite eatable—in a baker's shop here. Some way towards Walham Green the streets became clear of powder, and I passed a white terrace of houses on fire; the noise of the burning was an absolute relief. Going on towards Brompton, the streets were quiet again.

Here I came once more upon the black powder in the streets and upon dead bodies. I saw altogether about a dozen in the length of the Fulham Road. They had been dead many days, so that I hurried quickly past them. The black powder covered them over, and softened their outlines. One or two had been disturbed by dogs.

Where there was no black powder, it was curiously like a Sunday in the City, with the closed shops, the houses locked up and the blinds drawn, the desertion, and the stillness. In some places plunderers had been at work, but rarely at other than the provision and wine shops. A jeweller's window had been broken open in one place, but apparently the thief had been disturbed, and a number of gold chains and a watch lay scattered on the pavement. I did not trouble to touch them. Farther on was a tattered woman in a heap on a doorstep; the hand that hung over her knee was gashed and bled down her rusty brown dress, and a smashed magnum of champagne formed a pool across the pavement. She seemed asleep, but she was dead.

The farther I penetrated into London, the profounder grew the stillness. But it was not so much the stillness of death—it was the stillness of suspense, of expectation. At any time the destruction that had already singed the northwestern borders of the metropolis, and had annihilated Ealing and Kilburn, might strike

among these houses and leave them smoking ruins. It was a city condemned and derelict...

In South Kensington the streets were clear of dead and of black powder. It was near South Kensington that I first heard the howling. It crept almost imperceptibly upon my senses. It was a sobbing alternation of two notes, "Ulla, ulla, ulla, ulla," keeping on perpetually. When I passed streets that ran northward it grew in volume, and houses and buildings seemed to deaden and cut it off again. It came in a full tide down Exhibition Road. I stopped, staring towards Kensington Gardens, wondering at this strange, remote wailing. It was as if that mighty desert of houses had found a voice for its fear and solitude.

"Ulla, ulla, ulla, ulla," wailed that superhuman note—great waves of sound sweeping down the broad, sunlit roadway, between the tall buildings on each side. I turned northwards, marvelling, towards the iron gates of Hyde Park. I had half a mind to break into the Natural History Museum and find my way up to the summits of the towers, in order to see across the park. But I decided to keep to the ground, where quick hiding was possible, and so went on up the Exhibition Road. All the large mansions on each side of the road were empty and still, and my footsteps echoed against the sides of the houses. At the top, near the park gate, I came upon a strange sight—a bus overturned, and the skeleton of a horse picked clean. I puzzled over this for a time, and then went on to the bridge over the Serpentine. The voice grew stronger and stronger, though I could see nothing above the housetops on the north side of the park, save a haze of smoke to the northwest.

"Ulla, ulla, ulla, ulla," cried the voice, coming, as it seemed to me, from the district about Regent's Park. The desolating cry worked upon my mind. The mood that had sustained me passed. The wailing took possession of me. I found I was intensely weary, footsore, and now again hungry and thirsty.

It was already past noon. Why was I wandering alone in this city of the dead? Why was I alone when all London was lying in state, and in its black shroud? I felt intolerably lonely. My mind ran on old friends that I had forgotten for years. I thought of the poisons in the chemists' shops, of the liquors the wine merchants stored; I recalled the two sodden creatures of despair, who so far as I knew, shared the city with myself...

I came into Oxford Street by the Marble Arch, and here again were black powder and several bodies, and an evil, ominous smell from the gratings of the cellars of some of the houses. I grew very thirsty after the heat of my long walk. With infinite trouble I managed to break into a public-house and get food and drink. I was weary after eating, and went into the parlour behind the bar, and slept on a black horsehair sofa I found there.

I awoke to find that dismal howling still in my ears, "Ulla, ulla, ulla, ulla." It was now dusk, and after I had routed out some biscuits and a cheese in the bar—there was a meat safe, but it contained nothing but maggots —I wandered on through the silent residential squares to Baker Street —Portman Square is the only one I can name—and so came out at last upon Regent's Park. And as I emerged from the top of Baker Street, I saw far away over the trees in the clearness of the

sunset the hood of the Martian giant from which this howling proceeded. I was not terrified. I came upon him as if it were a matter of course. I watched him for some time, but he did not move. He appeared to be standing and yelling, for no reason that I could discover.

I tried to formulate a plan of action. That perpetual sound of "Ulla, ulla, ulla, ulla," confused my mind. Perhaps I was too tired to be very fearful. Certainly I was more curious to know the reason of this monotonous crying than afraid. I turned back away from the park and struck into Park Road, intending to skirt the park, went along under the shelter of the terraces, and got a view of this stationary, howling Martian from the direction of St. John's Wood. A couple of hundred yards out of Baker Street I heard a yelping chorus, and saw, first a dog with a piece of putrescent red meat in his jaws coming headlong towards me, and then a pack of starving mongrels in pursuit of him. He made a wide curve to avoid me, as though he feared I might prove a fresh competitor. As the yelping died away down the silent road, the wailing sound of "Ulla, ulla, ulla, ulla," reasserted itself.

I came upon the wrecked handling-machine halfway to St. John's Wood station. At first I thought a house had fallen across the road. It was only as I clambered among the ruins that I saw, with a start, this mechanical Samson lying, with its tentacles bent and smashed and twisted, among the ruins it had made. The forepart was shattered. It seemed as if it had driven blindly straight at the house, and had been overwhelmed in its overthrow. It seemed to me then that this might have happened by a handling-machine escaping from the guidance of its Martian. I could not clamber among the ruins to see it, and the twilight was now so far advanced that the blood with which its seat was smeared, and the gnawed gristle of the Martian that the dogs had left, were invisible to me.

Wondering still more at all that I had seen, I pushed on towards Primrose Hill. Far away, through a gap in the trees, I saw a second Martian, as motionless as the first, standing in the park towards the Zoological Gardens, and silent. A little beyond the ruins about the smashed handling-machine I came upon the red weed again, and found the Regent's Canal, a spongy mass of dark- red vegetation.

As I crossed the bridge, the sound of "Ulla, ulla, ulla, ulla," ceased. It was, as it were, cut off. The silence came like a thunderclap.

The dusky houses about me stood faint and tall and dim; the trees towards the park were growing black. All about me the red weed clambered among the ruins, writhing to get above me in the dimness. Night, the mother of fear and mystery, was coming upon me. But while that voice sounded the solitude, the desolation, had been endurable; by virtue of it London had still seemed alive, and the sense of life about me had upheld me. Then suddenly a change, the passing of something—I knew not what—and then a stillness that could be felt. Nothing but this gaunt quiet.

London about me gazed at me spectrally. The windows in the white houses were like the eye sockets of skulls. About me my imagination found a thousand noiseless enemies moving. Terror seized me, a horror of my temerity. In front of me the road became pitchy black as though it was tarred, and I saw a contorted

shape lying across the pathway. I could not bring myself to go on. I turned down St. John's Wood Road, and ran headlong from this unendurable stillness towards Kilburn. I hid from the night and the silence, until long after midnight, in a cabmen's shelter in Harrow Road. But before the dawn my courage returned, and while the stars were still in the sky I turned once more towards Regent's Park. I missed my way among the streets, and presently saw down a long avenue, in the half-light of the early dawn, the curve of Primrose Hill. On the summit, towering up to the fading stars, was a third Martian, erect and motionless like the others.

An insane resolve possessed me. I would die and end it. And I would save myself even the trouble of killing myself. I marched on recklessly towards this Titan, and then, as I drew nearer and the light grew, I saw that a multitude of black birds was circling and clustering about the hood. At that my heart gave a bound, and I began running along the road.

I hurried through the red weed that choked St. Edmund's Terrace (I waded breast-high across a torrent of water that was rushing down from the waterworks towards the Albert Road), and emerged upon the grass before the rising of the sun. Great mounds had been heaped about the crest of the hill, making a huge redoubt of it—it was the final and largest place the Martians had made—and from behind these heaps there rose a thin smoke against the sky. Against the sky line an eager dog ran and disappeared. The thought that had flashed into my mind grew real, grew credible. I felt no fear, only a wild, trembling exultation, as I ran up the hill towards the motionless monster. Out of the hood hung lank shreds of brown, at which the hungry birds pecked and tore.

In another moment I had scrambled up the earthen rampart and stood upon its crest, and the interior of the redoubt was below me. A mighty space it was, with gigantic machines here and there within it, huge mounds of material and strange shelter places. And scattered about it, some in their overturned war- machines, some in the now rigid handling-machines, and a dozen of them stark and silent and laid in a row, were the Martians—*dead*!—slain by the putrefactive and disease bacteria against which their systems were unprepared; slain as the red weed was being slain; slain, after all man's devices had failed, by the humblest things that God, in his wisdom, has put upon this earth.

For so it had come about, as indeed I and many men might have foreseen had not terror and disaster blinded our minds. These germs of disease have taken toll of humanity since the beginning of things—taken toll of our prehuman ancestors since life began here. But by virtue of this natural selection of our kind we have developed resisting power; to no germs do we succumb without a struggle, and to many—those that cause putrefaction in dead matter, for instance—our living frames are altogether immune. But there are no bacteria in Mars, and directly these invaders arrived, directly they drank and fed, our microscopic allies began to work their overthrow. Already when I watched them they were irrevocably doomed, dying and rotting even as they went to and fro. It was inevitable. By the toll of a billion deaths man has bought his birthright of the earth, and it is his

against all comers; it would still be his were the Martians ten times as mighty as they are. For neither do men live nor die in vain.

Here and there they were scattered, nearly fifty altogether, in that great gulf they had made, overtaken by a death that must have seemed to them as incomprehensible as any death could be. To me also at that time this death was incomprehensible. All I knew was that these things that had been alive and so terrible to men were dead. For a moment I believed that the destruction of Sennacherib had been repeated, that God had repented, that the Angel of Death had slain them in the night.

I stood staring into the pit, and my heart lightened gloriously, even as the rising sun struck the world to fire about me with his rays. The pit was still in darkness; the mighty engines, so great and wonderful in their power and complexity, so unearthly in their tortuous forms, rose weird and vague and strange out of the shadows towards the light. A multitude of dogs, I could hear, fought over the bodies that lay darkly in the depth of the pit, far below me. Across the pit on its farther lip, flat and vast and strange, lay the great flying-machine with which they had been experimenting upon our denser atmosphere when decay and death arrested them. Death had come not a day too soon. At the sound of a cawing overhead I looked up at the huge fighting- machine that would fight no more for ever, at the tattered red shreds of flesh that dripped down upon the overturned seats on the summit of Primrose Hill.

I turned and looked down the slope of the hill to where, enhaloed now in birds, stood those other two Martians that I had seen overnight, just as death had overtaken them. The one had died, even as it had been crying to its companions; perhaps it was the last to die, and its voice had gone on perpetually until the force of its machinery was exhausted. They glittered now, harmless tripod towers of shining metal, in the brightness of the rising sun.

All about the pit, and saved as by a miracle from everlasting destruction, stretched the great Mother of Cities. Those who have only seen London veiled in her sombre robes of smoke can scarcely imagine the naked clearness and beauty of the silent wilderness of houses.

Eastward, over the blackened ruins of the Albert Terrace and the splintered spire of the church, the sun blazed dazzling in a clear sky, and here and there some facet in the great wilderness of roofs caught the light and glared with a white intensity.

Northward were Kilburn and Hampsted, blue and crowded with houses; westward the great city was dimmed; and southward, beyond the Martians, the green waves of Regent's Park, the Langham Hotel, the dome of the Albert Hall, the Imperial Institute, and the giant mansions of the Brompton Road came out clear and little in the sunrise, the jagged ruins of Westminster rising hazily beyond. Far away and blue were the Surrey hills, and the towers of the Crystal Palace glittered like two silver rods. The dome of St. Paul's was dark against the sunrise, and injured, I saw for the first time, by a huge gaping cavity on its western side.

And as I looked at this wide expanse of houses and factories and churches, silent and abandoned; as I thought of the multitudinous hopes and efforts, the innumerable hosts of lives that had gone to build this human reef, and of the swift and ruthless destruction that had hung over it all; when I realised that the shadow had been rolled back, and that men might still live in the streets, and this dear vast dead city of mine be once more alive and powerful, I felt a wave of emotion that was near akin to tears.

The torment was over. Even that day the healing would begin. The survivors of the people scattered over the country—leaderless, lawless, foodless, like sheep without a shepherd—the thousands who had fled by sea, would begin to return; the pulse of life, growing stronger and stronger, would beat again in the empty streets and pour across the vacant squares. Whatever destruction was done, the hand of the destroyer was stayed. All the gaunt wrecks, the blackened skeletons of houses that stared so dismally at the sunlit grass of the hill, would presently be echoing with the hammers of the restorers and ringing with the tapping of their trowels. At the thought I extended my hands towards the sky and began thanking God. In a year, thought I—in a year...

With overwhelming force came the thought of myself, of my wife, and the old life of hope and tender helpfulness that had ceased for ever.

CHAPTER NINE - WRECKAGE

And now comes the strangest thing in my story. Yet, perhaps, it is not altogether strange. I remember, clearly and coldly and vividly, all that I did that day until the time that I stood weeping and praising God upon the summit of Primrose Hill. And then I forget.

Of the next three days I know nothing. I have learned since that, so far from my being the first discoverer of the Martian overthrow, several such wanderers as myself had already discovered this on the previous night. One man—the first—had gone to St. Martin's-le-Grand, and, while I sheltered in the cabmen's hut, had contrived to telegraph to Paris. Thence the joyful news had flashed all over the world; a thousand cities, chilled by ghastly apprehensions, suddenly flashed into frantic illuminations; they knew of it in Dublin, Edinburgh, Manchester, Birmingham, at the time when I stood upon the verge of the pit. Already men, weeping with joy, as I have heard, shouting and staying their work to shake hands and shout, were making up trains, even as near as Crewe, to descend upon London. The church bells that had ceased a fortnight since suddenly caught the news, until all England was bell-ringing. Men on cycles, lean-faced, unkempt, scorched along every country lane shouting of unhoped deliverance, shouting to gaunt, staring figures of despair. And for the food! Across the Channel, across the Irish Sea, across the Atlantic, corn, bread, and meat were tearing to our relief. All the shipping in the world seemed going Londonward in those days. But of all this I have no memory. I drifted—a demented man. I found myself in a house of kindly people, who had found me on the third day wandering, weeping, and raving through the streets of St. John's Wood. They have told me since that I was singing some insane doggerel about "The Last Man Left Alive! Hurrah! The Last Man Left Alive!" Troubled as they were with their own affairs, these people, whose name, much as I would like to express my gratitude to them, I may not even give here, nevertheless cumbered themselves with me, sheltered me, and protected me from myself. Apparently they had learned something of my story from me during the days of my lapse.

Very gently, when my mind was assured again, did they break to me what they had learned of the fate of Leatherhead. Two days after I was imprisoned it had been destroyed, with every soul in it, by a Martian. He had swept it out of existence, as it seemed, without any provocation, as a boy might crush an ant hill, in the mere wantonness of power.

I was a lonely man, and they were very kind to me. I was a lonely man and a sad one, and they bore with me. I remained with them four days after my recovery. All that time I felt a vague, a growing craving to look once more on whatever remained of the little life that seemed so happy and bright in my past. It was a mere hopeless desire to feast upon my misery. They dissuaded me. They did all they could to divert me from this morbidity. But at last I could resist the impulse no longer, and, promising faithfully to return to them, and parting, as I will confess, from these four-day friends with tears, I went out again into the streets that had lately been so dark and strange and empty.

Already they were busy with returning people; in places even there were shops open, and I saw a drinking fountain running water.

I remember how mockingly bright the day seemed as I went back on my melancholy pilgrimage to the little house at Woking, how busy the streets and vivid the moving life about me. So many people were abroad everywhere, busied in a thousand activities, that it seemed incredible that any great proportion of the population could have been slain. But then I noticed how yellow were the skins of the people I met, how shaggy the hair of the men, how large and bright their eyes, and that every other man still wore his dirty rags. Their faces seemed all with one of two expressions—a leaping exultation and energy or a grim resolution. Save for the expression of the faces, London seemed a city of tramps. The vestries were indiscriminately distributing bread sent us by the French government. The ribs of the few horses showed dismally. Haggard special constables with white badges stood at the corners of every street. I saw little of the mischief wrought by the Martians until I reached Wellington Street, and there I saw the red weed clambering over the buttresses of Waterloo Bridge.

At the corner of the bridge, too, I saw one of the common contrasts of that grotesque time—a sheet of paper flaunting against a thicket of the red weed, transfixed by a stick that kept it in place. It was the placard of the first newspaper to resume publication—the *Daily Mail.* I bought a copy for a blackened shilling I found in my pocket. Most of it was in blank, but the solitary compositor who did the thing had amused himself by making a grotesque scheme of advertisement stereo on the back page. The matter he printed was emotional; the news organisation had not as yet found its way back. I learned nothing fresh except that already in one week the examination of the Martian mechanisms had yielded astonishing results. Among other things, the article assured me what I did not believe at the time, that the "Secret of Flying," was discovered. At Waterloo I found the free trains that were taking people to their homes. The first rush was already over. There were few people in the train, and I was in no mood for casual conversation. I got a compartment to myself, and sat with folded arms, looking greyly at the sunlit devastation that flowed past the windows. And just outside the terminus the train jolted over temporary rails, and on either side of the railway the houses were blackened ruins. To Clapham Junction the face of London was grimy with powder of the Black Smoke, in spite of two days of thunderstorms and rain, and at Clapham Junction the line had been wrecked again; there were hundreds of out-of-

work clerks and shopmen working side by side with the customary navvies, and we were jolted over a hasty relaying.

All down the line from there the aspect of the country was gaunt and unfamiliar; Wimbledon particularly had suffered. Walton, by virtue of its unburned pine woods, seemed the least hurt of any place along the line. The Wandle, the Mole, every little stream, was a heaped mass of red weed, in appearance between butcher's meat and pickled cabbage. The Surrey pine woods were too dry, however, for the festoons of the red climber. Beyond Wimbledon, within sight of the line, in certain nursery grounds, were the heaped masses of earth about the sixth cylinder. A number of people were standing about it, and some sappers were busy in the midst of it. Over it flaunted a Union Jack, flapping cheerfully in the morning breeze. The nursery grounds were everywhere crimson with the weed, a wide expanse of livid colour cut with purple shadows, and very painful to the eye. One's gaze went with infinite relief from the scorched greys and sullen reds of the foreground to the blue-green softness of the eastward hills.

The line on the London side of Woking station was still undergoing repair, so I descended at Byfleet station and took the road to Maybury, past the place where I and the artilleryman had talked to the hussars, and on by the spot where the Martian had appeared to me in the thunderstorm. Here, moved by curiosity, I turned aside to find, among a tangle of red fronds, the warped and broken dog cart with the whitened bones of the horse scattered and gnawed. For a time I stood regarding these vestiges...

Then I returned through the pine wood, neck-high with red weed here and there, to find the landlord of the Spotted Dog had already found burial, and so came home past the College Arms. A man standing at an open cottage door greeted me by name as I passed.

I looked at my house with a quick flash of hope that faded immediately. The door had been forced; it was unfast and was opening slowly as I approached.

It slammed again. The curtains of my study fluttered out of the open window from which I and the artilleryman had watched the dawn. No one had closed it since. The smashed bushes were just as I had left them nearly four weeks ago. I stumbled into the hall, and the house felt empty. The stair carpet was ruffled and discoloured where I had crouched, soaked to the skin from the thunderstorm the night of the catastrophe. Our muddy footsteps I saw still went up the stairs.

I followed them to my study, and found lying on my writing-table still, with the selenite paper weight upon it, the sheet of work I had left on the afternoon of the opening of the cylinder. For a space I stood reading over my abandoned arguments. It was a paper on the probable development of Moral Ideas with the development of the civilising process; and the last sentence was the opening of a prophecy: "In about two hundred years," I had written, "we may expect—" The sentence ended abruptly. I remembered my inability to fix my mind that morning, scarcely a month gone by, and how I had broken off to get my *Daily Chronicle* from the newsboy. I remembered how I went down to the garden gate as he came along, and how I had listened to his odd story of "Men from Mars."

I came down and went into the dining room. There were the mutton and the bread, both far gone now in decay, and a beer bottle overturned, just as I and the artilleryman had left them. My home was desolate. I perceived the folly of the faint hope I had cherished so long. And then a strange thing occurred. "It is no use," said a voice. "The house is deserted. No one has been here these ten days. Do not stay here to torment yourself. No one escaped but you."

I was startled. Had I spoken my thought aloud? I turned, and the French window was open behind me. I made a step to it, and stood looking out.

And there, amazed and afraid, even as I stood amazed and afraid, were my cousin and my wife—my wife white and tearless. She gave a faint cry.

"I came," she said. "I knew—knew—"

She put her hand to her throat—swayed. I made a step forward, and caught her in my arms.

CHAPTER TEN - THE EPILOGUE

I cannot but regret, now that I am concluding my story, how little I am able to contribute to the discussion of the many debatable questions which are still unsettled. In one respect I shall certainly provoke criticism. My particular province is speculative philosophy. My knowledge of comparative physiology is confined to a book or two, but it seems to me that Carver's suggestions as to the reason of the rapid death of the Martians is so probable as to be regarded almost as a proven conclusion. I have assumed that in the body of my narrative.

At any rate, in all the bodies of the Martians that were examined after the war, no bacteria except those already known as terrestrial species were found. That they did not bury any of their dead, and the reckless slaughter they perpetrated, point also to an entire ignorance of the putrefactive process. But probable as this seems, it is by no means a proven conclusion.

Neither is the composition of the Black Smoke known, which the Martians used with such deadly effect, and the generator of the Heat-Rays remains a puzzle. The terrible disasters at the Ealing and South Kensington laboratories have disinclined analysts for further investigations upon the latter. Spectrum analysis of the black powder points unmistakably to the presence of an unknown element with a brilliant group of three lines in the green, and it is possible that it combines with argon to form a compound which acts at once with deadly effect upon some constituent in the blood. But such unproven speculations will scarcely be of interest to the general reader, to whom this story is addressed. None of the brown scum that drifted down the Thames after the destruction of Shepperton was examined at the time, and now none is forthcoming.

The results of an anatomical examination of the Martians, so far as the prowling dogs had left such an examination possible, I have already given. But everyone is familiar with the magnificent and almost complete specimen in spirits at the Natural History Museum, and the countless drawings that have been made from it; and beyond that the interest of their physiology and structure is purely scientific.

A question of graver and universal interest is the possibility of another attack from the Martians. I do not think that nearly enough attention is being given to this aspect of the matter. At present the planet Mars is in conjunction, but with every return to opposition I, for one, anticipate a renewal of their adventure. In any case, we should be prepared. It seems to me that it should be possible to define the position of the gun from which the shots are discharged, to keep a

sustained watch upon this part of the planet, and to anticipate the arrival of the next attack.

In that case the cylinder might be destroyed with dynamite or artillery before it was sufficiently cool for the Martians to emerge, or they might be butchered by means of guns so soon as the screw opened. It seems to me that they have lost a vast advantage in the failure of their first surprise. Possibly they see it in the same light.

Lessing has advanced excellent reasons for supposing that the Martians have actually succeeded in effecting a landing on the planet Venus. Seven months ago now, Venus and Mars were in alignment with the sun; that is to say, Mars was in opposition from the point of view of an observer on Venus. Subsequently a peculiar luminous and sinuous marking appeared on the unillumined half of the inner planet, and almost simultaneously a faint dark mark of a similar sinuous character was detected upon a photograph of the Martian disk. One needs to see the drawings of these appearances in order to appreciate fully their remarkable resemblance in character.

At any rate, whether we expect another invasion or not, our views of the human future must be greatly modified by these events. We have learned now that we cannot regard this planet as being fenced in and a secure abiding place for Man; we can never anticipate the unseen good or evil that may come upon us suddenly out of space. It may be that in the larger design of the universe this invasion from Mars is not without its ultimate benefit for men; it has robbed us of that serene confidence in the future which is the most fruitful source of decadence, the gifts to human science it has brought are enormous, and it has done much to promote the conception of the commonweal of mankind. It may be that across the immensity of space the Martians have watched the fate of these pioneers of theirs and learned their lesson, and that on the planet Venus they have found a securer settlement. Be that as it may, for many years yet there will certainly be no relaxation of the eager scrutiny of the Martian disk, and those fiery darts of the sky, the shooting stars, will bring with them as they fall an unavoidable apprehension to all the sons of men.

The broadening of men's views that has resulted can scarcely be exaggerated. Before the cylinder fell there was a general persuasion that through all the deep of space no life existed beyond the petty surface of our minute sphere. Now we see further. If the Martians can reach Venus, there is no reason to suppose that the thing is impossible for men, and when the slow cooling of the sun makes this earth uninhabitable, as at last it must do, it may be that the thread of life that has begun here will have streamed out and caught our sister planet within its toils.

Dim and wonderful is the vision I have conjured up in my mind of life spreading slowly from this little seed bed of the solar system throughout the inanimate vastness of sidereal space. But that is a remote dream. It may be, on the other hand, that the destruction of the Martians is only a reprieve. To them, and not to us, perhaps, is the future ordained.

I must confess the stress and danger of the time have left an abiding sense of doubt and insecurity in my mind. I sit in my study writing by lamplight, and suddenly I see again the healing valley below set with writhing flames, and feel the house behind and about me empty and desolate. I go out into the Byfleet Road, and vehicles pass me, a butcher boy in a cart, a cabful of visitors, a workman on a bicycle, children going to school, and suddenly they become vague and unreal, and I hurry again with the artilleryman through the hot, brooding silence. Of a night I see the black powder darkening the silent streets, and the contorted bodies shrouded in that layer; they rise upon me tattered and dog-bitten. They gibber and grow fiercer, paler, uglier, mad distortions of humanity at last, and I wake, cold and wretched, in the darkness of the night.

I go to London and see the busy multitudes in Fleet Street and the Strand, and it comes across my mind that they are but the ghosts of the past, haunting the streets that I have seen silent and wretched, going to and fro, phantasms in a dead city, the mockery of life in a galvanised body. And strange, too, it is to stand on Primrose Hill, as I did but a day before writing this last chapter, to see the great province of houses, dim and blue through the haze of the smoke and mist, vanishing at last into the vague lower sky, to see the people walking to and fro among the flower beds on the hill, to see the sight-seers about the Martian machine that stands there still, to hear the tumult of playing children, and to recall the time when I saw it all bright and clear-cut, hard and silent, under the dawn of that last great day...

And strangest of all is it to hold my wife's hand again, and to think that I have counted her, and that she has counted me, among the dead.

THE SHAPE OF THINGS TO COME

TO JOSÉ ORTEGA Y GASSET - EXPLORADOR

First UK edition: Hutchinson & Co., London, 1933
First US edition: Macmillan & Co., New York, 1933

INTRODUCTION - THE DREAM BOOK OF DR. PHILIP RAVEN

The unexpected death of Dr. Philip Raven at Geneva in November 1930 was a very grave loss to the League of Nations Secretariat. Geneva lost a familiar figure—the long bent back, the halting gait, the head quizzically on one side—and the world lost a stimulatingly aggressive mind. His incessant devoted work, his extraordinary mental vigour, were, as his obituary notices testified, appreciated very highly by a world-wide following of distinguished and capable admirers. The general public was suddenly made aware of him.

It is rare that anyone outside the conventional areas of newspaper publicity produces so great a stir by dying; there were accounts of him in nearly every paper of importance from Oslo to New Zealand and from Buenos Aires to Japan—and the brief but admirable memoir by Sir Godfrey Cliffe gave the general reader a picture of an exceptionally simple, direct, devoted and energetic personality. There seems to have been only two extremely dissimilar photographs available for publication: an early one in which he looks like a blend of Shelley and Mr. Maxton, and a later one, a snapshot, in which he leans askew on his stick and talks to Lord Parmoor in the entrance hall of the Assembly. One of his lank hands is held out in a characteristic illustrative gesture.

Incessantly laborious though he was, he could nevertheless find time to assist in, share and master all the broader problems that exercised his colleagues, and now they rushed forward with their gratitude. One noticeable thing in that posthumous eruption of publicity was the frequent acknowledgments of his aid and advice. Men were eager to testify to his importance and resentful at the public ignorance of his work. Three memorial volumes of his more important papers, reports, memoranda and addresses were arranged for and are still in course of publication.

Personally, although I was asked to do so in several quarters, and though I was known to have had the honour of his friendship, I made no contribution to that obituary chorus. My standing in the academic world did not justify my writing him a testimonial, but under normal circumstances that would not have deterred me from an attempt to sketch something of his odd personal ease and charm. I did not do so, however, because I found myself in a position of extraordinary embarrassment. His death was so unforeseen that we had embarked upon a very peculiar joint undertaking without making the slightest provision for that risk. It is only now after an interval of nearly three years, and after some very difficult discus-

sions with his more intimate friends, that I have decided to publish the facts and the substance of this peculiar cooperation of ours.

It concerns the matter of this present book. All this time I have been holding back a manuscript, or rather a collection of papers and writings, entrusted to me. It is a collection about which, I think, a considerable amount of hesitation was, and perhaps is still, justifiable. It is, or at least it professes to be, a Short History of the World for about the next century and a half. (I can quite understand that the reader will rub his eyes at these words and suspect the printer of some sort of agraphia.) But that is exactly what this manuscript is. It is a Short History of the Future. It is a modern Sibylline book. Only now that the events of three years have more than justified everything stated in this anticipatory history have I had the courage to associate the reputation of my friend with the incredible claims of this work, and to find a publisher for it.

Let me tell very briefly what I know of its origin and how it came into my hands. I made the acquaintance of Dr. Raven, or to be more precise, he made mine, in the closing year of the war. It was before he left Whitehall for Geneva. He was always an eager amateur of ideas, and he had been attracted by some suggestions about money I had made in a scrappy little book of forecasts called What is Coming? published in 1916. In this I had thrown out the suggestion that the waste of resources in the war, combined with the accumulation of debts that had been going on, would certainly leave the world as a whole bankrupt, that is to say it would leave the creditor class in a position to strangle the world, and that the only method to clear up this world bankruptcy and begin again on a hopeful basis would be to scale down all debts impartially, by a reduction of the amount of gold in the pound sterling and proportionally in the dollar and all other currencies based on gold. It seemed to me then an obvious necessity. It was, I recognize now, a crude idea— evidently I had not even got away from the idea of intrinsically valuable money —but none of us in those days had had the educational benefit of the monetary and credit convulsions that followed the Peace of Versailles. We were without experience, it wasn't popular to think about money, and at best we thought like precocious children. Seventeen years later this idea of appreciating gold is accepted as an obvious suggestion by quite a number of people. Then it was received merely as the amateurish comment of an ignorant writer upon what was still regarded as the mysterious business of "monetary experts." But it attracted the attention of Raven, who came along to talk over that and one or two other post-war possibilities I had started, and so he made my acquaintance.

Raven was as free from intellectual pompousness as William James; as candidly receptive to candid thinking. He could talk about his subject to an artist or a journalist; he would have talked to an errand boy if he thought he would get a fresh slant in that way. "Obvious" was the word he brought with him. "The thing, my dear fellow"—he called me my dear fellow in the first five minutes —"is so obvious that everybody will be too clever to consider it for a moment. Until it is belated. It is impossible to persuade anybody responsible that there is going to be a tremendous financial and monetary mix-up after this war. The victors will exact

vindictive penalties and the losers of course will undertake to pay, but none of them realizes that money is going to do the most extraordinary things to them when they begin upon that. What they are going to do to each other is what occupies them, and what money is going to do to the whole lot of them is nobody's affair."

I can still see him as he said that in his high-pitched remonstrating voice. I will confess that for perhaps our first half-hour, until I was accustomed to his flavour, I did not like him. He was too full, too sure, too rapid and altogether too vivid for my slower Anglo-Saxon make-up. I did not like the evident preparation of his talk, nor the fact that he assisted it by the most extraordinary gestures. He would not sit down; he limped about my room, peering at books and pictures while he talked in his cracked forced voice, and waving those long lean hands of his about almost as if he was swimming through his subject. I have compared him to Maxton plus Shelley, rather older, but at the first outset I was reminded of Svengali in Du Maurier's once popular Trilby. A shaven Svengali. I felt he was FOREIGN, and my instincts about foreigners are as insular as my principles are cosmopolitan. It always seemed to me a little irreconcilable that he was a Balliol scholar, and had been one of the brightest ornaments of our Foreign Office staff before he went to Geneva.

At bottom I suppose much of our essential English shyness is an exaggerated wariness. We suspect the other fellow of our own moral subtleties. We restrain ourselves often to the point of insincerity. I am a rash man with a pen perhaps, but I am as circumspect and evasive as any other of my fellow countrymen when it comes to social intercourse. I found something almost indelicate in Raven's direct attack upon my ideas.

He wanted to talk about my ideas beyond question. But at least equally he wanted to talk about his own. I had more than a suspicion that he had, in fact, come to me in order to talk to himself and hear how it sounded—against me as a sounding-board.

He called me then a Dealer in the Obvious, and he repeated that not very flattering phrase on various occasions when we met. "You have," he said, "defects that are almost gifts: a rapid but inexact memory for particulars, a quick grasp of proportions, and no patience with detail. You hurry on to wholes. How men of affairs must hate you—if and when they hear of you! They must think you an awful mug, you know—and yet you get there! Complications are their life. YOU try to get all these complications out of the way. You are a stripper, a damned impatient stripper. I would be a stripper too if I hadn't the sort of job I have to do. But it is really extraordinarily refreshing to spend these occasional hours, stripping events in your company."

The reader must forgive my egotism in quoting these comments upon myself; they are necessary if my relations with Raven are to be made clear and if the spirit of this book is to be understood.

I was, in fact, an outlet for a definite mental exuberance of his which it had hitherto distressed him to suppress. In my presence he could throw off Balliol and

the Foreign Office—or, later on, the Secretariat—and let himself go. He could become the Eastern European Cosmopolitan he was by nature and descent. I became, as it were, an imaginative boon companion for him, his disreputable friend, a sort of intelligent butt, his Watson. I got to like the relationship. I got used to his physical exoticism, his gestures. I sympathized more and more with his irritation and distress as the Conference at Versailles unfolded. My instinctive racial distrust faded before the glowing intensity of his intellectual curiosity. We found we supplemented each other. I had a ready unclouded imagination and he had knowledge. We would go on the speculative spree together.

Among other gifted and original friends who, at all too rare intervals, honour me by coming along for a gossip, is Mr. J. W. Dunne, who years ago invented one of the earliest and most "different" of aeroplanes, and who has since done a very considerable amount of subtle thinking upon the relationship of time and space to consciousness. Dunne clings to the idea that in certain ways we may anticipate the future, and he has adduced a series of very remarkable observations indeed to support that in his well-known Experiment with Time. That book was published in 1927, and I found it so attractive and stimulating that I wrote about it in one or two articles that were syndicated very extensively throughout the world. It was so excitingly fresh.

And among others who saw my account of this Experiment with Time, and who got the book and read it and then wrote to me about it, was Raven. Usually his communications to me were the briefest of notes, saying he would be in London, telling me of a change of address, asking about my movements, and so forth; but this was quite a long letter. Experiences such as Dunne's, he said, were no novelty to him. He could add a lot to what was told in the book, and indeed he could EXTEND the experience. The thing anticipated between sleeping and waking —Dunne's experiments dealt chiefly with the premonitions in the dozing moment between wakefulness and oblivion—need not be just small affairs of tomorrow or next week; they could have a longer range. If, that is, you had the habit of long-range thinking. But these were days when scepticism had to present a hard face to greedy superstition, and it was one's public duty to refrain from rash statements about these flimsy intimations, difficult as they were to distinguish from fantasies—except in one's own mind. One might sacrifice a lot of influence if one betrayed too lively an interest in this sort of thing.

He wandered off into such sage generalizations and concluded abruptly. The letter had an effect of starting out to tell much more than he did.

Then he turned up in London, dropped into my study unexpectedly and made a clean breast of it.

"This Dunne business," he began.

"Well?" said I.

"He has a way of snatching the fleeting dream between unconscious sleep and waking."

"Yes."

"He keeps a notebook by his bedside and writes down his dream the very instant he is awake."

"That's the procedure."

"And he finds that a certain percentage of his dream items are—sometimes quite plainly—anticipations of things that will come into his mind out of reality, days, weeks, and even years ahead."

"That's Dunne."

"It's nothing."

"But how—nothing?"

"Nothing to what I have been doing for a long time."

"And that is—?"

He stared at the backs of my books. It was amusing to find Raven for once at a loss for words.

"Well?" I said.

He turned and looked at me with a reluctant expression that broke into a smile. Then he seemed to rally his candour.

"How shall I put it? I wouldn't tell anyone but you. For some years, off and on—between sleeping and waking—I've been—in effect—reading a book. A non-existent book. A dream book if you like. It's always the same book. Always. And it's a history."

"Of the past?"

"There's a lot about the past. With all sorts of things I didn't know and all sorts of gaps filled in. Extraordinary things about North India and Central Asia, for instance. And also—it goes on. It's going on. It keeps on going on."

"Going on?"

"Right past the present time."

"Sailing away into the future?"

"Yes."

"Is it—is it a PAPER book?"

"Not quite paper. Rather like that newspaper of your friend Brownlow. Not quite print as we know it. Vivid maps. And quite easy to read, in spite of the queer letters and spelling."

He paused. "I know it's nonsense."

He added. "It's frightfully real."

"Do you turn the pages?"

He thought for a moment. "No, I don't turn the pages. That would wake me up."

"It just goes on?"

"Yes."

"Until you realize you are doing it?"

"I suppose—yes, it is like that."

"And then you wake up?"

"Exactly. And it isn't there!"

"And you are always READING?"

"Generally—very definitely."

"But at times?"

"Oh—just the same as reading a book when one is awake. If the matter is vivid one SEES the events. As if one was looking at a moving picture on the page."

"But the book is still there?"

"Yes—always. I think it's there always."

"Do you by any chance make notes?"

"I didn't at first. Now I do."

"At once?"

"I write a kind of shorthand.... Do you know—I've piles of notes THAT high."

He straddled my fireplace and stared at me.

"Now you've told me," I said.

"Now I've told you."

"Illegible, my dear sir—except to me. You don't know my shorthand. I can hardly read it myself after a week or so. But lately I've been writing it out— some I've dictated.

"You see," he went on, standing up and walking about my room, "if it's—a reality, it's the most important thing in the world. And I haven't an atom of proof. Not an atom. Do you—? Do you believe this sort of thing is possible?"

"POSSIBLE?" I considered. "I'm inclined to think I do. Though what exactly this kind of thing may be, I don't know."

"I can't tell anyone but you. How could I? Naturally they would say I had gone cranky—or that I was an impostor. You know the sort of row. Look at Oliver Lodge. Look at Charles Richet. It would smash my work, my position. And yet, you know, it's such credible stuff.... I tell you I believe in it."

"If you wrote some of it out. If I could see some of it."

"You shall."

He seemed to be consulting my opinion. "The worst thing against it is that I always believe in what the fellow says. That's rather as though it was ME, eh?"

He did not send me any of his notes, but when next I met him, it was at Berne, he gave me a spring-backed folder filled with papers. Afterwards he gave me two others. Pencilled sheets they were mostly, but some were evidently written at his desk in ink and perhaps fifty pages had been typed, probably from his dictation. He asked me to take great care of them, to read them carefully, have typed copies made and return a set to him. The whole thing was to be kept as a secret between us. We were both to think over the advisability of a possibly anonymous publication. And meanwhile events might either confirm or explode various statements made in this history and so set a definite value, one way or the other, upon its authenticity.

Then he died.

He died quite unexpectedly as the result of a sudden operation. Some dislocation connected with his marked spinal curvature had developed abruptly into an acute crisis.

As soon as I heard of his death I hurried off to Geneva and told the story of the dream book to his heir and executor, Mr. Montefiore Renaud. I am greatly indebted to that gentleman for his courtesy and quick understanding of the situation. He was at great pains to get every possible scrap of material together and to place it all at my disposal. In addition to the three folders Raven had already given me there were a further folder in longhand and a drawerful of papers in his peculiar shorthand evidently dealing with this History. The fourth folder contained the material which forms the concluding book of this present work. The shorthand notes, of which even the pages were not numbered, have supplied the material for the penultimate book, which has had to be a compilation of my own. Generally, Raven seems to have scribbled down his impressions of the dream book as soon as he could, before the memory faded, and as he intended to recopy it all himself he had no consideration for any prospective reader. This material was just for his own use. It is a mixture of very cursive (and inaccurate) shorthand, and for proper names and so forth, longhand. Punctuation is indicated by gaps, and often a single word stands for a whole sentence and even a paragraph. About a third of the shorthand stuff was already represented by longhand or typescript copy in the folders. That was my Rosetta Stone. If it were not for the indications conveyed by that I do not think it would have been possible to decipher any of the remainder. As it is, I found it impossible to make a flowing narrative, altogether of a piece with the opening and closing parts of this history. Some passages came out fairly clear and then would come confusion and obscurity. I have transcribed what I could and written-up the intervals when transcription was hopeless. I think I have made a comprehensible story altogether of the course of events during the struggles and changes in world government that went on between 1980 and 2059, at which date the Air Dictatorship, properly so called, gave place to that world-wide Modern State which was still flourishing when the history was published. The reader will find large gaps, or rather he will find large abbreviations, in that portion, but none that leave the main lines of the history of world consolidation in doubt.

And now let me say a word or so more about the real value of this queer "Outline of the Future".

Certain minor considerations weigh against the idea that this history that follows is merely the imaginative dreaming of a brilliant publicist. I put them before the reader, but I will not press them. First of all this history has now received a certain amount of confirmation. The latest part of the MS. dates from September 20th, 1930, and much of it is earlier. And yet it alludes explicitly to the death of Ivar Kreuger a year later, to the tragic kidnapping of the Lindbergh baby, which happened in the spring of 1932, to the Mollison world flights of the same year, to the American debt discussions in December 1932, to the Hitlerite régime in Germany, and Japanese invasion of China proper in 1933, the election of President Roosevelt II and the World Economic Conference in London. These anticipations in detail I find a little difficult to explain away. I do not think that they are of such a nature that they could have been foretold. They are not events that were deduci-

ble from any preceding situation. How could Raven have known about them in 1930?

And another thing that troubles me much more than it will trouble the reader is the fact that there was no reason at all why Raven should have attempted a mystification upon me. There was no reason on earth or heaven why he should have lied about the way in which this material came to him and he wrote it down.

If it were not for these considerations, I think I should be quite prepared to fall in with what will no doubt be the general opinion, that the writing of this History was deliberately chosen by Raven as an imaginative outlet. That it is indeed a work of fiction by a late member of the Geneva Secretariat with unusual opportunities for forming judgments upon the trend of things. Or, let us say, a conditional prophecy in the Hebrew manner produced in a quasi- inspired mood. The style in which it is written is recognizably Raven's style, and there are few of those differences in vocabulary and locutions that one might reasonably expect in our language a hundred and seventy odd years from now. On the other hand, the attitude revealed is entirely inconsistent with Raven's fully conscious public utterances. The idiom of thought at least is not his, whatever the idiom of expression. Either his marginal vision transcended his waking convictions or we have here a clear case of suppressions making their way to the surface. Is that what history is going to be?

I must admit that at first, while I was still under the impression that the whole thing was a speculative exercise, I was tempted to annotate Raven's text rather extensively. I wanted to take a hand in the game. In fact I did some months' work upon it. Until my notes were becoming more bulky than his history. But when I revised them I came to the conclusion that many of them were fussy obtrusions and very few of them likely to be really helpful to an intelligent and well-informed contemporary reader. The more attracted he was by the book, the more likely he was to make his observations for himself; the less he appreciated it, the less he was likely to appreciate a superincumbent mass of elucidation. My notes might have proved as annoying as the pencillings one finds at times in public library books to-day. If the history is merely a speculative history, even then they would have been impertinent; if there is anything more in it than speculation, then they would be a very grave impertinence indeed. In the end I scrapped the entire accumulation.

But I have had also to arrange these chapters in order, and that much intervention was unavoidable and must remain. I have had indeed to arrange and rearrange them after several trials, because they do not seem to have been read and written down by Raven in their proper chronological sequence. I have smoothed out the transitions. Later on I hope to publish a special edition of Raven's notes exactly as he left them.

We begin here with what is evidently the opening of a fresh book in the history, though it was not actually the first paper in the folders handed to me. It reviews very conveniently the course of worldly events in recent years, and it does so in what is, to me, a novel and very persuasive way. It analyses the main

factors of the great war from a new angle. From that review the story of the "Age of Frustration", in the opening years of which we are now living, flows on in a fairly consecutive fashion. Apart from this introduction the period covered by the actual narrative is roughly from about 1929 A.D. to the end of the year 2105. The last recorded event is on New Year's Day 2106; there is a passing mention of the levelling of the remaining "skeletons" of the famous "Skyscrapers" of Lower New York on that date. The printing and publication probably occurred early in the new year; occurred—or should I write "will occur"?

H. G. W.

BOOK THE FIRST - TODAY AND TOMORROW: THE AGE OF FRUSTRATION DAWNS

1. A CHRONOLOGICAL NOTE

In the nineteenth and twentieth centuries the story of mankind upon this planet undergoes a change of phase. It broadens out. It unifies. It ceases to be a tangle of more and more interrelated histories and it becomes plainly and consciously one history. There is a complete confluence of racial, social and political destinies. With that a vision of previously unsuspected possibilities opens to the human imagination. And that vision brings with it an immense readjustment of ideas.

The first phase of that readjustment is necessarily destructive. The conceptions of life and obligation that have served and satisfied even the most vigorous and intelligent personalities hitherto, conceptions that were naturally partial, sectarian and limited, begin to lose, decade by decade, their credibility and their directive force. They fade, they become attenuated. It is an age of increasing mental uneasiness, of forced beliefs, hypocrisy, cynicism, abandon and impatience. What has been hitherto a final and impenetrable background of conviction in the rightness of the methods of behaviour characteristic of the national or local culture of each individual, becomes, as it were, a dissolving and ragged curtain. Behind it appear, vague and dim at first, and refracted and distorted by the slow dissolution of the traditional veils, the intimations of the type of behaviour necessary to that single world community in which we live to-day.

Until the Chronological Institute has completed its present labours of revision and defined the cardinal dates in our social evolution, it is best to refer our account of the development of man's mind and will throughout this hectic period of human experience to the clumsy and irrelevant computation by centuries before and after the Christian Era, that is still current. As we have explained more fully in a previous book[1], we inherit this system of historical pigeonholes from Christendom; that arbitrary chequerwork of hundred- year blocks was imposed upon the entire Mediterranean and Atlantic literatures for two thousand years, and it

[1] Nothing of this is to be found in Raven's notes.—ED.

still distorts the views of history of all but the alertest minds. The young student needs to be constantly on his guard against its false divisions. As Peter Lightfoot has remarked, we talk of the "eighteenth century", and we think of fashions and customs and attitudes that are characteristic of a period extending from the Treaty of Westphalia in C.E. [Christian Era] 1642 to the Napoleonic collapse in C.E. 1815; we talk of the "nineteenth century", and the pictures and images evoked are those of the gas- lighting and steam-transport era, from after the distressful years of post- Napoleonic recovery to the immense shock of the World War in C.E. 1914. The phase "twentieth century", again, calls forth images of the aeroplane, the electrification of the world and so forth; but an aeroplane was an extremely rare object in the air until 1914 (the first got up in 1905), and the replacement of the last steam railway train and the last steamship was not completed until the nineteen-forties. It is a tiresome waste of energy to oblige each generation of young minds to learn first of all in any unmeaning pattern of centuries and then to correct that first crude arrangement, so that this long-needed revision of our chronology is one that will be very welcome to every teacher. Then from the very outset he or she will be able to block out the story of our race in significant masses.

The Chronological Institute is setting about its task with a helpful publicity, inviting discussion from every angle. It is proposing to divide up as much of the known history of our race as is amenable to annual reckoning, into a series of eras of unequal length. Naturally the choice of these eras is the cause of some extremely lively and interesting interchanges; most of us have our own private estimates of the values of events, and many issues affecting the earlier civilized communities remain in a state of animated unsettlement. Our chronology is now fairly sure as to the year for most important events in the last 4,000 years, and, thanks largely to the minute and patient labours of the Selwyn-Cornford Committee for Alluvial Research, to the decade for another hundred centuries. So far as the last 3,000 years are concerned, little doubt remains now that the main dividing points to be adopted will be FIRST the epoch of Alexander and the Hellenic conquests which will begin the phase of the great Helleno-Latin monetary imperialism in the western world, the Helleno-Latin Era. This will commence at the crossing of the Hellespont by Alexander the Great and end either with the Battle of the Yarmuk (636 C.E.) or the surrender of Jerusalem to the Caliph Omar (638 C.E.). NEXT will come the epoch of Moslem and Mongol pressure on the West which opened the era of feudal Christendom vis-à-vis with feudal Islam: the Era of Asiatic Predominance. This ends with the Battle of Lepanto (1571 C.E.). Then THIRDLY there will follow the epoch of the Protestant and the Catholic (counter) Reformations, which inaugurated the era of the competing sovereign states with organized standing armies: the Era of European Predominance, or, as it may also be called, the Era of National Sovereignty. Finally comes the catastrophe of the World War of 1914, when the outward drive of the new economic methods the Atlantic civilizations had developed gave way under the internal stresses of European nationalism. That war, and its long-drawn sequelae, released the human

mind to the potentialities and dangers of an imperfectly Europeanized world—a world which had unconsciously become one single interlocking system, while still obsessed by the Treaty of Westphalia and the idea of competing sovereign states. This mental shock and release marks the beginning of the Era of the Modern State. The opening phase of this latest era is this Age of Frustration with which we are now about to deal. That is the first age of the Era of the Modern State. A second age, but not a new era, began with the Declaration of Mégève which was accepted by the general commonsense of mankind forty-seven years ago. This closed the Age of Frustration, which lasted therefore a little short of a century and a half.

The date upon the title-page for the first publication of this History is C.E. 2106. Before many editions have been exhausted that will be changed to Modern Era (M.E.) 192 or M.E. 189 or M.E. 187, according to whether our chronologists decide upon 1914, the date of the outbreak of the Great War, or 1917, the beginning of the social revolution in Russia, or 1919, the signing of the Treaty of Versailles, as the conclusive opening of the Age of Frustration and the conflict for world unity. The second date seems at present to be the more practicable one.

In C.E. 1914 the concept of an organized world order did not seem to be within the sphere of human possibility; in C.E. 1919 it was an active power in a steadily increasing proportion of human brains. The Modern State had been conceived. It was germinating. One system, the Soviet system in Russia, was already claiming to be a world system. To most of the generation which suffered it, the Great War seemed to be purely catastrophe and loss; to us who see those hideous years in perspective and in proportion to the general dulness and baseness of apprehension out of which that conflict arose, the destruction of life and substance, unprecedented as they were, has none of that overwhelming quality. We see it as a clumsy, involuntary release from outworn assumptions by their reduction to tragic absurdity, and as a practically unavoidable step therefore in the dialectic of human destiny.

2. HOW THE IDEA AND HOPE OF THE MODERN WORLD STATE FIRST APPEARED

The essential difference between the world before the Great War and the world after it lay in this, that before that storm of distress and disillusionment the clear recognition that a worldwide order and happiness, in spite of contemporary distresses, was within the reach of mankind was confined to a few exceptional persons, while after the catastrophe it had spread to an increasing multitude, it had become a desperate hope and desire, and at last a working conviction that made organized mass action possible.

Even those who apprehended this idea before the epoch of the Great War seem to have propounded it with what impresses us today as an almost inexplicable timidity and feebleness. Apart from the great star of Shelley, which shines the brighter as his successors dwindle in perspective, there is a flavour of unreality about all these pre-war assertions of a possible world order. In most of them the Victorian terror of "extravagance" is dominant, and the writer simpers and laughs at his own suggestions in what was evidently supposed to be a very disarming manner. Hardly any of these prophets dared believe in their own reasoning. Maxwell Brown has recently disinterred a pamphlet, The Great Analysis,[1] dated 1912, in which a shrewd and reasoned forecast of the primary structure of the Modern State, quite amazingly prescient for the time, was broached with the utmost timidity, without even an author's name. It was a scheme to revolutionize the world, and the writer would not put his name to it, he confesses, because it might make him ridiculous.

Maxwell Brown's entertaining Modern State Prophets Before the Great War is an exhaustive study of the psychological processes by which this idea, which is now the foundation of our contemporary life, gradually ousted its opposite of combative patriotism and established itself as a practicable and necessary form of action for men of good-will a century and a half ago. He traces the idea almost to its germ; he shows that its early manifestations, so far from being pacific, were dreams of universal conquest. He tells of its age- long struggle with everyday us-

[1] Here for once the editor knows better than the writer of the history. This pamphlet was written by William Archer, the dramatic critic, and reprinted under its author's name with a preface by Gilbert Murray in 1931. Apparently the book collectors of the years ahead are going to miss this book.—ED.

age and practical commonsense. In the first of his huge supplementary volumes he gives thousands of quotations going back far beyond the beginnings of the Christian Era. All the monotheistic religions were, in spirit, world-state religions. He examines the Tower of Babel myth as the attempt of some primordial cosmopolitan, some seer before the dawn, to account for the divisions of mankind. (There is strong reason now for ascribing this story to Emesal Gudeka of Nippur, the early Sumerian fabulist.)

Maxwell Brown shows how the syncretic religious developments, due to the growth of the early empires and the official pooling of gods, led necessarily to monotheism. From at least the time of Buddha onward, the sentiment, if not the living faith, in human brotherhood, always existed somewhere in the world. But its extension from a mere sentiment and a fluctuating sympathy for the stranger to the quality of a practicable enterprise was a very recent process indeed. The necessary conditions were not satisfied.

In the briefer studies of human innovations that preceded his more important contributions to human history, Maxwell Brown has shown how for the past ten thousand years at least, since the Cro-Magnards stamped their leather robes and tents, the art of printing reappeared and disappeared again and again, never culminating in the printed book and all its consequences, never obtaining a primary importance in human doings, until the fifteenth century (C.E.); he has assembled the evidence for man's repeated abortive essays in flying, from the fourth dynasty gliders recently found at Bedrashen, the shattered Yu-chow machine and the interesting wreckage, ornaments and human remains found last year in Mirabella Bay. (These last were first remarked in 2104 C.E. after an earthquake in the deep sea photographs of the survey aeroplane Crawford, and they were subsequently sought and recovered by the divers of the submarine Salvemini belonging to the Naples Biological Station. They have now been identified by Professor Giulio Marinetti as the remains of the legendary glider of Daedalus and Icarus.) Maxwell Brown has also traced the perpetual discovery and rediscovery of America from the days of the Aalesund tablets and the early Chinese inscriptions in the caves near Bahia Coqui to the final establishment of uninterrupted communications across the Atlantic by the Western Europeans in the fifteenth century C.E. In all there are sixteen separate ineffectual discoveries of America either from the east or from the west now on record, and there may have been many others that left no trace behind them.

These earlier cases of human enterprise and inadequacy help us to understand the long struggle of the Age of Frustration and the difficulty our ancestors found in achieving what is now so obviously the only sane arrangement of human affairs upon this planet.

The fruitlessness of all these premature inventions is very easily explained. First in the case of the Transatlantic passage; either the earlier navigators who got to America never got back, or, if they did get back, they were unable to find the necessary support and means to go again before they died, or they had had enough of hardship, or they perished in a second attempt. Their stories were distorted into

fantastic legends and substantially disbelieved. It was, indeed, a quite futile adventure to get to America until the keeled sailing ship, the science of navigation, and the mariner's compass had been added to human resources.

Then again, in the matter of printing, it was only when the Chinese had developed the systematic manufacture of abundant cheap paper sheets in standard sizes that the printed book—and its consequent release of knowledge—became practically possible. Finally the delay in the attainment of flying was inevitable because before men could progress beyond precarious gliding it was necessary for metallurgy to reach a point at which the internal combustion engine could be made. Until then they could build nothing strong enough and light enough to battle with the eddies of the air.

In an exactly parallel manner, the conception of one single human community organized for collective service to the common weal had to wait until the rapid evolution of the means of communication could arrest and promise to defeat the disintegrative influence of geographical separation. That rapid evolution came at last in the nineteenth century, and it has been described already in a preceding chapter of this world history[1]. Steam power, oil power, electric power, the railway, the steamship, the aeroplane, transmission by wire and aerial transmission followed each other very rapidly. They knit together the human species as it had never been knit before. Insensibly, in less than a century, the utterly impracticable became not merely a possible adjustment but an urgently necessary adjustment if civilization was to continue.

Now the cardinal prominence of the Great War in history lies in this, that it demonstrated the necessity of that adjustment. It was never considered to be necessary before. Recognition lagged behind accomplishment. None of the pre-war World-State Prophets betrays any sense of necessity. They make their polite and timid gestures towards human unity as something nice and desirable indeed but anything but imperative. The clearest demand for world-wide cooperation before the war, came from the Second International. And even after the war, and after the vague and vacillating adumbration of a federal super- state by the League of Nations at Geneva, most of even the most advanced writers seem to have been still under the impression that the utmost adjustment needed was some patching up of the current system so as to prevent or mitigate war and restrain the insurrectionary urge of the unprosperous.

Even the Communist movement which, as we had told already, had been able by a conspiracy of accidents to seize upon Russia and demonstrate the value of its theories there, lapsed from, rather than advanced towards, cosmopolitan socialism. Its theories, as we have shown, were hopelessly inadequate for its practical needs. The development of its ideology was greatly hampered by the conservative dogmatism imposed upon it by the incurable egotism of Marx. His intolerance, his innate bad manners, his vain insistence that he had produced a final doctrine to put beside Darwinism, cast a long shadow of impatience and obduracy upon the

[1] Not Recorded by Raven.—ED.

subsequent development of Communism. He was bitterly jealous of the Utopian school of socialism, and so, until Lenin faced the urgencies of power, the "orthodox" Marxist took a quite idiotic pride in a planless outlook. "Overthrow capitalism", he said, and what could happen but millennial bliss? Communism insisted indeed upon the necessity of economic socialization but— until it attained power in Russia—without a glance at its technical difficulties. It produced its belated and ill-proportioned Five Year Plan only in 1928 C.E., eleven years after its accession to power. Until then it had no comprehensive working scheme whatever for the realization of socialism. Thrown back on experiment, it was forced to such desperately urgent manoeuvres, improvisations and changes of front, and defended by such tawdry and transparent apologetics, that the general world movement passed out of its ken.

The reader of this world history knows already how the moral and intellectual force of the Communist Party proved unequal, after the death of Lenin, to control or resist the dictatorship of that forcible, worthy, devoted and limited man, the Georgian, Stalin. The premature death of the creative and adaptable Lenin and the impatient suppression by Stalin of such intelligent, troublesome, but necessary types as Trotsky—a man who, but for lack of tact and essential dignity, might well have been Lenin's successor—crippled whatever hope there may have been that the Modern State would first emerge in Russia. Terrible are the faithful disciples of creative men. Lenin relaxed and reversed the dogmatism of Marx, Stalin made what he imagined to be Leninism into a new and stiffer dogmatism. Thereafter the political doctrinaire dominated and crippled the technician in a struggle that cried aloud for technical competence. Just as theological disputes impoverished and devastated Europe through the long centuries of Christendom, and reduced the benefits of its unifying influence to zero, so in Russia efficiency of organization was prevented by the pedantries of political theorists. The young were trained to a conceit and a xenophobia, indistinguishable in its practical effects from the gross patriotism of such countries as France, Germany, Italy or Scotland.

Because of this subordination of its mental development to Politics, Russia passed into a political and social phase comparable, as Rostovtzeff pointed out at the time in his Social and Economic History of the Roman Empire, in its universal impoverishment and its lack of any critical vigour, to the well- meaning but devitalizing autocracy of the Emperor Diocletian. From its very start the Russian revolution failed in its ambition to lead mankind. Its cosmopolitanism lasted hardly longer than the cosmopolitanism of the great French revolution a dozen decades earlier.

This almost inevitable lag of the constructive movement in Russia behind Western developments was foreseen by the shrewd and penetrating brain of Lenin even in the phase of its apparent leadership (see No. 3090 in the thirteenth series of the Historical Documents Collection, Left Wing Communism). But his observation found little or no echo in the incurably illiberal thought of the Marxian tradition.

It was in Western Europe especially that the conception of the organized and disciplined World-State as a revolutionary objective, ultimately grew to its full proportions. At first it grew obscurely. In 1933, any observer might have been misled by the fact of the Fascist régime in Italy, by the tumult of the Nazi party in Germany, by similar national-socialist movements in other countries, and by the increase in tariff barriers and other restraints upon trade everywhere, to conclude that the cosmopolitan idea was everywhere in retreat before the obsessions of race, creed and nationalism. Yet all the while the germs of the Modern State were growing, everywhere its votaries were learning and assembling force.

It needed the financial storm of the years 1928 and 1929 C.E. and the steadily progressive collapse of the whole world's economic life, of which this storm was the prelude, to give the World-State prophets the courage of their convictions. Then indeed they began to speak out. Instead of the restrained, partial and inconclusive criticism of public affairs which had hitherto contented them, they now insisted plainly upon the need of a world- wide reconstruction, that is to say of a world revolution—though "revolution" was still a word they shirked. The way in which this increased definition of aim and will came about is characteristic of the changing quality of social life. It was not that one or two outstanding men suddenly became audible and conspicuous as leaders in this awakening. There were no leaders. It was a widespread movement in human thought.

The conclusions upon which intelligent people were converging may be briefly stated. They had arrived at the realization that human society had become one indivisible economic system with novel and enormous potentialities of well- being. By 1931 C.E. this conception becomes visible even in the obstinately intellectualist mind of France—for example, in the parting speech to America of an obscure and transitory French Prime Minister, Laval, who crossed the Atlantic on some new undiscoverable mission in that year; and we find it promptly echoed by such prominent loud speakers as President Hoover of America and Mr. Ramsay MacDonald the British Prime Minister.

That idea at any rate had already become sufficiently popular for the politicians to render it lip service. But it was still only the intelligent minority who went on to the logical consequences of its realization; that is to say, the necessity of disavowing the sovereignty of contemporary governments, of setting up authoritative central controls to supplement or supersede them, and of putting the production of armaments, the production of the main economic staples and the protection of workers from destructive under-payment, beyond the reach of profit-seeking manipulation.

Yet by 1932-33 this understanding minority was speaking very plainly. These immense changes were no longer being presented as merely desirable things; they were presented as urgently necessary things if civilization was to be saved from an immense catastrophe. And not merely saved. The alternative to disaster, they saw even then, was not just a bleak and terrified security. That was the last thing possible. There was no alternative to disorder and wretchedness, but "such an abundance, such a prosperity and richness of opportunity", as man had never

known before. (These words are quoted from a Scottish newspaper of the year 1929.) Enlightened people in 1932 C.E. were as assured of the possibility of world order, universal sufficiency and ever increasing human vitality as are we who live to-day in ample possession of our lives amidst the practical realization of that possibility.

Clearness of vision did not make for the happiness of the enlightened. Their minds were tormented not simply by contemporary fears and miseries, but by the sure knowledge of a possible world of free activity within the reach of man and, as it were, magically withheld. They saw hundreds of millions of lives cramped and crippled, meagrely lived, sacrificed untimely, and they could not see any primary necessity for this blighting and starvation of human life. They saw youthful millions drifting to lives of violence, mutilation and premature and hideous deaths. And beyond was our security, our eventfulness and our freedom.

Maxwell Brown, in a chapter called "Tantalus 1932", cites forty instances of these realizations. But the legendary Tantalus was put within apparent reach of the unattainable by the inexorable decrees of the gods. Mankind was under no such pitiless destiny. The world-wide Modern State shone bright upon the living imaginations of our race within a decade of the Great War, absurdly near, fantastically out of reach. For a century of passionate confusion and disorder, that modern state was not to be released from potentiality into actuality.

It is to the story of these battling, lost and suffering generations, the "generations of the half light", that we must now proceed.

When now we look back to the scattered and diverse individuals who first give expression to this idea of the modern World-State which was dawning upon the human intelligence, when we appraise their first general efforts towards its realization, we need, before we can do them anything like justice, to attempt some measure of the ignorances, prejudices and other inertias, the habits of concession and association, the herd love and the herd fear, with which they had to struggle not only in the society in which they found themselves, but within themselves. It is not a conflict of light and darkness we have to describe; it is the struggle of the purblind among the blind. We have to realize that for all that they were haunted by a vision of the civilized world of to-day, they still belonged not to our age but to their own. The thing imagined in their minds was something quite distinct from their present reality. Maxwell Brown has devoted several chapters, and a third great supplementary volume, to a special selection of early Modern State Prophets who followed public careers. He showed conclusively that in the third and fourth decades of the twentieth century (C.E.) there was a rapidly increasing number of men and women with a clear general conception of the possibilities of the modern world. He gives their written and spoken words, often astoundingly prescient and explicit. And then he traces out the tenor of their lives subsequent to these utterances. The discrepancy of belief and effort is a useful and indeed a startling reminder of the conditional nature of the individual life.

As he writes: "In the security and serenity of the study, these men and women could see plainly. In those hours of withdrawal, the fragile delicate brain matter

could escape from immediacy, apprehended causation in four dimensions, reach forward to the permanent values of social events in the space- time framework. But even to the study there penetrated the rumble of the outer disorder. And directly the door was opened, forthwith the uproar of contemporary existence, the carnival, the riot, the war and the market, beat in triumphantly. The raging question of what had to be done that day, scattered the fine thought of our common destiny to the four winds of heaven."

Maxwell Brown adds a vivid illustration to this passage. It is the facsimile of the first draft by Peter Raut, the American progressive leader, of the Revolutionary Manifesto of 1937. It was indisputably a very inspiring document in its time and Raut gave the last proof of loyalty to the best in his mind, by a courageous martyrdom. But in the margin of this draft one's attention is caught by a maze of little figures; little sums in multiplication and addition. By his almost inspired gift for evidence and through the industry of his group of research assistants, Maxwell Brown has been able to demonstrate exactly what these sums were. They show that even while Raut, so far as his foresight permitted, was planning our new world, his thoughts were not wholly fixed on that end. They wandered. For a time the manifesto was neglected while he did these sums. He was gambling in industrial equities, and a large and active portion of his brain was considering whether the time had arrived to sell.

3. THE ACCUMULATING DISPROPORTIONS OF THE OLD ORDER

Let us consider some of the main appearances that disposed many minds to expect a world community in the early twentieth century. In the first place a very considerable financial unity had been achieved. The credit of the City of London ran to the ends of the earth and the gold sovereign was for all practical purposes a world coin, exchangeable locally for local expenditure within relatively slight fluctuations. Economic life was becoming very generalized. Over great areas trade moved with but small impediments, and the British still hoped to see their cosmopolitan conception of Free Trade accepted by the whole world. The International Institute of Agriculture in Rome was developing an annual census of staple production and reaching out towards a world control of commodity transport. Considerable movements and readjustments of population were going on, unimpeded by any government interference. Swarms of Russian Poles, for instance, drifted into Eastern Germany for the harvest work and returned; hundreds of thousands of Italians went to work in the United States for a few years and then came back with their earnings to their native villages. An ordinary traveller might go all over the more settled parts of the earth and never be asked for a passport unless he wanted to obtain a registered letter at a post office or otherwise prove his identity.

A number of minor but significant federal services had also come into existence and had a sound legal standing throughout the world, the Postal Union for example. Before 1914 C.E. a written document was delivered into the hands of the addressee at almost every point upon the planet, almost as surely as, if less swiftly than, it is to-day. (The Historical Documents Board has recently reprinted a small book, International Government, prepared for the little old Fabian Society during the Great War period by L. S. Woolf, which gives a summary of such arrangements. He lists twenty-three important world unions dealing at that time with trade, industry, finance, communications, health, science, art, literature, drugs, brothels, criminals, emigration and immigration and minor political affairs.) These world-wide cooperations seemed —more particularly to the English-speaking peoples—to presage a direct and comparatively smooth transition from the political patchwork of the nineteenth century, as the divisions of the patchwork grew insensibly fainter, to a stable confederation of mankind. The idea of a coming World-State was quite familiar at the time—one finds it, for instance, as early as Lord Tennyson's Locksley Hall (published in 1842); but there was no

effort whatever to achieve it, and indeed no sense of the need of such effort. The World-State was expected to come about automatically by the inherent forces in things.

That belief in some underlying benevolence in uncontrolled events was a common error, one might almost say THE common error, of the time. It affected every school of thought. In exactly the same fashion the followers of Marx (before the invigorating advent of Lenin and the Bolshevist reconstruction of Communism) regarded their dream of world communism as inevitable, and the disciples of Herbert Spencer found a benevolent Providence in "free competition". "Trust Evolution", said the extreme Socialist and the extreme Individualist, as piously as the Christians put their trust in God. It was the Bolshevik movement in the twentieth century which put will into Communism. The thought of the nineteenth century revolutionary and reactionary alike was saturated with that confident irresponsible laziness. As Professor K. Chandra Sen has remarked, hope in the Victorian period was not a stimulant but an opiate.

We who live in a disciplined order, the chastened victors of a hard- fought battle, understand how superficial and unsubstantial were all those hopeful appearances. The great processes of mechanical invention, which have been described in our general account of the release of experimental science from deductive intellectualism, were increasing the power and range of every operating material force quite irrespective of its fitness or unfitness for the new occasions of mankind. With an equal impartiality they were bringing world- wide understanding and world-wide massacre into the range of human possibility.

It was through no fault of these inventors and investigators that the new opportunities they created were misused. That was outside their range. They had as yet no common culture of their own. Nor, since each worked in his own field, were they responsible for the fragmentary irregularity of their discoveries. Biological and especially social invention were lagging far behind the practical advances of the exacter, simpler sciences. Their application was more difficult; the matters they affected were so much more deeply embedded in ordinary use and wont, variation was more intimate, novelties could not be inserted with the same freedom. It was easy to supplant the coach and horses on the macadamized road by the steam-engine or the railway, because it was not necessary to do anything to the road or the coach and horses to bring about the change. They were just left alone to run themselves out as the railroad (and later the automobile on the rubber-glass track) superseded them. But men cannot set up new social institutions, new social and political and industrial relationships, side by side with the old in that fashion. It must be an altogether tougher and slower job. It is a question not of ousting but of reconstruction. The old must be converted into the new without ceasing for a moment to be a going concern. The over-running of the biologically old by the mechanically new, due to these differences in timing, was inevitable, and it reached its maximum in the twentieth century.

A pathological analogy may be useful here. In the past, before the correlation of development in living organisms began to be studied, people used to suffer

helplessly and often very dreadfully from all sorts of irregularities of growth in their bodies. The medical services of the time, such as they were, were quite unable to control them. One of these, due to what is called the Nurmi ratios in the blood, was a great overproduction of bone, either locally or generally. The suffered gradually underwent distortion into a clumsy caricature of his former self; his features became coarse and massive, his skull bones underwent a monstrous expansion; the proportions of his limbs altered, and the leverage of his muscles went askew. He was made to look grotesque; he was crippled and at last killed. Something strictly parallel happened to human society in the hundred years before the Great War. Under the stimulus of mechanical invention and experimental physics it achieved, to pursue our metaphor, a hypertrophy of bone, muscle and stomach, without any corresponding enlargement of its nervous controls.

Long before the Great War this progressive disproportion had been dimly recognized by many observers. The favourite formula was to declare that "spiritual"—for the naïve primordial opposition of spirit and matter was still accepted in those days—had not kept pace with "material" advance. This was usually said with an air of moral superiority to the world at large. Mostly there was a vague implication that if these other people would only refrain from using modern inventions so briskly, or go to church more, or marry earlier and artlessly, or read a more "spiritual" type of literature, or refrain from mixed bathing, or work harder and accept lower wages, or be more respectful and obedient to constituted authority, all might yet be well. Beyond this sort of thing there was little recognition of the great and increasing disharmonies of the social corpus until after the Great War.

The young reader will ask, "But where was the Central Observation Bureau? Where was the professorial and student body which should have been recording these irregularities and producing plans for adjustment?"

There was no Central Observation Bureau. That did not exist for another century. That complex organization of discussion, calculation, criticism and forecast was undreamt of. Those cities of thought, full of serene activities, came into existence only after the organization of the Record and Library Network under the Air Dictatorship between 2010 and 2030. Even the mother thought-city, the World Encyclopaedia Establishment, was not founded until 2012. In the early twentieth century there was still no adequate estimate of economic forces and their social reactions. There were only a few score professors and amateurs of these fundamentally important studies scattered throughout the earth. They were scattered in every sense; even their communications were unsystematic. They had no powers of enquiry, no adequate statistics, little prestige; few people heeded what they thought or said.

Maybe they deserved nothing better. They bickered stupidly with and discredited each other. They ignored or wilfully misunderstood each other. It is impossible to read such social and economic literature as the period produced without realizing the extraordinary backwardness of that side of the world's intellectual life. It is difficult to believe nowadays that the writers of these

publications, at once tediously copious and incredibly jejune, were living at the same time as the lively multitude of workers in the experimental sciences which were daily adding to and reshaping knowledge to achieve fresh practical triumphs. From 1812 C.E., when public gas-lighting was first organized, to the outbreak of the Great War, while the world was being made over anew by gas, by steam, by oil, and then by the swift headlong development of electrical science, while the last terrae incognitae were being explored and mapped, while a multitude of hitherto unthought-of elements and compounds and hundreds of thousands of new substances were coming into use, while epidemic diseases were being restrained and driven back, while the death rate was being halved, and the average duration of life increased by a score of years, the social and political sciences remained practically stagnant and unserviceable. Throughout that century of material achievement there is no single instance of the successful application of a social, economic or educational generalization.

Because of this belatedness of the social sciences, the progressive dislocation of the refined if socially limited and precarious civilization of the more advanced of the eighteenth and nineteenth century sovereign states went on without any effectual contemporary understanding of what was straining it to pieces. The Europeans and the Americans of the early twentieth century apprehended the social and political forces that ravaged their lives hardly more clearly than the citizens of the Roman Empire during its collapse. Plenty and the appearance of security HAPPENED; then débâcle HAPPENED. There was no analysis of operating causes. For years even quite bold and advanced thinkers were chased by events. They did not grasp what was occurring at the time. They only realized what had really occurred long afterwards. And so they never foresaw. There was no foresight, and therefore still less could there be any understanding control.

4. EARLY ATTEMPTS TO UNDERSTAND AND DEAL WITH THESE DISPROPORTIONS; THE CRITICISMS OF KARL MARX AND HENRY GEORGE

There are, however, one or two exceptions to this general absence of diagnosis in the affairs of the nineteenth and twentieth century of the Christian Era, which even the student of general history cannot ignore. Prominent among them is the analysis and forecasts of economic development made by Karl Marx and his associates.

In any case Marxism would have demanded our attention as a curious contemporary realization of the self-destroying elements in the business methods of the nineteenth century; but its accidental selection as the ostensible creed of revolutionary Russia after the Tzarist collapse gives it an almost primary importance in the history of kinetic ideas.

Karl Marx (1818-1883) was the son of a christianized Jewish lawyer of Treves, of considerable social pretensions; he had an excellent university career at Bonn and Berlin, assimilated the radical thought of his time and became the lifelong friend of the far more modest and gifted Friedrich Engels (1820-1895), a Lancashire calico dealer. Under the inspiration of Engels and the English socialist movement of Robert Owen, Marx elaborated the theory of economic development which is the substance of Marxism. It is embodied in a huge unfinished work, Das Kapital, and summarized in a Communist Manifesto (1848) drawn up by Engels and himself. (These, and indeed all his writings, together with an able digest and summary, are to be found in the Library of Historical Thought, vols. 17252-9.) His chief merit lies in his clear recognition of the ultimate dependence of social and political forms and reactions upon physical necessity. ("The Materialist Conception of History".) His chief fault was his insane hatred of the middle classes (bourgeoisie), due mainly to his pose as a needy aristocrat and embittered, it may be, by his material and intellectual dependence on the trader Engels. His own attempts to apply his theories by conspiracy and political action were inept and futile. He died in London a disappointed and resentful man, quite unaware of the posthumous fame that awaited his doctrines. It was the organization of his followers into the disciplined Communist Party and the modernization of his doctrines by the genius of Lenin that made his name a cardinal one in history.

It is interesting to consider his general propositions now in the light of accomplished events and note the hits and misses of those heroic speculations— heroic, that is to say, measured by the mental courage of the time.

Nowadays every schoolboy knows that the essential and permanent conflict in life is a conflict between the past and the future, between the accomplished past and the forward effort. He is made to realize this conflict in his primary biological course. Therein he comes to see and in part to understand the continual automatic struggle of the thing achieved, to hold the new, the new- born individual, the new-born idea, the widening needs of the species, in thrall. This conflict he is shown runs through all history. In the old classical mythology Saturn, the Conservative head-god, devoured all his children until at last one escaped to become Jove. And of how Jove bound Prometheus in his turn every lover of Shelley can tell. We need only refer the student to the recorded struggles in the histories of Republican Rome and Judaea between debtor and creditor; to the plebeian Secessions of the former and the year of Jubilee of the latter; to the legend of Joseph in Egypt (so richly interpreted now through the minute study of contemporary Egyptian documents by the students of the Breasted Commemoration Fund); to the English Statute of Mortmain; to Austen Livewright's lucid study of Bankruptcy Through the Ages (1979), to remind him of this perennial struggle of life against the creditor and the dead hand. But Marx, like most of his contemporaries, was profoundly ignorant of historical science, and addicted to a queer "dialectic" devised by the pseudo-philosopher Hegel; his ill-equipped mind apprehended this perennial antagonism only in terms of the finance of the industrial production about him; the entrepreneur, the capitalist, became the villain of his piece, using the prior advantage of his capital to appropriate the "surplus value" of production, so that his share of purchasing power became more and more disproportionately great.

Marx seems never to have distinguished clearly between restrictive and productive possessions, which nowadays we recognize as a difference of fundamental importance. Exploitation for profit and strangulation for dominance, the radical son and the conservative father, were all one to him. And his proposals for expropriating the profit-seeking "Capitalist" were of the vaguest; he betrayed no conception whatever of the real psychology of economic activities, and he had no sense of the intricate organization of motives needed if the coarse incentive of profit was to be superseded. Indeed, he had no practical capacity at all, and one is not surprised to learn that for his own part he never earned a living. He claimed all the privileges of a prophet and all the laxity and indolence of a genius, and he never even completed his great book.

It was the far abler and finer-minded Lenin (1870-1924, in power in Russia after 1917), rather than Marx, who gave a practical organization to the revolutionary forces of Communism and made the Communist Party for a time, until Stalin overtook it, the most vital creative force in the world. The essential intellectual difference between these two men is explained very clearly by Max Eastman (1895-1980), whose compact and scholarly Marx and Lenin is still quite readable by the contemporary student. In his time Lenin had to pose as the disciple and exponent of Marx; it was only later that criticism revealed the subtle brilliance of his effort to wrest a practical commonsense out of the time-worn doctrines of the older prophet.

Another nineteenth-century writer, with perhaps a clearer realization of the strangulating effect of restrictive property as distinguished from the stimulating effect of exploitation, was Henry George (1839-1897), an American printer who rose to great popularity as a writer upon economic questions. He saw the life of mankind limited and dwarfed by the continual rise in rents. His naïve remedy was to tax the landowner, as Marx's naïve remedy was to expropriate the capitalist, and just as Marx never gave his disciples the ghost of an idea for a competent administration of the expropriated economic plant and resources of the world, so Henry George never indicated how, in the world of implacable individualism he advocated, the taxing authority was to find a use for its ever-increasing tax receipts.

We can smile to-day at the limitations of these early pioneers. But we smile only because we live later than they did, and are two centuries and more to the good in our experience. We owe them enormous gratitude for the valiant disinterestedness of their life work.

Our debt is on the whole rather for what they got rid of than for what they did. The broad outlines of the world's economic life are fairly simple as we see them frankly exposed to-day, but these men were born into an atmosphere of uncriticized usage, secrecy, time-honoured misconceptions, fetishisms, working fictions—which often worked very badly—and almost insane suppressions of thought and statement. The very terms they were obliged to use were question-begging terms; the habitual assumptions of the world they addressed were crooked and only to be apprehended with obliquity and inconsistency. They were forcing their minds towards the expression of reality through an intricate mental and moral tangle. They destroyed the current assumption of permanence in established institutions and usages, and though that seems a small thing to us now, it was a profoundly important release at the time. The infantile habit of assuming the fixity of the Thing that Is was almost universal in their day.

The Marxist doctrines did at least indicate that a term was necessarily set to economic development through profit-seeking, by the concentration of controlling ownership, by the progressive relative impoverishment of larger and larger sections of the world population and by the consequent final dwindling of markets. The rapid coagulation of human activities after 1928 C.E. was widely recognized as a confirmation of the Marxian forecast, and by one of those rapid mental leaps characteristic of the time, as a complete endorsement of the Communist pretension to have solved the social problem.

Unembarrassed as we are now by the mental clutter of our forefathers, the fundamental processes at work during the distressful years of the third and fourth decade of the century appear fairly simple. We know that it is a permanent condition of human well-being that the general level of prices should never fall, and we have in the Currency Council a fairly efficient and steadily improving world-organ to ensure that end. A dollar, as we know it to-day, means practically the same thing in goods, necessities and satisfactions from one year's end to another. Its diminution in value is infinitesimal. No increase is ever allowed to occur. For

the owner of an unspent dollar there is neither un- earnt increment nor unmerited loss. As the productive energy of our species rises, the dollar value of the total wealth is arranged to increase steadily in proportion, and neither is the creditor enriched nor robbed of his substantial expectation nor the debtor confronted with payments beyond his powers.

There remains no way now of becoming passively wealthy. Gambling was ruthlessly eradicated under the Air Dictatorship and has never returned. Usury ranks with forgery as a monetary offence. Money is given to people to get what they want and not as a basis for further acquisition, and we realize that the gambling spirit is a problem for the educationist and mental expert. It implies a fundamental misunderstanding of life. We have neither speculators, shareholders, private usurers or rent lords. All these "independent" types have vanished from the earth. Land and its natural resources are now owned and administered either directly or by delegation, by a hierarchy of administrative boards representing our whole species; there are lease-holding cultivators and exploiting corporations with no right to sublet, but there is no such thing as a permanent private ownership of natural resources making an automatic profit by the increment of rent. And since there is, and probably always will be now, a continual advance in our average individual productive efficiency by which the whole community profits, there follows a continual extension of our collective enterprises, a progressive release of leisure and a secular raising of the standard of individual life, to compensate for what would otherwise be a progressive diminution in the number of brains and hands needed to carry on the work of the world. Human society, so long as productive efficiency increases, is OBLIGED to raise its standards of consumption and extend its activities year by year, or collapse. And if its advance does not go on it will drop into routine, boredom, viciousness and decay. Steadfastly the quantity and variety of things MUST increase.

These imperative conditions, which constitute the A B C of the existing order, seem so obvious to-day, that it is with difficulty we put ourselves in the place of these twentieth century folk to whom they were strange and novel. They were not yet humanized en masse; they still had the mentality of the "struggle for existence". It is only by a considerable mental effort, and after a careful study of the gradual evolution of the civilized mentality out of the chaotic impulses and competition of an originally very unsocial animal, that we can even begin to see matters with the eyes of our predecessors of a century and a half ago.

5. THE WAY IN WHICH COMPETITION AND MONETARY INEFFICIENCY STRAINED THE OLD ORDER

In the twentieth century of the Christian era there was still no common currency by which to measure and carry on the world's economic exchanges. Those transactions were not merely apprehended inexactly because of this; they were falsified, and it did not seem possible that there would ever be an effective simplification. It is true that during what is known as the First Period of General Prosperity, from 1850 C.E. until 1914, there was a kind of working world system of currency and credit, centring upon the City of London and based on the gold pound; but this was a purely accidental growth, made workable by successive gold discoveries which prevented too disastrous a fall in prices as productive efficiency increased, and by the circumstances that gave the insular English a lead in the development of steam transport on land and sea and real incentives towards a practical propaganda of world free trade.

That first gleam of cosmopolitan sunlight waned as it had waxed, without any contemporary apprehension of the real forces at work, much less any attempt to seize upon them and organize them in permanence. The financial ascendency and initiative of the City of London crumbled away after the war and nothing appeared to take its place. In any case, this quasi-cosmopolitan system based on the gold sovereign, and owing its modicum of success to continual increments in the available gold, would have wilted as the world's gold supplies gave out, but the strangulation of the world's industry after the war was greatly accelerated by the gold hoarding of the Americans and French.

And during all that phase of opportunity there was no substantial effort to take hold of the land, sea and natural resources of the planet and bring them from a state of fragmentary, chaotic and wasteful exploitation into a general scheme. There remained sixty-odd "sovereign" governments, each claiming a supreme control of all the natural wealth of the areas within its frontiers, and under these governments, under conditions that varied with each, there were private corporations and individuals with a right to deal more or less freely with the fragment upon which they had established a grip. Everywhere the guiding principle in the exploitation of the minerals, sunshine and power resources of the globe was the profit of single or associated private individuals, and the patchwork governments of the time interfered in the profit scramble only in favour of their nationals against their foreign rivals. Yet for nearly a hundred years, because of the fortu-

nate influx of gold and inventions, this profit-seeking system, linked to the metallic monetary system, sufficed to sustain a very great expansion and enlargement of human life, and it was hard to convince the mass of men, and still harder to convince the prosperous manufacturers, traders, miners, cultivators and financiers who dominated public affairs, that this was not a permanent system and that the world already needed very essential modifications of its economic methods. A considerable measure of breakdown, a phase of display, fear and distress, was necessary before they could be disillusioned.

The nineteenth century had for its watchwords "individual enterprise and free competition". But the natural end of all competition is the triumph of one competitor. It was in America that the phenomena of Big Business first appeared and demonstrated the force of this truism; at a score of points triumphant organizations capable of crushing out new competitors and crippling and restraining new initiatives that threatened their predominance appeared. In Europe there was little governmental resistance to industrial alliances and concentrations in restraint of competition, and they speedily developed upon a scale that transcended political frontiers, but in the United States of America there was a genuine effort to prevent enterprises developing on a monopolistic scale. The conspicuous leader of this preventive effort was the first President Roosevelt (1858-1919) and its chief fruit the Sherman Anti-Trust Act (1890), which proved a rich mine for lawyers in the subsequent decades.

These great consolidations, which closed the phase of free competition, were so far effective in controlling trade and arresting new developments that Hilary Hooker, in his Studies in Business Coagulation During the First Period of General Prosperity, is able to cite rather more than two thousand instances, ranging from radium and new fruits and foodstuffs to gramophones, automobiles, reconstructed households, artificial moonlight for the roadways by the countryside, and comfortable and economical railway plant, in which ample supplies or beneficial improvements were successfully kept off the market in the interests of established profit-making systems. After 1900 C.E. again there was a world-wide cessation of daily newspaper initiative and a consequent systole of free speech. Distribution, paper supply and news services had fallen into the hands of powerful groups able and willing to crush out any new types of periodical, or any inimical schools of public suggestion. They set about stereotyping the public mind.

These same profit-making systems in possession also played a large part in arresting competition from countries in which they were less completely in control, by subsidized political action for the maintenance of protective tariffs. Long before the world break-down became manifest, the experience of the ordinary consumer so far belied the sanguine theory that free competition was a mode of endless progress, that he was still living in a house, wearing clothes, using appliances, travelling about in conveyances, and being fed with phrases and ideas that by the standard of the known and worked-out inventions of the time should have been discarded on an average, Hooker computes, from a quarter to half a century before. There was labour unemployed and abundant material available to remedy

all this, but its utilization was held up by the rent-exacting and profit-earning systems already in possession.

This lag in modernization added greatly to the effects of increased productive efficiency in the disengagement of those vast masses of destitute unemployed and unemploying people which began to appear almost everywhere, like the morbid secretion of a diseased body, as the twentieth century passed on into its third decade.

6. THE PARADOX OF OVER-PRODUCTION AND ITS RELATION TO WAR

This so-called "paradox of over-production" which figures so largely in the loose discussions of the "post-war" period was in its essence a very simple affair indeed. Just as the inevitable end of a process of free competition was a consolidation of successful competitors and an arrest of enterprise, so the inevitable end of a search for profit in production was a steady reduction of costs through increased efficiency—that is to say, a steady decrease of the ratio of employment to output. These things lie so much on the surface of the process that it is almost incredible to us that, wilfully or not, our ancestors disregarded them. Equally inevitable was it that these necessary contractions of enterprise and employment should lead to an increase in the proportion of unemployable people. Geographical expansion and a rising standard of life among both the employed and possessing classes, together with the stimulating effect of a steady influx of gold, masked and tempered for half a century this squeezing-out of an increasing fraction of the species from its general economic life. There were nevertheless fluctuations, "cycles of trade" as they were called, when the clogging machinery threatened to stall and was then relieved and went on again. But by the opening of the twentieth century, the fact that the method of running human affairs as an open competition for profit, was in its nature a terminating method, was forcing itself upon the attention even of those who profited most by it and had the most excuse for disregarding it, and who, as a class, knew nothing of the Marxian analysis.

We know now that the primary task of world administration is to arrest this squeezing out of human beings from active economic life, by the continual extension of new collective enterprises, but such ideas had still to be broached at that time. The common folk, wiser in their instincts than the political economists in their intellectualism, were disposed to approve of waste and extravagance because money was "circulated" and workers "found employment". And the reader will not be able to understand the world-wide tolerance of growing armaments and war preparations during this period unless he realizes the immediate need inherent in the system for unremunerative public expenditure. Somewhere the energy economized had to come out. The world of private finance would not tolerate great rehousing, great educational and socially constructive enterprises, on the part of the relatively feeble governments of the time. All that had to be reserved for the profit accumulator. And so the ever-increasing productivity of the race

found its vent in its ancient traditions of warfare, which admitted the withdrawal of a large proportion of the male population from employment for a year or so and secreted that vast accumulation of forts, battleships, guns, submarines, explosives, barracks and the like, which still amazes us. Without this cancer growth of armies and navies, the paradox of over-production latent in competitive private enterprise would probably have revealed itself in an overwhelming mass of unemployment before even the end of the nineteenth century. A social revolution might have occurred then.

Militarism, however, alleviated these revolutionary stresses, by providing vast profit-yielding channels of waste. And it also strengthened the forces of social repression. The means of destruction accumulated on a scale that well-nigh kept pace with the increase in the potential wealth of mankind. The progressive enslavement of the race to military tyranny was an inseparable aspect, therefore, of free competition for profits. The latter system conditioned and produced the former. It needed the former so as to have ballast to throw out to destruction and death whenever it began to sink. The militarist phase of the early twentieth century and the paradox of over-production are correlated facets of the same reality, the reality of the planless hypertrophy of the social body.

It is interesting to note how this morbid accumulation of energy in belligerence and its failure to find vent in other directions became more and more evident in the physiognomy of the world as the twentieth century progressed. The gatherings of mankind became blotched with uniforms. Those admirable albums of coloured pictures, Historical Scenes in a Hundred Volumes, which are now placed in all our schools and show-places and supplied freely to any home in which there are children, display very interestingly the advent, predominance and disappearance of military preoccupations in the everyday life of our ancestors. These pictures are all either reproductions of actual paintings, engravings or photographs, or, in the case of the earlier volumes, they are elaborate reconditionings to the more realistic methods of our time of such illustrations as were available. Military operations have always attracted the picture-maker at all times, and there are plentiful pictures of battles from every age, from the little cricket-field battle of the Middle Ages to the hundred mile fights of the last Great War, but our interest here is not with battles but with the general facies of social life. Even in the war-torn seventeenth century the general stream of life went on without any manifest soldiering. War was a special occupation. While the battles of the English Civil War, which set up the first English Republic (1649-1660), were in progress, we have evidence that hunting and hawking parties were busy almost within sound of the guns. The novels of Jane Austen (England, 1775-1817) pursue their even way without the faintest echo of the land and sea campaigns in progress. Goethe in Weimar (the German literary "Great Man" during the "Great Man" period of literary thought in Europe, 1749-1832) could not be bothered by requests for supplies of wood and food for the German troops before the battle of Jena, and was very pleased to meet his "enemy alien" Napoleon socially during that campaign.

We rarely see the monarchs of the eighteenth century depicted in military guise; the fashion was for robes and majesty rather than for the spurs and feathers of the Bantam warrior-king. It was the unprecedented vehemence of the Napoleonic adventure that splashed the social life of Europe with uniforms, infected feminine fashions, and even set plump princess colonels, frogged with gold lace and clutching bare sabres, joggling unsteadily at the heads of regiments. There was a brief return towards civilian attire with the accession of the "domesticated monarchs", Louis Philippe in France and Victoria in Great Britain; they marked a transient reaction from Napoleonic fashions; but from the middle of the nineteenth century onward the prestige of the soldier resumed its advance and the military uniform became increasingly pervasive. Flags became more abundant in the towns and "flag-days" dotted the calendar. There was never a crowd pictured in Europe after 1870 without a soldier or so.

The Great War greatly intensified the military element in the street population, not only in Europe but America. Various corps of feminine auxiliaries were enrolled during that time and paraded the world thereafter in appetising soldierly outfits. In the United States, except at Washington, or when there was a parade of civil war veterans, a soldier in uniform had been hitherto the rarest of birds. He would have felt strange and uncomfortable. He would have offended the susceptibilities of a consciously liberated people. The Great War changed all that. When Germany was disarmed after the war, a Nazi movement and a Reichsbanner movement supplied the needed colour until a German's freedom to get into properly recognized livery was restored. The pattern of half-military, half-civilian organizations in uniform had already been spread about the world between the South African War (1899-1901) and the Great War, by the Boy Scout movement.

Of the Nazi movement, the Italian Fascisti and the Polish Brotherhood at least there will be more to tell later. The black and brown shirts may be cited here as instances of the visible breaking-down of the boundaries between military and civil life that went on during and after the World War.

Hitherto war had been a marginal business, fought upon "fronts", and the ordinary citizen had lived in comparative security behind the front, but the bombing, gas-diffusing aeroplane, and later the long-range air torpedo, changed all that. The extended use of propaganda as a weapon, and the increasing danger of social mutiny under war stress, had also its share in making the entire surface of a belligerent country a war area and abolishing any vestiges of civil liberty, first during actual warfare and then in view of warfare. The desirability of getting everyone under orders, under oath, and subject to prompt disciplinary measures, became more and more manifest to governments.

So within a century the appearance of the human crowd changed over from a varied assembly of incoordinated free individuals to a medley of uniforms. Everybody's dress at last indicated function, obligation and preparedness. The militarization of the European multitude reached a maximum during the Polish wars. About 1942 gas masks, either actually worn or hanging from the neck, were common for a time, and so, too, were the small sheath- knives which were to be

used in disposing of fallen aviators who might still be alive. Patella metal hats and metal epaulettes to protect the head and body against a rain of poisoned needles also appeared. Some civilians became far more formidable- looking than any soldiers.

The military authorities of those days were much perplexed by the problem of giving the general population protective apparatus and light weapons that would be effective against the military enemy and yet useless for the purposes of insurrection. For in spite of the most strenuous suppression of agitation in those troubled decades, the possible revolt of humanity against warfare, the possibility of complete "loss of morale", however illogical and incoherent, was felt by the professional soldiers as an increasing menace.

Along the streets of most of the old-world cities there presently appeared the characteristic yellow (or in France blue, and in America red-and- white-striped) air-raid pillars with their glass faces, only to be broken into and used after an official alarm, which contained respirators and first-aid sets for possible gas victims. It is also to the same period we have to ascribe the multiplication of vivid and abundant direction signs at every street corner, set so as to throw a minimum of light upward and pointing the way to gas chambers and hospitals. It was a "gas-minded" world in the 'forties. The practical suppression of other vivid and illuminated street signs was a natural corollary to this preoccupation.

In the first half of the twentieth century the cities blazed with advertisement. It was the period of maximum advertisement. The pictures of the Great White Way of New York, Piccadilly Circus, the Grands Boulevards of Paris and so forth, with their polychromatic visual clamour, still strike us as distractingly picturesque. There was much flood-lighting after 1928. Then progressively the lights were turned down again and that visual clamour died away. As the air threat returned, "lights out" became at last imperative, except for the vivid furtive indications of refuge and first aid we have just mentioned.

War fear spread very rapidly after 1930. Darkness recaptured the nocturnal town. "Night-life" became stealthy and obscure, with an increasing taint of criminality. All civil hospitals and all private doctors had disappeared from the world by 1945 and the health services were only legally demilitarized again after 2010. The amalgamation of the military and civil hospital and medical services began in France as early as 1933. By 1945 every doctor in the Old World was, in theory at least, on a quasi-military footing; he wore a distinctive uniform, was subject to stringent discipline, and his premises, as well as the hospitals, bore the characteristic black-and-yellow chequerwork. All nurses were similarly enrolled. Finally the general public was enrolled for health treatment as common patients under oath. By 1948 in such towns as had sufficiently survived the general social demoralization to enforce such regulations, it was impossible to take a chill or break an ankle without at once falling into the category of patients and being numbered, put into a black- and-yellow uniform and marched or carried off for treatment. Theoretically this system of treatment was universal. In practice neither the uniforms nor the doctors were available. For regulation and militarization were going

on in that period against an immense counter-drive towards social disintegration. The more humanity got into uniform, the shabbier the uniforms became.

Before the Polish struggle, general architecture was very little affected by military needs. The militarization of costume preceded the militarization of scenery. Even barracks and such-like army buildings were erected by army architects as a simple vulgarization of ordinary housing patterns, a mere stiffening up, so to speak, of the common "jerry-built" house. There still survive for our astonishment pictures of Victorian Military Gothic and Victorian Military Tudor, produced under the British War Office. They display homes fit for drill-sergeants. The military mind had to be roused by the experiences of the Polish conflict to the profound reconstruction of the ordinary town that had become necessary if it was still to be taken seriously. Before then, fortification scarcely affected the urban scene at all, even in the case of a fortified town. Previously a fortress had been just an ordinary civil town surrounded at distances of from three to fifty miles by forts, strong points, trench systems and the like. Now it was realized, first in Berlin, and then in Danzig, Warsaw, Paris and Turin, and after that by the whole world, that air warfare demanded not merely fortification round a town, but much more imperatively, fortification OVER a town. The world, which had been far too stupid to realize in 1930 that the direct way out of its economic difficulties lay in the modernization and rebuilding of its houses, set itself, in a state of war panic after 1942, to as complete a revision of its architecture in the face of bombs and gas as its deepening impoverishment permitted. What it would not do for prosperity, it attempted belatedly out of fear.

The first most obvious undertaking was the construction of those immense usually ill-built concrete cavern systems for refuge, whose vestiges are still to be visited by the curious tourist at Paris and Berlin (the London ones have all fallen in, the collapse beginning after the great landslip and fire), and close upon this came the cessation of tall building and the concentration of design upon the vast (and often dangerous) carapace roof and its gigantic supporting pillars and foundation rafts. Only the ever-deepening poverty, the increasing industrial disorganization and the transitoriness of that last war- phase saved all the towns in the world from being thrust completely under such squat massive coverings.

So strong were the influences of that time that even up to 2020 the tendency of architectural design was to crouch. Hardly any mass of buildings erected between 1945 and the end of the century lifts up its head and looks the world in the face. That period has been called, not unjustly, Second Egyptian. And this was so in spite of the multiplying opportunities for grace and lightness afforded by the supersession of steel frame buildings by the strong and flexible neo-concrete materials that were already available. How timidly they were used! We grovel no longer because we are ceasing to fear each other. The soaring, ever improving homes in which we live to-day would have sent our great- grandfathers scurrying to their cellars in an ecstasy of terror.

7. THE GREAT WAR OF 1914-1918

There is a monstrous tedious accumulation of records concerned with the World War. The Catalogue of Historical Material stored at Atacama gives a list of 2,362,705 books and gross files, up to date, and of these over 182,000 deal exclusively or largely with the causation of the war. Nothing could bring home to the student the profound difference in mental equipment between ourselves and the men and women of that period than a visit to the long silent galleries of that great library of dead disputes and almost completely forgotten records. He will see hardly a visitor along the vistas of that shining framework of shelves; a quiet cleaner or duster perhaps will be visible, scrutinizing the condition of the material, or a young revisionist student patiently checking some current summary—or a black cat. For the rest, above, below, to right and left is a clean and luminous stillness; papers at rest.

In one large section of this sere honeycomb the student will find the records of the "war guilt controversy" that agitated the world for decades after the Peace of Versailles. Let him draw out a seat anywhere and take down a file or so at hazard and turn over its pages. He will be able to read almost all of it nowadays, whatever the original language, because practically all the collection has now been interleaved with translations into Basic English. And it will seem to him that he is reading the outpourings of lunatics, so completely have the universal obsessions of that time been exorcized since.

Had "Germany" planned the war? Was "France" the guilty party? Had "Britain" much to answer for? With difficulty will the student let down his mind into the fantastic world of extinct imaginations in which these strange personifications, as monstrous and incredible as the ancient gods of India, were treated as real and morally responsible individuals, hated, trusted, feared and loved. The war was, in immediate fact, an aimless and fruitless slaughter upon the altars of these stupendous deities, the wounding and mutilation of perhaps twenty million human beings, and a vast burning-up of material wealth. In the crazy fancy of our ancestors it was a noble and significant struggle. Happily we need not revive their craziness here. The question of "war guilt" was never settled. It ceased to be pursued, it was neglected, it floated away into the absurd, and little but those three hundred feet or so of forgotten books and gross files remain to testify to its vanished importance.

The causation of the struggle was, indeed, perfectly simple. It arose naturally and necessarily from that irregular and disproportionate growth of human appli-

ances as compared with the extension of political and social intelligence we have already described.

The new means of communication and transport, and the new economic life which demanded the products of every zone and soil for its purposes, were necessitating the reorganization of human affairs as a World-State, and since the world was already parcelled up among sixty-odd competing sovereign governments there were only two possible courses open to mankind, either to arrange the coalescence of these governments by treaty and rational arrangements to meet the new need, or to allow a steadily intensified mutual pressure to develop into more or less thinly disguised attempts at world conquest. In the decades before the war the British, French, German, Russian, Japanese and American systems were all, as the word went then, "imperialist"— all, that is, attempting to become World-States on a planet on which obviously there was room only for one single World-State. Nothing of the sort had been apparent when the methods of European statescraft had been devised. These vaster possibilities had yawned open afterwards. The eighteenth and nineteenth centuries were centuries of small restricted wars for limited advantages. In the twentieth century the scale of war expanded beyond any limit and the advantages to be won by it disappeared. But the politicians and diplomatists played their time-honoured game against each other with a sort of terrified inevitability. They were driven; they had no control, or at least none of them seemed to have had the vigour and imagination to attempt a control. They were driven by the economic necessity we have explained in the previous section. They had to arm preposterously. They had to threaten. They had to go through with the business.

These forces account for the outbreak and universality of the Great War, but they do not account for its peculiar frightfulness. For that it is necessary to realize that though governments expanded only against an enormous pressure of mutual restraint, no limitations had been set to the hypertrophy of financial and industrial enterprises. These last were under the sway of a relentless and unrestrained progress; they expanded, invented, urged and sold; they brought weapons of a strange and terrible effectiveness to the settlement of what were in comparison small and antiquated disputes. To that hypertrophy of the armourer we will return presently, because the Great War was really only a first revelation of this particular disproportion between economics and politics, and the evil still went on in an exaggerated form after the formal conclusion of the struggle at the Peace of Versailles (1919). But let us first tell what needs to be known of the details of the Great War.

How little that is now! There is a vast literature both of fiction based on experience and of personal reminiscence about it, and some of it is admirably written; almost any of it may be read for interest and edification and hardly any of it need be read with scholarly precision. The picture of the outbreak of the war still touches us. There was a curious unconsciousness of the grossness of the menace in events, even on the part of myriads doomed to suffer and die in a few months' time. Many of the stories told begin with a holiday party or a country-house gath-

ering or some such bright setting. The weather that August (1914) was exceptionally fine.

The details of the struggle itself were as horrible and distressing as they were inconsequent, and there is no need whatever for anyone but the specialist to master their sequence in detail. The old-fashioned history, with its lists of names, dates, battles and so on, was designed rather to supply easily marked material for examinations than to give any sense of the historical process. Examinations have long passed out of educational practice; they have gone to join the "globes" and the abacus, the slate and the cane in the scholastic limbo, but their memory is preserved in the popular game of "examination papers", when people write down as fast as they can and as much as they can about some suddenly selected subject.

Few of us could write even a brief account now of the World War. The names of such generals as Haig, Kitchener, French, Joffre, Foch and Ludendorff, to take names at random, and such battles as Tannenberg, the Marne, the Somme, Paschendaele, the Falkland Isles, Jutland and so forth, mean nothing and need mean nothing to the ordinary citizen to-day. He does not know whether French was really French or not, nor whether Foch was a Frenchman or a German. He inclines to the latter view. He does not know who won or lost these conflicts and he does not care. He has not even a sporting interest in it. They were not lively fights. Nearly all the commanders concerned had dull and unattractive personalities and the business was altogether too unwieldy for them. Most of their operations were densely stupid, muddled both in conception and execution. One would as soon listen to a child reciting not very accurately and at endless length the deals and tricks of some game of cards it has played, or imagines it has played, as read their memoirs—packed as they too often are with self- exculpation, personal resentments and malice. Faint, faded, immense and far-off tragedies, these struggles that were to have astounded posterity have already gone far towards complete effacement in any but a few specializing minds, are hardly more vivid now in our collective consciousness than the battles of the Peloponnesian War—or the campaigns and conquests of Tamerlane. They had nothing of the primary historical importance and strategic splendour which have restored the gigantic military conceptions of Genghis Khan to an integral place in our ordinary educational curriculum.

For the rodomontade of the conflict the curious cannot do better than glance through the eager narrative of Winston Churchill's World Crisis. There one finds all the stereotyped flourishes and heroisms of nineteenth- century history from the British point of view; the "drama of history" in rich profusion, centred upon one of the most alert personalities in the conflict. He displays a vigorous naïve puerility that still gives his story an atoning charm. He has the insensitiveness of a child of thirteen. His soldiers are toy soldiers and he loves to knock over a whole row of them. He enjoyed the war. He takes himself and all the now forgotten generals and statesmen of the war with a boyish seriousness. He passes grave judgments on their tragic fooleries and distributes compliments and blame, often in the most gracious manner, convinced that he is writing for a meticulously admiring and

envious posterity. They would read, they would marvel. He was the sort of man who believed that when he begot children he created an audience. He was misled by the excitement of his own reading of history. He not only measures for us the enormous gulf between the mentality of his times and our own, but he enables us to bridge that gulf with an amused and forgiving sympathy.

A less attractive spirit displays itself in the memoirs of such figures as Ludendorff, Bülow, Clemenceau, Fisher, Foch, and so through the whole category of war leaders. The war was the supreme event in the lives of most of these men and apparently they were never able to think of anything else afterwards. They had none of the recuperative innocence of Churchill, his terrier-like interest in everything. They all took to writing furiously in their declining years and no other pens could have damned them so completely. They are grown-up and yet underdeveloped persons; as adult as old chimpanzees; they cannot claim Churchill's benefit of schoolboy, and there is a real horror in their wrinkled meannesses and envies, their gross enthusiasms and their sincere bloodthirstiness and hate. Most of their mutual recriminations are too incomprehensible to be of the slightest interest now; spite and twaddle are still spite and twaddle even if drenched with blood. The most accessible sample for the contemporary reader is The Life and Diaries of Field-Marshal Sir Henry Wilson, Bart., G.C.B., D.S.O., a lean, unsightly man of infinite energy, gusto and vanity, who played a very prominent rôle in bringing about and carrying out the catastrophe. It is the latest reprint in the Historical Documents Series; it is richly illustrated and abundantly annotated, and with it are bound up the brilliantly scornful criticisms of Wilson's contemporary, Sir Andrew Macphail, and Stephen Freudheim's more scientific analysis of him as the supreme type of the "soldierly mind".

For the grimmer actualities of the struggle there is a vast and sombre literature. It has been summarized in the last fifteen years by the Historical Bureau in its War Pictures for Posterity by Pen, Pencil and Camera. Everyone should turn over those strange incredible records of endurance, callousness, devotion and insane courage, to learn something of the extremes to which men and women like ourselves can be pushed by the grim forces of social compulsion.

The earlier volumes deal chiefly with the psychology of the more than half civilized citizens of the Atlantic and North European states suddenly precipitated into a maelstrom of destruction. We see the urban crowds demonstrating and cheering in the streets of the capital cities, the floods of youths coming from their work to "join up", the wonder and unimaginative fierceness and heroism of the opening stage. Then come the first contacts, villages in flames, the wild shooting of curious bystanders as spies and guerillas, realizations of horror and a wave of fear, the invaded populations in flight, black crowds with their pitiful impedimenta streaming along darkling roads, going they know not whither. The rifles and machine-guns rattle, the guns thud, and the cheering adventurousness of the advancing armies as they blunder heavily into contact passes into a phase of astounded violence and hardship. The new war was like no war that had ever been before. The French upon their eastern front went forward to the attack with im-

mense élan, in bright uniforms and to the historical inspiration of the "Marseillaise". They were massacred. They lost a third of a million men in three weeks. The Germans poured through Belgium, more than a million strong, to be stopped and stunned with Paris almost within their grasp. The pictures show the smiling landscape of eastern Belgium, France and east Prussia in July 1914, and the same countryside a couple of months later—torn, scored and trenched, defiled with bloody heaps of litter that were once clothed bodies, an anguish of countless thousands of unclean, hungry, exhausted, cruelty-wrung human beings.

These bands of contact, these regions of filthy pain and tumult, spread. Presently there were "war zones" reaching from the North Sea to the Alps and across Eastern Europe, strange regions in which every house was a ruin, every tree a splintered trunk, where millions of crouching men went to and fro in trenches and ditches furtively like rats, and the ragged dead lay unburied. There day and night the superfluous energy of a profiteering economic system, denied all other outlet by its own preconceptions and the rigid historical traditions in which it was blinkered, blew itself away in the incessant concussions of mines, bombs and guns and a continued destruction of human life.

Presently newly invented weapons, hitherto untried, came to extend and intensify the struggle. The aeroplane, and that primitive "navigable" the Zeppelin, carried the war behind the fronts and attacked the civilian population in the cities. We see the explosive and incendiary bombs bursting into the dirty little urban homes of the time, blowing to rags the bed-rid grandmother and the baby in the cradle; we see the panic-stricken crowds seeking the shelter of cellars and excavations and the drainlike railway "tubes" of the time. In the early stages of the air-war only explosives and inflammatory substances were used, but as the struggle progressed the art of using gas bombs developed, and an agonizing suffocation was added to the nocturnal chances of flame and explosion and death among fallen ruins for the non-combatant at home. The submarine, also, was a novelty of the Great War, and a very searching novelty. It was used first to sink fighting ships and then it was turned against all sea-going craft. We have vivid descriptions of the sinking of the Lusitania without warning and the drowning of 1,198 men, women and children. She was, by the standards of the time, a great and luxurious ship, and a sort of symbolism was found by the writers of this period in this sudden descent from light, comfort and confidence into a desperate and hopeless struggle in the waters of the night. All the achievements of nineteenth-century civilization seemed to many to be following in the downward wake of the Lusitania.

Service in these early submarines strained men to the breaking point. They were essentially engines of war, they had all the defects of inventions at an early stage, and none of the security and comfort of the great submarine barges that are used to-day for the Mediterranean and Atlantic Ridge mines and for general deep sea exploration. These, with their beautifully adjusted pressure systems and their limitless vertical range, are calculated rather to mislead than enlighten us as to the capabilities of the primitive submarines of the Great War. The latter were able to

descend safely only to a depth of a hundred metres; below that the pressure became too much for them and their plates gave and leaked. When they leaked the salt water was apt to affect the accumulators and chlorine gas was released to torment and suffocate the crews. Below a hundred and fifty metres these fragile contrivances crumpled up altogether and were destroyed. The air in them became foul when they submerged, in spite of the compressed oxygen they carried, and the continual condensation of exhaled moisture gave them a peculiar clammy discomfort. They could move about under water for a couple of days by means of their electric batteries, but then it was necessary to come to the surface and run their oil combustion engines for some hours to recharge. Armed with guns and packed with mines, bombs, torpedoes and other explosives, they set out to harass and destroy the surface shipping of the enemy.

It was a difficult and almost fantastically dangerous task. Submerged, they were invisible, but also they were blind. Near the surface they could get a limited view of what was going on by means of a periscope. On the surface they had the range of outlook of any other surface boat, but at all the risks a surface boat must take. So under conditions of extreme discomfort and partial asphyxiation the crews of these strangely formidable and strangely fragile contrivances groped their way towards their victims. To see the quarry fairly they had to come to the surface, and that exposed them to gunfire. If their thin steel skins were pierced by a single shot they could no longer go under. Often when submerged they betrayed their whereabouts unwittingly by bubbles of gas and escapes of oil.

At first, in spite of their limitations, the submarines proved a very deadly weapon, more particularly in the hands of the Central European Powers. They destroyed a great multitude of ships and drowned many score thousands of men. Then slowly the methods used against them improved. They were hunted by a special flotilla, and among other ships by the "Q" boats, armed vessels disguised as harmless merchantmen. These lured them to the surface and then let down sham bulwarks and opened fire upon them, so that after a time they no longer dared emerge to challenge even the most harmless-looking craft. Explosive mines were moored in their possible tracks and mine-armed nets set across harbours and channels. They were also watched for by aeroplanes and special airships whose signals guided the destroyers to their quarry. Ingenious listening contrivances were invented to locate them. They were shot at on the surface, rammed, and pursued by "depth charges" which could strain their plates and disable them even when exploded scores of metres away.

Such, briefly, were the conditions of submarine warfare in the years 1917- 18. And yet to the very end of the war men could be found to carry it on, to destroy and drown and be in their turn hunted and destroyed. The building and launching of submersibles never ceased. Men went down in them to chilly confinement, to the perpetual anxiety of mine or ram, to the quivering menace of the distant depth charge, to the reasonable probability of a frightful death beyond all human aid. Few submarines returned to harbour ten times; many went out new upon their first voyage never to return. Two hundred of them were lost by the Germans alone;

each loss a tragedy of anguish and dismay in the deeps. Towards the end it was claimed by their antagonists that the crews were losing morale. Once or twice an undamaged submarine that had been cornered surrendered, and the new commanders showed a growing tendency to return to port for minor repairs or other slight pretexts. But on the whole, such is the unimaginative heroic submissiveness of our species, the service was sustained. The Germans supplied most of the flesh for this particular altar; willing and disciplined, their youngsters saluted and carried their kit down the ladder into this gently swaying clumsy murder mechanism which was destined to become their coffin.

Their obedience brings us to one of the most fundamental lessons that the Great War has for us: the extreme slowness with which the realization of even the most obvious new conditions pierces through the swathings of habitual acceptance. Millions of human beings went open-eyed to servitude, bullying, hardship, suffering and slaughter, without a murmur, with a sort of fatalistic pride. In obedience to the dictates of the blindest prejudices and the most fatuous loyalties they did their utmost to kill men against whom they had no conceivable grievance, and they were in their turn butchered gallantly, fighting to the last. The War Pictures volumes dismay our imaginations by portraying a series of wholesale butcheries, many of them on a stupendous scale, of men who died facing their enemies. After the great slaughter of the French at the outset of the war, and a mighty killing of Russians at the Battles of Tannenberg and the Masurian Lakes, there was during what was called the deadlock period, the period of trench warfare, a diminution of the losses upon the West. Hostilities sank down to a gusty conflict of shell-fire, rifle assassinations, and raids with bombs and bludgeons. In the East, however, the Russians ran out of ammunition, and held their trenches only by a great martyrdom of men; they lost well over a million before the end of 1914, and yet they continued to obey orders. A series of minor campaigns broke out in regions remote from the main centres of contact. There is a horrible account in the Pictures of the sufferings of some thousands of British common soldiers taken prisoners at Kut, in Mesopotamia. (Their generals and other officers, however, who had arranged that particular capitulation, were honourably and comfortably entertained by their captors the Turks.) There is no effective expression of resentment by the British troops on record.

In 1916 and 1917 there were spasmodic renewals of hostilities on a large scale by the British and French in France. Newly trained British armies were made to advance in close formation by generals who, unless they were imbeciles, could have had no doubts of the fate to which they were sending their men. If they were not imbeciles then they were criminally unwilling to learn and soul- blind to suffering and waste. The mentality of these men is still a matter for discussion. The poor boys they commanded were marched forward shoulder to shoulder in successive waves of attack, and so advancing they were shot to pieces by the enemy machine-guns. Out of battalions of six or seven hundred, perhaps a hundred would struggle through the defensive fire and come to bomb- throwing, bayonet-thrusts and surrender in the German trenches. Small isolated groups of them in

shell-holes and captured positions fought on for days. So perished the flower of an entire school generation, collected from hundreds of thousands of homes, more or less loved, more or less cared for and more or less educated; it had been enlisted, trained, sent out to the battlefields at enormous cost, to be left at last in the desolated spaces between the armies, lying in heaps and swathes to rot and be rat-eaten. For months afterwards, as the photographs show, thousands of them were to be seen sprawling in formation as they fell, just as if their ranks were still waiting to leap again to the attack. But as the observer drew nearer he realized their corruption. He discovered bony hands, eyeless sockets, faces far gone in decay.

The British commander-in-chief in his despatches did not fail to extol the courage of his lost battalions and to represent this monstrous exploit as a victory. Some mile or so of ground had been gained in that July offensive and less than 12,000 prisoners had been taken. Twice as many British were left prisoners in German hands, but this the despatches ignored.

The appalling nature of this particular disaster leaked out only very slowly. The British censorship at least was efficient and the generals, however incapable in other respects, lied magnificently. The Channel crossing made it particularly easy to hide events from the British public. And it had a peculiar effect on the British troops; it gave them a feeling of being in another and a different world from "home", a war-world in which such cruel and fantastic things could be natural. This monstrous massacre was, indeed, contrived and carried through, not simply without a revolt, but with scarcely an audible protest on the part of either the parents, relations, friends or surviving comrades of those hosts of wasted victims.

The commanders of the Russian armies in Austria, Armenia and elsewhere were announcing equally costly and heroic triumphs and the Germans and Austrians were issuing the most valiant and excessive contradictions of their claims. They, too, were losing hideously enough, though in a lesser proportion than their opponents. The next year (1917), the British, gallant and docile as ever, with only very slightly improved tactics, were going again into great offensives.

But now the French troops began to manifest a livelier intelligence. They were amidst familiar things, nearer their homes and less cut off from subversive influences than the British. A certain General Nivelle, at that time French Commander-in-Chief, made what Churchill calls an "experiment", which resulted altogether in the loss of nearly a couple of hundred thousand men. It involved the advance of masses of infantry into intense fields of fire. In an hour, said Lieutenant Ybarnegaray (in a debate in the French Chamber, June 1917), they were reduced to a crowd "running like madmen", all formations and distinctions lost. Provision had been made for less than 15,000 wounded. There were seven times as many. Most of the casualties never received the most elementary attention for three days. The result was gangrene, amputation and death for thousands. Then came the first intimation that there were limits to human obedience. A French division ordered into action to continue this futile holocaust refused to march. Churchill says this was "deeply disquieting" to the authorities, and no doubt it

pained and distressed every intelligent amateur of war. This particular division was cajoled into a change of mind. It took part in the fighting, says Churchill, "without discredit", but the spirit of its resistance spread.

The next sign of sanity in this world torture was the collapse of the grotesque Russian autocracy. We have already told of the mental and moral decay of the Tzardom in our general study of the degeneration of monarchy. [Non inventus.—ED.] Abruptly this profoundly rotten government collapsed into nothing; its vast domains became a various disorder, and for some months phantom imitations of Western revolutionaries, inspired by memories of the first French revolution or by legends of British parliamentary wisdom, occupied the capital. The one certain fact in the situation was the accumulated disinclination of the Russian people for any further warfare. But this first republican government under an eloquent lawyer politician, of no great directive force, Alexandre Kerensky, was unable either to carry on the war or to end it. A subdued but spreading clamour for "peace by negotiation" in all the combatant countries ensued, a clamour that active repression and the most rigorous concealment in the Press failed to silence. There was an attempt to call a sort of peace conference of Radicals at Stockholm, and then a second revolution in Russia which carried a small and resolute Communist organization to power—carried it to power simply and solely because there was no other organized alternative, and because it promised peace plainly and surely—peace on any terms. The Russian armies melted away at its signal; the men streamed home. The German military authorities in the East found the trenches before them undefended, and with every courtesy of war, as one soldier to another, welcomed the Russian officers of the old régime, taking refuge from the belated resentment of their own men.

In 1917 mankind seemed already to be awakening from the war-nightmare. Mutinies broke out in sixteen separate French army corps, 115 regiments were involved, divisions elected soldiers' councils and whole regiments set out for Paris to demand a reasonable wind-up of the struggle. The one last hope of the despairing soldiers, said Pierre Laval, had been Stockholm. That disappointment had made life unbearable. But the storm abated with the entry of the United States of America into the war, and the powers in control of the Western World were still able to pursue their dreadful obsessions for another year.

War Pictures for Posterity by Pen, Pencil and Camera devotes a whole volume (xxi) to the tragedy of a special Russian infantry corps in France. Fifteen thousand Russians had been sent thither in 1916 to be equipped and armed and put into the line with the French armies. Many of these poor lads scarcely knew the difference between a Frenchman and a German, and the ostensible objects of the war were quite beyond their understanding. But they heard of the revolution in their own country and they resolved to consider their attitude with regard to it. They elected representatives and put it to the vote whether they should continue to fight, which meant for them to take part in that "experiment" of Nivelle's known to be in preparation at the time. They chose what seemed to them the generous part and went into the battle. The French command used them ruthlessly, and nearly 6,000 were

killed or wounded. The rest came out of the line and mutinied. They would fight no more. Thereupon these defenceless men were surrounded by trustworthy French troops, a great concentration of guns was assembled, fire was opened upon them suddenly and they were massacred. Horrible photographs of the details of this—photographs hidden away at the time from the authorities and brought to light later—are given in the summary already cited.

For nearly a year the French lost confidence in the morale of their own men and dared make no more great attacks, but their allies offered up another 400,000 men in the battle of Paschendaele and accounted for 300,000 Germans, and in the spring the Germans made a vast multitudinous attack in the West which succeeded at first and then collapsed, whereupon their antagonists, reinforced by new armies from America, waded back through blood to a dreadful final victory. The last nine months of the conflict saw more slaughter than any preceding year. From March 21st, 1918, to November 11th in the same year the British suffered 830,000 casualties, the French and Belgians 964,000 and the Germans 1,470,000. There were also 2,000,000 American troops brought to Europe before the end, and of these more than half were actually engaged in the fighting. Their casualties were certainly not less than 350,000. Portuguese and other contingents from the most unexpected quarters also contributed to that culminating death-roll, but it is impossible for us now to give exact numbers for these minor forces.

These are the gross figures of warfare. But War Pictures devotes three volumes, perhaps the most horrible of all, to the presentation of various details of the fighting in which these vast multitudes suffered and perished. These three volumes are like the microscopic slides in a specimen book of anatomy, which show us from a selected scrap of tissue the texture of the whole. Little figures stand out enlarged, chosen by the hazard that they wrote or talked or carried a camera, to represent the nameless millions who have left no record. We have accounts of men who were left to lie out for days between the lines, tortured by thirst and stifled by the stench of their own corruption, and yet who survived to tell the tale. We have the stories of men who fell into heaps of rotting dead, and lay there choking, and of men who were gassed. The tortures of gas were already many and various, and most of the mixtures then used left tormenting weaknesses in the system for the rest of life. We have descriptions of the rude surgery of the time and abstracts of the mental disorders through which minds fled from reality. There are also some dreadful pictures of mutilated men, faceless, crippled, grotesquely distorted, and an autobiography of one of the blinded (Outstaying My Welcome, by Fritz Schiff, 1923). Scores of thousands of unhappy fragments of humanity had to be hidden away in special institutions until they died, they were at once so terrifying and so pitiful and hopeless. The world forgot them even while they lived.

The distortion of souls was even more dreadful than the distortion of bodies. One of the most lurid items in that dreadful assemblage of realities is a lecture on the use of the bayonet, which chanced to be printed, reprinted later by anti-war propagandists and so preserved for us, delivered by a certain Sergeant-Major Franklin to some English cadets in London. To us he is incredible in his ferocity;

we are almost forced to believe he was drunk or mad, until we realize from the "laughter" that punctuated his utterances, from the hearty thanks of his commanding officer, and the "three cheers" which rewarded him at the conclusion of his discourse, that he was merely expressing the spirit of war service as it was then understood.

"If you see a wounded German," he said, "shove him out and have no nonsense about it."

He was all against taking prisoners—and for murdering them after surrender. He told with sympathy and approval of how a corporal under him butchered a group of German boys. "Can I do these blokes in, sir?" asked the corporal, pointing to a bunch of disarmed enemies.

"Please yourself," said the sergeant-major....

When they had been "done in", the honest corporal, a released convict from Dartmoor prison, came back to the sergeant-major very gratified and honoured, and, still in favour, discussed the technical difficulties of withdrawing a bayonet quickly in order to be ready for the "next fellow".

That was, that is, the spirit to which war brings a human being. Sergeant- Major Franklin had his abundant equivalents in every army engaged. We are able to quote an English document, freely published. Participants in many other countries had less freedom. On the whole the English were as gentle as any other soldiers. But fear and bloodlust, it is plain, wipe out all the slowly acquired restraints and tolerance of social order very quickly and completely from any breed of men. History must not be written in pink and gilt. Prisoners and wounded were not simply neglected and ill-treated and "shoved out". Many were actually tortured to death—either by way of reprisals or in sheer wanton cruelty. There is also a series of photographs of foully mutilated bodies, mutilated and indecently displayed while they were dying or immediately after they were dead. Those millions marched indeed right out of civilization, right out of any sort of human life as we know it to-day, marched down to something viler than mere bestiality, when they marched into the war zone.

After the summer of 1918, which brought with it the certainty of ultimate defeat, the combatant energy of Germany evaporated. Everywhere there was distress and hunger due to a rigorous blockade. The discipline of the land relaxed; the country behind the front was infested by stragglers; the Higher German Command found itself now, like its antagonists, unable to rely upon the men to advance, found itself unable to rely upon their resistance to an enemy attack. They became eager to surrender—taking the off-chance of meeting experimental corporals from Dartmoor on the way.

Wherever there was still loyalty and obedience, however, men were still callously sacrificed by the Higher Command. War Pictures (vol. xxvii, 23842 et seq,) show the German machine-gunners in their pits, on the defensive against advancing British and American troops. These men allowed themselves to be drugged and chained to their weapons, and so continued to fire and kill until the attack came up to them. Then they found small mercy. They were bayoneted or

their brains were beaten out. They paid for the inventions of their masters. They paid for the hatred of Germany the introduction of poison gas had evoked in every attacking army. Such residues of senseless devotion availed nothing against the massive pressures that were at last exhausting Germany. In November the Kaiser, the War Lord, was in flight; a humiliating Armistice had been concluded and the German armies were streaming home in disorder, incoherently revolutionary.

Upon that phrase, "incoherently revolutionary", our account of the main war may very well end. Here we will only allude to the defeat and demoralization of the Italian armies after the battle of Caporetto, when 800,000 were either killed, wounded, taken prisoner, or (sensible fellows) "went home". Nor will we describe the naval battles, of which the chief and last was Jutland. It was the last, because afterwards the German admirals were faced by the threat of mutiny if they essayed another fight. Whether it was or was not a victory for the British was never exactly determined. The controversy died out during the Polish wars.

The War Pictures volumes give many photographs and accounts of these naval encounters. We have, for example, a whole series of snapshots of a British cruiser in the Battle of Jutland, the Defence steaming at full-speed- ahead to attack and finish up a smashed and sinking German battleship, the Wiesbaden. The onrush of that fierce mechanism is terrific. It seems invincible and overpowering. It has an undeniable splendour. Then suddenly a series of blinding flashes show the Defence has been hit by the fire of some other German battleship coming to the help of her sister ship, and in a moment she has blown up and gone; she is no more than a mounting unfolding column of smoke and flying fragments, including, we realize with an effort, the torn and scalded bodies of eight hundred men. Then a welter of littered tumbled water....

There is no end to the multitude of such pictures.

But let us return to our phrase "incoherently revolutionary". That is the key to the whole human situation at that time. The distaste for the war throughout the world was enormous, if not in its opening phases, then certainly before the second year was reached. It bored; it disgusted. Its events had none of the smashing decisiveness that seizes the imagination. Even the great naval battle of Jutland was, from the point of view of spectacle, a complete failure. None the less, for a very simple reason a comparatively small minority of resolutely belligerent persons was able to keep this vast misery going. On the one hand the war was in accordance with the ruling ideas of the time, while on the other the hundreds of millions whose astonishment and dismay deepened daily, as horror unfolded beyond horror, had no conception of any alternative pattern of life to which they could turn as a refuge from its relentless sequences.

To cry "End the war" ended nothing, because it gave no intimations of what had to replace belligerent governments in the control of human affairs. The peace the masses craved for was as yet only a featureless negative. But peace must be a positive thing, designed and sustained, for peace is less natural than warfare. We who have at last won through to the Pax Mundi know how strong and resolute, how powerfully equipped and how vigilant, the keepers of the peace must be.

8. THE IMPULSE TO ABOLISH WAR; THE EPISODE OF THE FORD PEACE SHIP

One quaint expedition, grotesque and childish and yet an augury of greater things to come, flits very illuminatingly across the dreadful record of these war years. It is the voyage of a passenger steamship from New York to Norway. The dark curtains of oblivion fall in heavier and heavier folds before the thundering battleships of the twilit Battle of Jutland; their forgotten names sink back into a vague general impression of huge flame-spouting masses that rush through smoke and mist to their fate; only a specialist can tell us now whether the Lützow or the Friedrich der Grosse, the Lion, or the Iron Duke, the Vanguard or the Colossus perished with its complement of men or staggered out of that battle. They have become monstrous irrelevances. There is nothing but their size, and the smashing and drowning of hundreds of men in them, to make them more significant to us now than an exploding casket of fireworks. But steaming its way across the Atlantic a few months before Jutland was fought came this other ship, a passenger boat of the Scandinavian-American line, the Oscar II, whose voyage remains to this day important and interesting, because in the most simple and artless fashion it mingled the new conceptions of life that were coming into being, with all the prevalent weaknesses of the time. The Oscar II is better known in history as the Peace Ship of Henry Ford. It is a gleam of tragic comedy amidst the universal horror.

This Henry Ford was a very natural-minded mechanical genius, without much education or social sophistication, a great friend of, and kindred spirit with, that Edison whose career has been traced in the chapter of human history dealing with the development and exploitations of inventions at the close of the nineteenth and the beginning of the twentieth century. Born and brought up in a period of economic expansion, Ford took economic expansion as if it were a necessity inherent in things, and never began to doubt continual progress until he was a man of over seventy. That was his good fortune. That gave him the confidence to design an automobile as sound and good and cheap as could be done at that time, and to organize the mass production of his pattern with extraordinary energy and skill, because his mind was untroubled by the thought that there could be a limit to the number of possible purchasers. He marketed his "flivver", or "tin lizzie", as it was affectionately called, in enormous quantities, and in consequence he revolutionized the road transport and town planning of America. He changed the shape of every growing town by enabling the small householder to live further from the

work and business centre than had ever been possible before. He did more than any other single man to drive the horse not only from the road but, by making farm tractors, from the fields. He created factories at Dearborn that even to-day seem vast. He became enormously rich and an outstanding "character" in the world, and particularly in America. And he remained curiously simple and direct in his outlook upon life.

The first effect of the Great War upon him, as on a vast proportion of the English-speaking peoples, was incredulous amazement. He had known there were armies and sovereign nations in the world, but apparently he had never supposed they would fight. He felt there must be some mistake. He exchanged views with other Americans in a similar phase of astonishment. By the beginning of 1915 they had accumulated a sufficient mass of evidence from the belligerent countries to convince them that great masses of people in these countries were as amazed and as anxious to end the widening bloodshed and brutalization as the neutral onlookers. There had been deputations to the President (President Wilson), who was at that time, in harmony with his country, highly pacificist, and there was a widespread ambition that the United States should evoke some sort of permanent arbitration council alone, or in concert with the other Powers still neutral, which should stand, so to speak, on the edge of the battlefield and continue to offer its mediatory services to the warring governments until they were accepted. There was the suggestion of a deputation to Europe to further this idea, and the question arose how should it go across the Atlantic. Ford offered to charter a ship to take it.

Then his peculiar imagination seized upon his own offer. He would make this ship a spectacular ship; it should be the "Peace Ship". It should take a complement of chosen delegates to Europe in such a blaze of publicity that at its coming the war would be, as it were, arrested, to look at it. Its mere appearance would recall infuriated Europe to its senses. "I want to get those boys out of the trenches," said Ford. "They don't want to fight, and would be only too glad to shake hands with each other." At the back of his mind there seems to have been an idea of calling a general strike at the fronts. "Out of the trenches by Christmas, never to return again," was his brief speech at a public meeting in Washington in November. All sorts of eminent and energetic people were invited to join the mission. He sought the overt approval of the President, but the President was far too seasoned a politician to squander his publicity upon this "gesture" of Henry Ford's. He was meditating a gesture of his own later on.

American life at that time had its conspicuous popular stars, who embodied its ideals of greatness and goodness. Some of them are still for various reasons remembered by the historian, Jane Addams and Thomas Edison, for example, William Jennings Bryan (the "Last Creationist") and Luther Burbank. These names are still to be found even in the Lower School Encyclopaedia. Ford tried to include them all in one meteoric shipload. The governors of all the states in the Union were also invited, groups of representative university students, and so on. The Historical Collection at Atacama has gathered all the surviving originals or replicas of Ford's invitations, and the replies in which these outstanding individu-

als hesitated over or evaded his proposals. Several were only prevented by sudden attacks of ill-health at the very last moment from joining him. And there was a number of newspaper reporters, cinema operators and other photographers, stenographers, typists, translators, interpreters, baggage masters and publicity agents who made no trouble about coming. A certain Madame Rosika Schwimmer, an Hungarian lady, gleams forth and vanishes again from history as the organizing spirit of this selection. A vast multitude of adventurers and crazy people offered to assist when Ford's project was made public, and many were only prevented with the utmost difficulty from coming aboard the Oscar II.

There is still material for a great writer in the details of that expedition, but our interest here is neither with the expedition as a whole nor with Ford or the other persons concerned in it as personalities, but with this idea that flamed and faded, this idea of 'an appeal against war to human sanity'. And with the vicissitudes of that idea.

The first thing to note is that it evoked response, and a very wide response. Eminent people, both in America and Europe, with their popularity to consider, found it advisable to be sympathetic, even if unhelpful. President Wilson, for example, was sympathetic but unhelpful. All the pretentious weathercocks of the Western World swung round towards it. We have every indication indeed of a very considerable drive towards a world pax in these years. But presently the weathercocks began to waver and swing away.

Why did they waver? From the first there was a sustained, malignant antagonism to the project. This grew in force and vigour. The American Press, and in its wake the European Press, set itself to magnify and distort every weakness, every slight absurdity, in the expedition and to invent further weaknesses and absurdities. A campaign of ridicule began, so skilful and persistent that it stripped away one blushing celebrity after another from the constellation, and smothered the essential sanity of the project in their wilting apologies. While Ford and his surviving missioners discussed and discoursed on their liner, the newspaper men they had brought with them concocted lies and absurd stories about their host—as though they were under instructions.

We know now they were under instructions. The Historical Documents Series makes this perfectly plain.

As our students disentangle strand after strand of that long hidden story, we realize more and more clearly the tortuous dishonesty, the confused double-mindedness, of the times. The export trade of the United States was flourishing under war conditions as it had never flourished before. Munitions of every sort were being sold at enormously enhanced prices to the belligerents. Such great banking houses as Morgan and Co. were facilitating the financial subjugation of Europe to America, through debts for these supplies. It is clear that American finance and American Big Business had not foreseen this. They had no exceptional foresight. But suddenly they found themselves in a position of great advantage, and by all their traditions they were bound to make use of that advantage. And

Ford in his infinite artlessness, "butting in", as they said, "on things that were not his business", was setting out to destroy this favourable state of affairs.

There was just enough plausibility in this endeavour to make it seem dangerous. Ford could not be ignored; his available publicity was too great for that. He was by no means beneath contempt; so he had to be made contemptible. With an earnestness worthy of a better cause, the American Press was launched against him. And it was one of the strange traditions of the American Press that a newsman should have no scruples. The ordinary reporter was a moral invert taking a real pride in his degradation. No expedient was too mean, no lie, no trick too contemptible if only it helped thwart and disillusion Ford.

And they did thwart and disillusion him. They got him wrong with himself. This half-baked man of genius, deserted by his friends, lost confidence in his project. He began to suspect his allies and believe his enemies.

We have to accept the evidence preserved for us, but even with that evidence before us, some of the details of that Press campaign appear incredible. There are a hundred gross files of newspaper cuttings at Atacama, and some of the most amazing are reproduced in the selected Historical Documents. The reporters and writers, who were abroad as Ford's guests, invented and sent home by wireless fantastic reports of free fights among the members of the mission, of disputes among the leaders, of Ford being chained to his bed by his secretary, of mutinies and grotesque happenings. Ford was told of and could have prevented these radio messages being sent—it was his ship for the time being—but a kind of fanaticism for free opinion—even if in practice that meant free lying —restrained him. "Let them do their darnedest," he said, still valiant. "Our work will speak for itself."

But presently he caught the influenza, a lowering disease long since extinct but very rife in that period and, under clumsy medical attention of the day, he arrived in Europe deflated and tired, physically and morally, prepared now to believe that there was something essentially foolish in the whole affair. He had been drenched in ridicule beyond his powers of resistance, and he was giving way. He gave way.

"Guess I had better go home to mother," said Mr. Ford, sick in bed in Christiania, and kept to his room, though all Norway was agog to greet and cheer him.

But his movement went on by the inertia it had gained. His delegation was received with great enthusiasm in Norway and subsequently in Sweden, Switzerland, Denmark and Holland, those small sovereign European states which contrived so dexterously to keep out of the conflict to the end. People in those countries were evidently only too eager to believe that this novel intervention might help to end the war. If Ford was discouraged, some of his associates were of more persistent material. They held great public meetings in Sweden, Holland and Switzerland, and the repercussion of their activities certainly had a heartening effect on the peace movement in Germany and Britain. They contrived to get speech with a number of politicians and statesmen, and they roused the watchful hostility of the German and British War authorities— for the military chiefs of both sides regarded this mission very properly as an attack on war morale. A Neutral Conference for Continuous Mediation came into being—very precarious

being—in Stockholm. It is claimed that it checked a movement to bring Sweden into the war on the side of the Germans.

Then gradually the Ford Organization for Peace lost prominence. It was overshadowed by greater movements towards negotiation, and more particularly by the large uncertain gestures of President Wilson, who, re-elected as "the man who kept the United States out of the war," brought his people from a phase of hypocritical pacificism and energetic armament into the war in 1917. Before that culmination the Peace Ship bladder had collapsed altogether. Its last typist and photographer and clerk had been paid off, and Ford himself was already doing all that was humanly possible to draw a blanket of oblivion over that unforgettable Peace Ship. But the records have been too much for him.

He had not led his expeditionary force in Europe, even nominally, for more than five weeks. He had kept to his Norwegian hotel, avoided his more enthusiastic associates, started a vigorous reduction of his financial commitments, and finally bolted home. He deserted. He left his hotel at Christiania, stealthily, at five o'clock in the morning, and, in spite of the pleadings of those of his party who, warned at the last minute, tumbled out of bed to protest, he got away. Before the year was out he had ceased even financial support, and the various men and women who had abandoned careers and positions and faced ridicule and odium in complete faith in his simplicity were left to find their way back to their former niches or discover fresh ones.

Now what had happened to his great idea? What strange reversal of motive had occurred in the brain and heart of this Peace Crusader? There the curious historian must needs speculate, for that brain and heart have gone now beyond all closer scrutiny.

It has to be noted first that while the Peace Ship was on the Atlantic something very significant was going on at Washington. The swiftly growing munition industries of America had discovered that a home market for their products, a home market of superior solvency, might be added to the vast demands of the fighting nations overseas. America, it was argued, might keep out of the war—well and good—but nevertheless America must be "prepared." The United States must arm. The President had weighed this proposal with a due regard for the votes and Press support that would come to him at the next election; he had weighed it very carefully as became a politician, and after some resistance he consented that America should be "prepared". Munitions should be assembled, troops should be drilled. Flags began to wave—and the United States flag was a very intoxicating one—and drums and trumpets to sound. Military excitement stirred through that vast pacific population and rose.

And Ford had a mighty industrial plant hitherto engaged in pouring out motorcars and agricultural material, but capable of rapid adaptation to the production of war material. It was his creation; it was his embodiment. It was all that made him visibly different from any other fellow in the street. His friends and family had certainly watched his abandonment of business for world affairs with profound misgiving. It may have been plain to them before it was plain to him, that if he

stood out of this "preparedness" movement as he threatened to do, other great plants would arise beside his own, to produce war material indeed at first, but capable when the war was over of a reverse transformation into great factories for the mass production of motorcars and the like. In France this transference from munitions to automobiles was actually foreseen and carried out by the Citröen organization. It is impossible that this prospect could have escaped Ford.

But in his haste he had declared himself against preparedness. He had threatened to hoist an "international flag" over his works in the place of the Stars and Stripes....

It is clear that in that one lively brain all the main forces of the time were at work. It had responded vividly and generously to the new drive towards a world-pax. Lochner (America's Don Quixote, 1924) reports him thus on his sailing from New York:

"Have you any last word to say?" a journalist enquired.

"Yes," he replied. "Tell the people to cry peace and fight preparedness."

"What if this expedition fails?" ventured another.

"If this expedition fails I'll start another," he flashed without a moment's hesitation.

"People say you are not sincere," commented a third....

"We've got peace-talk going now, and I'll pound it to the end."

And afterwards came those second thoughts. When, in 1917, the United States entered the war, the Peace Ship was a stale old joke and the vast Ford establishments were prepared and ready for the production of munitions.

Ford was a compendium of his age. That is why we give him this prominence in our history. The common man of the twentieth century was neither a pacifist nor a war-monger. He was both—and Ford was just a common man made big by accident and exceptional energy.

The main thread in the history of the twentieth century is essentially the drama of the indecisions manifested in their elementary plainness by Ford on board his Peace Ship. That voyage comes therefore like a tin-whistle solo by way of overture, to the complex orchestration of human motive in the great struggle for human unity that lay ahead.

9. THE DIRECT ACTION OF THE ARMAMENT INDUSTRIES IN MAINTAINING WAR STRESSES

We must now say something about the direct activities of the hypertrophied "armament firms" in bringing about and sustaining the massacres of the Great War. A proper understanding of that influence is essential if the stresses and martyrdoms of the middle years of the twentieth century are to be understood.

These "armament firms" were an outcome of the iron and steel industry, which in a few score years between 1700 and 1850 grew up—no man objecting—from a modest activity of artisans to relatively gigantic possibilities of production. This industry covered the world with a network of railways, and produced iron and then steel steamships to drive the wooden sailing ships off the seas. And at an early stage (all this is traced in full detail in Luke Zimmern's Entwickelung und Geschichte von Kruppismus, 1913; Hist. Doc. 394112) it turned its attention to the weapons in the world.

In a perpetual progress in the size and range of great guns, in a vast expansion of battleships that were continually scrapped in favour of larger or more elaborate models, it found a most important and inexhaustible field of profit. The governments of the world were taken unawares, and in a little while the industry, by sound and accepted methods of salesmanship, was able to impose its novelties upon these ancient institutions with their tradition of implacable mutual antagonism. It was realized very soon that any decay of patriotism and loyalty would be inimical to this great system of profits, and the selling branch of the industry either bought directly or contrived to control most of the great newspapers of the time, and exercised a watchful vigilance on the teaching of belligerence in schools. Following the established rules and usages for a marketing industrialism, and with little thought of any consequences but profits, the directors of these huge concerns built up the new warfare that found its first exposition in the Great War of 1914-18, and gave its last desperate and frightful convulsions in the Polish wars of 1940 and the subsequent decades.

Even at its outset in 1914-18 this new warfare was extraordinarily uncongenial to humanity. It did not even satisfy man's normal combative instincts. What an angry man wants to do is to beat and bash another living being, not to be shot at from ten miles distance or poisoned in a hole. Instead of drinking delight of battle with their peers, men tasted all the indiscriminating terror of an earthquake. The war literature stored at Atacama, to which we have already referred, is full of futile protest against the horror, the unsportsmanlike quality, the casual filthiness

and indecency, the mechanical disregard of human dignity of the new tactics. But such protest itself was necessarily futile, because it did not go on to a clear indictment of the forces that were making, sustaining and distorting war. The child howled and wept and they did not even attempt to see what it was had tormented it.

To us nowadays it seems insane that profit-making individuals and companies should have been allowed to manufacture weapons and sell the apparatus of murder to all comers. But to the man of the late nineteenth and early twentieth centuries it seemed the most natural thing in the world. It had grown up in an entirely logical and necessary way, without any restraint upon the normal marketing methods of peace-time commerce, from the continually more extensive application of new industrial products to warfare. Even after the World War catastrophe, after that complete demonstration of the futility of war, men still allowed themselves to be herded like sheep into the barracks, to be trained to consume, and be consumed, by new lines of slaughter goods produced and marketed by the still active armament traders. And the accumulation of a still greater and still more dangerous mass of war material continued.

There is a queer little pseudo-scientific essay by a Bengali satirist (Professor K. Chondra Sen, 1897-1942) among the India series of reprints, professing to be a study of the relative stupidity of the more intelligent animals up to and including man. He is concerned by the fatuity with which the mass of humanity watched the preparation of its own destruction during this period. He considers the fate of various species of penguins which were then being swept out of the world—the twentieth century was an age of extermination for hundreds of species—and infers a similar destiny for mankind. He begins with the slaughter of the penguins; he gives photographs of these extraordinary creatures in their multitudes, gathered on the beaches of Oceanic islands and watching the advance of their slayers. One sees them scattered over a long sloping shore, standing still, or waddling about or flapping their stumpy wings while the massacre goes on. They seem to be vaguely interested in the killing of their fellows, but in no way stirred either to flight or resistance. (No thorough scientific observations, we may note, were ever made of penguin mentality, the revival of experimental psychology comes too late for that, and we are left now to guess at what went on in these queer brains of theirs during these raids. There is evidence to show that these creatures had curiosity, kindliness, sympathy and humour; and they were eminently teachable. They stood quite high in the scale of bird intelligence. And yet they permitted their own extinction.) They were not so much a-mental, Professor Sen insists, half seriously, half mockingly, as defective and wrong. They were capable of many idea systems but not of the idea of social preservation. He suggests, too, that the same was true of the sea elephants which were also very rapidly destroyed. (The last of these were murdered later "to make a record" by a Japanese lunatic with a craving for an "immortal Name" when the protective patrol was withdrawn during the "revolt of the sea pirates" in C.E. 1985.) But after Professor Sen has weighed every possible case, he still awards the palm for complaisant social stupidity to man.

With a fine parody of the social research methods of that time, he gives various photographs of what he calls the "human penguins" of that early Twentieth Century, waddling in their sleek thousands to see battleships launched, to rejoice over reviews and parades, to watch their army aeroplanes stunting in the sky. Side by side he gives photographs of penguin assemblies that, either by happy accident or skilful rearrangement, are absurdly parallel. He gives lists of shareholders in the armament firms, including the current Bishop of Hereford, the current President of the Free Church Council, a great multitude of clergymen, artists, judges and every sort of gentlefolk. He quotes extensively from the Hansard records of various debates in the British House of Commons (in a debate on the Naval Estimates early in 1914, Philip Snowden, the radical socialist who afterwards became Viscount Snowden, was particularly explicit), showing that the nature of the danger was clearly seen and clearly and publicly stated. Only it was not FELT. It is upon that little difference between factual apprehension and the kind of apprehension that leads to effective action that our interest concentrates here.

Why did humanity gape at the guns and do nothing? And why, after the Great War, after that generation had seen over twenty million human beings perish painfully and untimely did it still go on, doing nothing adequate to the occasion? With the preparations still mounting up and the horrible possibilities of war increasing under its eyes? The great Cradle of Bethlehem Steel Corporation of America in 1929 was revealed as actively opposing naval disarmament at the Geneva Conference of 1927. At any rate it was associated with three shipbuilding companies who were sued by a Mr. Shearer, who claimed to have been given that task, for fees alleged to be due to him. There seems to have been little dispute that he had been so employed; the case turned upon the extent of his services and the amount of his fees. Nothing was done by the penguins either to the companies concerned or to Mr. Shearer. A few expressed indignation; that was all. Just as now and then no doubt a bird or so squawked at the oil hunters. For a detailed account and references see The Navy: Defence or Portent by C. A. Beard, 1930, reprinted Hist. Doc. Series 4,270,112.

The clue lies in the fact that there was practically no philosophical education at all in the world, no intelligent criticism of generalizations and general ideas. There was no science of social processes at all. People were not trained to remark the correlations of things; for the most part they were not aware that there was any correlation between things; they imagined this side of life might change and that remain unaltered. The industrialists and financiers built up these monstrous armaments and imposed them on the governments of the time, with a disregard of consequences that seems now absolutely imbecile. Most of these armament propagandists were admirable in their private lives: gentle lovers, excellent husbands, fond of children and animals, good fellows, courteous to inferiors, and so on. Sir Basil Zaharoff, the greatest of munition salesmen, as one sees him in the painting (ascribed to Orpen) recently discovered in Paris, with his three-cornered hat, his neat little moustaches and beardlet, and the ribbon of some Order of Chivalry about his neck, looks quite a nice, if faintly absurd, little gentleman. Those share-

holding bishops and clergy may, for anything we know to the contrary, have had charming personalities. But they wanted their dividends. And in order to pay them those dividends, the dread of war and the need of war had to be kept alive in the public mind.

That was done most conveniently through the Press. You could buy a big newspaper in those days, lock, stock and barrel, for five or ten million dollars, and the profits made on one single battleship came to more than that. Naturally, and according to the best business traditions, the newspapers hired or sold themselves to the war salesmen. What was wrong in that? Telling the news in those days was a trade, not a public duty. A daily paper that had dealt faithfully with this accumulating danger would quite as naturally and necessarily have found its distribution impeded, have found itself vigorously outdone by more richly endowed competitors, able because of their wealth to buy up all the most attractive features, able to outdo it in every way with the common reader.

It wasn't that the newspaper owners and the munition dealers wanted anyone hurt. They only wanted to sell equipment and see it used up. Nor was it that the newspapers desired the wholesale mangling and butchering of human beings. They wanted sales and advertisements. The butchery was quite by the way, an unfortunate side issue to legitimate business. Shortsightedness is not diabolical, even if it produces diabolical results.

And even those soldiers? Freudheim, in his analysis of the soldierly mind, shows a picture of that Sir Henry Wilson we have already mentioned, arrayed in shirt-sleeves and digging modestly in the garden of his villa during a phase of retirement, and the same individual smirking in all his glory, buttons, straps and "decorations", as a director of military operations. It is an amazing leap from the suburban insignificance of a retired clerk to godlike importance. In peace time, on the evidence of his own diaries, this Wilson was a tiresome nobody, an opinionated bore; in war he passed beyond criticism and became a god. One understands at once what a vital matter employment and promotion must have been to him. But so far as we can tell he desired no killing AS killing. If he had been given blood to drink he would probably have been sick. Yet he lived upon tanks of blood.

These professional soldiers thought of slaughter as little as possible. It is preposterous to say they desired it, much less that they gloated over it. It might have fared better with their men if they had thought of it more. They had an age-old sentimental devotion to their country, a solemn sense of great personal worth in their services, an orgiastic delight of battle. And they did not see, nor want to see, what was beyond their occupation. Their religious teachers were quite ready to assure them they were correct in all they did and were.

The senescent Christian Churches of that age had indeed a very direct interest in war. A marked tendency to ignore or ridicule the current religious observances had become manifest, but under the stresses of loss and death people turned again to the altar. It is easily traceable in the fiction of the time. The despised curate of the tea-cups and croquet lawn became the implicitly heroic "padre" of the sentimental war stories.

The problem that confronted the growing minority that was waking up to the perils and possibilities of our species in the third and fourth decades of the twentieth century was this: How in the first place to concentrate the minds of people onto this state of distraction and diffusion, how to bring them to bear upon the crude realities before them, and then how to organize the gigantic effort needed to shake off that intermittent and ever more dangerous fever of war and that chronic onset of pauperization which threatened the whole world with social dissolution.

There was no central antagonist, no ruling devil, for those anxious spirits to fight. That would have made it a straight, understandable campaign. But the Press with a certain flavouring of pious intentions was practically against them. Old social and political traditions, whatever the poses they assumed, were tacitly against them. History was against them, for it could but witness that war had always gone on since its records began. Not only the current Bishop of Hereford, and the current President of the Free Church Council, caught with their dividends upon them, but their Churches and the Catholic Church, and indeed all the Christian Churches, in spite of their allegiance to the Prince of Peace, were quietly competitive with, or antagonistic to, the secular world controls that alone could make a healthy world peace possible. The admission of the insufficiency of their own creeds to comfort or direct would have been the necessary prelude to a new moral effort.

And the idea of the naturalness and inevitability of war was not only everywhere in the world around those few forward-looking men who knew better, it was in their blood and habits. They were seeking how to attack not a fortress, but what seemed a perpetually recuperative jungle of mixed motives, tangled interests and cross-purposes, within themselves as without.

10. VERSAILLES: SEED BED OF DISASTERS

The formal war, against the Central Powers, the "World War", ended on November 11, 1918, C.E. in the defeat and submission of the Central Powers. There was a conference at Versailles, in the same palace in which triumphant Germans had dictated peace to France after a previous war in 1870-71. There was a needlessly dramatic flavour in this reversal of the rôles of the two countries. It was now France and her allies who dictated, and naturally the ideas of a romantic restoration and a stern and righteous judgment dominated the situation. The assembled Powers sat down to right the wrongs and punish the misdeeds of their grandparents. Even at the time it seemed a little belated. But threading their proceedings we do find quite plainly evident the developing conflict between historical tradition and the quickening sense of human unity in the world. If the World-State was not present at the conference, its voice was at any rate "heard without".

By this time (1919 C.E.) there was indeed quite a considerable number of intelligent people in the world who had realized the accumulating necessity of a world government, and a still larger multitude, like that Henry Ford we have described, who had apprehended it instinctively and sentimentally, but there was no one yet who had had the intellectual vigour to attack in earnest the problem of substituting a world system for the existing governments. Men's minds and hearts quailed before that undertaking. And yet, as we now know so clearly, it was the only thing for them to do. It was the sole alternative to an ever-broadening and deepening series of disasters. But its novelty and vastness held them back. Irrational habit kept them in the ancient currents of history.

To us they seem like drowning men who were willing to attempt to save themselves by rallies of swimming, floating, holding on to straws and bubbles, but who refused steadfastly, in spite of the proximity of a ladder, to clamber out of the water for good and all.

Hardly any of them in their ideas of a world system dared go beyond a purely political agreement for the avoidance of war. Five decades of human distress were still needed before there was to be any extensive realization that belligerence was only one symptom, and by no means the gravest symptom, of human disunion.

The American President Woodrow Wilson, of all the delegates to the Peace Conference, was the most susceptible to the intimations of the future. The defects and limitations of his contributions to that settlement give us a measure of the political imagination of those days. He brought what was left of the individualistic

liberalism that had created the American Republics to the solution of the world problem. None of the other participants in these remarkable discussions—Clemenceau (France), Lloyd George (Britain), Sonnino (Italy), Saionji (Japan), Hymans (Belgium), Paderewski (Poland), Bratianu (Roumania), Benes (Bohemia), Venezelos (Greece), Feisal (Hedjaz), and so on through a long list of now fading names—seemed aware that, apart from any consideration of national advantage, humanity as a whole might claim an interest in the settlement. They were hard-shell "representatives", national advocates. For a brief interval Wilson stood alone for mankind. Or at least he seemed to stand for mankind. And in that brief interval there was a very extraordinary and significant wave of response to him throughout the earth. So eager was the situation that all humanity leapt to accept and glorify Wilson— for a phrase, for a gesture. It seized upon him as its symbol. He was transfigured in the eyes of men. He ceased to be a common statesman; he became a Messiah. Millions believed him as the bringer of untold blessings; thousands would gladly have died for him. That response was one of the most illuminating events in the early twentieth century. Manifestly the World-State had been conceived then, and now it stirred in the womb. It was alive.

And then for some anxious decades it ceased to stir.

Amidst different scenery and in different costumes, the story of Wilson repeats the story of Ford, the story of a man lifted by an idea too great for him, thrown up into conspicuousness for a little while and then dropped, as a stray leaf may be spun up and dropped by a gust of wind before a gale. The essential Wilson, the world was soon to learn, was vain and theatrical, with no depth of thought and no wide generosity. So far from standing for all mankind, he stood indeed only for the Democratic Party in the United States—and for himself. He sacrificed the general support of his people in America to party considerations and his prestige in Europe to a craving for social applause. For a brief season he was the greatest man alive. Then for a little while he remained the most conspicuous. He visited all the surviving courts of Europe and was fêted and undone in every European capital. That triumphal procession to futility need not occupy us further here. Our concern is with his idea.

Manifestly he wanted some sort of a world pax. But it is doubtful if at any time he realized that a world pax means a world control of all the vital common interests of mankind. He seems never to have thought out this job to which he set his hand so confidently. He did not want, or, if he did, he did not dare to ask for, any such centralized world controls as we now possess. They were probably beyond the range of his reading and understanding. His project from first to last was purely a politician's project.

The pattern conceived by him was a naïve adaptation of the parliamentary governments of Europe and America to a wider union. His League, as it emerged from the Versailles Conference, was a typical nineteenth-century government enlarged to planetary dimensions and greatly faded in the process; it had an upper chamber, the Council, and a lower chamber, the Assembly, but, in ready deference to national susceptibilities, it had no executive powers, no certain revenues,

no army, no police, and practically no authority to do anything at all. And even as a political body it was remote and ineffective; it was not in any way representative of the peoples of the earth as distinguished from the governments of the earth. Practically nothing was done to make the common people of the world feel that the League was theirs. Its delegates were appointed by the Foreign Offices of the very governments its only conceivable rôle was to supersede. They were national politicians and they were expected to go to Geneva to liquidate national politics. The League came into being at last, a solemn simulacrum to mock, cheat and dispel the first desire for unity that mankind had ever betrayed.

Yet what else was possible then? If Wilson seemed to embody the formless aspirations of mankind, there can be no dispute that he impressed the politicians with whom he had to deal as a profoundly insincere visionary. They dealt with him as that and they beat him as that. The only way to have got anything more real than this futile League would have been a revolutionary appeal to the war-weary peoples of the earth against their governments, to have said, as indeed he could have said in 1918, to the whole world that the day of the World-State had come. That would have reverberated to the ends of the earth.

He was not the man to do that. He had not that power of imagination. He had not that boldness with governments. He had the common politician's way of regarding great propositions as a means to small ends. If he had been bolder and greater, he might have failed, he might have perished; but he failed and perished anyhow; and a bolder bid for world unity might have put the real issue before mankind for ever and shortened the Age of Frustration by many decades.

What he did do was to reap an immediate harvest of popular applause, to present to human hope a white face rigid with self-approval, bowing from processional carriages and decorated balconies, retiring gravely into secret conference with the diplomatists and politicians of the old order and emerging at last with this League of Nations, that began nothing and ended nothing and passed in a couple of decades out of history.

It was a League not to end sovereignties but preserve them. It stipulated that the extraordinarily ill-contrived boundaries established by the Treaty in which it was incorporated should be guaranteed by the League for EVERMORE. Included among other amiable arrangements were clauses penalizing Germany and her allies as completely as Carthage was penalized by Rome after the disaster of Zamia— penalizing her in so overwhelming a way as to make default inevitable and afford a perennial excuse for her continued abasement. It was not a settlement, it was a permanent punishment. The Germans were to become the penitent helots of the conquerors; a generation, whole generations, were to be born and die in debt, and to ensure the security of this arrangement Germany was to be effectually disarmed and kept disarmed.

Delenda est Germanic was the sole idea of the French (see Morris Henbane's Study of Pertinax, 1939) and the representatives of the other Allies who were gathered together in the Paris atmosphere, and, working amidst the vindictive memories of Versailles, were only too ready to fall in with this punitive concep-

tion of their task. It was the easiest conception; it put a hundred difficult issues into a subordinate place. It always looks so much easier to men of poor imagination to put things back than to carry them on. If the French dreaded a resurrection of the German armies, the British feared a resurrection of the German fleet and of German industrial competition. Japan and Italy, seeking their own compensations elsewhere, were content to see the German- speaking peoples, who constituted the backbone of the continent, divided and reduced to vassalage.

The antiquated form of Wilson's ideas produced still more mischievous consequences in the multiplication of sovereign governments in the already congested European area. Deluded by the vague intimations of unity embodied in the League, Wilson lent himself readily to a reconstruction of the map of Europe upon strictly nationalist lines. The Polish nation was restored. Our history has already studied the successive divisions of this country in the eighteenth century. It is a great region of the Central Plain, whose independent existence became more and more inconvenient as the trade and commerce of Europe developed. Geography fought against it. It was a loose-knit union of individualistic equestrian aristocrats dominating a peasantry. But its partition between Russia, Prussia and Austria was achieved with the utmost amount of brutality, and after the Napoleonic wars a romantic legend about this lost kingdom of Poland seized upon the sentiment of France, Britain and America. These rude nobles and their serfs, so roughly incorporated by the adjacent states, were transfigured into a delicate, brave and altogether wonderful people, a people with a soul torn asunder and trampled underfoot by excessively booted oppressors. The restoration of Poland—the excessive restoration of Poland—was one of the brightest ambitions of President Wilson.

Poland was restored. But instead of a fine-spirited and generous people emerging from those hundred and twenty years of subjugation, and justifying the sympathy and hopes of liberalism throughout the world, there appeared a narrowly patriotic government, which presently developed into an aggressive, vindictive and pitiless dictatorship, and set itself at once to the zestful persecution of the unfortunate ethnic minorities (about a third of the entire population) caught in the net of its all too ample boundaries. The real Poland of the past had been a raiding and aggressive nation which had ridden and harried to the very walls of Moscow. It had not changed its nature. The Lithuanian city of Vilna was now grabbed by a coup de main and the southeastern boundary pushed forward in Galicia. In the treatment of the Ukrainians and Ruthenians involved in liberation, Poland equalled any of the atrocities which had been the burden of her song during her years of martyrdom. In 1932 one- third of the budget of this new militant Power was for armament.

Not only was Poland thus put back upon the map. As a result of a sedulous study of historical sentimentalities, traditions, dialects and local feelings, a whole cluster of new sovereign Powers, Czechoslovakia, Jugoslavia, Finland, Esthonia, Latvia, Lithuania, an attenuated Hungary and an enlarged Roumania, was evoked to crowd and complicate the affairs of mankind by their sovereign liberties, their

ambitions, hostilities, alliances, understandings, misunderstandings, open and secret treaties, tariffs, trade wars and the like. Russia was excluded from the first attempt at a World Parliament because she had repudiated her vast war debts—always a matter of grave solicitude to the Western creditor, and—strangest fact of all in this strange story—the United States, the Arbitrator and Restorer of Nations, stood out from the League, because President Wilson's obstinate resolve to monopolize the immortal glory of World Salvation for himself and his party had estranged a majority of his senators.

The Senate, after some attempts at compromise, rejected the Covenant of the League altogether, washed its hands of world affairs, and the President, instead of remaining for ever Prince of Everlasting Peace and Wonder of the Ages, shrank again very rapidly to human proportions and died a broken and disappointed man. Like Ford, the United States returned to normal business and the Profit and Loss Account, and the Europeans were left with the name of Wilson written all over their towns, upon streets, avenues, esplanades, railway stations, parks and squares, to make what they could of this emasculated League he had left about among their affairs.

If Russia and Germany in their character of Bad Peoples were excluded from the League, such remote peoples as the Chinese and the Japanese were included as a matter of course. It was assumed, apparently, that they were "just fellows" of the universal Treaty-of-Westphalia pattern. The European world knew practically nothing of the mental processes of these remote and ancient communities, and it seems hardly to have dawned upon the conferring statesmen that political processes rest entirely upon mental facts. The League, after much difficulty, and after some years' delay, did indeed evolve a Committee of Intellectual Cooperation, but so far as its activities can now be traced, this was concerned with dilettante intellectualism only; there is no indication that it ever interested itself in the League as an idea.

Considering all things in the light of subsequent events, it would have been well if the League of Nations had committed hara-kiri directly the United States Senate refused participation, and if the European Powers, realizing their failure to stabilize the planet at one blow, had set themselves at once to the organization of a League of Conciliation and Cooperation within the European area. The League's complete inability to control or even modify the foreign policy of Japan (modelled on the best nineteenth-century European patterns) was the decisive factor in its declension to a mere organization of commentary upon current affairs.

As its authority declined the courage and pungency of its reports increased. Some of the later ones are quite admirable historical documents. Gradually the member governments discontinued their subsidies and the secretariat dwindled to nothing. Like the Hague Tribunal, the League faded out of existence before or during the Famished Fifties. It does not figure in history after the first Polish war, but its official buildings were intact in 1965, and in 1968, and for some years later, they were used as auxiliary offices by the Western branch of the Transport Union.

The imposition of vast monetary payments upon Germany was the only part of the settlement of Versailles that dealt with the financial and economic life of our race. Astounding as this seems to us to-day, it was the most natural oversight possible to the Versailles politicians. Political life was still deep in the old purely combatant tradition, still concentrated upon boundaries and strategic advantages; and it was extraordinarily innocent in the face of economic realities. The mighty forces demanding economic unification, albeit they were, as we have shown, the real causes of the Great War, were ignored at Versailles as completely as if they had never existed.

Only one outstanding voice, that of the British economist J. M. Keynes (Economic Consequences of the Peace, 1919), was audible at the time in protest and warning against the preposterous dislocation of credit and trade involved in the reparation payments. There was no arrangement whatever for the liquidation of the debts piled up by the Allies AGAINST EACH OTHER (!), and no economic parallel to the political League of Nations. No control of economic warfare was even suggested. The Americans, Wilson included, were still in a stage of financial individualism; they thought money-getting was an affair of individual smartness within the limits of the law, and the American conception of law was of something that presented interesting obstacles rather than effectual barriers to enlightened self-seeking. The contemporary American form of mutual entertainment was a poker party, and that great people therefore found nothing inimical in sitting down after the war to play poker, with France and Great Britain as its chief opponents, for the gold and credit of the world.

It was only slowly during the decade following after the war that the human intelligence began to realize that the Treaty of Versailles had not ended the war at all. It had set a truce to the bloodshed, but it had done so only to open a more subtle and ultimately more destructive phase in the traditional struggle of the sovereign states. The existence of independent sovereign states IS war, white or red, and only an elaborate mis-education blinded the world to this elementary fact. The peoples of the defeated nations suffered from a real if not very easily defined sense of injustice in this Treaty, which was framed only for them to sign, and sign in the rôle of wrongdoers brought to book. Very naturally they were inspired by an ill-concealed resolve to revise, circumvent or disregard its provisions at the earliest possible opportunity. The conquering Powers, on the other hand, were conscious of having not only humiliated their defeated enemies but thrust them into a state of exasperated disadvantage. The thought of a revanche was equally present therefore to the victors, and instead of disarming as the Germans were compelled to do, they broke the obligations of the Treaty and retained and increased their military establishments.

The armament firms and their newspapers naturally did all they could to intensify this persistence in an armed "security". Any disposition on the part of the French public, for instance, to lay aside its weapons was promptly checked by tales of secret arsenals and furtive drilling in Germany. And the narrow patriotic forces that guided France not only kept her extravagantly armed against her fallen

foe, but carried on a subtle but ruthless financial warfare that, side by side with the American game, overcame every effort of Germany to recover socially or economically.

Moreover, the conquering Powers, so soon as they considered their former antagonists conclusively disposed of, turned themselves frankly, in full accordance with the traditions of the sovereign state system, to the task of getting the better of each other in the division of the spoils. Their "Alliances" had brought about no sense of community. Already within a year of the signing of the Peace Treaty of Versailles heavy fighting was going on in Asia Minor between the Greeks and the Turks. The Greeks had British encouragement; the French and Italians had supported the Turks. It was a war of catspaws. This war culminated in a disastrous rout of the Greeks and the burning of the town of Smyrna. This last was a quite terrible massacre; multitudes of women and children were outraged, men and boys gouged, emasculated or killed; all but the Turkish quarter was looted and burnt. The quays in front of the flaming town were dense with terror-stricken crowds, hoping against hope to get away upon some ship before they were fallen upon, robbed, butchered, or thrust into the water.

A little before this the Turks had driven the French out of the ancient province of Cilicia, and had completed the extermination of that ancient people the Hittites or Armenians. During the war or after the war mattered little to the Armenians, for fire and sword pursued them still. Over two million died— for the most part violent deaths.

Fighting still went on after the Great Peace in the north and south of Russia and in eastern Siberia; and China became a prey to armies of marauders. Poland seized Vilna, invaded eastern Galicia and fought Russia in the Ukraine, and a raid of patriotic Italians expelled a mixed Allied garrison from Fiume.

Presently there was a dreadful famine in south-east Russia which neither America nor Europe was able to alleviate. Always before the war a famine in any part of the world had exercised the philanthropic element in the Anglo-Saxon community. But philanthropy had lost heart. There was a faint but insufficient flutter of the old habits in America but none in Britain.

Such was the peace and union of the world immediately achieved by the Conference of Versailles.

A number of unsatisfactory appendices and patches had presently to be made to correct the most glaring defects and omissions of the Treaty. Constantinople, which had been taken from the Turks and held by a mixed force of the Allies, was restored to them in 1923 after the Smyrna massacre and some warlike gesticulation between them and the British.

In drawing the boundaries of the new and revised states of the European patchwork there was the utmost disregard of economic commonsense; peasants would find themselves cut off from winter or summer pasture or from market towns which had been developed by their needs. Great foundries and chemical and metallurgical works were separated from the ores and deposits on which they relied. Vienna, once the financial and business centre of all south-east Central

Europe, was decapitated. Most fantastic and, as it proved, most disastrous of all the follies of Versailles, was the creation of the free city of Danzig and what was called the Polish Corridor.

Let us note a point or so about this latter tangle to illustrate the mental quality of the Conference at its worst. Here more than anywhere else did the simple romantic idea that the Germans were Bad, and that anyone opposed to the Germans was without qualification Good, rule the situation. The Poles were Good, and they were the chosen of the Allies, the particular protégés of the sentimental historian from America. He had come to put down the mighty from their seats and to exalt the humble and the meek. The hungry and eager were to be filled with good things and the rich, the erstwhile rich, were to be sent empty away. Germany, like Dives in hell, was to look up and see Poland like Lazarus in Woodrow Wilson's bosom. Not only were the Good Poles to be given dominion over Ruthenians, Ukrainians, Jews (whom particularly they detested), Lithuanians, White Russians and Germans, they were to have also something of profound economic importance—"access to the sea".

On that President Wilson had been very insistent. Switzerland had done very well in pre-war Europe without access to the sea, but that was another story. The difficulty was that by no stretch of ethnic map-colouring could Poland be shown to border on the sea. A belt of Pomeranians and Germans stretched across the mouth of the Vistula, and the only possibility of a reasonable trading outlet to the sea, so far as Poland needed such an outlet—for most of its trade was with its immediate neighbours—was through an understanding with that belt of people. That would have been easy enough to arrange. At the mouth of the Vistula stood the entirely German city of Danzig. It lived mainly as an outlet for Polish trade, and it could prosper in no other way. There was no reason to suppose it would put any difficulties in the way of Polish imports and exports. It was an ancient, honest, clean and prosperous German city. Ninety-six per cent of its inhabitants were German.

This was the situation to which the Conference of Versailles, under the inspiration of that magic phrase "access to the sea", turned its attention. Even the profound belief of the Conquerors that there were no Germans but bad Germans could not justify their turning over Danzig itself to Polish rule. But they separated it from Germany and made it into a "free city", and to the west of it they achieved that "access to the sea" of Wilson's, by annexing a broad band of Pomeranian territory to Poland. (This was the actual "Corridor" of the controversies.) It had no port to compare with Danzig, but the Poles set themselves to create a rival in Gdynia, which should be purely Polish, and which should ultimately starve the trading Germans out of Danzig.

And to keep the waters of the Vistula as pure and sweet for Poland as the existence of Danzig at the estuary allowed, the peace-makers ran the Vistula boundary between Poland and east Prussia, not in the usual fashion midway along the stream, but at a little distance on the east Prussian side. (Jacques Kayser, La Paix en Péril, 1931; Hist. Doc., 711711.) So that the east German population, the

peasant cultivator, the erstwhile fisherman, the shepherd with his flocks to water, was pulled up by a line of frontier posts and a Polish rifle within sight of the stream. Moreover, that eastward country was flat and low-lying and had hitherto been protected from floods and a relapse to marsh conditions by a line of dykes. The frontier cut that line five times, and since the Poles had no interest whatever in these defences, they fell rapidly out of repair. Further along the boundary cut off the great towns of Garnsee and Bischofswerder from their railway station.

But we must not lose ourselves in the details of this exasperating settlement. The maximum of irritation developed in the absurd Corridor itself. The current of traffic had hitherto run to and fro between east and west, the trend of the railways was in that direction; the traffic in the north and south direction had come to Danzig along the great river. Now the Poles set themselves to obstruct both these currents and to wrench round all the communications into a north and south direction avoiding Danzig. Every German going east or west found himself subjected to a series of frontier examinations, to tariff payments, to elaborate delays, to such petty but memorable vexations as that all the windows of an express train passing across the Corridor should be closed, and so forth, and the city of Danzig, cut off from German trade, found its Polish business being steadily diverted to Gdynia. French capital was poured into Gdynia and into its new railway to the south, so that French financial interests were speedily entangled in the dispute.

The indignity and menace of Danzig burnt into the German imagination. That Corridor fretted it as nothing else in the peace settlement had fretted it. It became a dominant political issue. There was an open sore of a similar character in Upper Silesia; there was a sore in the Saar Valley; there was the sore of an enforced detachment from Austria; there were many other bitter memories and grievances, but this was so intimate, so close to Berlin, that it obsessed all German life.

Within a dozen years of the signing of the Treaty of Versailles the Polish Corridor was plainly the most dangerous factor in the European situation. It mocked every projection of disarmament. It pointed the hypnotized and impotent statescraft of Europe straight towards a resumption of war. A fatalistic attitude towards war as something terrible indeed but inevitable, which had already been evident among the politicians of Europe before 1914, reappeared and spread.

History had an air of repeating itself. Nobody made any definite suggestions about any of these open sores, but there was scarcely a politician of the period who could not claim to have been very eloquent on various occasions against war—with, of course, a skilful avoidance of anything that could be considered specific, controversial, unpatriotic or likely to wound the susceptibilities of the Powers immediately concerned.

11. THE IMPULSE TO ABOLISH WAR: WHY THE LEAGUE OF NATIONS FAILED TO PACIFY THE WORLD

Before we leave that bleak and futile idealist, Woodrow Wilson, altogether, we will draw the attention of the student to the essential factors of his failure. The defects of his personality must not blind us to the impossibility of his ambition. His narrow egotism, the punitive treatment of the Central Powers and so forth, merely emphasized a disadvantage that would have been fatal to the launching of any League of Nations at that time. There had been an insufficient mental preparation for a world system to operate. No ideology existed to sustain it. The World-State, the Modern State, was still only a vaguely apprehended suggestion; it had not been worked out with any thoroughness and the League was the most hasty of improvisations.

It needed the life scheming of de Windt and his associates, which we shall presently describe; it needed a huge development and application of the science of social psychology, before the supersession of the chaos of sovereign states by a central control was even a remote possibility. Wilson thought he could get together with a few congenial spirits and write a recipe for human unity. He had not the slightest inkling of the gigantic proportions, the intricacy, intimacy and profundity, of the task that was opening before him. He attempted to patch up the outworn system of his time and pass it off as a new one. He did not dream of the monetary reconstruction, the need for a thorough- going socialism throughout the world, and for a complete revolution in education, before the peace and security of mankind could be established. Yet, narrow and blind as he was, he seems to have been in advance of the general thought of his age.

This premature and ineffectual League was a hindrance rather than a help to the achievement of world peace. It got in the way. It prevented people from thinking freely about the essentials of the problem. Organizations of well- meaning folk, the British League of Nations Union, for example, came into existence to support it, and resisted rather than helped any effectual criticism of its constitution and working. They would say that it was "better than nothing", whereas a false start is very much worse than nothing. In the post-war decade, the amount of vigorous constructive thought in the general mind about world politics was extraordinarily small. It was only when the insufficiency of the League had passed beyond any possibility of dispute that men began to take up the abandoned search for world unification again.

A dozen years later the Modern State movement was still only foreshadowed in sketchy attempts to find a comprehensive set of general formulae for liberal progressive effort. The pacificists, communists, socialists and every other sort of "ists" who gave a partial and confused expression to human discontent had still to be drawn together into understanding and cooperation. Most of their energy was wasted in obscure bickerings, mutual suspicion and petty and partial tentatives. The middle of the century had been passed before there was any considerable body of Modern State propaganda and education on earth.

12. THE BREAKDOWN OF "FINANCE" AND SOCIAL MORALE AFTER VERSAILLES

The unprecedented range and destruction of the World War were, we have pointed out, largely ascribable to the hypertrophy of the world's iron and steel industry relatively to the political and social concepts of the race. But in the first "post-war" decade the stresses of other disproportionate developments began to make themselves manifest at various other weak points in the loosely linked association of our species. The war from the economic point of view had been the convulsive using up of an excess of production that the race had no other method of distributing and consuming. But the necessities of the struggle, and particularly its interference with international trading, which had evoked factories and finishing processes in many undeveloped regions hitherto yielding only raw or unfinished materials, had added greatly to the gross bulk of productive plant throughout the world, and so soon as the open war-furnaces ceased to burn up the surplus and hold millions of men out of the labour market, this fact became more and more oppressively apparent. The postwar increase in war preparation, which went on in spite of endless palavering about disarmament, did not destroy men, nor scrap and destroy material, in sufficient quantity to relieve the situation.

Moreover, the expansion of productive energy was being accompanied by a positive contraction of the distributive arrangements which determined consumption. The more efficient the output, the fewer were the wages-earners. The more stuff there was, the fewer consumers there were. The fewer the consumers, the smaller the trading profits, and the less the gross spending power of the shareholders and individual entrepreneurs. So buying dwindled at both ends of the process and the common investor suffered with the wages- earner. This was the "Paradox of Overproduction" which so troubled the writers and journalists of the third decade of the twentieth century.

It is easy for the young student to-day to ask "Why did they not adjust?" But let him ask himself who there was to adjust. Our modern superstructure of applied economic science, the David Lubin Bureau and the General Directors' Board, with its vast recording organization, its hundreds of thousands of stations and observers, directing, adjusting, apportioning and distributing, had not even begun to exist. Adjustment was left to blind and ill- estimated forces. It was the general interest of mankind to be prosperous, but it was nobody's particular interest to keep affairs in a frame of prosperity. Manifestly a dramatic revision of the liberties of enterprise was necessary, but the enterprising people who controlled

politics, so far as political life was controlled, were the very last people to undertake such a revision.

With the hypertrophy of productive activities there had been a concurrent hypertrophy of banking and financial organization generally, but it had been a flabby hypertrophy, a result of the expansion of material production rather than a compensatory and controlling development.

It is so plain to us to-day that the apportionment of the general product of the world for enterprise or consumption is a department of social justice and policy, and can be dealt with only in the full light of public criticism and upon grounds of claim and need, that it is difficult for us to understand the twentieth century attitude to these things. We should no more dream of leaving the effectual control in these matters in private profit-seeking hands than we should leave our law courts or our schools to the private bidder. But nothing of the sort was plain in 1935 C.E. That lesson had still to be learnt.

The story of banking and money in the early twentieth century has so much in it verging upon the incredible, that it has become one of the most attractive and fruitful fields for the student of historical psychology. The system had grown up as a tangle of practice. It was evolved, not designed. There was never any attempt to gauge the justice or the ultimate consequences of any practice, so long as it worked at the time. Men tried this and that, did this and that, and concealed their opinions of what the results might be. Reserve was essential in the system. So little was the need for publicity in this universal interest understood, that the most fundamental decisions affecting the common man's purchasing power and the credit of industrial undertakings were made in secret, and the restriction and stimulation of trade and work went on in the profoundest obscurity. Neither in the ordinary courses of the schools and universities was there any instruction in these essential facts. The right of private enterprise to privacy was respected in the Churches, the law courts and private practice alike. Men found themselves employed or unemployed, cheated of their savings or better off, they knew not why. Instead of the clear knowledge of economic pressures and movements that we have to-day, strange Mystery Men were dimly visible through a fog of baffling evasions and mis-statements, manipulating prices and exchanges.

Prominent among these Mystery Men was a certain Mr. Montagu Norman, Governor of the Bank of England from 1920 to 1935. He is among the least credible figures in all history, and a great incrustation of legends has accumulated about him. In truth the only mystery about him was that he was mysterious. His portrait shows a slender, bearded man, dressed more like a successful artist or musician than the conventional banker of the time. He was reputed to be shy and, in the phraseology of the time, "charming", and he excited the popular imagination by a habit of travelling about under assumed names and turning up in unexpected places. Why he did so, nobody now knows. Perhaps he did it for the fun of doing it. He gave evidence before an enquiry into finance in 1930 (the Macmillan Committee), and from that and from one or two of his public speeches that have been preserved, it is plain that he had what we should now consider an

entirely inadequate education for the veiled activities in which he was engaged. Of human ecology he betrays no knowledge, and his ideas of social and economic processes are not what we should now recognize as adequate general ideas even for an ordinary citizen. Indeed his chief qualification for his darkly responsible post was some practical experience acquired in association with various private banking firms before he entered the service of the Bank of England. This experience was acquired during what we know now to have been a period of quite accidental and transitory expansion of human wealth. Plainly he did not even bring a blank mind to his task. He had a mind warped and prejudiced by gainful banking under abnormal conditions. Yet for a time he was regarded as an "expert" of almost magical quality, and during the convulsions of the post-war period he was able to dictate or defeat arrangements that enriched or impoverished millions of people in every country in Europe.

Another big obscure financial force in the war and post-war periods was the complex of great private banking ganglia, of which Morgan and Co., with its associated firms, was the most central and most typical. This particular firm carried on its business upon a scale that completely overshadowed many minor governments. The loans it made or refused, confirmed or shattered régimes. Its founder, J. P. Morgan, a queer combination of Yankee "gentleman" and German junker, whose innate acquisitiveness overflowed in great collections of pictures and "art" objects generally, had died before the outbreak of the war, but a phrase he used in a dispute with President Roosevelt the First was taken up later and made into a deadly critical weapon against the whole private banking world. "Roosevelt", he protested, "wants all of us to have glass pockets!"

A second President Roosevelt was presently to revive that demand.

Nothing could better betray the habit of deep gainful manoeuvrings than that phrase. Morgan was never dishonest and always disingenuous. That was the rule of his game. Opaque pockets he insisted upon, and hidden motives, but also the punctual performance of a bargain. His tradition lived after him. His firm became an octopus of credit. The interweaving bargains it made hung like a shadowy group of spiders' webs about European life. It did its work of strangulation by its nature and without malice, as a spider spins. No contemporary could apprehend it. The particulars of any particular situation could only be unravelled vaguely by a normal enquirer after many months of study.

Interacting with such mystery systems as these of the banking world were other dark figures and groups, controlling vast industrial activities, obsessing and perverting spending power. There was, for example, that Mystery Man of Mystery Men, Sir Basil Zaharoff, the armaments salesman, still the delight of our schoolboy novelists, and Ivar Kreuger, who created an almost world-wide system of lucifer match monopolies, lent great sums to governments and was finally caught forging big parcels of bonds. He then staged a suicide in Paris to escape the penalty of fraud. (We have to remember that in those days the lucifer matches we now see in museums were consumed by the billion. There was no other handy source of fire, and their manufacture and distribution was on the scale of a prima-

ry industry.) Kreuger, unlike Morgan, was not a man of the acquisitive type; he neither hoarded nor collected; he kept nothing, not even the law, but he built lavishly and gave away money for scientific research. (The discovery of Pekin Man, a memorable incident in early archaeology, was, for instance, made possible by his gifts.) Morgan forestalled and accumulated; Kreuger robbed and gave. When Morgan spent his gains he bought "Old Masters", manuscripts and suchlike indisputably genuine and valuable junk; when Kreuger dispersed the moneys that had been entrusted to him he made the most extraordinary experiments in decorative art, in electric lighting and fantastic building. But each operated unchecked. So obscure was the financial machinery of the time that for some months Kreuger was able to pass off as genuine a package of forged Italian bonds amounting to about half a million dollars, and to obtain advances upon them from reputable lenders. To- day a trick of such a character would be detected, were it possible, in the course of a single day by the ordinary checking of the Transactions Bureau. But nowadays no one would have any reason for attempting anything of the sort. The lives of these Mystery Men and of the various groups of speculators (the Balkan Gang, e.g.) who manipulated the exchanges of the various national currencies of Eastern Europe, and of a great number of other profit-seeking groups and individuals who were thrusting about amidst the machinery of exchange, are to be found in the Lives of Mischief (Financial Volumes) taken out of the Dictionary of Biography. The very best of them were men who waylaid gain or sought adventures in a fog. Most of them were as active and as blind to the consequences of their activities as moles who perforate a dyke.

In the files of the financial papers of this period, when the movements of gold were of vital significance to the prices of commodities and the credit of everyone in the world, one sees such headings as "Unknown Buyer Takes Two Millions in Gold" or, less exactly, "Gold Bought by Unknown Buyer". Then all the little manipulators of money would be set peering and spying and guessing and rigging their business to the possible shift of equilibrium this dark intimation might portend.

Other Mystery Men, Mystery Men ex officio, were the various Ministers of Finance, of whom perhaps the British Chancellor of the Exchequer was most typical. Every year there was a vast amount of whispering and hinting, peeping and calculating and going to and fro, about the National Budget and the readjustment of taxation for another twelvemonth. An arithmetical mystery called "balancing the Budget" had to be performed. Business would be held up as the great revelation drew near; gambling operations, insurance operations, would multiply. The wife, the family, the intimates and secretaries of the Man of Destiny, went about the world sealed, enigmatical, oracular, profoundly important with his reflected importance. At last the great day dawned. The legislature would assemble in unusual force, excited and curious. The Witch Doctor, with his portfolios of Obi, would take his place in the House of Commons, rise portentously, begin the "Budget Speech".

No Budget Speech was complete without its "surprises". Could anything witness more vividly to the chaotic casualness of the twentieth century? Anything might be taxed; anything might be relieved; anyone might shift the weights about. In the economic darkness of the time it did not seem to matter. The marvel is that the system staggered on for so long.

How amazing, how fantastic, was that condition of affairs! It is as if one of the great transatlantic liners of the period had careered across the ocean with its passenger decks and cabins brightly lit, its saloons and bars in full swing, while down below, its essential machinery, manifestly with something going wrong with it, had no arrangements for illumination at all and was served by men (some of them masked), working without a foreman or any general directions, by the light of an occasional match or a treasured but rather worn- out electric torch, or altogether in the dark, upon the great cranks and swiftly sliding shafts that beat and circled about them.

From the very cessation of the fighting in 1918 and onward it was manifest that this machinery was seriously out of gear. The economic history of the time is a story of swerves and fluctuations of the most alarming kind, each one more disconcerting and disastrous than its predecessor. In the decades before the war, though there were certainly variations in the real value of the different currencies, they were variations within moderate limits, and the rise or fall went on through comparatively long periods, but after the war there commenced a series of movements in exchange and prices unprecedented throughout the whole period of prosperity. Currencies rose and towered above others and broke like Atlantic waves, and people found the good money in their banks changed to useless paper in a period of a few months. It became more and more difficult to carry on foreign trade because of the increasing uncertainty of payment, and since there was scarcely a manufacturing industry that had not to obtain some material from abroad, the entanglement of foreign trade often involved a strangulation of production at home. Trade and industry sickened and lost heart more and more in this disastrous uncertainty; it was like being in an earthquake, when it seems equally unsafe to stand still or run away; and the multitudes of unemployed increased continually. The economically combatant nations entrenched themselves behind tariffs, played each other tricks with loans, repudiations, sudden inflations and deflations, and no power in the world seemed able to bring them into any concerted action to arrest and stop their common dégringolade.

The opening years of the second third of the twentieth century saw Homo sapiens in the strangest plight. The planet had a healthier and more abundant human population than it had ever carried before, and it lacked nothing in its available resources to give the whole of this population full and happy lives. That was already the material reality of the position. But through nothing in the world but a universal, various muddle-headedness, our species seemed unable to put out its hand and take the abundance within its reach. As we turn over the periodicals and literature of the time the notes of apprehension and distress increase and deepen. The war period of 1914-1918 was full of suffering, but also it was full of excite-

ment; even the dying on the battlefields believed that a compensatory peace and happiness lay close ahead. The survivors were promised "homes fit for heroes." But the Depression of 1930 and onward was characterized by its inelasticity; it was a phase of unqualified disappointment and hopelessly baffled protest. One lived, as one contemporary writer put it, "in a world bewitched".

The economic consequences of this monetary disorganization followed hard upon it, but the deeper-lying destruction of social morale and its effects were manifested less immediately. The whole world system heretofore had been sustained by the general good behavior of common men, by the honesty and punctuality of clerks, workers of every sort, traders, professional men. General security depended upon habitual decent behaviour in the street and on the countryside. But the common man behaved well because he had faith that his pay was a safe, if sometimes a scanty, assurance of a certain comfort and dignity in his life. He imagined an implicit bargain between himself and society that he should be given employment and security in exchange for his law- abiding subordination, and that society would keep faith with his savings. He assumed that the governments would stand by the money they issued and see that it gave him the satisfactions it promised him. He was not a good boy for nothing. Nobody is. But now in various terms and phrases all over the world millions of men and women were asking themselves whether it "paid" to be industrious, skilful and law-abiding. The cement of confidence in the social fabric from 1918 onward was more and more plainly decaying and changing to dust. The percentage of criminal offences, which had been falling through all the period of prosperity, rose again.

13. 1933: "PROGRESS" COMES TO A HALT

So we bring the history of mankind to that great pause in social expansion which concluded the first third of the twentieth century. The year 1933 closed in a phase of dismayed apprehension. It was like that chilly stillness, that wordless interval of suspense, that comes at times before the breaking of a storm. The wheels of economic life were turning only reluctantly and uncertainly; the millions of unemployed accumulated and became more and more plainly a challenge and a menace. All over the world the masses were sinking down through distress and insufficiency to actual famine. And collectively they were doing nothing effectual in protest or struggle. Insurrectionary socialism lurked and muttered in every great agglomeration. But insurrection alone could remedy nothing without constructive ideas, and there was no power and energy yet behind any such constructive ideas as had appeared. The merely repressive forces, whatever their feebleness in the face of criminality, were still fully capable of restraining popular insurrection. They could keep misery stagnant and inoperative.

Everywhere, in everything, there was an ebb of vitality. A decline in the public health was becoming perceptible. A diminishing resistance to infections and a rise in the infantile death-rate was already very evident in the vital statistics after 1933.

War was manifestly drawing nearer, in Eastern Asia, in Eastern Europe; it loitered, it advanced, it halted, and no one displayed the vigour or capacity needed to avert its intermittent, unhurrying approach.

Still the immense inertias of the old order carried things on. Under a darkling sky, the majority of people were going about their business according to use and wont. The unprofitable industries still carried on with reduced staffs; the shopkeepers opened their shops to a dwindling tale of customers; the unemployed queued up at the Labour Exchanges by force of habit, and some at least got a job; the landlord's agent no longer collected the rent that was due but called for an instalment of his arrears; the unfed or ill-fed children went sniffing to chilly schools to be taught by dispirited teachers on reduced salaries, but still the schools were not closed; the bankrupt railways and steamship lines ran diminished but punctual services; hotels stayed open not to make profits but to mitigate losses; the road traffic lost something of its newness and smartness and swiftness, but still it flowed; the crowds in the streets moved less briskly, but, if anything, these sluggish crowds were more numerous, and the police, if less alertly vigilant, maintained order.

There had been a considerable if inadequate building boom after the Peace of Versailles, but after 1930 new construction fell off more and more. Yet some builders found work, necessary repairs were attended to, burnt-out houses were reconditioned, for example. In 1935 and 1937 the world was swept by influenza epidemics of unusual virulence. The lowered resistance, already noted by the statisticians, was now made conspicuous by this return towards mediaeval conditions; but the doctors and nurses stuck to their duties stoutly and the druggists and undertakers, whose affairs had long since been reorganized on Big Business lines, profited.

Pictures of life in the shadows during this phase of devitalization are not very abundant, nor do they convey the essential misery into which a whole generation was born, in which it lived and died. One sees the rows of dilapidated houses, the wretched interiors and shabbily clad men and women standing about. In these pictures they seem always to be just standing about. Descriptive journalism brings the student nearer to the realities of a life without space, colour, movement, hope or opportunity. There were a number of "enquiries" made, more particularly by the British, American and French newspapers, and the tale they tell is always a tale of wheels slowing down to a stoppage, of factory gates being closed, of smokeless chimneys and rusting rails. Here is a vivid contemporary vignette, to show how things were with millions of human beings during this strange phase of human experience. It is from the pen of H. M. Tomlinson (1873-1969) one of the best of English descriptive writers.

"I chanced upon a little town above Cardiff last week. It was by pure chance; I had never before heard of the place. It is typical of these valleys, so never mind its name. It could have many names. Its population is, or was, about 6,000. Its people have faced trouble before—less than twenty years ago over 300 of its men perished in a mine explosion. We won't say the town got over that, for I spoke to those for whom the calamity is an abiding horror. It was a terrific defeat for them in the war upon Nature, but survivors returned to the struggle and said no more about it.

"When first I saw the town from a distance, with the bleak, bare uplands about it, I was reminded of the towns, once familiar, that were too near the battleline in France. It was midday, and sunny, yet this colliery town was silent and so still that it seemed under a spell.

"As a fact it IS under a spell. It is, in a way, dead. But its people cling to the empty shell of it. Where else can they go?

"At first sight no people could have been there. Buildings in the foreground were in ruins. The gaunt pit-head gearing evidently had not moved for an age. The gaps in the blackened walls of the power-house suggested a home of bats and owls.

"The first man I met when I reached the end of its main street and saw then that the shops were not only closed, but abandoned, was standing on the kerb, a man in the middle years, shrewd, but haggard, his clothes brushed till they were threadbare.

"'What's the matter with this town?' I asked.

"'On the dole.'

"'Are you out too?'

"'Of course I'm out.'

"'How long?'

"He was silent. He held up five fingers.

"'Months?'

"'Years.'

"'Are all the men here the same?'

"'Most of them. And won't go back.'

"He led me up a mound of refuse, where a goat was eating paper, and we had a near view of the colliery itself. 'That's the reason we won't go down again,' he said. 'How would you work it?'

"Whether by design or rust a steel footbridge had fallen across the wide railway track which went to the pit-head. A deflected stream guttered down between the metals, which were overgrown with grass and stagnant marsh stuff. The outbuildings were a huddle of dilapidations. It looked haunted. 'Some men I knew,' muttered my guide, 'are still down there. There they'll stop. They've been there nineteen years now. Would you call them lucky?'

"Two thousand five hundred men came out of the principal colliery five years ago. That is why the shops are shut, long rows of them with whitewashed windows and doorways filled with dust and straws. The woodwork of many houses has been taken for firewood. Even the Cooperative store is shut, as well as the pawnshop. Thrift and thriftlessness mean the same thing in this town, where I noticed that even Nonconformist chapels, with broken windows, had been left to the rats and birds.

"Worse than the dismal shops and broken buildings are the groups of shabby men, all neat and tidy, standing listless and silent at the street corners, waiting.

"Waiting for what? Nothing. There is nothing to come....

"They are doomed, these parents, to watch a generation grow up with thin bones and a shadow on its mind. Their children learn the signs of the slow death about them when they should be at play; children that have no childhood.

"Their homes are in a graveyard of human aspiration...."

The Press and literature of that period make curious reading. It varied between a bleak insincere optimism and hopeless desperation. An undignified viciousness and a jeering humour invaded popular art and literature; "strong" in manner and in flavour rather than in any grasp upon the realities of contemporary life. There was also an abundant production and consumption of reassuring and deliberately "cheerful" books, a movement towards religious mysticism and other-worldliness and a marked tendency towards repressive puritanism. Excesses of libertinism provoke censorious and superstitious suppression; the two things are correlated aspects of a decline in human dignity. In the face of its financial and political perplexities mankind was becoming neurasthenic.

All neurasthenia has apparently unaccountable elements. To us to-day, it seems incredible that the way out of all these distresses was not plainly seen and boldly taken. There was a blindness and an effortlessness that still exercise the mind of the social psychologist. The way was so plain that it was visible, it was indicated by hundreds of intelligent and detached observers as early as the thirties of the twentieth century. Maxwell Brown, in his study of the Modern State idea, has two supplementary volumes of citations to this effect. Such phrases, for example, as "Cosmopolis, Inflation and Public Employment" (from a British provincial newspaper article in 1932) do state, in general terms at any rate, the line of escape for the race. These are crude, ill- defined terms, but manifestly they have in them the shape of the ultimate reconstruction. "Cosmopolis" foreshadows our rational world controls, "Inflation" was a plain indication of our present complete restraint upon the aggravation of debts and fluctuations of price level; "Public Employment" was our ancestors' conception of socialist enterprise.

But before the exodus to peace and freedom could be achieved, such scattered flashes of understanding had to ignite a steadier illumination. The conception of revolutionary world reconstruction had to spread from the few to the many, spread to them not merely as an idea and as a suggestion, but in such force as to saturate their minds and determine their lives. Then, and then only, could the necessary will-power be marshalled and directed to the effective reorganization of earthly affairs.

A struggle for sanity had to take place in the racial brain, a great casting- out of false assumptions, conventional distortions, hitherto uncriticized maxims and impossible "rights," a great clearing-up of ideas about moral, material and biological relationships; it was a struggle that, as we shall see, involved the passing of three generations. To an analysis of the factors and decisive forces in this struggle our history must next address itself.

Something between eight and ten thousand million human lives in all were lived out during the Age of Frustration. Compared with the average lives of today, they were shorter and far less healthy; nearly all of them had long phases of such infection, maladjustment and enfeeblement as are now almost outside man's experience. The great majority of them were passed laboriously in squalid or dingy surroundings, in huts, hovels, cottages, tenements and cellars almost as dismal as the ancestral cave and nearly as insanitary. A minority who could command the services of "domestics" lived in relative comfort and even with a certain freedom and luxury, at an enormous cost to the rest. This prosperous minority dwindled after 1931. It had vanished in Russia after 1917.

There was a diminishing sense of personal security in the world, an enervating fear and uncertainty about the morrow, through the ensuing years. There was what we find now an almost incredible amount of mutual distrust, suspicion, irritation and quarrelling. Only a small proportion of the world's population lived to be peacefully and gracefully old in this phase of deterioration. Disease or a violent death became the common end again. One of the first general histories that was ever written was called The Martyrdom of Man (Winwood Reade, 1871). In

the Age of Frustration it seemed to many that that martyrdom was mounting to a final hopeless agony.

Yet in the welter there were also laughter, sympathy, helpfulness and courage. Those fretted and painful lives interwove with threads of great brightness. Out of that medley of human distresses, out of the brains of men stressed out of indolence and complacency by the gathering darkness and suffering about them, there came first the hope, then the broad plan and the effort, and at last the achievement of that fruitful order, gathering beauty and happy assurance, in which we live to-day.

BOOK THE SECOND - THE DAYS AFTER TOMORROW: THE AGE OF FRUSTRATION

1. THE LONDON CONFERENCE: THE CROWNING FAILURE OF THE OLD GOVERNMENTS; THE SPREAD OF DICTATORSHIPS AND FASCISMS

In the preceding chapters we have explained how the old order of the nineteenth century, the Capitalist System as it was called, came to disaster in the second and third decades of the twentieth century because of the disproportionate development of its industrial production, the unsoundness and vulnerability of its monetary nexus, and its political inadaptability. It had no inherent power of recovery, and there was no idea of a new order, sufficiently developed, to replace it. Necessarily therefore the tale of disaster went on.

The only mechanisms in existence for collective action, and that only in disconnected spurts, were the various sovereign governments. Most of these at the outset of the war were either parliamentary monarchies or parliamentary republics. The parliaments were elected upon a very preposterous system by the bulk or all of the population. The age was called the Age of Democracy. Democracy did not mean then what it means now, an equal opportunity for every human being according to his ability and the faculty to which he belongs, to serve and have a voice in collective affairs. Nor did it mean the fraternal equality of a small community. It expressed a political fiction of a very extraordinary kind: that every subject of the contemporary state was equally capable of making whatever collective decisions had to be made.

The great republics of a remoter antiquity, the Carthaginian, the Athenian, the Roman, for example, were all essentially aristocratic. Democratic republics, that is to say republics in which every man was supposed to share equally in the government, in the rare instances when they occurred at all before the end of the eighteenth century, were, like, Uri, Unterwalden or Andorra, small and poor and perched in inaccessible places. The world at large knew nothing of them. Their affairs were equally small and well within the scope of a common citizen's understanding.

Then with the Era of European Predominance came a turning-point in human affairs, that outbreak of books and discussion in the fifteenth century, a period of great animation and confusion when the destructive criticism of faiths and loyalties got loose. The release of new economic forces strained the old feudal order to breaking. Exploration and merchandising, new financial conditions, industrial development, created new types of men, uncertain of their powers, needing and demanding free play. They did not know clearly what they wanted; they did not know clearly how they differed from the men of the old order, nor had they any conception that such a structural reform of human relations as Plato had already pictured nearly two thousand years before them. His plan for a devoted and trained order of rulers was unknown to them, though More had tried to revive it. They were simply responding to the facts about them. They chafed under an hereditary aristocracy, and they distrusted an absolute king.

Essentially the movement that evolved the phraseology of nineteenth- century democracy was a revolt against "birth" and "privilege", against the monopolization of direction and advantages by restricted and generally hereditary classes in accordance with definitely established dogmas. Because this revolt was the revolt of a very miscellaneous number of energetic and resentful individuals not definitely organized, mentally or socially, it came about that at a quite early stage of the new movement it took the form of an assertion of the equal political rights of all men.

It was not that these sixteenth and seventeenth-century Radicals were for government by the general mass; it was that they were antagonistic to established classes and rulers. They constituted a vigorous insurgent minority rousing, so far as it could, and trailing after it the apathetic majority of submissive mankind. That was always the character of these democratic movements of the Age of European Predominance. The multitude was supposed to be demanding and deciding—and all the time it was being pushed or led. The individuality of the popular "leaders" of those centuries stands out far more vividly than the kings and ecclesiastics of the period. Only one or two such hereditary monarchs as William Prince of Orange, or Frederick the Great of Prussia, figure as conspicuously on the record as—to cite a miscellany of new types— Cromwell, Voltaire, Mirabeau, Washington, Gladstone, Robespierre, Bonaparte or Marx.

Later on (in England, America, Scandinavia, Germany, Finland, e.g.) in just the same way a minority of dissatisfied and aggressive women struggling for a rôle in affairs inflicted the vote upon the indifferent majority of women. But their achievement ended with that. Outside that sexual vindication, women at that time had little to contribute to the solution of the world's problems, and as a matter of fact they contributed nothing.

Research in social psychology is still only beginning to unravel the obscure processes by which faith in "democracy" became for the better part of a century the ruling cant of practically all America and the greater part of Europe. There was often a profound internal disingenuousness even in those who were known as "Thinkers" in that age. They were afraid in their hearts of stark realities; they tried

instinctively to adapt even their heresies to what seemed to them invincibly established prejudices. Their primary conception of democracy was of some far-away simple little republic of stout upstanding men, all similar, all practically equal in fortune and power, managing the affairs of the canton in a folk-meeting, by frank speech and acclamation. All the old- world democracies, up to and including the Republic of Rome, were ruled, in theory at least, by such meetings of all the citizens. The people, it was imagined, watched, listened, spoke, and wisdom ensued.

The extension of this ideal to the large communities of the new world that was replacing the feudal order, involved such manifest difficulties and even such absurdities that mysticism was inevitable if the people was still to be supposed the sovereign of the community. But there was so strong and widespread a dread that if this supposition was not maintained privilege, restriction, tyranny would come back that the mystical interpretation was boldly adopted. At any cost those old inequalities must not return, said the adventurers of the dawning capitalist age, and, flying from one subjugation, they hurried on to another.

They found the doctrine of man's natural virtue as expounded by Rousseau extraordinarily helpful and effective. The common man, when he is not beguiled by Priest or King, is always right. The Common People became therefore a mystical sympathetic being, essentially a God, whose altar was the hustings and whose oracle the ballot box. A little slow and lumpish was this God of the Age of European Predominance, but, though his mills ground slowly, men were assured that they ground with ultimate exactitude. And meanwhile business could be carried on. You could fool some of the people all the time and all the people some of the time, said Abraham Lincoln, but you could not fool all the people all the time. Yet for such crucial purposes as bringing about a war or exploiting an economic situation, this was manifestly a quite disastrous degree of foolability.

And the situation naturally evolved a Press of the very highest fooling capacity.

This belatedly inevitable Divinity proved now to be altogether too slow- witted for the urgent political and economic riddles, with ruin and death at hand, which pressed upon our race as the twentieth century unfolded. The experience of the futile Disarmament and Economic Conferences of 1932 and 1933, the massive resistance in every national legislature to any but the most narrow egotism in foreign policy, the inability of the world as a whole to establish any unanimity of action in face of swift economic collapse, revealed the final bankruptcy of Parliamentary Democracy.

The inability of the world's nominal rulers to shake off their lifelong habit of speaking to, or at, a vaguely conceived crowd of prejudiced voters, and their invincible repugnance from clear statement, frustrated every effort towards realism. They recoiled from any suggestion of definitive or novel action on the plea that their function was purely representative. Behind them all the reader feels the sprawling uneasy presence of that poor invertebrate mass deity of theirs, the Voter, easily roused to panic and frantic action against novel, bold or radical measures, very amenable to patriotic claptrap, very easily scared and maddened

into war, and just as easily baffled to distrust and impotence by delays, side issues, and attacks on the personalities of decisive people he might otherwise have trusted. An entirely irresponsible Press, mercenary or partisan, played upon his baser emotions, which were so easy to play upon, and made no appeal whatever to his intelligence or his conscience.

The Voter, the Mass, which was neither educated nor led, the Voter without any sincere organizations of leadership anywhere, is the basal explanation of the impotence of those culminating conferences. The World Economic Conference in London was by far the more significant of the two. Armament and disarmament are symptoms and superficial, but economic life is fundamental. This London gathering has been made the subject of a thousand studies by our social psychologists. Many of its contradictions still perplex us profoundly. The men who assembled had just as good brains as anyone to-day, and, as an exhaustive analysis by Moreton Canby of the various projects advanced at the Conference proves, they had a substantial understanding of the needs of the world situation, yet collectively, and because of their haunting paralysing sense of the Mass and Press behind them and of their incalculable impulses and resentments, they achieved an effect of fatuity far beyond the pompous blunderings of Versailles.

Primarily the London Conference was a belated effort to repair the vast omissions of that earlier gathering, to supplement the well-meaning political patchwork of Wilson by some readjustment of the monetary and economic dislocations he had been too limited to foresee or too weak to avoid. Wraithlike conceptions of some vague monetary League of Nations at Bâle, and some Tariff Council and Assembly, drifted through the mists of the opening meeting. And History, with its disposition to inexact repetition made one of the principal figures of this second world assembly also a President of the United States, belonging also to the Democratic Party and according to the ritual of that Party invoking the name of Jefferson as the Communists invoked the name of Marx or the Moslim, Mahomet. This was Roosevelt II. He leaves a less vivid impression than his predecessor because he did not impend for so long upon the European scene. But for some months at least before and after his election as American President and the holding of the London Conference there was again a whispering hope in the world that a real "Man" had arisen, who would see simply and clearly, who would speak plainly to all mankind and liberate the world from the dire obsessions and ineptitudes under which it suffered and to which it seemed magically enslaved. But the one thing he failed to do was to speak plainly.

Drawing wisdom from Wilson's personal failure, he did not come to London and expose himself and his conversation to too close a scrutiny. He preferred to deal with the fluctuating crises in London from his yacht, Amberjack II, in Nantucket Harbour, through intermittent messages and through more or less completely authorized intermediaries. Amberjack II has become almost as significant a ship in the history of human affairs as the Ford Peace Ship. Significant equally in its intentions and in its inadequacies.

Everywhere as the Conference drew near men were enquiring about this possible new leader for them. "Is this at last the Messiah we seek, or shall we look for another?" Every bookshop in Europe proffered his newly published book of utterances, Looking Forward, to gauge what manner of mind they had to deal with. It proved rather disconcerting reading for their anxious minds. Plainly the man was firm, honest and amiable, as the frontispiece portrait with its clear frank eyes and large resolute face showed, but the text of the book was a politician's text, saturated indeed with good will, seasoned with much vague modernity, but vague and wanting in intellectual grip. "He's good," they said, "but is this good enough?"

Nevertheless hope fought a stout fight. There was no other personality visible who even promised to exorcize the spell that lay upon the economic life of the race. It was Roosevelt's Conference or nothing. And in spite of that disappointing book there remained some sound reasons for hope. In particular the President, it was asserted, had a "Brain Trust". A number of indisputably able and modern-minded men were his associates, such men as Professors Tugwell, Moley and Dickinson, men whose later work played a significant part in that reconstruction of legal and political method which was America's particular contribution to Modern State ideas. This "last hope of mankind", it was credibly reported, called these intimates by their Christian names and they called him "Guv'nor." He was said to have the modesty and greatness to defer to their studied and matured opinions. Observers, still hopeful, felt that if he listened to these advisors things might not go so badly after all. He was at any rate one point better than the European politicians and heads of States who listened only to bankers and big- business men.

But was he listening? Did he grasp the threefold nature of the problem in hand? He understood, it seemed, the need for monetary inflation to reduce the burthen of debt and over-capitalization; he was apparently alive to the need for a progressive expansion of public employment; and so far he was sound. Unless, which is not quite clear, he wavered between "public" and "publicly assisted", which was quite another matter. But was he sound upon the necessity that these measures should be world-wide or practically world-wide? He made some unexpected changes of attitude in these respects. Were these changes inconstancies or were they tactical manoeuvres veiling a profoundly consistent and resolute purpose? Was it wise to be tactical when all the world was in need of plain speech and simple directive ideas? His treatment took on a disconcertingly various quality. He listened, it seemed, to his advisors; but was he not also listening to everybody? He was flirting with bimetallism. No medicine, it seemed, was to be spared.

The Conference opened with a stout determination to be brilliant and eventful; the hotels were full, the streets beflagged, the programme of entertainments was admirable, and even the English weather seemed to make an effort. The opening addresses by the King of England and his Prime Minister Ramsay MacDonald make very curious reading to-day. They express an acute recognition of the crucial condition of human affairs. They state in so many words that the failure of the

Conference will precipitate world disaster. They insist upon the necessity for world cooperation, for monetary simplification and a resumption of employment; and in all that we admit they had the truth of the matter. But they make not the faintest intimation of how these desirable ends are to be obtained. They made gestures that are incomprehensible to us unless they had an inkling of the primary elements of the situation. And then immediately they turned away to other things. That mixture of resolve and failure to attack is what perplexes us most. If they saw the main essentials of the situation they certainly did not see them as a connected whole; they did not see any line of world action before them.

Cordell Hull, the chief of the United States delegation, was equally large and fine. The grave and splendid words—shot with piety in the best American tradition—that he inscribed upon the roll of history were as follows: "Selfishness must be banished. If—which God forbid!—any nation should wreck this Conference, with the notion that its local interests might profit, that nation would merit the execration of mankind."

Again Daladier, the French Prime Minister, opened with extremely broad and sane admissions. He insisted strongly on a necessity which the two opening English speeches had minimized, the necessity, the urgent necessity, for a progressive development of great public works throughout the world to absorb the unemployed and restore consumption. The Americans in the second week seemed to be coming in line with that. But after this much of lucidity the Conference fell away to minor issues. Apparently it could not keep at so high a level of reality. The pressure of the Mass and the Press behind each delegate began to tell upon him. The national representatives began to insist with increasing explicitness that national interests must not be sacrificed to the general good, and in a little time it became doubtful if there could be such a thing as the general good. The World Economic Conference became by imperceptible transitions a World Economic Conflict just as the League of Nations had become a diplomatic bargain mart. All the fine preluding of the first séances withered to fruitlessness because the mind of the world had still to realize the immense moral and educational effort demanded by those triple conditions that were dawning upon its apprehension, and because it was still unwilling to accept the immense political pooling they indicated. The amount of self- abnegation involved was an insurmountable psychological barrier in the way of the representatives present. It would have meant a sacrifice of the very conditions that had made them. How could men appointed as national representatives accept a pooling of national interests? They were indeed fully prepared to revolutionize the world situation and change gathering misery to hope, plenty and order, but only on the impossible condition that they were not to change themselves and that nothing essential to their importance changed. The leading ideas of the Conference were cloudily true, but the disintegrative forces of personal, party and national egotism were too strong for them.

It is a very curious thing that the representatives of Soviet Russia did nothing to enlighten the obscurity of the world riddle. It is still argued by many writers that the Bolshevik régime was the direct precursor of our Modern World-State as

it exists to-day. But there was no direct continuity. The Modern State arose indeed out of the same social imperatives and the same constructive impulses that begot Marxism and Leninism, but as an independent, maturer, and sounder revolutionary conception. The Soviet system certainly anticipated many of the features of our present order in its profession of internationalism, in its very real socialism, and particularly in the presence of a devoted controlling organization, the Communist Party, which foreshadowed our Modern State Fellowship. But there was always a wide divergence in Russia between theory and practice, and Litvinoff, who spoke on behalf of that first great experiment in planning, was too preoccupied with various particular points at issue between his country and the western world, trading embargoes and difficulties of credit, for example, to use the occasion as he might have done, for a world-wide appeal. He did nothing to apply the guiding principles of Communism to the world situation. Here was a supreme need for planning, but he said nothing for a Five Year or Ten Year Plan for all the world. Here was a situation asking plainly for collective employment, and he did not even press the inevitability of world-socialism. Apparently he had forgotten the world considered as a whole as completely as any of the capitalist delegates. He was thinking of Russia versus the other States of the world as simply as if he were an ordinary capitalist patriot.

The claims of the other delegations were even more shortsighted and uninspired. Since there was a time-limit set to their speeches, they compressed their assertions of general humanitarian benevolence to a phrase or so and then came to business. Only Senator Connolly, from the Irish Free State, protested against the blinkered outlooks of his fellow speakers and pleaded for a consideration of "every possible theory, however unorthodox." But his own speech propounded no substantial constructive ideas. He was too obsessed by an embargo that England had put upon Irish exports, and to that he settled down...

The whole idea of the Modern World-State, Moreton Canby insists, is to be traced, albeit in a warped and sterilized form, alike in the expressed idea- systems of the Americans, the British, the French and the Russians at the Conference. In the American statements it is wrapped about and hidden by individualist phrases and precautions, in the British it is overlaid by imperialist assumptions, in the Russian it is made unpalatable by the false psychology and harsh jargon of Marxism. In the first the business man refuses to change and get out of the way, in the second the imperialist administrator, and in the third the doctrinaire party man. Athwart every assertion of general principles drive the misty emotions of patriotism, party and personal association. Yet for all that it is indisputable that the Modern World-State was definitely adumbrated at London in 1933. Like a ghost out of the future its presence was felt by nearly everyone, though the worst phases of the Age of Frustration had still to come, though generations of suffering had still to lapse, before it could appear as the living reality of human political life.

The ghost, says Canby, did not materialise because there was no material. Every large country in the world was feeling its way towards the essentials of a permanently progressive world-state but none was yet within reach even of its

partial and local realisation. Roosevelt II and his eleventh hour effort to reconstruct America, he finds particularly interesting. The President was clearly aware of the need to relieve debt by inflation, but he was unable to check the dissipation of the liberated energy in speculation. He was dealing with men, trained and saturated in the tradition of poker, to whom a solemn cunning had become a second nature, and he was asking them (with occasional fierce threats) to display an open-faced helpfulness. He had no proper civil service available to control large public works; it was impossible to change the American technicians at one blow from quasi-financial operators to a candid, devoted public salariat. So he tried to induce profiteers to forego profits and organise their industries on altruistic lines by dire threats of socialisation which he had no managing class to enforce. And he was as ignorant of British or European mentality and as little able to get to an understanding with it as Wilson had been before him. It was a mutual misunderstanding, but his manners were self-righteous and provocative. He began to scold long before the Conference was over. By 1935 everyone was pointing to a sort of contrasted parallelism between America and Russia. Each was manifestly struggling towards a more scientifically organised state, and each was finding the same difficulty in reconciling productive efficiency in the general interest with primarily political control. Technician and politician had still to be assimilated one to the other. Each great dictatorship was at war with the speculator and the profiteer. Each professed a faint hope of cosmopolitan cooperation and then concentrated practically and urgently upon the establishment of an internal prosperity. But they started towards that common objective from opposite poles of productive efficiency and social assumption. Roosevelt started from the standpoint of democratic individualism and Stalin from that of Marxist communism. The British system and the other intermediate countries of the world struggled to be conservative in the chaos of financial collapse. No solvent had yet been devised to synthesise the good will in the world.

The London Conference rose to no such dramatic climax as the signing of the Peace Treaty at Versailles. It rose to nothing. It began at its highest point and steadily declined. If Versailles produced a monster, London produced nothing at all. Never did so valiant a beginning peter out so completely.

There are abundant intimations in the Press of the time (see Habwright's The Sense of Catastrophe in the Nineteen Thirties, a summary of quotations in the Historical Documents Series 173,192) of a realization that the political and economic morale of that age was played out, and that almost any casual selection of men would have been at least as adequate as this gathering of old- world political personages to face the vast impending disasters before our race. For at any rate these men had already been tried and tested and found wanting. Mr. Ramsay MacDonald indeed, the British premier, the fine flower and summary of professional politics, rolled his r's and his eyes over the Conference and seemed still to be hoping that some favourable accident out of the void might save him and his like from the damning dissection of history. For a time, in the opening glow of the assembly, with the clicking photographers recording every studied gesture, with

the attentive microphones spreading out and pickling for ever his fine voice and his rich accent, with bustling secretaries in sedulous attendance, with the well-trained gravity of the delegates and particularly the well-matured high seriousness of those adepts in public appearance, the Americans, to sustain him, this last sublimation of democratic statesmanship may really have believed that some kind of favourable incantation was in progress under his direction. He must have felt that or he could not have remained there talking. Incantations had made him. By the sheer use of voice and gesture he had clambered from extreme obscurity to world prominence. If he did not believe in incantation there was nothing left for him to believe in. He must have clung to that persuasion to the end. But if that was his state of mind at the time, it could hardly have survived the comments and criticisms of the next few months. Surely then he had some sleepless nights in which even his private incantations failed.

The World Economic Conference lost its brilliance in a week or so. The City, which had been so flushed with hope that for a time its price lists, all pluses, looked like war-time cemeteries, relapsed into depression. The World Slump did not wait for the Conference to disperse before it resumed. At the outset London had been all blown up and distended by bright anticipations, so that it was like one of those little squeaking bladders children play with, and like one of those bladders, so soon as the blowing ceased, it shrank and shrivelled and ended in a dying wail of despair.

As Habwright puts it, by July 1933 intelligent men and women everywhere were saying two things. Of the assembled rulers and delegates they were saying: "These people can do nothing for us. They do worse than nothing. They intensify the disaster." And in the second place it was demanded with a sort of astonishment: "Why have historians, sociologists and economists nothing to tell us now? There may indeed be some excuse for the failure of politicians under democratic conditions. But have our universities been doing nothing about it? Is there indeed no science of these things? Is there no knowledge? Has history learnt nothing of causes, and is there no analysis of the social processes that are destroying us?"

To which the professors, greatly preoccupied at that particular date in marking honours papers in history and social and political science, made no audible reply.

Before the end of the thirties it was plain to all the world that a world- wide social catastrophe was now inevitably in progress, that the sanest thing left for intelligent men to do was to set about upon some sort of Noah's Ark to salvage whatever was salvageable of civilization, so that there should be a new beginning after the rising deluge of misfortune had spent itself. A few prescient spirits had been saying as much for some years, but now this idea of salvage spread like an epidemic. It prepared the way for the Modern State Movement on which our present order rests. At the time, however, the general pessimism was little mitigated by any real hope of recovery. One writer, quoted by Habwright, compared man to a domesticated ape, "which has had the intelligence and ability to drag its straw mattress up to the fire when it is cold, but has had neither the wit nor the foresight to escape the consequent blaze". Habwright's brief summary of the financial oper-

ations that went on as the sense of catastrophe grew justifies that grim image very completely.

The conviction that Parliamentary Democracy had come to an end spread everywhere in that decade. Already in the period between the vacillation in international affairs after Versailles and the warfare of the Forties, men had been going about discussing and scheming and plotting for some form of government that should be at least decisive. And now their efforts took on a new urgency. There was a world-wide hysteria to change governments and officials.

At its first onset this craving for decisiveness had produced some extremely crude results. An epidemic of tawdry "dictatorships" had run over Europe from Poland to Spain immediately after the war. For the most part these adventures followed the pattern of the pronunciamentos of the small South American republics, and were too incidental and inconsequent for the student of general history to be troubled about them now. But there followed a world-wide development of directive or would-be directive political associations which foreshadowed very plainly the organization of the Modern State Fellowship upon which our present world order rests.

The Fascist dictatorship of Mussolini in Italy had something in it of a more enduring type than most of the other supersessions of parliamentary methods. It rose not as a personal usurpation but as the expression of an organization with a purpose and a sort of doctrine of its own. The intellectual content of Fascism was limited, nationalist and romantic; its methods, especially in its opening phase, were violent and dreadful; but at least it insisted upon discipline and public service for its members. It appeared as a counter movement to a chaotic labour communism, but its support of the still- surviving monarchy and the Church was qualified by a considerable boldness in handling education and private property for the public benefit. Fascism indeed was not an altogether bad thing; it was a bad good thing; and Mussolini has left his mark on history.

In Russia something still more thorough and broader came into operation after 1917. This was the Communist Party. It was the invention of Lenin; he continued to modify and adapt its organization and doctrine until his untimely death in 1924. While he lived Russia's experiment really seemed to be leading the world in its flight towards a new order from the futile negations and paralysis of Parliamentary government. It is still profoundly interesting to note the modernity of many aspects of the early Bolshevik régime.

This modernity achieved under the stress of urgent necessities and Lenin's guidance was attained in spite of many grave difficulties created by the Marxist tradition. Marx, who was a man of what the psychologists of the middle twenty-first century used to call "blinkered originality", never saw through the democratic sentimentalities of the period in which he lived. There had been a tendency to exclude the privileged classes from the True Democracy of Common Men even at the dawn of the modern democratic idea, and he and his followers intensified and stereotyped this tendency in their own particular version of deified democracy,

the Proletariat. The Proletariat was just Pure Masses, and mystical beyond measure.

But at the outset the actual Russian revolution was under the control of the intensely practical and intensely middle-class Lenin, and he took care that the great social reconstruction he had in mind was equally secured against the risk of paralysis through mass inertia and the risk of overthrow through mass panic. His ostensibly "democratic" government of Soviets, the Soviet pyramid, was built up on a hierarchic scheme that brought the administration face to face only with seasoned representatives who had been filtered through an ascendant series of bodies. Moreover, he established a very complete control of education and the Press, to keep the thought of the nominally sovereign masses upon the right lines. And to animate and control the whole machine he had his invention of the Communist Party.

This Communist Party, like the Italian Fascisti, owes its general conception to that germinal idea of the Modern State, the Guardians in Plato's Republic. For if anyone is to be called the Father of the Modern State it is Plato. The Members of the Communist Party were extremely like those Guardians. As early as 1900 critics of democratic institutions were discussing the possibility of creating a cult primarily devoted to social and political service, self- appointed, self-trained and self-disciplined. The English- speaking Socialist movement was debating projects of that kind in 1909-10 (see Fabian News in Historical Documents for those years), but it needed the dangers and stresses of the postwar European situation to produce types of workers and young people sufficiently detached, desperate and numerous, to unite effectively into a permanent revolutionary control.

From its beginnings the Communist Party, though it was not divided into "faculties" and remained political rather than technical in spirit, resembled our own Modern State Fellowship in its insistence upon continuous learning and training throughout life, upon free criticism within the limits of the party, upon accessibility (under due limitations) to all who wished to serve in it, and upon the right to resignation from its privileges and severities of all who wished to return to comparative irresponsibility. But the conditions which created the Russian Communist Party made it inevitably Marxist, and even after a thorough Leninization, Communism, that characteristic final product of middle- nineteenth-century radicalism, still retained many of its old sentimentalities, reverting indeed more and more towards them after Lenin's death and the rule of the devoted but unoriginal, suspicious and overbearing Stalin.

There was a heavy load of democratic and equalitarian cant upon the back of the Russian system, just as there was a burthen of patriotic and religious cant upon the Italian Fascist. Even the United States Constitution did not profess democratic equality and insist upon the inspired wisdom of the untutored more obstinately than the new Russian régime. Although hardly any of the ruling group of Russians were of peasant or working-class origin—there were far more politicians from that social level in the public life of Western Europe and America—there was a universal pretence of commonness about them all. They spat, they

went unshaved and collarless. They pretended to be indifferent to bourgeois comfort. It was ordained that at the phrase "Class-War" every knee should bow. When the Communist leaders quarrelled among themselves, "bourgeois" or "petty bourgeois" was the favourite term of abuse, none the less deadly because it was almost invariably true. Long years were to pass before any movement whatever in the direction of the Modern State System was quite free from this heritage of cant.

One unfortunate aspect of this entanglement of the new experiment in Russia with the social envies and hatreds of the old order was its inability to assimilate competent technicians, organizers and educators into its direction. In its attempt to modernize, it refused the assistance of just the most characteristically modern types in the community. But since these types had a special education and knew things not generally known, it was difficult to accord them proletarian standing. In Russia therefore, as in America, the politician with his eloquence and his necessary and habitual disingenuousness still intervened and obstructed, if he did not actually bar, the way to a scientific development of a new economic and social order.

Manifestly Stalin learnt much from his difficulties with the Five Year Plan of the evil of subordinating technical to political ability, and a speech of his upon the Old and New Technical Intelligentzia made in June 1931 (Historical Documents Series, Stalinism, XM 327,705) is a very frank admission of the primary necessity in the modern community of the "non-party" man of science and of special knowledge. Unhappily the hand of the party politician in Russia was strengthened by the untrammelled activities of those strange protectors of Marxist authority the Checka, which became later the G.P.U. So from 1928, the date of the First Five Year Plan, in spite of a great driving- force of enthusiastic devotion, Russia went clumsily, heavily and pretentiously—a politician's dictatorship, propaganding rather than performing, disappointing her well-wishers abroad and thwarting the best intelligences she produced. When her plans went wrong through her lack of precise material foresight, she accused, and imprisoned or shot, engineers and suchlike technical workers.

A further bad result of this ineradicable democratic taint of the Soviet system was the widening estrangement of the Russian process from Western creative effort. Instead of being allies they became opponents. As the challenge of social disintegration became more urgent in the Atlantic countries, it became plainer and plainer that such hope as there was for the salvaging of a reconstructed civilization from a welter of disaster lay in the coordinate effort of intelligent, able and energetic individuals of every nation, race, type and class. A revolution was certainly needed, but not a revolution according to the time-worn formula of street battles and barricades, not a class war. A revolution in the very character of revolutions had to occur. There was no need for insurrectionary revolution any longer, since now the system was destroying itself. The phase for boldly constructive revolution had arrived, and at every point where constructive effort was made the nagging antagonism of the Class War fanatic appeared, to impede and divide. (See, for example, Upton Sinclair on this conflict, in The Way Out, 1933, in the

series of reprints under his name, Historical Documents Series, History of Opinion.)

The waste of creative energy was enormous, not only in Russia but all over the world. Multitudes of young men and women in every civilized community, the living hope of the race, dissipated their generous youth and vigour in bitter conflicts upon a purely doctrinaire issue. The poison of nationalism was abroad to complicate their reactions. Many turned against progress altogether and sought to thrust the world back to some imaginary lost age of virtue. So they became Ku Klux Klansmen, Nationalists, Nazis. All felt the natural youthful impulse towards large, effective, vehement action. All meant well. They were one in spirit though they suffered from a confusion of tongues. The idea of the Modern State could not for a long time make itself clear to their imaginations largely because the conspicuous self-contradictions of Russia stood in the way.

Russia seemed to lead, it sought to lead in its acts and deeds, and it lied. Meanwhile, surviving very largely because of this distraction of creative forces, the elderly methods of Parliamentary Democracy and the elderly Nationalist Diplomacy remained in possession of the greater part of the Western World, and the social collapse it was powerless to arrest continued.

2. THE SLOUGHING OF THE OLD EDUCATIONAL TRADITION

Faber in his interesting and suggestive Historical Analyses (2103) discusses how far the wars, depressions, pestilences, phases of semi-famine and periods of actual starvation, in the hundred years before 2014, were necessary, and how far, with the resources then available, they might have been avoided by mankind. He takes the view that the encumbrance of tradition was so great that for all that period this martyrdom of our kind was inevitable. He argues that without the sufferings of these generations men's minds could never have been sufficiently purged of their obstinate loyalties, jealousies, fears and superstitions; men's wills never roused to the efforts, disciplines and sacrifices that were demanded for the establishment of the Modern State.

Faber applies his criticism more particularly to this so-called decadence of education after (circa) 1930. It has hitherto been usual to treat the ebb of school-building and schooling that took place then as a real retrogression, to rank it with the fall in the general standard of life and the deterioration of public health. But he advanced some excellent reasons for supposing that, so far from being an evil, the starvation and obliteration of the old-world teaching machinery was a necessary preliminary to social recovery.

The common school, he insists, had to be born again, had to be remade fundamentally. And before that could happen it had to be broken up and wellnigh destroyed. He sweeps aside almost contemptuously the claim that the nineteenth century was an educational century. We are misled, he argues, by a mere resemblance between the schools and universities of the past and the schools and post-school education of the modern period. Both occupy the time of the young, and we do not sufficiently appreciate the fact that what they are doing with the young is something entirely different. Our education is an introduction to the continual revolutionary advance of life. But education before the twenty-first century was essentially a conservative process. It was so rigorously and completely traditional that its extensive disorganization was an inevitable preliminary to the foundation of a new world.

The word education has come now to cover almost all intellectual activities throughout life except research and artistic creation. That was not its original meaning. It meant originally the preparation of the young for life. It did not go on even in extreme cases beyond three or four and twenty, and usually it was over by fourteen! But we draw no line at any age, as our ancestors did, when learning

ceases. The general information of the public, public discussion and collective decisions, all fall within the scope of our educational directorate. All that was outside what passed for education in the early Twentieth Century.

What people knew in those days they knew in the most haphazard way. The privately owned newspapers of the period told the public what their readers or their proprietors desired; the diffusion of facts and ideas by the early cinema, the sound radio and so on was entirely commercialized for the advertisement of goods in America, and controlled and directed in the interests of influential politicians in Great Britain; book-publishing, even the publication of scientific works, was mainly speculative and competitive, and there was no such thing as a Centre of Knowledge in the world.

It is remarkable to note how long mankind was able to carry on without any knowledge organization whatever. No encyclopaedia, not even a bookseller's encyclopaedia, had existed before the seventeenth century, for the so-called Chinese Encyclopaedia was a literary miscellany, and there was no permanent organization of record even on the part of such mercenary encyclopaedias as came into existence after that date. Nor was there any conception of the need of a permanent system of ordered knowledge, continually revised until the twentieth century was nearing its end. To the people of the Age of Frustration our interlocking research, digest, discussion, verification, notification and informative organizations, our Fundamental Knowledge System, that is, with its special stations everywhere, its regional bureaus, its central city at Barcelona, its seventeen million active workers and its five million correspondents and reserve enquirers, would have seemed incredibly vast. It would have seemed incredibly vast to them in spite of the fact that the entirely unproductive armies and military establishments they sustained in those days of universal poverty were practically as huge.

We are still enlarging this Brain of Mankind, still increasing its cells, extending its records and making its interactions more rapid and effective. A vast independent literature flourishes beside it. Compared with today our species in the Age of Frustration was as a whole brainless: it was collectively invertebrate with a few scattered ill-connected ganglia; it was lethargically ignorant; it had still to develop beyond the crude rudiments of any coordinated knowledge at all.

But not only was general knowledge rudimentary, casual, erroneous and bad. Faber's case against the old education is worse than that. Knowledge was explicitly outside education, outside formal schooling altogether. The need for a sound common ideology is a Modern State idea. The old, so called "Elementary" schools, Faber shows, did not pretend to give knowledge. So far as directive ideas were concerned, they disavowed this intention. He quotes a very revealing contemporary survey of the situation in America by Dr. G. S. Counts (The American Road to Culture, 1930) in which the complete ideological sterilization of the common schools of the Republic is demonstrated beyond question. The sterilization was deliberate. So far as the giving of comprehensive information about life went, says Faber, there was absolutely nothing valuable destroyed during this period of educational collapse because nothing valuable had as yet got into the

curricula. The history taught in these popular schools was pernicious patriotic twaddle; the biology, non-existent or prudish and childish —the "facts of sex", as they were called, were for example TAUGHT by dissecting flowers—and there was no economic instruction whatever. The nineteenth-century "education" was not enlightenment; it was anti- enlightenment. Parents, political and religious organizations watched jealously that this should be so. He quotes school time-tables and public discussions and gives samples of the textbooks in use.

The decline in scientific research, moreover, during this age of systole, Faber insists, has been greatly exaggerated. Although there was certainly a considerable diminution in the number of actual workers through the destruction of private endowments and what was called "economy", and although there was also a considerable interference with the international exchange of ideas and a slacking down in pace at which ideas grew, there was no absolute interruption in the advance of ordered science even through the worst phases of the social breakdown. Research displayed a protean adaptability and indestructibility. It shifted from the patronage of the millionaire to the patronage of the war lord; it took refuge in Russia, Spain and South America; it betook itself to the aeroplane hangars, to rise again in due time to its present world-predominance. It had never been pampered under the régime of private capitalism. All through that First Age of Prosperity pure research had lived from hand to mouth. As soon as it paid, says Sinclair Lewis in Martin Arrowsmith, it was commercialized and it degenerated. When the bad times came the parasites of science fell away, but the genuine scientific worker, accustomed to scanty supplies, tightened his belt a little more and in all sorts of out-of-the-way places stuck to his job.

What really did break up in this period between 1930 and 1950 was a systematic schooling of the masses which had developed steadily during the nineteenth century. Beyond the elements of reading, speech and counting, this was no more and no less than a drilling in tradition. There had been some reforms, more particularly in method, some advance in the teaching of infants (though this was sacrificed early in the economy flurry), and a few exceptional schools emerged, but this was the character of the typical school of the time. A progressive multiplication of this kind of school had indeed gone on in nearly every country in the world even up to the outbreak of the Great War. The proportion of "literates" who could at least read increased steadily. After that the rate of advance (except in Russia after 1917, where popular teaching was only beginning) fell stage by stage to zero. But what was ebbing was not really knowledge or instruction at all, but a training in the binding traditions of the old society.

The story of what used to be called "the conflict between religion and science" belongs mainly to the history of the nineteenth century, and we will not tell again here how the fairly stable structure of Christian belief and disciplines was weakened by the changes in values that ensued from the revelation of geological and biological horizons in that period. Before 1850 more than ninety-nine per cent of the population of Europe and America believed unquestioningly that the universe had been created in the year 4004 B.C. Their intellectual lives were all cramped to

the dimensions of that petty cellule of time. It was rather frightening for them to break out. They succumbed to mental agoraphobia. The student knows already of the difficulties experienced by the Christian ministry during those years of mental release and expansion in "symbolizing" the Fall and Atonement, which had hitherto been taught as historical facts, and of the loss of confidence and authority that came through this unavoidable ambiguity. The ensuing controversies thundered and died away into mutterings and ironies, but the consequences of these disputes became more and more evident in the succeeding generations. They evinced themselves in a universal moral indefiniteness. The new and old cancelled out.

The accepted Christian world outlook, both that prescribed by the Catholic Church and that of the various dissentient Protestant sects, had carried with it a coarse but fairly effective moral imperative. Hell was the ultima ratio of good behaviour. The Churches, although badly damaged in argument, were well endowed and powerfully entrenched in the educational organization. Their practical resistance to the new views proved to be more effective than their controversial efforts. People had the social habit of belonging to them and entrusting their children to them. There were no other teachers ready; no other schools. So the traditional orthodoxies were able to obstruct the development of a modern ethic in harmony with the new realizations of man's place in space and time, in spite of the loss of much of their former power of unquestionable conviction.

Gradually throughout the First Age of General Prosperity the relative value of their endowments diminished, and they lost intellectual and moral prestige. But it was only with the economic landslides of the post-war period that their material foundations gave way completely. For a time these great organizations share in the common disaster, and when at last under new auspices a restoration of production occurred they recovered nothing of their proportional importance. Their old investments had vanished. They suffered with other landlords in the general resumption of estates by the community. By 1965 C.E. it was no longer possible for an ordinary young man to get a living as a minister of any Church. Holy orders, since they implied an old-world outlook, were also a grave encumbrance for an ambitious teacher. It was extraordinary with what facility the priests and parsons changed their collars and vanished into the crowd with the progressive disappearance of their endowments. The organized Christian Churches pass out of history at last almost as quickly as the priesthood of Baal vanished after the Persian conquest. There is considerable plausibility in Faber's contention that they could have disappeared in no other way.

It had been usual to treat the extensive destruction of social morale which characterized this period as due to the interregnum between the fading out of the Christian ethic and the moral and intellectual establishment of modern conduct. Faber questions that boldly. He admits that the morale of Western civilization was built up very largely by Christian agencies, but he denies that they were sustaining it. He ascribes its evaporation almost entirely to the destruction of social confidence which we have noted already as a natural consequence of the wild

fluctuations of economic security and monetary values at that time. Men ceased to respect society because they felt they were being cheated and betrayed by society.

3. DISINTEGRATION AND CRYSTALLIZATION IN THE SOCIAL MAGMA. THE GANGSTER AND MILITANT POLITICAL ORGANIZATIONS

The dissolutions and regroupings of people that were going on through this period have always attracted the attention of the social philosopher. The common man had lost his faith in a friendly God, his confidence in social justice and his educational and social services. He was out of employment and stirred by unsatisfied appetites. The time-honoured life of work and family interests had become impossible for a growing majority.

What we now call social nucleation was failing; the grouping of human beings in families and working communities was not going on. They became restive and troublesome. The social confidence and discipline that had prevailed throughout the nineteenth century deteriorated very rapidly. There was a swift fall in social security.

Phases of fever have occurred time without number in human history, phases of unsettlement and confused motivation, clottings and drives and migrations of population. Periods of tranquil assurance are the exception throughout the ages. But in the past it has usually been the exhaustion of food supplies, pestilence or some cruel invasion that has broken up the social texture and made humanity lawless again. This new disintegration was of a different character. It was due in the first place to an increase rather than a diminution of material and energy in the social scheme. It was a process of expansion which went wrong through the inadequacy of traditional law and government.

The disintegrative forces were already evident in the eighteenth century; they became very conspicuous in the French Revolution and the subsequent social and political disturbances but they only rose to a plain domination of the controlling forces after the World War.

In the seventeenth century, when population was thin and hardly anyone moved about, it had been possible to keep order by means of a village constable, to try the malefactor by a local magistrate and jury which knew him thoroughly and understood his position and motives. Dogberry and Shallow sufficed. But the economic growth of the eighteenth century increased the size of towns and the traffic on the newly made roads between them without any corresponding increase in the forces of order. It produced, therefore, the urban mob, the footpad, the highwayman and the brigand. The local constable was unequal to these new

demands; the local magistrate as inadequate. There was a phase of increasing crime.

After the failure of a régime of savage punishment uncertainly inflicted, after the excesses of the first French Revolution, after phases of mob violence in every European capital, and endless other manifestations of this outpacing of social control, the machinery of government did by an effort adjust itself to the new conditions. More or less modernized police forces appeared throughout the world and inaugurated a new phase of order and security, a phase which reached its maximum in the years before the Great War. For a time then the world, or at any rate very considerable areas of it, was almost as safe as it is today. An unarmed man could go about in reasonable security in most of Europe, India, China, America. Nobody offered him violence or attempted open robbery. Even the policeman in the English-speaking and Western European communities carried no weapon but a truncheon.

But the World War broke down many of the inhibitions of violence and bloodshed that had been built up during the progressive years of the nineteenth century and an accumulating number of intelligent, restless unemployed men, in a new world of motor-cars, telephones, plate-glass shop windows, unbarred country houses and trustful social habits, found themselves faced with illegal opportunities far more attractive than any legal behaviour-system now afforded them. And now after the world slump that insanity of public economy which runs like a disease through the story of the age prevented any prompt enlargement and modernization of the existing educational, legal or police organizations. The scale and prestige of the law-court and police-court dwindled as the problems presented to them by the vast irregular developments of that period of stress and perplexity increased.

So the stage was set for a lawless phase. The criminal was liberated from parochialism and reactionary economies long before his antagonist the policeman, and he experienced all the invigoration and enlargement of that release. The criminal grew big while the law, pot-bound in its traditional swathings, was unable to keep pace with him.

The criminal records of this disorderly interlude make strange reading today. Things that were terrible enough at the time appear to us now as they recede into the past through a thickening, highly retractile veil of grotesqueness and picturesque absurdity. We read about them, as we read about mediaeval tortures or cannibal feasts or war atrocities or human sacrifice, with a startled incredulity. We laugh now; it is all so IMPOSSIBLE. Few of us actually realize these were flesh-and-blood sufferings that living men and women went through only a century and a half ago.

The criminals of the more fortunate countries of the European system, during that First Age of General Prosperity before the World War, like the few cases of intolerable behaviour with which society deals today, had constituted a small abnormal and diminishing minority for the most part mental defectives or at best very inferior types. The majority of their offences were emotional or brutish of-

fences. There was some stealing and a steady proportion of swindling in business, not sufficient to disturb the social order at all seriously. But as the morale of the old order dissolved, this ceased to be the case. Increasing numbers of intelligent and enterprising people found themselves in conflict with society because, as they argued very reasonably, society had cheated them. Patriotism too, they felt, had cheated them and given them nothing but poverty and war. They had never had a fair chance. They looked after themselves and left the community to look after itself. They fell back on the nearer loyalties of their immediate associates.

Your "pal" at any rate was close at hand. If he "let you down", you had a fair chance to "get at" him. Little gang-nuclei came into existence, therefore, wherever unassimilated elements of the population were congested and humiliated or wherever intelligent men festered in unemployment and need.

In 1900 European society in particular was still nucleated about the family group in relation to a generally understood code of lawful behaviour. In 1950 its individuals were either nucleated into gangs, groups or societies or dissolved into crowds, and the influence and pretence of any universally valid standard of good conduct had disappeared.

Robbery is the first great division in the catalogue of anti-social offences. Every efficient government in the past reserved to itself the sole right of dispossession, and every intelligent government exercised the right with extreme discretion. In the past of unregulated private ownership the filching of portable objects and raids upon unguarded possessions were always going on. In Great Britain, in which country the highest levels of social order were attained during the First Age of General Prosperity, stealing (with which we may include various forms of embezzlement and fraud) remained the chief offence upon the list. Almost all the others had become exceptional. But whenever there was a dip in the common prosperity, more active methods of robbery appeared to supplement the ordinary theft. The snatcher began to take his chance with bags and watches. The enterprise of the burglar increased. Then came the simple hold- up under threats, or robbery with assault. In a world of general confidence, unarmed and unaccompanied people were going about everywhere wearing valuable jewellery and carrying considerable sums of money. But that atmosphere of confidence could be rapidly chilled. Even in later- nineteenth-century Britain there were epidemics of robbery by single men or by men in couples, the "garrotters" of the sixties, for example, who assaulted suddenly from behind and seized the watch and pocketbook. They would clap a pitch plaster over their victim's mouth. There were brief phases when the suburban regions even of London and Paris became unsafe, and at no time were any but the more central regions of some of the great American cities secure. This kind of thing increased notably everywhere after the World War.

There were manifest limits to this hold-up business. It was something that extinguished itself. There had to be a general feeling of practical security for that type of robbery to prosper. There had to be people to rob. Robbery from the person is an acute and not a chronic disease of communities. So soon as the footpad

became too prevalent people ceased to carry so many valuables, they shunned lonely or dark streets and roads, they went about in company and began to bear arms. The epidemic of hold-ups passed its maximum and declined.

The criminally disposed soon learnt the importance of association for the exploitation of new lines of effort. With a more alert and defensive and less solitary type of victim, the casual criminal developed into the planning criminal. In every country multiplying nuclei of crime began to work out the problems of that terroristic gang discipline which is imperative upon those who combine to defy the law. In Europe the intensifying tariff wars put an increasing premium upon the enterprise of the smuggler, and in smuggling enterprises men readily developed those furtive secret loyalties, those sub- laws of the underworld, which proved so readily applicable to more aggressive efforts. In America the repressive laws against alcohol had already created the necessary conditions for a similar morbid organization 'of gang systems, which had become readily confluent with the older associations for political corruption and terrorism. As the economic breakdown proceeded throughout the thirties and forties of the twentieth century, ordinary social security diminished even more rapidly in America than in Europe. But everywhere a parallel dégringolade was going on. Now it would be the criminal forces in one country and now those in another which were leading in novel attacks upon the law-abiding citizen of the decaying order.

The hold-up in force became bolder and more frequent. History repeated itself with variations. In the place of the highwayman of the seventeenth and eighteenth centuries came the motor-car bandit and the train-robber. Trains-de- luxe were successfully held up by armed bands, first of all in Eastern Europe and America and then very generally. These were operations involving the concerted action of a dozen men or more, who had to be sure of their "get away" and with a market for their loot. Country houses and country clubs full of wealthy guests presently began to be attacked—the telephones cut and the whole place systematically looted. Restaurants, gambling-clubs and other resorts of people with full pocketbooks were also raided with increasing efficiency. Local banks and bank branches became insecure. Until the nineteen- thirties a town bank had a large open handsome office with swinging doors, low counters and glass partitions. Ten years later the face of the bank had changed: the clerks were protected by steel defences, they were armed with revolvers, and they parleyed with the customer through small pigeonholes that could be promptly closed.

This change in the scale and quality of aggressive crime was reflected in public manners and display. The wearing of jewellery, gold watch-chains, expensive studs and suchlike challenges to poverty declined, costume became more "buttoned up" and restrained. Hip-pocket weapons spread from America to Europe. Women's dress and ornaments, though if anything they improved in their artistic quality, diminished in intrinsic value. Everywhere there was a diminution of social ostentation. Houses with narrow exterior windows and well equipped with steel doors, locks, bolts and bars, were preferred to those candidly exposed to sun-

light and exterior observation. The window displays of the town shops became more guarded.

The need for protection and the dread of conspicuousness affected automobile design. The common automobile of the middle twentieth century was a sullen-looking pugnacious beast. And its occupants were in harmony with it. Before the World War the spectacle of a broken-down vehicle or any such trouble by the wayside would induce almost any passing car to stop and offer assistance. Under the new conditions people feared a decoy. They would refuse to stop after twilight, and even in the daytime they sometimes hurried on, though injured or apparently injured people might be lying by the roadside.

Travel diminished very rapidly under such conditions. There is some difficulty about the statistics, but between 1928 and 1938 the number of pleasure travellers upon the roads and railways of continental Europe fell by something over, rather than under, eighty per cent. There were, of course, other causes at work besides the general insecurity of movement in producing this decline; there was a general impoverishment also which disposed people to stay at home. But the major factor was insecurity.

The roads were less and less frequented as they became unsafe. Many fell out of repair, and the old road-signs and petrol pumps, now dear to our school- museum collectors, vanished one by one from the landscape.

Improvements in robbery were only one group of the criminal developments in progress. A much more distressful aspect was the organization of terroristic blackmail, at first directed against individuals and then against whole classes in the community. As people ceased to travel to be robbed, the robber had to pursue them to their homes. Here again American inventiveness and enterprise led the world. By imperceptible degrees the ordinary prosperous citizen found his life enmeshed in a tangle of threats and vague anxieties. Even during the prosperous period there had been an element of menace in the lives of the American well-to-do; their securities had never been quite secure and their positions never perfectly stable. But now over and above the ever increasing instability of possessions and income came the increasing need to buy off molestation. Breaking through the now inadequate protection of the police appeared silently and grimly and more and more openly the blackmailer, the kidnapper and the gang terrorist.

A particularly cruel form of attack upon unprotected private people was the threatening and kidnapping of young children. It had a minor grotesque side in the stealing and ransoming of pet animals. Many hundreds of children had been stolen, hidden away, and brought back for reward before the abduction and murder of the child of Colonel Lindbergh, a long-distance aviator very popular in America, called general attention to this increasing nuisance. Nothing effective, however, was done to control these practices, and in the bad years that followed 1930 kidnapping and the threat of kidnapping increased very greatly, and spread to the old world. It was organised. Men and women were spirited away, intimidated by threats of torture, held captive. If the pursuit was pressed too hard they disappeared and were heard of no more. Assassinations multiplied. Bodies of men

set themselves up almost without concealment under such names as Citizens' Protection Societies, or Civil Order Associations. The man who wanted to be left alone in peace, he and his household, was pressed to pay his tribute to the gang. Or he would not be left in peace. And even if his particular "protectors" left him in peace, there might still be other gangs about for whom they disavowed responsibility and with whom he had to make a separate deal.

It was not merely the well-to-do who were worried and levied upon in this fashion. An increasing proportion of minor workers and traders found it necessary to pay a percentage of their gains or earnings to escape systematic persecution. "Trouble" was the characteristic American word. "You don't want to have trouble," said the blackmailer, gently but insistently.

The new generation grew up into a world of secret compromises and underhand surrenders. The common man picked his way discreetly through a world of possible trouble. No one dared live who was not a member (and servant) of a Union of some kind. It was a return to very ancient conditions, conditions that had prevailed for ages in China, for instance, and in Sicily and Southern Italy. But it was a relapse from the freedom and confidence of the better days at the close of the nineteenth century. It was a contraction of everyday human happiness.

Kidnapping was not confined to kidnapping for ransom. There had always been a certain irrepressible trade in the beguiling and stealing of young persons for sexual prostitution, and this also increased again. Workers were kidnapped, and the intimidation of workers in factories became bolder and less formally legal. There was a great release of violence in personal quarrels, and in particular crimes of revenge multiplied. In a phase of dwindling confidence and happiness, people of spirit no longer recoiled from the tragic ending of oppressive situations. They took the law into their own hands. They began to fight and kill, and they were no longer inevitably overtaken by the law.

The remaining rich, the financial adventurers who still appeared, the prominent political leaders, the transitory "kings" of the underworld, all surrounded themselves with bodyguards. Types recalling the hired "bravos" of the Italian cities of the later Middle Ages and the Samurai of the Japanese noblemen reappeared as the hefty private attendants of the wealthier Americans. After the economic slump had fairly set in the posse of needy retainers became a universal practice with all who could afford it. They protected the person and the home. They supplemented the police.

The transition from a protective to an aggressive bodyguard was inevitable. Leading American bootleggers were the chief offenders, but the example was contagious. "Brawling" of retainers reappeared first in America, Germany and Ireland. These brawls were usually small street battles, or conflicts at race meetings and suchlike gatherings, or side issues to political meetings and processions. It was a courageous politician who would face an audience after 1938 unless he knew that his men were about him and posted at strategically important points in the meeting. And he would be wearing a mail undervest or suchlike protection of his more vital parts. There are hundreds of such garments in our museums.

No man, woman or child that "mattered" went about "unshadowed" after 1940. After the middle nineteenth century women had made great advances toward personal freedom. About 1912 a pretty girl in her teens might have taken a knapsack and marched off alone through the northern states of Europe or America in perfect safety, unmolested. All this freedom vanished during the age of insecurity. Women ceased to go about without an escort even in the towns. It was not until 2014 that there was any real return towards the former common liberties of the young and weak and gentle. There was on the part of women, as the novels of the time reveal, a survival of social fear in human life, the fear of going alone, until the middle of the twenty-first century.

After 1945 a fresh aspect of insecurity appears in the records. There is mention of unsafe roadside hotels, and a great increase not simply of streets, but of whole districts and villages where "things happened", people disappeared, and it was inadvisable for strangers to go. Some of these criminally infected areas did not recover their reputations for three quarters of a century. The DANGEROUS big hotel with its secret lifts, passages, ambushes and sinister private rooms is still the delight of our popular romancers; it loses nothing in elaboration as it recedes into the past.

The psychology of the twentieth-century policeman has been made the subject of a whole group of historical studies. There was no connection in those days between the policeman and either the educational or medical services. This association which appears so inevitable to us today would have seemed insane to the organizers of the first police forces in the eighteenth and nineteenth centuries. The policeman, for them, was to be an animated barrier and signpost, capable of leaping into action at the sight of assault, petty larceny or unseemly behaviour. Beyond that very little initiative was expected from him. He took into custody people who were "given in charge". Above him were officers, usually of a different class, and associated with the force was a group of criminal enquiry experts, who were quite capable of handling most of the offences against the law that prevailed in the era before the extensive introduction of rapid transit, power machinery and mass production. This pattern of police force worked fairly well up to the beginning of the twentieth century. Except in districts where sexual prostitution was rife it remained fairly honest. It maintained a fairly high level of liberty, security of property and social order for a century. Only when the control of morals or political intervention was thrust upon it did it prove unequal to the strain.

And then, as the greater community of the World State began to struggle clumsily and painfully out of traditional forms, we see police control again outpaced by its task. It gives way. "Why," the student asks, "was this police organization unable to keep pace with the new stresses? Why were the ruling people of that time so incapable of fitting it to the new demands upon it?" We have already indicated the main lines of the answer. Just when the need for a fundamental refashioning of the police of the world was becoming urgent, came also, first that exacerbation of international hostilities, of "secret service" and espio-

nage to render any broad international handling of the problem impossible, and secondly that desperately foolish sacrifice of life to the creditor which seems to be the inevitable conclusion of any social system based on acquisition.

The Profit-Capitalist System was absolutely incapable of controlling the unemployment it had evoked and the belligerence it stimulated. It stagnated on its hoards. It fought against inflation and it fought against taxation. It died frothing economies at the mouth. It killed the schools on which public acquiescence rested. Impartially it restricted employment and the relief of the unemployed. Even on this plain issue of its police protection it economized. Impossible, it said, to plan a new police when we cannot even pay for the police we have.

And so the desperate fight of an essentially nineteenth-century pattern of police organization, under-financed, inadequately equipped, divided up, controlled by small-scale, antiquated national or parochial authorities, in many cases rotten with corruption, against the monstrous forces of disorganization released by the irregular hypertrophies to social development was added to the other conflicts of that distressful age.

In spite of a notable amount of corruption and actual descents into criminality, the general will of most of the police forces seems to have remained sound. Most but not all. Most of these organizations did keep up a fight for order even when they were in a process of dissolution. They did keep up their traditional war against crime. But their methods underwent a considerable degeneration, which was shared, and shared for the same reason, by the criminal law of the period. Police and prosecutor both felt that the dice were loaded against them, that they were battling against unfair odds. Their war against crime became a feud. It grew less and less like a serene control, and more and more like a gang conflict. They were working in an atmosphere in which witnesses were easily intimidated and local sympathy more often than not against the law. This led to an increasing unscrupulousness on their part in the tendering and treatment of evidence. In many cases (see Aubrey Wilkinson's The Natural History of the Police Frame-up, 1991) the police deliberately manufactured evidence against criminals they had good reason to believe guilty, and perjured themselves unhesitatingly. Wilkinson declares that in the early twentieth century hundreds of thousands of wrongdoers were "justly condemned on false evidence", and that they could have been condemned in no other way.

But the apologetics of Wilkinson for the police break down when he comes to the next aspect of their degeneration under stress. We have all read with horror of the use of torture in mediaeval practice and shuddered at the fact that there were even special machines and instruments in those days, the rack, the thumbscrew, the boot and so forth, for the infliction of pain. But there remains little doubt now that the police of the twentieth century, fighting with their backs to the wall against enormous odds, did go very far towards a revival of torture against those they believed to be social dangers. It is a difficult as well as an ugly task to disentangle this story now, but sufficient fact emerges to show us that in the general decay of behaviour that was going on, not merely casual blows and roughness of

handling, but the systematic exhaustion, pestering, ill-treatment and actual torment of persons under arrest in order to extort confessions and incriminating statements, became prevalent.

There is no real distinction in nature between the processes that led up to this chaotic nucleation of human beings about gangs and organizations for frankly criminal purposes and those which led to protective associations for the illegal maintenance of security and order and again to those much wider allegiances within the state such as the nationalist Sokols in the Austrian provinces that became Szecho Slovakia, the Irish Republican organizations, the Ku Klux Klan in America, the multitudinous secret societies of India, China, and Japan, the Communist Party which captured Russia, the Fascist who captured Italy, the Nazis who captured Germany, all of which pursued on bolder and bolder scales large intimidatory and revolutionary economic and political ends. All these were structurally great gangster systems. Instead of specific immediate blackmail they sought larger satisfactions; that is all the difference. Even when the organisation as a whole had large conceptions of its function, it was apt to degenerate locally into a mere boss or bully rule. All these forms of recrystallization within the community, large and small, arose because of the inadaptability and want of vigour and cooperation in the formal governing, economically directive and educational systems. Because there was no foresight to ensure continuity in the growth of institutions, there were these unpremeditated and often morbid growths, expressive of the accumulating discomfort and discontent and of the need for a more intimate, energetic and fruitful form of human association.

It is paradoxical but true that the civilized human society of the later nineteenth and earlier twentieth centuries broke up because of the imperative need of human beings to live in active combination. It was pulled to pieces by its own new cohesions. Until there was a complete, satisfactory and vigorous World-State organization potentially in being, the continuation of this breaking up and reassembling of social energy was inevitable. It was like the break-up of caterpillar organs in the cocoon to form the new structures of the imago.

Even the Modern State Fellowship itself, so far as many of its nuclei were concerned, was at first of this nature, a coalescence of all these varied technicians who realized that employment would vanish, that everything they valued in life would vanish, with the spread of social disorder. They constituted protective and aggressive gangs with an unexampled power of world- wide cooperation. Their confluence became the new world.

The demoralization of the world's sea life, thanks to the surviving vestiges of naval power, was far less rapid and complete than the spread of disorder on the land. It was only after the series of naval mutinies towards the end of the last European war that the ancient practice of piracy was resumed. Even then ships could still be policed and a recalcitrant ship brought to book much more easily than the black streets of a town. One or two pleasure liners were boarded and held up in out-of-the-way ports in the thirties, but in no case did the assailants get away with their plunder. In 1933 the Chinese fleet had disintegrated into shipfuls of adven-

turers offering their services by wireless to the various governments who divided the country. But these stray warships did little mischief before they were bought, captured or sunk by the Japanese.

A Canadian pleasure liner, The King of the Atlantic, on one of the last holiday voyages to be made, was seized on the high seas by an armed gang in 1939, and an attempt was made to hold its passengers to ransom. They were all to be killed if the pursuit was pressed home. In the face, however, of a combined attack by American sea and air forces, at that time still efficient though greatly in arrears with their pay, the hearts of the gangsters failed them and they surrendered ignominiously.

No ship of over 9,000 tons was ever captured by pirates. This relative maintenance of orderliness at sea was due to special conditions—the then recent discovery of radio communications, for example. It outlasted the practical cessation of shipbuilding in the forties and an immense shrinkage in the world's shipping.

Nor did new types of criminal appear in the air until after the third European conflict, and then not overwhelmingly. Here again was a field of human activity, essentially simple and controllable. For a time indeed the aeroplane was the safest as well as the swiftest method of getting about the world. For some years after the practical cessation of general land travel the infrequent aviator still hummed across the sky, over dangerous city and deserted highroad, over ruined country houses and abandoned cultivations, recalling the memory of former disciplines and the promise of an orderly future.

There were fewer aeroplanes just as there were fewer ships, and, because of the general discouragement of enterprise, there was little change of type, yet the skies, like the high seas, remained practically outside the range of the general social debacle until well past the middle of the century. The need for aerodromes, for repairing and fuelling, held the dwindling body of aviators together. Air outrages at the worst phase were still scattered and disconnected events. And it was in the air at last and along the air routes that the sword of a new order reappeared.

4. CHANGES IN WAR PRACTICE AFTER THE WORLD WAR

The science and practice of warfare during this Age of Frustration, having now no adequate directing and controlling forces over it, pursued, in its development, a preposterous and dreadful logic of its own.

In 1914, at the outbreak of the World War, military science had been a pretentious and backward lore. The War Offices, as we have told, had allowed the armament industry to put enormously outsize weapons into their hands, but they had made none of the necessary mental adjustments needed to meet this change of scale. All the land commanders engaged in that struggle with scarcely an exception were still fighting clumsily according to the obsolete tradition of nineteenth-century warfare. They were still thinking in terms of frontal attack, outflanking, the break-through and so-forth. We have told as briefly as we could the horrors of the ensuing harvest. The Admiralties, forewarned perhaps by their engineers, showed a livelier discretion and for the most part hid away their costly fleets from the disasters of combat in strongly defended harbours, and allowed them to emerge only on one or two wild occasions for battle so inconclusive that they were prolonged as controversies for years afterwards and remain undecided to this day. The submarine, the minefield, the aeroplane, the primitive "tank", organized propaganda to weaken war will, a tentative use of gas, and the replacement of many of the elder commanders as the war proceeded did something to modify land fighting, but to the very last, when the general collapse of "morale" led to the armistice, the professional soldiers were clinging to the idea that nothing fundamental had happened to the methods of their ancient and honoured profession.

All this changed after the Peace of Versailles. A spirit of unrest entered into both the War Offices and Foreign Offices of the world. They were invaded by a consciousness of great changes none the less potent because it was belated and had accumulated. The younger generals who had been through the war could not put out of their minds memories of attacks from overhead, gas attacks, tank actions, and, above all, the loose ungentlemanly comments of temporary officers of practical ability and unmilitary habits of mind. These younger generals aged in their turn, and as they aged they succeeded to positions of authority. They came into power repeating perpetually: "We must keep pace with the times."

A phase of extreme innovation succeeded the conservatism of the older generation. Everywhere the War Offices stirred with novel conceptions of strange inventions, secret novelties and furtive systematic research. Everywhere the ob-

scure reports of spies and informants, carefully fostered by the armament dealers affected, stimulated this forced inventiveness.

It was realized that the old warfare had in fact perished in a state of lumpish hypertrophy in the trenches. It had indeed been a "war to end war"— and the old war was done for. The new warfare had to replace it—and quickly. The Foreign Offices demanded it. They could not do without war of some sort. Sovereignty was war. The traditional state was an organization against foreigners resting on the ultimate sanction of belligerence. They could imagine no other state of affairs, for to begin with that would have involved imagining themselves non-existent. The thirties and forties of the century teemed with furtive and grotesquely hideous researches to discover and develop the methods of the New Warfare. For the only alternative to further war was the abandonment of state sovereignty, and for that men's minds were altogether unprepared.

The changes in war method that went on between 1900 and 1950 C.E., with the possible exception of the introduction of firearms between the twelfth and sixteenth centuries, were far greater than anything that had ever happened since the earliest men hit and scuffled in their first rude group encounters. For endless ages the main conflict had been the "battle", the encounter of bodies of men on foot or on horseback. The infantry had been the traditional backbone of the army, and (except when the Huns and the Mongols refused to play according to the rules) the cavalry was secondary. Artillery was used only for "preparation" before the attack. So fought Rameses, so Alexander, so Caesar, so Napoleon. The glorious victories during the romantic ages of human warfare all amounted to battles of practically the same pattern, to a great central battering with pikes, swords, bayonets, maces or suchlike implements, a swiping, pushing, punching, pelting, stabbing, poking and general clapperclawing amidst a shower of comparatively light missiles, that went on at longest for a few hours, and ended in a break, a flight, a cavalry pursuit and a massacre. This "open warfare" alternated, it is true, with long sieges, less sportsmanlike phases, in which the contending hosts refused battle and squatted unwholesomely in excavations and behind walls, annoying each other by raids and attempts to storm and break through, until hunger, pestilence, the decay of discipline under boredom, or the exasperation of the surrounding population broke up the party. Non-combatants suffered considerable temporary and incidental molestation during warfare, there was a certain amount of raping and looting, devastation to destroy supplies, pressed labour and spy-hunting on a scale which amounted in most cases to little more than an exacerbation of normal criminality. Wholesale devastation, such as the break-up of the irrigation of Mesopotamia by the Mongols, or the laying waste of Northumbria by William the Conqueror of England, was, when it occurred, a measure of policy rather than a war measure. War had to go on for many decades before it could produce such disorganisation as that of Asia Minor in the wars between Byzantium and Persia. The Islamic invasions were at first made additionally disagreeable by religious propaganda, but this was speedily replaced by discriminatory taxation. The long distance campaigns of Roman, Hunnish and Mongol armies again

spread various once localized infectious and contagious diseases very widely; but the total influence of the old warfare upon human destiny was enormously exaggerated by the nationalist historians of the old régime. It was of infinitely less importance than migration. The peasant life went on unchangingly, squalid and laborious, as it had been going on for the majority of human beings since agriculture began. The various "Decisive Battles of the World" were high points in that fantasy of the pedants, the great "drama of the empires", with which they befogged the human mind for so long during its gropings from the peasant state of life towards a sane and orderly way of living.

But with the Napoleonic wars, the soldier began to invade and modify the texture of normal life as he had never done before, by conscription, by unprecedented monetary levies, indemnities and taxes that dislocated economic processes; and conversely, quite uninvited by the soldier, as we have shown, the expanding forces of power industrialism and of mass manipulation through journalistic and other sorts of propaganda, invaded both the military field and the common life. War, which had been like the superficial ploughing of our ancestors, became a subsoil plough, an excavator that went deeper and deeper, that began presently to deflect underground springs and prepare extensive landslides.

The Generals of the World War were all in the position of inexperienced amateurs in charge of vast mechanisms beyond their power of control. War, which formerly had been fought on the flat along a "front", suddenly reached through and over the contending armies, and allowed no one to stand out of it any more. The New Warfare, it was already being remarked by 1918, was a war of whole populations, from which all respect for the non-combatant was vanishing. People said this, and some few even tried to understand in detail what it meant. And now all over the world military gentlemen, many of them still adorned with the spurs, epaulettes, froggings, buttons, stripes, ribbons, medals, residual scraps of armour and suchlike pretty glories of the good old times, set themselves most valiantly to work out the possibilities and methods of the New Warfare.

Courage was always the better part of the military tradition, and nothing could exceed the courage with which these men set themselves throughout this period to overtake the march of invention, to master engineering and engineers, chemistry and chemists, war correspondents and newspaper editors, biology, medicine, and even finance, in their efforts to keep that ancient war idea, the idea of the battling sovereign state, alive. As we have seen, the schools stood loyally by them; they had the support of the armament industries, and, less whole-heartedly perhaps, the approval of the old religions and of the old royalties and loyalties. Their activities were profoundly stupid, but the grotesque horror of their achievements, the distress and unhappiness of three generations of our race, are still recent enough to mask their ludicrous quality.

The literature of the military science of this period is a copious one, and perhaps the best survey of it all is Fuller-Metsch's The Ideas of the New Warfare in the Middle Twentieth Century (2001). Therein the writer sets himself to three enquiries: "For what did they suppose they were going to fight?" "How were they

going to fight?" And "What did they consider would constitute a definitive end and winding-up of their fighting?"

The answer he gives is a composite one. No single individual seems to have grasped the New Warfare in its entirety. With a solemn pedantry, a pretentious modesty, each "expert" dealt with his own department and left it to Fate to put the assembled parts together into a whole. But what the composite soldier of 1935 was contemplating rather foggily seems to have been very much as follows. He conceived the world as divided up among a number of governments or Powers. These were the sovereign states as the Treaty of Westphalia (1642) presented them. All these powers were competitive and passively or actively hostile. The intervals when the hostility was active were wars. The intervals of recuperation and preparation were peace. War was a cessation of a truce between the belligerents, a cessation arising out of an irreconcilable dispute or clash of interests, and the objective then of each Power was to impose its Will upon its enemy. In the days before the twentieth century this imposition of Will was done more or less professionally by the governments and armies. One or other Power took the offensive, crossed its borders and marched on the enemy seat of government. After various operations and battles the capital would be captured or the invader driven back to his own, and a peace made and a treaty signed more or less in accordance with the Will of the victor. Boundaries would be adjusted in accordance with that Will, colonies transferred, indemnities arranged for; the victorious Power expanded and the defeated shrivelled. The people of the unsuccessful Power would be very much ashamed of themselves. To the end of the nineteenth century this formula was observed.

But by the time of the World War much more than the disappearance of the "front" and the increasing entanglement of the erstwhile non-combatants was happening to this procedure. The Powers were losing their definite identities. The fine question of what constituted a responsible government capable of imposing a Will, or giving in to it, arose. In Russia, for example, was the new Communist régime responsible for the obligations of the Autocracy? Was Germany, were all the Germans, to be held responsible for Krupp-Kaiser militarism? Was a dummy Sultan in Constantinople, or Kemal Pasha in Angora, the proper authority to consent to the dismemberment of Turkey? Again, the United States of America had come gaily into the war and then declined effective participation in President Wilson's settlement. He had not, it seemed, been a plenipotentiary. Was that behaving as a Power should behave?

Still further perplexities arose about the laws of war. If the front was abolished, if civilians were to be bombed from the air, what became of the right of professional soldiers to shoot franc-tireurs and destroy their homes? It was as if the arena of a football match were invaded by the spectators, who began kicking the ball about, chasing the referee, and declining to keep any score as between the original sides in the game.

The military authority recoiled from these devastating riddles of the new age. Such issues, he decided, were not for him. There had always been sides in a war,

and there must still be sides. It was for the politicians to define them. He fell back on his fundamental conception of a Power "imposing its Will" upon another Power, but using now, in addition to the old invasion and march on the capital, the new methods of propaganda, blockades and attacks behind the front, and all the latest chemical and aerial devices to "undermine the morale" of the enemy population and dispose its government to yield. In the end there must be a march, if only a concluding professional march, through the goal or capital of the losing side. He refused to entertain the inevitable problem of an enemy government not yielding but collapsing, and leaving no responsible successor. That was not his affair. Presumably in that case the war would continue indefinitely.

Nor was it his business to enter into the financial aspects of the matter, to estimate any ratio whatever between the costs of the New Warfare and the material advantages to be exacted when the Will of the conqueror was imposed. In that regard he was excessively modest. He could not be expected to think of everything. His business was to prepare the best and most thorough war possible, with all the latest improvements, and quite regardless of cost, for his Power. It was for his government to find out how to pay for and use the war he had prepared for it. Or to use it partially. War, just war itself, was the limit of his task.

Research for the latest improvements soon led the now almost morbidly progressive military mind to some horrifying discoveries. Some of the soldiers concerned were certainly badly scared by the realization of what evils it was now possible to inflict in warfare. It leaked out in their speeches and books. But they kept on. They kept on partly because they had a stout-hearted tradition and refused to be dismayed, but mainly no doubt for the same reason that the Christian priests and bishops who had lost their faith still stuck to their Churches—because it was the only job they could do. Throughout the three decades that followed the Congress of Versailles, thousands of highly intelligent men, specialist soldiers, air soldiers, engineering soldiers, chemical, medical soldiers and the like, a far ampler and more energetic personnel than that devoted to the solution of the much more urgent and important financial riddles of the time, were working out, with unstinted endowments and the acquiescence and approval of their prospective victims, patiently, skilfully, thoroughly, almost inconceivably, abominable novelties for the surprise and torture of human beings.

None of these experts seems to have been more than mediocre; it was an age of mental and moral mediocrities; and even within the accepted limitation we have already noted, none of them seems to have worked out the New Warfare as a whole complete process. Groups of men working in secrecy, immune from outer criticism, naturally conspire not only against the foreigner but against each other, and most of the men in decisive positions were rather men skilled in securing appointments and promotion than inspired specialists. A certain lumbering quality in their devices ensued.

In Great Britain a group of these experts became exceedingly busy in what was called mechanical warfare. The British had first invented, and then made a great mess of, the tank in the World War, and they were a tenacious people. The au-

thorities stuck to it belatedly but doggedly. In a time of deepening and ever bitterer parsimony their War Office spared no expense in this department. It was the last of all to feel the pinch. The funny land ironclads of all sizes these military "inventors" produced, from a sort of armoured machine-gunner on caterpillar wheels up to very considerable mobile forts, are still among the queerest objects in the sheds of the vast war dumps which constitute the Aldershot Museum. They are fit peers for Admiral Fisher's equally belated oil Dreadnoughts.

The British dream of the next definitive war seems to have involved a torrent of this ironmongery tearing triumphantly across Europe. In some magic way (too laborious to think out) these armoured Wurms were to escape traps, gas poison belts, mines and gunfire. There were even "tanks" that were intended to go under water, and some that could float. Hansen even declared (see The Last War Preparations, xxiv, 1076) that he had found (rejected) plans of tanks to fly and burrow. Most of these contrivances never went into action. That throws a flavour of genial absurdity over this particular collection that is sadly lacking from most war museums.

The British and the French experts, and presently the Germans, also worked very hard at the fighting aeroplane—the British and Germans with the greatest success; the aerial torpedo, controllable at immense distances, was perfected almost simultaneously by the Italians and the Japanese. The French mind, for all its native brilliance, was hampered by its characteristic reluctance to scrap old plant for new. It was the German, American and Russian experts who went furthest with the possibilities of chemical attack. The disarmament of Germany necessarily forced its military authorities to concentrate on an arm that could be studied, experimented upon and prepared unknown to the outer world, and the Russians were forced to take up parallel enquiries because of their relative industrial poverty. The Germans had been first to use gas in the Great War, and they remained for a long time the war gas pioneers. But after the Great War much attention was given to this arm in America through the influence of the chemical industry. Biological warfare, that is to say the distribution of infectious diseases, was also extensively studied, America and the Central Europeans in this case leading the way.

Even before the Central European fighting in 1940 and the subsequent years, the distribution of various disease germs was no longer a merely theoretical possibility. Little containers, made to look like fountain pens, were already being manufactured. The caps could be removed to expose soluble ends, and then they could be dropped into reservoirs or running streams. Glass bombs also existed for use from aeroplanes, railway-train windows and so forth, which would break on hitting water. There are specimens in the Aldershot Museum. The enrolment and territorial organization of medical men and trained assistants to inoculate threatened populations went on with increasing vigour after 1932.

But there was a certain hesitation about the use of disease germs. It is easy to distribute them but hard to limit their field of action, and if prisoners (military or civilian) were still to be taken and towns and territory occupied, a well launched

pestilence might conceivably recoil with deadly effect upon its users. Bacterial warfare seemed, even to the specialists who studied it, a very improbable method for any but an heroically vindictive population in the hour of defeat. Nevertheless it was thought best to have it worked out. Except for the distribution of malignant influenza in Kan-su and Shensi by the Japanese during their efforts to tranquillize North China in 1936, "without proceeding to extremities", its use was never officially admitted. Other alleged instances of its deliberate employment by responsible Powers have been shown by the researches of the Historical Bureau to have been due either to the unauthorized zeal of subordinates or to the activities of those religious fanatics who became so prevalent during the period of confusion after 1945. The acclimatization of the mosquito transmitting yellow fever in India in 1950, which did so much to diminish the population of that peninsula, has never been explained. It is generally supposed to have been accidental.

So far as method and invention went, what was called "Gas Warfare" ran very parallel to bacterial warfare. Its beginning and end is now a closed chapter in the history of the human intelligence and will. It is surely one of the strangest. It set its stamp upon the clothing and urban architecture of the age. It ranks in horror with the story of judicial torture or the story of ritual cannibalism, but its inhumanity is more striking because of its nearness to our own times. Like those older instances, it brings home to us the supreme need for sound common general ideas to hold together human activities. It tells how thousands of clear and active minds, each indisputably sane, could, in an atmosphere obsessed by plausible false assumptions about patriotic duty and honour, cooperate to produce a combined result fantastically futile and cruel.

The people engaged in this business were, on the whole, exceptionally grave, industrious and alert-minded. Could they revisit the world to-day individually we should probably find them all respectable, companionable, intelligible persons. Yet in the aggregate they amounted to an organization of dangerous lunatics. They inflicted dreadful deaths, hideous sufferings or tormented lives upon, it is estimated, about a million of their fellow creatures.

Most of the lethal substances prepared for gas warfare purposes have passed altogether out of general knowledge. They are either never manufactured now or they are produced upon rare occasions and under proper control for the purposes of physiological research. The old devices and appliances for their distribution seem, nowadays, like grotesque anticipations of many of the features of the large scale agricultural and hygienic operations that are carried out to-day. The treatment of locust swarms by air attack, the spraying of the reafforested regions against various tree diseases, the regular cleansing and stimulation of our grain and root crops are all subsequent rationalizations of these practices of the Age of Frustration.

Faber, that Calvinistic optimist, with his doctrine that the bad is all to the good in this maddest of all conceivable worlds, thinks that all these big scale methods were "enormously stimulated" by the crazy inventiveness of the war period. But then he has also suggested that the aeroplane would not have come into general

use for many years without war stimulation. We venture to think he carries his doctrine of the attainment of wisdom through imbecility too far. It is really only a modernization of Charles Lamb's story of the invention of the roast pig. It had the touch of Rasputinism, this revival of the ancient heresy that one must sin THOROUGHLY before one can be saved.

Much more after the gas-war pattern were the campaigns (2033 and 2035) against rats and mice, that finally cleansed the world of the lurking poison of that medieval terror, bubonic plague, and the distributions of "festivity gas", that were permitted in various regions in 2060. The countervailing use of benign- gases as a subsidiary to the suppression of the depressing cometary toxins of 2080 will also occur to the reader. The oxygenation of council chambers, factories, playing-fields and similar loci demanding special brightness and activity, and the use of Padanath Tagore's Lotus Gas in the Himalayan rest valleys, we may note, are also claimed by Faber as part of the legacy of gas warfare.

One or two of the offensive substances actually manufactured for war purposes are now utilized in relation to very special and specially protected processes in our industrial plants. The preparation of some of them is a major felony. They were a very various miscellany, for every chemical possibility was ransacked to find them. Very few of them were actually gases. Many were volatile liquids or even finely divided solids, which were to be sprayed or dusted over positions in enemy occupation. Dr. Gertrud Woker, in a paper on this subject contributed to an enquiry by the Interparliamentary Union in 1931, gave a useful summary of the existing state of knowledge at that time. In conjunction with various colleagues (What Would Be the Character of a New War? Historical Documents 937,205), she allows us to form an estimate of what was actually being contemplated by contemporary military experts. Except for one important exception, her list covers all the main types of poison gas substances that were actually prepared. This spate of investigation culminated about 1938. By that time the entire field had been explored. After that there were improvements but no major innovations.

After 1940 even military research was restricted by the increasing financial paralysis. In 1960 no plants capable of producing material for gas warfare on a sufficiently abundant scale were operating.

Of gases actually tried out in the World War itself, the chief seem to have been chlorine and various chlorine compounds (phosgene, Green Cross gas, chloropicrin and so forth). These attacked and destroyed the lung tissue. Chlorine was used by the Germans as early as April 1915 at Ypres when 6,000 men were killed by it; it was soon abandoned, because it was so immediately irritating that its presence was detected at once, and precautionary measures could be taken. The other gases in this class got to work less frankly. Presently the victim began to cough. Then as the destruction of the bronchioles and alveoli of the lungs went on he retched and suffocated and coughed up blood and tissue. He died amidst his expectorations with a visage blue and bloated and bloodstained froth on his lips. If by good luck he survived, he survived with his lungs so injured that he easily fell a victim to tuberculosis or suchlike disease. Most of this group of gases had their own char-

acteristic complications. One series, for instance, would attack the nervous system, causing wild excitement, terror, convulsions, screams and paralysis. Thousands of men had already died in agony from Green Cross gas during the World War, and the plans of some of these experts involved the massacre of whole populations in the same atrocious fashion. Green Cross gas was used, but not in sufficient strength to be very deadly, in the Polish bombing of Berlin in May 1940, and in a more concentrated form in the aerial torpedoes that were sent from Germany to Warsaw. It had been used also at Nankin in 1935 and in the Chinese reprisal at Osaka.

Yellow Cross gas, or mustard gas, was much more insidious and also more cruel and murderous. It was not really a gas; it was a volatile liquid. When cold, it spread unsuspected in a thin film over the ground, getting on to boots and clothing, being carried hither and thither. Slowly, as it vaporized, its presence was revealed. Discomfort came, a horrible suspicion, fear and then coughing and retching. It involved quite frightful and hopeless suffering. Steadily but surely it killed every living substance with which it came into contact; it burnt it, blistered it, rotted it away. One part of mustard gas in five million of air was sufficient to affect the lungs. It ate into the skin, inflamed the eyes; it turned the muscles into decaying tissue. It became a creeping disease of the body, enfeebling every function, choking, suffocating. It is doubtful if any of those affected by it were ever completely cured. Its maximum effect was rapid torture and death; its minimum prolonged misery and an abbreviated life. The gases used in the fighting in North China in 1934-37 and in the Chinese raids upon Japan were mostly of this group. And an evacuation of Berlin in 1946 was brought about by the threat of Yellow Cross bombs[1].

Allied rather than competing with these gases of the Green and Yellow Cross categories, Dr. Woker cites the Blue Cross group. These substances were essentially direct nervous irritants in the form of an almost impalpable dust. They could penetrate most of the gas masks then in use, and produced such pain, so violent a sneezing and nausea, and such a loss of self-control that the victim would tear off his mask, so exposing himself to the Green or Yellow vapours with which Blue Cross was usually associated.

All these torments had been extensively inflicted already during the World War, but after its conclusion the secret activities of the various poison gas departments were sustained with great energy. It took them nearly twenty years even to open up the main possibilities of their speciality. One substance, which played a large part in the discussions of the time, was "Lewisite", the discovery of a Pro-

[1] They were actually dropped, but either through accident or by the insubordination of the chemists employed by the Poles, they smashed ineffectively. It was one of the most striking instances of what appears to have been the pacificist sabotage that helped to end the formal warfare in Central Europe. Five of the chemical workers concerned were shot and seventeen given long sentences of imprisonment, but none of the records of their trial has survived.

fessor Lewis of Chicago, which came too late for actual use before the end of 1918. This was one of a group or arsenical compounds. One part of it in ten millions of air was sufficient to put a man out of action. It was inodorous, tasteless; you only knew you had it when it began to work upon you. It blistered as much as mustard gas and produced a violent sickness.

Other war poisons followed upon this invention, still more deadly: merciful poisons that killed instantly and cruel and creeping poisons that implacably rotted the brain. Some produced convulsions and a knotting up of the muscles a hundred times more violent than the once dreaded tetanus. There is a horrible suggestiveness in the description of the killing of a flock of goats for experimental purposes in these researches: "All succumbed to the effect of the gas except three, which dashed their brains out against the enclosure." And to assist these chemicals in their task of what Dr. Woker calls "mass murder" there was a collateral research into incendiary substances and high explosives, to shatter and burn any gas attack shelter to which a frightened crowd might resort.

Dr. Woker's summary does not include Kovoet's invention of the permanent Death Gas in 1934. Its composition is still a secret and its very complicated preparation a felony. This compound, although not absolutely permanent, decomposed with extreme slowness. It was in itself neither a gas nor a poison. It was a heavy, rather coarse-grained powder. It evaporated as camphor does, and as it evaporated it combined with oxygen to form a poison effective when diluted with fifty million times its volume of air. Its action was essentially of the Lewisite type. This was actually used in the first Polish War to cut off East Prussia. A zone of territory from a mile to three miles wide along the whole frontier was evacuated and dusted with Permanent Death Gas. East Prussia became a peninsula accessible only from Lithuania or by sea. In spite of the heaviness of the grains, the winds finally widened this band of death to about fifteen miles in width and carried its lethal influence into the suburbs of Danzig.

This murdered region was not re-entered, except by a few specially masked explorers, until after 1960, and then it was found to be littered with the remains not only of the human beings, cattle and dogs who had strayed into it, but with the skeletons and scraps of skin and feathers of millions of mice, rats, birds and suchlike small creatures. In some places they lay nearly a metre deep. War Pictures has two photographs of this strange deposit. Vegetation was not so completely destroyed; trees died and remained bare and pickled; some grasses suffered, but others of the ranker sort flourished, and great areas were covered by a carpet of dwarfed and stunted corn-cockles and elecampane set in grey fluff.

A curious by-product of Permanent Death Gas is what is now known as the Sterilizing Inhalation. This was first made by accident. A Chinese Vindication Society organized an air raid on Osaka and Tokio in 1935 after the great Green Cross raid on Nankin in that year. It was intended to strike terror into the Japanese mind. Permanent Death Powder was to have been used, but because of the haste and danger of the preparations the Chinese had not tested it out, and here again, either by accident or design, things went wrong; the formula, it seems, had been

falsified. Consequently, when the raid was made—all the machines employed were brought down on their way home—nothing ensued but a temporary fever accompanied by retching and purging.

There was much derision of the unfortunate aviators in Japan. It was only some months after that the Western World learnt that the medical services of both towns were reporting a complete cessation of early pregnancies. Not a litter of kittens or puppies had appeared for weeks, mares were no longer foaling nor cows in calf. Mice and rats vanished. The sterilization in all cases was permanent. But birds were not affected for reasons that Crayford- Huxley has since made clear. The sparrows multiplied enormously and the hens still clucked triumphantly in these childless cities.

In some way the Chinese chemists had blundered upon one of those rare sub-radiant gases known as Pabst's Kinetogens, which affect the genes. A whole series of these are now known to biologists, chiefly through the work of Pabst and his assistants, and most of the more extraordinary flower sports and new aberrant animal types in our experimental gardens are due to their employment; but for a long time, until indeed Pabst took up the subject with an insight all his own, only the Sterilization Inhalation was known. Most of the campaigns in the Forties of the twenty-first century against contagious rodents made an extensive use of this gas wherever regions could be isolated from human intrusion, and the day may not be distant when it will have important eugenic applications.

But the Japanese experience produced even a greater sensation throughout the world than the actual slaughter of the victims would have occasioned. The militarist class in Japan was as deeply sentimental as the Western equivalent in Europe, and as resolute that the common people should not only die but breed fresh battle fodder for their country. Until the patriots realized that the Chinese supply of this stuff was limited, they lived in horror. They saw themselves stripped bare of subject lives. They saw themselves extinct in the hour of victory. There was a great clamour about the world for the extensive application of this new find during the fiercer war years; there are proposals on record (Hate Eugenics, Historical Documents 5752890 and seq.) to apply it from the air to Palestine, Arabia, Ireland, the whole of China and the African Continent in part or as a whole. But mankind was saved from any such catastrophe by the fact that the first production of Sterilizing Inhalation was essentially accidental. It had been prepared furtively, its makers were untraceable, and the proper formula was not worked out and made controllable until our insane world was well in the grip of the harsh humanity of the Air Dictatorship.

How all these hideous devices of the New Warfare were to be brought together to effect the definitive subjugation of the Will of a belligerent Power was apparently never thought out, or, if it was, the plans were kept so secret that now they have perished with their makers. After the millions had choked, after the cities were a stench of dead bodies—what then?

Perhaps the artistic interest of the business precluded such remote considerations. All we can disentangle now of this gas warfare, as its experts contemplated

it, consists of projects of mere mischief and torture. They seem imbued with much the same wanton destructiveness as that displayed by some of the younger specimens among the Loando-Mobi chimpanzee hybrids.

Yet some of these plans are amazingly thorough up to a certain point—up to the point when one asks, "But WHY?" For instance, in the Marine War Museum in the Torcello Lagoon there are no fewer than half a dozen raider submarines built for four different great Powers, and all specially designed as long- distance bases for gas warfare. They carried no guns nor ordinary fighting equipment. They had practically unlimited cruising range, and within them from five to nine aeroplanes were packed with a formidable supply of gas bombs. One of them carried thirty long-range air torpedoes with all the necessary directional apparatus. There were four different types of gas mixture in the bombs, but they differed little in character and efficiency. The smallest of these raiders carried enough of such stuff to "prepare" about eight hundred square miles of territory. Completely successful, it could have turned most of the London or New York of that time, after some clamour and running and writhing and choking, into a cityful of distorted corpses. These vessels made London vulnerable from Japan, Tokio vulnerable from Dublin; they abolished the last corners of safety in the world.

These six sinister monsters gleam now in the great gallery side by side, their poison fangs drawn, their mission abandoned, the grim vestiges, the uncontrovertible evidence of one nightmare among the many nightmares of hate and evil that afflicted the human brain during the Age of Frustration. There they are. Men made them—as men made the instruments of torture during the previous dark ages. Even amidst the happy confidence of our present life it is well that we should remember that, given different conditions, men technically as sane as ourselves could design and make these things.

There is something revolting in these details. We have given enough for our purpose. History must not be made a feast of horror. From first to last gas warfare destroyed very painfully between one and one and a quarter million lives that might have been fruitful and happy. That much mischief was done. They suffered and they have gone. The gist of our story is that, after the humiliation and quickening of the military mind by the ineptitudes of the World War, belligerent science did not so much progress as lose itself in the multiplicity of its own inventions. It developed one frightful and monstrous contrivance after another, to dismay and torment mankind, to spread ill health and hate, to demoralize and destroy industrial life, to make whole countries uninhabitable and loosen every band that held men together in orderly societies, but it made no steps at all to any comprehensive and decisive conduct of war. With no plan for the future, with no vision of the world as a whole at all, these thousands of furtive specialists, these "damned ingenious patriots", as Isaac Burtonshaw (1913-2003) called them, went on accumulating, here frightful explosives, there stores of disgusting disease germs, and there again stores of this or that fantastically murderous gas.

No comprehensive plan held any of these centres of evil together into one premeditated whole, as, for instance, the military preparations of the Hohenzol-

lern Empire were held together by a clear and deliberate scheme of conclusive warfare. Beneath the vulgar monarchist claptrap of the German effort of 1914 there was indeed a real scheme for the reorganization and modernization of civilization about a Teutonic nucleus according to Teutonic ideals. It may have had its fatuous elements, but it was logical and complete. But war planning never recovered that completeness after 1914; never got back to the same logical foundations. After that belligerence lost its head. It still went on as everything else went on in those days—by inertia. But it had no longer any idea of what it was up to.

Yet over all the world these incoherent mines were prepared, and they might well have exploded, had their release been simultaneous, into such an outbreak of disorderly evil as staggers the contemporary imagination. It is conceivable that they might have destroyed mankind. It would have needed no change in the essential conditions but only a rearrangement of the determining accidents to have brought about that final catastrophe.

This menace of a chaos of disasters and aimless cruelties hung over a disorganized and unprotected world for three-quarters of a century. It is what some historians call the Period of Maximum Insecurity, from 1935 to 1965. Here and there quite monstrous things occurred—at Nankin, Pekin, Osaka, Berlin, Warsaw, for instance; things terrible enough to hearten and steel the better elements in humanity for the achievement of that world peace towards which all these forces were urging it. Fortunately for mankind the two fundamental evils of traditionalism were just sufficient to neutralize each other during this long period of the incubation of the Modern State. The greed of the creditor balanced the greed of the armament dealer. As armaments grew more and more costly, the possible purchasers grew poorer and poorer. If Economy starved and hampered many good things in human life, it did at least finally take all vigour and confidence out of the development of the New Warfare. The Chemical Armament industry followed the other typical institutions of the old order into the general social liquidation which wound up the bankruptcy of Private Profit Capitalism.

5. THE FADING VISION OF A WORLD PAX: JAPAN REVERTS TO WARFARE

We have shown already how Parliamentary Democracy necessarily abolished real leaders in public affairs and substituted a strange type of pseudo-leader, men who were essentially RESULTANTS, who made nothing, created no forces, met no emergencies, but simply manoeuvred for position, prestige and the pettier rewards of power. They followed the collapse of the decaying order without an effort to arrest its decay. Why indeed should they have made an effort? They were representatives of the popular will, and if there was no popular will...

We have already considered the behaviour of this amazingly ineffective collection of men in face of the financial dislocation that was choking the economic life of the race. It is doubtful if a single one of them ever gave a month's continuous study to the plain realities of that situation. And in the face of the accumulating stresses created by the maladjustments of Versailles, this galaxy of humbugs to whom democracy had entrusted the direction of human beings—humbugs unavoidably, for the system insisted upon it regardless of the best intentions—was equally enigmatical and impotent. Along the eastern frontiers of Italy and Germany the open sores festered. No one sought to heal them. In the Far East the conflict between Japan and China, failing a European protest, became frankly a formal war. Every world event cried louder than the last for collective action, and there was no collective action. The League of Nations appointed commissions of enquiry and produced often quite admirable analyses of hopeless situations.

No one knew how to arrest the grim development of the situation. The chief of states repeated the traditional gestures, as though these were all that could be expected of them. But the patterns of history served them no more. They found themselves like men who attempt to gesticulate and find their limbs have changed to cloud and rock.

Of all the "Powers" of that time the behaviour of Japan was the most decisive. In 1931 an internal revolution in that country had put political power into the hands of a patriotic military group, diplomatically unscrupulous and grossly sentimental according to the distinctive Japanese tradition, and this coterie set itself now with extraordinary energy and an equally extraordinary lack of authentic vision to caricature the aggressive imperialisms of the nineteenth- century Europeans. The mind of this ruling group was still intensely romantic, still obsessed by those ideas of national dominance and glory which had passed already so fatally over the intelligence of Christendom. Their military initiatives were

quasi-Napoleonic, their diplomatic pretences and evasions modelled on the best European precedents. It was "Japan's turn" now.

The investigation of just what these Japanese Imperialists imagined they were doing has greatly exercised our historical research department. But it is indeed only a special instance of the general riddle of what any "Power", regarded as a mentality in itself, imagined it was doing in that age. Only a century and a half has passed since those Japanese columns were marching into one Chinese town after another, and today our psychologists confess themselves baffled by an enterprise that was manifestly undertaken by men like ourselves and yet had already assumed a quality of absolute insanity. Why did these very intelligent people behave in that fashion?

The clue lies in the extraordinary ease with which distasteful reality can be repressed by the human mind, and in the atmosphere of grotesque but flattering illusions in which these people were living. Just as in the West the bankers, economic experts, responsible statesmen would not realize the complete smash to which their fiscal and financial methods were plainly heading until the smash had actually come, so these Japanese militarists could not see the inevitable consequences of their continental adventures. They could not see behind them a miserable peasantry breeding itself down to the basest subsistence; a miserable urban proletariat deteriorating physically and morally; they could not estimate the mutterings of revolt in all their sweated and driven industrial centres; they could not understand the protests of their own fine and growing intelligentzia.

Even the steady fall of the national credit abroad and the increasing economic stresses of the land aroused no misgivings of hallucination. Japan in her headlong pursuit of Western precedents was rapidly reproducing all the revolutionary conditions of the West. All that was lost upon her leaders. The one thing they could see clearly was that China was disorganized, that she was struggling with great difficulty to discover a new method of collective living to replace her ancient slack imperialism, and that by all the rules of the international game this was Japan's opportunity. They thought that, in very much the same way that the disorganization of the Empire of the Great Mogul had laid India bare to the piratical enterprise of the Europeans and permitted the establishment of the unstable aimless Indian Empire of the British, so now Fate had invited them to an equally glorious opportunity, to a parallel Japanese domination of the most or all of Asia. Who could tell where their imperial adventure would end—or whether it would have an end? The mirage of limitless power and glory opened out before them, as it has opened out to all empire builders since the world began.

They were reckoning without the New Warfare, reckoning without modern industrialism, without the paradoxical self-destructiveness of Private Capitalist enterprise, without Russia, without America, without the superior mass, the traditional unity and mental obduracy of the Chinese population. They were thinking as a Pomeranian Junker or a British general from that "hot-bed of Imperialists", Ulster, might have thought before 1914. It was an archaic megalomania—that led

to the killing of about three million combatants, an extreme social disintegration in China, and the final collapse of the Japanese monarchy.

In the special histories of this struggle, the student who needs or desires the knowledge may find the detailed particulars of the Japanese aggressions from 1931 onward which grew at last into the formal invasion of China proper; the tentative of Shanghai, the invasion of Manchuria and the establishment of the puppet kingdom of Manchukuo (1932), the attack on Shanhaikwan which led to the penetration of the Great Wall, the invasion of China Proper from the north and the march on Pekin. The operations up to that point were largely on the pattern of the old warfare as it had been practised up to 1914. The Chinese were poorly equipped and had little modern material; the Japanese found it unnecessary to make any excessively expensive efforts to attain their objectives.

All this earlier fighting went on to an accompaniment of protests from the quite powerless League of Nations at Geneva. A "Lytton Report" prepared by a commission of enquiry is to be found in the Historical Documents Series (2067111). But counterbalancing these remonstrances were the ambiguous utterances of the British Foreign Office, the support of the French armament industry and its Press, the overt support of a great group of American banks and their newspapers. In view of these divisions, the Japanese militarists had every reason to disregard Western criticism altogether.

In 1935 the Japanese occupied Pekin and Tientsin. They set up a second puppet monarchy in Pekin. But they found very great difficulty in holding the country, particularly to the south and west of these centres. Manchuria, Inner Mongolia and Shansi remained seething with bandits and rebel bands, and the still unoccupied valley of the Yang-tsze-kiang remained fighting with an increasing unity under the leadership of the reorganized Kuomintang. In no part of China or Manchuria was it safe for a Japanese to go about alone, and a rigorous economic boycott, sustained by an omnipresent terrorism, continued. The Kuomintang was a directive association created by the great Chinese revolutionary Sun Yat Sen, and it had gone through various vicissitudes; it had a rough general resemblance to the Communist Party and the various European fascisms, and, like them, it sustained a core of conscious purpose throughout its community. It had no vital centre, no formal head; it was a thing of the mind, unquenchable by military operations. And under the stress of this resistance it had become violently patriotic and xenophobic.

In 1936 Japan already had more than a million and a half men scattered between the Manchurian frontier and Canton, where a third landing had been made and still her hold upon China hardly extended beyond the range of her guns and the glitter of her bayonets. She had bombed Nankin twice on an extensive scale, Pekin before its surrender, and Wuchang and Hankow, with Yellow Cross bombs. Hundreds of thousands of people had been slaughtered, but the great invertebrate body of China seemed able to endure such losses with a stoicism impossible in a more highly organized state. In return the "Vindication of China" Society aston-

ished the world by suddenly bombing and, through an error in the gas mixture, STERILIZING Osaka and Tokio.

No one knew of these Chinese air forces until they appeared in action. The machines had come from Sweden by way of Russia. But nearly every Western country was supplying contraband of war to the Chinese. Unaccountable hostile aeroplanes with untraceable bombs appeared in the sky and came humming over the sea to Japan. Then in 1935 a Japanese transport blew up and sank in the Gulf of Pe-chih-li. In 1936, three Japanese liners were destroyed by mines of unknown origin within fifty miles of port. War supplies of all sorts got into China from Soviet Russia in the north and from the French and British possessions in the south, and the help and sympathy of America became more and more manifest as the vast imperial ambitions of the Japanese leaders became unmistakable. Western feeling had at first been acutely divided between distrust of Japan and the desire to see China restored to order on capitalist lines and saved from Communism. But with every Japanese advance European and American feeling veered back towards China. Australia and New Zealand appealed to the Washington Government for a joint guarantee to supplement the Imperial tie in 1937. They were advocating a mutual guarantee of all the Europeanized regions of the Pacific. For a time it seemed as though the Western world might be guided to a sort of unity by the flares of Japan. But the unforgettable humiliations inflicted upon Central Europe after the war still rankled sufficiently to prevent that.

Even before the launching of the definitive conquest of China there had been considerable economic and social stress in Japan. The earlier successes, the easy capture of Pekin and the failure of an adequate Chinese army to materialize, had filled the island empire with patriotic enthusiasm and hope; the war was brought to a victorious conclusion three times, and each time it broke out again. No invader ever conquered Russia to the end, and no one ever completed the conquest of China. Always beyond the subjugated provinces appeared other provinces swarming with hostility. Szechwan and the south supplied inexhaustible support and supplies for the Kuomintang resistance. It seemed at last as though there could be no peace any more in China until the invaders fought their way through to Tibet.

War weariness descended upon Nippon. The peasants saw their sons marching off, never to return, and shortages of ordinary commodities deepened to famine. There was already vigorous "Stop the War" agitation in Japan in 1935; there were continual strikes in Nagoya and hundreds of casualties, and afterwards there began a frantic dumping of accumulated goods abroad, to pay not merely for munitions but for such now vitally essential imports as Australian meat and Canadian and American corn. The war was starving the home fields of men and it was destroying the productivity of large areas of China. The social structure of Japan proved to be far too primitive to emulate the miracles of economy performed by the Germans during the World War. The confidence and credit of Japan sank steadily. Foreign loans became no longer possible even at such exorbitant rates as 14 or 15 per cent. And still there was no end in sight.

The Japanese militarists had gone too far to recede. Behind them they had a suffering population that might rapidly become vindictive, and about the arena of the struggle watched Russia, America and Europe. According to the best traditions of their culture, these national leaders resolved on a supreme military effort, a march in overwhelming force into the central province of Hupeh. Colossal preparations were made, and every able-bodied Japanese who was not already enrolled was called up. This was to be "a blow at the heart".

A convergent march from Nankin, Shantung and Canton was planned. This dispersal of the bases was justified by the necessity for living on the country as far as that remained possible. There were railways in existence from Canton and Shantung, but they were difficult to protect, and, apart from them, there was such an utter want of practicable roads that by the time the Japanese were in Hupeh a third of their forces were trailed out upon their lines of communication making roads, and the equipment of heavy guns and munitions they had been able to bring up was very little superior to that of the Chinese, who were still fighting with all the wealth of Szechwan at their backs and the almost overt sympathy of the West. The three great Japanese armies effected their junction in a loose ring round Wuchang—a ring that was for a time slowly drawn tighter and then ceased to contract. A deadlock ensued, a deadlock of mutual exhaustion. Neither up nor down the river was the closure of the ring complete. Throughout 1938, Japan waited for good news from the long crescents of trenches about Wuchang, and waited in vain. Pestilence broke out in July and defeated the utmost sanitary and medical efforts of the invaders. Then early in 1939 they began their retreat to Nankin, with transport disorganized, with mutiny growing, with all the country rising about them.

The horrors of that retreat have never been fully told. The three Japanese armies at their maximum strength had numbered well over two million of men; but probably about a million or less remained fit enough for the retreat. Famine was far more deadly with them than the Chinese guerillas; the exhausted wretches fell out along the line of march and waited stoically for the end; few prisoners were taken; the Chinese had no food even if they had had mercy to give quarter, and the fallen were left to perish in their own time. The broken remnant that assembled at Nankin did not greatly exceed a hundred thousand, and still smaller bodies from the lines of communication fought their way homeward to the north and south. The rest of these two million lay in the vast cemeteries of Puki and Kichow, or they had been drowned in the floods, or their bodies were littered as they had dropped and crawled over the sad monotonous landscape of the Chinese hills. At Nankin the weary and dispirited survivors realized that Japan was now also at war with the United States and that Osaka and Nagoya were in the hands of Communist Committees.

For some weeks the Japanese army sprawled inactive in its former cantonments to the west of Nankin. Then it revolted, shot many of its officers, declared for the social revolution and fraternized with the Chinese Red Army which had marched in under its nose from Hangchow and taken control of the city proper.

The entry of the United States into the Eastern War, which did so much to complete the demoralization of militarist Japan, was the climax of a prolonged wrangle about the supply of mines and submarines to the Chinese, that became more and more acute after the sinking of a Japanese transport in the gulf of Pe-chih-li.

It is only recently that the full history—which is also a very tedious and disputatious history—of the sea war against Japan has been worked out. Every contemporary record was falsified at the time; every event hidden completely or elaborately camouflaged. It is now fairly evident that not merely did private firms manufacture mines and build submarine mine-layers but that the various European navies under the plea of economy sold out a large proportion of quite modern and valid under-sea craft for "breaking up" to agents and dealers acting for South American intermediaries. The submarines, either intact or so "broken up" that they could easily be reconstructed, went to various Peruvian and Chilian ports and thence found their way across the Pacific to the Philippines. The Philippine Islands were quasi-independent, but the Manila declaration of President Roosevelt II in 1937 had practically extended to them the protection of the Monroe Doctrine, and the Japanese had never had the surplus energy necessary to challenge this informal protectorate. Now these islands became the base for vexatious attacks upon their overseas trade and sea communications.

The naval situation in the Pacific was a complicated one. To the east of the Philippines lie the Ladrones, a scattered group of volcanic islands, of which the largest, Guam, had been assigned to the United States of America by the Treaty of Versailles and was administered as a part of the American navy, while the rest were held by Japan under a mandate. (The Powers previously in possession had been first Spain and, after 1899, Germany.) The Japanese were bound by treaty not to fortify their holdings, but as the situation grew tense they seem to have ignored this restriction, at least to the extent of establishing submarine bases. Now that the situation was growing tenser the state of affairs above and under water between the Ladrones, the Philippines and the Asiatic mainland became darker and more dangerous. There was a threatening concentration of the American Fleet between Guam and the Philippines to ensure the neutrality of the latter, a patrolling concentration of the Japanese along the Chinese coast, and an obscure activity of privateering submarines and ambiguous shipping, which smuggled munitions and supplies and raided weak points of the Japanese communications.

Above water a submarine, like any other ship, can fly a flag and claim the respect due to its nationality, but mines fly no flags, and under water a submarine may be able to recognize the coded signals of a co-national but has no means at all of distinguishing a neutral from an enemy. Mistakes and pseudo- mistakes were inevitable. Two American submarines disappeared in 1936. Then several Japanese submarines vanished from the Ladrone archipelago. Disputes that broke out in neutral cafés came to a murderous end in the depths. The American navy took matters into its own hands. By 1937 an informal naval war had developed in the Western Pacific.

Neither Power hurried on to an actual declaration of war. America, in spite of, or perhaps because of, the bold experimenting of Roosevelt II, was in a state of deepening economic and political disorder, and Japan was putting forth her utmost strength for that disastrous "blow at the heart" in China. But many of the more conservative influences in the United States saw in a Pacific war a saving distraction of public attention and public energy. There was an agitation to re-annex the Philippines, and after the Japanese failure to hold Wuchang the drive towards open war became uncontrollable.

The particulars of the brief, destructive and indecisive naval war that followed need not occupy us here. The battle fleets met in the Western Pacific and separated after two days of gunfire and heavy losses. Ammunition gave out, it seems, on the Japanese side. At any rate they drew off in the twilight under a smokescreen. The Americans claimed the victory because they were able to go on to Manila, while the Japanese withdrew to the protection of their minefields and submarines and were never able to emerge again for lack of material. Both Powers were now in a state of deepening domestic stress, and their war, in a technical sense, never ended. That is to say, there was no final treaty as between two Powers, because both had in effect collapsed. They fell apart. Social revolution swept the conflict off the stage.

[The student will be reminded, by this inconclusive termination, of the almost incessant, dreary and futile wars of Byzantine and Sassanid, that devastated Asia Minor for three centuries and did not so much come to an end as suffer effacement from history by the sponge of Islam.]

The social disintegration of Japan, once it had begun, was very rapid. The great mass of the population, the peasants, had been scarcely affected by the process of Westernization, and they lapsed very readily into the same unprogressive variant of Communism as their equivalents in Kwantung, Chekiang and Fukien had adopted. A small Westernized intelligentzia with many internal feuds and doctrinal disputes struggled, not very effectively, in the larger towns to turn this merely insurgent Communism into modern and constructive paths after the Moscow pattern. Fragmentation when it came was swift and thorough. Militarism degenerated into brigandage and local feudalism. Here and there some scion of the old nobility reappeared with his attendant Samurai as a gangster boss.

In the space of a few years all Asia from the Pacific to Persia seemed to be sliding back to political and social chaos, to hand-to-mouth cultivation, destitution and endemic pestilence. For the greater part of India and most of Further India were also now drifting back to barbarism. There also the phrases and the insubordination, if not the spirit and methods, of Communism had captured vast multitudes who had remained completely unaffected by other European ideas. It was Communism without any Five Year Plan or indeed any conception of a plan. It was the class-war in its ultimate crudity. It killed money-lenders and tax-collectors with gusto and elaboration. It evolved strange religious fanaticisms, and it abandoned sanitation as "boujawai", the accursed thing. The imperial power in India was not overthrown; rather it was stripped of effective prestige and receded

to an immense distance. The princes remained formally "loyal", though in some cases they tacitly annexed "disturbed districts" adjacent to their proper dominions. Localities and local adventurers improvised a sort of social order at a low level and with a continually completer disregard of any central authority.

6. THE WESTERN GRIP ON ASIA RELAXES

The recession of the directive influence of the half modernized European imperialisms in Asia went on steadily. Even as early as 1929 the spread of a peasant communism similar to that which had obtained so strong a hold upon the popular imagination in China was causing grave alarm to the Indian Government. The seizure and trial of a group of British and Indian agitators at Meerut, and the extravagantly heavy sentences passed upon them in 1933, showed both the gravity of these fears and the unintelligent clumsiness with which the situation was being met.

For the British Empire there was to be no such decline and fall as happened to Rome. Instead it relaxed, as we shall now describe, to nothing.

Unhappily, before it relaxed in India it had, as in Ireland, a brief convulsive phase of "firmness"....

[Here several sheets from Raven's MS. appear to be missing.]

7. THE MODERN STATE AND GERMANY

A question of primary importance in human history is this: Why were the lessons of the Great War, and the subsequent economic and social disorders, lessons which seem to us to-day to be as starkly plain as lessons could be— why were these lessons lost upon every one of the great communities of thought into which the world was divided? British thought, French thought, American thought, German, Russian, Italian thought, seem in our retrospect to ring the changes upon every conceivable sequence of prejudice and stupidity. Why was Wilson's start towards world unification not followed up? Why after 1932 was there no vigour to reconstruct the League of Nations, when all the world was crying for some central authority to unify money and economic life? Why did the Age of Frustration last so long? We have already noted some of the controlling causes, the mercenary Press, the vast anti-social private interests, the heavy weight of tradition, the reactionary quality of schoolmasters, the social disintegration due to economic demoralization. But even these malignant influences, taken all together, do not seem sufficient for this blindness in the general intelligence of our race towards the obvious elements of its situation.

Behind all these conditions making for failure there was something else: there was an intrinsic weakness in the forces of reconstruction, there was a fundamental lack. It was impossible for the world to get out of its difficulties because it had no definite complete idea of what it wanted to get out to. It had ideas, yes, more than enough, but they were confused and often mutually contradictory ideas. A drowning man cannot save himself by swimming unless he has something solid to which he can swim. The deficiency was not moral nor material, it was intellectual. There was the will for salvation and the material for salvation, but there was no plan of salvation. The world has no definition of an objective. That had still to be made plain to it.

It will make this matter clearer if we consider the mental and emotional phases of one typical culture community of central importance at that time, the German. Stories similar in essence, if widely different in detail, could be given of the French, Anglo-Saxon, Russian and Spanish-speaking communities. The feature they had in common was this, a failure to realize that there could be no salvation now unless it was a comprehensive salvation. They were attempting to do severally and with a jostling competitiveness what could only be done with the utmost difficulty in unison. That meant for every one of them the paralysing influence of a war threat, extreme economic instability, incapacity for dealing with morbid

financial conditions, and a consequent state of mental "worry" that made every move inaccurate and untimely.

It is only when we realize the sapping of that aggressive energy that had well-nigh Europeanized the whole world before the World War that we can understand the length of the Age of Frustration. Certain facts of fundamental importance to the continued health of our world community have to be stressed. Europe could not lead the world to unity when the world seemed dying to be led to unity, because Europe itself was profoundly disunited. The World War was merely the explosion of tensions that had been straining below the surface throughout the whole First Period of World Prosperity. Before the European peoples, who by 1920 amounted to a quarter of the whole human race, could resume the exploring, experimenting and civilizing rôle they had played for two centuries, it was necessary that they should be purged of a chronic mental disease—a disease which had, it seemed, to rise to an acute phase and run its enfeebling and devastating course before it could be treated: the disease of hate.

Although each year in the Thirties saw the international tension in Europe increasing, it was only in 1940 that actual warfare broke out. All Europe was "mined" for ten years before that time, but the very consciousness of that fact, if it did not hold back the drift towards war, increased the gravity of its onset. That ingenious contrivance of President Wilson's, the Polish Corridor, Poland's "access to the sea", was the particular mine that exploded first. But it was only one of a series of accumulating detonations which were destined to blow the still creaking ineffective League of Nations, and indeed nearly every vestige of the unfortunate Treaty of Versailles and its subordinate "settlements", out of the way of human readjustment.

The mental phases of that great body of Europeans who used the German language summarize the world situation. The history of Europe from 1900 to 1950 could be told in a study of the German brain alone, its torment and the reactions it evoked in the peoples about it. It was a brain of outstanding vigour and crudity. It aroused admiration, envy and fear. Its achievements in material science were magnificent; its energy of industrial organization was unparalleled. Its mathematical and psychological ineptitudes were redeemed by the Jewish intelligences entangled in its meshes. Compared with the Anglo-Saxon brain its political thought was unsupple, and it had neither the extreme lucidity of the French intelligence, the boldness of the Italian, nor the poetic power of Spain and Russia. It had these conspicuous limitations. Its obstinate association with a stupidly arrogant monarchism and a woolly tangle of preposterous racial pretensions stood in the way of sympathetic cooperation with any other cultural system. It had failed conspicuously to assimilate the non-German subject populations involved in its political web. It had intensified the defensive nationalism of the French; its tactless challenge upon the sea had terrified and exasperated the British; it had roused even America to a wary disapproval and a final hostility. Russia it had never won, but then in the huge carcass of pre-revolutionary Russia there was very little to be won anyhow. (There was indeed no real national self-consciousness in Russia

before the Soviet régime; there was only Dostoievsky and the Tzar.) Assertive ungraciousness had been the chief factor in Germany's isolation and the cause of its defeat in the World War.

Yet after defeat this afflicted German mentality, if only on account of a certain toughness and vigour it possessed, remained still the central reality and the central perplexity of the European system. War and disaster could not alter the fact that the backbone of Europe, the most skilled, industrious, teachable and intelligent block of its population, spoke and thought German. What might happen to it, what would happen to it, should have been the primary preoccupation of every intelligent statesman. For if Germany had gone right everything would have gone right. But there were no statesmen sufficiently intelligent to consider anything of the sort. Germany had had a phase of pride and megalomania. It had been immensely disillusioned, it had thrown off its glittering imperialist headship, it had accepted military defeat. It had even passed through a phase of humility. At first it did not hate conspicuously. Amidst great difficulties the new republic displayed creative courage, moderation, a dawning sense of the significance of world politics.

Creative, forward-looking minds turned to Germany with an entirely pathetic hopefulness. "Now we shall see what Germany can do," they said. "Be patient with Germany." All the world scolded France for her inveterate distrust. Given courage and generosity abroad and leadership at home this great mass of Teutonic brains might have taken up the task of the Modern State then, and fallen into co-operation with the rest of a disillusioned but renascent world. It might even have led in the work of reconstruction, and 1918 might have been the opening year of a phase of world renewal.

But that was not to be. The world had still to reap a harvest of disunion through sixty tragic years. At home leadership came to Germany too late. Stresemann mastered his lesson too slowly and died too soon. Brüning was betrayed by Hindenburg's mental decay. And abroad it seemed to the Germans that there was nothing but war-strained and vindictive enemies. They looked for friends and saw only Foreign Offices. We have told already how the rôle of only sinner in a world of outraged saints was thrust upon Germany by the Conference of Versailles. She was to be permanently enfeebled, restrained and humiliated. German babies yet unborn were expected to be born penitent about the war. They were to gasp for their first breath under the smacks of an unforgiving world.

How all the good effort in Germany was thwarted, how the nets of suspicion held her down, would make a long and intricate story. At last these losers of the World War became as violent and frantic as stifled creatures fighting for air. Only by a feat of imagination can we now put ourselves in their places. Everything seemed to be making for the strangulation of Central Europe. The young energetic men in the defeated countries were to be given no share in the rebuilding of their shattered world. That was to be reserved for the new generation of the conquerors. They were to live in an atmosphere of punishment, toiling, heavily taxed, and out-

lawed from the advancement of civilization to the very end of their days. That they should recover prosperity or achieve great things would be an offence.

Naturally life so circumscribed was bitter and lapsed very easily towards vice, apathy or blind revolt. There is a remarkable novel in the Historical Documents Series (Fabian, by Erich Kastner, 1932) which renders the individual aspect of this phase of German life very vividly. Another novel almost equally vivid and illuminating is Kleiner Mann, was nun? by Hans Fallada, 1932.

These conditions of mind, this tied and stifled outlook upon life, were, it must be admitted, by no means confined to the German-speaking peoples. The intelligent and ambitious young Indian or Egyptian or negro, the intelligent young man of any subordinated, handicapped and restrained people or class—and this covered perhaps two-thirds of the youth of our race in these days— participated in the same distress of a foreordained inferiority and futility. But the young German had recent memories of hope and pride and a greater fund of resentment and aggressive energy. He had no tradition of inferiority and subservient adjustment.

Unhappily no teachers or leaders arose to point him on to his legitimate rôle in the replacement of the current disorder by the Modern World State. The Hohenzollern régime and the stresses of the war had stood in the way of his attaining anything like the cosmopolitanism of, say, the English and Americans. His new republicanism was superficial and half-hearted, and in the schools and universities the teachers and leaders of the old militarist régime were still living, active and malignant. The Press and all the organizations of instruction and suggestion stood out of the revolution and showed themselves only too eager and skilful in restoring a pre-war fierceness. The futility of the new Germany was their text. "This is not German" they insisted. "Go back to the old Imperialism," they said, "and try again." The spirit of the women about the new generation, mothers and sweethearts alike, was for the most part one of passionate indignation.

An acute contemporary observer, L. B. Namier, pointed out that it was almost a law in history that war-strained and defeated countries should relapse towards violent patriotism between twelve and fifteen years after the war in which they suffered concluded. He suggested that this was precisely the time when the children who, without any participation in the realities of warfare, had felt all the strain and bitterness of defeat and all the hatred of the enemy would have grown up to manhood. These children became the energetic stratum in the population by 1933.

It was at this phase in European history that the rise of Hitlerism occurred. Adolf Hitler, as the decisive product of Germany in labour, is one of the most incredible figures in the whole of history. He must have astonished even the teachers and writers who had evoked him. We can study his personal presence from a hundred different angles in Vol. 30112 of the Historical Portrait Gallery, and it is that of an entirely commonplace man, void of dignity, void of fine quality. We can hear his voice, we can hear him persuading, exhorting and attempting to reason from the numerous steel-tape records that were made of his speeches. It is a raucous, strained voice, talking violently but incoherently. It is the voice of a

vulgar, limited, illiterate man, lashing himself to fierceness, shouting, threatening, beating his fists at the window, smashing the furniture about him, to escape from perplexity and despair. He was perfectly simple and honest in his quality. And that was perhaps the secret of his career. He gave vent to the German overstrain. He is the voice of Germany losing control.

He denounced foreigners, Jews, Cosmopolitans, Communists, Republicans, owners of property and leaders in finance with raucous impartiality, and nothing is so pleasing to perplexed unhappy people as the denunciation of others. Not their fault, their troubles. They have been betrayed. To Fallada's question, "Little Man, what now?" his answer was, "Massacre Jews, expel foreigners, arm and get more arms, be German, utterly German, and increase and multiply."

One has to remember that he never carried with him even an absolute voting majority of the German public. But the people permitted him to seize power and shatter their republic, stifle public discussion and destroy their liberties. They had no energy to resist him. They had no conception left in their fagged and hope-starved brains of any finer rôle than that which his bawling nationalism, his violent campaign against Communists and imaginary Communistic plots, against Jews, speculators and Liberals, presented to them. The treason of the senile Hindenburg to the Republic that had trusted him, conduced inestimably to the adventurer's success.

Hitler's exploit in seizing Germany and turning it back towards reaction was modelled on Mussolini's precedent. But intellectually he was far inferior to that strange figure. He took all that was worst in the Fascist régime and never rose to the real constructive effort or the competent industry of his prototype. One little point that illustrates his general ignorance and essential feeble-mindedness was the adoption of the Swastika, the running cross, as the emblem of his Nazis. This brisk, silly little sign is of very old origin, and, as we have noted in the earlier stages of this summary of history, its ornamental use was one of the associated characteristics of that type of Neolithic culture, that culture of brownish and dark-white warm-water peoples, from which the early civilizations sprang. It is hardly known in connexion with the so-called "Nordics" or with the negro peoples, and it is in no way expressive of an "Aryan" culture. Old writers used to declare it was the "symbol" of the sun, but it seems to have signified little beyond a certain cheerfulness. It took the place of an idea in the muddled heads of the Nazis and they treated it with immense solemnity and wore it on their banners, clothes, proclamations and wherever else they could. Arden Essenden, when it was revived in Europe during the struggle for the air control, called it the "idiot's own trade mark", and it has certainly had a fatal attraction for many second-rate imaginative types.

So for a time, under a hubbub of young blackguards in brown shirts and Swastika badges, Germany, just when her rather heavy but persistent and faithful mind would have been of primary value in mankind's struggle with the world problem, passed out of the intellectual commonweal of mankind. Her real mind went into exile, in America, in England, in Switzerland, in irony or in hiding. She missed

her proper share in the unification of mankind in the twentieth century, just as she missed her share in the Europeanization of the world in the eighteenth and nineteenth. At home this National Socialism sought destructively to construct, sought to restore her former scientific prestige and industrial efficiency by boasting, exhortation, intolerance, outrage and compulsion. It was a pitiful and tragic phase, the dementia of a great nation. The story of German life during this interval is a rowdy and unhappy story—a story of faction fights and street encounters, demonstrations and counter- demonstrations, of a complicating tyranny of blackmailing officials, and at last of an ill managed and unsuccessful war, that belied the innate orderliness of the Teutonic peoples. There was a progressive increase of secret vice and furtive dishonesty, the outcome of hopelessness. The number of people killed or seriously injured in riots and civil conflicts in Germany, or murdered for political reasons, between 1932 and 1936 amounted to something over rather than under thirty thousand.

8. A NOTE ON HATE AND CRUELTY

[This section was in a detached fascicle, but its place seems to be here.—ED.]

The student of history will find it almost impossible to understand the peculiar difficulties of political life as it was lived until about a hundred years ago, nor will he grasp the essential differences between what was called education in those days and the educational processes we are still developing to-day, unless he masters the broad facts about these systems of hatred that dominated the group relationships of mankind right up to the assertion of the Modern State. We have given the main particulars of the issue between the Germans and the Poles, but that is only one striking and historically important instance of a general condition. We could give fifty such chapters. Nearly everywhere populations were to be found steeped in and moved by mass hatreds of a volume and obduracy outside any contemporary human experience.

All these hatreds arose out of the same essential causes. Two or more population groups, each with its own special narrow and inadaptable culture and usually with a distinctive language or dialect, had been by the change of scale in human affairs jammed together or imposed one upon another. A sort of social dementia ensued. In the absence of a common idea of community, civilized motives gave place to instinctive hostilities and spasmodic impulses.

Wherever there were mingled populations these hates were found and, except in the Basque country, Wales and Lapland, they were intense enough to be of primary political importance. South and east of Bohemia there seemed no boundary to the realms of hate. The Magyar hated the Slav, the Slav the Italian, the Roumanian the Russian. Religious differences, the mischief of priests, cut up even racial solidarities; the Catholic Slav hated the Orthodox Slav and the Orthodox Greeks in Macedonia were hopelessly divided among themselves. Over all the ancient domain of the Sultan, through Persia, through India, hates extended. Islam was rent by two ancient hate systems. These mass hatreds were accepted in a kind of despair by even the wisest. They defied the policies of statesmen absolutely. They were supposed to be beyond human control.

It is extraordinary how recent is the intelligent mitigation and suppression of hatred. Our ancestors did not envisage this as a controllable mental disease. They did not know that it was possible to get through life without hatred, just as they did not know that the coughs and colds that afflicted them and most of the phenomena of senility were avoidable.

But it is amazing to think how submissively human beings allowed their lives to be spoilt by controllable things—until almost within living memory. It was not only against hate and envy that they made no effort. They left their poor nerves bare and unprotected from an endless persecution by man- made afflictions. Up to 2010 they lived in towns that were crazy with noise; there was practically no control of offensive sounds, and the visual clamour of advertisements died out only in the needy decades that preceded the Air Dictatorship. But then it was still hardly more than a century that there had been sufficient light upon the towns and highways to drive away the blackness of night and overcast weather. In northern climates in the winter before the twentieth century people lived between the nocturnal dark and a dismal grey half-light which they called daylight, not seeing the sun often for weeks together.

And before the nineteenth century it is clear to anyone who can read between the lines that mankind STANK. One has only to study the layout and drainage of their houses and towns, their accommodation for washing, their exiguous wardrobes, the absence of proper laundry organization and of destructors for outworn objects, to realize that only usage saved them from a perpetual disgust and nausea. No wonder that, quite apart from their bad food and loathsome cooking, they coughed, spat, ached, went deaf and blind and feeble, in a continual alternation of lassitude and mutual irritation.

These conditions of life have gone one after another and almost imperceptibly. Few of us realize how different it was to be a human being only a few hundred years ago. It is only when we take our imaginations with us back into the past that we realize how evil to nose, eye, ear and soul the congregation of human beings could be. And necessarily, inevitably, because of the ill-interpreted protests of body and mind against this mode of existence, they hated—almost at haphazard. We have in Swift's Gulliver's Travels (1726) the cry of one man of exceptional intelligence and sensibility who discovered himself imprisoned as it were in the life of the eighteenth century and could find neither outlet nor opiate. The reek of the kennels of a medieval town was nothing to the stench of hatred in the popular Press of the twentieth century. The ordinary newspaper of that time was not so much a news sheet as a poison rag. Every morning the common man took in fresh suggestions of suspicion and resentment and gratified his spite with bad news and malicious gossip.

Hatred, we know, is a morbid, infectious and preventable relapse to which the mammalian cerebrum, and particularly the cerebrum of the social types, is prone. It is a loss of rational control. It is caused normally by small repeated irritations of the cerebral cortex. The contagion may occur at any phase before or after maturity, and acute attacks predispose the brain for recurrence and may run together at last into a chronic condition of vindictive disapproval.

Once hatred has established itself to that extent it seems to be ineradicable. The patient seeks, often with the greatest ingenuity, occasion for offence, and finds a profound satisfaction in the nursing of resentment and the search for reprisals and revenges. He has what he calls his "proper pride". He disapproves of

his fellow creatures and grudges them happiness. Our current education is framed very largely to avert and anticipate this facile contagion, but the Press of that time subsisted by its dissemination, in the interests of reactionary forces. We are as sedulous now for cleanliness and ventilation in our mental as in our physical atmosphere. The contrast between a contemporary crowd and the crowds depicted by Hogarth or Raphael is not simply in the well- clad, well-grown, well-nourished and well-exercised bodies, the absence of rags and cripples, but in the candid interested faces that replace the introverted, suspicious and guarded expressions of those unhappy times. It is only in the light of this universal malaria that human history can be made comprehensible.

And now this great German mind stretching across the centre of Europe in seventy million brains was incapable of autotherapy, and let its sickness have its way with it. It would not recognize that it suffered from anything but a noble resentment. Least of all peoples was it able to entertain those ideas of a world-wide cooperation of the World-State, which were still seeking their proper form and instrument. It was a deeper hate altogether than the fear- begotten hate of the French. In both these antagonized countries cosmopolitan sanity went begging, but most so in Germany.

The fluctuations in German hatred during the Thirties were curiously affected by subconscious currents of discretion. Though Germany was fiercely belligerent in spirit, her armament still lagged behind that of her neighbours; her Hitlerites snarled and threatened, but rather against Poland than France, and when the tension became too great it found relief by outrages upon Communists, Pacificists and intellectuals and by an exacerbated persecution of those whipping-boys of the Western civilization, the Jews. From the accession of Hitler to the chancellorship of the Reich in 1933 onward, not only looting and massacre, but legalized outrage, became an ever present menace in the life of the German Jew.

Faber speaks in his studies of political psychology of the "hate map" of the world. The intensity of the colouring of such a map would vary widely. The English-speaking states (except for Ireland, that erstwhile "island of evergreen malice", which is now the most delightful and welcoming of summer resorts) and the Spanish-speaking communities felt hate far less intensely than the peoples of the continental European patchwork. They were less congested, they were free from acute alien interference, they had more space to move about in, and the infection was not so virulent. For two decades Spain and Spanish South America (after the Peruvian Settlement) sustained indeed a more liberal and creative mentality than any other region of the world. The Spanish contribution, beginning with Unamuno and Ortega y Gasset and going onward through a long list of great names, was of increasing importance in the building up of the Modern World-State.

Russia, we may note, was never so constructive mentally as Spain. She had not now the same wealth of freely thinking and writing men. She had no surplus of mental energy to philosophize. She ecstasized, prophesied or dogmatized. Such brain discipline as she had was used up in her sprawling technical efforts. But she

again was not a malignant country. Young Russia was taught to hate indeed, but to hate a dissolving enemy, the Wicked Imperialist. Even in that hate there was an element of humorous caricature. When in due course the Wicked Imperialist faded away to the quality of a nursery Ogre, he took with him most of the hatred out of Russia. Hate, except in brief vivid spurts, does not seem congenial to the Russian temperament.

Few people in 1940 realized that the essential political trouble in the world, as distinguished from its monetary malaise, was this endemic disease, and still fewer had the boldness of mind even to think of the drastic cleansing and destruction of infected social institutions and economic interests and accumulations that was needed if the disease was ever to be stamped out. Meanwhile along the tangled frontiers of Central and Eastern Europe the sores festered and the inflammation increased.

Among the more frequent methods of releasing hatred in the more troubled communities were aggressive demonstrations inviting or involving violence, attacks on representative buildings, such as embassies and consulates, the defilement of flags, statues and other symbols (in India the slaughter of sacred or forbidden animals such as cows or pigs in holy places), quarrels picked in cafés and restaurants, beatings-up, assassinations, the throwing of bombs and crackers into parties and gatherings of the objectionable nationality, or into law courts, religious buildings and other unsuitable places for an explosion, firing at sentinels and across boundaries. Along the Adriatic coast it would appear there was an exceptionally strong disposition to insult the characteristic Italian respect for statues and pictures.

This was of recent origin. At the Congress of Versailles Italy had been bilked by her French and British Allies of a considerable amount of the Dalmatian coastline—to which indeed neither she nor they had any right, but which nevertheless had been promised to her in the secret engagements that had brought her into the World War. Her patriots had never ceased to resent this broken promise, nor the Jugo-Slav peoples, who held the coveted districts, to fear a forcible annexation. There had been much propaganda about the dispute. One prominent argument on the Italian side was that the Republic of Venice (of which Rome was the natural heir) had formerly dominated this coast, and, in proof of this, appeal was made to the public buildings in the towns of the disputed regions, which everywhere bore the insignia of their Italian founders and particularly the distinctive lion of Venice. For that was the Fascist fantasy: wherever the Venetian lion had made its lair or the Roman eagles cast their shadows, from Hadrian's Wall in England to Mesopotamia, the Fascisti claimed to rule.

This contention, though taken calmly enough by the English, French, Spanish, Turks and other emancipated peoples, was bitterly resented by the populations more immediately threatened, and particularly did it arouse resentment and hatred along the Dalmatian coast. For the young and excitable Slav, those sculptured lions and archaic eagles, those antique vestiges, were robbed of their artistic and historical charm; they took on an arrogant contemporary quality and seemed to

demand an answer to their challenge. His response was to deface or mutilate them.

Already in 1932 there were bitter recriminations between Rome and Belgrade on this score, and in 1935 and again in 1937 fresh trouble arose. The later occasions were not simply matters of chipping and breaking. These heraldic and highly symbolic animals were now painted, and painted in such a manner as to bring them into grave contempt. And the outrages were not confined to heraldic animals. Portraits and images of Mussolini were also adorned all too often with pencilled moustaches, formidable whiskers, a red nose and other perversions of his vigorous personality.

Such vexatious modes of expression were in constant evidence in all the inflamed areas. To us they seem trivial, imbecile, preposterous, but then they were steeped in tragic possibility.

The reader must picture for himself, if he can, how things went in the brain of some youngster growing to manhood in one of these hate regions, the constant irritation of restrictions, the constant urge to do some vivid expressive thing, the bitter, unconsoling mockery against the oppressor, and at last the pitiful conspiracy, the still more pitiful insult. He must think of the poor excitement of getting the paint-pot and the ladder, of watching the receding police patrol, the tremulous triumph of smearing the hated object. That perhaps was the poor crown of life for that particular brain. Then the alarm, the conflict, the flight, a shot, a wound, straw and filth in a prison cell, the beatings and the formal punishment, the intensified resolve to carry on the resistance. There was nothing to think of then but the next outrage, the next riot. So very often the story went on to wounds and death, the body crumpled up on a street pavement and trampled under foot or put against a wall to be shot, and then the rotting away and dispersal of that particular human brain with all the gifts and powers it possessed. That was all that life could be for hundreds of thousands of those hate-drenched brains. For that they came into being, like flowers that open in a rain of filth.

A Natural History of Cruelty has recently been published by Otto Jaspers (2085 —), a lineal descendant of that Professor Jaspers of Heidelberg University under whom De Windt studied and to whose Die geistiger Situation der Gegenwart De Windt was greatly indebted. Cruelty in the Twentieth Century is treated in considerable detail, and it makes very terrible reading indeed. Happily it is not considered a necessary part of a general education to probe under those dark processes of the human mind which make the infliction of horrible pain and injuries a relief to otherwise intolerable mental distresses. The psychologist, however, must acquaint himself with all those facts; he cannot fully understand our intricate minds without them, and the practical disappearance of deliberate cruelty from our world to-day makes the horror literature of the World War and World Slump periods a mine of essential material for his investigations. One or two glimpses we have given the student. If he has any imagination he will be able to expand those hints for himself into an infinitude of mutilations, tortures and wanton violence.

The older psychologists were disposed to classify cruelty as a form of sexual aberration—in ordinary speech we still use their old word Sadistic—but this attribution is no longer respected by contemporary authorities. Cruelty goes far beyond the sexual field. Just as hate is now understood to be a combative fear compound, the stiffening up of a faltering challenge, which may become infectious, so cruelty is regarded as a natural development of effort against resistance, so soon as the apprehension of frustration exceeds a certain limit. It is a transformation of our attempt to subdue something, usually a living thing, to our will, under the exasperation of actual or anticipated obduracy.

This interpretation makes it plain why the breakdown of the private capital economic and political system and the world-wide uncertainty, dismay and want which ensued was followed by wave after wave of unprecedented cruelty. In 1900, a visitor from another sphere might reasonably have decided that man, as one met him in Europe or America, was a kindly, merciful and generous creature. In 1940 he might have decided, with an equal show of justice, that this creature was diabolically malignant. And yet it was the same creature, under different conditions of stress.

There were many thousands of suicides between 1930 and 1940—suicides of sensitive men and women, who could endure the dreadful baseness and cruelty of life no longer. Yet in the records of the reviving world of 1980 there is scarcely a mention of atrocious conduct towards human beings or animals. It was not a change of nature; it was a change of phase. Millions of people who had actually killed, massacred, tortured, were still alive—and they were behaving now quite reasonably and well. Most of them had forgotten their own deeds more or less completely. Hope had returned to human life. The frantic years were past.

9. THE LAST WAR CYCLONE, 1940- 50

The drift to war in Europe became more powerful with the elimination of Japan and the United States from the possibility of intervention, and with the deepening preoccupation of Britain with Indian disorder and with the Black Revolt in South Africa. The last restraints upon continental hatreds had gone. The issues simplified.

War came at last in 1940. The particular incident that led to actual warfare in Europe was due to a Polish commercial traveller, a Pole of Jewish origin, who was so ill advised as to have trouble with an ill-fitting dental plate during the halt of his train in Danzig. He seems to have got this plate jammed in such a fashion that he had to open his mouth wide and use both hands to struggle with it, and out of deference to his fellow passengers he turned his face to the window during these efforts at readjustment. He was a black- bearded man with a long and prominent nose, and no doubt the effect of his contortions was unpleasing. Little did he realize that his clumsy hands were to release the dogs of war from the Pyrenees to Siberia.

The primary irritant seems to have been either an orange-pip or a small fragment of walnut.

Unhappily, a young Nazi was standing on the platform outside and construed the unfortunate man's facial disarrangement into a hostile comment upon his uniform. For many of these youths were of an extreme innate sensibility. The flames of patriotic indignation shot up in his heart. He called up three fellow guards and two policemen—for like the Italian Fascisti these young heroes rarely acted alone—and boarded the train in a swift and exemplary mood. There was a furious altercation, rendered more difficult by the facts that the offending Pole knew little or no German and was still in effect gagged. Two fellow travellers, however, came to his help, others became involved, vociferation gave place to pushing and punching, and the Nazis, outnumbered, were put off the train.

Whereupon the young man who had started all the trouble, exasperated, heated and dishevelled, and seeing that now altogether intolerable Jew still making unsatisfactory passes with his hands and face at the window, drew a revolver and shot him dead. Other weapons flashed into action, and the miniature battle was brought to an end only by the engine-driver drawing his train out of the station. The matter was complicated politically by the fact that the exact status of the Danzig police was still in dispute and that the Nazis had no legal authority upon the Danzig platform.

By itself this distressing incident might have been arranged without the outbreak of a European war. The moribund League of Nations might have been invoked or even the mummified Hague Tribunal galvanized into activity; either institution was still fully capable of dealing with, let us say, a Polish dentist who might have been treated as the culpable party, traced, punished and made the scapegoat of Europe. But that would have needed a certain goodwill on the part of the Powers directly involved, and at that time no such goodwill was forthcoming.

For eight years now the German mind had been working up for a fight over the Corridor, and the rearmament of Germany, overt and secret, had been going on. Both France and Poland had been watching the military recovery of Germany with ever-deepening apprehension, and the military authorities of both countries were urgent that a blow should be struck while they were still disproportionately stronger. Time after time it seemed that the crisis had come, and time after time nothing more than a stock-exchange tornado had occurred. Now the last reasons for patience had disappeared. The tension had risen to a point at which disaster seemed like relief and Europe was free to tear itself to fragments.

Such a situation was the inevitable climax to every "armed peace" in the old belligerent world. At some point there was an irresistible logic in "Strike now before they get too strong". That had been an underlying motive of primary force in the British readiness to fight in 1914. They were eager to strike before the ever-growing German fleet equalled their own. So they ended an intolerable tension. The Germans had "asked for it", they said. "Better now than to-morrow."

Now again Germany has "asked for it" and Poland was leaping to the occasion. The War Offices pressed their bell buttons. The printing machines of Paris, London and New York were still busy with various misstatements about the murdered commercial traveller, while the Polish and German air patrols were in conflict all along the fatal boundary. That dental plate apparently began to feel uncomfortable about one o'clock in the afternoon of Friday, January 4th, 1940. On Saturday, about three o'clock in the afternoon, Michael Koreniovsky, the Polish ace, after a brilliant fight with three antagonists, fell flaming out of the sky into the crowded Langgasse of Danzig and set fire to the Rathaus.

The first Polish air raid on Berlin and the unresisted "demonstration flight" of two hundred French air squadrons in formation over Bavaria and West Prussia followed. The Germans seem to have been taken completely by surprise by this display of immense and immediate preparedness. They had not thought it of the French. But they had the quickness of apprehension to decline an air battle against odds, and the French flew home again. The fighting on the Polish-German frontier continued.

The authorities in Paris were uncertain whether they were disappointed or relieved by the non-resistance of their old enemies. A smashing air victory over Germany would have been very satisfactory and conclusive, but these aeroplanes were also wanted at home to cow the ever-increasing domestic discontent. An indecisive battle—and that was always possible in the air— might have produced serious internal stresses.

For a week of years from the resumption of armament by Germany in 1933, the diplomatic centres of the world had been watching the steady onset of this conflict and had been doing nothing to avert it. Now London, Washington, Madrid and Geneva became hysterically active. There was a mighty running to and fro of ambassadors and foreign ministers. "Delay," said Geneva; though there had already been twenty years of delay.

"Localize the conflict" was a phrase that leapt into vivid prominence. It found favour not only in the neutral countries, but in Paris and Berlin. In effect "localize the conflict" meant this: it meant that Paris should scrap her engagements to Poland and leave the Poles to make what sort of arrangements they could between Germany and Russia. For Russia now, by an enigmatical silence combined with a prompt mobilization of the Red Army, became almost immediately an important piece in the developing international game.

And Paris had soon very excellent reasons for not pushing a conflict with Berlin to extremities. The first Frenchman to be killed in the New Warfare had been killed already. And he had been killed in the Maritime Alps, shot by the bullet of an Italian patrol.

On Sunday night, January the 6th, while the Polish aeroplanes were dropping gas bombs on Berlin, the Italians were administering the same treatment to Belgrade. At the same time an identical note had been dispatched from Rome to all the Powers giving Italy's reasons for this decisive blow. It seemed that between Friday evening and Sunday morning there had been a violent recrudescence of Yugo-Slav irreverence. The Fascist agents who had to supply the material for grievance and indignation had in fact overdone their task to the pitch of caricature. On Saturday the entire Italian population found itself roused from its normal preoccupation with its daily budget by the terrible intelligence of Mussolini everywhere made bibulous and ophthalmious with red paint, of Venetian lions coloured as indelicately as baboons and of shamefully overdecorated Roman eagles. Eloquent and dishevelled young Fascists, often in tears, protested at every street corner against these intolerable indignities and called for war. The cup of Yugo-Slav iniquity was full. It was only in later years that astounded students, tracing these outrages to their sources, realized how excessively that cup had been filled to justify the Fascist invasion.

Once the Polish and Italian forces had crossed their boundaries the other states of Eastern Europe did not wait even to produce an insult before launching their offensives. The whole crazy patchwork of Versailles dissolved into fighting—the joyless, frantic fighting of peoples full of hate and fear, led blindly to no ends that anyone could foresee. For two straining years the theory of localizing the conflict held Russia and France out of the fight. A "formula" was found by which France undertook not to intervene on the side of her erstwhile allies, on the understanding that Russia by way of compensation also refrained from any action against them. Moreover, the trade in munitions was to be carried on "impartially". It was a flimsy formula to justify a diplomatic default, but it kept warfare away from the Western front of Germany for two distressful years. The persistent shooting by

Italians over the French boundary was difficult to explain away, and indeed it was not so much explained away as quietly disregarded. The air fleets of France paraded at intervals, to the increasing irritation of all her immediate neighbours, but on the whole as a restraining influence. The demonstration chilled the foreigner and assuaged the hotheads at home.

From the outset there was far less enthusiasm for this "localized" European war of 1940 than had been displayed by the populations of the belligerent countries in 1914. What enthusiasm was displayed was confined to the inexperienced young of the middle and upper classes, the youth of the Fascisti, Nazi, "public schoolboy" and scoutmaster type. They went about, shouting and urgent, in a heavy, sullen and apprehensive atmosphere. No nation "leapt to arms". The common soldiers deserted and "fell out" incessantly, and these shirkers were difficult to punish, since the "deserter mentality" was so widespread, more particularly in the peasant armies of Eastern Europe, that it was impossible to shoot offenders. One Posen battalion went into battle near Lodz with thirty-nine officers and fifty-seven men.

From the first "economies" marched with the troops. From the first there was a threadbare needy quality about the struggle. General orders insisted upon "a restrained use of ammunition".

The actual fighting was, however, on a much higher level, mechanically and scientifically, than the Japanese war in China. The military authorities had good roads, automobiles, camions, railways, rolling stock, electrical material, guns of all sorts, and great air forces available. Behind the fronts were chemical and other munition factories in good working order. If there were no longer infantry battles there were some brilliant conflicts of technicians. The prompt cutting off of East Prussia from any help from main Germany by the Permanent Death Gas was an operation far above the technical level of any Eastern operations. It was strategically silly but technically very successful.

The first offensive against Berlin was also planned with modern equipment and the maximum of contemporary military science. It was to be another "blow at the heart", and the Polish general staff relied upon it as firmly as the Germans in 1914 had relied upon their march on Paris. Unfortunately for the Poles, it had been necessary to consult a number of "experts" in preparing this advance; there were leakages through France, through the Czech and Swedish munition makers, through Russia, and through domestic treason, and the broad outline of the plan was as well known and understood in Berlin as it was in Warsaw. The great gas raid on Berlin was indeed terrifying and devastating, but the rush of tanks, great caterpillar guns and troops in motor transport was held and checked within sixty miles of the German capital by an ingenious system of poison-gas barriers—chiefly Lewisite and Blue Cross—wired mines and "slime pits" of a novel type in the roads and open fields. A cavalry raid to the north between Berlin and the sea failed disastrously amidst wire, gas and machine- guns; nearly forty thousand men were killed, wounded or taken prisoner. Moreover, there had been mistakes in the manufacture of the gas masks worn by the Polish troops, and several brigades

gave way to the persuasion that they had been sold and betrayed. The main Polish masses never came into actual contact with the German troops, and only their great numerical superiority in aeroplanes saved their repulse from becoming a rout.

The Polish armies rallied and, according to the secondary plan prepared for any such failure, extended themselves and dug themselves in along a line between Stettin and the Bohemian frontier. Behind the barrier they began a systematic reduction of Silesia. Every night an air battle raged over both Berlin and Warsaw. It was often an indecisive battle. The Poles had the numerical superiority, but the German machines were more efficient and better handled. But the Poles had far more of the new aerial torpedoes—which could go to an assigned spot two hundred miles away, drop a large bomb and return— than their adversaries.

Bohemia, like France, had mobilized but did not immediately enter the war. The Czecho-Slovak armies remained in their mountain quadrilateral or lined out along the Hungarian front, awaiting the next turn in the game. Austria also remained excited but neutral.

The Southern war opened brilliantly for the Italians, and for some weeks it went on without any formal connexion with the Polish conflict. Bulgaria, Albania and Hungary also declared war upon Yugo-Slavia, the Italian air forces "darkened the sky", and few of the towns in Croatia and Serbia escaped an aerial bombardment. The Italian fleet set itself to capture the ports and islands of Dalmatia. But the advance of the Italian troops into the hills of Slavonia and Croatia was not as rapid as had been expected. Six weeks passed before they were able to fight their way to Zagreb.

The country was a difficult one, ill adapted to the use of gas or mechanism, there was no central point at which a decisive blow could be struck, and the population had a long tradition of mountain warfare. It did not affect these sturdy peasants whether the townsmen were bombed or not. They never gave battle; they never exposed themselves in masses, but their bullets flew by day and night into the Italian encampments. Many of them went to and fro between their fields and the front. Munitions poured in for them through Roumania, which, with a big Red Army on its Bessarabian frontier and its own peasants recalcitrant, remained also ambiguously, dangerously, and yet for a time profitably, out of the struggle. The Hungarians crossed the Yugo-Slav frontier and threatened Belgrade, but the mass of their forces faced towards Czecho- Slovakia and awaited further events.

A curious pause in the fighting occurred at the end of the year. The frantic efforts of Prague, London and Paris to call a halt were temporarily successful. The invaders of Germany and Yugo-Slavia remained upon enemy territory, but neutral zones were improvised and there was a cessation of hostilities. An eleventh-hour attempt was made to stop the war by negotiation and keep the two conflicts from coalescence. There were weeks during which this seemed possible. Both Germany and Poland were of two minds about continuing the war now that the Polish advance was held, and Italy hoped to be left in possession of Dalmatia without an irksome campaign of further conquest. It was as if the spirit of civilization had

once more come near to awakening from its hallucinations and had asked, "Why on earth is this happening to us?"

The British Cabinet thought the occasion opportune for a conference at Vevey to revise the Treaty of Versailles "finally". The pacific speeches of Duff- Cooper, Hore-Belisha, Ellen Wilkinson and Randolph Churchill echoed throughout Europe and were brilliantly supported by Benito Caruso and Corliss Lamont in America. The Pope, the Archbishop of Canterbury, the Non-conformist Churches, the President of the Swiss Republic and the able and venerable President Benes swelled the chorus of remonstrance. France, which had been growing steadily more pacificist after her social conflicts in 1934-35, found able spokesmen in Louchère and Chavanne. Once again we are reminded of the impulses of Henry Ford and Wilson. Once again the concept of a World Pax flickered in the human imagination and vanished. This time it was a fuller, more explicit and more unanimous chorus than that which had cried aloud in 1916- 17. Yet at the time it was hardly more effective. Vevey prolonged the truce throughout 1941 until June, but it could settle nothing. The military authorities, having had a breathing-time, became impatient. With a mutually destructive malice the fighting was resumed "before the harvest could be gathered".

Vevey failed because the constructive conception of the Modern State had no representative there. It was just another gathering of national diplomatists who professed to seek peace, and yet who set about the business with all those antiquated assumptions of sovereignty that were bound to lead to a revival of the conflict. The fantasy of some "balance of power" was as near as they ever came to a peace idea. Such a balance was bound to sway from year to year and from day to day. Whatever the common people and men of intelligence were thinking, the experts now wanted to see the war fought to a finish. "The Germans hadn't been beaten enough" was all too acceptable to the munition dealers and the Press in France and Scandinavia. "The Italians have their hands full in Yugo-Slavia."

The British and Americans, who hoped to keep out of the conflict to the end, had experienced an exhilarating revival of exports and found their bills against the belligerents mounting very hopefully. Once more Tyneside echoed to hammering; steel, iron and chemical shares boomed and the iron and steel industry, like some mangy, toothless old tiger, roused itself for the only quarry it had now the vigour to pursue—man-eating. It had long ceased to dream of new liners or bridges or railways or steel-framed houses. But it could still make guns and kill. It could not look far enough ahead to reckon whether at last there would be any meat on the man's bones. The only countries that really wanted peace, enduring peace, were Czecho-Slovakia and Austria, which stretched out between the two combatant systems and had possible enemy frontiers on every hand. The human will for peace as it found expression at Vevey was still a tangled and ineffective will.

The fighting revived almost simultaneously in the Polish Ukraine, where the peasants had revolted and were evidently fighting with Soviet officers and equipment, and in a vigorous surprise attack upon the Polish lines to free the German soil from the invader. The Germans had been working night and day during the

truce to equalize conditions in the air; they produced new and swifter aeroplanes and a particularly effective machine-gun, and for some weeks there was such aerial fighting as was never seen before or since.

Gradually the Germans established a sufficient ascendancy to bring their bombers and gas into play. Lodz and Warsaw were terrorized and the civilian population evacuated and the Polish line broken so as to restore communications with Silesia. And then the conflict broadened. Lithuania, evidently with Russian encouragement, seized her old city of Wilna, and Austria linked the Northern and the Southern struggle by entering both wars as the ally of Germany and Italy. Germany declared her final union with Austria. Very swiftly now the remaining European states followed one another into the cauldron. Hungary attacked Eastern Czecho-Slovakia without a declaration of war "to restore her legitimate boundaries", and brought the army frameworks of Roumania into the field against her. Thereupon Russia announced the impossibility of maintaining her understanding with France in the face of these events, and the Red Army advanced on Lemberg. Macedonia was already a seething mass of fighting, village against village; Bulgaria entered the "South Slav" alliance and assailed Albania, and Greece seized Rhodes, which had been up to that time held by Italy.

So France saw her ancient policy of "security", of setting state to balance state and allying herself with a countervailing state at the back of every antagonistic neighbour, work out to its necessary conclusion. Gladly would her business men and her peoples now have rested behind her immensely fortified frontiers and shared the profits of neutrality and munition-selling with the British and Americans, but her engagements were too binding. After one last ambiguous attempt on the part of London, Washington and Geneva to avert the disaster, France declared war against the Central European alliance in 1943.

On the face of it the new war resembled the World War of 1914-18. It seemed to be an attempt to reverse or confirm the Versailles settlement. It had an air of being the same sort of siege of Central Europe. But now Italy was in close alliance with the Teutonic powers; Belgium, in a state of extreme industrial distress, was out of the war; Britain stood aloof; and in the place of her former Allies France had to help—rather than be helped—by the band of states from the Corridor to the Black Sea and the Balkans which the Quai d'Orsay had toiled so painfully to knit into an anti-German alliance.

Russia, however, was a doubtful ally of the Central Powers; she was not operating in concert with them; she was simply supporting the new Soviet republics in Eastern Poland and Bessarabia. There the Red Army halted. The old enthusiasm for a World Revolution had faded out of the Russian imagination. Marxism had become so Russianized that it feared now to take in too large a contingent of Western adherents. The Kremlin was content to consolidate the kindred Slav Soviets and then rest. Japan and China and the American continent remained out of the mêlée, concentrated on their own social difficulties.

It would be possible for a superficial student to regard all this merely as a rearrangement of the familiar counters of sovereign state politics. But, in reality, the

forces in collision were profoundly different. France, in spite of her internal social stresses, was still a capitalist community of the Nineteenth Century type, with democratic parliamentary forms and irresponsible finance and industrialism. Save for the teaching of a sentimental patriotism, her young people were mentally unorganized. Her allies were peasant states with governments of the royal or parliamentary form, and, if anything, more old- fashioned. But the Central Powers were all of the new Fascist pattern, more closely knit in its structure and dominated by an organization of the younger spirits, which claimed to be an élite.

Except for the fundamentally important fact that these Fascisti were intensely nationalist, this control by a self-appointed, self-disciplined élite was a distinct step towards our Modern State organization. These various Fascisti were destined to destroy their own states and disappear because of their essentially shallow and sentimental mentality, their inability to get outside nationalist traditions and coalesce; there is no direct continuity between them and our modern educational and administrative system; but there was nothing like them in the World War of 1914-18 anywhere, and they are noteworthy, as the Russian Communist Party (in spite of its proletarian formula) is noteworthy, for their partial but very real advance on democratic institutions. Amidst the chaos, that organized "devotion of the young" on which our modern community rests was clearly foreshadowed in these Central European states. The idea of disciplined personal participation in human government was being driven into the mentality of the new generation.

Until something more convincing appeared, it had to crystallize, disastrously enough, about such strange nuclei as the theatrical Mussolini and the hysterical Hitler. It had to be patriotic because that was the only form in which the State then presented itself. But after these first crystallizations had been shattered and dissolved in the war disasters that now ensued, the idea was still there, this idea of banded cooperation ready to be directed to greater ends. Youth had ceased to be irresponsible in all the Fascist countries.

Not only were these new wars unlike their predecessors in the fact that they were not, so far as the Central Powers were concerned, wars of the democratic masses, but also they were quite unprecedented in the range and quality of the fighting. We have already indicated some of the main differences between the New Warfare and the Old. These now became accentuated by the extraordinary way in which the boundaries of the battling states interdigitated. In the first spurt of conflict there was indeed a "front" between Poland and Germany; but after 1943 there was no front, no main objective, and no central idea to the storming destruction that spread over Europe.

The Poles tried to draw a line of Permanent Death Gas across East Brandenburg before their withdrawal to Posen, but their collapse came too swiftly, and they were able only to poison three small areas of no strategic importance. After 1943 the war became mainly a war in the air, with an increasing use of gas and landing raids, raids rather than invasions, to seize, organize and hold advantageous positions. A bitter and intense naval struggle went on in the Mediterranean

to cut off reinforcements and supplies between North Africa and France, but there was little molestation of the Atlantic traffic of France.

There was never an Aerial Trafalgar, never an Air Ecnomus. War in three dimensions does not afford those channels, straits, narrow seas, passes, main roads, by which an inferior force may be brought to a decisive battle, and indeed to this day it is uncertain which side was absolutely predominant in the air. It was a war of raids and reprisals, and no large decisive operations were attempted. A big German infantry push into Posen was held by gas and slimes, and a French invasion of Italy got no further than Turin.

The complete exhaustion of the adversary, materially and morally, became the only possible road to any sort of victory. Once more the tormented populations were urged to sustain a "war of attrition". "It is the man who holds out half an hour longer than the other who wins" was translated into every European language. The attacks on social order increased in malignancy as the impossibility of any military decision became manifest. Crops and forests were deliberately fired, embankments smashed, low-lying regions flooded, gas and water supplies destroyed. The aviators would start off to look for a crowd and bomb it. It became as cruel as the fighting of ferrets.

There was still, in spite of a decade of financial dislocation and industrial depression, a vast amount of mechanical material in Europe; everywhere there were factories strongly protected against air attack and skilfully camouflaged. Moreover, all the chief belligerents had sufficiently open frontiers for the importation of material, so long as anything compact and valuable could be wrung out of their nationals by tax or levy, to pay for such supplies. The goods crossed the frontier at night; the cargoes were piloted into unlit harbours. Every able-bodied adult not actually in the fighting forces was pressed to work at excavations for bomb shelters and the reconstitution of buildings against gas and high explosive. Much of this also was night work. Recalcitrance and shirking were punished by a deprivation of rations. There is a grim picture by Eglon Callet called "Security at Last", of which the reader may have seen reproductions. A chain gang of emaciated and ragged Frenchmen is working under the lash in a tunnel. In the foreground one who has fainted is being given a stimulant; another, past help, dies untended.

In comparison with the abundant literature of personal experiences in the World War, at least so far as the Western front was concerned, there are remarkably few records either of combatant or non-combatant adventures during the Fighting Forties. The big air raids seem to have been altogether horrible. They were much more dreadful than the air raids of the World War. They began with a nightmare of warning maroons, sirens, hooters and the shrill whistles of cyclist scouts, then swarms of frantic people running to and fro, all pride and dignity gone, seeking the nearest shelter and aid, and they ended for most of their victims in an extremity of physical suffering.

We have already given some intimation of the nature of those torture deaths. In nearly every case the organization of refuges and gas masks broke down. In many cases there had never been a real provision, but only sham visors and sham

bomb-proof buildings to allay "premature" panic and "keep up the popular morale". None of these great raids was ever reported in the newspapers that still struggled on into the war years. Even in America the publication of any detail was treated as "pacificist propaganda against recruiting".

There is a descriptive letter from Berlin after an air raid, undated and signed "Sinclair", which is believed by most competent critics to have been written by Sinclair Lewis the novelist (1885-1990). One passage may be quoted:

"We went down Unter den Linden and along the Sieges Allee, and the bodies of people were lying everywhere, men, women and children, not scattered evenly, but bunched together very curiously in heaps, as though their last effort had been to climb on to each other for help. This attempt to get close up to someone seems to be characteristic of death by this particular gas. Something must happen in the mind. Everyone was crumpled up in the same fashion and nearly all had vomited blood. The stench was dreadful, although all this multitude had been alive twenty-four hours ago. The body corrupts at once. The archway into the park was almost impassable...."

So we get one glimpse of how peaceful town-bred people might die a century and a half ago.

The individual stories of the actual fighting in that last warfare are no more ample than the non-combatant descriptions. There was little inducement for anyone to write about it in the subsequent decades; there was not the same high proportion of literate men as there was in the Western armies during the Great War; there was a less artless interest in what was happening and more running away, desertion, apathy, drunkenness, raping, plundering and malignant cruelty, which are not things of which men leave records. The whole world was less sensitive than it had been thirty years before; if it suffered more grossly it suffered less acutely. In 1914-15 many of the British and German rankers kept diaries from day to day. This shows a sense of personality and a receptiveness to events quite outside the sullen fatalism, shot with gleams of primitive exaltation or fury, which seems to have been the prevalent state of mind in the armies of the Forties.

In the Historical Documents Series there is a diary of a Japanese officer who was killed in the retreat from Wuchang. Failing any European material of the same kind, it may perhaps be quoted here to show how it felt to fight in the last wars of all. It is not, however, a very vivid document. He was an intellectual, a socialist and a strong believer in the League of Nations, and his record is mainly a series of hostile criticisms in cypher of the superior command. But in the latter half these dissertations die out. The diary becomes a broken record of what he found to eat and drink and how he fought against influenza and dysentery. He seems to have had a company of men with him; he notes twice when he contrived a haul of food for them, and he jots down names as they are killed or missing. There are also figures that may be a note of his diminishing ammunition. He was already badly starved when he was killed. As he weakened he seems to have found his rather complicated cypher too difficult to use, and he lapsed first into

bad English and then into plain Japanese. The very last item is an unfinished poem, a fragment in the old style, which might be rendered as follows:

Almond blossom in the spring sunshine, Fuji-Yama gracious lady, Island treasure home of lovely things, Shall I never see you again?...

Something, death perhaps, prevented the completion of his naive verses. He and his detachment were probably overtaken and done to death near Kai- feng.

In none of these later war memoirs is there anything to recall that queer quality of the 1914-18 stories, of men who felt they were going out from absolutely sure and stable homes and cities, to which with reasonable good fortune they would return—and live happily ever afterwards. The mood then was often extraordinarily brave and tender. The men of this later cycle of wars felt that there would be no such home-coming. They knew that they went out to misery and left misery in active possession at home. Their war was not an expedition; it was a change for ever. The memoirs of the airmen who did so much destruction are amazingly empty. They note fights, but quite flatly. "Put down two Polaks", for example; "a close shave"; but they do not seem to have had an inkling of the effect of the bombs they dropped upon the living flesh below. Many of these young men survived to become Modern State aviators and to serve the Air and Sea Control after 1965. But though some wrote well of their later experiences, none of them has left any useful documents for the history of the war time. The historian turns to his dates, maps and totals again from this meagre salvage of the hopes, fears, dreads, curiosities and agonies of the millions who went through that age of cruel disaster, doubtful whether he is sorry or thankful that most of that welter of feeling and suffering has vanished now as completely as though it had never been.

After 1945 the signs of exhaustion multiplied. Such despair had come to the souls of men that even defensive energy failed. They lay starving in their beds and hovels and let the bombs fall about them. But a whiff of gas could still cause a panic, a headlong rush of tormented people coughing and spitting through the streets to the shelter pits. Influenza with its peculiar intensity of mental depression came again repeatedly after 1942, and in 1945 came cholera. These epidemics, though they seemed grave enough at the time, were the mere first scouts of that great "Raid of the Germs" which was in preparation for disunited humanity. It was as if they were testing the defensive organization of mankind.

Except for air warfare, Britain and the North European neutrals were suffering almost as acutely as if they were actually at war. They had poured munitions into Europe and reaped a harvest of bad debts. After the first economic exhilaration due to this state of employment, the exports from Great Britain, which had once been the pioneer of free world trade and cosmopolitan thought, dwindled to insignificance; the erstwhile creditor of the world could not collect such debts as were still due to her, and could not pay therefore for the food supply of her dwindling but still excessive population. Her former sanitation had rotted to filthiness under a régime of relentless saving. Housing in that disagreeable climate had passed from congestion to horror. The first cholera epidemic found her in the throes not only of famine but of civil disorder, controlled and suppressed by her highly

mechanized army and by the still very powerful habits of orderliness and subordination in her people. Never, since the Black Death of the Fifteenth Century, had the British Isles known such a pestilence. They had believed the days of pestilence were past for ever. And yet that cholera was only the precursor of the still more terrible experiences that were to follow it in the subsequent decade.

Slowly but surely the spirit of protest and mutiny spread through Europe. That growing despairful insubordination that had done so much to bring about the winding up of the World War in 1918 reappeared in new forms. But because now war was no longer primarily an infantryman's business, mass mutiny, such as had crippled the French offensives after 1917, taken Russia out of the war, and led to the final German collapse, had not now the same disabling effect. There were not the same big aggregations of men under exasperating discipline and in touch with "subversive" suggestions. Power had passed over to the specialized forces —to the aviators and war technicians. By the use of small bombs, machine- guns and the milder gases they could "handle" and disperse mass meetings and "tranquillize" insurgent districts in a manner that would have been inconceivable to the street barricade revolutionaries of the later Eighteenth Century.

Even strikes in the munition factories were no longer so effective as they had been, because even there the increased efficiency of power production had ousted the comparatively unskilled worker in his multitudes. For the same reason the propaganda of insurrectionary class-war communism, though it now dominated the thought of nine-tenths of the European peasants and workers, found unexpected obstacles in its attempts to seize control of affairs. It could not repeat the Russian social revolution because the new conditions were entirely different. The Bolshevik success had been possible only through the backwardness of Russia and the absence of a technically educated social stratum. The unrest and insubordination of the common people in Central and Western Europe could and did produce immense passive resistances and local revolutionary movements, but it found opposed to it a whole system of aviators, mechanics, technicians, scientific workers and so forth who had learnt from Red Russia what sort of direction and planning to expect from a proletariat led by party politicians. Whatever they thought about their own governments—and already they were beginning to think in a very fresh and vigorous fashion about them—it was not towards democratic communism that the minds of the scientific and technical workers were turning.

Nevertheless, with the help of organizers from Russia, the protest of humanity against the prolongation of the New Warfare took for a time the form of communist risings. In 1947, in Marseilles, St. Etienne, Paris, Barcelona, Milan, Naples, Hamburg, Lodz and Glasgow there were mutinies of troops under arms and risings sufficiently formidable to sustain provisional Soviets for periods varying from a week to several months. The Hamburg and Glasgow Soviets were the best organized and held out longest, collapsing only after considerable bloodshed. Almost everywhere there were minor incidents of the same character. And the formal suspension of the war by the responsible governments concerned was certainly due more than anything else to their terror of a general social revolt. As the

material organization of the system was shattered, as the behaviour of the technicians became uncertain, the threatening visage of the class-vindictive proletarian drew nearer and nearer to the face of the stockbroker, the war-monger, the banker, the traditional ruler.

It took nearly three years to end the last war. The Conference of London in 1947 did its best to work out a stable settlement of Europe on the lines of the Versailles Treaty, but the politicians and diplomatists were still incapable of the frankness and generosity needed. Face-saving was so much more important than life-saving to these creatures that they actually allowed the now pointless hostilities to be renewed in 1948.

In the spring of 1949, however, at Prague, President Benes achieved what had seemed to be the impossible, and brought the fighting to an end. He did this by inventing a phrase and suggesting, instead of a treaty, a "Suspension of Hostilities". Each Power was to remain in possession of the territory it occupied, and there was to be no further fighting pending the assembly of an unspecified Conference to be organized later. Influenza, cholera, and at last maculated fever, the progressive enfeeblement of economic life and new developments of human relationship, prevented that Conference from ever meeting. The Benes Suspension of Hostilities became a permanent suspension. It endures to this day.

10. THE RAID OF THE GERMS

That same dearth of detailed description which takes the colour out of the history of the last wars becomes even more apparent in the records of the epidemics that made any resumption of that warfare impossible. Diaries, letters and descriptive writing were out of fashion; there were other things to do and no surplus energy in the brain. It is as if the micro-organisms had taken a leaf out of the book of the Foreign Offices and found in mankind's confusion an opportunity for restoring the long-lost empire of the germs.

The attack began in the best style without a declaration of war. The first line of advance consisted of a variety of influenzas, impoverishing fevers, that were highly infectious and impossible to control under war conditions. The depleted strength of the belligerent populations, a depletion due to their reduced and disorganised nourishment and the collapse of their sanitary services, gave these infections full scope; they killed some millions and diminished the already lowered vitality of the great populations still further. That lowering of the general vitality was far more important than the actual mortality. Cholera and bubonic plague followed, and then, five years and more later, when the worst seemed to have passed, came the culminating attack by maculated fever.

This obscure disease, hitherto known only as a disease of captive baboons, seems to have undergone some abrupt adaptation to the kindred habitat of the human body; possibly there was some intermediate host which prepared the bacilli for their attack on mankind. Or it may be that the preceding epidemics had changed some hitherto defensive element in human blood. We are still quite in the dark upon these points because at that time there were no doctors or biologists with the leisure to record observations, even had they had time to make them, and scientific publications had ceased to appear anywhere.

The disease appeared first in the vicinity of the London Zoological Gardens and spread thence with incredible rapidity. It discoloured the face and skin, produced a violent fever, cutaneous irritation and extreme mental distress, causing an uncontrollable desire to wander. Then the bodily energy vanished in collapse and the victim lay down and died. The fever was not simply infectious through water, but transmitted by the almost impalpable scabs scratched off by the sufferer. Wind, water and the demented sick carried it everywhere. About half humanity was vulnerable, and so far as we know now all who were vulnerable took it, and all who took it died.

So the world's malaise culminated in the terrible eighteen months between May 1955 and November 1956, at which latter date Nature with a pitiless but antiseptic winter came to the rescue of the human remnant. No effectual cure was ever devised for this fever and no helpful palliative. It swept the whole world and vanished as enigmatically as it came. It is still a riddle for pathologists. It no longer affects even the surviving baboon population, so that investigators can make no cultures, nor attempt any experiments. There is no material. It came, it destroyed, and it seems to have at last committed suicide with some unknown anti-body of its production. Or the real disease, as Mackensen believes, may have been not the maculated fever at all, but the state of vulnerability to its infection. That vulnerability had spread unsuspected throughout the world, he thinks, in the warring forties. The actual pestilence was not the disease but the harvest of a weakness already prepared.

History is like the individual memory in this, that it tends to obliterate disagreeable experiences. One of the most nonsensical things that was ever said was that a country is happy that has no history. On the contrary, it is only the really secure and prosperous phases that have left anything like sufficient material for historical reconstruction. We know of the pleasant social life of all the centuries of abundance in Egypt; we know the greatness and conquests of Assyria; the court-life of Ajanta and Central Asia is pictured for us to share; but the days of military disaster leave nothing but a band of ashes, and the years of pestilence merely break the continuities of the record. There is a good account of the Plague of London (1665) written by Defoe (1659- 1731), and the unwary reader has to be warned that that account was compiled and fabricated many years after the event by an ingenious writer who was not even an eye-witness. There is a painting by Raphael of the plague in Rome which is similarly reminiscent. Most of the great plagues of history took their dead and departed unportrayed. What concerns history is the subsequent social and economic dislocation. On that Clio becomes copious again. What goes on again matters to her, but what is dead is dead.

The flowering prosperity of the nineteenth and early twentieth centuries has left us an almost uncontrollable mass of record about people who knew nothing except by hearsay of the more frightful experiences of mankind. We have novels, letters, diaries, memoirs, pictures, photographs and so on by the million. But there survives hardly a letter, no pictures, and not a book or newspaper to throw light on those years 1955 and 1956, little more than a century and a third ago, which were certainly the most terrible through which our race ever passed. What was written at the time was destroyed as infectious. Afterwards it was left for a new generation of Defoes and Stephen Cranes to contrive a picture.

The descriptions of Cable, Nath Dass, Bodesco and Martini seem to be fairly justifiable, and to these fictions the reader is referred. They ring the changes upon not only villages but towns and cities with none but dead men and women in them; people lying unburied and gnawed by packs of hungry dogs and solitary cats; in India the tigers and in Africa the lions came into the desolate streets, and in Brazil the dead population of whole districts was eaten chiefly by wild hog,

which multiplied excessively. Rats swarmed, and with an unwonted boldness threatened even the immune.

One terror which is never omitted is the wandering of the infected. Nothing would induce them to remain in bed or hospital; nothing could keep them from entering towns and houses that were as yet immune. Thousands of these dying wanderers were shot by terror-stricken people whom they approached. That dreadful necessity horrifies us to-day as much as that other grim act of self- protection: the survivors in the boats of the big steamship Titanic which struck an iceberg in 1912, beating at the knuckles of the drowning men and women who clung to the sides and threatened to swamp them. For awhile, under such desperate and revealing stresses, man ceased to obey the impulses of a social animal. Those of the population who resisted the infection—and with maculated fever the alternatives were immunity or death—gave way to a sort of despair and hatred against the filthy suffering around them. Only a few men with medical, military, priestly or police training seem to have made head against the disaster and tried to maintain a sort of order. Many plundered. On the whole, so far as the evidence can be sifted, women behaved better than men, but some few women who joined the looters were terrible.

This nightmare came and passed.

In January 1957, people were walking about in the deserted towns, breaking into empty houses, returning to abandoned homes, exploring back streets littered with gnawed bones or fully-clad skeletons, and they were still unable to realize that the wrath of Nature was over and life still before them.

Maculated fever had put gas warfare in its place. It had halved the population of the world.

11. EUROPE IN 1960

The more advanced student of history finds it necessary to work out in detail the local variations of the process by which the great patchwork of empires and nationalist states, set up during the Age of European Predominance, lost its defining lines, lost its contrasted cultures and its elaborated traditions, and ceased to divide the allegiance and devotion of men of goodwill. It was still standing—a hollow shell in 1933; in 1966 it had gone. It crumpled up, it broke down; its forms melted together and disappeared.

For the purposes of general education, the intricate interplay of personalities and accidents in this world débâcle can be passed over, as we pass over the details of the Great War or of Napoleon's various military campaigns, and as Gibbon, the author of the Decline and Fall of the Roman Empire (published between 1776 and 1788) passed over a thousand years of Byzantine court life. Nowadays that sort of history has become a mine for those admirable biographical studies which are ousting the old romantic novel from the entertainment of our leisure so soon as our imaginations have passed beyond the purely romantic stage. All that is needed for our present purpose is some understanding of the broader forces that were operating through this lush jungle of human reactions.

The tempo of human affairs increases continually, and the main difference between the decline and fall of the Roman system and the decline and fall of the world rule of private-profit capitalism in the Twentieth Century lies in the far more rapid onset and development of the later collapse. A second important difference is the much livelier understanding of what was happening on the part of the masses involved. Each of these two great depressions in the record of human well-being was primarily a monetary breakdown, due to the casual development of financial and proprietary law and practice without any reference to a comprehensive well-being, and to the lag in political and educational adaptation which left the whole system at last completely without guidance. But while the former débâcle went to the pace of the horse on the paved road and of the written and spoken word, the phases of the new downfall flashed about the globe instantaneously and evoked a body of thought and reaction out of all comparison greater than the Roman precedent. So we see only a much compressed and abbreviated parallelism. From the demoralization of the deflated Roman Empire by the great plagues at the end of the second century of the Christian era, to the reappearance of commerce, industry, art and politeness in the cities of the thirteenth and fourteenth centuries, was well over a thousand nerveless years; from the invasion of

Belgium by the Germans in 1914 to the return of general material prosperity under the Air Dictatorship after 2010 was roughly a century.

The mental process, if for this reason alone, was much more continuous. It got to its conclusions while still in contact with its premises. The first world collapse was spread over a number of generations, each one oblivious of the experiences of its predecessor, but the larger and swifter part of the second world collapse fell well within the compass of a single long life. People who could remember the plentiful and relatively stable times between 1924 and 1928 as young men and women were still only at the riper end of middle age in 1960. Many who were children at the onset of the Hoover Slump were taking an active part in affairs in the days of the first international police, the Police of the Air and Sea Ways. It was possible to grasp what was happening as one whole. It is doubtful if any Roman citizen under the Empire ever grasped what was happening.

Nevertheless in each case there was a parallel obliteration of old ideas, the same effacement of boundaries, the same destruction of time-honoured traditions, the lapsing of debts and obligations, the disappearance of religious and educational organizations, the impoverishment of favoured and privileged classes, the recrudescence of lawlessness, the cleansing disillusionment. Each was the effectual liquidation of a bankrupt civilization preparatory to a drastic reconstruction.

We will now take a sort of rough cross-section of the world at about the date of 1960 C.E., and consider the condition of the main masses of the world's population and the great forces at work among them. In the light of subsequent events we can realize that there was already a very considerable convergence of conditions going on throughout the middle decades of the century. But it may be doubted whether that was evident at the time. The goal towards which the fundamental bionomic forces were driving was everywhere the same, but the particulars varied widely with the geographical, ethnic and traditional circumstances, and their immediate interpretations were even more diverse.

We have viewed the events of the Era of European Predominance as the outcome of an uncontrolled irregularity in growth, of economic hypertrophy in a phase of political and cultural atrophy. An immense increase in the energy of human society had occurred which had relieved itself partly in a great multiplication of the human population (Europe from 180 to 420 millions between 1800 and 1914, says Werner Sombart, in spite of a great emigration), partly in a monstrous exaggeration of warfare, and less considerably in an increased fullness and speed of the individual life. But, as we have related, the forces of conservativism and functional resistance embodied in the creditor and legal systems were presently able to give pause to the release of fresh energy. For the second time in human experience the inadaptable quality of the financial and proprietary organization produced a strangulation and an arrest.

The money and credit organization of the prosperity of the nineteenth century differed in many respects from, and was more elaborate than, the Roman, but its life history was essentially the same. It wound itself up in the same fashion. First came a vast expansion and increase of private fortunes and then destructive taxa-

tion. So far history repeated itself. The European system, like the Roman system before it, impoverished itself finally by the violent expenditure of its vast windfall of energy. It repeated the same blind story of wastage, but with the unprecedented headlong facilities science afforded it. It ran through its available fortune and was helplessly in debt in a few decades. The height of its expenditure was between 1914 and 1950. Thereafter the pace was less catastrophic.

Regarded even as destruction the New Warfare proved in the end to be a failure. It went to pieces when it was attempted. It did not kill as it might have killed—which is why the reader is alive to read this history. The actual battles of the European wars in the Forties—the purely military operations, that is to say—in all their ramifications cost mankind hardly a quarter of the battle slaughters of 1914-1918. And yet they mark the highest level of scientific fighting ever attained by mankind. The Asiatic troubles had been more destructive because they were nearer the barbaric level, but even there the actual deaths in warfare are estimated as under nine million. Of these, nearly five million are to be ascribed to the final offensive of Japan in 1938, the deadlock in Central China, the desperate fighting with the Kuomintang levies west of Hankow, and the subsequent retreat.

Man had fallen as short as all that of the magnificent horrors he had anticipated. He had failed to raise war to its ultimate mechanical level. The social and political dislocation following upon these two main struggles was indeed proportionately far greater than the disorder of 1917-1919, but warfare was its prelude rather than its cause. This New Warfare, which the prophets had said would end in a scientific massacre of mankind, passed insensibly into a squalor of political fiascos, unpayable debts, unsubscribed loans, scrapped machinery, insurrection, guerilla and bandit conflicts, universal hunger and the great pestilences. Gas Warfare and Air War faded out of the foreground of human experience, dwarfed and overwhelmed by the more primitive realities of panic, famine and fever. The ultimate victor in the middle twentieth century was the germ of maculated fever. The main causes in the fall of the world's population from about two thousand million in 1930 to a little under half that total in 1960 were diseases or simple starvation, arising directly from the complete economic collapse. Where war slew its millions in a few great massacres, pestilence slew its hundreds of millions in a pitiless pursuit that went on by day and night for two terrific years.

As Imhoff has said, there is no single European history of these Famished and Pestilential Fifties which followed so swiftly on the war years; there are ten million histories. The various governments created by the Treaty of Versailles were for the most part still legally in existence throughout this age, but with the monetary cessation they had become so faded and ineffective that they had ceased to have any great influence on everyday life. Some, like the British and the French, limited their activities to efforts—generally quite futile efforts, at tax-collecting; they went on finally in a way which will remind the student of the old tribute-levying Empires before the Helleno- Latin period. They interfered spasmodically with local affairs, but for the most part they let them drift. They ignored or compromised with active resistance. The British government was still, it seems,

paying arrears upon its various loans, in 1952, to such stockholders as it was able to trace. The records are obscure; the payments seem to have been made in a special paper currency without real purchasing power. Other governments, like the Italian and Spanish, carried on as real administrative bodies within restricted areas. Rome, for instance, remained in fairly effective control of the triangle marked out by Genoa, Florence and the Mediterranean Coast, and Barcelona and Madrid kept order throughout most of the Peninsula except the Sovietized Spanish Riviera, Portugal and Andalusia.

The process in America was roughly parallel. Detachment was easier so soon as the bankrupt railways ceased to operate there, because the distances between population centres were greater and the capacity of the people for local autonomy much greater. They were still not a century from pioneering. The railways never resumed after the pestilence. The authority of the Federal Government of the United States shrank to Washington, very much as the Eastern Empire shrank to Byzantium, but Washington had none of the vitality of Byzantium, and it was already a merely historical capital long before the revival of tourism towards 2000. Germany as a unity did not survive the Polish wars, and Berlin dwindled rapidly to the status of a group of villages amidst the ruins of the Polish aerial bombardments.

The practical effacement of these bankrupt political systems in a few years, the equally rapid drying up of general transport and communications, the crescendo of the monetary breakdown, the speedy degeneration of military organizations, threw back the tasks of social order upon such local and regional leading as still existed. They found themselves astonishingly called upon. In Europe, as all over the world throughout this extraordinary decade, towns, cities, rural districts, discovered themselves obliged to "carry on" by themselves. The plague only drove home that imperative need. The municipal authorities organized such health services as they could against the infection, or gave way to emergency bodies that took things out of their hands. When the plague disappeared, they were like shipwrecked sailors on a strange island; they had to reconstitute their shrunken economic life. They used old authority for new needs and old terms for new things. Here it would be an energetic leader who called himself the Mayor or the Duke, here a resolute little band, self-styled the Town Council or the Citizens' Union. Here "advanced" terminology prevailed, and it was a "Soviet of Workers" which took control. In effect the latter would be very similar to a Citizens' Union. Its chief distinction was its consciousness of being in a new social phase.

There was the most extraordinary variation in the political structure of this phase of dislocation, and a flat contradiction between the actual and the "legal" controls. Across South Germany, Poland and North France, the prevalent impression was one of social revolution, and Soviets were in fashion. But they were very different in character from the original local Russian Soviets. It was possible to find a Communist district referring itself vaguely to Moscow, lying side by side with another that was under the control of its former owners and employers and professed to be, and often was, still in communication with the national govern-

ment in the capital. An uneasy truce would be maintained between these theoretically antagonistic systems. Deputations would go for authority in various disputes—arrears of taxes in hand—to Westminster, Paris or Rome, very much as the barbarian chiefs of the Early Mediaeval period would upon due occasion refer to Byzantium or Rome. Local conflicts and revolutions were constantly occurring. They were recognized at the capitals only as local riots and municipal readjustments.

Scattered through this disarticulating Europe were the vestiges of the old militarism, broken fragments of unpaid armies with irreplaceable weapons and a dwindling supply of ammunition. They consisted of the officers who were soldiers by profession, and the levies who had not been disbanded or who had refused to be disbanded because there was no employment for them outside the ranks. These men had their officers very much under control because of the great facilities for desertion. In some cases these shrivelled military forces were in contact with the capital and the old legal government, and conducted, or attempted to conduct, tax requisitions and suchlike surviving functions of the old order; in other instances they became frankly brigand forces, though often with high-sounding titles, Public Order Guards of the Emergency Army. Most merged with the local police of aggressive Mayors or councils. Small wars of conquest went on in the early Sixties. Old empires and sovereign states reappeared, in duplicate or triplicate, and vanished or became something else. After 1960 there were even quasi-military forces levying contributions, keeping a sort of order, and professing to be Modern State nuclei. They would occupy the old barracks and accommodation of garrison towns.

In the Forties these soldiers had been raw recruits. In the following decades those who remained in their old formations became formidable middle- aged rascals in patched and shabby and supplemented uniforms. Some of the commandants had gained control of local aerodromes and local munition factories, but everywhere the military found themselves more and more out of sympathy with the technical workers they needed to make these acquisitions effective. They degenerated to the level of the nineteenth century infantry and were at last glad to get even a few thousand roughly made cartridges to replenish their supply.

Under the necessity of doing things for themselves, people did things for themselves that they had left to the central government for a century. Even during the World War, and in the year or so of stress that followed it, various French Chambers of Commerce had supplemented the deficiency in small change by local token coinages. Now this practice reappeared widely. Today our museums contain hundreds of thousands of specimens of these improvised European coins of lead, nickel, tin and all sorts of alloys, jetons or checks of wood, and tons of signed, printed paper notes, useful in the local market, acceptable for rents and local taxes, but of no avail at all at a distance of a few score miles. The local bank manager as often as not would improvise a local credit system in cooperation with the local solicitor; the doctors would contrive a way of getting along without the

Home Office. There were still printers' establishments in most centres of population, and for some years local periodicals, often of considerable originality, appearing weekly or monthly and printed on the roughest and most variable paper, supplied all that remained alive of the European Press. But their foreign news amounted to little more than rumour. The great Press agencies were bankrupt and dead; the telegraph organization was out of gear.

Save in a few exceptional centres, the diffusion of news by radio died out completely. The manufacture of receiving sets was entirely disorganized. From 1930 to 1970 the "ether" for all except the special purposes of air transport was still. There is a long and interesting study in the Historical Record Series of the vicissitudes of posts, telegraphs and telephones between 1950 and 1980. There seem to have been extraordinary survivals. Apparently London, Paris and Rome were in telephonic communication almost without a break, and the news of the great London landslide was telephoned to Madrid and thence radioed to Buenos Ayres in 1968. But that may have been a revival connected with the new Sea and Air Control.

The disappearance not only of radio sets but of an enormous variety of small conveniences and appliances was extraordinarily rapid after the collapse of world trade. Photography, for instance, was wiped out almost at once. The bicycle became rare, and the old pneumatic tyre was replaced by a thin solid one of often very badly adulterated "remade" rubber. Electric lighting flickered out and vanished for want of the proper material for filaments. All electrical material deteriorated, and tramway systems either fell into complete disuse or returned to horse traction.

Ordinary life had been lowering its standards bit by bit from the World War onward. First one thing went and then another. Neither in the British nor the French provinces did the housing of the common people recover from the cessation of building during the actual warfare. Except in places like Berlin or Vienna where there had been a vigorous outbreak of post-war building which provided accommodation in excess for the shrunken population, the mass of Europeans were even more congested and dirty in their domestic accommodation than they had been before the conflict, though indeed they never sank to the immemorial squalor and poverty of the Chinese and Indian towns. Cleanliness diminished at such a pace as to be noted even by the newspapers after 1933. There are constant complaints of the dirtiness of the streets and the bad repair of the roads, and regretful comparisons with the trim orderliness of twenty years before.

Clothing declined with housing. The clothing trade shrank steadily per head of population for nearly forty years. The city crowds, in spite of the more and more abundant uniforms (until 1950), lost nearly all their former brightness and élan. People patched up their old clothing for want of new, and rags became increasingly common. The supply of boots was very restricted. The mass production of boots had been commandeered at the outbreak of the war and was never turned back to commercial use because of the complete financial ruin that ensued. But the old-fashioned shoemakers had been driven off the face of Europe long before

by this mass production, and so throughout the Famished Fifties the Europeans were very painfully shod. Spain had the best boots and France and Britain took to sandals—and chilblains. A certain manufacture of footwear went on in some centre in Bohemia, now untraceable, and next to Spain ranked Central Europe in the order of shoe welfare. There was an extreme scarcity of hats everywhere.

There was also a universal decline in the little comforts and accessories of life to which the world had grown accustomed. Except in a few favoured regions where it was actually grown, tobacco disappeared. The mass production of cigarettes died out, and those who smoked, smoked pipes of substitute. Real tea became a great rarity, and sugar was scarce. Dietetic diseases and diseases of under-nutrition increased.

During the strain and effort of the Great War most of the Europeans had already learnt something of contrivance and makeshift. Now they were to have a decade of domestic management under difficulties. The Germans were already familiar with the word Ersatz; there was much technical knowledge and ability diffused among them; and it is indisputable that they contrived to keep much nearer comfort than the rest of the world during these dismal years. They devised substitute leather, substitute cotton, substitute coffee and tea, substitute tobacco, substitute quinine and opium, and a very respectable list of other substitute drugs.

At the other extreme were the shiftless Irish. Until the return of production their physical misery was very great indeed. One observer doubted if there were a million yards of new cloth produced in that country between 1950 and 1960. "They live," he reported, "on buttermilk, potatoes, whisky and political excitement. They have contrived garments of woven straw, often very picturesquely dyed, which they call Early Erse and of which they boast inordinately, and they warm themselves by means of fires of peat and dung and a great warmth of mutual invective." This sounds quite barbaric. Yet it is to this period that we owe the graceful—though, according to a recent Historical Documents report, rather rickety—Church of the Atonement, built on the site of the Dublin Royal College of Science after that had been suppressed by the Censorship of 1939 for "teaching biology in a manner tending to disintegrate the Holy Trinity".

The student must be more or less familiar with the representations of this period in that useful compilation Historical Scenes in a Hundred Volumes, and he has probably read a number of romances and stories of this time. Actual photographs are least abundant in the later fifties and early sixties. There were still plenty of cameras in the world, but the supply of films seems to have died out after 1955, and there are hardly any but slow wet-plate exposures after that time for nearly ten years. We get only a few score of such animated snapshots as were abundant during the preceding decades, and there are no European cinematograph films at all. Neither was there much sketching except of single figures, and so the editors have had to supplement their material by very carefully studied drawings and photographed restorations made at a later date.

There are six interesting snapshots of scenes in Lyons in 1959. Someone seems to have found a spool of film and been able to develop it. One shows the

big central square, the Place Bellecour as it was called, on a market day. Earlier pictures show a big bronze equestrian figure of Louis XIV, but this had already disappeared, probably it had been melted for its metal; and the windows of some of the big buildings, formerly hotels and hospitals, in the background have the empty frameless look of gutted houses. But the scene is quite a busy one. It was probably the monthly market, and there is a considerable amount of cattle, numerous horses being traded, hurdled sheep, many goats and a row of pig-pens. The people are mostly peasants wearing straw hats and either very old coats or in some cases shawls wrapped about them. Townspeople are still wearing the clothing of the 'thirties, shabby and patched, and there are three market officials or magistrates in the old-world top hat. In the foreground a bearded man leads a couple of oxen harnessed to a small "runabout" car in which a corpulent woman sits in front with a crate of ducklings while behind is a netted calf. The lady smiles broadly at the camera, unaware that she is smiling at posterity.

Another of these snapshots shows a bowls competition in the deserted railway station. It is clearly a festive occasion, and several games are in progress. The rails have disappeared from the tracks, which have been levelled for the game, and the ponies and mules of the players are tethered on the platform in a long line. The doors of the various bureaus have been taken away but the inscriptions Chef de Gare, Salle d'Attente, Restaurant, are still faintly visible. There are two long tables on one of the middle platforms on which simple refreshments are being served. A third picture shows a crowd staring at the ruins of a row of houses which have just collapsed down a steep slope in what is apparently the district known as Fourvière. Here two bearded men in the unmistakable uniform of the old Alpini are keeping order. We know as a matter of fact that the Lyons municipality at that time had three regiments of these soldiers quartered in barracks. They are wearing sandals supplemented by cloth strips that are twisted round their legs, and their cloaks are in good condition.

Three others of these photographs give us a glimpse of the state of affairs in a disused silk factory. Up to the time of the economic collapse, the silk manufactured at Lyons was still largely that produced by the silkworm, but the supply of raw material seems to have died out more or less completely in the Rhône valley, and the shrinkage of trade and then the war diminished the importation of the reeled-up thread. But silk was needed in the manufacture of shells, and probably there were special efforts to maintain the supply up to the last. This particular establishment seems to have been carrying on a diminished output until the Lyons commune in 1951. Then no doubt it was abruptly abandoned. One photograph shows a great heap of paper litter among weaving-machines and a number of petrol cans. Apparently there was an attempt to fire the place. Another gives a vista of winding-machines shrouded in spiders' webs and fine dust. In a third a wild cat crouches among the spindles of a spinning-machine and spits at the unwanted intruder. The machinery has all the complicated clumsiness characteristic of twentieth- century mechanism. Apparently a window of some sort was opened or a blind drawn back to make this particular photograph, for the picture is blurred

with a multitude of whirling moths, most of them out of focus, evidently just stirred up.

These particular pictures are valuable because of their authenticity. There are also two contemporary dry-plate pictures of the Café Royal, the big restaurant of the Grand Hotel of Stockholm, deserted and still intact. They are oddly suggestive of two pictures of the ruins of the Baths of Caracalla in Rome as they appeared a hundred years earlier. And there is also a photograph of the remains of the old dining-room of the Hotel Métropole at Brighton in England before it was undermined and fell into the sea. But all the rest of the pictures given in Historical Scenes between 1955 and 1963 are arranged pictures. The Transport organization was running scores of aeroplanes and radio communications were restored long before the complex manufacture of photographic apparatus and material was set going again.

There are some very interesting restorations of conditions in London showing the empty streets and the vacant tumbledown warehouses of the city after the pestilence. The pictures of the corridors of the hotels in the Strand turned into hospital wards are very impressive. So too is the sketch of a great fight between the cow-keepers and the potato-growers for the possession of Hyde Park and Kensington Gardens in which three hundred people were killed. The dreadful pictures of the bodies of plague victims floating down the Thames and accumulating in the Pool of London, however, are now said to be exaggerated.

We try in the midst of our present securities to imagine the phases of anxiety, loss, incredulity and reluctant acquiescence through which the minds of hundreds of millions of Europeans passed, day by day, from the general comfort of the Twenties, through the shocks, fear, horror, rage and excitement of the war cycle, into this phase of universal impotence and destitution. The poor perhaps had a less vivid apprehension of disaster than the rich. Even in the days of General Prosperity, as it is called, they had at the best what we should consider very dull, drab, irksome lives. Even though they mostly ate sufficiently, they ate badly, and there was never a stage of universal decent housing at any time for them. They went from bad to worse. They passed from toil to unemployment and lethargy. But the middling sort passed from good to bad, from something one might almost consider tolerable living to the hopeless neediness of the masses.

A class that went through great unhappiness everywhere during this period was the class of elderly and "retired" persons and persons of "independent means" (and no responsibilities) which had expanded so enormously during the First Age of General Prosperity. This superfluity of prosperous humanity had spread itself out very pleasantly over the world, oblivious of the exertions that sustained social discipline and ensured its security. Insensibly it had taken the place of the old administrative and directive noblesse and country gentry. The investment system during its period of steady efficiency had relieved this social stratum of every bother. There were great areas of agreeable country, residential districts, given up to this "well-off" society, to its gardens, which were often delightful, its golf-courses, race-courses, mountain sport centres, parks, country clubs, plages, and

hotels. It wilted a little during the World War, but revived again very hopefully in the decade of hectic and uncertain expansion that followed. Then, as the Great Slump developed its grim phases, this life of leisure passed away.

The Phase of Economy is really a misnomer. There was really no economy; there was strangulation and inaction through a cessation of expenditure. Nobody— unless it was a dexterous speculator on a falling market—grew richer, or even relatively richer. The only profits appeared in bank balance sheets. As the malady of arrest spread, traffics declined, enterprise died out, borrowing states and corporations suspended payments, and these children of good fortune, these well-off people, found themselves confronted at the same time by a suspension of payments and more and more urgent charitable appeals. Their bankers and solicitors informed them that first this trusted prop and then that was in arrears or in default. The waters of repudiation rose, submerging security after security. If they sold out and hoarded, some fluctuation in exchange might still engulf great fractions of their capital. "Whatever else may be falling off, sleepless nights are on the increase," a financial paper remarked in 1933. The head full of self-reproach that tossed on the crumpled pillow in the villa marked time with the fretting of the unemployed who worried in the stuffy cold of the slum.

We have the Diary of Titus Cobbett, who rode on a bicycle from Rome and along the Riviera to Bordeaux in 1958. He had begun life as an art dealer, and had served the British Inland Revenue for some years as a valuer of furniture, pictures and the like. His tour seems to have been a journey of curiosity. He complains bitterly of the difficulty of changing money between Genoa and Bordeaux. He seems to have had some obscure diplomatic or consular function, but of that he is too discreet to speak. Perhaps he was sent to make a report, but if so there is no record of his instructions.

His description of that smitten coast is still very interesting reading. He had, as a young man with good connections, known Monte Carlo well in the twenties, and the places he visited were often those at which he had stayed as a guest. He records the abandonment of hundreds of lovely châteaux, locked-up, unsaleable, abandoned, in the keeping perhaps of some old domestic, or frankly looted by the people of the district, once delightful gardens whose upkeep had become impossible, blind tangles of roses, oleanders, pomegranates, oranges, cypresses, palm trees, agaves, cacti and weeds; unremunerative hotels allowed to fall into ruins, broken-down water-conduits washing away the roads, bungalows taken over by the peasants. Something of the same swift desolation must have come upon the Campagna and the villadom of the Bay of Naples during the ebb of Roman vitality, but this had been a swifter decline. The roads, he says, were very variable, but a great number of the road signs and roadside advertisements were still making their mute appeal to a vanished traffic. As he rode along wondering whether he would find a reasonably clean and hospitable shelter for the night, he read, he says, picked out in metallic knobs that answered brightly to his oil lamp:

H TEL S LEN ID
CU SINE RENOM

T T LE C NFOR M RNE

Whither had host and guests departed? Where were the owners and tenants of these villas and gardens; the bright clientele of the pleasure resorts? Many of them no doubt were already dead, for the Riviera owners had been mostly middle- aged and oldish people. The rest were back in their own countries leading impoverished lives, full of tiresome reminiscences, lost in the universal indigence.

Cobbett visited the ruins of the old Casino at Monte Carlo, and the younger Sports Club. The ceiling of the American Bar had fallen in a few days before his visit. "They looked small," he says. "When I was young they had seemed tremendous places."

The celebrated garden in which suicidal gamblers used to put an end to their troubles was overgrown with mesembryanthemum.

Yet there was one exception to this general decadence, and our observer stresses the significance of that. Air traffic was still going on. Between Rome and Marseilles he notes very precisely that he saw thirteen aeroplanes going east or west, besides two that he heard before he got up in the morning. "I doubt if I should have seen so many twenty-five years ago," he writes, and goes on to enlarge, very illuminatingly, on the revival of trade and the possible revival of order these throbbing mechanisms portended. At Nice and at Marseilles he noted there was shipping—"not mere fishing boats but ships of a thousand tons or more"; and at Nice they were building a bigger ship—he estimated it as a three-thousand tonner. We have no other records of shipbuilding between 1947 and 1962. Long before 1940 the building of very big ships had ceased to be a "paying proposition" and it is fairly certain that no sea-going ships whatever, big or little, were built anywhere in the world in the early fifties. Year by year the transport system of the bankrupt planet had been sinking into disuse. It is only nowadays that our historical students are attempting to work out statistical charts of that swift decadence.

Cobbett also notes with surprise and hope a stretch of railway (operated by lever trolleys and a petrol engine or so) between the port of Marseilles and some inland quarries. He was clearly under the impression that no railways were operating in the world any longer. So soon as the traffic had sunken to a level below the possibility of paying subsistence wages, maintaining the permanent way and meeting running expenses, it had been impossible even for speculative buyers to handle these once valuable properties. They had become old junk on the landscape, tracks of torn and rusty rails smothered in agaves and wild flowers. He mentions the beauty of the viaducts of the old Sud de France, and tells how he bicycled along the footworn side-path of the Paris-Lyon- Méditerranée in preference to the road. The peasants had used the derelict railway as a convenient iron-mine, and few rails remained. Most of the sleepers had been used for fuel.

At Fréjus there was an aerodrome, and here he describes a very illuminating conversation with a Spanish-American aviator who had served first with the Poles, then with the Germans, and finally with the French during the warfare. Cobbett was impressed by the evident revival of trade, and surprised to find rubber, spices, mercury and block-tin among the commodities coming by air from the

East, while clocks, watches, compasses, knives, needles, buttons, hardened glass and the like were going back in exchange. Most of the trade was barter, and the profits were so considerable that there seemed every reason to expect a steady expansion of the service.

He seems to have learnt for the first time of the developing combination of air-merchants who were mostly aviators surviving from the war. They had already organized a loose world union, it seems, and were keeping the airways and air lights in order.

Cobbett remarked on the shipping revival he had noted.

"We shall have to watch that," said the aviator significantly.

"You take passengers?"

"When they can pay a passage."

"But this is civilization coming back!" cried Cobbett.

"Don't believe it! It's a new civilization beginning."

And he seems to have opened Cobbett's eyes for the first time to some of the ideas that were already taking shape in such brains as his. "World Empire?" he said. "That's an old idea! The men who hold the air and the transport hold the world. What do we want with empires and that stuff any more?"

Cobbett was greatly impressed by this conversation. He went on across France to Bordeaux, where it seems some sort of money awaited him, thinking this over and jotting down his thoughts. He makes one sound and interesting parallel between this new World Transport Organization and those Hansa Merchants who played such an important rôle in the revival of civilization about the Baltic and North Europe generally after the Roman collapse. "After all," reflects Cobbett, "we have never given organized transport and trading its proper importance in history."

At Bordeaux he sold his bicycle and was able to get a passage in an aeroplane to Le Bourget (an aerodrome of old origin near the ruins of Paris) and thence to fly to Hendon. His 'plane landed at Le Mans for an exchange of goods. His delight to escape from the rough roads he had been riding is infectious.

He describes the recovery of the devastated French forests in the form of scrub, and he peered down at the little peasants' clearings that were appearing in groups and patches round the old towns. He sees the aviators and mechanics at the aerodromes with new eyes, and he learns from them of the way in which World Transport was picking up and reinstating metallurgical and electrical works. He has an eye for the beauty of Le Mans cathedral, which he had seen and admired in his student days, and which he rejoices to find intact, and he describes that early monument to the pioneers of aviation in the Place below which still survives. Amiens cathedral also was uninjured at that time.

His diary ends on a melancholy note. Apparently he had not visited England for some years, and he is shocked by the ruinous desolation of the outer suburbs of London. Plainly he had lived in and loved London as a boy. A part of Hyde Park, in spite of the opposition of the squatter cultivators, had been converted into an aerodrome, but he found the rebuilding of the central region haphazard and

unpleasing. He objects to the crowding of heavy buildings, with their vast anti-aircraft carapaces of cement, at the centre, due to the decay of suburban traffic facilities. It looked, he says, like a cluster of "diseased" mushrooms. "When shall we English learn to plan?" he asks, and then with an odd prophetic gleam he doubts whether the northern slope of the Thames depression, so ill drained and so soft in its subsoil, can carry this lumpish mass of unsound new buildings to which the life of the old city was shrinking.

Only ten years later his fears were to be justified. The bed of the Thames buckled up and the whole of the Strand, Fleet Street, Cornhill and, most regrettable of all, the beautiful St. Paul's Cathedral of Sir Christopher Wren, so familiar to us in the pictures and photographs of that age, collapsed in ruin and perished in flame. The reader who has pored over Historical Scenes in a Hundred Volumes,—and what child has not?—will remember the peculiar appearance of the old Waterloo Bridge, crumpled up to a pent-house shape, and the grotesque obliquity of the Egyptian obelisk, once known as Cleopatra's Needle, that venerable slab of hieroglyphics, cracked and splintered by air- raid shrapnel, which slanted incredibly for some years before it fell into the banked-up water of the Lambeth-Chelsea lake.

12. AMERICA IN LIQUIDATION

The preceding sections have given a general view of the course of history in the Old World during the middle decades of the twentieth century. Even in Europe certain regions, as we have noted, stand rather aloof from the essential drama, following a line of development of their own, less tragic and intense than that of the leading Powers. Spain, for example, the new Spain that was born in 1931, has the rôle of an onlooker, an onlooker much preoccupied with his own affairs. Still more noticeable is the non-participation of both Latin- and English-speaking America in these passionate and violent happenings. They suffered parallel economic, political and social stresses, but within their own limits. After the financial storms of the Early Thirties, the shocks that came to them from the European troubles affected them less and less. They took up their particular aspect of the decline and fall of private capitalism and worked it out in their own way.

Yet the fact they did share in that decline and fall brings out very clearly a fact that was sometimes disputed in the past: the immediate causes of the world collapse in the twentieth century were first monetary inadaptability, secondly the disorganization of society through increased productivity, and thirdly the great pestilence. War was not a direct cause. The everyday life of man is economic, not belligerent, and it was strangled by the creditor. Had the world been already one state in 1900, and had it still been an economy of private accumulation with a deflating currency, it would have collapsed in very much the same fashion that it did collapse. Had it been cut up into a hundred belligerent states at that time, but with a monetary system that restrained the creditor and allowed industrial development without limit, it might have released sufficient energy to have gone on with its wars for another century or so before it reached the goal of mutual extermination. The monetary collapse was the most immediate factor in the world's disorganization, enfeeblement and famine. Without it man might have pursued a far longer and more strenuous career to massacre and suffocation. On the whole it was perhaps well for him that progress tumbled over finance in the nineteen-thirties.

The futility of all the early anti-war movements becomes understandable only when we grasp the essential importance of a sane monetary nexus. On this we have insisted throughout, we have elucidated the connexion of the creditor and traditional antagonisms from half a dozen angles, and nothing could emphasize and drive home the lesson more than the parallelism of the American and Old-World experiences.

From the days of their first political separation from the European system the American communities had gone through their own series of developmental phases, independent of and out of rhythm with the course of events in the Old-World. Independent—and yet not completely independent, because they were upon the same planet. Throughout the nineteenth century the American mind, in north and south alike, was saturated with the idea of ISOLATION. It was taught in the schools, in the Press, in every political utterance of a general import, that the New World was indeed a new world, an escape from the tyranny of ancient traditions to peace, liberty, opportunity and a fresh life for mankind. It had to avoid all "entangling alliances" with Old-World states and policies, forget the inveterate quarrels and hatreds of Europe even at the price of forgetting kinship and breaking with a common culture, and work out and set the example of a more generous way of living. From the days of George Washington to the days of Woodrow Wilson, in spite of the Civil War and much grave economic trouble, the American mind never abandoned its belief in its own exemplary quality and its conception that towards the rest of the world its attitude must be missionary and philanthropic. It realized that it knew many things very simply, but it had no doubt it knew better.

Throughout the nineteenth century both America and Europe expanded enormously, economically, biologically. America was profoundly impressed by her own growth and disposed to disregard the equal pace of European progress. Assisted by a tremendous immigration from Europe, the population of the United States increased by about 80 millions in a hundred years. But in spite of that tremendous emigration, Europe during that period added 240 millions to her multitudes. The American cherished a delusion that he had "got on" relatively to Europe. His life had in fact expanded, concurrently with the European's, and through the working of ideas and inventions and the importation of human energy from the older centres. In his unimpeded continent the different elements in the expansion increased at rates that did not correspond with the European process. He was living in a similar progressive system, but he was more and more out of phase with Transatlantic developments.

And throughout that century inventions in transport and communications were "abolishing distance" and bringing points that had formerly been months apart into a few hours' or a few moments' distance from one another.

The resulting alternations of intimacy and remoteness across the Atlantic constitute one of the outstanding aspects of twentieth-century history. It is like two great and growing tops that spin side by side. They approach, they touch and clash, they wabble and fly apart. Or it is like two complexes of machinery, destined ultimately to combine into one world mechanism, whose spinning wheels attempt to mesh and fail to mesh and jar with a great shower of sparks and splinters and separate again. From the end of the nineteenth century onward the unifying forces of life were tending to gear America with Europe. By the middle of the twentieth century any observer might have been forgiven the conclusion that the intergearing had failed.

We have already given great prominence in this history to the figures of Henry Ford, Woodrow Wilson, and the second Roosevelt, Franklin Roosevelt. We have told of the magnificent advance upon Europe and the subsequent recoil of America within and about them. A brief but competent contemporary book by an American publicist, Frank H. Simonds, Can America stay at Home? (1933) surveys the question of isolation very illuminatingly as it appeared in the opening years of the great economic slump which closed down for good and all the wild freedoms of Acquisitive Private Capitalism. He shows how the phases of approach and repulsion succeeded one another from the first imperialist enterprises of Roosevelt I (Theodore Roosevelt, 1901-1909) onward; how impossible it seemed for America either to keep out of Old-World affairs or to mingle frankly in them. It expressed its virtuous opinions and would not back them. It insisted upon moral judgments and would not take responsibility. In European eyes, to quote Simonds' new historical phrase, "American concern for peace appeared a transparent endeavour to combine the mission of John the Baptist with the method of Pontius Pilate." The explanation lay in just that mixture of liberal modernity and naive crudity in the American intelligence on which we have laid stress.

From its beginning the American republic was a break with history, a new thing, far newer, having regard to its period, than the Soviet Republic of Lenin, and from its beginning it was failing to go on with its newness, failing to develop and intensify its ideas. It evolved a body of higher schools and cultivated men to think itself out only after more than a century of independence; in the interim it left its mass education to underpaid teachers and repetitive women. It grew bodily, immensely, and for more than a century it lived on imported brain-food. The result was this rawness, this immense sense of its mission and this want of any subtlety or vigour in its conduct. Wilson's foolish preachments and arrangements, so foolish and yet so saturated with the wisdom of world peace, were perhaps the highest expression of the American mind of his time.

The American mind even in the nineteenth century was not an ignorant mind; it was an immensely uneducated mind. If it was clumsy, it was also free. Its religious "revivalism" was exactly parallel to its political fluctuations. We find in the stories and studies of authentic American life such features as camp-meetings and organized emotional campaigns for repentance and conversion. We think of firelit scenes, of harsh preaching and lusty chanting. These waves of popular feeling, these gatherings, often in the woods, with their hymn- singing, their exhortation, their shouts of penitence and exultant belief, the mindless exaltation and the subsequent mindless deflation of American spiritual life, were precisely reflected in these booms and slumps of the American world mission. Only with the shock of world economic disaster did the real social and political thinking of America rise to its full vigour. The retreat of the United States from the imbroglio of European affairs as the great depression intensified was marked by a new, more vigorous determination to grip the essentials of social life.

And certainly there was everything to stimulate thought in the internal situation. The dégringolade was at first more rapid even than in Europe. The industrial

edifice had been reared to giddier heights of mass production and fell more heavily. In 1928 the United States of America still believed itself the most prosperous country in the world; in 1933 its unemployed were more hopeless and formidable than those of any other continent. But they made no organized effort of revolt; they had no revolutionary formula to bring them together. They revolted as individuals and gangs and became criminals. Society was not overthrown, but it crumbled rapidly to dust and disorder. The crime wave, the financial stress, the frantic efforts to economize, and all the consequent strangulation of popular education and the dissolution of confidence, order and intercommunication—that sequence which we have already traced in general terms manifested itself most severely and typically in this vast, comparatively unhistorical area. Roosevelt II struggled gallantly but he came too late to stop the rot.

In America as in Europe a phase of fragmentation set in. It was not a smash to which one can give a definite date, but every day there was something happening in the direction of dissolution. In America as in Europe State governments became insolvent phantoms making feebler and feebler efforts to collect taxes, and the Federal authority in Washington faded away, if not as completely as the League of Nations in Europe, at any rate in a comparable manner. We have the same phenomena of municipalities becoming autonomous, and provisional controls, Citizens' Unions, Law and Order Societies, Workers' Protection Associations and plain Workers' Soviets (in New Mexico and Arizona) springing into activity here, there and everywhere. In the Blue Mountains and on the Pacific coast small republics had already isolated themselves in 1945 and were carrying out a strange blend of Methodism, "Technocracy" and the Douglas Plan, and Utah had become a practically autonomous Single-Tax State and had restored Mormonism of the original type as the State religion. But there had been no formal secession from the Federal Union anywhere.

There is in the Records a description of Washington in the year 1958, by a former attaché of the British Embassy there. (All the Ambassadors of the British Empire had been replaced by "consolidated consuls" in 1946.) He describes a visit to the White House, where he was entertained at lunch by President Benito Caruso. The President was carrying on although his term had expired because his successor elect had disappeared on his way to the capital in the Allegheny Mountains. There had been considerable confusion about the last election, and two Secession Presidents who were disputing possession of the State of New York after a conflict over the Yonkers Ballot Boxes had cut off communications with New England altogether.

The President received his visitor very cordially and asked many very sympathetic and intelligent questions about the European situation. He spoke very hopefully of the American outlook. The "return to Normalcy", he said, was at last in sight. There had been a restoration of the steamboat traffic on the Mississippi, and cotton was going through to the north again in spite of the political unrest. A hundred and forty automobiles had been sent to South America alone in the year 1956-7 in the place of only seventy-two for the previous year. The new quinine-

coffee barter system was working well. He looked forward now to a steady upward movement in business affairs. The Hoover Slump had, he admitted, lasted much longer and had gone much lower than had been expected, and it had tried the people to the utmost, but they had faced their trials in a manner worthy of the fathers of the republic. He concluded with the compliments usual then between the two great divisions of the English-speaking peoples.

The lunch was plain but ample. There was excellent pork and a variety of vegetables which the President with genuine democratic frankness boasted he had raised himself with the help of his negro "secretariat" in the pig-pens and garden at the back of the White House. The duties of the secretariat seem to have been in the household rather than the office. They had been appointed for abstruse political reasons, and several of them were unable to read. Mrs. Caruso, a very pleasant lady of Irish extraction, was disposed to dwell on the difficulties of housekeeping in Washington in view of the increasing unpunctuality in the collection of the Federal revenue, but the President checked her, evidently considering these domestic matters a reflection upon the solvency of the nation.

At that time only about a third of the States were actually represented by Congressmen in the Assembly. The rest had found it either too expensive or unnecessary to send delegates. A member was in possession of the house, a tattered individual, reciting some lengthy grievance; there were no reporters visible, and nobody was listening to him. Apparently this man was trying to "talk out" some legislative proposal, but the visitor could not find anyone who could explain the situation precisely.

The visitor dined on the following day with the eloquent, vital and venerable Senator Borah from Idaho (1865-1970). He was in excellent form, and talked throughout the meal. Indeed, he talked so ably that his visitor was unable to ask him several questions previously prepared for him. He too was extremely hopeful for his country. He admitted that there had been a marked decline in the grosser welfare of America during his lifetime. He would not quarrel with statistics. In tons of coal and steel, in miles of railway run, in the mass production of motorcars and commodities generally, it was possible to institute unfavourable comparisons with the past. "But man does not live by bread alone," said America's Grand Old Man. "Let us look a little nearer the heart of things."

That heart, it seemed, had never been sounder. The pestilence, like everything that came from God, had been "wholesome". The standard of life was, he maintained, higher than it ever had been, having regard to the nobler aspects of things. Fewer bathrooms there might be, at least in working order, but there was far more purity of mind. In his younger days there had been a lamentable lapse into luxurious indulgence and carelessness on the part of the free people of the States, but all that was past. America was nearer now to the old Colonial simplicity, honesty and purity than she had ever been.

A little inconsecutively the Senator went on to denounce the dishonesty of Europe and the disingenuousness of European and particularly of British diplomacy. He seemed for a time to be repeating long-remembered speeches and to have for-

gotten how completely British diplomacy had lapsed. He had apparently heard the word "attaché" before he began to talk, and that had sent his mind back to old times. He returned to the present situation. The United States, he insisted, had gone through far blacker phases in its early history. A hundred and fifty-four years ago Washington had been burnt by a victorious British army. Nothing of the sort had occurred during the present depression—if it could still be spoken of as a depression. Even at the darkest hour in this great Hoover Slump nobody had ever thought of burning Washington.

Later on this same traveller visited the University of Chicago, Columbia University, Harvard and a number of other centres of intellectual activity. His comments are shrewd and intelligent, and fall in very conveniently with our examination of the mental reactions that even then were rapidly producing a new and more sinewy American consciousness amidst the ruins of its ancient laxity.

These institutions were naturally in a most varied state of adjustment to the new conditions. Not all were progressive. Harvard reminded him of what he had read of the ancient lamaseries of Tibet. There was practically no paper to be got for note-taking or exercises, and the teaching was entirely oral and the learning done by heart. The libraries were closely guarded against depredations, and the more important books were only to be inspected in locked glass cases. A page was turned daily. The teachers varied in prestige with the number of their following. They either sat in class-rooms and under trees and lectured, or they went for long walks discoursing as they went to a rabble of disciples. They varied not only in prestige but physical well-being, because it was the rôle of these students to cultivate food for their masters and themselves in the college grounds and produce woven clothing and sandals in the Technical and Art Buildings. Some literary production was going on. The more gifted students wrote verses on slates and these, if they were sufficiently esteemed by the teaching staff, were written up on the walls or ceilings of the building. The atmosphere was one of archaic simplicity and studied leisure. The visitor was entertained by President Eliot, a tall distinguished-looking elderly man in a toga, who had inherited his position from his grandfather. There was a large open fire in the room, which was lit by tallow candles which two undergraduates continually snuffed. The President talked very beautifully over his simple soup, his choice Maryland claret and a cornucopia of fruit and nuts, and the conversation went on until a late hour.

The impression of Nicholson, the visitor, was one of an elegant impracticability. The simple graciousness of the life he could not deny, but it seemed to him also profoundly futile. He seems, however, to have concealed this opinion from the President and allowed him to talk unchallenged of how Harvard had achieved the ultimate purification and refinement of the Anglican culture, that blend of classicism and refined Christianity, with a graceful monarchist devotion.

"There is a King here?" asked the visitor.

"Not actually a King," said the President regretfully. "We have decided that the Declaration of Independence is inoperative, but we have been unable to locate

the legitimate King of England, and so there has been no personal confirmation of our attitude. But we have an attitude of loyalty. We cherish that."

The chief subjects of study seem to have been the Ptolemaic cosmogony, the Homeric poems, the authentic plays of Shakespeare and theology. The scanty leisure of the students did not admit of a very high standard of gymnastics, and they seem to have abandoned those typical American college sports of baseball and football altogether. The President spoke of these games as "late innovations". One chief out-of-door employment seems to have been wood-cutting and felling.

This glimpse of graceful and idealistic pedantry is interesting because it left so few traces for later times. It depended very much on the personality of the President himself, and after his death at an advanced age, and the hard winters of 1981 and 1983, this ancient foundation seems to have been completely deserted and allowed to fall into ruin.

Both Columbia University and Chicago were in violent contrast to Harvard. Here the influence of the new De Windt school of thought was very evident, and the traditions of Dewey, Robinson, Harry Elmer Barnes, Raymond Fosdick, the Beard couple and their associates were still alive. Although New York City was already abandoned and dangerous because of the instability of its huge unoccupied skyscrapers, there was still considerable trading on the Hudson River and some manufacturing activity. The great iron bridges were still quite practicable for pack horses and mules, and, affording as they did a North and South line of communication of quite primary value, they gave the place a unique commercial importance. The industrial workers there and in Chicago were in close contact with the college staffs, and they were working with very great energy at what they called "The General Problem of Recovery".

"They don't", writes Nicholson, "admit that civilization has broken down. They talk here just as they did in Washington, of the Hoover Slump. I never met people so confident that somehow and in some fashion things will pick up again. There is nothing like this at home. One night there was a tremendous crash and an earthquake. A huge pile called 'Radio City' had collapsed in the night. In the bright keen morning I went out to the Pantheon, and there a crowd of people was watching the clouds of dust that were still rising, and listening to the occasional concussions that marked minor fallings- in. Were they in the least downhearted? Not at all. 'There's a bit more liquidation,' said a man near me. 'We have to get these things off our hands somehow.'"

Nicholson gives a fairly full account of the curricula of both Columbia and Chicago. He is greatly struck by the equipment of the scientific laboratories and the relative importance of experimental work. "I felt almost as though I was back in 1930," he says, "when I visited the Rockefeller chemical laboratory." But still more was he struck by the advanced state of the sociological work. "They are producing a sort of lawyers who are not litigators," he writes. "I think the new law stuff they are doing here is the most interesting thing about the place. It isn't what my father would have recognized as law at all. It's the physiology and pathology of society and social therapeutics arising therefrom. There are one or two men

here, Hooper Hamilton and Rin Kay for instance, whose talk is a liberal education. They won't hear any of the rot we deal out at home about the Sunset of Mankind."

That was his key observation, so to speak. But it is interesting to note that the reduction of Basic English to practicable use was also being made. Spanish and English were already on their way to become the interchangeable languages they remained throughout all the earlier twenty-first century. The teaching of French had fallen off very greatly, and the old classical studies (Greek and Latin) to judge by his complete silence about them, had been completely abandoned.

Our tourist flew from Chicago to the Ford Aerodrome at Dearborn, saw the ruins of the main factories and the reconstructed settlement, and spent some days with the Technological School there and in the still very imperfectly arranged Museum of American Life. It was startling to see some scores of square miles of closely cultivated land round the open space of the Aerodrome and to learn that an old Ford idea of dividing the time of the staff between agricultural production and mechanical work was still in effective operation. There were associated textile and boot factories in Detroit. There was still an output of some thousand-odd automobiles a year and a "few hundred" (!) aeroplanes. And there was a small but healthy radio department.

"We keep in touch," said the Director. "We don't interfere with people, and we are not interfered with. We are running all that is left of the distance letter post.... Yes, Canada and Mexico as well. Nobody bothers us now about the boundaries, and we don't bother. When trade was at its worst we sat tight, cultivated our farms, and did experiments."

The Henry Ford, that "great original" whose adventure of the Peace Ship has been chosen to mark a turning-point in our history, had long since played out his part, but the Director mentioned in these papers seems to have been his son Edsel, carrying on the initiatives of his finely simple-minded parent.

That the place was able to "sit tight and carry on" was no empty boast. The visitor from a slovenly world dwells on the "tidiness" of everything. The Edison workshop was still in the original state as it had been re-erected by Henry Ford; there or in the Museum Nicholson was shown the first phonograph and the first telephone ever made, and the earliest experimental automobiles and aeroplanes.

"It is as recent as that," he tells us he said. "In the lifetime of ourselves and our fathers we have seen the beginning, the triumph, and the collapse of the greatest civilization that the world has ever seen. We have spanned the whole history of mechanical mass production."

"Not a bit of it," said the Director. "It's hardly begun."

There followed a long conversation the gist of which the visitor seems to have written down immediately in dialogue form. Its interest for the student of history lies in the fact that here again we have evidence of the way in which amidst the world-wide collapse into misery, disorder and incoherent peasant life the vitality of the mechanical transport system was manifesting itself. We can put the talk of the Dearborn director side by side with that of the European aviator reported by

Titus Cobbett. There is the same realization of the final death of the old order. "All that king business and congress business is as dead as mutton," said the Dearborn director. "And the banking business is deader."

"And what is coming?" asked the visitor.

"THAT," said the director, and pointed to a mounting aeroplane inaudible and almost invisible in the blue.

BOOK THE THIRD - THE WORLD RENASCENCE: THE BIRTH OF THE MODERN STATE

1. THE PLAN OF THE MODERN STATE IS WORKED OUT

In the preceding chapters the culmination, the dislocation and the collapse of the private capitalist civilization has been told. It has been a chronicle of disaster, wherein particular miseries, the torment and frustration of thousands of millions, are more than overshadowed by its appalling general aimlessness. We have seen the urge towards unity and order, appearing and being frustrated, reappearing and again being defeated. At last it reappeared—and won. The problem had been solved.

The world was not able to unify before 1950 for a very simple reason: there was no comprehensive plan upon which it could unify; it was able to unify within another half century because by that time the entire problem had been stated, the conditions of its solution were known and a social class directly interested in the matter had differentiated out to achieve it. From a vague aspiration the Modern World-State became a definite and so a realizable plan.

It was no great moral impulse turned mankind from its drift towards chaos. It was an intellectual recovery. Essentially what happened was this: social and political science overtook the march of catastrophe.

Obscure but persistent workers in these decades of disaster pieced together the puzzle bit by bit. There is a fantastic disproportion between the scale of the labourers and the immense consequences they released. The psychology of association, group psychology, was a side of social biology that had been disregarded almost entirely before the time of which we are writing. People had still only the vaguest ideas about the origins and working processes of the social structure in and by which they lived. They accepted the most arbitrary and simple explanations of their accumulated net of relationships, and were oblivious even to fundamental changes in that net. Wild hopes, delusions and catastrophes ensued inevitably.

If you had interrogated an ordinary European of the year 1925 about the motives for his political activities and associations and his general social behaviour, he would probably have betrayed a feeling that your enquiry was slightly indelicate, and if you overcame that objection, he would have talked either some nonsense about the family as the nucleus of social organization, a sort of expansion of brothers and cousins, kith and kin to the monarch, the Sire of the whole system, or he would have gone off in an entirely different direction and treated you to a crude version of Rousseau's Social Contract in which he and the other fellows had combined under agreed-upon rules for mutual defence and aid. The betting would have been quite even as to which of these flatly contradictory explanations he would have given.

He would have said nothing about religious ties in 1925, though fifty years earlier he might have based his whole description on the Divine Will. He would have betrayed no lucid apprehension of the part played by the money nexus in gearing relationships; he would have been as unconscious as his Roman predecessor of the primary social importance of properly adjusted money. He would have thought it was just stuff you earnt and handed out and got things for, and he might have added rather irrelevantly that it was "the root of all evil". He would certainly have referred to the family idea when his patriotism was touched upon, if not before, to justify that tangle of hates, fears and consequent and subordinate loyalties; he would have talked of "mother country" or "fatherland". If he practised any craft or skill, he might or might not have had his mind organized in relation to his profession or trade union, but there would be no measure between that and his patriotism, either might override the other, and either might give way before some superstitious or sexual complex in his make-up.

Incidentally he would have revealed extensive envy systems and social suspicion and distrust systems, growing up at every weak point like casual fungi. Everything would be flavoured more or less with the chronic hatred endemic everywhere. And all these disconnected associations from which flowed his judgments and impulses he would have regarded as natural—as natural as the shape of his ears; he would have been blankly unconscious that the education of school and circumstances had had anything to do with his accumulation.

On millions of minds equipped in this fragmentary fashion, uninformed or misinformed and with no internal connectedness, the institutions of the world were floating right up to the middle of the Twentieth Century. Tossing at last, rather than merely floating. Men called themselves individualist or socialist, and they had not the beginnings of an idea how the individual was and might be related to society; they were nationalist and patriotic, and none of them could tell what a nation was. It was only when these institutions began to batter against each other, and leak and heel over, and show every disposition to go down altogether, that even intelligent men began to realize how haphazard, sentimental and insincere were their answers to the all-important question: "What holds us together and sustains our cooperations?"

This prevalent superficiality and ignorance about socializing forces was the necessary reflection of a backwardness and want of vigour in academic circles and the intellectual world. The common man, busied about his petty concerns, did not know nor think about collective affairs because at the time there existed no knowledge or ordered thought in an assimilable form to reach down and stimulate his mind. The social body was mentally embryonic from the top downward. That it was possible to demonstrate a complete system of social reactions and to state the necessary idea of the Modern State in convincing and practically applicable terms, had still to penetrate to the minds not merely of the politicians and statesmen, but of the psychologists, historians and so- called "economists" of the time.

In 1932 Group Psychology was at about the same level of development as was physical science in the days of the Marquess of Worcester's Century of Inventions (1663). It was still in that vague inconclusive phase of "throwing out" ideas. It was no more capable of producing world order than the physical science of 1663 could have produced an aeroplane or a steam turbine. The ordinary man seeking guidance in the dismay of the Great Slump (see Emil Desaguliers' Ideas in Chaos and Society in Collapse, 2017) was confronted with a sort of intellectual rummage sale. He had believed that somewhere somebody knew; he discovered that nobody had ever yet bothered to know. A dozen eminent authorities with the utmost mutual civility were giving him every possible and impossible counsel in his difficulties, suavely but flatly contradicting each other. They were able to do so because they were all floating on independent arbitrary first assumptions without any structural reference to the primary facts of human ecology.

Nevertheless certain primary matters were being rapidly analysed at that time. The general understanding of money, for example, was increasing rapidly. Desaguliers notes about a hundred and eighty names, including the too-little-honoured name of that choleric but interesting amateur, Major C. H. Douglas (Works in the Historical Documents, Economic Section B. 178200), who were engaged in clearing away the conception of a metallic standard as a monetary basis. They were making it plain that the only possible money for a progressive world must keep pace with the continually increasing real wealth of that world. They were getting this into the general consciousness as a matter of primary importance.

But they were proposing the most diverse methods of realizing this conception. The "Douglas Plan" appealed to the general social credit, but was limited by the narrow political outlook of the worthy Major, who could imagine bankers abolished but not boundaries. In America an interesting movement known as "Technocracy" was attracting attention. Essentially that was a soundly scientific effort to restate economics on a purely physical basis. But it was exploited in a journalistic fashion and presented to a remarkably receptive public as a cut-and-dried scheme for a new social order in which social and economic life was to be treated as an energy system controlled by "experts". The explicit repudiation of democratic control by the Technologists at that date is very notable. The unit of energy was to be the basis of a new currency. So every power station became a

mint and every waterfall a potential "gold- mine", and the money and the energy in human affairs remained practically in step. Another important school, represented by such economists as Irving Fisher and J. M. Keynes, was winning an increased adherence to the idea of a price index controlling the issue of currency.

It was a phase of disconnected mental fermentation. Many of those who were most lucid about monetary processes were, like Douglas and Keynes, still in blinkers about national and imperial boundaries; they wanted to shut off some existing political system by all sorts of artificial barriers and restraints from the world at large, in order to develop their peculiar system within its confines. They disregarded the increasing flimsiness of the traditional political structure altogether. They were in too much of a hurry with their particular panacea to trouble about that. And if the money reformers were not as a rule cosmopolitans, the cosmopolitans were equally impatient with the money reformers and blind to the primary importance of money.

A third class of intelligences stressed the urgent necessity for great public enterprises to correct the paradoxical increase of unemployment consequent upon the increase of productivity that had taken the shiftless world by surprise. That was an independent maladjustment. But thinkers of this school were apt to disregard the importance of monetary rectification. As to who was to control the more complicated methods of mutual service proposed, the world money and the world socialism and so forth, there was an even greater diversity of outlook and an even greater conflict of mental limitations. As Desaguliers says in his summary: "People could not get out of the sinking social vessels in which they found themselves for the simple reason that nothing but the imperfectly assembled phantom of a salvage ship was yet in sight, a large rudderless, powerless promise, so to speak, standing by."

Only very knowledgeable people could have foretold then how nearly this phase of throwing out bright but disconnected ideas was drawing to its end, and how rapidly the consolidation of social and educational science into an applicable form was to go forward, once that it had begun. The rush of correlated social discoveries and inventions to the rescue of mankind, when at last it was fairly started, was even more rapid and remarkable than the release of steam and electrical energy in the nineteenth century.

It went on under difficulties. Perhaps it was quickened and purified by those very difficulties.

Gustave De Windt's great work, Social Nucleation (1942), was the first exhaustive study of the psychological laws underlying team play and esprit de corps, disciplines of criminal gangs, spirit of factory groups, crews, regiments, political parties, churches, professionalisms, aristocracies, patriotisms, class consciousness, organized research and constructive cooperation generally. It did for the first time correlate effectively the increasing understanding of individual psychology, with new educational methods and new concepts of political life. In spite of its unattractive title and a certain wearisomeness in the exposition, his book became a definite backbone for the constructive effort of the new time.

De Windt worked under all the handicap of the intellectual worker in that uncomfortable time. Much of his writing, like that of Marx and Lenin, was done in the British Museum in London, but he was expelled from England during a phase of xenophobia in 1939, and he was not allowed to return from Holland to his "beloved Bloomsbury" until 1941. He was slightly gassed during the ninth Polish air raid on Berlin, and this no doubt accelerated his death in Bloomsbury, the tuberculous London slum in which his book was completed.

Much has been done since to elaborate and correct the broad generalizations he established. But his name stands with those of Plato, Galileo, Newton, Darwin and Robert Owen as marking a real step forward in the expression and expansion of human ideas. Such men are all in their various dimensions something more than themselves, like stones that have become surveyors' datum marks. After 1950 De Windt's doctrines and formulae spread with great rapidity, in spite of the disturbed state of the world—assisted and enforced indeed by the disturbed state of the world.

Few people read De Windt nowadays, just as few people read Plato or Bacon or Charles Darwin or Adam Smith or Karl Marx, but what he thought has been built into the general outlook of mankind. What he established is now platitude, but in his time very much of what he had to say would still have seemed heresy and fantasy, if it had not been for the patient massiveness, the Darwinesque patience, with which he built up his points.

The most important features of his teaching were, first, that he insisted with an irrefutable rigidity upon the entirely artificial nature of the content of the social side of a human being. Men are born but citizens are made. A child takes to itself what is brought to it. It accepts example, usage, tradition and general ideas. All the forms of its social reactions and most of its emotional interpretations are provided by its education.

"Obviously," the reader will say. But it is essential to the understanding of history to realize that before De Windt's time this was not obvious. Moral values, bias and prejudice, hatreds and so forth were supposed to come "by nature." And consequently the generation about him had grown up in a clotted mass of outworn explanations, metaphors, mythologies and misleading incentives, and the misshapen minds reflected and condoned the misshapen social order. His rôle in intellectual history is primarily that of a strong arm sweeping a terrible litter of encumbrance aside, and replacing it by a clearly defined structure. He restored again to credibility what Plato had first asserted: that, however difficult, it was possible to begin again at the beginning with uninfected minds. And having cleared his ground in this way he proceeded to build up the imperatives of that sane progressive education and life for mankind which now opens out about us.

He brought home clearly to the general intelligence firstly that the monetary method of relationship was essential to any complex productive society, since it was the only device that could give personal choice and freedom in return for service. It liberated economic relationships. But money was not a thing in itself, it was a means to an end, and its treatment was to be judged entirely by its attain-

ment of that end. It had indeed grown out of a barterable commodity, a thing in itself, silver or gold or the like, but it had ceased to be this, and it was the difficulties in the transition of money from the former to the latter status that had released those diseases of the economic system which had in succession first destroyed the Roman imperialism and then the European sovereign states. A completely abstract money, a money as abstract and free from association with any material substance as weight or measure, had to be contrived for mankind. Human society could not be saved from chaos without it. It had to be of worldwide validity; its tokens,and notes had to be issued to maintain a practically invariable price index, and it had to be protected by the most stringent laws against any form of profit-making manipulation. He demonstrated that not merely forgery, but every form of gambling and speculation, had to be made major offences under a criminal code. He showed that usury was unnecessary. He unravelled the old entanglements by which new production had hitherto been saddled with permanent debts for its promotion and experiments. He made profit-making banking, that Old Man of the Sea, get off the back of enterprise. He eliminated every excuse for its profits. Banking was a public function. The distribution of credit was a vital part of government.

The New Banking of the Twenty-first Century grew up along the lines he established for it. To-day it is our system of public book-keeping, a part of our state statistical organization, a clearing-house of obligations and a monetary record of the accumulating surplus of racial energy, which the world- controls apportion to our ever expanding enterprises. It is entirely public and entirely gratuitous. It is hard to realize that it was ever allowed to be a source of private and secret profit. We register a man's earnings and spending as we register births and deaths. Our money is fundamentally a check on these publicly kept private accounts.

But this desiratum of a sufficiency of invariable money was only a "foundation need," a quantitative basis for the establishment of vital relationships, or, in De Windt's terminology, for "social nucleation." So soon as money was put in order it ceased to be necessary to trouble about money, just as it is needless to think about light and air in a properly lit and ventilated room.

For a couple of centuries before De Windt, the family, which had been the common social cellule throughout the whole agricultural age of mankind, had been losing its distinctness, had been dissolving into larger systems of relationship, more especially in the Northern and Western communities. It had been losing its economic, its mental, and its emotional autonomy at the same time. In the nineteenth century this dissolution of the family had gone on very rapidly indeed. The domestication of women, and their concentration upon children and the home, had diminished greatly.

By general sentiment, the instinctive factor in family unification had always been overrated. In effect, that instinctive bond dissolves long before the children are thirteen or fourteen. After that age the binding force of parent to child and vice versa is not instinct, but affection, convenience, habit, and tradition. And that convenience, usage, and tradition had dwindled. Put to the test of exterior attrac-

tions, family solidarity had weakened not only in the West, but also, as Asia had been Westernized, in Turkey, India, China, and Japan. This was so essentially, even more than apparently. The family home remained generally as a meeting-place and common domicile for parents and children, but it ceased to be a vehicle of tradition, it ceased to train and discipline. It ceased to do so for the simple reason that these functions were now discharged with far more emphasis, if with less intensity, by exterior agencies. Citizens were begotten in the home but they were no longer MADE in the home.

De Windt drew a vivid contrast between the home life of a Central European family in the late eighteenth century, with the father reading the Bible to his assembled offspring, conducting daily prayer, watching over, reproving and chastizing his sons and daughters up to the age of sixteen or seventeen and even controlling their marriage, and the loosely associated family structure in the early twentieth century.

This structural dissolution was universally recognized long before the time of De Windt, but it was left for him to emphasize the need for a planned "renucleation" in the social magma that arose out of this dissolution. The popular school, the experiences and associations of industrialized production, the daily paper and so forth, had knocked the strength out of the mental and moral education of the home and put nothing in its place. The sapping forces had not, in their turn, been converted into "organic forces." In default of these, minds were lapsing towards crude and base self-seeking and entirely individualistic aims.

These contemporary emotional suggestions and haphazard ideologies were not good enough, he preached, to make a human being a tolerable social unit. Social tissue was not to be made and coordinated on such lines. The stars in their courses were pointing our race towards the organized world community, the Modern State, and if ever that goal was to be attained, if the reorganization of the species was not to collapse, degenerate, and perish by the wayside, then the individual mind throughout the world had to be educated, had to be disciplined and equipped, definitely and sufficiently to this end. That would not come by nature. The social side of the individual had to be oriented deliberately. "Society is an educational product."

For the race to get to this Modern State as a whole it had to get there as so many hundreds of millions of human beings, all individually aware of that as the general objective at which their lives aimed. The Modern State could not arrive as an empty form with all humanity left behind it. Every teacher, every writer, every talker, every two friends who talked together constituted a potential primary nucleus in a renascent social system. These nuclei had to be organized. Their existence had to be realized, and they had to be brought into effective cooperation. It is hard nowadays to realize that once upon a time such commonplaces as these were not commonplaces, and that in the very days when De Windt was writing, multitudes of well-meaning people were attempting to assemble "movements" for social reconstruction and world revolution out of the raw, unprepared miscellany of the contemporary crowd. It was with extreme reluctance

that impatient reformers turned their minds from impossible coups d'état and pronunciamentos, strikes against war and booby millennia, to this necessary systematic preliminary renucleation of the world. The immediate task seemed too narrow and intense for them and its objective too high and remote. "It is no good asking people what they want," wrote De Windt. "That is the error of democracy. You have first to think out what they ought to want if society is to be saved. Then you have to tell them what they want and see that they get it."

And further, he urged, if you cannot start nucleation everywhere, then at least you can start it close at hand. "Get the nuclei going. Be yourself a nucleus." From the beginning of life, nuclei have begotten nuclei. The Modern State, which had to be evoked everywhere, could be begun anywhere.

Another point that was new in his time, so far as Western civilization went, was his insistence upon the greater importance of adolescent education and his denial of the primary right of the parent to shape his offspring according to his fancy. The "renucleation" of society had to be complete. The "nuclei" which were ultimately to become the sole educational and disciplinary units of a new- born society would be in the first place, and usually, intensive study circles and associations for moral and physical training. Their social and political activities were to be secondary exercises, subordinated to a primary mental, moral and bodily training. He searched the social disorder about him for favourable conditions for the pioneer nucleations. He looked to factories, laboratories, technical schools, public services, hospital staffs, to banded men and women of all sorts, for the material for his nucleation. He insisted that the impulse to build up a social order was instinctive. Wherever there was social confusion the crude efforts to get together into a new directive order appeared.

He pointed to the Sokols, Nazis, Fascists, Communist Party members, Kuomintang members of his time, as the first primitive intimations of the greater organization that was coming. They had the spirit of an élite class, although they wasted it more or less upon the loyalties and prejudices of the past. People are not leading these young men, he argued; "they are taking advantage of the instinctive needs of these young men. Try to realize what it is that they are—however blindly—seeking."

Like St. Paul, the founder of Christianity, speaking to the Athenians—he quotes the passage—he said: "That Unknown God, whom ignorantly ye worship, him declare I unto you." He was declaring the as yet unknown Modern State.

Intensively De Windt's teaching was a theory of education; extensively it was the assertion of the Modern State. These were inseparable aspects of the same thing. "A community is an education in action," he declared. And with a complete continuity he carried up his scheme of social structure through every variety of productive organization, control and enterprise. Men were to "fall in and serve this end."

Borrowing a word from Ortega y Gasset, but going boldly beyond that original thinker, he declared that "plenitude" of life was now only to be attained by living in relation to the Modern State. All other living was "waste, discontent and sor-

row." It was becoming impossible to retain self- respect, to be happy within oneself, unless one was "all in" upon that one sound objective. The old loyalties, to flag, to nation, to class, were outworn and discredited. They had become unreal. They did not call out all that was in a man, because now we saw their limitations. They could no longer keep up the "happy turgidity" of life. They could not be served "with a sure and untroubled soul". They would certainly leave a man in the end "deflated, collapsed into an aimless self". In the past men could live and live fully within their patriotisms and their business enterprises, because they knew no better. But now they knew better.

Finally De Windt set himself diametrically against one of the direst concepts of Parliamentary Democracy, a concept that still had enormous influence in his time, and that was the idea of the "Opposition." "Criticize," he wrote, "yes, but do not obstruct." If a directive organization is fundamentally bad, he taught, break it and throw it away, but rid your minds altogether of a conception of see-saw and give and take as a proper method in human affairs. The Parliamentary gang Governments, that were then in their last stage of ineptitude, were rotten with the perpetual amendment and weakening of measures, with an endless blocking and barring of projects, with enfeebling bargains and blackmailing concessions. Against every directive body, every party in power, sat another devoting itself to misrepresenting, thwarting, delaying, and spoiling, often for no reason or for the flimsiest reasons, merely for the sake of misrepresenting, thwarting, delaying and spoiling what the governing body was attempting to do, in the hope of degrading affairs to such a pitch of futility as to provoke a change of government that would bring the opposition into power. The opportunities of profit and advancement afforded in such a mental atmosphere to a disingenuous careerist were endless.

All this tangle of ideas had to be swept aside. "About most affairs there can be no two respectable and antagonistic opinions," said De Windt. "It is nonsense to pretend there can be. There is one sole right way and there are endless wrong ways of doing things. A government is trying to go the right way or it is criminal. Sabotage must cease. It has always been one of the ugliest vices of advanced movements. It is a fundamental social vice."

His discussion of the difference between Criticism and Opposition is one of those classics that few people read. It is a pity, because it is a very good specimen of twentieth-century English prose. The right to criticize and the duty of well-wrought criticism are fundamental to modern citizenship. He considered how that right and duty had been ignored by the shallow mentality of Italian Fascism and how fatally they had been entangled with the suppression of malignancy in Russia. He analysed the reckless irresponsibility of censorship in the Western communities. There was no law anywhere to restrain conspiracies, on the part of religious, political, or business bodies, for the suppression of publications. His warnings against the suppression of opinion were not so immediately effective as his general revolutionary project. Many people did not realize what he was driving at. In practice the conflict of world order with the opposition spirit, during the struggle to maintain the Air Dictatorship, was to lapse again and again into the

suppression of honest criticism. In practice it was found that criticism and suggestion passed by insensible degrees into incitement and insurrectionary propaganda.

This clear-cut revolutionary scheme of De Windt's was vividly new and tonic to the energetic young men of the middle twentieth century. We summarize here its main constructive conceptions in spite of its present platitudinousness. It is unnecessary to tell in any detail his far-sighted schemes to link his nuclei into a world propaganda, because by insensible degrees that organization has grown into the educational system of our world to- day. This history and indeed every text book in use in the world could well be dedicated to him. And his complex and very detailed anticipations of the process of a world revolution need not detain us here (his Book V, The New World in the Body of the Old contains most of this), because we can now tell of that vast reconstruction itself.

In some respects he was remarkably prescient, in others he estimated human reactions inaccurately and even incorrectly. The reconstruction of human affairs involved some very rough work from which he would have recoiled. None the less he put all the main structural factors in the establishment of the Modern State so plainly and convincingly before his fellow-men that soon thousands and presently millions were living for that vision, were bringing it out of thought into reality. He made it seem so like destiny, that it became destiny.

For some years his views spread very slowly. An increasing number of people knew about them, but at first very few made serious efforts to realize them. One man after another would say, "But this is right!" and then "But this is impossible!" De Windt was dead before his school of thought became a power in the world. Like Karl Marx, he was never to know of the harvest he had sown.

In our description of the failure of the League of Nations we have noted how foredoomed that experiment was, because nowhere among either the influential men of the time nor among the masses was there any sense of the necessity and the necessary form of a new world order. The statesmen, diplomatists and politicians of the time impress us as almost incredibly blind to things that are as plain as daylight to us now, and it is hard for us to believe that that blindness was not wilful. It was not. They could not see it. We read their speeches at conference after conference until their voices die away at last in the rising tide of disaster and we almost cry out as we read: "You idiots! Wasn't world control there just under your noses? And was anything else but disaster possible?"

The answer is that it was not precisely under their noses. Slowly, laboriously, with perpetual repetitions and slight variations, the Obvious had to be got into and spread and diffused in the human mind. It is De Windt's peculiar claim to human gratitude, not that he discovered anything fresh, but that he so built up and fortified the Obvious, that not the most subtle and disingenuous mind, nor the biggest fool who ever sentimentalized and spouted, could escape honestly from its inexorable imperatives.

2. THOUGHT AND ACTION: THE NEW MODEL OF REVOLUTION

It is a wholesome check upon individual pride that no single man and indeed no single type of man is able both to conceive and carry through the simplest of our social operations. Even the man who cultivates the earth and grows food cannot make the productive implements he uses or select the seeds and plants that yield him increase. Defoe's queer story of Robinson Crusoe is an impossibly hopeful estimate of what a single man, with only a little flotsam and jetsam from the outer world, and in unusually benign climatic conditions, on a desert island could contrive to do for his own comfort and security. Still more does this interdependence of men and different types apply to the complex processes that now, in this Age of Maximum Insecurity, were demanded, if the new generation was to escape from the economic and institutional wreckage amidst which it found itself, and create the social order in which we live to- day.

First came the intellectuals, men living aloof from responsibility, men often devoid of the qualities of leadership and practical organization. Like De Windt they planned everything and achieved no more than a plan. Such men are primarily necessary in the human adventure, because they build up a sound diagnosis of events; they reveal more and more clearly and imperatively the course that lies before the race and in that task their lives are spent and justified. Then it is that the intelligent executive type, capable of concentration upon a complex idea once it is grasped, and resisting discursiveness as a drag on efficiency, comes into action. Their imaginative limitation is a necessary virtue for the task they have to do. No man can administer a province successfully if he is always wandering beyond its frontiers. The rather unimaginative forcible type is the necessary executive of a revolution, and the benefit of the revolution is entirely dependent upon the soundness of the ideology with which he has been loaded.

Because of this necessity for complementary types of revolutionary, history does not produce any modern equivalents to the legendary figures of Solon, Moses or Confucius in its story of the coming of the Modern State. De Windt was not so much a creator as a summarizer, a concentrator, a lens that gathered to a burning focus the accumulating mental illumination of his day.

The light of understanding that lit the fires of this last revolution came from no single brain. It came from ten thousand active and devoted minds, acting and reacting upon one another, without order or precedence; it was like the growth of physical and biological science that preceded it, something that happened as a

whole, something that happened not in any single consciousness but in the consciousness of the race.

We have already noted how far back the first germination of the World- State idea can be traced; we have shown how the forces of economic life drove towards it in the nineteenth century. We have displayed it working as a quasi- instinctive aspiration in the brains of Henry Ford and Woodrow Wilson. With De Windt's Social Nucleation we see it made concrete, with all its essential structures projected and all its necessary conditions laid down, a practicable proposal. The World-State has ceased to be a cloudy aspiration and it has become a plan. Forceful men could adopt it.

A distinct change in the quality of those who were promoting the movement for the Modern State became very evident even before the War Cycle of the Forties. It was now sufficiently "thought out" for men of resolute character to incorporate it in their personal lives. It was passing over from the reflective to the energetic types. Its earliest propagandists had been largely reflective and practically ineffective individuals; a miscellany of pacificists whose dread and detestation of war was overwhelming and who had the intelligence to realize that war can only be avoided by establishing a World Pax; a number of writers, "pure" scientific workers, young sociologists, economists and the like and "intellectuals" from the working class movement. Now a multitude of engineers, architects, skilled foremen and industrial organizers, technicians of all sorts, business men and captains of industry, were also beginning to "talk Modern State" and put in an increasing proportion of their time and attention to its advocacy.

The transition is easily explicable. The increasing social disorder was driving men of the vigorous practical type out of satisfactory employment. During the First Age of Prosperity, and during the false recovery after the World War, such men had been able to find ample work agreeable to their temperaments in the immense industrial developments of the time. They had organized great businesses, vast production; they had exploited the incessant stream of inventions; they had opened up the natural resources of hitherto backward regions. They had carried production far beyond the consuming power of human society. So long as all this enterprise could go on, it did not seem necessary to them to trouble about the political and monetary methods of their world. Now and then some of them showed a certain restiveness at the banking network; our typical original-minded industrial Henry Ford, for instance, had two vigorous tussles with the bankers during his career; but generally the phenomena of political and financial strangulation only began to compel their serious attention after the great Hoover Slump (the Thirty Year Slump) was well under way.

Then they began to think, talk and write about the social order with the energy of men accustomed to handle large affairs and work for immediate tangible results. The vast experiment of Soviet Russia aroused their technical jealousy and a sort of envious impatience both at its opportunities and its incapacities. And the young men coming on from the abundant technical schools of the time, stirred by the books and talk and omnipresent hopes and memories of the immediate past,

and looking for adventure and achievement in material enterprise, realized very rapidly that the lights of opportunity upon their paths were being turned down in a manner at once mysterious and exasperating.

The revolutionary movement in the nineteenth century had seemed to such men a tiresomeness of slacking workers, aided and abetted by critics like Ruskin, artists like William Morris, playwrights like Bernard Shaw and suchlike impracticable and unconvincing people. It was associated in their minds with sham Gothic, yellow-green draperies, long hair, anti-vivisection and vegetarianism. There was scarcely a man of scientific or technical eminence on the revolutionary side before 1900. But by the third decade of the twentieth century two-thirds of the technicians, scientific workers and able business organizers were talking active revolution. It was no longer to be a class insurrection of hands; it was to be a revolt of the competent. Their minds were feeling round for ideas. They found in such books as De Windt's exactly what they wanted. They began to set about the evocation of the Modern World- State in no uncertain fashion.

A revolution in revolutionary ideas had occurred. The protean spirit of Revolution had cut its hair, put on blue overalls, made blue prints for itself, created a New Model, and settled down to work in a systematic fashion.

3. THE TECHNICAL REVOLUTIONARY

The existence of this large number of scientific and technical workers in the Western communities and their rapid and lively apprehension of the breakdown about them is one of the profoundest differences between the second and the first Decline and Fall.

We find no real equivalent at all to them in the Roman story. There were great numbers of artisans without any science, steeped in tradition; and quite out of touch with these artisans there were a few small groups of ineffective philosophers whose speculations were finally swamped by the synthesis of Christianity. Artisan and philosopher were in different worlds. The philosopher has left it on record that he despised the artisan. Probably the artisan despised the philosopher in equal measure so far as he knew about him; but he has not left it on record. Neither artisan nor philosopher seem to have had any awareness of the broad social forces that were destroying the common security in which they went about their affairs, and turning the Empire into a battling ground for barbarian adventurers.

It is doubtful if at any time the imperial court or the imperial civil service had any real conception of any sustained decline. Nineteenth—and twentieth- Century historians, as Ogilvy and Freud point out in their Roman History (2003 and revised by Pan Chow Liang 2047), were all too apt to imagine an up-to-date intelligence for such emperors as Julius Caesar, Octavius, Marcus Aurelius or Domitian. They represented them as scheming and planning on almost modern lines. But there is no proof of any such awareness in the Latin record. One large element in that old Roman world that would surely have displayed some sense of the needs of the time, if anywhere there had been that sense, was the universally present building industry. It did hold on in a way throughout the decline and fall, but consciously it did nothing politically.

Students are still working out the preservation and continuation of the art and mystery of the masons into the middle ages. There was a great loss of knowledge but also a real survival. The medieval free-masons who built those flimsy but often quite beautiful Gothic cathedrals it is now such a task to conserve, carried on a tradition that had never really broken with that of the pyramid builders. But they had no sense of politics. They had a tradition of protective guild association similar to the Trade Unions of the Capitalist age, they interfered in local affairs in order to make jobs for themselves, but there is no sign that at any time they con-

cerned themselves with the order and stability of the community as a whole. Their horizons were below that level of intelligence.

Now the skilled and directive men of the collapsing order of the twentieth century were of an altogether livelier quality. Their training was not traditional but progressive, far more progressive than that of any other class. They were inured to fundamental changes in scope, method and material. They ceased to be acquiescent in the political and financial life about them directly they found their activities seriously impeded. Simultaneously with the outbreak of that very expressive and significant word "Technocracy" in the world's Press (1932-33) we find, for instance, a Professor of Engineering, Professor Miles Walker, at a meeting of the British Association for the Advancement of Science, boldly arraigning the whole contemporary order by the standards of engineering efficiency. Everywhere in that decadence, amidst that twilight of social order, engineers, industrialists and professors of physical science were writing and talking constructive policies. They were invading politics. We have already noted the name of Professor Soddy as one of the earlier men of science who ceased to "mind his own business", and took up business psychology.

At first these technicians and business men were talking at large. They did not immediately set about doing things; they still assumed that the politicians and monetary authorities were specialists with sound and thorough knowledge in their own departments, as capable of invention and adaptation as themselves; so that they did no more than clamour for decisive action—not realizing that the very conditions under which bankers and politicians lived made them incapable of varying their methods in any fundamental fashion. But this grew plain as disaster followed disaster. A new type had to assume authority if new methods were to be given a fair chance. New methods of government must oust the old. An increasing proportion of the younger men, abandoning all ideas of loyalty to or cooperation with the old administrative institutions, and with an ever clearer consciousness of their objective, set themselves to organize nuclei after the De Windt pattern and to link these up with other nuclei.

The movement spread from workshop to workshop and from laboratory to laboratory with increasing rapidity all over the world. Al Haran estimated that already in 1960 seven-eighths of the aviators were Modern State men, and most of the others he says were "at least infected with these same ideas". Such infection went far and deep.

Wherever there was little or no repression the development of this movement to salvage civilization went on openly. But to begin with it encountered some very serious antagonisms. The military element had always been disposed to regard the man of science and the technician as a gifted sort of inferior. The soldier in his panoply ordered them to do their tricks, and they did their tricks. That was the idea. The behaviour of both types during the World War did much to confirm this assumption of their docility. The Peace of Versailles came before there was any serious disillusionment. The nineteenth- century scientific man had been a

very lopsided man; often he had proved himself a poor conventional snob outside his particular investigations.

"The sciences," as Simon Azar remarked, "came before Science"; the scientific outlook was a late result and not a primary cause of the systematic pursuit of knowledge. It was a discovery and not a starting point. Science taught the men who served it, and the pupil learnt more than the teacher knew. There was and is an incessant conflict in the scientific world between achievement and fresh enquiry, and in the nineteenth and early twentieth centuries it was acute. The older men suspected younger men with broader ideas and hindered their advancement. They wanted them all to work in specialist blinkers. But after the World War the world of pure and applied science found itself obliged to think about things in general, and, as the Great Slump went on without surcease, it thought hard. The technicians, because of their closer approach to business and practical affairs generally, were considerably in advance of the "pure" scientific investigators in this application of constructive habits of thought to political and social organization.

Even during the Chinese warfare there were intimations that chemists, engineers and doctors might have different ideas from the military. After the Tokio sterilization fiasco, and still more so after the failure of the eleventh gas offensive upon Wuchang to produce adequate results, the Japanese military authorities began to enquire into the possibility of "expert sabotage", and their enquiries had a certain repercussion upon the relations of "scientific" military men to real scientific and technical experts in Europe. There was an attempt to distinguish between experts who were "loyal" and experts who were "subversive". More often than not it was the latter who were the brilliant and inventive men. Uncritical loyalty was found to go with a certain general dullness. The authorities found themselves in a dilemma between men who could not do what was wanted of them and men who would not.

A campaign against pacificist, disturbing and revolutionary ideas had been gathering force during the thirties. It became a confused and tiresome persecution in the later forties. But it was ineffective because it was incoherent. Attempts to weed the staffs and students of technical schools and to reduce the teaching profession to docility failed, because there seemed to be no way of distinguishing what was essential science from what was treasonable thought. The attempt to destroy freedom in one part of a man's brain while leaving other parts to move freely and creatively was doomed to failure from the outset.

4. PROPHETS, PIONEERS, FANATICS AND MURDERED MEN

History, especially general history, is prone to deal too much with masses and outlines. We write that "all Germany" resented an insult, or the "hopes of Asia" fell. But the living facts of history are changes in thought, emotion and reaction in the minds of thousands of millions of lives.

In the preceding sections we have spoken in general terms of "concepts of combination" developing; of ideologies dissolving and giving place to other ideologies like clouds that gather and melt and pass across the mental skies of mankind. In the books before those sections we traced the growing awareness of a possible World-State in the thoughts of men throughout two thousand years of slow awakening. But the presentation is incomplete until we have turned our attention, for a chapter at least, from the broad sweep of opinion and the changing determination of the collective will, to the texture of individual experiences, the brain storms, the tormented granules, which shaped out these massive structural developments.

One must draw upon the naive materials of one's own childhood to conceive, however remotely, the states of mind of those rare spirits who looked first towards human brotherhood. One must consider the life of some animal, one's dog, one's cheetah or one's pony, to realize the bounded, definite existence of a human being in the early civilizations. The human life then was just as set in its surroundings as any animal's. There was the town, the river, the cultivations, the distant hills, the temple, near friends and strange distant enemies constituting a complete and satisfying ALL. The gods were credible and responsible, taking all ultimate responsibility off your shoulders; the animals had souls like yourself, as understandable as yourself, and the darkness and shadows were haunted by spirits. In that sort of setting innumerable generations lived and loved and hated and died. Everything was made familiar and understandable by the trick of personification. You brought the stranger into your family; you made it a member of your group. Earth was a mother and the sun a great father of glory marching across the sky.

It is a marvellous intricate history to trace how the human mind began to doubt, to pry and question, to penetrate the curtains of assurance and fancied security that enclosed it. Perhaps it was rather torn out of its confidence than that it fretted its way out by any urgency of its own.

The Hebrew Bible, which Christianity preserved for us, is a precious record of uneasy souls amidst the limited conditions of these ages before mechanism or travel or logical analysis. It tells how man came out of the Eden of unquestioning acceptance and found perplexity. It gives us intimate glimpses of states of mind that were typical of what went on in hundreds of thousands of struggling brains. They were beginning to note thorns and weeds, toil and the insecurity of life. They made great efforts to explain their growing sense that all was not right with the world. They had to dramatize the story. They had as yet only "personification" as a means of apprehending relations and causes. They had no way of getting hold of a general idea except by imagining it as a person. Strange thoughts frightened them. They seemed exterior to them. They dared not even say "I think"; they had to say "I heard a voice" or the "Word of the Lord came to me". Enormous effort therefore was needed to pass from the thought of a patriarchal tribal God to a mightier overriding God. Men did not unite communities; they identified their Gods. Monotheism was the first form of the World-State in men's minds.

What a desperate deed it was for some inwardly terrified man to lift up his voice against the local elders and the local idol, proclaiming "There is no God but God." The reactions of his fellows, living still within the framework of accepted beliefs, to this attempt to break out to wide relations, were scorn, amusement, irritation, dislike or horror and superstitious fear. We have the story of Mohammed recorded, and of his fight with the gods of Mecca, but that was a late and sophisticated instance of something that happened in innumerable times and places; the challenge of the man "inspired" by his new idea to the social mental nest out of which he was breaking.

Men who saw the light and spoke, were only one species of a larger genus of human beings whose minds worked differently from the common man's or were simply more feverishly active. The others were eccentrics or downright madmen. One sort was hardly to be told from another, for both were sayers of incredible things.

The beginning of written record in the millennium before Christ shows a long tradition already established for the treatment of these odd, disturbing exceptions. So far as we can peer into the past we find the tranquillity of the everyday community broken by these troubled troublesome individuals who went about, living queerly, saying unusual and disconcerting things, inciting people to behave strangely, threatening divine anger, foreboding evils. There was a disposition to buy them off with a sort of reverence—and disregard. Inferior and unhappy people might find an interest and excitement in their strange announcements and suggestions. But rulers did not like them, comfortable people disliked and feared them. They irritated, they terrified contented people. They seemed perverse, and many of them plainly were perverse. If they went too far mankind turned on them and they were ill-treated and mobbed and ridiculed; they were cast into prisons; beaten and killed.

The ones that mattered most seemed always, by our present standards, to have had something to say that was at once profoundly important and yet not quite true

or not quite truly said. Disciples, sometimes in great multitude, respond to their enigmatical utterances. When they died or were killed men were left asking, "What exactly did he say? What exactly did he mean?" The inspired words became very readily riddles for interpreters and matter for pedantry. They were phrased and rephrased, applied and misapplied, tried out in every possible and impossible way.

Nowadays we find a common quality in all these madmen, prophets, teachers and disturbers of the mental peace. The species was learning to talk and use language. The race was, as it were, trying to think something out; was attempting to say something new and enlarging to itself. It was doing this against great resistance. Its intellectual enterprise was playing against its instinctive fear of novelty. Some of these teachers died terribly, were flayed or burnt or tortured to death. One hung on a cross and died of physical weakness some hours before the two felons who were his hardier fellow sufferers, leaving a teaching compounded of such sweet and fine ideas of conduct, such mystical incomprehensibleness, such misleading inconsistency, that it remained a moral stimulus and an intellectual perplexity, a jungle for heresies and discoveries, for millions of souls for two millennia.

Vainly does one try nowadays to put ourself into the mind of the prophet led to execution. We know the value of what he did, it is true, but what did he think he was doing? The secret of such personifying, urgently seeking brains seems hidden from us now for ever.

In the busier and more prosperous social phases of history such disturbers are less evident; in times of change, and especially when there was also a release of social energy, when conflicting traditions ground and wore upon each other, these troubled and troublesome minds seemed to have multiplied. The days of the vast unstable Roman imperialism abounded in efforts to say something new and profound about life. Everywhere there were new worships, because a worship still seemed the only form in which a new idea and way of life could be conveyed from mind to mind. Everywhere the puzzled sprawling human race was trying to say something, some magic word to resolve its perplexities and guide it to peace.

With the Renascence of learning and the onset of organized science the actual number and the actual proportion of enquiring and innovating minds increased greatly. The effort of the racial mind to master the conditions of its being was renewed on a multitudinous scale. But now the disturbers of equanimity no longer appear as wild-eyed prophets; they no longer claim that the Word of the Lord is upon them. Abstract and logical thought has pervaded the mind of the race and such personification is no longer needed. They do not denounce the old gods; they analyse them. Moreover, now that we approach modern times and deal with more and more abundantly recorded events, we begin to realize with a living understanding and sympathy what was going on in the minds of the innovators and to feel in touch with the immeasurable heroisms and innumerable tragedies of those later pioneers, those rebels, critics, revolutionaries who were thrusting, more or

less intelligently, against the acceptances and inertias amidst which they lived, towards a saner, more comprehensive and more clearly apprehended racial idea.

So far no completely masterly digest has been made of the millions of biographies and tons of other material that tell of the mental seething of the world from the seventeenth century of the Christian Era onward. If the old world prophets are too rare and remote for our understanding, the modern revolutionaries are almost too close and abundant for us to stand back and see them clearly. Vast studies have been organized of various portions of the field; Roger Cuddington and his associates' Studies of Protestant Thought in Holland, the Rhineland, Switzerland and Britain from the Seventeenth to the Nineteenth Century give, for instance, a picture of one wide area and period, in which the fermentation arose first in a religious form and owed much to the clash of Jew and Gentile; while Margrim's Early Forms of Anarchism and Socialism is a very successful attempt to realize the ideas and personalities from which the modern criticism of rule and property derived. With the help of such works as these, and with some luck among the biographies, we do contrive at last to get down close to an imaginative participation in those individual reactions, which in the aggregate remade the human community in the form we know to-day.

Every one of these personal stories, if it were told completely, would have to begin with a child, taking the world for granted, believing its home, its daddy and mummy to be right and eternal. It confronted a fixed and established world with no standard of comparison in past or future. It was told its place in life and what it had to do. Bad luck, discomfort, some shock or some innate unrest was needed to put a note of interrogation against these certainties. Then for those whom destiny has marked for disturbance comes the suspicion: "This that they have told me isn't true." Still more disturbing came the possibility: "This that they do and want me to do isn't right." And then with a widening reference: "Things could be better than this." So the infected individual drifted out of easy vulgar living with his fellows, out of a natural animal- like acceptance of the established thing, to join the fermenting and increasing minority of troubled minds that made trouble.

He began talking to his fellows or he made notes in secret of his opinions. He asked awkward questions. He attempted little comments and ironies. We could conjure up hundreds of thousands of pictures of such doubters beginning to air their opinions in the eighteenth-century world, in the little workshops of the time, in shabby, needy homes, in market places, in village inns, daring to say something, hardly daring to say anything, unable often to join up the vague objections they were making into any orderly criticism. But in the brown libraries and studies of the period other men were sitting, poring over books, writing with something furtive in their manner, while the pride of contemporary life brayed and trumpeted along the roadway outside. "What is being told to the people is not true. Things could be better than this." Men ventured on strange suggestions in university classes; brought out startlingly unorthodox theses.

The infectious interrogations spread. Constituted authority got wind of these questionings and itself came questioning in search of heresy and sedition, with

rack and thumbscrew. When we read the books and pamphlets of that awakening phase, writings which seem amidst profuse apologies to half say next to nothing, we get the measure of the reasonable timidities of the time. Men might pay in sweating agony and death for that next-to-nothing they had said.

At first they raised not so much the substance as the form of an interrogation. In the sixteenth century you would have found a number of local accumulations of heresies, but hardly any inkling of the Modern State. Except for some scholar's echo to the Republic or Laws of Plato, there was no one at all reading and comparing in the field of social and political structure before the seventeenth century. The eighteenth century was, in comparison with its predecessor, an age of voluminous revolutionary thought. Men began calling fundamental ideas and political institutions in question as they had never been challenged since the onset of Christianity. They went into exile for their innovations; their books were burnt; censorships were established to suppress these new ideas. Still they spread and multiplied. The authoritative claim of aristocracy, the divinity of monarchy, tarnished, dwindled, became ineffective under these dripping notes of interrogation. Republics appeared and the first embryonic intimations of socialism.

In our account of the first French Revolution and the revolutionary perturbation of the eighteenth century[1] we have had to discriminate between the economic and social forces that were forcing political readjustment on the one hand, and the influence of new ideas on the other. We have shown how little these formal changes were planned, and how small a share in these events is to be ascribed to creative intention or mental processes generally. Nevertheless the questioning was drawing closer to reality and the scope of the planning was spreading. We will not tell again of the profound change in men's ideas about private property, private freedom and monetary relationship, that began to find expression in the socialist and communist movements of the age. Our concern here is to emphasize the billions of small wrangles that were altering the collective thought, to summon out of the past, for an instant, an elfin clamour of now silenced voices that prepared the soil for revolution, the not- at-all- lucid propagandists at street corners, the speakers in little meeting- houses, in open spaces and during work intermissions; to recall the rustle of queer newspapers that were not quite ordinary newspapers; and the handicapped book publications that were everywhere fighting traditional and instinctive resistances. Everywhere the leaven of the Modern State was working—confusedly.

As we have seen, the new conception of a single world society did not come at one blow, perfect and effective, into the human mind. It was not completed even in outline until the days of De Windt, and before that time it was represented by a necessary confusion of contributory material, incomplete bits of it and illogical and misleading extensions of those bits. It had to begin like that; it had to begin in fragments and rashly. There was always a fierce disposition manifested to apply the new incomplete ideas, headlong and violently. The more the sense of insuffi-

[1] No traces of this account are to be found in Raven's papers.—Ed.

ciency gnaws at a man's secret consciousness, the more he is in conflict with an inner as well as an outer antagonist, the more emphatic, dogmatic and final he is apt to be. That disposition to bring the new ideas to the test of reality, the urge to assert by experiment, was the chief source of trouble for these ever increasing multitudes, of innovating minds. Constituted authority, established usage, have no quarrel with ideas as such; it is only when these ideas become incitation, when they sought incarnation in act and reality, that conflict began.

So all over the world throughout the nineteenth century men were to be found contriving trouble for authority and devising outrages on usage. The light of world reconstruction lit their souls, but often it filtered through thick veils of misconception and had the colourings of some epidemic hate. They dreamt of insurrections, of seizures of power, of organized terror; in practice their efforts dwindled down too often to stupid little murders—often completely irrelevant murders—to shouting and swarming in the streets, to peltings and window-breaking, to blowing in the front doors of government houses and embassies, to the casting of explosives amidst the harmless spectators at public ceremonies.

Before the French Revolution there was not nearly so much of such sporadic violence as afterwards. There were a few assassinations by religious or racial fanatics, but usually the older type of political crime was definitely connected with some conspiracy to change the personnel rather than the nature of a régime. The "Anarchist" outrages of the nineteenth century, however clumsy, were by comparison social criticisms. Behind them, even though vague, exaggerated and distorted, was the hope of a new world order.

Linked inseparably with all these premature expressions of the desire for a new life were the activities of more extensive revolutionary systems: printing-presses in cellars, furtive distribution of papers, secret meetings, the savage discipline of fear-ruled illegal societies, the going to and fro of emissaries —men often with narrow and ill-assorted minds, but nevertheless men with everything to lose and little to gain or hope for by such activities. After we have allowed for every sort of resentment and bitter impulse in them, the fact remains such men were devotees. They were a necessary ferment for the spread of thought.

That increasing revolutionary ferment, in all its tentative aspects, used to be called The Extreme Left. There had never been anything quite like it in the world before. For the most part these men had broken not only with the political and social order of their time, but with its religious beliefs. Between 1788 and 1965, hundreds of thousands of men and thousands of women, far braver than any Moslem fanatics, sustained by no hope of a future life, no hope of any greeting after the sudden blankness of their untimely deaths, and, so far as we can gather now, not even with a clear vision of the full and ordered social life for which they died, stood up sullenly or with a certain sad exaltation to face the firing party or the halter. A hundred times as many endured exile, prisons, ostracisms, beatings, gross humiliations and the direst poverty for the still dimly apprehended cause of human liberation.

They had not even the assurance of unanimity. They were all convinced that there had to be a better world, but they had not the knowledge, they had not the facilities for free and open discussion, to clear up and work out the inevitable outline of their common need. They formulated their ideas dully and clumsily; they went a certain way to truth and then stopped short; they suspected all other formulae than the ones they themselves had hit upon; they quarrelled endlessly, bitterly, murderously, among themselves. Nearly all sooner or later were infected by hate. Often it happened that two men, each of whom had roughly half the justice of things in him, killed each other, when indeed they needed only to put their prepossessions together to get the full outline of a working reconstruction.

Da Silva has called all those who made the revolutions and revolutionary efforts that occurred between 1788 and 1948 the "revolutionaries of the half- light". His studies of the tangled history of the new social concepts that broke through to open popular discussion, only after the establishment of the Soviet régime in Russia in 1917, constitute a very brilliant work of elucidation and simplification. It is a history of twilight that ends at dawn. In the twenties and thirties of the twentieth century the ordinary man in the street was discussing, cheaply perhaps, but freely, ideas, possibilities and courses of action that no one would have dared to whisper about, would scarcely have dared to think about, two centuries before. He scarcely knew a single name of the pioneers, fanatics and desperadoes who had won this freedom for his mind.

The nature of the conflict was changing. That was very plain by 1940. Where there had been pioneers, there were now systematic explorers and surveyors; the teeming multitudes of our race were still producing devoted and sacrificial types, but the half light was now a cloudy daylight and the ordered analyses and plans of such men as De Windt were making understandings and cooperations possible that would have been incredible in the nineteenth century. In the nineteenth century revolution was suspected, forbidden, dark, criminal, desperate and hysterical. In the twentieth century it became candid and sympathetic. The difference was essentially an intellectual one; after a vast period of stormy disputation the revolutionary idea had cleared up. The sun of the Modern State broke through.

Revolution still demanded its martyrs, but the martyrdoms were henceforth of a different character. Biographies of revolutionists before the Great War go on by night, amidst a scenery of back streets, cellars, prisons, suspicions and betrayals. Biographies of revolutionists in the final struggle to establish the Modern State go on in full daylight. It is reaction now which has taken to the darkness, to plots, assassinations, and illegal measures. The Modern State propagandist became less and less like an insurgent individual of some alien subject race; he became more and more like a missionary in savage country, ill- armed or unarmed, and at an immediate disadvantage, but with the remote incalculable prestige of a coming power behind him.

The later death-roll of revolutionaries has fewer and fewer executions in it and an increasing tale of assassinations and deaths in public conflict. A larger and larger proportion of those who died for it were killed either by mobs or in fair and

open fighting. And soon the idea of the Modern State had become so pervasive that the battles ceased to be for it or against it; they became, rather, misunderstandings between impatient zealots with a common end. In many conflicts the historian is still perplexed to determine which side, if either, can be counted as fighting for the Modern State.

The analyses of De Windt made immense charities of understanding possible. Creative-minded men, though they hardened against the liar and the cheat, became less and less willing to fight the puerile adherent and the honest fanatic with a tiresome but honestly intended formula. "There," they said, "but for certain misconceptions and resolvable obsessions go our men," and set themselves at any risk or loss to the task of conversion. Just as Fascism in its time seized upon the ancient terroristic and blackmailing Mafia in Sicily and partly annexed it, partly changed it and so superseded it, just as the Nazi movement incorporated large chunks of the Communist party in its efforts to reformulate Germany, so now the Modern State fellowship grappled with the world- wide series of organizations which had superseded democratic institutions nearly everywhere, made every effort to capture the imaginations of their adherents, and showed the most unscrupulous boldness in seizing their direction whenever it could. The Modern State Movement differed from every preceding revolutionary movement in its immense assimilating power, due to the clearness of the objectives it set before men's minds.

The difference between the revolutionary before the Great War and the revolutionary after that illuminating crisis is closely parallel to the difference between the old alchemist and the modern man of science; the former haunted by demons, goblins and spirits, warped by symbolic obsessions and cabalistic words and numbers, terribly alone with himself, obsessed with religious fears, by fear of the inquisitor, by fear of the ruler above and of the rabble below, perpetually baffled in his attempts to achieve great things, but full of a dangerous unpremeditated knowledge of poisons and mischievous devices; the latter with a mind released by centuries of analysis and simplification, reassured by the incessant tale of scientific victories, stoically indifferent to popular misrepresentation and equally sure of his universe and himself.

5. THE FIRST CONFERENCE AT BASRA: 1965

The conference of scientific and technical workers at Basra in 1965 is regarded by historians as a cardinal date in the emergence of the Modern State. It was organized by the Transport Union, which had begun as a loose association of the surviving aeroplane and shipping operators for mutual aid and protection. The ideas formulated at this conference—and even those were still formulated with a certain tentative or tactful incompleteness—had been gathering force and definition for some time. But this conference was the first to draw up a definite plan of the general human outlook and initiate an organization to carry it out. It marked the transition from thought to action in general affairs.

The idea of using air transport as the combining and directive force for a new synthesis of civilization was already an old and familiar one. It had been in men's thoughts for at least thirty years. A popular story published in 1933, Man's Mortality (by the English romancer Michael Arlen, 1895-1990), for instance, is an amusing fantasy of the world dominated by an air-transport syndicate. It is still a very readable book and interesting in showing the limitations of the educated imagination at that time. The belief in the possibilities of invention is unbounded; air velocities and air fighting are described on a scale that still seems preposterously exaggerated to-day; while on the other hand the inflated stock buying and selling of that period, although it had grown from the merest germ in about a century and a half, is represented as still going on unchanged, and the world's air dictators are gambling dishonestly in stock, and at last "crash" financially and bolt as though they were just contemporary politicians and mystery men rather than lords of the whole power of the air. In a world of incredible metals, explosives and swiftness, the Stock Exchange, the Bourses, still survive. And there are still Powers and Foreign Policies! Nothing could illustrate better the inability of people at that time to realize the economic and political changes that were then actually tumbling upon them. For some obscure reason mental and moral progress and institutional invention seemed absolutely impossible to them.

An interesting little London periodical of the same time, Essential News, has recently been reprinted for graduate students of history in the Students' Reprint Series. Its fourth issue (February 4th, 1933) contains a summary of contemporary thought about World Air Control. It cites a complete scheme for the "International" control of aviators, drawn up by a small French group at the suggestion of M. Henri de Jouvenal under the presidency of M. Pierre Denis. A Union Aéronautique Internationale is proposed, a cosmopolitan air transport company.

Linked with this and controlled by the poor League of Nations, an "Air Force for Mutual Assistance" was to police the atmosphere. The proposals are so plainly Utopian and impracticable in the face of the sovereign state system as to seem insincere. It was only thirty years later, after the common suicide of the sovereign Powers of Europe, that the assembled technicians at Basra could revive the broad conception of this proposal.

This first conference at Basra was distinguished from its predecessors first by its universality and then by the extremely bold and comprehensive proposals for united action it accepted—proposals which were in effect, if not in form, the project for the modern World-State. It was the first of these gatherings attended by considerable American, Chinese and Japanese contingents, as well as the customary European representatives, and the Russian technicians were present in unprecedented strength and unexpectedly united and independent of the political controllers who accompanied them. New Zealand also had reappeared in the world's affairs. There were even two representatives (two schoolmasters in the Social Psychology section) from Iceland, which for most practical purposes had been cut off from the world for over five years. And one has only to compare the agenda of this and previous assemblies to feel at once the stride forward in the scope and courage of scientific and technical thought that had occurred.

It was a young gathering; the average age is estimated by Amen Rihani as about thirty-three, and five or six women attended in the social and educational branches. A third but very significant feature was the extensive use of that simple and convenient lingua franca of the aviators, Basic English. Even the native English-speaking people present did their best to keep their speeches within the limitations of that ingenious idiom.

The master section was still that of General Transport. The body which had organized the gathering was, as has been said already, the Transport Union, originally a purely business body, but the inspiration was that of the Modern State movement, and technicians in medicine, education, agriculture and every main type of industrial production were present. There was much discussion of the upkeep of the world routes and the administrative tasks arising out of that. Nothing could give the student a more vivid sense of the derelict state of the world at that time than the boldness with which this Control took possession of things and pushed its activities into new fields. It was decided, for instance, that all existing aerodromes and landmarks, lights and lighting fields, should be directly under its management. There was no question of purchase; it took them over. Every aeroplane in the world was to be registered, was to carry a distinctive number, respect the common tariff of charges and pay a registration fee to the Control. Airships and aeroplanes which did not do this were to be treated as pirates, denied the use of aerodromes and filling stations, and "driven out of the air". They were to be driven out of the air if necessary by an "air police" which the Control was to organize. Aerodromes or regions that harboured such recalcitrants were to be boycotted.

These proposals were not accepted without discussion. But there was very little protest against what was certainly, from the older point of view, an illegal usurpation of authority. The political members of the Russian contingent offered the chief resistance, and what other opposition appeared was not from aviators, engineers, chemists, biologists or men of that type, but from sociologists and economists of the less advanced schools. The main objection took the form of a question: "But what will governments say to this?" So far as the Westerners and Chinese were concerned there was a disposition to disregard the possibility of political intervention. "Wait till it comes," they said cheerfully. But Soviet Russia and Soviet Japan were at that time much more rankly political than the rest of the world, and they at least had politicians as well as men of skill and science present at this gathering. A long speech was made by the commissar Vladimir Peshkoff, full of the menace of later trouble. He denounced the projected Control as an insidious attempt to restore a capitalist trust in the world. Its psychology would be bourgeois and capitalist. Moscow would never consent to the passage of controlled machines over the vast territories under Soviet control nor allow the exploitation of the resources of Russia in oil and minerals by any outside organization.

"And how will Moscow prevent it?" asked Ivan Englehart, a Russian aviator and aeroplane builder, rising as Peshkoff sat down. "Is it a nationalism of this sort that the Third International is to end?"

By way of reply Peshkoff leant towards him and spat out in Russian, "Wait until you return to Moscow."

"I may have to wait a little time," said Englehart. "I am a citizen of the world, and I shall go back to Russia in my own time and in my own fashion."

"This is treason. Wait until Moscow hears of this!"

"And how and when will Moscow hear of this?"

"Very soon."

Englehart was standing a few yards from Peshkoff. He shook his head with a sceptical smile. He spoke gently, like a man who had long prepared himself for such an occasion.

"You flew here, Tavarish Peshkoff, in my squadron. How do you propose to return?"

Peshkoff rose to his feet, realized the blank want of sympathy in the gathering, spluttered and sat down again in unconcealed dismay.

Englehart waited for a moment or so and then went on, choosing his words with quiet deliberation, to assure the meeting of the adhesion of the Russian technicians to the projected Control. "That phantom Proletarian of yours fades with all the other empires and kingdoms," he said to the political delegates his colleagues. "We are only giving shape to a new world order that is already born."

His speech set the key for most of the subsequent debate.

That establishment of the Control was the backbone discussion, but it was no more than the backbone of a plan that covered the whole future organization of society; upon it was articulated a whole framework of structural proposals. The

central section dealt not only with the air network but with the organization of every type of communication. The lighthouses, lightships, sea marks, channels and harbours of the world were suffering from a decade of economy, a decade of wartime destruction and a decade of chaos and decay. The meteorological services were no longer operative. All this had to be restored. The definite abandonment of every type of railroad was accepted as a matter of course. Railways were buried at Basra forever. And the restoration and reconstruction of production in a hundred essential industries followed also as a necessary consequence of these primary resolutions.

The more the reader scrutinizes the agenda, the more is he impressed by the mildness of the official title of the gathering: "A Conference on Scientific and Mercantile Communications and Associated Questions". It is clear that the conveners resolved to press on with their task of world reorganization as far as they possibly could, without rousing the enfeebled and moribund political organizations of the past to obstruction and interference. The language throughout is that of understatement; the shape of the projects is fearlessly bold. A committee of experts had prepared a very good general survey of the natural resources of the planet, including those of the already suspicious Russia, and the conference set itself unhesitatingly to work out the problems of a resumption of production generally, with an entire disregard of the various proprietary claims that might arise to challenge the realization of these schemes. There was no provocative discussion of these claims; they were ignored. The Sea and Air Ways Control evidently meant to take effective possession not only of all derelict ports, aerodromes, coal-mines, oil wells, power stations and mines, but to bring those in which a certain vitality still lingered into line with its schemes by hook or by crook, by persuasion or pressure. Its confidence in its solidarity with the skilled men working these latter establishments was absolute. Such a solidarity would have been inconceivable thirty years before. Financial adventure had been washed out of the minds of the new generation of technicians altogether. They simply wanted to "get things going again". Ideas of personal enrichment were swamped in their universal conviction that their class must now either work together and master the world, or leave it.

So with a modest air of logical necessity, of being driven rather than driving, the Conference spread its planning far beyond the material and mechanism of world intercommunication.

What is this reconstructed transport to carry? How is it to be fed—and paid for? About the air-ports everywhere were tracts and regions sinking back to that primordial peasant cultivation which had been the basis of all the barbaric civilizations of the past. The question of the expropriation of the peasant and the modernization of agricultural production was taken up at Basra at the point where Lenin and Stalin had laid it down, defeated. The Conference was lucidly aware that upon the same planet at the same time you cannot have both an aviator and a starveling breeding peasantry, toiling endlessly and forever in debt. One or other has to go, and the fundamental objective of the Conference was to make the world

safe for the former. The disappearance of the latter followed, not as a sought-after end but as a necessary consequence. And the disappearance of as much of the institutions of the past as were interwoven with it.

In the ideas of their relations to each other and to the world as a whole, these Basra technicians were all what the nineteenth century would have called socialistic. They were so fundamentally socialistic that they did not even raise the question of socialism. It is doubtful if the word was ever used before. They took it for granted that this Control that was growing like a limitless polyp in their minds would be the effectual owner and exploiter of all the aeroplanes, routes, industrial townships, factories, mines, cultivations that were falling into place in their Plan. It would have seemed as unnatural to them that a new Ford or a new Rockefeller should arise to own a factory or a mine personally, as that anyone should try to steal the ocean or the air. There it was for the common good, and just as much was industrial plant for the common good.

All these men it must be remembered, almost without exception, were men of the salaried type of mind. They had been born and brought up in a tradition in which money was a secondary matter. From the beginning of the mechanical age, the men of science, the technical experts, the inventors and discoverers, the foremen and managers and organizers, had been essentially of the salariat. Some few had dabbled in finance and grown rich, but they were exceptions. Before the World War indeed these sort of men had been accustomed to accept the acquisitive and gambling types, the powerful rich and owning people, as a necessary evil. Now they were manifestly a totally unnecessary evil, and without the least vindictiveness or animosity plans were made to do without them and prevent their return. The Basra Conference would as soon have considered a return of Foreign Offices or of Kings or Divinities.

But they had to consider—and this was the work of a powerful section upon which the Americans were exceptionally active—how the wealth of the world that they meant to restore had to be distributed for consumption, and how a close-knit world organization was to be reconciled with personal freedom and particularly with artistic and literary initiatives. This was entitled the Section of Wages, Charges and Supply.

There seems to have been the completest agreement that the only way of combining service with private liberty is by the use of money. Without money there is necessarily a dictation of consumption and a dictation of movement to the worker. He would be given "what was good for him". But money generalized the claim of the worker as worker, and the claim of the citizen as shareholder in the commonweal, upon the goods, pleasures, facilities and liberties of life. You take your money and you buy this or that, or go here or there, or do whatever you please. But there were dangers in this invention; twice in history money had failed mankind and a money-linked order had crashed. This time, they thought, mankind had learnt its lesson, and a new money had to be devised that would be, in any large sense, fool-proof, sneak-proof and scoundrel-proof. So much lay beneath the intention of the Section of Wages, Charges and Supply.

This section carried the question of money into regions that would have seemed quite outside its scope thirty years before. In the Twenties and Thirties of the century, and indeed into the war troubles of the Forties, there had been a great volume of discussion about money. Men had realized its dangers and set themselves, with the energy born of a sense of crisis, to the analysis of its progresses and the invention of new methods that should prevent the gross accumulation of ownership, the mischievous manipulation of credit, the relative impoverishment of the worker and the strangulation of enterprise that had wrecked the second monetary civilization. Gradually it had been realized that there could be no Theory of Money that was not in fact a complete theory of social organization. The Conference set itself now to a prepared and simplified task.

The interdependence of monetary theory with the general theory of property and social structure, which had hardly been suspected by their fathers, was now universally recognized. There was a considerable contingent of young lawyers present, though it would have amazed the previous generation beyond measure to find them in the ranks of technologists and men of science. They knocked the dust of centuries off the idea of ownership in these very pregnant debates. We have already mentioned the surprise of Nicholson at the new sort of law schools he found in America. At Basra the products of these schools were very much to the fore, together with several older teachers from the London School of Economics, which flourished until the landslide of 1968. These new lawyers, with their fundamentally scientific habits of mind, were amazingly unlike their professional predecessors—those obstinate, cunning and terrible old sinners who played so large a part in the economic strangulation of the United States and the frustration of all the high hopes of their founders. They had completely abandoned the pretence that the business of the law was to protect private property, exact debts and maintain a false appearance of equity between man and man. They knew that justice without equality of status and opportunity can be nothing more than a sham, and their ideas were already completely based on our current conception of law as the regulative system in the network of relationships between the human commonweal and its subordinate corporations and individuals. They were entirely contemptuous of any claims, contracts, rules and precedents that impeded the free expansion of human welfare. Among all the various types that gathered at Basra, these younger lawyers, in close touch with the new economists on the one hand and the group psychologists on the other, and inspired by a political constructiveness of the boldest sort, were certainly the most remarkable.

It is chiefly to them that we owe the firm assertion by the Basra Conference of the principle that in a modern community there can be no individual property in anything but personal belongings and money. This was thrown out as something too obvious to discuss. Houses and lands were henceforth to be held on leases of a not too lengthy period, life tenure being the longest. All other tangible things, they assumed, belonged inalienably to the world commonweal—in the usufruct of which every human being was manifestly a shareholder. And it was these younger lawyers also who did the greater part of that task of disentanglement and simplifi-

cation, which reduced money to its present and only proper use as a check for consumable goods and services, either paid out to the individual, or, in the case of minors and incapables, to the individual's guardians, either as a part of the racial inheritance or else as wages for work in the common service. The world was to be reborn without usury or monetary speculation.

The monetary methods of the world at that time were in a state of such complete chaos that there was no effective system in working order anywhere to present an immediate resistance to the operation of the new ideas. Every region was running its own, often very arbitrary and primitive, system of tokens and checks. But the revival of communications that had made Basra possible was already giving an increasing prestige to what was known as the "air-dollar". This was not a metallic coin at all; it was a series of paper notes, which represented distance, weight, bulk, and speed. Each note was good for so many kilograms in so much space, for so many kilometres at such a pace. The value of an air-dollar had settled down roughly to a cubic metre weighing ten kilograms and travelling two hundred kilometres at a hundred kilometres an hour.

This was already an energy unit and not a unit of substance, such as the old world standards had always been. It marked very definitely that the old static conceptions of human life with limited resources were giving place to kinetic ideas of a continually expanding life. The air-dollar was a unit of energy in terms of transport, and its transformation into the energy dollar of our daily life to-day was already sketched out clearly by the Basra experts, although the actual change over was not accomplished until ten years later.

It was the plain, if unformulated, intention of the new Air and Sea Control to gain possession and exploit all the available sources of energy in the world as soon as possible, to frame its human balance sheet, scale its wages and declare its dividends as the common trustee of mankind, but manifestly if the threat of Peshkoff materialized, and the Russian Soviet system (or indeed any other owning group) was able to remain in effective control of its territorial wealth, the energy dollar would afford a just unambiguous medium for whatever trade was necessary between the competing administrations.

The planning of a new political, industrial, and monetary world scheme still does not measure the full achievement of this First Basra Conference. There was also a strong and vigorous educational section working in close touch with the technicians and the social psychologists. It made plans not only for the coordination of the surviving colleges and technical schools in the world and for the revivification of those that had lapsed, but it set itself definitely to the task of that propaganda of the idea of the Modern State which is the substantial content of our existing fundamental education. This was dealt with by the Section of Training and Advertisement. Basic English was to lay the foundations of a world lingua franca. Evidently wherever the influence of the Air and Sea Control extended, a new propaganda, a new Press, and new common schools were to extend. There can be little doubt that most of the teachers at Basra already saw quite clearly ahead of them the world-wide mental and social order in which we live to-day.

They knew what they were doing. They went back from this gathering encouraged and confirmed, to give themselves to the terrific and exalting adventure before them, to the evocation day by day, and idea by idea, of a new civilization amidst the distressful, slovenly, and still living wreckage of the old.

When the Conference at last dispersed two new realities had appeared in the world, so unobtrusively that it was only slowly that the mass of mankind realized their significance. One was the Central Board, known also as the Sea and Air Control, consolidating the Transport Union, linking with it the other Controls and sections, and having its permanent offices at Basra; the other was the Police of the Air and Sea Ways, at first a modest organization with about 3,000 aeroplanes, a handful of seaplanes, a hundred patrol ships, and a personnel of about 25,000 men. It was a small body judged by the standards either of preceding or subsequent times, but at that period it was by far the most powerful armed force in the world.

6. THE GROWTH OF RESISTANCE TO THE SEA AND AIR WAYS CONTROL

For nearly ten years the Air and Sea Control was able to grow and extend its methods and influence without any general conflict. The little breeze between the Russian political control and the technicians did not rise to a storm; instead it died away. Russia was learning wisdom at last and weakening in her resolve to subordinate the modern scientific type of man to his old- fashioned demagogic rival. She had suffered so severely by the miscalculations and convulsive direction of her party chiefs; she was still so ill equipped mechanically, and so poorly provided with aviators, that the old and now mentally weary dictatorship recoiled from a new struggle with these and their associated technical experts. It is to be noted that, in spite of the closest espionage, the creed of the Russian aviators, engineers, and men of science was already the Modern State and not the Dictatorship of the Proletariat, and that her political rulers were beginning to understand this.

So that the Air and Sea Control, sustained by a multitude of nuclei on De Windt's pattern scattered throughout the world, very much as the Bolshevik political organization had been sustained by the Communist Party, came into existence and spread its ever-growing network about the planet without an immediate struggle. Its revolutionary nature was understood by few people other than its promoters. It grew rapidly. As the Esthonian proverb says: "One must be born before one's troubles begin."

The recovery of human prosperity in that decade between 1965 and 1975 was very rapid. It went on side by side with the expansion of the Transport system. By 1970 the Transport Control, the chief of the subsidiaries of the general Air and Sea Control, was running world-wide services that had as many as 25,000 aeroplanes aloft at the same time; it had possessed itself of shipyards on the Tyne, in Belfast, Hamburg, and a number of other points, and was building steel cargo ships by the score; it was creating a new system of high roads for which a number of the old main railway tracks were taken over, and it was running water-power stations, substituting our present chemical treatment of carboniferous strata for the terrible hand coal-mining of the older economy, and it was working oil. It had developed a subsidiary body, the Supply Control, which was rapidly becoming a vaster organization than its parent. This was engaged in producing iron and steel, producing or purchasing rubber, metals, cotton, wool and vegetable substances, and restoring the mass production of clothing of all sorts, electrical material,

mechanisms, and a vast variety of chemicals of which the output had been dormant in some instances for twenty years or more.

Never very clearly cut off from the Supply Control was the Food Control, which began ostensibly with the victualling of the Transport Services, and was soon carrying on a vast barter in food materials, its own surplus supplies and commodities generally throughout the world. In all its ramifications these three bodies were in 1970 employing about two million people, to whom wages were paid in the new modern dollars, energy dollars, good for units in Transport, housing, and for all the priced commodities handled by the Controls.

The property of all these Controls was vested in the Modern State Society, which consisted at this time of about a quarter of a million Fellows, who had to be qualified up to a certain level of technical efficiency, who submitted to the Society disciplines during their years of active participation, and received wages varying by about 200 per cent above or below a mean standard, according to their standing. About a quarter of the other employees were student apprentices aspiring to fellowship, and of these the proportion was increasing. The Society had already developed the organization it was to retain for a century. The Fellows were divided into faculties for technical purposes; they voted by localized groups upon local issues and they had a general vote for the faculty delegations to the central council of the Society, which had its first seat at Basra contiguous to the central offices of the Three Controls. The relation of the Society to the Controls was not unlike the relation of the Communist Party to the Moscow Government in the early days of the Soviet system; it was a collateral activity of much the same people.

It was the Society itself which at first directed the educational activities of the Modern State Movement. Wherever it had either its own "nuclei" or found employees of the Controls, it provided an elementary education of the new pattern, which involved a very clear understanding of the history and aims of the Modern State idea, and wherever it had works and factories and a sufficient supply of students, it founded and equipped science schools and technical schools, which included psychology, medicine, group psychology and administration. Gradually a special section of Training and Education was developed under the Air and Sea Control, and this grew into a separate Educational Control. But it never became as distinct from, and collateral to, the Modern State Fellowship as the rest of the Control organizations. One may figure the whole of this world system as a vast business octopus, with the Air and Sea Control as its head and the other Controls as its tentacles. The account-keeping of this octopus centred at Basra, but a rapid development of subsidiary record and statistical bureaus also occurred. Side by side grew the intelligence and research services. By 1970, the world meteorological service was far in advance of anything that had ever existed before.

But already this restoration of communications and circulation was producing effects far beyond the Fellowship and the power of employment of the associated Controls. The ebb in the vitality of human life had already passed its maximum and now began a restoration of activity everywhere, a fresh movement in the de-

caying towns, a new liveliness upon the countryside, a general reawakening of initiative, that were to confront the direction of this fast growing nexus of the Modern State, with challenges, difficulties, and menaces, that grew rapidly to tremendous proportions.

It had been comparatively easy to spread throughout a prostrate and bankrupt world the new system of air and sea communications and trading that had been evolved. That world was too exhausted by war, famine, and pestilence and too impoverished to support extensive and aggressive political organizations. It was altogether another problem, even with the spreading "nuclei", the new schools and propaganda, to control and assimilate the populations that now, no longer living in want and insecurity, were beginning to feel a fresh strength and a renewed vigour of desire.

Let us review the world situation about 1975. The Transport Control had usurped a monopoly of air and sea transport and was also monopolizing the use of its own new great roads. This gave it a practical ownership of the trade in staple products throughout the world. It was turning all the surplus products of its activities back, when its salaries had been paid, into strengthening its grip upon the general economy of mankind. By 1975 the Modern State Society counted just over a million Fellows, and in addition it was employing and training two million candidates, it was simply employing another three million and it had between seven and eight million youngsters in its new schools. They were all, we may note, not only given a sound training in physical science and biology, but were learning world history and so acquiring a world outlook in the place of the more limited views that had hitherto framed the ordinary political imagination, and they were being taught Basic English as a lingua franca. In ten wonderful years the Transport Control had grown far beyond the scale of any of the great Trusts or Controls of the opening years of the century. It had created a world currency. But it was still far from "owning the earth". Its own produce did not exceed an eighth of all the outside stuff that it bought and sold. Its own production was mainly fuel, metals and mechanisms. Food it bought, timber, vegetable oils, crude rubber, for example. Several hundred millions of human beings were still self-subsisting, quite out of its scheme, or dealing with it only for a few manufactured articles and mass produced commodities. And other hundreds of millions were rapidly developing, or rather recovering, a collateral productivity in relation to or in rivalry with its activities.

The chief difficulties before the Modern State movement arose out of this parallel to its own rapid success. It was calling into existence a mass of exterior prosperity far beyond its immediate power of assimilation. Propagandists and teachers, advisory traders and competent directive agents are not made in a day. The strain upon the supply of ability, loyalty, and complete understanding in the movement was already being noted in 1970. In 1972 we hear of a "scrutiny of qualifications", and new rules were made for the lapsing and expulsion of incompetent and unsatisfactory Fellows. The controlling staff had to be enlarged continually, and the supply of men with the necessary character, knowledge of

group psychology and understanding of the constructive theory of the movement was limited.

"Let us serve", said Fedor Galland, who was already becoming a leading spirit upon the World Council, in a speech that was circulated in 1973; "let us not fall into factions; let us not group ourselves. We cannot afford bickering; we must not thwart and waste each other. We have done no more as yet than make a start. Remember the strangulation of Russia by Stalin. Remember those excellent chapters of De Windt against the spirit of opposition. The struggle for the Modern State has only begun."

Here we have the clearest indication that growth strains were already apparent within the structure of the still infantile Modern State.

But if the movement found difficulty in sustaining its internal unanimity, there was at least this in its favour, that, outside it, there was no single world-wide framework in which antagonisms could concentrate. The old international banking system was dead and gone, and the new order issued its new money and was free to create and dominate the financial organization of things. The old armament-dealing interests were dead and buried. The old nationalist Press systems were dead and already forgotten. It is extraordinary with what rapidity this latter aspect of social life was forgotten, seeing that up to 1940 at any rate it was the primary medium of collective thought and opinion. To-day a copy of a newspaper of any date between 1890 and 1970 is a rare and precious thing, which has to be protected from carbonization in an air- proof wrapper. The Central Board controlled most of the new paper supplies as well as the now rapidly reviving telegraphic, telephonic and air transmission systems.

The resistances and antagonisms it had to encounter, within its organization and without, were certainly immense, but they were extremely various; the dangers they developed never came together into one united danger, never rose to a simultaneous maximum and produced a supreme crisis. In this respect or that the advance of the Modern State might be fought to a standstill and held, but it was never put entirely upon the defensive, and since it held trade, money and its ever-spreading efficient common schools in its hands, time was always on its side. "If not to-day, to-morrow," said Arden Essenden. "But better to-day," said Fedor Galland.

The rapidity with which the Transport Control of 1965 expanded into the Modern State octopus of 1975 accounts for quite another group of difficulties, as well as this initial difficulty of creating a personnel to keep pace with the perpetually elaborated task. This second group of troubles came from the fact that in habit and spirit the old order of things, the old ideas, the old methods, had not had time to die. That old world, blinded and enfeebled by its own errors, had staggered and fallen down in the Thirties and Forties, had lain in a coma in the Fifties. Throughout the Sixties the new world had come into existence. But in the brains of all the men and women alive who were more than forty years old, and in a great majority of those younger, more or less of the old world survived. The revival of human vitality in the Seventies involved not merely a renascence but a

restoration. Old things came back to find their habitations still very imperfectly occupied by the new.

Let us consider what form this opposition had taken and what were the more serious survivals of the old order—old "state of affairs" rather than "order" —still in active existence about 1975. We shall then have a clue to the history of the next seventy-five years.

The task before the Air and Sea Control was essentially to leaven the whole world to its own pattern. Within its far-flung tentacles it embraced and sought to permeate with its own nature, with the concepts and methods of a commonweal of mutual service, a mass of some thousands and a half million human beings, still carried on by inertias established during thousands of generations. Morowitz calculates that in 1976 about sixty per cent of this mass was living directly upon the seasonal cultivation of the soil, and that two- thirds of this, throughout the temperate zone, was producing mainly for its own consumption and not for trade. He thinks this was a relapse from the state of affairs that obtained about 1910-1920. An emancipation from the soil, an abolition of the peasant, had then been in progress for more than a century. Large-scale production, with an abundant use of machines, had so increased the output per head as to liberate (if it can be called liberation) a growing proportion of hands for industrial work or unemployment. But this process had been reversed after 1940. From that date onward there was a drift back of workers to the land, to live very incompetently and wretchedly.

The abolition of the self-subsisting peasant had been the conscious objective of Lenin and Stalin in Russia. The cultivator, with increasing ease, was to produce fundamental foodstuffs far beyond his own needs and to receive for his surplus an ever increasing variety of helps, comforts and amenities. Millions of the cultivators in 1910 were cultivating entirely for the market; they produced cotton, hemp, rubber or what not, and were as dependent on the provision shop for their food as any townsman. The social crash had ended all that. In the Famished Fifties, as Morowitz says, everyone was "scratching for food in his own patch". In the Sixties the common way of life throughout the world was again immediate production and consumption. Only under the direction and stimulus of the Transport Control did the workers upon the soil begin to recover the confidence and courage needed to produce beasts only for sale and crops only for marketing.

The ambition of the Modern State Fellowship was to become the landlord of the planet and either to mine, afforest, pasture, and cultivate directly or to have these tasks performed by responsible tenants, or groups and associations of tenants under its general control. But at the outset it had neither the personnel nor the power to carry out so fundamental a reconstruction of human affairs. The comparative failure of the two Five Year Plans in Russia had been a useful warning against extravagant propositions.

The Modern State did not mean, as the old saying goes, "to bite off more than it could chew". Its chief missionaries were its traders. They were more abundant than, and they did not need the same amount of training as, the Modern State schoolmasters and propagandists. They went offering contracts and prices to ex-

isting or potential food growers, cotton growers, rubber planters and operable mines; the Control did its best to guarantee sales and prices to any surviving factories, and it trusted to the selective power it had through transport, the new monetary issues, research and technical education to strengthen its grip as time went on and enable it to establish a general order in this worldwide mélange of bankrupt producers and impoverished customers it was restoring to activity.

At first it made no enquiry as to the ownership of goods that were brought to its depots; it paid cash and observed its contracts; it attempted no discriminations between man and man so long as they delivered the goods and traded square. Its nuclei and schools were still propagandist schools in 1975 and quasi independent of the trading, transport and industrial organizations that endowed them. But this was only the first stage in the Modern State undertaking. The next was to be more difficult.

The student of history must always keep in mind the importance of lifetime periods in social and political change. Between 1935 and 1975 was only forty years. Everywhere old systems of ideas were still dominating men's brains and still being transmitted to the young. Old habits of thought, old values, old patterns of conduct, that had been put aside, as it were, just as jewels and fine clothes and many polite usages had been put aside, during the days of dire need and immediate fear, returned with returning self-respect. During the Famished Fifties the full creative scheme of the Modern State won its way to dominate the imaginations of at most a few score thousand minds, whose scientific and technical education had prepared them for it. After that the propaganda had been vigorous, but still, even after the Conference of Basra in 1965, the number of brains that could be reckoned as primarily Modern State makers probably numbered less than a couple of hundred thousand.

The subsequent propaganda was still more swift and urgent, but the new membership was not always of the same thorough quality as the old. The society wanted the services of every man or woman it could incorporate with its Fellowship, but it did not want an inrush of half prepared adherents, refugees from moral perplexity requiring guidance, ambitious careerists. Every new religion, every church, every organized movement has known this conflict between the desire for expansion and the dread of dilution. On the one hand the Modern State recalled the headlong shallow mass conversions of Christianity and Islam, which had reduced those great faiths to a mere superstitious veneer upon barbarism, and on the other there was the more recent warning of Soviet Russia, morally and intellectually sterilized at last by the eternal espionage, censorship and "purges" of the G.P.U. The central brain of the Modern State octopus had to steer its world system of organization between the extremes of rash receptiveness and black suspicion. It had to go steadfastly and discreetly and yet it had to go swiftly. If, on the one hand, it found presently that its own Fellowship was not altogether as free as it had been at first from reactionary weaknesses and traditional sentiments, on the other it found that its leading ideas, by virtue of its material successfulness

and of continual explicit statement, were spreading far beyond the limits of its nuclei and its organized teaching.

In the economic realm there appeared, even from the first, intimations of a revival of prosperity, a number of developments that the Society, had it had the necessary resources, would gladly have nipped in the bud. It wanted to deal directly with every primary producer. To-day that is how things are. But so soon as there was a new demand for cotton, for rubber, for pork, wheat, rice and the like, a multitude of obliging intermediaries appeared between the negro cotton growers in America, the Sudanese cotton growers, the local folk who went into the largely abandoned rubber plantations to collect rubber again, the wheat farmers and swineherds and ranchmen, and set themselves to collect and handle the produce for the Control buyers and to distribute Control goods by retail in return.

These people, the former business men of the world, emerged from the slums of decaying towns, from municipal offices, from their own reluctantly cultivated corners of land, from the dingy retreats of predatory bands, from small local trading establishments, full of the sense of trade revival. They organized loans to the peasants, contrived advances of material to them, advised them shrewdly, went officiously to the Control agents for instructions.

This sort of intervention did not stop at individuals, nor with advices and promises. In many parts of the world, in townships and counties and small states, where a Town Council or Workers' Soviet or Mayor or Lord of the Manor was in authority, or where mines or plantations lay abandoned and neglected, the reviving breeze of buying produced a violent desire in the minds of men to set other people working for their profit. There were "Getting to Work Again" fêtes in America in 1969 to "stimulate local business".

By 1975, from Manchuria to Cape Colony and from Vancouver to Java, the old state of affairs—peasants in debt, peasants working to pay rent, peasants bringing in goods in arrears, fishermen, miners, factory and gang workers generally, collectors and hunters, the old immemorial economic life of mankind —was recovering vigour. Debt serfdom was returning everywhere. Rents were rising everywhere. Everywhere the increasing surplus product was being intercepted according to time-honoured patterns. Even slavery was reappearing in thinly disguised forms.

It had always been a strong tendency in the old order to utilize the labour of offenders against the law. Forced labour seemed so just and reasonable a punishment that whenever the possibility of using it profitably appeared the authorities set themselves to multiply indictable offences and bring luckless people into unpaid servitude. In the "classic" age most mines were worked and most galleys propelled by convicts. In the late Middle Ages the Mediterranean shipping waited on the magistrate, and if offenders did not appear in sufficient numbers they had to be sought for. Out of the dimness of the Fifties and Sixties into the returning publicity and activity of this phase of recovery there appeared everywhere local bosses, chiefs and political gangs inciting and driving people to the production of marketable goods. The Supply Control Report of 1976 on "Conditions of Labour

Supplying Goods to Us" notes the existence of convict labour in North and South America, on the West Coast of Africa, in Soviet Russia, Central India, North China, Japan, Java and elsewhere, and states that in many districts it is hardly distinguishable from kidnapping.

"The cheapness of human beings", runs the Report, "is once more impeding the efficient organization of mechanical production. Outside the range of our own services and factories, there are vast and increasing masses of people now living at a standard of life too low and under stresses too urgent for them even to begin to understand the objectives of the Modern State, and, drawing its sustenance from their degradation, there is arising again an intricate tangle of exploiting classes, entrepreneurs, wholesalers, retailers, money- lenders (lending the local coinages and exchanging against our notes), politicians, private and corporation lawyers, investors and landowners, of the most varied types, but all having one common characteristic, that they put profit before service and will resist and drive as hard a bargain as they can with our expanding organization. These things are returning about as fast as we are growing."

The Transport Control Report of the same year notes another system of troubles arising. Here the attack on Modern State development was more direct. "We are finding the question of way-leaves an increasing difficulty in the extension of our road net for local and heavy traffic. The world, we are told more plainly every day, is not ours to do with as we like. Everywhere claimants are springing up, renascent corporations, local authorities or private individuals who profess ownership of the soil and demand rents or monetary compensation from us. In some cases, where the local authority was of such a character as to afford a reasonable hope of its ultimate absorption by our organization, we have been able to come to an arrangement by which it has taken over the making and maintenance of the route within the area of its alleged jurisdiction, but in the majority of instances the resistance is much more frankly in the nature of a hold-up. The enquiries of our social psychologists show a widespread desire for simple or disguised bribery on the part of the obstructives, though it has to be admitted that there are many genuine cases of quite disinterested stupidity. Few of them realize clearly that they are demanding bribes or exacting blackmail. They are obsessed by old-fashioned ideas of property; almost anything in existence they imagine can be appropriated as a man's 'own', and then he has an absolute right to do what he likes with his 'own', deny its use to the commonweal, destroy it, let it at a rack rent, hold it for some exorbitant price.

"Rarely have these obstructives the whole-hearted support of their communities behind them—so much has to be conceded to the propaganda of the Modern State and to the general diffusion of our ideas and the spontaneous appearance of fresh and kindred idea systems. We are preparing a schedule of obstructives. They vary in scale from the single tiresome litigious individual with an old- fashioned clutching mind, through a long range of associations, cities and provincial councils, to the resuscitated sovereign governments of the war period. Two royal families have been exhumed from their retirement in the German-speaking part of

Europe and more, it is said, are to follow. On various of our routes, notably on the Bordeaux-Black Sea road, the old Chinese claim for 'likin' has reappeared. Our lorries have been held up at Ventimiglia, where a 'dogana' has been erected by the Fascist government in Rome, a barrier has been put across the track, and payments have been demanded in the name of the King of Italy. There have also been demands for Octroi dues outside some French and Italian towns.

"A legal committee of the Modern State Faculty of Social Psychology is taking up the question of these new impediments to world revival and unification, and it will prepare a plan of action in the course of the next month. This attempt to revive the proprietary strangulation which ended the old order is irritating and may develop into very grave obstruction. The former world system of ownership and administration was in complete liquidation before 1960, and we have no intention of buying it out at anything above scrap rates. We deny absolutely any claim to enhanced values created by our restoration of production and commerce."

7. INTELLECTUAL ANTAGONISM TO THE MODERN STATE

The earliest known histories are dynastic. They are little more than lists of priest-kings and kings and tribes and contributions. With Herodotus history became political. It was only in the eighteenth century (C.E.) that economic processes came into the story, and only after the time of Karl Marx that their essential importance was recognized. Later still, climatic, biological and geographical changes were woven into the historical tapestry. Not until the last hundred years have education, cultural influences and psychological sequences generally been given their proper rôle in the human drama.

The most difficult thing in our understanding of the past is to realize, even in the most elementary form, the mental states of those men and women, who seem so deceptively like ourselves. They had bodies on exactly the same pattern as ours, if not so well exercised, well nourished and uniformly healthy; they had brains as capable as ours and as complicated. It is only when we compare their conduct with ours that we realize that, judged by their contents and their habits of reaction, those brains might almost have belonged to another species of creature.

We read incredulously about the public burning of religious heretics, of the torture of criminals to enforce confession, of murders and outrages, of the offence of rape, of the hunting and tormenting of animals for "sport", of men and women paying money for the pleasure of throwing sticks at a tethered cock until it died, and it is hard to resist the persuasion that our ancestors were insane. Most of us, were we suddenly put back into the London of King Henry VIII, would be as frightened, and frightened in the same way, as if we were put into a ward of unattended criminal lunatics. But the brains of these people were no more diseased than ours. Their mental habit systems had been built up on a different framework; and that is the whole difference.

It was perfectly sane men who made the World War, who allowed the private capitalist system to smash itself to fragments in spite of reiterated warnings, and who came near to destroying mankind. If the reader were sent back only for the hundred and seventy years between now and 1933, he would still feel a decided uneasiness about what people might or might not do next. Yet as he fought down his alarm and went about among them he would have found them as completely satisfied of the sanity of their own mental shapes as he was.

Presently he would have found himself trying to adapt himself to those mental shapes. In the end he might come to realize that, in his own case also, it might be

that the things he felt compelled to believe and do, and the things he found impossible to believe and do, though they had served his everyday purposes in his own time fairly well, were no more final in the scheme of things than the ideology that framed the motives and acts of a Roman emperor or a Sumerian slave.

The difficulty in the comparison and understanding of past mental states with our own increases rather than diminishes as we approach the present, because the differences become more subtle and more interwoven with familiar phrases and with values we accept. We cannot keep in mind that meanings are perpetually being expanded or whittled away. We live to-day so saturated in our circumstances, so full of the security, abundance and vitalizing activity of our world-commonweal, that it is hard to realize how recently it was possible for minds of the highest intelligence to call the most fundamental conceptions of our present order in question. Even in the middle Twentieth Century, ideas that now seem so natural and necessary to us that we cannot imagine them disputed, appeared extravagant, impossible and offensive to brains that were in their essential quality just as good as the best alive to-day.

In the early half of the Twentieth Century a great majority of educated and intelligent men and women had no faith whatever in the Modern State; they hated it, feared it and opposed it, and it is doubtful whether the balance was redressed until the Twenty-first Century was well under way. The Modern State was built up, by comparatively mediocre men, upon whom the necessary group of ideas happened to strike with compelling force. As H. Levy insisted in his Universe of Science as early as 1932 (Historical Documents: General Ideas Series, 192301), science is a "social venture" rather than an accumulation of individual triumphs. Both the scientific idea and the idea of the human community were not individual but social products. And the Modern State prevailed because its logic steadily conquered not this man in particular nor that man in particular, but the sense of fitness in the general human intelligence.

Maxwell Brown, in his monumental studies of the growth of the Modern State idea, has made a fairly exhaustive review of the art and literature of the early Twentieth Century. Except in the writings of a few such sociologists as J. A. Hodson, Harry Elmer Barnes, James Harvey Robinson, C. A. and Mary Beard, Raymond B. Fosdick and a few American and English journalists, and in such alarmist fantasies as Aldous Huxley's Brave New World, there is no sense whatever of the immense revolutionary changes that were occurring in the social structure. Bernard Shaw, for example, though classed as a revolutionary writer, never, except in his preposterous Back to Methuselah, anticipated. The mass of his work was a witty and destructive commentary upon contemporary things, ending in that petition in bankruptcy, Too True to be Good. He had to a supreme degree the opposition mentality of the Irish.

This estrangement of literature from the Modern State movement became more marked throughout the nineteen twenties and thirties. As reality became urgent, as war and insolvency descended upon social life, literature, art and criticism recoiled into studies and studios and their own bitter and peculiar Bo-

hemia; they became elaborately stylistic and "rare", or brilliantly or brutally smutty.

This decadence of literature, says Maxwell Brown, was an inevitable expression of the economic decadence of the Thirties and Forties. He draws an illuminating contrast between the type of mind primarily directed towards aestheticism and the type of mind primarily directed towards science. The "aesthetic producer", he insists, is dominated by acceptance; he writes for response. The scientific worker aims at knowledge and is quite indifferent whether people like or dislike the knowledge he produces. Aesthetic life therefore is conditioned by the times; science conditions the times.

Literature and art are necessarily time-servers, either abjectly so or aggressively and pretentiously so. They deflect real moods or speculate upon possible moods in the community. It is no good writing books that people will not read or painting pictures from which they merely turn away. Psychology in those days had not developed sufficiently to permit of a scientific analysis of creative work, and such criticism as there was, when it was not a simple release of spite, was essentially an effort either to persuade or to browbeat people into buying books and pictures or listening to music of a type fancied by the critic. It was more bitterly partisan and propagandist than political discussion.

In the expansive phase of the later nineteenth century the general confidence of the prosperous classes was reflected in a large, hopeful, forward- looking complacent literature, and every critic was, so to speak, an uncle, a prosperous uncle, sitting by the fire, but the sense of contraction and advancing dangers that troubled the patrons of art and literature as the twentieth century unfolded threw a defensive quality over the intellectual world, outside the spheres of science and invention. The progressive note was popular no longer. The reading offered to the people was pervaded by a nagging hostility to new things, by lamentations for imaginary lost loyalties and vanished virtues.

It was not so much that the writers of the time desired civilization to retrace its steps, as that they wished that no more steps should be taken. They wanted things to stop—oh, they wanted them to stop! The underlying craving was for consolidation and rest before more was lost. There was little coherent system in the objections taken; it was objection at large. Mass production was very generally reprehended; science rarely got a good word; war—with modern weapons—was condemned, though much was to be said for the "chivalrous" warfare of the past; there were proposals to "abolish" aeroplanes and close all the laboratories in the world; it was assumed that hygiene, and especially sexual hygiene, "robbed life of romance"; the decay of good manners since the polished days of Hogarth, Sir Charles Grandison and Tony Lumpkin was deplored, and the practical disappearance of anything that could be called Style. As one nineteenth-century American writer lamented, in suitably archaic English:

"How life hath cheapened, and how blank The Worlde is! like a fen Where long ago unstained sank The starrie gentlemen: Since Marston Moor and Newbury drank King Charles his gentlemen."

That was the dominant note.

Maxwell Brown gives a volume of material, quotations (Literature Hangs Back; Historical Documents: General Ideas Series 311002) from about four thousand representative books and papers.

As the world emerged again from the sheer desolation of the Famished Fifties and the great pestilence, this purely opposition mentality revived in hundreds of thousands of elderly literate people whose brains had been fitted and turned round in that way for good. It revived because it was all there was to revive in them; and it met with all too ready and natural an acceptance among those endless myriads of cleverish active people who were now trying to get private businesses and private profit systems going before it became too late for ever, between the expanding system—of the Transport Control and its collaterals above, and the inarticulate and still needy masses below. They did not realize how much the revival of prosperity was due to the new organization. It was not in their type of mind to want to account for revivals of prosperity. What they desired to do was to take advantage of the "turn of luck". To them from the first the Transport Control appeared as a formidable competitor, harsh in spirit and still harsher in method, which had set itself to prevent smaller brighter folk making hay while the sun shone. They were only too eager to see it as a huge, cheap, nasty, vulgar menace to all the jolly little profits and rewards and assurances that were peeping up again in life. For the loyalty and obedience of servants, it offered them ingenious mechanical arrangements; for the labour of respectful toilers, it suggested indifferent and dangerous power machinery. Are we not wise and virtuous enough in ourselves, they asked, that this World Control should come "tidying us up"?

Manifestly the new order was resolved to "incorporate" (hateful word!), if it could, all these would-be privileged, would-be irresponsible people. Its face was hard towards them. Its hygienic and educational activities threatened an increasing regulation of their lives. It proposed to rob them of the natural excitements and adventure of gambling and speculation; to deprive them of the legitimate advantages of their foresight and business flair. It threatened them with service; service and ever more service—a rôle, they insisted, that would be unendurably "monotonous". They wanted to be good sometimes and bad sometimes and jump from this to that. A "soulless uniformity" became the bugbear of these recalcitrant minds.

The workers often resented Modern State methods almost as much as their immediate employers. Men have always been difficult to educate and reluctant to submit themselves to discipline, and there was a curious suggestion of the schoolmaster about these fellows of the Modern State nuclei. Dislike of what was at hand helped to conjure up fears of what might lie beyond. Once freedom of business had gone, what rules and regulations might not presently enmesh the wilful individual under the thumb of this one world employer? For instance, the Modern State centres were talking of a control of population; it was easy to see in that a hideous invasion of the most private moments in life. Weights and measures and money to-day, and wives and parentage tomorrow!

These widely diffused repugnances, fears and antagonisms were enhanced by the difficulties put in the way of aspirants to the Modern State Fellowship and to positions of responsibility in the service of the Controls. Jobs were not for everyone. Rejected candidates to the Fellowship were among the most energetic of Modern State antagonists. By 1970, all over the world, wherever the remains of the old prosperous and educated classes of "independent" and business people were to be found, appeared associations to combat the activities of the Modern State nuclei. There were Liberty Clubs and Free Trade Associations; there were Leagues of Citizens, Trade Protection Chambers and "Return to Legality" societies. There were organized religious and patriotic revivals. The Modern State schools were discovered to be immoral, unpatriotic and anti-religious. It was extraordinary how the money-changers hurried to the deserted temples and clamoured for the return of Christ.

Every town and city found someone or other—as often as not it was some elderly lawyer or politician from the old days—keen to revive and protect its privileges. The world heard once more of the rights of peoples and nations to be free and sovereign within their borders. A hundred different flags fluttered more abundantly every day about the reviving earth in the sacred name of freedom. Even men who were engaged in organizing debt-serf cultivation and debt- serf industrialism in the American cotton districts, in the old rubber plantations and in the factories of India, China and South Italy, appeared as generous supporters of and subscribers to the sacred cause of individual liberty.

The behaviour of the inferior masses showed a wide divergence of reactions. The widespread communist propaganda of the War Years and the Famished Fifties had intensified their natural hostility to the profit-seeking bourgeoisie, and there was little chance of their making common cause with them; but the Modern State Society, with the lessons of Russia before it, had no disposition to exacerbate the class war for its own ends. It knew quite clearly that to appeal to the mere insurrectionary impulse of the downtrodden was to invite the specialist demagogue, sustained by his gang and his heelers, his spies and secret police, to take the chair in the council chamber.

De Windt had driven that point well home. "Creative revolution cannot cooperate with insurrectionary revolution." There was to be no flattery of ignorance and inferiority as though they were the keys to an instinctive wisdom; no incitement to envy and jealousy against knowledge and ability. The Modern State meant to abolish toil, and that meant to abolish any toiling class, proletariat, labour mass, serf or slave, whatever it was called, but it had no intention of flattering and using the oafish mental as well as physical limitations it meant to liberate from existence altogether. It took the risk that the forces of reaction would organize strikes and mass resistance against its regulations, its economies of employment, its mechanization, its movements of population and the like, among the other inevitable difficulties of its task.

So the world-stage was set for the triangular drama of the late Twentieth and early Twenty-first Centuries, in which reaction in a thousand forms, and Modern

State organization in one, struggled against each other to subjugate or assimilate the more or less passive majority of mankind.

We write in outline, and necessarily in an elementary history it is only the primary lines that can be given. But just as when we enlarge our scale of observation, the broad divisions of a map vanish and countries and divisions become hills, valleys, buildings, forests, roads, and at last, when we come to earth, stones, pebbles, blades of grass and flowers, so this rough division of humanity into three intermingled and intensely interacting multitudes was in reality qualified by a thousand million individual complications.

On the whole the content of people's minds was far more intricate then than it is now. That is a principle the student of history must never forget. The intellectual progress of mankind had been a continual disentanglement and simplification leading to increased grasp and power. These closing decades of the Age of Frustration were still, in comparison with our own time, a time of uncertainties, inaccuracies, mixed motives, irrational surprises and bitter late realizations. There was scarcely an unskilled toiler in the world who was really no more than a passive clod in the hands of his exploiters and employers. There was scarcely a reactionary who did not in some fashion want tidiness and efficiency. And, conversely, there was hardly a Fellow of the Modern State organization, man or woman, who had not spasms of acute self- seeking and vanity, who could not be doctrinaire, intolerant and vindictive on occasion, who could not be touched by the sentimental and aesthetic values of the old order, and who did not like, love and react to scores of people incurably shaped to the opposition pattern.

The New Fiction of the Eighties and Nineties is enormously preoccupied with this universal battle of ideas and mental habits in people's minds. The simpler novels of the earlier past and the novels of the present day tell of individual character in a set battle between good and bad in a world of undisputed standards; but the novels of those years of social conflict tell of a wild confusion between two sorts of good and two sorts of bad and of innate character distorted in a thousand ways. It was a difficult age. Life still has its endless ironies and ambiguities, but they are as nothing to those amidst which the men of 1970 had to steer their courses.

8. THE SECOND CONFERENCE AT BASRA, 1978

The second Conference at Basra, though many of its prominent figures had already played leading rôles in the earlier gathering in 1965, was very different in scale, scope and spirit from that assembly. It was an older gathering. The average age, says Amen Rihani, was a full ten years higher. Young men were still coming into the Fellowship abundantly, but there had also been accessions—and not always very helpful accessions—of older men who had been radical and revolutionary leaders in the war period. Their frame of experience had shaped them for irresponsible resistance. Their mental disposition was often obstructively critical and insubordinate. Many had had no sort of technical experience. They were disposed to throw an anarchistic flavour over schools and propaganda.

Moreover, the great scheme of the Modern State had now lost something of its first compelling freshness. The "young men of '65" had had ten years of responsible administrative work. They had been in contact with urgent detail for most of that period. They had had to modify De Windt's generalizations in many particulars, and the large splendour of the whole project no longer had the same dominating power over their minds. They had lost something of the professional esprit de corps, the close intimate confidence with each other, with which they had originally embarked upon the great adventure of the Modern State. Many had married women of the older social tradition and formed new systems of gratification and friendship. They had ceased to be enthusiastic young men and they had become men of the world. The consequent loss of a sure touch upon primary issues was particularly evident in the opening sessions.

Moreover, the atmosphere of the 1965 gathering had been purely a Modern State atmosphere. Except for the Russian political representatives, there had been no antagonism at all to its general purposes, and there had been few people in Basra who were not Fellows of the Modern State Society or closely sympathetic with its aims. But now the reviving nationalisms, the resuscitating social and commercial interests of the moribund old world system, were acutely aware of the immense significance of events at Basra, and there had gathered an assemblage of delegations, reporters, adventurers, friends and camp followers of every description, far exceeding the numbers of the actual Fellows. They crowded the Control rest houses that clustered about the aerodrome, they invaded the offices and residences of the Controls, they stimulated the private enterprise hotels and restaurants that had recently sprung up among the date palms and rice fields of the environs, to an unprecedented congestion and liveliness, and multitudes of them

had to be accommodated in tents and houseboats. A number of thirty-year-old hulls of passenger liners were fitted for their accommodation. Observers were reminded of the tourist period of the First Age of General Prosperity when they saw these uninvited visitors, chaffering with the old-world Bagdad carpet traders and Arab nomads who had also been attracted by the gathering.

There would probably have been a far greater multitude drawn to Basra if the Transport Control had not realized in time the social and hygienic dangers of too great a gathering, and had refused passages and limited bookings. Casual individuals were eliminated as much as possible, and all over the world groups of stranded pilgrims found themselves unable to get further on the journey.

The most serious of these invaders were the delegations of enquiry sent by the reawakening sovereign governments of the old order. These were half diplomatic, half official-expert, teams, and they came with the declared intention of challenging the activities of the Controls in their several territories. They proposed to legalize and regulate the Controls. They had no formal standing in the Conference; they had invited themselves and given the Conference organizers notice of their coming. "Better now than later," said the Modern State officials, and accepted notice and provided accommodation. "We have to have things out with them," Williams Kapek wrote to Isabel Garden (The Kapek Garden Letters. Historical Documents Series: Basra II 9376).

Beside these "old government" agencies there were a number of parties claiming to represent various new business combines and interests that were setting up in frank competition with the Control monopolies. There were a number of lawyers of the older type, men in sharp contrast and antagonism to the younger legists of the new American school. The contrast of the two types, the older all pomp and dodges and the younger all candour and science, is dwelt upon lengthily by Kapek.

"This Conference is essentially a conference on Scientific and Mercantile Communications and Associated Questions, similar to that held at Basra in 1965"; so ran a printed notice circulated to all the visitors who could claim any representative status. "Its discussions are open only to the Fellows of the faculties of the Modern State Society. They are not public discussions and their reports are for the use of Fellows only. But it would be disingenuous to deny that the decisions arrived at may affect the general welfare of mankind profoundly, and since you come to present criticisms, claims and proposals presumably in that interest, the committee of organization of the Conference will do all it can to facilitate meetings between your group and the faculty or faculties affected. Unfortunately the accommodation for meetings in Basra will be greatly strained by the needs of the actual Conference, and the committee can do little to arrange conferences between the immense variety of accredited bodies that have made an appearance, much less to arrange for their pleasures and comforts during the period of this assembly. The committee regrets that it does not consider the proposal of the committee of Bagdad citizens, claiming to represent the government of Irak, to police this unexpected World Fair with 300 Arab policemen, a camel corps of seventy-nine

men and six machine-guns, as a practicable one. It has removed this body painlessly to comfortable quarters in the Island of Ormuz, and the Police of the Air and Sea Ways in its recognizable uniform will be alone responsible for order in the ancient province of Bassorah."

Explicit details of information bureaus, hospital organization, supply and available accommodation followed.

It is difficult to see how else the Central Control could have dealt with this unexpectedly abundant eruption of the old system, but the various delegations and commissions professed to be extremely indignant at their reception. They were of such various and unequal value, that they found it impossible to fall into any combined scheme of action. Since their theory was that the Controls and the Modern State organization were nothing more than a sort of world cooperative society, none of them could behave as diplomatic missions to a sovereign power. And consequently they could not regard each other as diplomatic missions. Their powers and authorizations were extremely ill- defined. The bland refusal of the Conference authorities to concede them meeting-places and anything but a very limited use of telephonic, cable and radio communications embarrassed them extremely.

"I met Sir Horatio Porteous, the British Imperial representative, in the street," writes Williams Kapek. "He was very eager to get my advice upon a point of etiquette. It seems that we have seized the province of Bassorah from the government of Irak and made prisoners of an alleged local police—those fifty lousy camels and the rest of it I told you about in my last—and that Irak is a mandatory protectorate under Great Britain. He wished to put in a protest somewhere. 'But WHERE?' said he.

"I adopted a sympathetic tone. 'You see,' said Sir Horatio, 'this Central Control of yours isn't any damned thing at all! If it was a provisional government or something...'

"I suggested a call on the Air and Sea Police.

"'But they are acting under orders. Who gives the orders? It's all so damned irregular!...'"

There was a flutter of calls between the delegations, some "serious talks" and much drafting of more or less futile minutes, reports and protests. The weather was exceptionally hot and dry and such space and apparatus as was available for exercise and recreation was monopolized by the more energetic Fellows who were taking part in the Conference proper. It was difficult to keep cool, difficult to keep calm; still more difficult to keep well and hopeful. Some few of the intrusive delegates and commissioners took to drinking hard, but the supply of alcohol was severely limited and the police had turned practically all the professional ministers of pleasure out of the province. On the other hand, the Transport Control, in a mood of friendly indulgence, started a special service of pleasure steamers to Bubiyan, outside the jurisdiction of its police, and there a floating little mushroom town of cafés, restaurants, houses of pleasure, music halls and

shows of every sort speedily sprung up to minister to the unofficial overflow of the Conference.

"Bubiyan is draining us quite pleasantly," wrote Williams Kapek, "and they say there is quite a boom in entertainment for man and beast in Babylon and Bagdad. The old British institution of the long week-end flourishes and Babylon gets more and more Babylonian."

But there were still plenty of outsiders left in Basra to keep the faculties busy.

Meanwhile the Conference was going on behind closed doors. It was clearly recognized that this curious mélange of agents, delegates and officials from without its organization was only the first intimation of the confused antagonisms that were gathering against the new order. The policy of expansion and quiet disregard had lasted long enough. The pretence of being a Conference upon communications and associated matters had to be dropped. The time had come for the Modern State to define itself and clear up its relations to the past out of which it had arisen, and to all this world of tradition which was now rapping at its doors.

"Before we disperse," said Arden Essenden, who presided at the first plenary session, "we must admit some at least of these delegations, hear them and give them answers to take home with them. But first we have to know our mind much more clearly. What are we now and what do we intend to do? The days before us begin a new chapter in human history. It is for us to choose the heading and plan that chapter now."

9. "THREE COURSES OF ACTION"

There was no dominant individual of the De Windt character and quality at the second Basra Conference. There was no prophetic direction of the deliberations. But there was no want of what used to be called "leadership", and a number of interesting personalities, the politic Hooper Hamilton; the frank, emphatic William Ryan; the intricate Shi-lung-tang; M'bangoi, the East African biologist; Rin Kay, the social psychologist—perhaps the finest mind in the gathering; Mohini L. Tagore; Morowitz, the mystical humanist; and Arden Essenden, the fanatic of action, gave point and definition to the differences of opinion.

They were interesting rather than outstanding men because the general level of intelligence was a high one. The gathering had a personality of its own, wary, resolved to be well informed and to weigh considerations, but essentially determined. The presence of that miscellany of delegations and commissions which besieged the Conference dramatized the world situation and pressed for decisions. "I feel like one of those old world jurymen," wrote Williams Kapek, "who used to be locked up together until they returned a verdict. And you cannot imagine how hot and dry Basra can sometimes contrive to be."

De Windt and his school of writers had planned the framework of a new world and shown to what social elements one had to look for its evocation, but he had given only the most scanty suggestions for getting rid of the body of the old. Already in 1965 the Modern State people had had a fairly distinct vision of our present order. But few of them had anticipated the diffused toughness of the old corpus and its capacity for counter-revolutionary exertion. That had become oppressively evident by 1975.

Reports on the general situation had been very carefully prepared. They dealt with the various centres at which the spirit of opposition was being organized. Most serious of these were those former sovereign governments and legal systems, which had seemed effaced, moribund or prostrate during the desolation of the Famished and Fever-stricken Fifties. In 1965 the only government actively antagonistic to the Controls had been the Soviet government in Russia. That antagonism, curiously enough, was not so great as it had been at first. The technicians of the sovietized regions were ousting the politicians; there was now indeed a working cooperation of Russian transport, communications and production with the world system under the Controls, and there seemed a reasonable prospect of ultimate assimilation. There was no objection being made to people nominally communists who were also Fellows of the Modern State, and many

Russian scientific and technical workers were Modern State Fellows and not members of the communist party at all. The reports discussed hopefully and analytically the possibility of some similar process in America and the Far East. There also the political and legal structures did not present insurmountable obstacles to assimilation. The decline of humbug in America was bringing out the fundamental constructive energy of that great synthesis of Western peoples. But elsewhere there was increasing evidence that the sovereign state system and the system of private ownership were fundamentally irreconcilable with the new conceptions.

The reports gave information, that was in many particulars new to most of the assembled Fellows, of the very strenuous attempts that were being made by the reviving national governments in Germany, France, Italy and Great Britain to resume the manufacture of aeroplanes and war material. Whether there was a common agreement among them was doubtful, but the intention to put up air forces and organize aerodromes that should be able to ignore the regulations and refuse the services of the Air and Sea Control was quite plain. They were finding great difficulty in securing the services of competent engineers, mechanics and aviators, but the thing was going on. Every student in the technical schools of the Control who failed a test or an examination, or was penalized for misbehaviour or rejected from the Modern State Fellowship, would turn up presently as a national government expert. And the governments were now setting up their own national technical schools and attempting to bring the schools and laboratories of the Control into the "national" educational organization. Not only was there a disposition to set up a competing system side by side with the Controls system, but there was a growing tendency to annex the organizations, roads, plant, mines, factories, aerodromes, schools, colleges, laboratories and personnel of the Control that chanced to be within the jurisdiction of the sovereign government concerned. The new Bavarian government, the Windsor Parliament and the government in Rome were all "arranging to take over" these things within their territories. They were becoming more explicit about it every year. They persisted in regarding the interlocking Controls as a dangerous international Trust.

This was the burthen of the national missions of observation and enquiry which were stewing in the sunshine outside the doors of the Conference—"in a state of tentative menace", as Williams Kapek put it.

The minor delegations representing groups of owners and organized local interests had this much in common with the national missions, that they proposed more or less frankly to resume possession of properties the Controls had taken hold of and revived, or to impose burthensome charges. They varied like the inmates of a zoological garden in scale and power, but they had one quality in common: an obstructive litigiousness.

In the frankness of its privacy behind its closed doors, the Conference sized up these antagonisms and discussed their treatment. "There are just three lines of treatment possible," said Ryan brutally. "We can treat with 'em, bribe 'em, or rule 'em. I'm for a straight rule."

"Or combine those ingredients," said Hooper Hamilton.

The method of treaty-making and a modus vivendi was already in operation in regard to Russia. There indeed it was hard to say whether the communist party or the Modern State movement was in control, so far had assimilation gone. And the new spirit in the old United States was now so "Modern", that the protests of Washington and of various state governors against the Controls were received hilariously. Aeroplanes from Dearborn circled over the capital and White House and dropped parodies of the President's instructions to dissolve the Air and Food Trust of America. All over that realist continent, indeed, the Controls expanded as a self-owned business with a complete disregard of political formalities. But the European situation was more perplexing.

"Most of these European sovereign governments are no more than scarecrows," said William Ryan. "There's no living people behind them any longer. Leastway, no living people that matter. Call their bluff on them and you'll hear no more about them."

It was Shi-lung-tang who argued against defiance and stated the case for Bribery.

Bribery in his suave exposition, bribery combined with treaties and tact, became a highly moral amelioration of direct action. He asked the Conference to realize how specialized and rare as yet was its new forward-looking habit of mind. When all the work of the propaganda and schools had been accounted for, it was doubtful if a twentieth part of the race accepted, or if a tenth understood, even in the most general terms, the difference between minds trained to creative conceptions and minds brought up in an atmosphere of defensive acquisitiveness and property accumulation. It would take three or four generations to convert the world to a forward-looking attitude. Either the Modern State movement had to seize power openly now and inaugurate a tyranny that would have to last as long as it took to turn round the great majority of intelligences into the new direction, or it had to propitiate, compromise and persuade these outer masses—UPON THEIR OWN LINES.

"These people will never see things as we see them," he insisted, making strange gestures and repeating his words to emphasize their importance. "They have to live and die, ON THEIR OWN LINES. It is not just to impose too much upon them. It is only as they die out that the Modern State form of mind can hope to be in a dominant majority. Their mental vices are incurable. Meet them half way, make things easy for them. You will save the world three generations of suffering and bitter conflict."

He unfolded his Machiavellian project. A greedy acquisitiveness was part of the make-up of every energetic old world-type. They were as incurably voracious as dogs. And yet we made good friends and helpers out of dogs. Their loyalties were at best gang loyalties; they were none the less greedy because they did at times hunt in packs. But they had no fundamental instinctive hostility to the Modern State. It was only when the Modern State thwarted their established habits of behaviour that they snarled at it and began to fear it. They could never make a

solid front against the Modern State. They could always be played off against each other, one against another; they could be neutralized. The lesson of Russia's harsh repression of her bourgeoisie and professional classes in the Twenties and Thirties was a warning against the miseries and social damage of too sudden and forcible an attempt to change ideals of behaviour. Let the Modern State go more softly and more kindly.

He went on to detailed suggestions. With Russia, Spain and America, bribery need play but a minor rôle. The ruling mentality in these countries was now such that the present working agreements would pass naturally into assimilation in a little while. Elsewhere there was really no permanent harm in recognizing the old claims to sovereign and proprietary rights, and securing such a hold upon leading men that they would keep their hands off the Modern State propaganda and schools and be content with handsome subsidies from the Control services and industries. It would be cheaper than war. "If they want a little war now and then among themselves—"

In spite of Shi-lung-tang's smiling face, there was audible disapproval at this point.

When he had done, his case for tact and insinuating corruption was knocked to pieces by Rin Kay. "If we were a Society of Moral Supermen," he said, "we might venture to be as disingenuous as this." But Mr. Shi-lung-tang forgot that every Fellow in the Modern State society had two enemies: the acquisitive man outside and the acquisitive man within. The point their Chinese friend missed was the fact that it was much more natural to adopt the behaviour patterns of the old world than to acquire those of the Modern State. The old dispositions were something that was; the new dispositions were something that had to be made and sustained. The inner life of a Modern State Fellow was a sustained effort to be simple and serve simply. That should take him all his time. He could not afford to be intricate and politic. "We have a difficult enough task before us just to do what we have to do, plainly and honestly. We cannot afford to say and do THIS and mean THAT." William Ryan supported that with vigour, but Hooper Hamilton spoke long and elaborately on the other side. The spirit of the society was plainly with Kay.

M. L. Tagore, an economic botanist, introduced a new line of thought into the discussion, or rather he revived the line of thought of nineteenth-century mystical liberalism. He said he was equally against bribery, insincere treaties or any use of force. He was old-fashioned enough to be a democrat and a believer in the innate wisdom of the unsophisticated man. And also he believed in the supreme value of truth and inaggressiveness. We must not outrage the sense of right in man, even if that meant the abandonment of our immediate objectives. We had to persuade him. And we had no right to assume that he did not hold himself to be right because his conception of conduct differed from ours. Let the Modern State society go on with the scientific organization of the world, yes, and let us go on with the propaganda of its doctrines in every land. But let it not lift a hand to compel, not even to resist evil. He appealed to the missionary successes of early Buddhism and Christianity as evidence of the practical successfulness of spiritual urgency

and physical passivity. He concluded in a glow of religious enthusiasm, that did not spare him the contemptuous criticisms of the social psychologists who fell upon him tooth and nail so soon as he had done.

These speeches, which are to be found in full in the Basra Conference Reports, vols. 371 and 372, were the three salient types of opinion in that gathering. The immense majority were for the active line, for frankness and rule. A not inconsiderable minority, however, wavered behind the leadership of Hooper Hamilton. They felt that there were elaborations and refinements that did not find expression in the more aggressive speeches, that the use of force could be tempered by tact and that lucidity towards an objective was compatible with kindliness and concession.

In a number of speeches some of them tried to express this rather elusive conception of compromise; some of them were not too skilful as speakers, they went too far in the opposite direction, and on the whole they tended to drive the movement towards a harder assertiveness than it might otherwise have expressed. The problems of the Russian system and America were abundantly discussed. Russia now was represented only by technicians and there was abundant evidence that the repressive influence of the Og-pu had waned. Ivan Englehart was again a leading figure. He assured the Conference that there would be no trouble from Moscow. "Russia," he said, "is ready to assimilate. Is eager to assimilate."

Arden Essenden spoke late in the general discussion; he spoke with a harsh enthusiasm and passionate faith; he carried all the younger men and most of the older ones with him and he shaped the ultimate decisions.

Some of his phrases are, as people used to say, "historical". He said, "The World-State is not a thing of the Future. It is here and now. It has always been here and now, since ever men said they had a common God above them, or talked, however timidly, of the brotherhood of mankind. The man who serves a particular state or a particular ownership in despite of the human commonweal is a Traitor. Men who did that have always been Traitors and men who tolerated them nursed treason in their hearts. In the past the World-State had been torn up among three-score-and-ten anarchies and a countless myriad of proprietors and creditors, and the socialists and cosmopolitans, the true heirs of the race, were hunted like criminals and persecuted and killed.

"Now, through the utter failure of those robbers even to maintain their own social order and keep at peace among themselves, the world has fallen into our hands. Power has deserted them, and we, we here, have Power. If we do not use it, if we do not use it to the fullest, we are traitors in our turn. Are we to tolerate even a temporary revival of the old system? In the name of reason, why? If their brains have got into the wrong grooves—well, we can make fresh brains. Are we to connive with, and indulge this riffraff that waits outside our doors? Go out and look at them. Look at their insincere faces! Look at their furtive hands. Weigh what they say. Weigh the offers they will make you!"

To us to-day that seems platitudinous and over emphatic, but it conveyed the sense of the Conference and it led directly to the general decision with which its

proceedings concluded. The most significant of these was the increase of the Police of the Air and Sea Ways to a million men, and the apportionment of a greatly increased amount of energy to the improvement of their equipment. There was also to be a great intensification and speeding up of Modern State education and propaganda. Provision was also made for the enlistment of auxiliary forces and services as they might be needed for the preservation of order; these auxiliaries were to renounce any allegiance except to the Transport or other Control that might enlist them. The Controls were reorganized, and a central committee, which speedily became known as the World Council, was appointed by them to act as the speaking head of the whole system. The ideas of treaties and contracts with exterior administrations and of any diplomatic dealings with dissentients were abandoned. Instead it was determined that this central committee, the World Council, should openly declare itself the sole government of the world and proceed to make the associated Controls the administrative organization of the planet.

Accordingly a proclamation was prepared to this effect and issued very widely. It was broadcast as well as printed and reprinted from a multitude of centres. It was "put upon the ether" everywhere to the exclusion of other matter. For now the world had its wireless again in as great abundance already as in the early Thirties. So simultaneously the whole planet received it. It whipped up the awaiting miscellany at Basra into a foam of excited enquiry. All over the world city crowds or solitary workers received it, open-mouthed. At first there was very little discussion. The effect was too stunning for that. People began to talk after a day or so.

We give it as it was issued: a singularly poor piece of prose when we consider the magnificence of its matter. It seems to have been drafted by Arden Essenden, with some assistance from Hamilton and amended in a few particulars by the Council.

"The Council for World Affairs, constituted by the Air and Sea Control and its associates, declares:

"That between 1950 and 1965 this planet became derelict through the incapacity of its ostensible rulers and property owners to keep the peace, regulate production and distribution, and conserve and guide the common life of mankind;

"That chaos ensued, and

"That it became urgently necessary to build up a new world administration amidst the ruins.

"This the Air and Sea Control did.

"This administration has now been organized about a Central Council for World Affairs, which is making this statement to you.

"It is the only sovereign upon this planet. There is now no other primary authority from end to end of the earth. All other sovereignty and all proprietary rights whatever that do not conduce directly to the general welfare of mankind ceased to exist during the period of disorder, and cannot be revived.

"The Council has its air and sea ways, its airports, dockyards, factories, mines, plantations, laboratories, colleges and schools throughout the world. These are

administered by its officials and protected by its own police, and the latter are instructed to defend these organizations whenever and wherever it may be necessary against the aggression of unauthorized persons.

"In every centre of population there are now Modern State nuclei and Control agents conducting the educational work of the Council and in reasonable contact with the local economic life, with local enterprises, local authorities and individuals not yet affiliated to the Modern State organization. The time has come for all these various quasi independent organs of business and administration to place themselves in orderly relations to the new Government of the Whole World.

"We are constituting a Bureau of Transition, for the simplification and modernization of the business activities, the educational and hygienic services, production, distribution and the preservation of order and security throughout our one home and garden, our pleasure ground and the source of all our riches—the earth, our Mother Earth, our earth and yours.

"Without haste or injustice and without delay, with a due regard to your comfort, your welfare and your wishes, the Bureau will set itself to bring your life into sound and permanent correlation with the one human commonweal."

"It is usurpation!" cried a voice, when the declaration was put to the vote as a whole.

"You decide upon Force," said Shi-lung-tang. "I did my best—"

"But this means War!" cried Tagore.

"No," said Arden Essenden. "There is no more War. This is not War—nor Revolution. This is the recognition of a Revolution and Government again."

10. THE LIFE-TIME PLAN

It is still a debatable question how far that hard decisive declaration of the Socialist World-State at Basra was not premature. There are those who consider it the most timely of acts; there are some who believe it should have been made as early as the first Conference in 1965. The discussion became involved with the intellectual and moral conflicts that went on under the Air Dictatorship. It mingles with the controversies of to-day. But certainly, from 1978 onward, the Modern State movement lost something of its pristine mental freshness, lost openness, lost much of that almost irresponsible adventurousness that had flung the network of transport and trading controls so swiftly about the earth. "We have swallowed the world, but now we have to digest it," said Arden Essenden. The old defiant repudiation of the past was replaced by a firm and sometimes rather heavy insistence upon the order of the future.

There was nowhere any immediate uprising in response to the proclamation of a World Government. Although it had been plainly coming for some years, although it had been endlessly feared and murmured against, it found no opposition prepared anywhere. Thirteen years had wrought a profound change in Soviet Russia and the large areas of China in association with Moscow. The practical assimilation of Soviet Transport and Communications was almost tacitly accepted. The details of the amalgamation were entrusted to committees flying between Moscow and Basra. All over the world, wherever there was any sort of governing or managing body not already associated with the Modern State System, it fell to debating just how and to what extent it could be incorporated or how it could resist incorporation. Everywhere there were Modern State nuclei ready to come into conference and fully informed upon local or regional issues. The plain necessity for a systematic "renucleation" of the world became evident. The "Section of Training and Advertisement" had long since worked out the broad lines of a modus vivendi between the old and the new.

That modus vivendi is called variously The Life Time Plan or—with a memory of that pioneer effort in planning, The Five Year Plan of the Russian Dictatorship—The Thirty Year Plan. Independent businesses that respected certain standards of treatment by the workers, which would accept a certain amount of exterior control, technical and financial, and which maintained a certain standard of efficiency, were to be accorded not simply tolerance but a reasonable protection. Even if their methods were suddenly superseded by new devices, they were to be kept running until they could be wound up, their products were still to be

taken by the Controls. This was far better treatment than was ever accorded superseded producers under the smash-and-grab conditions of the competitive system. In the same way, whenever possible the small owning peasant or the agricultural tenant was not dispossessed; he was given a fixed price for his output, counselled or directed in the matter of improvements and so merged by bearable degrees into the class of agricultural workers. This, as Rupert Bordinesco put it (Brief Explanation: Historical Documents Series 1969), gave them "time to die out". Because it was an integral part of the Life Time Plan that the new generation should be educated to develop a service mentality in the place of a proprietary mentality. There were to be no independent merchants or independent cultivators under twenty in 1980, none under thirty in 1990 and none under forty in 2000. This not only gave the old order time to die out; it gave the new order time to develop the more complex system of direction, mechanism and delivery it needed soundly and healthily. The lesson of the mental discords and tragic disproportions in the headlong development of the first Russian Five Year Plan—disproportions as monstrous and distressful as the hypertrophies and atrophies of the planless "Capitalist System" of the nineteenth century—had been marked and learnt.

It did not trouble the World Council that to retain millions of small businesses and tens of millions of small cultivators the whole world over for so long meant a much lower efficiency of production. "These older people have to be fed and employed," wrote Bordinesco, "and now they will never learn or be able to adapt themselves to a novel routine of life. Help them to do their job a little better. Save them from the smart people who want to prey upon them— usurers, mortgagers, instalment salesmen, intimidators, religious or secular; and for the rest—leave them in peace."

The Brief Explanation also drew a moral from the "Period of Glut" in the Twenties, which preceded the collapse of the Thirties, when the whole world was full of unconsumed goods and unemployed people. This, Bordinesco pointed out, was the inevitable consequence of an unregulated progressive system of private enterprise. "There is no sense in throwing a man out of an employment, however old-fashioned, unless there is a new job for him. There is no sense in bringing children into the world unless there is education, training and useful work for them to do. We have to see that each new generation is arranged numerically in different categories of training and objective from those of its predecessor. The Russians learnt this necessity in their great experiment. As we progress towards a scientific production of primary substances, the actual proportion of agricultural workers, miners, forest wardens, fishermen and so forth in the community must fall. So also the proportion of ordinary industrial workers must fall. The heavy industries will precede the light in that. A certain compensation will be caused by a steady rise in the standard of living and particularly by what De Windt called 'the rebuilding of the world', new cities, new roads, continually renewed houses everywhere." (This was foreshadowed to a certain extent by the French plan for "Outillage National" and the German housing schemes in operation as early as the late Twenties, plans and schemes ultimately strangled by the budget-balancing

fanatics.) But even that diversion of energy from the production of basic materials and small commodities to big structural undertakings would not suffice to use up the continually released human power in the community. At this point appeared what Bordinesco called the "enlarging categories", which were to consume more than they gave. There had to be increasing numbers of people engaged in education, in the developing and ordering of knowledge, in experimental science, in artistic production, in making life more abundant and ample. To that expansion no limit could be set.

"We men have a lease of this planet," runs the Brief Explanation, "for some millions of years. It is foolish not to press on to better life, but it is more foolish to hurry frantically and cruelly. The history of the past two centuries is one sustained warning against the disemployment of men and women for whom there is no other use. Before we teach, our teachers have to learn; before we direct comprehensively, we must have experience in direction. We must always be attempting a little more than we can do, but we must not be attempting the impossible. We must advance without needless delay, but without waste, hurry, or cruelty. Do not be fearful or jealous of the advent of the new conditions. No honest worker, man or woman, has anything to fear from the coming of the Modern State."

11. THE REAL STRUGGLE FOR GOVERNMENT BEGINS

But the rulers of the new World-State, as their enlargements of the Air and Sea Police made manifest, were under no illusion that the new order could be established in the world by declarations and "Brief Explanations", and hard upon its proposals for conferences and assimilations came the organization of its local constabularies and the regulations that made the reorganized nuclei the sole means of communication of independent local authorities, businesses and individuals with the central Controls. In nearly every part of the earth the nuclei had prepared a personnel of sympathizers and auxiliaries, varying in character with local conditions, outside the ranks of the Fellowship. The khaki uniform of the street and road guardians, differing very little then from the one familiar to us today, appeared as if by magic all over the world, and the symbol of the winged disc broke out upon aeroplanes, post offices, telephone and telegraph booths, road signs, transport vehicles and public buildings. There was still no discord with Russia; there the blazon of the wings was put up side by side with the old hammer and sickle.

Nowhere at first was there any armed insurrectionary movement. We realize from this how complete had been the collapse of the organized patriotic states of the World War period. They had no national newspapers, no diplomats, no Foreign Offices any more. There had been no paper for the former and there had been no salaries for the latter. Lacking vocal organs, nationalism as such was silenced. There were, however, protests, in a considerable variety of ineffectiveness, from local self-appointed bodies, and much passive resistance and failure to comply. But even the removal of the winged sign was infrequent, and usually where that occurred nothing further ensued when the air police came whirring out of the sky to replace it.

This phase of tacit acquiescence was, however, only temporary, until the opposition could gather itself into new forms and phases and discover methods of organization. The elements of antagonism were abundant enough. The Fascist garrison in Rome, claiming to be the government of all Italy, was one of the earliest to make its challenge. It had a number of airmen, unlicensed for various reasons by the Transport Control, and it now sent a detachment of its Black Shirts to occupy the new aeroplane factory outside the old Roman town of Turin, and to seize a small aerodrome and whatever air material was to be found in it at Ostia. The winged disc at these two places was replaced by the national fasces. A proc-

lamation was made and disseminated as widely as the restricted means of publication permitted, calling for an assembly of the old League of Nations and reviving a long defunct phrase of President Wilson's, "the self-determination of peoples." The King of Italy, after a diligent search, was found inoffensively farming in Piedmont, and the long closed palace of the Quirinal was reopened and made habitable for him.

The new air police had been waiting with a certain impatience for provocation of this sort. It had been equipped with a new type of gas bomb releasing a gas called Pacificin, which rendered the victim insensible for about thirty-six hours and was said to have no further detrimental effect. With this it now proceeded to "treat" the long resented customs house at Ventimiglia and the factory and aerodrome in dispute.

At Ostia the police planes found a complication of the situation.

An extraordinary ceremony was in progress in the aerodrome. Three new aeroplanes had just been brought thither from the Turin factory, and they were being blessed by the Pope (Pope Alban III).

For the still vital Catholic Church had always been given to the blessing of implements, shops, boats, bridges, automobiles, flags, guns, battleships, new buildings and the like. It was a ceremony that advertised the Church, gratified the faithful, and did no perceptible harm to the objects blessed. And this particular occasion had been made something of a demonstration against the World Council. The Pope had come; the King and the reigning Duce were present. Sound films made only a few minutes before the arrival of the air police show a gathering as brilliant, with its uniforms and canonicals, as anything that might have occurred before the World War. Choristers in cassocks and charming little lace collars chant, acolytes swing censers; the venerable Holy Father sits on a throne under a canopy, on a large crimson-draped platform. There was a muster of at least three thousand Black Shirts.

The action of the Council commander, Luigi Roselli, was precipitate.

The subsequent enquiry intimates pretty clearly that he betrayed anti- clerical bias. He had been chosen for this task because he was himself an Italian, and so, it was thought, less likely to exacerbate any latent nationalist feeling. (It is an interesting sidelight on the times that the Fascist commandatore on the ground was Mario Roselli, his elder half-brother.) His general instructions had been to seize the aerodrome and the aeroplanes with as little violence as possible. The Pacificin was only to be used in case of armed resistance. But the sight of the cassocks, the birettas, the canopies and ornaments and robes, the sound of chanting and the general ecclesiastical atmosphere were too much for the young man's prejudices. His squadron circled in formation over the aerodrome. The ceremony proceeded with dignity in spite of the noise of his propellers. For it seemed incredible that any human being would dare to gas the Pope.

"Let go," said Luigi Roselli, too malicious to realize the brutality of his outrage.

The gas containers came crashing into the arena.

"Just for a moment," says one of the aviators concerned, in a memorable letter, "the chanting rose louder. They showed pluck, those priests. Hardly one of them broke ranks. Then they crumpled up in their places, drifting down on their knees for the most part. It was queer the way you saw the gas spreading among them; it was like a bed of flowers dying and the death spreading out from a lot of centres. The old boy on the throne didn't turn a hair. He had his hands together and his head bowed. You couldn't tell when it took him. The Fascist guard and the King's party weren't anything like so dignified. They gesticulated, they yelled. They were defiant and all that. And some ran about a bit before the stuff got them.

"Of course, you must understand, the whole lot thought they were being killed. None of them could have known anything of this new stuff. WE didn't know until a fortnight ago.

"We had no gas masks on our bird, so I didn't take part in the landing party which seized the new 'planes.

"The last I saw of that aerodrome, it looked like some old Turkish carpet, gone threadbare in places but still with some brightish patches. Perfect garden of sleep. I hope nobody robbed any of them before they came to. But Roselli, I believe, dropped proper instructions about it all in Rome...."

Unhappily the raid had not been so completely bloodless as this young man supposed. A youthful priest, Odet Buanarotti, had been struck on the head by one of the glass containers and killed outright. He was subsequently canonized; the last saint and martyr to be inscribed in the Latin hagiography....

At this point Raven's written transcript breaks off abruptly.

BOOK THE FOURTH - THE MODERN STATE MILITANT

1. GAP IN THE TEXT

So far I have been transcribing, with very little correction and no alteration, the text of Raven's dream book as he left it fully written out. But at this point, that fully written out history breaks off. The record of the next seventy or eighty years is represented only by an untidy mass of notes in the perfectly abominable private shorthand Raven used. Then comes the concluding chapter fully written out again.

I cannot say with any certainty why Raven left this very vital part of his story obscure and confused while he went on to the very last part of all. But I have my own ideas of what happened in his brain. In the first place he had a very human impulse to realize the issue of this world revolution that was unfolding in these notes, and it was easier, therefore, because it was more attractive, for him to write out the later part first. And in the next the intervening matter was really much more intricate for him to handle. It had, if I may use the expression, "come through his mind" with difficulty and against resistances. His general ideas had been prepared for the new wars, for the post- war breakdown and for a world rule based on air power, and they had also been prepared for the steadily progressive World-State of the final phase. But they had not been prepared for the profound and complex mental and spiritual struggles of three-quarters of a century which inaugurated the new order. Those he had not thought out.

Whether it was really a clairvoyant vision he had of a real future text book of history, or whether all this matter was an eruption from his subconscious mind, hardly affects the manifest fact that all this part came against the grain. One of the strongest arguments for the view that this Outline of the Future was evolved by Raven from his inner consciousness is the fact that there are several passages in which he seems to argue with himself, and that the quiet unhurrying assurance of the earlier and later narratives is not sustained in these middle parts.

I do not think it was mere chance that pulled him up precisely at the point when he came to the gassing of the Pope and the martyrdom of Saint Odet of Ostia. I think that this incident struck him as cardinal, as marking a supremely significant corner which humanity was turning. It was something that had to hap-

pen and it was something he had never let his mind dwell upon. It ended a practical truce that had endured for nearly three centuries in the matter of moral teaching, in the organization of motive, in what was then understood as religion. It was the first killing in a new religious conflict. The new government meant to rule not only the planet but the human will. One thing meant the other. It had realized that to its own surprise. And Raven, with an equal surprise, had realized that so it had to be.

Nearly a year earlier the One World-State had been declared at Basra. There already it had been asserted plainly that a new order must insist upon its own specific education, and that it could not tolerate any other forms of training for the world-wide lives it contemplated. But to say a thing like that is not to realize its meaning. Things of that sort had been said before, and passed like musical flourishes across the minds of men. The new government did not apprehend the fullness of its own intentions until this unpremeditated act of supreme sacrilege forced decision upon it. But now it had struck down the very head of Catholic Christianity and killed an officiating priest in the midst of his ministrations. It had gripped that vast world organization, the Catholic Church, and told it in effect to be still for evermore. It was now awake to its own purpose. It might have retreated or compromised. It decided to go on.

Ten days later air guards descended upon Mecca and closed the chief holy places. A number of religious observances were suppressed in India, and the slaughter-houses in which kosher food was prepared in an antiquated and unpleasant manner for orthodox Jews were closed throughout the world. An Act of Uniformity came into operation everywhere. There was now to be one faith only in the world, the moral expression of the one world community.

Raven was taken unawares, as the world of 1978 was taken unawares, by this swift unfolding of a transport monopoly into a government, a social order and a universal faith. And yet the experiment of Soviet Russia and the practical suppression of any other religion than the so-called communism that had been forced upon it might well have prepared his mind for the realization that for any new social order there must be a new education of all who were to live willingly and helpfully in it, and that the core of an education is a religion. Plainly he had not thought out all that such a statement means. Like almost all the liberal-minded people of our time, he had disbelieved in every form of contemporary religion, and he had tolerated them all. It had seemed to him entirely reasonable that minds could be left to take the mould of any pattern and interpretation of life that chanced upon them without any serious effect upon their social and political reactions. It is extraordinary how such contradictory conceptions of living still exist side by side in our present world with only a little mutual nagging. But very evidently that is not going to be accepted by the generations that are coming. They are going to realize that there can be only one right way of looking at the world for a normal human being and only one conception of a proper scheme of social reactions, and that all others must be wrong and misleading and involve destructive distortions of conduct.

Raven's dream book, as it unfolded the history of the last great revolution in human affairs to him, shattered all the evasive optimism, all the kindly disastrous toleration and good fellowship of our time, in his mind. If there was to be peace on earth and any further welfare for mankind, if there was to be an end to wars, plunderings, poverty and bitter universal frustration, not only the collective organization of the race but the moral making of the individual had to begin anew. The formal revolution that had taken place was only the prelude to the real revolution; it provided only the frame, the Provisional Government, within which the essential thing, mental reconstruction, had now to begin.

That precarious first world government with its few millions of imperfectly assimilated adherents, which now clutched the earth, had to immobilize or destroy every facile system of errors, misinterpretations, compensations and self-consolations that still survived to confuse the minds of men; it had to fight a battle against fear, indolence, greed and jealousy in every soul in the world, the souls of its own people most of all, and win. Or it had to lapse. It had to do that within a definite time. If it did not win within that time, then dissension and relapse were inevitable and one more century of blundering and futility would have to be added to the long record of man's martyrdom. This new régime had to clean up the racial mind or fail, and if it failed then in all probability it would leave the race to drift back again to animal individualism, and so through chaos to extinction. Failures in the past had been possible without general disaster, because they were partial and local, but this was the decisive world effort.

2. MELODRAMATIC INTERLUDE

I have remarked already how impersonal is this school history of the year 2006 in comparison with the histories of our own time. Politicians and statesmen pass like the shadows of general forces, royalties peep and vanish like mice behind the wainscot. They vanish at last altogether—unobtrusively. Now and then this history picks out individuals, Henry Ford for instance, or De Windt, Winston Churchill or Woodrow Wilson, not as heroes and leaders but as types and witnesses. They manifest streams of tendency in the social brain, systems of ideas at a point of maximum effectiveness.

Then suddenly at this point the history lapses into something like melodrama. For a phase personalities assume such an importance as to seem to dominate the world's affairs, as Caesar and Cleopatra did or Mirabeau and Marie Antoinette. I think some explanatory links must be missing here, some comments that might have pointed the value of this episode in illuminating the play of motive that led to the Air Dictatorship. But let me give it as it came to me.

The Air and Sea Control and the organization of the associated subsidiary Controls had been the work of a group of keen young men, moved to action by the growing disorder of life and directly inspired by De Windt and his school of writers. They had been full of generosity, enthusiasm and confidence. The first World Council elected in 1978 included most of these leaders of '65, now coming to middle age, one or two older acquisitions and only two additions from among the younger men. Arden Essenden, with his vigour of initiative, was not only the chairman but the natural leader of the first World Council. Only Ivan Englehart could compare with him in power of personality. There were finer and nobler minds present, but none others so emphatic and so available for the crude uses of popular admiration.

There was, it seems, a curiosity in the world about Essenden; his name was better known than any of his colleagues; his portrait, though indeed through nothing worse than acquiescence on his part, got into circulation, as newspapers began to abound again. It was the method of the new world government to have no presidential or secretarial signatures to its public announcements; it was stated simply that the "Control", whichever it was, or the Council suggested, stated, proposed or had decided, and the World-State seal with its winged disc authenticated the document. But the idea spread by impalpable means that Essenden, who was known to have made the decisive speech for immediate world government at the second Basra Conference, might well have put his name whenever that seal appeared. His

prestige grew and came back to his ears. There can be no doubt that his consciousness of a vague exterior support affected his attitude towards his colleagues and their common task.

The historians of our text book, so far as some difficult passages in the stenography can be deciphered, weigh the good and bad effects of this reinforcement of Essenden's natural impatient decisiveness. They bring in other instances and compare him with other dictators. Indisputably there are crises in human affairs so urgent that many worthy considerations and qualifications are better disregarded and overborne rather than that action should be delayed. These critics of our time study the amount of justification that can be made out for Mussolini, for Stalin, Kemal, Hitler and the various other dictators during the economic debacle of the West, and I find this judgment of posterity very discordant with my own profoundly liberal and Anglo- Saxon prejudices. They stress the hopeless indeterminateness of the preceding parliamentary régime more than I should do.

They do not extend anything like the same charity to Essenden that they do to the earlier dictators. He played the "strong man" rôle half a century too late. The pattern of development, they decide, had been fully provided by De Windt and his fellow theorists. Essenden, they insist, did not so much lead as "speak first", and with a needless haste, when the general decision was imminent. He induced the committee to strike too soon and too harshly at the old religious and political traditions that seemed to stand in the way of the Modern State. He found some of his colleagues slow in grasping things that seemed obvious to him. He was impatient and overbearing.

Quite early after the declaration of world sovereignty there were altercations in the committee meetings between him on the one hand and William Ryan and Hooper Hamilton on the other. Shi-lung-tang also becomes an inexplicable thorn in Essenden's side, an enervating influence full of insidious depreciation. We find Rin Kay intervening with a gentle firmness in these disputes and Englehart fretting openly at their dissensions.

This new world government, one must realize, was carrying on under conditions that were often saturated with emotion. There was still much uncertainty in the outlook; and this perhaps let in adventure and romance. The World Council was in effective possession of world power, but not in unchallenged possession. Even in 2000 C.E., nineteen-twentieths of mankind were still unassimilated to the organization. If the world was not rebellious it was mutinous, and there were plenty of alert and intelligent people in opposition, estranged people or people shaped to forms of thought altogether uncongenial to the reconditioning of human affairs on Modern State lines.

It was inevitable that these disharmonies between the leading figures at the centre of things, and the similar veins of discord that broke the solidarity of the Fellowship with a thousand intricate streaks and patches of weakness, should find echoes and misinterpretations in the greater world outside the machine. That greater world was still prepared for heroes and villains, ready for blind partisanships and storms of suspicion. It wanted drama in its government. A legend came

into being which exaggerated a supposed want of sympathy on the part of Essenden for the "priggishness" and "petty tyrannies" of the various Controls. He was supposed to be nobler stuff. He was credited with the intention of taking things into his own hands altogether and ruling the world in a more generous and popular spirit. As the history puts it: "An autocrat has always been the imaginative refuge of the crowd from hard and competent aristocracy."

That Arden Essenden ever plotted to realize these dreams there is no evidence at all. No word, much less any deed, is on record to show that he was unfaithful to the Modern State. But there can be no doubt that he felt that he was a fine figure and very necessary to the World Republic. He felt, as Stalin had done before him, that men could not do without him.

And then abruptly women come back into the history. We find a love intrigue flung across the stream of history. I did not notice until I came to this part of the world story how small a part women had played in the drama that began with the World War. In most countries they had been emancipated and given equal political rights with men before that disaster. That achieved, they vanish out of the picture throughout four decades of violence. There were indeed women leaders in the early stages of the Russian Revolution, but none filled a decisive rôle. And for all the leadership women exercised between the Twenties and the Eighties they might have been every one of them in kitchen, nursery, hospital, or harem. They lost what little political significance they had when queens went out of fashion. A considerable proportion of the Modern State Fellowship was feminine, but no women occupied decisive positions in the scheme. There were none on the World Council. They were doing vitally important work, educational, secretarial, executive, and the like, but it was ancillary work that did not lead to individual distinction.

But at this point the historian of the year 2106 breaks his inadvertent taboo and two women's names appear, the names of Elizabeth Horthy and Jean Essenden, and we find the threads of human destiny running askew about a story of passionate love and passionate misbehaviour.

Elizabeth Horthy, who caused the downfall and execution of Arden Essenden, was evidently a woman of splendid appearance and unfaltering conduct. She was an air pilot, and she seems to have liked to wear her uniform on occasions when most women would have been in a robe. She knew, says the history, what suited her. She was tall and evidently beautifully made; she "lifted her chin", it seems; she had a "broad brow" and a "serene" face. This I learn from quotations that are given from Essenden's letters to her. They are the letters of a man quite artlessly in love. But there is nothing in the notes to tell us whether she was dark or fair, what colour of eyes looked out from under that "broad brow", nor what sort of voice she had. Her love letters seem to have been pithy and extraordinarily indiscreet. Of her charm and distinction there can be no doubt. She was one of those women who seem radiant to men. She was "like sunshine"; she was "like heartening music". Again I quote Essenden. She made men her friends, except for Hooper Hamilton, who manifestly felt some obscure resentment against her.

Now this young woman, with her obvious "bravery" and a powerful disposition for romance, seems to have come to Basra in the train of William Ryan. It is possible but improbable that she was his mistress. Apparently she took little or no interest in the immense task of the World Revolution except as a suitable background for her exciting personal adventure. She seems to have fallen in love with Essenden at sight and he with her. It may be she came to Basra intending to do that. Something theatrical about him was not too theatrical for her. They were both theatrical. She liked things to be magnificent, and perhaps her taste for magnificence was stronger than her critical powers.

She seems to have given herself to him without hesitation or qualification or concealment. Theirs was—again I quote those artless letters of his—"the sort of love that flaunts itself like a flag".

But there was a third principal in this primitive drama, the wife of Essenden, a woman of great energy, great possessiveness and obtrusive helpfulness. It had been her vanity to "inspire" Essenden. And in the cast of the drama was Ryan, loudly resentful at Essenden "stealing" his "air girl", and Hooper Hamilton, inexplicably malignant. We are left to guess at the incidents and details of the drama, which was after all a very commonplace drama, only that it was magnified to the scale of the world stage. It culminated in Jean Essenden bringing a charge before the World Council against her husband of being concerned in a reactionary plot against the Modern State. She had, she said, intercepted letters, though none were ever produced. The historian of the year 2106, reviewing the particulars of the case, declared that there was no real evidence at all of any guilty associations of either Elizabeth Horthy or Essenden with the widespread movement that certainly existed for a monarchist and individualist reaction. But at the time the accusation was all too plausible. In some of her scrawled notes to him it seems Elizabeth called him "my King".

Moreover, Jean Essenden repeated the most incredible conversations with her husband: boasts of future glory, dark threats at his colleagues, strange replies to her remonstrances. She at least was an inflexible Modern Republican. Afterwards in a storm of remorse she retracted all this evidence, but only when it was too late. Probably it was half true. Probably it was reality a little refracted in her mind.

It was Hamilton who sealed Essenden's fate. He presided over the Special Court that had been formed to try the case. "Some of the evidence may be given with a motive," he said, looking at the white face of the accusing wife. "But it is a small matter that Essenden should or should not be a party in this conspiracy. His real offence is that he should have allowed this situation to develop, that he should have permitted his attention to wander from the services of the Republic to personal gratifications—personal gratifications and displays. At least he has been guilty of egotism. He has sacrificed himself and the interest of the world that has wrapped about him to an intensely personal drama. The question of his specific guilt is an altogether minor matter. The question before us is not, 'What has Essenden done?' but, 'What are we going to do about Essenden?' There is need for repression coming; civil war and bloodshed are plainly upon us. This is no time

for Great Lovers. Essenden has become ambiguous. He cannot lead us, and—how can we do without him? Things have come to this, Essenden, you are INCONVENIENT. Apart from this quarrel of the women, YOU ARE IN THE WAY."

The notes quote these words from the gramophone records of the trial. For it appears that the historian of the year 2106 could sit at his desk and listen to the steel-band record of the proceedings; note the speeches and mark the inflexions of the voices.

There was a pause, and then Essenden cleared his throat. "I see that I am in the way."

It was decided that there should be no open trial and condemnation. That would have precipitated the revolt. A tabloid was to be given to him, and he was to take it privately. He might "sit in the spring sunshine amidst flowers and green trees" and take it in his own time.

The record was cut deep, it seems, by the scream of Jean Essenden, protesting that that last half-hour should not be spent by the two lovers together.

Through all the years to come those steel ribbons will preserve the shrill intonations of those distressful moments. "I can't bear THAT!" cried Jean Essenden—down to the end of time.

"No," Elizabeth's actual words are given; "there is no need for you to be hurt any more. Don't be distressed, Jean, any more. It's over. It's all over for ever. I will go now. Out of the court now. I never meant to hurt Arden in this way. How was I to know? There is no need at all for us two even to say Good-Bye or be together any more. Jean, you couldn't help yourself. You had to do what you have done. But I never meant to hurt you. Or him."

Those are her words as the shorthand notes give them, but we shall never hear the sound of them. But the man who wrote them down, a century after they were spoken, heard them as he wrote, heard her voice weaken, if it weakened. Was she speaking or was she making a speech? We are left guessing how far these words of hers betrayed her sense of drama or whether it had indeed the simple generosity it may have had.

There is no description of the last moments of Arden Essenden, the man who had drafted the proclamation that founded the World-State. Possibly he did sit for awhile in some sunlit garden and then quietly swallowed his tabloid. He may have thought about his life of struggle, of his early days in the years of devastation and of the long battle for the World-State for which he had fought so stubbornly. Or perhaps according to all the rules of romance he thought only of Elizabeth. Much more probably he was too tired and baffled to think coherently and sat dully in the sunshine staring at those flowers which make the colophon to his story. Then the book closed for him. He died somewhere in the North of France, but the notes do not say precisely where.

They are more explicit about the fate of Elizabeth Horthy, who killed herself that day. There was no tabloid for her. She took her nearest way out of the world by flying her machine to an immense height and throwing herself out. She went

up steeply. It was as though she was trying to fly right away from a planet which had done with romance. "The aeroplane ceased to climb; it hung motionless, a quivering speck in the sky, and then began to waver and fall like a dead leaf. It was too high for anyone to see that its pilot had leapt free from it and was also falling through the air. A mere tattered rag of body was found amidst the branches of a little thicket of oak near Chantilly."

A fortnight after Hooper Hamilton also succumbed to "egotism" and took an overdose of sleeping-draught at his summer-house in the Aland Isles.

And with that this novelette-like interlude ends. It is elementary in its crudity. It is out of key with all that precedes it and all that follows. We are told there were other "stories" about the men of the First Council, but these other stories after this one sample are left to our imaginations. Its immense irrelevance tears the fabric of our history. But through the gap we see the pitiful imagination of humanity straining for a supreme intensity of personal passion.

Did that young woman as she stepped out upon nothingness above the cirrus clouds feel that her life had been worth while? The history calls her, "that last romantic".

3. FUTILE INSURRECTION

The notes show the historians of 2106 convinced that there was no real complicity between Elizabeth Horthy and the leaders of the Federated Nationalists who now broke out into open revolt. The impression of her character made by her recorded words and deeds is, they argue, quite incompatible with the idea that if she had indeed been a revolutionary, she would have abandoned her fellow conspirators for a melodramatic suicide because of the execution of Essenden. Far more like her would it have been for her to fly to the rebels in Germany and give herself passionately to avenge and vindicate his memory. But plainly she did not care a rap for the monarchist conspiracy, and it is possible that she did not know of its existence. Both she and Essenden, there can be little doubt, lived and died loyal, in intention at least, to the Modern State.

But it suited the revolt to seize upon her tragedy and use her as one of its symbols, and it was long believed that Essenden had retracted the socialist cosmopolitanism of the Basra Conference in favour of Federated Nationalism. It is interesting to find the legend of the poor old League of Nations presently become more powerful than its living reality, and ironical that it should supply the formula for an attempt to divide up the world again into "sovereign" fragments. The declaration of the so-called Prince Manfred of Bavaria put the League into the forefront of his promises. Alternatively he spoke of it as a World Federation of Free Peoples, and he promised Freedom of Thought, Freedom of Teaching, Freedom of Trade and Enterprise, Freedom of Religious Profession, Freedom from Basic English, Freedom from Alien Influence everywhere. As a foretaste of these good things, he released a little pogrom in the Frankfurt district where a few professing Jews still lingered.

[From this point to another which I shall indicate when I reach it I am able to give a fairly trustworthy transcription of the notes—ED.]

There was never anything that amounted to actual war during this period of disturbance; nothing that could be called a battle. The World Council had the supreme advantage of holding all communications in its hands, and, as military and naval experts could have told the rebels, there is no warfare without communications. Prince Manfred issued some valiant proclamations "to the World" before he took his tabloid, but since Basic English was repudiated by his movement, they were translated into only a few local languages, printed on stolen paper by hidden hand-presses, and sought after chiefly by collectors. The jamming of the public radio service was mischief rather than revolt. At first there was a certain revival of

the manufacture of munitions in factories that had been seized by rebel bands, but generally these ended their output after at most a few weeks under the soporific influence of Pacificin. There were a few deserters from the Air Police and a certain number of small private aeroplanes in nationalist hands; but the net work of registration, vigilant police patrols, and the absence of independent aerodromes soon swept rebellion out of the air.

There remained the bomb, the forbidden pistol, the dagger and the ambush. It was these that made the revolt formidable, forced espionage, search raids, restriction of private movement and counter violence upon the World Control, and rendered the last stages of the struggle a grim and indeed a terrible chapter in human history. In narrow streets, in crowds and conferences, in the bureaus of administrations and upon the new roads, lurked the death-dealing patriot. He merged insensibly with the merely criminal organizations of blackmail and crime.

It was this murder campaign, the "Warfare of the Silenced and Disarmed", as Prince Manfred put it, which stiffened the face and hardened the heart of the Modern State for half a century. It took to "preventive" measures; it began to suspect and test; that horrible creature, the agent provocateur, was already busy again before 2000. He was busy for another decade; he did not certainly vanish from the world until the Declaration of Mégève in 2059, but there is no record of his activity after 2030. And the government which had begun its killing with Arden Essenden and Prince Manfred came to realize the extreme decisiveness and facility of the lethal tabloid. For the grosser forms of execution had given place to this polite method, and every condemned man could emulate the Death of Socrates, assemble his friends if he chose, visit some lovely place, or retire to his bureau. In vain the veteran Rin Kay protested in the committee that, just as he had argued long ago that men were not good enough to be Machiavellian, so now he declared they were not good enough to be given powers of life or death, incarceration or relief over their fellows. "You murder yourselves when you kill," he said.

The rebels, however, were killing with considerable vigour and persistence, and their victims had no such calm and grace in their last moments. They were stabbed, shot, waylaid and beaten to death.

"For a terror," wrote Kramer, "death must be terrible."

"For murder," said Antoine Ayala, "death must be inevitable."

In the end the penal code did seem to achieve its end. There were 5703 political murders in 2005, and 1114 in 2007. The last recorded occurred in 2034. The total is over 120,000. But during these twenty-nine years there were 47,066 political executions! Rihani estimates that more than seven per cent of these were carried out upon anonymous, circumstantial, or otherwise unsatisfactory evidence. Most were practically sentences by courts martial. The millennium arrived in anything but millennial fashion.

4. THE SCHOOLING OF MANKIND

And now again the shorthand notes are troubled, disturbed and almost unreadable, and the resistances of Raven rise up and mingle with the proper text.

It was the age-long issue between faith in compulsion and faith in the goodwill of the natural man that had invaded the record. It affects me as I transcribe now; I do not see how it can fail to affect any contemporary writer or reader. I get again that flavour, that slight but perceptible flavour of— what can I call it but INHUMANITY?—in the historian's contribution. These men whom we anticipate here are different in their fundamental ideas. This short transition of a hundred and seventy years is marked by a subtle change in the human heart. I wonder if the same kind of difference might not arise if we could bring a good contemporary mind of the early eighteenth century into untempered contact with our thoughts to-day. Would not such a mind find us nowadays rather hard and sceptical about things respected, rather harshly frank about things biological, rather misshapen in our sentimentalities?

It is an old joke to revive such literary characters as Dr. Johnson or Addison and make them discuss contemporary things, but generally the fun goes no further than clothing modern reactions in old-fashioned phrases and costume. But in the light of my own response to the harshly lucid, cold, and faintly contemptuous criticism of our present resistances by the writer or writers of this 2106 document I find myself reviewing these old juxtapositions. I see that if we could indeed revive Johnson he would not only strike us as an ill- mannered, offensive, inadaptable and tiresome old gentleman who smelt unpleasantly and behaved worse, whose comments on life and events would be wide of the mark and discoloured with the echoes of antiquated controversies, but we should find that his contact with us would be pervaded by an incurable distress at our pace, at our strangely different values, our inhuman humanitarianism, as it would have seemed to him, and our cruel rationality. He who had sat so sturdily against his background of accepted and acceptable institutions, customs, and interpretations would find that background vanished and himself like a poor martyr in the arena with eyes upon him from every direction. Of course he would be hustled off to meet Mr. G. K. Chesterton, and that might prove the most painful of all his encounters. For Mr. Chesterton, who is posed so often as an avatar of the old doctor belongs to his own time quite as much as the most futuristic of us all.

I am a hostile critic of present conditions and a revolutionary in essence; nevertheless, I can get on with the people about me because, even though my song is

a song of revolt, it is in the same key and tempo as theirs; but I perceive that if I were transferred to this infinitely happier and more spacious world the history of Raven's reveals I should be continually and irreparably, in small things and great things alike, discordant. I should find nobody to get the point of my intelligent observations; I should laugh incomprehensively, fail to see the jokes that pleased these larger, more vigorous people, and the business of life would hurry past me. All sorts of things I had hoped for and forecast might be there—but in some essential way different and alien to me.

It is one of the things that Raven's notes have taught me that a human mind, an adult human mind anyhow, is much less easily transplanted to a new time and climate than I had been wont to assume. To me, the story of Arden Essenden's bold leadership, his acute self-consciousness, and his uncontrolled love for Elizabeth Horthy seem matter for such another story, let us say, as Meredith's Tragic Comedians; but the historian of the year 2106 finds him and her only material from which to dissect out the treacherous egotism of passion. Something in me rebels against that, just as it rebels against the assumption that the World War was a process of sheer waste, its heroisms and sacrifices blind blundering, and its significance out of all proportion less than the social and economic dislocations that caused it.

And now that I come to these disconnected records of the harshly rational schooling of human motives under the Air Dictatorship, records that even Raven found no zest in copying, my distaste is as ineradicable as it is unreasonable. I feel that, but for "the accidents of space and time", I should have been one of the actively protesting spirits who squirmed in the pitilessly benevolent grip of the Air Dictatorship. But whether it suits my temperament or not, this story, as it came through Raven to me, has to be told.

The men who made the great revolution and unified the world between 1965 and 1978 were men of practically the same mental assumptions as our own. They were in direct mental and moral continuity with our contemporaries. While the reader turns the page, if there is any truth in this history, De Windt, still absolutely unknown, must be working either in Berlin or London upon that Theory of the Nucleated Modern State which was the decisive plan of that final consolidation, publishers must already have read and rejected the preliminary scheme of his great work, and in a year or so from now some Mrs. Essenden will be choosing the name of Arden for her boy. It is as close to us as that. The men of the first World Council, therefore, saw both sides of the business and wavered in feeling between our tradition and the new order they were creating. But the subsequent generation which constituted the Air Dictatorship had been shaped from the beginning in the aggressive bright new schools of the Modern State nuclei, they had fed on a new literature, they looked out upon fresh horizons, and their ideology had been determined more than anything else by the social psychologists and "new lawyers" of the American school. They were starkly constructive. Nuance to them was obscurity and compromise weakness.

It is plain that so far as the future was concerned the first World Council with its rivalries and politics was far less effective than the unobtrusive Educational Control which worked under it during its régime and gradually drew together police, hygiene, schooling, and literature into one powerful nexus of direction. While the World Council was fighting for and directing and carrying on the unified World-State, the Educational Control was remoulding mankind. With the opening years of the twenty-first century (C.E.) the erstwhile leading figures of the revolution fall back into secondary places or vanish from the limelight altogether, and a simpler-minded, more determined group of rules comes to the front.

[I resume my transcription here.]

"The world is various enough without artificial variety," was a leading maxim of the Educational Control which created the men of the Air Dictatorship; and a variant of this maxim was: "It does not increase the interest of the human assembly to suffer avoidable mental cripples and defectives." So this body of teachers set themselves to guard new lives, beginning even with prenatal circumstances, from what they esteemed to be physical and mental distortion. There was no shadow of doubt upon this score for the Educational Control. Every possible human being had to be brought into the new communion. Everyone was to be exposed to the contagion of modernity. Every year now increased the power of the Modern State Fellowship; by 2000 it numbered five million; by 2010 thirteen. Every increase enabled the Educational Control to thrust its enquiring and compelling fingers more and more intimately into the recesses of human life. It had more men and women made to its pattern and a greater force of teachers and inspectors it could trust.

There can be no denying the excellence of the immediate physical results. Historical Scenes in a Hundred Volumes witnesses from 1990 onward, not only to the resumption of the advance in the technique of picture-making and the abundance of pictures, but to the restoration of physical welfare. As the student turns over the pages he sees man straighten himself again, grow physically, become more alert. The slouching foot-dragging men and women, the aimless faces, the fattish and lumpish figures of improperly nourished people, the wretched clothing and ignoble makeshift gear of the Second Decline and Fall, disappear; after 1990 clothing is fresh and simple, and after 2010 it begins to be austerely beautiful.

And this being achieved very largely through what the liberal thought of the nineteenth century would certainly have called "persecution". It is plain that the earlier World Council was all too disposed to leave great areas of the planet that did not "give trouble" alone. The new World Council, which is known also as the Air Dictatorship, would have none of that. There began a systematic attack upon the "lapsed regions", as they were called from the year 2006 onward. The government set itself in that year to "tidy up" the still half- barbaric peasant populations of Hayti, Ireland, West and Central Africa, South Italy, American Georgia and its associated states, Georgia in the Caucasus, Eastern Bengal, regions where traditional superstitions, secret societies, magic cults or sacrificial practices showed an obstinate persistence. There was a definite hunt for medicine

men, sorcerers, priests, religious teachers, and organizers of sedition; they would be fined or exiled, and parents and others would be fined for "impeding" the education of their children at the cosmopolitan schools.

Many critics of the Air Dictatorship are of opinion that this was a needless pursuit of dying customs and beliefs that might well have been left to fade out into mere fantasies and affectations. But the new generation of rulers took life too seriously for that. It is an issue that can never be settled, since we can only know what actually occurred.

The old Catholic Church, it seems, was still in existence in these days, the last surviving Christian organization, but it was greatly impoverished, and it had suffered severely from schisms, evidently the result of imperfect communications throughout the dark decades. There was a Pope in Dublin and another in Rome and a coloured Pope in Pernambuco. From the legal point of view the Irish Pope was the most legitimate successor of St. Peter. He had been duly elected by the Conclave, but the Fascist organization objected that he was not of Italian origin, his original surname being O'Dowd and his Italian accent imperfect, and the cardinals were intimidated into a new election. Some feud between rival gang organizations in America seems to have been involved in this split, but the details are obscure and need not occupy the student's time here. There was in consequence a division of the American Catholic world between the Dublin and the Roman communion, and this led to a murderous series of feuds, riots, and small local wars. "Down with the Wop Pope!" said the Irish. One is reminded of that earlier splitting of the Church through the rivalry of the French monarchy and the Central European imperial system that set up a rival Pope in Avignon.

Ireland was the last stronghold of Christianity. The Catholic religion had been compulsory in South Ireland from 1944 until 1980, and the Erse language, although that was largely corrupted by unavoidable English words and locutions, had also been made obligatory. Overt Birth Control knowledge had been successfully banned, though this produced no effect in the decline in population, and the Modern State nuclei had been boycotted more effectually there than in any other part of the world. The Dictatorship found itself fighting one of its most difficult battles for power with this tenacious people. The Irish came out in revolt all over the world. In Ireland after the maculated fever the population never rose above two millions, but there was a widespread Irish tradition throughout the English-speaking world. Some of the more brilliant and formidable antagonists of this schooling and drilling of our race that was going on, Paidrick Lynd, Arthur Fitzgerald, and Bernard O'Dwyer for example, came from Ireland. Oddly enough none of these three was a Catholic, and Fitzgerald at any rate had suffered a term of imprisonment for blasphemy, but the spirit of opposition was either innate in them or it had become ingrained in their natures.

Let the student note the open alternative at the end of the preceding paragraph. It raises a question that remains unsettled to this day. It is the clue to our contemporary moral problem. The Air Dictatorship, with what was still a very underdeveloped science of social psychology at its disposal, had come upon one of the

obscurest and most debatable of educational problems, the variability of mental resistance to direction and the limits set by nature to the ideal of an acquiescent co-operative world. De Windt, preoccupied by his gigantic schemes for world organization, had treated the "spirit of opposition" as purely evil, as a vice to be guarded against, as a trouble in the machinery that was to be minimized as completely as possible. The Air Dictatorship was carrying out and did carry out its world settlements on those assumptions. One may well believe that the world could have been unified into one enduring Pax Mundi in no other way. And yet they were faulty assumptions, and in the end they had to be abandoned for subtler and better conceptions of social interaction.

As every practising teacher understands, resistance is a necessary factor in teaching. Soft non-resistant material takes an imprint very readily only to lose it again very quickly. Easy pupils make teaching slipshod. The difficulty but also the soundness of teaching increases with the amount of reaction in the learner. And also resistance involves a certain element of collaboration; the thing learnt becomes a resultant, incorporating elements introduced in the struggle. It is easier to carve cheese than a good piece of wood; every piece of wood has a bias, it has to be dealt with on its own terms, it has to be managed and humoured, but in the end there is no comparison in quality and interest between carved cheese and wood-carving. These are the commonplaces of our educationists. But the defence of the work of the Educational Control is that its repressive measures were aimed not at intrinsic but at artificial resistances left over from the pre-revolutionary age.

In the old world of the early twentieth century there was a vast amount of crude generalization about what were called "racial" characteristics. There were generalizations about arbitrarily chosen agglomerations of mixed population—the Spanish for example, or "the West", "Russia", or the Jews; such generalizations were always unjust and inaccurate and often extremely mischievous. Nowadays we do not write of races any more, but we recognize groups of characteristics, evidently transmitted en bloc as a rule by associated genes, and anthropologists are steadily developing a scientific classification of human types. In few aspects do human beings vary more widely than in their recalcitrance. It is not a simple case that some people are more resistant and some less. There is a wide variation in the life cycle in this respect. Recalcitrance varies with age and sex. It varies with diet. Some types are obdurate as children but afterwards become more reasonable. Some reach a maximum of insubordination in adolescence. Generally speaking, passive resistance, unteachableness and obstinacy, but not insurrectionary energy, increase rapidly with age. And in certain populations, of which the Irish was one, there was a powerful access of resistance after adolescence in the male. It rose to the level of absolute refractoriness.

Now the apologists for the "persecutions" of the Air Dictatorship maintain that its missionary teachers were already quite prepared with the sympathy and finesse needed to teach every type of human being they would encounter in the world. So long as resistance was personal between teacher and learner they welcomed it. At least they said they welcomed it. But when it came to the systematic organization

of young people who would otherwise have had indifferent minds, so as to present a mass resistance and subversive opposition to the world order, the Educational Control, it is argued, was justified in hindering and suppressing books, meetings, teachings, agitations. It had the whip hand, and it would have been a sin not to have made use of that advantage. "We do not suppress individuality; we do not destroy freedom; we destroy obsessions and remove temptations. The world is still full of misleading doctrines, dangerous imitations and treacherous suggestions, and it is the duty of government to erase these"; so ran the uncompromising memorandum issued by the Educational Council in 2017.

"We have to get a common vision of existence, a common idea of right and wrong, established throughout the whole population of the world, and SPEEDILY," this memorandum declares. "Natural instinct is no help in a labyrinth of artificialities. It has to be supplemented by either training or discipline. The better we train, the less need for oppression; the more thoroughly we crush out false presentations and agitations, the more freely, as well as safely, men can live. Things are rushing back headlong to prosperity, and we cannot face abundance and leisure with the present morale of the race. It has to be stiffened up; it has to be drilled to keep ranks."

In 1955 humanity was suffering throughout the globe from disorder, famine and pestilence; its numbers were declining, and it might well have been supposed that it was driving towards extinction. The change of fortune was swift beyond precedent. As early as 2017 we have this clear intimation that its guides and rulers were contemplating the advance of plenty and an excess of leisure with terror.

EDITOR'S NOTE

I think that it may make things clearer for the reader here if I give a compact summary of the political forms assumed by the developing world government between 1965 and 2106. The writer of this history of Raven's, writing for his contemporaries, assumed them to be familiar with many institutions for which the readers of this book will be altogether unprepared. Fortunately the relations of the Communist and Fascist Parties to their respective governments give us a helpful parallel to the relations to the World Council, the actual world government after 1965, of what was called the Modern State Movement. It was its incentive and its conscience.

The political structure of the world developed in this fashion:

After the chaos of the war (1940-50) and the subsequent pestilence and "social fragmentation" (1950-60) there arose, among other attempts to again reconstitute a larger society, a combine of the surviving aviators and the men employed upon the ground plant of their trade and transport. This combine was called The Transport Union. It does not appear to have realized its full potentialities in the beginning, in spite of the forecasts of De Windt.

It initiated various conferences of technicians and at last one in 1965, when it was reorganized as The Air and Sea Control and produced as subsidiary organs The Supply Control, The Transport (and Trading) Control, an Educational and Advertisement Control and other Controls which varied from time to time.

It was this Air and Sea Control which ultimately gave rise in 1978 at the Second Conference of Basra to the World Council. This was the first declared and formal supreme government of the world. The Air and Sea Control then disappeared, but its subordinate Controls remained, and coalesced and multiplied as ministries do in existing governments, under the supreme direction of the World Council.

There was no further change in essential political structure between 1978 and 2059, but there was a great change in the spirit and method of that supreme government, the World Council. A new type of administrator grew up, harder, more devoted and more resolute than the extremely various men of the two Basra Conferences. These younger men constituted what our historian calls here the Second Council, though it was continuous with the first. There was a struggle for power involving the deaths of several of the earlier councillors, but no formal change of régime; there continued to be a World Council constituting the supreme government of the world. This Second Council is also referred to as the Air Dictatorship in its earlier years, and later on as the Puritan Tyranny. These are not exact constitutional terms but loose descriptive phrases. The membership of the World Council changed by individuals coming and going, but its character remained singularly uniform for over forty years. It grew more elderly in spite of a few youthful accessions. In 2045 its average age was 61.

This Second World Council endured until a Conference at Mégève in Savoy (2059) reconstituted the world government on lines which are drawn out fairly plainly in the following chapters.

And now for the relations of this series of governing bodies to the World-State Movement.

The ideological developments that inspired these changes were initiated by a group of writers of whom De Windt was the outstanding figure. He built up the project for a world-state in all its essentials in a book on Social Nucleation published in 1942. The intrinsic quality of this book has been entirely overshadowed by its importance as a datum point in history. It is a slow laborious book.

It was the seed of the Modern State Movement which furnished the plans of the Air and Sea Control. The Modern State Movement was never a formally constituted government nor anything in the nature of a public administration; it was the propaganda and development of a system of ideas, and this system of ideas produced its own forms of government. The "Movement" was initially a propaganda and research, and then a propaganda, research, and educational organization. Its active full members were called Fellows; it had a class of dormant members, whose relationship to the active category varied under different conditions and at different periods; and it had a class of neophytes or apprentices, as numerous or more numerous than its active Fellows. It ultimately incorporated the mass of adult mankind (and womankind) in its Fellowship.

It was never divided up into regional bodies. Its Fellows were acceptable at any local centre they happened to visit. Naturally it began mainly as localized nuclei, but those localizations were merely for convenience of propaganda, teaching,

and local purposes. The effective subdivision of the Fellowship was into FACULTIES, and these again were subdivided into sections and departments. There was to begin with a faculty of scientific research, a faculty of interpretation and education, a health faculty, a faculty of social order, a supply and trading faculty, a number of productive faculties, agricultural, mineral and so on. There were splits and coalescences among these faculties. Their splits and coalescences had a frequent relationship to the splits and coalescences of the Controls, because it was obviously a mental convenience for a faculty or faculties to correspond with one or more Controls.

The faculties and their subdivisions, their sections and departments, possessed electoral central councils, but there never seems to have been a general directorate of the Modern State Movement after the early days in which it was one simple system of propaganda and enquiry nuclei; its nuclei almost from the outset differentiated naturally into faculties, each viewing human affairs from its own angle; the movement as a whole did not require a continuing directive council; there were only conferences when concerted action between diverse faculties was desirable.

There never seems to have been any difficulty in the way of a man or woman belonging to two or more faculties at the same time, and this greatly facilitated the melting of one faculty into another. The Modern State Movement was an "open order" attack on social structures; it was a solvent and not a mould. The moulds were the Controls.

The faculties and their sections, departments, and so forth developed very unequally; some dwindled to insignificance, and some on the other hand grew to unanticipated proportions and created their own distinctive organization and machinery. This was particularly the case with the social psychology department of the faculty of science, which annexed the whole faculty of training and advertisement by a sheer community of subject. This social psychology department of the faculty of science was given the legal and responsible direction of the Educational Control.

This body of social psychologists and their associates became a great critical and disciplinary organism side by side with the World Council, which ultimately, as will be explained in the following chapters, it superseded.

The world then ceased, it seems, to have any single permanent government at all. It remained under a series of primary Controls dealing with each other by the method of conference, namely the Controls of transport, natural products, staple manufactures, population (housing and increase), social sanitation (police and medicine), education (these two latter were later merged as the Behaviour Control), and the ever expanding activities of scientific research and creative work. So the world which had once been divided among territorial Great Powers became divided among functional Great Powers.

Later a Bureau of Reconciliation and Cooperation seems to have grown up, which decided upon the necessity and method of inter-Control conferences. It was something rather in the nature of a Supreme Court than of a ruling council.

Most of the old faculties of the Modern State Movement dissolved into technical organizations under these Controls, with the one exception of that former department of the science faculty the department of social psychology, which by 2106 had become, so to speak, the whole literature, philosophy, and general thought of the world. It was the surviving vital faculty of the Modern State Movement, the reasoning soul in the body of the race.

In the end it becomes something like what the early nineteenth century used to think existed under the name of Public Opinion, the consensus of active thought and imagination throughout the world. It is plain that by 2106 this rule by a pervasive intelligence had become an unchallenged success. It was all that was left by way of King, President, or Supreme government on earth.

This assembling and clearing-up of statements which are otherwise scattered rather perplexingly through the text under consideration will not, I hope, annoy such readers as have already grasped what I have summarized here. I will now return to that text itself.

5. THE TEXT RESUMES: THE TYRANNY OF THE SECOND COUNCIL

The Air Dictatorship is also called by some historians the Puritan Tyranny. We may perhaps give a section to it from this point of view.

"Puritan" is a misused word. Originally invented to convey a merely doctrinal meticulousness among those Protestants who "protested" against the Roman version of Catholicism, it came to be associated with a severely self- disciplined and disciplinary life, a life in which the fear of indolence and moral laxity was the dominant force. At its best it embodied an honourable realization: "I shall do nothing worth while and nothing worth while will be done unless I pull myself together and stiffen up my conduct." If the new Air Dictatorship was schooling the world with considerable austerity, it was certainly schooling itself much more so.

The code of the first makers of the World-State had been a simple one. "Tell the truth," they insisted; "maintain the highest technical standards, control money and do not keep it, give your powers ungrudgingly to the service of the World-State." That seemed to leave them free for a good deal of refreshing self- indulgence, and it did. They ate, drank, and were merry, made love very freely, envied and competed with one another for power and distinction, and set no adequate guard upon the growth of rivalries and resentments. Our history has glanced at the fall and death of Essenden, but this is only one episode in the long and complicated history of the private lives of the first world committee. Slowly the details are being elucidated and analysed by a body of historical students. Except that the victims are dead, and cannot hear, the results are as pitiless as the old Christian fancy of the Recording Angel and his Book on Resurrection Day.

They appear as very pitifully human; their sins happened to them, they were taken unawares in phases of fatigue, by resentment, by sensuality or flattery. Women were attracted by their prestige and offered the reassurance of love to their weaker moments. In many cases the moral downfall was due to the very limitlessness of the devotion with which they first gave themselves to their world task. They worked without rest. Then they would suddenly find themselves worn bare, bankrupt of moral energy. They had made no proper balance between the public task and the inward desire. Outbreaks of evil temper would follow, or phases of indolence or gross indulgence. The Fellowship was disconcerted; the outer world ran with scandal. "These Fellows," said their critics, "are no better than the pretenders and rascals of the old régime. Rin Kay, the wise, is consumed

with affection for his little friend, and Ardasher of the experimental aeroplanes makes his young men do dangerous stunts to please a girl. Morovitz is collecting Persian miniatures quite unscrupulously and Fedor Galland spends half his time now making a garden at Babylon."

The ambitious young men who were little boys when the first conference at Basra was held were educated by teachers who were none the less harshly zealous because they were doing relatively inconspicuous work and had no little friends nor miniatures nor gardens to amuse them. These teachers had a lively sense of their leaders' defects and of their own modest but real moral superiority. The youngsters under their teaching were saturated with constructive enthusiasm, but they were trained also to judge and condemn the weaknesses of their spent and tired predecessors. They learnt that the brightness of this new world that had been made for them was in danger from the very men who had made it. The technically more skilful and intensive teaching that had been given them had made them more self-conscious and wary in their behaviour, and far more capable of managing the detail of their lives. They were simple in principle and hard in detail. They had a modern wisdom about diet and indulgence; they regarded lack of fitness as a crime.

The difference is evident in Historical Pictures, where one usually sees the older generation dressed either carelessly or picturesquely and often either self-consciously or gracelessly posed, while the younger men and women in the simpler and plainer clothing that was coming into fashion carry themselves like athletes. Austerity has become a second nature to them. Devotion and the sacrifice of the individual they carried to such a pitch that, for instance, it was considered unseemly for them to have portraits made, and there was no record kept of the names of the chairmen and of the movers of motions in the central committee during their ascendency. It has needed special research to rescue some of the names of this second generation of world rulers, who set up the Puritan Tyranny and made the Socialist World-State secure. One of the moving spirits was certainly Han H'su and another Antoine Ayala.

They ousted their predecessors without any coup d'état, one by one, through sheer superiority in energy and working power. The great revolution was over; the World-State was in being. But it was not secure. It was a time for just such continuous detailed work as only a naturally able and energetic type with a hard training could hope to do. They were not selected by any voting or politics to fill the Council, they were selected by their own staying and driving power. The milder or subtler types could not keep the pace and fell into less authoritative positions. The influence of certain teachers and groups of teachers was very considerable. Three schools, the Unamuno Foundation at Coimbra, the Columbia University of New York, and the Tokio Social College, accounted for more than a third of the World Council in 2017.

For nearly forty years the new Council, with occasional renewals, worked and kept a whole generation of men and women working. As Aldous Huxley (1894-

2004), one of the most brilliant of reactionary writers, foretold of them, they "tidied up" the world.

There can be no denying the purification and rarefaction of the human scene that was achieved during their sway. They tightened up the disciplines of the Modern State Fellowship, and nevertheless the proportion of the Fellowship increased until it bade fair to become the larger moiety of adult mankind. The mental habits of the Fellowship, its habitual bearing, extended through the whole population. The Tyranny, says Vordin, altered the human face for ever. It closed the mouth and made the lips firmer, made the eyes steadier and more candid, opened the brow, altered the poise of the head, obliterated a number of wrinkles and habits of expression. Portraits of the earlier and later time confirm this generalization. One type of odd-character after another became rare and began to disappear from the human comedy. Rascals and recalcitrants grew old, sat in the sun for a time rather protestingly and vanished. They took many disagreeable and some whimsical casts of countenance with them. Sexual prostitution ceased and eliminated a characteristic defiance from feminine carriage. The trader found he had nothing to trade with and came into the employment of the Supply Control. Gambling, horse-racing, sport, generally went out of fashion, and those queer oblongs of pasteboard, "playing cards", retired to museums, never to emerge again. Every one of these vanishing interests or practices took its own scores of social types, of "reaction systems", to use the modern phrase, away with it. Faces ceased to be masks.

Every year the world grew safer for the candid. The need for cunning and wary self-restraint diminished enormously, the habit of making a face a "mask". Humanity was extroverted. A lively self-forgetful interest in external things becomes more and more patent. The "worried" look of the introspective habit of mind disappears. "Everyone must know plainly," said the new rulers. "Men must be perplexed no more." The old religions could not emulate the moral prestige of the new cult, and even the resentments of the persecution that deprived them of their last shreds of educational influence could not preserve them. For nearly forty years this rule of the new saints, this resolute simplification and smoothing out of life, went on.

History becomes a record of increasingly vast engineering undertakings, and cultivations, of the pursuit of minerals and of the first deep borings into the planet. New mechanisms appeared, multiplied, and were swept away by better mechanisms. The face of the earth changed. The scientific redistribution of population began. Yet there was little likeness to the world of to-day, as we know it. No age in human history has left us such strange and uncongenial pictures.

Costume was not unpleasant during this period, because of its simplicity; the human figures in the scene at least are tolerable; but these scientific Puritans also produced some of the clumsiest architecture, the most gaunt and ungainly housing blocks, the dullest forests, endless vistas of straight stems, and the vastest, most hideous dams and power-stations, pylon-lines, pipe-lines, and so forth that the planet has ever borne. But at any rate they flooded the Sahara and made the North

African littoral the loveliest land in the world. The productivity of mankind was now advancing by leaps and bounds, in spite of the severe restraint presently put upon the introduction of fresh labour-saving devices; and yet these Puritans were consumed by an overwhelming fear of leisure both for themselves and others. They found it morally necessary to keep going and to keep everybody else going. They INVENTED work for the Fellowship and all the world. Earth became an ant-hill under their dominion clean and orderly but needlessly "busy". So harshly had they reacted against the weaknesses of their seniors and so unable were they to mitigate their own self- imposed severities.

Let us cast up the good mankind can attribute to this strange phase of sternness and grim repression. For all the faint masochist and sadistic flavour of its closing years, the good was beyond all measure greater than the evil. "The obliteration of out-of-date moral values" (the phrase is Antoine Ayala's) "and the complete establishment of a code of rigorous and critical self- control, of habitual service, creative activity, cooperation, of public as well as private good manners, and invariable truthfulness, were achieved for all time. We grow up so easily now into one free, abundant, and happy world that we do not realize the effort still needed even in the year 2000 to keep life going upon what seem now to us the most natural and simple lines possible. We find it almost impossible to imagine the temptations to slacken at work, loiter, do nothing, 'look for trouble', seek 'amusement', feel bored and take to trivial or mischievous 'time-killing' occupations, that pursued the ill-trained under- vitalized, objectless common citizen before 2000 C.E. Still more difficult is it to realize how subtly these temptations were diffused through the mass and how hard they made a well-directed life. We have to trust the psychological experts about that."

The New Puritans "disinfected" the old literature, for example. It is hard to see that now as an urgent necessity. These old stories, plays, and poems seem to us to convey the quaintest and most inexplicable systems of motivation conceivable, and we cannot imagine people being deflected by them; they might as easily be led astray by the figures on a Chinese screen or an Hellenic sarcophagus; but before the persecution those books were, as one censor called them, "fever rags". They stood then for "real life". They provided patterns for behaviour and general conduct. That queer clowning with insults and repartees, that insincerely sympathetic mocking of inferiors, that denigration of superiors, which constituted "humour" in the old days, strikes us as either fatuous or malicious. We cannot understand, for instance, the joy our ancestors found in the little blunders and misconceptions of ill-educated people. But then they also laughed at the cripples who still abounded in the world! Equally distasteful now is most of their "romance" with its false stresses, its unnecessary sacrifices and desperations. "Romance", says Paul Hennessey, "is essentially the violent and miserable reaction of weak spirits to prohibitions they cannot fairly overcome."

We find the books glorifying war and massacre, and the tangled masses of suggestion that elaborated the innate hostility and excitement caused by difference of racial type, so unconvincing that it is difficult to believe that they ever

gripped. But they did grip and compel. They drove innumerable men to murders, lynchings, deliberate torture. They dressed the foulest and cruellest of crimes in heroic colours. There had to be a break with these traditions before they could be seen as we see them now. It needed the heroic "priggishness" of the Air Dictatorship, putting away the old literature and drama for a time, suppressing the suggestion systems of the old religions and superstitions, jailing and segregating men and women for "hate incitement", ruthlessly eliminating sexual incitation from the lives of the immature and insisting upon a universal frank sexual hygiene, to cleanse the human mind for good and all and inaugurate the unconstrained civilization of to-day. There was no other way to Renaissance.

Joseph Koreniovsky has called the Puritan Tyranny "the cold bath that braced up mankind after the awakening". Man, he says, was still "frowsty- minded" and "half asleep" in the early twenty-first century, still in urgent danger of a relapse into the confused nightmare living of the Age of Frustration. You may call it a tyranny, but it was in fact a release; it did not suppress men, but obsessions. None of us now can fully realize the value of that "disentanglement from tradition", because now we are all disentangled.

And next to this ruthless "mental disinfection" of the world, and indeed inseparable from it, we must put the physical disinfection of mankind to the credit of the Air Dictatorship. Between 2000 and 2040 every domicile in the world was either destroyed and replaced, or reconditioned and exhaustively disinfected. There was an immense loss of "picturesqueness" in that process, and we shiver nowadays when we look at pictures of the white bare streets, the mobile rural living-boxes, the bleakly "cheerful" public buildings, the plain cold interiors with their metallic furniture, which everywhere replaced the huts, hovels, creeper-clad cottages and houses, old decaying stone and brick town halls, market houses, churches, mosques, factories and railway stations in which our tough if ill-proportioned and undersized forefathers assembled about their various archaic businesses.

But between the same years the following diseases, the names of which abound in the old histories, and the nature of which we can hardly imagine, vanish from the human records: catarrh, influenza, whooping cough, sleeping sickness, cholera, typhus, typhoid, bubonic plague, measles, and a score of other infectious scourges. (Only yellow fever remained as a serious infection after 2050. That demanded the special effort of 2079 for its extirpation.) Syphilis and indeed all those diseases known as venereal, were stamped out completely in two generations; they were afflictions so horrible and disgusting that their description is not now considered suitable for the general reader. There was a similar worldwide attack on plant diseases and distortions, but of that the student will learn in his Botanical History.

The psychologists who are rewriting human history have still many open questions to settle about the training and early influences that gave the world this peculiar group of rulers, and so the account of its hardening and deterioration remains incomplete. They admit that the Tyranny was in essence a liberation, but they insist that it left vitally important desires in the human make-up unsatisfied.

Old traditions and mischievous obsessions were rooted in these desires, and the Tyranny had not been content with an eradication of the old traditions. It had denied the desires. It had pulled up the soil with the weeds. It had exalted incessant, even if pointless, activity above everything else in life.

Overwork, a strained strenuousness, has been a common characteristic of the rulers of mankind in the past. It shows through the Edicts of Asoka, for example, and particularly in Rock Edict VI (Asoka, D. R. Bhandarkar, 1932, Classical Historical Studies, 21-118). "I am never satisfied," runs the Edict, "with the exertion or with dispatch of business. The welfare of the whole world is an esteemed duty with me. And the root of that, again, is this, namely, exertion and dispatch of business." A great majority of the successful Caesars and Autocrats from Shi-Hwang-Ti to Hitler have the same strenuousness— Alexander the Great perhaps was the chief exception, but then his father had done the work before him. Mussolini, the realizer of Italian Fascismo, in his Talks to Ludwig (Historical Documents Series 100, 319) betrays an equal disposition for single-handed accomplishment and an equal disinclination to relinquish responsibility.

All the chief figures of the Air Dictatorship betray, upon scrutiny, signs of the same drive to do too much and still to do more. They display all the traits of a collective weary conqueror, unable to desist and think and adapt himself. They went on ruling and fighting when their victory was won. They had tidied up the world for ever and still they went on tidying. After their first real successes they manifest an extreme reluctance to bring new blood into the responsible administrative task. They had arisen to power as a group by their usefulness, because they were unavoidably necessary to those original founders of the World-State whom they first served and then by sheer insistence upon performance pushed out of authority and replaced. The three virtues in a ruler according to Han H'su were punctuality, precision, and persistence. But it was a dictum of Paidrick Lynd's that "indolence is the mother of organization". They had none of that blessed gift of indolence. When the legacy of work that the first world revolution had left them was exhausted, they brought things at last to the necessity for a final revolution through their sheer inability to organize a direct succession to themselves or to invent fresh undertakings.

That final revolution was the most subtle of all the substitutions of power that have occurred in human affairs, the most subtle and so far the last. The Dictatorship could suppress overt resistance; it could impose obedience to its myriads of injunctions and rules. But it could not suppress the development of general psychology nor the penetration of its own legislative and administrative activities by enquiry and criticism.

The Department of General Psychology had grown rapidly until it had become the most vigorous system of activities in the scientific faculty of the Modern State Fellowship. In its preparatory stages it had taken the place of the various "Arts" and Law curricula of the old régime. It was the modernization of the "humanities". The founders of the World-State had given this particular department of the scientific faculty almost as great a directive and modifying power over both the

Educational and Legal Controls as it exercises to-day. Even then it was formally recognized as the responsible guardian in the theory of Modern State organization. It more than realized the intentions of De Windt. It became the thought, as the World Council had become the will, of mankind acting as a whole. And since the education and legal adjustment of the World-State was thus under the direction of a department of research continually advancing, they differed diametrically in character from the education and teaching of the old world order.

The student cannot keep this difference, this flat contrast, too clearly in mind. He will never understand the historical process without it. The Old Education existed to preserve traditions and institutions. Progressive forces arose as a dissent from it and operated outside its machinery. In the eighteenth, nineteenth, and early twentieth century education was always a generation or so behind living contemporary ideas and the schoolmaster was a drag on mankind. But the New Education, based on a swiftly expanding science of relationship, was no longer the preservation of a tradition, but instead the explanation of a creative effort in the light of a constantly most penetrating criticism of contemporary things. The new schoolmaster showed the way, and the new education kept steadily ahead of contemporary social fact. The difference of the New Law and the Old Law was strictly parallel. If a man of the year 1900 had been told of a progressive revolution led by lawyers and schoolmasters inspired by scientific ideas, he would have taken it as a rather preposterous joke, but to-day we ask, "How else can the continuity of a progressive revolution be sustained?"

The failure of the German revolution of 1918 and the relapse of that unfortunate country into the puerility and brutish follies of Hitlerism was entirely due to the disregard of the elementary principle that no revolution could be a real and assured revolution until it has completely altered the educational system of the community. Every effective old-world revolution was a revolt against an established education and against the established law.

The rôle of the modern Education Control in preserving, correcting, and revivifying the progressive process in human affairs had already been manifested by the supersession of the leading personalities of the Basra conference in the World Council by their successors who became the Air Dictatorship. Now these men in their turn found the instruments of government becoming recalcitrant in their hands and obeying the impulse of unfamiliar ideas. They had cleared and cleansed the site while social science had been preparing the idea of the new structures that were to stand upon it, and now they found themselves confronted by an impulse towards creation and enrichment entirely discordant with their habits of administration. Their subordinates began to send back the instructions given them as "insufficient and not in accordance with the psychology of the workers"—or other people—"concerned". Schemes were condemned by those to whom they were entrusted as unnecessarily toilsome or needlessly ungracious. Workers took matters into their own hands and demanded more pleasant processes or more beautiful results. The committee was disposed at first to insist upon unquestioning

obedience. Thereupon the Education Control produced a masterful argument to show "the social harmfulness of unquestioning obedience".

There could be no greater contrast in the world than that between the older revolutionary crises in human affairs and this later conflict of wills. The old revolutions were at best frantic, bawling, sentimental affairs in which there was much barricading of roads and destruction of property; people were shot abundantly and carelessly and a new régime stumbled clumsily to responsibility on the ruin and reversal of its predecessor. Such revolutions were insurrections of discontent against established institutions. But this last revolution was the cool and effectual indictment of the world executive by a great world wide educational system. It was not an insurrection; it was a collateral intervention. The new order arose beside its predecessor, took matters out of its hands and replaced it.

The need for an intolerant militant stage of the World-State had passed. The very reason for the disciplines of the Puritan Tyranny had been dissolved away in the completeness of its victory. But the last men to realize this were the old men who now sat trying to find tasks to keep humanity out of mischief in the bureau of the World Council.

6. AESTHETIC FRUSTRATION: THE NOTE-BOOKS OF ARISTON THEOTOCOPULOS

It is a growing custom of historians, and we have already followed it freely, to vivify their general statements by quotations from contemporary descriptive writers. As histories have disentangled themselves from their primitive obsession about rulers and their policies, they have made a more and more extensive use of private memoirs, diaries, novels, plays, letters, sketches, pictures and the like. Once upon a time washing bills and memorandum books were below the "dignity of history". Now we esteem them far above acts of parliament or diplomatic memoranda. And certainly there is no more convenient source of information about current ideas and feeling under the Air Dictatorship than the cipher Note Books of that gifted painter and designer Ariston Theotocopulos (1997-2062). For thirty-seven years until his death, he wrote in these books almost daily, making his own shrewd comments on current events, describing many odd and curious occurrences, noting very particularly his own emotional reactions, and adorning them all with a wealth of sketches, dreams, caricatures and the like, which make the full edition in facsimile, with a translation, among the greatest delights of the book-lover. The bulk of this matter does not concern the student of general history at all, and yet it is possible to pick out from it material for a far clearer realization of life under the second Council than could be derived from a score of abstract descriptions.

The earlier of these volumes are coloured by the irritation of the writer with three particular things: the restrictions upon private flying, his difficulties in finding scope for his genius, and the general want of beauty and graciousness in life. At that time there were no privately owned aeroplanes and no one could act as an air pilot who was not an active Fellow of the Modern State organization and subject to its rules and disciplines. Theotocopulos had an anarchistic soul, and his desire to wander freely above the mountains and clouds, to go whither he liked at his own sweet will, unhampered by any thought of immediate "service", became an obsession with him. "If they would let me alone I would give the world something," he scribbles. "But what on earth is the good of those blighted old Master Decorators telling me to do this and that? Did I come into the world to imitate and repeat things done already?"

And in another place he notes: "Some damned official flying overhead on his way to preventing something. It spoilt the day for me. I couldn't THINK any more."

Then comes a cry of agony. "The lay-out of all this terracing is wrong. What is the good of putting me to do a frieze of elephants on a wall that ought to come down again? If I do anything good that wall will stay where it is. The better I do it, the more likely they are to keep that wall. And it's wrong. It's wrong. It's wrong."

A few pages on, one word is all alone by itself: "ELEPHANTS!"

Then follows a string of caricatures of that animal which Li has characterized as acute biological criticism. Theotocopulos had been vividly interested in elephants, but now he had tired of them. He represents them as diaphanous or altogether transparent, and reveals the distresses of their internal lives. And there is a whole page of incredibly wicked elephants' eyes.

He was working on the rather deliberate decoration of the main-road system then in course of construction, running from Cape Finisterre through North Italy and along the North Black-Sea Dyke to the Crimea and Caucasia. That system has since been deflected from the Ligurian coast northward, but at that time it was made to follow by the sea to Genoa, and thence passed in a great cutting through the mountains to the plain of the Po and so to the still existing Chioggia viaduct. It was one of a not very ably conceived system of world roads that was greatly modified before its completion in our own time, and it was carried out with a massiveness and a solidity of ornamentation that witness to the World Council's incapacity to realize that Change was still going on. Those roads seem to have been planned for all time. They indicate mental coagulation.

Theotocopulos was engaged upon the coast section between the old town of Nice to the old port of Genoa. It was driven in a series of flattened curves that straightened out in places to a right line, cutting brutally through headlands and leaping gulfs and bays in vast viaducts. Above and below the slopes were terraced with natural or imitation marble walls and the terraces were planted with oranges, lemons, vines, roses, olives and agaves. These terraces went up, as Theotocopulos says, "relentlessly" to the old Corniche Road above, broken only by a few masses of evergreen trees. The ruins of the villas and gardens of the Capitalist era and most of the towns along the coast that Titus Cobbett had visited and described seventy-odd years before had now been cleared away; a few groups of residential buildings occurred here and there, and pretentious staircases, which were rarely used because of the lifts they masked, led down to beaches and holiday places and harbours for pleasure boats and fishermen. These holiday places and the residential buildings were low and solid-looking, after the fashion of the time, and they provoked Theotocopulos to frenzy. He caricatured them and spotted his drawings with indecent words. It is amazing how truthfully he drew them and how ingeniously he distorted them. He represented them as cowering into the earth like the late buildings of the war years, from which they certainly derived their squatness.

"We still dream of air raids and war in the air," he said, and he speaks elsewhere of "the inmates of those fortifications.... If only I could get hold of an aeroplane and a bomb! Perhaps after all there is some sense in keeping intelligent people like me out of the air, with this sort of stuff about."

His task unhappily kept him in close contact with all this squat architectural magnificence. He had won distinction at an unusually early age for his brilliant drawings of men and animals; he had a grotesque facility for seeing into bodies and conveying his sense of internal activities; before his time the only anatomy known to artists had been muscular anatomy; and he was set to "decorate" an ungainly stretch of wall near Alassio with a frieze of elephants. It is necessary to explain that in those days there was the completest divorce in people's minds between aesthetic and mechanical considerations. First you made a thing, they thought, and then you decorated it. It seems almost incredible now, but the engineers of the Air Dictatorship were supposed and expected to disregard all thought of beauty in what they did. If they made something frightful, then the artist was called in to sugar the pill. There, as in so many things, the restless sensitive mind of Theotocopulos anticipated the ideas of to-day. "Engineers ought to be artists," he says, "anyhow; and artists ought to be engineers or leave structural work alone." This wall of his still exists; his decoration has preserved it, even as he foresaw. It just remains for his sake, a lesson for students and a monument to his still incomparable talent.

"Took a holiday," he notes one day, "and rowed about five miles out to sea. These disproportions grow worse as one gets away from them. Never before have I seen anything that got uglier as it receded in perspective. This coast does. The road is too broad and big. There will never be that much traffic. The population of the world isn't increasing and on the whole it rushes about less than it did. One hundred and twelve metres of width! What is this coming torrent of traffic from Finisterre to God knows where? Not a sign of it as yet. Nor ever will be. The little lizards get lost across that glassy surface and die and dry up. Artless earthworms crawl out upon it and perish. One sees them by the thousand after wet weather. No shade for miles. The terraces are badly spaced and the walls that sustain them look gaunt. There is no sympathy in all this straight stuff with the line and movement of the hills behind. They LIVE. And this accursed habit of building houses close to the ground! Damn it, don't we build to get away from the ground?"

And then suddenly in big capitals comes one word: "PROPORTION!"

After that he meditated with his pencil in hand, jotting down his thoughts. "The clue to life. Not simply beauty. There is no evil but WANT OF PROPORTION. Pain? Pain arises out of a disproportion between sensations. Dishonesty? Cruelty? It is all want of proportion between impulse and control...."

It is interesting to trace in the notebooks how he tries over ideas that are now familiar to everyone. He worries between the ideas of proportion and harmony. Then he hits on the discovery that all history is a record of fluctuations in proportion. To-day, of course, that is a commonplace. We have told the economic and political history of the twentieth century, for instance, almost entirely as the story of an irregular growth of the elements of life, hypertrophy of economic material going on concurrently with a relative arrest of educational, legal, and political adjustment. The first dim realizations of these disharmonies were manifested by the appearance of "planning", those various crude attempts to make estimates of

quantities in social life of which the Russian Five Year Plan was the first. After 1930, the world was full of Plans, and most of them were amazingly weak and headlong plans.

We learn from these notebooks of Theotocopulos how imperfectly this idea of really deliberate quantitative preparation in the activities of our species was apprehended even in the early twenty-first century. Just as the war complex ran away with men's minds in the war period, so now political unity and uniformity and an extravagant concentration of enterprise upon productive efficiency had outrun reason. The interest of these notebooks lies exactly in the fact that they are not the writings of a scientific social psychologist, but of a man who was, except for his peculiar genius and energy of expression, a very ordinary personality. They tell us how common people were taking the peculiar drive of the times, how the general mind was puzzling out its new set of perplexities and asking why after having abolished war, restored order, secured plenty, defeated the fears and realized the wildest hopes of the martyr generations, it was still so far from tranquillity and happiness.

"Growing pains," he writes abruptly. "That was old Lenin's phrase. Is a certain want of proportion unavoidable?"

After that flash in the pan, the notebook wanders off into a dissertation upon Levels of Love, of no importance for our present purpose. But that idea of "Growing Pains" was working under the surface all the time. Suddenly appear pages of sketches of strange embryos, of babies and kittens and puppies, all cases of morbid hypertrophy. "Is want of proportion inevitable in all growth? Nature seems to find it so, but she always has been a roundabout fumbler. She starts out to make a leg, and when it comes out a wing she says, 'Eureka! I MEANT to do that.' But in DESIGNED WORK? In engineering for example?"

His mind goes off to the making of castings, the waste in grinding, the problems that arise in assembling a machine.

"Nature corrects the disproportions of growth by varying the endocrines," he reflects. "And when a house has got its frames set up and its walls built, we turn out the masons and put in the plasterers and painters. So now. A change of régime in the world's affairs is indicated. New endocrinals. Fresh artisans."

This particular entry in the notebook is dated April 7, 2027. It is one of the earliest appearances of what presently became a current phrase, "change of régime".

The preoccupations of Theotocopulos with the physical and mental aspects of love, his extraordinary knack of linking physiological processes with the highest emotional developments, need not concern us here, important as they are in the history of aesthetic analysis. For a year or so he is concentrated upon his great "Desire Frieze" in the Refectory of the Art Library at Barcelona, and he thinks no more of politics. He likes the architects with whom he is associated; he approves of the developments at Barcelona, and he is given a free hand. "These fellows do as they like," he remarks. "A great change from all those damned committees, 'sanctioning' this or asking you to 'reconsider' that." Then he comes under the influence of that very original young woman from Argentina, also in her way a

great artist, Juanita Mackail. Sketches of her, memoranda of poses and gestures, introduce her. Then he remarks: "This creature thinks." So far he has never named her. Then she appears as "J" and becomes more and more frequent.

"There is something that frightens me about a really intelligent woman. Was it Poe or De Quincey—it must have been De Quincey—who dreamt of a woman with breasts that suddenly opened and became eyes? Horrid! To find you are being looked at like that."

Following this a page has been torn out by him, the only page he ever tore out, and we are left guessing about it.

An abrupt return to political speculation in the notebooks follows. A number of entries begin, "J says", or end, "This is J's idea."

Then some pages later he repeats: "This creature thinks. Do I? Only with my fingers. Language is too abstract for me. Or is it true, as she says, that I am mentally lazy. MENTALLY LAZY—after I had been talking continuously to her for three hours!

"It seems all my bright little thoughts don't amount to anything compared with the stuff these social psychologists are doing. I have a lot to learn. I suppose J would schoolmistress anybody."

The notebooks keep the fragile grace and mental vigour of Juanita Mackail alive to this day. She was the sort of woman who would have been a socialist revolutionary in the nineteenth century, a commissar in Early Soviet Russia or a hard worker for the Modern State in the middle twentieth century. Now she was giving all the time her strongly decorative idiosyncrasy left free to the peculiar politics of the period. It is plain that before she met Theotocopulos she was already politically minded. She had had a feeling that the world was in some way not going right, but her clear perception of what had to be done about it came only with her liaison with him. The notebooks with their frankness and brutality tell not only a very exceptional love story, but what is perhaps inseparable from every worthwhile love story, a mutual education. Theotocopulos was her first and only lover. To begin with he had treated her as casually as he had treated the many other women in his life, and then it is plain that, as he began to find her out, his devotion to her became by degrees as great or greater than her devotion to him.

He studied her. He made endless notes about her. We know exactly how she affected him. How he affected her we are left to guess, but it is plain that for her there was at once the magnificence of his gifts and the appeal of his wayward childishness. The former overwhelmed her own. It is plain in her surviving work. The earlier work is the best. He asks twice, "Am I swamping J? Her stuff is losing character. She is borrowing my eyes. That last cartoon. Am I to blame? It WAS such lovely stuff. Once upon a time." And he writes: "This maternity specialization is Nature's meanest trick on women. If they are not going to be mothers, if they CAN'T be mothers, why on earth should they be saturated with motherhood? Why should J think more about getting me a free hand to do what I please than she does about her own work? She does. I haven't asked her. Or have I, in some unconscious way, asked her? No, it's just her innate vicious mothering. I am her

beloved son and lover and the round world is my brother, and every day her proper work deteriorates and she gets more political and social-psychological on our account."

From that point onward the trend of these notebooks towards politics becomes very strong. The early volumes express the resentments of an isolated man of extreme creative power who finds himself singlehanded and powerless in an unsympathetically ordered world. The late show that same individuality broadening to a conception of the whole world as plastic material, sustained by a sense of understanding and support, coming into relationship and cooperation with an accumulating movement of kindred minds. At last it is not so much Theotocopulos who thinks as the awakening aesthetic consciousness of the world community.

"The change of régime has to be like a chick breaking out of its egg. The shell has to be broken. BUT THE SHELL HAD TO BE THERE. Let us be just. There is proportion in time as well as in space. If the shell is broken too soon there is nothing to be done but make a bad omelette. But if it isn't broken at the proper time, the chick dies and stinks."

The forty-seventh notebook is devoted almost entirely to a replanning of the subject of his early animadversions, the Ligurian coast. That notebook proved to be so richly suggestive that to-day some of his sketches seem to be actual drawings of present conditions, the treatment of the Monaco headland for example, and the reduction of the terraces. But his dreams of orange-groves are already quaint, because he knew nothing of the surprises in tree form that the experimental botanists were preparing. The forty-ninth booknote is also devoted to planning. "Plans for a world," he writes on the first page. "Contributions." He seems to have amused himself with this book at irregular intervals. There are some brilliant anticipations in it and also some incredible fantasies. Occasionally, like every prophet, he finds detail too much for him and lapses into burlesque.

There is a very long note of a very modern spirited discussion about individuality which he had with Juanita when apparently they were staying together at Montserrat. The notes are the afterthoughts of this talk, "shots at statement" as he would have called them, and they bring back to the reader a picture of that vanished couple who strolled just sixty years ago among the tumbled rocks and fragrant shrubs beneath the twisted pines of that high resort, both of them so acutely responsive to the drift of ideas that made the ultimate revolution—she intent and critical, holding on to her argument against his plunging suggestions, like someone who flies a kite in a high wind.

"The individual is for the species; but equally the species is for the individual.

"Man lives for the State in order to live by and through—and in spite of— the State.

"Life is a pendulum that swings between service and assertion. Resist, obey, resist, obey.

"Order, discipline, health, are nothing except to make the world safe for the aesthetic life."

"We are Stoics that we may be Epicureans."

"Exercise and discipline are the cookery but not the meal of life.

"Here as ever—PROPORTION. But how can proportion be determined except aesthetically?

"The core of life is wilfulness."

So they were thinking in 2046. Have we really got very much further to- day?

7. THE DECLARATION OF MÉGÈVE

Theotocopulos and his Juanita were present at the Conference at Mégève which wound up the second World Council. They both seem to have been employed upon the decoration of the temporary town that was erected for this purpose on those upland meadows. The notebooks, in addition to some very beautiful designs for metal structures, contain sketches of various members of the Council and some brilliant impressions of crowd effects in the main pavilion. There is also a sketch of a painting Theotocopulos afterwards made; it appears in all our picture-books of history: the tall presence of old Antoine Ayala, standing close to the aeroplane in which he departed for his chosen retreat in the Sierra Nevada; he is looking back with an expression of thoughtful distrust at the scene of his resignation. The pilot waits patiently behind him. "Well, well," he seems to say. "So be it." The sinking sun is shining in his eyes, so that they peer but do not seem to see.

The drawing of nine of the World Councillors listening intently to the statement of Emil Donadieu, the secretary of the Education Faculty, is almost equally well known.

It was the most gentle of all revolutions. It might have been a thousand years away from the fighting and barricading, the pursuits and shootings and loose murderings, of the older revolutionary changes. The Council suffered not overthrow but apotheosis. Creation asserted itself over formal construction and conservation. For a decade and more the various Controls had been showing a greater and greater disregard of the Central Council; they had been dealing directly with one another, working out their immense cooperations without the intervention—which was more and more inhibition—of the overriding body. It was the Education Faculty of the Control of Health and Behaviour that had at last provoked the gathering. It had in its own authority set aside the prohibitions on naked athleticism which had been imposed by the Council in its "general rules of conduct" thirty years before. The matter was a trifling one, but the attention of the Council was drawn to it; and it was decided to choose the occasion for a definite assertion of the Council's authority. Was there still a Supreme Government in the world? was the question posed by the veteran ruling body. Probably it seemed to them quite imperative that there should be a supreme overriding body, and the bland exposition of Emil Donadieu which dispelled this assumption must have been an illuminating revelation to them of the march of human ideas since those

days of youthful zeal and vigour when they found themselves directing the still militant World-State.

In those days the need for concentrated leadership had prevailed over every other human consideration. It had been necessary to fight and destroy for ever vast systems of loyalties and beliefs that divided, misled and wasted the energies of mankind. It had been necessary to replace a chaos of production and distribution for individual profit by an ordered economic world system. But once this vast change-over was made and its permanence assured by the reconstruction of education on a basis of world history and social science, the task of a militant World-State was at an end. The task of the World Council was at an end.

"But then who is to govern the world?" asked Eric Gunnarsson, the youngest and most ambitious member of the Council.

"No need to govern the world," said Donadieu. "We have made war impossible; we have liberated ourselves from the great anti-social traditions that set man against man; we have made the servitude of man to man through poverty impossible. The faculties of health, education, and behaviour will sustain the good conduct of the race. The controls of food, housing, transport, clothing, supply, initiative, design, research, can do their own work. There is nothing left for a supreme government to do. Except look up the world it has made and see that it is good. And bless it."

"Yes," said Eric Gunnarsson, "but—"

These words are registered in the phonograph record of the debate. And with these two words Eric Gunnarsson, the ambitious young man who may have dreamt at one time of being President of the World, vanishes from history.

Donadieu went on to a brief history of government in human affairs, how at first man could only think in personifications and had to conceive a tribal God and a tribal King because he could not conceive of organized cooperation in any other way; how Kings remained all too individual and all too little social for anything but the narrowest tribal and national ends, and how therefore they had to be controlled and superseded by councils, assemblies and congresses, which in their turn became unnecessary. These ruling bodies clamped men together through ages of discord until at last the race could be held together in assured permanence by the cement of a universal education.

But the gist of that debate was embodied in the "Declaration of Mégève" with which the Conference concluded its deliberations.

"The World-State now follows all the subordinate states it swallowed up to extinction; the supreme sovereign government, which conquered and absorbed all minor sovereignties, vanishes from human affairs. The long, and often blind and misdirected, effort of our race for peace and security has at length succeeded, thanks to this great Council that now retires. It retires with the applause and gratitude of all mankind. And now in serenity and security we can survey the property it has redeemed from waste, this planet and its possibilities, our own undeveloped possibilities too, and all the fullness of life that lies before us. This is the day, this is the hour of sunrise for united manhood. The Martyrdom of Man is at an end.

From pole to pole now there remains no single human being upon the planet without a fair prospect of self- fulfilment, of health, interest, and freedom. There are no slaves any longer; no poor; none doomed by birth to an inferior status; none sentenced to long unhelpful terms of imprisonment; none afflicted in mind or body who are not being helped with all the powers of science and the services of interested and able guardians. The world is all before us to do with as we will, within the measure of our powers and imaginations. The struggle for material existence is over. It has been won. The need for repressions and disciplines has passed. The struggle for truth and that indescribable necessity which is beauty begins now, unhampered by any of the imperatives of the lower struggle. No one now need live less nor be less than his utmost.

"We must respect the race and each other, but that has been made easy for us by our upbringing. We must be loyal to the conventions of money, of open witness, of responsibility for the public peace and health and decency: these are the common obligations of the citizen by which the commonweal is sustained. We must contribute our modicum of work to the satisfaction of the world's needs. And, for the rest, now WE CAN LIVE. No part of the world, no work in the world, no pleasure, except such pleasure as may injure others, is denied us. Thanks to you, Heroic Council; thanks beyond limit to you."

BOOK THE FIFTH - THE MODERN STATE IN CONTROL OF LIFE

1. MONDAY MORNING IN THE CREATION OF A NEW WORLD

With the Declaration of Mégève in 2059 C.E. the Age of Frustration, the opening phase of the Era of the Modern State, came to an end. Let us recapitulate that history in its barest outline. The World-State had appeared dimly and evasively, as an aspiration, as a remote possibility, as the suggestion of a League of Nations, during the World War of 1914-18; it had gathered experience and definition throughout the decades of collapse and disaster; it had formally invaded human politics at the Conference of Basra in 1965 as manifestly the only possible solution of the human problem, and now it had completed its conquest of mankind.

The systematic consolidation of that conquest had begun in earnest after the Second Conference of Basra in 1978. Then the World Council had set itself to certain tasks that had been so inconceivable hitherto that not the most daring sociologists had looked them in the face. They had contented themselves with pious aspirations, and taken refuge in the persuasion that, if they were sufficiently disregarded, these tasks would somehow do themselves. They were tasks of profound mental reconstruction, reconstruction going deeper into the substratum of the individual life than anything that had ever been attempted before. In the first place traditions of nationality had to be cleared away for good, and racial prejudice replaced by racial understanding. This was a positive job against immense resistances. Next a lingua-franca had to be made universal and one or other of the great literature-bearing languages rendered accessible to everyone. This again was not to be done for the wishing. And thirdly, and most evaded of all three obstacles that had to be surmounted, issue had to be joined with the various quasi-universal religious and cultural systems, Christianity, Jewry, Islam, Buddhism and so forth, which right up to the close of the twentieth century were still in active competition with the Modern State movement for the direction of the individual life and the control of human affairs. While these competing cultures remained in being they were bound to become refuges and rallying-shelters for all

the opposition forces that set themselves to cripple and defeat the new order of the world.

We have told already how that issue was joined, and shown how necessary it was to bring all the moral and intellectual training of the race into direct and simple relations with the Modern State organization. After 2020 there is no record of any schools being open in the world except the Modern State schools. Christianity where it remained sacerdotal and intractable was suppressed, but over large parts of the world it was not so much abolished as watered down to modernity. Everywhere its endowments had vanished in the universal slump; it could find no supply of educated men to sustain its ministry; the majority of its churches stood neglected and empty, and when the great rebuilding of the world began most of them vanished with all the other old edifices that lacked beauty or interest. They were cleared away like dead leaves.

The story of Islam was closely parallel. It went more readily even than Christianity because its school organization was weaker. It was pinned very closely to the teaching of Arabic. The decadence of that language shattered its solidarity much as the disuse of Latin disintegrated Western Christianity. It left a few-score beautiful mosques as Christianity left a few-score beautiful chapels, churches and cathedrals. And patterns, legends, memories remained over in abundance, more gracious and lovely by far than the realities from which they were distilled.

There had been a widespread belief in the tenacity and solidarity of Judaism. The Jews had been able to keep themselves a people apart, eating peculiar food and following distinctive religious practices, a nation within the nation, in every state in the world. They had been a perpetual irritant to statesmen, a breach in the collective solidarity everywhere. They had played a peculiar in- and-out game of social relationship. One could never tell whether a Jew was being a citizen or whether he was being just a Jew. They married, they traded preferentially. They had their own standards of behaviour. Wherever they abounded their peculiarities aroused bitter resentment.

It might have been supposed that a people so widely dispersed would have developed a cosmopolitan mentality and formed a convenient linking organization for many world purposes, but their special culture of isolation was so intense that this they neither did nor seemed anxious to attempt. After the World War the orthodox Jews played but a poor part in the early attempts to formulate the Modern State, being far more preoccupied with a dream called Zionism, the dream of a fantastic independent state all of their own in Palestine, which according to their Babylonian legend was the original home of all this synthesis of Semitic-speaking peoples. Only a psycho-analyst could begin to tell for what they wanted this Zionist state. It emphasized their traditional wilful separation from the main body of mankind. It irritated the world against them, subtly and incurably.

On another score also the unpopularity of Israel intensified in the early twentieth century. The core of the slump process was manifestly monetary. Something was profoundly rotten with money and credit. The Jews had always had and cultivated the reputation of a peculiar understanding and cleverness in monetary

processes. Yet in the immense difficulties of that time no authoritative direction came from the Jews. The leading minds of the time who grappled with the intricate problems of monetary reconstruction and simplification were almost all Gentiles. It was natural for the common man to ask, "Where are the Jews?" It was easy for him to relapse into suspicion and persecution. Were they speculating unobtrusively? It was an obvious thing for Gentile speculators to shift suspicion to this race which gloried in and suffered by its obstinate resolve to remain a "peculiar people".

And yet between 1940 and 2059, in little more than a century, this antiquated obdurate culture disappeared. It and its Zionist state, its kosher food, the Law and all the rest of its paraphernalia, were completely merged in the human community. The Jews were not suppressed; there was no extermination; there were worldwide pogroms during the political and social breakdown of the Famished Fifties, but under the Tyranny there was never any specific persecution at all; yet they were educated out of their oddity and racial egotism in little more than three generations. Their attention was distracted from Moses and the Promise to Abraham and the delusion that God made his creation for them alone, and they were taught the truth about their race. The world is as full as ever it was of men and women of Semitic origin, but they belong no more to "Israel".

This success—the people of the nineteenth century would have deemed it a miracle—is explicable because of two things. The first of them is that the Modern State revolution was from the first educational and only secondarily political; it ploughed deeper than any previous revolution. And next it came about under new and more favourable conditions. In the nineteenth century the family group had ceased to be the effective nucleus in either economic or cultural life. And all the odd exclusiveness of the Jew had been engendered in his closed and guarded prolific home. There is an immense collection of fiction written by Jews for Jews in the early twentieth century, in which the relaxation of this immemorial close home-training and the clash of the old and modernizing generations is described. The dissolution of Israel was beginning even then.

The task of making the mind of the next generation had been abandoned almost unconsciously, for Jew and Gentile alike, to external influences, and particularly to the newspaper and the common school. After 1940 this supersession of home training was renewed in an extensive form. The Modern State movement had from the outset gripped the teachers, re-created popular education after the dark decades upon its own lines, and arrested every attempt to revive competing schools. Even had he desired it the Jew could no longer be peculiar in the food either of his body or his mind.

The complete solidarity of mankind in 2059, the disappearance of the last shadows of dislike and distrust between varied cults, races, and language groups, witnesses to the profound truth of what Falaise, one of De Windt's editors, has called the Mental Conception of History. The Age of Frustration was essentially an age of struggle to achieve certain plainly possible things against the resistances of a muddled human mind. The Declaration of Mégève was not simply an asser-

tion of victory and freedom for the race, it was the demonstration of its achieved lucidity.

As the curtain of separatist dreams, racial fantasies and hate nightmares thinned out and passed away, what was presented to that awakening human brain? A little sunlit planet, for its external material, bearing what we now realize is not a tithe of its possible flora and fauna, a ball crammed with unused and unsuspected resources; and for the internal stuff of that brain almost limitless possibilities of mental achievement. All that had been done hitherto by man was like the scribbling of a little child before eye and hand have learnt sufficient co-ordination to draw. It was like the pawing and crawling of a kitten before it begins to see. And now man's eyes were open.

This little planet of which he was now at last in mentally untroubled possession was not simply still under-developed and waste; its surface was everywhere scarred and disfigured by the long wars he had waged so blindly for its mastery. Everywhere in 2059 the scenery of the earth still testified to the prolonged war, the state of siege to establish a unified mastery, that had now come to an end. If most of the divisions and barriers of the period of the sovereign states had disappeared, if there were no longer castles, fortifications, boundaries and strategic lines to be traced, there were still many indications that the world was under control and still not quite sure of its own good behaviour. The carefully planned system of aerodromes to prevent any untoward developments of the free private flying that had been tolerated after 2040 was such an indication, and so was the strategic import plainly underlying the needlessly wide main roads that left no possible region of insurrection inaccessible. From the air or on a map it was manifest that the world was still "governed". The road system was like a net cast over a dangerous beast.

And equally visible still was the quality of recent conquest in the social and economic fields. As Theotocopulos complained, the Second Council overdid its embankments. It was distrustful even of the waters of the earth. Its reservoirs and rivers had, he says, "a bullied air". If the jostling little fields and misshapen ill-proportioned farms, the untidy mines, refuse-heaps, factories, workers, slums and hovels and all the dire squalor of competitive industrialism had long since disappeared from the spectacle, there was still effort visible at every point in the layout of twenty-first-century exploitation. The stripping and burning of forests that had devastated the world so extensively in the middle decades of the preceding hundred years had led to strenuous reafforestation. Strenuous is the word. "Grow," said the Council, "and let there be no nonsense about it." At the end of the Age of Frustration a tree that was not lined up and lopped and drilled was an exception in the landscape.

Everywhere there was still this suggestion of possible insubordination and the sense of an underlying threat. Man had struggled desperately and had won, but it was only now that he was finding time to consider any but the most immediate and superficial possibilities of his planet.

The air-view as the dispersing delegates from Mégève saw it forty-seven years ago was indeed in the vividest contrast to the world garden in which we live to-day. That clumsy rationality, that real dread of aestheticism, that had haunted the Council to its end, had made the artificial factors in the landscape inelegant and emphatic almost without exception. Bridges and roads "got there", as Theotocopulos said, "like charging rhinoceroses". True that the disposition to squat forms, which came from the age of the air raids, no longer prevailed, but there was a general tendency to make buildings too solid and too big; they had sometimes a certain grandiose boldness, but more often than not there was a touch of military stupidity in the appearance of their piled-up masses. They stood to attention. There was a needlessly lavish abundance of pylons, and they were generally too sturdy.

The enrichment of vegetation which is now world-wide was in operation at that time only in a few experimental areas; in most regions there was still hardly more forest or cultivation than had existed a century and a half before. If the devastation of fellings and fires during the last wars had been replaced by the new straight-ruled, squared-out forests, there was as yet no perceptible rise in the level of the plant community anywhere; what had previously been forest was plantation or forest again, and what had been prairie was still prairie, differing only from the grass prairies of older days in the dwindling contingent of weeds and wild flowers. In spite of the self-complacency of the forestry department of that time, many trees distorted by disease survived, and most were by our standards stunted. To young eyes to-day this world of our fathers, as they see it in picture book and panorama, has not merely a regimented but a barren look, and its cultivation seems laborious and poor.

Yet compared with the landscape of two centuries ago its aspect was relatively prosperous, spacious and orderly. There is something very touching in the freely expressed response of the nineteenth-century folk to both urban and country landscape and to natural scenery generally. They did not dream how meagre their descendants were to find the spectacle before them. They had, at any rate, as good cloudscapes and sunsets as we have, and such natural coast scenery as that of Western Scotland was practically the same then as it is to- day. They would endure irksome travel to see sunlit snowy mountain masses or get to some viewpoint that caught the rhythm of a distant chain. They loved water and woodlands and distant fields in a wide view, and towns they admired chiefly as piled up accumulations seen from a distance. Also they delighted very greatly in the close brightness of flowering hedges, sheets of bluebells, primrose rides, green moss and tendrils and any sort of flower. They pick these things out for appreciation so persistently in their literature and paintings that it is only with an effort we realize how much they were "picked out", and how dull and repetitive were endless miles of their normal roads and countryside and how flatly forbidding the ordinary aspects of their habitations.

So far as we can reconstruct it now the prevalent note of the nineteenth century scene was weak insipidity, degenerating very easily into a distressful mean un-

gainliness. America was frostbitten in the north and slovenly in the south and unkempt everywhere. Happily the shorter-lived, not very healthy or vigorous folk of these days had no standards of comparison, and actual intimations of discontent with nature and the countryside were rare. There is scarcely an admission in nineteenth-century literature that the larger part of the natural world was gaunt, unsatisfactory and utterly unsympathetic. Writers and poets did not dare to admit as much because they had neither the hope nor the energy to make things better. They would not see it in obedience to an elementary psychological law.

But under the Second Council, the criticism not only of man's achievement but of natural insufficiency had become voluminous because neither was felt any longer to be final. It was not only the heavy engineering, the massive buildings and the over-emphasied roadways that those returning delegates threatened with their minds. Much of the land was still unsettled. They looked down on areas of marsh and scrub, bare wildernesses of rock, rainless regions, screes and avalanche slopes. For them as for us it was a world of promise still to be fulfilled.

"Now we can begin on all this," they said. "Now we have really to begin."

2. KEYING UP THE PLANET

It had long been known that the vegetation of earth and sea, on which the volume and vigour of all other life depends, was not nearly commensurate with the available moisture and sunlight. As early as the nineteen thirties it was being pointed out by an English economic botanist, Frederick Keeble (1870-1975, Collective Works in the Science section of the Reprints), that there were delays and arrests in the multiplication of diatoms, seasonal grass crops, and other extensive primary vegetable growths, arrests due to the fact that while all other conditions were favourable the supply of assimilable nitrogen was too slow to keep up the growth process. He applied the agricultural lesson of manuring to the whole spectacle of life and insisted that we were living in a "nitrogen-starved world". Nitrogen is yielded up by the inorganic world to the uses of life with extreme reluctance. This observation of Keeble's threw a new light for most people on the alleged bounty of nature. Other workers in the same field spread their observations to other elements. Carlos Metom (1927- 2014), in a striking passage, compared life on our planet to "a starveling foal on a barren patch that has never learnt to look for green pasture".

This fundamental poverty of terrestrial existence can be traced through most of the geological record. Life has been a stinted thing. There were a few periods of exuberance, the period of the Coal Measures for example, when life seemed really to pour upward; but for most of recorded time life nibbled round the outside of a ball of limitless mineral wealth to which it had no key. No individual intelligence could ever penetrate that hidden hoard of plenty. It was only when the collective mentality of Science had arisen and was going on deathlessly from one clarification to another that a far more abundant vegetable basis for animal and human existence came within the range of possibility, and only now that the waste of human energy in warfare and uncoordinated trading and money-getting was at an end for ever, that the realization of that possibility could be attempted. But hundreds of thousands of brains are now alight with the prospect of evoking such a plenty and wealth of life on our planet as the whole universe had never dreamed of before this time.

The Second Council, in the beginning of its long reign, had not a sufficient knowledge of the latent powers of applied biology to anticipate this fundamental enrichment of life. It conceived its rôle to be the working- out of the logical consequences of mechanical invention during the nineteenth and twentieth centuries. The greatest of these consequences were the abolition of distance and the super-

session of toil by power machinery. The goal of the Council was to confirm and establish human unity for ever, and to set up a frame of progressive public activities that should provide universal employment and universal purchasing power in the face of a continually increasing industrial efficiency. At first it was preoccupied by the persecuting activities that were needed to secure the world against any reaction towards private monopolization, romantic nationalism, religious eccentricism, and social fission. Then, as its success in this direction passed beyond challenge, as the world community was plainly assured, it found itself confronted by an ever more portentous problem of leisure.

It seemed a natural outlet for the surplus of human energy to provide among other things for an enormous development of scientific research and an exploration of the deeper mineral resources of the earth's crust. The Council assigned something like a third of the resources available for science to biological work, and it does not seem to have occurred to these rulers of the world, preoccupied as they were with the suppression, the excessive suppression, the obliteration even, of deleterious and antiquated separatist doctrines and the refashioning of economic life, that this huge growth of biological enquiry would result in anything more than the extinction of plant and animal diseases, and improvements and economies in cultivation. It was outside the range of their imaginations to anticipate a spate of biological invention that put the spate of mechanical invention which revolutionized the conditions of human life in the nineteenth and twentieth centuries altogether in the shade. Biological knowledge outgrew them just as aesthetic sensibility outgrew them.

From the thirties of the twenty-first century onward the conservatism of the Second Council had held back an increasing amount of scientific discoveries from practical application. The world was unified; it was supporting its population (which was being kept well below the modest safety line of 2000 million) with absolute ease; its health was at a higher level than nature had ever known before; and it was, so far as the powers in being could manage it, marking time. It was like an adolescent who is still treated as a child. Even the new possibilities of exuberant vegetation were not being released. The areas needed for food supply could have been halved before 2050, but the Council decided that the consequent dislocation of the population would be likely to strain social order, and it kept four or five million people at the healthy but not very entertaining work of agricultural production, while it promoted enquiries for the "industrial application of marginal excesses of foodstuffs". It was not only producing, but distributing, staples in 2050 on precisely the lines adopted in 2020. It was restraining educational developments and innovations in building. It had made the world safe for humanity, and it meant to keep the world at that.

In 2047 Homer Lee Pabst published his remarkable researches on the effect upon chromosomes of certain gases derived from the old Sterilizing Inhalation made from Permanent Death Gas. These gases are known now as Pabst's Kinetogens, and there is a whole series of them. Their general effect is to produce mutations of various types. They bring about, abundantly and controllably, a vari-

ability in life which has hitherto been caused only with comparative rarity by cosmic radiations. By 2050 the biological world was confronted by a score of absolutely new species of plants and—queer first- fruits in the animal world— by two new and very destructive species of rodent. The artificial evolution of new creatures had come within the range of human possibility.

Limitless possibilities opened before the human imagination. The Council gave way to panic. It saw the world it had taken such pains to put in order given over to uncontrollable vegetable and animal monstrosities. A nightmare of evil weeds and strange beasts dismayed it. Even the human type, it realized, was threatened. The laws restraining experiments upon animals were extended, and every animal novelty produced by Pabst was to be reported upon and destroyed. Plant novelties of decorative or economic value were, however, to be tolerated. Within his laboratory and experimental grounds Pabst ignored these prohibitions, and the faculty of science increased the endowment of the new experimental genetics. And now that the Supreme Council could no longer interfere, the Transport and General Distribution Control, the newly developed section of the Behaviour Control and the Health Services took up Pabst's results and arranged a conference (2060) for their proper exploitation. A general plan for the directed evolution of life upon the planet was drawn up, a plan which, with various amendments, is in operation to this day.

Most of the "wild beasts" of our ancestors are now under control in their special enclosures and reservations. There are fifteen Major Parks of over five hundred square miles in which various specially interesting faunas and floras flourish without human interference, except for the occasional passage of some qualified observer on foot or the transit of a specially licensed aeroplane overhead. Adventurous holiday-makers are excluded. The creatures in these areas are less affected by man than were their predecessors. They form a valuable reserve control of the genetic tentatives that are being made upon their more or less captive brethren. The most startling result of these experiments is Dumoric's claim to have restored, by means of carefully bred crosses and the cultivation of atavistic types, extinct ancestral forms of the fallow deer.

One beneficial result of the preoccupation of the Second Council with the problem of employment for idle hands and minds had been the very great advances made in both mineralogical and meteorological science. It did not realize that the systematic observation of winds and rainfall could possibly upset its orderly world. Indeed, the prospect of forbidding the wind to blow where it listed was entirely after the Council's heart. So, too, the possibility of controlling or drying up volcanoes and earthquakes appealed very strongly to it. Before 2000, man's knowledge of the composition of what he used to call the earth's "crust" and the mineral resources of the planet beneath that crust was extraordinarily superficial. Geologists relied almost entirely for their knowledge upon surface features, chance exposures, and industrial excavations. But the ever increasing resources available for research made a systematic probing and exploration of the deeper layers increasingly possible. The student will find in any contemporary textbook

of Geology an account of the series of beautiful contrivances such as the Shansi borer, the Hull and Watkins "diviner," and the Noguchi petrograph, which have now made, so to speak, hidden things visible to a depth of twenty-five miles, and there too he will find a description of a score of ingenious devices for isolating blocks of deep-lying rock and bringing their desirable ingredients to the surface. Until a hundred years ago nothing of this sort was even imagined. Instead of employing the energy imprisoned underground to drive what was needed to the surface, the scanty product of the old-world mines was HAULED up by human or mechanical power from above and the ores and coal and salt were actually hewn out in situ by hordes of sweating underpaid human beings.

Equally rapid was the progress of meteorology once the Second Council gave its mind to that subject. Practical meteorology was of very recent date. Except for a little work with the barometer from 1643 onward, forecasting began only in the nineteenth century and was not systematically attempted until 1850. An infinitesimal tampering with the composition of the air began in the early twentieth century. Then man found himself able to withdraw nitrogen from it, but this was done only to provide fertilizers, and in such small quantities as to make no appreciable effect upon the composition of the atmosphere. Little more was attempted until the last war, when the local use of substances like the so-called Permanent Death Gas was carried out on a sufficiently big scale to amount to a transitory readjustment of the air over the region poisoned. Then in the thirties of the twenty-first century there was an extensive use of gas on a large scale to destroy locusts, rodents, and various insect pests. Considerable enthusiasm was shown at the time, but one or two unfortunate accidents cooled the zeal of the Council. It was realized that air-mixing for anything but stimulating and purifying purposes must wait upon the achievement of wind control. Air-mixing was put back into the pigeonholes with a gathering number of other gifts from science that the Council deemed premature.

The Joint Commission for replanning the world found itself therefore with three correlated groups of possibility challenging its spirit of adventure. A new flora of several thousand species was awaiting release from the experimental grounds, and this was only the easiest of the apparently limitless possibilities of animal and vegetable variation that experimental biology was taking up. A huge and hitherto unsuspected wealth of mineral substances was ready to come out of the deep-lying rocks and refresh the rather limited and jaded resources of the contemporary soil. And alterations in the composition and movements of the atmosphere were no longer inaccessibly beyond human effort. The obstruction of individual ownership and localized governments had been swept away for ever. In that respect the Second Council had beyond question triumphed. But the very vigour with which it had done its task for man and the world as they were, and still in effect are, had cleared the ground for such an unprecedented inventiveness as is now rapidly altering not only the face but the very substance of life.

The Replanning Commission set about its task with the leisurely energy of a body under no stress of necessity. "Life is quite good as it is," runs the Introduc-

tion to its Draft Plan. "But it is part of the fundamental goodness of life that we have as much incessant novelty as we desire at our disposal. Due proportion must be our perpetual care. Want of proportion in the development of new things was the general cause of the great bulk of human suffering and frustration during the past five centuries. We have now an organization of controls that can restrain anything like the spasmodic mercenary enterprise, without plan or balance, that let loose disaster in the early twentieth century. We can afford to look before we leap and measure within quite close limits the tale of consequences we set going. In the end we may find that there was very considerable justification for the restraint put by our Supreme Council upon the immediate application of recent inventions, and particularly of recent biological inventions, which might otherwise have precipitated very similar but even more fundamental and catastrophic disproportions to those which overwhelmed the capitalist civilization of the nineteenth century.

"The particular field in which we propose a continuation of restraint is in the application of the rapidly advancing science of genetics to the increase of variability so far as human beings, and probably some other of the higher mammals, are concerned. We believe that the general feeling of the race is against any such experimentation at present. Under the Second Council the painless destruction of monsters and the more dreadful and pitiful sorts of defective was legalized, and also the sterilization of various types that would otherwise have transmitted tendencies that were plainly undesirable. This is as far, we think, as humanity should go in directing its racial heredity, until our knowledge of behaviour has been greatly amplified. For an age or so we can be content with humanity as it now is, humanity no longer distressed and driven to cruelty by overcrowding, under-nourishment, infections, mental and physical poisons of every sort. There is a rich mine of still greatly underdeveloped capacity in the human brain as it is, and this we may very happily explore by means of artistic effort, by scientific investigations, by living freely and gaily, for the next few generations. Normal human life can be cleansed, extended and amplified. With that we propose to content ourselves. Even upon this planet we have millions of years ahead before there can be any fundamental change in our environment.

"Directly we turn from humanity to other forms of life it is manifest that a most attractive realm is opening to us. We may have new and wonderful forests; we may have new plants; we may replace the weedy and scanty greensward of the past by a subtler and livelier texture. Undreamt-of fruits and blossoms may be summoned out of non-existence. The insect world, on which so much of the rest of life depends, may be made more congenial to mankind. The smaller fry of life and the little beasts and the birds can be varied now until they all come into a tolerable friendship with ourselves. As our hands lose their clumsiness we may interfere more and more surely with the balance of life. There is no longer fear of abundance now that man is sane.

"Our planning of human activities for the next few generations will involve no fundamental changes at all for humanity. It will be a keying-up of the sort of life for which our race, however darkly, confusedly and unsuccessfully, has always

striven. At present deliberate weather-control is too big a task for us, but we believe that a sure weather calendar for a year or so ahead is now becoming possible. An immense series of enterprises to change the soil, lay- out, vegetation and fauna, first of this region and then of that, will necessitate a complete rearrangement of the mines, deep quarries, road network and heavy sea transport of the globe. None of this need be ugly or repulsive, even in the doing; it can all be made intensely interesting. Engineering structure, which was once clumsy and monstrous, is now becoming as graceful as a panther. Industrial enterprises that formerly befouled the world with smoke, refuse and cinder heaps, are now cleaner in their habits than a well-trained cat. The world lay-out of the Second Council, designed apparently for a static society, will be to a large extent swept aside by our new operations. And no doubt our achievements in their turn will give way to still bolder and lovelier enterprises."

So ran the Introduction to what is known as the Keying-up Plan of 2060. Today we are most of us still immersed in its realization. It has given the world occupation without servitude and leisure without boredom. When we have had enough of our own work for a time we fly off—or walk round the corner—to see what other people are doing. The world is full of interest and delight, from the forest gardens of the Amazons with their sloths, monkeys and occasional pumas and alligators to that playground of the world, the snowfields of the Himalayas. We can arrange to take a turn with the meteorological observers in the upper air, or tune our lungs for a spell in the deep-sea galleries below the rafts of Atlantis. There we can see the great cephalopods of the middle levels coming for their food or watch the headlong growth of a giant pearl.

We are already so accustomed to grace, beauty and variety in all the details and general forms about us that it is only by turning over the pictures and records of seventy years ago that we realize how relatively uneventful were the first decades of human unity. At first man seems to have been so exhausted by his escape from massacre, disease, economic waste and general futility, and so terrified by the thought of any relapse into the old confusions, conflicts and economic cannibalism, that he was capable of nothing but order. But he gathers courage. It is not only our world that is being keyed up, but ourselves.

3. GEOGONIC PLANNING

Among the "deferred projects" that lie behind our current activities, and second only to the system of schemes for inducing and directing a great increase in human variability, is the complex of plans that have been drawn out to alter the terrestrial contours. Here again is something far too great and dangerous for our present wisdom, but something which it seems inevitable our race will ultimately attempt.

At present, and for many generations yet, we are still the creatures and subjects of geography; the oceans and great mountain chains condition our lives. They determine habitats, which again determine the human type best adapted to live for the greater part of its life in this or that region. Every kind of us, dark or fair, thick-set or slender, black or buff, has its own distinctive best place in which to rear its children and work and rest. It may roam the earth as it will, but only in certain regions is it altogether at home. No type is at home everywhere. There is no universal man. A universal type of man would be possible only on a flat and uniform earth. There is a necessary variety in humanity which no one now desires to diminish.

But the question the modern geographer puts to us is whether there is not a classification of habitats possible into very desirable, desirable, undesirable, and inimical, and whether a certain modification of the planet- levels operating in conjunction with the restoration of forests now in progress would not greatly increase the desirable habitats, by a redistribution of rainfall, a change in the fall of the surface waters, protection from winds and so forth. A not very considerable rise in the Appennines, for instance, would bring them up to the permanent snow-line and change the character of the entire Italian peninsula. And an increase in desirable habitats may bring with it an increase in the variety of desirable human types.

Yesterday this sort of thing was called "chimerical," to-day it is impracticable and unnecessary, because of the volcanic forces that might be released. So for the present the geogonist, like the geneticist, must content himself with dreams—in his case dreams of moulding a fire-spouting, quivering planet closer to the expanding needs of man. His turn to remodel the world will come perhaps in a thousand years or so. There is plenty of time for that.

4. CHANGES IN THE CONTROL OF BEHAVIOUR

The past forty-eight years have seen very great modifications in the social control of individual behaviour. There has been a very great increase in the science, skill and quality of the teachers throughout the world, but quite apart from that the character and purpose of education and police have changed profoundly.

Education as we understand it to-day began about the middle of the twentieth century. It had only the slenderest continuity with the education of the preceding age, just as the education of Christendom had only the slenderest continuity with the education of the pagan world. Reading, writing, and counting were taught in all three systems, but beyond that the very objectives were different. Modern education began as propaganda after the time of De Windt, as the propaganda of the Modern State. It sought to establish a new complete ideology and a new spirit which would induce the individual to devote himself and to shape all his activities to one definite purpose, to the attainment and maintenance of a progressive world-socialism, using an efficient monetary system as its normal medium of relationship.

This seemed, and was, a gigantic undertaking. It faced colossal obstacles in ordinary human nature. But it was supremely necessary if human civilization was to continue. The alternative was a relapse through chaotic barbarism to animal casualness and final extinction. Thought and behaviour patterns had to be shaped therefore to subserve this objective, to the relative disregard of any other conceivable purpose. The Modern State became the whole duty of man. This propaganda passed necessarily into a training for public service and a universal public education. The Modern State Fellowship was a trained body pledged to impose its own type of training upon all the world. It proposed to be the New Humanity. It would accept no compromises. It made the whole educational framework militant. No other type of school and no other system of teaching was tolerated for more than half a century. Never before was man so directed and disciplined.

The educationists of this period of the First Council and the Air Dictatorship were particularly sedulous to restrain what they called "aberrant motives." Austerity in eating and drinking, hardiness, severity in exercise, a jealousy of leisure, and a profound distrust of aesthetic and sensuous gratification, and particularly of sexual excitement, marked the educational ideals of these men who set out to demodel the world. In the early stages of progressive and revolutionary thought in the nineteenth century there had been considerable laxity of private conduct. There had been a revolt against what was called "Christian morality," and a dispo-

sition not simply to condone but encourage indulgence in forms that had hitherto been prohibited. Most of this "liberalism" in conduct had vanished from revolutionary circles by the second or third decade of the twentieth century. The Modern State movement, as it developed, was pervaded by a disapproval of every sort of sensuous or emotional affection. The business in hand could not suffer it. It wasted time; it wasted energy. It let in too much intrigue. It undermined the common loyalty. Not even Christianity in its most militant stages was so set against the dissipation of energy in this direction. The new sexual puritanism differed from the old in its toleration of birth control, its disregard of formal marriage, and a certain charity towards the first excesses of youth, but it insisted with even greater vigour upon public decency and upon the desirability of sexual seriousness, enduring connexions, and complete loyalty between lovers. As a result the world was far more monogamous, more decorous, and decently busy after 2000 C.E., than it had ever been before.

Many critics to-day are disposed to consider the repressions of that time excessive. We are now in a different phase; the militant age is past. They allege that there was a vast amount of secret and solitary vice and moral and mental distortion beneath the cold surface of things during these disciplined years, and they consider that the undeniable harshness and obstinacy of the Second Council as it grew old was a direct result of its puritanism. They do not hesitate to use such terms as masochist and sadist. But this is by no means a unanimous opinion. Equally reputable authorities deny that there was any such seething pit of stifled desires and thwarted motives under the orderly and healthy activities of the constructive time as this new school pretends. In no psychological problem are we still so inadequately informed as in the quantitative estimate of sexual impulse and restraint.

Our investigators work at literature, biographies, diaries, pictorial art, police reports in their intricate attempt to recover the vanished mental states of these departed generations. There seems to be a sort of rhythm in these things. The contrast between present conditions and conditions seventy years ago is paralleled in history by the contrast between English social life in 1855 and 1925. There also we have a phase of extreme restraint and decorum giving way to one of remarkable freedom. We can trace every phase. Every phase is amply documented. There are not the slightest grounds for supposing that the earlier period was one of intense nervous strain and misery. There was a general absence of vivid excitation, and the sexual life flowed along in an orderly fashion. It did not get into politics or the control of businesses. It appears in plays and novels like a tame animal which is not to be made too much of. It goes out of the room whenever necessary. By comparison England in 1920 was out for everything it could do sexually. It did everything and boasted about it and incited the young. As the gravity of economic and political problems increased and the structural unsoundness of the world became more manifest, sexual preoccupations seem to have afforded a sort of refuge from the mental strain demanded by the struggle. People distracted themselves from the immense demands of the situation by making a great noise about the in-

tensifications and aberrations of the personal life. There was a real propaganda of drugs and homosexuality among the clever young. Literature, always so responsive to its audience, stood on its head and displayed its private parts. It produced a vast amount of solemn pornography, facetious pornography, sadistic incitement, re-sexualized religiosity and verbal gibbering in which the rich effectiveness of obscene words was abundantly exploited. It is all available for the reader to-day who cares to examine it. He will find it neither shocking, disgusting, exciting or interesting. He will find it comically pretentious and pitifully silly.

It is small wonder that the scattered workers for the Modern State, who were struggling heroically with the huge problems of social dislocation and social reconstruction, developed an antipathy against these aesthetic and sexual preoccupations which robbed them of the help and service of so many hopeful youngsters. The Modern State Movement was unobtrusively puritanical from the outset. After the romantic lapses of the First World Council it became oppressively puritanical.

It was the precedent of the moral disorder of the early twentieth century to which the Educational Control appealed, a hundred and twenty years later, to justify its sustained regulation of private morals and repression of stimulation. It failed to realize the profound difference of the new conditions. The florid ebullition of sexual troubles, sexual refinements and sexual grossnesses in the Age of Frustration had been a natural consequence of frustration. Everywhere in the face of challenges too huge to face, rich and poor alike found themselves aimless, unoccupied, menaced. Ill health was increasing. Drugs, alcohol and sex were available to excite and soothe and deaden their distressed nerves. Good-looking youth, which could not sell its brains or labour, could still find a market for its person. About every nucleus of unjustly acquired wealth or demoralized power prostitution and parasitism festered. What else was there to do in that ugly, unhappy and dangerous world? But the world of 2040 was a busy, keenly interested and healthy world again.

We cannot detail in this general review of history the reluctant lifting of one prohibition after another. We may now go naked, love as we like, eat, drink and amuse ourselves with our work or as we will, subject only to a proper respect for unformed minds. And no harm has been done at all. When the Puritanical Tyranny began, its directors felt they had imprisoned a tiger that would otherwise consume all the plenty and safety they achieved. Very reluctantly indeed, bit by bit and after endless disputes, were their prohibitions relaxed. And no tiger appeared. Properly nourished people do not take to gluttony, properly interested people are not overwhelmed by sex. Instead of a tiger appeared a harmless, quiet, unobtrusive and not unpleasing pussy-cat, which declined to be in any way notable.

Humanity was changing. The threatened outbreak of pornography, abnormality and sex excitation did not occur. But anyone who studies the fiction and drama of the past half-century and compares it with the similar literature of the old world will realize that there are far more personal love and far more happy lovers than

ever before, and that physical love to demonstrate loyalty, show preference, enrich association and seal friendship was never so direct and beautiful. Jealousy we have, but it is rarely malicious; desire, but it is rarely vicious. In this as in so many other things progress has meant simplification. The souls we read about of two centuries ago strike us as grotesquely tangled, tormented and nasty souls. Hate mingled with their desires; mercenary considerations were an ever present defilement; they paired dishonestly and mated insincerely.

But while there has been this release from the strait-laced sexual morals of the militant period, in another field there has been no relaxation. The new order can tolerate no tampering with the monetary-property system that holds us all together. Not only is our police incessantly alert against robbery and cheating as the old world understood it, but many gainful practices that 1920 would have considered tolerable or even admirable are suppressed, and are likely to be suppressed for all time. Gambling, the mean desire and device to get the spending of someone else's earnings, is punished as heavily as the forgery of money checks; and all those speculative activities which seemed to be the very texture of the nineteenth-century social order dare not reappear now in any disguise at all. Money is a check for our personal needs, or for the giving of graceful presents. There must be no misuse of money to gain an advantage over another human being, even with that other human being's connivance. There we are still bound. That sort of thing is the vice of cannibalism. Beyond that liberty increases daily.

With a sound education of mind and body and a rigorous and exact protection of property and money from dishonourable impulses, we have found that it is possible to give every human being such a liberty of movement and general behaviour as would have seemed incredible to those militant socialists who ruled the world during the earlier decades of the last century. But it is just because of their stern and thorough cleansing of human life that we can now live in freedom. We may go anywhere in the world now, we may do practically anything that we can possibly desire to do.

5. ORGANIZATION OF PLENTY

Just as it becomes increasingly difficult for the teacher of history to convey to each new generation what human feelings and motives were like in a world of morbid infections and unwholesome bodily habits or in a heavily sentimentalized atmosphere of general distrust and insecurity, so also he has to make a most vigorous imaginative effort to recover even the faintest shadow of the pervading vexation, humiliations and straining anxiety that resulted from an almost universal deficiency of common things. Everybody, except a small minority, went short until the close of the twentieth century. Even the rich had to be wary cunning buyers to satisfy all their fancies and desires. The simplified economic order of our world to-day runs so smoothly that we hardly think at all about our ordinary needs. Housing, food and clothing wait upon us wherever we go. It is so easily done that we fail to realize the immense cleansing away of obstructive difficulties that had to occur before it could be made so easy.

One of the results of abundance that our ancestors would have found paradoxical is the abolition of encumbrance. But the less there was in the past the more you had to have and hold. Men had to appropriate things because there was not enough to go round. Your home was not simply the place to which you retired for solitude or intimacy; it was a store house. In the sixteenth or seventeenth century it was even fortified by bars, locks and bolts against robbers. You got with difficulty, and what you got you kept. The successful man of those days was imprisoned and smothered in accumulations upon which he dared not relax his watchfulness and grip. They were as indestructible as he could make them, for once destroyed or ignored they might prove irreplaceable. Everybody was keeping things, keeping them rather than using them. If they were not wanted now they might be wanted presently. If that successful man desired to vary his urban life he had to possess a country house. In these establishments there had to be a miniature social economy. Much of the food was not only prepared in the personal household, but produced on the private estate. All this had to be managed and watched to prevent waste, slackness and dishonesty. All the clothes the prosperous man might want to wear had to be stored and preserved in presses and wardrobes; his household needed gear against any possible emergency; and all his accumulations had to be guarded against robbers. It was almost as anxious and wearing a job to be rich as to be poor in those days of general insufficiency. And if the rich man travelled, he had to travel in his own coach with his attendants, taking a great burthen of clothing and general luggage with him.

In the relatively plentiful days of the later nineteenth century, which in so many details foreshadowed and yet failed to complete and generalize the conditions of our own time, there was for the prosperous at least a certain alleviation of the burthen of property. The temporary achievement of a limited cosmopolitanism of money and credit, the multiplication of the bourgeoisie, the liquidation of ownership by joint-stock undertakings, the increased facilities for communication and movement, made successful people less disposed to sit down amidst their possessions. There was a sustained general effort, which we now find grotesque and irrational, to keep property and at the same time not to be bothered by property. The ideal of success was no longer concrete ownership but purchasing power. Houses, furnishings and so forth changed hands with increased readiness.

Instead of living in great complete houses and dining at home, people lived in smaller houses or flats and dined in collective dining-rooms or restaurants. They gave up having country houses of their own and travelled freely and variously, evoking a vast industry of hotels and hired villas. They travelled lighter—in comparison with preceding centuries, that is. As retail trade organized itself upon big-business lines, the need for the private storage of gear diminished. People bought things when they wanted them, because now they could do so. The big "stores" of the early twentieth century carried an enormous and greatly varied stock.

In the days of Shakespeare new clothes, new furniture, new houses, new things of all sorts were infrequent; in the early twentieth century there were already intimations of the general fresh newness of our own times. The facilities for scrapping were still poorly developed, and there was much congestion and endless litter about, but renewal and replacement for those who had purchasing power were already well developed. If it had not been for the social catastrophe due to ignorance, individualism, monetary deflation and nationalism that overwhelmed that phase of civilization, the distributing organization of the world might very probably have developed straight on from the system of linked stores as it flourished in America in 1925 to our present conditions. And similarly there was an expansion of hotel life and a belated beginning of portable country houses, clearly foreshadowing our current arrangements.

After the disasters and new beginnings of the middle decades of the twentieth century it was to the patterns of big business at the close of the First Age of Abundance that the direction of the Transport Union recurred. We have told how easily and necessarily that Union became the trading monopoly and finally, as the Air and Sea Control, the actual government of the renascent world. Its counting-houses issuing and receiving its energy notes became the New Banking; its Trading Council became the New Retailing; its Supply Control took over, at last, the productive activities of the world. From the first the new powers were instinct with the idea of mobility. They had no vestiges in their composition of the skimping and saving traditions of the ages of insufficiency. They set about providing as ample and various accommodation for everybody as the ever-increasing production of the planet permitted.

The great distributing stores of the previous age provided the patterns from which the new distribution developed in that age of recovery. Wherever old towns and cities were being reconstructed or new ones appearing about new centres of productive activity the architects of the Air and Sea Control erected their great establishments, at first big and handsome after the old fashion and then more finely planned. At first these stores sold things according to the old method, then gradually in regard to a number of things, to clothing for example, they organized the modern system of exchanging new things for old; the new shoes or garment would be made and fitted to the customer and the old taken away and pulped or otherwise disposed of. Nothing is cobbled nowadays; nothing is patched or repaired. By degrees this method abolished that ancient institution the laundry altogether. That line of fluttering patched and tattered garments so characteristic of old-world village scenery vanished from the earth. New rapid methods of measuring and fitting replaced the tape, scissors and sewing of the old days. In the time of the Hoover Slump men would wear their underclothes for years, having them painfully washed out, dried, ironed and returned weekly, and they would wear their complex outer garments with all the old fastenings, buttons, straps, buckles and so forth, sometimes for many years. They had to be made of dark fabrics with broken patterns to conceal their griminess. The clothing of the Middle Ages was still filthier. Nowadays the average life of our much simpler and brighter outer garments with their convenient zip fastenings is about a week, and such light underclothes as we wear last about three days. We keep no wardrobes of them; the stores are our wardrobes. If the weather changes the stores are ready for us everywhere with wraps or heavier or lighter materials. It must be a remote expedition indeed that needs a change of raiment. We wear less clothing than our ancestors, partly because of our healthier condition, partly because we do not like to hide lovely bodies, but mainly because in the past men wrapped themselves up against every contingency. They wore hats whenever they were not under a roof, socks inside their boots, buttons on their sleeve-cuffs, collars and ties. It seems as though these elaborations became necessary to social prestige because of the general shortage. In an age of scarcity it was a testimonial to one's worth to be fully clad. In the nineteenth century the well-to-do wore gold watch-chains and gloves, which they carried in their hands in hot weather, as further evidence of substantial means.

Housing again, under the Air and Sea Control, took off from the point where the hotel-flat had left it in 1930. There was never any attempt to resume the building of those small permanent houses which were spread so abundantly over England, for example, after the World War. The first task of the new world control was mainly sanitary. Infection lurked everywhere; four decades of social disorder had made every building a decaying disease-trap for the young that were born into it. The Housing Control rebuilt the housing quarters of the rotten old towns in the form of blocks of dwellings, clean, spacious and convenient, but, to our eyes now, very squat and dull. They went from ten to twelve stories high, and very soundly and honestly made. Everywhere they had water, lighting, heating in

the colder climates, and sanitation. The picturesquely clustering rural villages were replaced all over the earth by the same type of concentrated house-block, the style and material varying only so far as conditions of climate required it. The villages were literally swept up into these piles. Even where small private cultivation was still going on, the concentration into these mansions occurred and the peasants bicycled out to their properties. Every block had its crèche, its school, its store and its general meeting-rooms.

As we look back on it this supersession of the single separate unlit, undrained and waterless hut or hovel, cottage or little steading seems to have been a swift business, but in reality it took from 1980 to 2030, much more than half the average lifetime, to spread this new conception of housing over most of the world, and by that time in the more advanced regions the older blocks were already being replaced by more beautiful and convenient creations.

Historical Pictures shows us the whole process. We see the jumbling growths of the early phase of the twentieth century; towering apartment-houses and hotels struggling up, far above the churches, mosques, pagodas and public buildings, out of a dense undergrowth of slums. Then come arrest and decline. The pictures become as full of ruins, sheds and makeshift buildings as the drawings of Albrecht Dürer. Amidst these appear air-raid shelters with their beetling covers, first-aid pillars with their chequered markings, and anti-aircraft forts. Further ruin ensues and we see life disorganized by the Great Plague.

Then suddenly these stout, squat, virtuous new blocks thrust into the scene and the battered past vanishes. A new Age has begun. The towns grow larger, finer and more varied. The housing blocks are grouped with the expanding stores, public clubs and hotels in parks and gardens near to the aerodrome, and convenient for whatever industry gives the agglomeration its importance. The public club became prominent after C.E. 2000, both architecturally and socially. That again was the revival of two old ideas; it was a combination of the idea of the English or American club with the idea of the Baths to which the Roman citizens resorted. Here from the start were grouped the gymnastic and sports halls, dancing-floors, conference rooms, the perpetual news cinema, libraries, reading-rooms, small studies, studios and social centres of the reviving social life.

The twenty-first century rediscovered an experience of the nineteenth and of the first centuries of the Christian Era, a discovery that was also made by Alexander the Great, that it is much easier to build great modern cities in new places than to modernize the old centres of activity. And the more vital these old centres remained the more difficult was their reconstruction, because it meant the interruption and transfer of important activities to new quarters. New York was typical of this lag in rebuilding. Up to quite recently Lower New York has been the most old-fashioned city in the world, unique in its gloomy antiquity. The last of the ancient skyscrapers, the Empire State Building, is even now under demolition in C.E. 2106!

This was not because New York has fallen out of things, but, on the contrary, because it was in the van of the new movement. We have already quoted Nichol-

son's account of its reviving importance in 1960. A year or so later it became the headquarters of the American branch of the Sea and Air Control, a western equivalent to Basra. The swiftly expanding activities of the new government needed immediate housing, and the gaunt surviving piles of Lower New York were adapted hastily to its accommodation. This kept them going for a time, and then arose a prolonged controversy between rival schools of planning for the reconstruction of that strangely vital city. It is not only true that the poorer the world was the more it was encumbered by property, but also that the more vigorously a place or a building is being used in progressive work the more difficult it is to keep it up to date.

Since the middle of the twenty-first century there has been a world-wide reappearance of the individual home, more particularly on the countryside, by the sea, and amidst forests and mountain scenery. But it has reappeared in a new form. It is not really the same thing as the old cottage and country house.

The idea of a home made of portable material, constructed at some convenient industrial centre and sent to any desired site, was already in the minds of such restless innovators as Henry Ford before the Decline and Fall. The country college, the country house, is an imaginative outlet. For great numbers of men and women comes a phase when the desire for that little peculiar place, with its carefully chosen site, its distinctive long-coveted amenities, its outlet upon the woods, the mountain, the jungle or the sea, has an overpowering appeal. There they will live, dream, work and be happy. Few of the many who had that dream could satisfy it in the old days. Some rare, rich persons were able to buy land, build elaborately after their desires, make gardens. When they died or became bankrupt other people without the leisure to make their own homes bought the abandoned home. They would far rather have made a place for themselves, but there stood the predecessor's desire in brick or stone, solid and irremovable, and they did what they could, by means of alterations, to eliminate the taste of him.

But as plenty and mechanical power increased, as the new road system made more and more of the earth accessible, as power-cables and water supply spread everywhere, it became easy not only to clear away and obliterate the traces of houses that were done for, but to bring a pleasant individualized country house within the purchasing power of an increasing proportion of the population. The mastery of power in our time is manifested almost as much by its swift scrapping and scavenging as by its limitless productivity. Nowadays a man or woman may hit upon an unoccupied site, spend a few pleasant weeks planning and revising projects and designs, and give his order. In a month his home is ready, in a day or so more the foundation has been laid, and in three or four weeks the dream is realized; the house stands as he wished it to stand, connected to the power mains, supplied with water, furnished to his taste smiling and ready. It is hardly more trouble than ordering an aeroplane or an automobile.

In its earlier stages the evocation of the preconstructed house was not so rapid, but from the first it was far quicker than the laborious piling up of the old-world builder.

And with an equal facility now a house is cleared away. We no longer think it meet to wear another man's abandoned house any more than we think it proper to wear the clothes of the dead. Clearing away, says Michael Kemal, is the primary characteristic of the Modern Age. The Age of Frustration was essentially an age that could not clear away, either debts, sovereignties, patriotisms, old classes, old boundaries, old buildings, old scores or old grievances. It is only in the past century that man has learnt the real lesson of plenty, that far more important than getting things is getting rid of things. We are rich universally because we are no longer rich personally.

We have mentioned the travelling wealthy man of the seventeenth century, for then only the wealthy aristocrats could travel freely, and we have glanced at the cumbersome impedimenta of his voyage. Compare him with any ordinary man today who decides to take a holiday and go to the ends of the earth. He may arrange with a travel bureau overnight for one or two special accommodations, then off he goes in the clothes he wears. He takes a wallet with his money account, his identification papers and perhaps a memorandum book. He may wear, as many people do, a personal ornament or so that has taken a hold upon his imagination. He may carry something to read or a specimen he wants to show. Whatever else he is likely to want on his way he will find on his way. He needs no other possessions because his possessions are everywhere. We have solved the problem of socializing property, the problem the early twentieth century was unable to solve. We have the use and consumption of material goods without the burthen of ownership.

6. THE AVERAGE MAN GROWS OLDER AND WISER

The numbers and the quality of the human population have changed very greatly in the past two centuries. Always these things have varied; every animal and vegetable species fluctuates continually in the numbers and quality of its individuals; but it is only recently that these movements have been recorded and examined systematically. The anti-progressives of the early twentieth century loved to assert that "human nature" never altered; to imagine that the men of the Stone Age felt and thought like bank clerks picnicking in a cave, and that the ideas of Confucius and Buddha were easily interchangeable with the ideas of Rousseau, Karl Marx or De Windt. They were not simply ignorant but misinformed about almost every essential fact in the past experiences and present situation of the race. Only when the twenty-first century was well under way did any consciousness of the primary operating forces in human biology appear in the discussion and conduct of world affairs.

In the year 1800 the total population of the world was under 900 millions, and the average age was about 22. In 1900 the population had doubled and the average age had risen by nearly ten years. In 1935 a maximum was attained of 2000 millions and the average age had mounted to nearly 40. In a hundred years the facilities for intercommunication and physical reaction had increased beyond all measure. But the statesmen, educators and lawyers of that age, as we have shown very plainly in this history, were unaware of any of these differences that had occurred since their methods were developed. They drooled along according to precedent. A set-back for adjustment was therefore inevitable. We have told the broad facts of the crash that began with the war massacres of 1914-18 and culminated in the cycle of pestilences before 1957. In thirty years the population of the earth fell to about one thousand millions or less, and the average age receded to something about 23. This was a stupendous recession, not merely in numbers but in the maturity of the average mind.

Then came the Air and Sea Control and the First and the Second Council with their restoration of hygienic conditions and their scientific planning. The increase of population was watched and restrained for a century, but the average age extended until now it is 62 and still rising. The population total crept back to 1500 millions in 2060 and reached 2000 millions again in 2085. It has become manifest that such a population is no longer unwieldy, and that with the scientific education and behaviour control we now possess a considerable further increase can be contemplated without dismay.

The population of the earth is now 2500 millions, and it will probably be let up to 4000 millions as rapidly as the world is keyed up for its full support and happiness. The danger of such a population swarming dangerously or getting into panics, mental jams, crushes and insanitary congestions grows less and less. The opinion of contemporary authorities is that 4000 millions is an optimum, and that before many decades have passed it will be possible to keep most of those born actively and happily alive to something like 90 years of age. But the question of the possibility and advisability of prolonging the individual life more than three or four decades beyond the "threescore and ten" of the Biblical barbarian is still an open one. It is possible that there is a limit to the memories a brain can carry and to its power of taking new interest in fresh events. There may be a natural death for most people in the future about the age of a hundred or a little more, as painless and acceptable as going to bed and sleeping after a long and interesting day.

These quantitative biological alterations involve the profoundest differences in the quality of every life concerned. It is not simply that each individual has now a justifiable faith that he will live out his life to the end, but that the conditions in which he lives call out quite a different reaction system from that evoked in the past. Before the Middle Ages people thought of their grandparents as older and mightier people, but we think of our ancestors as younger and feebler people. Those earlier generations were like fresh-water fish, living in shallow, saline and readily dried-up water, in comparison with others of the same species living in a deep, abundant, well- aerated and altogether congenial lake. They were continually uncomfortable, constantly stranded by circumstances; they flapped about wildly and died early. Although they were the same in essence, their behaviour, their very movements, were like the behaviour of a different species of being.

Consider the existence of a young man in Shakespeare's time. If he did not die young he aged rapidly. He would be heavy, old and pompous at forty. A swarm of ailments lay in wait for him to emphasize and accelerate his decay. Youth was stuff that would not endure. The beauty and vitality of women were even more evanescent. So they snatched at love and adventure. The world was full of Romeos and Juliets at the crest of their passionate lives in their teens, who nowadays would be in the college stage of education, a score of years away from any conclusive drama. The literature of the time witnesses to a universal normal swift transitoriness. The simple precipitate love story, the jealousy, the headlong revenge and so on makes the substances of drama, romance and poem. That and the grab at spendable wealth: El Dorado, treasure trove or robbery attempted and defeated. A career was made or marred by a week's folly, and there was little time to recover it before the end. It is extraordinarily interesting to note all the things in life that are left out by the Elizabethan literature, and so to measure that smaller brighter circle of interest in that age.

The changing biological conditions between 1840 and 1940 mirror themselves faithfully in the art and reading of the decades. The novel, which is at first pervaded by a gay hello to life, which accepts everything as cheerfully as a young animal, which laughs, caricatures and incites, becomes reflective, analytical, pur-

poseful. Life no longer ends at the first rush. The proportion of novels to other books diminishes. The penetration of the individual consciousness by the great social and economic processes that were going on becomes more and more evident. When literature revived at the close of the twentieth century it was an adult literature, expressing the mentality of readers and writers who were fully grown men and women in a planning world that had ceased to be accidental and incoherent. In the novel as it then reappeared there is much more about personal love and the interplay of character, but far less (and the proportion continues to diminish) about the primary love adventure.

That diminution of haste and avidity, of the quick egotism and swift uncritical judgment of youth, still continues. The deliberation, serenity and breadth of reference in the normal life increase. The years from thirty to seventy were formerly a sort of dump for the consequences of the first three decades; now they are the main part of life, the years of work, expression and complete self-discovery, to which these earlier stages are the bright, delightful prelude. There was a time when the man or woman over forty felt something of a survivor; he was "staying on"; relatively the world swarmed with youth, with the swiftness, rivalries and shallowness of youth: the fitness of the ill-protected body had gone already; the elderly people who were "getting on for fifty" moved slowly and had duller if sounder apprehensions. But now most of us are in the graver years with our bodies and apprehensions unimpaired, and there is no longer the same effect of being rather in the way of a juvenile treat. The juvenile treat, the age when even the old aped the young, ended in the World War and the economic collapse. After that came a struggle, at first unconscious and then open and declared, between youth and mental maturity.

In the bad years after the World War for a couple of generations there was a very unhappy relapse towards youthful predominance. The old people had failed to avert the collapse, the legitimate seniors for the new period were dead and broken and morally disorganized, and there was a sort of poetic justice in the stormy release of puerility that ensued. Italy was scourged by its hobbledehoys in black shirts; Russia was ruled by the blue-chinned Young; Ireland was devastated by hooligan patriots; presently Germany, after brooding over its defeat for ten years, had a convulsive relapse to fiercely crazy boyishness in the Nazis. Indian patriotism had a kindred immaturity. The tender years of many of the young revolutionaries executed by the British, outrage our standards of toleration. Everywhere was youthful ignorance with lethal weapons in its hands, conceited, self-righteous, exalted, blind to the tale of consequences. Breaking up things is the disposition of youth, and making is not yet in its experience. Liberalism and the middle-aged had a phase of unprecedented ineffectiveness. There seemed to be no judgment left in the world, and the young, in masks and requisitioned cars, making nocturnal raids, indulging in punitive cruelties, beating, torturing, displaying in equal measure physical recklessness and moral panic, came near to wrecking the whole civilizing process.

It is an interesting task to trace the gradual maturing of these adolescent organizers that seized so much of the control of the world in that age of transitional disorder. There are voluminous books in which Fascism in 1920, Fascism in 1930, and Fascism in 1940, or again Communism in the same decades, is elaborately compared with itself. After all their impatience and sentimentality, their rank patriotism and reactionary cant, we find these youth movements unobtrusively sneaking back to planning, discipline, and scientific methods. Millions of young men who began Fascist, Nazi, Communist and the like, blind nationalists and irrational partisans, became Modern State men in their middle years. They became at last instruments to realize the plans and visions of the very men they had hunted, maltreated and murdered in the crude zeal of their first beginnings.

But now youth is well in hand for ever, and when we speak of a man to-day we really mean a different being from a nineteenth-century man. Bodily he is sounder and fitter, almost completely free from disease; mentally he is clear and clean and educated to a pitch that was still undreamt of two centuries ago. He is over fifty instead of being under thirty. He is less gregarious in his instincts and less suggestible because he is further away from the "home and litter" mentality, but he is far more social and unselfish in his ideology and mental habits. He is, in fact, for all the identity of his heredity, a different animal. He is bigger and stronger, more clear-headed, with more self- control and more definitely related to his fellow creatures.

This is manifest everywhere, but it is particularly visible in such regions as Bengal and Central China. There we find the direct descendants of shrill, unhappy, swarming, degenerate, undernourished, under-educated, underbred and short-lived populations among the finest, handsomest, longest- lived and ablest of contemporary humanity. This has been achieved without any attempt at Positive Eugenics; it has resulted from the honest application of the Obvious to health, education, and economic organization, within little more than a hundred years. These populations were terribly weeded by the pestilences of the age of disorder and grimly disciplined by the Tyranny. They are now, after that pruning and training bearing as fine flowers of literary and scientific achievement as any other racial masses.

7. LANGUAGE AND MENTAL GROWTH

(I print this section exactly as Raven wrote it down. It is, the reader will remark, in very ordinary twentieth-century English. Yet plainly if it is a part of a twenty-second-century textbook of general history it cannot have been written originally in our contemporary idiom. It insists upon a refinement and enlargement of language as if it had already occurred, but no such refinement is evident. It must have been translated by Raven as he dreamt it into the prose of to-day. If he saw that book of his at all, he saw it not with his eyes but with his mind. The actual page could have had neither our lettering, our spelling, our phrasing nor our vocabulary.)

One of the unanticipated achievements of the twenty-first century was the rapid diffusion of Basic English as the lingua franca of the world and the even more rapid modification, expansion and spread of English in its wake. The English most of us speak and write today is a very different tongue from the English of Shakespeare, Addison, Bunyan or Shaw; it has shed the last traces of such archaic elaborations as a subjunctive mood; it has simplified its spelling, standardized its pronunciation, adopted many foreign locutions, and naturalized and assimilated thousands of foreign words. No deliberate attempt was made to establish it as the world language. It had many natural advantages over its chief competitors, Spanish, French, Russian, German and Italian. It was simpler, subtler, more flexible and already more widely spoken, but it was certainly the use of Basic English which gave it its final victory over these rivals.

Basic English was the invention of an ingenious scholar of Cambridge in England, C. K. Ogden (1889-1990), who devoted a long and industrious life to the simplification of expression and particularly to this particular simplification. It is interesting to note that he was a contemporary of James Joyce (1882-1955), who also devoted himself to the task of devising a new sort of English. But while Ogden sought scientific simplification, Joyce worked aesthetically for elaboration and rich suggestion, and vanished at last from the pursuit of his dwindling pack of readers in a tangled prose almost indistinguishable from the gibbering of a lunatic. Nevertheless he added about twenty-five words to the language which are still in use. Ogden, after long and industrious experimentation in the reverse direction, emerged with an English of 850 words and a few rules of construction which would enable any foreigner to express practically any ordinary idea simply and clearly. It became possible for an intelligent foreigner to talk or correspond in understandable English in a few weeks. On the whole it was more difficult to train

English speakers to restrict themselves to the forms and words selected than to teach outsiders the whole of Basic. It was a teacher of languages, Rudolph Boyle (1910-1959), who contrived the method by which English speakers learnt to confine themselves, when necessary, to Basic limitations.

This convenience spread like wildfire after the First Conference of Basra. It was made the official medium of communication throughout the world by the Air and Sea Control, and by 2020 there was hardly anyone in the world who could not talk and understand it.

It is from phonetically spelt Basic English as a new starting-point that the language we write and speak to-day developed, chiefly by the gradual resumption of verbs and idioms from the mother tongue and by the assimilation of foreign terms and phrases. We speak a language of nearly two million words nowadays, a synthetic language in fact, into which roots, words and idioms from every speech in the world have been poured. K. Wang in a recent essay has shown that there are still specializations of vocabulary. The vocabulary of a score of recent writers of Italian origin chosen haphazard shows a marked preference for words derived from the Latin, in comparison with twenty Eastern Asiatic writers whose bias is Chinese and American. Yet they can all understand one another and they are all in one undivided cultural field.

There are few redundancies in the new English of today and tomorrow, and there is an increasing disposition to take synonyms, and what used to be classified as "rare" or "obsolete" terms, and re-define them to convey some finer shade of meaning. Criticism, in the form of the Dictionary Bureau, scrutinizes, but permits desirable additions. One can feel little doubt about the increasing delicacy and precision of expression to-day if we compare a contemporary book with some English classic of the eighteenth or nineteenth century. That is still quite understandable to us, but in its bareness and occasional ineptitudes it seems halfway back to the limitations and lumberingness of Early English or Gothic.

The fuller the terminology the finer the mind. There can be very little doubt that the brain of a twentieth-century man compared with the brain of an ordinary man to-day, though in no way intrinsically inferior, was a far less polished and well-adjusted implement. It was warped by bad habits, cumbered with a tangle of unsound associations, clogged with unresolved complexes; it was like a fine piece of machinery in a state of dirt and neglect. The modern brain is far more neatly packed and better arranged, cleaner and better lubricated. It not only holds much more, but it uses the larger keyboard of our contemporary language more efficiently. The common man to-day is apt to find the philosophers and "thinkers" of two centuries ago unaccountably roundabout, tedious and encumbered. It is not so much that he finds them obscure, but that when at last he has dragged the meanings out of their jungles of statement into the light of day he finds he has thought all round them.

An interesting and valuable group of investigators, whose work still goes on, appeared first in a rudimentary form in the nineteenth century. The leader of this group was a certain Lady Welby (1837-1912), who was frankly considered by

most of her contemporaries as an unintelligible bore. She corresponded copiously with all who would attend to her, harping perpetually on the idea that language could be made more exactly expressive, that there should be a "Science of Significs". C. K. Ogden and a fellow Fellow of Magdalene College, I. A. Richards (1893-1977), were among the few who took her seriously. These two produced a book, The Meaning of Meaning, in 1923 which counts as one of the earliest attempts to improve the language mechanism. Basic English was a by- product of these enquiries. The new Science was practically unendowed, it attracted few workers, and it was lost sight of during the decades of disaster. It was revived only in the early twenty-first century.

Then Carl Ratan became the centre of a group of workers inspired by the idea of making English more lucid and comprehensive and a truly universal language. His work has expanded into the voluminous organization of the Language Bureau as we know it to-day. The work of that Bureau has been compared to the work of the monetary experts who finally made money exact a hundred and fifty years ago. Just as civilization was held back for some centuries by the imperfections of the money nexus, so we begin to realize to-day that our intellectual progress is by no means so rapid as it might be because of the endless flaws and looseness of the language nexus.

An interesting compilation in hand, which promises to become a veritable history of philosophy and knowledge is the Language Discard. This project was originally set going by the Dictionary Section of the Language Bureau, as a mere account rendered of obsolete or obsolescent terms or terms which have become greatly altered from their original meaning; but the enquiry into the reasons for these changings and preferences and abandonments led very directly into an exhaustive analysis of the primary processes of human thought. A series of words, "soul spirit, matter, force, essence", for example, were built into the substance of Aryan and Semitic thought almost from their beginnings, and it was only quite recently that the exhaustive analyses by Yuan Shan and his associates of these framework terms made it clear that the processes of Chinese and Negro thinking were by no means parallel. Translation between languages, in all matters except matters of material statement, is always a little loose and rough, but between the ideology underlying the literature of Eastern Asia or the attempts of Africans to express themselves and that embodied in the ruling language of to-day the roughness approaches violence. That clash, as it is examined, is likely to produce very extensive innovations in our philosophical (general scientific) and technical nomenclature. We are speaking and writing a provisional language to-day. Our great-grandchildren will no more think of using many of our terms and turns of expression to-day than we should think of resorting again to the railway train, the paddle steamboat and the needle telegraph.

This rearrangement of the association systems of the human brain which is now in progress brings with it—long before we begin to dream of eugenic developments—the prospect of at present inconceivable extensions of human mental capacity. It will involve taking hold of issues that are at present quite outside our

grasp. There was a time when early man was no more capable of drawing a sketch or threading a needle than a cow; it was only as his thumb and fingers became opposable that the powers of craftsmanship and mechanism came within his grip. Similarly we may anticipate an enormous extension of research and a far deeper penetration into reality as language, our intellectual hand, is brought to a new level of efficiency.

There is not only this sharpening and refinement of the brain going on, but there has been what our great grandparents would have considered an immense increase in the amount, the quality, and the accessibility of knowledge. As the individual brain quickens and becomes more skilful, there also appears a collective Brain, the Encyclopaedia, the Fundamental Knowledge System which accumulates, sorts, keeps in order and renders available everything that is known. The Encyclopaedic organization, which centres upon Barcelona, with its seventeen million active workers is the Memory of Mankind. Its tentacles spread out in one direction to millions of investigators, checkers and correspondents, and in another to keep the educational process in living touch with mental advance. It is growing rapidly as the continual advance in productive efficiency liberates fresh multitudes of workers for its services. The mental mechanism of mankind is as yet only in its infancy.

Adolescence perhaps rather than infancy. It is because the mind of man is growing up that for the first time it realizes that it is young.

8. SUBLIMATION OF INTEREST

Not only is the average man to-day an older and graver creature than his ancestor of three centuries ago, but he is very differently employed. There has been a great diversion of his interest from the primary necessities of life.

Three centuries ago, well over ninety per cent of the human population was absorbed either in the direct production of necessities or in the scramble to get them from their original producers. Direct producers, the peasants and toilers, the entrepreneurs and their managers and directors, and direct distributors accounted for upward of eighty per cent of the human total; the rest were the millions of interveners, usurers, claim-makers, landowners, rentiers, solicitors, speculators, parasites, robbers, and thieves who were deemed necessary to ginger up the economic process. The forces of law, order and education, excluding temporary conscription and levies for military ends, took up five or six per cent of the residue, and a small minority, something under five per cent of the total population, supplied all the artistic effort, the scientific enquiry, the social and political thought, the living soul of the entire social body.

The systems of interest of most people were therefore restricted almost entirely to work and the struggle to possess. They had to think continually of the work they did either for their own profit or for the personal profit, comfort or fantasy of some employer. They had to think of keeping their jobs or of getting fresh ones, and this, in the days of narrowing employment after the Hoover Slump, became at last a monstrous obsession of the brain. What they earned they had to spend carefully or guard carefully, for the rascaldom of business was everywhere seeking to give nothing for something. Sometimes, sick of their narrow lives, they would gamble in the desperate hope of a convulsive enlargement, and for most of them gambling meant disappointment and self- reproach. Add to these worries a little love, a good deal of hate, and a desperate struggle to see it all in a hopeful and honourable light, a desperate hunger to be flattered and reassured, and you have the content of ninety-nine per cent of the human brains that made the world of 1930. They could no more escape from this restricted circle of urgently clamorous interests, hardly ampler than the circle of an animal's interest, than the animals can.

The Modern State has broken this cramping circle of interests for every human being. We are still creatures with brains like our forefathers, corresponding ganglia to ganglia and fibre to fibre, but WE ARE NOT USING THOSE BRAINS FOR THE SAME PURPOSES. The Modern State, by ensuring plenty and con-

trolling the increase of population, has taken all the interests of the food- hunt and the food-scramble, and all the interests of the struggle to down-and- out our human competitors, away from the activities of the individual brain. A relatively small number of specialized workers keep the necessary Controls of these primary preoccupations going. We worry about food, drink, clothing, health and personal freedom no more. The work we MUST do is not burthensome in amount, and it is the most congenial our educational guardians can find for us and help us to find. When it is done we are sure of the result; nobody is left in the world to cheat us or rob us of our pay. We are still competitive, more so perhaps than ever; jealousy still wars with generosity in us; the story of our personal affections is rarely a simple story; but the interest we feel in our work is a masterful interest and not a driven interest, and our competition is for distinction, appreciation and self-approval and not for mutual injury. There has been a release of by far the larger moiety of the mental energy of the normal man from its former inescapable preoccupations.

This steady obliteration of primary motives is manifested most illuminatingly by the statistics of what used to be "Crime and Punishment", figures of the offences, insubordinations and deliberate outrages upon social order and the consequent punishments and corrective proceedings that are issued by the disciplinary organization of the Behaviour Control. Statistics for the years of decadence are not forthcoming, but there is plentiful material from the comparatively orderly and prosperous period between 1890 and 1930. Great Britain then constituted the healthiest and most law-abiding community in the world, but the figures that emerge to the student of history present what seems to us an appalling welter of crime. Stealing, cheating of every sort, forgery, burglary, robbery with violence, poisoning and other forms of murder, occurred daily. It did not seem as though that thick defilement of wrongdoing about property could ever cease. Innumerable suicides occurred through pecuniary worry. Yet now all these crimes, which filled the jails, arising out of the scramble for money and property in an age of insufficiency, have almost completely vanished from human life. The Behaviour Control Report for 2104 (2105 is not yet available) records 715 cases of stealing for the whole world. In nearly every case the object stolen was some personal work of art, some small jewel, a piece of embroidery, a pet animal, several children, and—in one instance—the bulb of a new variety of lily that aroused the instinct to possess and care for. It is doubtful whether there were many undetected or unreported thefts.

There has not, however, been anything like the same abolition of personal offences. They have diminished. But while the property offences have diminished to the scale of one-ten-millionth of the old-world figures, these others show a reduction in the nature of single instances to former hundreds. Many types in our population are still very easily turned toward sexual lawlessness. Beautiful and attractive people and particularly attractive children are not yet perfectly immune from undesired solicitation, personal persecution, annoying assault and resentful injury. Jealousy is still a dangerous passion, more particularly below the age of

forty. The Behaviour Control ascribes nearly 520,000 offences to this group of urgencies, mostly assaults of varying degree of malignity, culminating in 67 murders. There were also 2192 suicides in the total. These figures show only a slight improvement upon the annual average for the previous decade.

Another difficult class of offence which finds no exact parallel in the criminal statistics of former times, unless the British offence of "malignant mischief" is to be put in this group, are acts of annoyance, destruction, assault and so forth, due to competitive jealousy and the exasperation aroused, often quite unwittingly, by the bearing or achievements of one's fellow creatures. This sort of misbehaviour varies in degree from the black hatred and fury of an uncontrolled egotism to what verges in some cases upon justifiable criticism of slightly fatuous or self-complacent behaviour. Four murders, some hundreds of assaults and acts of wanton destruction in this category, witness to the fact that this world is still not a Paradise for every type of individual. Either they are bitter by some inner necessity or they have been embittered. Yet when we take the grand total of every misdeed that had to be dealt with last year, counting even the most petty occasions for restoration, warning or reproof, and find it is just three quarters of a million in a world of 2500 million people, we have a quantitative measure of human progress in two brief centuries that justifies a very stalwart confidence in the human outlook. The imagination of man's heart is no longer evil continually. It is only evil occasionally, and the practical task of our social psychologists is to reduce those occasions and provocations.

The abundant release of brain-stuff, the mental plenty which has resulted from the organization of material plenty, is of necessity being directed into new channels. That meagre half per cent or less of creative workers of the old régime, the few curious men who played about with novel ideas, the odd men of leisure who collected "rarities" and inventions, has grown into a mighty body of enquiry, experiment, verification and record which is becoming now the larger part of the world's population.

We know now certainly what the people of three centuries ago never suspected, that the human brain released from hunger, fear and the other primary stresses is very easily amenable not only to creative and directive desire but also to kindly and helpful impulses. Almost all the people who keep our productive, our distributing and transport services going are there because they find the work entertaining, because they like making the machine work well and helping people. There is a satisfaction in being able to do things skilfully for others that they could not do nearly so well for themselves. The barbers, shoemakers, tailors, dressmakers, hatters, outfitters and so forth in the great stores to- day are very different people from the rather obsequious, deferential "inferiors" who made our great-great-grandfathers presentable to the world. Their essential interest is to make their customers sightly and comfortable and not to earn a profit for an employer. The old literature reeks with contempt for barbers and tailors and cobblers, often the contempt of profound resentment. If the common man despised the cobbler, the cobbler pinched his toe and chafed his heel. The barber, it

seemed, did no more than cut hair rather badly, and the tailor cut clothes. Except by accident, the barber had ceased to be a barber-surgeon. But nowadays the old-world barber would scarcely recognize himself in the barber-dentist, the kindly expert who sees to our coiffure, gives attention to our teeth, scrutinizes our mouth, hair and skin to detect any evidence of failing health, and sends us on our way refreshed, encouraged or warned. Often his friend the tailor or dressmaker will call in while he deals with us to consider our general bravery and improvement, and suggest variations of our exercise and habits.

The old distributing trades have lost their sharp demarcation from the advisory professions. They are in touch with the guardians of development who have replaced the schoolmasters, nurses, governesses, tutors and so forth of the old time, and with the general advisers who have taken on the tasks of the family solicitor, religious minister, private confessor and general practitioner of the past. These advisory and directive professions probably number two or three times as big a proportion of the whole population as the lawyers, educationists and doctors of the nineteenth century. They merge again into another stratum, the specialist teachers, concerned with developing and imparting skills and building up and maintaining the common ideology. This class again passes by insensible degrees into the worlds of technical work, art, literature and scientific research.

The primary producers and elaborators of material, our agriculturalists, engineers, chemists, transport men and industrial directors, also do their work because they like doing it. It satisfies them. They like their materials, they like their difficulties, they like the order of their days. In spite of an increasing output per head of population and an increasing variety and elaboration of the things we use, socially or individually, the numerical proportion of this section of the human population does not increase. Efficiency still outruns need and desire. The two and a half years of compulsory public service, which is an integral part of our education, supplies a larger and larger proportion of such toil as is still unavoidable.

This release of human energy from primary needs is a process that seems likely to continue indefinitely. And all the forces that have made our world- wide social life and keep it going direct that released energy towards the achievement of fresh knowledge and the accumulation and rendering of fresh experience. There is a continual sublimation of interest. Man becomes more curious, more excited, more daring, skilful, and pleasantly occupied every year. The more we learn of the possibilities of our world and the possibilities of ourselves, the richer, we learn, is our inheritance. This planet, which seemed so stern a mother to mankind, is discovered to be inexhaustible in its bounty. And the greatest discovery man has made has been the discovery of himself. Leonardo da Vinci with his immense breadth of vision, his creative fervour, his curiosity, his power of intensive work, was the precursor of the ordinary man, as the world is now producing him.

9. A NEW PHASE IN THE HISTORY OF LIFE

From the point of view of the ecologist the establishment of the Modern State marks an epoch in biological history. It has been an adaptation, none too soon, of our species to changing conditions that must otherwise have destroyed it. The immense developments and disasters of the nineteenth and twentieth centuries show us mankind scrambling on the verge of irreparable disaster.

The infinite toil of millions of tormented brains, the devotion and persistence of countless forgotten devotees, gave form and clear purpose in time to what were at first mere flounderings and clutchings towards safety. The threatened race did not fall back into that abyss of extinction which has swallowed up so many of the bolder experiments of life. In pain and uncertainty it clambered past its supreme danger phase, and now it has struggled to such a level of assurance, understanding and safety as no living substance has ever attained before.

By means of education and social discipline the normal human individual to-day acquires characteristics without which his continued existence would be impossible. In the future, as the obscurer processes of selection are accelerated and directed by eugenic effort, these acquired characteristics will be incorporated with his inherent nature, and his educational energy will be released for further adaptations. He will become generation by generation a new species, differing more widely from that weedy, tragic, pathetic, cruel, fantastic, absurd and sometimes sheerly horrible being who christened himself in a mood of oafish arrogance Homo sapiens.

The differences of the coming man from the man of the past will be multitudinous and intricate, but certain broad lines of comparison appear already. We have noted already the difference in the age cycle between ourselves and our ancestors, which has prolonged the youthful phase and shifted on the valid years towards the thirty-five to eighty period, and we have cited also the completer physical development, due to the release of vital energy from the task of resisting various infections, poisons and morbidities of growth. We are probably only in the beginning of very much more considerable physical modification. The aesthetic ideals of the past are likely to play a large part in determining the direction in which these modifications will take us. But these physical developments, important though they must ultimately be, are as yet much less important than the changes in moral form that are manifestly in progress. A brief consideration of these will make a fitting conclusion to this general outline of history.

Essentially they constitute a readjustment of the individual to the racial life. When we go back in time for a million years or so we find our ancestor species in a phase of almost fundamental individualism. Except where sexual life and the instinct system to protect offspring came in, the subman shifted for himself. He had no associates in the food hunt, no allies for defence. He was as solitary an animal as the tiger. From that he passed through stages of increasing sociability. The onset of these stages was made practicable by the retention of immature characteristics into adult life. The same thing is happening to the remnant of the lions today. They remain cubbish and friendly now to a much later age than they did a few-score thousand years ago. Man passed through a stage when he was as sociable as a modern lion and on to a phase when he was as sociable as a wolf or hunting dog.

But he did not rest at that. All the conditions of his life favoured the formation of still-larger communities and still-closer interdependence. He became a cultivator, an economic animal, and his communities expanded to thousands and scores of thousands of individuals held together by mutual service. He produced language and religion to bind the will and activities of these aggregations into an effective common policy. The history of mankind, as we unfold it to the contemporary student, is a story of ever increasing communication and ever increasing interdependence. Insensibly the material side of individual freedom was modified into unavoidable cooperation with the community.

Stress must be laid upon that word material. The physical subjugation and socialization of the human animal far outran his moral subjection. The history of mankind is also a history of education and compulsion. It is a record of give and take. Man almost up to the present day has remained at heart still the early savage, caring only for himself, for his sexual life, and, during the few years of their helplessness, his children. He has been willing to associate for aggression or for defence, but only very reluctantly for a common happiness. He has had to barter his freedom for the advantages of collective action, but he has done so against the grain, needing persuasion, pressure and helpful delusions.

The history of mankind has had to be very largely the history of a succession of religious and emotional inventions and reconstructions, to override the inherent distaste in the individual for subordination and self- sacrifice. At every opportunity the individual has sought to recover its personal initiatives. Its egotism has battled instinctively of necessity to get the best of the bargain and receive with as little giving as possible.

Man's natural self struggles to do that now as strongly as ever he did. But he struggles now in a better light and more intelligently; he realizes what is impossible, and the long conflict of individualism with society has arrived at a rational compromise. We have learnt how to catch and domesticate the ego at an early stage and train it for purposes greater than itself.

What has happened during the past three and a half centuries to the human consciousness has been a sublimation of individuality. That phase is the quintessence of modern history. A large part of the commonplace life of man, the food-

hunt, the shelter-hunt, the safety- hunt, has been lifted out of the individual sphere and socialized for ever. To that the human egotism has given its assent perforce. It has abandoned gambling and profit-seeking and all the wilder claims of property. It has ceased altogether to snatch, scramble and oust for material ends. And the common man has also been deprived of any weapons for his ready combativeness and of any liberty in its release. Nowadays even children do not fight each other. Gentleness in difference has become our second nature.

All that part of man's life and interests has been socialized entirely against his natural disposition in the matter. In all those concerns the whole race is now confluent; it is becoming as much a colonial organism as any branching coral or polyp, though the ties that link us are not fleshly bands, but infinitely elastic and invisible and subtle. In the later chapters of this world history we have examined and displayed, with particular attention because of its culminating character, the essential individualism of the World War process, and we have told how, with what difficulty and after what scourgings, our race has been brought to its present phase of organized self- control. This present phase is the victory of creative power working through the individualities of a more intelligent minority, in the face of universal confusion, taking indeed advantage of that confusion to inaugurate our present order. That wilful minority has opened the gates to a power and abundance of existence beyond all former dreaming. But our Modern State has neither absorbed nor destroyed individuality, which now, accepting the necessary restrictions upon its material aggressiveness, resumes at every opportunity its freedom and enterprise upon a higher level of life.

The individuality deprived, or relieved if you will, of its primary instinctive preoccupations with getting and keeping, disillusioned about precedence, personal display and suchlike barbaric vanities, growing continually and swiftly in wisdom and knowledge, has now to go further afield to find itself. No longer a self-sufficient being, at war with all its kind, it has become a responsible part of a species. It has become an experiment in feeling, knowing, making and response.

The body of mankind is now one single organism of nearly two thousand five hundred million persons, and the individual differences of every one of these persons is like an exploring tentacle thrust out to test and learn, to savour life in its fullness and bring in new experiences for the common stock. We are all members of one body[1]. Only in the dimmest analogy has anything of this sort happened in

[1] This was the phrase of that interesting mystic St. Paul (Saul) of Tarsus (2- 62 C.E. Epistles with analysis and commentary by Hirsch and Potter in the Historical Reprints: Development of Ideas Series), who did so much to pervert and enlarge the simpler cosmopolitan fraternalism of Jesus of Nazareth (-4-30 C.E.) before it was finally over-overwhelmed and lost in the sacrificial sacerdotalism of formal Christianity. For a brief period before it relapsed the Pauline cult had a curious flavour of Modern State feeling. There was, however, a politic disingenuousness in Paul which betrayed his undeniable intellectual power. He was ambiguous about blood sacrifices, immortality, private property and slavery, to the eternal injury of the Christian movement. It was completely

the universe as we knew it before. Our sense of our individual difference makes our realization of our common being more acute. We work, we think, we explore, we dispute, we take risks and suffer—for there seems no end to the difficult and dangerous adventures individual men and women may attempt; and more and more plain does it become to us that it is not our little selves, but Man the Undying who achieves these things through us.

As the slower processes of heredity seize upon and confirm these social adaptations, as the confluence of wills supersedes individual motives and loses its present factors of artificiality, the history of life will pass into a new phase, a phase with a common consciousness and a common will. We in our time are still rising towards the crest of that transition. And when that crest is attained what grandeur of life may not open out to Man! Eye hath not seen, nor ear heard; nor hath it entered into the mind of man to conceive.... For now we see as in a glass darkly....

At this point Raven's copied-out manuscript comes to an end—it seems to me a little abruptly. But it is the end; he has written the word "Finis" here. I will add only one word or so by way of comment. I have called that manuscript a dream book. Was it a dream book or was it indeed, as he declared and believed it to be, a vision of the shape of things to come? Or—there is a third possibility. As dreaming, this book is far too coherent; as vision, incredulity creeps in. But was Raven, too busily employed and too obsessed by the sense of urgency to embark upon a detailed analysis of world development, was he trying nevertheless to sketch out in this fantastic form a general thesis at least about the condition of things to come? If this is neither a dream book nor a Sibylline history, then it is a theory of world revolution. Plainly the thesis is that history must now continue to be a string of accidents with an increasingly disastrous trend until a comprehensive faith in the modernized World-State, socialistic, cosmopolitan and creative, takes hold of the human imagination. When the existing governments and ruling theories of life, the decaying religious and the decaying political forms of to- day, have sufficiently lost prestige through failure and catastrophe, then and then only will world-wide reconstruction be possible. And it must needs be the work, first of all, of an aggressive order of religiously devoted men and women who will try out and establish and impose a new pattern of living upon our race.

prostituted to usage before the first century was over. See Ivan Mackenzie, General Elements of Religion 2103. Mackenzie has an excellent chapter on the anticipation of Modern State ideas by ancient writers, and is particularly interesting on the Superior Person (Generalized or Super Man) of Confucius (551- 478 B.C.) and the City of God of St. Augustine (354-430).

THE INVISIBLE MAN
A GROTESQUE ROMANCE

Serialised in *Pearson's Weekly*, Jun-Jul 1897
First book edition: C. Arthur Pearson, London, 1897

CHAPTER I - THE STRANGE MAN'S ARRIVAL

The stranger came early in February, one wintry day, through a biting wind and a driving snow, the last snowfall of the year, over the down, walking from Bramblehurst railway station, and carrying a little black portmanteau in his thickly gloved hand. He was wrapped up from head to foot, and the brim of his soft felt hat hid every inch of his face but the shiny tip of his nose; the snow had piled itself against his shoulders and chest, and added a white crest to the burden he carried. He staggered into the "Coach and Horses" more dead than alive, and flung his portmanteau down. "A fire," he cried, "in the name of human charity! A room and a fire!" He stamped and shook the snow from off himself in the bar, and followed Mrs. Hall into her guest parlour to strike his bargain. And with that much introduction, that and a couple of sovereigns flung upon the table, he took up his quarters in the inn.

Mrs. Hall lit the fire and left him there while she went to prepare him a meal with her own hands. A guest to stop at Iping in the wintertime was an unheard-of piece of luck, let alone a guest who was no "haggler," and she was resolved to show herself worthy of her good fortune. As soon as the bacon was well under way, and Millie, her lymphatic aid, had been brisked up a bit by a few deftly chosen expressions of contempt, she carried the cloth, plates, and glasses into the parlour and began to lay them with the utmost *eclat*. Although the fire was burning up briskly, she was surprised to see that her visitor still wore his hat and coat, standing with his back to her and staring out of the window at the falling snow in the yard. His gloved hands were clasped behind him, and he seemed to be lost in thought. She noticed that the melting snow that still sprinkled his shoulders dripped upon her carpet. "Can I take your hat and coat, sir?" she said, "and give them a good dry in the kitchen?"

"No," he said without turning.

She was not sure she had heard him, and was about to repeat her question.

He turned his head and looked at her over his shoulder. "I prefer to keep them on," he said with emphasis, and she noticed that he wore big blue spectacles with sidelights, and had a bush side-whisker over his coat-collar that completely hid his cheeks and face.

"Very well, sir," she said. "*As* you like. In a bit the room will be warmer."

He made no answer, and had turned his face away from her again, and Mrs. Hall, feeling that her conversational advances were ill-timed, laid the rest of the table things in a quick staccato and whisked out of the room. When she returned

he was still standing there, like a man of stone, his back hunched, his collar turned up, his dripping hat-brim turned down, hiding his face and ears completely. She put down the eggs and bacon with considerable emphasis, and called rather than said to him, "Your lunch is served, sir."

"Thank you," he said at the same time, and did not stir until she was closing the door. Then he swung round and approached the table with a certain eager quickness.

As she went behind the bar to the kitchen she heard a sound repeated at regular intervals. Chirk, chirk, chirk, it went, the sound of a spoon being rapidly whisked round a basin. "That girl!" she said. "There! I clean forgot it. It's her being so long!" And while she herself finished mixing the mustard, she gave Millie a few verbal stabs for her excessive slowness. She had cooked the ham and eggs, laid the table, and done everything, while Millie (help indeed!) had only succeeded in delaying the mustard. And him a new guest and wanting to stay! Then she filled the mustard pot, and, putting it with a certain stateliness upon a gold and black tea-tray, carried it into the parlour.

She rapped and entered promptly. As she did so her visitor moved quickly, so that she got but a glimpse of a white object disappearing behind the table. It would seem he was picking something from the floor. She rapped down the mustard pot on the table, and then she noticed the overcoat and hat had been taken off and put over a chair in front of the fire, and a pair of wet boots threatened rust to her steel fender. She went to these things resolutely. "I suppose I may have them to dry now," she said in a voice that brooked no denial.

"Leave the hat," said her visitor, in a muffled voice, and turning she saw he had raised his head and was sitting and looking at her.

For a moment she stood gaping at him, too surprised to speak.

He held a white cloth—it was a serviette he had brought with him —over the lower part of his face, so that his mouth and jaws were completely hidden, and that was the reason of his muffled voice. But it was not that which startled Mrs. Hall. It was the fact that all his forehead above his blue glasses was covered by a white bandage, and that another covered his ears, leaving not a scrap of his face exposed excepting only his pink, peaked nose. It was bright, pink, and shiny just as it had been at first. He wore a dark- brown velvet jacket with a high, black, linen-lined collar turned up about his neck. The thick black hair, escaping as it could below and between the cross bandages, projected in curious tails and horns, giving him the strangest appearance conceivable. This muffled and bandaged head was so unlike what she had anticipated, that for a moment she was rigid.

He did not remove the serviette, but remained holding it, as she saw now, with a brown gloved hand, and regarding her with his inscrutable blue glasses. "Leave the hat," he said, speaking very distinctly through the white cloth.

Her nerves began to recover from the shock they had received. She placed the hat on the chair again by the fire. "I didn't know, sir," she began, "that—" and she stopped embarrassed.

"Thank you," he said drily, glancing from her to the door and then at her again.

"I'll have them nicely dried, sir, at once," she said, and carried his clothes out of the room. She glanced at his white-swathed head and blue goggles again as she was going out of the door; but his napkin was still in front of his face. She shivered a little as she closed the door behind her, and her face was eloquent of her surprise and perplexity. "I *never*," she whispered. "There!" She went quite softly to the kitchen, and was too preoccupied to ask Millie what she was messing about with *now*, when she got there.

The visitor sat and listened to her retreating feet. He glanced inquiringly at the window before he removed his serviette, and resumed his meal. He took a mouthful, glanced suspiciously at the window, took another mouthful, then rose and, taking the serviette in his hand, walked across the room and pulled the blind down to the top of the white muslin that obscured the lower panes. This left the room in a twilight. This done, he returned with an easier air to the table and his meal.

"The poor soul's had an accident or an op'ration or somethin'," said Mrs. Hall. "What a turn them bandages did give me, to be sure!"

She put on some more coal, unfolded the clothes-horse, and extended the traveller's coat upon this. "And they goggles! Why, he looked more like a divin' helmet than a human man!" She hung his muffler on a corner of the horse. "And holding that handkerchief over his mouth all the time. Talkin' through it! ... Perhaps his mouth was hurt too—maybe."

She turned round, as one who suddenly remembers. "Bless my soul alive!" she said, going off at a tangent; "ain't you done them taters *yet*, Millie?"

When Mrs. Hall went to clear away the stranger's lunch, her idea that his mouth must also have been cut or disfigured in the accident she supposed him to have suffered, was confirmed, for he was smoking a pipe, and all the time that she was in the room he never loosened the silk muffler he had wrapped round the lower part of his face to put the mouthpiece to his lips. Yet it was not forgetfulness, for she saw he glanced at it as it smouldered out. He sat in the corner with his back to the window-blind and spoke now, having eaten and drunk and being comfortably warmed through, with less aggressive brevity than before. The reflection of the fire lent a kind of red animation to his big spectacles they had lacked hitherto.

"I have some luggage," he said, "at Bramblehurst station," and he asked her how he could have it sent. He bowed his bandaged head quite politely in acknowledgment of her explanation. "To-morrow?" hc said. "There is no speedier delivery?" and seemed quite disappointed when she answered, "No." Was she quite sure? No man with a trap who would go over?

Mrs. Hall, nothing loath, answered his questions and developed a conversation. "It's a steep road by the down, sir," she said in answer to the question about a trap; and then, snatching at an opening, said, "It was there a carriage was upsetted, a year ago and more. A gentleman killed, besides his coachman. Accidents, sir, happen in a moment, don't they?"

But the visitor was not to be drawn so easily. "They do," he said through his muffler, eyeing her quietly through his impenetrable glasses.

"But they take long enough to get well, don't they? ... There was my sister's son, Tom, jest cut his arm with a scythe, tumbled on it in the 'ayfield, and, bless me! he was three months tied up sir. You'd hardly believe it. It's regular given me a dread of a scythe, sir."

"I can quite understand that," said the visitor.

"He was afraid, one time, that he'd have to have an op'ration—he was that bad, sir."

The visitor laughed abruptly, a bark of a laugh that he seemed to bite and kill in his mouth. "*Was* he?" he said.

"He was, sir. And no laughing matter to them as had the doing for him, as I had—my sister being took up with her little ones so much. There was bandages to do, sir, and bandages to undo. So that if I may make so bold as to say it, sir—"

"Will you get me some matches?" said the visitor, quite abruptly. "My pipe is out."

Mrs. Hall was pulled up suddenly. It was certainly rude of him, after telling him all she had done. She gasped at him for a moment, and remembered the two sovereigns. She went for the matches.

"Thanks," he said concisely, as she put them down, and turned his shoulder upon her and stared out of the window again. It was altogether too discouraging. Evidently he was sensitive on the topic of operations and bandages. She did not "make so bold as to say," however, after all. But his snubbing way had irritated her, and Millie had a hot time of it that afternoon.

The visitor remained in the parlour until four o'clock, without giving the ghost of an excuse for an intrusion. For the most part he was quite still during that time; it would seem he sat in the growing darkness smoking in the firelight—perhaps dozing.

Once or twice a curious listener might have heard him at the coals, and for the space of five minutes he was audible pacing the room. He seemed to be talking to himself. Then the armchair creaked as he sat down again.

CHAPTER II - MR. TEDDY HENFREY'S FIRST IMPRESSIONS

At four o'clock, when it was fairly dark and Mrs. Hall was screwing up her courage to go in and ask her visitor if he would take some tea, Teddy Henfrey, the clock-jobber, came into the bar. "My sakes! Mrs. Hall," said he, "but this is terrible weather for thin boots!" The snow outside was falling faster.

Mrs. Hall agreed, and then noticed he had his bag with him. "Now you're here, Mr. Teddy," said she, "I'd be glad if you'd give th' old clock in the parlour a bit of a look. 'Tis going, and it strikes well and hearty; but the hour-hand won't do nuthin' but point at six."

And leading the way, she went across to the parlour door and rapped and entered.

Her visitor, she saw as she opened the door, was seated in the armchair before the fire, dozing it would seem, with his bandaged head drooping on one side. The only light in the room was the red glow from the fire—which lit his eyes like adverse railway signals, but left his downcast face in darkness—and the scanty vestiges of the day that came in through the open door. Everything was ruddy, shadowy, and indistinct to her, the more so since she had just been lighting the bar lamp, and her eyes were dazzled. But for a second it seemed to her that the man she looked at had an enormous mouth wide open—a vast and incredible mouth that swallowed the whole of the lower portion of his face. It was the sensation of a moment: the white-bound head, the monstrous goggle eyes, and this huge yawn below it. Then he stirred, started up in his chair, put up his hand. She opened the door wide, so that the room was lighter, and she saw him more clearly, with the muffler held up to his face just as she had seen him hold the serviette before. The shadows, she fancied, had tricked her.

"Would you mind, sir, this man a-coming to look at the clock, sir?" she said, recovering from the momentary shock.

"Look at the clock?" he said, staring round in a drowsy manner, and speaking over his hand, and then, getting more fully awake, "certainly."

Mrs. Hall went away to get a lamp, and he rose and stretched himself. Then came the light, and Mr. Teddy Henfrey, entering, was confronted by this bandaged person. He was, he says, "taken aback."

"Good afternoon," said the stranger, regarding him—as Mr. Henfrey says, with a vivid sense of the dark spectacles—"like a lobster."

"I hope," said Mr. Henfrey, "that it's no intrusion."

"None whatever," said the stranger. "Though, I understand," he said turning to Mrs. Hall, "that this room is really to be mine for my own private use."

"I thought, sir," said Mrs. Hall, "you'd prefer the clock—"

"Certainly," said the stranger, "certainly—but, as a rule, I like to be alone and undisturbed.

"But I'm really glad to have the clock seen to," he said, seeing a certain hesitation in Mr. Henfrey's manner. "Very glad." Mr. Henfrey had intended to apologise and withdraw, but this anticipation reassured him. The stranger turned round with his back to the fireplace and put his hands behind his back. "And presently," he said, "when the clock-mending is over, I think I should like to have some tea. But not till the clock-mending is over."

Mrs. Hall was about to leave the room—she made no conversational advances this time, because she did not want to be snubbed in front of Mr. Henfrey—when her visitor asked her if she had made any arrangements about his boxes at Bramblehurst. She told him she had mentioned the matter to the postman, and that the carrier could bring them over on the morrow. "You are certain that is the earliest?" he said.

She was certain, with a marked coldness.

"I should explain," he added, "what I was really too cold and fatigued to do before, that I am an experimental investigator."

"Indeed, sir," said Mrs. Hall, much impressed.

"And my baggage contains apparatus and appliances."

"Very useful things indeed they are, sir," said Mrs. Hall.

"And I'm very naturally anxious to get on with my inquiries."

"Of course, sir."

"My reason for coming to Iping," he proceeded, with a certain deliberation of manner, "was ... a desire for solitude. I do not wish to be disturbed in my work. In addition to my work, an accident—"

"I thought as much," said Mrs. Hall to herself.

"—necessitates a certain retirement. My eyes—are sometimes so weak and painful that I have to shut myself up in the dark for hours together. Lock myself up. Sometimes—now and then. Not at present, certainly. At such times the slightest disturbance, the entry of a stranger into the room, is a source of excruciating annoyance to me—it is well these things should be understood."

"Certainly, sir," said Mrs. Hall. "And if I might make so bold as to ask—"

"That I think, is all," said the stranger, with that quietly irresistible air of finality he could assume at will. Mrs. Hall reserved her question and sympathy for a better occasion.

After Mrs. Hall had left the room, he remained standing in front of the fire, glaring, so Mr. Henfrey puts it, at the clock-mending. Mr. Henfrey not only took off the hands of the clock, and the face, but extracted the works; and he tried to work in as slow and quiet and unassuming a manner as possible. He worked with the lamp close to him, and the green shade threw a brilliant light upon his hands, and upon the frame and wheels, and left the rest of the room shadowy. When he

looked up, coloured patches swam in his eyes. Being constitutionally of a curious nature, he had removed the works—a quite unnecessary proceeding—with the idea of delaying his departure and perhaps falling into conversation with the stranger. But the stranger stood there, perfectly silent and still. So still, it got on Henfrey's nerves. He felt alone in the room and looked up, and there, grey and dim, was the bandaged head and huge blue lenses staring fixedly, with a mist of green spots drifting in front of them. It was so uncanny to Henfrey that for a minute they remained staring blankly at one another. Then Henfrey looked down again. Very uncomfortable position! One would like to say something. Should he remark that the weather was very cold for the time of year?

He looked up as if to take aim with that introductory shot. "The weather—" he began.

"Why don't you finish and go?" said the rigid figure, evidently in a state of painfully suppressed rage. "All you've got to do is to fix the hour- hand on its axle. You're simply humbugging—"

"Certainly, sir—one minute more. I overlooked—" and Mr. Henfrey finished and went.

But he went feeling excessively annoyed. "Damn it!" said Mr. Henfrey to himself, trudging down the village through the thawing snow; "a man must do a clock at times, surely."

And again "Can't a man look at you?—Ugly!"

And yet again, "Seemingly not. If the police was wanting you you couldn't be more wrapped and bandaged."

At Gleeson's corner he saw Hall, who had recently married the stranger's hostess at the "Coach and Horses," and who now drove the Iping conveyance, when occasional people required it, to Sidderbridge Junction, coming towards him on his return from that place. Hall had evidently been "stopping a bit" at Sidderbridge, to judge by his driving. "'Ow do, Teddy?" he said, passing.

"You got a rum un up home!" said Teddy.

Hall very sociably pulled up. "What's that?" he asked.

"Rum-looking customer stopping at the 'Coach and Horses,'" said Teddy. "My sakes!"

And he proceeded to give Hall a vivid description of his grotesque guest. "Looks a bit like a disguise, don't it? I'd like to see a man's face if I had him stopping in *my* place," said Henfrey. "But women are that trustful —where strangers are concerned. He's took your rooms and he ain't even given a name, Hall."

"You don't say so!" said Hall, who was a man of sluggish apprehension.

"Yes," said Teddy. "By the week. Whatever he is, you can't get rid of him under the week. And he's got a lot of luggage coming to-morrow, so he says. Let's hope it won't be stones in boxes, Hall."

He told Hall how his aunt at Hastings had been swindled by a stranger with empty portmanteaux. Altogether he left Hall vaguely suspicious. "Get up, old girl," said Hall. "I s'pose I must see 'bout this."

Teddy trudged on his way with his mind considerably relieved.

Instead of "seeing 'bout it," however, Hall on his return was severely rated by his wife on the length of time he had spent in Sidderbridge, and his mild inquiries were answered snappishly and in a manner not to the point. But the seed of suspicion Teddy had sown germinated in the mind of Mr. Hall in spite of these discouragements. "You wim' don't know everything," said Mr. Hall, resolved to ascertain more about the personality of his guest at the earliest possible opportunity. And after the stranger had gone to bed, which he did about half-past nine, Mr. Hall went very aggressively into the parlour and looked very hard at his wife's furniture, just to show that the stranger wasn't master there, and scrutinised closely and a little contemptuously a sheet of mathematical computations the stranger had left. When retiring for the night he instructed Mrs. Hall to look very closely at the stranger's luggage when it came next day.

"You mind you own business, Hall," said Mrs. Hall, "and I'll mind mine."

She was all the more inclined to snap at Hall because the stranger was undoubtedly an unusually strange sort of stranger, and she was by no means assured about him in her own mind. In the middle of the night she woke up dreaming of huge white heads like turnips, that came trailing after her, at the end of interminable necks, and with vast black eyes. But being a sensible woman, she subdued her terrors and turned over and went to sleep again.

CHAPTER III - THE THOUSAND AND ONE BOTTLES

So it was that on the twenty-ninth day of February, at the beginning of the thaw, this singular person fell out of infinity into Iping village. Next day his luggage arrived through the slush—and very remarkable luggage it was. There were a couple of trunks indeed, such as a rational man might need, but in addition there were a box of books—big, fat books, of which some were just in an incomprehensible handwriting—and a dozen or more crates, boxes, and cases, containing objects packed in straw, as it seemed to Hall, tugging with a casual curiosity at the straw—glass bottles. The stranger, muffled in hat, coat, gloves, and wrapper, came out impatiently to meet Fearenside's cart, while Hall was having a word or so of gossip preparatory to helping being them in. Out he came, not noticing Fearenside's dog, who was sniffing in a *dilettante* spirit at Hall's legs. "Come along with those boxes," he said. "I've been waiting long enough."

And he came down the steps towards the tail of the cart as if to lay hands on the smaller crate.

No sooner had Fearenside's dog caught sight of him, however, than it began to bristle and growl savagely, and when he rushed down the steps it gave an undecided hop, and then sprang straight at his hand. "Whup!" cried Hall, jumping back, for he was no hero with dogs, and Fearenside howled, "Lie down!" and snatched his whip.

They saw the dog's teeth had slipped the hand, heard a kick, saw the dog execute a flanking jump and get home on the stranger's leg, and heard the rip of his trousering. Then the finer end of Fearenside's whip reached his property, and the dog, yelping with dismay, retreated under the wheels of the waggon. It was all the business of a swift half-minute. No one spoke, everyone shouted. The stranger glanced swiftly at his torn glove and at his leg, made as if he would stoop to the latter, then turned and rushed swiftly up the steps into the inn. They heard him go headlong across the passage and up the uncarpeted stairs to his bedroom.

"You brute, you!" said Fearenside, climbing off the waggon with his whip in his hand, while the dog watched him through the wheel. "Come here," said Fearenside—"You'd better."

Hall had stood gaping. "He wuz bit," said Hall. "I'd better go and see to en," and he trotted after the stranger. He met Mrs. Hall in the passage. "Carrier's darg," he said "bit en."

He went straight upstairs, and the stranger's door being ajar, he pushed it open and was entering without any ceremony, being of a naturally sympathetic turn of mind.

The blind was down and the room dim. He caught a glimpse of a most singular thing, what seemed a handless arm waving towards him, and a face of three huge indeterminate spots on white, very like the face of a pale pansy. Then he was struck violently in the chest, hurled back, and the door slammed in his face and locked. It was so rapid that it gave him no time to observe. A waving of indecipherable shapes, a blow, and a concussion. There he stood on the dark little landing, wondering what it might be that he had seen.

A couple of minutes after, he rejoined the little group that had formed outside the "Coach and Horses." There was Fearenside telling about it all over again for the second time; there was Mrs. Hall saying his dog didn't have no business to bite her guests; there was Huxter, the general dealer from over the road, interrogative; and Sandy Wadgers from the forge, judicial; besides women and children, all of them saying fatuities: "Wouldn't let en bite *me*, I knows"; "'Tasn't right *have* such dargs"; "Whad *'e* bite 'n for, than?" and so forth.

Mr. Hall, staring at them from the steps and listening, found it incredible that he had seen anything so very remarkable happen upstairs. Besides, his vocabulary was altogether too limited to express his impressions.

"He don't want no help, he says," he said in answer to his wife's inquiry. "We'd better be a-takin' of his luggage in."

"He ought to have it cauterised at once," said Mr. Huxter; "especially if it's at all inflamed."

"I'd shoot en, that's what I'd do," said a lady in the group.

Suddenly the dog began growling again.

"Come along," cried an angry voice in the doorway, and there stood the muffled stranger with his collar turned up, and his hat-brim bent down. "The sooner you get those things in the better I'll be pleased." It is stated by an anonymous bystander that his trousers and gloves had been changed.

"Was you hurt, sir?" said Fearenside. "I'm rare sorry the darg—"

"Not a bit," said the stranger. "Never broke the skin. Hurry up with those things."

He then swore to himself, so Mr. Hall asserts.

Directly the first crate was, in accordance with his directions, carried into the parlour, the stranger flung himself upon it with extraordinary eagerness, and began to unpack it, scattering the straw with an utter disregard of Mrs. Hall's carpet. And from it he began to produce bottles—little fat bottles containing powders, small and slender bottles containing coloured and white fluids, fluted blue bottles labeled Poison, bottles with round bodies and slender necks, large green-glass bottles, large white-glass bottles, bottles with glass stoppers and frosted labels, bottles with fine corks, bottles with bungs, bottles with wooden caps, wine bottles, salad-oil bottles —putting them in rows on the chiffonnier, on the mantel, on the table under the window, round the floor, on the bookshelf—everywhere. The

chemist's shop in Bramblehurst could not boast half so many. Quite a sight it was. Crate after crate yielded bottles, until all six were empty and the table high with straw; the only things that came out of these crates besides the bottles were a number of test-tubes and a carefully packed balance.

And directly the crates were unpacked, the stranger went to the window and set to work, not troubling in the least about the litter of straw, the fire which had gone out, the box of books outside, nor for the trunks and other luggage that had gone upstairs.

When Mrs. Hall took his dinner in to him, he was already so absorbed in his work, pouring little drops out of the bottles into test-tubes, that he did not hear her until she had swept away the bulk of the straw and put the tray on the table, with some little emphasis perhaps, seeing the state that the floor was in. Then he half turned his head and immediately turned it away again. But she saw he had removed his glasses; they were beside him on the table, and it seemed to her that his eye sockets were extraordinarily hollow. He put on his spectacles again, and then turned and faced her. She was about to complain of the straw on the floor when he anticipated her.

"I wish you wouldn't come in without knocking," he said in the tone of abnormal exasperation that seemed so characteristic of him.

"I knocked, but seemingly—"

"Perhaps you did. But in my investigations—my really very urgent and necessary investigations—the slightest disturbance, the jar of a door—I must ask you—"

"Certainly, sir. You can turn the lock if you're like that, you know. Any time."

"A very good idea," said the stranger.

"This stror, sir, if I might make so bold as to remark—"

"Don't. If the straw makes trouble put it down in the bill." And he mumbled at her—words suspiciously like curses.

He was so odd, standing there, so aggressive and explosive, bottle in one hand and test-tube in the other, that Mrs. Hall was quite alarmed. But she was a resolute woman. "In which case, I should like to know, sir, what you consider—"

"A shilling—put down a shilling. Surely a shilling's enough?"

"So be it," said Mrs. Hall, taking up the table-cloth and beginning to spread it over the table. "If you're satisfied, of course—"

He turned and sat down, with his coat-collar toward her.

All the afternoon he worked with the door locked and, as Mrs. Hall testifies, for the most part in silence. But once there was a concussion and a sound of bottles ringing together as though the table had been hit, and the smash of a bottle flung violently down, and then a rapid pacing athwart the room. Fearing "something was the matter," she went to the door and listened, not caring to knock.

"I can't go on," he was raving. "I *can't* go on. Three hundred thousand, four hundred thousand! The huge multitude! Cheated! All my life it may take me! ... Patience! Patience indeed! ... Fool! fool!"

There was a noise of hobnails on the bricks in the bar, and Mrs. Hall had very reluctantly to leave the rest of his soliloquy. When she returned the room was silent again, save for the faint crepitation of his chair and the occasional clink of a bottle. It was all over; the stranger had resumed work.

When she took in his tea she saw broken glass in the corner of the room under the concave mirror, and a golden stain that had been carelessly wiped. She called attention to it.

"Put it down in the bill," snapped her visitor. "For God's sake don't worry me. If there's damage done, put it down in the bill," and he went on ticking a list in the exercise book before him.

"I'll tell you something," said Fearenside, mysteriously. It was late in the afternoon, and they were in the little beer-shop of Iping Hanger.

"Well?" said Teddy Henfrey.

"This chap you're speaking of, what my dog bit. Well—he's black. Leastways, his legs are. I seed through the tear of his trousers and the tear of his glove. You'd have expected a sort of pinky to show, wouldn't you? Well —there wasn't none. Just blackness. I tell you, he's as black as my hat."

"My sakes!" said Henfrey. "It's a rummy case altogether. Why, his nose is as pink as paint!"

"That's true," said Fearenside. "I knows that. And I tell 'ee what I'm thinking. That marn's a piebald, Teddy. Black here and white there—in patches. And he's ashamed of it. He's a kind of half-breed, and the colour's come off patchy instead of mixing. I've heard of such things before. And it's the common way with horses, as any one can see."

CHAPTER IV - MR. CUSS INTERVIEWS THE STRANGER

I have told the circumstances of the stranger's arrival in Iping with a certain fulness of detail, in order that the curious impression he created may be understood by the reader. But excepting two odd incidents, the circumstances of his stay until the extraordinary day of the club festival may be passed over very cursorily. There were a number of skirmishes with Mrs. Hall on matters of domestic discipline, but in every case until late April, when the first signs of penury began, he over-rode her by the easy expedient of an extra payment. Hall did not like him, and whenever he dared he talked of the advisability of getting rid of him; but he showed his dislike chiefly by concealing it ostentatiously, and avoiding his visitor as much as possible. "Wait till the summer," said Mrs. Hall sagely, "when the artisks are beginning to come. Then we'll see. He may be a bit overbearing, but bills settled punctual is bills settled punctual, whatever you'd like to say."

The stranger did not go to church, and indeed made no difference between Sunday and the irreligious days, even in costume. He worked, as Mrs. Hall thought, very fitfully. Some days he would come down early and be continuously busy. On others he would rise late, pace his room, fretting audibly for hours together, smoke, sleep in the armchair by the fire. Communication with the world beyond the village he had none. His temper continued very uncertain; for the most part his manner was that of a man suffering under almost unendurable provocation, and once or twice things were snapped, torn, crushed, or broken in spasmodic gusts of violence. He seemed under a chronic irritation of the greatest intensity. His habit of talking to himself in a low voice grew steadily upon him, but though Mrs. Hall listened conscientiously she could make neither head nor tail of what she heard.

He rarely went abroad by daylight, but at twilight he would go out muffled up invisibly, whether the weather were cold or not, and he chose the loneliest paths and those most overshadowed by trees and banks. His goggling spectacles and ghastly bandaged face under the penthouse of his hat, came with a disagreeable suddenness out of the darkness upon one or two home-going labourers, and Teddy Henfrey, tumbling out of the "Scarlet Coat" one night, at half-past nine, was scared shamefully by the stranger's skull-like head (he was walking hat in hand) lit by the sudden light of the opened inn door. Such children as saw him at nightfall dreamt of bogies, and it seemed doubtful whether he disliked boys more than

they disliked him, or the reverse; but there was certainly a vivid enough dislike on either side.

It was inevitable that a person of so remarkable an appearance and bearing should form a frequent topic in such a village as Iping. Opinion was greatly divided about his occupation. Mrs. Hall was sensitive on the point. When questioned, she explained very carefully that he was an "experimental investigator," going gingerly over the syllables as one who dreads pitfalls. When asked what an experimental investigator was, she would say with a touch of superiority that most educated people knew such things as that, and would thus explain that he "discovered things." Her visitor had had an accident, she said, which temporarily discoloured his face and hands, and being of a sensitive disposition, he was averse to any public notice of the fact.

Out of her hearing there was a view largely entertained that he was a criminal trying to escape from justice by wrapping himself up so as to conceal himself altogether from the eye of the police. This idea sprang from the brain of Mr. Teddy Henfrey. No crime of any magnitude dating from the middle or end of February was known to have occurred. Elaborated in the imagination of Mr. Gould, the probationary assistant in the National School, this theory took the form that the stranger was an Anarchist in disguise, preparing explosives, and he resolved to undertake such detective operations as his time permitted. These consisted for the most part in looking very hard at the stranger whenever they met, or in asking people who had never seen the stranger, leading questions about him. But he detected nothing.

Another school of opinion followed Mr. Fearenside, and either accepted the piebald view or some modification of it; as, for instance, Silas Durgan, who was heard to assert that "if he choses to show enself at fairs he'd make his fortune in no time," and being a bit of a theologian, compared the stranger to the man with the one talent. Yet another view explained the entire matter by regarding the stranger as a harmless lunatic. That had the advantage of accounting for everything straight away.

Between these main groups there were waverers and compromisers. Sussex folk have few superstitions, and it was only after the events of early April that the thought of the supernatural was first whispered in the village. Even then it was only credited among the women folk.

But whatever they thought of him, people in Iping, on the whole, agreed in disliking him. His irritability, though it might have been comprehensible to an urban brain-worker, was an amazing thing to these quiet Sussex villagers. The frantic gesticulations they surprised now and then, the headlong pace after nightfall that swept him upon them round quiet corners, the inhuman bludgeoning of all tentative advances of curiosity, the taste for twilight that led to the closing of doors, the pulling down of blinds, the extinction of candles and lamps—who could agree with such goings on? They drew aside as he passed down the village, and when he had gone by, young humourists would up with coat- collars and down with hatbrims, and go pacing nervously after him in imitation of his occult bearing. There

was a song popular at that time called "The Bogey Man". Miss Statchell sang it at the schoolroom concert (in aid of the church lamps), and thereafter whenever one or two of the villagers were gathered together and the stranger appeared, a bar or so of this tune, more or less sharp or flat, was whistled in the midst of them. Also belated little children would call "Bogey Man!" after him, and make off tremulously elated.

Cuss, the general practitioner, was devoured by curiosity. The bandages excited his professional interest, the report of the thousand and one bottles aroused his jealous regard. All through April and May he coveted an opportunity of talking to the stranger, and at last, towards Whitsuntide, he could stand it no longer, but hit upon the subscription-list for a village nurse as an excuse. He was surprised to find that Mr. Hall did not know his guest's name. "He give a name," said Mrs. Hall—an assertion which was quite unfounded—"but I didn't rightly hear it." She thought it seemed so silly not to know the man's name.

Cuss rapped at the parlour door and entered. There was a fairly audible imprecation from within. "Pardon my intrusion," said Cuss, and then the door closed and cut Mrs. Hall off from the rest of the conversation.

She could hear the murmur of voices for the next ten minutes, then a cry of surprise, a stirring of feet, a chair flung aside, a bark of laughter, quick steps to the door, and Cuss appeared, his face white, his eyes staring over his shoulder. He left the door open behind him, and without looking at her strode across the hall and went down the steps, and she heard his feet hurrying along the road. He carried his hat in his hand. She stood behind the door, looking at the open door of the parlour. Then she heard the stranger laughing quietly, and then his footsteps came across the room. She could not see his face where she stood. The parlour door slammed, and the place was silent again.

Cuss went straight up the village to Bunting the vicar. "Am I mad?" Cuss began abruptly, as he entered the shabby little study. "Do I look like an insane person?"

"What's happened?" said the vicar, putting the ammonite on the loose sheets of his forth-coming sermon.

"That chap at the inn—"

"Well?"

"Give me something to drink," said Cuss, and he sat down.

When his nerves had been steadied by a glass of cheap sherry—the only drink the good vicar had available—he told him of the interview he had just had. "Went in," he gasped, "and began to demand a subscription for that Nurse Fund. He'd stuck his hands in his pockets as I came in, and he sat down lumpily in his chair. Sniffed. I told him I'd heard he took an interest in scientific things. He said yes. Sniffed again. Kept on sniffing all the time; evidently recently caught an infernal cold. No wonder, wrapped up like that! I developed the nurse idea, and all the while kept my eyes open. Bottles—chemicals—everywhere. Balance, test-tubes in stands, and a smell of —evening primrose. Would he subscribe? Said he'd consider it. Asked him, point-blank, was he researching. Said he was. A long

research? Got quite cross. 'A damnable long research,' said he, blowing the cork out, so to speak. 'Oh,' said I. And out came the grievance. The man was just on the boil, and my question boiled him over. He had been given a prescription, most valuable prescription—what for he wouldn't say. Was it medical? 'Damn you! What are you fishing after?' I apologised. Dignified sniff and cough. He resumed. He'd read it. Five ingredients. Put it down; turned his head. Draught of air from window lifted the paper. Swish, rustle. He was working in a room with an open fireplace, he said. Saw a flicker, and there was the prescription burning and lifting chimneyward. Rushed towards it just as it whisked up the chimney. So! Just at that point, to illustrate his story, out came his arm."

"Well?"

"No hand—just an empty sleeve. Lord! I thought, *that's* a deformity! Got a cork arm, I suppose, and has taken it off. Then, I thought, there's something odd in that. What the devil keeps that sleeve up and open, if there's nothing in it? There was nothing in it, I tell you. Nothing down it, right down to the joint. I could see right down it to the elbow, and there was a glimmer of light shining through a tear of the cloth. 'Good God!' I said. Then he stopped. Stared at me with those black goggles of his, and then at his sleeve."

"Well?"

"That's all. He never said a word; just glared, and put his sleeve back in his pocket quickly. 'I was saying,' said he, 'that there was the prescription burning, wasn't I?' Interrogative cough. 'How the devil,' said I, 'can you move an empty sleeve like that?' 'Empty sleeve?' 'Yes,' said I, 'an empty sleeve.'

"'It's an empty sleeve, is it? You saw it was an empty sleeve?' He stood up right away. I stood up too. He came towards me in three very slow steps, and stood quite close. Sniffed venomously. I didn't flinch, though I'm hanged if that bandaged knob of his, and those blinkers, aren't enough to unnerve any one, coming quietly up to you.

"'You said it was an empty sleeve?' he said. 'Certainly,' I said. At staring and saying nothing a barefaced man, unspectacled, starts scratch. Then very quietly he pulled his sleeve out of his pocket again, and raised his arm towards me as though he would show it to me again. He did it very, very slowly. I looked at it. Seemed an age. 'Well?' said I, clearing my throat, 'there's nothing in it.'

"Had to say something. I was beginning to feel frightened. I could see right down it. He extended it straight towards me, slowly, slowly—just like that—until the cuff was six inches from my face. Queer thing to see an empty sleeve come at you like that! And then—"

"Well?"

"Something—exactly like a finger and thumb it felt—nipped my nose."

Bunting began to laugh.

"There wasn't anything there!" said Cuss, his voice running up into a shriek at the "there." "It's all very well for you to laugh, but I tell you I was so startled, I hit his cuff hard, and turned around, and cut out of the room—I left him—"

Cuss stopped. There was no mistaking the sincerity of his panic. He turned round in a helpless way and took a second glass of the excellent vicar's very inferior sherry. "When I hit his cuff," said Cuss, "I tell you, it felt exactly like hitting an arm. And there wasn't an arm! There wasn't the ghost of an arm!"

Mr. Bunting thought it over. He looked suspiciously at Cuss. "It's a most remarkable story," he said. He looked very wise and grave indeed. "It's really," said Mr. Bunting with judicial emphasis, "a most remarkable story."

CHAPTER V - THE BURGLARY AT THE VICARAGE

The facts of the burglary at the vicarage came to us chiefly through the medium of the vicar and his wife. It occurred in the small hours of Whit Monday, the day devoted in Iping to the Club festivities. Mrs. Bunting, it seems, woke up suddenly in the stillness that comes before the dawn, with the strong impression that the door of their bedroom had opened and closed. She did not arouse her husband at first, but sat up in bed listening. She then distinctly heard the pad, pad, pad of bare feet coming out of the adjoining dressing-room and walking along the passage towards the staircase. As soon as she felt assured of this, she aroused the Rev. Mr. Bunting as quietly as possible. He did not strike a light, but putting on his spectacles, her dressing-gown and his bath slippers, he went out on the landing to listen. He heard quite distinctly a fumbling going on at his study desk downstairs, and then a violent sneeze.

At that he returned to his bedroom, armed himself with the most obvious weapon, the poker, and descended the staircase as noiselessly as possible. Mrs. Bunting came out on the landing.

The hour was about four, and the ultimate darkness of the night was past. There was a faint shimmer of light in the hall, but the study doorway yawned impenetrably black. Everything was still except the faint creaking of the stairs under Mr. Bunting's tread, and the slight movements in the study. Then something snapped, the drawer was opened, and there was a rustle of papers. Then came an imprecation, and a match was struck and the study was flooded with yellow light. Mr. Bunting was now in the hall, and through the crack of the door he could see the desk and the open drawer and a candle burning on the desk. But the robber he could not see. He stood there in the hall undecided what to do, and Mrs. Bunting, her face white and intent, crept slowly downstairs after him. One thing kept Mr. Bunting's courage; the persuasion that this burglar was a resident in the village.

They heard the chink of money, and realised that the robber had found the housekeeping reserve of gold—two pounds ten in half sovereigns altogether. At that sound Mr. Bunting was nerved to abrupt action. Gripping the poker firmly, he rushed into the room, closely followed by Mrs. Bunting. "Surrender!" cried Mr. Bunting, fiercely, and then stooped amazed. Apparently the room was perfectly empty.

Yet their conviction that they had, that very moment, heard somebody moving in the room had amounted to a certainty. For half a minute, perhaps, they stood gaping, then Mrs. Bunting went across the room and looked behind the screen,

while Mr. Bunting, by a kindred impulse, peered under the desk. Then Mrs. Bunting turned back the window-curtains, and Mr. Bunting looked up the chimney and probed it with the poker. Then Mrs. Bunting scrutinised the waste- paper basket and Mr. Bunting opened the lid of the coal-scuttle. Then they came to a stop and stood with eyes interrogating each other.

"I could have sworn—" said Mr. Bunting.

"The candle!" said Mr. Bunting. "Who lit the candle?"

"The drawer!" said Mrs. Bunting. "And the money's gone!"

She went hastily to the doorway.

"Of all the strange occurrences—"

There was a violent sneeze in the passage. They rushed out, and as they did so the kitchen door slammed. "Bring the candle," said Mr. Bunting, and led the way. They both heard a sound of bolts being hastily shot back.

As he opened the kitchen door he saw through the scullery that the back door was just opening, and the faint light of early dawn displayed the dark masses of the garden beyond. He is certain that nothing went out of the door. It opened, stood open for a moment, and then closed with a slam. As it did so, the candle Mrs. Bunting was carrying from the study flickered and flared. It was a minute or more before they entered the kitchen.

The place was empty. They refastened the back door, examined the kitchen, pantry, and scullery thoroughly, and at last went down into the cellar. There was not a soul to be found in the house, search as they would.

Daylight found the vicar and his wife, a quaintly-costumed little couple, still marvelling about on their own ground floor by the unnecessary light of a guttering candle.

CHAPTER VI - THE FURNITURE THAT WENT MAD

Now it happened that in the early hours of Whit Monday, before Millie was hunted out for the day, Mr. Hall and Mrs. Hall both rose and went noiselessly down into the cellar. Their business there was of a private nature, and had something to do with the specific gravity of their beer. They had hardly entered the cellar when Mrs. Hall found she had forgotten to bring down a bottle of sarsaparilla from their joint-room. As she was the expert and principal operator in this affair, Hall very properly went upstairs for it.

On the landing he was surprised to see that the stranger's door was ajar. He went on into his own room and found the bottle as he had been directed.

But returning with the bottle, he noticed that the bolts of the front door had been shot back, that the door was in fact simply on the latch. And with a flash of inspiration he connected this with the stranger's room upstairs and the suggestions of Mr. Teddy Henfrey. He distinctly remembered holding the candle while Mrs. Hall shot these bolts overnight. At the sight he stopped, gaping, then with the bottle still in his hand went upstairs again. He rapped at the stranger's door. There was no answer. He rapped again; then pushed the door wide open and entered.

It was as he expected. The bed, the room also, was empty. And what was stranger, even to his heavy intelligence, on the bedroom chair and along the rail of the bed were scattered the garments, the only garments so far as he knew, and the bandages of their guest. His big slouch hat even was cocked jauntily over the bedpost.

As Hall stood there he heard his wife's voice coming out of the depth of the cellar, with that rapid telescoping of the syllables and interrogative cocking up of the final words to a high note, by which the West Sussex villager is wont to indicate a brisk impatience. "George! You gart whad a wand?"

At that he turned and hurried down to her. "Janny," he said, over the rail of the cellar steps, "'tas the truth what Henfrey sez. 'E's not in uz room, 'e en't. And the front door's onbolted."

At first Mrs. Hall did not understand, and as soon as she did she resolved to see the empty room for herself. Hall, still holding the bottle, went first. "If 'e en't there," he said, "'is close are. And what's 'e doin' 'ithout 'is close, then? 'Tas a most curious business."

As they came up the cellar steps they both, it was afterwards ascertained, fancied they heard the front door open and shut, but seeing it closed and nothing there, neither said a word to the other about it at the time. Mrs. Hall passed her

husband in the passage and ran on first upstairs. Someone sneezed on the staircase. Hall, following six steps behind, thought that he heard her sneeze. She, going on first, was under the impression that Hall was sneezing. She flung open the door and stood regarding the room. "Of all the curious!" she said.

She heard a sniff close behind her head as it seemed, and turning, was surprised to see Hall a dozen feet off on the topmost stair. But in another moment he was beside her. She bent forward and put her hand on the pillow and then under the clothes.

"Cold," she said. "He's been up this hour or more."

As she did so, a most extraordinary thing happened. The bed-clothes gathered themselves together, leapt up suddenly into a sort of peak, and then jumped headlong over the bottom rail. It was exactly as if a hand had clutched them in the centre and flung them aside. Immediately after, the stranger's hat hopped off the bed-post, described a whirling flight in the air through the better part of a circle, and then dashed straight at Mrs. Hall's face. Then as swiftly came the sponge from the washstand; and then the chair, flinging the stranger's coat and trousers carelessly aside, and laughing drily in a voice singularly like the stranger's, turned itself up with its four legs at Mrs. Hall, seemed to take aim at her for a moment, and charged at her. She screamed and turned, and then the chair legs came gently but firmly against her back and impelled her and Hall out of the room. The door slammed violently and was locked. The chair and bed seemed to be executing a dance of triumph for a moment, and then abruptly everything was still.

Mrs. Hall was left almost in a fainting condition in Mr. Hall's arms on the landing. It was with the greatest difficulty that Mr. Hall and Millie, who had been roused by her scream of alarm, succeeded in getting her downstairs, and applying the restoratives customary in such cases.

"'Tas sperits," said Mrs. Hall. "I know 'tas sperits. I've read in papers of en. Tables and chairs leaping and dancing..."

"Take a drop more, Janny," said Hall. "'Twill steady ye."

"Lock him out," said Mrs. Hall. "Don't let him come in again. I half guessed—I might ha' known. With them goggling eyes and bandaged head, and never going to church of a Sunday. And all they bottles—more'n it's right for any one to have. He's put the sperits into the furniture... My good old furniture! 'Twas in that very chair my poor dear mother used to sit when I was a little girl. To think it should rise up against me now!"

"Just a drop more, Janny," said Hall. "Your nerves is all upset."

They sent Millie across the street through the golden five o'clock sunshine to rouse up Mr. Sandy Wadgers, the blacksmith. Mr. Hall's compliments and the furniture upstairs was behaving most extraordinary. Would Mr. Wadgers come round? He was a knowing man, was Mr. Wadgers, and very resourceful. He took quite a grave view of the case. "Arm darmed if thet ent witchcraft," was the view of Mr. Sandy Wadgers. "You warnt horseshoes for such gentry as he."

He came round greatly concerned. They wanted him to lead the way upstairs to the room, but he didn't seem to be in any hurry. He preferred to talk in the pas-

sage. Over the way Huxter's apprentice came out and began taking down the shutters of the tobacco window. He was called over to join the discussion. Mr. Huxter naturally followed over in the course of a few minutes. The Anglo-Saxon genius for parliamentary government asserted itself; there was a great deal of talk and no decisive action. "Let's have the facts first," insisted Mr. Sandy Wadgers. "Let's be sure we'd be acting perfectly right in bustin' that there door open. A door onbust is always open to bustin', but ye can't onbust a door once you've busted en."

And suddenly and most wonderfully the door of the room upstairs opened of its own accord, and as they looked up in amazement, they saw descending the stairs the muffled figure of the stranger staring more blackly and blankly than ever with those unreasonably large blue glass eyes of his. He came down stiffly and slowly, staring all the time; he walked across the passage staring, then stopped.

"Look there!" he said, and their eyes followed the direction of his gloved finger and saw a bottle of sarsaparilla hard by the cellar door. Then he entered the parlour, and suddenly, swiftly, viciously, slammed the door in their faces.

Not a word was spoken until the last echoes of the slam had died away. They stared at one another. "Well, if that don't lick everything!" said Mr. Wadgers, and left the alternative unsaid.

"I'd go in and ask'n 'bout it," said Wadgers, to Mr. Hall. "I'd d'mand an explanation."

It took some time to bring the landlady's husband up to that pitch. At last he rapped, opened the door, and got as far as, "Excuse me—"

"Go to the devil!" said the stranger in a tremendous voice, and "Shut that door after you." So that brief interview terminated.

CHAPTER VII - THE UNVEILING OF THE STRANGER

The stranger went into the little parlour of the "Coach and Horses" about half-past five in the morning, and there he remained until near midday, the blinds down, the door shut, and none, after Hall's repulse, venturing near him.

All that time he must have fasted. Thrice he rang his bell, the third time furiously and continuously, but no one answered him. "Him and his 'go to the devil' indeed!" said Mrs. Hall. Presently came an imperfect rumour of the burglary at the vicarage, and two and two were put together. Hall, assisted by Wadgers, went off to find Mr. Shuckleforth, the magistrate, and take his advice. No one ventured upstairs. How the stranger occupied himself is unknown. Now and then he would stride violently up and down, and twice came an outburst of curses, a tearing of paper, and a violent smashing of bottles.

The little group of scared but curious people increased. Mrs. Huxter came over; some gay young fellows resplendent in black ready-made jackets and *pique* paper ties—for it was Whit Monday—joined the group with confused interrogations. Young Archie Harker distinguished himself by going up the yard and trying to peep under the window-blinds. He could see nothing, but gave reason for supposing that he did, and others of the Iping youth presently joined him.

It was the finest of all possible Whit Mondays, and down the village street stood a row of nearly a dozen booths, a shooting gallery, and on the grass by the forge were three yellow and chocolate waggons and some picturesque strangers of both sexes putting up a cocoanut shy. The gentlemen wore blue jerseys, the ladies white aprons and quite fashionable hats with heavy plumes. Wodger, of the "Purple Fawn," and Mr. Jaggers, the cobbler, who also sold old second-hand ordinary bicycles, were stretching a string of union-jacks and royal ensigns (which had originally celebrated the first Victorian Jubilee) across the road.

And inside, in the artificial darkness of the parlour, into which only one thin jet of sunlight penetrated, the stranger, hungry we must suppose, and fearful, hidden in his uncomfortable hot wrappings, pored through his dark glasses upon his paper or chinked his dirty little bottles, and occasionally swore savagely at the boys, audible if invisible, outside the windows. In the corner by the fireplace lay the fragments of half a dozen smashed bottles, and a pungent twang of chlorine tainted the air. So much we know from what was heard at the time and from what was subsequently seen in the room.

About noon he suddenly opened his parlour door and stood glaring fixedly at the three or four people in the bar. "Mrs. Hall," he said. Somebody went sheepishly and called for Mrs. Hall.

Mrs. Hall appeared after an interval, a little short of breath, but all the fiercer for that. Hall was still out. She had deliberated over this scene, and she came holding a little tray with an unsettled bill upon it. "Is it your bill you're wanting, sir?" she said.

"Why wasn't my breakfast laid? Why haven't you prepared my meals and answered my bell? Do you think I live without eating?"

"Why isn't my bill paid?" said Mrs. Hall. "That's what I want to know."

"I told you three days ago I was awaiting a remittance—"

"I told you two days ago I wasn't going to await no remittances. You can't grumble if your breakfast waits a bit, if my bill's been waiting these five days, can you?"

The stranger swore briefly but vividly.

"Nar, nar!" from the bar.

"And I'd thank you kindly, sir, if you'd keep your swearing to yourself, sir," said Mrs. Hall.

The stranger stood looking more like an angry diving-helmet than ever. It was universally felt in the bar that Mrs. Hall had the better of him. His next words showed as much.

"Look here, my good woman—" he began.

"Don't 'good woman' *me*," said Mrs. Hall.

"I've told you my remittance hasn't come."

"Remittance indeed!" said Mrs. Hall.

"Still, I daresay in my pocket—"

"You told me three days ago that you hadn't anything but a sovereign's worth of silver upon you."

"Well, I've found some more—"

"'Ul-lo!" from the bar.

"I wonder where you found it," said Mrs. Hall.

That seemed to annoy the stranger very much. He stamped his foot. "What do you mean?" he said.

"That I wonder where you found it," said Mrs. Hall. "And before I take any bills or get any breakfasts, or do any such things whatsoever, you got to tell me one or two things I don't understand, and what nobody don't understand, and what everybody is very anxious to understand. I want to know what you been doing t'my chair upstairs, and I want to know how 'tis your room was empty, and how you got in again. Them as stops in this house comes in by the doors—that's the rule of the house, and that you *didn't* do, and what I want to know is how you *did* come in. And I want to know—"

Suddenly the stranger raised his gloved hands clenched, stamped his foot, and said, "Stop!" with such extraordinary violence that he silenced her instantly.

"You don't understand," he said, "who I am or what I am. I'll show you. By Heaven! I'll show you." Then he put his open palm over his face and withdrew it. The centre of his face became a black cavity. "Here," he said. He stepped forward and handed Mrs. Hall something which she, staring at his metamorphosed face, accepted automatically. Then, when she saw what it was, she screamed loudly, dropped it, and staggered back. The nose—it was the stranger's nose! pink and shining—rolled on the floor.

Then he removed his spectacles, and everyone in the bar gasped. He took off his hat, and with a violent gesture tore at his whiskers and bandages. For a moment they resisted him. A flash of horrible anticipation passed through the bar. "Oh, my Gard!" said some one. Then off they came.

It was worse than anything. Mrs. Hall, standing open-mouthed and horror-struck, shrieked at what she saw, and made for the door of the house. Everyone began to move. They were prepared for scars, disfigurements, tangible horrors, but nothing! The bandages and false hair flew across the passage into the bar, making a hobbledehoy jump to avoid them. Everyone tumbled on everyone else down the steps. For the man who stood there shouting some incoherent explanation, was a solid gesticulating figure up to the coat-collar of him, and then—nothingness, no visible thing at all!

People down the village heard shouts and shrieks, and looking up the street saw the "Coach and Horses" violently firing out its humanity. They saw Mrs. Hall fall down and Mr. Teddy Henfrey jump to avoid tumbling over her, and then they heard the frightful screams of Millie, who, emerging suddenly from the kitchen at the noise of the tumult, had come upon the headless stranger from behind. These increased suddenly.

Forthwith everyone all down the street, the sweetstuff seller, cocoanut shy proprietor and his assistant, the swing man, little boys and girls, rustic dandies, smart wenches, smocked elders and aproned gipsies—began running towards the inn, and in a miraculously short space of time a crowd of perhaps forty people, and rapidly increasing, swayed and hooted and inquired and exclaimed and suggested, in front of Mrs. Hall's establishment. Everyone seemed eager to talk at once, and the result was Babel. A small group supported Mrs. Hall, who was picked up in a state of collapse. There was a conference, and the incredible evidence of a vociferous eye-witness. "O Bogey!" "What's he been doin', then?" "Ain't hurt thc girl, 'as 'e?" "Run at en with a knife, I believe." "No 'ed, I tell ye. I don't mean no manner of speaking. I mean *marn 'ithout a 'ed*!" "Narnsense! 'tis some conjuring trick." "Fetched off 'is wrapping, 'e did—"

In its struggles to see in through the open door, the crowd formed itself into a straggling wedge, with the more adventurous apex nearest the inn. "He stood for a moment, I heerd the gal scream, and he turned. I saw her skirts whisk, and he went after her. Didn't take ten seconds. Back he comes with a knife in uz hand and a loaf; stood just as if he was staring. Not a moment ago. Went in that there door. I tell 'e, 'e ain't gart no 'ed at all. You just missed en—"

There was a disturbance behind, and the speaker stopped to step aside for a little procession that was marching very resolutely towards the house; first Mr. Hall, very red and determined, then Mr. Bobby Jaffers, the village constable, and then the wary Mr. Wadgers. They had come now armed with a warrant.

People shouted conflicting information of the recent circumstances. "'Ed or no 'ed," said Jaffers, "I got to 'rest en, and 'rest en I *will*."

Mr. Hall marched up the steps, marched straight to the door of the parlour and flung it open. "Constable," he said, "do your duty."

Jaffers marched in. Hall next, Wadgers last. They saw in the dim light the headless figure facing them, with a gnawed crust of bread in one gloved hand and a chunk of cheese in the other.

"That's him!" said Hall.

"What the devil's this?" came in a tone of angry expostulation from above the collar of the figure.

"You're a damned rum customer, mister," said Mr. Jaffers. "But 'ed or no 'ed, the warrant says 'body,' and duty's duty—"

"Keep off!" said the figure, starting back.

Abruptly he whipped down the bread and cheese, and Mr. Hall just grasped the knife on the table in time to save it. Off came the stranger's left glove and was slapped in Jaffers' face. In another moment Jaffers, cutting short some statement concerning a warrant, had gripped him by the handless wrist and caught his invisible throat. He got a sounding kick on the shin that made him shout, but he kept his grip. Hall sent the knife sliding along the table to Wadgers, who acted as goalkeeper for the offensive, so to speak, and then stepped forward as Jaffers and the stranger swayed and staggered towards him, clutching and hitting in. A chair stood in the way, and went aside with a crash as they came down together.

"Get the feet," said Jaffers between his teeth.

Mr. Hall, endeavouring to act on instructions, received a sounding kick in the ribs that disposed of him for a moment, and Mr. Wadgers, seeing the decapitated stranger had rolled over and got the upper side of Jaffers, retreated towards the door, knife in hand, and so collided with Mr. Huxter and the Sidderbridge carter coming to the rescue of law and order. At the same moment down came three or four bottles from the chiffonnier and shot a web of pungency into the air of the room.

"I'll surrender," cried the stranger, though he had Jaffers down, and in another moment he stood up panting, a strange figure, headless and handless —for he had pulled off his right glove now as well as his left. "It's no good," he said, as if sobbing for breath.

It was the strangest thing in the world to hear that voice coming as if out of empty space, but the Sussex peasants are perhaps the most matter-of-fact people under the sun. Jaffers got up also and produced a pair of handcuffs. Then he stared.

"I say!" said Jaffers, brought up short by a dim realization of the incongruity of the whole business, "Darn it! Can't use 'em as I can see."

The stranger ran his arm down his waistcoat, and as if by a miracle the buttons to which his empty sleeve pointed became undone. Then he said something about his shin, and stooped down. He seemed to be fumbling with his shoes and socks.

"Why!" said Huxter, suddenly, "that's not a man at all. It's just empty clothes. Look! You can see down his collar and the linings of his clothes. I could put my arm—"

He extended his hand; it seemed to meet something in mid-air, and he drew it back with a sharp exclamation. "I wish you'd keep your fingers out of my eye," said the aerial voice, in a tone of savage expostulation. "The fact is, I'm all here—head, hands, legs, and all the rest of it, but it happens I'm invisible. It's a confounded nuisance, but I am. That's no reason why I should be poked to pieces by every stupid bumpkin in Iping, is it?"

The suit of clothes, now all unbuttoned and hanging loosely upon its unseen supports, stood up, arms akimbo.

Several other of the men folks had now entered the room, so that it was closely crowded. "Invisible, eh?" said Huxter, ignoring the stranger's abuse. "Who ever heard the likes of that?"

"It's strange, perhaps, but it's not a crime. Why am I assaulted by a policeman in this fashion?"

"Ah! that's a different matter," said Jaffers. "No doubt you are a bit difficult to see in this light, but I got a warrant and it's all correct. What I'm after ain't no invisibility,—it's burglary. There's a house been broke into and money took."

"Well?"

"And circumstances certainly point—"

"Stuff and nonsense!" said the Invisible Man.

"I hope so, sir; but I've got my instructions."

"Well," said the stranger, "I'll come. I'll *come*. But no handcuffs."

"It's the regular thing," said Jaffers.

"No handcuffs," stipulated the stranger.

"Pardon me," said Jaffers.

Abruptly the figure sat down, and before any one could realise what was being done, the slippers, socks, and trousers had been kicked off under the table. Then he sprang up again and flung off his coat.

"Here, stop that," said Jaffers, suddenly realising what was happening. He gripped at the waistcoat; it struggled, and the shirt slipped out of it and left it limply and empty in his hand. "Hold him!" said Jaffers, loudly. "Once he gets the things off—"

"Hold him!" cried everyone, and there was a rush at the fluttering white shirt which was now all that was visible of the stranger.

The shirt-sleeve planted a shrewd blow in Hall's face that stopped his open-armed advance, and sent him backward into old Toothsome the sexton, and in another moment the garment was lifted up and became convulsed and vacantly flapping about the arms, even as a shirt that is being thrust over a man's head. Jaffers clutched at it, and only helped to pull it off; he was struck in the mouth out

of the air, and incontinently threw his truncheon and smote Teddy Henfrey savagely upon the crown of his head.

"Look out!" said everybody, fencing at random and hitting at nothing. "Hold him! Shut the door! Don't let him loose! I got something! Here he is!" A perfect Babel of noises they made. Everybody, it seemed, was being hit all at once, and Sandy Wadgers, knowing as ever and his wits sharpened by a frightful blow in the nose, reopened the door and led the rout. The others, following incontinently, were jammed for a moment in the corner by the doorway. The hitting continued. Phipps, the Unitarian, had a front tooth broken, and Henfrey was injured in the cartilage of his ear. Jaffers was struck under the jaw, and, turning, caught at something that intervened between him and Huxter in the melee, and prevented their coming together. He felt a muscular chest, and in another moment the whole mass of struggling, excited men shot out into the crowded hall.

"I got him!" shouted Jaffers, choking and reeling through them all, and wrestling with purple face and swelling veins against his unseen enemy.

Men staggered right and left as the extraordinary conflict swayed swiftly towards the house door, and went spinning down the half-dozen steps of the inn. Jaffers cried in a strangled voice—holding tight, nevertheless, and making play with his knee—spun around, and fell heavily undermost with his head on the gravel. Only then did his fingers relax.

There were excited cries of "Hold him!" "Invisible!" and so forth, and a young fellow, a stranger in the place whose name did not come to light, rushed in at once, caught something, missed his hold, and fell over the constable's prostrate body. Half-way across the road a woman screamed as something pushed by her; a dog, kicked apparently, yelped and ran howling into Huxter's yard, and with that the transit of the Invisible Man was accomplished. For a space people stood amazed and gesticulating, and then came panic, and scattered them abroad through the village as a gust scatters dead leaves.

But Jaffers lay quite still, face upward and knees bent, at the foot of the steps of the inn.

CHAPTER VIII - IN TRANSIT

The eighth chapter is exceedingly brief, and relates that Gibbons, the amateur naturalist of the district, while lying out on the spacious open downs without a soul within a couple of miles of him, as he thought, and almost dozing, heard close to him the sound as of a man coughing, sneezing, and then swearing savagely to himself; and looking, beheld nothing. Yet the voice was indisputable. It continued to swear with that breadth and variety that distinguishes the swearing of a cultivated man. It grew to a climax, diminished again, and died away in the distance, going as it seemed to him in the direction of Adderdean. It lifted to a spasmodic sneeze and ended. Gibbons had heard nothing of the morning's occurrences, but the phenomenon was so striking and disturbing that his philosophical tranquillity vanished; he got up hastily, and hurried down the steepness of the hill towards the village, as fast as he could go.

CHAPTER IX - MR. THOMAS MARVEL

You must picture Mr. Thomas Marvel as a person of copious, flexible visage, a nose of cylindrical protrusion, a liquorish, ample, fluctuating mouth, and a beard of bristling eccentricity. His figure inclined to embonpoint; his short limbs accentuated this inclination. He wore a furry silk hat, and the frequent substitution of twine and shoe-laces for buttons, apparent at critical points of his costume, marked a man essentially bachelor.

Mr. Thomas Marvel was sitting with his feet in a ditch by the roadside over the down towards Adderdean, about a mile and a half out of Iping. His feet, save for socks of irregular open-work, were bare, his big toes were broad, and pricked like the ears of a watchful dog. In a leisurely manner —he did everything in a leisurely manner—he was contemplating trying on a pair of boots. They were the soundest boots he had come across for a long time, but too large for him; whereas the ones he had were, in dry weather, a very comfortable fit, but too thin-soled for damp. Mr. Thomas Marvel hated roomy shoes, but then he hated damp. He had never properly thought out which he hated most, and it was a pleasant day, and there was nothing better to do. So he put the four shoes in a graceful group on the turf and looked at them. And seeing them there among the grass and springing agrimony, it suddenly occurred to him that both pairs were exceedingly ugly to see. He was not at all startled by a voice behind him.

"They're boots, anyhow," said the Voice.

"They are—charity boots," said Mr. Thomas Marvel, with his head on one side regarding them distastefully; "and which is the ugliest pair in the whole blessed universe, I'm darned if I know!"

"H'm," said the Voice.

"I've worn worse—in fact, I've worn none. But none so owdacious ugly—if you'll allow the expression. I've been cadging boots—in particular—for days. Because I was sick of *them*. They're sound enough, of course. But a gentleman on tramp sees such a thundering lot of his boots. And if you'll believe me, I've raised nothing in the whole blessed country, try as I would, but *them*. Look at 'em! And a good country for boots, too, in a general way. But it's just my promiscuous luck. I've got my boots in this country ten years or more. And then they treat you like this."

"It's a beast of a country," said the Voice. "And pigs for people."

"Ain't it?" said Mr. Thomas Marvel. "Lord! But them boots! It beats it."

He turned his head over his shoulder to the right, to look at the boots of his interlocutor with a view to comparisons, and lo! where the boots of his interlocutor should have been were neither legs nor boots. He was irradiated by the dawn of a great amazement. "Where *are* yer?" said Mr. Thomas Marvel over his shoulder and coming on all fours. He saw a stretch of empty downs with the wind swaying the remote green-pointed furze bushes.

"Am I drunk?" said Mr. Marvel. "Have I had visions? Was I talking to myself? What the—"

"Don't be alarmed," said a Voice.

"None of your ventriloquising *me*," said Mr. Thomas Marvel, rising sharply to his feet. "Where *are* yer? Alarmed, indeed!"

"Don't be alarmed," repeated the Voice.

"*You'll* be alarmed in a minute, you silly fool," said Mr. Thomas Marvel. "Where *are* yer? Lemme get my mark on yer...

"Are yer *buried*?" said Mr. Thomas Marvel, after an interval.

There was no answer. Mr. Thomas Marvel stood bootless and amazed, his jacket nearly thrown off.

"Peewit," said a peewit, very remote.

"Peewit, indeed!" said Mr. Thomas Marvel. "This ain't no time for foolery." The down was desolate, east and west, north and south; the road with its shallow ditches and white bordering stakes, ran smooth and empty north and south, and, save for that peewit, the blue sky was empty too. "So help me," said Mr. Thomas Marvel, shuffling his coat on to his shoulders again. "It's the drink! I might ha' known."

"It's not the drink," said the Voice. "You keep your nerves steady."

"Ow!" said Mr. Marvel, and his face grew white amidst its patches. "It's the drink!" his lips repeated noiselessly. He remained staring about him, rotating slowly backwards. "I could have *swore* I heard a voice," he whispered.

"Of course you did."

"It's there again," said Mr. Marvel, closing his eyes and clasping his hand on his brow with a tragic gesture. He was suddenly taken by the collar and shaken violently, and left more dazed than ever. "Don't be a fool," said the Voice.

"I'm—off—my—blooming—chump," said Mr. Marvel. "It's no good. It's fretting about them blarsted boots. I'm off my blessed blooming chump. Or it's spirits."

"Neither one thing nor the other," said the Voice. "Listen!"

"Chump," said Mr. Marvel.

"One minute," said the Voice, penetratingly, tremulous with self- control.

"Well?" said Mr. Thomas Marvel, with a strange feeling of having been dug in the chest by a finger.

"You think I'm just imagination? Just imagination?"

"What else *can* you be?" said Mr. Thomas Marvel, rubbing the back of his neck.

"Very well," said the Voice, in a tone of relief. "Then I'm going to throw flints at you till you think differently."

"But where *are* yer?"

The Voice made no answer. Whizz came a flint, apparently out of the air, and missed Mr. Marvel's shoulder by a hair's-breadth. Mr. Marvel, turning, saw a flint jerk up into the air, trace a complicated path, hang for a moment, and then fling at his feet with almost invisible rapidity. He was too amazed to dodge. Whizz it came, and ricochetted from a bare toe into the ditch. Mr. Thomas Marvel jumped a foot and howled aloud. Then he started to run, tripped over an unseen obstacle, and came head over heels into a sitting position.

"*Now*," said the Voice, as a third stone curved upward and hung in the air above the tramp. "Am I imagination?"

Mr. Marvel by way of reply struggled to his feet, and was immediately rolled over again. He lay quiet for a moment. "If you struggle any more," said the Voice, "I shall throw the flint at your head."

"It's a fair do," said Mr. Thomas Marvel, sitting up, taking his wounded toe in hand and fixing his eye on the third missile. "I don't understand it. Stones flinging themselves. Stones talking. Put yourself down. Rot away. I'm done."

The third flint fell.

"It's very simple," said the Voice. "I'm an invisible man."

"Tell us something I don't know," said Mr. Marvel, gasping with pain. "Where you've hid—how you do it—I *don't* know. I'm beat."

"That's all," said the Voice. "I'm invisible. That's what I want you to understand."

"Anyone could see that. There is no need for you to be so confounded impatient, mister. *Now* then. Give us a notion. How are you hid?"

"I'm invisible. That's the great point. And what I want you to understand is this—"

"But whereabouts?" interrupted Mr. Marvel.

"Here! Six yards in front of you."

"Oh, *come*! I ain't blind. You'll be telling me next you're just thin air. I'm not one of your ignorant tramps—"

"Yes, I am—thin air. You're looking through me."

"What! Ain't there any stuff to you. *Vox et*—what is it? —jabber. Is it that?"

"I am just a human being—solid, needing food and drink, needing covering too—But I'm invisible. You see? Invisible. Simple idea. Invisible."

"What, real like?"

"Yes, real."

"Let's have a hand of you," said Marvel, "if you *are* real. It won't be so darn out-of-the-way like, then—*Lord*!" he said, "how you made me jump!—gripping me like that!"

He felt the hand that had closed round his wrist with his disengaged fingers, and his fingers went timorously up the arm, patted a muscular chest, and explored a bearded face. Marvel's face was astonishment.

"I'm dashed!" he said. "If this don't beat cock-fighting! Most remarkable!—And there I can see a rabbit clean through you, 'arf a mile away! Not a bit of you visible—except—"

He scrutinised the apparently empty space keenly. "You 'aven't been eatin' bread and cheese?" he asked, holding the invisible arm.

"You're quite right, and it's not quite assimilated into the system."

"Ah!" said Mr. Marvel. "Sort of ghostly, though."

"Of course, all this isn't half so wonderful as you think."

"It's quite wonderful enough for *my* modest wants," said Mr. Thomas Marvel. "Howjer manage it! How the dooce is it done?"

"It's too long a story. And besides—"

"I tell you, the whole business fairly beats me," said Mr. Marvel.

"What I want to say at present is this: I need help. I have come to that —I came upon you suddenly. I was wandering, mad with rage, naked, impotent. I could have murdered. And I saw you—"

"*Lord*!" said Mr. Marvel.

"I came up behind you—hesitated—went on—"

Mr. Marvel's expression was eloquent.

"—then stopped. 'Here,' I said, 'is an outcast like myself. This is the man for me.' So I turned back and came to you—you. And—"

"*Lord*!" said Mr. Marvel. "But I'm all in a tizzy. May I ask —How is it? And what you may be requiring in the way of help?—Invisible!"

"I want you to help me get clothes—and shelter—and then, with other things. I've left them long enough. If you won't—well! But you *will—must*."

"Look here," said Mr. Marvel. "I'm too flabbergasted. Don't knock me about any more. And leave me go. I must get steady a bit. And you've pretty near broken my toe. It's all so unreasonable. Empty downs, empty sky. Nothing visible for miles except the bosom of Nature. And then comes a voice. A voice out of heaven! And stones! And a fist—Lord!"

"Pull yourself together," said the Voice, "for you have to do the job I've chosen for you."

Mr. Marvel blew out his cheeks, and his eyes were round.

"I've chosen you," said the Voice. "You are the only man except some of those fools down there, who knows there is such a thing as an invisible man. You have to be my helper. Help me—and I will do great things for you. An invisible man is a man of power." He stopped for a moment to sneeze violently.

"But if you betray me," he said, "if you fail to do as I direct you—" He paused and tapped Mr. Marvel's shoulder smartly. Mr. Marvel gave a yelp of terror at the touch. "I don't want to betray you," said Mr. Marvel, edging away from the direction of the fingers. "Don't you go a-thinking that, whatever you do. All I want to do is to help you—just tell me what I got to do. (Lord!) Whatever you want done, that I'm most willing to do."

CHAPTER X - MR. MARVEL'S VISIT TO IPING

After the first gusty panic had spent itself Iping became argumentative. Scepticism suddenly reared its head—rather nervous scepticism, not at all assured of its back, but scepticism nevertheless. It is so much easier not to believe in an invisible man; and those who had actually seen him dissolve into air, or felt the strength of his arm, could be counted on the fingers of two hands. And of these witnesses Mr. Wadgers was presently missing, having retired impregnably behind the bolts and bars of his own house, and Jaffers was lying stunned in the parlour of the "Coach and Horses." Great and strange ideas transcending experience often have less effect upon men and women than smaller, more tangible considerations. Iping was gay with bunting, and everybody was in gala dress. Whit Monday had been looked forward to for a month or more. By the afternoon even those who believed in the Unseen were beginning to resume their little amusements in a tentative fashion, on the supposition that he had quite gone away, and with the sceptics he was already a jest. But people, sceptics and believers alike, were remarkably sociable all that day.

Haysman's meadow was gay with a tent, in which Mrs. Bunting and other ladies were preparing tea, while, without, the Sunday-school children ran races and played games under the noisy guidance of the curate and the Misses Cuss and Sackbut. No doubt there was a slight uneasiness in the air, but people for the most part had the sense to conceal whatever imaginative qualms they experienced. On the village green an inclined strong, down which, clinging the while to a pulley-swung handle, one could be hurled violently against a sack at the other end, came in for considerable favour among the adolescent, as also did the swings and the cocoanut shies. There was also promenading, and the steam organ attached to a small roundabout filled the air with a pungent flavour of oil and with equally pungent music. Members of the club, who had attended church in the morning, were splendid in badges of pink and green, and some of the gayer-minded had also adorned their bowler hats with brilliant- coloured favours of ribbon. Old Fletcher, whose conceptions of holiday-making were severe, was visible through the jasmine about his window or through the open door (whichever way you chose to look), poised delicately on a plank supported on two chairs, and white-washing the ceiling of his front room.

About four o'clock a stranger entered the village from the direction of the downs. He was a short, stout person in an extraordinarily shabby top hat, and he appeared to be very much out of breath. His cheeks were alternately limp and

tightly puffed. His mottled face was apprehensive, and he moved with a sort of reluctant alacrity. He turned the corner of the church, and directed his way to the "Coach and Horses." Among others old Fletcher remembers seeing him, and indeed the old gentleman was so struck by his peculiar agitation that he inadvertently allowed a quantity of whitewash to run down the brush into the sleeve of his coat while regarding him.

This stranger, to the perceptions of the proprietor of the cocoanut shy, appeared to be talking to himself, and Mr. Huxter remarked the same thing. He stopped at the foot of the "Coach and Horses" steps, and, according to Mr. Huxter, appeared to undergo a severe internal struggle before he could induce himself to enter the house. Finally he marched up the steps, and was seen by Mr. Huxter to turn to the left and open the door of the parlour. Mr. Huxter heard voices from within the room and from the bar apprising the man of his error. "That room's private!" said Hall, and the stranger shut the door clumsily and went into the bar.

In the course of a few minutes he reappeared, wiping his lips with the back of his hand with an air of quiet satisfaction that somehow impressed Mr. Huxter as assumed. He stood looking about him for some moments, and then Mr. Huxter saw him walk in an oddly furtive manner towards the gates of the yard, upon which the parlour window opened. The stranger, after some hesitation, leant against one of the gate-posts, produced a short clay pipe, and prepared to fill it. His fingers trembled while doing so. He lit it clumsily, and folding his arms began to smoke in a languid attitude, an attitude which his occasional glances up the yard altogether belied.

All this Mr. Huxter saw over the canisters of the tobacco window, and the singularity of the man's behaviour prompted him to maintain his observation.

Presently the stranger stood up abruptly and put his pipe in his pocket. Then he vanished into the yard. Forthwith Mr. Huxter, conceiving he was witness of some petty larceny, leapt round his counter and ran out into the road to intercept the thief. As he did so, Mr. Marvel reappeared, his hat askew, a big bundle in a blue table-cloth in one hand, and three books tied together—as it proved afterwards with the Vicar's braces—in the other. Directly he saw Huxter he gave a sort of gasp, and turning sharply to the left, began to run. "Stop, thief!" cried Huxter, and set off after him. Mr. Huxter's sensations were vivid but brief. He saw the man just before him and spurting briskly for the church corner and the hill road. He saw the village flags and festivities beyond, and a face or so turned towards him. He bawled, "Stop!" again. He had hardly gone ten strides before his shin was caught in some mysterious fashion, and he was no longer running, but flying with inconceivable rapidity through the air. He saw the ground suddenly close to his face. The world seemed to splash into a million whirling specks of light, and subsequent proceedings interested him no more.

CHAPTER XI - IN THE "COACH AND HORSES"

Now in order clearly to understand what had happened in the inn, it is necessary to go back to the moment when Mr. Marvel first came into view of Mr. Huxter's window.

At that precise moment Mr. Cuss and Mr. Bunting were in the parlour. They were seriously investigating the strange occurrences of the morning, and were, with Mr. Hall's permission, making a thorough examination of the Invisible Man's belongings. Jaffers had partially recovered from his fall and had gone home in the charge of his sympathetic friends. The stranger's scattered garments had been removed by Mrs. Hall and the room tidied up. And on the table under the window where the stranger had been wont to work, Cuss had hit almost at once on three big books in manuscript labelled "Diary."

"Diary!" said Cuss, putting the three books on the table. "Now, at any rate, we shall learn something." The Vicar stood with his hands on the table.

"Diary," repeated Cuss, sitting down, putting two volumes to support the third, and opening it. "H'm—no name on the fly-leaf. Bother!—cypher. And figures."

The vicar came round to look over his shoulder.

Cuss turned the pages over with a face suddenly disappointed. "I'm —dear me! It's all cypher, Bunting."

"There are no diagrams?" asked Mr. Bunting. "No illustrations throwing light—"

"See for yourself," said Mr. Cuss. "Some of it's mathematical and some of it's Russian or some such language (to judge by the letters), and some of it's Greek. Now the Greek I thought *you*—"

"Of course," said Mr. Bunting, taking out and wiping his spectacles and feeling suddenly very uncomfortable—for he had no Greek left in his mind worth talking about; "yes—the Greek, of course, may furnish a clue."

"I'll find you a place."

"I'd rather glance through the volumes first," said Mr. Bunting, still wiping. "A general impression first, Cuss, and *then*, you know, we can go looking for clues."

He coughed, put on his glasses, arranged them fastidiously, coughed again, and wished something would happen to avert the seemingly inevitable exposure. Then he took the volume Cuss handed him in a leisurely manner. And then something did happen.

The door opened suddenly.

Both gentlemen started violently, looked round, and were relieved to see a sporadically rosy face beneath a furry silk hat. "Tap?" asked the face, and stood staring.

"No," said both gentlemen at once.

"Over the other side, my man," said Mr. Bunting. And "Please shut that door," said Mr. Cuss, irritably.

"All right," said the intruder, as it seemed in a low voice curiously different from the huskiness of its first inquiry. "Right you are," said the intruder in the former voice. "Stand clear!" and he vanished and closed the door.

"A sailor, I should judge," said Mr. Bunting. "Amusing fellows, they are. Stand clear! indeed. A nautical term, referring to his getting back out of the room, I suppose."

"I daresay so," said Cuss. "My nerves are all loose to-day. It quite made me jump—the door opening like that."

Mr. Bunting smiled as if he had not jumped. "And now," he said with a sigh, "these books."

Someone sniffed as he did so.

"One thing is indisputable," said Bunting, drawing up a chair next to that of Cuss. "There certainly have been very strange things happen in Iping during the last few days—very strange. I cannot of course believe in this absurd invisibility story—"

"It's incredible," said Cuss—"incredible. But the fact remains that I saw—I certainly saw right down his sleeve—"

"But did you—are you sure? Suppose a mirror, for instance—hallucinations are so easily produced. I don't know if you have ever seen a really good conjuror—"

"I won't argue again," said Cuss. "We've thrashed that out, Bunting. And just now there's these books—Ah! here's some of what I take to be Greek! Greek letters certainly."

He pointed to the middle of the page. Mr. Bunting flushed slightly and brought his face nearer, apparently finding some difficulty with his glasses. Suddenly he became aware of a strange feeling at the nape of his neck. He tried to raise his head, and encountered an immovable resistance. The feeling was a curious pressure, the grip of a heavy, firm hand, and it bore his chin irresistibly to the table. "Don't move, little men," whispered a voice, "or I'll brain you both!" He looked into the face of Cuss, close to his own, and each saw a horrified reflection of his own sickly astonishment.

"I'm sorry to handle you so roughly," said the Voice, "but it's unavoidable."

"Since when did you learn to pry into an investigator's private memoranda," said the Voice; and two chins struck the table simultaneously, and two sets of teeth rattled.

"Since when did you learn to invade the private rooms of a man in misfortune?" and the concussion was repeated.

"Where have they put my clothes?"

"Listen," said the Voice. "The windows are fastened and I've taken the key out of the door. I am a fairly strong man, and I have the poker handy —besides being invisible. There's not the slightest doubt that I could kill you both and get away quite easily if I wanted to—do you understand? Very well. If I let you go will you promise not to try any nonsense and do what I tell you?"

The vicar and the doctor looked at one another, and the doctor pulled a face. "Yes," said Mr. Bunting, and the doctor repeated it. Then the pressure on the necks relaxed, and the doctor and the vicar sat up, both very red in the face and wriggling their heads.

"Please keep sitting where you are," said the Invisible Man. "Here's the poker, you see."

"When I came into this room," continued the Invisible Man, after presenting the poker to the tip of the nose of each of his visitors, "I did not expect to find it occupied, and I expected to find, in addition to my books of memoranda, an outfit of clothing. Where is it? No—don't rise. I can see it's gone. Now, just at present, though the days are quite warm enough for an invisible man to run about stark, the evenings are quite chilly. I want clothing—and other accommodation; and I must also have those three books."

CHAPTER XII - THE INVISIBLE MAN LOSES HIS TEMPER

It is unavoidable that at this point the narrative should break off again, for a certain very painful reason that will presently be apparent. While these things were going on in the parlour, and while Mr. Huxter was watching Mr. Marvel smoking his pipe against the gate, not a dozen yards away were Mr. Hall and Teddy Henfrey discussing in a state of cloudy puzzlement the one Iping topic.

Suddenly there came a violent thud against the door of the parlour, a sharp cry, and then—silence.

"Hul-lo!" said Teddy Henfrey.

"Hul-lo!" from the Tap.

Mr. Hall took things in slowly but surely. "That ain't right," he said, and came round from behind the bar towards the parlour door.

He and Teddy approached the door together, with intent faces. Their eyes considered. "Summat wrong," said Hall, and Henfrey nodded agreement. Whiffs of an unpleasant chemical odour met them, and there was a muffled sound of conversation, very rapid and subdued.

"You all right thur?" asked Hall, rapping.

The muttered conversation ceased abruptly, for a moment silence, then the conversation was resumed, in hissing whispers, then a sharp cry of "No! no, you don't!" There came a sudden motion and the oversetting of a chair, a brief struggle. Silence again.

"What the dooce?" exclaimed Henfrey, *sotto voce*.

"You—all—right thur?" asked Mr. Hall, sharply, again.

The Vicar's voice answered with a curious jerking intonation: "Quite ri- right. Please don't—interrupt."

"Odd!" said Mr. Henfrey.

"Odd!" said Mr. Hall.

"Says, 'Don't interrupt,'" said Henfrey.

"I heerd'n," said Hall.

"And a sniff," said Henfrey.

They remained listening. The conversation was rapid and subdued. "I *can't*," said Mr. Bunting, his voice rising; "I tell you, sir, I *will* not."

"What was that?" asked Henfrey.

"Says he wi' nart," said Hall. "Warn't speaking to us, wuz he?"

"Disgraceful!" said Mr. Bunting, within.

"'Disgraceful,'" said Mr. Henfrey. "I heard it—distinct."

"Who's that speaking now?" asked Henfrey.

"Mr. Cuss, I s'pose," said Hall. "Can you hear—anything?"

Silence. The sounds within indistinct and perplexing.

"Sounds like throwing the table-cloth about," said Hall.

Mrs. Hall appeared behind the bar. Hall made gestures of silence and invitation. This aroused Mrs. Hall's wifely opposition. "What yer listenin' there for, Hall?" she asked. "Ain't you nothin' better to do—busy day like this?"

Hall tried to convey everything by grimaces and dumb show, but Mrs. Hall was obdurate. She raised her voice. So Hall and Henfrey, rather crestfallen, tiptoed back to the bar, gesticulating to explain to her.

At first she refused to see anything in what they had heard at all. Then she insisted on Hall keeping silence, while Henfrey told her his story. She was inclined to think the whole business nonsense—perhaps they were just moving the furniture about. "I heerd'n say 'disgraceful'; *that* I did," said Hall.

"*I* heerd that, Mrs. Hall," said Henfrey.

"Like as not—" began Mrs. Hall.

"Hsh!" said Mr. Teddy Henfrey. "Didn't I hear the window?"

"What window?" asked Mrs. Hall.

"Parlour window," said Henfrey.

Everyone stood listening intently. Mrs. Hall's eyes, directed straight before her, saw without seeing the brilliant oblong of the inn door, the road white and vivid, and Huxter's shop-front blistering in the June sun. Abruptly Huxter's door opened and Huxter appeared, eyes staring with excitement, arms gesticulating. "Yap!" cried Huxter. "Stop thief!" and he ran obliquely across the oblong towards the yard gates, and vanished.

Simultaneously came a tumult from the parlour, and a sound of windows being closed.

Hall, Henfrey, and the human contents of the tap rushed out at once pell- mell into the street. They saw someone whisk round the corner towards the road, and Mr. Huxter executing a complicated leap in the air that ended on his face and shoulder. Down the street people were standing astonished or running towards them.

Mr. Huxter was stunned. Henfrey stopped to discover this, but Hall and the two labourers from the Tap rushed at once to the corner, shouting incoherent things, and saw Mr. Marvel vanishing by the corner of the church wall. They appear to have jumped to the impossible conclusion that this was the Invisible Man suddenly become visible, and set off at once along the lane in pursuit. But Hall had hardly run a dozen yards before he gave a loud shout of astonishment and went flying headlong sideways, clutching one of the labourers and bringing him to the ground. He had been charged just as one charges a man at football. The second labourer came round in a circle, stared, and conceiving that Hall had tumbled over of his own accord, turned to resume the pursuit, only to be tripped

by the ankle just as Huxter had been. Then, as the first labourer struggled to his feet, he was kicked sideways by a blow that might have felled an ox.

As he went down, the rush from the direction of the village green came round the corner. The first to appear was the proprietor of the cocoanut shy, a burly man in a blue jersey. He was astonished to see the lane empty save for three men sprawling absurdly on the ground. And then something happened to his rear-most foot, and he went headlong and rolled sideways just in time to graze the feet of his brother and partner, following headlong. The two were then kicked, knelt on, fallen over, and cursed by quite a number of over-hasty people.

Now when Hall and Henfrey and the labourers ran out of the house, Mrs. Hall, who had been disciplined by years of experience, remained in the bar next the till. And suddenly the parlour door was opened, and Mr. Cuss appeared, and without glancing at her rushed at once down the steps toward the corner. "Hold him!" he cried. "Don't let him drop that parcel."

He knew nothing of the existence of Marvel. For the Invisible Man had handed over the books and bundle in the yard. The face of Mr. Cuss was angry and resolute, but his costume was defective, a sort of limp white kilt that could only have passed muster in Greece. "Hold him!" he bawled. "He's got my trousers! And every stitch of the Vicar's clothes!"

"'Tend to him in a minute!" he cried to Henfrey as he passed the prostrate Huxter, and, coming round the corner to join the tumult, was promptly knocked off his feet into an indecorous sprawl. Somebody in full flight trod heavily on his finger. He yelled, struggled to regain his feet, was knocked against and thrown on all fours again, and became aware that he was involved not in a capture, but a rout. Everyone was running back to the village. He rose again and was hit severely behind the ear. He staggered and set off back to the "Coach and Horses" forthwith, leaping over the deserted Huxter, who was now sitting up, on his way.

Behind him as he was halfway up the inn steps he heard a sudden yell of rage, rising sharply out of the confusion of cries, and a sounding smack in someone's face. He recognised the voice as that of the Invisible Man, and the note was that of a man suddenly infuriated by a painful blow.

In another moment Mr. Cuss was back in the parlour. "He's coming back, Bunting!" he said, rushing in. "Save yourself!"

Mr. Bunting was standing in the window engaged in an attempt to clothe himself in the hearth-rug and a *West Surrey Gazette*. "Who's coming?" he said, so startled that his costume narrowly escaped disintegration.

"Invisible Man," said Cuss, and rushed on to the window. "We'd better clear out from here! He's fighting mad! Mad!"

In another moment he was out in the yard.

"Good heavens!" said Mr. Bunting, hesitating between two horrible alternatives. He heard a frightful struggle in the passage of the inn, and his decision was made. He clambered out of the window, adjusted his costume hastily, and fled up the village as fast as his fat little legs would carry him.

From the moment when the Invisible Man screamed with rage and Mr. Bunting made his memorable flight up the village, it became impossible to give a consecutive account of affairs in Iping. Possibly the Invisible Man's original intention was simply to cover Marvel's retreat with the clothes and books. But his temper, at no time very good, seems to have gone completely at some chance blow, and forthwith he set to smiting and overthrowing, for the mere satisfaction of hurting.

You must figure the street full of running figures, of doors slamming and fights for hiding-places. You must figure the tumult suddenly striking on the unstable equilibrium of old Fletcher's planks and two chairs—with cataclysmic results. You must figure an appalled couple caught dismally in a swing. And then the whole tumultuous rush has passed and the Iping street with its gauds and flags is deserted save for the still raging unseen, and littered with cocoanuts, overthrown canvas screens, and the scattered stock in trade of a sweetstuff stall. Everywhere there is a sound of closing shutters and shoving bolts, and the only visible humanity is an occasional flitting eye under a raised eyebrow in the corner of a window pane.

The Invisible Man amused himself for a little while by breaking all the windows in the "Coach and Horses," and then he thrust a street lamp through the parlour window of Mrs. Gribble. He it must have been who cut the telegraph wire to Adderdean just beyond Higgins' cottage on the Adderdean road. And after that, as his peculiar qualities allowed, he passed out of human perceptions altogether, and he was neither heard, seen, nor felt in Iping any more. He vanished absolutely.

But it was the best part of two hours before any human being ventured out again into the desolation of Iping street.

CHAPTER XIII - MR. MARVEL DISCUSSES HIS RESIGNATION

When the dusk was gathering and Iping was just beginning to peep timorously forth again upon the shattered wreckage of its Bank Holiday, a short, thick-set man in a shabby silk hat was marching painfully through the twilight behind the beechwoods on the road to Bramblehurst. He carried three books bound together by some sort of ornamental elastic ligature, and a bundle wrapped in a blue table-cloth. His rubicund face expressed consternation and fatigue; he appeared to be in a spasmodic sort of hurry. He was accompanied by a voice other than his own, and ever and again he winced under the touch of unseen hands.

"If you give me the slip again," said the Voice, "if you attempt to give me the slip again—"

"Lord!" said Mr. Marvel. "That shoulder's a mass of bruises as it is."

"On my honour," said the Voice, "I will kill you."

"I didn't try to give you the slip," said Marvel, in a voice that was not far remote from tears. "I swear I didn't. I didn't know the blessed turning, that was all! How the devil was I to know the blessed turning? As it is, I've been knocked about—"

"You'll get knocked about a great deal more if you don't mind," said the Voice, and Mr. Marvel abruptly became silent. He blew out his cheeks, and his eyes were eloquent of despair.

"It's bad enough to let these floundering yokels explode my little secret, without *your* cutting off with my books. It's lucky for some of them they cut and ran when they did! Here am I ... No one knew I was invisible! And now what am I to do?"

"What am *I* to do?" asked Marvel, *sotto voce*.

"It's all about. It will be in the papers! Everybody will be looking for me; everyone on their guard—" The Voice broke off into vivid curses and ceased.

The despair of Mr. Marvel's face deepened, and his pace slackened.

"Go on!" said the Voice.

Mr. Marvel's face assumed a greyish tint between the ruddier patches.

"Don't drop those books, stupid," said the Voice, sharply—overtaking him.

"The fact is," said the Voice, "I shall have to make use of you... You're a poor tool, but I must."

"I'm a *miserable* tool," said Marvel.

"You are," said the Voice.

"I'm the worst possible tool you could have," said Marvel.

"I'm not strong," he said after a discouraging silence.

"I'm not over strong," he repeated.

"No?"

"And my heart's weak. That little business—I pulled it through, of course—but bless you! I could have dropped."

"Well?"

"I haven't the nerve and strength for the sort of thing you want."

"*I'll* stimulate you."

"I wish you wouldn't. I wouldn't like to mess up your plans, you know. But I might—out of sheer funk and misery."

"You'd better not," said the Voice, with quiet emphasis.

"I wish I was dead," said Marvel.

"It ain't justice," he said; "you must admit... It seems to me I've a perfect right—"

"*Get* on!" said the Voice.

Mr. Marvel mended his pace, and for a time they went in silence again.

"It's devilish hard," said Mr. Marvel.

This was quite ineffectual. He tried another tack.

"What do I make by it?" he began again in a tone of unendurable wrong.

"Oh! *shut up*!" said the Voice, with sudden amazing vigour. "I'll see to you all right. You do what you're told. You'll do it all right. You're a fool and all that, but you'll do—"

"I tell you, sir, I'm not the man for it. Respectfully—but it *is* so—"

"If you don't shut up I shall twist your wrist again," said the Invisible Man. "I want to think."

Presently two oblongs of yellow light appeared through the trees, and the square tower of a church loomed through the gloaming. "I shall keep my hand on your shoulder," said the Voice, "all through the village. Go straight through and try no foolery. It will be the worse for you if you do."

"I know that," sighed Mr. Marvel, "I know all that."

The unhappy-looking figure in the obsolete silk hat passed up the street of the little village with his burdens, and vanished into the gathering darkness beyond the lights of the windows.

CHAPTER XIV - AT PORT STOWE

Ten o'clock the next morning found Mr. Marvel, unshaven, dirty, and travel-stained, sitting with the books beside him and his hands deep in his pockets, looking very weary, nervous, and uncomfortable, and inflating his cheeks at infrequent intervals, on the bench outside a little inn on the outskirts of Port Stowe. Beside him were the books, but now they were tied with string. The bundle had been abandoned in the pine-woods beyond Bramblehurst, in accordance with a change in the plans of the Invisible Man. Mr. Marvel sat on the bench, and although no one took the slightest notice of him, his agitation remained at fever heat. His hands would go ever and again to his various pockets with a curious nervous fumbling.

When he had been sitting for the best part of an hour, however, an elderly mariner, carrying a newspaper, came out of the inn and sat down beside him. "Pleasant day," said the mariner.

Mr. Marvel glanced about him with something very like terror. "Very," he said.

"Just seasonable weather for the time of year," said the mariner, taking no denial.

"Quite," said Mr. Marvel.

The mariner produced a toothpick, and (saving his regard) was engrossed thereby for some minutes. His eyes meanwhile were at liberty to examine Mr. Marvel's dusty figure, and the books beside him. As he had approached Mr. Marvel he had heard a sound like the dropping of coins into a pocket. He was struck by the contrast of Mr. Marvel's appearance with this suggestion of opulence. Thence his mind wandered back again to a topic that had taken a curiously firm hold of his imagination.

"Books?" he said suddenly, noisily finishing with the toothpick.

Mr. Marvel started and looked at them. "Oh, yes," he said. "Yes, they're books."

"There's some extra-ordinary things in books," said the mariner.

"I believe you," said Mr. Marvel.

"And some extra-ordinary things out of 'em," said the mariner.

"True likewise," said Mr. Marvel. He eyed his interlocutor, and then glanced about him.

"There's some extra-ordinary things in newspapers, for example," said the mariner.

"There are."

"In *this* newspaper," said the mariner.

"Ah!" said Mr. Marvel.

"There's a story," said the mariner, fixing Mr. Marvel with an eye that was firm and deliberate; "there's a story about an Invisible Man, for instance."

Mr. Marvel pulled his mouth askew and scratched his cheek and felt his ears glowing. "What will they be writing next?" he asked faintly. "Ostria, or America?"

"Neither," said the mariner. "*Here*."

"Lord!" said Mr. Marvel, starting.

"When I say *here*," said the mariner, to Mr. Marvel's intense relief, "I don't of course mean here in this place, I mean hereabouts."

"An Invisible Man!" said Mr. Marvel. "And what's *he* been up to?"

"Everything," said the mariner, controlling Marvel with his eye, and then amplifying, "every—blessed—thing."

"I ain't seen a paper these four days," said Marvel.

"Iping's the place he started at," said the mariner.

"In-*deed*!" said Mr. Marvel.

"He started there. And where he came from, nobody don't seem to know. Here it is: 'Pe-culiar Story from Iping.' And it says in this paper that the evidence is extra-ordinary strong—extra-ordinary."

"Lord!" said Mr. Marvel.

"But then, it's an extra-ordinary story. There is a clergyman and a medical gent witnesses—saw 'im all right and proper—or leastways didn't see 'im. He was staying, it says, at the 'Coach an' Horses,' and no one don't seem to have been aware of his misfortune, it says, aware of his misfortune, until in an Altercation in the inn, it says, his bandages on his head was torn off. It was then ob-served that his head was invisible. Attempts were At Once made to secure him, but casting off his garments, it says, he succeeded in escaping, but not until after a desperate struggle, in which he had inflicted serious injuries, it says, on our worthy and able constable, Mr. J. A. Jaffers. Pretty straight story, eh? Names and everything."

"Lord!" said Mr. Marvel, looking nervously about him, trying to count the money in his pockets by his unaided sense of touch, and full of a strange and novel idea. "It sounds most astonishing."

"Don't it? Extra-ordinary, *I* call it. Never heard tell of Invisible Men before, I haven't, but nowadays one hears such a lot of extra- ordinary things—that—"

"That all he did?" asked Marvel, trying to seem at his ease.

"It's enough, ain't it?" said the mariner.

"Didn't go Back by any chance?" asked Marvel. "Just escaped and that's all, eh?"

"All!" said the mariner. "Why!—ain't it enough?"

"Quite enough," said Marvel.

"I should think it was enough," said the mariner. "I should think it was enough."

"He didn't have any pals—it don't say he had any pals, does it?" asked Mr. Marvel, anxious.

"Ain't one of a sort enough for you?" asked the mariner. "No, thank Heaven, as one might say, he didn't."

He nodded his head slowly. "It makes me regular uncomfortable, the bare thought of that chap running about the country! He is at present At Large, and from certain evidence it is supposed that he has—taken—*took*, I suppose they mean—the road to Port Stowe. You see we're right *in* it! None of your American wonders, this time. And just think of the things he might do! Where'd you be, if he took a drop over and above, and had a fancy to go for you? Suppose he wants to rob—who can prevent him? He can trespass, he can burgle, he could walk through a cordon of policemen as easy as me or you could give the slip to a blind man! Easier! For these here blind chaps hear uncommon sharp, I'm told. And wherever there was liquor he fancied—"

"He's got a tremenjous advantage, certainly," said Mr. Marvel. "And —well..."

"You're right," said the mariner. "He *has*."

All this time Mr. Marvel had been glancing about him intently, listening for faint footfalls, trying to detect imperceptible movements. He seemed on the point of some great resolution. He coughed behind his hand.

He looked about him again, listened, bent towards the mariner, and lowered his voice: "The fact of it is—I happen—to know just a thing or two about this Invisible Man. From private sources."

"Oh!" said the mariner, interested. "*You*?"

"Yes," said Mr. Marvel. "Me."

"Indeed!" said the mariner. "And may I ask—"

"You'll be astonished," said Mr. Marvel behind his hand. "It's tremenjous."

"Indeed!" said the mariner.

"The fact is," began Mr. Marvel eagerly in a confidential undertone. Suddenly his expression changed marvellously. "Ow!" he said. He rose stiffly in his seat. His face was eloquent of physical suffering. "Wow!" he said.

"What's up?" said the mariner, concerned.

"Toothache," said Mr. Marvel, and put his hand to his ear. He caught hold of his books. "I must be getting on, I think," he said. He edged in a curious way along the seat away from his interlocutor. "But you was just a-going to tell me about this here Invisible Man!" protested the mariner. Mr. Marvel seemed to consult with himself. "Hoax," said a Voice. "It's a hoax," said Mr. Marvel.

"But it's in the paper," said the mariner.

"Hoax all the same," said Marvel. "I know the chap that started the lie. There ain't no Invisible Man whatsoever—Blimey."

"But how 'bout this paper? D'you mean to say—?"

"Not a word of it," said Marvel, stoutly.

The mariner stared, paper in hand. Mr. Marvel jerkily faced about. "Wait a bit," said the mariner, rising and speaking slowly, "D'you mean to say —?"

"I do," said Mr. Marvel.

"Then why did you let me go on and tell you all this blarsted stuff, then? What d'yer mean by letting a man make a fool of himself like that for? Eh?"

Mr. Marvel blew out his cheeks. The mariner was suddenly very red indeed; he clenched his hands. "I been talking here this ten minutes," he said; "and you, you little pot-bellied, leathery-faced son of an old boot, couldn't have the elementary manners—"

"Don't you come bandying words with *me*," said Mr. Marvel.

"Bandying words! I'm a jolly good mind—"

"Come up," said a Voice, and Mr. Marvel was suddenly whirled about and started marching off in a curious spasmodic manner. "You'd better move on," said the mariner. "Who's moving on?" said Mr. Marvel. He was receding obliquely with a curious hurrying gait, with occasional violent jerks forward. Some way along the road he began a muttered monologue, protests and recriminations.

"Silly devil!" said the mariner, legs wide apart, elbows akimbo, watching the receding figure. "I'll show you, you silly ass—hoaxing *me*! It's here—on the paper!"

Mr. Marvel retorted incoherently and, receding, was hidden by a bend in the road, but the mariner still stood magnificent in the midst of the way, until the approach of a butcher's cart dislodged him. Then he turned himself towards Port Stowe. "Full of extra-ordinary asses," he said softly to himself. "Just to take me down a bit—that was his silly game—It's on the paper!"

And there was another extraordinary thing he was presently to hear, that had happened quite close to him. And that was a vision of a "fist full of money" (no less) travelling without visible agency, along by the wall at the corner of St. Michael's Lane. A brother mariner had seen this wonderful sight that very morning. He had snatched at the money forthwith and had been knocked headlong, and when he had got to his feet the butterfly money had vanished. Our mariner was in the mood to believe anything, he declared, but that was a bit *too* stiff. Afterwards, however, he began to think things over.

The story of the flying money was true. And all about that neighbourhood, even from the august London and Country Banking Company, from the tills of shops and inns—doors standing that sunny weather entirely open—money had been quietly and dexterously making off that day in handfuls and rouleaux, floating quietly along by walls and shady places, dodging quickly from the approaching eyes of men. And it had, though no man had traced it, invariably ended its mysterious flight in the pocket of that agitated gentleman in the obsolete silk hat, sitting outside the little inn on the outskirts of Port Stowe.

It was ten days after—and indeed only when the Burdock story was already old—that the mariner collated these facts and began to understand how near he had been to the wonderful Invisible Man.

CHAPTER XV - THE MAN WHO WAS RUNNING

In the early evening time Dr. Kemp was sitting in his study in the belvedere on the hill overlooking Burdock. It was a pleasant little room, with three windows—north, west, and south—and bookshelves covered with books and scientific publications, and a broad writing-table, and, under the north window, a microscope, glass slips, minute instruments, some cultures, and scattered bottles of reagents. Dr. Kemp's solar lamp was lit, albeit the sky was still bright with the sunset light, and his blinds were up because there was no offence of peering outsiders to require them pulled down. Dr. Kemp was a tall and slender young man, with flaxen hair and a moustache almost white, and the work he was upon would earn him, he hoped, the fellowship of the Royal Society, so highly did he think of it.

And his eye, presently wandering from his work, caught the sunset blazing at the back of the hill that is over against his own. For a minute perhaps he sat, pen in mouth, admiring the rich golden colour above the crest, and then his attention was attracted by the little figure of a man, inky black, running over the hill-brow towards him. He was a shortish little man, and he wore a high hat, and he was running so fast that his legs verily twinkled.

"Another of those fools," said Dr. Kemp. "Like that ass who ran into me this morning round a corner, with the "Visible Man a-coming, sir!' I can't imagine what possess people. One might think we were in the thirteenth century."

He got up, went to the window, and stared at the dusky hillside, and the dark little figure tearing down it. "He seems in a confounded hurry," said Dr. Kemp, "but he doesn't seem to be getting on. If his pockets were full of lead, he couldn't run heavier."

"Spurted, sir," said Dr. Kemp.

In another moment the higher of the villas that had clambered up the hill from Burdock had occulted the running figure. He was visible again for a moment, and again, and then again, three times between the three detached houses that came next, and then the terrace hid him.

"Asses!" said Dr. Kemp, swinging round on his heel and walking back to his writing-table.

But those who saw the fugitive nearer, and perceived the abject terror on his perspiring face, being themselves in the open roadway, did not share in the doctor's contempt. By the man pounded, and as he ran he chinked like a well- filled purse that is tossed to and fro. He looked neither to the right nor the left, but his dilated eyes stared straight downhill to where the lamps were being lit, and the

people were crowded in the street. And his ill-shaped mouth fell apart, and a glairy foam lay on his lips, and his breath came hoarse and noisy. All he passed stopped and began staring up the road and down, and interrogating one another with an inkling of discomfort for the reason of his haste.

And then presently, far up the hill, a dog playing in the road yelped and ran under a gate, and as they still wondered something—a wind—a pad, pad, pad,—a sound like a panting breathing, rushed by.

People screamed. People sprang off the pavement: It passed in shouts, it passed by instinct down the hill. They were shouting in the street before Marvel was halfway there. They were bolting into houses and slamming the doors behind them, with the news. He heard it and made one last desperate spurt. Fear came striding by, rushed ahead of him, and in a moment had seized the town.

"The Invisible Man is coming! The Invisible Man!"

CHAPTER XVI - IN THE "JOLLY CRICKETERS"

The "Jolly Cricketers" is just at the bottom of the hill, where the tram- lines begin. The barman leant his fat red arms on the counter and talked of horses with an anaemic cabman, while a black-bearded man in grey snapped up biscuit and cheese, drank Burton, and conversed in American with a policeman off duty.

"What's the shouting about!" said the anaemic cabman, going off at a tangent, trying to see up the hill over the dirty yellow blind in the low window of the inn. Somebody ran by outside. "Fire, perhaps," said the barman.

Footsteps approached, running heavily, the door was pushed open violently, and Marvel, weeping and dishevelled, his hat gone, the neck of his coat torn open, rushed in, made a convulsive turn, and attempted to shut the door. It was held half open by a strap.

"Coming!" he bawled, his voice shrieking with terror. "He's coming. The 'Visible Man! After me! For Gawd's sake! 'Elp! 'Elp! 'Elp!"

"Shut the doors," said the policeman. "Who's coming? What's the row?" He went to the door, released the strap, and it slammed. The American closed the other door.

"Lemme go inside," said Marvel, staggering and weeping, but still clutching the books. "Lemme go inside. Lock me in—somewhere. I tell you he's after me. I give him the slip. He said he'd kill me and he will."

"*You're* safe," said the man with the black beard. "The door's shut. What's it all about?"

"Lemme go inside," said Marvel, and shrieked aloud as a blow suddenly made the fastened door shiver and was followed by a hurried rapping and a shouting outside. "Hullo," cried the policeman, "who's there?" Mr. Marvel began to make frantic dives at panels that looked like doors. "He'll kill me—he's got a knife or something. For Gawd's sake—!"

"Here you are," said the barman. "Come in here." And he held up the flap of the bar.

Mr. Marvel rushed behind the bar as the summons outside was repeated. "Don't open the door," he screamed. "*Please* don't open the door. *Where* shall I hide?"

"This, this Invisible Man, then?" asked the man with the black beard, with one hand behind him. "I guess it's about time we saw him."

The window of the inn was suddenly smashed in, and there was a screaming and running to and fro in the street. The policeman had been standing on the set-

tee staring out, craning to see who was at the door. He got down with raised eyebrows. "It's that," he said. The barman stood in front of the bar-parlour door which was now locked on Mr. Marvel, stared at the smashed window, and came round to the two other men.

Everything was suddenly quiet. "I wish I had my truncheon," said the policeman, going irresolutely to the door. "Once we open, in he comes. There's no stopping him."

"Don't you be in too much hurry about that door," said the anaemic cabman, anxiously.

"Draw the bolts," said the man with the black beard, "and if he comes—" He showed a revolver in his hand.

"That won't do," said the policeman; "that's murder."

"I know what country I'm in," said the man with the beard. "I'm going to let off at his legs. Draw the bolts."

"Not with that blinking thing going off behind me," said the barman, craning over the blind.

"Very well," said the man with the black beard, and stooping down, revolver ready, drew them himself. Barman, cabman, and policeman faced about.

"Come in," said the bearded man in an undertone, standing back and facing the unbolted doors with his pistol behind him. No one came in, the door remained closed. Five minutes afterwards when a second cabman pushed his head in cautiously, they were still waiting, and an anxious face peered out of the bar-parlour and supplied information. "Are all the doors of the house shut?" asked Marvel. "He's going round—prowling round. He's as artful as the devil."

"Good Lord!" said the burly barman. "There's the back! Just watch them doors! I say—!" He looked about him helplessly. The bar-parlour door slammed and they heard the key turn. "There's the yard door and the private door. The yard door—"

He rushed out of the bar.

In a minute he reappeared with a carving-knife in his hand. "The yard door was open!" he said, and his fat underlip dropped. "He may be in the house now!" said the first cabman.

"He's not in the kitchen," said the barman. "There's two women there, and I've stabbed every inch of it with this little beef slicer. And they don't think he's come in. They haven't noticed—"

"Have you fastened it?" asked the first cabman.

"I'm out of frocks," said the barman.

The man with the beard replaced his revolver. And even as he did so the flap of the bar was shut down and the bolt clicked, and then with a tremendous thud the catch of the door snapped and the bar-parlour door burst open. They heard Marvel squeal like a caught leveret, and forthwith they were clambering over the bar to his rescue. The bearded man's revolver cracked and the looking- glass at the back of the parlour starred and came smashing and tinkling down.

As the barman entered the room he saw Marvel, curiously crumpled up and struggling against the door that led to the yard and kitchen. The door flew open while the barman hesitated, and Marvel was dragged into the kitchen. There was a scream and a clatter of pans. Marvel, head down, and lugging back obstinately, was forced to the kitchen door, and the bolts were drawn.

Then the policeman, who had been trying to pass the barman, rushed in, followed by one of the cabmen, gripped the wrist of the invisible hand that collared Marvel, was hit in the face and went reeling back. The door opened, and Marvel made a frantic effort to obtain a lodgment behind it. Then the cabman collared something. "I got him," said the cabman. The barman's red hands came clawing at the unseen. "Here he is!" said the barman.

Mr. Marvel, released, suddenly dropped to the ground and made an attempt to crawl behind the legs of the fighting men. The struggle blundered round the edge of the door. The voice of the Invisible Man was heard for the first time, yelling out sharply, as the policeman trod on his foot. Then he cried out passionately and his fists flew round like flails. The cabman suddenly whooped and doubled up, kicked under the diaphragm. The door into the bar-parlour from the kitchen slammed and covered Mr. Marvel's retreat. The men in the kitchen found themselves clutching at and struggling with empty air.

"Where's he gone?" cried the man with the beard. "Out?"

"This way," said the policeman, stepping into the yard and stopping.

A piece of tile whizzed by his head and smashed among the crockery on the kitchen table.

"I'll show him," shouted the man with the black beard, and suddenly a steel barrel shone over the policeman's shoulder, and five bullets had followed one another into the twilight whence the missile had come. As he fired, the man with the beard moved his hand in a horizontal curve, so that his shots radiated out into the narrow yard like spokes from a wheel.

A silence followed. "Five cartridges," said the man with the black beard. "That's the best of all. Four aces and a joker. Get a lantern, someone, and come and feel about for his body."

CHAPTER XVII - DR. KEMP'S VISITOR

Dr. Kemp had continued writing in his study until the shots aroused him. Crack, crack, crack, they came one after the other.

"Hullo!" said Dr. Kemp, putting his pen into his mouth again and listening. "Who's letting off revolvers in Burdock? What are the asses at now?"

He went to the south window, threw it up, and leaning out stared down on the network of windows, beaded gas-lamps and shops, with its black interstices of roof and yard that made up the town at night. "Looks like a crowd down the hill," he said, "by 'The Cricketers,'" and remained watching. Thence his eyes wandered over the town to far away where the ships' lights shone, and the pier glowed—a little illuminated, facetted pavilion like a gem of yellow light. The moon in its first quarter hung over the westward hill, and the stars were clear and almost tropically bright.

After five minutes, during which his mind had travelled into a remote speculation of social conditions of the future, and lost itself at last over the time dimension, Dr. Kemp roused himself with a sigh, pulled down the window again, and returned to his writing desk.

It must have been about an hour after this that the front-door bell rang. He had been writing slackly, and with intervals of abstraction, since the shots. He sat listening. He heard the servant answer the door, and waited for her feet on the staircase, but she did not come. "Wonder what that was," said Dr. Kemp.

He tried to resume his work, failed, got up, went downstairs from his study to the landing, rang, and called over the balustrade to the housemaid as she appeared in the hall below. "Was that a letter?" he asked.

"Only a runaway ring, sir," she answered.

"I'm restless to-night," he said to himself. He went back to his study, and this time attacked his work resolutely. In a little while he was hard at work again, and the only sounds in the room were the ticking of the clock and the subdued shrillness of his quill, hurrying in the very centre of the circle of light his lampshade threw on his table.

It was two o'clock before Dr. Kemp had finished his work for the night. He rose, yawned, and went downstairs to bed. He had already removed his coat and vest, when he noticed that he was thirsty. He took a candle and went down to the dining-room in search of a syphon and whiskey.

Dr. Kemp's scientific pursuits have made him a very observant man, and as he recrossed the hall, he noticed a dark spot on the linoleum near the mat at the foot

of the stairs. He went on upstairs, and then it suddenly occurred to him to ask himself what the spot on the linoleum might be. Apparently some subconscious element was at work. At any rate, he turned with his burden, went back to the hall, put down the syphon and whiskey, and bending down, touched the spot. Without any great surprise he found it had the stickiness and colour of drying blood.

He took up his burden again, and returned upstairs, looking about him and trying to account for the blood-spot. On the landing he saw something and stopped astonished. The door-handle of his own room was blood-stained.

He looked at his own hand. It was quite clean, and then he remembered that the door of his room had been open when he came down from his study, and that consequently he had not touched the handle at all. He went straight into his room, his face quite calm—perhaps a trifle more resolute than usual. His glance, wandering inquisitively, fell on the bed. On the counterpane was a mess of blood, and the sheet had been torn. He had not noticed this before because he had walked straight to the dressing-table. On the further side the bedclothes were depressed as if someone had been recently sitting there.

Then he had an odd impression that he had heard a low voice say, "Good Heavens!—Kemp!" But Dr. Kemp was no believer in voices.

He stood staring at the tumbled sheets. Was that really a voice? He looked about again, but noticed nothing further than the disordered and blood- stained bed. Then he distinctly heard a movement across the room, near the wash- hand stand. All men, however highly educated, retain some superstitious inklings. The feeling that is called "eerie" came upon him. He closed the door of the room, came forward to the dressing-table, and put down his burdens. Suddenly, with a start, he perceived a coiled and blood-stained bandage of linen rag hanging in mid-air, between him and the wash-hand stand.

He stared at this in amazement. It was an empty bandage, a bandage properly tied but quite empty. He would have advanced to grasp it, but a touch arrested him, and a voice speaking quite close to him.

"Kemp!" said the Voice.

"Eh?" said Kemp, with his mouth open.

"Keep your nerve," said the Voice. "I'm an Invisible Man."

Kemp made no answer for a space, simply stared at the bandage. "Invisible Man," he said.

"I am an Invisible Man," repeated the Voice.

The story he had been active to ridicule only that morning rushed through Kemp's brain. He does not appear to have been either very much frightened or very greatly surprised at the moment. Realisation came later.

"I thought it was all a lie," he said. The thought uppermost in his mind was the reiterated arguments of the morning. "Have you a bandage on?" he asked.

"Yes," said the Invisible Man.

"Oh!" said Kemp, and then roused himself. "I say!" he said. "But this is nonsense. It's some trick." He stepped forward suddenly, and his hand, extended towards the bandage, met invisible fingers.

He recoiled at the touch and his colour changed.

"Keep steady, Kemp, for God's sake! I want help badly. Stop!"

The hand gripped his arm. He struck at it.

"Kemp!" cried the Voice. "Kemp! Keep steady!" and the grip tightened.

A frantic desire to free himself took possession of Kemp. The hand of the bandaged arm gripped his shoulder, and he was suddenly tripped and flung backwards upon the bed. He opened his mouth to shout, and the corner of the sheet was thrust between his teeth. The Invisible Man had him down grimly, but his arms were free and he struck and tried to kick savagely.

"Listen to reason, will you?" said the Invisible Man, sticking to him in spite of a pounding in the ribs. "By Heaven! you'll madden me in a minute!

"Lie still, you fool!" bawled the Invisible Man in Kemp's ear.

Kemp struggled for another moment and then lay still.

"If you shout, I'll smash your face," said the Invisible Man, relieving his mouth.

"I'm an Invisible Man. It's no foolishness, and no magic. I really am an Invisible Man. And I want your help. I don't want to hurt you, but if you behave like a frantic rustic, I must. Don't you remember me, Kemp? Griffin, of University College?"

"Let me get up," said Kemp. "I'll stop where I am. And let me sit quiet for a minute."

He sat up and felt his neck.

"I am Griffin, of University College, and I have made myself invisible. I am just an ordinary man—a man you have known—made invisible."

"Griffin?" said Kemp.

"Griffin," answered the Voice. A younger student than you were, almost an albino, six feet high, and broad, with a pink and white face and red eyes, who won the medal for chemistry."

"I am confused," said Kemp. "My brain is rioting. What has this to do with Griffin?"

"I *am* Griffin."

Kemp thought. "It's horrible," he said. "But what devilry must happen to make a man invisible?"

"It's no devilry. It's a process, sane and intelligible enough—"

"It's horrible!" said Kemp. "How on earth—?"

"It's horrible enough. But I'm wounded and in pain, and tired ... Great God! Kemp, you are a man. Take it steady. Give me some food and drink, and let me sit down here."

Kemp stared at the bandage as it moved across the room, then saw a basket chair dragged across the floor and come to rest near the bed. It creaked, and the

seat was depressed the quarter of an inch or so. He rubbed his eyes and felt his neck again. "This beats ghosts," he said, and laughed stupidly.

"That's better. Thank Heaven, you're getting sensible!"

"Or silly," said Kemp, and knuckled his eyes.

"Give me some whiskey. I'm near dead."

"It didn't feel so. Where are you? If I get up shall I run into you? *There*! all right. Whiskey? Here. Where shall I give it to you?"

The chair creaked and Kemp felt the glass drawn away from him. He let go by an effort; his instinct was all against it. It came to rest poised twenty inches above the front edge of the seat of the chair. He stared at it in infinite perplexity. "This is—this must be—hypnotism. You have suggested you are invisible."

"Nonsense," said the Voice.

"It's frantic."

"Listen to me."

"I demonstrated conclusively this morning," began Kemp, "that invisibility—"

"Never mind what you've demonstrated!—I'm starving," said the Voice, "and the night is chilly to a man without clothes."

"Food?" said Kemp.

The tumbler of whiskey tilted itself. "Yes," said the Invisible Man rapping it down. "Have you a dressing-gown?"

Kemp made some exclamation in an undertone. He walked to a wardrobe and produced a robe of dingy scarlet. "This do?" he asked. It was taken from him. It hung limp for a moment in mid-air, fluttered weirdly, stood full and decorous buttoning itself, and sat down in his chair. "Drawers, socks, slippers would be a comfort," said the Unseen, curtly. "And food."

"Anything. But this is the insanest thing I ever was in, in my life!"

He turned out his drawers for the articles, and then went downstairs to ransack his larder. He came back with some cold cutlets and bread, pulled up a light table, and placed them before his guest. "Never mind knives," said his visitor, and a cutlet hung in mid-air, with a sound of gnawing.

"Invisible!" said Kemp, and sat down on a bedroom chair.

"I always like to get something about me before I eat," said the Invisible Man, with a full mouth, eating greedily. "Queer fancy!"

"I suppose that wrist is all right," said Kemp.

"Trust me," said the Invisible Man.

"Of all the strange and wonderful—"

"Exactly. But it's odd I should blunder into *your* house to get my bandaging. My first stroke of luck! Anyhow I meant to sleep in this house to- night. You must stand that! It's a filthy nuisance, my blood showing, isn't it? Quite a clot over there. Gets visible as it coagulates, I see. It's only the living tissue I've changed, and only for as long as I'm alive... I've been in the house three hours."

"But how's it done?" began Kemp, in a tone of exasperation. "Confound it! The whole business—it's unreasonable from beginning to end."

"Quite reasonable," said the Invisible Man. "Perfectly reasonable."

He reached over and secured the whiskey bottle. Kemp stared at the devouring dressing gown. A ray of candle-light penetrating a torn patch in the right shoulder, made a triangle of light under the left ribs. "What were the shots?" he asked. "How did the shooting begin?"

"There was a real fool of a man—a sort of confederate of mine —curse him!— who tried to steal my money. *Has* done so."

"Is *he* invisible too?"

"No."

"Well?"

"Can't I have some more to eat before I tell you all that? I'm hungry —in pain. And you want me to tell stories!"

Kemp got up. "*You* didn't do any shooting?" he asked.

"Not me," said his visitor. "Some fool I'd never seen fired at random. A lot of them got scared. They all got scared at me. Curse them!—I say —I want more to eat than this, Kemp."

"I'll see what there is to eat downstairs," said Kemp. "Not much, I'm afraid."

After he had done eating, and he made a heavy meal, the Invisible Man demanded a cigar. He bit the end savagely before Kemp could find a knife, and cursed when the outer leaf loosened. It was strange to see him smoking; his mouth, and throat, pharynx and nares, became visible as a sort of whirling smoke cast.

"This blessed gift of smoking!" he said, and puffed vigorously. "I'm lucky to have fallen upon you, Kemp. You must help me. Fancy tumbling on you just now! I'm in a devilish scrape—I've been mad, I think. The things I have been through! But we will do things yet. Let me tell you—"

He helped himself to more whiskey and soda. Kemp got up, looked about him, and fetched a glass from his spare room. "It's wild—but I suppose I may drink."

"You haven't changed much, Kemp, these dozen years. You fair men don't. Cool and methodical—after the first collapse. I must tell you. We will work together!"

"But how was it all done?" said Kemp, "and how did you get like this?"

"For God's sake, let me smoke in peace for a little while! And then I will begin to tell you."

But the story was not told that night. The Invisible Man's wrist was growing painful; he was feverish, exhausted, and his mind came round to brood upon his chase down the hill and the struggle about the inn. He spoke in fragments of Marvel, he smoked faster, his voice grew angry. Kemp tried to gather what he could.

"He was afraid of me, I could see that he was afraid of me," said the Invisible Man many times over. "He meant to give me the slip—he was always casting about! What a fool I was!"

"The cur!

"I should have killed him!"

"Where did you get the money?" asked Kemp, abruptly.

The Invisible Man was silent for a space. "I can't tell you to-night," he said.

He groaned suddenly and leant forward, supporting his invisible head on invisible hands. "Kemp," he said, "I've had no sleep for near three days, except a couple of dozes of an hour or so. I must sleep soon."

"Well, have my room—have this room."

"But how can I sleep? If I sleep—he will get away. Ugh! What does it matter?"

"What's the shot wound?" asked Kemp, abruptly.

"Nothing—scratch and blood. Oh, God! How I want sleep!"

"Why not?"

The Invisible Man appeared to be regarding Kemp. "Because I've a particular objection to being caught by my fellow-men," he said slowly.

Kemp started.

"Fool that I am!" said the Invisible Man, striking the table smartly. "I've put the idea into your head."

CHAPTER XVIII - THE INVISIBLE MAN SLEEPS

Exhausted and wounded as the Invisible Man was, he refused to accept Kemp's word that his freedom should be respected. He examined the two windows of the bedroom, drew up the blinds and opened the sashes, to confirm Kemp's statement that a retreat by them would be possible. Outside the night was very quiet and still, and the new moon was setting over the down. Then he examined the keys of the bedroom and the two dressing-room doors, to satisfy himself that these also could be made an assurance of freedom. Finally he expressed himself satisfied. He stood on the hearth rug and Kemp heard the sound of a yawn.

"I'm sorry," said the Invisible Man, "if I cannot tell you all that I have done tonight. But I am worn out. It's grotesque, no doubt. It's horrible! But believe me, Kemp, in spite of your arguments of this morning, it is quite a possible thing. I have made a discovery. I meant to keep it to myself. I can't. I must have a partner. And you... We can do such things ... But to-morrow. Now, Kemp, I feel as though I must sleep or perish."

Kemp stood in the middle of the room staring at the headless garment. "I suppose I must leave you," he said. "It's—incredible. Three things happening like this, overturning all my preconceptions—would make me insane. But it's real! Is there anything more that I can get you?"

"Only bid me good-night," said Griffin.

"Good-night," said Kemp, and shook an invisible hand. He walked sideways to the door. Suddenly the dressing-gown walked quickly towards him. "Understand me!" said the dressing-gown. "No attempts to hamper me, or capture me! Or—"

Kemp's face changed a little. "I thought I gave you my word," he said.

Kemp closed the door softly behind him, and the key was turned upon him forthwith. Then, as he stood with an expression of passive amazement on his face, the rapid feet came to the door of the dressing-room and that too was locked. Kemp slapped his brow with his hand. "Am I dreaming? Has the world gone mad—or have I?"

He laughed, and put his hand to the locked door. "Barred out of my own bedroom, by a flagrant absurdity!" he said.

He walked to the head of the staircase, turned, and stared at the locked doors. "It's fact," he said. He put his fingers to his slightly bruised neck. "Undeniable fact!

"But—"

He shook his head hopelessly, turned, and went downstairs.

He lit the dining-room lamp, got out a cigar, and began pacing the room, ejaculating. Now and then he would argue with himself.

"Invisible!" he said.

"Is there such a thing as an invisible animal? ... In the sea, yes. Thousands—millions. All the larvae, all the little nauplii and tornarias, all the microscopic things, the jelly-fish. In the sea there are more things invisible than visible! I never thought of that before. And in the ponds too! All those little pond-life things—specks of colourless translucent jelly! But in air? No!

"It can't be.

"But after all—why not?

"If a man was made of glass he would still be visible."

His meditation became profound. The bulk of three cigars had passed into the invisible or diffused as a white ash over the carpet before he spoke again. Then it was merely an exclamation. He turned aside, walked out of the room, and went into his little consulting-room and lit the gas there. It was a little room, because Dr. Kemp did not live by practice, and in it were the day's newspapers. The morning's paper lay carelessly opened and thrown aside. He caught it up, turned it over, and read the account of a "Strange Story from Iping" that the mariner at Port Stowe had spelt over so painfully to Mr. Marvel. Kemp read it swiftly.

"Wrapped up!" said Kemp. "Disguised! Hiding it! 'No one seems to have been aware of his misfortune.' What the devil *is* his game?"

He dropped the paper, and his eye went seeking. "Ah!" he said, and caught up the *St. James' Gazette*, lying folded up as it arrived. "Now we shall get at the truth," said Dr. Kemp. He rent the paper open; a couple of columns confronted him. "An Entire Village in Sussex goes Mad" was the heading.

"Good Heavens!" said Kemp, reading eagerly an incredulous account of the events in Iping, of the previous afternoon, that have already been described. Over the leaf the report in the morning paper had been reprinted.

He re-read it. "Ran through the streets striking right and left. Jaffers insensible. Mr. Huxter in great pain—still unable to describe what he saw. Painful humiliation—vicar. Woman ill with terror! Windows smashed. This extraordinary story probably a fabrication. Too good not to print—*cum grano*!"

He dropped the paper and stared blankly in front of him. "Probably a fabrication!"

He caught up the paper again, and re-read the whole business. "But when does the Tramp come in? Why the deuce was he chasing a tramp?"

He sat down abruptly on the surgical bench. "He's not only invisible," he said, "but he's mad! Homicidal!"

When dawn came to mingle its pallor with the lamp-light and cigar smoke of the dining-room, Kemp was still pacing up and down, trying to grasp the incredible.

He was altogether too excited to sleep. His servants, descending sleepily, discovered him, and were inclined to think that over-study had worked this ill on him. He gave them extraordinary but quite explicit instructions to lay breakfast

for two in the belvedere study—and then to confine themselves to the basement and ground-floor. Then he continued to pace the dining-room until the morning's paper came. That had much to say and little to tell, beyond the confirmation of the evening before, and a very badly written account of another remarkable tale from Port Burdock. This gave Kemp the essence of the happenings at the "Jolly Cricketers," and the name of Marvel. "He has made me keep with him twenty-four hours," Marvel testified. Certain minor facts were added to the Iping story, notably the cutting of the village telegraph-wire. But there was nothing to throw light on the connexion between the Invisible Man and the Tramp; for Mr. Marvel had supplied no information about the three books, or the money with which he was lined. The incredulous tone had vanished and a shoal of reporters and inquirers were already at work elaborating the matter.

Kemp read every scrap of the report and sent his housemaid out to get everyone of the morning papers she could. These also he devoured.

"He is invisible!" he said. "And it reads like rage growing to mania! The things he may do! The things he may do! And he's upstairs free as the air. What on earth ought I to do?"

"For instance, would it be a breach of faith if—? No."

He went to a little untidy desk in the corner, and began a note. He tore this up half written, and wrote another. He read it over and considered it. Then he took an envelope and addressed it to "Colonel Adye, Port Burdock."

The Invisible Man awoke even as Kemp was doing this. He awoke in an evil temper, and Kemp, alert for every sound, heard his pattering feet rush suddenly across the bedroom overhead. Then a chair was flung over and the wash-hand stand tumbler smashed. Kemp hurried upstairs and rapped eagerly.

CHAPTER XIX - CERTAIN FIRST PRINCIPLES

"What's the matter?" asked Kemp, when the Invisible Man admitted him.

"Nothing," was the answer.

"But, confound it! The smash?"

"Fit of temper," said the Invisible Man. "Forgot this arm; and it's sore."

"You're rather liable to that sort of thing."

"I am."

Kemp walked across the room and picked up the fragments of broken glass. "All the facts are out about you," said Kemp, standing up with the glass in his hand; "all that happened in Iping, and down the hill. The world has become aware of its invisible citizen. But no one knows you are here."

The Invisible Man swore.

"The secret's out. I gather it was a secret. I don't know what your plans are, but of course I'm anxious to help you."

The Invisible Man sat down on the bed.

"There's breakfast upstairs," said Kemp, speaking as easily as possible, and he was delighted to find his strange guest rose willingly. Kemp led the way up the narrow staircase to the belvedere.

"Before we can do anything else," said Kemp, "I must understand a little more about this invisibility of yours." He had sat down, after one nervous glance out of the window, with the air of a man who has talking to do. His doubts of the sanity of the entire business flashed and vanished again as he looked across to where Griffin sat at the breakfast-table—a headless, handless dressing-gown, wiping unseen lips on a miraculously held serviette.

"It's simple enough—and credible enough," said Griffin, putting the serviette aside and leaning the invisible head on an invisible hand.

"No doubt, to you, but—" Kemp laughed.

"Well, yes; to me it seemed wonderful at first, no doubt. But now, great God! ... But we will do great things yet! I came on the stuff first at Chesilstowe."

"Chesilstowe?"

"I went there after I left London. You know I dropped medicine and took up physics? No; well, I did. *Light* fascinated me."

"Ah!"

"Optical density! The whole subject is a network of riddles—a network with solutions glimmering elusively through. And being but two-and- twenty and full

of enthusiasm, I said, 'I will devote my life to this. This is worth while.' You know what fools we are at two-and-twenty?"

"Fools then or fools now," said Kemp.

"As though knowing could be any satisfaction to a man!

"But I went to work—like a slave. And I had hardly worked and thought about the matter six months before light came through one of the meshes suddenly—blindingly! I found a general principle of pigments and refraction—a formula, a geometrical expression involving four dimensions. Fools, common men, even common mathematicians, do not know anything of what some general expression may mean to the student of molecular physics. In the books—the books that tramp has hidden—there are marvels, miracles! But this was not a method, it was an idea, that might lead to a method by which it would be possible, without changing any other property of matter—except, in some instances colours—to lower the refractive index of a substance, solid or liquid, to that of air—so far as all practical purposes are concerned."

"Phew!" said Kemp. "That's odd! But still I don't see quite ... I can understand that thereby you could spoil a valuable stone, but personal invisibility is a far cry."

"Precisely," said Griffin. "But consider, visibility depends on the action of the visible bodies on light. Either a body absorbs light, or it reflects or refracts it, or does all these things. If it neither reflects nor refracts nor absorbs light, it cannot of itself be visible. You see an opaque red box, for instance, because the colour absorbs some of the light and reflects the rest, all the red part of the light, to you. If it did not absorb any particular part of the light, but reflected it all, then it would be a shining white box. Silver! A diamond box would neither absorb much of the light nor reflect much from the general surface, but just here and there where the surfaces were favourable the light would be reflected and refracted, so that you would get a brilliant appearance of flashing reflections and translucencies—a sort of skeleton of light. A glass box would not be so brilliant, not so clearly visible, as a diamond box, because there would be less refraction and reflection. See that? From certain points of view you would see quite clearly through it. Some kinds of glass would be more visible than others, a box of flint glass would be brighter than a box of ordinary window glass. A box of very thin common glass would be hard to see in a bad light, because it would absorb hardly any light and refract and reflect very little. And if you put a sheet of common white glass in water, still more if you put it in some denser liquid than water, it would vanish almost altogether, because light passing from water to glass is only slightly refracted or reflected or indeed affected in any way. It is almost as invisible as a jet of coal gas or hydrogen is in air. And for precisely the same reason!"

"Yes," said Kemp, "that is pretty plain sailing."

"And here is another fact you will know to be true. If a sheet of glass is smashed, Kemp, and beaten into a powder, it becomes much more visible while it is in the air; it becomes at last an opaque white powder. This is because the powdering multiplies the surfaces of the glass at which refraction and reflection occur.

In the sheet of glass there are only two surfaces; in the powder the light is reflected or refracted by each grain it passes through, and very little gets right through the powder. But if the white powdered glass is put into water, it forthwith vanishes. The powdered glass and water have much the same refractive index; that is, the light undergoes very little refraction or reflection in passing from one to the other.

"You make the glass invisible by putting it into a liquid of nearly the same refractive index; a transparent thing becomes invisible if it is put in any medium of almost the same refractive index. And if you will consider only a second, you will see also that the powder of glass might be made to vanish in air, if its refractive index could be made the same as that of air; for then there would be no refraction or reflection as the light passed from glass to air."

"Yes, yes," said Kemp. "But a man's not powdered glass!"

"No," said Griffin. "He's more transparent!"

"Nonsense!"

"That from a doctor! How one forgets! Have you already forgotten your physics, in ten years? Just think of all the things that are transparent and seem not to be so. Paper, for instance, is made up of transparent fibres, and it is white and opaque only for the same reason that a powder of glass is white and opaque. Oil white paper, fill up the interstices between the particles with oil so that there is no longer refraction or reflection except at the surfaces, and it becomes as transparent as glass. And not only paper, but cotton fibre, linen fibre, wool fibre, woody fibre, and *bone*, Kemp, *flesh*, Kemp, *hair*, Kemp, *nails* and *nerves*, Kemp, in fact the whole fabric of a man except the red of his blood and the black pigment of hair, are all made up of transparent, colourless tissue. So little suffices to make us visible one to the other. For the most part the fibres of a living creature are no more opaque than water."

"Great Heavens!" cried Kemp. "Of course, of course! I was thinking only last night of the sea larvae and all jelly-fish!"

"*Now* you have me! And all that I knew and had in mind a year after I left London—six years ago. But I kept it to myself. I had to do my work under frightful disadvantages. Oliver, my professor, was a scientific bounder, a journalist by instinct, a thief of ideas—he was always prying! And you know the knavish system of the scientific world. I simply would not publish, and let him share my credit. I went on working; I got nearer and nearer making my formula into an experiment, a reality. I told no living soul, because I meant to flash my work upon the world with crushing effect and become famous at a blow. I took up the question of pigments to fill up certain gaps. And suddenly, not by design but by accident, I made a discovery in physiology."

"Yes?"

"You know the red colouring matter of blood; it can be made white—colourless—and remain with all the functions it has now!"

Kemp gave a cry of incredulous amazement.

The Invisible Man rose and began pacing the little study. "You may well exclaim. I remember that night. It was late at night—in the daytime one was bothered with the gaping, silly students—and I worked then sometimes till dawn. It came suddenly, splendid and complete in my mind. I was alone; the laboratory was still, with the tall lights burning brightly and silently. In all my great moments I have been alone. 'One could make an animal —a tissue—transparent! One could make it invisible! All except the pigments—I could be invisible!' I said, suddenly realising what it meant to be an albino with such knowledge. It was overwhelming. I left the filtering I was doing, and went and stared out of the great window at the stars. 'I could be invisible!' I repeated.

"To do such a thing would be to transcend magic. And I beheld, unclouded by doubt, a magnificent vision of all that invisibility might mean to a man —the mystery, the power, the freedom. Drawbacks I saw none. You have only to think! And I, a shabby, poverty-struck, hemmed-in demonstrator, teaching fools in a provincial college, might suddenly become—this. I ask you, Kemp if *you* ... Anyone, I tell you, would have flung himself upon that research. And I worked three years, and every mountain of difficulty I toiled over showed another from its summit. The infinite details! And the exasperation! A professor, a provincial professor, always prying. 'When are you going to publish this work of yours?' was his everlasting question. And the students, the cramped means! Three years I had of it—

"And after three years of secrecy and exasperation, I found that to complete it was impossible—impossible."

"How?" asked Kemp.

"Money," said the Invisible Man, and went again to stare out of the window.

He turned around abruptly. "I robbed the old man—robbed my father.

"The money was not his, and he shot himself."

CHAPTER XX - AT THE HOUSE IN GREAT PORTLAND STREET

For a moment Kemp sat in silence, staring at the back of the headless figure at the window. Then he started, struck by a thought, rose, took the Invisible Man's arm, and turned him away from the outlook.

"You are tired," he said, "and while I sit, you walk about. Have my chair."

He placed himself between Griffin and the nearest window.

For a space Griffin sat silent, and then he resumed abruptly:

"I had left the Chesilstowe cottage already," he said, "when that happened. It was last December. I had taken a room in London, a large unfurnished room in a big ill-managed lodging-house in a slum near Great Portland Street. The room was soon full of the appliances I had bought with his money; the work was going on steadily, successfully, drawing near an end. I was like a man emerging from a thicket, and suddenly coming on some unmeaning tragedy. I went to bury him. My mind was still on this research, and I did not lift a finger to save his character. I remember the funeral, the cheap hearse, the scant ceremony, the windy frost-bitten hillside, and the old college friend of his who read the service over him—a shabby, black, bent old man with a snivelling cold.

"I remember walking back to the empty house, through the place that had once been a village and was now patched and tinkered by the jerry builders into the ugly likeness of a town. Every way the roads ran out at last into the desecrated fields and ended in rubble heaps and rank wet weeds. I remember myself as a gaunt black figure, going along the slippery, shiny pavement, and the strange sense of detachment I felt from the squalid respectability, the sordid commercialism of the place.

"I did not feel a bit sorry for my father. He seemed to me to be the victim of his own foolish sentimentality. The current cant required my attendance at his funeral, but it was really not my affair.

"But going along the High Street, my old life came back to me for a space, for I met the girl I had known ten years since. Our eyes met.

"Something moved me to turn back and talk to her. She was a very ordinary person.

"It was all like a dream, that visit to the old places. I did not feel then that I was lonely, that I had come out from the world into a desolate place. I appreciated my loss of sympathy, but I put it down to the general inanity of things. Re-entering my room seemed like the recovery of reality. There were the things I

knew and loved. There stood the apparatus, the experiments arranged and waiting. And now there was scarcely a difficulty left, beyond the planning of details.

"I will tell you, Kemp, sooner or later, all the complicated processes. We need not go into that now. For the most part, saving certain gaps I chose to remember, they are written in cypher in those books that tramp has hidden. We must hunt him down. We must get those books again. But the essential phase was to place the transparent object whose refractive index was to be lowered between two radiating centres of a sort of ethereal vibration, of which I will tell you more fully later. No, not those Roentgen vibrations—I don't know that these others of mine have been described. Yet they are obvious enough. I needed two little dynamos, and these I worked with a cheap gas engine. My first experiment was with a bit of white wool fabric. It was the strangest thing in the world to see it in the flicker of the flashes soft and white, and then to watch it fade like a wreath of smoke and vanish.

"I could scarcely believe I had done it. I put my hand into the emptiness, and there was the thing as solid as ever. I felt it awkwardly, and threw it on the floor. I had a little trouble finding it again.

"And then came a curious experience. I heard a miaow behind me, and turning, saw a lean white cat, very dirty, on the cistern cover outside the window. A thought came into my head. 'Everything ready for you,' I said, and went to the window, opened it, and called softly. She came in, purring—the poor beast was starving—and I gave her some milk. All my food was in a cupboard in the corner of the room. After that she went smelling round the room, evidently with the idea of making herself at home. The invisible rag upset her a bit; you should have seen her spit at it! But I made her comfortable on the pillow of my truckle-bed. And I gave her butter to get her to wash."

"And you processed her?"

"I processed her. But giving drugs to a cat is no joke, Kemp! And the process failed."

"Failed!"

"In two particulars. These were the claws and the pigment stuff, what is it?—at the back of the eye in a cat. You know?"

"*Tapetum*."

"Yes, the *tapetum*. It didn't go. After I'd given the stuff to bleach the blood and done certain other things to her, I gave the beast opium, and put her and the pillow she was sleeping on, on the apparatus. And after all the rest had faded and vanished, there remained two little ghosts of her eyes."

"Odd!"

"I can't explain it. She was bandaged and clamped, of course—so I had her safe; but she woke while she was still misty, and miaowed dismally, and someone came knocking. It was an old woman from downstairs, who suspected me of vivisecting—a drink-sodden old creature, with only a white cat to care for in all the world. I whipped out some chloroform, applied it, and answered the door. 'Did I hear a cat?' she asked. 'My cat?' 'Not here,' said I, very politely. She was a little

doubtful and tried to peer past me into the room; strange enough to her no doubt—bare walls, uncurtained windows, truckle- bed, with the gas engine vibrating, and the seethe of the radiant points, and that faint ghastly stinging of chloroform in the air. She had to be satisfied at last and went away again."

"How long did it take?" asked Kemp.

"Three or four hours—the cat. The bones and sinews and the fat were the last to go, and the tips of the coloured hairs. And, as I say, the back part of the eye, tough, iridescent stuff it is, wouldn't go at all.

"It was night outside long before the business was over, and nothing was to be seen but the dim eyes and the claws. I stopped the gas engine, felt for and stroked the beast, which was still insensible, and then, being tired, left it sleeping on the invisible pillow and went to bed. I found it hard to sleep. I lay awake thinking weak aimless stuff, going over the experiment over and over again, or dreaming feverishly of things growing misty and vanishing about me, until everything, the ground I stood on, vanished, and so I came to that sickly falling nightmare one gets. About two, the cat began miaowing about the room. I tried to hush it by talking to it, and then I decided to turn it out. I remember the shock I had when striking a light—there were just the round eyes shining green—and nothing round them. I would have given it milk, but I hadn't any. It wouldn't be quiet, it just sat down and miaowed at the door. I tried to catch it, with an idea of putting it out of the window, but it wouldn't be caught, it vanished. Then it began miaowing in different parts of the room. At last I opened the window and made a bustle. I suppose it went out at last. I never saw any more of it.

"Then—Heaven knows why—I fell thinking of my father's funeral again, and the dismal windy hillside, until the day had come. I found sleeping was hopeless, and, locking my door after me, wandered out into the morning streets."

"You don't mean to say there's an invisible cat at large!" said Kemp.

"If it hasn't been killed," said the Invisible Man. "Why not?"

"Why not?" said Kemp. "I didn't mean to interrupt."

"It's very probably been killed," said the Invisible Man. "It was alive four days after, I know, and down a grating in Great Titchfield Street; because I saw a crowd round the place, trying to see whence the miaowing came."

He was silent for the best part of a minute. Then he resumed abruptly:

"I remember that morning before the change very vividly. I must have gone up Great Portland Street. I remember the barracks in Albany Street, and the horse soldiers coming out, and at last I found the summit of Primrose Hill. It was a sunny day in January—one of those sunny, frosty days that came before the snow this year. My weary brain tried to formulate the position, to plot out a plan of action.

"I was surprised to find, now that my prize was within my grasp, how inconclusive its attainment seemed. As a matter of fact I was worked out; the intense stress of nearly four years' continuous work left me incapable of any strength of feeling. I was apathetic, and I tried in vain to recover the enthusiasm of my first inquiries, the passion of discovery that had enabled me to compass even the downfall of my father's grey hairs. Nothing seemed to matter. I saw pretty clearly

this was a transient mood, due to overwork and want of sleep, and that either by drugs or rest it would be possible to recover my energies.

"All I could think clearly was that the thing had to be carried through; the fixed idea still ruled me. And soon, for the money I had was almost exhausted. I looked about me at the hillside, with children playing and girls watching them, and tried to think of all the fantastic advantages an invisible man would have in the world. After a time I crawled home, took some food and a strong dose of strychnine, and went to sleep in my clothes on my unmade bed. Strychnine is a grand tonic, Kemp, to take the flabbiness out of a man."

"It's the devil," said Kemp. "It's the palaeolithic in a bottle."

"I awoke vastly invigorated and rather irritable. You know?"

"I know the stuff."

"And there was someone rapping at the door. It was my landlord with threats and inquiries, an old Polish Jew in a long grey coat and greasy slippers. I had been tormenting a cat in the night, he was sure—the old woman's tongue had been busy. He insisted on knowing all about it. The laws in this country against vivisection were very severe—he might be liable. I denied the cat. Then the vibration of the little gas engine could be felt all over the house, he said. That was true, certainly. He edged round me into the room, peering about over his German-silver spectacles, and a sudden dread came into my mind that he might carry away something of my secret. I tried to keep between him and the concentrating apparatus I had arranged, and that only made him more curious. What was I doing? Why was I always alone and secretive? Was it legal? Was it dangerous? I paid nothing but the usual rent. His had always been a most respectable house—in a disreputable neighbourhood. Suddenly my temper gave way. I told him to get out. He began to protest, to jabber of his right of entry. In a moment I had him by the collar; something ripped, and he went spinning out into his own passage. I slammed and locked the door and sat down quivering.

"He made a fuss outside, which I disregarded, and after a time he went away.

"But this brought matters to a crisis. I did not know what he would do, nor even what he had the power to do. To move to fresh apartments would have meant delay; altogether I had barely twenty pounds left in the world, for the most part in a bank—and I could not afford that. Vanish! It was irresistible. Then there would be an inquiry, the sacking of my room.

"At the thought of the possibility of my work being exposed or interrupted at its very climax, I became very angry and active. I hurried out with my three books of notes, my cheque-book—the tramp has them now —and directed them from the nearest Post Office to a house of call for letters and parcels in Great Portland Street. I tried to go out noiselessly. Coming in, I found my landlord going quietly upstairs; he had heard the door close, I suppose. You would have laughed to see him jump aside on the landing as came tearing after him. He glared at me as I went by him, and I made the house quiver with the slamming of my door. I heard him come shuffling up to my floor, hesitate, and go down. I set to work upon my preparations forthwith.

"It was all done that evening and night. While I was still sitting under the sickly, drowsy influence of the drugs that decolourise blood, there came a repeated knocking at the door. It ceased, footsteps went away and returned, and the knocking was resumed. There was an attempt to push something under the door —a blue paper. Then in a fit of irritation I rose and went and flung the door wide open. 'Now then?' said I.

"It was my landlord, with a notice of ejectment or something. He held it out to me, saw something odd about my hands, I expect, and lifted his eyes to my face.

"For a moment he gaped. Then he gave a sort of inarticulate cry, dropped candle and writ together, and went blundering down the dark passage to the stairs. I shut the door, locked it, and went to the looking-glass. Then I understood his terror... My face was white—like white stone.

"But it was all horrible. I had not expected the suffering. A night of racking anguish, sickness and fainting. I set my teeth, though my skin was presently afire, all my body afire; but I lay there like grim death. I understood now how it was the cat had howled until I chloroformed it. Lucky it was I lived alone and untended in my room. There were times when I sobbed and groaned and talked. But I stuck to it... I became insensible and woke languid in the darkness.

"The pain had passed. I thought I was killing myself and I did not care. I shall never forget that dawn, and the strange horror of seeing that my hands had become as clouded glass, and watching them grow clearer and thinner as the day went by, until at last I could see the sickly disorder of my room through them, though I closed my transparent eyelids. My limbs became glassy, the bones and arteries faded, vanished, and the little white nerves went last. I gritted my teeth and stayed there to the end. At last only the dead tips of the fingernails remained, pallid and white, and the brown stain of some acid upon my fingers.

"I struggled up. At first I was as incapable as a swathed infant—stepping with limbs I could not see. I was weak and very hungry. I went and stared at nothing in my shaving-glass, at nothing save where an attenuated pigment still remained behind the retina of my eyes, fainter than mist. I had to hang on to the table and press my forehead against the glass.

"It was only by a frantic effort of will that I dragged myself back to the apparatus and completed the process.

"I slept during the forenoon, pulling the sheet over my eyes to shut out the light, and about midday I was awakened again by a knocking. My strength had returned. I sat up and listened and heard a whispering. I sprang to my feet and as noiselessly as possible began to detach the connections of my apparatus, and to distribute it about the room, so as to destroy the suggestions of its arrangement. Presently the knocking was renewed and voices called, first my landlord's, and then two others. To gain time I answered them. The invisible rag and pillow came to hand and I opened the window and pitched them out on to the cistern cover. As the window opened, a heavy crash came at the door. Someone had charged it with the idea of smashing the lock. But the stout bolts I had screwed up some days be-

fore stopped him. That startled me, made me angry. I began to tremble and do things hurriedly.

"I tossed together some loose paper, straw, packing paper and so forth, in the middle of the room, and turned on the gas. Heavy blows began to rain upon the door. I could not find the matches. I beat my hands on the wall with rage. I turned down the gas again, stepped out of the window on the cistern cover, very softly lowered the sash, and sat down, secure and invisible, but quivering with anger, to watch events. They split a panel, I saw, and in another moment they had broken away the staples of the bolts and stood in the open doorway. It was the landlord and his two step-sons, sturdy young men of three or four and twenty. Behind them fluttered the old hag of a woman from downstairs.

"You may imagine their astonishment to find the room empty. One of the younger men rushed to the window at once, flung it up and stared out. His staring eyes and thick-lipped bearded face came a foot from my face. I was half minded to hit his silly countenance, but I arrested my doubled fist. He stared right through me. So did the others as they joined him. The old man went and peered under the bed, and then they all made a rush for the cupboard. They had to argue about it at length in Yiddish and Cockney English. They concluded I had not answered them, that their imagination had deceived them. A feeling of extraordinary elation took the place of my anger as I sat outside the window and watched these four people—for the old lady came in, glancing suspiciously about her like a cat, trying to understand the riddle of my behaviour.

"The old man, so far as I could understand his *patois*, agreed with the old lady that I was a vivisectionist. The sons protested in garbled English that I was an electrician, and appealed to the dynamos and radiators. They were all nervous about my arrival, although I found subsequently that they had bolted the front door. The old lady peered into the cupboard and under the bed, and one of the young men pushed up the register and stared up the chimney. One of my fellow lodgers, a coster-monger who shared the opposite room with a butcher, appeared on the landing, and he was called in and told incoherent things.

"It occurred to me that the radiators, if they fell into the hands of some acute well-educated person, would give me away too much, and watching my opportunity, I came into the room and tilted one of the little dynamos off its fellow on which it was standing, and smashed both apparatus. Then, while they were trying to explain the smash, I dodged out of the room and went softly downstairs.

"I went into one of the sitting-rooms and waited until they came down, still speculating and argumentative, all a little disappointed at finding no 'horrors,' and all a little puzzled how they stood legally towards me. Then I slipped up again with a box of matches, fired my heap of paper and rubbish, put the chairs and bedding thereby, led the gas to the affair, by means of an india- rubber tube, and waving a farewell to the room left it for the last time."

"You fired the house!" exclaimed Kemp.

"Fired the house. It was the only way to cover my trail—and no doubt it was insured. I slipped the bolts of the front door quietly and went out into the street. I

was invisible, and I was only just beginning to realise the extraordinary advantage my invisibility gave me. My head was already teeming with plans of all the wild and wonderful things I had now impunity to do."

CHAPTER XXI - IN OXFORD STREET

"In going downstairs the first time I found an unexpected difficulty because I could not see my feet; indeed I stumbled twice, and there was an unaccustomed clumsiness in gripping the bolt. By not looking down, however, I managed to walk on the level passably well.

"My mood, I say, was one of exaltation. I felt as a seeing man might do, with padded feet and noiseless clothes, in a city of the blind. I experienced a wild impulse to jest, to startle people, to clap men on the back, fling people's hats astray, and generally revel in my extraordinary advantage.

"But hardly had I emerged upon Great Portland Street, however (my lodging was close to the big draper's shop there), when I heard a clashing concussion and was hit violently behind, and turning saw a man carrying a basket of soda- water syphons, and looking in amazement at his burden. Although the blow had really hurt me, I found something so irresistible in his astonishment that I laughed aloud. 'The devil's in the basket,' I said, and suddenly twisted it out of his hand. He let go incontinently, and I swung the whole weight into the air.

"But a fool of a cabman, standing outside a public house, made a sudden rush for this, and his extending fingers took me with excruciating violence under the ear. I let the whole down with a smash on the cabman, and then, with shouts and the clatter of feet about me, people coming out of shops, vehicles pulling up, I realised what I had done for myself, and cursing my folly, backed against a shop window and prepared to dodge out of the confusion. In a moment I should be wedged into a crowd and inevitably discovered. I pushed by a butcher boy, who luckily did not turn to see the nothingness that shoved him aside, and dodged behind the cab-man's four-wheeler. I do not know how they settled the business, I hurried straight across the road, which was happily clear, and hardly heeding which way I went, in the fright of detection the incident had given me, plunged into the afternoon throng of Oxford Street.

"I tried to get into the stream of people, but they were too thick for me, and in a moment my heels were being trodden upon. I took to the gutter, the roughness of which I found painful to my feet, and forthwith the shaft of a crawling hansom dug me forcibly under the shoulder blade, reminding me that I was already bruised severely. I staggered out of the way of the cab, avoided a perambulator by a convulsive movement, and found myself behind the hansom. A happy thought saved me, and as this drove slowly along I followed in its immediate wake, trembling and astonished at the turn of my adventure. And not only trembling, but

shivering. It was a bright day in January and I was stark naked and the thin slime of mud that covered the road was freezing. Foolish as it seems to me now, I had not reckoned that, transparent or not, I was still amenable to the weather and all its consequences.

"Then suddenly a bright idea came into my head. I ran round and got into the cab. And so, shivering, scared, and sniffing with the first intimations of a cold, and with the bruises in the small of my back growing upon my attention, I drove slowly along Oxford Street and past Tottenham Court Road. My mood was as different from that in which I had sallied forth ten minutes ago as it is possible to imagine. This invisibility indeed! The one thought that possessed me was—how was I to get out of the scrape I was in.

"We crawled past Mudie's, and there a tall woman with five or six yellow- labelled books hailed my cab, and I sprang out just in time to escape her, shaving a railway van narrowly in my flight. I made off up the roadway to Bloomsbury Square, intending to strike north past the Museum and so get into the quiet district. I was now cruelly chilled, and the strangeness of my situation so unnerved me that I whimpered as I ran. At the northward corner of the Square a little white dog ran out of the Pharmaceutical Society's offices, and incontinently made for me, nose down.

"I had never realised it before, but the nose is to the mind of a dog what the eye is to the mind of a seeing man. Dogs perceive the scent of a man moving as men perceive his vision. This brute began barking and leaping, showing, as it seemed to me, only too plainly that he was aware of me. I crossed Great Russell Street, glancing over my shoulder as I did so, and went some way along Montague Street before I realised what I was running towards.

"Then I became aware of a blare of music, and looking along the street saw a number of people advancing out of Russell Square, red shirts, and the banner of the Salvation Army to the fore. Such a crowd, chanting in the roadway and scoffing on the pavement, I could not hope to penetrate, and dreading to go back and farther from home again, and deciding on the spur of the moment, I ran up the white steps of a house facing the museum railings, and stood there until the crowd should have passed. Happily the dog stopped at the noise of the band too, hesitated, and turned tail, running back to Bloomsbury Square again.

"On came the band, bawling with unconscious irony some hymn about 'When shall we see His face?' and it seemed an interminable time to me before the tide of the crowd washed along the pavement by me. Thud, thud, thud, came the drum with a vibrating resonance, and for the moment I did not notice two urchins stopping at the railings by me. 'See 'em,' said one. 'See what?' said the other. 'Why—them footmarks—bare. Like what you makes in mud.'

"I looked down and saw the youngsters had stopped and were gaping at the muddy footmarks I had left behind me up the newly whitened steps. The passing people elbowed and jostled them, but their confounded intelligence was arrested. 'Thud, thud, thud, when, thud, shall we see, thud, his face, thud, thud.' 'There's a

barefoot man gone up them steps, or I don't know nothing,' said one. 'And he ain't never come down again. And his foot was a-bleeding.'

"The thick of the crowd had already passed. 'Looky there, Ted,' quoth the younger of the detectives, with the sharpness of surprise in his voice, and pointed straight to my feet. I looked down and saw at once the dim suggestion of their outline sketched in splashes of mud. For a moment I was paralysed.

"'Why, that's rum,' said the elder. 'Dashed rum! It's just like the ghost of a foot, ain't it?' He hesitated and advanced with outstretched hand. A man pulled up short to see what he was catching, and then a girl. In another moment he would have touched me. Then I saw what to do. I made a step, the boy started back with an exclamation, and with a rapid movement I swung myself over into the portico of the next house. But the smaller boy was sharp-eyed enough to follow the movement, and before I was well down the steps and upon the pavement, he had recovered from his momentary astonishment and was shouting out that the feet had gone over the wall.

"They rushed round and saw my new footmarks flash into being on the lower step and upon the pavement. 'What's up?' asked someone. 'Feet! Look! Feet running!'

"Everybody in the road, except my three pursuers, was pouring along after the Salvation Army, and this blow not only impeded me but them. There was an eddy of surprise and interrogation. At the cost of bowling over one young fellow I got through, and in another moment I was rushing headlong round the circuit of Russell Square, with six or seven astonished people following my footmarks. There was no time for explanation, or else the whole host would have been after me.

"Twice I doubled round corners, thrice I crossed the road and came back upon my tracks, and then, as my feet grew hot and dry, the damp impressions began to fade. At last I had a breathing space and rubbed my feet clean with my hands, and so got away altogether. The last I saw of the chase was a little group of a dozen people perhaps, studying with infinite perplexity a slowly drying footprint that had resulted from a puddle in Tavistock Square, a footprint as isolated and incomprehensible to them as Crusoe's solitary discovery.

"This running warmed me to a certain extent, and I went on with a better courage through the maze of less frequented roads that runs hereabouts. My back had now become very stiff and sore, my tonsils were painful from the cabman's fingers, and the skin of my neck had been scratched by his nails; my feet hurt exceedingly and I was lame from a little cut on one foot. I saw in time a blind man approaching me, and fled limping, for I feared his subtle intuitions. Once or twice accidental collisions occurred and I left people amazed, with unaccountable curses ringing in their ears. Then came something silent and quiet against my face, and across the Square fell a thin veil of slowly falling flakes of snow. I had caught a cold, and do as I would I could not avoid an occasional sneeze. And every dog that came in sight, with its pointing nose and curious sniffing, was a terror to me.

"Then came men and boys running, first one and then others, and shouting as they ran. It was a fire. They ran in the direction of my lodging, and looking back down a street I saw a mass of black smoke streaming up above the roofs and telephone wires. It was my lodging burning; my clothes, my apparatus, all my resources indeed, except my cheque-book and the three volumes of memoranda that awaited me in Great Portland Street, were there. Burning! I had burnt my boats—if ever a man did! The place was blazing."

The Invisible Man paused and thought. Kemp glanced nervously out of the window. "Yes?" he said. "Go on."

CHAPTER XXII - IN THE EMPORIUM

"So last January, with the beginning of a snowstorm in the air about me —and if it settled on me it would betray me!—weary, cold, painful, inexpressibly wretched, and still but half convinced of my invisible quality, I began this new life to which I am committed. I had no refuge, no appliances, no human being in the world in whom I could confide. To have told my secret would have given me away—made a mere show and rarity of me. Nevertheless, I was half-minded to accost some passer-by and throw myself upon his mercy. But I knew too clearly the terror and brutal cruelty my advances would evoke. I made no plans in the street. My sole object was to get shelter from the snow, to get myself covered and warm; then I might hope to plan. But even to me, an Invisible Man, the rows of London houses stood latched, barred, and bolted impregnably.

"Only one thing could I see clearly before me—the cold exposure and misery of the snowstorm and the night.

"And then I had a brilliant idea. I turned down one of the roads leading from Gower Street to Tottenham Court Road, and found myself outside Omniums, the big establishment where everything is to be bought—you know the place: meat, grocery, linen, furniture, clothing, oil paintings even—a huge meandering collection of shops rather than a shop. I had thought I should find the doors open, but they were closed, and as I stood in the wide entrance a carriage stopped outside, and a man in uniform—you know the kind of personage with 'Omnium' on his cap—flung open the door. I contrived to enter, and walking down the shop—it was a department where they were selling ribbons and gloves and stockings and that kind of thing—came to a more spacious region devoted to picnic baskets and wicker furniture.

"I did not feel safe there, however; people were going to and fro, and I prowled restlessly about until I came upon a huge section in an upper floor containing multitudes of bedsteads, and over these I clambered, and found a resting-place at last among a huge pile of folded flock mattresses. The place was already lit up and agreeably warm, and I decided to remain where I was, keeping a cautious eye on the two or three sets of shopmen and customers who were meandering through the place, until closing time came. Then I should be able, I thought, to rob the place for food and clothing, and disguised, prowl through it and examine its resources, perhaps sleep on some of the bedding. That seemed an acceptable plan. My idea was to procure clothing to make myself a muffled but acceptable figure, to get money, and then to recover my books and parcels where

they awaited me, take a lodging somewhere and elaborate plans for the complete realisation of the advantages my invisibility gave me (as I still imagined) over my fellow-men.

"Closing time arrived quickly enough. It could not have been more than an hour after I took up my position on the mattresses before I noticed the blinds of the windows being drawn, and customers being marched doorward. And then a number of brisk young men began with remarkable alacrity to tidy up the goods that remained disturbed. I left my lair as the crowds diminished, and prowled cautiously out into the less desolate parts of the shop. I was really surprised to observe how rapidly the young men and women whipped away the goods displayed for sale during the day. All the boxes of goods, the hanging fabrics, the festoons of lace, the boxes of sweets in the grocery section, the displays of this and that, were being whipped down, folded up, slapped into tidy receptacles, and everything that could not be taken down and put away had sheets of some coarse stuff like sacking flung over them. Finally all the chairs were turned up on to the counters, leaving the floor clear. Directly each of these young people had done, he or she made promptly for the door with such an expression of animation as I have rarely observed in a shop assistant before. Then came a lot of youngsters scattering sawdust and carrying pails and brooms. I had to dodge to get out of the way, and as it was, my ankle got stung with the sawdust. For some time, wandering through the swathed and darkened departments, I could hear the brooms at work. And at last a good hour or more after the shop had been closed, came a noise of locking doors. Silence came upon the place, and I found myself wandering through the vast and intricate shops, galleries, show-rooms of the place, alone. It was very still; in one place I remember passing near one of the Tottenham Court Road entrances and listening to the tapping of boot-heels of the passers-by.

"My first visit was to the place where I had seen stockings and gloves for sale. It was dark, and I had the devil of a hunt after matches, which I found at last in the drawer of the little cash desk. Then I had to get a candle. I had to tear down wrappings and ransack a number of boxes and drawers, but at last I managed to turn out what I sought; the box label called them lambswool pants, and lambswool vests. Then socks, a thick comforter, and then I went to the clothing place and got trousers, a lounge jacket, an overcoat and a slouch hat—a clerical sort of hat with the brim turned down. I began to feel a human being again, and my next thought was food.

"Upstairs was a refreshment department, and there I got cold meat. There was coffee still in the urn, and I lit the gas and warmed it up again, and altogether I did not do badly. Afterwards, prowling through the place in search of blankets—I had to put up at last with a heap of down quilts—I came upon a grocery section with a lot of chocolate and candied fruits, more than was good for me indeed—and some white burgundy. And near that was a toy department, and I had a brilliant idea. I found some artificial noses —dummy noses, you know, and I thought of dark spectacles. But Omniums had no optical department. My nose had been a difficulty indeed—I had thought of paint. But the discovery set my mind running on wigs

and masks and the like. Finally I went to sleep in a heap of down quilts, very warm and comfortable.

"My last thoughts before sleeping were the most agreeable I had had since the change. I was in a state of physical serenity, and that was reflected in my mind. I thought that I should be able to slip out unobserved in the morning with my clothes upon me, muffling my face with a white wrapper I had taken, purchase, with the money I had taken, spectacles and so forth, and so complete my disguise. I lapsed into disorderly dreams of all the fantastic things that had happened during the last few days. I saw the ugly little Jew of a landlord vociferating in his rooms; I saw his two sons marvelling, and the wrinkled old woman's gnarled face as she asked for her cat. I experienced again the strange sensation of seeing the cloth disappear, and so I came round to the windy hillside and the sniffing old clergyman mumbling 'Earth to earth, ashes to ashes, dust to dust,' at my father's open grave.

"'You also,' said a voice, and suddenly I was being forced towards the grave. I struggled, shouted, appealed to the mourners, but they continued stonily following the service; the old clergyman, too, never faltered droning and sniffing through the ritual. I realised I was invisible and inaudible, that overwhelming forces had their grip on me. I struggled in vain, I was forced over the brink, the coffin rang hollow as I fell upon it, and the gravel came flying after me in spadefuls. Nobody heeded me, nobody was aware of me. I made convulsive struggles and awoke.

"The pale London dawn had come, the place was full of a chilly grey light that filtered round the edges of the window blinds. I sat up, and for a time I could not think where this ample apartment, with its counters, its piles of rolled stuff, its heap of quilts and cushions, its iron pillars, might be. Then, as recollection came back to me, I heard voices in conversation.

"Then far down the place, in the brighter light of some department which had already raised its blinds, I saw two men approaching. I scrambled to my feet, looking about me for some way of escape, and even as I did so the sound of my movement made them aware of me. I suppose they saw merely a figure moving quietly and quickly away. 'Who's that?' cried one, and 'Stop, there!' shouted the other. I dashed around a corner and came full tilt—a faceless figure, mind you!—on a lanky lad of fifteen. He yelled and I bowled him over, rushed past him, turned another corner, and by a happy inspiration threw myself behind a counter. In another moment feet went running past and I heard voices shouting, 'All hands to the doors!' asking what was 'up,' and giving one another advice how to catch me.

"Lying on the ground, I felt scared out of my wits. But—odd as it may seem—it did not occur to me at the moment to take off my clothes as I should have done. I had made up my mind, I suppose, to get away in them, and that ruled me. And then down the vista of the counters came a bawling of 'Here he is!'

"I sprang to my feet, whipped a chair off the counter, and sent it whirling at the fool who had shouted, turned, came into another round a corner, sent him spinning, and rushed up the stairs. He kept his footing, gave a view hallo, and came

up the staircase hot after me. Up the staircase were piled a multitude of those bright-coloured pot things—what are they?"

"Art pots," suggested Kemp.

"That's it! Art pots. Well, I turned at the top step and swung round, plucked one out of a pile and smashed it on his silly head as he came at me. The whole pile of pots went headlong, and I heard shouting and footsteps running from all parts. I made a mad rush for the refreshment place, and there was a man in white like a man cook, who took up the chase. I made one last desperate turn and found myself among lamps and ironmongery. I went behind the counter of this, and waited for my cook, and as he bolted in at the head of the chase, I doubled him up with a lamp. Down he went, and I crouched down behind the counter and began whipping off my clothes as fast as I could. Coat, jacket, trousers, shoes were all right, but a lambswool vest fits a man like a skin. I heard more men coming, my cook was lying quiet on the other side of the counter, stunned or scared speechless, and I had to make another dash for it, like a rabbit hunted out of a wood-pile.

"'This way, policeman!' I heard someone shouting. I found myself in my bedstead storeroom again, and at the end of a wilderness of wardrobes. I rushed among them, went flat, got rid of my vest after infinite wriggling, and stood a free man again, panting and scared, as the policeman and three of the shopmen came round the corner. They made a rush for the vest and pants, and collared the trousers. 'He's dropping his plunder,' said one of the young men. 'He *must* be somewhere here.'

"But they did not find me all the same.

"I stood watching them hunt for me for a time, and cursing my ill-luck in losing the clothes. Then I went into the refreshment-room, drank a little milk I found there, and sat down by the fire to consider my position.

"In a little while two assistants came in and began to talk over the business very excitedly and like the fools they were. I heard a magnified account of my depredations, and other speculations as to my whereabouts. Then I fell to scheming again. The insurmountable difficulty of the place, especially now it was alarmed, was to get any plunder out of it. I went down into the warehouse to see if there was any chance of packing and addressing a parcel, but I could not understand the system of checking. About eleven o'clock, the snow having thawed as it fell, and the day being finer and a little warmer than the previous one, I decided that the Emporium was hopeless, and went out again, exasperated at my want of success, with only the vaguest plans of action in my mind."

CHAPTER XXIII - IN DRURY LANE

"But you begin now to realise," said the Invisible Man, "the full disadvantage of my condition. I had no shelter—no covering—to get clothing was to forego all my advantage, to make myself a strange and terrible thing. I was fasting; for to eat, to fill myself with unassimilated matter, would be to become grotesquely visible again."

"I never thought of that," said Kemp.

"Nor had I. And the snow had warned me of other dangers. I could not go abroad in snow—it would settle on me and expose me. Rain, too, would make me a watery outline, a glistening surface of a man—a bubble. And fog—I should be like a fainter bubble in a fog, a surface, a greasy glimmer of humanity. Moreover, as I went abroad—in the London air —I gathered dirt about my ankles, floating smuts and dust upon my skin. I did not know how long it would be before I should become visible from that cause also. But I saw clearly it could not be for long.

"Not in London at any rate.

"I went into the slums towards Great Portland Street, and found myself at the end of the street in which I had lodged. I did not go that way, because of the crowd halfway down it opposite to the still smoking ruins of the house I had fired. My most immediate problem was to get clothing. What to do with my face puzzled me. Then I saw in one of those little miscellaneous shops—news, sweets, toys, stationery, belated Christmas tomfoolery, and so forth —an array of masks and noses. I realised that problem was solved. In a flash I saw my course. I turned about, no longer aimless, and went—circuitously in order to avoid the busy ways, towards the back streets north of the Strand; for I remembered, though not very distinctly where, that some theatrical costumiers had shops in that district.

"The day was cold, with a nipping wind down the northward running streets. I walked fast to avoid being overtaken. Every crossing was a danger, every passenger a thing to watch alertly. One man as I was about to pass him at the top of Bedford Street, turned upon me abruptly and came into me, sending me into the road and almost under the wheel of a passing hansom. The verdict of the cab-rank was that he had had some sort of stroke. I was so unnerved by this encounter that I went into Covent Garden Market and sat down for some time in a quiet corner by a stall of violets, panting and trembling. I found I had caught a fresh cold, and had to turn out after a time lest my sneezes should attract attention.

"At last I reached the object of my quest, a dirty, fly-blown little shop in a by-way near Drury Lane, with a window full of tinsel robes, sham jewels, wigs, slippers, dominoes and theatrical photographs. The shop was old-fashioned and low and dark, and the house rose above it for four storeys, dark and dismal. I peered through the window and, seeing no one within, entered. The opening of the door set a clanking bell ringing. I left it open, and walked round a bare costume stand, into a corner behind a cheval glass. For a minute or so no one came. Then I heard heavy feet striding across a room, and a man appeared down the shop.

"My plans were now perfectly definite. I proposed to make my way into the house, secrete myself upstairs, watch my opportunity, and when everything was quiet, rummage out a wig, mask, spectacles, and costume, and go into the world, perhaps a grotesque but still a credible figure. And incidentally of course I could rob the house of any available money.

"The man who had just entered the shop was a short, slight, hunched, beetle-browed man, with long arms and very short bandy legs. Apparently I had interrupted a meal. He stared about the shop with an expression of expectation. This gave way to surprise, and then to anger, as he saw the shop empty. 'Damn the boys!' he said. He went to stare up and down the street. He came in again in a minute, kicked the door to with his foot spitefully, and went muttering back to the house door.

"I came forward to follow him, and at the noise of my movement he stopped dead. I did so too, startled by his quickness of ear. He slammed the house door in my face.

"I stood hesitating. Suddenly I heard his quick footsteps returning, and the door reopened. He stood looking about the shop like one who was still not satisfied. Then, murmuring to himself, he examined the back of the counter and peered behind some fixtures. Then he stood doubtful. He had left the house door open and I slipped into the inner room.

"It was a queer little room, poorly furnished and with a number of big masks in the corner. On the table was his belated breakfast, and it was a confoundedly exasperating thing for me, Kemp, to have to sniff his coffee and stand watching while he came in and resumed his meal. And his table manners were irritating. Three doors opened into the little room, one going upstairs and one down, but they were all shut. I could not get out of the room while he was there; I could scarcely move because of his alertness, and there was a draught down my back. Twice I strangled a sneeze just in time.

"The spectacular quality of my sensations was curious and novel, but for all that I was heartily tired and angry long before he had done his eating. But at last he made an end and putting his beggarly crockery on the black tin tray upon which he had had his teapot, and gathering all the crumbs up on the mustard stained cloth, he took the whole lot of things after him. His burden prevented his shutting the door behind him—as he would have done; I never saw such a man for shutting doors—and I followed him into a very dirty underground kitchen and scullery. I had the pleasure of seeing him begin to wash up, and then, finding no

good in keeping down there, and the brick floor being cold on my feet, I returned upstairs and sat in his chair by the fire. It was burning low, and scarcely thinking, I put on a little coal. The noise of this brought him up at once, and he stood aglare. He peered about the room and was within an ace of touching me. Even after that examination, he scarcely seemed satisfied. He stopped in the doorway and took a final inspection before he went down.

"I waited in the little parlour for an age, and at last he came up and opened the upstairs door. I just managed to get by him.

"On the staircase he stopped suddenly, so that I very nearly blundered into him. He stood looking back right into my face and listening. 'I could have sworn,' he said. His long hairy hand pulled at his lower lip. His eye went up and down the staircase. Then he grunted and went on up again.

"His hand was on the handle of a door, and then he stopped again with the same puzzled anger on his face. He was becoming aware of the faint sounds of my movements about him. The man must have had diabolically acute hearing. He suddenly flashed into rage. 'If there's anyone in this house—' he cried with an oath, and left the threat unfinished. He put his hand in his pocket, failed to find what he wanted, and rushing past me went blundering noisily and pugnaciously downstairs. But I did not follow him. I sat on the head of the staircase until his return.

"Presently he came up again, still muttering. He opened the door of the room, and before I could enter, slammed it in my face.

"I resolved to explore the house, and spent some time in doing so as noiselessly as possible. The house was very old and tumble-down, damp so that the paper in the attics was peeling from the walls, and rat infested. Some of the door handles were stiff and I was afraid to turn them. Several rooms I did inspect were unfurnished, and others were littered with theatrical lumber, bought second-hand, I judged, from its appearance. In one room next to his I found a lot of old clothes. I began routing among these, and in my eagerness forgot again the evident sharpness of his ears. I heard a stealthy footstep and, looking up just in time, saw him peering in at the tumbled heap and holding an old-fashioned revolver in his hand. I stood perfectly still while he stared about open-mouthed and suspicious. 'It must have been her,' he said slowly. 'Damn her!'

"He shut the door quietly, and immediately I heard the key turn in the lock. Then his footsteps retreated. I realised abruptly that I was locked in. For a minute I did not know what to do. I walked from door to window and back, and stood perplexed. A gust of anger came upon me. But I decided to inspect the clothes before I did anything further, and my first attempt brought down a pile from an upper shelf. This brought him back, more sinister than ever. That time he actually touched me, jumped back with amazement and stood astonished in the middle of the room.

"Presently he calmed a little. 'Rats,' he said in an undertone, fingers on lips. He was evidently a little scared. I edged quietly out of the room, but a plank creaked. Then the infernal little brute started going all over the house, revolver in hand and

locking door after door and pocketing the keys. When I realised what he was up to I had a fit of rage—I could hardly control myself sufficiently to watch my opportunity. By this time I knew he was alone in the house, and so I made no more ado, but knocked him on the head."

"Knocked him on the head?" exclaimed Kemp.

"Yes—stunned him—as he was going downstairs. Hit him from behind with a stool that stood on the landing. He went downstairs like a bag of old boots."

"But—I say! The common conventions of humanity—"

"Are all very well for common people. But the point was, Kemp, that I had to get out of that house in a disguise without his seeing me. I couldn't think of any other way of doing it. And then I gagged him with a Louis Quatorze vest and tied him up in a sheet."

"Tied him up in a sheet!"

"Made a sort of bag of it. It was rather a good idea to keep the idiot scared and quiet, and a devilish hard thing to get out of—head away from the string. My dear Kemp, it's no good your sitting glaring as though I was a murderer. It had to be done. He had his revolver. If once he saw me he would be able to describe me—"

"But still," said Kemp, "in England—to-day. And the man was in his own house, and you were—well, robbing."

"Robbing! Confound it! You'll call me a thief next! Surely, Kemp, you're not fool enough to dance on the old strings. Can't you see my position?"

"And his too," said Kemp.

The Invisible Man stood up sharply. "What do you mean to say?"

Kemp's face grew a trifle hard. He was about to speak and checked himself. "I suppose, after all," he said with a sudden change of manner, "the thing had to be done. You were in a fix. But still—"

"Of course I was in a fix—an infernal fix. And he made me wild too—hunting me about the house, fooling about with his revolver, locking and unlocking doors. He was simply exasperating. You don't blame me, do you? You don't blame me?"

"I never blame anyone," said Kemp. "It's quite out of fashion. What did you do next?"

"I was hungry. Downstairs I found a loaf and some rank cheese—more than sufficient to satisfy my hunger. I took some brandy and water, and then went up past my impromptu bag—he was lying quite still—to the room containing the old clothes. This looked out upon the street, two lace curtains brown with dirt guarding the window. I went and peered out through their interstices. Outside the day was bright—by contrast with the brown shadows of the dismal house in which I found myself, dazzlingly bright. A brisk traffic was going by, fruit carts, a hansom, a four-wheeler with a pile of boxes, a fishmonger's cart. I turned with spots of colour swimming before my eyes to the shadowy fixtures behind me. My excitement was giving place to a clear apprehension of my position again. The room was full of a faint scent of benzoline, used, I suppose, in cleaning the garments.

"I began a systematic search of the place. I should judge the hunchback had been alone in the house for some time. He was a curious person. Everything that

could possibly be of service to me I collected in the clothes storeroom, and then I made a deliberate selection. I found a handbag I thought a suitable possession, and some powder, rouge, and sticking-plaster.

"I had thought of painting and powdering my face and all that there was to show of me, in order to render myself visible, but the disadvantage of this lay in the fact that I should require turpentine and other appliances and a considerable amount of time before I could vanish again. Finally I chose a mask of the better type, slightly grotesque but not more so than many human beings, dark glasses, greyish whiskers, and a wig. I could find no underclothing, but that I could buy subsequently, and for the time I swathed myself in calico dominoes and some white cashmere scarfs. I could find no socks, but the hunchback's boots were rather a loose fit and sufficed. In a desk in the shop were three sovereigns and about thirty shillings' worth of silver, and in a locked cupboard I burst in the inner room were eight pounds in gold. I could go forth into the world again, equipped.

"Then came a curious hesitation. Was my appearance really credible? I tried myself with a little bedroom looking-glass, inspecting myself from every point of view to discover any forgotten chink, but it all seemed sound. I was grotesque to the theatrical pitch, a stage miser, but I was certainly not a physical impossibility. Gathering confidence, I took my looking-glass down into the shop, pulled down the shop blinds, and surveyed myself from every point of view with the help of the cheval glass in the corner.

"I spent some minutes screwing up my courage and then unlocked the shop door and marched out into the street, leaving the little man to get out of his sheet again when he liked. In five minutes a dozen turnings intervened between me and the costumier's shop. No one appeared to notice me very pointedly. My last difficulty seemed overcome."

He stopped again.

"And you troubled no more about the hunchback?" said Kemp.

"No," said the Invisible Man. "Nor have I heard what became of him. I suppose he untied himself or kicked himself out. The knots were pretty tight."

He became silent and went to the window and stared out.

"What happened when you went out into the Strand?"

"Oh!—disillusionment again. I thought my troubles were over. Practically I thought I had impunity to do whatever I chose, everything—save to give away my secret. So I thought. Whatever I did, whatever the consequences might be, was nothing to me. I had merely to fling aside my garments and vanish. No person could hold me. I could take my money where I found it. I decided to treat myself to a sumptuous feast, and then put up at a good hotel, and accumulate a new outfit of property. I felt amazingly confident; it's not particularly pleasant recalling that I was an ass. I went into a place and was already ordering lunch, when it occurred to me that I could not eat unless I exposed my invisible face. I finished ordering the lunch, told the man I should be back in ten minutes, and went out exasperated. I don't know if you have ever been disappointed in your appetite."

"Not quite so badly," said Kemp, "but I can imagine it."

"I could have smashed the silly devils. At last, faint with the desire for tasteful food, I went into another place and demanded a private room. 'I am disfigured,' I said. 'Badly.' They looked at me curiously, but of course it was not their affair—and so at last I got my lunch. It was not particularly well served, but it sufficed; and when I had had it, I sat over a cigar, trying to plan my line of action. And outside a snowstorm was beginning.

"The more I thought it over, Kemp, the more I realised what a helpless absurdity an Invisible Man was—in a cold and dirty climate and a crowded civilised city. Before I made this mad experiment I had dreamt of a thousand advantages. That afternoon it seemed all disappointment. I went over the heads of the things a man reckons desirable. No doubt invisibility made it possible to get them, but it made it impossible to enjoy them when they are got. Ambition—what is the good of pride of place when you cannot appear there? What is the good of the love of woman when her name must needs be Delilah? I have no taste for politics, for the blackguardisms of fame, for philanthropy, for sport. What was I to do? And for this I had become a wrapped- up mystery, a swathed and bandaged caricature of a man!"

He paused, and his attitude suggested a roving glance at the window.

"But how did you get to Iping?" said Kemp, anxious to keep his guest busy talking.

"I went there to work. I had one hope. It was a half idea! I have it still. It is a full blown idea now. A way of getting back! Of restoring what I have done. When I choose. When I have done all I mean to do invisibly. And that is what I chiefly want to talk to you about now."

"You went straight to Iping?"

"Yes. I had simply to get my three volumes of memoranda and my cheque-book, my luggage and underclothing, order a quantity of chemicals to work out this idea of mine—I will show you the calculations as soon as I get my books—and then I started. Jove! I remember the snowstorm now, and the accursed bother it was to keep the snow from damping my pasteboard nose."

"At the end," said Kemp, "the day before yesterday, when they found you out, you rather—to judge by the papers—"

"I did. Rather. Did I kill that fool of a constable?"

"No," said Kemp. "He's expected to recover."

"That's his luck, then. I clean lost my temper, the fools! Why couldn't they leave me alone? And that grocer lout?"

"There are no deaths expected," said Kemp.

"I don't know about that tramp of mine," said the Invisible Man, with an unpleasant laugh.

"By Heaven, Kemp, you don't know what rage *is*! ... To have worked for years, to have planned and plotted, and then to get some fumbling purblind idiot messing across your course! ... Every conceivable sort of silly creature that has ever been created has been sent to cross me.

"If I have much more of it, I shall go wild—I shall start mowing 'em.

"As it is, they've made things a thousand times more difficult."
"No doubt it's exasperating," said Kemp, drily.

CHAPTER XXIV - THE PLAN THAT FAILED

"But now," said Kemp, with a side glance out of the window, "what are we to do?"

He moved nearer his guest as he spoke in such a manner as to prevent the possibility of a sudden glimpse of the three men who were advancing up the hill road—with an intolerable slowness, as it seemed to Kemp.

"What were you planning to do when you were heading for Port Burdock? *Had* you any plan?"

"I was going to clear out of the country. But I have altered that plan rather since seeing you. I thought it would be wise, now the weather is hot and invisibility possible, to make for the South. Especially as my secret was known, and everyone would be on the lookout for a masked and muffled man. You have a line of steamers from here to France. My idea was to get aboard one and run the risks of the passage. Thence I could go by train into Spain, or else get to Algiers. It would not be difficult. There a man might always be invisible—and yet live. And do things. I was using that tramp as a money box and luggage carrier, until I decided how to get my books and things sent over to meet me."

"That's clear."

"And then the filthy brute must needs try and rob me! He *has* hidden my books, Kemp. Hidden my books! If I can lay my hands on him!"

"Best plan to get the books out of him first."

"But where is he? Do you know?"

"He's in the town police station, locked up, by his own request, in the strongest cell in the place."

"Cur!" said the Invisible Man.

"But that hangs up your plans a little."

"We must get those books; those books are vital."

"Certainly," said Kemp, a little nervously, wondering if he heard footsteps outside. "Certainly we must get those books. But that won't be difficult, if he doesn't know they're for you."

"No," said the Invisible Man, and thought.

Kemp tried to think of something to keep the talk going, but the Invisible Man resumed of his own accord.

"Blundering into your house, Kemp," he said, "changes all my plans. For you are a man that can understand. In spite of all that has happened, in spite of this

publicity, of the loss of my books, of what I have suffered, there still remain great possibilities, huge possibilities—"

"You have told no one I am here?" he asked abruptly.

Kemp hesitated. "That was implied," he said.

"No one?" insisted Griffin.

"Not a soul."

"Ah! Now—" The Invisible Man stood up, and sticking his arms akimbo began to pace the study.

"I made a mistake, Kemp, a huge mistake, in carrying this thing through alone. I have wasted strength, time, opportunities. Alone—it is wonderful how little a man can do alone! To rob a little, to hurt a little, and there is the end.

"What I want, Kemp, is a goal-keeper, a helper, and a hiding-place, an arrangement whereby I can sleep and eat and rest in peace, and unsuspected. I must have a confederate. With a confederate, with food and rest—a thousand things are possible.

"Hitherto I have gone on vague lines. We have to consider all that invisibility means, all that it does not mean. It means little advantage for eavesdropping and so forth—one makes sounds. It's of little help —a little help perhaps—in housebreaking and so forth. Once you've caught me you could easily imprison me. But on the other hand I am hard to catch. This invisibility, in fact, is only good in two cases: It's useful in getting away, it's useful in approaching. It's particularly useful, therefore, in killing. I can walk round a man, whatever weapon he has, choose my point, strike as I like. Dodge as I like. Escape as I like."

Kemp's hand went to his moustache. Was that a movement downstairs?

"And it is killing we must do, Kemp."

"It is killing we must do," repeated Kemp. "I'm listening to your plan, Griffin, but I'm not agreeing, mind. *Why* killing?"

"Not wanton killing, but a judicious slaying. The point is, they know there is an Invisible Man—as well as we know there is an Invisible Man. And that Invisible Man, Kemp, must now establish a Reign of Terror. Yes; no doubt it's startling. But I mean it. A Reign of Terror. He must take some town like your Burdock and terrify and dominate it. He must issue his orders. He can do that in a thousand ways—scraps of paper thrust under doors would suffice. And all who disobey his orders he must kill, and kill all who would defend them."

"Humph!" said Kemp, no longer listening to Griffin but to the sound of his front door opening and closing.

"It seems to me, Griffin," he said, to cover his wandering attention, "that your confederate would be in a difficult position."

"No one would know he was a confederate," said the Invisible Man, eagerly. And then suddenly, "Hush! What's that downstairs?"

"Nothing," said Kemp, and suddenly began to speak loud and fast. "I don't agree to this, Griffin," he said. "Understand me, I don't agree to this. Why dream of playing a game against the race? How can you hope to gain happiness? Don't

be a lone wolf. Publish your results; take the world—take the nation at least—into your confidence. Think what you might do with a million helpers—"

The Invisible Man interrupted—arm extended. "There are footsteps coming upstairs," he said in a low voice.

"Nonsense," said Kemp.

"Let me see," said the Invisible Man, and advanced, arm extended, to the door.

And then things happened very swiftly. Kemp hesitated for a second and then moved to intercept him. The Invisible Man started and stood still. "Traitor!" cried the Voice, and suddenly the dressing-gown opened, and sitting down the Unseen began to disrobe. Kemp made three swift steps to the door, and forthwith the Invisible Man—his legs had vanished—sprang to his feet with a shout. Kemp flung the door open.

As it opened, there came a sound of hurrying feet downstairs and voices.

With a quick movement Kemp thrust the Invisible Man back, sprang aside, and slammed the door. The key was outside and ready. In another moment Griffin would have been alone in the belvedere study, a prisoner. Save for one little thing. The key had been slipped in hastily that morning. As Kemp slammed the door it fell noisily upon the carpet.

Kemp's face became white. He tried to grip the door handle with both hands. For a moment he stood lugging. Then the door gave six inches. But he got it closed again. The second time it was jerked a foot wide, and the dressing- gown came wedging itself into the opening. His throat was gripped by invisible fingers, and he left his hold on the handle to defend himself. He was forced back, tripped and pitched heavily into the corner of the landing. The empty dressing-gown was flung on the top of him.

Halfway up the staircase was Colonel Adye, the recipient of Kemp's letter, the chief of the Burdock police. He was staring aghast at the sudden appearance of Kemp, followed by the extraordinary sight of clothing tossing empty in the air. He saw Kemp felled, and struggling to his feet. He saw him rush forward, and go down again, felled like an ox.

Then suddenly he was struck violently. By nothing! A vast weight, it seemed, leapt upon him, and he was hurled headlong down the staircase, with a grip on his throat and a knee in his groin. An invisible foot trod on his back, a ghostly patter passed downstairs, he heard the two police officers in the hall shout and run, and the front door of the house slammed violently.

He rolled over and sat up staring. He saw, staggering down the staircase, Kemp, dusty and disheveled, one side of his face white from a blow, his lip bleeding, and a pink dressing-gown and some underclothing held in his arms.

"My God!" cried Kemp, "the game's up! He's gone!"

CHAPTER XXV - THE HUNTING OF THE INVISIBLE MAN

For a space Kemp was too inarticulate to make Adye understand the swift things that had just happened. They stood on the landing, Kemp speaking swiftly, the grotesque swathings of Griffin still on his arm. But presently Adye began to grasp something of the situation.

"He is mad," said Kemp; "inhuman. He is pure selfishness. He thinks of nothing but his own advantage, his own safety. I have listened to such a story this morning of brutal self-seeking... He has wounded men. He will kill them unless we can prevent him. He will create a panic. Nothing can stop him. He is going out now—furious!"

"He must be caught," said Adye. "That is certain."

"But how?" cried Kemp, and suddenly became full of ideas. "You must begin at once. You must set every available man to work; you must prevent his leaving this district. Once he gets away, he may go through the countryside as he wills, killing and maiming. He dreams of a reign of terror! A reign of terror, I tell you. You must set a watch on trains and roads and shipping. The garrison must help. You must wire for help. The only thing that may keep him here is the thought of recovering some books of notes he counts of value. I will tell you of that! There is a man in your police station—Marvel."

"I know," said Adye, "I know. Those books—yes. But the tramp..."

"Says he hasn't them. But he thinks the tramp has. And you must prevent him from eating or sleeping; day and night the country must be astir for him. Food must be locked up and secured, all food, so that he will have to break his way to it. The houses everywhere must be barred against him. Heaven send us cold nights and rain! The whole country-side must begin hunting and keep hunting. I tell you, Adye, he is a danger, a disaster; unless he is pinned and secured, it is frightful to think of the things that may happen."

"What else can we do?" said Adye. "I must go down at once and begin organising. But why not come? Yes—you come too! Come, and we must hold a sort of council of war—get Hopps to help—and the railway managers. By Jove! it's urgent. Come along—tell me as we go. What else is there we can do? Put that stuff down."

In another moment Adye was leading the way downstairs. They found the front door open and the policemen standing outside staring at empty air. "He's got away, sir," said one.

"We must go to the central station at once," said Adye. "One of you go on down and get a cab to come up and meet us—quickly. And now, Kemp, what else?"

"Dogs," said Kemp. "Get dogs. They don't see him, but they wind him. Get dogs."

"Good," said Adye. "It's not generally known, but the prison officials over at Halstead know a man with bloodhounds. Dogs. What else?"

"Bear in mind," said Kemp, "his food shows. After eating, his food shows until it is assimilated. So that he has to hide after eating. You must keep on beating. Every thicket, every quiet corner. And put all weapons—all implements that might be weapons, away. He can't carry such things for long. And what he can snatch up and strike men with must be hidden away."

"Good again," said Adye. "We shall have him yet!"

"And on the roads," said Kemp, and hesitated.

"Yes?" said Adye.

"Powdered glass," said Kemp. "It's cruel, I know. But think of what he may do!"

Adye drew the air in sharply between his teeth. "It's unsportsmanlike. I don't know. But I'll have powdered glass got ready. If he goes too far..."

"The man's become inhuman, I tell you," said Kemp. "I am as sure he will establish a reign of terror—so soon as he has got over the emotions of this escape—as I am sure I am talking to you. Our only chance is to be ahead. He has cut himself off from his kind. His blood be upon his own head."

CHAPTER XXVI - THE WICKSTEED MURDER

The Invisible Man seems to have rushed out of Kemp's house in a state of blind fury. A little child playing near Kemp's gateway was violently caught up and thrown aside, so that its ankle was broken, and thereafter for some hours the Invisible Man passed out of human perceptions. No one knows where he went nor what he did. But one can imagine him hurrying through the hot June forenoon, up the hill and on to the open downland behind Port Burdock, raging and despairing at his intolerable fate, and sheltering at last, heated and weary, amid the thickets of Hintondean, to piece together again his shattered schemes against his species. That seems to most probable refuge for him, for there it was he re-asserted himself in a grimly tragical manner about two in the afternoon.

One wonders what his state of mind may have been during that time, and what plans he devised. No doubt he was almost ecstatically exasperated by Kemp's treachery, and though we may be able to understand the motives that led to that deceit, we may still imagine and even sympathise a little with the fury the attempted surprise must have occasioned. Perhaps something of the stunned astonishment of his Oxford Street experiences may have returned to him, for he had evidently counted on Kemp's co-operation in his brutal dream of a terrorised world. At any rate he vanished from human ken about midday, and no living witness can tell what he did until about half-past two. It was a fortunate thing, perhaps, for humanity, but for him it was a fatal inaction.

During that time a growing multitude of men scattered over the countryside were busy. In the morning he had still been simply a legend, a terror; in the afternoon, by virtue chiefly of Kemp's drily worded proclamation, he was presented as a tangible antagonist, to be wounded, captured, or overcome, and the countryside began organising itself with inconceivable rapidity. By two o'clock even he might still have removed himself out of the district by getting aboard a train, but after two that became impossible. Every passenger train along the lines on a great parallelogram between Southampton, Manchester, Brighton and Horsham, travelled with locked doors, and the goods traffic was almost entirely suspended. And in a great circle of twenty miles round Port Burdock, men armed with guns and bludgeons were presently setting out in groups of three and four, with dogs, to beat the roads and fields.

Mounted policemen rode along the country lanes, stopping at every cottage and warning the people to lock up their houses, and keep indoors unless they were armed, and all the elementary schools had broken up by three o'clock, and the

children, scared and keeping together in groups, were hurrying home. Kemp's proclamation—signed indeed by Adye—was posted over almost the whole district by four or five o'clock in the afternoon. It gave briefly but clearly all the conditions of the struggle, the necessity of keeping the Invisible Man from food and sleep, the necessity for incessant watchfulness and for a prompt attention to any evidence of his movements. And so swift and decided was the action of the authorities, so prompt and universal was the belief in this strange being, that before nightfall an area of several hundred square miles was in a stringent state of siege. And before nightfall, too, a thrill of horror went through the whole watching nervous countryside. Going from whispering mouth to mouth, swift and certain over the length and breadth of the country, passed the story of the murder of Mr. Wicksteed.

If our supposition that the Invisible Man's refuge was the Hintondean thickets, then we must suppose that in the early afternoon he sallied out again bent upon some project that involved the use of a weapon. We cannot know what the project was, but the evidence that he had the iron rod in hand before he met Wicksteed is to me at least overwhelming.

Of course we can know nothing of the details of that encounter. It occurred on the edge of a gravel pit, not two hundred yards from Lord Burdock's lodge gate. Everything points to a desperate struggle—the trampled ground, the numerous wounds Mr. Wicksteed received, his splintered walking- stick; but why the attack was made, save in a murderous frenzy, it is impossible to imagine. Indeed the theory of madness is almost unavoidable. Mr. Wicksteed was a man of forty-five or forty-six, steward to Lord Burdock, of inoffensive habits and appearance, the very last person in the world to provoke such a terrible antagonist. Against him it would seem the Invisible Man used an iron rod dragged from a broken piece of fence. He stopped this quiet man, going quietly home to his midday meal, attacked him, beat down his feeble defences, broke his arm, felled him, and smashed his head to a jelly.

Of course, he must have dragged this rod out of the fencing before he met his victim—he must have been carrying it ready in his hand. Only two details beyond what has already been stated seem to bear on the matter. One is the circumstance that the gravel pit was not in Mr. Wicksteed's direct path home, but nearly a couple of hundred yards out of his way. The other is the assertion of a little girl to the effect that, going to her afternoon school, she saw the murdered man "trotting" in a peculiar manner across a field towards the gravel pit. Her pantomime of his action suggests a man pursuing something on the ground before him and striking at it ever and again with his walking- stick. She was the last person to see him alive. He passed out of her sight to his death, the struggle being hidden from her only by a clump of beech trees and a slight depression in the ground.

Now this, to the present writer's mind at least, lifts the murder out of the realm of the absolutely wanton. We may imagine that Griffin had taken the rod as a weapon indeed, but without any deliberate intention of using it in murder. Wicksteed may then have come by and noticed this rod inexplicably moving through

the air. Without any thought of the Invisible Man—for Port Burdock is ten miles away—he may have pursued it. It is quite conceivable that he may not even have heard of the Invisible Man. One can then imagine the Invisible Man making off—quietly in order to avoid discovering his presence in the neighbourhood, and Wicksteed, excited and curious, pursuing this unaccountably locomotive object—finally striking at it.

No doubt the Invisible Man could easily have distanced his middle-aged pursuer under ordinary circumstances, but the position in which Wicksteed's body was found suggests that he had the ill luck to drive his quarry into a corner between a drift of stinging nettles and the gravel pit. To those who appreciate the extraordinary irascibility of the Invisible Man, the rest of the encounter will be easy to imagine.

But this is pure hypothesis. The only undeniable facts—for stories of children are often unreliable—are the discovery of Wicksteed's body, done to death, and of the blood-stained iron rod flung among the nettles. The abandonment of the rod by Griffin, suggests that in the emotional excitement of the affair, the purpose for which he took it—if he had a purpose—was abandoned. He was certainly an intensely egotistical and unfeeling man, but the sight of his victim, his first victim, bloody and pitiful at his feet, may have released some long pent fountain of remorse which for a time may have flooded whatever scheme of action he had contrived.

After the murder of Mr. Wicksteed, he would seem to have struck across the country towards the downland. There is a story of a voice heard about sunset by a couple of men in a field near Fern Bottom. It was wailing and laughing, sobbing and groaning, and ever and again it shouted. It must have been queer hearing. It drove up across the middle of a clover field and died away towards the hills.

That afternoon the Invisible Man must have learnt something of the rapid use Kemp had made of his confidences. He must have found houses locked and secured; he may have loitered about railway stations and prowled about inns, and no doubt he read the proclamations and realised something of the nature of the campaign against him. And as the evening advanced, the fields became dotted here and there with groups of three or four men, and noisy with the yelping of dogs. These men-hunters had particular instructions in the case of an encounter as to the way they should support one another. But he avoided them all. We may understand something of his exasperation, and it could have been none the less because he himself had supplied the information that was being used so remorselessly against him. For that day at least he lost heart; for nearly twenty-four hours, save when he turned on Wicksteed, he was a hunted man. In the night, he must have eaten and slept; for in the morning he was himself again, active, powerful, angry, and malignant, prepared for his last great struggle against the world.

CHAPTER XXVII - THE SIEGE OF KEMP'S HOUSE

Kemp read a strange missive, written in pencil on a greasy sheet of paper.

"You have been amazingly energetic and clever," this letter ran, "though what you stand to gain by it I cannot imagine. You are against me. For a whole day you have chased me; you have tried to rob me of a night's rest. But I have had food in spite of you, I have slept in spite of you, and the game is only beginning. The game is only beginning. There is nothing for it, but to start the Terror. This announces the first day of the Terror. Port Burdock is no longer under the Queen, tell your Colonel of Police, and the rest of them; it is under me—the Terror! This is day one of year one of the new epoch —the Epoch of the Invisible Man. I am Invisible Man the First. To begin with the rule will be easy. The first day there will be one execution for the sake of example—a man named Kemp. Death starts for him to-day. He may lock himself away, hide himself away, get guards about him, put on armour if he likes—Death, the unseen Death, is coming. Let him take precautions; it will impress my people. Death starts from the pillar box by midday. The letter will fall in as the postman comes along, then off! The game begins. Death starts. Help him not, my people, lest Death fall upon you also. To-day Kemp is to die."

Kemp read this letter twice, "It's no hoax," he said. "That's his voice! And he means it."

He turned the folded sheet over and saw on the addressed side of it the postmark Hintondean, and the prosaic detail "2d. to pay."

He got up slowly, leaving his lunch unfinished—the letter had come by the one o'clock post—and went into his study. He rang for his housekeeper, and told her to go round the house at once, examine all the fastenings of the windows, and close all the shutters. He closed the shutters of his study himself. From a locked drawer in his bedroom he took a little revolver, examined it carefully, and put it into the pocket of his lounge jacket. He wrote a number of brief notes, one to Colonel Adye, gave them to his servant to take, with explicit instructions as to her way of leaving the house. "There is no danger," he said, and added a mental reservation, "to you." He remained meditative for a space after doing this, and then returned to his cooling lunch.

He ate with gaps of thought. Finally he struck the table sharply. "We will have him!" he said; "and I am the bait. He will come too far."

He went up to the belvedere, carefully shutting every door after him. "It's a game," he said, "an odd game—but the chances are all for me, Mr. Griffin, in spite of your invisibility. Griffin *contra mundum* ... with a vengeance."

He stood at the window staring at the hot hillside. "He must get food every day—and I don't envy him. Did he really sleep last night? Out in the open somewhere—secure from collisions. I wish we could get some good cold wet weather instead of the heat.

"He may be watching me now."

He went close to the window. Something rapped smartly against the brickwork over the frame, and made him start violently back.

"I'm getting nervous," said Kemp. But it was five minutes before he went to the window again. "It must have been a sparrow," he said.

Presently he heard the front-door bell ringing, and hurried downstairs. He unbolted and unlocked the door, examined the chain, put it up, and opened cautiously without showing himself. A familiar voice hailed him. It was Adye.

"Your servant's been assaulted, Kemp," he said round the door.

"What!" exclaimed Kemp.

"Had that note of yours taken away from her. He's close about here. Let me in."

Kemp released the chain, and Adye entered through as narrow an opening as possible. He stood in the hall, looking with infinite relief at Kemp refastening the door. "Note was snatched out of her hand. Scared her horribly. She's down at the station. Hysterics. He's close here. What was it about?"

Kemp swore.

"What a fool I was," said Kemp. "I might have known. It's not an hour's walk from Hintondean. Already?"

"What's up?" said Adye.

"Look here!" said Kemp, and led the way into his study. He handed Adye the Invisible Man's letter. Adye read it and whistled softly. "And you—?" said Adye.

"Proposed a trap—like a fool," said Kemp, "and sent my proposal out by a maid servant. To him."

Adye followed Kemp's profanity.

"He'll clear out," said Adye.

"Not he," said Kemp.

A resounding smash of glass came from upstairs. Adye had a silvery glimpse of a little revolver half out of Kemp's pocket. "It's a window, upstairs!" said Kemp, and led the way up. There came a second smash while they were still on the staircase. When they reached the study they found two of the three windows smashed, half the room littered with splintered glass, and one big flint lying on the writing table. The two men stopped in the doorway, contemplating the wreckage. Kemp swore again, and as he did so the third window went with a snap like a pistol, hung starred for a moment, and collapsed in jagged, shivering triangles into the room.

"What's this for?" said Adye.

"It's a beginning," said Kemp.

"There's no way of climbing up here?"

"Not for a cat," said Kemp.

"No shutters?"

"Not here. All the downstairs rooms—Hullo!"

Smash, and then whack of boards hit hard came from downstairs. "Confound him!" said Kemp. "That must be—yes—it's one of the bedrooms. He's going to do all the house. But he's a fool. The shutters are up, and the glass will fall outside. He'll cut his feet."

Another window proclaimed its destruction. The two men stood on the landing perplexed. "I have it!" said Adye. "Let me have a stick or something, and I'll go down to the station and get the bloodhounds put on. That ought to settle him! They're hard by—not ten minutes—"

Another window went the way of its fellows.

"You haven't a revolver?" asked Adye.

Kemp's hand went to his pocket. Then he hesitated. "I haven't one—at least to spare."

"I'll bring it back," said Adye, "you'll be safe here."

Kemp, ashamed of his momentary lapse from truthfulness, handed him the weapon.

"Now for the door," said Adye.

As they stood hesitating in the hall, they heard one of the first-floor bedroom windows crack and clash. Kemp went to the door and began to slip the bolts as silently as possible. His face was a little paler than usual. "You must step straight out," said Kemp. In another moment Adye was on the doorstep and the bolts were dropping back into the staples. He hesitated for a moment, feeling more comfortable with his back against the door. Then he marched, upright and square, down the steps. He crossed the lawn and approached the gate. A little breeze seemed to ripple over the grass. Something moved near him. "Stop a bit," said a Voice, and Adye stopped dead and his hand tightened on the revolver.

"Well?" said Adye, white and grim, and every nerve tense.

"Oblige me by going back to the house," said the Voice, as tense and grim as Adye's.

"Sorry," said Adye a little hoarsely, and moistened his lips with his tongue. The Voice was on his left front, he thought. Suppose he were to take his luck with a shot?

"What are you going for?" said the Voice, and there was a quick movement of the two, and a flash of sunlight from the open lip of Adye's pocket.

Adye desisted and thought. "Where I go," he said slowly, "is my own business." The words were still on his lips, when an arm came round his neck, his back felt a knee, and he was sprawling backward. He drew clumsily and fired absurdly, and in another moment he was struck in the mouth and the revolver wrested from his grip. He made a vain clutch at a slippery limb, tried to struggle up and fell back. "Damn!" said Adye. The Voice laughed. "I'd kill you now if it

wasn't the waste of a bullet," it said. He saw the revolver in mid- air, six feet off, covering him.

"Well?" said Adye, sitting up.

"Get up," said the Voice.

Adye stood up.

"Attention," said the Voice, and then fiercely, "Don't try any games. Remember I can see your face if you can't see mine. You've got to go back to the house."

"He won't let me in," said Adye.

"That's a pity," said the Invisible Man. "I've got no quarrel with you."

Adye moistened his lips again. He glanced away from the barrel of the revolver and saw the sea far off very blue and dark under the midday sun, the smooth green down, the white cliff of the Head, and the multitudinous town, and suddenly he knew that life was very sweet. His eyes came back to this little metal thing hanging between heaven and earth, six yards away. "What am I to do?" he said sullenly.

"What am *I* to do?" asked the Invisible Man. "You will get help. The only thing is for you to go back."

"I will try. If he lets me in will you promise not to rush the door?"

"I've got no quarrel with you," said the Voice.

Kemp had hurried upstairs after letting Adye out, and now crouching among the broken glass and peering cautiously over the edge of the study window sill, he saw Adye stand parleying with the Unseen. "Why doesn't he fire?" whispered Kemp to himself. Then the revolver moved a little and the glint of the sunlight flashed in Kemp's eyes. He shaded his eyes and tried to see the source of the blinding beam.

"Surely!" he said, "Adye has given up the revolver."

"Promise not to rush the door," Adye was saying. "Don't push a winning game too far. Give a man a chance."

"You go back to the house. I tell you flatly I will not promise anything."

Adye's decision seemed suddenly made. He turned towards the house, walking slowly with his hands behind him. Kemp watched him—puzzled. The revolver vanished, flashed again into sight, vanished again, and became evident on a closer scrutiny as a little dark object following Adye. Then things happened very quickly. Adye leapt backwards, swung around, clutched at this little object, missed it, threw up his hands and fell forward on his face, leaving a little puff of blue in the air. Kemp did not hear the sound of the shot. Adye writhed, raised himself on one arm, fell forward, and lay still.

For a space Kemp remained staring at the quiet carelessness of Adye's attitude. The afternoon was very hot and still, nothing seemed stirring in all the world save a couple of yellow butterflies chasing each other through the shrubbery between the house and the road gate. Adye lay on the lawn near the gate. The blinds of all the villas down the hill-road were drawn, but in one little green summer-house was a white figure, apparently an old man asleep. Kemp scrutinised the surround-

ings of the house for a glimpse of the revolver, but it had vanished. His eyes came back to Adye. The game was opening well.

Then came a ringing and knocking at the front door, that grew at last tumultuous, but pursuant to Kemp's instructions the servants had locked themselves into their rooms. This was followed by a silence. Kemp sat listening and then began peering cautiously out of the three windows, one after another. He went to the staircase head and stood listening uneasily. He armed himself with his bedroom poker, and went to examine the interior fastenings of the ground-floor windows again. Everything was safe and quiet. He returned to the belvedere. Adye lay motionless over the edge of the gravel just as he had fallen. Coming along the road by the villas were the housemaid and two policemen.

Everything was deadly still. The three people seemed very slow in approaching. He wondered what his antagonist was doing.

He started. There was a smash from below. He hesitated and went downstairs again. Suddenly the house resounded with heavy blows and the splintering of wood. He heard a smash and the destructive clang of the iron fastenings of the shutters. He turned the key and opened the kitchen door. As he did so, the shutters, split and splintering, came flying inward. He stood aghast. The window frame, save for one crossbar, was still intact, but only little teeth of glass remained in the frame. The shutters had been driven in with an axe, and now the axe was descending in sweeping blows upon the window frame and the iron bars defending it. Then suddenly it leapt aside and vanished. He saw the revolver lying on the path outside, and then the little weapon sprang into the air. He dodged back. The revolver cracked just too late, and a splinter from the edge of the closing door flashed over his head. He slammed and locked the door, and as he stood outside he heard Griffin shouting and laughing. Then the blows of the axe with its splitting and smashing consequences, were resumed.

Kemp stood in the passage trying to think. In a moment the Invisible Man would be in the kitchen. This door would not keep him a moment, and then —

A ringing came at the front door again. It would be the policemen. He ran into the hall, put up the chain, and drew the bolts. He made the girl speak before he dropped the chain, and the three people blundered into the house in a heap, and Kemp slammed the door again.

"The Invisible Man!" said Kemp. "He has a revolver, with two shots —left. He's killed Adye. Shot him anyhow. Didn't you see him on the lawn? He's lying there."

"Who?" said one of the policemen.

"Adye," said Kemp.

"We came in the back way," said the girl.

"What's that smashing?" asked one of the policemen.

"He's in the kitchen—or will be. He has found an axe—"

Suddenly the house was full of the Invisible Man's resounding blows on the kitchen door. The girl stared towards the kitchen, shuddered, and retreated into

the dining-room. Kemp tried to explain in broken sentences. They heard the kitchen door give.

"This way," said Kemp, starting into activity, and bundled the policemen into the dining-room doorway.

"Poker," said Kemp, and rushed to the fender. He handed the poker he had carried to the policeman and the dining-room one to the other. He suddenly flung himself backward.

"Whup!" said one policeman, ducked, and caught the axe on his poker. The pistol snapped its penultimate shot and ripped a valuable Sidney Cooper. The second policeman brought his poker down on the little weapon, as one might knock down a wasp, and sent it rattling to the floor.

At the first clash the girl screamed, stood screaming for a moment by the fireplace, and then ran to open the shutters—possibly with an idea of escaping by the shattered window.

The axe receded into the passage, and fell to a position about two feet from the ground. They could hear the Invisible Man breathing. "Stand away, you two," he said. "I want that man Kemp."

"We want you," said the first policeman, making a quick step forward and wiping with his poker at the Voice. The Invisible Man must have started back, and he blundered into the umbrella stand.

Then, as the policeman staggered with the swing of the blow he had aimed, the Invisible Man countered with the axe, the helmet crumpled like paper, and the blow sent the man spinning to the floor at the head of the kitchen stairs. But the second policeman, aiming behind the axe with his poker, hit something soft that snapped. There was a sharp exclamation of pain and then the axe fell to the ground. The policeman wiped again at vacancy and hit nothing; he put his foot on the axe, and struck again. Then he stood, poker clubbed, listening intent for the slightest movement.

He heard the dining-room window open, and a quick rush of feet within. His companion rolled over and sat up, with the blood running down between his eye and ear. "Where is he?" asked the man on the floor.

"Don't know. I've hit him. He's standing somewhere in the hall. Unless he's slipped past you. Doctor Kemp—sir."

Pause.

"Doctor Kemp," cried the policeman again.

The second policeman began struggling to his feet. He stood up. Suddenly the faint pad of bare feet on the kitchen stairs could be heard. "Yap!" cried the first policeman, and incontinently flung his poker. It smashed a little gas bracket.

He made as if he would pursue the Invisible Man downstairs. Then he thought better of it and stepped into the dining-room.

"Doctor Kemp—" he began, and stopped short.

"Doctor Kemp's a hero," he said, as his companion looked over his shoulder.

The dining-room window was wide open, and neither housemaid nor Kemp was to be seen.

The second policeman's opinion of Kemp was terse and vivid.

CHAPTER XXVIII - THE HUNTER HUNTED

Mr. Heelas, Mr. Kemp's nearest neighbour among the villa holders, was asleep in his summer house when the siege of Kemp's house began. Mr. Heelas was one of the sturdy minority who refused to believe "in all this nonsense" about an Invisible Man. His wife, however, as he was subsequently to be reminded, did. He insisted upon walking about his garden just as if nothing was the matter, and he went to sleep in the afternoon in accordance with the custom of years. He slept through the smashing of the windows, and then woke up suddenly with a curious persuasion of something wrong. He looked across at Kemp's house, rubbed his eyes and looked again. Then he put his feet to the ground, and sat listening. He said he was damned, but still the strange thing was visible. The house looked as though it had been deserted for weeks—after a violent riot. Every window was broken, and every window, save those of the belvedere study, was blinded by the internal shutters.

"I could have sworn it was all right"—he looked at his watch —"twenty minutes ago."

He became aware of a measured concussion and the clash of glass, far away in the distance. And then, as he sat open-mouthed, came a still more wonderful thing. The shutters of the drawing-room window were flung open violently, and the housemaid in her outdoor hat and garments, appeared struggling in a frantic manner to throw up the sash. Suddenly a man appeared beside her, helping her — Dr. Kemp! In another moment the window was open, and the housemaid was struggling out; she pitched forward and vanished among the shrubs. Mr. Heelas stood up, exclaiming vaguely and vehemently at all these wonderful things. He saw Kemp stand on the sill, spring from the window, and reappear almost instantaneously running along a path in the shrubbery and stooping as he ran, like a man who evades observation. He vanished behind a laburnum, and appeared again clambering over a fence that abutted on the open down. In a second he had tumbled over and was running at a tremendous pace down the slope towards Mr. Heelas.

"Lord!" cried Mr. Heelas, struck with an idea; "it's that Invisible Man brute! It's right, after all!"

With Mr. Heelas to think things like that was to act, and his cook watching him from the top window was amazed to see him come pelting towards the house at a good nine miles an hour. There was a slamming of doors, a ringing of bells, and the voice of Mr. Heelas bellowing like a bull. "Shut the doors, shut the win-

dows, shut everything!—the Invisible Man is coming!" Instantly the house was full of screams and directions, and scurrying feet. He ran himself to shut the French windows that opened on the veranda; as he did so Kemp's head and shoulders and knee appeared over the edge of the garden fence. In another moment Kemp had ploughed through the asparagus, and was running across the tennis lawn to the house.

"You can't come in," said Mr. Heelas, shutting the bolts. "I'm very sorry if he's after you, but you can't come in!"

Kemp appeared with a face of terror close to the glass, rapping and then shaking frantically at the French window. Then, seeing his efforts were useless, he ran along the veranda, vaulted the end, and went to hammer at the side door. Then he ran round by the side gate to the front of the house, and so into the hill-road. And Mr. Heelas staring from his window—a face of horror—had scarcely witnessed Kemp vanish, ere the asparagus was being trampled this way and that by feet unseen. At that Mr. Heelas fled precipitately upstairs, and the rest of the chase is beyond his purview. But as he passed the staircase window, he heard the side gate slam.

Emerging into the hill-road, Kemp naturally took the downward direction, and so it was he came to run in his own person the very race he had watched with such a critical eye from the belvedere study only four days ago. He ran it well, for a man out of training, and though his face was white and wet, his wits were cool to the last. He ran with wide strides, and wherever a patch of rough ground intervened, wherever there came a patch of raw flints, or a bit of broken glass shone dazzling, he crossed it and left the bare invisible feet that followed to take what line they would.

For the first time in his life Kemp discovered that the hill-road was indescribably vast and desolate, and that the beginnings of the town far below at the hill foot were strangely remote. Never had there been a slower or more painful method of progression than running. All the gaunt villas, sleeping in the afternoon sun, looked locked and barred; no doubt they were locked and barred—by his own orders. But at any rate they might have kept a lookout for an eventuality like this! The town was rising up now, the sea had dropped out of sight behind it, and people down below were stirring. A tram was just arriving at the hill foot. Beyond that was the police station. Was that footsteps he heard behind him? Spurt.

The people below were staring at him, one or two were running, and his breath was beginning to saw in his throat. The tram was quite near now, and the "Jolly Cricketers" was noisily barring its doors. Beyond the tram were posts and heaps of gravel—the drainage works. He had a transitory idea of jumping into the tram and slamming the doors, and then he resolved to go for the police station. In another moment he had passed the door of the "Jolly Cricketers," and was in the blistering fag end of the street, with human beings about him. The tram driver and his helper—arrested by the sight of his furious haste—stood staring with the tram horses unhitched. Further on the astonished features of navvies appeared above the mounds of gravel.

His pace broke a little, and then he heard the swift pad of his pursuer, and leapt forward again. "The Invisible Man!" he cried to the navvies, with a vague indicative gesture, and by an inspiration leapt the excavation and placed a burly group between him and the chase. Then abandoning the idea of the police station he turned into a little side street, rushed by a greengrocer's cart, hesitated for the tenth of a second at the door of a sweetstuff shop, and then made for the mouth of an alley that ran back into the main Hill Street again. Two or three little children were playing here, and shrieked and scattered at his apparition, and forthwith doors and windows opened and excited mothers revealed their hearts. Out he shot into Hill Street again, three hundred yards from the tram-line end, and immediately he became aware of a tumultuous vociferation and running people.

He glanced up the street towards the hill. Hardly a dozen yards off ran a huge navvy, cursing in fragments and slashing viciously with a spade, and hard behind him came the tram conductor with his fists clenched. Up the street others followed these two, striking and shouting. Down towards the town, men and women were running, and he noticed clearly one man coming out of a shop- door with a stick in his hand. "Spread out! Spread out!" cried some one. Kemp suddenly grasped the altered condition of the chase. He stopped, and looked round, panting. "He's close here!" he cried. "Form a line across—"

He was hit hard under the ear, and went reeling, trying to face round towards his unseen antagonist. He just managed to keep his feet, and he struck a vain counter in the air. Then he was hit again under the jaw, and sprawled headlong on the ground. In another moment a knee compressed his diaphragm, and a couple of eager hands gripped his throat, but the grip of one was weaker than the other; he grasped the wrists, heard a cry of pain from his assailant, and then the spade of the navvy came whirling through the air above him, and struck something with a dull thud. He felt a drop of moisture on his face. The grip at his throat suddenly relaxed, and with a convulsive effort, Kemp loosed himself, grasped a limp shoulder, and rolled uppermost. He gripped the unseen elbows near the ground. "I've got him!" screamed Kemp. "Help! Help—hold! He's down! Hold his feet!"

In another second there was a simultaneous rush upon the struggle, and a stranger coming into the road suddenly might have thought an exceptionally savage game of Rugby football was in progress. And there was no shouting after Kemp's cry—only a sound of blows and feet and heavy breathing.

Then came a mighty effort, and the Invisible Man threw off a couple of his antagonists and rose to his knees. Kemp clung to him in front like a hound to a stag, and a dozen hands gripped, clutched, and tore at the Unseen. The tram conductor suddenly got the neck and shoulders and lugged him back.

Down went the heap of struggling men again and rolled over. There was, I am afraid, some savage kicking. Then suddenly a wild scream of "Mercy! Mercy!" that died down swiftly to a sound like choking.

"Get back, you fools!" cried the muffled voice of Kemp, and there was a vigorous shoving back of stalwart forms. "He's hurt, I tell you. Stand back!"

There was a brief struggle to clear a space, and then the circle of eager faces saw the doctor kneeling, as it seemed, fifteen inches in the air, and holding invisible arms to the ground. Behind him a constable gripped invisible ankles.

"Don't you leave go of en," cried the big navvy, holding a blood-stained spade; "he's shamming."

"He's not shamming," said the doctor, cautiously raising his knee; "and I'll hold him." His face was bruised and already going red; he spoke thickly because of a bleeding lip. He released one hand and seemed to be feeling at the face. "The mouth's all wet," he said. And then, "Good God!"

He stood up abruptly and then knelt down on the ground by the side of the thing unseen. There was a pushing and shuffling, a sound of heavy feet as fresh people turned up to increase the pressure of the crowd. People now were coming out of the houses. The doors of the "Jolly Cricketers" stood suddenly wide open. Very little was said.

Kemp felt about, his hand seeming to pass through empty air. "He's not breathing," he said, and then, "I can't feel his heart. His side—ugh!"

Suddenly an old woman, peering under the arm of the big navvy, screamed sharply. "Looky there!" she said, and thrust out a wrinkled finger.

And looking where she pointed, everyone saw, faint and transparent as though it was made of glass, so that veins and arteries and bones and nerves could be distinguished, the outline of a hand, a hand limp and prone. It grew clouded and opaque even as they stared.

"Hullo!" cried the constable. "Here's his feet a-showing!"

And so, slowly, beginning at his hands and feet and creeping along his limbs to the vital centres of his body, that strange change continued. It was like the slow spreading of a poison. First came the little white nerves, a hazy grey sketch of a limb, then the glassy bones and intricate arteries, then the flesh and skin, first a faint fogginess, and then growing rapidly dense and opaque. Presently they could see his crushed chest and his shoulders, and the dim outline of his drawn and battered features.

When at last the crowd made way for Kemp to stand erect, there lay, naked and pitiful on the ground, the bruised and broken body of a young man about thirty. His hair and brow were white—not grey with age, but white with the whiteness of albinism—and his eyes were like garnets. His hands were clenched, his eyes wide open, and his expression was one of anger and dismay.

"Cover his face!" said a man. "For Gawd's sake, cover that face!" and three little children, pushing forward through the crowd, were suddenly twisted round and sent packing off again.

Someone brought a sheet from the "Jolly Cricketers," and having covered him, they carried him into that house. And there it was, on a shabby bed in a tawdry, ill-lighted bedroom, surrounded by a crowd of ignorant and excited people, broken and wounded, betrayed and unpitied, that Griffin, the first of all men to make himself invisible, Griffin, the most gifted physicist the world has ever seen, ended in infinite disaster his strange and terrible career.

THE EPILOGUE - So ends the story of the strange and evil experiments of the Invisible Man. And if you would learn more of him you must go to a little inn near Port Stowe and talk to the landlord. The sign of the inn is an empty board save for a hat and boots, and the name is the title of this story. The landlord is a short and corpulent little man with a nose of cylindrical proportions, wiry hair, and a sporadic rosiness of visage. Drink generously, and he will tell you generously of all the things that happened to him after that time, and of how the lawyers tried to do him out of the treasure found upon him.

"When they found they couldn't prove who's money was which, I'm blessed," he says, "if they didn't try to make me out a blooming treasure trove! Do I *look* like a Treasure Trove? And then a gentleman gave me a guinea a night to tell the story at the Empire Music 'All—just to tell 'em in my own words—barring one."

And if you want to cut off the flow of his reminiscences abruptly, you can always do so by asking if there weren't three manuscript books in the story. He admits there were and proceeds to explain, with asseverations that everybody thinks *he* has 'em! But bless you! he hasn't. "The Invisible Man it was took 'em off to hide 'em when I cut and ran for Port Stowe. It's that Mr. Kemp put people on with the idea of *my* having 'em."

And then he subsides into a pensive state, watches you furtively, bustles nervously with glasses, and presently leaves the bar.

He is a bachelor man—his tastes were ever bachelor, and there are no women folk in the house. Outwardly he buttons—it is expected of him —but in his more vital privacies, in the matter of braces for example, he still turns to string. He conducts his house without enterprise, but with eminent decorum. His movements are slow, and he is a great thinker. But he has a reputation for wisdom and for a respectable parsimony in the village, and his knowledge of the roads of the South of England would beat Cobbett.

And on Sunday mornings, every Sunday morning, all the year round, while he is closed to the outer world, and every night after ten, he goes into his bar parlour, bearing a glass of gin faintly tinged with water, and having placed this down, he locks the door and examines the blinds, and even looks under the table. And then, being satisfied of his solitude, he unlocks the cupboard and a box in the cupboard and a drawer in that box, and produces three volumes bound in brown leather, and places them solemnly in the middle of the table. The covers are weather-worn and tinged with an algal green—for once they sojourned in a ditch and some of the pages have been washed blank by dirty water. The landlord sits down in an armchair, fills a long clay pipe slowly—gloating over the books the while. Then he pulls one towards him and opens it, and begins to study it—turning over the leaves backwards and forwards.

His brows are knit and his lips move painfully. "Hex, little two up in the air, cross and a fiddle-de-dee. Lord! what a one he was for intellect!"

Presently he relaxes and leans back, and blinks through his smoke across the room at things invisible to other eyes. "Full of secrets," he says. "Wonderful secrets!"

"Once I get the haul of them—*Lord*!"

"I wouldn't do what *he* did; I'd just—well!" He pulls at his pipe.

So he lapses into a dream, the undying wonderful dream of his life. And though Kemp has fished unceasingly, no human being save the landlord knows those books are there, with the subtle secret of invisibility and a dozen other strange secrets written therein. And none other will know of them until he dies.

THE ISLAND OF DOCTOR MOREAU

First published by William Heinemann, London, 1896

NOTE. The substance of the chapter entitled "Doctor Moreau Explains," which contains the essential idea of the story, appeared as a middle article in *The Saturday Review* in January, 1895. This is the only portion of this story that has been previously published, and it has been entirely recast to adapt it to the narrative form.

INTRODUCTION

On February the First, 1887, the "Lady Vain" was lost by collision with a derelict when about the latitude 1° S. and longitude 107° W.

On January the Fifth, 1888—that is eleven months and four days after—my uncle, Edward Prendick, a private gentleman, who certainly went aboard the Lady Vain at Callao, and who had been considered drowned, was picked up in latitude 5° 3' S. and longitude 101° W. in a small open boat of which the name was illegible, but which is supposed to have belonged to the missing schooner Ipecacuanha. He gave such a strange account of himself that he was supposed demented. Subsequently he alleged that his mind was a blank from the moment of his escape from the Lady Vain. His case was discussed among psychologists at the time as a curious instance of the lapse of memory consequent upon physical and mental stress. The following narrative was found among his papers by the undersigned, his nephew and heir, but unaccompanied by any definite request for publication.

The only island known to exist in the region in which my uncle was picked up is Noble's Isle, a small volcanic islet and uninhabited. It was visited in 1891 by H. M. S. Scorpion. A party of sailors then landed, but found nothing living thereon except certain curious white moths, some hogs and rabbits, and some rather peculiar rats. So that this narrative is without confirmation in its most essential particular. With that understood, there seems no harm in putting this strange story before the public in accordance, as I believe, with my uncle's intentions. There is at least this much in its behalf: my uncle passed out of human knowledge about latitude 5° S. and longitude 105° E., and reappeared in the same part of the ocean after a space of eleven months. In some way he must have lived during the interval. And it seems that a schooner called the Ipecacuanha with a drunken captain, John Davies, did start from Africa with a puma and certain other animals aboard in January, 1887, that the vessel was well known at several ports in the South Pacific, and that it finally disappeared from those seas (with a considerable amount of copra aboard), sailing to its unknown fate from Bayna in December, 1887, a date that tallies entirely with my uncle's story.

CHARLES EDWARD PRENDICK.

THE STORY WRITTEN BY EDWARD PRENDICK

I. IN THE DINGEY OF THE "LADY VAIN"

I do not propose to add anything to what has already been written concerning the loss of the "Lady Vain." As everyone knows, she collided with a derelict when ten days out from Callao. The longboat, with seven of the crew, was picked up eighteen days after by H. M. gunboat "Myrtle," and the story of their terrible privations has become quite as well known as the far more horrible "Medusa" case. But I have to add to the published story of the "Lady Vain" another, possibly as horrible and far stranger. It has hitherto been supposed that the four men who were in the dingey perished, but this is incorrect. I have the best of evidence for this assertion: I was one of the four men.

But in the first place I must state that there never were four men in the dingey,—the number was three. Constans, who was "seen by the captain to jump into the gig,"[1] luckily for us and unluckily for himself did not reach us. He came down out of the tangle of ropes under the stays of the smashed bowsprit, some small rope caught his heel as he let go, and he hung for a moment head downward, and then fell and struck a block or spar floating in the water. We pulled towards him, but he never came up.

I say lucky for us he did not reach us, and I might almost say luckily for himself; for we had only a small breaker of water and some soddened ship's biscuits with us, so sudden had been the alarm, so unprepared the ship for any disaster. We thought the people on the launch would be better provisioned (though it seems they were not), and we tried to hail them. They could not have heard us, and the next morning when the drizzle cleared,—which was not until past midday,—we could see nothing of them. We could not stand up to look about us, because of the pitching of the boat. The two other men who had escaped so far with me were a man named Helmar, a passenger like myself, and a seaman whose name I don't know,—a short sturdy man, with a stammer.

[1] Daily News, March 17, 1887.

We drifted famishing, and, after our water had come to an end, tormented by an intolerable thirst, for eight days altogether. After the second day the sea subsided slowly to a glassy calm. It is quite impossible for the ordinary reader to imagine those eight days. He has not, luckily for himself, anything in his memory to imagine with. After the first day we said little to one another, and lay in our places in the boat and stared at the horizon, or watched, with eyes that grew larger and more haggard every day, the misery and weakness gaining upon our companions. The sun became pitiless. The water ended on the fourth day, and we were already thinking strange things and saying them with our eyes; but it was, I think, the sixth before Helmar gave voice to the thing we had all been thinking. I remember our voices were dry and thin, so that we bent towards one another and spared our words. I stood out against it with all my might, was rather for scuttling the boat and perishing together among the sharks that followed us; but when Helmar said that if his proposal was accepted we should have drink, the sailor came round to him.

I would not draw lots however, and in the night the sailor whispered to Helmar again and again, and I sat in the bows with my clasp-knife in my hand, though I doubt if I had the stuff in me to fight; and in the morning I agreed to Helmar's proposal, and we handed halfpence to find the odd man. The lot fell upon the sailor; but he was the strongest of us and would not abide by it, and attacked Helmar with his hands. They grappled together and almost stood up. I crawled along the boat to them, intending to help Helmar by grasping the sailor's leg; but the sailor stumbled with the swaying of the boat, and the two fell upon the gunwale and rolled overboard together. They sank like stones. I remember laughing at that, and wondering why I laughed. The laugh caught me suddenly like a thing from without.

I lay across one of the thwarts for I know not how long, thinking that if I had the strength I would drink sea-water and madden myself to die quickly. And even as I lay there I saw, with no more interest than if it had been a picture, a sail come up towards me over the sky-line. My mind must have been wandering, and yet I remember all that happened, quite distinctly. I remember how my head swayed with the seas, and the horizon with the sail above it danced up and down; but I also remember as distinctly that I had a persuasion that I was dead, and that I thought what a jest it was that they should come too late by such a little to catch me in my body.

For an endless period, as it seemed to me, I lay with my head on the thwart watching the schooner (she was a little ship, schooner-rigged fore and aft) come up out of the sea. She kept tacking to and fro in a widening compass, for she was sailing dead into the wind. It never entered my head to attempt to attract attention, and I do not remember anything distinctly after the sight of her side until I found myself in a little cabin aft. There's a dim half-memory of being lifted up to the gangway, and of a big round countenance covered with freckles and surrounded with red hair staring at me over the bulwarks. I also had a disconnected impression of a dark face, with extraordinary eyes, close to mine; but that I thought was

a nightmare, until I met it again. I fancy I recollect some stuff being poured in between my teeth; and that is all.

II. THE MAN WHO WAS GOING NOWHERE.

The cabin in which I found myself was small and rather untidy. A youngish man with flaxen hair, a bristly straw-coloured moustache, and a dropping nether lip, was sitting and holding my wrist. For a minute we stared at each other without speaking. He had watery grey eyes, oddly void of expression. Then just overhead came a sound like an iron bedstead being knocked about, and the low angry growling of some large animal. At the same time the man spoke. He repeated his question,—"How do you feel now?"

I think I said I felt all right. I could not recollect how I had got there. He must have seen the question in my face, for my voice was inaccessible to me.

"You were picked up in a boat, starving. The name on the boat was the 'Lady Vain,' and there were spots of blood on the gunwale."

At the same time my eye caught my hand, so thin that it looked like a dirty skin-purse full of loose bones, and all the business of the boat came back to me.

"Have some of this," said he, and gave me a dose of some scarlet stuff, iced.

It tasted like blood, and made me feel stronger.

"You were in luck," said he, "to get picked up by a ship with a medical man aboard." He spoke with a slobbering articulation, with the ghost of a lisp.

"What ship is this?" I said slowly, hoarse from my long silence.

"It's a little trader from Arica and Callao. I never asked where she came from in the beginning,—out of the land of born fools, I guess. I'm a passenger myself, from Arica. The silly ass who owns her,—he's captain too, named Davies,—he's lost his certificate, or something. You know the kind of man,—calls the thing the 'Ipecacuanha,' of all silly, infernal names; though when there's much of a sea without any wind, she certainly acts according."

(Then the noise overhead began again, a snarling growl and the voice of a human being together. Then another voice, telling some "Heaven-forsaken idiot" to desist.)

"You were nearly dead," said my interlocutor. "It was a very near thing, indeed. But I've put some stuff into you now. Notice your arm's sore? Injections. You've been insensible for nearly thirty hours."

I thought slowly. (I was distracted now by the yelping of a number of dogs.) "Am I eligible for solid food?" I asked.

"Thanks to me," he said. "Even now the mutton is boiling."

"Yes," I said with assurance; "I could eat some mutton."

"But," said he with a momentary hesitation, "you know I'm dying to hear of how you came to be alone in that boat. Damn that howling!" I thought I detected a certain suspicion in his eyes.

He suddenly left the cabin, and I heard him in violent controversy with some one, who seemed to me to talk gibberish in response to him. The matter sounded as though it ended in blows, but in that I thought my ears were mistaken. Then he shouted at the dogs, and returned to the cabin.

"Well?" said he in the doorway. "You were just beginning to tell me."

I told him my name, Edward Prendick, and how I had taken to Natural History as a relief from the dulness of my comfortable independence.

He seemed interested in this. "I've done some science myself. I did my Biology at University College,—getting out the ovary of the earthworm and the radula of the snail, and all that. Lord! It's ten years ago. But go on! go on! tell me about the boat."

He was evidently satisfied with the frankness of my story, which I told in concise sentences enough, for I felt horribly weak; and when it was finished he reverted at once to the topic of Natural History and his own biological studies. He began to question me closely about Tottenham Court Road and Gower Street. "Is Caplatzi still flourishing? What a shop that was!" He had evidently been a very ordinary medical student, and drifted incontinently to the topic of the music halls. He told me some anecdotes.

"Left it all," he said, "ten years ago. How jolly it all used to be! But I made a young ass of myself,—played myself out before I was twenty- one. I daresay it's all different now. But I must look up that ass of a cook, and see what he's done to your mutton."

The growling overhead was renewed, so suddenly and with so much savage anger that it startled me. "What's that?" I called after him, but the door had closed. He came back again with the boiled mutton, and I was so excited by the appetising smell of it that I forgot the noise of the beast that had troubled me.

After a day of alternate sleep and feeding I was so far recovered as to be able to get from my bunk to the scuttle, and see the green seas trying to keep pace with us. I judged the schooner was running before the wind. Montgomery—that was the name of the flaxen-haired man—came in again as I stood there, and I asked him for some clothes. He lent me some duck things of his own, for those I had worn in the boat had been thrown overboard. They were rather loose for me, for he was large and long in his limbs. He told me casually that the captain was three-parts drunk in his own cabin. As I assumed the clothes, I began asking him some questions about the destination of the ship. He said the ship was bound to Hawaii, but that it had to land him first.

"Where?" said I.

"It's an island, where I live. So far as I know, it hasn't got a name."

He stared at me with his nether lip dropping, and looked so wilfully stupid of a sudden that it came into my head that he desired to avoid my questions. I had the discretion to ask no more.

III. THE STRANGE FACE

We left the cabin and found a man at the companion obstructing our way. He was standing on the ladder with his back to us, peering over the combing of the hatchway. He was, I could see, a misshapen man, short, broad, and clumsy, with a crooked back, a hairy neck, and a head sunk between his shoulders. He was dressed in dark-blue serge, and had peculiarly thick, coarse, black hair. I heard the unseen dogs growl furiously, and forthwith he ducked back,—coming into contact with the hand I put out to fend him off from myself. He turned with animal swiftness.

In some indefinable way the black face thus flashed upon me shocked me profoundly. It was a singularly deformed one. The facial part projected, forming something dimly suggestive of a muzzle, and the huge half-open mouth showed as big white teeth as I had ever seen in a human mouth. His eyes were blood-shot at the edges, with scarcely a rim of white round the hazel pupils. There was a curious glow of excitement in his face.

"Confound you!" said Montgomery. "Why the devil don't you get out of the way?"

The black-faced man started aside without a word. I went on up the companion, staring at him instinctively as I did so. Montgomery stayed at the foot for a moment. "You have no business here, you know," he said in a deliberate tone. "Your place is forward."

The black-faced man cowered. "They—won't have me forward." He spoke slowly, with a queer, hoarse quality in his voice.

"Won't have you forward!" said Montgomery, in a menacing voice. "But I tell you to go!" He was on the brink of saying something further, then looked up at me suddenly and followed me up the ladder.

I had paused half way through the hatchway, looking back, still astonished beyond measure at the grotesque ugliness of this black-faced creature. I had never beheld such a repulsive and extraordinary face before, and yet—if the contradiction is credible—I experienced at the same time an odd feeling that in some way I *had* already encountered exactly the features and gestures that now amazed me. Afterwards it occurred to me that probably I had seen him as I was lifted aboard; and yet that scarcely satisfied my suspicion of a previous acquaintance. Yet how one could have set eyes on so singular a face and yet have forgotten the precise occasion, passed my imagination.

Montgomery's movement to follow me released my attention, and I turned and looked about me at the flush deck of the little schooner. I was already half prepared by the sounds I had heard for what I saw. Certainly I never beheld a deck so dirty. It was littered with scraps of carrot, shreds of green stuff, and indescribable filth. Fastened by chains to the mainmast were a number of grisly staghounds, who now began leaping and barking at me, and by the mizzen a huge puma was cramped in a little iron cage far too small even to give it turning room. Farther under the starboard bulwark were some big hutches containing a number of rabbits, and a solitary llama was squeezed in a mere box of a cage forward. The dogs were muzzled by leather straps. The only human being on deck was a gaunt and silent sailor at the wheel.

The patched and dirty spankers were tense before the wind, and up aloft the little ship seemed carrying every sail she had. The sky was clear, the sun midway down the western sky; long waves, capped by the breeze with froth, were running with us. We went past the steersman to the taffrail, and saw the water come foaming under the stern and the bubbles go dancing and vanishing in her wake. I turned and surveyed the unsavoury length of the ship.

"Is this an ocean menagerie?" said I.

"Looks like it," said Montgomery.

"What are these beasts for? Merchandise, curios? Does the captain think he is going to sell them somewhere in the South Seas?"

"It looks like it, doesn't it?" said Montgomery, and turned towards the wake again.

Suddenly we heard a yelp and a volley of furious blasphemy from the companion hatchway, and the deformed man with the black face came up hurriedly. He was immediately followed by a heavy red-haired man in a white cap. At the sight of the former the staghounds, who had all tired of barking at me by this time, became furiously excited, howling and leaping against their chains. The black hesitated before them, and this gave the red-haired man time to come up with him and deliver a tremendous blow between the shoulder-blades. The poor devil went down like a felled ox, and rolled in the dirt among the furiously excited dogs. It was lucky for him that they were muzzled. The red-haired man gave a yawp of exultation and stood staggering, and as it seemed to me in serious danger of either going backwards down the companion hatchway or forwards upon his victim.

So soon as the second man had appeared, Montgomery had started forward. "Steady on there!" he cried, in a tone of remonstrance. A couple of sailors appeared on the forecastle. The black-faced man, howling in a singular voice rolled about under the feet of the dogs. No one attempted to help him. The brutes did their best to worry him, butting their muzzles at him. There was a quick dance of their lithe grey-figured bodies over the clumsy, prostrate figure. The sailors forward shouted, as though it was admirable sport. Montgomery gave an angry exclamation, and went striding down the deck, and I followed him. The black-faced man scrambled up and staggered forward, going and leaning over the bul-

wark by the main shrouds, where he remained, panting and glaring over his shoulder at the dogs. The red-haired man laughed a satisfied laugh.

"Look here, Captain," said Montgomery, with his lisp a little accentuated, gripping the elbows of the red-haired man, "this won't do!"

I stood behind Montgomery. The captain came half round, and regarded him with the dull and solemn eyes of a drunken man. "Wha' won't do?" he said, and added, after looking sleepily into Montgomery's face for a minute, "Blasted Sawbones!"

With a sudden movement he shook his arms free, and after two ineffectual attempts stuck his freckled fists into his side pockets.

"That man's a passenger," said Montgomery. "I'd advise you to keep your hands off him."

"Go to hell!" said the captain, loudly. He suddenly turned and staggered towards the side. "Do what I like on my own ship," he said.

I think Montgomery might have left him then, seeing the brute was drunk; but he only turned a shade paler, and followed the captain to the bulwarks.

"Look you here, Captain," he said; "that man of mine is not to be ill- treated. He has been hazed ever since he came aboard."

For a minute, alcoholic fumes kept the captain speechless. "Blasted Sawbones!" was all he considered necessary.

I could see that Montgomery had one of those slow, pertinacious tempers that will warm day after day to a white heat, and never again cool to forgiveness; and I saw too that this quarrel had been some time growing. "The man's drunk," said I, perhaps officiously; "you'll do no good."

Montgomery gave an ugly twist to his dropping lip. "He's always drunk. Do you think that excuses his assaulting his passengers?"

"My ship," began the captain, waving his hand unsteadily towards the cages, "was a clean ship. Look at it now!" It was certainly anything but clean. "Crew," continued the captain, "clean, respectable crew."

"You agreed to take the beasts."

"I wish I'd never set eyes on your infernal island. What the devil —want beasts for on an island like that? Then, that man of yours—understood he was a man. He's a lunatic; and he hadn't no business aft. Do you think the whole damned ship belongs to you?"

"Your sailors began to haze the poor devil as soon as he came aboard."

"That's just what he is—he's a devil! an ugly devil! My men can't stand him. *I* can't stand him. None of us can't stand him. Nor *you* either!"

Montgomery turned away. "*You* leave that man alone, anyhow," he said, nodding his head as he spoke.

But the captain meant to quarrel now. He raised his voice. "If he comes this end of the ship again I'll cut his insides out, I tell you. Cut out his blasted insides! Who are you, to tell me what I'm to do? I tell you I'm captain of this ship,—captain and owner. I'm the law here, I tell you,—the law and the prophets. I bar-

gained to take a man and his attendant to and from Arica, and bring back some animals. I never bargained to carry a mad devil and a silly Sawbones, a—"

Well, never mind what he called Montgomery. I saw the latter take a step forward, and interposed. "He's drunk," said I. The captain began some abuse even fouler than the last. "Shut up!" I said, turning on him sharply, for I had seen danger in Montgomery's white face. With that I brought the downpour on myself.

However, I was glad to avert what was uncommonly near a scuffle, even at the price of the captain's drunken ill-will. I do not think I have ever heard quite so much vile language come in a continuous stream from any man's lips before, though I have frequented eccentric company enough. I found some of it hard to endure, though I am a mild-tempered man; but, certainly, when I told the captain to "shut up" I had forgotten that I was merely a bit of human flotsam, cut off from my resources and with my fare unpaid; a mere casual dependant on the bounty, or speculative enterprise, of the ship. He reminded me of it with considerable vigour; but at any rate I prevented a fight.

IV. AT THE SCHOONER'S RAIL

That night land was sighted after sundown, and the schooner hove to. Montgomery intimated that was his destination. It was too far to see any details; it seemed to me then simply a low-lying patch of dim blue in the uncertain blue-grey sea. An almost vertical streak of smoke went up from it into the sky. The captain was not on deck when it was sighted. After he had vented his wrath on me he had staggered below, and I understand he went to sleep on the floor of his own cabin. The mate practically assumed the command. He was the gaunt, taciturn individual we had seen at the wheel. Apparently he was in an evil temper with Montgomery. He took not the slightest notice of either of us. We dined with him in a sulky silence, after a few ineffectual efforts on my part to talk. It struck me too that the men regarded my companion and his animals in a singularly unfriendly manner. I found Montgomery very reticent about his purpose with these creatures, and about his destination; and though I was sensible of a growing curiosity as to both, I did not press him.

We remained talking on the quarter deck until the sky was thick with stars. Except for an occasional sound in the yellow-lit forecastle and a movement of the animals now and then, the night was very still. The puma lay crouched together, watching us with shining eyes, a black heap in the corner of its cage. Montgomery produced some cigars. He talked to me of London in a tone of half-painful reminiscence, asking all kinds of questions about changes that had taken place. He spoke like a man who had loved his life there, and had been suddenly and irrevocably cut off from it. I gossiped as well as I could of this and that. All the time the strangeness of him was shaping itself in my mind; and as I talked I peered at his odd, pallid face in the dim light of the binnacle lantern behind me. Then I looked out at the darkling sea, where in the dimness his little island was hidden.

This man, it seemed to me, had come out of Immensity merely to save my life. To-morrow he would drop over the side, and vanish again out of my existence. Even had it been under commonplace circumstances, it would have made me a trifle thoughtful; but in the first place was the singularity of an educated man living on this unknown little island, and coupled with that the extraordinary nature of his luggage. I found myself repeating the captain's question, What did he want with the beasts? Why, too, had he pretended they were not his when I had remarked about them at first? Then, again, in his personal attendant there was a bizarre quality which had impressed me profoundly. These circumstances threw a

haze of mystery round the man. They laid hold of my imagination, and hampered my tongue.

Towards midnight our talk of London died away, and we stood side by side leaning over the bulwarks and staring dreamily over the silent, starlit sea, each pursuing his own thoughts. It was the atmosphere for sentiment, and I began upon my gratitude.

"If I may say it," said I, after a time, "you have saved my life."

"Chance," he answered. "Just chance."

"I prefer to make my thanks to the accessible agent."

"Thank no one. You had the need, and I had the knowledge; and I injected and fed you much as I might have collected a specimen. I was bored and wanted something to do. If I'd been jaded that day, or hadn't liked your face, well —it's a curious question where you would have been now!"

This damped my mood a little. "At any rate," I began.

"It's a chance, I tell you," he interrupted, "as everything is in a man's life. Only the asses won't see it! Why am I here now, an outcast from civilisation, instead of being a happy man enjoying all the pleasures of London? Simply because eleven years ago—I lost my head for ten minutes on a foggy night."

He stopped. "Yes?" said I.

"That's all."

We relapsed into silence. Presently he laughed. "There's something in this starlight that loosens one's tongue. I'm an ass, and yet somehow I would like to tell you."

"Whatever you tell me, you may rely upon my keeping to myself—if that's it."

He was on the point of beginning, and then shook his head, doubtfully.

"Don't," said I. "It is all the same to me. After all, it is better to keep your secret. There's nothing gained but a little relief if I respect your confidence. If I don't—well?"

He grunted undecidedly. I felt I had him at a disadvantage, had caught him in the mood of indiscretion; and to tell the truth I was not curious to learn what might have driven a young medical student out of London. I have an imagination. I shrugged my shoulders and turned away. Over the taffrail leant a silent black figure, watching the stars. It was Montgomery's strange attendant. It looked over its shoulder quickly with my movement, then looked away again.

It may seem a little thing to you, perhaps, but it came like a sudden blow to me. The only light near us was a lantern at the wheel. The creature's face was turned for one brief instant out of the dimness of the stern towards this illumination, and I saw that the eyes that glanced at me shone with a pale- green light. I did not know then that a reddish luminosity, at least, is not uncommon in human eyes. The thing came to me as stark inhumanity. That black figure with its eyes of fire struck down through all my adult thoughts and feelings, and for a moment the forgotten horrors of childhood came back to my mind. Then the effect passed as it had come. An uncouth black figure of a man, a figure of no particular import,

hung over the taffrail against the starlight, and I found Montgomery was speaking to me.

"I'm thinking of turning in, then," said he, "if you've had enough of this."

I answered him incongruously. We went below, and he wished me good-night at the door of my cabin.

That night I had some very unpleasant dreams. The waning moon rose late. Its light struck a ghostly white beam across my cabin, and made an ominous shape on the planking by my bunk. Then the staghounds woke, and began howling and baying; so that I dreamt fitfully, and scarcely slept until the approach of dawn.

V. THE MAN WHO HAD NOWHERE TO GO

In the early morning (it was the second morning after my recovery, and I believe the fourth after I was picked up), I awoke through an avenue of tumultuous dreams,—dreams of guns and howling mobs,—and became sensible of a hoarse shouting above me. I rubbed my eyes and lay listening to the noise, doubtful for a little while of my whereabouts. Then came a sudden pattering of bare feet, the sound of heavy objects being thrown about, a violent creaking and the rattling of chains. I heard the swish of the water as the ship was suddenly brought round, and a foamy yellow-green wave flew across the little round window and left it streaming. I jumped into my clothes and went on deck.

As I came up the ladder I saw against the flushed sky—for the sun was just rising—the broad back and red hair of the captain, and over his shoulder the puma spinning from a tackle rigged on to the mizzen spanker- boom.

The poor brute seemed horribly scared, and crouched in the bottom of its little cage.

"Overboard with 'em!" bawled the captain. "Overboard with 'em! We'll have a clean ship soon of the whole bilin' of 'em."

He stood in my way, so that I had perforce to tap his shoulder to come on deck. He came round with a start, and staggered back a few paces to stare at me. It needed no expert eye to tell that the man was still drunk.

"Hullo!" said he, stupidly; and then with a light coming into his eyes, "Why, it's Mister—Mister?"

"Prendick," said I.

"Prendick be damned!" said he. "Shut-up,—that's your name. Mister Shut-up."

It was no good answering the brute; but I certainly did not expect his next move. He held out his hand to the gangway by which Montgomery stood talking to a massive grey-haired man in dirty-blue flannels, who had apparently just come aboard.

"That way, Mister Blasted Shut-up! that way!" roared the captain.

Montgomery and his companion turned as he spoke.

"What do you mean?" I said.

"That way, Mister Blasted Shut-up,—that's what I mean! Overboard, Mister Shut-up,—and sharp! We're cleaning the ship out,—cleaning the whole blessed ship out; and overboard you go!"

I stared at him dumfounded. Then it occurred to me that it was exactly the thing I wanted. The lost prospect of a journey as sole passenger with this quarrelsome sot was not one to mourn over. I turned towards Montgomery.

"Can't have you," said Montgomery's companion, concisely.

"You can't have me!" said I, aghast. He had the squarest and most resolute face I ever set eyes upon.

"Look here," I began, turning to the captain.

"Overboard!" said the captain. "This ship aint for beasts and cannibals and worse than beasts, any more. Overboard you go, Mister Shut-up. If they can't have you, you goes overboard. But, anyhow, you go—with your friends. I've done with this blessed island for evermore, amen! I've had enough of it."

"But, Montgomery," I appealed.

He distorted his lower lip, and nodded his head hopelessly at the grey- haired man beside him, to indicate his powerlessness to help me.

"I'll see to *you*, presently," said the captain.

Then began a curious three-cornered altercation. Alternately I appealed to one and another of the three men,—first to the grey-haired man to let me land, and then to the drunken captain to keep me aboard. I even bawled entreaties to the sailors. Montgomery said never a word, only shook his head. "You're going overboard, I tell you," was the captain's refrain. "Law be damned! I'm king here." At last I must confess my voice suddenly broke in the middle of a vigorous threat. I felt a gust of hysterical petulance, and went aft and stared dismally at nothing.

Meanwhile the sailors progressed rapidly with the task of unshipping the packages and caged animals. A large launch, with two standing lugs, lay under the lea of the schooner; and into this the strange assortment of goods were swung. I did not then see the hands from the island that were receiving the packages, for the hull of the launch was hidden from me by the side of the schooner. Neither Montgomery nor his companion took the slightest notice of me, but busied themselves in assisting and directing the four or five sailors who were unloading the goods. The captain went forward interfering rather than assisting. I was alternately despairful and desperate. Once or twice as I stood waiting there for things to accomplish themselves, I could not resist an impulse to laugh at my miserable quandary. I felt all the wretcheder for the lack of a breakfast. Hunger and a lack of blood-corpuscles take all the manhood from a man. I perceived pretty clearly that I had not the stamina either to resist what the captain chose to do to expel me, or to force myself upon Montgomery and his companion. So I waited passively upon fate; and the work of transferring Montgomery's possessions to the launch went on as if I did not exist.

Presently that work was finished, and then came a struggle. I was hauled, resisting weakly enough, to the gangway. Even then I noticed the oddness of the brown faces of the men who were with Montgomery in the launch; but the launch was now fully laden, and was shoved off hastily. A broadening gap of green water appeared under me, and I pushed back with all my strength to avoid falling headlong. The hands in the launch shouted derisively, and I heard Montgomery curse

at them; and then the captain, the mate, and one of the seamen helping him, ran me aft towards the stern.

The dingey of the "Lady Vain" had been towing behind; it was half full of water, had no oars, and was quite unvictualled. I refused to go aboard her, and flung myself full length on the deck. In the end, they swung me into her by a rope (for they had no stern ladder), and then they cut me adrift. I drifted slowly from the schooner. In a kind of stupor I watched all hands take to the rigging, and slowly but surely she came round to the wind; the sails fluttered, and then bellied out as the wind came into them. I stared at her weather-beaten side heeling steeply towards me; and then she passed out of my range of view.

I did not turn my head to follow her. At first I could scarcely believe what had happened. I crouched in the bottom of the dingey, stunned, and staring blankly at the vacant, oily sea. Then I realised that I was in that little hell of mine again, now half swamped; and looking back over the gunwale, I saw the schooner standing away from me, with the red-haired captain mocking at me over the taffrail, and turning towards the island saw the launch growing smaller as she approached the beach.

Abruptly the cruelty of this desertion became clear to me. I had no means of reaching the land unless I should chance to drift there. I was still weak, you must remember, from my exposure in the boat; I was empty and very faint, or I should have had more heart. But as it was I suddenly began to sob and weep, as I had never done since I was a little child. The tears ran down my face. In a passion of despair I struck with my fists at the water in the bottom of the boat, and kicked savagely at the gunwale. I prayed aloud for God to let me die.

VI. THE EVIL-LOOKING BOATMEN

But the islanders, seeing that I was really adrift, took pity on me. I drifted very slowly to the eastward, approaching the island slantingly; and presently I saw, with hysterical relief, the launch come round and return towards me. She was heavily laden, and I could make out as she drew nearer Montgomery's white-haired, broad-shouldered companion sitting cramped up with the dogs and several packing-cases in the stern sheets. This individual stared fixedly at me without moving or speaking. The black-faced cripple was glaring at me as fixedly in the bows near the puma. There were three other men besides, —three strange brutish-looking fellows, at whom the staghounds were snarling savagely. Montgomery, who was steering, brought the boat by me, and rising, caught and fastened my painter to the tiller to tow me, for there was no room aboard.

I had recovered from my hysterical phase by this time and answered his hail, as he approached, bravely enough. I told him the dingey was nearly swamped, and he reached me a piggin. I was jerked back as the rope tightened between the boats. For some time I was busy baling.

It was not until I had got the water under (for the water in the dingey had been shipped; the boat was perfectly sound) that I had leisure to look at the people in the launch again.

The white-haired man I found was still regarding me steadfastly, but with an expression, as I now fancied, of some perplexity. When my eyes met his, he looked down at the staghound that sat between his knees. He was a powerfully-built man, as I have said, with a fine forehead and rather heavy features; but his eyes had that odd drooping of the skin above the lids which often comes with advancing years, and the fall of his heavy mouth at the corners gave him an expression of pugnacious resolution. He talked to Montgomery in a tone too low for me to hear.

From him my eyes travelled to his three men; and a strange crew they were. I saw only their faces, yet there was something in their faces—I knew not what—that gave me a queer spasm of disgust. I looked steadily at them, and the impression did not pass, though I failed to see what had occasioned it. They seemed to me then to be brown men; but their limbs were oddly swathed in some thin, dirty, white stuff down even to the fingers and feet: I have never seen men so wrapped up before, and women so only in the East. They wore turbans too, and thereunder peered out their elfin faces at me, —faces with protruding lower-jaws and bright eyes. They had lank black hair, almost like horsehair, and seemed as they sat to

exceed in stature any race of men I have seen. The white-haired man, who I knew was a good six feet in height, sat a head below any one of the three. I found afterwards that really none were taller than myself; but their bodies were abnormally long, and the thigh-part of the leg short and curiously twisted. At any rate, they were an amazingly ugly gang, and over the heads of them under the forward lug peered the black face of the man whose eyes were luminous in the dark. As I stared at them, they met my gaze; and then first one and then another turned away from my direct stare, and looked at me in an odd, furtive manner. It occurred to me that I was perhaps annoying them, and I turned my attention to the island we were approaching.

It was low, and covered with thick vegetation,—chiefly a kind of palm, that was new to me. From one point a thin white thread of vapour rose slantingly to an immense height, and then frayed out like a down feather. We were now within the embrace of a broad bay flanked on either hand by a low promontory. The beach was of dull-grey sand, and sloped steeply up to a ridge, perhaps sixty or seventy feet above the sea-level, and irregularly set with trees and undergrowth. Half way up was a square enclosure of some greyish stone, which I found subsequently was built partly of coral and partly of pumiceous lava. Two thatched roofs peeped from within this enclosure. A man stood awaiting us at the water's edge. I fancied while we were still far off that I saw some other and very grotesque-looking creatures scuttle into the bushes upon the slope; but I saw nothing of these as we drew nearer. This man was of a moderate size, and with a black negroid face. He had a large, almost lipless, mouth, extraordinary lank arms, long thin feet, and bow-legs, and stood with his heavy face thrust forward staring at us. He was dressed like Montgomery and his white-haired companion, in jacket and trousers of blue serge. As we came still nearer, this individual began to run to and fro on the beach, making the most grotesque movements.

At a word of command from Montgomery, the four men in the launch sprang up, and with singularly awkward gestures struck the lugs. Montgomery steered us round and into a narrow little dock excavated in the beach. Then the man on the beach hastened towards us. This dock, as I call it, was really a mere ditch just long enough at this phase of the tide to take the longboat. I heard the bows ground in the sand, staved the dingey off the rudder of the big boat with my piggin, and freeing the painter, landed. The three muffled men, with the clumsiest movements, scrambled out upon the sand, and forthwith set to landing the cargo, assisted by the man on the beach. I was struck especially by the curious movements of the legs of the three swathed and bandaged boatmen, —not stiff they were, but distorted in some odd way, almost as if they were jointed in the wrong place. The dogs were still snarling, and strained at their chains after these men, as the white-haired man landed with them. The three big fellows spoke to one another in odd guttural tones, and the man who had waited for us on the beach began chattering to them excitedly—a foreign language, as I fancied—as they laid hands on some bales piled near the stern. Somewhere I had heard such a voice before, and I could not think where. The white-haired man stood, holding in a tumult of

six dogs, and bawling orders over their din. Montgomery, having unshipped the rudder, landed likewise, and all set to work at unloading. I was too faint, what with my long fast and the sun beating down on my bare head, to offer any assistance.

Presently the white-haired man seemed to recollect my presence, and came up to me.

"You look," said he, "as though you had scarcely breakfasted." His little eyes were a brilliant black under his heavy brows. "I must apologise for that. Now you are our guest, we must make you comfortable,—though you are uninvited, you know." He looked keenly into my face. "Montgomery says you are an educated man, Mr. Prendick; says you know something of science. May I ask what that signifies?"

I told him I had spent some years at the Royal College of Science, and had done some researches in biology under Huxley. He raised his eyebrows slightly at that.

"That alters the case a little, Mr. Prendick," he said, with a trifle more respect in his manner. "As it happens, we are biologists here. This is a biological station—of a sort." His eye rested on the men in white who were busily hauling the puma, on rollers, towards the walled yard. "I and Montgomery, at least," he added. Then, "When you will be able to get away, I can't say. We're off the track to anywhere. We see a ship once in a twelve- month or so."

He left me abruptly, and went up the beach past this group, and I think entered the enclosure. The other two men were with Montgomery, erecting a pile of smaller packages on a low-wheeled truck. The llama was still on the launch with the rabbit hutches; the staghounds were still lashed to the thwarts. The pile of things completed, all three men laid hold of the truck and began shoving the ton-weight or so upon it after the puma. Presently Montgomery left them, and coming back to me held out his hand.

"I'm glad," said he, "for my own part. That captain was a silly ass. He'd have made things lively for you."

"It was you," said I, "that saved me again".

"That depends. You'll find this island an infernally rum place, I promise you. I'd watch my goings carefully, if I were you. *He*—" He hesitated, and seemed to alter his mind about what was on his lips. "I wish you'd help me with these rabbits," he said.

His procedure with the rabbits was singular. I waded in with him, and helped him lug one of the hutches ashore. No sooner was that done than he opened the door of it, and tilting the thing on one end turned its living contents out on the ground. They fell in a struggling heap one on the top of the other. He clapped his hands, and forthwith they went off with that hopping run of theirs, fifteen or twenty of them I should think, up the beach.

"Increase and multiply, my friends," said Montgomery. "Replenish the island. Hitherto we've had a certain lack of meat here."

As I watched them disappearing, the white-haired man returned with a brandy-flask and some biscuits. "Something to go on with, Prendick," said he, in a far more familiar tone than before. I made no ado, but set to work on the biscuits at once, while the white-haired man helped Montgomery to release about a score more of the rabbits. Three big hutches, however, went up to the house with the puma. The brandy I did not touch, for I have been an abstainer from my birth.

VII. THE LOCKED DOOR

The reader will perhaps understand that at first everything was so strange about me, and my position was the outcome of such unexpected adventures, that I had no discernment of the relative strangeness of this or that thing. I followed the llama up the beach, and was overtaken by Montgomery, who asked me not to enter the stone enclosure. I noticed then that the puma in its cage and the pile of packages had been placed outside the entrance to this quadrangle.

I turned and saw that the launch had now been unloaded, run out again, and was being beached, and the white-haired man was walking towards us. He addressed Montgomery.

"And now comes the problem of this uninvited guest. What are we to do with him?"

"He knows something of science," said Montgomery.

"I'm itching to get to work again—with this new stuff," said the white-haired man, nodding towards the enclosure. His eyes grew brighter.

"I daresay you are," said Montgomery, in anything but a cordial tone.

"We can't send him over there, and we can't spare the time to build him a new shanty; and we certainly can't take him into our confidence just yet."

"I'm in your hands," said I. I had no idea of what he meant by "over there."

"I've been thinking of the same things," Montgomery answered. "There's my room with the outer door—"

"That's it," said the elder man, promptly, looking at Montgomery; and all three of us went towards the enclosure. "I'm sorry to make a mystery, Mr. Prendick; but you'll remember you're uninvited. Our little establishment here contains a secret or so, is a kind of Blue-Beard's chamber, in fact. Nothing very dreadful, really, to a sane man; but just now, as we don't know you—"

"Decidedly," said I, "I should be a fool to take offence at any want of confidence."

He twisted his heavy mouth into a faint smile—he was one of those saturnine people who smile with the corners of the mouth down,—and bowed his acknowledgment of my complaisance. The main entrance to the enclosure was passed; it was a heavy wooden gate, framed in iron and locked, with the cargo of the launch piled outside it, and at the corner we came to a small doorway I had not previously observed. The white-haired man produced a bundle of keys from the pocket of his greasy blue jacket, opened this door, and entered. His keys, and the elaborate locking-up of the place even while it was still under his eye, struck me as peculi-

ar. I followed him, and found myself in a small apartment, plainly but not uncomfortably furnished and with its inner door, which was slightly ajar, opening into a paved courtyard. This inner door Montgomery at once closed. A hammock was slung across the darker corner of the room, and a small unglazed window defended by an iron bar looked out towards the sea.

This the white-haired man told me was to be my apartment; and the inner door, which "for fear of accidents," he said, he would lock on the other side, was my limit inward. He called my attention to a convenient deck-chair before the window, and to an array of old books, chiefly, I found, surgical works and editions of the Latin and Greek classics (languages I cannot read with any comfort), on a shelf near the hammock. He left the room by the outer door, as if to avoid opening the inner one again.

"We usually have our meals in here," said Montgomery, and then, as if in doubt, went out after the other. "Moreau!" I heard him call, and for the moment I do not think I noticed. Then as I handled the books on the shelf it came up in consciousness: Where had I heard the name of Moreau before? I sat down before the window, took out the biscuits that still remained to me, and ate them with an excellent appetite. Moreau!

Through the window I saw one of those unaccountable men in white, lugging a packing-case along the beach. Presently the window-frame hid him. Then I heard a key inserted and turned in the lock behind me. After a little while I heard through the locked door the noise of the staghounds, that had now been brought up from the beach. They were not barking, but sniffing and growling in a curious fashion. I could hear the rapid patter of their feet, and Montgomery's voice soothing them.

I was very much impressed by the elaborate secrecy of these two men regarding the contents of the place, and for some time I was thinking of that and of the unaccountable familiarity of the name of Moreau; but so odd is the human memory that I could not then recall that well-known name in its proper connection. From that my thoughts went to the indefinable queerness of the deformed man on the beach. I never saw such a gait, such odd motions as he pulled at the box. I recalled that none of these men had spoken to me, though most of them I had found looking at me at one time or another in a peculiarly furtive manner, quite unlike the frank stare of your unsophisticated savage. Indeed, they had all seemed remarkably taciturn, and when they did speak, endowed with very uncanny voices. What was wrong with them? Then I recalled the eyes of Montgomery's ungainly attendant.

Just as I was thinking of him he came in. He was now dressed in white, and carried a little tray with some coffee and boiled vegetables thereon. I could hardly repress a shuddering recoil as he came, bending amiably, and placed the tray before me on the table. Then astonishment paralysed me. Under his stringy black locks I saw his ear; it jumped upon me suddenly close to my face. The man had pointed ears, covered with a fine brown fur!

"Your breakfast, sair," he said.

I stared at his face without attempting to answer him. He turned and went towards the door, regarding me oddly over his shoulder. I followed him out with my eyes; and as I did so, by some odd trick of unconscious cerebration, there came surging into my head the phrase, "The Moreau Hollows"—was it? "The Moreau—" Ah! It sent my memory back ten years. "The Moreau Horrors!" The phrase drifted loose in my mind for a moment, and then I saw it in red lettering on a little buff-coloured pamphlet, to read which made one shiver and creep. Then I remembered distinctly all about it. That long-forgotten pamphlet came back with startling vividness to my mind. I had been a mere lad then, and Moreau was, I suppose, about fifty,—a prominent and masterful physiologist, well-known in scientific circles for his extraordinary imagination and his brutal directness in discussion.

Was this the same Moreau? He had published some very astonishing facts in connection with the transfusion of blood, and in addition was known to be doing valuable work on morbid growths. Then suddenly his career was closed. He had to leave England. A journalist obtained access to his laboratory in the capacity of laboratory-assistant, with the deliberate intention of making sensational exposures; and by the help of a shocking accident (if it was an accident), his gruesome pamphlet became notorious. On the day of its publication a wretched dog, flayed and otherwise mutilated, escaped from Moreau's house. It was in the silly season, and a prominent editor, a cousin of the temporary laboratory- assistant, appealed to the conscience of the nation. It was not the first time that conscience has turned against the methods of research. The doctor was simply howled out of the country. It may be that he deserved to be; but I still think that the tepid support of his fellow-investigators and his desertion by the great body of scientific workers was a shameful thing. Yet some of his experiments, by the journalist's account, were wantonly cruel. He might perhaps have purchased his social peace by abandoning his investigations; but he apparently preferred the latter, as most men would who have once fallen under the overmastering spell of research. He was unmarried, and had indeed nothing but his own interest to consider.

I felt convinced that this must be the same man. Everything pointed to it. It dawned upon me to what end the puma and the other animals—which had now been brought with other luggage into the enclosure behind the house —were destined; and a curious faint odour, the halitus of something familiar, an odour that had been in the background of my consciousness hitherto, suddenly came forward into the forefront of my thoughts. It was the antiseptic odour of the dissecting-room. I heard the puma growling through the wall, and one of the dogs yelped as though it had been struck.

Yet surely, and especially to another scientific man, there was nothing so horrible in vivisection as to account for this secrecy; and by some odd leap in my thoughts the pointed ears and luminous eyes of Montgomery's attendant came back again before me with the sharpest definition. I stared before me out at the green sea, frothing under a freshening breeze, and let these and other strange memories of the last few days chase one another through my mind.

What could it all mean? A locked enclosure on a lonely island, a notorious vivisector, and these crippled and distorted men?

VIII. THE CRYING OF THE PUMA

Montgomery interrupted my tangle of mystification and suspicion about one o'clock, and his grotesque attendant followed him with a tray bearing bread, some herbs and other eatables, a flask of whiskey, a jug of water, and three glasses and knives. I glanced askance at this strange creature, and found him watching me with his queer, restless eyes. Montgomery said he would lunch with me, but that Moreau was too preoccupied with some work to come.

"Moreau!" said I. "I know that name."

"The devil you do!" said he. "What an ass I was to mention it to you! I might have thought. Anyhow, it will give you an inkling of our—mysteries. Whiskey?"

"No, thanks; I'm an abstainer."

"I wish I'd been. But it's no use locking the door after the steed is stolen. It was that infernal stuff which led to my coming here,—that, and a foggy night. I thought myself in luck at the time, when Moreau offered to get me off. It's queer—"

"Montgomery," said I, suddenly, as the outer door closed, "why has your man pointed ears?"

"Damn!" he said, over his first mouthful of food. He stared at me for a moment, and then repeated, "Pointed ears?"

"Little points to them," said I, as calmly as possible, with a catch in my breath; "and a fine black fur at the edges?"

He helped himself to whiskey and water with great deliberation. "I was under the impression—that his hair covered his ears."

"I saw them as he stooped by me to put that coffee you sent to me on the table. And his eyes shine in the dark."

By this time Montgomery had recovered from the surprise of my question. "I always thought," he said deliberately, with a certain accentuation of his flavouring of lisp, "that there *was* something the matter with his ears, from the way he covered them. What were they like?"

I was persuaded from his manner that this ignorance was a pretence. Still, I could hardly tell the man that I thought him a liar. "Pointed," I said; "rather small and furry,—distinctly furry. But the whole man is one of the strangest beings I ever set eyes on."

A sharp, hoarse cry of animal pain came from the enclosure behind us. Its depth and volume testified to the puma. I saw Montgomery wince.

"Yes?" he said.

"Where did you pick up the creature?"

"San Francisco. He's an ugly brute, I admit. Half-witted, you know. Can't remember where he came from. But I'm used to him, you know. We both are. How does he strike you?"

"He's unnatural," I said. "There's something about him—don't think me fanciful, but it gives me a nasty little sensation, a tightening of my muscles, when he comes near me. It's a touch—of the diabolical, in fact."

Montgomery had stopped eating while I told him this. "Rum!" he said. "I can't see it." He resumed his meal. "I had no idea of it," he said, and masticated. "The crew of the schooner must have felt it the same. Made a dead set at the poor devil. You saw the captain?"

Suddenly the puma howled again, this time more painfully. Montgomery swore under his breath. I had half a mind to attack him about the men on the beach. Then the poor brute within gave vent to a series of short, sharp cries.

"Your men on the beach," said I; "what race are they?"

"Excellent fellows, aren't they?" said he, absentmindedly, knitting his brows as the animal yelled out sharply.

I said no more. There was another outcry worse than the former. He looked at me with his dull grey eyes, and then took some more whiskey. He tried to draw me into a discussion about alcohol, professing to have saved my life with it. He seemed anxious to lay stress on the fact that I owed my life to him. I answered him distractedly.

Presently our meal came to an end; the misshapen monster with the pointed ears cleared the remains away, and Montgomery left me alone in the room again. All the time he had been in a state of ill-concealed irritation at the noise of the vivisected puma. He had spoken of his odd want of nerve, and left me to the obvious application.

I found myself that the cries were singularly irritating, and they grew in depth and intensity as the afternoon wore on. They were painful at first, but their constant resurgence at last altogether upset my balance. I flung aside a crib of Horace I had been reading, and began to clench my fists, to bite my lips, and to pace the room. Presently I got to stopping my ears with my fingers.

The emotional appeal of those yells grew upon me steadily, grew at last to such an exquisite expression of suffering that I could stand it in that confined room no longer. I stepped out of the door into the slumberous heat of the late afternoon, and walking past the main entrance—locked again, I noticed—turned the corner of the wall.

The crying sounded even louder out of doors. It was as if all the pain in the world had found a voice. Yet had I known such pain was in the next room, and had it been dumb, I believe—I have thought since—I could have stood it well enough. It is when suffering finds a voice and sets our nerves quivering that this pity comes troubling us. But in spite of the brilliant sunlight and the green fans of the trees waving in the soothing sea- breeze, the world was a confusion, blurred

with drifting black and red phantasms, until I was out of earshot of the house in the chequered wall.

IX. THE THING IN THE FOREST

I strode through the undergrowth that clothed the ridge behind the house, scarcely heeding whither I went; passed on through the shadow of a thick cluster of straight-stemmed trees beyond it, and so presently found myself some way on the other side of the ridge, and descending towards a streamlet that ran through a narrow valley. I paused and listened. The distance I had come, or the intervening masses of thicket, deadened any sound that might be coming from the enclosure. The air was still. Then with a rustle a rabbit emerged, and went scampering up the slope before me. I hesitated, and sat down in the edge of the shade.

The place was a pleasant one. The rivulet was hidden by the luxuriant vegetation of the banks save at one point, where I caught a triangular patch of its glittering water. On the farther side I saw through a bluish haze a tangle of trees and creepers, and above these again the luminous blue of the sky. Here and there a splash of white or crimson marked the blooming of some trailing epiphyte. I let my eyes wander over this scene for a while, and then began to turn over in my mind again the strange peculiarities of Montgomery's man. But it was too hot to think elaborately, and presently I fell into a tranquil state midway between dozing and waking.

From this I was aroused, after I know not how long, by a rustling amidst the greenery on the other side of the stream. For a moment I could see nothing but the waving summits of the ferns and reeds. Then suddenly upon the bank of the stream appeared Something—at first I could not distinguish what it was. It bowed its round head to the water, and began to drink. Then I saw it was a man, going on all-fours like a beast. He was clothed in bluish cloth, and was of a copper-coloured hue, with black hair. It seemed that grotesque ugliness was an invariable character of these islanders. I could hear the suck of the water at his lips as he drank.

I leant forward to see him better, and a piece of lava, detached by my hand, went pattering down the slope. He looked up guiltily, and his eyes met mine. Forthwith he scrambled to his feet, and stood wiping his clumsy hand across his mouth and regarding me. His legs were scarcely half the length of his body. So, staring one another out of countenance, we remained for perhaps the space of a minute. Then, stopping to look back once or twice, he slunk off among the bushes to the right of me, and I heard the swish of the fronds grow faint in the distance and die away. Long after he had disappeared, I remained sitting up staring in the direction of his retreat. My drowsy tranquillity had gone.

I was startled by a noise behind me, and turning suddenly saw the flapping white tail of a rabbit vanishing up the slope. I jumped to my feet. The apparition of this grotesque, half-bestial creature had suddenly populated the stillness of the afternoon for me. I looked around me rather nervously, and regretted that I was unarmed. Then I thought that the man I had just seen had been clothed in bluish cloth, had not been naked as a savage would have been; and I tried to persuade myself from that fact that he was after all probably a peaceful character, that the dull ferocity of his countenance belied him.

Yet I was greatly disturbed at the apparition. I walked to the left along the slope, turning my head about and peering this way and that among the straight stems of the trees. Why should a man go on all-fours and drink with his lips? Presently I heard an animal wailing again, and taking it to be the puma, I turned about and walked in a direction diametrically opposite to the sound. This led me down to the stream, across which I stepped and pushed my way up through the undergrowth beyond.

I was startled by a great patch of vivid scarlet on the ground, and going up to it found it to be a peculiar fungus, branched and corrugated like a foliaceous lichen, but deliquescing into slime at the touch; and then in the shadow of some luxuriant ferns I came upon an unpleasant thing,—the dead body of a rabbit covered with shining flies, but still warm and with the head torn off. I stopped aghast at the sight of the scattered blood. Here at least was one visitor to the island disposed of! There were no traces of other violence about it. It looked as though it had been suddenly snatched up and killed; and as I stared at the little furry body came the difficulty of how the thing had been done. The vague dread that had been in my mind since I had seen the inhuman face of the man at the stream grew distincter as I stood there. I began to realise the hardihood of my expedition among these unknown people. The thicket about me became altered to my imagination. Every shadow became something more than a shadow,—became an ambush; every rustle became a threat. Invisible things seemed watching me. I resolved to go back to the enclosure on the beach. I suddenly turned away and thrust myself violently, possibly even frantically, through the bushes, anxious to get a clear space about me again.

I stopped just in time to prevent myself emerging upon an open space. It was a kind of glade in the forest, made by a fall; seedlings were already starting up to struggle for the vacant space; and beyond, the dense growth of stems and twining vines and splashes of fungus and flowers closed in again. Before me, squatting together upon the fungoid ruins of a huge fallen tree and still unaware of my approach, were three grotesque human figures. One was evidently a female; the other two were men. They were naked, save for swathings of scarlet cloth about the middle; and their skins were of a dull pinkish-drab colour, such as I had seen in no savages before. They had fat, heavy, chinless faces, retreating foreheads, and a scant bristly hair upon their heads. I never saw such bestial-looking creatures.

They were talking, or at least one of the men was talking to the other two, and all three had been too closely interested to heed the rustling of my approach. They swayed their heads and shoulders from side to side. The speaker's words came thick and sloppy, and though I could hear them distinctly I could not distinguish what he said. He seemed to me to be reciting some complicated gibberish. Presently his articulation became shriller, and spreading his hands he rose to his feet. At that the others began to gibber in unison, also rising to their feet, spreading their hands and swaying their bodies in rhythm with their chant. I noticed then the abnormal shortness of their legs, and their lank, clumsy feet. All three began slowly to circle round, raising and stamping their feet and waving their arms; a kind of tune crept into their rhythmic recitation, and a refrain,—"Aloola," or "Balloola," it sounded like. Their eyes began to sparkle, and their ugly faces to brighten, with an expression of strange pleasure. Saliva dripped from their lipless mouths.

Suddenly, as I watched their grotesque and unaccountable gestures, I perceived clearly for the first time what it was that had offended me, what had given me the two inconsistent and conflicting impressions of utter strangeness and yet of the strangest familiarity. The three creatures engaged in this mysterious rite were human in shape, and yet human beings with the strangest air about them of some familiar animal. Each of these creatures, despite its human form, its rag of clothing, and the rough humanity of its bodily form, had woven into it—into its movements, into the expression of its countenance, into its whole presence—some now irresistible suggestion of a hog, a swinish taint, the unmistakable mark of the beast.

I stood overcome by this amazing realisation and then the most horrible questionings came rushing into my mind. They began leaping in the air, first one and then the other, whooping and grunting. Then one slipped, and for a moment was on all-fours,—to recover, indeed, forthwith. But that transitory gleam of the true animalism of these monsters was enough.

I turned as noiselessly as possible, and becoming every now and then rigid with the fear of being discovered, as a branch cracked or a leaf rustled, I pushed back into the bushes. It was long before I grew bolder, and dared to move freely. My only idea for the moment was to get away from these foul beings, and I scarcely noticed that I had emerged upon a faint pathway amidst the trees. Then suddenly traversing a little glade, I saw with an unpleasant start two clumsy legs among the trees, walking with noiseless footsteps parallel with my course, and perhaps thirty yards away from me. The head and upper part of the body were hidden by a tangle of creeper. I stopped abruptly, hoping the creature did not see me. The feet stopped as I did. So nervous was I that I controlled an impulse to headlong flight with the utmost difficulty. Then looking hard, I distinguished through the interlacing network the head and body of the brute I had seen drinking. He moved his head. There was an emerald flash in his eyes as he glanced at me from the shadow of the trees, a half- luminous colour that vanished as he turned his head again. He was motionless for a moment, and then with a noiseless

tread began running through the green confusion. In another moment he had vanished behind some bushes. I could not see him, but I felt that he had stopped and was watching me again.

What on earth was he,—man or beast? What did he want with me? I had no weapon, not even a stick. Flight would be madness. At any rate the Thing, whatever it was, lacked the courage to attack me. Setting my teeth hard, I walked straight towards him. I was anxious not to show the fear that seemed chilling my backbone. I pushed through a tangle of tall white-flowered bushes, and saw him twenty paces beyond, looking over his shoulder at me and hesitating. I advanced a step or two, looking steadfastly into his eyes.

"Who are you?" said I.

He tried to meet my gaze. "No!" he said suddenly, and turning went bounding away from me through the undergrowth. Then he turned and stared at me again. His eyes shone brightly out of the dusk under the trees.

My heart was in my mouth; but I felt my only chance was bluff, and walked steadily towards him. He turned again, and vanished into the dusk. Once more I thought I caught the glint of his eyes, and that was all.

For the first time I realised how the lateness of the hour might affect me. The sun had set some minutes since, the swift dusk of the tropics was already fading out of the eastern sky, and a pioneer moth fluttered silently by my head. Unless I would spend the night among the unknown dangers of the mysterious forest, I must hasten back to the enclosure. The thought of a return to that pain-haunted refuge was extremely disagreeable, but still more so was the idea of being overtaken in the open by darkness and all that darkness might conceal. I gave one more look into the blue shadows that had swallowed up this odd creature, and then retraced my way down the slope towards the stream, going as I judged in the direction from which I had come.

I walked eagerly, my mind confused with many things, and presently found myself in a level place among scattered trees. The colourless clearness that comes after the sunset flush was darkling; the blue sky above grew momentarily deeper, and the little stars one by one pierced the attenuated light; the interspaces of the trees, the gaps in the further vegetation, that had been hazy blue in the daylight, grew black and mysterious. I pushed on. The colour vanished from the world. The tree-tops rose against the luminous blue sky in inky silhouette, and all below that outline melted into one formless blackness. Presently the trees grew thinner, and the shrubby undergrowth more abundant. Then there was a desolate space covered with a white sand, and then another expanse of tangled bushes. I did not remember crossing the sand-opening before. I began to be tormented by a faint rustling upon my right hand. I thought at first it was fancy, for whenever I stopped there was silence, save for the evening breeze in the tree-tops. Then when I turned to hurry on again there was an echo to my footsteps.

I turned away from the thickets, keeping to the more open ground, and endeavouring by sudden turns now and then to surprise something in the act of creeping upon me. I saw nothing, and nevertheless my sense of another presence

grew steadily. I increased my pace, and after some time came to a slight ridge, crossed it, and turned sharply, regarding it steadfastly from the further side. It came out black and clear-cut against the darkling sky; and presently a shapeless lump heaved up momentarily against the sky-line and vanished again. I felt assured now that my tawny-faced antagonist was stalking me once more; and coupled with that was another unpleasant realisation, that I had lost my way.

For a time I hurried on hopelessly perplexed, and pursued by that stealthy approach. Whatever it was, the Thing either lacked the courage to attack me, or it was waiting to take me at some disadvantage. I kept studiously to the open. At times I would turn and listen; and presently I had half persuaded myself that my pursuer had abandoned the chase, or was a mere creation of my disordered imagination. Then I heard the sound of the sea. I quickened my footsteps almost into a run, and immediately there was a stumble in my rear.

I turned suddenly, and stared at the uncertain trees behind me. One black shadow seemed to leap into another. I listened, rigid, and heard nothing but the creep of the blood in my ears. I thought that my nerves were unstrung, and that my imagination was tricking me, and turned resolutely towards the sound of the sea again.

In a minute or so the trees grew thinner, and I emerged upon a bare, low headland running out into the sombre water. The night was calm and clear, and the reflection of the growing multitude of the stars shivered in the tranquil heaving of the sea. Some way out, the wash upon an irregular band of reef shone with a pallid light of its own. Westward I saw the zodiacal light mingling with the yellow brilliance of the evening star. The coast fell away from me to the east, and westward it was hidden by the shoulder of the cape. Then I recalled the fact that Moreau's beach lay to the west.

A twig snapped behind me, and there was a rustle. I turned, and stood facing the dark trees. I could see nothing—or else I could see too much. Every dark form in the dimness had its ominous quality, its peculiar suggestion of alert watchfulness. So I stood for perhaps a minute, and then, with an eye to the trees still, turned westward to cross the headland; and as I moved, one among the lurking shadows moved to follow me.

My heart beat quickly. Presently the broad sweep of a bay to the westward became visible, and I halted again. The noiseless shadow halted a dozen yards from me. A little point of light shone on the further bend of the curve, and the grey sweep of the sandy beach lay faint under the starlight. Perhaps two miles away was that little point of light. To get to the beach I should have to go through the trees where the shadows lurked, and down a bushy slope.

I could see the Thing rather more distinctly now. It was no animal, for it stood erect. At that I opened my mouth to speak, and found a hoarse phlegm choked my voice. I tried again, and shouted, "Who is there?" There was no answer. I advanced a step. The Thing did not move, only gathered itself together. My foot struck a stone. That gave me an idea. Without taking my eyes off the black form before me, I stooped and picked up this lump of rock; but at my motion the Thing

turned abruptly as a dog might have done, and slunk obliquely into the further darkness. Then I recalled a schoolboy expedient against big dogs, and twisted the rock into my handkerchief, and gave this a turn round my wrist. I heard a movement further off among the shadows, as if the Thing was in retreat. Then suddenly my tense excitement gave way; I broke into a profuse perspiration and fell a-trembling, with my adversary routed and this weapon in my hand.

It was some time before I could summon resolution to go down through the trees and bushes upon the flank of the headland to the beach. At last I did it at a run; and as I emerged from the thicket upon the sand, I heard some other body come crashing after me. At that I completely lost my head with fear, and began running along the sand. Forthwith there came the swift patter of soft feet in pursuit. I gave a wild cry, and redoubled my pace. Some dim, black things about three or four times the size of rabbits went running or hopping up from the beach towards the bushes as I passed.

So long as I live, I shall remember the terror of that chase. I ran near the water's edge, and heard every now and then the splash of the feet that gained upon me. Far away, hopelessly far, was the yellow light. All the night about us was black and still. Splash, splash, came the pursuing feet, nearer and nearer. I felt my breath going, for I was quite out of training; it whooped as I drew it, and I felt a pain like a knife at my side. I perceived the Thing would come up with me long before I reached the enclosure, and, desperate and sobbing for my breath, I wheeled round upon it and struck at it as it came up to me,—struck with all my strength. The stone came out of the sling of the handkerchief as I did so. As I turned, the Thing, which had been running on all-fours, rose to its feet, and the missile fell fair on its left temple. The skull rang loud, and the animal-man blundered into me, thrust me back with its hands, and went staggering past me to fall headlong upon the sand with its face in the water; and there it lay still.

I could not bring myself to approach that black heap. I left it there, with the water rippling round it, under the still stars, and giving it a wide berth pursued my way towards the yellow glow of the house; and presently, with a positive effect of relief, came the pitiful moaning of the puma, the sound that had originally driven me out to explore this mysterious island. At that, though I was faint and horribly fatigued, I gathered together all my strength, and began running again towards the light. I thought I heard a voice calling me.

X. THE CRYING OF THE MAN

As I drew near the house I saw that the light shone from the open door of my room; and then I heard coming from out of the darkness at the side of that orange oblong of light, the voice of Montgomery shouting, "Prendick!" I continued running. Presently I heard him again. I replied by a feeble "Hullo!" and in another moment had staggered up to him.

"Where have you been?" said he, holding me at arm's length, so that the light from the door fell on my face. "We have both been so busy that we forgot you until about half an hour ago." He led me into the room and sat me down in the deck chair. For awhile I was blinded by the light. "We did not think you would start to explore this island of ours without telling us," he said; and then, "I was afraid—But—what—Hullo!"

My last remaining strength slipped from me, and my head fell forward on my chest. I think he found a certain satisfaction in giving me brandy.

"For God's sake," said I, "fasten that door."

"You've been meeting some of our curiosities, eh?" said he.

He locked the door and turned to me again. He asked me no questions, but gave me some more brandy and water and pressed me to eat. I was in a state of collapse. He said something vague about his forgetting to warn me, and asked me briefly when I left the house and what I had seen.

I answered him as briefly, in fragmentary sentences. "Tell me what it all means," said I, in a state bordering on hysterics.

"It's nothing so very dreadful," said he. "But I think you have had about enough for one day." The puma suddenly gave a sharp yell of pain. At that he swore under his breath. "I'm damned," said he, "if this place is not as bad as Gower Street, with its cats."

"Montgomery," said I, "what was that thing that came after me? Was it a beast or was it a man?"

"If you don't sleep to-night," he said, "you'll be off your head to- morrow."

I stood up in front of him. "What was that thing that came after me?" I asked.

He looked me squarely in the eyes, and twisted his mouth askew. His eyes, which had seemed animated a minute before, went dull. "From your account," said he, "I'm thinking it was a bogle."

I felt a gust of intense irritation, which passed as quickly as it came. I flung myself into the chair again, and pressed my hands on my forehead. The puma began once more.

Montgomery came round behind me and put his hand on my shoulder. "Look here, Prendick," he said, "I had no business to let you drift out into this silly island of ours. But it's not so bad as you feel, man. Your nerves are worked to rags. Let me give you something that will make you sleep. *That* —will keep on for hours yet. You must simply get to sleep, or I won't answer for it."

I did not reply. I bowed forward, and covered my face with my hands. Presently he returned with a small measure containing a dark liquid. This he gave me. I took it unresistingly, and he helped me into the hammock.

When I awoke, it was broad day. For a little while I lay flat, staring at the roof above me. The rafters, I observed, were made out of the timbers of a ship. Then I turned my head, and saw a meal prepared for me on the table. I perceived that I was hungry, and prepared to clamber out of the hammock, which, very politely anticipating my intention, twisted round and deposited me upon all-fours on the floor.

I got up and sat down before the food. I had a heavy feeling in my head, and only the vaguest memory at first of the things that had happened over night. The morning breeze blew very pleasantly through the unglazed window, and that and the food contributed to the sense of animal comfort which I experienced. Presently the door behind me—the door inward towards the yard of the enclosure—opened. I turned and saw Montgomery's face.

"All right," said he. "I'm frightfully busy." And he shut the door.

Afterwards I discovered that he forgot to re-lock it. Then I recalled the expression of his face the previous night, and with that the memory of all I had experienced reconstructed itself before me. Even as that fear came back to me came a cry from within; but this time it was not the cry of a puma. I put down the mouthful that hesitated upon my lips, and listened. Silence, save for the whisper of the morning breeze. I began to think my ears had deceived me.

After a long pause I resumed my meal, but with my ears still vigilant. Presently I heard something else, very faint and low. I sat as if frozen in my attitude. Though it was faint and low, it moved me more profoundly than all that I had hitherto heard of the abominations behind the wall. There was no mistake this time in the quality of the dim, broken sounds; no doubt at all of their source. For it was groaning, broken by sobs and gasps of anguish. It was no brute this time; it was a human being in torment!

As I realised this I rose, and in three steps had crossed the room, seized the handle of the door into the yard, and flung it open before me.

"Prendick, man! Stop!" cried Montgomery, intervening.

A startled deerhound yelped and snarled. There was blood, I saw, in the sink,—brown, and some scarlet—and I smelt the peculiar smell of carbolic acid. Then through an open doorway beyond, in the dim light of the shadow, I saw something bound painfully upon a framework, scarred, red, and bandaged; and then blotting this out appeared the face of old Moreau, white and terrible. In a moment he had gripped me by the shoulder with a hand that was smeared red, had twisted me off my feet, and flung me headlong back into my own room. He lifted

me as though I was a little child. I fell at full length upon the floor, and the door slammed and shut out the passionate intensity of his face. Then I heard the key turn in the lock, and Montgomery's voice in expostulation.

"Ruin the work of a lifetime," I heard Moreau say.

"He does not understand," said Montgomery. and other things that were inaudible.

"I can't spare the time yet," said Moreau.

The rest I did not hear. I picked myself up and stood trembling, my mind a chaos of the most horrible misgivings. Could it be possible, I thought, that such a thing as the vivisection of men was carried on here? The question shot like lightning across a tumultuous sky; and suddenly the clouded horror of my mind condensed into a vivid realisation of my own danger.

XI. THE HUNTING OF THE MAN

It came before my mind with an unreasonable hope of escape that the outer door of my room was still open to me. I was convinced now, absolutely assured, that Moreau had been vivisecting a human being. All the time since I had heard his name, I had been trying to link in my mind in some way the grotesque animalism of the islanders with his abominations; and now I thought I saw it all. The memory of his work on the transfusion of blood recurred to me. These creatures I had seen were the victims of some hideous experiment. These sickening scoundrels had merely intended to keep me back, to fool me with their display of confidence, and presently to fall upon me with a fate more horrible than death,—with torture; and after torture the most hideous degradation it is possible to conceive,—to send me off a lost soul, a beast, to the rest of their Comus rout.

I looked round for some weapon. Nothing. Then with an inspiration I turned over the deck chair, put my foot on the side of it, and tore away the side rail. It happened that a nail came away with the wood, and projecting, gave a touch of danger to an otherwise petty weapon. I heard a step outside, and incontinently flung open the door and found Montgomery within a yard of it. He meant to lock the outer door! I raised this nailed stick of mine and cut at his face; but he sprang back. I hesitated a moment, then turned and fled, round the corner of the house. "Prendick, man!" I heard his astonished cry, "don't be a silly ass, man!"

Another minute, thought I, and he would have had me locked in, and as ready as a hospital rabbit for my fate. He emerged behind the corner, for I heard him shout, "Prendick!" Then he began to run after me, shouting things as he ran. This time running blindly, I went northeastward in a direction at right angles to my previous expedition. Once, as I went running headlong up the beach, I glanced over my shoulder and saw his attendant with him. I ran furiously up the slope, over it, then turning eastward along a rocky valley fringed on either side with jungle I ran for perhaps a mile altogether, my chest straining, my heart beating in my ears; and then hearing nothing of Montgomery or his man, and feeling upon the verge of exhaustion, I doubled sharply back towards the beach as I judged, and lay down in the shelter of a canebrake. There I remained for a long time, too fearful to move, and indeed too fearful even to plan a course of action. The wild scene about me lay sleeping silently under the sun, and the only sound near me was the thin hum of some small gnats that had discovered me. Presently I became aware of a drowsy breathing sound, the soughing of the sea upon the beach.

After about an hour I heard Montgomery shouting my name, far away to the north. That set me thinking of my plan of action. As I interpreted it then, this island was inhabited only by these two vivisectors and their animalised victims. Some of these no doubt they could press into their service against me if need arose. I knew both Moreau and Montgomery carried revolvers; and, save for a feeble bar of deal spiked with a small nail, the merest mockery of a mace, I was unarmed.

So I lay still there, until I began to think of food and drink; and at that thought the real hopelessness of my position came home to me. I knew no way of getting anything to eat. I was too ignorant of botany to discover any resort of root or fruit that might lie about me; I had no means of trapping the few rabbits upon the island. It grew blanker the more I turned the prospect over. At last in the desperation of my position, my mind turned to the animal men I had encountered. I tried to find some hope in what I remembered of them. In turn I recalled each one I had seen, and tried to draw some augury of assistance from my memory.

Then suddenly I heard a staghound bay, and at that realised a new danger. I took little time to think, or they would have caught me then, but snatching up my nailed stick, rushed headlong from my hiding-place towards the sound of the sea. I remember a growth of thorny plants, with spines that stabbed like pen-knives. I emerged bleeding and with torn clothes upon the lip of a long creek opening northward. I went straight into the water without a minute's hesitation, wading up the creek, and presently finding myself kneedeep in a little stream. I scrambled out at last on the westward bank, and with my heart beating loudly in my ears, crept into a tangle of ferns to await the issue. I heard the dog (there was only one) draw nearer, and yelp when it came to the thorns. Then I heard no more, and presently began to think I had escaped.

The minutes passed; the silence lengthened out, and at last after an hour of security my courage began to return to me. By this time I was no longer very much terrified or very miserable. I had, as it were, passed the limit of terror and despair. I felt now that my life was practically lost, and that persuasion made me capable of daring anything. I had even a certain wish to encounter Moreau face to face; and as I had waded into the water, I remembered that if I were too hard pressed at least one path of escape from torment still lay open to me,—they could not very well prevent my drowning myself. I had half a mind to drown myself then; but an odd wish to see the whole adventure out, a queer, impersonal, spectacular interest in myself, restrained me. I stretched my limbs, sore and painful from the pricks of the spiny plants, and stared around me at the trees; and, so suddenly that it seemed to jump out of the green tracery about it, my eyes lit upon a black face watching me. I saw that it was the simian creature who had met the launch upon the beach. He was clinging to the oblique stem of a palm-tree. I gripped my stick, and stood up facing him. He began chattering. "You, you, you," was all I could distinguish at first. Suddenly he dropped from the tree, and in another moment was holding the fronds apart and staring curiously at me.

I did not feel the same repugnance towards this creature which I had experienced in my encounters with the other Beast Men. "You," he said, "in the boat." He was a man, then,—at least as much of a man as Montgomery's attendant,—for he could talk.

"Yes," I said, "I came in the boat. From the ship."

"Oh!" he said, and his bright, restless eyes travelled over me, to my hands, to the stick I carried, to my feet, to the tattered places in my coat, and the cuts and scratches I had received from the thorns. He seemed puzzled at something. His eyes came back to my hands. He held his own hand out and counted his digits slowly, "One, two, three, four, five—eigh?"

I did not grasp his meaning then; afterwards I was to find that a great proportion of these Beast People had malformed hands, lacking sometimes even three digits. But guessing this was in some way a greeting, I did the same thing by way of reply. He grinned with immense satisfaction. Then his swift roving glance went round again; he made a swift movement—and vanished. The fern fronds he had stood between came swishing together,

I pushed out of the brake after him, and was astonished to find him swinging cheerfully by one lank arm from a rope of creepers that looped down from the foliage overhead. His back was to me.

"Hullo!" said I.

He came down with a twisting jump, and stood facing me.

"I say," said I, "where can I get something to eat?"

"Eat!" he said. "Eat Man's food, now." And his eye went back to the swing of ropes. "At the huts."

"But where are the huts?"

"Oh!"

"I'm new, you know."

At that he swung round, and set off at a quick walk. All his motions were curiously rapid. "Come along," said he.

I went with him to see the adventure out. I guessed the huts were some rough shelter where he and some more of these Beast People lived. I might perhaps find them friendly, find some handle in their minds to take hold of. I did not know how far they had forgotten their human heritage.

My ape-like companion trotted along by my side, with his hands hanging down and his jaw thrust forward. I wondered what memory he might have in him. "How long have you been on this island?" said I.

"How long?" he asked; and after having the question repeated, he held up three fingers.

The creature was little better than an idiot. I tried to make out what he meant by that, and it seems I bored him. After another question or two he suddenly left my side and went leaping at some fruit that hung from a tree. He pulled down a handful of prickly husks and went on eating the contents. I noted this with satisfaction, for here at least was a hint for feeding. I tried him with some other

questions, but his chattering, prompt responses were as often as not quite at cross purposes with my question. Some few were appropriate, others quite parrot-like.

I was so intent upon these peculiarities that I scarcely noticed the path we followed. Presently we came to trees, all charred and brown, and so to a bare place covered with a yellow-white incrustation, across which a drifting smoke, pungent in whiffs to nose and eyes, went drifting. On our right, over a shoulder of bare rock, I saw the level blue of the sea. The path coiled down abruptly into a narrow ravine between two tumbled and knotty masses of blackish scoriae. Into this we plunged.

It was extremely dark, this passage, after the blinding sunlight reflected from the sulphurous ground. Its walls grew steep, and approached each other. Blotches of green and crimson drifted across my eyes. My conductor stopped suddenly. "Home!" said he, and I stood in a floor of a chasm that was at first absolutely dark to me. I heard some strange noises, and thrust the knuckles of my left hand into my eyes. I became aware of a disagreeable odor, like that of a monkey's cage ill-cleaned. Beyond, the rock opened again upon a gradual slope of sunlit greenery, and on either hand the light smote down through narrow ways into the central gloom.

XII. THE SAYERS OF THE LAW

Then something cold touched my hand. I started violently, and saw close to me a dim pinkish thing, looking more like a flayed child than anything else in the world. The creature had exactly the mild but repulsive features of a sloth, the same low forehead and slow gestures.

As the first shock of the change of light passed, I saw about me more distinctly. The little sloth-like creature was standing and staring at me. My conductor had vanished. The place was a narrow passage between high walls of lava, a crack in the knotted rock, and on either side interwoven heaps of sea- mat, palm-fans, and reeds leaning against the rock formed rough and impenetrably dark dens. The winding way up the ravine between these was scarcely three yards wide, and was disfigured by lumps of decaying fruit-pulp and other refuse, which accounted for the disagreeable stench of the place.

The little pink sloth-creature was still blinking at me when my Ape-man reappeared at the aperture of the nearest of these dens, and beckoned me in. As he did so a slouching monster wriggled out of one of the places, further up this strange street, and stood up in featureless silhouette against the bright green beyond, staring at me. I hesitated, having half a mind to bolt the way I had come; and then, determined to go through with the adventure, I gripped my nailed stick about the middle and crawled into the little evil-smelling lean-to after my conductor.

It was a semi-circular space, shaped like the half of a bee-hive; and against the rocky wall that formed the inner side of it was a pile of variegated fruits, cocoanuts among others. Some rough vessels of lava and wood stood about the floor, and one on a rough stool. There was no fire. In the darkest corner of the hut sat a shapeless mass of darkness that grunted "Hey!" as I came in, and my Ape-man stood in the dim light of the doorway and held out a split cocoa-nut to me as I crawled into the other corner and squatted down. I took it, and began gnawing it, as serenely as possible, in spite of a certain trepidation and the nearly intolerable closeness of the den. The little pink sloth-creature stood in the aperture of the hut, and something else with a drab face and bright eyes came staring over its shoulder.

"Hey!" came out of the lump of mystery opposite. "It is a man."

"It is a man," gabbled my conductor, "a man, a man, a five-man, like me."

"Shut up!" said the voice from the dark, and grunted. I gnawed my cocoa- nut amid an impressive stillness.

I peered hard into the blackness, but could distinguish nothing.

"It is a man," the voice repeated. "He comes to live with us?"

It was a thick voice, with something in it—a kind of whistling overtone—that struck me as peculiar; but the English accent was strangely good.

The Ape-man looked at me as though he expected something. I perceived the pause was interrogative. "He comes to live with you," I said.

"It is a man. He must learn the Law."

I began to distinguish now a deeper blackness in the black, a vague outline of a hunched-up figure. Then I noticed the opening of the place was darkened by two more black heads. My hand tightened on my stick.

The thing in the dark repeated in a louder tone, "Say the words." I had missed its last remark. "Not to go on all-fours; that is the Law," it repeated in a kind of sing-song.

I was puzzled.

"Say the words," said the Ape-man, repeating, and the figures in the doorway echoed this, with a threat in the tone of their voices.

I realised that I had to repeat this idiotic formula; and then began the insanest ceremony. The voice in the dark began intoning a mad litany, line by line, and I and the rest to repeat it. As they did so, they swayed from side to side in the oddest way, and beat their hands upon their knees; and I followed their example. I could have imagined I was already dead and in another world. That dark hut, these grotesque dim figures, just flecked here and there by a glimmer of light, and all of them swaying in unison and chanting,

"Not to go on all-fours; that is the Law. Are we not Men? "Not to suck up Drink; that is the Law. Are we not Men? "Not to eat Fish or Flesh; that is the Law. Are we not Men? "Not to claw the Bark of Trees; that is the Law. Are we not Men? "Not to chase other Men; that is the Law. Are we not Men?"

And so from the prohibition of these acts of folly, on to the prohibition of what I thought then were the maddest, most impossible, and most indecent things one could well imagine. A kind of rhythmic fervour fell on all of us; we gabbled and swayed faster and faster, repeating this amazing Law. Superficially the contagion of these brutes was upon me, but deep down within me the laughter and disgust struggled together. We ran through a long list of prohibitions, and then the chant swung round to a new formula.

"*His* is the House of Pain. "*His* is the Hand that makes. "*His* is the Hand that wounds. "*His* is the Hand that heals."

And so on for another long series, mostly quite incomprehensible gibberish to me about *Him*, whoever he might be. I could have fancied it was a dream, but never before have I heard chanting in a dream.

"*His* is the lightning flash," we sang. "*His* is the deep, salt sea."

A horrible fancy came into my head that Moreau, after animalising these men, had infected their dwarfed brains with a kind of deification of himself. However, I was too keenly aware of white teeth and strong claws about me to stop my chanting on that account.

"*His* are the stars in the sky."

At last that song ended. I saw the Ape-man's face shining with perspiration; and my eyes being now accustomed to the darkness, I saw more distinctly the figure in the corner from which the voice came. It was the size of a man, but it seemed covered with a dull grey hair almost like a Skye- terrier. What was it? What were they all? Imagine yourself surrounded by all the most horrible cripples and maniacs it is possible to conceive, and you may understand a little of my feelings with these grotesque caricatures of humanity about me.

"He is a five-man, a five-man, a five-man—like me," said the Ape- man.

I held out my hands. The grey creature in the corner leant forward.

"Not to run on all-fours; that is the Law. Are we not Men?" he said.

He put out a strangely distorted talon and gripped my fingers. The thing was almost like the hoof of a deer produced into claws. I could have yelled with surprise and pain. His face came forward and peered at my nails, came forward into the light of the opening of the hut and I saw with a quivering disgust that it was like the face of neither man nor beast, but a mere shock of grey hair, with three shadowy over-archings to mark the eyes and mouth.

"He has little nails," said this grisly creature in his hairy beard. "It is well."

He threw my hand down, and instinctively I gripped my stick.

"Eat roots and herbs; it is His will," said the Ape-man.

"I am the Sayer of the Law," said the grey figure. "Here come all that be new to learn the Law. I sit in the darkness and say the Law."

"It is even so," said one of the beasts in the doorway.

"Evil are the punishments of those who break the Law. None escape."

"None escape," said the Beast Folk, glancing furtively at one another.

"None, none," said the Ape-man,—"none escape. See! I did a little thing, a wrong thing, once. I jabbered, jabbered, stopped talking. None could understand. I am burnt, branded in the hand. He is great. He is good!"

"None escape," said the grey creature in the corner.

"None escape," said the Beast People, looking askance at one another.

"For every one the want that is bad," said the grey Sayer of the Law. "What you will want we do not know; we shall know. Some want to follow things that move, to watch and slink and wait and spring; to kill and bite, bite deep and rich, sucking the blood. It is bad. 'Not to chase other Men; that is the Law. Are we not Men? Not to eat Flesh or Fish; that is the Law. Are we not Men?'"

"None escape," said a dappled brute standing in the doorway.

"For every one the want is bad," said the grey Sayer of the Law. "Some want to go tearing with teeth and hands into the roots of things, snuffing into the earth. It is bad."

"None escape," said the men in the door.

"Some go clawing trees; some go scratching at the graves of the dead; some go fighting with foreheads or feet or claws; some bite suddenly, none giving occasion; some love uncleanness."

"None escape," said the Ape-man, scratching his calf.

"None escape," said the little pink sloth-creature.

"Punishment is sharp and sure. Therefore learn the Law. Say the words."

And incontinently he began again the strange litany of the Law, and again I and all these creatures began singing and swaying. My head reeled with this jabbering and the close stench of the place; but I kept on, trusting to find presently some chance of a new development.

"Not to go on all-fours; that is the Law. Are we not Men?"

We were making such a noise that I noticed nothing of a tumult outside, until some one, who I think was one of the two Swine Men I had seen, thrust his head over the little pink sloth-creature and shouted something excitedly, something that I did not catch. Incontinently those at the opening of the hut vanished; my Ape-man rushed out; the thing that had sat in the dark followed him (I only observed that it was big and clumsy, and covered with silvery hair), and I was left alone. Then before I reached the aperture I heard the yelp of a staghound.

In another moment I was standing outside the hovel, my chair-rail in my hand, every muscle of me quivering. Before me were the clumsy backs of perhaps a score of these Beast People, their misshapen heads half hidden by their shoulder-blades. They were gesticulating excitedly. Other half-animal faces glared interrogation out of the hovels. Looking in the direction in which they faced, I saw coming through the haze under the trees beyond the end of the passage of dens the dark figure and awful white face of Moreau. He was holding the leaping staghound back, and close behind him came Montgomery revolver in hand.

For a moment I stood horror-struck. I turned and saw the passage behind me blocked by another heavy brute, with a huge grey face and twinkling little eyes, advancing towards me. I looked round and saw to the right of me and a half-dozen yards in front of me a narrow gap in the wall of rock through which a ray of light slanted into the shadows.

"Stop!" cried Moreau as I strode towards this, and then, "Hold him!"

At that, first one face turned towards me and then others. Their bestial minds were happily slow. I dashed my shoulder into a clumsy monster who was turning to see what Moreau meant, and flung him forward into another. I felt his hands fly round, clutching at me and missing me. The little pink sloth- creature dashed at me, and I gashed down its ugly face with the nail in my stick and in another minute was scrambling up a steep side pathway, a kind of sloping chimney, out of the ravine. I heard a howl behind me, and cries of "Catch him!" "Hold him!" and the grey-faced creature appeared behind me and jammed his huge bulk into the cleft. "Go on! go on!" they howled. I clambered up the narrow cleft in the rock and came out upon the sulphur on the westward side of the village of the Beast Men.

That gap was altogether fortunate for me, for the narrow chimney, slanting obliquely upward, must have impeded the nearer pursuers. I ran over the white space and down a steep slope, through a scattered growth of trees, and came to a low-lying stretch of tall reeds, through which I pushed into a dark, thick undergrowth that was black and succulent under foot. As I plunged into the reeds, my foremost pursuers emerged from the gap. I broke my way through this under-

growth for some minutes. The air behind me and about me was soon full of threatening cries. I heard the tumult of my pursuers in the gap up the slope, then the crashing of the reeds, and every now and then the crackling crash of a branch. Some of the creatures roared like excited beasts of prey. The staghound yelped to the left. I heard Moreau and Montgomery shouting in the same direction. I turned sharply to the right. It seemed to me even then that I heard Montgomery shouting for me to run for my life.

Presently the ground gave rich and oozy under my feet; but I was desperate and went headlong into it, struggled through kneedeep, and so came to a winding path among tall canes. The noise of my pursuers passed away to my left. In one place three strange, pink, hopping animals, about the size of cats, bolted before my footsteps. This pathway ran up hill, across another open space covered with white incrustation, and plunged into a canebrake again. Then suddenly it turned parallel with the edge of a steep-walled gap, which came without warning, like the ha-ha of an English park,—turned with an unexpected abruptness. I was still running with all my might, and I never saw this drop until I was flying headlong through the air.

I fell on my forearms and head, among thorns, and rose with a torn ear and bleeding face. I had fallen into a precipitous ravine, rocky and thorny, full of a hazy mist which drifted about me in wisps, and with a narrow streamlet from which this mist came meandering down the centre. I was astonished at this thin fog in the full blaze of daylight; but I had no time to stand wondering then. I turned to my right, down-stream, hoping to come to the sea in that direction, and so have my way open to drown myself. It was only later I found that I had dropped my nailed stick in my fall.

Presently the ravine grew narrower for a space, and carelessly I stepped into the stream. I jumped out again pretty quickly, for the water was almost boiling. I noticed too there was a thin sulphurous scum drifting upon its coiling water. Almost immediately came a turn in the ravine, and the indistinct blue horizon. The nearer sea was flashing the sun from a myriad facets. I saw my death before me; but I was hot and panting, with the warm blood oozing out on my face and running pleasantly through my veins. I felt more than a touch of exultation too, at having distanced my pursuers. It was not in me then to go out and drown myself yet. I stared back the way I had come.

I listened. Save for the hum of the gnats and the chirp of some small insects that hopped among the thorns, the air was absolutely still. Then came the yelp of a dog, very faint, and a chattering and gibbering, the snap of a whip, and voices. They grew louder, then fainter again. The noise receded up the stream and faded away. For a while the chase was over; but I knew now how much hope of help for me lay in the Beast People.

XIII. A PARLEY

I turned again and went on down towards the sea. I found the hot stream broadened out to a shallow, weedy sand, in which an abundance of crabs and long- bodied, many-legged creatures started from my footfall. I walked to the very edge of the salt water, and then I felt I was safe. I turned and stared, arms akimbo, at the thick green behind me, into which the steamy ravine cut like a smoking gash. But, as I say, I was too full of excitement and (a true saying, though those who have never known danger may doubt it) too desperate to die.

Then it came into my head that there was one chance before me yet. While Moreau and Montgomery and their bestial rabble chased me through the island, might I not go round the beach until I came to their enclosure,—make a flank march upon them, in fact, and then with a rock lugged out of their loosely-built wall, perhaps, smash in the lock of the smaller door and see what I could find (knife, pistol, or what not) to fight them with when they returned? It was at any rate something to try.

So I turned to the westward and walked along by the water's edge. The setting sun flashed his blinding heat into my eyes. The slight Pacific tide was running in with a gentle ripple. Presently the shore fell away southward, and the sun came round upon my right hand. Then suddenly, far in front of me, I saw first one and then several figures emerging from the bushes,—Moreau, with his grey stag-hound, then Montgomery, and two others. At that I stopped.

They saw me, and began gesticulating and advancing. I stood watching them approach. The two Beast Men came running forward to cut me off from the undergrowth, inland. Montgomery came, running also, but straight towards me. Moreau followed slower with the dog.

At last I roused myself from my inaction, and turning seaward walked straight into the water. The water was very shallow at first. I was thirty yards out before the waves reached to my waist. Dimly I could see the intertidal creatures darting away from my feet.

"What are you doing, man?" cried Montgomery.

I turned, standing waist deep, and stared at them. Montgomery stood panting at the margin of the water. His face was bright-red with exertion, his long flaxen hair blown about his head, and his dropping nether lip showed his irregular teeth. Moreau was just coming up, his face pale and firm, and the dog at his hand barked at me. Both men had heavy whips. Farther up the beach stared the Beast Men.

"What am I doing? I am going to drown myself," said I.

Montgomery and Moreau looked at each other. "Why?" asked Moreau.

"Because that is better than being tortured by you."

"I told you so," said Montgomery, and Moreau said something in a low tone.

"What makes you think I shall torture you?" asked Moreau.

"What I saw," I said. "And those—yonder."

"Hush!" said Moreau, and held up his hand.

"I will not," said I. "They were men: what are they now? I at least will not be like them."

I looked past my interlocutors. Up the beach were M'ling, Montgomery's attendant, and one of the white-swathed brutes from the boat. Farther up, in the shadow of the trees, I saw my little Ape-man, and behind him some other dim figures.

"Who are these creatures?" said I, pointing to them and raising my voice more and more that it might reach them. "They were men, men like yourselves, whom you have infected with some bestial taint,—men whom you have enslaved, and whom you still fear.

"You who listen," I cried, pointing now to Moreau and shouting past him to the Beast Men,—"You who listen! Do you not see these men still fear you, go in dread of you? Why, then, do you fear them? You are many—"

"For God's sake," cried Montgomery, "stop that, Prendick!"

"Prendick!" cried Moreau.

They both shouted together, as if to drown my voice; and behind them lowered the staring faces of the Beast Men, wondering, their deformed hands hanging down, their shoulders hunched up. They seemed, as I fancied, to be trying to understand me, to remember, I thought, something of their human past.

I went on shouting, I scarcely remember what,—that Moreau and Montgomery could be killed, that they were not to be feared: that was the burden of what I put into the heads of the Beast People. I saw the green-eyed man in the dark rags, who had met me on the evening of my arrival, come out from among the trees, and others followed him, to hear me better. At last for want of breath I paused.

"Listen to me for a moment," said the steady voice of Moreau; "and then say what you will."

"Well?" said I.

He coughed, thought, then shouted: "Latin, Prendick! bad Latin, schoolboy Latin; but try and understand. Hi non sunt homines; sunt animalia qui nos habemus—vivisected. A humanising process. I will explain. Come ashore."

I laughed. "A pretty story," said I. "They talk, build houses. They were men. It's likely I'll come ashore."

"The water just beyond where you stand is deep—and full of sharks."

"That's my way," said I. "Short and sharp. Presently."

"Wait a minute." He took something out of his pocket that flashed back the sun, and dropped the object at his feet. "That's a loaded revolver," said he. "Mont-

gomery here will do the same. Now we are going up the beach until you are satisfied the distance is safe. Then come and take the revolvers."

"Not I! You have a third between you."

"I want you to think over things, Prendick. In the first place, I never asked you to come upon this island. If we vivisected men, we should import men, not beasts. In the next, we had you drugged last night, had we wanted to work you any mischief; and in the next, now your first panic is over and you can think a little, is Montgomery here quite up to the character you give him? We have chased you for your good. Because this island is full of inimical phenomena. Besides, why should we want to shoot you when you have just offered to drown yourself?"

"Why did you set—your people onto me when I was in the hut?"

"We felt sure of catching you, and bringing you out of danger. Afterwards we drew away from the scent, for your good."

I mused. It seemed just possible. Then I remembered something again. "But I saw," said I, "in the enclosure—"

"That was the puma."

"Look here, Prendick," said Montgomery, "you're a silly ass! Come out of the water and take these revolvers, and talk. We can't do anything more than we could do now."

I will confess that then, and indeed always, I distrusted and dreaded Moreau; but Montgomery was a man I felt I understood.

"Go up the beach," said I, after thinking, and added, "holding your hands up."

"Can't do that," said Montgomery, with an explanatory nod over his shoulder. "Undignified."

"Go up to the trees, then," said I, "as you please."

"It's a damned silly ceremony," said Montgomery.

Both turned and faced the six or seven grotesque creatures, who stood there in the sunlight, solid, casting shadows, moving, and yet so incredibly unreal. Montgomery cracked his whip at them, and forthwith they all turned and fled helter-skelter into the trees; and when Montgomery and Moreau were at a distance I judged sufficient, I waded ashore, and picked up and examined the revolvers. To satisfy myself against the subtlest trickery, I discharged one at a round lump of lava, and had the satisfaction of seeing the stone pulverised and the beach splashed with lead. Still I hesitated for a moment.

"I'll take the risk," said I, at last; and with a revolver in each hand I walked up the beach towards them.

"That's better," said Moreau, without affectation. "As it is, you have wasted the best part of my day with your confounded imagination." And with a touch of contempt which humiliated me, he and Montgomery turned and went on in silence before me.

The knot of Beast Men, still wondering, stood back among the trees. I passed them as serenely as possible. One started to follow me, but retreated again when Montgomery cracked his whip. The rest stood silent—watching. They may once have been animals; but I never before saw an animal trying to think.

XIV. DOCTOR MOREAU EXPLAINS

"And now, Prendick, I will explain," said Doctor Moreau, so soon as we had eaten and drunk. "I must confess that you are the most dictatorial guest I ever entertained. I warn you that this is the last I shall do to oblige you. The next thing you threaten to commit suicide about, I shan't do,—even at some personal inconvenience."

He sat in my deck chair, a cigar half consumed in his white, dexterous- looking fingers. The light of the swinging lamp fell on his white hair; he stared through the little window out at the starlight. I sat as far away from him as possible, the table between us and the revolvers to hand. Montgomery was not present. I did not care to be with the two of them in such a little room.

"You admit that the vivisected human being, as you called it, is, after all, only the puma?" said Moreau. He had made me visit that horror in the inner room, to assure myself of its inhumanity.

"It is the puma," I said, "still alive, but so cut and mutilated as I pray I may never see living flesh again. Of all vile—"

"Never mind that," said Moreau; "at least, spare me those youthful horrors. Montgomery used to be just the same. You admit that it is the puma. Now be quiet, while I reel off my physiological lecture to you."

And forthwith, beginning in the tone of a man supremely bored, but presently warming a little, he explained his work to me. He was very simple and convincing. Now and then there was a touch of sarcasm in his voice. Presently I found myself hot with shame at our mutual positions.

The creatures I had seen were not men, had never been men. They were animals, humanised animals,—triumphs of vivisection.

"You forget all that a skilled vivisector can do with living things," said Moreau. "For my own part, I'm puzzled why the things I have done here have not been done before. Small efforts, of course, have been made,—amputation, tongue-cutting, excisions. Of course you know a squint may be induced or cured by surgery? Then in the case of excisions you have all kinds of secondary changes, pigmentary disturbances, modifications of the passions, alterations in the secretion of fatty tissue. I have no doubt you have heard of these things?"

"Of course," said I. "But these foul creatures of yours—"

"All in good time," said he, waving his hand at me; "I am only beginning. Those are trivial cases of alteration. Surgery can do better things than that. There is building up as well as breaking down and changing. You have heard, perhaps,

of a common surgical operation resorted to in cases where the nose has been destroyed: a flap of skin is cut from the forehead, turned down on the nose, and heals in the new position. This is a kind of grafting in a new position of part of an animal upon itself. Grafting of freshly obtained material from another animal is also possible,—the case of teeth, for example. The grafting of skin and bone is done to facilitate healing: the surgeon places in the middle of the wound pieces of skin snipped from another animal, or fragments of bone from a victim freshly killed. Hunter's cock-spur —possibly you have heard of that—flourished on the bull's neck; and the rhinoceros rats of the Algerian zouaves are also to be thought of, —monsters manufactured by transferring a slip from the tail of an ordinary rat to its snout, and allowing it to heal in that position."

"Monsters manufactured!" said I. "Then you mean to tell me—"

"Yes. These creatures you have seen are animals carven and wrought into new shapes. To that, to the study of the plasticity of living forms, my life has been devoted. I have studied for years, gaining in knowledge as I go. I see you look horrified, and yet I am telling you nothing new. It all lay in the surface of practical anatomy years ago, but no one had the temerity to touch it. It is not simply the outward form of an animal which I can change. The physiology, the chemical rhythm of the creature, may also be made to undergo an enduring modification,—of which vaccination and other methods of inoculation with living or dead matter are examples that will, no doubt, be familiar to you. A similar operation is the transfusion of blood,—with which subject, indeed, I began. These are all familiar cases. Less so, and probably far more extensive, were the operations of those mediaeval practitioners who made dwarfs and beggar-cripples, show-monsters,—some vestiges of whose art still remain in the preliminary manipulation of the young mountebank or contortionist. Victor Hugo gives an account of them in 'L'Homme qui Rit.'—But perhaps my meaning grows plain now. You begin to see that it is a possible thing to transplant tissue from one part of an animal to another, or from one animal to another; to alter its chemical reactions and methods of growth; to modify the articulations of its limbs; and, indeed, to change it in its most intimate structure.

"And yet this extraordinary branch of knowledge has never been sought as an end, and systematically, by modern investigators until I took it up! Some such things have been hit upon in the last resort of surgery; most of the kindred evidence that will recur to your mind has been demonstrated as it were by accident,—by tyrants, by criminals, by the breeders of horses and dogs, by all kinds of untrained clumsy-handed men working for their own immediate ends. I was the first man to take up this question armed with antiseptic surgery, and with a really scientific knowledge of the laws of growth. Yet one would imagine it must have been practised in secret before. Such creatures as the Siamese Twins—And in the vaults of the Inquisition. No doubt their chief aim was artistic torture, but some at least of the inquisitors must have had a touch of scientific curiosity."

"But," said I, "these things—these animals talk!"

He said that was so, and proceeded to point out that the possibility of vivisection does not stop at a mere physical metamorphosis. A pig may be educated. The mental structure is even less determinate than the bodily. In our growing science of hypnotism we find the promise of a possibility of superseding old inherent instincts by new suggestions, grafting upon or replacing the inherited fixed ideas. Very much indeed of what we call moral education, he said, is such an artificial modification and perversion of instinct; pugnacity is trained into courageous self-sacrifice, and suppressed sexuality into religious emotion. And the great difference between man and monkey is in the larynx, he continued,—in the incapacity to frame delicately different sound-symbols by which thought could be sustained. In this I failed to agree with him, but with a certain incivility he declined to notice my objection. He repeated that the thing was so, and continued his account of his work.

I asked him why he had taken the human form as a model. There seemed to me then, and there still seems to me now, a strange wickedness for that choice.

He confessed that he had chosen that form by chance. "I might just as well have worked to form sheep into llamas and llamas into sheep. I suppose there is something in the human form that appeals to the artistic turn of mind more powerfully than any animal shape can. But I've not confined myself to man- making. Once or twice—" He was silent, for a minute perhaps. "These years! How they have slipped by! And here I have wasted a day saving your life, and am now wasting an hour explaining myself!"

"But," said I, "I still do not understand. Where is your justification for inflicting all this pain? The only thing that could excuse vivisection to me would be some application—"

"Precisely," said he. "But, you see, I am differently constituted. We are on different platforms. You are a materialist."

"I am *not* a materialist," I began hotly.

"In my view—in my view. For it is just this question of pain that parts us. So long as visible or audible pain turns you sick; so long as your own pains drive you; so long as pain underlies your propositions about sin, —so long, I tell you, you are an animal, thinking a little less obscurely what an animal feels. This pain—"

I gave an impatient shrug at such sophistry.

"Oh, but it is such a little thing! A mind truly opened to what science has to teach must see that it is a little thing. It may be that save in this little planet, this speck of cosmic dust, invisible long before the nearest star could be attained—it may be, I say, that nowhere else does this thing called pain occur. But the laws we feel our way towards—Why, even on this earth, even among living things, what pain is there?"

As he spoke he drew a little penknife from his pocket, opened the smaller blade, and moved his chair so that I could see his thigh. Then, choosing the place deliberately, he drove the blade into his leg and withdrew it.

"No doubt," he said, "you have seen that before. It does not hurt a pin- prick. But what does it show? The capacity for pain is not needed in the muscle, and it is not placed there,—is but little needed in the skin, and only here and there over the thigh is a spot capable of feeling pain. Pain is simply our intrinsic medical adviser to warn us and stimulate us. Not all living flesh is painful; nor is all nerve, not even all sensory nerve. There's no taint of pain, real pain, in the sensations of the optic nerve. If you wound the optic nerve, you merely see flashes of light,—just as disease of the auditory nerve merely means a humming in our ears. Plants do not feel pain, nor the lower animals; it's possible that such animals as the starfish and crayfish do not feel pain at all. Then with men, the more intelligent they become, the more intelligently they will see after their own welfare, and the less they will need the goad to keep them out of danger. I never yet heard of a useless thing that was not ground out of existence by evolution sooner or later. Did you? And pain gets needless.

"Then I am a religious man, Prendick, as every sane man must be. It may be, I fancy, that I have seen more of the ways of this world's Maker than you, —for I have sought his laws, in *my* way, all my life, while you, I understand, have been collecting butterflies. And I tell you, pleasure and pain have nothing to do with heaven or hell. Pleasure and pain—bah! What is your theologian's ecstasy but Mahomet's houri in the dark? This store which men and women set on pleasure and pain, Prendick, is the mark of the beast upon them,—the mark of the beast from which they came! Pain, pain and pleasure, they are for us only so long as we wriggle in the dust.

"You see, I went on with this research just the way it led me. That is the only way I ever heard of true research going. I asked a question, devised some method of obtaining an answer, and got a fresh question. Was this possible or that possible? You cannot imagine what this means to an investigator, what an intellectual passion grows upon him! You cannot imagine the strange, colourless delight of these intellectual desires! The thing before you is no longer an animal, a fellow-creature, but a problem! Sympathetic pain,—all I know of it I remember as a thing I used to suffer from years ago. I wanted—it was the one thing I wanted—to find out the extreme limit of plasticity in a living shape."

"But," said I, "the thing is an abomination—"

"To this day I have never troubled about the ethics of the matter," he continued. "The study of Nature makes a man at last as remorseless as Nature. I have gone on, not heeding anything but the question I was pursuing; and the material has—dripped into the huts yonder. It is nearly eleven years since we came here, I and Montgomery and six Kanakas. I remember the green stillness of the island and the empty ocean about us, as though it was yesterday. The place seemed waiting for me.

"The stores were landed and the house was built. The Kanakas founded some huts near the ravine. I went to work here upon what I had brought with me. There were some disagreeable things happened at first. I began with a sheep, and killed it after a day and a half by a slip of the scalpel. I took another sheep, and made a

thing of pain and fear and left it bound up to heal. It looked quite human to me when I had finished it; but when I went to it I was discontented with it. It remembered me, and was terrified beyond imagination; and it had no more than the wits of a sheep. The more I looked at it the clumsier it seemed, until at last I put the monster out of its misery. These animals without courage, these fear-haunted, pain-driven things, without a spark of pugnacious energy to face torment,—they are no good for man- making.

"Then I took a gorilla I had; and upon that, working with infinite care and mastering difficulty after difficulty, I made my first man. All the week, night and day, I moulded him. With him it was chiefly the brain that needed moulding; much had to be added, much changed. I thought him a fair specimen of the negroid type when I had finished him, and he lay bandaged, bound, and motionless before me. It was only when his life was assured that I left him and came into this room again, and found Montgomery much as you are. He had heard some of the cries as the thing grew human,—cries like those that disturbed *you* so. I didn't take him completely into my confidence at first. And the Kanakas too, had realised something of it. They were scared out of their wits by the sight of me. I got Montgomery over to me—in a way; but I and he had the hardest job to prevent the Kanakas deserting. Finally they did; and so we lost the yacht. I spent many days educating the brute,—altogether I had him for three or four months. I taught him the rudiments of English; gave him ideas of counting; even made the thing read the alphabet. But at that he was slow, though I've met with idiots slower. He began with a clean sheet, mentally; had no memories left in his mind of what he had been. When his scars were quite healed, and he was no longer anything but painful and stiff, and able to converse a little, I took him yonder and introduced him to the Kanakas as an interesting stowaway.

"They were horribly afraid of him at first, somehow,—which offended me rather, for I was conceited about him; but his ways seemed so mild, and he was so abject, that after a time they received him and took his education in hand. He was quick to learn, very imitative and adaptive, and built himself a hovel rather better, it seemed to me, than their own shanties. There was one among the boys a bit of a missionary, and he taught the thing to read, or at least to pick out letters, and gave him some rudimentary ideas of morality; but it seems the beast's habits were not all that is desirable.

"I rested from work for some days after this, and was in a mind to write an account of the whole affair to wake up English physiology. Then I came upon the creature squatting up in a tree and gibbering at two of the Kanakas who had been teasing him. I threatened him, told him the inhumanity of such a proceeding, aroused his sense of shame, and came home resolved to do better before I took my work back to England. I have been doing better. But somehow the things drift back again: the stubborn beast-flesh grows day by day back again. But I mean to do better things still. I mean to conquer that. This puma —

"But that's the story. All the Kanaka boys are dead now; one fell overboard of the launch, and one died of a wounded heel that he poisoned in some way with

plant-juice. Three went away in the yacht, and I suppose and hope were drowned. The other one—was killed. Well, I have replaced them. Montgomery went on much as you are disposed to do at first, and then—

"What became of the other one?" said I, sharply,—"the other Kanaka who was killed?"

"The fact is, after I had made a number of human creatures I made a Thing—" He hesitated.

"Yes?" said I.

"It was killed."

"I don't understand," said I; "do you mean to say—"

"It killed the Kanaka—yes. It killed several other things that it caught. We chased it for a couple of days. It only got loose by accident —I never meant it to get away. It wasn't finished. It was purely an experiment. It was a limbless thing, with a horrible face, that writhed along the ground in a serpentine fashion. It was immensely strong, and in infuriating pain. It lurked in the woods for some days, until we hunted it; and then it wriggled into the northern part of the island, and we divided the party to close in upon it. Montgomery insisted upon coming with me. The man had a rifle; and when his body was found, one of the barrels was curved into the shape of an S and very nearly bitten through. Montgomery shot the thing. After that I stuck to the ideal of humanity—except for little things."

He became silent. I sat in silence watching his face.

"So for twenty years altogether—counting nine years in England —I have been going on; and there is still something in everything I do that defeats me, makes me dissatisfied, challenges me to further effort. Sometimes I rise above my level, sometimes I fall below it; but always I fall short of the things I dream. The human shape I can get now, almost with ease, so that it is lithe and graceful, or thick and strong; but often there is trouble with the hands and the claws,—painful things, that I dare not shape too freely. But it is in the subtle grafting and reshaping one must needs do to the brain that my trouble lies. The intelligence is often oddly low, with unaccountable blank ends, unexpected gaps. And least satisfactory of all is something that I cannot touch, somewhere—I cannot determine where —in the seat of the emotions. Cravings, instincts, desires that harm humanity, a strange hidden reservoir to burst forth suddenly and inundate the whole being of the creature with anger, hate, or fear. These creatures of mine seemed strange and uncanny to you so soon as you began to observe them; but to me, just after I make them, they seem to be indisputably human beings. It's afterwards, as I observe them, that the persuasion fades. First one animal trait, then another, creeps to the surface and stares out at me. But I will conquer yet! Each time I dip a living creature into the bath of burning pain, I say, 'This time I will burn out all the animal; this time I will make a rational creature of my own!' After all, what is ten years? Men have been a hundred thousand in the making." He thought darkly. "But I am drawing near the fastness. This puma of mine—" After a silence, "And they revert. As soon as my hand is taken from them the beast begins to creep back, begins to assert itself again." Another long silence.

"Then you take the things you make into those dens?" said I.

"They go. I turn them out when I begin to feel the beast in them, and presently they wander there. They all dread this house and me. There is a kind of travesty of humanity over there. Montgomery knows about it, for he interferes in their affairs. He has trained one or two of them to our service. He's ashamed of it, but I believe he half likes some of those beasts. It's his business, not mine. They only sicken me with a sense of failure. I take no interest in them. I fancy they follow in the lines the Kanaka missionary marked out, and have a kind of mockery of a rational life, poor beasts! There's something they call the Law. Sing hymns about 'all thine.' They build themselves their dens, gather fruit, and pull herbs—marry even. But I can see through it all, see into their very souls, and see there nothing but the souls of beasts, beasts that perish, anger and the lusts to live and gratify themselves.—Yet they're odd; complex, like everything else alive. There is a kind of upward striving in them, part vanity, part waste sexual emotion, part waste curiosity. It only mocks me. I have some hope of this puma. I have worked hard at her head and brain—

"And now," said he, standing up after a long gap of silence, during which we had each pursued our own thoughts, "what do you think? Are you in fear of me still?"

I looked at him, and saw but a white-faced, white-haired man, with calm eyes. Save for his serenity, the touch almost of beauty that resulted from his set tranquillity and his magnificent build, he might have passed muster among a hundred other comfortable old gentlemen. Then I shivered. By way of answer to his second question, I handed him a revolver with either hand.

"Keep them," he said, and snatched at a yawn. He stood up, stared at me for a moment, and smiled. "You have had two eventful days," said he. "I should advise some sleep. I'm glad it's all clear. Good-night." He thought me over for a moment, then went out by the inner door.

I immediately turned the key in the outer one. I sat down again; sat for a time in a kind of stagnant mood, so weary, emotionally, mentally, and physically, that I could not think beyond the point at which he had left me. The black window stared at me like an eye. At last with an effort I put out the light and got into the hammock. Very soon I was asleep.

XV. CONCERNING THE BEAST FOLK

I woke early. Moreau's explanation stood before my mind, clear and definite, from the moment of my awakening. I got out of the hammock and went to the door to assure myself that the key was turned. Then I tried the window-bar, and found it firmly fixed. That these man-like creatures were in truth only bestial monsters, mere grotesque travesties of men, filled me with a vague uncertainty of their possibilities which was far worse than any definite fear.

A tapping came at the door, and I heard the glutinous accents of M'ling speaking. I pocketed one of the revolvers (keeping one hand upon it), and opened to him.

"Good-morning, sair," he said, bringing in, in addition to the customary herb-breakfast, an ill-cooked rabbit. Montgomery followed him. His roving eye caught the position of my arm and he smiled askew.

The puma was resting to heal that day; but Moreau, who was singularly solitary in his habits, did not join us. I talked with Montgomery to clear my ideas of the way in which the Beast Folk lived. In particular, I was urgent to know how these inhuman monsters were kept from falling upon Moreau and Montgomery and from rending one another. He explained to me that the comparative safety of Moreau and himself was due to the limited mental scope of these monsters. In spite of their increased intelligence and the tendency of their animal instincts to reawaken, they had certain fixed ideas implanted by Moreau in their minds, which absolutely bounded their imaginations. They were really hypnotised; had been told that certain things were impossible, and that certain things were not to be done, and these prohibitions were woven into the texture of their minds beyond any possibility of disobedience or dispute.

Certain matters, however, in which old instinct was at war with Moreau's convenience, were in a less stable condition. A series of propositions called the Law (I had already heard them recited) battled in their minds with the deep- seated, ever-rebellious cravings of their animal natures. This Law they were ever repeating, I found, and ever breaking. Both Montgomery and Moreau displayed particular solicitude to keep them ignorant of the taste of blood; they feared the inevitable suggestions of that flavour. Montgomery told me that the Law, especially among the feline Beast People, became oddly weakened about nightfall; that then the animal was at its strongest; that a spirit of adventure sprang up in them at the dusk, when they would dare things they never seemed to dream about by day. To that I owed my stalking by the Leopard-man, on the night of my arri-

val. But during these earlier days of my stay they broke the Law only furtively and after dark; in the daylight there was a general atmosphere of respect for its multifarious prohibitions.

And here perhaps I may give a few general facts about the island and the Beast People. The island, which was of irregular outline and lay low upon the wide sea, had a total area, I suppose, of seven or eight square miles.{2} It was volcanic in origin, and was now fringed on three sides by coral reefs; some fumaroles to the northward, and a hot spring, were the only vestiges of the forces that had long since originated it. Now and then a faint quiver of earthquake would be sensible, and sometimes the ascent of the spire of smoke would be rendered tumultuous by gusts of steam; but that was all. The population of the island, Montgomery informed me, now numbered rather more than sixty of these strange creations of Moreau's art, not counting the smaller monstrosities which lived in the undergrowth and were without human form. Altogether he had made nearly a hundred and twenty; but many had died, and others—like the writhing Footless Thing of which he had told me—had come by violent ends. In answer to my question, Montgomery said that they actually bore offspring, but that these generally died. When they lived, Moreau took them and stamped the human form upon them. There was no evidence of the inheritance of their acquired human characteristics. The females were less numerous than the males, and liable to much furtive persecution in spite of the monogamy the Law enjoined.

{2} This description corresponds in every respect to Noble's Isle. —C. E. P.

It would be impossible for me to describe these Beast People in detail; my eye has had no training in details, and unhappily I cannot sketch. Most striking, perhaps, in their general appearance was the disproportion between the legs of these creatures and the length of their bodies; and yet—so relative is our idea of grace—my eye became habituated to their forms, and at last I even fell in with their persuasion that my own long thighs were ungainly. Another point was the forward carriage of the head and the clumsy and inhuman curvature of the spine. Even the Ape-man lacked that inward sinuous curve of the back which makes the human figure so graceful. Most had their shoulders hunched clumsily, and their short forearms hung weakly at their sides. Few of them were conspicuously hairy, at least until the end of my time upon the island.

The next most obvious deformity was in their faces, almost all of which were prognathous, malformed about the ears, with large and protuberant noses, very furry or very bristly hair, and often strangely-coloured or strangely- placed eyes. None could laugh, though the Ape-man had a chattering titter. Beyond these general characters their heads had little in common; each preserved the quality of its particular species: the human mark distorted but did not hide the leopard, the ox, or the sow, or other animal or animals, from which the creature had been moulded. The voices, too, varied exceedingly. The hands were always malformed; and though some surprised me by their unexpected human appearance, almost all were deficient in the number of the digits, clumsy about the finger-nails, and lacking any tactile sensibility.

The two most formidable Animal Men were my Leopard-man and a creature made of hyena and swine. Larger than these were the three bull-creatures who pulled in the boat. Then came the silvery-hairy-man, who was also the Sayer of the Law, M'ling, and a satyr-like creature of ape and goat. There were three Swine-men and a Swine-woman, a mare-rhinoceros-creature, and several other females whose sources I did not ascertain. There were several wolf-creatures, a bear-bull, and a Saint-Bernard-man. I have already described the Ape-man, and there was a particularly hateful (and evil-smelling) old woman made of vixen and bear, whom I hated from the beginning. She was said to be a passionate votary of the Law. Smaller creatures were certain dappled youths and my little sloth-creature. But enough of this catalogue.

At first I had a shivering horror of the brutes, felt all too keenly that they were still brutes; but insensibly I became a little habituated to the idea of them, and moreover I was affected by Montgomery's attitude towards them. He had been with them so long that he had come to regard them as almost normal human beings. His London days seemed a glorious, impossible past to him. Only once in a year or so did he go to Arica to deal with Moreau's agent, a trader in animals there. He hardly met the finest type of mankind in that seafaring village of Spanish mongrels. The men aboard-ship, he told me, seemed at first just as strange to him as'the Beast Men seemed to me,—unnaturally long in the leg, flat in the face, prominent in the forehead, suspicious, dangerous, and cold-hearted. In fact, he did not like men: his heart had warmed to me, he thought, because he had saved my life. I fancied even then that he had a sneaking kindness for some of these metamorphosed brutes, a vicious sympathy with some of their ways, but that he attempted to veil it from me at first.

M'ling, the black-faced man, Montgomery's attendant, the first of the Beast Folk I had encountered, did not live with the others across the island, but in a small kennel at the back of the enclosure. The creature was scarcely so intelligent as the Ape-man, but far more docile, and the most human-looking of all the Beast Folk; and Montgomery had trained it to prepare food, and indeed to discharge all the trivial domestic offices that were required. It was a complex trophy of Moreau's horrible skill,—a bear, tainted with dog and ox, and one of the most elaborately made of all his creatures. It treated Montgomery with a strange tenderness and devotion. Sometimes he would notice it, pat it, call it half-mocking, half-jocular names, and so make it caper with extraordinary delight; sometimes he would ill-treat it, especially after he had been at the whiskey, kicking it, beating it, pelting it with stones or lighted fusees. But whether he treated it well or ill, it loved nothing so much as to be near him.

I say I became habituated to the Beast People, that a thousand things which had seemed unnatural and repulsive speedily became natural and ordinary to me. I suppose everything in existence takes its colour from the average hue of our surroundings. Montgomery and Moreau were too peculiar and individual to keep my general impressions of humanity well defined. I would see one of the clumsy bovine-creatures who worked the launch treading heavily through the undergrowth,

and find myself asking, trying hard to recall, how he differed from some really human yokel trudging home from his mechanical labours; or I would meet the Fox-bear woman's vulpine, shifty face, strangely human in its speculative cunning, and even imagine I had met it before in some city byway.

Yet every now and then the beast would flash out upon me beyond doubt or denial. An ugly-looking man, a hunch-backed human savage to all appearance, squatting in the aperture of one of the dens, would stretch his arms and yawn, showing with startling suddenness scissor-edged incisors and sabre-like canines, keen and brilliant as knives. Or in some narrow pathway, glancing with a transitory daring into the eyes of some lithe, white-swathed female figure, I would suddenly see (with a spasmodic revulsion) that she had slit-like pupils, or glancing down note the curving nail with which she held her shapeless wrap about her. It is a curious thing, by the bye, for which I am quite unable to account, that these weird creatures—the females, I mean—had in the earlier days of my stay an instinctive sense of their own repulsive clumsiness, and displayed in consequence a more than human regard for the decency and decorum of extensive costume.

XVI. HOW THE BEAST FOLK TASTE BLOOD

My inexperience as a writer betrays me, and I wander from the thread of my story.

After I had breakfasted with Montgomery, he took me across the island to see the fumarole and the source of the hot spring into whose scalding waters I had blundered on the previous day. Both of us carried whips and loaded revolvers. While going through a leafy jungle on our road thither, we heard a rabbit squealing. We stopped and listened, but we heard no more; and presently we went on our way, and the incident dropped out of our minds. Montgomery called my attention to certain little pink animals with long hind-legs, that went leaping through the undergrowth. He told me they were creatures made of the offspring of the Beast People, that Moreau had invented. He had fancied they might serve for meat, but a rabbit-like habit of devouring their young had defeated this intention. I had already encountered some of these creatures, —once during my moonlight flight from the Leopard-man, and once during my pursuit by Moreau on the previous day. By chance, one hopping to avoid us leapt into the hole caused by the uprooting of a wind-blown tree; before it could extricate itself we managed to catch it. It spat like a cat, scratched and kicked vigorously with its hind-legs, and made an attempt to bite; but its teeth were too feeble to inflict more than a painless pinch. It seemed to me rather a pretty little creature; and as Montgomery stated that it never destroyed the turf by burrowing, and was very cleanly in its habits, I should imagine it might prove a convenient substitute for the common rabbit in gentlemen's parks.

We also saw on our way the trunk of a tree barked in long strips and splintered deeply. Montgomery called my attention to this. "Not to claw bark of trees, *that* is the Law," he said. "Much some of them care for it!" It was after this, I think, that we met the Satyr and the Ape-man. The Satyr was a gleam of classical memory on the part of Moreau,—his face ovine in expression, like the coarser Hebrew type; his voice a harsh bleat, his nether extremities Satanic. He was gnawing the husk of a pod-like fruit as he passed us. Both of them saluted Montgomery.

"Hail," said they, "to the Other with the Whip!"

"There's a Third with a Whip now," said Montgomery. "So you'd better mind!"

"Was he not made?" said the Ape-man. "He said—he said he was made."

The Satyr-man looked curiously at me. "The Third with the Whip, he that walks weeping into the sea, has a thin white face."

"He has a thin long whip," said Montgomery.

"Yesterday he bled and wept," said the Satyr. "You never bleed nor weep. The Master does not bleed or weep."

"Ollendorffian beggar!" said Montgomery, "you'll bleed and weep if you don't look out!"

"He has five fingers, he is a five-man like me," said the Ape-man.

"Come along, Prendick," said Montgomery, taking my arm; and I went on with him.

The Satyr and the Ape-man stood watching us and making other remarks to each other.

"He says nothing," said the Satyr. "Men have voices."

"Yesterday he asked me of things to eat," said the Ape-man. "He did not know."

Then they spoke inaudible things, and I heard the Satyr laughing.

It was on our way back that we came upon the dead rabbit. The red body of the wretched little beast was rent to pieces, many of the ribs stripped white, and the backbone indisputably gnawed.

At that Montgomery stopped. "Good God!" said he, stooping down, and picking up some of the crushed vertebrae to examine them more closely. "Good God!" he repeated, "what can this mean?"

"Some carnivore of yours has remembered its old habits," I said after a pause. "This backbone has been bitten through."

He stood staring, with his face white and his lip pulled askew. "I don't like this," he said slowly.

"I saw something of the same kind," said I, "the first day I came here."

"The devil you did! What was it?"

"A rabbit with its head twisted off."

"The day you came here?"

"The day I came here. In the undergrowth at the back of the enclosure, when I went out in the evening. The head was completely wrung off."

He gave a long, low whistle.

"And what is more, I have an idea which of your brutes did the thing. It's only a suspicion, you know. Before I came on the rabbit I saw one of your monsters drinking in the stream."

"Sucking his drink?"

"Yes."

"'Not to suck your drink; that is the Law.' Much the brutes care for the Law, eh? when Moreau's not about!"

"It was the brute who chased me."

"Of course," said Montgomery; "it's just the way with carnivores. After a kill, they drink. It's the taste of blood, you know.—What was the brute like?" he continued. "Would you know him again?" He glanced about us, standing astride over the mess of dead rabbit, his eyes roving among the shadows and screens of greenery, the lurking-places and ambuscades of the forest that bounded us in. "The taste of blood," he said again.

He took out his revolver, examined the cartridges in it and replaced it. Then he began to pull at his dropping lip.

"I think I should know the brute again," I said. "I stunned him. He ought to have a handsome bruise on the forehead of him."

"But then we have to *prove* that he killed the rabbit," said Montgomery. "I wish I'd never brought the things here."

I should have gone on, but he stayed there thinking over the mangled rabbit in a puzzle-headed way. As it was, I went to such a distance that the rabbit's remains were hidden.

"Come on!" I said.

Presently he woke up and came towards me. "You see," he said, almost in a whisper, "they are all supposed to have a fixed idea against eating anything that runs on land. If some brute has by any accident tasted blood—"

We went on some way in silence. "I wonder what can have happened," he said to himself. Then, after a pause again: "I did a foolish thing the other day. That servant of mine—I showed him how to skin and cook a rabbit. It's odd—I saw him licking his hands—It never occurred to me."

Then: "We must put a stop to this. I must tell Moreau."

He could think of nothing else on our homeward journey.

Moreau took the matter even more seriously than Montgomery, and I need scarcely say that I was affected by their evident consternation.

"We must make an example," said Moreau. "I've no doubt in my own mind that the Leopard-man was the sinner. But how can we prove it? I wish, Montgomery, you had kept your taste for meat in hand, and gone without these exciting novelties. We may find ourselves in a mess yet, through it."

"I was a silly ass," said Montgomery. "But the thing's done now; and you said I might have them, you know."

"We must see to the thing at once," said Moreau. "I suppose if anything should turn up, M'ling can take care of himself?"

"I'm not so sure of M'ling," said Montgomery. "I think I ought to know him."

In the afternoon, Moreau, Montgomery, myself, and M'ling went across the island to the huts in the ravine. We three were armed; M'ling carried the little hatchet he used in chopping firewood, and some coils of wire. Moreau had a huge cowherd's horn slung over his shoulder.

"You will see a gathering of the Beast People," said Montgomery. "It is a pretty sight!"

Moreau said not a word on the way, but the expression of his heavy, white-fringed face was grimly set.

We crossed the ravine down which smoked the stream of hot water, and followed the winding pathway through the canebrakes until we reached a wide area covered over with a thick, powdery yellow substance which I believe was sulphur. Above the shoulder of a weedy bank the sea glittered. We came to a kind of shallow natural amphitheatre, and here the four of us halted. Then Moreau sounded the horn, and broke the sleeping stillness of the tropical afternoon. He must

have had strong lungs. The hooting note rose and rose amidst its echoes, to at last an ear-penetrating intensity.

"Ah!" said Moreau, letting the curved instrument fall to his side again.

Immediately there was a crashing through the yellow canes, and a sound of voices from the dense green jungle that marked the morass through which I had run on the previous day. Then at three or four points on the edge of the sulphurous area appeared the grotesque forms of the Beast People hurrying towards us. I could not help a creeping horror, as I perceived first one and then another trot out from the trees or reeds and come shambling along over the hot dust. But Moreau and Montgomery stood calmly enough; and, perforce, I stuck beside them.

First to arrive was the Satyr, strangely unreal for all that he cast a shadow and tossed the dust with his hoofs. After him from the brake came a monstrous lout, a thing of horse and rhinoceros, chewing a straw as it came; then appeared the Swine-woman and two Wolf-women; then the Fox-bear witch, with her red eyes in her peaked red face, and then others,—all hurrying eagerly. As they came forward they began to cringe towards Moreau and chant, quite regardless of one another, fragments of the latter half of the litany of the Law,—"His is the Hand that wounds; His is the Hand that heals," and so forth. As soon as they had approached within a distance of perhaps thirty yards they halted, and bowing on knees and elbows began flinging the white dust upon their heads.

Imagine the scene if you can! We three blue-clad men, with our misshapen black-faced attendant, standing in a wide expanse of sunlit yellow dust under the blazing blue sky, and surrounded by this circle of crouching and gesticulating monstrosities,—some almost human save in their subtle expression and gestures, some like cripples, some so strangely distorted as to resemble nothing but the denizens of our wildest dreams; and, beyond, the reedy lines of a canebrake in one direction, a dense tangle of palm-trees on the other, separating us from the ravine with the huts, and to the north the hazy horizon of the Pacific Ocean.

"Sixty-two, sixty-three," counted Moreau. "There are four more."

"I do not see the Leopard-man," said I.

Presently Moreau sounded the great horn again, and at the sound of it all the Beast People writhed and grovelled in the dust. Then, slinking out of the canebrake, stooping near the ground and trying to join the dust-throwing circle behind Moreau's back, came the Leopard-man. The last of the Beast People to arrive was the little Ape-man. The earlier animals, hot and weary with their grovelling, shot vicious glances at him.

"Cease!" said Moreau, in his firm, loud voice; and the Beast People sat back upon their hams and rested from their worshipping.

"Where is the Sayer of the Law?" said Moreau, and the hairy-grey monster bowed his face in the dust.

"Say the words!" said Moreau.

Forthwith all in the kneeling assembly, swaying from side to side and dashing up the sulphur with their hands,—first the right hand and a puff of dust, and then

the left,—began once more to chant their strange litany. When they reached, "Not to eat Flesh or Fish, that is the Law," Moreau held up his lank white hand.

"Stop!" he cried, and there fell absolute silence upon them all.

I think they all knew and dreaded what was coming. I looked round at their strange faces. When I saw their wincing attitudes and the furtive dread in their bright eyes, I wondered that I had ever believed them to be men.

"That Law has been broken!" said Moreau.

"None escape," from the faceless creature with the silvery hair. "None escape," repeated the kneeling circle of Beast People.

"Who is he?" cried Moreau, and looked round at their faces, cracking his whip. I fancied the Hyena-swine looked dejected, so too did the Leopard-man. Moreau stopped, facing this creature, who cringed towards him with the memory and dread of infinite torment.

"Who is he?" repeated Moreau, in a voice of thunder.

"Evil is he who breaks the Law," chanted the Sayer of the Law.

Moreau looked into the eyes of the Leopard-man, and seemed to be dragging the very soul out of the creature.

"Who breaks the Law—" said Moreau, taking his eyes off his victim, and turning towards us (it seemed to me there was a touch of exultation in his voice).

"Goes back to the House of Pain," they all clamoured,—"goes back to the House of Pain, O Master!"

"Back to the House of Pain,—back to the House of Pain," gabbled the Ape-man, as though the idea was sweet to him.

"Do you hear?" said Moreau, turning back to the criminal, "my friend — Hullo!"

For the Leopard-man, released from Moreau's eye, had risen straight from his knees, and now, with eyes aflame and his huge feline tusks flashing out from under his curling lips, leapt towards his tormentor. I am convinced that only the madness of unendurable fear could have prompted this attack. The whole circle of threescore monsters seemed to rise about us. I drew my revolver. The two figures collided. I saw Moreau reeling back from the Leopard-man's blow. There was a furious yelling and howling all about us. Every one was moving rapidly. For a moment I thought it was a general revolt. The furious face of the Leopard-man flashed by mine, with M'ling close in pursuit. I saw the yellow eyes of the Hyena-swine blazing with excitement, his attitude as if he were half resolved to attack me. The Satyr, too, glared at me over the Hyena-swine's hunched shoulders. I heard the crack of Moreau's pistol, and saw the pink flash dart across the tumult. The whole crowd seemed to swing round in the direction of the glint of fire, and I too was swung round by the magnetism of the movement. In another second I was running, one of a tumultuous shouting crowd, in pursuit of the escaping Leopard-man.

That is all I can tell definitely. I saw the Leopard-man strike Moreau, and then everything spun about me until I was running headlong. M'ling was ahead, close in pursuit of the fugitive. Behind, their tongues already lolling out, ran the Wolf-

women in great leaping strides. The Swine folk followed, squealing with excitement, and the two Bull-men in their swathings of white. Then came Moreau in a cluster of the Beast People, his wide-brimmed straw hat blown off, his revolver in hand, and his lank white hair streaming out. The Hyena-swine ran beside me, keeping pace with me and glancing furtively at me out of his feline eyes, and the others came pattering and shouting behind us.

The Leopard-man went bursting his way through the long canes, which sprang back as he passed, and rattled in M'ling's face. We others in the rear found a trampled path for us when we reached the brake. The chase lay through the brake for perhaps a quarter of a mile, and then plunged into a dense thicket, which retarded our movements exceedingly, though we went through it in a crowd together,—fronds flicking into our faces, ropy creepers catching us under the chin or gripping our ankles, thorny plants hooking into and tearing cloth and flesh together.

"He has gone on all-fours through this," panted Moreau, now just ahead of me.

"None escape," said the Wolf-bear, laughing into my face with the exultation of hunting. We burst out again among rocks, and saw the quarry ahead running lightly on all-fours and snarling at us over his shoulder. At that the Wolf Folk howled with delight. The Thing was still clothed, and at a distance its face still seemed human; but the carriage of its four limbs was feline, and the furtive droop of its shoulder was distinctly that of a hunted animal. It leapt over some thorny yellow-flowering bushes, and was hidden. M'ling was halfway across the space.

Most of us now had lost the first speed of the chase, and had fallen into a longer and steadier stride. I saw as we traversed the open that the pursuit was now spreading from a column into a line. The Hyena-swine still ran close to me, watching me as it ran, every now and then puckering its muzzle with a snarling laugh. At the edge of the rocks the Leopard-man, realising that he was making for the projecting cape upon which he had stalked me on the night of my arrival, had doubled in the undergrowth; but Montgomery had seen the manoeuvre, and turned him again. So, panting, tumbling against rocks, torn by brambles, impeded by ferns and reeds, I helped to pursue the Leopard-man who had broken the Law, and the Hyena-swine ran, laughing savagely, by my side. I staggered on, my head reeling and my heart beating against my ribs, tired almost to death, and yet not daring to lose sight of the chase lest I should be left alone with this horrible companion. I staggered on in spite of infinite fatigue and the dense heat of the tropical afternoon.

At last the fury of the hunt slackened. We had pinned the wretched brute into a corner of the island. Moreau, whip in hand, marshalled us all into an irregular line, and we advanced now slowly, shouting to one another as we advanced and tightening the cordon about our victim. He lurked noiseless and invisible in the bushes through which I had run from him during that midnight pursuit.

"Steady!" cried Moreau, "steady!" as the ends of the line crept round the tangle of undergrowth and hemmed the brute in.

"Ware a rush!" came the voice of Montgomery from beyond the thicket.

I was on the slope above the bushes; Montgomery and Moreau beat along the beach beneath. Slowly we pushed in among the fretted network of branches and leaves. The quarry was silent.

"Back to the House of Pain, the House of Pain, the House of Pain!" yelped the voice of the Ape-man, some twenty yards to the right.

When I heard that, I forgave the poor wretch all the fear he had inspired in me. I heard the twigs snap and the boughs swish aside before the heavy tread of the Horse-rhinoceros upon my right. Then suddenly through a polygon of green, in the half darkness under the luxuriant growth, I saw the creature we were hunting. I halted. He was crouched together into the smallest possible compass, his luminous green eyes turned over his shoulder regarding me.

It may seem a strange contradiction in me,—I cannot explain the fact,—but now, seeing the creature there in a perfectly animal attitude, with the light gleaming in its eyes and its imperfectly human face distorted with terror, I realised again the fact of its humanity. In another moment other of its pursuers would see it, and it would be overpowered and captured, to experience once more the horrible tortures of the enclosure. Abruptly I slipped out my revolver, aimed between its terror-struck eyes, and fired. As I did so, the Hyena-swine saw the Thing, and flung itself upon it with an eager cry, thrusting thirsty teeth into its neck. All about me the green masses of the thicket were swaying and cracking as the Beast People came rushing together. One face and then another appeared.

"Don't kill it, Prendick!" cried Moreau. "Don't kill it!" and I saw him stooping as he pushed through under the fronds of the big ferns.

In another moment he had beaten off the Hyena-swine with the handle of his whip, and he and Montgomery were keeping away the excited carnivorous Beast People, and particularly M'ling, from the still quivering body. The hairy-grey Thing came sniffing at the corpse under my arm. The other animals, in their animal ardour, jostled me to get a nearer view.

"Confound you, Prendick!" said Moreau. "I wanted him."

"I'm sorry," said I, though I was not. "It was the impulse of the moment." I felt sick with exertion and excitement. Turning, I pushed my way out of the crowding Beast People and went on alone up the slope towards the higher part of the headland. Under the shouted directions of Moreau I heard the three white-swathed Bull-men begin dragging the victim down towards the water.

It was easy now for me to be alone. The Beast People manifested a quite human curiosity about the dead body, and followed it in a thick knot, sniffing and growling at it as the Bull-men dragged it down the beach. I went to the headland and watched the bull-men, black against the evening sky as they carried the weighted dead body out to sea; and like a wave across my mind came the realisation of the unspeakable aimlessness of things upon the island. Upon the beach among the rocks beneath me were the Ape-man, the Hyena-swine, and several other of the Beast People, standing about Montgomery and Moreau. They were all still intensely excited, and all overflowing with noisy expressions of their loyalty to the Law; yet I felt an absolute assurance in my own mind that the Hyena-swine

was implicated in the rabbit-killing. A strange persuasion came upon me, that, save for the grossness of the line, the grotesqueness of the forms, I had here before me the whole balance of human life in miniature, the whole interplay of instinct, reason, and fate in its simplest form. The Leopard- man had happened to go under: that was all the difference. Poor brute!

Poor brutes! I began to see the viler aspect of Moreau's cruelty. I had not thought before of the pain and trouble that came to these poor victims after they had passed from Moreau's hands. I had shivered only at the days of actual torment in the enclosure. But now that seemed to me the lesser part. Before, they had been beasts, their instincts fitly adapted to their surroundings, and happy as living things may be. Now they stumbled in the shackles of humanity, lived in a fear that never died, fretted by a law they could not understand; their mock-human existence, begun in an agony, was one long internal struggle, one long dread of Moreau—and for what? It was the wantonness of it that stirred me.

Had Moreau had any intelligible object, I could have sympathised at least a little with him. I am not so squeamish about pain as that. I could have forgiven him a little even, had his motive been only hate. But he was so irresponsible, so utterly careless! His curiosity, his mad, aimless investigations, drove him on; and the Things were thrown out to live a year or so, to struggle and blunder and suffer, and at last to die painfully. They were wretched in themselves; the old animal hate moved them to trouble one another; the Law held them back from a brief hot struggle and a decisive end to their natural animosities.

In those days my fear of the Beast People went the way of my personal fear for Moreau. I fell indeed into a morbid state, deep and enduring, and alien to fear, which has left permanent scars upon my mind. I must confess that I lost faith in the sanity of the world when I saw it suffering the painful disorder of this island. A blind Fate, a vast pitiless Mechanism, seemed to cut and shape the fabric of existence and I, Moreau (by his passion for research), Montgomery (by his passion for drink), the Beast People with their instincts and mental restrictions, were torn and crushed, ruthlessly, inevitably, amid the infinite complexity of its incessant wheels. But this condition did not come all at once: I think indeed that I anticipate a little in speaking of it now.

XVII. A CATASTROPHE

Scarcely six weeks passed before I had lost every feeling but dislike and abhorrence for this infamous experiment of Moreau's. My one idea was to get away from these horrible caricatures of my Maker's image, back to the sweet and wholesome intercourse of men. My fellow-creatures, from whom I was thus separated, began to assume idyllic virtue and beauty in my memory. My first friendship with Montgomery did not increase. His long separation from humanity, his secret vice of drunkenness, his evident sympathy with the Beast People, tainted him to me. Several times I let him go alone among them. I avoided intercourse with them in every possible way. I spent an increasing proportion of my time upon the beach, looking for some liberating sail that never appeared,—until one day there fell upon us an appalling disaster, which put an altogether different aspect upon my strange surroundings.

It was about seven or eight weeks after my landing,—rather more, I think, though I had not troubled to keep account of the time,—when this catastrophe occurred. It happened in the early morning—I should think about six. I had risen and breakfasted early, having been aroused by the noise of three Beast Men carrying wood into the enclosure.

After breakfast I went to the open gateway of the enclosure, and stood there smoking a cigarette and enjoying the freshness of the early morning. Moreau presently came round the corner of the enclosure and greeted me. He passed by me, and I heard him behind me unlock and enter his laboratory. So indurated was I at that time to the abomination of the place, that I heard without a touch of emotion the puma victim begin another day of torture. It met its persecutor with a shriek, almost exactly like that of an angry virago.

Then suddenly something happened,—I do not know what, to this day. I heard a short, sharp cry behind me, a fall, and turning saw an awful face rushing upon me,—not human, not animal, but hellish, brown, seamed with red branching scars, red drops starting out upon it, and the lidless eyes ablaze. I threw up my arm to defend myself from the blow that flung me headlong with a broken forearm; and the great monster, swathed in lint and with red- stained bandages fluttering about it, leapt over me and passed. I rolled over and over down the beach, tried to sit up, and collapsed upon my broken arm. Then Moreau appeared, his massive white face all the more terrible for the blood that trickled from his forehead. He carried a revolver in one hand. He scarcely glanced at me, but rushed off at once in pursuit of the puma.

I tried the other arm and sat up. The muffled figure in front ran in great striding leaps along the beach, and Moreau followed her. She turned her head and saw him, then doubling abruptly made for the bushes. She gained upon him at every stride. I saw her plunge into them, and Moreau, running slantingly to intercept her, fired and missed as she disappeared. Then he too vanished in the green confusion. I stared after them, and then the pain in my arm flamed up, and with a groan I staggered to my feet. Montgomery appeared in the doorway, dressed, and with his revolver in his hand.

"Great God, Prendick!" he said, not noticing that I was hurt, "that brute's loose! Tore the fetter out of the wall! Have you seen them?" Then sharply, seeing I gripped my arm, "What's the matter?"

"I was standing in the doorway," said I.

He came forward and took my arm. "Blood on the sleeve," said he, and rolled back the flannel. He pocketed his weapon, felt my arm about painfully, and led me inside. "Your arm is broken," he said, and then, "Tell me exactly how it happened—what happened?"

I told him what I had seen; told him in broken sentences, with gasps of pain between them, and very dexterously and swiftly he bound my arm meanwhile. He slung it from my shoulder, stood back and looked at me.

"You'll do," he said. "And now?"

He thought. Then he went out and locked the gates of the enclosure. He was absent some time.

I was chiefly concerned about my arm. The incident seemed merely one more of many horrible things. I sat down in the deck chair, and I must admit swore heartily at the island. The first dull feeling of injury in my arm had already given way to a burning pain when Montgomery reappeared. His face was rather pale, and he showed more of his lower gums than ever.

"I can neither see nor hear anything of him," he said. "I've been thinking he may want my help." He stared at me with his expressionless eyes. "That was a strong brute," he said. "It simply wrenched its fetter out of the wall." He went to the window, then to the door, and there turned to me. "I shall go after him," he said. "There's another revolver I can leave with you. To tell you the truth, I feel anxious somehow."

He obtained the weapon, and put it ready to my hand on the table; then went out, leaving a restless contagion in the air. I did not sit long after he left, but took the revolver in hand and went to the doorway.

The morning was as still as death. Not a whisper of wind was stirring; the sea was like polished glass, the sky empty, the beach desolate. In my half- excited, half-feverish state, this stillness of things oppressed me. I tried to whistle, and the tune died away. I swore again,—the second time that morning. Then I went to the corner of the enclosure and stared inland at the green bush that had swallowed up Moreau and Montgomery. When would they return, and how? Then far away up the beach a little grey Beast Man appeared, ran down to the water's edge and began splashing about. I strolled back to the doorway, then to the corner again, and

so began pacing to and fro like a sentinel upon duty. Once I was arrested by the distant voice of Montgomery bawling, "Coo-ee —Moreau!" My arm became less painful, but very hot. I got feverish and thirsty. My shadow grew shorter. I watched the distant figure until it went away again. Would Moreau and Montgomery never return? Three sea-birds began fighting for some stranded treasure.

Then from far away behind the enclosure I heard a pistol-shot. A long silence, and then came another. Then a yelling cry nearer, and another dismal gap of silence. My unfortunate imagination set to work to torment me. Then suddenly a shot close by. I went to the corner, startled, and saw Montgomery, —his face scarlet, his hair disordered, and the knee of his trousers torn. His face expressed profound consternation. Behind him slouched the Beast Man, M'ling, and round M'ling's jaws were some queer dark stains.

"Has he come?" said Montgomery.

"Moreau?" said I. "No."

"My God!" The man was panting, almost sobbing. "Go back in," he said, taking my arm. "They're mad. They're all rushing about mad. What can have happened? I don't know. I'll tell you, when my breath comes. Where's some brandy?"

Montgomery limped before me into the room and sat down in the deck chair. M'ling flung himself down just outside the doorway and began panting like a dog. I got Montgomery some brandy-and-water. He sat staring in front of him at nothing, recovering his breath. After some minutes he began to tell me what had happened.

He had followed their track for some way. It was plain enough at first on account of the crushed and broken bushes, white rags torn from the puma's bandages, and occasional smears of blood on the leaves of the shrubs and undergrowth. He lost the track, however, on the stony ground beyond the stream where I had seen the Beast Man drinking, and went wandering aimlessly westward shouting Moreau's name. Then M'ling had come to him carrying a light hatchet. M'ling had seen nothing of the puma affair; had been felling wood, and heard him calling. They went on shouting together. Two Beast Men came crouching and peering at them through the undergrowth, with gestures and a furtive carriage that alarmed Montgomery by their strangeness. He hailed them, and they fled guiltily. He stopped shouting after that, and after wandering some time farther in an undecided way, determined to visit the huts.

He found the ravine deserted.

Growing more alarmed every minute, he began to retrace his steps. Then it was he encountered the two Swine-men I had seen dancing on the night of my arrival; blood-stained they were about the mouth, and intensely excited. They came crashing through the ferns, and stopped with fierce faces when they saw him. He cracked his whip in some trepidation, and forthwith they rushed at him. Never before had a Beast Man dared to do that. One he shot through the head; M'ling flung himself upon the other, and the two rolled grappling. M'ling got his brute under and with his teeth in its throat, and Montgomery shot that too as it

struggled in M'ling's grip. He had some difficulty in inducing M'ling to come on with him. Thence they had hurried back to me. On the way, M'ling had suddenly rushed into a thicket and driven out an under-sized Ocelot-man, also blood-stained, and lame through a wound in the foot. This brute had run a little way and then turned savagely at bay, and Montgomery—with a certain wantonness, I thought—had shot him.

"What does it all mean?" said I.

He shook his head, and turned once more to the brandy.

XVIII. THE FINDING OF MOREAU

When I saw Montgomery swallow a third dose of brandy, I took it upon myself to interfere. He was already more than half fuddled. I told him that some serious thing must have happened to Moreau by this time, or he would have returned before this, and that it behoved us to ascertain what that catastrophe was. Montgomery raised some feeble objections, and at last agreed. We had some food, and then all three of us started.

It is possibly due to the tension of my mind, at the time, but even now that start into the hot stillness of the tropical afternoon is a singularly vivid impression. M'ling went first, his shoulder hunched, his strange black head moving with quick starts as he peered first on this side of the way and then on that. He was unarmed; his axe he had dropped when he encountered the Swine-man. Teeth were *his* weapons, when it came to fighting. Montgomery followed with stumbling footsteps, his hands in his pockets, his face downcast; he was in a state of muddled sullenness with me on account of the brandy. My left arm was in a sling (it was lucky it was my left), and I carried my revolver in my right. Soon we traced a narrow path through the wild luxuriance of the island, going northwestward; and presently M'ling stopped, and became rigid with watchfulness. Montgomery almost staggered into him, and then stopped too. Then, listening intently, we heard coming through the trees the sound of voices and footsteps approaching us.

"He is dead," said a deep, vibrating voice.

"He is not dead; he is not dead," jabbered another.

"We saw, we saw," said several voices.

"Hullo!" suddenly shouted Montgomery, "Hullo, there!"

"Confound you!" said I, and gripped my pistol.

There was a silence, then a crashing among the interlacing vegetation, first here, then there, and then half-a-dozen faces appeared,—strange faces, lit by a strange light. M'ling made a growling noise in his throat. I recognised the Ape-man: I had indeed already identified his voice, and two of the white-swathed brown-featured creatures I had seen in Montgomery's boat. With these were the two dappled brutes and that grey, horribly crooked creature who said the Law, with grey hair streaming down its cheeks, heavy grey eyebrows, and grey locks pouring off from a central parting upon its sloping forehead,—a heavy, faceless thing, with strange red eyes, looking at us curiously from amidst the green.

For a space no one spoke. Then Montgomery hiccoughed, "Who—said he was dead?"

The Monkey-man looked guiltily at the hairy-grey Thing. "He is dead," said this monster. "They saw."

There was nothing threatening about this detachment, at any rate. They seemed awestricken and puzzled.

"Where is he?" said Montgomery.

"Beyond," and the grey creature pointed.

"Is there a Law now?" asked the Monkey-man. "Is it still to be this and that? Is he dead indeed?"

"Is there a Law?" repeated the man in white. "Is there a Law, thou Other with the Whip?"

"He is dead," said the hairy-grey Thing. And they all stood watching us.

"Prendick," said Montgomery, turning his dull eyes to me. "He's dead, evidently."

I had been standing behind him during this colloquy. I began to see how things lay with them. I suddenly stepped in front of Montgomery and lifted up my voice:—"Children of the Law," I said, "he is *not* dead!" M'ling turned his sharp eyes on me. "He has changed his shape; he has changed his body," I went on. "For a time you will not see him. He is—there," I pointed upward, "where he can watch you. You cannot see him, but he can see you. Fear the Law!"

I looked at them squarely. They flinched.

"He is great, he is good," said the Ape-man, peering fearfully upward among the dense trees.

"And the other Thing?" I demanded.

"The Thing that bled, and ran screaming and sobbing,—that is dead too," said the grey Thing, still regarding me.

"That's well," grunted Montgomery.

"The Other with the Whip—" began the grey Thing.

"Well?" said I.

"Said he was dead."

But Montgomery was still sober enough to understand my motive in denying Moreau's death. "He is not dead," he said slowly, "not dead at all. No more dead than I am."

"Some," said I, "have broken the Law: they will die. Some have died. Show us now where his old body lies,—the body he cast away because he had no more need of it."

"It is this way, Man who walked in the Sea," said the grey Thing.

And with these six creatures guiding us, we went through the tumult of ferns and creepers and tree-stems towards the northwest. Then came a yelling, a crashing among the branches, and a little pink homunculus rushed by us shrieking. Immediately after appeared a monster in headlong pursuit, blood- bedabbled, who was amongst us almost before he could stop his career. The grey Thing leapt aside. M'ling, with a snarl, flew at it, and was struck aside. Montgomery fired and missed, bowed his head, threw up his arm, and turned to run. I fired, and the Thing still came on; fired again, point-blank, into its ugly face. I saw its features

vanish in a flash: its face was driven in. Yet it passed me, gripped Montgomery, and holding him, fell headlong beside him and pulled him sprawling upon itself in its death-agony.

I found myself alone with M'ling, the dead brute, and the prostrate man. Montgomery raised himself slowly and stared in a muddled way at the shattered Beast Man beside him. It more than half sobered him. He scrambled to his feet. Then I saw the grey Thing returning cautiously through the trees.

"See," said I, pointing to the dead brute, "is the Law not alive? This came of breaking the Law."

He peered at the body. "He sends the Fire that kills," said he, in his deep voice, repeating part of the Ritual. The others gathered round and stared for a space.

At last we drew near the westward extremity of the island. We came upon the gnawed and mutilated body of the puma, its shoulder-bone smashed by a bullet, and perhaps twenty yards farther found at last what we sought. Moreau lay face downward in a trampled space in a canebrake. One hand was almost severed at the wrist and his silvery hair was dabbled in blood. His head had been battered in by the fetters of the puma. The broken canes beneath him were smeared with blood. His revolver we could not find. Montgomery turned him over. Resting at intervals, and with the help of the seven Beast People (for he was a heavy man), we carried Moreau back to the enclosure. The night was darkling. Twice we heard unseen creatures howling and shrieking past our little band, and once the little pink sloth-creature appeared and stared at us, and vanished again. But we were not attacked again. At the gates of the enclosure our company of Beast People left us, M'ling going with the rest. We locked ourselves in, and then took Moreau's mangled body into the yard and laid it upon a pile of brushwood. Then we went into the laboratory and put an end to all we found living there.

XIX. MONTGOMERY'S "BANK HOLIDAY"

When this was accomplished, and we had washed and eaten, Montgomery and I went into my little room and seriously discussed our position for the first time. It was then near midnight. He was almost sober, but greatly disturbed in his mind. He had been strangely under the influence of Moreau's personality: I do not think it had ever occurred to him that Moreau could die. This disaster was the sudden collapse of the habits that had become part of his nature in the ten or more monotonous years he had spent on the island. He talked vaguely, answered my questions crookedly, wandered into general questions.

"This silly ass of a world," he said; "what a muddle it all is! I haven't had any life. I wonder when it's going to begin. Sixteen years being bullied by nurses and schoolmasters at their own sweet will; five in London grinding hard at medicine, bad food, shabby lodgings, shabby clothes, shabby vice, a blunder, —I didn't know any better,—and hustled off to this beastly island. Ten years here! What's it all for, Prendick? Are we bubbles blown by a baby?"

It was hard to deal with such ravings. "The thing we have to think of now," said I, "is how to get away from this island."

"What's the good of getting away? I'm an outcast. Where am *I* to join on? It's all very well for *you*, Prendick. Poor old Moreau! We can't leave him here to have his bones picked. As it is—And besides, what will become of the decent part of the Beast Folk?"

"Well," said I, "that will do to-morrow. I've been thinking we might make the brushwood into a pyre and burn his body—and those other things. Then what will happen with the Beast Folk?"

"*I* don't know. I suppose those that were made of beasts of prey will make silly asses of themselves sooner or later. We can't massacre the lot —can we? I suppose that's what *your* humanity would suggest? But they'll change. They are sure to change."

He talked thus inconclusively until at last I felt my temper going.

"Damnation!" he exclaimed at some petulance of mine; "can't you see I'm in a worse hole than you are?" And he got up, and went for the brandy. "Drink!" he said returning, "you logic-chopping, chalky-faced saint of an atheist, drink!"

"Not I," said I, and sat grimly watching his face under the yellow paraffine flare, as he drank himself into a garrulous misery.

I have a memory of infinite tedium. He wandered into a maudlin defence of the Beast People and of M'ling. M'ling, he said, was the only thing that had ever really cared for him. And suddenly an idea came to him.

"I'm damned!" said he, staggering to his feet and clutching the brandy bottle.

By some flash of intuition I knew what it was he intended. "You don't give drink to that beast!" I said, rising and facing him.

"Beast!" said he. "You're the beast. He takes his liquor like a Christian. Come out of the way, Prendick!"

"For God's sake," said I.

"Get—out of the way!" he roared, and suddenly whipped out his revolver.

"Very well," said I, and stood aside, half-minded to fall upon him as he put his hand upon the latch, but deterred by the thought of my useless arm. "You've made a beast of yourself,—to the beasts you may go."

He flung the doorway open, and stood half facing me between the yellow lamp-light and the pallid glare of the moon; his eye-sockets were blotches of black under his stubbly eyebrows.

"You're a solemn prig, Prendick, a silly ass! You're always fearing and fancying. We're on the edge of things. I'm bound to cut my throat to-morrow. I'm going to have a damned Bank Holiday to-night." He turned and went out into the moonlight. "M'ling!" he cried; "M'ling, old friend!"

Three dim creatures in the silvery light came along the edge of the wan beach,—one a white-wrapped creature, the other two blotches of blackness following it. They halted, staring. Then I saw M'ling's hunched shoulders as he came round the corner of the house.

"Drink!" cried Montgomery, "drink, you brutes! Drink and be men! Damme, I'm the cleverest. Moreau forgot this; this is the last touch. Drink, I tell you!" And waving the bottle in his hand he started off at a kind of quick trot to the westward, M'ling ranging himself between him and the three dim creatures who followed.

I went to the doorway. They were already indistinct in the mist of the moonlight before Montgomery halted. I saw him administer a dose of the raw brandy to M'ling, and saw the five figures melt into one vague patch.

"Sing!" I heard Montgomery shout,—"sing all together, 'Confound old Prendick!' That's right; now again, 'Confound old Prendick!'"

The black group broke up into five separate figures, and wound slowly away from me along the band of shining beach. Each went howling at his own sweet will, yelping insults at me, or giving whatever other vent this new inspiration of brandy demanded. Presently I heard Montgomery's voice shouting, "Right turn!" and they passed with their shouts and howls into the blackness of the landward trees. Slowly, very slowly, they receded into silence.

The peaceful splendour of the night healed again. The moon was now past the meridian and travelling down the west. It was at its full, and very bright riding through the empty blue sky. The shadow of the wall lay, a yard wide and of inky blackness, at my feet. The eastward sea was a featureless grey, dark and mysterious; and between the sea and the shadow the grey sands (of volcanic glass and

crystals) flashed and shone like a beach of diamonds. Behind me the paraffine lamp flared hot and ruddy.

Then I shut the door, locked it, and went into the enclosure where Moreau lay beside his latest victims,—the staghounds and the llama and some other wretched brutes,—with his massive face calm even after his terrible death, and with the hard eyes open, staring at the dead white moon above. I sat down upon the edge of the sink, and with my eyes upon that ghastly pile of silvery light and ominous shadows began to turn over my plans. In the morning I would gather some provisions in the dingey, and after setting fire to the pyre before me, push out into the desolation of the high sea once more. I felt that for Montgomery there was no help; that he was, in truth, half akin to these Beast Folk, unfitted for human kindred.

I do not know how long I sat there scheming. It must have been an hour or so. Then my planning was interrupted by the return of Montgomery to my neighbourhood. I heard a yelling from many throats, a tumult of exultant cries passing down towards the beach, whooping and howling, and excited shrieks that seemed to come to a stop near the water's edge. The riot rose and fell; I heard heavy blows and the splintering smash of wood, but it did not trouble me then. A discordant chanting began.

My thoughts went back to my means of escape. I got up, brought the lamp, and went into a shed to look at some kegs I had seen there. Then I became interested in the contents of some biscuit-tins, and opened one. I saw something out of the tail of my eye,—a red figure,—and turned sharply.

Behind me lay the yard, vividly black-and-white in the moonlight, and the pile of wood and faggots on which Moreau and his mutilated victims lay, one over another. They seemed to be gripping one another in one last revengeful grapple. His wounds gaped, black as night, and the blood that had dripped lay in black patches upon the sand. Then I saw, without understanding, the cause of my phantom,—a ruddy glow that came and danced and went upon the wall opposite. I misinterpreted this, fancied it was a reflection of my flickering lamp, and turned again to the stores in the shed. I went on rummaging among them, as well as a one-armed man could, finding this convenient thing and that, and putting them aside for to-morrow's launch. My movements were slow, and the time passed quickly. Insensibly the daylight crept upon me.

The chanting died down, giving place to a clamour; then it began again, and suddenly broke into a tumult. I heard cries of, "More! more!" a sound like quarrelling, and a sudden wild shriek. The quality of the sounds changed so greatly that it arrested my attention. I went out into the yard and listened. Then cutting like a knife across the confusion came the crack of a revolver.

I rushed at once through my room to the little doorway. As I did so I heard some of the packing-cases behind me go sliding down and smash together with a clatter of glass on the floor of the shed. But I did not heed these. I flung the door open and looked out.

Up the beach by the boathouse a bonfire was burning, raining up sparks into the indistinctness of the dawn. Around this struggled a mass of black figures. I heard Montgomery call my name. I began to run at once towards this fire, revolver in hand. I saw the pink tongue of Montgomery's pistol lick out once, close to the ground. He was down. I shouted with all my strength and fired into the air. I heard some one cry, "The Master!" The knotted black struggle broke into scattering units, the fire leapt and sank down. The crowd of Beast People fled in sudden panic before me, up the beach. In my excitement I fired at their retreating backs as they disappeared among the bushes. Then I turned to the black heaps upon the ground.

Montgomery lay on his back, with the hairy-grey Beast-man sprawling across his body. The brute was dead, but still gripping Montgomery's throat with its curving claws. Near by lay M'ling on his face and quite still, his neck bitten open and the upper part of the smashed brandy-bottle in his hand. Two other figures lay near the fire,—the one motionless, the other groaning fitfully, every now and then raising its head slowly, then dropping it again.

I caught hold of the grey man and pulled him off Montgomery's body; his claws drew down the torn coat reluctantly as I dragged him away. Montgomery was dark in the face and scarcely breathing. I splashed sea-water on his face and pillowed his head on my rolled-up coat. M'ling was dead. The wounded creature by the fire—it was a Wolf-brute with a bearded grey face—lay, I found, with the fore part of its body upon the still glowing timber. The wretched thing was injured so dreadfully that in mercy I blew its brains out at once. The other brute was one of the Bull-men swathed in white. He too was dead. The rest of the Beast People had vanished from the beach.

I went to Montgomery again and knelt beside him, cursing my ignorance of medicine. The fire beside me had sunk down, and only charred beams of timber glowing at the central ends and mixed with a grey ash of brushwood remained. I wondered casually where Montgomery had got his wood. Then I saw that the dawn was upon us. The sky had grown brighter, the setting moon was becoming pale and opaque in the luminous blue of the day. The sky to the eastward was rimmed with red.

Suddenly I heard a thud and a hissing behind me, and, looking round, sprang to my feet with a cry of horror. Against the warm dawn great tumultuous masses of black smoke were boiling up out of the enclosure, and through their stormy darkness shot flickering threads of blood-red flame. Then the thatched roof caught. I saw the curving charge of the flames across the sloping straw. A spurt of fire jetted from the window of my room.

I knew at once what had happened. I remembered the crash I had heard. When I had rushed out to Montgomery's assistance, I had overturned the lamp.

The hopelessness of saving any of the contents of the enclosure stared me in the face. My mind came back to my plan of flight, and turning swiftly I looked to see where the two boats lay upon the beach. They were gone! Two axes lay upon the sands beside me; chips and splinters were scattered broadcast, and the ashes of

the bonfire were blackening and smoking under the dawn. Montgomery had burnt the boats to revenge himself upon me and prevent our return to mankind!

A sudden convulsion of rage shook me. I was almost moved to batter his foolish head in, as he lay there helpless at my feet. Then suddenly his hand moved, so feebly, so pitifully, that my wrath vanished. He groaned, and opened his eyes for a minute. I knelt down beside him and raised his head. He opened his eyes again, staring silently at the dawn, and then they met mine. The lids fell.

"Sorry," he said presently, with an effort. He seemed trying to think. "The last," he murmured, "the last of this silly universe. What a mess—"

I listened. His head fell helplessly to one side. I thought some drink might revive him; but there was neither drink nor vessel in which to bring drink at hand. He seemed suddenly heavier. My heart went cold. I bent down to his face, put my hand through the rent in his blouse. He was dead; and even as he died a line of white heat, the limb of the sun, rose eastward beyond the projection of the bay, splashing its radiance across the sky and turning the dark sea into a weltering tumult of dazzling light. It fell like a glory upon his death-shrunken face.

I let his head fall gently upon the rough pillow I had made for him, and stood up. Before me was the glittering desolation of the sea, the awful solitude upon which I had already suffered so much; behind me the island, hushed under the dawn, its Beast People silent and unseen. The enclosure, with all its provisions and ammunition, burnt noisily, with sudden gusts of flame, a fitful crackling, and now and then a crash. The heavy smoke drove up the beach away from me, rolling low over the distant tree-tops towards the huts in the ravine. Beside me were the charred vestiges of the boats and these five dead bodies.

Then out of the bushes came three Beast People, with hunched shoulders, protruding heads, misshapen hands awkwardly held, and inquisitive, unfriendly eyes and advanced towards me with hesitating gestures.

XX. ALONE WITH THE BEAST FOLK

I faced these people, facing my fate in them, single-handed now,—literally single-handed, for I had a broken arm. In my pocket was a revolver with two empty chambers. Among the chips scattered about the beach lay the two axes that had been used to chop up the boats. The tide was creeping in behind me. There was nothing for it but courage. I looked squarely into the faces of the advancing monsters. They avoided my eyes, and their quivering nostrils investigated the bodies that lay beyond me on the beach. I took half-a-dozen steps, picked up the blood-stained whip that lay beneath the body of the Wolf- man, and cracked it. They stopped and stared at me.

"Salute!" said I. "Bow down!"

They hesitated. One bent his knees. I repeated my command, with my heart in my mouth, and advanced upon them. One knelt, then the other two.

I turned and walked towards the dead bodies, keeping my face towards the three kneeling Beast Men, very much as an actor passing up the stage faces the audience.

"They broke the Law," said I, putting my foot on the Sayer of the Law. "They have been slain,—even the Sayer of the Law; even the Other with the Whip. Great is the Law! Come and see."

"None escape," said one of them, advancing and peering.

"None escape," said I. "Therefore hear and do as I command." They stood up, looking questioningly at one another.

"Stand there," said I.

I picked up the hatchets and swung them by their heads from the sling of my arm; turned Montgomery over; picked up his revolver still loaded in two chambers, and bending down to rummage, found half-a-dozen cartridges in his pocket.

"Take him," said I, standing up again and pointing with the whip; "take him, and carry him out and cast him into the sea."

They came forward, evidently still afraid of Montgomery, but still more afraid of my cracking red whip-lash; and after some fumbling and hesitation, some whip-cracking and shouting, they lifted him gingerly, carried him down to the beach, and went splashing into the dazzling welter of the sea.

"On!" said I, "on! Carry him far."

They went in up to their armpits and stood regarding me.

"Let go," said I; and the body of Montgomery vanished with a splash. Something seemed to tighten across my chest.

"Good!" said I, with a break in my voice; and they came back, hurrying and fearful, to the margin of the water, leaving long wakes of black in the silver. At the water's edge they stopped, turning and glaring into the sea as though they presently expected Montgomery to arise therefrom and exact vengeance.

"Now these," said I, pointing to the other bodies.

They took care not to approach the place where they had thrown Montgomery into the water, but instead, carried the four dead Beast People slantingly along the beach for perhaps a hundred yards before they waded out and cast them away.

As I watched them disposing of the mangled remains of M'ling, I heard a light footfall behind me, and turning quickly saw the big Hyena-swine perhaps a dozen yards away. His head was bent down, his bright eyes were fixed upon me, his stumpy hands clenched and held close by his side. He stopped in this crouching attitude when I turned, his eyes a little averted.

For a moment we stood eye to eye. I dropped the whip and snatched at the pistol in my pocket; for I meant to kill this brute, the most formidable of any left now upon the island, at the first excuse. It may seem treacherous, but so I was resolved. I was far more afraid of him than of any other two of the Beast Folk. His continued life was I knew a threat against mine.

I was perhaps a dozen seconds collecting myself. Then cried I, "Salute! Bow down!"

His teeth flashed upon me in a snarl. "Who are *you* that I should—"

Perhaps a little too spasmodically I drew my revolver, aimed quickly and fired. I heard him yelp, saw him run sideways and turn, knew I had missed, and clicked back the cock with my thumb for the next shot. But he was already running headlong, jumping from side to side, and I dared not risk another miss. Every now and then he looked back at me over his shoulder. He went slanting along the beach, and vanished beneath the driving masses of dense smoke that were still pouring out from the burning enclosure. For some time I stood staring after him. I turned to my three obedient Beast Folk again and signalled them to drop the body they still carried. Then I went back to the place by the fire where the bodies had fallen and kicked the sand until all the brown blood- stains were absorbed and hidden.

I dismissed my three serfs with a wave of the hand, and went up the beach into the thickets. I carried my pistol in my hand, my whip thrust with the hatchets in the sling of my arm. I was anxious to be alone, to think out the position in which I was now placed. A dreadful thing that I was only beginning to realise was, that over all this island there was now no safe place where I could be alone and secure to rest or sleep. I had recovered strength amazingly since my landing, but I was still inclined to be nervous and to break down under any great stress. I felt that I ought to cross the island and establish myself with the Beast People, and make myself secure in their confidence. But my heart failed me. I went back to the beach, and turning eastward past the burning enclosure, made for a point where a shallow spit of coral sand ran out towards the reef. Here I could sit down and think, my back to the sea and my face against any surprise. And there I sat, chin on knees, the sun beating down upon my head and unspeakable dread in my mind,

plotting how I could live on against the hour of my rescue (if ever rescue came). I tried to review the whole situation as calmly as I could, but it was difficult to clear the thing of emotion.

I began turning over in my mind the reason of Montgomery's despair. "They will change," he said; "they are sure to change." And Moreau, what was it that Moreau had said? "The stubborn beast-flesh grows day by day back again." Then I came round to the Hyena-swine. I felt sure that if I did not kill that brute, he would kill me. The Sayer of the Law was dead: worse luck. They knew now that we of the Whips could be killed even as they themselves were killed. Were they peering at me already out of the green masses of ferns and palms over yonder, watching until I came within their spring? Were they plotting against me? What was the Hyena-swine telling them? My imagination was running away with me into a morass of unsubstantial fears.

My thoughts were disturbed by a crying of sea-birds hurrying towards some black object that had been stranded by the waves on the beach near the enclosure. I knew what that object was, but I had not the heart to go back and drive them off. I began walking along the beach in the opposite direction, designing to come round the eastward corner of the island and so approach the ravine of the huts, without traversing the possible ambuscades of the thickets.

Perhaps half a mile along the beach I became aware of one of my three Beast Folk advancing out of the landward bushes towards me. I was now so nervous with my own imaginings that I immediately drew my revolver. Even the propitiatory gestures of the creature failed to disarm me. He hesitated as he approached.

"Go away!" cried I.

There was something very suggestive of a dog in the cringing attitude of the creature. It retreated a little way, very like a dog being sent home, and stopped, looking at me imploringly with canine brown eyes.

"Go away," said I. "Do not come near me."

"May I not come near you?" it said.

"No; go away," I insisted, and snapped my whip. Then putting my whip in my teeth, I stooped for a stone, and with that threat drove the creature away.

So in solitude I came round by the ravine of the Beast People, and hiding among the weeds and reeds that separated this crevice from the sea I watched such of them as appeared, trying to judge from their gestures and appearance how the death of Moreau and Montgomery and the destruction of the House of Pain had affected them. I know now the folly of my cowardice. Had I kept my courage up to the level of the dawn, had I not allowed it to ebb away in solitary thought, I might have grasped the vacant sceptre of Moreau and ruled over the Beast People. As it was I lost the opportunity, and sank to the position of a mere leader among my fellows.

Towards noon certain of them came and squatted basking in the hot sand. The imperious voices of hunger and thirst prevailed over my dread. I came out of the bushes, and, revolver in hand, walked down towards these seated figures. One, a Wolf-woman, turned her head and stared at me, and then the others. None at-

tempted to rise or salute me. I felt too faint and weary to insist, and I let the moment pass.

"I want food," said I, almost apologetically, and drawing near.

"There is food in the huts," said an Ox-boar-man, drowsily, and looking away from me.

I passed them, and went down into the shadow and odours of the almost deserted ravine. In an empty hut I feasted on some specked and half-decayed fruit; and then after I had propped some branches and sticks about the opening, and placed myself with my face towards it and my hand upon my revolver, the exhaustion of the last thirty hours claimed its own, and I fell into a light slumber, hoping that the flimsy barricade I had erected would cause sufficient noise in its removal to save me from surprise.

XXI. THE REVERSION OF THE BEAST FOLK

In this way I became one among the Beast People in the Island of Doctor Moreau. When I awoke, it was dark about me. My arm ached in its bandages. I sat up, wondering at first where I might be. I heard coarse voices talking outside. Then I saw that my barricade had gone, and that the opening of the hut stood clear. My revolver was still in my hand.

I heard something breathing, saw something crouched together close beside me. I held my breath, trying to see what it was. It began to move slowly, interminably. Then something soft and warm and moist passed across my hand. All my muscles contracted. I snatched my hand away. A cry of alarm began and was stifled in my throat. Then I just realised what had happened sufficiently to stay my fingers on the revolver.

"Who is that?" I said in a hoarse whisper, the revolver still pointed.

"I—Master."

"Who are you?"

"They say there is no Master now. But I know, I know. I carried the bodies into the sea, O Walker in the Sea! the bodies of those you slew. I am your slave, Master."

"Are you the one I met on the beach?" I asked.

"The same, Master."

The Thing was evidently faithful enough, for it might have fallen upon me as I slept. "It is well," I said, extending my hand for another licking kiss. I began to realise what its presence meant, and the tide of my courage flowed. "Where are the others?" I asked.

"They are mad; they are fools," said the Dog-man. "Even now they talk together beyond there. They say, 'The Master is dead. The Other with the Whip is dead. That Other who walked in the Sea is as we are. We have no Master, no Whips, no House of Pain, any more. There is an end. We love the Law, and will keep it; but there is no Pain, no Master, no Whips for ever again.' So they say. But I know, Master, I know."

I felt in the darkness, and patted the Dog-man's head. "It is well," I said again.

"Presently you will slay them all," said the Dog-man.

"Presently," I answered, "I will slay them all,—after certain days and certain things have come to pass. Every one of them save those you spare, every one of them shall be slain."

"What the Master wishes to kill, the Master kills," said the Dog-man with a certain satisfaction in his voice.

"And that their sins may grow," I said, "let them live in their folly until their time is ripe. Let them not know that I am the Master."

"The Master's will is sweet," said the Dog-man, with the ready tact of his canine blood.

"But one has sinned," said I. "Him I will kill, whenever I may meet him. When I say to you, 'That is he,' see that you fall upon him. And now I will go to the men and women who are assembled together."

For a moment the opening of the hut was blackened by the exit of the Dog-man. Then I followed and stood up, almost in the exact spot where I had been when I had heard Moreau and his staghound pursuing me. But now it was night, and all the miasmatic ravine about me was black; and beyond, instead of a green, sunlit slope, I saw a red fire, before which hunched, grotesque figures moved to and fro. Farther were the thick trees, a bank of darkness, fringed above with the black lace of the upper branches. The moon was just riding up on the edge of the ravine, and like a bar across its face drove the spire of vapour that was for ever streaming from the fumaroles of the island.

"Walk by me," said I, nerving myself; and side by side we walked down the narrow way, taking little heed of the dim Things that peered at us out of the huts.

None about the fire attempted to salute me. Most of them disregarded me, ostentatiously. I looked round for the Hyena-swine, but he was not there. Altogether, perhaps twenty of the Beast Folk squatted, staring into the fire or talking to one another.

"He is dead, he is dead! the Master is dead!" said the voice of the Ape- man to the right of me. "The House of Pain—there is no House of Pain!"

"He is not dead," said I, in a loud voice. "Even now he watches us!"

This startled them. Twenty pairs of eyes regarded me.

"The House of Pain is gone," said I. "It will come again. The Master you cannot see; yet even now he listens among you."

"True, true!" said the Dog-man.

They were staggered at my assurance. An animal may be ferocious and cunning enough, but it takes a real man to tell a lie.

"The Man with the Bandaged Arm speaks a strange thing," said one of the Beast Folk.

"I tell you it is so," I said. "The Master and the House of Pain will come again. Woe be to him who breaks the Law!"

They looked curiously at one another. With an affectation of indifference I began to chop idly at the ground in front of me with my hatchet. They looked, I noticed, at the deep cuts I made in the turf.

Then the Satyr raised a doubt. I answered him. Then one of the dappled things objected, and an animated discussion sprang up round the fire. Every moment I began to feel more convinced of my present security. I talked now without the catching in my breath, due to the intensity of my excitement, that had troubled me

at first. In the course of about an hour I had really convinced several of the Beast Folk of the truth of my assertions, and talked most of the others into a dubious state. I kept a sharp eye for my enemy the Hyena-swine, but he never appeared. Every now and then a suspicious movement would startle me, but my confidence grew rapidly. Then as the moon crept down from the zenith, one by one the listeners began to yawn (showing the oddest teeth in the light of the sinking fire), and first one and then another retired towards the dens in the ravine; and I, dreading the silence and darkness, went with them, knowing I was safer with several of them than with one alone.

In this manner began the longer part of my sojourn upon this Island of Doctor Moreau. But from that night until the end came, there was but one thing happened to tell save a series of innumerable small unpleasant details and the fretting of an incessant uneasiness. So that I prefer to make no chronicle for that gap of time, to tell only one cardinal incident of the ten months I spent as an intimate of these half-humanised brutes. There is much that sticks in my memory that I could write,—things that I would cheerfully give my right hand to forget; but they do not help the telling of the story.

In the retrospect it is strange to remember how soon I fell in with these monsters' ways, and gained my confidence again. I had my quarrels with them of course, and could show some of their teeth-marks still; but they soon gained a wholesome respect for my trick of throwing stones and for the bite of my hatchet. And my Saint-Bernard-man's loyalty was of infinite service to me. I found their simple scale of honour was based mainly on the capacity for inflicting trenchant wounds. Indeed, I may say—without vanity, I hope —that I held something like pre-eminence among them. One or two, whom in a rare access of high spirits I had scarred rather badly, bore me a grudge; but it vented itself chiefly behind my back, and at a safe distance from my missiles, in grimaces.

The Hyena-swine avoided me, and I was always on the alert for him. My inseparable Dog-man hated and dreaded him intensely. I really believe that was at the root of the brute's attachment to me. It was soon evident to me that the former monster had tasted blood, and gone the way of the Leopard-man. He formed a lair somewhere in the forest, and became solitary. Once I tried to induce the Beast Folk to hunt him, but I lacked the authority to make them co-operate for one end. Again and again I tried to approach his den and come upon him unaware; but always he was too acute for me, and saw or winded me and got away. He too made every forest pathway dangerous to me and my ally with his lurking ambuscades. The Dog-man scarcely dared to leave my side.

In the first month or so the Beast Folk, compared with their latter condition, were human enough, and for one or two besides my canine friend I even conceived a friendly tolerance. The little pink sloth-creature displayed an odd affection for me, and took to following me about. The Monkey-man bored me, however; he assumed, on the strength of his five digits, that he was my equal, and was for ever jabbering at me,—jabbering the most arrant nonsense. One thing about him entertained me a little: he had a fantastic trick of coining new words.

He had an idea, I believe, that to gabble about names that meant nothing was the proper use of speech. He called it "Big Thinks" to distinguish it from "Little Thinks," the sane every-day interests of life. If ever I made a remark he did not understand, he would praise it very much, ask me to say it again, learn it by heart, and go off repeating it, with a word wrong here or there, to all the milder of the Beast People. He thought nothing of what was plain and comprehensible. I invented some very curious "Big Thinks" for his especial use. I think now that he was the silliest creature I ever met; he had developed in the most wonderful way the distinctive silliness of man without losing one jot of the natural folly of a monkey.

This, I say, was in the earlier weeks of my solitude among these brutes. During that time they respected the usage established by the Law, and behaved with general decorum. Once I found another rabbit torn to pieces,—by the Hyena-swine, I am assured,—but that was all. It was about May when I first distinctly perceived a growing difference in their speech and carriage, a growing coarseness of articulation, a growing disinclination to talk. My Monkey-man's jabber multiplied in volume but grew less and less comprehensible, more and more simian. Some of the others seemed altogether slipping their hold upon speech, though they still understood what I said to them at that time. (Can you imagine language, once clear-cut and exact, softening and guttering, losing shape and import, becoming mere lumps of sound again?) And they walked erect with an increasing difficulty. Though they evidently felt ashamed of themselves, every now and then I would come upon one or another running on toes and finger-tips, and quite unable to recover the vertical attitude. They held things more clumsily; drinking by suction, feeding by gnawing, grew commoner every day. I realised more keenly than ever what Moreau had told me about the "stubborn beast-flesh." They were reverting, and reverting very rapidly.

Some of them—the pioneers in this, I noticed with some surprise, were all females—began to disregard the injunction of decency, deliberately for the most part. Others even attempted public outrages upon the institution of monogamy. The tradition of the Law was clearly losing its force. I cannot pursue this disagreeable subject.

My Dog-man imperceptibly slipped back to the dog again; day by day he became dumb, quadrupedal, hairy. I scarcely noticed the transition from the companion on my right hand to the lurching dog at my side.

As the carelessness and disorganisation increased from day to day, the lane of dwelling places, at no time very sweet, became so loathsome that I left it, and going across the island made myself a hovel of boughs amid the black ruins of Moreau's enclosure. Some memory of pain, I found, still made that place the safest from the Beast Folk.

It would be impossible to detail every step of the lapsing of these monsters,—to tell how, day by day, the human semblance left them; how they gave up bandagings and wrappings, abandoned at last every stitch of clothing; how the hair began to spread over the exposed limbs; how their foreheads fell away and their

faces projected; how the quasi-human intimacy I had permitted myself with some of them in the first month of my loneliness became a shuddering horror to recall.

The change was slow and inevitable. For them and for me it came without any definite shock. I still went among them in safety, because no jolt in the downward glide had released the increasing charge of explosive animalism that ousted the human day by day. But I began to fear that soon now that shock must come. My Saint-Bernard-brute followed me to the enclosure every night, and his vigilance enabled me to sleep at times in something like peace. The little pink sloth-thing became shy and left me, to crawl back to its natural life once more among the tree-branches. We were in just the state of equilibrium that would remain in one of those "Happy Family" cages which animal-tamers exhibit, if the tamer were to leave it for ever.

Of course these creatures did not decline into such beasts as the reader has seen in zoological gardens,—into ordinary bears, wolves, tigers, oxen, swine, and apes. There was still something strange about each; in each Moreau had blended this animal with that. One perhaps was ursine chiefly, another feline chiefly, another bovine chiefly; but each was tainted with other creatures,—a kind of generalised animalism appearing through the specific dispositions. And the dwindling shreds of the humanity still startled me every now and then,—a momentary recrudescence of speech perhaps, an unexpected dexterity of the fore-feet, a pitiful attempt to walk erect.

I too must have undergone strange changes. My clothes hung about me as yellow rags, through whose rents showed the tanned skin. My hair grew long, and became matted together. I am told that even now my eyes have a strange brightness, a swift alertness of movement.

At first I spent the daylight hours on the southward beach watching for a ship, hoping and praying for a ship. I counted on the "Ipecacuanha" returning as the year wore on; but she never came. Five times I saw sails, and thrice smoke; but nothing ever touched the island. I always had a bonfire ready, but no doubt the volcanic reputation of the island was taken to account for that.

It was only about September or October that I began to think of making a raft. By that time my arm had healed, and both my hands were at my service again. At first, I found my helplessness appalling. I had never done any carpentry or suchlike work in my life, and I spent day after day in experimental chopping and binding among the trees. I had no ropes, and could hit on nothing wherewith to make ropes; none of the abundant creepers seemed limber or strong enough, and with all my litter of scientific education I could not devise any way of making them so. I spent more than a fortnight grubbing among the black ruins of the enclosure and on the beach where the boats had been burnt, looking for nails and other stray pieces of metal that might prove of service. Now and then some Beast-creature would watch me, and go leaping off when I called to it. There came a season of thunder-storms and heavy rain, which greatly retarded my work; but at last the raft was completed.

I was delighted with it. But with a certain lack of practical sense which has always been my bane, I had made it a mile or more from the sea; and before I had dragged it down to the beach the thing had fallen to pieces. Perhaps it is as well that I was saved from launching it; but at the time my misery at my failure was so acute that for some days I simply moped on the beach, and stared at the water and thought of death.

I did not, however, mean to die, and an incident occurred that warned me unmistakably of the folly of letting the days pass so,—for each fresh day was fraught with increasing danger from the Beast People.

I was lying in the shade of the enclosure wall, staring out to sea, when I was startled by something cold touching the skin of my heel, and starting round found the little pink sloth-creature blinking into my face. He had long since lost speech and active movement, and the lank hair of the little brute grew thicker every day and his stumpy claws more askew. He made a moaning noise when he saw he had attracted my attention, went a little way towards the bushes and looked back at me.

At first I did not understand, but presently it occurred to me that he wished me to follow him; and this I did at last,—slowly, for the day was hot. When we reached the trees he clambered into them, for he could travel better among their swinging creepers than on the ground. And suddenly in a trampled space I came upon a ghastly group. My Saint-Bernard-creature lay on the ground, dead; and near his body crouched the Hyena-swine, gripping the quivering flesh with its misshapen claws, gnawing at it, and snarling with delight. As I approached, the monster lifted its glaring eyes to mine, its lips went trembling back from its red-stained teeth, and it growled menacingly. It was not afraid and not ashamed; the last vestige of the human taint had vanished. I advanced a step farther, stopped, and pulled out my revolver. At last I had him face to face.

The brute made no sign of retreat; but its ears went back, its hair bristled, and its body crouched together. I aimed between the eyes and fired. As I did so, the Thing rose straight at me in a leap, and I was knocked over like a ninepin. It clutched at me with its crippled hand, and struck me in the face. Its spring carried it over me. I fell under the hind part of its body; but luckily I had hit as I meant, and it had died even as it leapt. I crawled out from under its unclean weight and stood up trembling, staring at its quivering body. That danger at least was over; but this, I knew was only the first of the series of relapses that must come.

I burnt both of the bodies on a pyre of brushwood; but after that I saw that unless I left the island my death was only a question of time. The Beast People by that time had, with one or two exceptions, left the ravine and made themselves lairs according to their taste among the thickets of the island. Few prowled by day, most of them slept, and the island might have seemed deserted to a newcomer; but at night the air was hideous with their calls and howling. I had half a mind to make a massacre of them; to build traps, or fight them with my knife. Had I possessed sufficient cartridges, I should not have hesitated to begin the killing. There could now be scarcely a score left of the dangerous carnivores; the

braver of these were already dead. After the death of this poor dog of mine, my last friend, I too adopted to some extent the practice of slumbering in the daytime in order to be on my guard at night. I rebuilt my den in the walls of the enclosure, with such a narrow opening that anything attempting to enter must necessarily make a considerable noise. The creatures had lost the art of fire too, and recovered their fear of it. I turned once more, almost passionately now, to hammering together stakes and branches to form a raft for my escape.

I found a thousand difficulties. I am an extremely unhandy man (my schooling was over before the days of Slojd); but most of the requirements of a raft I met at last in some clumsy, circuitous way or other, and this time I took care of the strength. The only insurmountable obstacle was that I had no vessel to contain the water I should need if I floated forth upon these untravelled seas. I would have even tried pottery, but the island contained no clay. I used to go moping about the island trying with all my might to solve this one last difficulty. Sometimes I would give way to wild outbursts of rage, and hack and splinter some unlucky tree in my intolerable vexation. But I could think of nothing.

And then came a day, a wonderful day, which I spent in ecstasy. I saw a sail to the southwest, a small sail like that of a little schooner; and forthwith I lit a great pile of brushwood, and stood by it in the heat of it, and the heat of the midday sun, watching. All day I watched that sail, eating or drinking nothing, so that my head reeled; and the Beasts came and glared at me, and seemed to wonder, and went away. It was still distant when night came and swallowed it up; and all night I toiled to keep my blaze bright and high, and the eyes of the Beasts shone out of the darkness, marvelling. In the dawn the sail was nearer, and I saw it was the dirty lug-sail of a small boat. But it sailed strangely. My eyes were weary with watching, and I peered and could not believe them. Two men were in the boat, sitting low down,—one by the bows, the other at the rudder. The head was not kept to the wind; it yawed and fell away.

As the day grew brighter, I began waving the last rag of my jacket to them; but they did not notice me, and sat still, facing each other. I went to the lowest point of the low headland, and gesticulated and shouted. There was no response, and the boat kept on her aimless course, making slowly, very slowly, for the bay. Suddenly a great white bird flew up out of the boat, and neither of the men stirred nor noticed it; it circled round, and then came sweeping overhead with its strong wings outspread.

Then I stopped shouting, and sat down on the headland and rested my chin on my hands and stared. Slowly, slowly, the boat drove past towards the west. I would have swum out to it, but something—a cold, vague fear—kept me back. In the afternoon the tide stranded the boat, and left it a hundred yards or so to the westward of the ruins of the enclosure. The men in it were dead, had been dead so long that they fell to pieces when I tilted the boat on its side and dragged them out. One had a shock of red hair, like the captain of the "Ipecacuanha," and a dirty white cap lay in the bottom of the boat.

As I stood beside the boat, three of the Beasts came slinking out of the bushes and sniffing towards me. One of my spasms of disgust came upon me. I thrust the little boat down the beach and clambered on board her. Two of the brutes were Wolf-beasts, and came forward with quivering nostrils and glittering eyes; the third was the horrible nondescript of bear and bull. When I saw them approaching those wretched remains, heard them snarling at one another and caught the gleam of their teeth, a frantic horror succeeded my repulsion. I turned my back upon them, struck the lug and began paddling out to sea. I could not bring myself to look behind me.

I lay, however, between the reef and the island that night, and the next morning went round to the stream and filled the empty keg aboard with water. Then, with such patience as I could command, I collected a quantity of fruit, and waylaid and killed two rabbits with my last three cartridges. While I was doing this I left the boat moored to an inward projection of the reef, for fear of the Beast People.

XXII. THE MAN ALONE

In the evening I started, and drove out to sea before a gentle wind from the southwest, slowly, steadily; and the island grew smaller and smaller, and the lank spire of smoke dwindled to a finer and finer line against the hot sunset. The ocean rose up around me, hiding that low, dark patch from my eyes. The daylight, the trailing glory of the sun, went streaming out of the sky, was drawn aside like some luminous curtain, and at last I looked into the blue gulf of immensity which the sunshine hides, and saw the floating hosts of the stars. The sea was silent, the sky was silent. I was alone with the night and silence.

So I drifted for three days, eating and drinking sparingly, and meditating upon all that had happened to me,—not desiring very greatly then to see men again. One unclean rag was about me, my hair a black tangle: no doubt my discoverers thought me a madman.

It is strange, but I felt no desire to return to mankind. I was only glad to be quit of the foulness of the Beast People. And on the third day I was picked up by a brig from Apia to San Francisco. Neither the captain nor the mate would believe my story, judging that solitude and danger had made me mad; and fearing their opinion might be that of others, I refrained from telling my adventure further, and professed to recall nothing that had happened to me between the loss of the "Lady Vain" and the time when I was picked up again, —the space of a year.

I had to act with the utmost circumspection to save myself from the suspicion of insanity. My memory of the Law, of the two dead sailors, of the ambuscades of the darkness, of the body in the canebrake, haunted me; and, unnatural as it seems, with my return to mankind came, instead of that confidence and sympathy I had expected, a strange enhancement of the uncertainty and dread I had experienced during my stay upon the island. No one would believe me; I was almost as queer to men as I had been to the Beast People. I may have caught something of the natural wildness of my companions. They say that terror is a disease, and anyhow I can witness that for several years now a restless fear has dwelt in my mind,—such a restless fear as a half-tamed lion cub may feel.

My trouble took the strangest form. I could not persuade myself that the men and women I met were not also another Beast People, animals half wrought into the outward image of human souls, and that they would presently begin to revert,—to show first this bestial mark and then that. But I have confided my case to a strangely able man,—a man who had known Moreau, and seemed half to credit my story; a mental specialist,—and he has helped me mightily, though I do

not expect that the terror of that island will ever altogether leave me. At most times it lies far in the back of my mind, a mere distant cloud, a memory, and a faint distrust; but there are times when the little cloud spreads until it obscures the whole sky. Then I look about me at my fellow-men; and I go in fear. I see faces, keen and bright; others dull or dangerous; others, unsteady, insincere,—none that have the calm authority of a reasonable soul. I feel as though the animal was surging up through them; that presently the degradation of the Islanders will be played over again on a larger scale. I know this is an illusion; that these seeming men and women about me are indeed men and women,—men and women for ever, perfectly reasonable creatures, full of human desires and tender solicitude, emancipated from instinct and the slaves of no fantastic Law, —beings altogether different from the Beast Folk. Yet I shrink from them, from their curious glances, their inquiries and assistance, and long to be away from them and alone. For that reason I live near the broad free downland, and can escape thither when this shadow is over my soul; and very sweet is the empty downland then, under the wind-swept sky.

When I lived in London the horror was well-nigh insupportable. I could not get away from men: their voices came through windows; locked doors were flimsy safeguards. I would go out into the streets to fight with my delusion, and prowling women would mew after me; furtive, craving men glance jealously at me; weary, pale workers go coughing by me with tired eyes and eager paces, like wounded deer dripping blood; old people, bent and dull, pass murmuring to themselves; and, all unheeding, a ragged tail of gibing children. Then I would turn aside into some chapel,—and even there, such was my disturbance, it seemed that the preacher gibbered "Big Thinks," even as the Ape-man had done; or into some library, and there the intent faces over the books seemed but patient creatures waiting for prey. Particularly nauseous were the blank, expressionless faces of people in trains and omnibuses; they seemed no more my fellow-creatures than dead bodies would be, so that I did not dare to travel unless I was assured of being alone. And even it seemed that I too was not a reasonable creature, but only an animal tormented with some strange disorder in its brain which sent it to wander alone, like a sheep stricken with gid.

This is a mood, however, that comes to me now, I thank God, more rarely. I have withdrawn myself from the confusion of cities and multitudes, and spend my days surrounded by wise books,—bright windows in this life of ours, lit by the shining souls of men. I see few strangers, and have but a small household. My days I devote to reading and to experiments in chemistry, and I spend many of the clear nights in the study of astronomy. There is—though I do not know how there is or why there is—a sense of infinite peace and protection in the glittering hosts of heaven. There it must be, I think, in the vast and eternal laws of matter, and not in the daily cares and sins and troubles of men, that whatever is more than animal within us must find its solace and its hope. I hope, or I could not live.

And so, in hope and solitude, my story ends.

EDWARD PRENDICK.

THE FIRST MEN IN THE MOON

Serialised in *The Cosmopolitan*, Nov 1900-Jun 1901
First US book edition: Bowen-Merrill, Indianapolis, 1901
First UK book edition: George Newnes, London, 1901

CHAPTER I - MR. BEDFORD MEETS MR. CAVOR AT LYMPNE

As I sit down to write here amidst the shadows of vine-leaves under the blue sky of southern Italy, it comes to me with a certain quality of astonishment that my participation in these amazing adventures of Mr. Cavor was, after all, the outcome of the purest accident. It might have been any one. I fell into these things at a time when I thought myself removed from the slightest possibility of disturbing experiences. I had gone to Lympne because I had imagined it the most uneventful place in the world. "Here, at any rate," said I, "I shall find peace and a chance to work!"

And this book is the sequel. So utterly at variance is destiny with all the little plans of men. I may perhaps mention here that very recently I had come an ugly cropper in certain business enterprises. Sitting now surrounded by all the circumstances of wealth, there is a luxury in admitting my extremity. I can admit, even, that to a certain extent my disasters were conceivably of my own making. It may be there are directions in which I have some capacity, but the conduct of business operations is not among these. But in those days I was young, and my youth among other objectionable forms took that of a pride in my capacity for affairs. I am young still in years, but the things that have happened to me have rubbed something of the youth from my mind. Whether they have brought any wisdom to light below it is a more doubtful matter.

It is scarcely necessary to go into the details of the speculations that landed me at Lympne, in Kent. Nowadays even about business transactions there is a strong spice of adventure. I took risks. In these things there is invariably a certain amount of give and take, and it fell to me finally to do the giving reluctantly enough. Even when I had got out of everything, one cantankerous creditor saw fit to be malignant. Perhaps you have met that flaming sense of outraged virtue, or perhaps you have only felt it. He ran me hard. It seemed to me, at last, that there was nothing for it but to write a play, unless I wanted to drudge for my living as a clerk. I have a certain imagination, and luxurious tastes, and I meant to make a vigorous fight for it before that fate overtook me. In addition to my belief in my powers as a business man, I had always in those days had an idea that I was equal to writing a very good play. It is not, I believe, a very uncommon persuasion. I knew there is nothing a man can do outside legitimate business transactions that has such opulent possibilities, and very probably that biased my opinion. I had,

indeed, got into the habit of regarding this unwritten drama as a convenient little reserve put by for a rainy day. That rainy day had come, and I set to work.

I soon discovered that writing a play was a longer business than I had supposed; at first I had reckoned ten days for it, and it was to have a pied-a- terre while it was in hand that I came to Lympne. I reckoned myself lucky in getting that little bungalow. I got it on a three years' agreement. I put in a few sticks of furniture, and while the play was in hand I did my own cooking. My cooking would have shocked Mrs. Bond. And yet, you know, it had flavour. I had a coffee-pot, a sauce-pan for eggs, and one for potatoes, and a frying-pan for sausages and bacon—such was the simple apparatus of my comfort. One cannot always be magnificent, but simplicity is always a possible alternative. For the rest I laid in an eighteen-gallon cask of beer on credit, and a trustful baker came each day. It was not, perhaps, in the style of Sybaris, but I have had worse times. I was a little sorry for the baker, who was a very decent man indeed, but even for him I hoped.

Certainly if any one wants solitude, the place is Lympne. It is in the clay part of Kent, and my bungalow stood on the edge of an old sea cliff and stared across the flats of Romney Marsh at the sea. In very wet weather the place is almost inaccessible, and I have heard that at times the postman used to traverse the more succulent portions of his route with boards upon his feet. I never saw him doing so, but I can quite imagine it. Outside the doors of the few cottages and houses that make up the present village big birch besoms are stuck, to wipe off the worst of the clay, which will give some idea of the texture of the district. I doubt if the place would be there at all, if it were not a fading memory of things gone for ever. It was the big port of England in Roman times, Portus Lemanis, and now the sea is four miles away. All down the steep hill are boulders and masses of Roman brickwork, and from it old Watling Street, still paved in places, starts like an arrow to the north. I used to stand on the hill and think of it all, the galleys and legions, the captives and officials, the women and traders, the speculators like myself, all the swarm and tumult that came clanking in and out of the harbour. And now just a few lumps of rubble on a grassy slope, and a sheep or two—and I. And where the port had been were the levels of the marsh, sweeping round in a broad curve to distant Dungeness, and dotted here and there with tree clumps and the church towers of old medical towns that are following Lemanis now towards extinction.

That outlook on the marsh was, indeed, one of the finest views I have ever seen. I suppose Dungeness was fifteen miles away; it lay like a raft on the sea, and farther westward were the hills by Hastings under the setting sun. Sometimes they hung close and clear, sometimes they were faded and low, and often the drift of the weather took them clean out of sight. And all the nearer parts of the marsh were laced and lit by ditches and canals.

The window at which I worked looked over the skyline of this crest, and it was from this window that I first set eyes on Cavor. It was just as I was struggling with my scenario, holding down my mind to the sheer hard work of it, and naturally enough he arrested my attention.

The sun had set, the sky was a vivid tranquillity of green and yellow, and against that he came out black—the oddest little figure.

He was a short, round-bodied, thin-legged little man, with a jerky quality in his motions; he had seen fit to clothe his extraordinary mind in a cricket cap, an overcoat, and cycling knickerbockers and stockings. Why he did so I do not know, for he never cycled and he never played cricket. It was a fortuitous concurrence of garments, arising I know not how. He gesticulated with his hands and arms, and jerked his head about and buzzed. He buzzed like something electric. You never heard such buzzing. And ever and again he cleared his throat with a most extraordinary noise.

There had been rain, and that spasmodic walk of his was enhanced by the extreme slipperiness of the footpath. Exactly as he came against the sun he stopped, pulled out a watch, hesitated. Then with a sort of convulsive gesture he turned and retreated with every manifestation of haste, no longer gesticulating, but going with ample strides that showed the relatively large size of his feet—they were, I remember, grotesquely exaggerated in size by adhesive clay—to the best possible advantage.

This occurred on the first day of my sojourn, when my play-writing energy was at its height and I regarded the incident simply as an annoying distraction — the waste of five minutes. I returned to my scenario. But when next evening the apparition was repeated with remarkable precision, and again the next evening, and indeed every evening when rain was not falling, concentration upon the scenario became a considerable effort. "Confound the man," I said, "one would think he was learning to be a marionette!" and for several evenings I cursed him pretty heartily. Then my annoyance gave way to amazement and curiosity. Why on earth should a man do this thing? On the fourteenth evening I could stand it no longer, and so soon as he appeared I opened the french window, crossed the verandah, and directed myself to the point where he invariably stopped.

He had his watch out as I came up to him. He had a chubby, rubicund face with reddish brown eyes—previously I had seen him only against the light. "One moment, sir," said I as he turned. He stared. "One moment," he said, "certainly. Or if you wish to speak to me for longer, and it is not asking too much—your moment is up—would it trouble you to accompany me?"

"Not in the least," said I, placing myself beside him.

"My habits are regular. My time for intercourse—limited."

"This, I presume, is your time for exercise?"

"It is. I come here to enjoy the sunset."

"You don't."

"Sir?"

"You never look at it."

"Never look at it?"

"No. I've watched you thirteen nights, and not once have you looked at the sunset—not once."

He knitted his brows like one who encounters a problem.

"Well, I enjoy the sunlight—the atmosphere—I go along this path, through that gate"—he jerked his head over his shoulder —"and round—"

"You don't. You never have been. It's all nonsense. There isn't a way. To-night for instance—"

"Oh! to-night! Let me see. Ah! I just glanced at my watch, saw that I had already been out just three minutes over the precise half-hour, decided there was not time to go round, turned—"

"You always do."

He looked at me—reflected. "Perhaps I do, now I come to think of it. But what was it you wanted to speak to me about?"

"Why, this!"

"This?"

"Yes. Why do you do it? Every night you come making a noise—"

"Making a noise?"

"Like this." I imitated his buzzing noise. He looked at me, and it was evident the buzzing awakened distaste. "Do I do that?" he asked.

"Every blessed evening."

"I had no idea."

He stopped dead. He regarded me gravely. "Can it be," he said, "that I have formed a Habit?"

"Well, it looks like it. Doesn't it?"

He pulled down his lower lip between finger and thumb. He regarded a puddle at his feet.

"My mind is much occupied," he said. "And you want to know why! Well, sir, I can assure you that not only do I not know why I do these things, but I did not even know I did them. Come to think, it is just as you say; I never *have* been beyond that field... And these things annoy you?"

For some reason I was beginning to relent towards him. "Not annoy," I said. "But—imagine yourself writing a play!"

"I couldn't."

"Well, anything that needs concentration."

"Ah!" he said, "of course," and meditated. His expression became so eloquent of distress, that I relented still more. After all, there is a touch of aggression in demanding of a man you don't know why he hums on a public footpath.

"You see," he said weakly, "it's a habit."

"Oh, I recognise that."

"I must stop it."

"But not if it puts you out. After all, I had no business—it's something of a liberty."

"Not at all, sir," he said, "not at all. I am greatly indebted to you. I should guard myself against these things. In future I will. Could I trouble you —once again? That noise?"

"Something like this," I said. "Zuzzoo, zuzzoo. But really, you know—"

"I am greatly obliged to you. In fact, I know I am getting absurdly absent-minded. You are quite justified, sir—perfectly justified. Indeed, I am indebted to you. The thing shall end. And now, sir, I have already brought you farther than I should have done."

"I do hope my impertinence—"

"Not at all, sir, not at all."

We regarded each other for a moment. I raised my hat and wished him a good evening. He responded convulsively, and so we went our ways.

At the stile I looked back at his receding figure. His bearing had changed remarkably, he seemed limp, shrunken. The contrast with his former gesticulating, zuzzoing self took me in some absurd way as pathetic. I watched him out of sight. Then wishing very heartily I had kept to my own business, I returned to my bungalow and my play.

The next evening I saw nothing of him, nor the next. But he was very much in my mind, and it had occurred to me that as a sentimental comic character he might serve a useful purpose in the development of my plot. The third day he called upon me.

For a time I was puzzled to think what had brought him. He made indifferent conversation in the most formal way, then abruptly he came to business. He wanted to buy me out of my bungalow.

"You see," he said, "I don't blame you in the least, but you've destroyed a habit, and it disorganises my day. I've walked past here for years—years. No doubt I've hummed... You've made all that impossible!"

I suggested he might try some other direction.

"No. There is no other direction. This is the only one. I've inquired. And now—every afternoon at four—I come to a dead wall."

"But, my dear sir, if the thing is so important to you—"

"It's vital. You see, I'm—I'm an investigator—I am engaged in a scientific research. I live—" he paused and seemed to think. "Just over there," he said, and pointed suddenly dangerously near my eye. "The house with white chimneys you see just over the trees. And my circumstances are abnormal—abnormal. I am on the point of completing one of the most important—demonstrations—I can assure you one of the most important demonstrations that have ever been made. It requires constant thought, constant mental ease and activity. And the afternoon was my brightest time!—effervescing with new ideas—new points of view."

"But why not come by still?"

"It would be all different. I should be self-conscious. I should think of you at your play—watching me irritated—instead of thinking of my work. No! I must have the bungalow."

I meditated. Naturally, I wanted to think the matter over thoroughly before anything decisive was said. I was generally ready enough for business in those days, and selling always attracted me; but in the first place it was not my bungalow, and even if I sold it to him at a good price I might get inconvenienced in the delivery of goods if the current owner got wind of the transaction, and in the second I was,

well—undischarged. It was clearly a business that required delicate handling. Moreover, the possibility of his being in pursuit of some valuable invention also interested me. It occurred to me that I would like to know more of this research, not with any dishonest intention, but simply with an idea that to know what it was would be a relief from play-writing. I threw out feelers.

He was quite willing to supply information. Indeed, once he was fairly under way the conversation became a monologue. He talked like a man long pent up, who has had it over with himself again and again. He talked for nearly an hour, and I must confess I found it a pretty stiff bit of listening. But through it all there was the undertone of satisfaction one feels when one is neglecting work one has set oneself. During that first interview I gathered very little of the drift of his work. Half his words were technicalities entirely strange to me, and he illustrated one or two points with what he was pleased to call elementary mathematics, computing on an envelope with a copying- ink pencil, in a manner that made it hard even to seem to understand. "Yes," I said, "yes. Go on!" Nevertheless I made out enough to convince me that he was no mere crank playing at discoveries. In spite of his crank-like appearance there was a force about him that made that impossible. Whatever it was, it was a thing with mechanical possibilities. He told me of a work-shed he had, and of three assistants—originally jobbing carpenters—whom he had trained. Now, from the work-shed to the patent office is clearly only one step. He invited me to see those things. I accepted readily, and took care, by a remark or so, to underline that. The proposed transfer of the bungalow remained very conveniently in suspense.

At last he rose to depart, with an apology for the length of his call. Talking over his work was, he said, a pleasure enjoyed only too rarely. It was not often he found such an intelligent listener as myself, he mingled very little with professional scientific men.

"So much pettiness," he explained; "so much intrigue! And really, when one has an idea—a novel, fertilising idea—I don't want to be uncharitable, but—"

I am a man who believes in impulses. I made what was perhaps a rash proposition. But you must remember, that I had been alone, play-writing in Lympne, for fourteen days, and my compunction for his ruined walk still hung about me. "Why not," said I, "make this your new habit? In the place of the one I spoilt? At least, until we can settle about the bungalow. What you want is to turn over your work in your mind. That you have always done during your afternoon walk. Unfortunately that's over—you can't get things back as they were. But why not come and talk about your work to me; use me as a sort of wall against which you may throw your thoughts and catch them again? It's certain I don't know enough to steal your ideas myself—and I know no scientific men—"

I stopped. He was considering. Evidently the thing, attracted him. "But I'm afraid I should bore you," he said.

"You think I'm too dull?"

"Oh, no; but technicalities—"

"Anyhow, you've interested me immensely this afternoon."

"Of course it would be a great help to me. Nothing clears up one's ideas so much as explaining them. Hitherto—"

"My dear sir, say no more."

"But really can you spare the time?"

"There is no rest like change of occupation," I said, with profound conviction.

The affair was over. On my verandah steps he turned. "I am already greatly indebted to you," he said.

I made an interrogative noise.

"You have completely cured me of that ridiculous habit of humming," he explained.

I think I said I was glad to be of any service to him, and he turned away.

Immediately the train of thought that our conversation had suggested must have resumed its sway. His arms began to wave in their former fashion. The faint echo of "zuzzoo" came back to me on the breeze...

Well, after all, that was not my affair...

He came the next day, and again the next day after that, and delivered two lectures on physics to our mutual satisfaction. He talked with an air of being extremely lucid about the "ether" and "tubes of force," and "gravitational potential," and things like that, and I sat in my other folding- chair and said, "Yes," "Go on," "I follow you," to keep him going. It was tremendously difficult stuff, but I do not think he ever suspected how much I did not understand him. There were moments when I doubted whether I was well employed, but at any rate I was resting from that confounded play. Now and then things gleamed on me clearly for a space, only to vanish just when I thought I had hold of them. Sometimes my attention failed altogether, and I would give it up and sit and stare at him, wondering whether, after all, it would not be better to use him as a central figure in a good farce and let all this other stuff slide. And then, perhaps, I would catch on again for a bit.

At the earliest opportunity I went to see his house. It was large and carelessly furnished; there were no servants other than his three assistants, and his dietary and private life were characterised by a philosophical simplicity. He was a water-drinker, a vegetarian, and all those logical disciplinary things. But the sight of his equipment settled many doubts. It looked like business from cellar to attic—an amazing little place to find in an out-of-the-way village. The ground-floor rooms contained benches and apparatus, the bakehouse and scullery boiler had developed into respectable furnaces, dynamos occupied the cellar, and there was a gasometer in the garden. He showed it to me with all the confiding zest of a man who has been living too much alone. His seclusion was overflowing now in an excess of confidence, and I had the good luck to be the recipient.

The three assistants were creditable specimens of the class of "handy- men" from which they came. Conscientious if unintelligent, strong, civil, and willing. One, Spargus, who did the cooking and all the metal work, had been a sailor; a second, Gibbs, was a joiner; and the third was an ex-jobbing gardener, and now general assistant. They were the merest labourers. All the intelligent work was

done by Cavor. Theirs was the darkest ignorance compared even with my muddled impression.

And now, as to the nature of these inquiries. Here, unhappily, comes a grave difficulty. I am no scientific expert, and if I were to attempt to set forth in the highly scientific language of Mr. Cavor the aim to which his experiments tended, I am afraid I should confuse not only the reader but myself, and almost certainly I should make some blunder that would bring upon me the mockery of every up-to-date student of mathematical physics in the country. The best thing I can do therefore is, I think to give my impressions in my own inexact language, without any attempt to wear a garment of knowledge to which I have no claim.

The object of Mr. Cavor's search was a substance that should be "opaque" — he used some other word I have forgotten, but "opaque" conveys the idea —to "all forms of radiant energy." "Radiant energy," he made me understand, was anything like light or heat, or those Rontgen Rays there was so much talk about a year or so ago, or the electric waves of Marconi, or gravitation. All these things, he said, *radiate* out from centres, and act on bodies at a distance, whence comes the term "radiant energy." Now almost all substances are opaque to some form or other of radiant energy. Glass, for example, is transparent to light, but much less so to heat, so that it is useful as a fire-screen; and alum is transparent to light, but blocks heat completely. A solution of iodine in carbon bisulphide, on the other hand, completely blocks light, but is quite transparent to heat. It will hide a fire from you, but permit all its warmth to reach you. Metals are not only opaque to light and heat, but also to electrical energy, which passes through both iodine solution and glass almost as though they were not interposed. And so on.

Now all known substances are "transparent" to gravitation. You can use screens of various sorts to cut off the light or heat, or electrical influence of the sun, or the warmth of the earth from anything; you can screen things by sheets of metal from Marconi's rays, but nothing will cut off the gravitational attraction of the sun or the gravitational attraction of the earth. Yet why there should be nothing is hard to say. Cavor did not see why such a substance should not exist, and certainly I could not tell him. I had never thought of such a possibility before. He showed me by calculations on paper, which Lord Kelvin, no doubt, or Professor Lodge, or Professor Karl Pearson, or any of those great scientific people might have understood, but which simply reduced me to a hopeless muddle, that not only was such a substance possible, but that it must satisfy certain conditions. It was an amazing piece of reasoning. Much as it amazed and exercised me at the time, it would be impossible to reproduce it here. "Yes," I said to it all, "yes; go on!" Suffice it for this story that he believed he might be able to manufacture this possible substance opaque to gravitation out of a complicated alloy of metals and something new—a new element, I fancy—called, I believe, *helium*, which was sent to him from London in sealed stone jars. Doubt has been thrown upon this detail, but I am almost certain it was *helium* he had sent him in sealed stone jars. It was certainly something very gaseous and thin. If only I had taken notes...

But then, how was I to foresee the necessity of taking notes?

Any one with the merest germ of an imagination will understand the extraordinary possibilities of such a substance, and will sympathise a little with the emotion I felt as this understanding emerged from the haze of abstruse phrases in which Cavor expressed himself. Comic relief in a play indeed! It was some time before I would believe that I had interpreted him aright, and I was very careful not to ask questions that would have enabled him to gauge the profundity of misunderstanding into which he dropped his daily exposition. But no one reading the story of it here will sympathise fully, because from my barren narrative it will be impossible to gather the strength of my conviction that this astonishing substance was positively going to be made.

I do not recall that I gave my play an hour's consecutive work at any time after my visit to his house. My imagination had other things to do. There seemed no limit to the possibilities of the stuff; whichever way I tried I came on miracles and revolutions. For example, if one wanted to lift a weight, however enormous, one had only to get a sheet of this substance beneath it, and one might lift it with a straw. My first natural impulse was to apply this principle to guns and ironclads, and all the material and methods of war, and from that to shipping, locomotion, building, every conceivable form of human industry. The chance that had brought me into the very birth-chamber of this new time—it was an epoch, no less—was one of those chances that come once in a thousand years. The thing unrolled, it expanded and expanded. Among other things I saw in it my redemption as a business man. I saw a parent company, and daughter companies, applications to right of us, applications to left, rings and trusts, privileges, and concessions spreading and spreading, until one vast, stupendous Cavorite company ran and ruled the world.

And I was in it!

I took my line straight away. I knew I was staking everything, but I jumped there and then.

"We're on absolutely the biggest thing that has ever been invented," I said, and put the accent on "we." "If you want to keep me out of this, you'll have to do it with a gun. I'm coming down to be your fourth labourer to- morrow."

He seemed surprised at my enthusiasm, but not a bit suspicious or hostile. Rather, he was self-depreciatory. He looked at me doubtfully. "But do you really think—?" he said. "And your play! How about that play?"

"It's vanished!" I cried. "My dear sir, don't you see what you've got? Don't you see what you're going to do?"

That was merely a rhetorical turn, but positively, he didn't. At first I could not believe it. He had not had the beginning of the inkling of an idea. This astonishing little man had been working on purely theoretical grounds the whole time! When he said it was "the most important" research the world had ever seen, he simply meant it squared up so many theories, settled so much that was in doubt; he had troubled no more about the application of the stuff he was going to turn out than if he had been a machine that makes guns. This was a possible substance, and he was going to make it! V'la tout, as the Frenchman says.

Beyond that, he was childish! If he made it, it would go down to posterity as Cavorite or Cavorine, and he would be made an F.R.S., and his portrait given away as a scientific worthy with Nature, and things like that. And that was all he saw! He would have dropped this bombshell into the world as though he had discovered a new species of gnat, if it had not happened that I had come along. And there it would have lain and fizzled, like one or two other little things these scientific people have lit and dropped about us.

When I realised this, it was I did the talking, and Cavor who said, "Go on!" I jumped up. I paced the room, gesticulating like a boy of twenty. I tried to make him understand his duties and responsibilities in the matter—*our* duties and responsibilities in the matter. I assured him we might make wealth enough to work any sort of social revolution we fancied, we might own and order the whole world. I told him of companies and patents, and the case for secret processes. All these things seemed to take him much as his mathematics had taken me. A look of perplexity came into his ruddy little face. He stammered something about indifference to wealth, but I brushed all that aside. He had got to be rich, and it was no good his stammering. I gave him to understand the sort of man I was, and that I had had very considerable business experience. I did not tell him I was an undischarged bankrupt at the time, because that was temporary, but I think I reconciled my evident poverty with my financial claims. And quite insensibly, in the way such projects grow, the understanding of a Cavorite monopoly grew up between us. He was to make the stuff, and I was to make the boom.

I stuck like a leech to the "we"—"you" and "I" didn't exist for me.

His idea was that the profits I spoke of might go to endow research, but that, of course, was a matter we had to settle later. "That's all right," I shouted, "that's all right." The great point, as I insisted, was to get the thing done.

"Here is a substance," I cried, "no home, no factory, no fortress, no ship can dare to be without—more universally applicable even than a patent medicine. There isn't a solitary aspect of it, not one of its ten thousand possible uses that will not make us rich, Cavor, beyond the dreams of avarice!"

"No!" he said. "I begin to see. It's extraordinary how one gets new points of view by talking over things!"

"And as it happens you have just talked to the right man!"

"I suppose no one," he said, "is absolutely *averse* to enormous wealth. Of course there is one thing—"

He paused. I stood still.

"It is just possible, you know, that we may not be able to make it after all! It may be one of those things that are a theoretical possibility, but a practical absurdity. Or when we make it, there may be some little hitch!"

"We'll tackle the hitch when it comes." said I.

CHAPTER II - THE FIRST MAKING OF CAVORITE

But Cavor's fears were groundless, so far as the actual making was concerned. On the 14th of October, 1899, this incredible substance was made!

Oddly enough, it was made at last by accident, when Mr. Cavor least expected it. He had fused together a number of metals and certain other things —I wish I knew the particulars now!—and he intended to leave the mixture a week and then allow it to cool slowly. Unless he had miscalculated, the last stage in the combination would occur when the stuff sank to a temperature of 60 degrees Fahrenheit. But it chanced that, unknown to Cavor, dissension had arisen about the furnace tending. Gibbs, who had previously seen to this, had suddenly attempted to shift it to the man who had been a gardener, on the score that coal was soil, being dug, and therefore could not possibly fall within the province of a joiner; the man who had been a jobbing gardener alleged, however, that coal was a metallic or ore-like substance, let alone that he was cook. But Spargus insisted on Gibbs doing the coaling, seeing that he was a joiner and that coal is notoriously fossil wood. Consequently Gibbs ceased to replenish the furnace, and no one else did so, and Cavor was too much immersed in certain interesting problems concerning a Cavorite flying machine (neglecting the resistance of the air and one or two other points) to perceive that anything was wrong. And the premature birth of his invention took place just as he was coming across the field to my bungalow for our afternoon talk and tea.

I remember the occasion with extreme vividness. The water was boiling, and everything was prepared, and the sound of his "zuzzoo" had brought me out upon the verandah. His active little figure was black against the autumnal sunset, and to the right the chimneys of his house just rose above a gloriously tinted group of trees. Remoter rose the Wealden Hills, faint and blue, while to the left the hazy marsh spread out spacious and serene. And then—

The chimneys jerked heavenward, smashing into a string of bricks as they rose, and the roof and a miscellany of furniture followed. Then overtaking them came a huge white flame. The trees about the building swayed and whirled and tore themselves to pieces, that sprang towards the flare. My ears were smitten with a clap of thunder that left me deaf on one side for life, and all about me windows smashed, unheeded.

I took three steps from the verandah towards Cavor's house, and even as I did so came the wind.

Instantly my coat tails were over my head, and I was progressing in great leaps and bounds, and quite against my will, towards him. In the same moment the discoverer was seized, whirled about, and flew through the screaming air. I saw one of my chimney pots hit the ground within six yards of me, leap a score of feet, and so hurry in great strides towards the focus of the disturbance. Cavor, kicking and flapping, came down again, rolled over and over on the ground for a space, struggled up and was lifted and borne forward at an enormous velocity, vanishing at last among the labouring, lashing trees that writhed about his house.

A mass of smoke and ashes, and a square of bluish shining substance rushed up towards the zenith. A large fragment of fencing came sailing past me, dropped edgeways, hit the ground and fell flat, and then the worst was over. The aerial commotion fell swiftly until it was a mere strong gale, and I became once more aware that I had breath and feet. By leaning back against the wind I managed to stop, and could collect such wits as still remained to me.

In that instant the whole face of the world had changed. The tranquil sunset had vanished, the sky was dark with scurrying clouds, everything was flattened and swaying with the gale. I glanced back to see if my bungalow was still in a general way standing, then staggered forwards towards the trees amongst which Cavor had vanished, and through whose tall and leaf-denuded branches shone the flames of his burning house.

I entered the copse, dashing from one tree to another and clinging to them, and for a space I sought him in vain. Then amidst a heap of smashed branches and fencing that had banked itself against a portion of his garden wall I perceived something stir. I made a run for this, but before I reached it a brown object separated itself, rose on two muddy legs, and protruded two drooping, bleeding hands. Some tattered ends of garment fluttered out from its middle portion and streamed before the wind.

For a moment I did not recognise this earthy lump, and then I saw that it was Cavor, caked in the mud in which he had rolled. He leant forward against the wind, rubbing the dirt from his eyes and mouth.

He extended a muddy lump of hand, and staggered a pace towards me. His face worked with emotion, little lumps of mud kept falling from it. He looked as damaged and pitiful as any living creature I have ever seen, and his remark therefore amazed me exceedingly.

"Gratulate me," he gasped; "gratulate me!"

"Congratulate you!" said I. "Good heavens! What for?"

"I've done it."

"You *have*. What on earth caused that explosion?"

A gust of wind blew his words away. I understood him to say that it wasn't an explosion at all. The wind hurled me into collision with him, and we stood clinging to one another.

"Try and get back—to my bungalow," I bawled in his ear. He did not hear me, and shouted something about "three martyrs—science," and also something about "not much good." At the time he laboured under the impression that his three at-

tendants had perished in the whirlwind. Happily this was incorrect. Directly he had left for my bungalow they had gone off to the public-house in Lympne to discuss the question of the furnaces over some trivial refreshment.

I repeated my suggestion of getting back to my bungalow, and this time he understood. We clung arm-in-arm and started, and managed at last to reach the shelter of as much roof as was left to me. For a space we sat in arm-chairs and panted. All the windows were broken, and the lighter articles of furniture were in great disorder, but no irrevocable damage was done. Happily the kitchen door had stood the pressure upon it, so that all my crockery and cooking materials had survived. The oil stove was still burning, and I put on the water to boil again for tea. And that prepared, I could turn on Cavor for his explanation.

"Quite correct," he insisted; "quite correct. I've done it, and it's all right."

"But," I protested. "All right! Why, there can't be a rick standing, or a fence or a thatched roof undamaged for twenty miles round..."

"It's all right—*really*. I didn't, of course, foresee this little upset. My mind was preoccupied with another problem, and I'm apt to disregard these practical side issues. But it's all right—"

"My dear sir," I cried, "don't you see you've done thousands of pounds' worth of damage?"

"There, I throw myself on your discretion. I'm not a practical man, of course, but don't you think they will regard it as a cyclone?"

"But the explosion—"

"It was not an explosion. It's perfectly simple. Only, as I say, I'm apt to overlook these little things. Its that zuzzoo business on a larger scale. Inadvertently I made this substance of mine, this Cavorite, in a thin, wide sheet..."

He paused. "You are quite clear that the stuff is opaque to gravitation, that it cuts off things from gravitating towards each other?"

"Yes," said I. "Yes."

"Well, so soon as it reached a temperature of 60 degrees Fahrenheit, and the process of its manufacture was complete, the air above it, the portions of roof and ceiling and floor above it ceased to have weight. I suppose you know — everybody knows nowadays—that, as a usual thing, the air *has* weight, that it presses on everything at the surface of the earth, presses in all directions, with a pressure of fourteen and a half pounds to the square inch?"

"I know that," said I. "Go on."

"I know that too," he remarked. "Only this shows you how useless knowledge is unless you apply it. You see, over our Cavorite this ceased to be the case, the air there ceased to exert any pressure, and the air round it and not over the Cavorite was exerting a pressure of fourteen pounds and a half to the square in upon this suddenly weightless air. Ah! you begin to see! The air all about the Cavorite crushed in upon the air above it with irresistible force. The air above the Cavorite was forced upward violently, the air that rushed in to replace it immediately lost weight, ceased to exert any pressure, followed suit, blew the ceiling through and the roof off...

"You perceive," he said, "it formed a sort of atmospheric fountain, a kind of chimney in the atmosphere. And if the Cavorite itself hadn't been loose and so got sucked up the chimney, does it occur to you what would have happened?"

I thought. "I suppose," I said, "the air would be rushing up and up over that infernal piece of stuff now."

"Precisely," he said. "A huge fountain—"

"Spouting into space! Good heavens! Why, it would have squirted all the atmosphere of the earth away! It would have robbed the world of air! It would have been the death of all mankind! That little lump of stuff!"

"Not exactly into space," said Cavor, "but as bad—practically. It would have whipped the air off the world as one peels a banana, and flung it thousands of miles. It would have dropped back again, of course—but on an asphyxiated world! From our point of view very little better than if it never came back!"

I stared. As yet I was too amazed to realise how all my expectations had been upset. "What do you mean to do now?" I asked.

"In the first place if I may borrow a garden trowel I will remove some of this earth with which I am encased, and then if I may avail myself of your domestic conveniences I will have a bath. This done, we will converse more at leisure. It will be wise, I think"—he laid a muddy hand on my arm —"if nothing were said of this affair beyond ourselves. I know I have caused great damage—probably even dwelling-houses may be ruined here and there upon the country-side. But on the other hand, I cannot possibly pay for the damage I have done, and if the real cause of this is published, it will lead only to heartburning and the obstruction of my work. One cannot foresee everything, you know, and I cannot consent for one moment to add the burthen of practical considerations to my theorising. Later on, when you have come in with your practical mind, and Cavorite is floated—floated is the word, isn't it?—and it has realised all you anticipate for it, we may set matters right with these persons. But not now—not now. If no other explanation is offered, people, in the present unsatisfactory state of meteorological science, will ascribe all this to a cyclone; there might be a public subscription, and as my house has collapsed and been burnt, I should in that case receive a considerable share in the compensation, which would be extremely helpful to the prosecution of our researches. But if it is known that *I* caused this, there will be no public subscription, and everybody will be put out. Practically I should never get a chance of working in peace again. My three assistants may or may not have perished. That is a detail. If they have, it is no great loss; they were more zealous than able, and this premature event must be largely due to their joint neglect of the furnace. If they have not perished, I doubt if they have the intelligence to explain the affair. They will accept the cyclone story. And if during the temporary unfitness of my house for occupation, I may lodge in one of the untenanted rooms of this bungalow of yours—"

He paused and regarded me.

A man of such possibilities, I reflected, is no ordinary guest to entertain.

"Perhaps," said I, rising to my feet, "we had better begin by looking for a trowel," and I led the way to the scattered vestiges of the greenhouse.

And while he was having his bath I considered the entire question alone. It was clear there were drawbacks to Mr. Cavor's society I had not foreseen. The absentmindedness that had just escaped depopulating the terrestrial globe, might at any moment result in some other grave inconvenience. On the other hand I was young, my affairs were in a mess, and I was in just the mood for reckless adventure—with a chance of something good at the end of it. I had quite settled in my mind that I was to have half at least in that aspect of the affair. Fortunately I held my bungalow, as I have already explained, on a three- year agreement, without being responsible for repairs; and my furniture, such as there was of it, had been hastily purchased, was unpaid for, insured, and altogether devoid of associations. In the end I decided to keep on with him, and see the business through.

Certainly the aspect of things had changed very greatly. I no longer doubted at all the enormous possibilities of the substance, but I began to have doubts about the gun-carriage and the patent boots. We set to work at once to reconstruct his laboratory and proceed with our experiments. Cavor talked more on my level than he had ever done before, when it came to the question of how we should make the stuff next.

"Of course we must make it again," he said, with a sort of glee I had not expected in him, "of course we must make it again. We have caught a Tartar, perhaps, but we have left the theoretical behind us for good and all. If we can possibly avoid wrecking this little planet of ours, we will. But—there must be risks! There must be. In experimental work there always are. And here, as a practical man, *you* must come in. For my own part it seems to me we might make it edgeways, perhaps, and very thin. Yet I don't know. I have a certain dim perception of another method. I can hardly explain it yet. But curiously enough it came into my mind, while I was rolling over and over in the mud before the wind, and very doubtful how the whole adventure was to end, as being absolutely the thing I ought to have done."

Even with my aid we found some little difficulty, and meanwhile we kept at work restoring the laboratory. There was plenty to do before it became absolutely necessary to decide upon the precise form and method of our second attempt. Our only hitch was the strike of the three labourers, who objected to my activity as a foreman. But that matter we compromised after two days' delay.

CHAPTER III - THE BUILDING OF THE SPHERE

I remember the occasion very distinctly when Cavor told me of his idea of the sphere. He had had intimations of it before, but at the time it seemed to come to him in a rush. We were returning to the bungalow for tea, and on the way he fell humming. Suddenly he shouted, "That's it! That finishes it! A sort of roller blind!"

"Finishes what?" I asked.

"Space—anywhere! The moon."

"What do you mean?"

"Mean? Why—it must be a sphere! That's what I mean!"

I saw I was out of it, and for a time I let him talk in his own fashion. I hadn't the ghost of an idea then of his drift. But after he had taken tea he made it clear to me.

"It's like this," he said. "Last time I ran this stuff that cuts things off from gravitation into a flat tank with an overlap that held it down. And directly it had cooled and the manufacture was completed all that uproar happened, nothing above it weighed anything, the air went squirting up, the house squirted up, and if the stuff itself hadn't squirted up too, I don't know what would have happened! But suppose the substance is loose, and quite free to go up?"

"It will go up at once!"

"Exactly. With no more disturbance than firing a big gun."

"But what good will that do?"

"I'm going up with it!"

I put down my teacup and stared at him.

"Imagine a sphere," he explained, "large enough to hold two people and their luggage. It will be made of steel lined with thick glass; it will contain a proper store of solidified air, concentrated food, water distilling apparatus, and so forth. And enamelled, as it were, on the outer steel—"

"Cavorite?"

"Yes."

"But how will you get inside?"

"There was a similar problem about a dumpling."

"Yes, I know. But how?"

"That's perfectly easy. An air-tight manhole is all that is needed. That, of course, will have to be a little complicated; there will have to be a valve, so that things may be thrown out, if necessary, without much loss of air."

"Like Jules Verne's thing in *A Trip to the Moon*."

But Cavor was not a reader of fiction.

"I begin to see," I said slowly. "And you could get in and screw yourself up while the Cavorite was warm, and as soon as it cooled it would become impervious to gravitation, and off you would fly—"

"At a tangent."

"You would go off in a straight line—" I stopped abruptly. "What is to prevent the thing travelling in a straight line into space for ever?" I asked. "You're not safe to get anywhere, and if you do—how will you get back?"

"I've just thought of that," said Cavor. "That's what I meant when I said the thing is finished. The inner glass sphere can be air-tight, and, except for the manhole, continuous, and the steel sphere can be made in sections, each section capable of rolling up after the fashion of a roller blind. These can easily be worked by springs, and released and checked by electricity conveyed by platinum wires fused through the glass. All that is merely a question of detail. So you see, that except for the thickness of the blind rollers, the Cavorite exterior of the sphere will consist of windows or blinds, whichever you like to call them. Well, when all these windows or blinds are shut, no light, no heat, no gravitation, no radiant energy of any sort will get at the inside of the sphere, it will fly on through space in a straight line, as you say. But open a window, imagine one of the windows open. Then at once any heavy body that chances to be in that direction will attract us—"

I sat taking it in.

"You see?" he said.

"Oh, I *see*."

"Practically we shall be able to tack about in space just as we wish. Get attracted by this and that."

"Oh, yes. That's clear enough. Only—"

"Well?"

"I don't quite see what we shall do it for! It's really only jumping off the world and back again."

"Surely! For example, one might go to the moon."

"And when one got there? What would you find?"

"We should see—Oh! consider the new knowledge."

"Is there air there?"

"There may be."

"It's a fine idea," I said, "but it strikes me as a large order all the same. The moon! I'd much rather try some smaller things first."

"They're out of the question, because of the air difficulty."

"Why not apply that idea of spring blinds—Cavorite blinds in strong steel cases—to lifting weights?"

"It wouldn't work," he insisted. "After all, to go into outer space is not so much worse, if at all, than a polar expedition. Men go on polar expeditions."

"Not business men. And besides, they get paid for polar expeditions. And if anything goes wrong there are relief parties. But this—it's just firing ourselves off the world for nothing."

"Call it prospecting."

"You'll have to call it that... One might make a book of it perhaps," I said.

"I have no doubt there will be minerals," said Cavor.

"For example?"

"Oh! sulphur, ores, gold perhaps, possibly new elements."

"Cost of carriage," I said. "You know you're not a practical man. The moon's a quarter of a million miles away."

"It seems to me it wouldn't cost much to cart any weight anywhere if you packed it in a Cavorite case."

I had not thought of that. "Delivered free on head of purchaser, eh?"

"It isn't as though we were confined to the moon."

"You mean?"

"There's Mars—clear atmosphere, novel surroundings, exhilarating sense of lightness. It might be pleasant to go there."

"Is there air on Mars?"

"Oh, yes!"

"Seems as though you might run it as a sanatorium. By the way, how far is Mars?"

"Two hundred million miles at present," said Cavor airily; "and you go close by the sun."

My imagination was picking itself up again. "After all," I said, "there's something in these things. There's travel—"

An extraordinary possibility came rushing into my mind. Suddenly I saw, as in a vision, the whole solar system threaded with Cavorite liners and spheres deluxe. "Rights of pre-emption," came floating into my head—planetary rights of pre-emption. I recalled the old Spanish monopoly in American gold. It wasn't as though it was just this planet or that—it was all of them. I stared at Cavor's rubicund face, and suddenly my imagination was leaping and dancing. I stood up, I walked up and down; my tongue was unloosened.

"I'm beginning to take it in," I said; "I'm beginning to take it in." The transition from doubt to enthusiasm seemed to take scarcely any time at all. "But this is tremendous!" I cried. "This is Imperial! I haven't been dreaming of this sort of thing."

Once the chill of my opposition was removed, his own pent-up excitement had play. He too got up and paced. He too gesticulated and shouted. We behaved like men inspired. We *were* men inspired.

"We'll settle all that!" he said in answer to some incidental difficulty that had pulled me up. "We'll soon settle that! We'll start the drawings for mouldings this very night."

"We'll start them now," I responded, and we hurried off to the laboratory to begin upon this work forthwith.

I was like a child in Wonderland all that night. The dawn found us both still at work—we kept our electric light going heedless of the day. I remember now exactly how these drawings looked. I shaded and tinted while Cavor drew—smudged and haste-marked they were in every line, but wonderfully correct. We got out the orders for the steel blinds and frames we needed from that night's work, and the glass sphere was designed within a week. We gave up our afternoon conversations and our old routine altogether. We worked, and we slept and ate when we could work no longer for hunger and fatigue. Our enthusiasm infected even our three men, though they had no idea what the sphere was for. Through those days the man Gibbs gave up walking, and went everywhere, even across the room, at a sort of fussy run.

And it grew—the sphere. December passed, January—I spent a day with a broom sweeping a path through the snow from bungalow to laboratory — February, March. By the end of March the completion was in sight. In January had come a team of horses, a huge packing-case; we had our thick glass sphere now ready, and in position under the crane we had rigged to sling it into the steel shell. All the bars and blinds of the steel shell—it was not really a spherical shell, but polyhedral, with a roller blind to each facet —had arrived by February, and the lower half was bolted together. The Cavorite was half made by March, the metallic paste had gone through two of the stages in its manufacture, and we had plastered quite half of it on to the steel bars and blinds. It was astonishing how closely we kept to the lines of Cavor's first inspiration in working out the scheme. When the bolting together of the sphere was finished, he proposed to remove the rough roof of the temporary laboratory in which the work was done, and build a furnace about it. So the last stage of Cavorite making, in which the paste is heated to a dull red glow in a stream of helium, would be accomplished when it was already on the sphere.

And then we had to discuss and decide what provisions we were to take — compressed foods, concentrated essences, steel cylinders containing reserve oxygen, an arrangement for removing carbonic acid and waste from the air and restoring oxygen by means of sodium peroxide, water condensers, and so forth. I remember the little heap they made in the corner—tins, and rolls, and boxes—convincingly matter-of-fact.

It was a strenuous time, with little chance of thinking. But one day, when we were drawing near the end, an odd mood came over me. I had been bricking up the furnace all the morning, and I sat down by these possessions dead beat. Everything seemed dull and incredible.

"But look here, Cavor," I said. "After all! What's it all for?"

He smiled. "The thing now is to go."

"The moon," I reflected. "But what do you expect? I thought the moon was a dead world."

He shrugged his shoulders.

"We're going to see."

"Are we?" I said, and stared before me.

"You are tired," he remarked. "You'd better take a walk this afternoon."

"No," I said obstinately; "I'm going to finish this brickwork."

And I did, and insured myself a night of insomnia. I don't think I have ever had such a night. I had some bad times before my business collapse, but the very worst of those was sweet slumber compared to this infinity of aching wakefulness. I was suddenly in the most enormous funk at the thing we were going to do.

I do not remember before that night thinking at all of the risks we were running. Now they came like that array of spectres that once beleaguered Prague, and camped around me. The strangeness of what we were about to do, the unearthliness of it, overwhelmed me. I was like a man awakened out of pleasant dreams to the most horrible surroundings. I lay, eyes wide open, and the sphere seemed to get more flimsy and feeble, and Cavor more unreal and fantastic, and the whole enterprise madder and madder every moment.

I got out of bed and wandered about. I sat at the window and stared at the immensity of space. Between the stars was the void, the unfathomable darkness! I tried to recall the fragmentary knowledge of astronomy I had gained in my irregular reading, but it was all too vague to furnish any idea of the things we might expect. At last I got back to bed and snatched some moments of sleep—moments of nightmare rather—in which I fell and fell and fell for evermore into the abyss of the sky.

I astonished Cavor at breakfast. I told him shortly, "I'm not coming with you in the sphere."

I met all his protests with a sullen persistence. "The thing's too mad," I said, "and I won't come. The thing's too mad."

I would not go with him to the laboratory. I fretted bout my bungalow for a time, and then took hat and stick and set out alone, I knew not whither. It chanced to be a glorious morning: a warm wind and deep blue sky, the first green of spring abroad, and multitudes of birds singing. I lunched on beef and beer in a little public-house near Elham, and startled the landlord by remarking apropos of the weather, "A man who leaves the world when days of this sort are about is a fool!"

"That's what I says when I heerd on it!" said the landlord, and I found that for one poor soul at least this world had proved excessive, and there had been a throat-cutting. I went on with a new twist to my thoughts.

In the afternoon I had a pleasant sleep in a sunny place, and went on my way refreshed. I came to a comfortable-looking inn near Canterbury. It was bright with creepers, and the landlady was a clean old woman and took my eye. I found I had just enough money to pay for my lodging with her. I decided to stop the night there. She was a talkative body, and among many other particulars learnt she had never been to London. "Canterbury's as far as ever I been," she said. "I'm not one of your gad-about sort."

"How would you like a trip to the moon?" I cried.

"I never did hold with them ballooneys," she said evidently under the impression that this was a common excursion enough. "I wouldn't go up in one —not for ever so."

This struck me as being funny. After I had supped I sat on a bench by the door of the inn and gossiped with two labourers about brickmaking, and motor cars, and the cricket of last year. And in the sky a faint new crescent, blue and vague as a distant Alp, sank westward over the sun.

The next day I returned to Cavor. "I am coming," I said. "I've been a little out of order, that's all."

That was the only time I felt any serious doubt our enterprise. Nerves purely! After that I worked a little more carefully, and took a trudge for an hour every day. And at last, save for the heating in the furnace, our labours were at an end.

CHAPTER IV - INSIDE THE SPHERE

"Go on," said Cavor, as I sat across the edge of the manhole, and looked down into the black interior of the sphere. We two were alone. It was evening, the sun had set, and the stillness of the twilight was upon everything.

I drew my other leg inside and slid down the smooth glass to the bottom of the sphere, then turned to take the cans of food and other impedimenta from Cavor. The interior was warm, the thermometer stood at eighty, and as we should lose little or none of this by radiation, we were dressed in shoes and thin flannels. We had, however, a bundle of thick woollen clothing and several thick blankets to guard against mischance.

By Cavor's direction I placed the packages, the cylinders of oxygen, and so forth, loosely about my feet, and soon we had everything in. He walked about the roofless shed for a time seeking anything we had overlooked, and then crawled in after me. I noted something in his hand.

"What have you got there?" I asked.

"Haven't you brought anything to read?"

"Good Lord! No."

"I forgot to tell you. There are uncertainties—The voyage may last—We may be weeks!"

"But—"

"We shall be floating in this sphere with absolutely no occupation."

"I wish I'd known—"

He peered out of the manhole. "Look!" he said. "There's something there!"

"Is there time?"

"We shall be an hour."

I looked out. It was an old number of *Tit-Bits* that one of the men must have brought. Farther away in the corner I saw a torn *Lloyd's News*. I scrambled back into the sphere with these things. "What have you got?" I said.

I took the book from his hand and read, "The Works of William Shakespeare".

He coloured slightly. "My education has been so purely scientific—" he said apologetically.

"Never read him?"

"Never."

"He knew a little, you know—in an irregular sort of way."

"Precisely what I am told," said Cavor.

I assisted him to screw in the glass cover of the manhole, and then he pressed a stud to close the corresponding blind in the outer case. The little oblong of twilight vanished. We were in darkness. For a time neither of us spoke. Although our case would not be impervious to sound, everything was very still. I perceived there was nothing to grip when the shock of our start should come, and I realised that I should be uncomfortable for want of a chair.

"Why have we no chairs?" I asked.

"I've settled all that," said Cavor. "We won't need them."

"Why not?"

"You will see," he said, in the tone of a man who refuses to talk.

I became silent. Suddenly it had come to me clear and vivid that I was a fool to be inside that sphere. Even now, I asked myself, is to too late to withdraw? The world outside the sphere, I knew, would be cold and inhospitable enough for me—for weeks I had been living on subsidies from Cavor —but after all, would it be as cold as the infinite zero, as inhospitable as empty space? If it had not been for the appearance of cowardice, I believe that even then I should have made him let me out. But I hesitated on that score, and hesitated, and grew fretful and angry, and the time passed.

There came a little jerk, a noise like champagne being uncorked in another room, and a faint whistling sound. For just one instant I had a sense of enormous tension, a transient conviction that my feet were pressing downward with a force of countless tons. It lasted for an infinitesimal time.

But it stirred me to action. "Cavor!" I said into the darkness, "my nerve's in rags. I don't think—"

I stopped. He made no answer.

"Confound it!" I cried; "I'm a fool! What business have I here? I'm not coming, Cavor. The thing's too risky. I'm getting out."

"You can't," he said.

"Can't! We'll soon see about that!"

He made no answer for ten seconds. "It's too late for us to quarrel now, Bedford," he said. "That little jerk was the start. Already we are flying as swiftly as a bullet up into the gulf of space."

"I—" I said, and then it didn't seem to matter what happened. For a time I was, as it were, stunned; I had nothing to say. It was just as if I had never heard of this idea of leaving the world before. Then I perceived an unaccountable change in my bodily sensations. It was a feeling of lightness, of unreality. Coupled with that was a queer sensation in the head, an apoplectic effect almost, and a thumping of blood vessels at the ears. Neither of these feelings diminished as time went on, but at last I got so used to them that I experienced no inconvenience.

I heard a click, and a little glow lamp came into being.

I saw Cavor's face, as white as I felt my own to be. We regarded one another in silence. The transparent blackness of the glass behind him made him seem as though he floated in a void.

"Well, we're committed," I said at last.

"Yes," he said, "we're committed."

"Don't move," he exclaimed, at some suggestion of a gesture. "Let your muscles keep quite lax—as if you were in bed. We are in a little universe of our own. Look at those things!"

He pointed to the loose cases and bundles that had been lying on the blankets in the bottom of the sphere. I was astonished to see that they were floating now nearly a foot from the spherical wall. Then I saw from his shadow that Cavor was no longer leaning against the glass. I thrust out my hand behind me, and found that I too was suspended in space, clear of the glass.

I did not cry out nor gesticulate, but fear came upon me. It was like being held and lifted by something—you know not what. The mere touch of my hand against the glass moved me rapidly. I understood what had happened, but that did not prevent my being afraid. We were cut off from all exterior gravitation, only the attraction of objects within our sphere had effect. Consequently everything that was not fixed to the glass was falling—slowly because of the slightness of our masses—towards the centre of gravity of our little world, which seemed to be somewhere about the middle of the sphere, but rather nearer to myself than Cavor, on account of my greater weight.

"We must turn round," said Cavor, "and float back to back, with the things between us."

It was the strangest sensation conceivable, floating thus loosely in space, at first indeed horribly strange, and when the horror passed, not disagreeable at all, exceeding restful; indeed, the nearest thing in earthly experience to it that I know is lying on a very thick, soft feather bed. But the quality of utter detachment and independence! I had not reckoned on things like this. I had expected a violent jerk at starting, a giddy sense of speed. Instead I felt—as if I were disembodied. It was not like the beginning of a journey; it was like the beginning of a dream.

CHAPTER V - THE JOURNEY TO THE MOON

Presently Cavor extinguished the light. He said we had not overmuch energy stored, and that what we had we must economise for reading. For a time, whether it was long or short I do not know, there was nothing but blank darkness.

A question floated up out of the void. "How are we pointing?" I said. "What is our direction?"

"We are flying away from the earth at a tangent, and as the moon is near her third quarter we are going somewhere towards her. I will open a blind—"

Came a click, and then a window in the outer case yawned open. The sky outside was as black as the darkness within the sphere, but the shape of the open window was marked by an infinite number of stars.

Those who have only seen the starry sky from the earth cannot imagine its appearance when the vague, half luminous veil of our air has been withdrawn. The stars we see on earth are the mere scattered survivors that penetrate our misty atmosphere. But now at last I could realise the meaning of the hosts of heaven!

Stranger things we were presently to see, but that airless, star-dusted sky! Of all things, I think that will be one of the last I shall forget.

The little window vanished with a click, another beside it snapped open and instantly closed, and then a third, and for a moment I had to close my eyes because of the blinding splendour of the waning moon.

For a space I had to stare at Cavor and the white-lit things about me to season my eyes to light again, before I could turn them towards that pallid glare.

Four windows were open in order that the gravitation of the moon might act upon all the substances in our sphere. I found I was no longer floating freely in space, but that my feet were resting on the glass in the direction of the moon. The blankets and cases of provisions were also creeping slowly down the glass, and presently came to rest so as to block out a portion of the view. It seemed to me, of course, that I looked "down" when I looked at the moon. On earth "down" means earthward, the way things fall, and "up" the reverse direction. Now the pull of gravitation was towards the moon, and for all I knew to the contrary our earth was overhead. And, of course, when all the Cavorite blinds were closed, "down" was towards the centre of our sphere, and "up" towards its outer wall.

It was curiously unlike earthly experience, too, to have the light coming up to one. On earth light falls from above, or comes slanting down sideways, but here it came from beneath our feet, and to see our shadows we had to look up.

At first it gave me a sort of vertigo to stand only on thick glass and look down upon the moon through hundreds of thousands of miles of vacant space; but this sickness passed very speedily. And then—the splendour of the sight!

The reader may imagine it best if he will lie on the ground some warm summer's night and look between his upraised feet at the moon, but for some reason, probably because the absence of air made it so much more luminous, the moon seemed already considerably larger than it does from earth. The minutest details of its surface were acutely clear. And since we did not see it through air, its outline was bright and sharp, there was no glow or halo about it, and the star-dust that covered the sky came right to its very margin, and marked the outline of its unilluminated part. And as I stood and stared at the moon between my feet, that perception of the impossible that had been with me off and on ever since our start, returned again with tenfold conviction.

"Cavor," I said, "this takes me queerly. Those companies we were going to run, and all that about minerals?"

"Well?"

"I don't see 'em here."

"No," said Cavor; "but you'll get over all that."

"I suppose I'm made to turn right side up again. Still, *this* —For a moment I could half believe there never was a world."

"That copy of *Lloyd's News* might help you."

I stared at the paper for a moment, then held it above the level of my face, and found I could read it quite easily. I struck a column of mean little advertisements. "A gentleman of private means is willing to lend money," I read. I knew that gentleman. Then somebody eccentric wanted to sell a Cutaway bicycle, "quite new and cost 15 pounds," for five pounds; and a lady in distress wished to dispose of some fish knives and forks, "a wedding present," at a great sacrifice. No doubt some simple soul was sagely examining these knives and forks, and another triumphantly riding off on that bicycle, and a third trustfully consulting that benevolent gentleman of means even as I read. I laughed, and let the paper drift from my hand.

"Are we visible from the earth?" I asked.

"Why?"

"I knew some one who was rather interested in astronomy. It occurred to me that it would be rather odd if—my friend—chanced to be looking through come telescope."

"It would need the most powerful telescope on earth even now to see us as the minutest speck."

For a time I stared in silence at the moon.

"It's a world," I said; "one feels that infinitely more than one ever did on earth. People perhaps—"

"People!" he exclaimed. "No! Banish all that! Think yourself a sort of ultra-arctic voyager exploring the desolate places of space. Look at it!"

He waved his hand at the shining whiteness below. "It's dead—dead! Vast extinct volcanoes, lava wildernesses, tumbled wastes of snow, or frozen carbonic acid, or frozen air, and everywhere landslip seams and cracks and gulfs. Nothing happens. Men have watched this planet systematically with telescopes for over two hundred years. How much change do you think they have seen?"

"None."

"They have traced two indisputable landslips, a doubtful crack, and one slight periodic change of colour, and that's all."

"I didn't know they'd traced even that."

"Oh, yes. But as for people—!"

"By the way," I asked, "how small a thing will the biggest telescopes show upon the moon?"

"One could see a fair-sized church. One could certainly see any towns or buildings, or anything like the handiwork of men. There might perhaps be insects, something in the way of ants, for example, so that they could hide in deep burrows from the lunar light, or some new sort of creatures having no earthly parallel. That is the most probable thing, if we are to find life there at all. Think of the difference in conditions! Life must fit itself to a day as long as fourteen earthly days, a cloudless sun-blaze of fourteen days, and then a night of equal length, growing ever colder and colder under these, cold, sharp stars. In that night there must be cold, the ultimate cold, absolute zero, 273 degrees Centigrade, below the earthly freezing point. Whatever life there is must hibernate through that, and rise again each day."

He mused. "One can imagine something worm-like," he said, "taking its air solid as an earth-worm swallows earth, or thick-skinned monsters—"

"By the bye," I said, "why didn't we bring a gun?"

He did not answer that question. "No," he concluded, "we just have to go. We shall see when we get there."

I remembered something. "Of course, there's my minerals, anyhow," I said; "whatever the conditions may be."

Presently he told me he wished to alter our course a little by letting the earth tug at us for a moment. He was going to open one earthward blind for thirty seconds. He warned me that it would make my head swim, and advised me to extend my hands against the glass to break my fall. I did as he directed, and thrust my feet against the bales of food cases and air cylinders to prevent their falling upon me. Then with a click the window flew open. I fell clumsily upon hands and face, and saw for a moment between my black extended fingers our mother earth—a planet in a downward sky.

We were still very near—Cavor told me the distance was perhaps eight hundred miles and the huge terrestrial disc filled all heaven. But already it was plain to see that the world was a globe. The land below us was in twilight and vague, but westward the vast gray stretches of the Atlantic shone like molten silver under the receding day. I think I recognised the cloud- dimmed coast-lines of France and Spain and the south of England, and then, with a click, the shutter closed

again, and I found myself in a state of extraordinary confusion sliding slowly over the smooth glass.

When at last things settled themselves in my mind again, it seemed quite beyond question that the moon was "down" and under my feet, and that the earth was somewhere away on the level of the horizon—the earth that had been "down" to me and my kindred since the beginning of things.

So slight were the exertions required of us, so easy did the practical annihilation of our weight make all we had to do, that the necessity for taking refreshment did not occur to us for nearly six hours (by Cavor's chronometer) after our start. I was amazed at that lapse of time. Even then I was satisfied with very little. Cavor examined the apparatus for absorbing carbonic acid and water, and pronounced it to be in satisfactory order, our consumption of oxygen having been extraordinarily slight. And our talk being exhausted for the time, and there being nothing further for us to do, we gave way to a curious drowsiness that had come upon us, and spreading our blankets on the bottom of the sphere in such a manner as to shut out most of the moonlight, wished each other good-night, and almost immediately fell asleep.

And so, sleeping, and sometimes talking and reading a little, and at times eating, although without any keenness of appetite,[1] but for the most part in a sort of quiescence that was neither waking nor slumber, we fell through a space of time that had neither night nor day in it, silently, softly, and swiftly down towards the moon.

[1] It is a curious thing, that while we were in the sphere we felt not the slightest desire for food, nor did we feel the want of it when we abstained. At first we forced our appetites, but afterwards we fasted completely. Altogether we did not consume one-hundredth part of the compressed provisions we had brought with us. The amount of carbonic acid we breathed was also unnaturally low, but why this was, I am quite unable to explain.

CHAPTER VI - THE LANDING ON THE MOON

I remember how one day Cavor suddenly opened six of our shutters and blinded me so that I cried aloud at him. The whole area was moon, a stupendous scimitar of white dawn with its edge hacked out by notches of darkness, the crescent shore of an ebbing tide of darkness, out of which peaks and pinnacles came glittering into the blaze of the sun. I take it the reader has seen pictures or photographs of the moon and that I need not describe the broader features of that landscape, those spacious ring-like ranges vaster than any terrestrial mountains, their summits shining in the day, their shadows harsh and deep, the gray disordered plains, the ridges, hills, and craterlets, all passing at last from a blazing illumination into a common mystery of black. Athwart this world we were flying scarcely a hundred miles above its crests and pinnacles. And now we could see, what no eye on earth will ever see, that under the blaze of the day the harsh outlines of the rocks and ravines of the plains and crater floor grew gray and indistinct under a thickening haze, that the white of their lit surfaces broke into lumps and patches, and broke again and shrank and vanished, and that here and there strange tints of brown and olive grew and spread.

But little time we had for watching then. For now we had come to the real danger of our journey. We had to drop ever closer to the moon as we spun about it, to slacken our pace and watch our chance, until at last we could dare to drop upon its surface.

For Cavor that was a time of intense exertion; for me it was an anxious inactivity. I seemed perpetually to be getting out of his way. He leapt about the sphere from point to point with an agility that would have been impossible on earth. He was perpetually opening and closing the Cavorite windows, making calculations, consulting his chronometer by means of the glow lamp during those last eventful hours. For a long time we had all our windows closed and hung silently in darkness hurling through space.

Then he was feeling for the shutter studs, and suddenly four windows were open. I staggered and covered my eyes, drenched and scorched and blinded by the unaccustomed splendour of the sun beneath my feet. Then again the shutters snapped, leaving my brain spinning in a darkness that pressed against the eyes. And after that I floated in another vast, black silence.

Then Cavor switched on the electric light, and told me he proposed to bind all our luggage together with the blankets about it, against the concussion of our descent. We did this with our windows closed, because in that way our goods

arranged themselves naturally at the centre of the sphere. That too was a strange business; we two men floating loose in that spherical space, and packing and pulling ropes. Imagine it if you can! No up nor down, and every effort resulting in unexpected movements. Now I would be pressed against the glass with the full force of Cavor's thrust, now I would be kicking helplessly in a void. Now the star of the electric light would be overhead, now under foot. Now Cavor's feet would float up before my eyes, and now we would be crossways to each other. But at last our goods were safely bound together in a big soft bale, all except two blankets with head holes that we were to wrap about ourselves.

Then for a flash Cavor opened a window moonward, and we saw that we were dropping towards a huge central crater with a number of minor craters grouped in a sort of cross about it. And then again Cavor flung our little sphere open to the scorching, blinding sun. I think he was using the sun's attraction as a brake. "Cover yourself with a blanket," he cried, thrusting himself from me, and for a moment I did not understand.

Then I hauled the blanket from beneath my feet and got it about me and over my head and eyes. Abruptly he closed the shutters again, snapped one open again and closed it, then suddenly began snapping them all open, each safely into its steel roller. There came a jar, and then we were rolling over and over, bumping against the glass and against the big bale of our luggage, and clutching at each other, and outside some white substance splashed as if we were rolling down a slope of snow...

Over, clutch, bump, clutch, bump, over...

Came a thud, and I was half buried under the bale of our possessions, and for a space everything was still. Then I could hear Cavor puffing and grunting, and the snapping of a shutter in its sash. I made an effort, thrust back our blanket-wrapped luggage, and emerged from beneath it. Our open windows were just visible as a deeper black set with stars.

We were still alive, and we were lying in the darkness of the shadow of the wall of the great crater into which we had fallen.

We sat getting our breath again, and feeling the bruises on our limbs. I don't think either of us had had a very clear expectation of such rough handling as we had received. I struggled painfully to my feet. "And now," said I, "to look at the landscape of the moon! But—! It's tremendously dark, Cavor!"

The glass was dewy, and as I spoke I wiped at it with my blanket. "We're half an hour or so beyond the day," he said. "We must wait."

It was impossible to distinguish anything. We might have been in a sphere of steel for all that we could see. My rubbing with the blanket simply smeared the glass, and as fast as I wiped it, it became opaque again with freshly condensed moisture mixed with an increasing quantity of blanket hairs. Of course I ought not to have used the blanket. In my efforts to clear the glass I slipped upon the damp surface, and hurt my shin against one of the oxygen cylinders that protruded from our bale.

The thing was exasperating—it was absurd. Here we were just arrived upon the moon, amidst we knew not what wonders, and all we could see was the gray and streaming wall of the bubble in which we had come.

"Confound it!" I said, "but at this rate we might have stopped at home;" and I squatted on the bale and shivered, and drew my blanket closer about me.

Abruptly the moisture turned to spangles and fronds of frost. "Can you reach the electric heater," said Cavor. "Yes—that black knob. Or we shall freeze."

I did not wait to be told twice. "And now," said I, "what are we to do?"

"Wait," he said.

"Wait?"

"Of course. We shall have to wait until our air gets warm again, and then this glass will clear. We can't do anything till then. It's night here yet; we must wait for the day to overtake us. Meanwhile, don't you feel hungry?"

For a space I did not answer him, but sat fretting. I turned reluctantly from the smeared puzzle of the glass and stared at his face. "Yes," I said, "I am hungry. I feel somehow enormously disappointed. I had expected—I don't know what I had expected, but not this."

I summoned my philosophy, and rearranging my blanket about me sat down on the bale again and began my first meal on the moon. I don't think I finished it —I forget. Presently, first in patches, then running rapidly together into wider spaces, came the clearing of the glass, came the drawing of the misty veil that hid the moon world from our eyes.

We peered out upon the landscape of the moon.

CHAPTER VII - SUNRISE ON THE MOON

As we saw it first it was the wildest and most desolate of scenes. We were in an enormous amphitheatre, a vast circular plain, the floor of the giant crater. Its cliff-like walls closed us in on every side. From the westward the light of the unseen sun fell upon them, reaching to the very foot of the cliff, and showed a disordered escarpment of drab and grayish rock, lined here and there with banks and crevices of snow. This was perhaps a dozen miles away, but at first no intervening atmosphere diminished in the slightest the minutely detailed brilliancy with which these things glared at us. They stood out clear and dazzling against a background of starry blackness that seemed to our earthly eyes rather a gloriously spangled velvet curtain than the spaciousness of the sky.

The eastward cliff was at first merely a starless selvedge to the starry dome. No rosy flush, no creeping pallor, announced the commencing day. Only the Corona, the Zodiacal light, a huge cone-shaped, luminous haze, pointing up towards the splendour of the morning star, warned us of the imminent nearness of the sun.

Whatever light was about us was reflected by the westward cliffs. It showed a huge undulating plain, cold and gray, a gray that deepened eastward into the absolute raven darkness of the cliff shadow. Innumerable rounded gray summits, ghostly hummocks, billows of snowy substance, stretching crest beyond crest into the remote obscurity, gave us our first inkling of the distance of the crater wall. These hummocks looked like snow. At the time I thought they were snow. But they were not—they were mounds and masses of frozen air.

So it was at first; and then, sudden, swift, and amazing, came the lunar day.

The sunlight had crept down the cliff, it touched the drifted masses at its base and incontinently came striding with seven-leagued boots towards us. The distant cliff seemed to shift and quiver, and at the touch of the dawn a reek of gray vapour poured upward from the crater floor, whirls and puffs and drifting wraiths of gray, thicker and broader and denser, until at last the whole westward plain was steaming like a wet handkerchief held before the fire, and the westward cliffs were no more than refracted glare beyond.

"It is air," said Cavor. "It must be air—or it would not rise like this—at the mere touch of a sun-beam. And at this pace..."

He peered upwards. "Look!" he said.

"What?" I asked.

"In the sky. Already. On the blackness—a little touch of blue. See! The stars seem larger. And the little ones and all those dim nebulosities we saw in empty space—they are hidden!"

Swiftly, steadily, the day approached us. Gray summit after gray summit was overtaken by the blaze, and turned to a smoking white intensity. At last there was nothing to the west of us but a bank of surging fog, the tumultuous advance and ascent of cloudy haze. The distant cliff had receded farther and farther, had loomed and changed through the whirl, and foundered and vanished at last in its confusion.

Nearer came that steaming advance, nearer and nearer, coming as fast as the shadow of a cloud before the south-west wind. About us rose a thin anticipatory haze.

Cavor gripped my arm. "What?" I said.

"Look! The sunrise! The sun!"

He turned me about and pointed to the brow of the eastward cliff, looming above the haze about us, scarce lighter than the darkness of the sky. But now its line was marked by strange reddish shapes, tongues of vermilion flame that writhed and danced. I fancied it must be spirals of vapour that had caught the light and made this crest of fiery tongues against the sky, but indeed it was the solar prominences I saw, a crown of fire about the sun that is forever hidden from earthly eyes by our atmospheric veil.

And then—the sun!

Steadily, inevitably came a brilliant line, came a thin edge of intolerable effulgence that took a circular shape, became a bow, became a blazing sceptre, and hurled a shaft of heat at us as though it was a spear.

It seemed verily to stab my eyes! I cried aloud and turned about blinded, groping for my blanket beneath the bale.

And with that incandescence came a sound, the first sound that had reached us from without since we left the earth, a hissing and rustling, the stormy trailing of the aerial garment of the advancing day. And with the coming of the sound and the light the sphere lurched, and blinded and dazzled we staggered helplessly against each other. It lurched again, and the hissing grew louder. I had shut my eyes perforce, I was making clumsy efforts to cover my head with my blanket, and this second lurch sent me helplessly off my feet. I fell against the bale, and opening my eyes had a momentary glimpse of the air just outside our glass. It was running—it was boiling—like snow into which a white-hot rod is thrust. What had been solid air had suddenly at the touch of the sun become a paste, a mud, a slushy liquefaction, that hissed and bubbled into gas.

There came a still more violent whirl of the sphere and we had clutched one another. In another moment we were spun about again. Round we went and over, and then I was on all fours. The lunar dawn had hold of us. It meant to show us little men what the moon could do with us.

I caught a second glimpse of things without, puffs of vapour, half liquid slush, excavated, sliding, falling, sliding. We dropped into darkness. I went down with

Cavor's knees in my chest. Then he seemed to fly away from me, and for a moment I lay with all the breath out of my body staring upward. A toppling crag of the melting stuff had splashed over us, buried us, and now it thinned and boiled off us. I saw the bubbles dancing on the glass above. I heard Cavor exclaiming feebly.

Then some huge landslip in the thawing air had caught us, and spluttering expostulation, we began to roll down a slope, rolling faster and faster, leaping crevasses and rebounding from banks, faster and faster, westward into the white-hot boiling tumult of the lunar day.

Clutching at one another we spun about, pitched this way and that, our bale of packages leaping at us, pounding at us. We collided, we gripped, we were torn asunder—our heads met, and the whole universe burst into fiery darts and stars! On the earth we should have smashed one another a dozen times, but on the moon, luckily for us, our weight was only one-sixth of what it is terrestrially, and we fell very mercifully. I recall a sensation of utter sickness, a feeling as if my brain were upside down within my skull, and then —

Something was at work upon my face, some thin feelers worried my ears. Then I discovered the brilliance of the landscape around was mitigated by blue spectacles. Cavor bent over me, and I saw his face upside down, his eyes also protected by tinted goggles. His breath came irregularly, and his lip was bleeding from a bruise. "Better?" he said, wiping the blood with the back of his hand.

Everything seemed swaying for a space, but that was simply my giddiness. I perceived that he had closed some of the shutters in the outer sphere to save me—from the direct blaze of the sun. I was aware that everything about us was very brilliant.

"Lord!" I gasped. "But this—"

I craned my neck to see. I perceived there was a blinding glare outside, an utter change from the gloomy darkness of our first impressions. "Have I been insensible long?" I asked.

"I don't know—the chronometer is broken. Some little time... My dear chap! I have been afraid..."

I lay for a space taking this in. I saw his face still bore evidences of emotion. For a while I said nothing. I passed an inquisitive hand over my contusions, and surveyed his face for similar damages. The back of my right hand had suffered most, and was skinless and raw. My forehead was bruised and had bled. He handed me a little measure with some of the restorative—I forget the name of it—he had brought with us. After a time I felt a little better. I began to stretch my limbs carefully. Soon I could talk.

"It wouldn't have done," I said, as though there had been no interval.

"No! it *wouldn't*."

He thought, his hands hanging over his knees. He peered through the glass and then stared at me.

"Good Lord!" he said. "No!"

"What has happened?" I asked after a pause. "Have we jumped to the tropics?"

"It was as I expected. This air has evaporated—if it is air. At any rate, it has evaporated, and the surface of the moon is showing. We are lying on a bank of earthy rock. Here and there bare soil is exposed. A queer sort of soil!"

It occurred to him that it was unnecessary to explain. He assisted me into a sitting position, and I could see with my own eyes.

CHAPTER VIII - A LUNAR MORNING

The harsh emphasis, the pitiless black and white of scenery had altogether disappeared. The glare of the sun had taken upon itself a faint tinge of amber; the shadows upon the cliff of the crater wall were deeply purple. To the eastward a dark bank of fog still crouched and sheltered from the sunrise, but to the westward the sky was blue and clear. I began to realise the length of my insensibility.

We were no longer in a void. An atmosphere had arisen about us. The outline of things had gained in character, had grown acute and varied; save for a shadowed space of white substance here and there, white substance that was no longer air but snow, the arctic appearance had gone altogether. Everywhere broad rusty brown spaces of bare and tumbled earth spread to the blaze of the sun. Here and there at the edge of the snowdrifts were transient little pools and eddies of water, the only things stirring in that expanse of barrenness. The sunlight inundated the upper two blinds of our sphere and turned our climate to high summer, but our feet were still in shadow, and the sphere was lying upon a drift of snow.

And scattered here and there upon the slope, and emphasised by little white threads of unthawed snow upon their shady sides, were shapes like sticks, dry twisted sticks of the same rusty hue as the rock upon which they lay. That caught one's thoughts sharply. Sticks! On a lifeless world? Then as my eye grew more accustomed to the texture of their substance, I perceived that almost all this surface had a fibrous texture, like the carpet of brown needles one finds beneath the shade of pine trees.

"Cavor!" I said.

"Yes."

"It may be a dead world now—but once—"

Something arrested my attention. I had discovered among these needles a number of little round objects. And it seemed to me that one of these had moved. "Cavor," I whispered.

"What?"

But I did not answer at once. I stared incredulous. For an instant I could not believe my eyes. I gave an inarticulate cry. I gripped his arm. I pointed. "Look!" I cried, finding my tongue. "There! Yes! And there!"

His eyes followed my pointing finger. "Eh?" he said.

How can I describe the thing I saw? It is so petty a thing to state, and yet it seemed so wonderful, so pregnant with emotion. I have said that amidst the stick-like litter were these rounded bodies, these little oval bodies that might have

passed as very small pebbles. And now first one and then another had stirred, had rolled over and cracked, and down the crack of each of them showed a minute line of yellowish green, thrusting outward to meet the hot encouragement of the newly-risen sun. For a moment that was all, and then there stirred, and burst a third!

"It is a seed," said Cavor. And then I heard him whisper very softly, "Life!"

"Life!" And immediately it poured upon us that our vast journey had not been made in vain, that we had come to no arid waste of minerals, but to a world that lived and moved! We watched intensely. I remember I kept rubbing the glass before me with my sleeve, jealous of the faintest suspicion of mist.

The picture was clear and vivid only in the middle of the field. All about that centre the dead fibres and seeds were magnified and distorted by the curvature of the glass. But we could see enough! One after another all down the sunlit slope these miraculous little brown bodies burst and gaped apart, like seed-pods, like the husks of fruits; opened eager mouths. that drank in the heat and light pouring in a cascade from the newly-risen sun.

Every moment more of these seed coats ruptured, and even as they did so the swelling pioneers overflowed their rent-distended seed-cases, and passed into the second stage of growth. With a steady assurance, a swift deliberation, these amazing seeds thrust a rootlet downward to the earth and a queer little bundle-like bud into the air. In a little while the whole slope was dotted with minute plantlets standing at attention in the blaze of the sun.

They did not stand for long. The bundle-like buds swelled and strained and opened with a jerk, thrusting out a coronet of little sharp tips, spreading a whorl of tiny, spiky, brownish leaves, that lengthened rapidly, lengthened visibly even as we watched. The movement was slower than any animal's, swifter than any plant's I have ever seen before. How can I suggest it to you—the way that growth went on? The leaf tips grew so that they moved onward even while we looked at them. The brown seed-case shrivelled and was absorbed with an equal rapidity. Have you ever on a cold day taken a thermometer into your warm hand and watched the little thread of mercury creep up the tube? These moon plants grew like that.

In a few minutes, as it seemed, the buds of the more forward of these plants had lengthened into a stem and were even putting forth a second whorl of leaves, and all the slope that had seemed so recently a lifeless stretch of litter was now dark with the stunted olive-green herbage of bristling spikes that swayed with the vigour of their growing.

I turned about, and behold! along the upper edge of a rock to the eastward a similar fringe in a scarcely less forward condition swayed and bent, dark against the blinding glare of the sun. And beyond this fringe was the silhouette of a plant mass, branching clumsily like a cactus, and swelling visibly, swelling like a bladder that fills with air.

Then to the westward also I discovered that another such distended form was rising over the scrub. But here the light fell upon its sleek sides, and I could see that its colour was a vivid orange hue. It rose as one watched it; if one looked

away from it for a minute and then back, its outline had changed; it thrust out blunt congested branches until in a little time it rose a coralline shape of many feet in height. Compared with such a growth the terrestrial puff- ball, which will sometimes swell a foot in diameter in a single night, would be a hopeless laggard. But then the puff-ball grows against a gravitational pull six times that of the moon. Beyond, out of gullies and flats that had been hidden from us, but not from the quickening sun, over reefs and banks of shining rock, a bristling beard of spiky and fleshy vegetation was straining into view, hurrying tumultuously to take advantage of the brief day in which it must flower and fruit and seed again and die. It was like a miracle, that growth. So, one must imagine, the trees and plants arose at the Creation and covered the desolation of the new-made earth.

Imagine it! Imagine that dawn! The resurrection of the frozen air, the stirring and quickening of the soil, and then this silent uprising of vegetation, this unearthly ascent of fleshiness and spikes. Conceive it all lit by a blaze that would make the intensest sunlight of earth seem watery and weak. And still around this stirring jungle, wherever there was shadow, lingered banks of bluish snow. And to have the picture of our impression complete, you must bear in mind that we saw it all through a thick bent glass, distorting it as things are distorted by a lens, acute only in the centre of the picture, and very bright there, and towards the edges magnified and unreal.

CHAPTER IX - PROSPECTING BEGINS

We ceased to gaze. We turned to each other, the same thought, the same question in our eyes. For these plants to grow, there must be some air, however attenuated, air that we also should be able to breathe.

"The manhole?" I said.

"Yes!" said Cavor, "if it is air we see!"

"In a little while," I said, "these plants will be as high as we are. Suppose—suppose after all—Is it certain? How do you know that stuff *is* air? It may be nitrogen—it may be carbonic acid even!"

"That's easy," he said, and set about proving it. He produced a big piece of crumpled paper from the bale, lit it, and thrust it hastily through the man- hole valve. I bent forward and peered down through the thick glass for its appearance outside, that little flame on whose evidence depended so much!

I saw the paper drop out and lie lightly upon the snow. The pink flame of its burning vanished. For an instant it seemed to be extinguished. And then I saw a little blue tongue upon the edge of it that trembled, and crept, and spread!

Quietly the whole sheet, save where it lay in immediate contact with the snow, charred and shrivelled and sent up a quivering thread of smoke. There was no doubt left to me; the atmosphere of the moon was either pure oxygen or air, and capable therefore—unless its tenuity was excessive—of supporting our alien life. We might emerge—and live!

I sat down with my legs on either side of the manhole and prepared to unscrew it, but Cavor stopped me. "There is first a little precaution," he said. He pointed out that although it was certainly an oxygenated atmosphere outside, it might still be so rarefied as to cause us grave injury. He reminded me of mountain sickness, and of the bleeding that often afflicts aeronauts who have ascended too swiftly, and he spent some time in the preparation of a sickly-tasting drink which he insisted on my sharing. It made me feel a little numb, but otherwise had no effect on me. Then he permitted me to begin unscrewing.

Presently the glass stopper of the manhole was so far undone that the denser air within our sphere began to escape along the thread of the screw, singing as a kettle sings before it boils. Thereupon he made me desist. It speedily became evident that the pressure outside was very much less than it was within. How much less it was we had no means of telling.

I sat grasping the stopper with both hands, ready to close it again if, in spite of our intense hope, the lunar atmosphere should after all prove too rarefied for us,

and Cavor sat with a cylinder of compressed oxygen at hand to restore our pressure. We looked at one another in silence, and then at the fantastic vegetation that swayed and grew visibly and noiselessly without. And ever that shrill piping continued.

My blood-vessels began to throb in my ears, and the sound of Cavor's movements diminished. I noted how still everything had become, because of the thinning of the air.

As our air sizzled out from the screw the moisture of it condensed in little puffs.

Presently I experienced a peculiar shortness of breath that lasted indeed during the whole of the time of our exposure to the moon's exterior atmosphere, and a rather unpleasant sensation about the ears and finger-nails and the back of the throat grew upon my attention, and presently passed off again.

But then came vertigo and nausea that abruptly changed the quality of my courage. I gave the lid of the manhole half a turn and made a hasty explanation to Cavor; but now he was the more sanguine. He answered me in a voice that seemed extraordinarily small and remote, because of the thinness of the air that carried the sound. He recommended a nip of brandy, and set me the example, and presently I felt better. I turned the manhole stopper back again. The throbbing in my ears grew louder, and then I remarked that the piping note of the outrush had ceased. For a time I could not be sure that it had ceased.

"Well?" said Cavor, in the ghost of a voice.

"Well?" said I.

"Shall we go on?"

I thought. "Is this all?"

"If you can stand it."

By way of answer I went on unscrewing. I lifted the circular operculum from its place and laid it carefully on the bale. A flake or so of snow whirled and vanished as that thin and unfamiliar air took possession of our sphere. I knelt, and then seated myself at the edge of the manhole, peering over it. Beneath, within a yard of my face, lay the untrodden snow of the moon.

There came a little pause. Our eyes met.

"It doesn't distress your lungs too much?" said Cavor.

"No," I said. "I can stand this."

He stretched out his hand for his blanket, thrust his head through its central hole, and wrapped it about him. He sat down on the edge of the manhole, he let his feet drop until they were within six inches of the lunar ground. He hesitated for a moment, then thrust himself forward, dropped these intervening inches, and stood upon the untrodden soil of the moon.

As he stepped forward he was refracted grotesquely by the edge of the glass. He stood for a moment looking this way and that. Then he drew himself together and leapt.

The glass distorted everything, but it seemed to me even then to be an extremely big leap. He had at one bound become remote. He seemed twenty or

thirty feet off. He was standing high upon a rocky mass and gesticulating back to me. Perhaps he was shouting—but the sound did not reach me. But how the deuce had he done this? I felt like a man who has just seen a new conjuring trick.

In a puzzled state of mind I too dropped through the manhole. I stood up. Just in front of me the snowdrift had fallen away and made a sort of ditch. I made a step and jumped.

I found myself flying through the air, saw the rock on which he stood coming to meet me, clutched it and clung in a state of infinite amazement.

I gasped a painful laugh. I was tremendously confused. Cavor bent down and shouted in piping tones for me to be careful.

I had forgotten that on the moon, with only an eighth part of the earth's mass and a quarter of its diameter, my weight was barely a sixth what it was on earth. But now that fact insisted on being remembered.

"We are out of Mother Earth's leading-strings now," he said.

With a guarded effort I raised myself to the top, and moving as cautiously as a rheumatic patient, stood up beside him under the blaze of the sun. The sphere lay behind us on its dwindling snowdrift thirty feet away.

As far as the eye could see over the enormous disorder of rocks that formed the crater floor, the same bristling scrub that surrounded us was starting into life, diversified here and there by bulging masses of a cactus form, and scarlet and purple lichens that grew so fast they seemed to crawl over the rocks. The whole area of the crater seemed to me then to be one similar wilderness up to the very foot of the surrounding cliff.

This cliff was apparently bare of vegetation save at its base, and with buttresses and terraces and platforms that did not very greatly attract our attention at the time. It was many miles away from us in every direction; we seemed to be almost at the centre of the crater, and we saw it through a certain haziness that drove before the wind. For there was even a wind now in the thin air, a swift yet weak wind that chilled exceedingly but exerted little pressure. It was blowing round the crater, as it seemed, to the hot illuminated side from the foggy darkness under the sunward wall. It was difficult to look into this eastward fog; we had to peer with half-closed eyes beneath the shade of our hands, because of the fierce intensity of the motionless sun.

"It seems to be deserted," said Cavor, "absolutely desolate."

I looked about me again. I retained even then a clinging hope of some quasi-human evidence, some pinnacle of building, some house or engine, but everywhere one looked spread the tumbled rocks in peaks and crests, and the darting scrub and those bulging cacti that swelled and swelled, a flat negation as it seemed of all such hope.

"It looks as though these plants had it to themselves," I said. "I see no trace of any other creature."

"No insects—no birds, no! Not a trace, not a scrap nor particle of animal life. If there was—what would they do in the night? ... No; there's just these plants alone."

I shaded my eyes with my hand. "It's like the landscape of a dream. These things are less like earthly land plants than the things one imagines among the rocks at the bottom of the sea. Look at that yonder! One might imagine it a lizard changed into a plant. And the glare!"

"This is only the fresh morning," said Cavor.

He sighed and looked about him. "This is no world for men," he said. "And yet in a way—it appeals."

He became silent for a time, then commenced his meditative humming.

I started at a gentle touch, and found a thin sheet of livid lichen lapping over my shoe. I kicked at it and it fell to powder, and each speck began to grow.

I heard Cavor exclaim sharply, and perceived that one of the fixed bayonets of the scrub had pricked him. He hesitated, his eyes sought among the rocks about us. A sudden blaze of pink had crept up a ragged pillar of crag. It was a most extraordinary pink, a livid magenta.

"Look!" said I, turning, and behold Cavor had vanished.

For an instant I stood transfixed. Then I made a hasty step to look over the verge of the rock. But in my surprise at his disappearance I forgot once more that we were on the moon. The thrust of my foot that I made in striding would have carried me a yard on earth; on the moon it carried me six—a good five yards over the edge. For the moment the thing had something of the effect of those nightmares when one falls and falls. For while one falls sixteen feet in the first second of a fall on earth, on the moon one falls two, and with only a sixth of one's weight. I fell, or rather I jumped down, about ten yards I suppose. It seemed to take quite a long time, five or six seconds, I should think. I floated through the air and fell like a feather, knee-deep in a snow-drift in the bottom of a gully of blue-gray, white-veined rock.

I looked about me. "Cavor!" I cried; but no Cavor was visible.

"Cavor!" I cried louder, and the rocks echoed me.

I turned fiercely to the rocks and clambered to the summit of them. "Cavor!" I cried. My voice sounded like the voice of a lost lamb.

The sphere, too, was not in sight, and for a moment a horrible feeling of desolation pinched my heart.

Then I saw him. He was laughing and gesticulating to attract my attention. He was on a bare patch of rock twenty or thirty yards away. I could not hear his voice, but "jump" said his gestures. I hesitated, the distance seemed enormous. Yet I reflected that surely I must be able to clear a greater distance than Cavor.

I made a step back, gathered myself together, and leapt with all my might. I seemed to shoot right up in the air as though I should never come down.

It was horrible and delightful, and as wild as a nightmare, to go flying off in this fashion. I realised my leap had been altogether too violent. I flew clean over Cavor's head and beheld a spiky confusion in a gully spreading to meet my fall. I gave a yelp of alarm. I put out my hands and straightened my legs.

I hit a huge fungoid bulk that burst all about me, scattering a mass of orange spores in every direction, and covering me with orange powder. I rolled over spluttering, and came to rest convulsed with breathless laughter.

I became aware of Cavor's little round face peering over a bristling hedge. He shouted some faded inquiry. "Eh?" I tried to shout, but could not do so for want of breath. He made his way towards me, coming gingerly among the bushes.

"We've got to be careful," he said. "This moon has no discipline. She'll let us smash ourselves."

He helped me to my feet. "You exerted yourself too much," he said, dabbing at the yellow stuff with his hand to remove it from my garments.

I stood passive and panting, allowing him to beat off the jelly from my knees and elbows and lecture me upon my misfortunes. "We don't quite allow for the gravitation. Our muscles are scarcely educated yet. We must practise a little, when you have got your breath."

I pulled two or three little thorns out of my hand, and sat for a time on a boulder of rock. My muscles were quivering, and I had that feeling of personal disillusionment that comes at the first fall to the learner of cycling on earth.

It suddenly occurred to Cavor that the cold air in the gully, after the brightness of the sun, might give me a fever. So we clambered back into the sunlight. We found that beyond a few abrasions I had received no serious injuries from my tumble, and at Cavor's suggestion we were presently looking round for some safe and easy landing-place for my next leap. We chose a rocky slab some ten yards off, separated from us by a little thicket of olive-green spikes.

"Imagine it there!" said Cavor, who was assuming the airs of a trainer, and he pointed to a spot about four feet from my toes. This leap I managed without difficulty, and I must confess I found a certain satisfaction in Cavor's falling short by a foot or so and tasting the spikes of the scrub. "One has to be careful you see," he said, pulling out his thorns, and with that he ceased to be my mentor and became my fellow-learner in the art of lunar locomotion.

We chose a still easier jump and did it without difficulty, and then leapt back again, and to and fro several times, accustoming our muscles to the new standard. I could never have believed had I not experienced it, how rapid that adaptation would be. In a very little time indeed, certainly after fewer than thirty leaps, we could judge the effort necessary for a distance with almost terrestrial assurance.

And all this time the lunar plants were growing around us, higher and denser and more entangled, every moment thicker and taller, spiked plants, green cactus masses, fungi, fleshy and lichenous things, strangest radiate and sinuous shapes. But we were so intent upon our leaping, that for a time we gave no heed to their unfaltering expansion.

An extraordinary elation had taken possession of us. Partly, I think, it was our sense of release from the confinement of the sphere. Mainly, however, the thin sweetness of the air, which I am certain contained a much larger proportion of oxygen than our terrestrial atmosphere. In spite of the strange quality of all about us, I felt as adventurous and experimental as a cockney would do placed for the

first time among mountains and I do not think it occurred to either of us, face to face though we were with the unknown, to be very greatly afraid.

We were bitten by a spirit of enterprise. We selected a lichenous kopje perhaps fifteen yards away, and landed neatly on its summit one after the other. "Good!" we cried to each other; "good!" and Cavor made three steps and went off to a tempting slope of snow a good twenty yards and more beyond. I stood for a moment struck by the grotesque effect of his soaring figure—his dirty cricket cap, and spiky hair, his little round body, his arms and his knicker-bockered legs tucked up tightly—against the weird spaciousness of the lunar scene. A gust of laughter seized me, and then I stepped off to follow. Plump! I dropped beside him.

We made a few gargantuan strides, leapt three or four times more, and sat down at last in a lichenous hollow. Our lungs were painful. We sat holding our sides and recovering our breath, looking appreciation to one another. Cavor panted something about "amazing sensations." And then came a thought into my head. For the moment it did not seem a particularly appalling thought, simply a natural question arising out of the situation.

"By the way," I said, "where exactly is the sphere?"

Cavor looked at me. "Eh?"

The full meaning of what we were saying struck me sharply.

"Cavor!" I cried, laying a hand on his arm, "where is the sphere?"

CHAPTER X - LOST MEN IN THE MOON

His face caught something of my dismay. He stood up and stared about him at the scrub that fenced us in and rose about us, straining upward in a passion of growth. He put a dubious hand to his lips. He spoke with a sudden lack of assurance. "I think," he said slowly, "we left it ... somewhere ... about *there*."

He pointed a hesitating finger that wavered in an arc.

"I'm not sure." His look of consternation deepened. "Anyhow," he said, with his eyes on me, "it can't be far."

We had both stood up. We made unmeaning ejaculations, our eyes sought in the twining, thickening jungle round about us.

All about us on the sunlit slopes frothed and swayed the darting shrubs, the swelling cactus, the creeping lichens, and wherever the shade remained the snow-drifts lingered. North, south, east, and west spread an identical monotony of unfamiliar forms. And somewhere, buried already among this tangled confusion, was our sphere, our home, our only provision, our only hope of escape from this fantastic wilderness of ephemeral growths into which we had come.

"I think after all," he said, pointing suddenly, "it might be over there."

"No," I said. "We have turned in a curve. See! here is the mark of my heels. It's clear the thing must be more to the eastward, much more. No—the sphere must be over there."

"I *think*," said Cavor, "I kept the sun upon my right all the time."

"Every leap, it seems to me," I said, "my shadow flew before me."

We stared into one another's eyes. The area of the crater had become enormously vast to our imaginations, the growing thickets already impenetrably dense.

"Good heavens! What fools we have been!"

"It's evident that we must find it again," said Cavor, "and that soon. The sun grows stronger. We should be fainting with the heat already if it wasn't so dry. And ... I'm hungry."

I stared at him. I had not suspected this aspect of the matter before. But it came to me at once—a positive craving. "Yes," I said with emphasis. "I am hungry too."

He stood up with a look of active resolution. "Certainly we must find the sphere."

As calmly as possible we surveyed the interminable reefs and thickets that formed the floor of the crater, each of us weighing in silence the chances of our finding the sphere before we were overtaken by heat and hunger.

"It can't be fifty yards from here," said Cavor, with indecisive gestures. "The only thing is to beat round about until we come upon it."

"That is all we can do," I said, without any alacrity to begin our hunt. "I wish this confounded spike bush did not grow so fast!"

"That's just it," said Cavor. "But it was lying on a bank of snow."

I stared about me in the vain hope of recognising some knoll or shrub that had been near the sphere. But everywhere was a confusing sameness, everywhere the aspiring bushes, the distending fungi, the dwindling snow banks, steadily and inevitably changed. The sun scorched and stung, the faintness of an unaccountable hunger mingled with our infinite perplexity. And even as we stood there, confused and lost amidst unprecedented things, we became aware for the first time of a sound upon the moon other than the air of the growing plants, the faint sighing of the wind, or those that we ourselves had made.

Boom... Boom... Boom.

It came from beneath our feet, a sound in the earth. We seemed to hear it with our feet as much as with our ears. Its dull resonance was muffled by distance, thick with the quality of intervening substance. No sound that I can imagine could have astonished us more, or have changed more completely the quality of things about us. For this sound, rich, slow, and deliberate, seemed to us as though it could be nothing but the striking of some gigantic buried clock.

Boom... Boom... Boom.

Sound suggestive of still cloisters, of sleepless nights in crowded cities, of vigils and the awaited hour, of all that is orderly and methodical in life, booming out pregnant and mysterious in this fantastic desert! To the eye everything was unchanged: the desolation of bushes and cacti waving silently in the wind, stretched unbroken to the distant cliffs, the still dark sky was empty overhead, and the hot sun hung and burned. And through it all, a warning, a threat, throbbed this enigma of sound.

Boom... Boom... Boom...

We questioned one another in faint and faded voices.

"A clock?"

"Like a clock!"

"What is it?"

"What can it be?"

"Count," was Cavor's belated suggestion, and at that word the striking ceased.

The silence, the rhythmic disappointment of the silence, came as a fresh shock. For a moment one could doubt whether one had ever heard a sound. Or whether it might not still be going on. Had I indeed heard a sound?

I felt the pressure of Cavor's hand upon my arm. He spoke in an undertone, as though he feared to wake some sleeping thing. "Let us keep together," he whis-

pered, "and look for the sphere. We must get back to the sphere. This is beyond our understanding."

"Which way shall we go?"

He hesitated. An intense persuasion of presences, of unseen things about us and near us, dominated our minds. What could they be? Where could they be? Was this arid desolation, alternately frozen and scorched, only the outer rind and mask of some subterranean world? And if so, what sort of world? What sort of inhabitants might it not presently disgorge upon us?

And then, stabbing the aching stillness as vivid and sudden as an unexpected thunderclap, came a clang and rattle as though great gates of metal had suddenly been flung apart.

It arrested our steps. We stood gaping helplessly. Then Cavor stole towards me.

"I do not understand!" he whispered close to my face. He waved his hand vaguely skyward, the vague suggestion of still vaguer thoughts.

"A hiding-place! If anything came..."

I looked about us. I nodded my head in assent to him.

We started off, moving stealthily with the most exaggerated precautions against noise. We went towards a thicket of scrub. A clangour like hammers flung about a boiler hastened our steps. "We must crawl," whispered Cavor.

The lower leaves of the bayonet plants, already overshadowed by the newer ones above, were beginning to wilt and shrivel so that we could thrust our way in among the thickening stems without serious injury. A stab in the face or arm we did not heed. At the heart of the thicket I stopped, and stared panting into Cavor's face.

"Subterranean," he whispered. "Below."

"They may come out."

"We must find the sphere!"

"Yes," I said; "but how?"

"Crawl till we come to it."

"But if we don't?"

"Keep hidden. See what they are like."

"We will keep together," said I.

He thought. "Which way shall we go?"

"We must take our chance."

We peered this way and that. Then very circumspectly, we began to crawl through the lower jungle, making, so far as we could judge, a circuit, halting now at every waving fungus, at every sound, intent only on the sphere from which we had so foolishly emerged. Ever and again from out of the earth beneath us came concussions, beatings, strange, inexplicable, mechanical sounds; and once, and then again, we thought we heard something, a faint rattle and tumult, borne to us through the air. But fearful as we were we dared essay no vantage- point to survey the crater. For long we saw nothing of the beings whose sounds were so abundant and insistent. But for the faintness of our hunger and the drying of our throats that

crawling would have had the quality of a very vivid dream. It was so absolutely unreal. The only element with any touch of reality was these sounds.

Picture it to yourself! About us the dream-like jungle, with the silent bayonet leaves darting overhead, and the silent, vivid, sun-splashed lichens under our hands and knees, waving with the vigour of their growth as a carpet waves when the wind gets beneath it. Ever and again one of the bladder fungi, bulging and distending under the sun, loomed upon us. Ever and again some novel shape in vivid colour obtruded. The very cells that built up these plants were as large as my thumb, like beads of coloured glass. And all these things were saturated in the unmitigated glare of the sun, were seen against a sky that was bluish black and spangled still, in spite of the sunlight, with a few surviving stars. Strange! the very forms and texture of the stones were strange. It was all strange, the feeling of one's body was unprecedented, every other movement ended in a surprise. The breath sucked thin in one's throat, the blood flowed through one's ears in a throbbing tide—thud, thud, thud, thud...

And ever and again came gusts of turmoil, hammering, the clanging and throb of machinery, and presently—the bellowing of great beasts!

CHAPTER XI - THE MOONCALF PASTURES

So we two poor terrestrial castaways, lost in that wild-growing moon jungle, crawled in terror before the sounds that had come upon us. We crawled, as it seemed, a long time before we saw either Selenite or mooncalf, though we heard the bellowing and gruntulous noises of these latter continually drawing nearer to us. We crawled through stony ravines, over snow slopes, amidst fungi that ripped like thin bladders at our thrust, emitting a watery humour, over a perfect pavement of things like puff-balls, and beneath interminable thickets of scrub. And ever more helplessly our eyes sought for our abandoned sphere. The noise of the mooncalves would at times be a vast flat calf-like sound, at times it rose to an amazed and wrathy bellowing, and again it would become a clogged bestial sound, as though these unseen creatures had sought to eat and bellow at the same time.

Our first view was but an inadequate transitory glimpse, yet none the less disturbing because it was incomplete. Cavor was crawling in front at the time, and he first was aware of their proximity. He stopped dead, arresting me with a single gesture.

A crackling and smashing of the scrub appeared to be advancing directly upon us, and then, as we squatted close and endeavoured to judge of the nearness and direction of this noise, there came a terrific bellow behind us, so close and vehement that the tops of the bayonet scrub bent before it, and one felt the breath of it hot and moist. And, turning about, we saw indistinctly through a crowd of swaying stems the mooncalf's shining sides, and the long line of its back loomed out against the sky.

Of course it is hard for me now to say how much I saw at that time, because my impressions were corrected by subsequent observation. First of all impressions was its enormous size; the girth of its body was some fourscore feet, its length perhaps two hundred. Its sides rose and fell with its laboured breathing. I perceived that its gigantic, flabby body lay along the ground, and that its skin was of a corrugated white, dappling into blackness along the backbone. But of its feet we saw nothing. I think also that we saw then the profile at least of the almost brainless head, with its fat-encumbered neck, its slobbering omnivorous mouth, its little nostrils, and tight shut eyes. (For the mooncalf invariably shuts its eyes in the presence of the sun.) We had a glimpse of a vast red pit as it opened its mouth to bleat and bellow again; we had a breath from the pit, and then the monster heeled over like a ship, dragged forward along the ground, creasing all its leathery

skin, rolled again, and so wallowed past us, smashing a path amidst the scrub, and was speedily hidden from our eyes by the dense interlacings beyond. Another appeared more distantly, and then another, and then, as though he was guiding these animated lumps of provender to their pasture, a Selenite came momentarily into ken. My grip upon Cavor's foot became convulsive at the sight of him, and we remained motionless and peering long after he had passed out of our range.

By contrast with the mooncalves he seemed a trivial being, a mere ant, scarcely five feet high. He was wearing garments of some leathery substance, so that no portion of his actual body appeared, but of this, of course, we were entirely ignorant. He presented himself, therefore, as a compact, bristling creature, having much of the quality of a complicated insect, with whip-like tentacles and a clanging arm projecting from his shining cylindrical body case. The form of his head was hidden by his enormous many-spiked helmet—we discovered afterwards that he used the spikes for prodding refractory mooncalves—and a pair of goggles of darkened glass, set very much at the side, gave a bird-like quality to the metallic apparatus that covered his face. His arms did not project beyond his body case, and he carried himself upon short legs that, wrapped though they were in warm coverings, seemed to our terrestrial eyes inordinately flimsy. They had very short thighs, very long shanks, and little feet.

In spite of his heavy-looking clothing, he was progressing with what would be, from the terrestrial point of view, very considerable strides, and his clanging arm was busy. The quality of his motion during the instant of his passing suggested haste and a certain anger, and soon after we had lost sight of him we heard the bellow of a mooncalf change abruptly into a short, sharp squeal followed by the scuffle of its acceleration. And gradually that bellowing receded, and then came to an end, as if the pastures sought had been attained.

We listened. For a space the moon world was still. But it was some time before we resumed our crawling search for the vanished sphere.

When next we saw mooncalves they were some little distance away from us in a place of tumbled rocks. The less vertical surfaces of the rocks were thick with a speckled green plant growing in dense mossy clumps, upon which these creatures were browsing. We stopped at the edge of the reeds amidst which we were crawling at the sight of them, peering out at then and looking round for a second glimpse of a Selenite. They lay against their food like stupendous slugs, huge, greasy hulls, eating greedily and noisily, with a sort of sobbing avidity. They seemed monsters of mere fatness, clumsy and overwhelmed to a degree that would make a Smithfield ox seem a model of agility. Their busy, writhing, chewing mouths, and eyes closed, together with the appetising sound of their munching, made up an effect of animal enjoyment that was singularly stimulating to our empty frames.

"Hogs!" said Cavor, with unusual passion. "Disgusting hogs!" and after one glare of angry envy crawled off through the bushes to our right. I stayed long enough to see that the speckled plant was quite hopeless for human nourishment, then crawled after him, nibbling a quill of it between my teeth.

Presently we were arrested again by the proximity of a Selenite, and this time we were able to observe him more exactly. Now we could see that the Selenite covering was indeed clothing, and not a sort of crustacean integument. He was quite similar in his costume to the former one we had glimpsed, except that ends of something like wadding were protruding from his neck, and he stood on a promontory of rock and moved his head this way and that, as though he was surveying the crater. We lay quite still, fearing to attract his attention if we moved, and after a time he turned about and disappeared.

We came upon another drove of mooncalves bellowing up a ravine, and then we passed over a place of sounds, sounds of beating machinery as if some huge hall of industry came near the surface there. And while these sounds were still about us we came to the edge of a great open space, perhaps two hundred yards in diameter, and perfectly level. Save for a few lichens that advanced from its margin this space was bare, and presented a powdery surface of a dusty yellow colour. We were afraid to strike out across this space, but as it presented less obstruction to our crawling than the scrub, we went down upon it and began very circumspectly to skirt its edge.

For a little while the noises from below ceased and everything, save for the faint stir of the growing vegetation, was very still. Then abruptly there began an uproar, louder, more vehement, and nearer than any we had so far heard. Of a certainty it came from below. Instinctively we crouched as flat as we could, ready for a prompt plunge into the thicket beside us. Each knock and throb seemed to vibrate through our bodies. Louder grew this throbbing and beating, and that irregular vibration increased until the whole moon world seemed to be jerking and pulsing.

"Cover," whispered Cavor, and I turned towards the bushes.

At that instant came a thud like the thud of a gun, and then a thing happened—it still haunts me in my dreams. I had turned my head to look at Cavor's face, and thrust out my hand in front of me as I did so. And my hand met nothing! I plunged suddenly into a bottomless hole!

My chest hit something hard, and I found myself with my chin on the edge of an unfathomable abyss that had suddenly opened beneath me, my hand extended stiffly into the void. The whole of that flat circular area was no more than a gigantic lid, that was now sliding sideways from off the pit it had covered into a slot prepared for it.

Had it not been for Cavor I think I should have remained rigid, hanging over this margin and staring into the enormous gulf below, until at last the edges of the slot scraped me off and hurled me into its depths. But Cavor had not received the shock that had paralysed me. He had been a little distance from the edge when the lid had first opened, and perceiving the peril that held me helpless, gripped my legs and pulled me backward. I came into a sitting position, crawled away from the edge for a space on all fours, then staggered up and ran after him across the thundering, quivering sheet of metal. It seemed to be swinging open with a steadily accelerated velocity, and the bushes in front of me shifted sideways as I ran.

I was none too soon. Cavor's back vanished amidst the bristling thicket, and as I scrambled up after him, the monstrous valve came into its position with a clang. For a long time we lay panting, not daring to approach the pit.

But at last very cautiously and bit by bit we crept into a position from which we could peer down. The bushes about us creaked and waved with the force of a breeze that was blowing down the shaft. We could see nothing at first except smooth vertical walls descending at last into an impenetrable black. And then very gradually we became aware of a number of very faint and little lights going to and fro.

For a time that stupendous gulf of mystery held us so that we forgot even our sphere. In time, as we grew more accustomed to the darkness, we could make out very small, dim, elusive shapes moving about among those needle-point illuminations. We peered amazed and incredulous, understanding so little that we could find no words to say. We could distinguish nothing that would give us a clue to the meaning of the faint shapes we saw.

"What can it be?" I asked; "what can it be?"

"The engineering!... They must live in these caverns during the night, and come out during the day."

"Cavor!" I said. "Can they be—that—it was something like —men?"

"*That* was not a man."

"We dare risk nothing!"

"We dare do nothing until we find the sphere!"

"We *can* do nothing until we find the sphere."

He assented with a groan and stirred himself to move. He stared about him for a space, sighed, and indicated a direction. We struck out through the jungle. For a time we crawled resolutely, then with diminishing vigour. Presently among great shapes of flabby purple there came a noise of trampling and cries about us. We lay close, and for a long time the sounds went to and fro and very near. But this time we saw nothing. I tried to whisper to Cavor that I could hardly go without food much longer, but my mouth had become too dry for whispering.

"Cavor," I said, "I must have food."

He turned a face full of dismay towards me. "It's a case for holding out," he said.

"But I *must*," I said, "and look at my lips!"

"I've been thirsty some time."

"If only some of that snow had remained!"

"It's clean gone! We're driving from arctic to tropical at the rate of a degree a minute..."

I gnawed my hand.

"The sphere!" he said. "There is nothing for it but the sphere."

We roused ourselves to another spurt of crawling. My mind ran entirely on edible things, on the hissing profundity of summer drinks, more particularly I craved for beer. I was haunted by the memory of a sixteen gallon cask that had swaggered in my Lympne cellar. I thought of the adjacent larder, and especially of

steak and kidney pie—tender steak and plenty of kidney, and rich, thick gravy between. Ever and again I was seized with fits of hungry yawning. We came to flat places overgrown with fleshy red things, monstrous coralline growths; as we pushed against them they snapped and broke. I noted the quality of the broken surfaces. The confounded stuff certainly looked of a biteable texture. Then it seemed to me that it smelt rather well.

I picked up a fragment and sniffed at it.

"Cavor," I said in a hoarse undertone.

He glanced at me with his face screwed up. "Don't," he said. I put down the fragment, and we crawled on through this tempting fleshiness for a space.

"Cavor," I asked, "why not?"

"Poison," I heard him say, but he did not look round.

We crawled some way before I decided.

"I'll chance it," said I.

He made a belated gesture to prevent me. I stuffed my mouth full. He crouched watching my face, his own twisted into the oddest expression. "It's good," I said.

"O Lord!" he cried.

He watched me munch, his face wrinkled between desire and disapproval, then suddenly succumbed to appetite and began to tear off huge mouthfuls. For a time we did nothing but eat.

The stuff was not unlike a terrestrial mushroom, only it was much laxer in texture, and, as one swallowed it, it warmed the throat. At first we experienced a mere mechanical satisfaction in eating; then our blood began to run warmer, and we tingled at the lips and fingers, and then new and slightly irrelevant ideas came bubbling up in our minds.

"Its good," said I. "Infernally good! What a home for our surplus population! Our poor surplus population," and I broke off another large portion. It filled me with a curiously benevolent satisfaction that there was such good food in the moon. The depression of my hunger gave way to an irrational exhilaration. The dread and discomfort in which I had been living vanished entirely. I perceived the moon no longer as a planet from which I most earnestly desired the means of escape, but as a possible refuge from human destitution. I think I forgot the Selenites, the mooncalves, the lid, and the noises completely so soon as I had eaten that fungus.

Cavor replied to my third repetition of my "surplus population" remark with similar words of approval. I felt that my head swam, but I put this down to the stimulating effect of food after a long fast. "Ess'lent discov'ry yours, Cavor," said I. "Se'nd on'y to the 'tato."

"Whajer mean?" asked Cavor. "'Scovery of the moon—se'nd on'y to the 'tato?"

I looked at him, shocked at his suddenly hoarse voice, and by the badness of his articulation. It occurred to me in a flash that he was intoxicated, possibly by the fungus. It also occurred to me that he erred in imagining that he had discovered the moon; he had not discovered it, he had only reached it. I tried to lay my

hand on his arm and explain this to him, but the issue was too subtle for his brain. It was also unexpectedly difficult to express. After a momentary attempt to understand me—I remember wondering if the fungus had made my eyes as fishy as his—he set off upon some observations on his own account.

"We are," he announced with a solemn hiccup, "the creashurs o' what we eat and drink."

He repeated this, and as I was now in one of my subtle moods, I determined to dispute it. Possibly I wandered a little from the point. But Cavor certainly did not attend at all properly. He stood up as well as he could, putting a hand on my head to steady I himself, which was disrespectful, and stood staring about him, quite devoid now of any fear of the moon beings.

I tried to point out that this was dangerous for some reason that was not perfectly clear to me, but the word "dangerous" had somehow got mixed with "indiscreet," and came out rather more like "injurious" than either; and after an attempt to disentangle them, I resumed my argument, addressing myself principally to the unfamiliar but attentive coralline growths on either side. I felt that it was necessary to clear up this confusion between the moon and a potato at once—I wandered into a long parenthesis on the importance of precision of definition in argument. I did my best to ignore the fact that my bodily sensations were no longer agreeable.

In some way that I have now forgotten, my mind was led back to projects of colonisation. "We must annex this moon," I said. "There must be no shilly- shally. This is part of the White Man's Burthen. Cavor—we are—hic—Satap—mean Satraps! Nempire Caesar never dreamt. B'in all the newspapers. Cavorecia. Bedfordecia. Bedfordecia—hic—Limited. Mean—unlimited! Practically."

Certainly I was intoxicated.

I embarked upon an argument to show the infinite benefits our arrival would confer on the moon. I involved myself in a rather difficult proof that the arrival of Columbus was, on the whole, beneficial to America. I found I had forgotten the line of argument I had intended to pursue, and continued to repeat "sim'lar to C'lumbus," to fill up time.

From that point my memory of the action of that abominable fungus becomes confused. I remember vaguely that we declared our intention of standing no nonsense from any confounded insects, that we decided it ill became men to hide shamefully upon a mere satellite, that we equipped ourselves with huge armfuls of the fungus—whether for missile purposes or not I do not know—and, heedless of the stabs of the bayonet scrub, we started forth into the sunshine.

Almost immediately we must have come upon the Selenites. There were six of them, and they were marching in single file over a rocky place, making the most remarkable piping and whining sounds. They all seemed to become aware of us at once, all instantly became silent and motionless, like animals, with their faces turned towards us.

For a moment I was sobered.

"Insects," murmured Cavor, "insects! And they think I'm going to crawl about on my stomach—on my vertebrated stomach!

"Stomach," he repeated slowly, as though he chewed the indignity.

Then suddenly, with a sort of fury, he made three vast strides and leapt towards them. He leapt badly; he made a series of somersaults in the air, whirled right over them, and vanished with an enormous splash amidst the cactus bladders. What the Selenites made of this amazing, and to my mind undignified irruption from another planet, I have no means of guessing. I seem to remember the sight of their backs as they ran in all directions, but I am not sure. All these last incidents before oblivion came are vague and faint in my mind. I know I made a step to follow Cavor, and tripped and fell headlong among the rocks. I was, I am certain, suddenly and vehemently ill. I seem to remember, a violent struggle and being gripped by metallic clasps...

My next clear recollection is that we were prisoners at we knew not what depths beneath the moon's surface; we were in darkness amidst strange distracting noises; our bodies were covered with scratches and bruises, and our heads racked with pain.

CHAPTER XII - THE SELENITE'S FACE

I found myself sitting crouched together in a tumultuous darkness. For a long time I could not understand where I was, nor how I had come to this perplexity. I thought of the cupboard into which I had been thrust at times when I was a child, and then of a very dark and noisy bedroom in which I had slept during an illness. But these sounds about me were not the noises I had known, and there was a thin flavour in the air like the wind of a stable. Then I supposed we must still be at work upon the sphere, and that somehow I had got into the cellar of Cavor's house. I remembered we had finished the sphere, and fancied I must still be in it and travelling through space.

"Cavor," I said, "cannot we have some light?"

There came no answer.

"Cavor!" I insisted.

I was answered by a groan. "My head!" I heard him say; "my head!"

I attempted to press my hands to my brow, which ached, and discovered they were tied together. This startled me very much. I brought them up to my mouth and felt the cold smoothness of metal. They were chained together. I tried to separate my legs and made out they were similarly fastened, and also that I was fastened to the ground by a much thicker chain about the middle of my body.

I was more frightened than I had yet been by anything in all our strange experiences. For a time I tugged silently at my bonds. "Cavor!" I cried out sharply. "Why am I tied? Why have you tied me hand and foot?"

"I haven't tied you," he answered. "It's the Selenites."

The Selenites! My mind hung on that for a space. Then my memories came back to me: the snowy desolation, the thawing of the air, the growth of the plants, our strange hopping and crawling among the rocks and vegetation of the crater. All the distress of our frantic search for the sphere returned to me... Finally the opening of the great lid that covered the pit!

Then as I strained to trace our later movements down to our present plight, the pain in my head became intolerable. I came to an insurmountable barrier, an obstinate blank.

"Cavor!"

"Yes?"

"Where are we?"

"How should I know?"

"Are we dead?"

"What nonsense!"

"They've got us, then!"

He made no answer but a grunt. The lingering traces of the poison seemed to make him oddly irritable.

"What do you mean to do?"

"How should I know what to do?"

"Oh, very well!" said I, and became silent. Presently, I was roused from a stupor. "O Lord!" I cried; "I wish you'd stop that buzzing!"

We lapsed into silence again, listening to the dull confusion of noises like the muffled sounds of a street or factory that filled our ears. I could make nothing of it, my mind pursued first one rhythm and then another, and questioned it in vain. But after a long time I became aware of a new and sharper element, not mingling with the rest but standing out, as it were, against that cloudy background of sound. It was a series of relatively very little definite sounds, tappings and rubbings, like a loose spray of ivy against a window or a bird moving about upon a box. We listened and peered about us, but the darkness was a velvet pall. There followed a noise like the subtle movement of the wards of a well-oiled lock. And then there appeared before me, hanging as it seemed in an immensity of black, a thin bright line.

"Look!" whispered Cavor very softly.

"What is it?"

"I don't know."

We stared.

The thin bright line became a band, and broader and paler. It took upon itself the quality of a bluish light falling upon a white-washed wall. It ceased to be parallel-sided; it developed a deep indentation on one side. I turned to remark this to Cavor, and was amazed to see his ear in a brilliant illumination—all the rest of him in shadow. I twisted my head round as well as my bonds would permit. "Cavor," I said, "it's behind!"

His ear vanished—gave place to an eye!

Suddenly the crack that had been admitting the light broadened out, and revealed itself as the space of an opening door. Beyond was a sapphire vista, and in the doorway stood a grotesque outline silhouetted against the glare.

We both made convulsive efforts to turn, and failing, sat staring over our shoulders at this. My first impression was of some clumsy quadruped with lowered head. Then I perceived it was the slender pinched body and short and extremely attenuated bandy legs of a Selenite, with his head depressed between his shoulders. He was without the helmet and body covering they wear upon the exterior.

He was a blank, black figure to us, but instinctively our imaginations supplied features to his very human outline. I, at least, took it instantly that he was somewhat hunchbacked, with a high forehead and long features.

He came forward three steps and paused for a time. His movements seemed absolutely noiseless. Then he came forward again. He walked like a bird, his feet

fell one in front of the other. He stepped out of the ray of light that came through the doorway, and it seemed as though he vanished altogether in the shadow.

For a moment my eyes sought him in the wrong place, and then I perceived him standing facing us both in the full light. Only the human features I had attributed to him were not there at all!

Of course I ought to have expected that, only I didn't. It came to me as an absolute, for a moment an overwhelming shock. It seemed as though it wasn't a face, as though it must needs be a mask, a horror, a deformity, that would presently be disavowed or explained. There was no nose, and the thing had dull bulging eyes at the side—in the silhouette I had supposed they were ears. There were no ears... I have tried to draw one of these heads, but I cannot. There was a mouth, downwardly curved, like a human mouth in a face that stares ferociously...

The neck on which the head was poised was jointed in three places, almost like the short joints in the leg of a crab. The joints of the limbs I could not see, because of the puttee-like straps in which they were swathed, and which formed the only clothing the being wore.

There the thing was, looking at us!

At the time my mind was taken up by the mad impossibility of the creature. I suppose he also was amazed, and with more reason, perhaps, for amazement than we. Only, confound him! he did not show it. We did at least know what had brought about this meeting of incompatible creatures. But conceive how it would seem to decent Londoners, for example, to come upon a couple of living things, as big as men and absolutely unlike any other earthly animals, careering about among the sheep in Hyde Park! It must have taken him like that.

Figure us! We were bound hand and foot, fagged and filthy; our beards two inches long, our faces scratched and bloody. Cavor you must imagine in his knickerbockers (torn in several places by the bayonet scrub) his Jaegar shirt and old cricket cap, his wiry hair wildly disordered, a tail to every quarter of the heavens. In that blue light his face did not look red but very dark, his lips and the drying blood upon my hands seemed black. If possible I was in a worse plight than he, on account of the yellow fungus into which I had jumped. Our jackets were unbuttoned, and our shoes had been taken off and lay at our feet. And we were sitting with our backs to this queer bluish light, peering at such a monster as Durer might have invented.

Cavor broke the silence; started to speak, went hoarse, and cleared his throat. Outside began a terrific bellowing, as if a mooncalf were in trouble. It ended in a shriek, and everything was still again.

Presently the Selenite turned about, flickered into the shadow, stood for a moment retrospective at the door, and then closed it on us; and once more we were in that murmurous mystery of darkness into which we had awakened.

CHAPTER XIII - MR. CAVOR MAKES SOME SUGGESTIONS

For a time neither of us spoke. To focus together all the things we had brought upon ourselves seemed beyond my mental powers.

"They've got us," I said at last.

"It was that fungus."

"Well—if I hadn't taken it we should have fainted and starved."

"We might have found the sphere."

I lost my temper at his persistence, and swore to myself. For a time we hated one another in silence. I drummed with my fingers on the floor between my knees, and gritted the links of my fetters together. Presently I was forced to talk again.

"What do you make of it, anyhow?" I asked humbly.

"They are reasonable creatures—they can make things and do things. Those lights we saw..."

He stopped. It was clear he could make nothing of it.

When he spoke again it was to confess, "After all, they are more human than we had a right to expect. I suppose—"

He stopped irritatingly.

"Yes?"

"I suppose, anyhow—on any planet where there is an intelligent animal—it will carry its brain case upward, and have hands, and walk erect."

Presently he broke away in another direction.

"We are some way in," he said. "I mean—perhaps a couple of thousand feet or more."

"Why?"

"It's cooler. And our voices are so much louder. That faded quality —it has altogether gone. And the feeling in one's ears and throat."

I had not noted that, but I did now.

"The air is denser. We must be some depths—a mile even, we may be —inside the moon."

"We never thought of a world inside the moon."

"No."

"How could we?"

"We might have done. Only one gets into habits of mind."

He thought for a time.

"Now," he said, "it seems such an obvious thing."

"Of course! The moon must be enormously cavernous, with an atmosphere within, and at the centre of its caverns a sea.

"One knew that the moon had a lower specific gravity than the earth, one knew that it had little air or water outside, one knew, too, that it was sister planet to the earth, and that it was unaccountable that it should be different in composition. The inference that it was hollowed out was as clear as day. And yet one never saw it as a fact. Kepler, of course—"

His voice had the interest now of a man who has discerned a pretty sequence of reasoning.

"Yes," he said, "Kepler with his sub-volvani was right after all."

"I wish you had taken the trouble to find that out before we came," I said.

He answered nothing, buzzing to himself softly, as he pursued his thoughts. My temper was going.

"What do you think has become of the sphere, anyhow?" I asked.

"Lost," he said, like a man who answers an uninteresting question.

"Among those plants?"

"Unless they find it."

"And then?"

"How can I tell?"

"Cavor," I said, with a sort of hysterical bitterness, "things look bright for my Company..."

He made no answer.

"Good Lord!" I exclaimed. "Just think of all the trouble we took to get into this pickle! What did we come for? What are we after? What was the moon to us or we to the moon? We wanted too much, we tried too much. We ought to have started the little things first. It was you proposed the moon! Those Cavorite spring blinds! I am certain we could have worked them for terrestrial purposes. Certain! Did you really understand what I proposed? A steel cylinder—"

"Rubbish!" said Cavor.

We ceased to converse.

For a time Cavor kept up a broken monologue without much help from me.

"If they find it," he began, "if they find it ... what will they do with it? Well, that's a question. It may be that's *the* question. They won't understand it, anyhow. If they understood that sort of thing they would have come long since to the earth. Would they? Why shouldn't they? But they would have sent something—they couldn't keep their hands off such a possibility. No! But they will examine it. Clearly they are intelligent and inquisitive. They will examine it—get inside it—trifle with the studs. Off! ... That would mean the moon for us for all the rest of our lives. Strange creatures, strange knowledge..."

"As for strange knowledge—" said I, and language failed me.

"Look here, Bedford," said Cavor, "you came on this expedition of your own free will."

"You said to me, 'Call it prospecting'."

"There's always risks in prospecting."

"Especially when you do it unarmed and without thinking out every possibility."

"I was so taken up with the sphere. The thing rushed on us, and carried us away."

"Rushed on *me*, you mean."

"Rushed on me just as much. How was I to know when I set to work on molecular physics that the business would bring me here—of all places?"

"It's this accursed science," I cried. "It's the very Devil. The medieval priests and persecutors were right and the Moderns are all wrong. You tamper with it—and it offers you gifts. And directly you take them it knocks you to pieces in some unexpected way. Old passions and new weapons—now it upsets your religion, now it upsets your social ideas, now it whirls you off to desolation and misery!"

"Anyhow, it's no use your quarrelling with me now. These creatures —these Selenites, or whatever we choose to call them—have got us tied hand and foot. Whatever temper you choose to go through with it in, you will have to go through with it... We have experiences before us that will need all our coolness."

He paused as if he required my assent. But I sat sulking. "Confound your science!" I said.

"The problem is communication. Gestures, I fear, will be different. Pointing, for example. No creatures but men and monkeys point."

That was too obviously wrong for me. "Pretty nearly every animal," I cried, "points with its eyes or nose."

Cavor meditated over that. "Yes," he said at last, "and we don't. There's such differences—such differences!"

"One might... But how can I tell? There is speech. The sounds they make, a sort of fluting and piping. I don't see how we are to imitate that. Is it their speech, that sort of thing? They may have different senses, different means of communication. Of course they are minds and we are minds; there must be something in common. Who knows how far we may not get to an understanding?"

"The things are outside us," I said. "They're more different from us than the strangest animals on earth. They are a different clay. What is the good of talking like this?"

Cavor thought. "I don't see that. Where there are minds they will have something similar—even though they have been evolved on different planets. Of course if it was a question of instincts, if we or they are no more than animals—"

"Well, are they? They're much more like ants on their hind legs than human beings, and who ever got to any sort of understanding with ants?"

"But these machines and clothing! No, I don't hold with you, Bedford. The difference is wide—"

"It's insurmountable."

"The resemblance must bridge it. I remember reading once a paper by the late Professor Galton on the possibility of communication between the planets. Unhappily, at that time it did not seem probable that that would be of any material

benefit to me, and I fear I did not give it the attention I should have done—in view of this state of affairs. Yet... Now, let me see!

"His idea was to begin with those broad truths that must underlie all conceivable mental existences and establish a basis on those. The great principles of geometry, to begin with. He proposed to take some leading proposition of Euclid's, and show by construction that its truth was known to us, to demonstrate, for example, that the angles at the base of an isosceles triangle are equal, and that if the equal sides be produced the angles on the other side of the base are equal also, or that the square on the hypotenuse of a right-angled triangle is equal to the sum of the squares on the two other sides. By demonstrating our knowledge of these things we should demonstrate our possession of a reasonable intelligence... Now, suppose I ... I might draw the geometrical figure with a wet finger, or even trace it in the air..."

He fell silent. I sat meditating his words. For a time his wild hope of communication, of interpretation, with these weird beings held me. Then that angry despair that was a part of my exhaustion and physical misery resumed its sway. I perceived with a sudden novel vividness the extraordinary folly of everything I had ever done. "Ass!" I said; "oh, ass, unutterable ass... I seem to exist only to go about doing preposterous things. Why did we ever leave the thing? ... Hopping about looking for patents and concessions in the craters of the moon!... If only we had had the sense to fasten a handkerchief to a stick to show where we had left the sphere!"

I subsided, fuming.

"It is clear," meditated Cavor, "they are intelligent. One can hypothecate certain things. As they have not killed us at once, they must have ideas of mercy. Mercy! at any rate of restraint. Possibly of intercourse. They may meet us. And this apartment and the glimpses we had of its guardian. These fetters! A high degree of intelligence..."

"I wish to heaven," cried I, "I'd thought even twice! Plunge after plunge. First one fluky start and then another. It was my confidence in you! Why didn't I stick to my play? That was what I was equal to. That was my world and the life I was made for. I could have finished that play. I'm certain ... it was a good play. I had the scenario as good as done. Then... Conceive it! leaping to the moon! Practically—I've thrown my life away! That old woman in the inn near Canterbury had better sense."

I looked up, and stopped in mid-sentence. The darkness had given place to that bluish light again. The door was opening, and several noiseless Selenites were coming into the chamber. I became quite still, staring at their grotesque faces.

Then suddenly my sense of disagreeable strangeness changed to interest. I perceived that the foremost and second carried bowls. One elemental need at least our minds could understand in common. They were bowls of some metal that, like our fetters, looked dark in that bluish light; and each contained a number of whitish fragments. All the cloudy pain and misery that oppressed me rushed together and took the shape of hunger. I eyed these bowls wolfishly, and, though it re-

turned to me in dreams, at that time it seemed a small matter that at the end of the arms that lowered one towards me were not hands, but a sort of flap and thumb, like the end of an elephant's trunk. The stuff in the bowl was loose in texture, and whitish brown in colour—rather like lumps of some cold souffle, and it smelt faintly like mushrooms. From a partially divided carcass of a mooncalf that we presently saw, I am inclined to believe it must have been mooncalf flesh.

My hands were so tightly chained that I could barely contrive to reach the bowl; but when they saw the effort I made, two of them dexterously released one of the turns about my wrist. Their tentacle hands were soft and cold to my skin. I immediately seized a mouthful of the food. It had the same laxness in texture that all organic structures seem to have upon the moon; it tasted rather like a gauffre or a damp meringue, but in no way was it disagreeable. I took two other mouthfuls. "I wanted—foo'!" said I, tearing off a still larger piece...

For a time we ate with an utter absence of self-consciousness. We ate and presently drank like tramps in a soup kitchen. Never before nor since have I been hungry to the ravenous pitch, and save that I have had this very experience I could never have believed that, a quarter of a million of miles out of our proper world, in utter perplexity of soul, surrounded, watched, touched by beings more grotesque and inhuman than the worst creations of a nightmare, it would be possible for me to eat in utter forgetfulness of all these things. They stood about us watching us, and ever and again making a slight elusive twittering that stood the suppose, in the stead of speech. I did not even shiver at their touch. And when the first zeal of my feeding was over, I could note that Cavor, too, had been eating with the same shameless abandon.

CHAPTER XIV - EXPERIMENTS IN INTERCOURSE

When at last we had made an end of eating, the Selenites linked our hands closely together again, and then untwisted the chains about our feet and rebound them, so as to give us a limited freedom of movement. Then they unfastened the chains about our waists. To do all this they had to handle us freely, and ever and again one of their queer heads came down close to my face, or a soft tentacle-hand touched my head or neck. I don't remember that I was afraid then or repelled by their proximity. I think that our incurable anthropomorphism made us imagine there were human heads inside their masks. The skin, like everything else, looked bluish, but that was on account of the light; and it was hard and shiny, quite in the beetle-wing fashion, not soft, or moist, or hairy, as a vertebrated animal's would be. Along the crest of the head was a low ridge of whitish spines running from back to front, and a much larger ridge curved on either side over the eyes. The Selenite who untied me used his mouth to help his hands.

"They seem to be releasing us," said Cavor. "Remember we are on the moon! Make no sudden movements!"

"Are you going to try that geometry?"

"If I get a chance. But, of course, they may make an advance first."

We remained passive, and the Selenites, having finished their arrangements, stood back from us, and seemed to be looking at us. I say seemed to be, because as their eyes were at the side and not in front, one had the same difficulty in determining the direction in which they were looking as one has in the case of a hen or a fish. They conversed with one another in their reedy tones, that seemed to me impossible to imitate or define. The door behind us opened wider, and, glancing over my shoulder, I saw a vague large space beyond, in which quite a little crowd of Selenites were standing. They seemed a curiously miscellaneous rabble.

"Do they want us to imitate those sounds?" I asked Cavor.

"I don't think so," he said.

"It seems to me that they are trying to make us understand something."

"I can't make anything of their gestures. Do you notice this one, who is worrying with his head like a man with an uncomfortable collar?"

"Let us shake our heads at him."

We did that, and finding it ineffectual, attempted an imitation of the Selenites' movements. That seemed to interest them. At any rate they all set up the same movement. But as that seemed to lead to nothing, we desisted at last and so did they, and fell into a piping argument among themselves. Then one of them, short-

er and very much thicker than the others, and with a particularly wide mouth, squatted down suddenly beside Cavor, and put his hands and feet in the same posture as Cavor's were bound, and then by a dexterous movement stood up.

"Cavor," I shouted, "they want us to get up!"

He stared open-mouthed. "That's it!" he said.

And with much heaving and grunting, because our hands were tied together, we contrived to struggle to our feet. The Selenites made way for our elephantine heavings, and seemed to twitter more volubly. As soon as we were on our feet the thick-set Selenite came and patted each of our faces with his tentacles, and walked towards the open doorway. That also was plain enough, and we followed him. We saw that four of the Selenites standing in the doorway were much taller than the others, and clothed in the same manner as those we had seen in the crater, namely, with spiked round helmets and cylindrical body- cases, and that each of the four carried a goad with spike and guard made of that same dull-looking metal as the bowls. These four closed about us, one on either side of each of us, as we emerged from our chamber into the cavern from which the light had come.

We did not get our impression of that cavern all at once. Our attention was taken up by the movements and attitudes of the Selenites immediately about us, and by the necessity of controlling our motion, lest we should startle and alarm them and ourselves by some excessive stride. In front of us was the short, thick-set being who had solved the problem of asking us to get up, moving with gestures that seemed, almost all of them, intelligible to us, inviting us to follow him. His spout-like face turned from one of us to the other with a quickness that was clearly interrogative. For a time, I say, we were taken up with these things.

But at last the great place that formed a background to our movements asserted itself. It became apparent that the source of much, at least, of the tumult of sounds which had filled our ears ever since we had recovered from the stupefaction of the fungus was a vast mass of machinery in active movement, whose flying and whirling parts were visible indistinctly over the heads and between the bodies of the Selenites who walked about us. And not only did the web of sounds that filled the air proceed from this mechanism, but also the peculiar blue light that irradiated the whole place. We had taken it as a natural thing that a subterranean cavern should be artificially lit, and even now, though the fact was patent to my eyes, I did not really grasp its import until presently the darkness came. The meaning and structure of this huge apparatus we saw I cannot explain, because we neither of us learnt what it was for or how it worked. One after another, big shafts of metal flung out and up from its centre, their heads travelling in what seemed to me to be a parabolic path; each dropped a sort of dangling arm as it rose towards the apex of its flight and plunged down into a vertical cylinder, forcing this down before it. About it moved the shapes of tenders, little figures that seemed vaguely different from the beings about us. As each of the three dangling arms of the machine plunged down, there was a clank and then a roaring, and out of the top of the vertical cylinder came pouring this incandescent substance that lit the place, and ran over as milk runs over a boiling pot, and dripped luminously into a tank of light

below. It was a cold blue light, a sort of phosphorescent glow but infinitely brighter, and from the tanks into which it fell it ran in conduits athwart the cavern.

Thud, thud, thud, thud, came the sweeping arms of this unintelligible apparatus, and the light substance hissed and poured. At first the thing seemed only reasonably large and near to us, and then I saw how exceedingly little the Selenites upon it seemed, and I realised the full immensity of cavern and machine. I looked from this tremendous affair to the faces of the Selenites with a new respect. I stopped, and Cavor stopped, and stared at this thunderous engine.

"But this is stupendous!" I said. "What can it be for?"

Cavor's blue-lit face was full of an intelligent respect. "I can't dream! Surely these beings—Men could not make a thing like that! Look at those arms, are they on connecting rods?"

The thick-set Selenite had gone some paces unheeded. He came back and stood between us and the great machine. I avoided seeing him, because I guessed somehow that his idea was to beckon us onward. He walked away in the direction he wished us to go, and turned and came back, and flicked our faces to attract our attention.

Cavor and I looked at one another.

"Cannot we show him we are interested in the machine?" I said.

"Yes," said Cavor. "We'll try that." He turned to our guide and smiled, and pointed to the machine, and pointed again, and then to his head, and then to the machine. By some defect of reasoning he seemed to imagine that broken English might help these gestures. "Me look 'im," he said, "me think 'im very much. Yes."

His behaviour seemed to check the Selenites in their desire for our progress for a moment. They faced one another, their queer heads moved, the twittering voices came quick and liquid. Then one of them, a lean, tall creature, with a sort of mantle added to the puttee in which the others were dressed, twisted his elephant trunk of a hand about Cavor's waist, and pulled him gently to follow our guide, who again went on ahead. Cavor resisted. "We may just as well begin explaining ourselves now. They may think we are new animals, a new sort of mooncalf perhaps! It is most important that we should show an intelligent interest from the outset."

He began to shake his head violently. "No, no," he said, "me not come on one minute. Me look at 'im."

"Isn't there some geometrical point you might bring in apropos of that affair?" I suggested, as the Selenites conferred again.

"Possibly a parabolic—" he began.

He yelled loudly, and leaped six feet or more!

One of the four armed moon-men had pricked him with a goad!

I turned on the goad-bearer behind me with a swift threatening gesture, and he started back. This and Cavor's sudden shout and leap clearly astonished all the Selenites. They receded hastily, facing us. For one of those moments that seem to last for ever, we stood in angry protest, with a scattered semicircle of these inhuman beings about us.

"He pricked me!" said Cavor, with a catching of the voice.

"I saw him," I answered.

"Confound it!" I said to the Selenites; "we're not going to stand that! What on earth do you take us for?"

I glanced quickly right and left. Far away across the blue wilderness of cavern I saw a number of other Selenites running towards us; broad and slender they were, and one with a larger head than the others. The cavern spread wide and low, and receded in every direction into darkness. Its roof, I remember, seemed to bulge down as if with the weight of the vast thickness of rocks that prisoned us. There was no way out of it—no way out of it. Above, below, in every direction, was the unknown, and these inhuman creatures, with goads and gestures, confronting us, and we two unsupported men!

CHAPTER XV - THE GIDDY BRIDGE

Just for a moment that hostile pause endured. I suppose that both we and the Selenites did some very rapid thinking. My clearest impression was that there was nothing to put my back against, and that we were bound to be surrounded and killed. The overwhelming folly of our presence there loomed over me in black, enormous reproach. Why had I ever launched myself on this mad, inhuman expedition?

Cavor came to my side and laid his hand on my arm. His pale and terrified face was ghastly in the blue light.

"We can't do anything," he said. "It's a mistake. They don't understand. We must go. As they want us to go."

I looked down at him, and then at the fresh Selenites who were coming to help their fellows. "If I had my hands free—"

"It's no use," he panted.

"No."

"We'll go."

And he turned about and led the way in the direction that had been indicated for us.

I followed, trying to look as subdued as possible, and feeling at the chains about my wrists. My blood was boiling. I noted nothing more of that cavern, though it seemed to take a long time before we had marched across it, or if I noted anything I forgot it as I saw it. My thoughts were concentrated, I think, upon my chains and the Selenites, and particularly upon the helmeted ones with the goads. At first they marched parallel with us, and at a respectful distance, but presently they were overtaken by three others, and then they drew nearer, until they were within arms length again. I winced like a beaten horse as they came near to us. The shorter, thicker Selenite marched at first on our right flank, but presently came in front of us again.

How well the picture of that grouping has bitten into my brain; the back of Cavor's downcast head just in front of me, and the dejected droop of his shoulders, and our guide's gaping visage, perpetually jerking about him, and the goad-bearers on either side, watchful, yet open-mouthed—a blue monochrome. And after all, I do remember one other thing besides the purely personal affair, which is, that a sort of gutter came presently across the floor of the cavern, and then ran along by the side of the path of rock we followed. And it was full of that same bright blue luminous stuff that flowed out of the great machine. I walked close

beside it, and I can testify it radiated not a particle of heat. It was brightly shining, and yet it was neither warmer nor colder than anything else in the cavern.

Clang, clang, clang, we passed right under the thumping levers of another vast machine, and so came at last to a wide tunnel, in which we could even hear the pad, pad, of our shoeless feet, and which, save for the trickling thread of blue to the right of us, was quite unlit. The shadows made gigantic travesties of our shapes and those of the Selenites on the irregular wall and roof of the tunnel. Ever and again crystals in the walls of the tunnel scintillated like gems, ever and again the tunnel expanded into a stalactitic cavern, or gave off branches that vanished into darkness.

We seemed to be marching down that tunnel for a long time. "Trickle, trickle," went the flowing light very softly, and our footfalls and their echoes made an irregular paddle, paddle. My mind settled down to the question of my chains. If I were to slip off one turn *so*, and then to twist it *so*...

If I tried to do it very gradually, would they see I was slipping my wrist out of the looser turn? If they did, what would they do?

"Bedford," said Cavor, "it goes down. It keeps on going down."

His remark roused me from my sullen pre-occupation.

"If they wanted to kill us," he said, dropping back to come level with me, "there is no reason why they should not have done it."

"No," I admitted, "that's true."

"They don't understand us," he said, "they think we are merely strange animals, some wild sort of mooncalf birth, perhaps. It will be only when they have observed us better that they will begin to think we have minds—"

"When you trace those geometrical problems," said I.

"It may be that."

We tramped on for a space.

"You see," said Cavor, "these may be Selenites of a lower class."

"The infernal fools!" said I viciously, glancing at their exasperating faces.

"If we endure what they do to us—"

"We've got to endure it," said I.

"There may be others less stupid. This is the mere outer fringe of their world. It must go down and down, cavern, passage, tunnel, down at last to the sea—hundreds of miles below."

His words made me think of the mile or so of rock and tunnel that might be over our heads already. It was like a weight dropping, on my shoulders. "Away from the sun and air," I said. "Even a mine half a mile deep is stuffy." remarked.

"This is not, anyhow. It's probable—Ventilation! The air would blow from the dark side of the moon to the sunlit, and all the carbonic acid would well out there and feed those plants. Up this tunnel, for example, there is quite a breeze. And what a world it must be. The earnest we have in that shaft, and those machines—"

"And the goad," I said. "Don't forget the goad!"

He walked a little in front of me for a time.

"Even that goad—" he said.

"Well?"

"I was angry at the time. But—it was perhaps necessary we should get on. They have different skins, and probably different nerves. They may not understand our objection—just as a being from Mars might not like our earthly habit of nudging."

"They'd better be careful how they nudge me."

"And about that geometry. After all, their way is a way of understanding, too. They begin with the elements of life and not of thought. Food. Compulsion. Pain. They strike at fundamentals."

"There's no doubt about that," I said.

He went on to talk of the enormous and wonderful world into which we were being taken. I realised slowly from his tone, that even now he was not absolutely in despair at the prospect of going ever deeper into this inhuman planet-burrow. His mind ran on machines and invention, to the exclusion of a thousand dark things that beset me. It wasn't that he intended to make any use of these things, he simply wanted to know them.

"After all," he said, "this is a tremendous occasion. It is the meeting of two worlds! What are we going to see? Think of what is below us here."

"We shan't see much if the light isn't better," I remarked.

"This is only the outer crust. Down below—On this scale—There will be everything. Do you notice how different they seem one from another? The story we shall take back!"

"Some rare sort of animal," I said, "might comfort himself in that way while they were bringing him to the Zoo... It doesn't follow that we are going to be shown all these things."

"When they find we have reasonable minds," said Cavor, "they will want to learn about the earth. Even if they have no generous emotions, they will teach in order to learn... And the things they must know! The unanticipated things!"

He went on to speculate on the possibility of their knowing things he had never hoped to learn on earth, speculating in that way, with a raw wound from that goad already in his skin! Much that he said I forget, for my attention was drawn to the fact that the tunnel along which we had been marching was opening out wider and wider. We seemed, from the feeling of the air, to be going out into a huge space. But how big the space might really be we could not tell, because it was unlit. Our little stream of light ran in a dwindling thread and vanished far ahead. Presently the rocky walls had vanished altogether on either hand. There was nothing to be seen but the path in front of us and the trickling hurrying rivulet of blue phosphorescence. The figures of Cavor and the guiding Selenite marched before me, the sides of their legs and heads that were towards the rivulet were clear and bright blue, their darkened sides, now that the reflection of the tunnel wall no longer lit them, merged indistinguishably in the darkness beyond.

And soon I perceived that we were approaching a declivity of some sort, because the little blue stream dipped suddenly out of sight.

In another moment, as it seemed, we had reached the edge. The shining stream gave one meander of hesitation and then rushed over. It fell to a depth at which the sound of its descent was absolutely lost to us. Far below was a bluish glow, a sort of blue mist—at an infinite distance below. And the darkness the stream dropped out of became utterly void and black, save that a thing like a plank projected from the edge of the cliff and stretched out and faded and vanished altogether. There was a warm air blowing up out of the gulf.

For a moment I and Cavor stood as near the edge as we dared, peering into a blue-tinged profundity. And then our guide was pulling at my arm.

Then he left me, and walked to the end of that plank and stepped upon it, looking back. Then when he perceived we watched him, he turned about and went on along it, walking as surely as though he was on firm earth. For a moment his form was distinct, then he became a blue blur, and then vanished into the obscurity. I became aware of some vague shape looming darkly out of the black.

There was a pause. "Surely!—" said Cavor.

One of the other Selenites walked a few paces out upon the plank, and turned and looked back at us unconcernedly. The others stood ready to follow after us. Our guide's expectant figure reappeared. He was returning to see why we had not advanced.

"What is that beyond there?" I asked.

"I can't see."

"We can't cross this at any price," said I.

"I could not go three steps on it," said Cavor, "even with my hands free."

We looked at each other's drawn faces in blank consternation.

"They can't know what it is to be giddy!" said Cavor.

"It's quite impossible for us to walk that plank."

"I don't believe they see as we do. I've been watching them. I wonder if they know this is simply blackness for us. How can we make them understand?"

"Anyhow, we must make them understand."

I think we said these things with a vague half hope the Selenites might somehow understand. I knew quite clearly that all that was needed was an explanation. Then as I saw their faces, I realised that an explanation was impossible. Just here it was that our resemblances were not going to bridge our differences. Well, I wasn't going to walk the plank, anyhow. I slipped my wrist very quickly out of the coil of chain that was loose, and then began to twist my wrists in opposite directions. I was standing nearest to the bridge, and as I did this two of the Selenites laid hold of me, and pulled me gently towards it.

I shook my head violently. "No go," I said, "no use. You don't understand."

Another Selenite added his compulsion. I was forced to step forward.

"I've got an idea," said Cavor; but I knew his ideas.

"Look here!" I exclaimed to the Selenites. "Steady on! It's all very well for you—"

I sprang round upon my heel. I burst out into curses. For one of the armed Selenites had stabbed me behind with his goad.

I wrenched my wrists free from the little tentacles that held them. I turned on the goad-bearer. "Confound you!" I cried. "I've warned you of that. What on earth do you think I'm made of, to stick that into me? If you touch me again—"

By way of answer he pricked me forthwith.

I heard Cavor's voice in alarm and entreaty. Even then I think he wanted to compromise with these creatures. "I say, Bedford," he cried, "I know a way!" But the sting of that second stab seemed to set free some pent-up reserve of energy in my being. Instantly the link of the wrist-chain snapped, and with it snapped all considerations that had held us unresisting in the hands of these moon creatures. For that second, at least, I was mad with fear and anger. I took no thought of consequences. I hit straight out at the face of the thing with the goad. The chain was twisted round my fist.

There came another of these beastly surprises of which the moon world is full.

My mailed hand seemed to go clean through him. He smashed like—like some softish sort of sweet with liquid in it! He broke right in! He squelched and splashed. It was like hitting a damp toadstool. The flimsy body went spinning a dozen yards, and fell with a flabby impact. I was astonished. I was incredulous that any living thing could be so flimsy. For an instant I could have believed the whole thing a dream.

Then it had become real and imminent again. Neither Cavor nor the other Selenites seemed to have done anything from the time when I had turned about to the time when the dead Selenite hit the ground. Every one stood back from us two, every one alert. That arrest seemed to last at least a second after the Selenite was down. Every one must have been taking the thing in. I seem to remember myself standing with my arm half retracted, trying also to take it in. "What next?" clamoured my brain; "what next?" Then in a moment every one was moving!

I perceived we must get our chains loose, and that before we could do this these Selenites had to be beaten off. I faced towards the group of the three goad-bearers. Instantly one threw his goad at me. It swished over my head, and I suppose went flying into the abyss behind.

I leaped right at him with all my might as the goad flew over me. He turned to run as I jumped, and I bore him to the ground, came down right upon him, and slipped upon his smashed body and fell. He seemed to wriggle under my foot.

I came into a sitting position, and on every hand the blue backs of the Selenites were receding into the darkness. I bent a link by main force and untwisted the chain that had hampered me about the ankles, and sprang to my feet, with the chain in my hand. Another goad, flung javelin-wise, whistled by me, and I made a rush towards the darkness out of which it had come. Then I turned back towards Cavor, who was still standing in the light of the rivulet near the gulf convulsively busy with his wrists, and at the same time jabbering nonsense about his idea.

"Come on!" I cried.

"My hands!" he answered.

Then, realising that I dared not run back to him, because my ill- calculated steps might carry me over the edge, he came shuffling towards me, with his hands held out before him.

I gripped his chains at once to unfasten them.

"Where are they?" he panted.

"Run away. They'll come back. They're throwing things! Which way shall we go?"

"By the light. To that tunnel. Eh?"

"Yes," said I, and his hands were free.

I dropped on my knees and fell to work on his ankle bonds. Whack came something—I know not what—and splashed the livid streamlet into drops about us. Far away on our right a piping and whistling began.

I whipped the chain off his feet, and put it in his hand. "Hit with that!" I said, and without waiting for an answer, set off in big bounds along the path by which we had come. I had a nasty sort of feeling that these things could jump out of the darkness on to my back. I heard the impact of his leaps come following after me.

We ran in vast strides. But that running, you must understand, was an altogether different thing from any running on earth. On earth one leaps and almost instantly hits the ground again, but on the moon, because of its weaker pull, one shot through the air for several seconds before one came to earth. In spite of our violent hurry this gave an effect of long pauses, pauses in which one might have counted seven or eight. "Step," and one soared off! All sorts of questions ran through my mind: "Where are the Selenites? What will they do? Shall we ever get to that tunnel? Is Cavor far behind? Are they likely to cut him off?" Then whack, stride, and off again for another step.

I saw a Selenite running in front of me, his legs going exactly as a man's would go on earth, saw him glance over his shoulder, and heard him shriek as he ran aside out of my way into the darkness. He was, I think, our guide, but I am not sure. Then in another vast stride the walls of rock had come into view on either hand, and in two more strides I was in the tunnel, and tempering my pace to its low roof. I went on to a bend, then stopped and turned back, and plug, plug, plug, Cavor came into view, splashing into the stream of blue light at every stride, and grew larger and blundered into me. We stood clutching each other. For a moment, at least, we had shaken off our captors and were alone.

We were both very much out of breath. We spoke in panting, broken sentences.

"You've spoilt it all!" panted Cavor. "Nonsense," I cried. "It was that or death!"

"What are we to do?"

"Hide."

"How can we?"

"It's dark enough."

"But where?"

"Up one of these side caverns."

"And then?"

"Think."

"Right—come on."

We strode on, and presently came to a radiating dark cavern. Cavor was in front. He hesitated, and chose a black mouth that seemed to promise good hiding. He went towards it and turned.

"It's dark," he said.

"Your legs and feet will light us. You're wet with that luminous stuff."

"But—"

A tumult of sounds, and in particular a sound like a clanging gong, advancing up the main tunnel, became audible. It was horribly suggestive of a tumultuous pursuit. We made a bolt for the unlit side cavern forthwith. As we ran along it our way was lit by the irradiation of Cavor's legs. "It's lucky," I panted, "they took off our boots, or we should fill this place with clatter." On we rushed, taking as small steps as we could to avoid striking the roof of the cavern. After a time we seemed to be gaining on the uproar. It became muffled, it dwindled, it died away.

I stopped and looked back, and I heard the pad, pad of Cavor's feet receding. Then he stopped also. "Bedford," he whispered; "there's a sort of light in front of us."

I looked, and at first could see nothing. Then I perceived his head and shoulders dimly outlined against a fainter darkness. I saw, also, that this mitigation of the darkness was not blue, as all the other light within the moon had been, but a pallid gray, a very vague, faint white, the daylight colour. Cavor noted this difference as soon, or sooner, than I did, and I think, too, that it filled him with much the same wild hope.

"Bedford," he whispered, and his voice trembled. "That light—it is possible—"

He did not dare to say the thing he hoped. Then came a pause. Suddenly I knew by the sound of his feet that he was striding towards that pallor. I followed him with a beating heart.

CHAPTER XVI - POINTS OF VIEW

The light grew stronger as we advanced. In a little time it was nearly as strong as the phosphorescence on Cavor's legs. Our tunnel was expanding into a cavern, and this new light was at the farther end of it. I perceived something that set my hopes leaping and bounding.

"Cavor," I said, "it comes from above! I am certain it comes from above!"

He made no answer, but hurried on.

Indisputably it was a gray light, a silvery light.

In another moment we were beneath it. It filtered down through a chink in the walls of the cavern, and as I stared up, drip, came a drop of water upon my face. I started and stood aside—drip, fell another drop quite audibly on the rocky floor.

"Cavor," I said, "if one of us lifts the other, he can reach that crack!"

"I'll lift you," he said, and incontinently hoisted me as though I was a baby.

I thrust an arm into the crack, and just at my finger tips found a little ledge by which I could hold. I could see the white light was very much brighter now. I pulled myself up by two fingers with scarcely an effort, though on earth I weigh twelve stone, reached to a still higher corner of rock, and so got my feet on the narrow ledge. I stood up and searched up the rocks with my fingers; the cleft broadened out upwardly. "It's climbable," I said to Cavor. "Can you jump up to my hand if I hold it down to you?"

I wedged myself between the sides of the cleft, rested knee and foot on the ledge, and extended a hand. I could not see Cavor, but I could hear the rustle of his movements as he crouched to spring. Then whack and he was hanging to my arm—and no heavier than a kitten! I lugged him up until he had a hand on my ledge, and could release me.

"Confound it!" I said, "any one could be a mountaineer on the moon;" and so set myself in earnest to the climbing. For a few minutes I clambered steadily, and then I looked up again. The cleft opened out steadily, and the light was brighter. Only—

It was not daylight after all.

In another moment I could see what it was, and at the sight I could have beaten my head against the rocks with disappointment. For I beheld simply an irregularly sloping open space, and all over its slanting floor stood a forest of little club-shaped fungi, each shining gloriously with that pinkish silvery light. For a moment I stared at their soft radiance, then sprang forward and upward among them.

I plucked up half a dozen and flung them against the rocks, and then sat down, laughing bitterly, as Cavor's ruddy face came into view.

"It's phosphorescence again!" I said. "No need to hurry. Sit down and make yourself at home." And as he spluttered over our disappointment, I began to lob more of these growths into the cleft.

"I thought it was daylight," he said.

"Daylight!" cried I. "Daybreak, sunset, clouds, and windy skies! Shall we ever see such things again?"

As I spoke, a little picture of our world seemed to rise before me, bright and little and clear, like the background of some old Italian picture. "The sky that changes, and the sea that changes, and the hills and the green trees and the towns and cities shining in the sun. Think of a wet roof at sunset, Cavor! Think of the windows of a westward house!" He made no answer.

"Here we are burrowing in this beastly world that isn't a world, with its inky ocean hidden in some abominable blackness below, and outside that torrid day and that death stillness of night. And all these things that are chasing us now, beastly men of leather—insect men, that come out of a nightmare! After all, they're right! What business have we here smashing them and disturbing their world! For all we know the whole planet is up and after us already. In a minute we may hear them whimpering, and their gongs going. What are we to do? Where are we to go? Here we are as comfortable as snakes from Jamrach's loose in a Surbiton villa!"

"It was your fault," said Cavor.

"My fault!" I shouted. "Good Lord!"

"I had an idea!"

"Curse your ideas!"

"If we had refused to budge—"

"Under those goads?"

"Yes. They would have carried us!"

"Over that bridge?"

"Yes. They must have carried us from outside."

"I'd rather be carried by a fly across a ceiling."

"Good Heavens!"

I resumed my destruction of the fungi. Then suddenly I saw something that struck me even then. "Cavor," I said, "these chains are of gold!"

He was thinking intently, with his hands gripping his cheeks. He turned his head slowly and stared at me, and when I had repeated my words, at the twisted chain about his right hand. "So they are," he said, "so they are." His face lost its transitory interest even as he looked. He hesitated for a moment, then went on with his interrupted meditation. I sat for a space puzzling over the fact that I had only just observed this, until I considered the blue light in which we had been, and which had taken all the colour out of the metal. And from that discovery I also started upon a train of thought that carried me wide and far. I forgot that I had just been asking what business we had in the moon. Gold...

It was Cavor who spoke first. "It seems to me that there are two courses open to us."

"Well?"

"Either we can attempt to make our way—fight our way if necessary —out to the exterior again, and then hunt for our sphere until we find it, or the cold of the night comes to kill us, or else—"

He paused. "Yes?" I said, though I knew what was coming.

"We might attempt once more to establish some sort of understanding with the minds of the people in the moon."

"So far as I'm concerned—it's the first."

"I doubt."

"I don't."

"You see," said Cavor, "I do not think we can judge the Selenites by what we have seen of them. Their central world, their civilised world will be far below in the profounder caverns about their sea. This region of the crust in which we are is an outlying district, a pastoral region. At any rate, that is my interpretation. These Selenites we have seen may be only the equivalent of cowboys and engine-tenders. Their use of goads—in all probability mooncalf goads—the lack of imagination they show in expecting us to be able to do just what they can do, their indisputable brutality, all seem to point to something of that sort. But if we endured—"

"Neither of us could endure a six-inch plank across the bottomless pit for very long."

"No," said Cavor; "but then—"

"I *won't*," I said.

He discovered a new line of possibilities. "Well, suppose we got ourselves into some corner, where we could defend ourselves against these hinds and labourers. If, for example, we could hold out for a week or so, it is probable that the news of our appearance would filter down to the more intelligent and populous parts—"

"If they exist."

"They must exist, or whence came those tremendous machines?"

"That's possible, but it's the worst of the two chances."

"We might write up inscriptions on walls—"

"How do we know their eyes would see the sort of marks we made?"

"If we cut them—"

"That's possible, of course."

I took up a new thread of thought. "After all," I said, "I suppose you don't think these Selenites so infinitely wiser than men."

"They must know a lot more—or at least a lot of different things."

"Yes, but—" I hesitated.

"I think you'll quite admit, Cavor, that you're rather an exceptional man."

"How?"

"Well, you—you're a rather lonely man—have been, that is. You haven't married."

"Never wanted to. But why—"

"And you never grew richer than you happened to be?"

"Never wanted that either."

"You've just rooted after knowledge?"

"Well, a certain curiosity is natural—"

"You think so. That's just it. You think every other mind wants to know. I remember once, when I asked you why you conducted all these researches, you said you wanted your F.R.S., and to have the stuff called Cavorite, and things like that. You know perfectly well you didn't do it for that; but at the time my question took you by surprise, and you felt you ought to have something to look like a motive. Really you conducted researches because you had to. It's your twist."

"Perhaps it is—"

"It isn't one man in a million has that twist. Most men want—well, various things, but very few want knowledge for its own sake. I don't, I know perfectly well. Now, these Selenites seem to be a driving, busy sort of being, but how do you know that even the most intelligent will take an interest in us or our world? I don't believe they'll even know we have a world. They never come out at night—they'd freeze if they did. They've probably never seen any heavenly body at all except the blazing sun. How are they to know there is another world? What does it matter to them if they do? Well, even if they have had a glimpse of a few stars, or even of the earth crescent, what of that? Why should people living inside a planet trouble to observe that sort of thing? Men wouldn't have done it except for the seasons and sailing; why should the moon people?...

"Well, suppose there are a few philosophers like yourself. They are just the very Selenites who'll never have heard of our existence. Suppose a Selenite had dropped on the earth when you were at Lympne, you'd have been the last man in the world to hear he had come. You never read a newspaper! You see the chances against you. Well, it's for these chances we're sitting here doing nothing while precious time is flying. I tell you we've got into a fix. We've come unarmed, we've lost our sphere, we've got no food, we've shown ourselves to the Selenites, and made them think we're strange, strong, dangerous animals; and unless these Selenites are perfect fools, they'll set about now and hunt us till they find us, and when they find us they'll try to take us if they can, and kill us if they can't, and that's the end of the matter. If they take us, they'll probably kill us, through some misunderstanding. After we're done for, they may discuss us perhaps, but we shan't get much fun out of that."

"Go on."

"On the other hand, here's gold knocking about like cast iron at home. If only we can get some of it back, if only we can find our sphere again before they do, and get back, then—"

"Yes?"

"We might put the thing on a sounder footing. Come back in a bigger sphere with guns."

"Good Lord!" cried Cavor, as though that was horrible.

I shied another luminous fungus down the cleft.

"Look here, Cavor," I said, "I've half the voting power anyhow in this affair, and this is a case for a practical man. I'm a practical man, and you are not. I'm not going to trust to Selenites and geometrical diagrams if I can help it. That's all. Get back. Drop all this secrecy—or most of it. And come again."

He reflected. "When I came to the moon," he said, "I ought to have come alone."

"The question before the meeting," I said, "is how to get back to the sphere."

For a time we nursed our knees in silence. Then he seemed to decide for my reasons.

"I think," he said, "one can get data. It is clear that while the sun is on this side of the moon the air will be blowing through this planet sponge from the dark side hither. On this side, at any rate, the air will be expanding and flowing out of the moon caverns into the craters... Very well, there's a draught here."

"So there is."

"And that means that this is not a dead end; somewhere behind us this cleft goes on and up. The draught is blowing up, and that is the way we have to go. If we try to get up any sort of chimney or gully there is, we shall not only get out of these passages where they are hunting for us—"

"But suppose the gully is too narrow?"

"We'll come down again."

"Ssh!" I said suddenly; "what's that?"

We listened. At first it was an indistinct murmur, and then one picked out the clang of a gong. "They must think we are mooncalves," said I, "to be frightened at that."

"They're coming along that passage," said Cavor.

"They must be."

"They'll not think of the cleft. They'll go past."

I listened again for a space. "This time," I whispered, "they're likely to have some sort of weapon."

Then suddenly I sprang to my feet. "Good heavens, Cavor!" I cried. "But they will! They'll see the fungi I have been pitching down. They'll—"

I didn't finish my sentence. I turned about and made a leap over the fungus tops towards the upper end of the cavity. I saw that the space turned upward and became a draughty cleft again, ascending to impenetrable darkness. I was about to clamber up into this, and then with a happy inspiration turned back.

"What are you doing?" asked Cavor.

"Go on!" said I, and went back and got two of the shining fungi, and putting one into the breast pocket of my flannel jacket, so that it stuck out to light our climbing, went back with the other for Cavor. The noise of the Selenites was now so loud that it seemed they must be already beneath the cleft. But it might be they would have difficulty in clambering in to it, or might hesitate to ascend it against our possible resistance. At any rate, we had now the comforting knowledge of the

enormous muscular superiority our birth in another planet gave us. In other minute I was clambering with gigantic vigour after Cavor's blue-lit heels.

CHAPTER XVII - THE FIGHT IN THE CAVE OF THE MOON BUTCHERS

I do not know how far we clambered before we came to the grating. It may be we ascended only a few hundred feet, but at the time it seemed to me we might have hauled and jammed and hopped and wedged ourselves through a mile or more of vertical ascent. Whenever I recall that time, there comes into my head the heavy clank of our golden chains that followed every movement. Very soon my knuckles and knees were raw, and I had a bruise on one cheek. After a time the first violence of our efforts diminished, and our movements became more deliberate and less painful. The noise of the pursuing Selenites had died away altogether. It seemed almost as though they had not traced us up the crack after all, in spite of the tell-tale heap of broken fungi that must have lain beneath it. At times the cleft narrowed so much that we could scarce squeeze up it; at others it expanded into great drusy cavities, studded with prickly crystals or thickly beset with dull, shining fungoid pimples. Sometimes it twisted spirally, and at other times slanted down nearly to the horizontal direction. Ever and again there was the intermittent drip and trickle of water by us. Once or twice it seemed to us that small living things had rustled out of our reach, but what they were we never saw. They may have been venomous beasts for all I know, but they did us no harm, and we were now tuned to a pitch when a weird creeping thing more or less mattered little. And at last, far above, came the familiar bluish light again, and then we saw that it filtered through a grating that barred our way.

We whispered as we pointed this out to one another, and became more and more cautious in our ascent. Presently we were close under the grating, and by pressing my face against its bars I could see a limited portion of the cavern beyond. It was clearly a large space, and lit no doubt by some rivulet of the same blue light that we had seen flow from the beating machinery. An intermittent trickle of water dropped ever and again between the bars near my face.

My first endeavour was naturally to see what might be upon the floor of the cavern, but our grating lay in a depression whose rim hid all this from our eyes. Our foiled attention then fell back upon the suggestion of the various sounds we heard, and presently my eye caught a number of faint shadows that played across the dim roof far overhead.

Indisputably there were several Selenites, perhaps a considerable number, in this space, for we could hear the noises of their intercourse, and faint sounds that I identified as their footfalls. There was also a succession of regularly repeated

sounds—chid, chid, chid—which began and ceased, suggestive of a knife or spade hacking at some soft substance. Then came a clank as if of chains, a whistle and a rumble as of a truck running over a hollowed place, and then again that chid, chid, chid resumed. The shadows told of shapes that moved quickly and rhythmically, in agreement with that regular sound, and rested when it ceased.

We put our heads close together, and began to discuss these things in noiseless whispers.

"They are occupied," I said, "they are occupied in some way."

"Yes."

"They're not seeking us, or thinking of us."

"Perhaps they have not heard of us."

"Those others are hunting about below. If suddenly we appeared here—"

We looked at one another.

"There might be a chance to parley," said Cavor.

"No," I said. "Not as we are."

For a space we remained, each occupied by his own thoughts.

Chid, chid, chid went the chipping, and the shadows moved to and fro.

I looked at the grating. "It's flimsy," I said. "We might bend two of the bars and crawl through."

We wasted a little time in vague discussion. Then I took one of the bars in both hands, and got my feet up against the rock until they were almost on a level with my head, and so thrust against the bar. It bent so suddenly that I almost slipped. I clambered about and bent the adjacent bar in the opposite direction, and then took the luminous fungus from my pocket and dropped it down the fissure.

"Don't do anything hastily," whispered Cavor, as I twisted myself up through the opening I had enlarged. I had a glimpse of busy figures as I came through the grating, and immediately bent down, so that the rim of the depression in which the grating lay hid me from their eyes, and so lay flat, signalling advice to Cavor as he also prepared to come through. Presently we were side by side in the depression, peering over the edge at the cavern and its occupants.

It was a much larger cavern than we had supposed from our first glimpse of it, and we looked up from the lowest portion of its sloping floor. It widened out as it receded from us, and its roof came down and hid the remoter portion altogether. And lying in a line along its length, vanishing at last far away in that tremendous perspective, were a number of huge shapes, huge pallid hulls, upon which the Selenites were busy. At first they seemed big white cylinders of vague import. Then I noted the heads upon them lying towards us, eyeless and skinless like the heads of sheep at a butcher's, and perceived they were the carcasses of mooncalves being cut up, much as the crew of a whaler might cut up a moored whale. They were cutting off the flesh in strips, and on some of the farther trunks the white ribs were showing. It was the sound of their hatchets that made that chid, chid, chid. Some way away a thing like a trolley cable, drawn and loaded with chunks of lax meat, was running up the slope of the cavern floor. This enormous long avenue of hulls that were destined to be food gave us a sense of the vast

populousness of the moon world second only to the effect of our first glimpse down the shaft.

It seemed to me at first that the Selenites must be standing on trestle- supported planks,[1] and then I saw that the planks and supports and the hatchets were really of the same leaden hue as my fetters had seemed before white light came to bear on them. A number of very thick-looking crowbars lay about the floor, and had apparently assisted to turn the dead mooncalf over on its side. They were perhaps six feet long, with shaped handles, very tempting- looking weapons. The whole place was lit by three transverse streams of the blue fluid.

We lay for a long time noting all these things in silence. "Well?" said Cavor at last.

I crouched over and turned to him. I had come upon a brilliant idea. "Unless they lowered those bodies by a crane," I said, "we must be nearer the surface than I thought."

"Why?"

"The mooncalf doesn't hop, and it hasn't got wings."

He peered over the edge of the hollow again. "I wonder now—" he began. "After all, we have never gone far from the surface—"

I stopped him by a grip on his arm. I had heard a noise from the cleft below us!

We twisted ourselves about, and lay as still as death, with every sense alert. In a little while I did not doubt that something was quietly ascending the cleft. Very slowly and quite noiselessly I assured myself of a good grip on my chain, and waited for that something to appear.

"Just look at those chaps with the hatchets again," I said.

"They're all right," said Cavor.

I took a sort of provisional aim at the gap in the grating. I could hear now quite distinctly the soft twittering of the ascending Selenites, the dab of their hands against the rock, and the falling of dust from their grips as they clambered.

Then I could see that there was something moving dimly in the blackness below the grating, but what it might be I could not distinguish. The whole thing seemed to hang fire just for a moment—then smash! I had sprung to my feet, struck savagely at something that had flashed out at me. It was the keen point of a spear. I have thought since that its length in the narrowness of the cleft must have prevented its being sloped to reach me. Anyhow, it shot out from the grating like the tongue of a snake, and missed and flew back and flashed again. But the second time I snatched and caught it, and wrenched it away, but not before another had darted ineffectually at me.

I shouted with triumph as I felt the hold of the Selenite resist my pull for a moment and give, and then I was jabbing down through the bars, amidst squeals

[1] I do not remember seeing any wooden things on the moon; doors tables, everything corresponding to our terrestrial joinery was made of metal, and I believe for the most part of gold, which as a metal would, of course, naturally recommend itself—other things being equal —on account of the ease in working it, and its toughness and durability.

from the darkness, and Cavor had snapped off the other spear, and was leaping and flourishing it beside me, and making inefficient jabs. Clang, clang, came up through the grating, and then an axe hurtled through the air and whacked against the rocks beyond, to remind me of the fleshers at the carcasses up the cavern.

I turned, and they were all coming towards us in open order waving their axes. They were short, thick, little beggars, with long arms, strikingly different from the ones we had seen before. If they had not heard of us before, they must have realised the situation with incredible swiftness. I stared at them for a moment, spear in hand. "Guard that grating, Cavor," I cried, howled to intimidate them, and rushed to meet them. Two of them missed with their hatchets, and the rest fled incontinently. Then the two also were sprinting away up the cavern, with hands clenched and heads down. I never saw men run like them!

I knew the spear I had was no good for me. It was thin and flimsy, only effectual for a thrust, and too long for a quick recover. So I only chased the Selenites as far as the first carcass, and stopped there and picked up one of the crowbars that were lying about. It felt comfortingly heavy, and equal to smashing any number of Selenites. I threw away my spear, and picked up a second crowbar for the other hand. I felt five times better than I had with the spear. I shook the two threateningly at the Selenites, who had come to a halt in a little crowd far away up the cavern, and then turned about to look at Cavor.

He was leaping from side to side of the grating, making threatening jabs with his broken spear. That was all right. It would keep the Selenites down —for a time at any rate. I looked up the cavern again. What on earth were we going to do now?

We were cornered in a sort of way already. But these butchers up the cavern had been surprised, they were probably scared, and they had no special weapons, only those little hatchets of theirs. And that way lay escape. Their sturdy little forms—ever so much shorter and thicker than the mooncalf herds—were scattered up the slope in a way that was eloquent of indecision. I had the moral advantage of a mad bull in a street. But for all that, there seemed a tremendous crowd of them. Very probably there was. Those Selenites down the cleft had certainly some infernally long spears. It might be they had other surprises for us... But, confound it! if we charged up the cave we should let them up behind us, and if we didn't those little brutes up the cave would probably get reinforced. Heaven alone knew what tremendous engines of warfare—guns, bombs, terrestrial torpedoes—this unknown world below our feet, this vaster world of which we had only pricked the outer cuticle, might not presently send up to our destruction. It became clear the only thing to do was to charge! It became clearer as the legs of a number of fresh Selenites appeared running down the cavern towards us.

"Bedford!" cried Cavor, and behold! he was halfway between me and the grating.

"Go back!" I cried. "What are you doing—"

"They've got—it's like a gun!"

And struggling in the grating between those defensive spears appeared the head and shoulders of a singularly lean and angular Selenite, bearing some complicated apparatus.

I realised Cavor's utter incapacity for the fight we had in hand. For a moment I hesitated. Then I rushed past him whirling my crowbars, and shouting to confound the aim of the Selenite. He was aiming in the queerest way with the thing against his stomach. "Chuzz!" The thing wasn't a gun; it went off like cross-bow more, and dropped me in the middle of a leap.

I didn't fall down, I simply came down a little shorter than I should have done if I hadn't been hit, and from the feel of my shoulder the thing might have tapped me and glanced off. Then my left hand hit again the shaft, and I perceived there was a sort of spear sticking half through my shoulder. The moment after I got home with the crowbar in my right hand, and hit the Selenite fair and square. He collapsed—he crushed and crumpled—his head smashed like an egg.

I dropped a crowbar, pulled the spear out of my shoulder, and began to jab it down the grating into the darkness. At each jab came a shriek and twitter. Finally I hurled the spear down upon them with all my strength, leapt up, picked up the crowbar again, and started for the multitude up the cavern.

"Bedford!" cried Cavor. "Bedford!" as I flew past him.

I seem to remember his footsteps coming on behind me.

Step, leap ... whack, step, leap... Each leap seemed to last ages. With each, the cave opened out and the number of Selenites visible increased. At first they seemed all running about like ants in a disturbed ant-hill, one or two waving hatchets and coming to meet me, more running away, some bolting sideways into the avenue of carcasses, then presently others came in sight carrying spears, and then others. I saw a most extraordinary thing, all hands and feet, bolting for cover. The cavern grew darker farther up.

Flick! something flew over my head. Flick! As I soared in mid-stride I saw a spear hit and quiver in one of the carcasses to my left. Then, as I came down, one hit the ground before me, and I heard the remote chuzz! with which their things were fired. Flick, flick! for a moment it was a shower. They were volleying!

I stopped dead.

I don't think I thought clearly then. I seem to remember a kind of stereotyped phrase running through my mind: "Zone of fire, seek cover!" I know I made a dash for the space between two of the carcasses, and stood there panting and feeling very wicked.

I looked round for Cavor, and for a moment it seemed as if he had vanished from the world. Then he came out of the darkness between the row of the carcasses and the rocky wall of the cavern. I saw his little face, dark and blue, and shining with perspiration and emotion.

He was saying something, but what it was I did not heed. I had realised that we might work from mooncalf to mooncalf up the cave until we were near enough to charge home. It was charge or nothing. "Come on!" I said, and led the way.

"Bedford!" he cried unavailingly.

My mind was busy as we went up that narrow alley between the dead bodies and the wall of the cavern. The rocks curved about—they could not enfilade us. Though in that narrow space we could not leap, yet with our earth- born strength we were still able to go very much faster than the Selenites. I reckoned we should presently come right among them. Once we were on them, they would be nearly as formidable as black beetles. Only there would first of all be a volley. I thought of a stratagem. I whipped off my flannel jacket as I ran.

"Bedford!" panted Cavor behind me.

I glanced back. "What?" said I.

He was pointing upward over the carcasses. "White light!" he said. "White light again!"

I looked, and it was even so; a faint white ghost of light in the remoter cavern roof. That seemed to give me double strength.

"Keep close," I said. A flat, long Selenite dashed out of the darkness, and squealed and fled. I halted, and stopped Cavor with my hand. I hung my jacket over my crowbar, ducked round the next carcass, dropped jacket and crowbar, showed myself, and darted back.

"Chuzz-flick," just one arrow came. We were close on the Selenites, and they were standing in a crowd, broad, short, and tall together, with a little battery of their shooting implements pointing down the cave. Three or four other arrows followed the first, then their fire ceased.

I stuck out my head, and escaped by a hair's-breadth. This time I drew a dozen shots or more, and heard the Selenites shouting and twittering as if with excitement as they shot. I picked up jacket and crowbar again.

"Now!" said I, and thrust out the jacket.

"Chuzz-zz-zz-zz! Chuzz!" In an instant my jacket had grown a thick beard of arrows, and they were quivering all over the carcass behind us. Instantly I slipped the crowbar out of the jacket, dropped the jacket—for all I know to the contrary it is lying up there in the moon now—and rushed out upon them.

For a minute perhaps it was massacre. I was too fierce to discriminate, and the Selenites were probably too scared to fight. At any rate they made no sort of fight against me. I saw scarlet, as the saying is. I remember I seemed to be wading among those leathery, thin things as a man wades through tall grass, mowing and hitting, first right, then left; smash. Little drops of moisture flew about. I trod on things that crushed and piped and went slippery. The crowd seemed to open and close and flow like water. They seemed to have no combined plan whatever. There were spears flew about me, I was grazed over the ear by one. I was stabbed once in the arm and once in the cheek, but I only found that out afterwards, when the blood had had time to run and cool and feel wet.

What Cavor did I do not know. For a space it seemed that this fighting had lasted for an age, and must needs go on for ever. Then suddenly it was all over, and there was nothing to be seen but the backs of heads bobbing up and down as their owners ran in all directions... I seemed altogether unhurt. I ran forward some paces, shouting, then turned about. I was amazed.

I had come right through them in vast flying strides, they were all behind me, and running hither and thither to hide.

I felt an enormous astonishment at the evaporation of the great fight into which I had hurled myself, and not a little exultation. It did not seem to me that I had discovered the Selenites were unexpectedly flimsy, but that I was unexpectedly strong. I laughed stupidly. This fantastic moon!

I glanced for a moment at the smashed and writhing bodies that were scattered over the cavern floor, with a vague idea of further violence, then hurried on after Cavor.

CHAPTER XVIII - IN THE SUNLIGHT

Presently we saw that the cavern before us opened upon a hazy void. In another moment we had emerged upon a sort of slanting gallery, that projected into a vast circular space, a huge cylindrical pit running vertically up and down. Round this pit the slanting gallery ran without any parapet or protection for a turn and a half, and then plunged high above into the rock again. Somehow it reminded me then one of those spiral turns of the railway through the Saint Gothard. It was all tremendously huge. I can scarcely hope to convey to you the Titanic proportion of all that place, the Titanic effect of it. Our eyes followed up the vast declivity of the pit wall, and overhead and far above we beheld a round opening set with faint stars, and half of the lip about it well nigh blinding with the white light of the sun. At that we cried aloud simultaneously.

"Come on!" I said, leading the way.

"But there?" said Cavor, and very carefully stepped nearer the edge of the gallery. I followed his example, and craned forward and looked down, but I was dazzled by that gleam of light above, and I could see only a bottomless darkness with spectral patches of crimson and purple floating therein. Yet if I could not see, I could hear. Out of this darkness came a sound, a sound like the angry hum one can hear if one puts one's ear outside a hive of bees, a sound out of that enormous hollow, it may be, four miles beneath our feet...

For a moment I listened, then tightened my grip on my crowbar, and led the way up the gallery.

"This must be the shaft we looked down upon," said Cavor. "Under that lid."

"And below there, is where we saw the lights."

"The lights!" said he. "Yes—the lights of the world that now we shall never see."

"We'll come back," I said, for now we had escaped so much I was rashly sanguine that we should recover the sphere.

His answer I did not catch.

"Eh?" I asked.

"It doesn't matter," he answered, and we hurried on in silence.

I suppose that slanting lateral way was four or five miles long, allowing for its curvature, and it ascended at a slope that would have made it almost impossibly steep on earth, but which one strode up easily under lunar conditions. We saw only two Selenites during all that portion of our flight, and directly they became aware of us they ran headlong. It was clear that the knowledge of our strength and

violence had reached them. Our way to the exterior was unexpectedly plain. The spiral gallery straightened into a steeply ascendent tunnel, its floor bearing abundant traces of the mooncalves, and so straight and short in proportion to its vast arch, that no part of it was absolutely dark. Almost immediately it began to lighten, and then far off and high up, and quite blindingly brilliant, appeared its opening on the exterior, a slope of Alpine steepness surmounted by a crest of bayonet shrub, tall and broken down now, and dry and dead, in spiky silhouette against the sun.

And it is strange that we men, to whom this very vegetation had seemed so weird and horrible a little time ago, should now behold it with the emotion a home-coming exile might feel at sight of his native land. We welcomed even the rareness of the air that made us pant as we ran, and which rendered speaking no longer the easy thing that it had been, but an effort to make oneself heard. Larger grew the sunlit circle above us, and larger, and all the nearer tunnel sank into a rim of indistinguishable black. We saw the dead bayonet shrub no longer with any touch of green in it, but brown and dry and thick, and the shadow of its upper branches high out of sight made a densely interlaced pattern upon the tumbled rocks. And at the immediate mouth of the tunnel was a wide trampled space where the mooncalves had come and gone.

We came out upon this space at last into a light and heat that hit and pressed upon us. We traversed the exposed area painfully, and clambered up a slope among the scrub stems, and sat down at last panting in a high place beneath the shadow of a mass of twisted lava. Even in the shade the rock felt hot.

The air was intensely hot, and we were in great physical discomfort, but for all that we were no longer in a nightmare. We seemed to have come to our own province again, beneath the stars. All the fear and stress of our flight through the dim passages and fissures below had fallen from us. That last fight had filled us with an enormous confidence in ourselves so far as the Selenites were concerned. We looked back almost incredulously at the black opening from which we had just emerged. Down there it was, in a blue glow that now in our memories seemed the next thing to absolute darkness, we had met with things like mad mockeries of men, helmet-headed creatures, and had walked in fear before them, and had submitted to them until we could submit no longer. And behold, they had smashed like wax and scattered like chaff, and fled and vanished like the creatures of a dream!

I rubbed my eyes, doubting whether we had not slept and dreamt these things by reason of the fungus we had eaten, and suddenly discovered the blood upon my face, and then that my shirt was sticking painfully to my shoulder and arm.

"Confound it!" I said, gauging my injuries with an investigatory hand, and suddenly that distant tunnel mouth became, as it were, a watching eye.

"Cavor!" I said; "what are they going to do now? And what are we going to do?"

He shook his head, with his eyes fixed upon the tunnel. "How can one tell what they will do?"

"It depends on what they think of us, and I don't see how we can begin to guess that. And it depends upon what they have in reserve. It's as you say, Cavor, we have touched the merest outside of this world. They may have all sorts of things inside here. Even with those shooting things they might make it bad for us...

"Yet after all," I said, "even if we don't find the sphere at once, there is a chance for us. We might hold out. Even through the night. We might go down there again and make a fight for it."

I stared about me with speculative eyes. The character of the scenery had altered altogether by reason of the enormous growth and subsequent drying of the scrub. The crest on which we sat was high, and commanded a wide prospect of the crater landscape, and we saw it now all sere and dry in the late autumn of the lunar afternoon. Rising one behind the other were long slopes and fields of trampled brown where the mooncalves had pastured, and far away in the full blaze of the sun a drove of them basked slumberously, scattered shapes, each with a blot of shadow against it like sheep on the side of a down. But never a sign of a Selenite was to be seen. Whether they had fled on our emergence from the interior passages, or whether they were accustomed to retire after driving out the mooncalves, I cannot guess. At the time I believed the former was the case.

"If we were to set fire to all this stuff," I said, "we might find the sphere among the ashes."

Cavor did not seem to hear me. He was peering under his hand at the stars, that still, in spite of the intense sunlight, were abundantly visible in the sky. "How long do you think we've have been here?" he asked at last.

"Been where?"

"On the moon."

"Two earthly days, perhaps."

"More nearly ten. Do you know, the sun is past its zenith, and sinking in the west. In four days' time or less it will be night."

"But—we've only eaten once!"

"I know that. And—But there are the stars!"

"But why should time seem different because we are on a smaller planet?"

"I don't know. There it is!"

"How does one tell time?"

"Hunger—fatigue—all those things are different. Everything is different—everything. To me it seems that since first we came out of the sphere has been only a question of hours—long hours —at most."

"Ten days," I said; "that leaves—" I looked up at the sun for a moment, and then saw that it was halfway from the zenith to the western edge of things. "Four days! ... Cavor, we mustn't sit here and dream. How do you think we may begin?"

I stood up. "We must get a fixed point we can recognise—we might hoist a flag, or a handkerchief, or something—and quarter the ground, and work round that."

He stood up beside me.

"Yes," he said, "there is nothing for it but to hunt the sphere. Nothing. We may find it—certainly we may find it. And if not—"

"We must keep on looking."

He look this way and that, glanced up at the sky and down at the tunnel, and astonished me by a sudden gesture of impatience. "Oh! but we have done foolishly! To have come to this pass! Think how it might have been, and the things we might have done!"

"We might do something yet."

"Never the thing we might have done. Here below out feet is a world. Think of what that world must be! Think of that machine we saw, and the lid and the shaft! They were just remote outlying things, and those creatures we have seen and fought with no more than ignorant peasants, dwellers in the outskirts, yokels and labourers half akin to brutes. Down below! Caverns beneath caverns, tunnels, structures, ways... It must open out, and be greater and wider and more populous as one descends. Assuredly. Right down at the last the central sea that washes round the core of the moon. Think of its inky waters under the spare lights—if, indeed, their eyes need lights! Think of the cascading tributaries pouring down their channels to feed it! Think of the tides upon its surface, and the rush and swirl of its ebb and flow! perhaps they have ships that go upon it, perhaps down there are mighty cities and swarming ways, and wisdom and order passing the wit of man. And we may die here upon it, and never see the masters who must be—ruling over these things! We may freeze and die here, and the air will freeze and thaw upon us, and then—! Then they will come upon us, come on our stiff and silent bodies, and find the sphere we cannot find, and they will understand at last too late all the thought and effort that ended here in vain!"

His voice for all that speech sounded like the voice of someone heard in a telephone, weak and far away.

"But the darkness," I said.

"One might get over that."

"How?"

"I don't know. How am I to know? One might carry a torch, one might have a lamp—The others—might understand."

He stood for a moment with his hands held down and a rueful face, staring out over the waste that defied him. Then with a gesture of renunciation he turned towards me with proposals for the systematic hunting of the sphere.

"We can return," I said.

He looked about him. "First of all we shall have to get to earth."

"We could bring back lamps to carry and climbing irons, and a hundred necessary things."

"Yes," he said.

"We can take back an earnest of success in this gold."

He looked at my golden crowbars, and said nothing for a space. He stood with his hands clasped behind his back, staring across the crater. At last he signed and spoke. "It was I found the way here, but to find a way isn't always to be master of

a way. If I take my secret back to earth, what will happen? I do not see how I can keep my secret for a year, for even a part of a year. Sooner or later it must come out, even if other men rediscover it. And then ... Governments and powers will struggle to get hither, they will fight against one another, and against these moon people; it will only spread warfare and multiply the occasions of war. In a little while, in a very little while, if I tell my secret, this planet to its deepest galleries will be strewn with human dead. Other things are doubtful, but that is certain. It is not as though man had any use for the moon. What good would the moon be to men? Even of their own planet what have they made but a battle-ground and theatre of infinite folly? Small as his world is, and short as his time, he has still in his little life down there far more than he can do. No! Science has toiled too long forging weapons for fools to use. It is time she held her hand. Let him find it out for himself again—in a thousand years' time."

"There are methods of secrecy," I said.

He looked up at me and smiled. "After all," he said, "why should one worry? There is little chance of our finding the sphere, and down below things are brewing. It's simply the human habit of hoping till we die that makes us think of return. Our troubles are only beginning. We have shown these moon folk violence, we have given them a taste of our quality, and our chances are about as good as a tiger's that has got loose and killed a man in Hyde Park. The news of us must be running down from gallery to gallery, down towards the central parts... No sane beings will ever let us take that sphere back to earth after so much as they have seen of us."

"We aren't improving our chances," said I, "by sitting here."

We stood up side by side.

"After all," he said, "we must separate. We must stick up a handkerchief on these tall spikes here and fasten it firmly, and from this as a centre we must work over the crater. You must go westward, moving out in semicircles to and fro towards the setting sun. You must move first with your shadow on your right until it is at right angles with the direction of your handkerchief, and then with your shadow on your left. And I will do the same to the east. We will look into every gully, examine every skerry of rocks; we will do all we can to find my sphere. If we see the Selenites we will hide from them as well as we can. For drink we must take snow, and if we feel the need of food, we must kill a mooncalf if we can, and eat such flesh as it has—raw—and so each will go his own way."

"And if one of us comes upon the sphere?"

"He must come back to the white handkerchief, and stand by it and signal to the other."

"And if neither?"

Cavor glanced up at the sun. "We go on seeking until the night and cold overtake us."

"Suppose the Selenites have found the sphere and hidden it?"

He shrugged his shoulders.

"Or if presently they come hunting us?"

He made no answer.

"You had better take a club," I said.

He shook his head, and stared away from me across the waste.

But for a moment he did not start. He looked round at me shyly, hesitated. "Au revoir," he said.

I felt an odd stab of emotion. A sense of how we had galled each other, and particularly how I must have galled him, came to me. "Confound it," thought I, "we might have done better!" I was on the point of asking him to shake hands — for that, somehow, was how I felt just then—when he put his feet together and leapt away from me towards the north. He seemed to drift through the air as a dead leaf would do, fell lightly, and leapt again. I stood for a moment watching him, then faced westward reluctantly, pulled myself together, and with something of the feeling of a man who leaps into icy water, selected a leaping point, and plunged forward to explore my solitary half of the moon world. I dropped rather clumsily among rocks, stood up and looked about me, clambered on to a rocky slab, and leapt again...

When presently I looked for Cavor he was hidden from my eyes, but the handkerchief showed out bravely on its headland, white in the blaze of the sun.

I determined not to lose sight of that handkerchief whatever might betide.

CHAPTER XIX - MR. BEDFORD ALONE

In a little while it seemed to me as though I had always been alone on the moon. I hunted for a time with a certain intentness, but the heat was still very great, and the thinness of the air felt like a hoop about one's chest. I came presently into a hollow basin bristling with tall, brown, dry fronds about its edge, and I sat down under these to rest and cool. I intended to rest for only a little while. I put down my clubs beside me, and sat resting my chin on my hands. I saw with a sort of colourless interest that the rocks of the basin, where here and there the crackling dry lichens had shrunk away to show them, were all veined and splattered with gold, that here and there bosses of rounded and wrinkled gold projected from among the litter. What did that matter now? A sort of languor had possession of my limbs and mind, I did not believe for a moment that we should ever find the sphere in that vast desiccated wilderness. I seemed to lack a motive for effort until the Selenites should come. Then I supposed I should exert myself, obeying that unreasonable imperative that urges a man before all things to preserve and defend his life, albeit he may preserve it only to die more painfully in a little while.

Why had we come to the moon?

The thing presented itself to me as a perplexing problem. What is this spirit in man that urges him for ever to depart from happiness and security, to toil, to place himself in danger, to risk even a reasonable certainty of death? It dawned upon me up there in the moon as a thing I ought always to have known, that man is not made simply to go about being safe and comfortable and well fed and amused. Almost any man, if you put the thing to him, not in words, but in the shape of opportunities, will show that he knob as much. Against his interest, against his happiness, he is constantly being driven to do unreasonable things. Some force not himself impels him, and go he must. But why? Why? Sitting there in the midst of that useless moon gold, amidst the things of another world, I took count of all my life. Assuming I was to die a castaway upon the moon, I failed altogether to see what purpose I had served. I got no light on that point, but at any rate it was clearer to me than it had ever been in my life before that I was not serving my own purpose, that all my life I had in truth never served the purposes of my private life. Whose purposes, what purposes, was I serving? ... I ceased to speculate on why we had come to the moon, and took a wider sweep. Why had I come to the earth? Why had I a private life at all? ... I lost myself at last in bottomless speculations...

My thoughts became vague and cloudy, no longer leading in definite directions. I had not felt heavy or weary—I cannot imagine one doing so upon the moon—but I suppose I was greatly fatigued. At any rate I slept.

Slumbering there rested me greatly, I think, and the sun was setting and the violence of the heat abating, through all the time I slumbered. When at last I was roused from my slumbers by a remote clamour, I felt active and capable again. I rubbed my eyes and stretched my arms. I rose to my feet —I was a little stiff— and at once prepared to resume my search. I shouldered my golden clubs, one on each shoulder, and went on out of the ravine of the gold-veined rocks.

The sun was certainly lower, much lower than it had been; the air was very much cooler. I perceived I must have slept some time. It seemed to me that a faint touch of misty blueness hung about the western cliff I leapt to a little boss of rock and surveyed the crater. I could see no signs of mooncalves or Selenites, nor could I see Cavor, but I could see my handkerchief far off, spread out on its thicket of thorns. I looked bout me, and then leapt forward to the next convenient view-point.

I beat my round in a semicircle, and back again in a still remoter crescent. It was very fatiguing and hopeless. The air was really very much cooler, and it seemed to me that the shadow under the westward cliff was growing broad. Ever and again I stopped and reconnoitred, but there was no sign of Cavor, no sign of Selenites; and it seemed to me the mooncalves must have been driven into the interior again—I could see none of them. I became more and more desirous of seeing Cavor. The winged outline of the sun had sunk now, until it was scarcely the distance of its diameter from the rim of the sky. I was oppressed by the idea that the Selenites would presently close their lids and valves, and shut us out under the inexorable onrush of the lunar night. It seemed to me high time that he abandoned his search, and that we took counsel together. I felt how urgent it was that we should decide soon upon our course. We had failed to find the sphere, we no longer had time to seek it, and once these valves were closed with us outside, we were lost men. The great night of space would descend upon us—that blackness of the void which is the only absolute death. All my being shrank from that approach. We must get into the moon again, though we were slain in doing it. I was haunted by a vision of our freezing to death, of our hammering with our last strength on the valve of the great pit.

I took no thought any more of the sphere. I thought only of finding Cavor again. I was half inclined to go back into the moon without him, rather than seek him until it was too late. I was already half-way back towards our handkerchief, when suddenly—

I saw the sphere!

I did not find it so much as it found me. It was lying much farther to the westward than I had gone, and the sloping rays of the sinking sun reflected from its glass had suddenly proclaimed its presence in a dazzling beam. For an instant I thought this was some new device of the Selenites against us, and then I understood.

I threw up my arms, shouted a ghostly shout, and set off in vast leaps towards it. I missed one of my leaps and dropped into a deep ravine and twisted my ankle, and after that I stumbled at almost every leap. I was in a state of hysterical agitation, trembling violently, and quite breathless long before I got to it. Three times at least I had to stop with my hands resting on my side and in spite of the thin dryness of the air, the perspiration was wet upon my face.

I thought of nothing but the sphere until I reached it, I forgot even my trouble of Cavor's whereabouts. My last leap flung me with my hands hard against its glass; then I lay against it panting, and trying vainly to shout, "Cavor! here is the sphere!" When I had recovered a little I peered through the thick glass, and the things inside seemed tumbled. I stooped to peer closer. Then I attempted to get in. I had to hoist it over a little to get my head through the manhole. The screw stopper was inside, and I could see now that nothing had been touched, nothing had suffered. It lay there as we had left it when we had dropped out amidst the snow. For a time I was wholly occupied in making and remaking this inventory. I found I was trembling violently. It was good to see that familiar dark interior again! I cannot tell you how good. Presently I crept inside and sat down among the things. I looked through the glass at the moon world and shivered. I placed my gold clubs upon the table, and sought out and took a little food; not so much because I wanted it, but because it was there. Then it occurred to me that it was time to go out and signal for Cavor. But I did not go out and signal for Cavor forthwith. Something held me to the sphere.

After all, everything was coming right. There would be still time for us to get more of the magic stone that gives one mastery over men. Away there, close handy, was gold for the picking up; and the sphere would travel as well half full of gold as though it were empty. We could go back now, masters of ourselves and our world, and then—

I roused myself at last, and with an effort got myself out of the sphere. I shivered as I emerged, for the evening air was growing very cold. I stood in the hollow staring about me. I scrutinised the bushes round me very carefully before I leapt to the rocky shelf hard by, and took once more what had been my first leap in the moon. But now I made it with no effort whatever.

The growth and decay of the vegetation had gone on apace, and the whole aspect of the rocks had changed, but still it was possible to make out the slope on which the seeds had germinated, and the rocky mass from which we had taken our first view of the crater. But the spiky shrub on the slope stood brown and sere now, and thirty feet high, and cast long shadows that stretched out of sight, and the little seeds that clustered in its upper branches were brown and ripe. Its work was done, and it was brittle and ready to fall and crumple under the freezing air, so soon as the nightfall came. And the huge cacti, that had swollen as we watched them, had long since burst and scattered their spores to the four quarters of the moon. Amazing little corner in the universe—the landing place of men!

Some day, thought I, I will have an inscription standing there right in the midst of the hollow. It came to me, if only this teeming world within knew of the full import of the moment, how furious its tumult would become!

But as yet it could scarcely be dreaming of the significance of our coming. For if it did, the crater would surely be an uproar of pursuit, instead of as still as death! I looked about for some place from which I might signal Cavor, and saw that same patch of rock to which he had leapt from my present standpoint, still bare and barren in the sun. For a moment I hesitated at going so far from the sphere. Then with a pang of shame at that hesitation, I leapt...

From this vantage point I surveyed the crater again. Far away at the top of the enormous shadow I cast was the little white handkerchief fluttering on the bushes. It was very little and very far, and Cavor was not in sight. It seemed to me that by this time he ought to be looking for me. That was the agreement. But he was nowhere to be seen.

I stood waiting and watching, hands shading my eyes, expecting every moment to distinguish him. Very probably I stood there for quite a long time. I tried to shout, and was reminded of the thinness of the air. I made an undecided step back towards the sphere. But a lurking dread of the Selenites made me hesitate to signal my whereabouts by hoisting one of our sleeping- blankets on to the adjacent scrub. I searched the crater again.

It had an effect of emptiness that chilled me. And it was still. Any sound from the Selenites in the world beneath had died away. It was as still as death. Save for the faint stir of the shrub about me in the little breeze that was rising, there was no sound nor shadow of a sound. And the breeze blew chill.

Confound Cavor!

I took a deep breath. I put my hands to the sides of my mouth. "Cavor!" I bawled, and the sound was like some manikin shouting far away.

I looked at the handkerchief, I looked behind me at the broadening shadow of the westward cliff I looked under my hand at the sun. It seemed to me that almost visibly it was creeping down the sky. I felt I must act instantly if I was to save Cavor. I whipped off my vest and flung it as a mark on the sere bayonets of the shrubs behind me, and then set off in a straight line towards the handkerchief. Perhaps it was a couple of miles away—a matter of a few hundred leaps and strides. I have already told how one seemed to hang through those lunar leaps. In each suspense I sought Cavor, and marvelled why he should be hidden. In each leap I could feel the sun setting behind me. Each time I touched the ground I was tempted to go back.

A last leap and I was in the depression below our handkerchief, a stride, and I stood on our former vantage point within arms' reach of it. I stood up straight and scanned the world about me, between its lengthening bars of shadow. Far away, down a long declivity, was the opening of the tunnel up which we had fled, and my shadow reached towards it, stretched towards it, and touched it, like a finger of the night.

Not a sign of Cavor, not a sound in all the stillness, only the stir and waving of the scrub and of the shadows increased. And suddenly and violently I shivered. "Cav—" I began, and realised once more the uselessness of the human voice in that thin air. Silence. The silence of death.

Then it was my eye caught something—a little thing lying, perhaps fifty yards away down the slope, amidst a litter of bent and broken branches. What was it? I knew, and yet for some reason I would not know. I went nearer to it. It was the little cricket-cap Cavor had worn. I did not touch it, I stood looking at it.

I saw then that the scattered branches about it had been forcibly smashed and trampled. I hesitated, stepped forward, and picked it up.

I stood with Cavor's cap in my hand, staring at the trampled reeds and thorns about me. On some, of them were little smears of something dark, something that I dared not touch. A dozen yards away, perhaps, the rising breeze dragged something into view, something small and vividly white.

It was a little piece of paper crumpled tightly, as though it had been clutched tightly. I picked it up, and on it were smears of red. My eye caught faint pencil marks. I smoothed it out, and saw uneven and broken writing ending at last in a crooked streak up on the paper.

I set myself to decipher this.

"I have been injured about the knee, I think my kneecap is hurt, and I cannot run or crawl," it began—pretty distinctly written.

Then less legibly: "They have been chasing me for some time, and it is only a question of"—the word "time" seemed to have been written here and erased in favour of something illegible—"before they get me. They are beating all about me."

Then the writing became convulsive. "I can hear them," I guessed the tracing meant, and then it was quite unreadable for a space. Then came a little string of words that were quite distinct: "a different sort of Selenite altogether, who appears to be directing the—" The writing became a mere hasty confusion again.

"They have larger brain cases—much larger, and slenderer bodies, and very short legs. They make gentle noises, and move with organized deliberation...

"And though I am wounded and helpless here, their appearance still gives me hope." That was like Cavor. "They have not shot at me or attempted... injury. I intend—"

Then came the sudden streak of the pencil across the paper, and on the back and edges—blood!

And as I stood there stupid, and perplexed, with this dumbfounding relic in my hand, something very soft and light and chill touched my hand for a moment and ceased to be, and then a thing, a little white speck, drifted athwart a shadow. It was a tiny snowflake, the first snowflake, the herald of the night.

I looked up with a start, and the sky had darkened almost to blackness, and was thick with a gathering multitude of coldly watchful stars. I looked eastward, and the light of that shrivelled world was touched with sombre bronze; westward, and the sun robbed now by a thickening white mist of half its heat and splendour,

was touching the crater rim, was sinking out of sight, and all the shrubs and jagged and tumbled rocks stood out against it in a bristling disorder of black shapes. Into the great lake of darkness westward, a vast wreath of mist was sinking. A cold wind set all the crater shivering. Suddenly, for a moment, I was in a puff of falling snow, and all the world about me gray and dim.

And then it was I heard, not loud and penetrating as at first, but faint and dim like a dying voice, that tolling, that same tolling that had welcomed the coming of the day: Boom!... Boom!... Boom!...

It echoed about the crater, it seemed to throb with the throbbing of the greater stars, the blood-red crescent of the sun's disc sank as it tolled out: Boom!... Boom!... Boom!...

What had happened to Cavor? All through that tolling I stood there stupidly, and at last the tolling ceased.

And suddenly the open mouth of the tunnel down below there, shut like an eye and vanished out of sight.

Then indeed was I alone.

Over me, around me, closing in on me, embracing me ever nearer, was the Eternal; that which was before the beginning, and that which triumphs over the end; that enormous void in which all light and life and being is but the thin and vanishing splendour of a falling star, the cold, the stillness, the silence —the infinite and final Night of space.

The sense of solitude and desolation became the sense of an overwhelming presence that stooped towards me, that almost touched me.

"No," I cried. "No! Not yet! not yet! Wait! Wait! Oh, wait!" My voice went up to a shriek. I flung the crumpled paper from me, scrambled back to the crest to take my bearings, and then, with all the will that was in me, leapt out towards the mark I had left, dim and distant now in the very margin of the shadow.

Leap, leap, leap, and each leap was seven ages.

Before me the pale serpent-girdled section of the sun sank and sank, and the advancing shadow swept to seize the sphere before I could reach it. I was two miles away, a hundred leaps or more, and the air about me was thinning out as it thins under an air-pump, and the cold was gripping at my joints. But had I died, I should have died leaping. Once, and then again my foot slipped on the gathering snow as I leapt and shortened my leap; once I fell short into bushes that crashed and smashed into dusty chips and nothingness, and once I stumbled as I dropped and rolled head over heels into a gully, and rose bruised and bleeding and confused as to my direction.

But such incidents were as nothing to the intervals, those awful pauses when one drifted through the air towards that pouring tide of night. My breathing made a piping noise, and it was as though knives were whirling in my lungs. My heart seemed to beat against the top of my brain. "Shall I reach it? O Heaven! Shall I reach it?"

My whole being became anguish.

"Lie down!" screamed my pain and despair; "lie down!"

The nearer I struggled, the more awfully remote it seemed. I was numb, I stumbled, I bruised and cut myself and did not bleed.

It was in sight.

I fell on all fours, and my lungs whooped.

I crawled. The frost gathered on my lips, icicles hung from my moustache, I was white with the freezing atmosphere.

I was a dozen yards from it. My eyes had become dim. "Lie down!" screamed despair; "lie down!"

I touched it, and halted. "Too late!" screamed despair; "lie down!"

I fought stiffly with it. I was on the manhole lip, a stupefied, half- dead being. The snow was all about me. I pulled myself in. There lurked within a little warmer air.

The snowflakes—the airflakes—danced in about me, as I tried with chilling hands to thrust the valve in and spun it tight and hard. I sobbed. "I will," I chattered in my teeth. And then, with fingers that quivered and felt brittle, I turned to the shutter studs.

As I fumbled with the switches—for I had never controlled them before—I could see dimly through the steaming glass the blazing red streamers of the sinking sun, dancing and flickering through the snowstorm, and the black forms of the scrub thickening and bending and breaking beneath the accumulating snow. Thicker whirled the snow and thicker, black against the light. What if even now the switches overcame me? Then something clicked under my hands, and in an instant that last vision of the moon world was hidden from my eyes. I was in the silence and darkness the inter-planetary sphere.

CHAPTER XX - MR. BEDFORD IN INFINITE SPACE

It was almost as though I had been killed. Indeed, I could imagine a man suddenly and violently killed would feel very much as I did. One moment, a passion of agonising existence and fear; the next darkness and stillness, neither light nor life nor sun, moon nor stars, the blank infinite. Although the thing was done by my own act, although I had already tasted this very of effect in Cavor's company, I felt astonished, dumbfounded, and overwhelmed. I seemed to be borne upward into an enormous darkness. My fingers floated off the studs, I hung as if I were annihilated, and at last very softly and gently I came against the bale and the golden chain, and the crowbars that had drifted to the middle of the sphere.

I do not know how long that drifting took. In the sphere of course, even more than on the moon, one's earthly time sense was ineffectual. At the touch of the bale it was as if I had awakened from a dreamless sleep. I immediately perceived that if I wanted to keep awake and alive I must get a light or open a window, so as to get a grip of something with my eyes. And besides, I was cold. I kicked off from the bale, therefore, clawed on to the thin cords within the glass, crawled along until I got to the manhole rim, and so got my bearings for the light and blind studs, took a shove off, and flying once round the bale, and getting a scare from something big and flimsy that was drifting loose, I got my hand on the cord quite close to the studs, and reached them. I lit the little lamp first of all to see what it was I had collided with, and discovered that old copy of *Lloyd's News* had slipped its moorings, and was adrift in the void. That brought me out of the infinite to my own proper dimensions again. It made me laugh and pant for a time, and suggested the idea of a little oxygen from one of the cylinders. After that I lit the heater until I felt warm, and then I took food. Then I set to work in a very gingerly fashion on the Cavorite blinds, to see if I could guess by any means how the sphere was travelling.

The first blind I opened I shut at once, and hung for a time flattened and blinded by the sunlight that had hit me. After thinking a little I started upon the windows at right angles to this one, and got the huge crescent moon and the little crescent earth behind it, the second time. I was amazed to find how far I was from the moon. I had reckoned that not only should I have little or none of the "kick-off" that the earth's atmosphere had given us at our start, but that the tangential "fly off" of the moon's spin would be at least twenty-eight times less than the earth's. I had expected to discover myself hanging over our crater, and on the edge

of the night, but all that was now only a part of the outline of the white crescent that filled the sky. And Cavor —?

He was already infinitesimal.

I tried to imagine what could have happened to him. But at that time I could think of nothing but death. I seemed to see him, bent and smashed at the foot of some interminably high cascade of blue. And all about him the stupid insects stared...

Under the inspiring touch of the drifting newspaper I became practical again for a while. It was quite clear to me that what I had to do was to get back to earth, but as far as I could see I was drifting away from it. Whatever had happened to Cavor, even if he was still alive, which seemed to me incredible after that blood-stained scrap, I was powerless to help him. There he was, living or dead behind the mantle of that rayless night, and there he must remain at least until I could summon our fellow men to his assistance. Should I do that? Something of the sort I had in my mind; to come back to earth if it were possible, and then as maturer consideration might determine, either to show and explain the sphere to a few discreet persons, and act with them, or else to keep my secret, sell my gold, obtain weapons, provisions, and an assistant, and return with these advantages to deal on equal terms with the flimsy people of the moon, to rescue Cavor, if that were still possible, and at any rate to procure a sufficient supply of gold to place my subsequent proceedings on a firmer basis. But that was hoping far; I had first to get back.

I set myself to decide just exactly how the return to earth could be contrived. As I struggled with that problem I ceased to worry about what I should do when I got there. At last my only care was to get back.

I puzzled out at last that my best chance would be to drop back towards the moon as near as I dared in order to gather velocity, then to shut my windows, and fly behind it, and when I was past to open my earthward windows, and so get off at a good pace homeward. But whether I should ever reach the earth by that device, or whether I might not simply find myself spinning about it in some hyperbolic or parabolic curve or other, I could not tell. Later I had a happy inspiration, and by opening certain windows to the moon, which had appeared in the sky in front of the earth, I turned my course aside so as to head off the earth, which it had become evident to me I must pass behind without some such expedient. I did a very great deal of complicated thinking over these problems—for I am no mathematician—and in the end I am certain it was much more my good luck than my reasoning that enabled me to hit the earth. Had I known then, as I know now, the mathematical chances there were against me, I doubt if I should have troubled even to touch the studs to make any attempt. And having puzzled out what I considered to be the thing to do, I opened all my moonward windows, and squatted down—the effort lifted me for a time some feet or so into the air, and I hung there in the oddest way—and waited for the crescent to get bigger and bigger until I felt I was near enough for safety. Then I would shut the windows, fly

past the moon with the velocity I had got from it—if I did not smash upon it — and so go on towards the earth.

And that is what I did.

At last I felt my moonward start was sufficient. I shut out the sight of the moon from my eyes, and in a state of mind that was, I now recall, incredibly free from anxiety or any distressful quality, I sat down to begin a vigil in that little speck of matter in infinite space that would last until I should strike the earth. The heater had made the sphere tolerably warm, the air had been refreshed by the oxygen, and except for that faint congestion of the head that was always with me while I was away from earth, I felt entire physical comfort. I had extinguished the light again, lest it should fail me in the end; I was in darkness, save for the earthshine and the glitter of the stars below me. Everything was so absolutely silent and still that I might indeed have been the only being in the universe, and yet, strangely enough, I had no more feeling of loneliness or fear than if I had been lying in bed on earth. Now, this seems all the stranger to me, since during my last hours in that crater of the moon, the sense of my utter loneliness had been an agony...

Incredible as it will seem, this interval of time that I spent in space has no sort of proportion to any other interval of time in my life. Sometimes it seemed as though I sat through immeasurable eternities like some god upon a lotus leaf, and again as though there was a momentary pause as I leapt from moon to earth. In truth, it was altogether some weeks of earthly time. But I had done with care and anxiety, hunger or fear, for that space. I floated, thinking with a strange breadth and freedom of all that we had undergone, and of all my life and motives, and the secret issues of my being. I seemed to myself to have grown greater and greater, to have lost all sense of movement; to be floating amidst the stars, and always the sense of earth's littleness and the infinite littleness of my life upon it, was implicit in my thoughts.

I can't profess to explain the things that happened in my mind. No doubt they could all be traced directly or indirectly to the curious physical conditions under which I was living. I set them down here just for what they are worth, and without any comment. The most prominent quality of it was a pervading doubt of my own identity. I became, if I may so express it, dissociate from Bedford; I looked down on Bedford as a trivial, incidental thing with which I chanced to be connected. I saw Bedford in many relations —as an ass or as a poor beast, where I had hitherto been inclined to regard him with a quiet pride as a very spirited or rather forcible person. I saw him not only as an ass, but as the son of many generations of asses. I reviewed his school-days and his early manhood, and his first encounter with love, very much as one might review the proceedings of an ant in the sand. Something of that period of lucidity I regret still hangs about me, and I doubt if I shall ever recover the full-bodied self satisfaction of my early days. But at the time the thing was not in the least painful, because I had that extraordinary persuasion that, as a matter of fact, I was no more Bedford than I was any one else, but only a mind floating in the still serenity of space. Why should I be disturbed about this Bedford's shortcomings? I was not responsible for him or them.

For a time I struggled against this really very grotesque delusion. I tried to summon the memory of vivid moments, of tender or intense emotions to my assistance; I felt that if I could recall one genuine twinge of feeling the growing severance would be stopped. But I could not do it. I saw Bedford rushing down Chancery Lane, hat on the back of his head, coat tails flying out, en route for his public examination. I saw him dodging and bumping against, and even saluting, other similar little creatures in that swarming gutter of people. Me? I saw Bedford that same evening in the sitting-room of a certain lady, and his hat was on the table beside him, and it wanted brushing badly, and he was in tears. Me? I saw him with that lady in various attitudes and emotions—I never felt so detached before... I saw him hurrying off to Lympne to write a play, and accosting Cavor, and in his shirt sleeves working at the sphere, and walking out to Canterbury because he was afraid to come! Me? I did not believe it.

I still reasoned that all this was hallucination due to my solitude, and the fact that I had lost all weight and sense of resistance. I endeavoured to recover that sense by banging myself about the sphere, by pinching my hands and clasping them together. Among other things, I lit the light, captured that torn copy of *Lloyd's*, and read those convincingly realistic advertisements about the Cutaway bicycle, and the gentleman of private means, and the lady in distress who was selling those "forks and spoons." There was no doubt *they* existed surely enough, and, said I, "This is your world, and you are Bedford, and you are going back to live among things like that for all the rest of your life." But the doubts within me could still argue: "It is not you that is reading, it is Bedford, but you are not Bedford, you know. That's just where the mistake comes in."

"Confound it!" I cried; "and if I am not Bedford, what am I?"

But in that direction no light was forthcoming, though the strangest fancies came drifting into my brain, queer remote suspicions, like shadows seen from away. Do you know, I had a sort of idea that really I was something quite outside not only the world, but all worlds, and out of space and time, and that this poor Bedford was just a peephole through which I looked at life?...

Bedford! However I disavowed him, there I was most certainly bound up with him, and I knew that wherever or whatever I might be, I must needs feel the stress of his desires, and sympathise with all his joys and sorrows until his life should end. And with the dying of Bedford—what then?...

Enough of this remarkable phase of my experiences! I tell it here simply to show how one's isolation and departure from this planet touched not only the functions and feeling of every organ of the body, but indeed also the very fabric of the mind, with strange and unanticipated disturbances. All through the major portion of that vast space journey I hung thinking of such immaterial things as these, hung dissociated and apathetic, a cloudy megalomaniac, as it were, amidst the stars and planets in the void of space; and not only the world to which I was returning, but the blue-lit caverns of the Selenites, their helmet faces, their gigantic and wonderful machines, and the fate of Cavor, dragged helpless into that world, seemed infinitely minute and altogether trivial things to me.

Until at last I began to feel the pull of the earth upon my being, drawing me back again to the life that is real for men. And then, indeed, it grew clearer and clearer to me that I was quite certainly Bedford after all, and returning after amazing adventures to this world of ours, and with a life that I was very likely to lose in this return. I set myself to puzzle out the conditions under which I must fall to earth.

CHAPTER XXI - MR. BEDFORD AT LITTLESTONE

My line of flight was about parallel with the surface as I came into the upper air. The temperature of sphere began to rise forthwith. I knew it behoved me to drop at once. Far below me, in a darkling twilight, stretched a great expanse of sea. I opened every window I could, and fell—out of sunshine into evening, and out of evening into night. Vaster grew the earth and vaster, swallowing up the stars, and the silvery translucent starlit veil of cloud it wore spread out to catch me. At last the world seemed no longer a sphere but flat, and then concave. It was no longer a planet in the sky, but the world of Man. I shut all but an inch or so of earthward window, and dropped with a slackening velocity. The broadening water, now so near that I could see the dark glitter of the waves, rushed up to meet me. The sphere became very hot. I snapped the last strip of window, and sat scowling and biting my knuckles, waiting for the impact...

The sphere hit the water with a huge splash: it must have sent it fathoms high. At the splash I flung the Cavorite shutters open. Down I went, but slower and slower, and then I felt the sphere pressing against my feet, and so drove up again as a bubble drives. And at the last I was floating and rocking upon the surface of the sea, and my journey in space was at an end.

The night was dark and overcast. Two yellow pinpoints far away showed the passing of a ship, and nearer was a red glare that came and went. Had not the electricity of my glow-lamp exhausted itself, I could have got picked up that night. In spite of the inordinate fatigue I was beginning to feel, I was excited now, and for a time hopeful, in a feverish, impatient way, that so my travelling might end.

But at last I ceased to move about, and sat, wrists on knees, staring at a distant red light. It swayed up and down, rocking, rocking. My excitement passed. I realised I had yet to spend another night at least in the sphere. I perceived myself infinitely heavy and fatigued. And so I fell asleep.

A change in my rhythmic motion awakened me. I peered through the refracting glass, and saw that I had come aground upon a huge shallow of sand. Far away I seemed to see houses and trees, and seaward a curve, vague distortion of a ship hung between sea and sky.

I stood up and staggered. My one desire was to emerge. The manhole was upward, and I wrestled with the screw. Slowly I opened the manhole. At last the air was singing in again as once it had sung out. But this time I did not wait until the

pressure was adjusted. In another moment I had the weight of the window on my hands, and I was open, wide open, to the old familiar sky of earth.

The air hit me on the chest so that I gasped. I dropped the glass screw. I cried out, put my hands to my chest, and sat down. For a time I was in pain. Then I took deep breaths. At last I could rise and move about again.

I tried to thrust my head through the manhole, and the sphere rolled over. It was as though something had lugged my head down directly it emerged. I ducked back sharply, or I should have been pinned face under water. After some wriggling and shoving I managed to crawl out upon sand, over which the retreating waves still came and went.

I did not attempt to stand up. It seemed to me that my body must be suddenly changed to lead. Mother Earth had her grip on me now—no Cavorite intervening. I sat down heedless of the water that came over my feet.

It was dawn, a gray dawn, rather overcast but showing here and there a long patch of greenish gray. Some way out a ship was lying at anchor, a pale silhouette of a ship with one yellow light. The water came rippling in in long shallow waves. Away to the right curved the land, a shingle bank with little hovels, and at last a lighthouse, a sailing mark and a point. Inland stretched a space of level sand, broken here and there by pools of water, and ending a mile away perhaps in a low shore of scrub. To the north-east some isolated watering-place was visible, a row of gaunt lodging-houses, the tallest things that I could see on earth, dull dabs against the brightening sky. What strange men can have reared these vertical piles in such an amplitude of space I do not know. There they are, like pieces of Brighton lost in the waste.

For a long time I sat there, yawning and rubbing my face. At last I struggled to rise. It made me feel that I was lifting a weight. I stood up.

I stared at the distant houses. For the first time since our starvation in the crater I thought of earthly food. "Bacon," I whispered, "eggs. Good toast and good coffee... And how the devil am I going to all this stuff to Lympne?" I wondered where I was. It was an east shore anyhow, and I had seen Europe before I dropped.

I heard footsteps crunching in the sand, and a little round-faced, friendly-looking man in flannels, with a bathing towel wrapped about his shoulders, and his bathing dress over his arm, appeared up the beach. I knew instantly that I must be in England. He was staring most intently at the sphere and me. He advanced staring. I dare say I looked a ferocious savage enough —dirty, unkempt, to an indescribable degree; but it did not occur to me at the time. He stopped at a distance of twenty yards. "Hul-lo, my man!" he said doubtfully.

"Hullo yourself!" said I.

He advanced, reassured by that. "What on earth is that thing?" he asked.

"Can you tell me where I am?" I asked.

"That's Littlestone," he said, pointing to the houses; "and that's Dungeness! Have you just landed? What's that thing you've got? Some sort of machine?"

"Yes."

"Have you floated ashore? Have you been wrecked or something? What is it?"

I meditated swiftly. I made an estimate of the little man's appearance as he drew nearer. "By Jove!" he said, "you've had a time of it! I thought you —Well— Where were you cast away? Is that thing a sort of floating thing for saving life?"

I decided to take that line for the present. I made a few vague affirmatives. "I want help," I said hoarsely. "I want to get some stuff up the beach—stuff I can't very well leave about." I became aware of three other pleasant-looking young men with towels, blazers, and straw hats, coming down the sands towards me. Evidently the early bathing section of this Littlestone.

"Help!" said the young man: "rather!" He became vaguely active. "What particularly do you want done?" He turned round and gesticulated. The three young men accelerated their pace. In a minute they there about me, plying me with questions I was indisposed to answer. "I'll tell all that later," I said. "I'm dead beat. I'm a rag."

"Come up to the hotel," said the foremost little man. "We'll look after that thing there."

I hesitated. "I can't," I said. "In that sphere there's two big bars of gold."

They looked incredulously at one another, then at me with a new inquiry. I went to the sphere, stooped, crept in, and presently they had the Selenites' crowbars and the broken chain before them. If I had not been so horribly fagged I could have laughed at them. It was like kittens round a beetle. They didn't know what to do with the stuff. The fat little man stooped and lifted the end of one of the bars, and then dropped it with a grunt. Then they all did.

"It's lead, or gold!" said one.

"Oh, it's gold!" said another.

"Gold, right enough," said the third.

Then they all stared at me, and then they all stared at the ship lying at anchor.

"I say!" cried the little man. "But where did you get that?"

I was too tired to keep up a lie. "I got it in the moon."

I saw them stare at one another.

"Look here!" said I, "I'm not going to argue now. Help me carry these lumps of gold up to the hotel—I guess, with rests, two of you can manage one, and I'll trail this chain thing—and I'll tell you more when I've had some food."

"And how about that thing?"

"It won't hurt there," I said. "Anyhow—confound it!—it must stop there now. If the tide comes up, it will float all right."

And in a state of enormous wonderment, these young men most obediently hoisted my treasures on their shoulders, and with limbs that felt like lead I headed a sort of procession towards that distant fragment of "sea-front." Half- way there we were reinforced by two awe-stricken little girls with spades, and later a lean little boy, with a penetrating sniff, appeared. He was, I remember, wheeling a bicycle, and he accompanied us at a distance of about a hundred yards on our right flank, and then I suppose, gave us up as uninteresting, mounted his bicycle and rode off over the level sands in the direction of the sphere.

I glanced back after him.

"He won't touch it," said the stout young man reassuringly, and I was only too willing to be reassured.

At first something of the gray of the morning was in my mind, but presently the sun disengaged itself from the level clouds of the horizon and lit the world, and turned the leaden sea to glittering waters. My spirits rose. A sense of the vast importance of the things I had done and had yet to do came with the sunlight into my mind. I laughed aloud as the foremost man staggered under my gold. When indeed I took my place in the world, how amazed the world would be!

If it had not been for my inordinate fatigue, the landlord of the Littlestone hotel would have been amusing, as he hesitated between my gold and my respectable company on the one and my filthy appearance on the other. But at last I found myself in a terrestrial bathroom once more with warm water to wash myself with, and a change of raiment, preposterously small indeed, but anyhow clean, that the genial little man had lent me. He lent me a razor too, but I could not screw up my resolution to attack even the outposts of the bristling beard that covered my face.

I sat down to an English breakfast and ate with a sort of languid appetite—an appetite many weeks old and very decrepit—and stirred myself to answer the questions of the four young men. And I told them the truth.

"Well," said I, "as you press me—I got it in the moon."

"The moon?"

"Yes, the moon in the sky."

"But how do you mean?"

"What I say, confound it!"

"Then you have just come from the moon?"

"Exactly! through space—in that ball." And I took a delicious mouthful of egg. I made a private note that when I went back to the moon I would take a box of eggs.

I could see clearly that they did not believe one word what I told them, but evidently they considered me the most respectable liar they had ever met. They glanced at one another, and then concentrated the fire of their eyes on me. I fancy they expected a clue to me in the way I helped myself to salt. They seemed to find something significant in my peppering my egg. These strangely shaped masses of gold they had staggered under held their minds. There the lumps lay in front of me, each worth thousands of pounds, and as impossible for any one to steal as a house or a piece of land. As I looked at their curious faces over my coffee-cup, I realised something of the enormous wilderness of explanations into which I should have to wander to render myself comprehensible again.

"You don't really mean—" began the youngest young man, in the tone of one who speaks to an obstinate child.

"Just pass me that toast-rack," I said, and shut him up completely.

"But look here, I say," began one of the others. "We're not going to believe that, you know."

"Ah, well," said I, and shrugged my shoulders.

"He doesn't want to tell us," said the youngest young man in a stage aside; and then, with an appearance of great sang-froid, "You don't mind if I take a cigarette?"

I waved him a cordial assent, and proceeded with my breakfast. Two of the others went and looked out of the farther window and talked inaudibly. I was struck by a thought. "The tide," I said, "is running out?"

There was a pause, a doubt who should answer me.

"It's near the ebb," said the fat little man.

"Well, anyhow," I said, "it won't float far."

I decapitated my third egg, and began a little speech. "Look here," I said. "Please don't imagine I'm surly or telling you uncivil lies, or anything of that sort. I'm forced almost, to be a little short and mysterious. I can quite understand this is as queer as it can be, and that your imaginations must be going it. I can assure you, you're in at a memorable time. But I can't make it clear to you now—it's impossible. I give you my word of honour I've come from the moon, and that's all I can tell you... All the same, I'm tremendously obliged to you, you know, tremendously. I hope that my manner hasn't in any way given you offence."

"Oh, not in the least!" said the youngest young man affably. "We can quite understand," and staring hard at me all the time, he heeled his chair back until it very nearly upset, and recovered with some exertion. "Not a bit of it," said the fat young man.

"Don't you imagine that!" and they all got up and dispersed, and walked about and lit cigarettes, and generally tried to show they were perfectly amiable and disengaged, and entirely free from the slightest curiosity about me and the sphere. "I'm going to keep an eye on that ship out there all the same," I heard one of them remarking in an undertone. If only they could have forced themselves to it, they would, I believe, even have gone out and left me. I went on with my third egg.

"The weather," the fat little man remarked presently, "has been immense, has it not? I don't know when we have had such a summer."

Phoo-whizz! Like a tremendous rocket!

And somewhere a window was broken...

"What's that?" said I.

"It isn't—?" cried the little man, and rushed to the corner window.

All the others rushed to the window likewise. I sat staring at them.

Suddenly I leapt up, knocked over my third egg, rushed for the window also. I had just thought of something. "Nothing to be seen there," cried the little man, rushing for the door.

"It's that boy!" I cried, bawling in hoarse fury; "it's that accursed boy!" and turning about I pushed the waiter aside—he was just bring me some more toast—and rushed violently out of the room and down and out upon the queer little esplanade in front of the hotel.

The sea, which had been smooth, was rough now with hurrying cat's-paws, and all about where the sphere had been was tumbled water like the wake of a

ship. Above, a little puff of cloud whirled like dispersing smoke, and the three or four people on the beach were bring up with interrogative faces towards the point of that unexpected report. And that was all! Boots and waiter and the four young men in blazers came rushing out behind me. Shouts came from windows and doors, and all sorts of worrying people came into sight—agape.

For a time I stood there, too overwhelmed by this new development to think of the people.

At first I was too stunned to see the thing as any definite disaster —I was just stunned, as a man is by some accidental violent blow. It is only afterwards he begins to appreciate his specific injury.

"Good Lord!"

I felt as though somebody was pouring funk out of a can down the back of my neck. My legs became feeble. I had got the first intimation of what the disaster meant for me. There was that confounded boy—sky high! I was utterly left. There was the gold in the coffee-room—my only possession on earth. How would it all work out? The general effect was of a gigantic unmanageable confusion.

"I say," said the voice of the little man behind. "I say, you know."

I wheeled about, and there were twenty or thirty people, a sort of irregular investment of people, all bombarding me with dumb interrogation, with infinite doubt and suspicion. I felt the compulsion of their eyes intolerably. I groaned aloud.

"I *can't*," I shouted. "I tell you I can't! I'm not equal to it! You must puzzle and—and be damned to you!"

I gesticulated convulsively. He receded a step as though I had threatened him. I made a bolt through them into the hotel. I charged back into the coffee- room, rang the bell furiously. I gripped the waiter as he entered. "D'ye hear?" I shouted. "Get help and carry these bars up to my room right away."

He failed to understand me, and I shouted and raved at him. A scared- looking little old man in a green apron appeared, and further two of the young men in flannels. I made a dash at them and commandeered their services. As soon as the gold was in my room I felt free to quarrel. "Now get out," I shouted; "all of you get out if you don't want to see a man go mad before your eyes!" And I helped the waiter by the shoulder as he hesitated in the doorway. And then, as soon as I had the door locked on them all, I tore off the little man's clothes again, shied them right and left, and got into bed forthwith. And there I lay swearing and panting and cooling for a very long time.

At last I was calm enough to get out of bed and ring up the round-eyed waiter for a flannel nightshirt, a soda and whisky, and some good cigars. And these things being procured me, after an exasperating delay that drove me several times to the bell, I locked the door again and proceeded very deliberately to look entire situation in the face.

The net result of the great experiment presented itself as an absolute failure. It was a rout, and I was the sole survivor. It was an absolute collapse, and this was the final disaster. There was nothing for it but to save myself, and as much as I

could in the way of prospects from our debacle. At one fatal crowning blow all my vague resolutions of return and recovery had vanished. My intention of going back to the moon, of getting a sphereful of gold, and afterwards of having a fragment of Cavorite analysed and so recovering the great secret—perhaps, finally, even of recovering Cavor's body—all these ideas vanished altogether.

I was the sole survivor, and that was all.

I think that going to bed was one of the luckiest ideas I have ever had in an emergency. I really believe I should either have got loose-headed or done some indiscreet thing. But there, locked in and secure from all interruptions, I could think out the position in all its bearings and make my arrangements at leisure.

Of course, it was quite clear to me what had happened to the boy. He had crawled into the sphere, meddled with the studs, shut the Cavorite windows, and gone up. It was highly improbable he had screwed the manhole stopper, and, even if he had, the chances were a thousand to one against his getting back. It was fairly evident that he would gravitate with my bales to somewhere near the middle of the sphere and remain there, and so cease to be a legitimate terrestrial interest, however remarkable he might seem to the inhabitants of some remote quarter of space. I very speedily convinced myself on that point. And as for any responsibility I might have in the matter, the more I reflected upon that, the clearer it became that if only I kept quiet about things, I need not trouble myself about that. If I was faced by sorrowing parents demanding their lost boy, I had merely to demand my lost sphere—or ask them what they meant. At first I had had a vision of weeping parents and guardians, and all sorts of complications; but now I saw that I simply had to keep my mouth shut, and nothing in that way could arise. And, indeed, the more I lay and smoked and thought, the more evident became the wisdom of impenetrability.

It is within the right of every British citizen, provided he does not commit damage nor indecorum, to appear suddenly wherever he pleases, and as ragged and filthy as he pleases, and with whatever amount of virgin gold he sees fit to encumber himself, and no one has any right at all to hinder and detain him in this procedure. I formulated that at last to myself, and repeated it over as a sort of private Magna Charta of my liberty.

Once I had put that issue on one side, I could take up and consider in an equable manner certain considerations I had scarcely dared to think of before, namely, those arising out of the circumstances of my bankruptcy. But now, looking at this matter calmly and at leisure, I could see that if only I suppressed my identity by a temporary assumption of some less well-known name, and if I retained the two months' beard that had grown upon me, the risks of any annoyance from the spiteful creditor to whom I have already alluded became very small indeed. From that to a definite course of rational worldly action was plain sailing. It was all amazingly petty, no doubt, but what was there remaining for me to do?

Whatever I did I was resolved that I would keep myself level and right side up.

I ordered up writing materials, and addressed a letter to the New Romney Bank—the nearest, the waiter informed me—telling the manager I wished to open

an account with him, and requesting him to send two trustworthy persons properly authenticated in a cab with a good horse to fetch some hundredweight of gold with which I happened to be encumbered. I signed the letter "Blake," which seemed to me to be a thoroughly respectable sort of name. This done, I got a Folkstone Blue Book, picked out an outfitter, and asked him to send a cutter to measure me for a dark tweed suit, ordering at the same time a valise, dressing bag, brown boots, shirts, hat (to fit), and so forth; and from a watchmaker I also ordered a watch. And these letters being despatched, I had up as good a lunch as the hotel could give, and then lay smoking a cigar, as calm and ordinary as possible, until in accordance with my instructions two duly authenticated clerks came from the bank and weighed and took away my gold. After which I pulled the clothes over my ears in order to drown any knocking, and went very comfortably to sleep.

I went to sleep. No doubt it was a prosaic thing for the first man back from the moon to do, and I can imagine that the young and imaginative reader will find my behaviour disappointing. But I was horribly fatigued and bothered, and, confound it! what else was there to do? There certainly was not the remotest chance of my being believed, if I had told my story then, and it would certainly have subjected me to intolerable annoyances. I went to sleep. When at last I woke up again I was ready to face the world as I have always been accustomed to face it since I came to years of discretion. And so I got away to Italy, and there it is I am writing this story. If the world will not have it as fact, then the world may take it as fiction. It is no concern of mine.

And now that the account is finished, I am amazed to think how completely this adventure is gone and done with. Everybody believes that Cavor was a not very brilliant scientific experimenter who blew up his house and himself at Lympne, and they explain the bang that followed my arrival at Littlestone by a reference to the experiments with explosives that are going on continually at the government establishment of Lydd, two miles away. I must confess that hitherto I have not acknowledged my share in the disappearance of Master Tommy Simmons, which was that little boy's name. That, perhaps, may prove a difficult item of corroboration to explain away. They account for my appearance in rags with two bars of indisputable gold upon the Littlestone beach in various ingenious ways—it doesn't worry me what they think of me. They say I have strung all these things together to avoid being questioned too closely as to the source of my wealth. I would like to see the man who could invent a story that would hold together like this one. Well, they must take it as fiction—there it is.

I have told my story—and now, I suppose, I have to take up the worries of this terrestrial life again. Even if one has been to the moon, one has still to earn a living. So I am working here at Amalfi, on the scenario of that play I sketched before Cavor came walking into my world, and I am trying to piece my life together as it was before ever I saw him. I must confess that I find it hard to keep my mind on the play when the moonshine comes into my room. It is full moon here, and last night I was out on the pergola for hours, staring away at the shining

blankness that hides so much. Imagine it! tables and chairs, and trestles and bars of gold! Confound it!—if only one could hit on that Cavorite again! But a thing like that doesn't come twice in a life. Here I am, a little better off than I was at Lympne, and that is all. And Cavor has committed suicide in a more elaborate way than any human being ever did before. So the story closes as finally and completely as a dream. It fits in so little with all the other things of life, so much of it is so utterly remote from all human experience, the leaping, the eating, the breathing, and these weightless times, that indeed there are moments when, in spite of my moon gold, I do more than half believe myself that the whole thing was a dream...

CHAPTER XXII - THE ASTONISHING COMMUNICATION OF MR. JULIUS WENDIGEE

When I had finished my account of my return to the earth at Littlestone, I wrote, "The End," made a flourish, and threw my pen aside, fully believing that the whole story of the First Men in the Moon was done. Not only had I done this, but I had placed my manuscript in the hands of a literary agent, had permitted it to be sold, had seen the greater portion of it appear in the *Strand Magazine*, and was setting to work again upon the scenario of the play I had commenced at Lympne before I realised that the end was not yet. And then, following me from Amalfi to Algiers, there reached me (it is now about six months ago) one of the most astounding communications I have ever been fated to receive. Briefly, it informed me that Mr. Julius Wendigee, a Dutch electrician, who has been experimenting with certain apparatus akin to the apparatus used by Mr. Tesla in America, in the hope of discovering some method of communication with Mars, was receiving day by day a curiously fragmentary message in English, which was indisputably emanating from Mr. Cavor in the moon.

At first I thought the thing was an elaborate practical joke by some one who had seen the manuscript of my narrative. I answered Mr. Wendigee jestingly, but he replied in a manner that put such suspicion altogether aside, and in a state of inconceivable excitement I hurried from Algiers to the little observatory upon the Monte Rosa in which he was working. In the presence of his record and his appliances—and above all of the messages from Cavor that were coming to hand—my lingering doubts vanished. I decided at once to accept a proposal he made to me to remain with him, assisting him to take down the record from day to day, and endeavouring with him to send a message back to the moon. Cavor, we learnt, was not only alive, but free, in the midst of an almost inconceivable community of these ant-like beings, these ant-men, in the blue darkness of the lunar caves. He was lamed, it seemed, but otherwise in quite good health—in better health, he distinctly said, than he usually enjoyed on earth. He had had a fever, but it had left no bad effects. But curiously enough he seemed to be labouring under a conviction that I was either dead in the moon crater or lost in the deep of space.

His message began to be received by Mr. Wendigee when that gentleman was engaged in quite a different investigation. The reader will no doubt recall the little excitement that began the century, arising out an announcement by Mr. Nikola Tesla, the American electrical celebrity, that he had received a message from Mars. His announcement renewed attention to fact that had long been familiar to

scientific people, namely: that from some unknown source in space, waves of electromagnetic disturbance, entirely similar those used by Signor Marconi for his wireless telegraphy, are constantly reaching the earth. Besides Tesla quite a number of other observers have been engaged in perfecting apparatus for receiving and recording these vibrations, though few would go so far to consider them actual messages from some extraterrestrial sender. Among that few, however, we must certainly count Mr. Wendigee. Ever since 1898 he had devoted himself almost entirely to this subject, and being a man of ample means he had erected an observatory on the flanks of Monte Rosa, in a position singularly adapted in every way for such observations.

My scientific attainments, I must admit, are not great, but so far as they enable me to judge, Mr. Wendigee's contrivances for detecting and recording any disturbances in the electromagnetic conditions of space are singularly original and ingenious. And by a happy combination of circumstances they were set up and in operation about two months before Cavor made his first attempt to call up the earth. Consequently we have fragments of his communication even from the beginning. Unhappily, they are only fragments, and the most momentous of all the things that he had to tell humanity—the instructions, that is, for the making of Cavorite, if, indeed, he ever transmitted them—have throbbed themselves away unrecorded into space. We never succeeded in getting a response back to Cavor. He was unable to tell, therefore, what we had received or what we had missed; nor, indeed, did he certainly know that any one on earth was really aware of his efforts to reach us. And the persistence he displayed in sending eighteen long descriptions of lunar affairs—as they would be if we had them complete—shows how much his mind must have turned back towards his native planet since he left it two years ago.

You can imagine how amazed Mr. Wendigee must have been when he discovered his record of electromagnetic disturbances interlaced by Cavor's straightforward English. Mr. Wendigee knew nothing of our wild journey moonward, and suddenly—this English out of the void!

It is well the reader should understand the conditions under which it would seem these messages were sent. Somewhere within the moon Cavor certainly had access for a time to a considerable amount of electrical apparatus, and it would seem he rigged up—perhaps furtively—a transmitting arrangement of the Marconi type. This he was able to operate at irregular intervals: sometimes for only half an hour or so, sometimes for three or four hours at a stretch. At these times he transmitted his earthward message, regardless of the fact that the relative position of the moon and points upon the earth's surface is constantly altering. As a consequence of this and of the necessary imperfections of our recording instruments his communication comes and goes in our records in an extremely fitful manner; it becomes blurred; it "fades out" in a mysterious and altogether exasperating way. And added to this is the fact that he was not an expert operator; he had partly forgotten, or never completely mastered, the code in general use, and as he became fatigued he dropped words and misspelt in a curious manner.

Altogether we have probably lost quite half of the communications he made, and much we have is damaged, broken, and partly effaced. In the abstract that follows the reader must be prepared therefore for a considerable amount of break, hiatus, and change of topic. Mr. Wendigee and I are collaborating in a complete and annotated edition of the Cavor record, which we hope to publish, together with a detailed account of the instruments employed, beginning with the first volume in January next. That will be the full and scientific report, of which this is only the popular transcript. But here we give at least sufficient to complete the story I have told, and to give the broad outlines of the state of that other world so near, so akin, and yet so dissimilar to our own.

CHAPTER XXIII - AN ABSTRACT OF THE SIX MESSAGES FIRST RECEIVED FROM MR. CAVOR

The two earlier messages of Mr. Cavor may very well be reserved for that larger volume. They simply tell, with greater brevity and with a difference in several details that is interesting, but not of any vital importance, the bare facts of the making of the sphere and our departure from the world. Throughout, Cavor speaks of me as a man who is dead, but with a curious change of temper as he approaches our landing on the moon. "Poor Bedford," he says of me, and "this poor young man," and he blames himself for inducing a young man, "by no means well equipped for such adventures," to leave a planet "on which he was indisputably fitted to succeed" on so precarious a mission. I think he underrates the part my energy and practical capacity played in bringing about the realisation of his theoretical sphere. "We arrived," he says, with no more account of our passage through space than if we had made a journey of common occurrence in a railway train.

And then he becomes increasingly unfair to me. Unfair, indeed, to an extent I should not have expected in a man trained in the search for truth. Looking back over my previously written account of these things, I must insist that I have been altogether juster to Cavor than he has been to me. I have extenuated little and suppressed nothing. But his account is:—

"It speedily became apparent that the entire strangeness of our circumstances and surroundings—great loss of weight, attenuated but highly oxygenated air, consequent exaggeration of the results of muscular effort, rapid development of weird plants from obscure spores, lurid sky —was exciting my companion unduly. On the moon his character seemed to deteriorate. He became impulsive, rash, and quarrelsome. In a little while his folly in devouring some gigantic vesicles and his consequent intoxication led to our capture by the Selenites—before we had had the slightest opportunity of properly observing their ways..."

(He says, you observe, nothing of his own concession to these same "vesicles.")

And he goes on from that point to say that "We came to a difficult passage with them, and Bedford mistaking certain gestures of theirs"—pretty gestures they were!—"gave way to a panic violence. He ran amuck, killed three, and perforce I had to flee with him after the outrage. Subsequently we fought with a number who endeavoured to bar our way, and slew seven or eight more. It says much for the tolerance of these beings that on my recapture I was not instantly slain. We

made our way to the exterior and separated in the crater of our arrival, to increase our chances of recovering our sphere. But presently I came upon a body of Selenites, led by two who were curiously different, even in form, from any of these we had seen hitherto, with larger heads and smaller bodies, and much more elaborately wrapped about. And after evading them for some time I fell into a crevasse, cut my head rather badly, and displaced my patella, and, finding crawling very painful, decided to surrender—if they would still permit me to do so. This they did, and, perceiving my helpless condition, carried me with them again into the moon. And of Bedford I have heard or seen nothing more, nor, so far as I can gather, any Selenite. Either the night overtook him in the crater, or else, which is more probable, he found the sphere, and, desiring to steal a march upon me, made off with it—only, I fear, to find it uncontrollable, and to meet a more lingering fate in outer space."

And with that Cavor dismisses me and goes on to more interesting topics. I dislike the idea of seeming to use my position as his editor to deflect his story in my own interest, but I am obliged to protest here against the turn he gives these occurrences. He said nothing about that gasping message on the blood-stained paper in which he told, or attempted to tell, a very different story. The dignified self-surrender is an altogether new view of the affair that has come to him, I must insist, since he began to feel secure among the lunar people; and as for the "stealing a march" conception, I am quite willing to let the reader decide between us on what he has before him. I know I am not a model man—I have made no pretence to be. But am I that?

However, that is the sum of my wrongs. From this point I can edit Cavor with an untroubled mind, for he mentions me no more.

It would seem the Selenites who had come upon him carried him to some point in the interior down "a great shaft" by means of what he describes as "a sort of balloon." We gather from the rather confused passage in which he describes this, and from a number of chance allusions and hints in other and subsequent messages, that this "great shaft" is one of an enormous system of artificial shafts that run, each from what is called a lunar "crater," downwards for very nearly a hundred miles towards the central portion of our satellite. These shafts communicate by transverse tunnels, they throw out abysmal caverns and expand into great globular places; the whole of the moon's substance for a hundred miles inward, indeed, is a mere sponge of rock. "Partly," says Cavor, "this sponginess is natural, but very largely it is due to the enormous industry of the Selenites in the past. The enormous circular mounds of the excavated rock and earth it is that form these great circles about the tunnels known to earthly astronomers (misled by a false analogy) as volcanoes."

It was down this shaft they took him, in this "sort of balloon" he speaks of, at first into an inky blackness and then into a region of continually increasing phosphorescence. Cavor's despatches show him to be curiously regardless of detail for a scientific man, but we gather that this light was due to the streams and cascades of water—"no doubt containing some phosphorescent organism"—that flowed

ever more abundantly downward towards the Central Sea. And as he descended, he says, "The Selenites also became luminous." And at last far below him he saw, as it were, a lake of heatless fire, the waters of the Central Sea, glowing and eddying in strange perturbation, "like luminous blue milk that is just on the boil."

"This Lunar Sea," says Cavor, in a later passage "is not a stagnant ocean; a solar tide sends it in a perpetual flow around the lunar axis, and strange storms and boilings and rushings of its waters occur, and at times cold winds and thunderings that ascend out of it into the busy ways of the great ant- hill above. It is only when the water is in motion that it gives out light; in its rare seasons of calm it is black. Commonly, when one sees it, its waters rise and fall in an oily swell, and flakes and big rafts of shining, bubbly foam drift with the sluggish, faintly glowing current. The Selenites navigate its cavernous straits and lagoons in little shallow boats of a canoe-like shape; and even before my journey to the galleries about the Grand Lunar, who is Master of the Moon, I was permitted to make a brief excursion on its waters.

"The caverns and passages are naturally very tortuous. A large proportion of these ways are known only to expert pilots among the fishermen, and not infrequently Selenites are lost for ever in their labyrinths. In their remoter recesses, I am told, strange creatures lurk, some of them terrible and dangerous creatures that all the science of the moon has been unable to exterminate. There is particularly the Rapha, an inextricable mass of clutching tentacles that one hacks to pieces only to multiply; and the Tzee, a darting creature that is never seen, so subtly and suddenly does it slay..."

He gives us a gleam of description.

"I was reminded on this excursion of what I have read of the Mammoth Caves; if only I had had a yellow flambeau instead of the pervading blue light, and a solid-looking boatman with an oar instead of a scuttle-faced Selenite working an engine at the back of the canoe, I could have imagined I had suddenly got back to earth. The rocks about us were very various, sometimes black, sometimes pale blue and veined, and once they flashed and glittered as though we had come into a mine of sapphires. And below one saw the ghostly phosphorescent fishes flash and vanish in the hardly less phosphorescent deep. Then, presently, a long ultramarine vista down the turgid stream of one of the channels of traffic, and a landing stage, and then, perhaps, a glimpse up the enormous crowded shaft of one of the vertical ways.

"In one great place heavy with glistening stalactites a number of boats were fishing. We went alongside one of these and watched the long-armed Selenites winding in a net. They were little, hunchbacked insects, with very strong arms, short, bandy legs, and crinkled face-masks. As they pulled at it that net seemed the heaviest thing I had come upon in the moon; it was loaded with weights—no doubt of gold—and it took a long time to draw, for in those waters the larger and more edible fish lurk deep. The fish in the net came up like a blue moonrise—a blaze of darting, tossing blue.

"Among their catch was a many-tentaculate, evil-eyed black thing, ferociously active, whose appearance they greeted with shrieks and twitters, and which with quick, nervous movements they hacked to pieces by means of little hatchets. All its dissevered limbs continued to lash and writhe in a vicious manner. Afterwards, when fever had hold of me, I dreamt again and again of that bitter, furious creature rising so vigorous and active out of the unknown sea. It was the most active and malignant thing of all the living creatures I have yet seen in this world inside the moon...

"The surface of this sea must be very nearly two hundred miles (if not more) below the level of the moon's exterior; all the cities of the moon lie, I learnt, immediately above this Central Sea, in such cavernous spaces and artificial galleries as I have described, and they communicate with the exterior by enormous vertical shafts which open invariably in what are called by earthly astronomers the 'craters' of the moon. The lid covering one such aperture I had already seen during the wanderings that had preceded my capture.

"Upon the condition of the less central portion of the moon I have not yet arrived at very precise knowledge. There is an enormous system of caverns in which the mooncalves shelter during the night; and there are abattoirs and the like—in one of these it was that I and Bedford fought with the Selenite butchers—and I have since seen balloons laden with meat descending out of the upper dark. I have as yet scarcely learnt as much of these things as a Zulu in London would learn about the British corn supplies in the same time. It is clear, however, that these vertical shafts and the vegetation of the surface must play an essential role in ventilating and keeping fresh the atmosphere of the moon. At one time, and particularly on my first emergence from my prison, there was certainly a cold wind blowing *down* the shaft, and later there was a kind of sirocco upward that corresponded with my fever. For at the end of about three weeks I fell ill of an indefinable sort of fever, and in spite of sleep and the quinine tabloids that very fortunately I had brought in my pocket, I remained ill and fretting miserably, almost to the time when I was taken into the presence of the Grand Lunar, who is Master of the Moon.

"I will not dilate on the wretchedness of my condition," he remarks, "during those days of ill-health." And he goes on with great amplitude with details I omit here. "My temperature," he concludes, "kept abnormally high for a long time, and I lost all desire for food. I had stagnant waking intervals, and sleep tormented by dreams, and at one phase I was, I remember, so weak as to be earth-sick and almost hysterical. I longed almost intolerably for colour to break the everlasting blue..."

He reverts again presently to the topic of this sponge-caught lunar atmosphere. I am told by astronomers and physicists that all he tells is in absolute accordance with what was already known of the moon's condition. Had earthly astronomers had the courage and imagination to push home a bold induction, says Mr. Wendigee, they might have foretold almost everything that Cavor has to say of the general structure of the moon. They know now pretty certainly that moon and

earth are not so much satellite and primary as smaller and greater sisters, made out of one mass, and consequently made of the same material. And since the density of the moon is only three-fifths that of the earth, there can be nothing for it but that she is hollowed out by a great system of caverns. There was no necessity, said Sir Jabez Flap, F.R.S., that most entertaining exponent of the facetious side of the stars, that we should ever have gone to the moon to find out such easy inferences, and points the pun with an allusion to Gruyere, but he certainly might have announced his knowledge of the hollowness of the moon before. And if the moon is hollow, then the apparent absence of air and water is, of course, quite easily explained. The sea lies within at the bottom of the caverns, and the air travels through the great sponge of galleries, in accordance with simple physical laws. The caverns of the moon, on the whole, are very windy places. As the sunlight comes round the moon the air in the outer galleries on that side is heated, its pressure increases, some flows out on the exterior and mingles with the evaporating air of the craters (where the plants remove its carbonic acid), while the greater portion flows round through the galleries to replace the shrinking air of the cooling side that the sunlight has left. There is, therefore, a constant eastward breeze in the air of the outer galleries, and an upflow during the lunar day up the shafts, complicated, of course, very greatly by the varying shape of the galleries, and the ingenious contrivances of the Selenite mind...

CHAPTER XXIV - THE NATURAL HISTORY OF THE SELENITES

The messages of Cavor from the sixth up to the sixteenth are for the most part so much broken, and they abound so in repetitions, that they scarcely form a consecutive narrative. They will be given in full, of course, in the scientific report, but here it will be far more convenient to continue simply to abstract and quote as in the former chapter. We have subjected every word to a keen critical scrutiny, and my own brief memories and impressions of lunar things have been of inestimable help in interpreting what would otherwise have been impenetrably dark. And, naturally, as living beings, our interest centres far more upon the strange community of lunar insects in which he was living, it would seem, as an honoured guest than upon the mere physical condition of their world.

I have already made it clear, I think, that the Selenites I saw resembled man in maintaining the erect attitude, and in having four limbs, and I have compared the general appearance of their heads and the jointing of their limbs to that of insects. I have mentioned, too, the peculiar consequence of the smaller gravitation of the moon on their fragile slightness. Cavor confirms me upon all these points. He calls them "animals," though of course they fall under no division of the classification of earthly creatures, and he points out "the insect type of anatomy had, fortunately for men, never exceeded a relatively very small size on earth." The largest terrestrial insects, living or extinct, do not, as a matter of fact, measure six inches in length; "but here, against the lesser gravitation of the moon, a creature certainly as much an insect as vertebrate seems to have been able to attain to human and ultra- human dimensions."

He does not mention the ant, but throughout his allusions the ant is continually being brought before my mind, in its sleepless activity, in its intelligence and social organisation, in its structure, and more particularly in the fact that it displays, in addition to the two forms, the male and the female form, that almost all other animals possess, a number of other sexless creatures, workers, soldiers, and the like, differing from one another in structure, character, power, and use, and yet all members of the same species. For these Selenites, also, have a great variety of forms. Of course, they are not only colossally greater in size than ants, but also, in Cavor's opinion at least, in intelligence, morality, and social wisdom are they colossally greater than men. And instead of the four or five different forms of ant that are found, there are almost innumerably different forms of Selenite. I had endeavoured to indicate the very considerable difference observable in such

Selenites of the outer crust as I happened to encounter; the differences in size and proportions were certainly as wide as the differences between the most widely separated races of men. But such differences as I saw fade absolutely to nothing in comparison with the huge distinctions of which Cavor tells. It would seem the exterior Selenites I saw were, indeed, mostly engaged in kindred occupations—mooncalf herds, butchers, fleshers, and the like. But within the moon, practically unsuspected by me, there are, it seems, a number of other sorts of Selenite, differing in size, differing in the relative size of part to part, differing in power and appearance, and yet not different species of creatures, but only different forms of one species, and retaining through all their variations a certain common likeness that marks their specific unity. The moon is, indeed, a sort of vast ant-hill, only, instead of there being only four or five sorts of ant, there are many hundred different sorts of Selenite, and almost every gradation between one sort and another.

It would seem the discovery came upon Cavor very speedily. I infer rather than learn from his narrative that he was captured by the mooncalf herds under the direction of these other Selenites who "have larger brain cases (heads?) and very much shorter legs." Finding he would not walk even under the goad, they carried him into darkness, crossed a narrow, plank-like bridge that may have been the identical bridge I had refused, and put him down in something that must have seemed at first to be some sort of lift. This was the balloon —it had certainly been absolutely invisible to us in the darkness —and what had seemed to me a mere plank-walking into the void was really, no doubt, the passage of the gangway. In this he descended towards constantly more luminous caverns of the moon. At first they descended in silence—save for the twitterings of the Selenites—and then into a stir of windy movement. In a little while the profound blackness had made his eyes so sensitive that he began to see more and more of the things about him, and at last the vague took shape.

"Conceive an enormous cylindrical space," says Cavor, in his seventh message, "a quarter of a mile across, perhaps; very dimly lit at first and then brighter, with big platforms twisting down its sides in a spiral that vanishes at last below in a blue profundity; and lit even more brightly—one could not tell how or why. Think of the well of the very largest spiral staircase or lift-shaft that you have ever looked down, and magnify that by a hundred. Imagine it at twilight seen through blue glass. Imagine yourself looking down that; only imagine also that you feel extraordinarily light, and have got rid of any giddy feeling you might have on earth, and you will have the first conditions of my impression. Round this enormous shaft imagine a broad gallery running in a much steeper spiral than would be credible on earth, and forming a steep road protected from the gulf only by a little parapet that vanishes at last in perspective a couple of miles below.

"Looking up, I saw the very fellow of the downward vision; it had, of course, the effect of looking into a very steep cone. A wind was blowing down the shaft, and far above I fancy I heard, growing fainter and fainter, the bellowing of the mooncalves that were being driven down again from their evening pasturage on the exterior. And up and down the spiral galleries were scattered numerous moon

people, pallid, faintly luminous beings, regarding our appearance or busied on unknown errands.

"Either I fancied it or a flake of snow came drifting down on the icy breeze. And then, falling like a snowflake, a little figure, a little man- insect, clinging to a parachute, drove down very swiftly towards the central places of the moon.

"The big-headed Selenite sitting beside me, seeing me move my head with the gesture of one who saw, pointed with his trunk-like 'hand' and indicated a sort of jetty coming into sight very far below: a little landing-stage, as it were, hanging into the void. As it swept up towards us our pace diminished very rapidly, and in a few moments, as it seemed, we were abreast of it, and at rest. A mooring-rope was flung and grasped, and I found myself pulled down to a level with a great crowd of Selenites, who jostled to see me.

"It was an incredible crowd. Suddenly and violently there was forced upon my attention the vast amount of difference there is amongst these beings of the moon.

"Indeed, there seemed not two alike in all that jostling multitude. They differed in shape, they differed in size, they rang all the horrible changes on the theme of Selenite form! Some bulged and overhung, some ran about among the feet of their fellows. All of them had a grotesque and disquieting suggestion of an insect that has somehow contrived to mock humanity; but all seemed to present an incredible exaggeration of some particular feature: one had a vast right fore-limb, an enormous antennal arm, as it were; one seemed all leg, poised, as it were, on stilts; another protruded the edge of his face mask into a nose-like organ that made him startlingly human until one saw his expressionless gaping mouth. The strange and (except for the want of mandibles and palps) most insect-like head of the mooncalf-minders underwent, indeed, the most incredible transformations: here it was broad and low, here high and narrow; here its leathery brow was drawn out into horns and strange features; here it was whiskered and divided, and there with a grotesquely human profile. One distortion was particularly conspicuous. There were several brain cases distended like bladders to a huge size, with the face mask reduced to quite small proportions. There were several amazing forms, with heads reduced to microscopic proportions and blobby bodies; and fantastic, flimsy things that existed, it would seem, only as a basis for vast, trumpet-like protrusions of the lower part of the mask. And oddest of all, as it seemed to me for the moment, two or three of these weird inhabitants of a subterranean world, a world sheltered by innumerable miles of rock from sun or rain, *carried umbrellas* in their tentaculate hands—real terrestrial looking umbrellas! And then I thought of the parachutist I had watched descend.

"These moon people behaved exactly as a human crowd might have done in similar circumstances: they jostled and thrust one another, they shoved one another aside, they even clambered upon one another to get a glimpse of me. Every moment they increased in numbers, and pressed more urgently upon the discs of my ushers"—Cavor does not explain what he means by this —"every moment fresh shapes emerged from the shadows and forced themselves upon my astounded attention. And presently I was signed and helped into a sort of litter, and lifted

up on the shoulders of strong-armed bearers, and so borne through the twilight over this seething multitude towards the apartments that were provided for me in the moon. All about me were eyes, faces, masks, a leathery noise like the rustling of beetle wings, and a great bleating and cricket-like twittering of Selenite voices."

We gather he was taken to a "hexagonal apartment," and there for a space he was confined. Afterwards he was given a much more considerable liberty; indeed, almost as much freedom as one has in a civilised town on earth. And it would appear that the mysterious being who is the ruler and master of the moon appointed two Selenites "with large heads" to guard and study him, and to establish whatever mental communications were possible with him. And, amazing and incredible as it may seem, these two creatures, these fantastic men insects, these beings of other world, were presently communicating with Cavor by means of terrestrial speech.

Cavor speaks of them as Phi-oo and Tsi-puff. Phi-oo, he says, was about 5 feet high; he had small slender legs about 18 inches long, and slight feet of the common lunar pattern. On these balanced a little body, throbbing with the pulsations of his heart. He had long, soft, many-jointed arms ending in a tentacled grip, and his neck was many-jointed in the usual way, but exceptionally short and thick. His head, says Cavor—apparently alluding to some previous description that has gone astray in space—"is of the common lunar type, but strangely modified. The mouth has the usual expressionless gape, but it is unusually small and pointing downward, and the mask is reduced to the size of a large flat nose-flap. On either side are the little eyes.

"The rest of the head is distended into a huge globe and the chitinous leathery cuticle of the mooncalf herds thins out to a mere membrane, through which the pulsating brain movements are distinctly visible. He is a creature, indeed, with a tremendously hypertrophied brain, and with the rest of his organism both relatively and absolutely dwarfed."

In another passage Cavor compares the back view of him to Atlas supporting the world. Tsi-puff it seems was a very similar insect, but his "face" was drawn out to a considerable length, and the brain hypertrophy being in different regions, his head was not round but pear-shaped, with the stalk downward. There were also litter-carriers, lopsided beings, with enormous shoulders, very spidery ushers, and a squat foot attendant in Cavor's retinue.

The manner in which Phi-oo and Tsi-puff attacked the problem of speech was fairly obvious. They came into this "hexagonal cell" in which Cavor was confined, and began imitating every sound he made, beginning with a cough. He seems to have grasped their intention with great quickness, and to have begun repeating words to them and pointing to indicate the application. The procedure was probably always the same. Phi-oo would attend to Cavor for a space, then point also and say the word he had heard.

The first word he mastered was "man," and the second "Mooney"—which Cavor on the spur of the moment seems to have used instead of "Selenite" for the

moon race. As soon as Phi-oo was assured of the meaning of a word he repeated it to Tsi-puff, who remembered it infallibly. They mastered over one hundred English nouns at their first session.

Subsequently it seems they brought an artist with them to assist the work of explanation with sketches and diagrams—Cavor's drawings being rather crude. "He was," says Cavor, "a being with an active arm and an arresting eye," and he seemed to draw with incredible swiftness.

The eleventh message is undoubtedly only a fragment of a longer communication. After some broken sentences, the record of which is unintelligible, it goes on:—

"But it will interest only linguists, and delay me too long, to give the details of the series of intent parleys of which these were the beginning, and, indeed, I very much doubt if I could give in anything like the proper order all the twistings and turnings that we made in our pursuit of mutual comprehension. Verbs were soon plain sailing—at least, such active verbs as I could express by drawings; some adjectives were easy, but when it came to abstract nouns, to prepositions, and the sort of hackneyed figures of speech, by means of which so much is expressed on earth, it was like diving in cork-jackets. Indeed, these difficulties were insurmountable until to the sixth lesson came a fourth assistant, a being with a huge football-shaped head, whose forte was clearly the pursuit of intricate analogy. He entered in a preoccupied manner, stumbling against a stool, and the difficulties that arose had to be presented to him with a certain amount of clamour and hitting and pricking before they reached his apprehension. But once he was involved his penetration was amazing. Whenever there came a need of thinking beyond Phi-oo's by no means limited scope, this prolate-headed person was in request, but he invariably told the conclusion to Tsi-puff, in order that it might be remembered; Tsi-puff was ever the arsenal for facts. And so we advanced again.

"It seemed long and yet brief—a matter of days—before I was positively talking with these insects of the moon. Of course, at first it was an intercourse infinitely tedious and exasperating, but imperceptibly it has grown to comprehension. And my patience has grown to meet its limitations, Phi-oo it is who does all the talking. He does it with a vast amount of meditative provisional 'M'm—M'm' and has caught up one or two phrases, 'If I may say,' 'If you understand,' and beads all his speech with them.

"Thus he would discourse. Imagine him explaining his artist.

"'M'm—M'm—he—if I may say—draw. Eat little—drink little—draw. Love draw. No other thing. Hate all who not draw like him. Angry. Hate all who draw like him better. Hate most people. Hate all who not think all world for to draw. Angry. M'm. All things mean nothing to him—only draw. He like you ... if you understand... New thing to draw. Ugly—striking. Eh?

"'He'—turning to Tsi-puff—'love remember words. Remember wonderful more than any. Think no, draw no—remember. Say'—here he referred to his gifted assistant for a word—'histories—all things. He hear once—say ever.'

"It is more wonderful to me than I dreamt that anything ever could be again, to hear, in this perpetual obscurity, these extraordinary creatures —for even familiarity fails to weaken the inhuman effect of their appearance—continually piping a nearer approach to coherent earthly speech—asking questions, giving answers. I feel that I am casting back to the fable-hearing period of childhood again, when the ant and the grasshopper talked together and the bee judged between them..."

And while these linguistic exercises were going on Cavor seems to have experienced a considerable relaxation of his confinement. "The first dread and distrust our unfortunate conflict aroused is being," he said, "continually effaced by the deliberate rationality of all I do... I am now able to come and go as I please, or I am restricted only for my own good. So it is I have been able to get at this apparatus, and, assisted by a happy find among the material that is littered in this enormous store-cave, I have contrived to despatch these messages. So far not the slightest attempt has been made to interfere with me in this, though I have made it quite clear to Phi-oo that I am signalling to the earth.

"'You talk to other?' he asked, watching me.

"'Others,' said I.

"'Others,' he said. 'Oh yes, Men?'

"And I went on transmitting."

Cavor was continually making corrections in his previous accounts of the Selenites as fresh facts flowed upon him to modify his conclusions, and accordingly one gives the quotations that follow with a certain amount of reservation. They are quoted from the ninth, thirteenth, and sixteenth messages, and, altogether vague and fragmentary as they are, they probably give as complete a picture of the social life of this strange community as mankind can now hope to have for many generations.

"In the moon," says Cavor, "every citizen knows his place. He is born to that place, and the elaborate discipline of training and education and surgery he undergoes fits him at last so completely to it that he has neither ideas nor organs for any purpose beyond it. 'Why should he?' Phi-oo would ask. If, for example, a Selenite is destined to be a mathematician, his teachers and trainers set out at once to that end. They check any incipient disposition to other pursuits, they encourage his mathematical bias with a perfect psychological skill. His brain grows, or at least the mathematical faculties of his brain grow, and the rest of him only so much as is necessary to sustain this essential part of him. At last, save for rest and food, his one delight lies in the exercise and display of his faculty, his one interest in its application, his sole society with other specialists in his own line. His brain grows continually larger, at least so far as the portions engaging in mathematics are concerned; they bulge ever larger and seem to suck all life and vigour from the rest of his frame. His limbs shrivel, his heart and digestive organs diminish, his insect face is hidden under its bulging contours. His voice becomes a mere stridulation for the stating of formula; he seems deaf to all but properly enunciated problems. The faculty of laughter, save for the sudden discovery of some

paradox, is lost to him; his deepest emotion is the evolution of a novel computation. And so he attains his end.

"Or, again, a Selenite appointed to be a minder of mooncalves is from his earliest years induced to think and live mooncalf, to find his pleasure in mooncalf lore, his exercise in their tending and pursuit. He is trained to become wiry and active, his eye is indurated to the tight wrappings, the angular contours that constitute a 'smart mooncalfishness.' He takes at last no interest in the deeper part of the moon; he regards all Selenites not equally versed in mooncalves with indifference, derision, or hostility. His thoughts are of mooncalf pastures, and his dialect an accomplished mooncalf technique. So also he loves his work, and discharges in perfect happiness the duty that justifies his being. And so it is with all sorts and conditions of Selenites —each is a perfect unit in a world machine...

"These beings with big heads, on whom the intellectual labours fall, form a sort of aristocracy in this strange society, and at the head of them, quintessential of the moon, is that marvellous gigantic ganglion the Grand Lunar, into whose presence I am finally to come. The unlimited development of the minds of the intellectual class is rendered possible by the absence of any bony skull in the lunar anatomy, that strange box of bone that clamps about the developing brain of man, imperiously insisting 'thus far and no farther' to all his possibilities. They fall into three main classes differing greatly in influence and respect. There are administrators, of whom Phi-oo is one, Selenites of considerable initiative and versatility, responsible each for a certain cubic content of the moon's bulk; the experts like the football-headed thinker, who are trained to perform certain special operations; and the erudite, who are the repositories of all knowledge. To the latter class belongs Tsi-puff, the first lunar professor of terrestrial languages. With regard to these latter, it is a curious little thing to note that the unlimited growth of the lunar brain has rendered unnecessary the invention of all those mechanical aids to brain work which have distinguished the career of man. There are no books, no records of any sort, no libraries or inscriptions. All knowledge is stored in distended brains much as the honey-ants of Texas store honey in their distended abdomens. The lunar Somerset House and the lunar British Museum Library are collections of living brains...

"The less specialised administrators, I note, do for the most part take a very lively interest in me whenever they encounter me. They will come out of the way and stare at me and ask questions to which Phi-oo will reply. I see them going hither and thither with a retinue of bearers, attendants, shouters, parachute-carriers, and so forth—queer groups to see. The experts for the most part ignore me completely, even as they ignore each other, or notice me only to begin a clamorous exhibition of their distinctive skill. The erudite for the most part are rapt in an impervious and apoplectic complacency, from which only a denial of their erudition can rouse them. Usually they are led about by little watchers and attendants, and often there are small and active- looking creatures, small females usually, that I am inclined to think are a sort of wife to them; but some of the profounder scholars are altogether too great for locomotion, and are carried from

place to place in a sort of sedan tub, wabbling jellies of knowledge that enlist my respectful astonishment. I have just passed one in coming to this place where I am permitted to amuse myself with these electrical toys, a vast, shaven, shaky head, bald and thin- skinned, carried on his grotesque stretcher. In front and behind came his bearers, and curious, almost trumpet-faced, news disseminators shrieked his fame.

"I have already mentioned the retinues that accompany most of the intellectuals: ushers, bearers, valets, extraneous tentacles and muscles, as it were, to replace the abortive physical powers of these hypertrophied minds. Porters almost invariably accompany them. There are also extremely swift messengers with spider-like legs and 'hands' for grasping parachutes, and attendants with vocal organs that could well nigh wake the dead. Apart from their controlling intelligence these subordinates are as inert and helpless as umbrellas in a stand. They exist only in relation to the orders they have to obey, the duties they have to perform.

"The bulk of these insects, however, who go to and fro upon the spiral ways, who fill the ascending balloons and drop past me clinging to flimsy parachutes are, I gather, of the operative class. 'Machine hands,' indeed, some of these are in actual nature—it is not figure of speech, the single tentacle of the mooncalf herd is profoundly modified for clawing, lifting, guiding, the rest of them no more than necessary subordinate appendages to these important mechanisms, have enormously developed auditory organs; some whose work lies in delicate chemical operations project a vast olfactory organ; others again have flat feet for treadles with anchylosed joints; and others —who I have been told are glassblowers—seem mere lung-bellows. But every one of these common Selenites I have seen at work is exquisitely adapted to the social need it meets. Fine work is done by fined-down workers, amazingly dwarfed and neat. Some I could hold on the palm of my hand. There is even a sort of turnspit Selenite, very common, whose duty and only delight it is to apply the motive power for various small appliances. And to rule over these things and order any erring tendency there might be in some aberrant natures are the most muscular beings I have seen in the moon, a sort of lunar police, who must have been trained from their earliest years to give a perfect respect and obedience to the swollen heads.

"The making of these various sorts of operative must be a very curious and interesting process. I am very much in the dark about it, but quite recently I came upon a number of young Selenites confined in jars from which only the fore-limbs protruded, who were being compressed to become machine- minders of a special sort. The extended 'hand' in this highly developed system of technical education is stimulated by irritants and nourished by injection, while the rest of the body is starved. Phi-oo, unless I misunderstood him, explained that in the earlier stages these queer little creatures are apt to display signs of suffering in their various cramped situations, but they easily become indurated to their lot; and he took me on to where a number of flexible- minded messengers were being drawn out and broken in. It is quite unreasonable, I know, but such glimpses of the educational methods of these beings affect me disagreeably. I hope, however, that may pass

off, and I may be able to see more of this aspect of their wonderful social order. That wretched-looking hand- tentacle sticking out of its jar seemed to have a sort of limp appeal for lost possibilities; it haunts me still, although, of course it is really in the end a far more humane proceeding than our earthly method of leaving children to grow into human beings, and then making machines of them.

"Quite recently, too—I think it was on the eleventh or twelfth visit I made to this apparatus—I had a curious light upon the lives of these operatives. I was being guided through a short cut hither, instead of going down the spiral, and by the quays to the Central Sea. From the devious windings of a long, dark gallery, we emerged into a vast, low cavern, pervaded by an earthy smell, and as things go in this darkness, rather brightly lit. The light came from a tumultuous growth of livid fungoid shapes—some indeed singularly like our terrestrial mushrooms, but standing as high or higher than a man.

"'Mooneys eat these?' said I to Phi-oo.

"'Yes, food.'

"'Goodness me!' I cried; 'what's that?'

"My eye had just caught the figure of an exceptionally big and ungainly Selenite lying motionless among the stems, face downward. We stopped.

"'Dead?' I asked. (For as yet I have seen no dead the moon, and I have grown curious.)

"'No!' exclaimed Phi-oo. 'Him—worker—no work to do. Get little drink then—make sleep—till we him want. What good him wake, eh? No want him walking about.'

"'There's another!' cried I.

"And indeed all that huge extent of mushroom ground was, I found, peppered with these prostrate figures sleeping under an opiate until the moon had need of them. There were scores of them of all sorts, and we were able to turn over some of them, and examine them more precisely than I had been able to previously. They breathed noisily at my doing so, but did not wake. One, I remember very distinctly: he left a strong impression, I think, because some trick the light and of his attitude was strongly suggestive a drawn-up human figure. His fore-limbs were long, delicate tentacles—he was some kind of refined manipulator—and the pose of his slumber suggested a submissive suffering. No doubt it was a mistake for me to interpret his expression in that way, but I did. And as Phi-oo rolled him over into the darkness among the livid fleshiness again I felt a distinctly unpleasant sensation, although as he rolled the insect in him was confessed.

"It simply illustrates the unthinking way in which one acquires habits of feeling. To drug the worker one does not want and toss him aside is surely far better than to expel him from his factory to wander starving in the streets. In every complicated social community there is necessarily a certain intermittency of employment for all specialised labour, and in this way the trouble of an 'unemployed' problem is altogether anticipated. And yet, so unreasonable are even scientifically trained minds, I still do not like the memory of those prostrate forms amidst those quiet, luminous arcades of fleshy growth, and I avoid that short cut

in spite of the inconveniences of the longer, more noisy, and more crowded alternative.

"My alternative route takes me round by a huge, shadowy cavern, very crowded and clamorous, and here it is I see peering out of the hexagonal openings of a sort of honeycomb wall, or parading a large open space behind, or selecting the toys and amulets made to please them by the dainty-tentacled jewellers who work in kennels below, the mothers of the moon world—the queen bees, as it were, of the hive. They are noble-looking beings, fantastically and sometimes quite beautifully adorned, with a proud carriage, and, save for their mouths, almost microscopic heads.

"Of the condition of the moon sexes, marrying and giving in marriage, and of birth and so forth among the Selenites, I have as yet been able to learn very little. With the steady progress of Phi-oo in English, however, my ignorance will no doubt as steadily disappear. I am of opinion that, as with the ants and bees, there is a large majority of the members in this community of the neuter sex. Of course on earth in our cities there are now many who never live that life of parentage which is the natural life of man. Here, as with the ants, this thing has become a normal condition of the race, and the whole of such eplacement as is necessary falls upon this special and by no means numerous class of matrons, the mothers of the moon-world, large and stately beings beautifully fitted to bear the larval Selenite. Unless I misunderstand an explanation of Phi-oo's, they are absolutely incapable of cherishing the young they bring into the moon; periods of foolish indulgence alternate with moods of aggressive violence, and as soon as possible the little creatures, who are quite soft and flabby and pale coloured, are transferred to the charge of celibate females, women 'workers' as it were, who in some cases possess brains of almost masculine dimensions."

Just at this point, unhappily, this message broke off. Fragmentary and tantalising as the matter constituting this chapter is, it does nevertheless give a vague, broad impression of an altogether strange and wonderful world —a world with which our own may have to reckon we know not how speedily. This intermittent trickle of messages, this whispering of a record needle in the stillness of the mountain slopes, is the first warning of such a change in human conditions as mankind has scarcely imagined heretofore. In that satellite of ours there are new elements, new appliances, traditions, an overwhelming avalanche of new ideas, a strange race with whom we must inevitably struggle for mastery—gold as common as iron or wood...

CHAPTER XXV - THE GRAND LUNAR

The penultimate message describes, with occasionally elaborate detail, the encounter between Cavor and the Grand Lunar, who is the ruler or master of the moon. Cavor seems to have sent most of it without interference, but to have been interrupted in the concluding portion. The second came after an interval of a week.

The first message begins: "At last I am able to resume this—" it then becomes illegible for a space, and after a time resumed in mid- sentence.

The missing words of the following sentence are probably "the crowd." There follows quite clearly: "grew ever denser as we drew near the palace of the Grand Lunar—if I may call a series of excavations a palace. Everywhere faces stared at me—blank, chitinous gapes and masks, eyes peering over tremendous olfactory developments, eyes beneath monstrous forehead plates; and undergrowth of smaller creatures dodged and yelped, and helmet faces poised on sinuous, long-jointed necks appeared craning over shoulders and beneath armpits. Keeping a welcome space about me marched a cordon of stolid, scuttle-headed guards, who had joined us on our leaving the boat in which we had come along the channels of the Central Sea. The quick-eyed artist with the little brain joined us also, and a thick bunch of lean porter-insects swayed and struggled under the multitude of conveniences that were considered essential to my state. I was carried in a litter during the final stage of our journey. This litter was made of some very ductile metal that looked dark to me, meshed and woven, and with bars of paler metal, and about me as I advanced there grouped itself a long and complicated procession.

"In front, after the manner of heralds, marched four trumpet-faced creatures making a devastating bray; and then came squat, resolute-moving ushers before and behind, and on either hand a galaxy of learned heads, a sort of animated encyclopedia, who were, Phi-oo explained, to stand about the Grand Lunar for purposes of reference. (Not a thing in lunar science, not a point of view or method of thinking, that these wonderful beings did not carry in their heads!) Followed guards and porters, and then Phi-oo's shivering brain borne also on a litter. Then came Tsi-puff in a slightly less important litter; then myself on a litter of greater elegance than any other, and surrounded by my food and drink attendants. More trumpeters came next, splitting the ear with vehement outcries, and then several big brains, special correspondents one might well call them, or historiographers, charged with the task of observing and remembering every detail of this epoch-

making interview. A company of attendants, bearing and dragging banners and masses of scented fungus and curious symbols, vanished in the darkness behind. The way was lined by ushers and officers in caparisons that gleamed like steel, and beyond their line, so far as my eyes could pierce the gloom, the heads of that enormous crowd extended.

"I will own that I am still by no means indurated to the peculiar effect of the Selenite appearance, and to find myself, as it were, adrift on this broad sea of excited entomology was by no means agreeable. Just for a space I had something very like what I should imagine people mean when they speak of the 'horrors.' It had come to me before in these lunar caverns, when on occasion I have found myself weaponless and with an undefended back, amidst a crowd of these Selenites, but never quite so vividly. It is, of course, as absolutely irrational a feeling as one could well have, and I hope gradually to subdue it. But just for a moment, as I swept forward into the welter of the vast crowd, it was only by gripping my litter tightly and summoning all my will- power that I succeeded in avoiding an outcry or some such manifestation. It lasted perhaps three minutes; then I had myself in hand again.

"We ascended the spiral of a vertical way for some time, and then passed through a series of huge halls dome-roofed and elaborately decorated. The approach to the Grand Lunar was certainly contrived to give one a vivid impression of his greatness. Each cavern one entered seemed greater and more boldly arched than its predecessor. This effect of progressive size was enhanced by a thin haze of faintly phosphorescent blue incense that thickened as one advanced, and robbed even the nearer figures of clearness. I seemed to advance continually to something larger, dimmer, and less material.

"I must confess that all this multitude made me feel extremely shabby and unworthy. I was unshaven and unkempt; I had brought no razor; I had a coarse beard over my mouth. On earth I have always been inclined to despise any attention to my person beyond a proper care for cleanliness; but under the exceptional circumstances in which I found myself, representing, as I did, my planet and my kind, and depending very largely upon the attractiveness of my appearance for a proper reception, I could have given much for something a little more artistic and dignified than the husks I wore. I had been so serene in the belief that the moon was uninhabited as to overlook such precautions altogether. As it was I was dressed in a flannel jacket, knickerbockers, and golfing stockings, stained with every sort of dirt the moon offered, slippers (of which the left heel was wanting), and a blanket, through a hole in which I thrust my head. (These clothes, indeed, I still wear.) Sharp bristles are anything but an improvement to my cast of features, and there was an unmended tear at the knee of my knickerbockers that showed conspicuously as I squatted in my litter; my right stocking, too, persisted in getting about my ankle. I am fully alive to the injustice my appearance did humanity, and if by any expedient I could have improvised something a little out of the way and imposing I would have done so. But I could hit upon nothing. I did what I

could with my blanket—folding it somewhat after the fashion of a toga, and for the rest I sat as upright as the swaying of my litter permitted.

"Imagine the largest hall you have ever been in, imperfectly lit with blue light and obscured by a gray-blue fog, surging with metallic or livid-gray creatures of such a mad diversity as I have hinted. Imagine this hall to end in an open archway beyond which is a still larger hall, and beyond this yet another and still larger one, and so on. At the end of the vista, dimly seen, a flight of steps, like the steps of Ara Coeli at Rome, ascend out of sight. Higher and higher these steps appear to go as one draws nearer their base. But at last I came under a huge archway and beheld the summit of these steps, and upon it the Grand Lunar exalted on his throne.

"He was seated in what was relatively a blaze of incandescent blue. This, and the darkness about him gave him an effect of floating in a blue-black void. He seemed a small, self-luminous cloud at first, brooding on his sombre throne; his brain case must have measured many yards in diameter. For some reason that I cannot fathom a number of blue search-lights radiated from behind the throne on which he sat, and immediately encircling him was a halo. About him, and little and indistinct in this glow, a number of body-servants sustained and supported him, and overshadowed and standing in a huge semicircle beneath him were his intellectual subordinates, his remembrancers and computators and searchers and servants, and all the distinguished insects of the court of the moon. Still lower stood ushers and messengers, and then all down the countless steps of the throne were guards, and at the base, enormous, various, indistinct, vanishing at last into an absolute black, a vast swaying multitude of the minor dignitaries of the moon. Their feet made a perpetual scraping whisper on the rocky floor, as their limbs moved with a rustling murmur.

"As I entered the penultimate hall the music rose and expanded into an imperial magnificence of sound, and the shrieks of the news-bearers died away...

"I entered the last and greatest hall...

"My procession opened out like a fan. My ushers and guards went right and left, and the three litters bearing myself and Phi-oo and Tsi-puff marched across a shiny darkness of floor to the foot of the giant stairs. Then began a vast throbbing hum, that mingled with the music. The two Selenites dismounted, but I was bidden remain seated—I imagine as a special honour. The music ceased, but not that humming, and by a simultaneous movement of ten thousand respectful heads my attention was directed to the enhaloed supreme intelligence that hovered above me.

"At first as I peered into the radiating glow this quintessential brain looked very much like an opaque, featureless bladder with dim, undulating ghosts of convolutions writhing visibly within. Then beneath its enormity and just above the edge of the throne one saw with a start minute elfin eyes peering out of the glow. No face, but eyes, as if they peered through holes. At first I could see no more than these two staring little eyes, and then below I distinguished the little dwarfed body and its insect-jointed limbs shrivelled and white. The eyes stared

down at me with a strange intensity, and the lower part of the swollen globe was wrinkled. Ineffectual-looking little hand- tentacles steadied this shape on the throne...

"It was great. It was pitiful. One forgot the hall and the crowd.

"I ascended the staircase by jerks. It seemed to me that this darkly glowing brain case above us spread over me, and took more and more of the whole effect into itself as I drew nearer. The tiers of attendants and helpers grouped about their master seemed to dwindle and fade into the night. I saw that shadowy attendants were busy spraying that great brain with a cooling spray, and patting and sustaining it. For my own part, I sat gripping my swaying litter and staring at the Grand Lunar, unable to turn my gaze aside. And at last, as I reached a little landing that was separated only by ten steps or so from the supreme seat, the woven splendour of the music reached a climax and ceased, and I was left naked, as it were, in that vastness, beneath the still scrutiny of the Grand Lunar's eyes.

"He was scrutinising the first man he had ever seen...

"My eyes dropped at last from his greatness to the ant figures in the blue mist about him, and then down the steps to the massed Selenites, still and expectant in their thousands, packed on the floor below. Once again an unreasonable horror reached out towards me... And passed.

"After the pause came the salutation. I was assisted from my litter, and stood awkwardly while a number of curious and no doubt deeply symbolical gestures were vicariously performed for me by two slender officials. The encyclopaedic galaxy of the learned that had accompanied me to the entrance of the last hall appeared two steps above me and left and right of me, in readiness for the Grand Lunar's need, and Phi-oo's pale brain placed itself about half-way up to the throne in such a position as to communicate easily between us without turning his back on either the Grand Lunar or myself. Tsi- puff took up position behind him. Dexterous ushers sidled sideways towards me, keeping a full face to the Presence. I seated myself Turkish fashion, and Phi- oo and Tsi-puff also knelt down above me. There came a pause. The eyes of the nearer court went from me to the Grand Lunar and came back to me, and a hissing and piping of expectation passed across the hidden multitudes below and ceased.

"That humming ceased.

"For the first and last time in my experience the moon was silent.

"I became aware of a faint wheezy noise. The Grand Lunar was addressing me. It was like the rubbing of a finger upon a pane of glass.

"I watched him attentively for a time, and then glanced at the alert Phi- oo. I felt amidst these slender beings ridiculously thick and fleshy and solid; my head all jaw and black hair. My eyes went back to the Grand Lunar. He had ceased; his attendants were busy, and his shining superfices was glistening and running with cooling spray.

"Phi-oo meditated through an interval. He consulted Tsi-puff. Then he began piping his recognisable English—at first a little nervously, so that he was not very clear.

"'M'm—the Grand Lunar—wished to say—wishes to say —he gathers you are—m'm—men—that you are a man from the planet earth. He wishes to say that he welcomes you—welcomes you—and wishes to learn—learn, if I may use the word—the state of your world, and the reason why you came to this.'

"He paused. I was about to reply when he resumed. He proceeded to remarks of which the drift was not very clear, though I am inclined to think they were intended to be complimentary. He told me that the earth was to the moon what the sun is to the earth, and that the Selenites desired very greatly to learn about the earth and men. He then told me no doubt in compliment also, the relative magnitude and diameter of earth and moon, and the perpetual wonder and speculation with which the Selenites had regarded our planet. I meditated with downcast eyes, and decided to reply that men too had wondered what might lie in the moon, and had judged it dead, little recking of such magnificence as I had seen that day. The Grand Lunar, in token of recognition, caused his long blue rays to rotate in a very confusing manner, and all about the great hall ran the pipings and whisperings and rustlings of the report of what I had said. He then proceeded to put to Phi-oo a number of inquiries which were easier to answer.

"He understood, he explained, that we lived on the surface of the earth, that our air and sea were outside the globe; the latter part, indeed, he already knew from his astronomical specialists. He was very anxious to have more detailed information of what he called this extraordinary state of affairs, for from the solidity of the earth there had always been a disposition regard it as uninhabitable. He endeavoured first to ascertain the extremes of temperature to which we earth beings were exposed, and he was deeply interested by my descriptive treatment of clouds and rain. His imagination was assisted by the fact that the lunar atmosphere in the outer galleries of the night side is not infrequently very foggy. He seemed inclined to marvel that we did not find the sunlight too intense for our eyes, and was interested in my attempt to explain that the sky was tempered to a bluish colour through the refraction of the air, though I doubt if he clearly understood that. I explained how the iris of the human eyes can contract the pupil and save the delicate internal structure from the excess of sunlight, and was allowed to approach within a few feet of the Presence in order that this structure might be seen. This led to a comparison of the lunar and terrestrial eyes. The former is not only excessively sensitive to such light as men can see, but it can also *see* heat, and every difference in temperature within the moon renders objects visible to it.

"The iris was quite a new organ to the Grand Lunar. For a time he amused himself by flashing his rays into my face and watching my pupils contract. As a consequence, I was dazzled and blinded for some little time...

"But in spite of that discomfort I found something reassuring by insensible degrees in the rationality of this business of question and answer. I could shut my eyes, think of my answer, and almost forget that the Grand Lunar has no face...

"When I had descended again to my proper place the Grand Lunar asked how we sheltered ourselves from heat and storms, and I expounded to him the arts of building and furnishing. Here we wandered into misunderstandings and cross-

purposes, due largely, I must admit, to the looseness of my expressions. For a long time I had great difficulty in making him understand the nature of a house. To him and his attendant Selenites it seemed, no doubt, the most whimsical thing in the world that men should build houses when they might descend into excavations, and an additional complication was introduced by the attempt I made to explain that men had originally begun their homes in caves, and that they were now taking their railways and many establishments beneath the surface. Here I think a desire for intellectual completeness betrayed me. There was also a considerable tangle due to an equally unwise attempt on my part to explain about mines. Dismissing this topic at last in an incomplete state, the Grand Lunar inquired what we did with the interior of our globe.

"A tide of twittering and piping swept into the remotest corners of that great assembly then it was last made clear that we men know absolutely nothing of the contents of the world upon which the immemorial generations of our ancestors had been evolved. Three times had I to repeat that of all the 4000 miles of distance between the earth and its centre men knew only to the depth of a mile, and that very vaguely. I understood the Grand Lunar to ask why had I come to the moon seeing we had scarcely touched our own planet yet, but he did not trouble me at that time to proceed to an explanation, being too anxious to pursue the details of this mad inversion of all his ideas.

"He reverted to the question of weather, and I tried to describe the perpetually changing sky, and snow, and frost and hurricanes. 'But when the night comes,' he asked, 'is it not cold?'

"I told him it was colder than by day.

"'And does not your atmosphere freeze?'

"I told him not; that it was never cold enough for that, because our nights were so short.

"'Not even liquefy?'

"I was about to say 'No,' but then it occurred to me that one part at least of our atmosphere, the water vapour of it, does sometimes liquefy and form dew, and sometimes freeze and form frost—a process perfectly analogous to the freezing of all the external atmosphere of the moon during its longer night. I made myself clear on this point, and from that the Grand Lunar went on to speak with me of sleep. For the need of sleep that comes so regularly every twenty-four hours to all things is part also of our earthly inheritance. On the moon they rest only at rare intervals, and after exceptional exertions. Then I tried to describe to him the soft splendours of a summer night, and from that I passed to a description of those animals that prowl by night and sleep by day. I told him of lions and tigers, and here it seemed as though we had come to a deadlock. For, save in their waters, there are no creatures in the moon not absolutely domestic and subject to his will, and so it has been for immemorial years. They have monstrous water creatures, but no evil beasts, and the idea of anything strong and large existing 'outside' in the night is very difficult for them..."

[The record is here too broken to transcribe for the space of perhaps twenty words or more.]

"He talked with his attendants, as I suppose, upon the strange superficiality and unreasonableness of (man) who lives on the mere surface of a world, a creature of waves and winds, and all the chances of space, who cannot even unite to overcome the beasts that prey upon his kind, and yet who dares to invade another planet. During this aside I sat thinking, and then at his desire I told him of the different sorts of men. He searched me with questions. 'And for all sorts of work you have the same sort of men. But who thinks? Who governs?'

"I gave him an outline of the democratic method.

"When I had done he ordered cooling sprays upon his brow, and then requested me to repeat my explanation conceiving something had miscarried.

"'Do they not do different things, then?' said Phi-oo.

"Some, I admitted, were thinkers and some officials; some hunted, some were mechanics, some artists, some toilers. 'But *all* rule,' I said.

"'And have they not different shapes to fit them to their different duties?'

"'None that you can see,' I said, 'except perhaps, for clothes. Their minds perhaps differ a little,' I reflected.

"'Their minds must differ a great deal,' said the Grand Lunar, 'or they would all want to do the same things.'

"In order to bring myself into a closer harmony with his preconceptions, I said that his surmise was right. 'It was all hidden in the brain,' I said; 'but the difference was there. Perhaps if one could see the minds and souls of men they would be as varied and unequal as the Selenites. There were great men and small men, men who could reach out far and wide, men who could go swiftly; noisy, trumpet-minded men, and men who could remember without thinking...'"

[The record is indistinct for three words.]

"He interrupted me to recall me to my previous statements. 'But you said all men rule?' he pressed.

"'To a certain extent,' I said, and made, I fear, a denser fog with my explanation.

"He reached out to a salient fact. 'Do you mean,' asked, 'that there is no Grand Earthly?'

"I thought of several people, but assured him finally there was none. I explained that such autocrats and emperors as we had tried upon earth had usually ended in drink, or vice, or violence, and that the large and influential section of the people of the earth to which I belonged, the Anglo- Saxons, did not mean to try that sort of thing again. At which the Grand Lunar was even more amazed.

"'But how do you keep even such wisdom as you have?' he asked; and I explained to him the way we helped our limited"

[A word omitted here, probably "brains."]

"with libraries of books. I explained to him how our science was growing by the united labours of innumerable little men, and on that he made no comment save that it was evident we had mastered much in spite of our social savagery, or

we could not have come to the moon. Yet the contrast was very marked. With knowledge the Selenites grew and changed; mankind stored their knowledge about them and remained brutes—equipped. He said this..."

[Here there is a short piece of the record indistinct.]

"He then caused me to describe how we went about this earth of ours, and I described to him our railways and ships. For a time he could not understand that we had had the use of steam only one hundred years, but when he did he was clearly amazed. (I may mention as a singular thing, that the Selenites use years to count by, just as we do on earth, though I can make nothing of their numeral system. That, however, does not matter, because Phi-oo understands ours.) From that I went on to tell him that mankind had dwelt in cities only for nine or ten thousand years, and that we were still not united in one brotherhood, but under many different forms of government. This astonished the Grand Lunar very much, when it was made clear to him. At first he thought we referred merely to administrative areas.

"'Our States and Empires are still the rawest sketches of what order will some day be,' I said, and so I came to tell him..."

[At this point a length of record that probably represents thirty or forty words is totally illegible.]

"The Grand Lunar was greatly impressed by the folly of men in clinging to the inconvenience of diverse tongues. 'They want to communicate, and yet not to communicate,' he said, and then for a long time he questioned me closely concerning war.

"He was at first perplexed and incredulous. 'You mean to say,' he asked, seeking confirmation, 'that you run about over the surface of your world —this world, whose riches you have scarcely begun to scrape—killing one another for beasts to eat?'

"I told him that was perfectly correct.

"He asked for particulars to assist his imagination.

"'But do not ships and your poor little cities get injured?' he asked, and I found the waste of property and conveniences seemed to impress him almost as much as the killing. 'Tell me more,' said the Grand Lunar; 'make me see pictures. I cannot conceive these things.'

"And so, for a space, though something loath, I told him the story of earthly War.

"I told him of the first orders and ceremonies of war, of warnings and ultimatums, and the marshalling and marching of troops. I gave him an idea of manoeuvres and positions and battle joined. I told him of sieges and assaults, of starvation and hardship in trenches, and of sentinels freezing in the snow. I told him of routs and surprises, and desperate last stands and faint hopes, and the pitiless pursuit of fugitives and the dead upon the field. I told, too, of the past, of invasions and massacres, of the Huns and Tartars, and the wars of Mahomet and the Caliphs, and of the Crusades. And as I went on, and Phi-oo translated, and the Selenites cooed and murmured in a steadily intensified emotion.

"I told them an ironclad could fire a shot of a ton twelve miles, and go through 20 feet of iron—and how we could steer torpedoes under water. I went on to describe a Maxim gun in action, and what I could imagine of the Battle of Colenso. The Grand Lunar was so incredulous that he interrupted the translation of what I had said in order to have my verification of my account. They particularly doubted my description of the men cheering and rejoicing as they went into battle.

"'But surely they do not like it!' translated Phi-oo.

"I assured them men of my race considered battle the most glorious experience of life, at which the whole assembly was stricken with amazement.

"'But what good is this war?' asked the Grand Lunar, sticking to his theme.

"'Oh! as for *good*!' said I; 'it thins the population!'

"'But why should there be a need—?'

"There came a pause, the cooling sprays impinged upon his brow, and then he spoke again."

[At this point a series of undulations that have been apparent as a perplexing complication as far back as Cavor's description of the silence that fell before the first speaking of the Grand Lunar become confusingly predominant in the record. These undulations are evidently the result of radiations proceeding from a lunar source, and their persistent approximation to the alternating signals of Cavor is curiously suggestive of some operator deliberately seeking to mix them in with his message and render it illegible. At first they are small and regular, so that with a little care and the loss of very few words we have been able to disentangle Cavor's message; then they become broad and larger, then suddenly they are irregular, with an irregularity that gives the effect at last of some one scribbling through a line of writing. For a long time nothing can be made of this madly zigzagging trace; then quite abruptly the interruption ceases, leaves a few words clear, and then resumes and continues for the rest of the message, completely obliterating whatever Cavor was attempting to transmit. Why, if this is indeed a deliberate intervention, the Selenites should have preferred to let Cavor go on transmitting his message in happy ignorance of their obliteration of its record, when it was clearly quite in their power and much more easy and convenient for them to stop his proceedings at any time, is a problem to which I can contribute nothing. The thing seems to have happened so, and that is all I can say. This last rag of his description of the Grand Lunar begins in mid- sentence.]

"...interrogated me very closely upon my secret. I was able in a little while to get to an understanding with them, and at last to elucidate what has been a puzzle to me ever since I realised the vastness of their science, namely, how it is they themselves have never discovered 'Cavorite.' I find they know of it as a theoretical substance, but they have always regarded it as a practical impossibility, because for some reason there is no helium in the moon, and helium..."

[Across the last letters of helium slashes the resumption of that obliterating trace. Note that word "secret," for that, and that alone, I base my interpretation of the message that follows, the last message, as both Mr. Wendigee and myself now believe it to be, that he is ever likely to send us.]

CHAPTER XXVI - THE LAST MESSAGE CAVOR SENT TO THE EARTH

On this unsatisfactory manner the penultimate message of Cavor dies out. One seems to see him away there in the blue obscurity amidst his apparatus intently signalling us to the last, all unaware of the curtain of confusion that drops between us; all unaware, too, of the final dangers that even then must have been creeping upon him. His disastrous want of vulgar common sense had utterly betrayed him. He had talked of war, he had talked of all the strength and irrational violence of men, of their insatiable aggressions, their tireless futility of conflict. He had filled the whole moon world with this impression of our race, and then I think it is plain that he made the most fatal admission that upon himself alone hung the possibility—at least for a long time—of any further men reaching the moon. The line the cold, inhuman reason of the moon would take seems plain enough to me, and a suspicion of it, and then perhaps some sudden sharp realisation of it, must have come to him. One imagines him about the moon with the remorse of this fatal indiscretion growing in his mind. During a certain time I am inclined to guess the Grand Lunar was deliberating the new situation, and for all that time Cavor may have gone as free as ever he had gone. But obstacles of some sort prevented his getting to his electromagnetic apparatus again after that message I have just given. For some days we received nothing. Perhaps he was having fresh audiences, and trying to evade his previous admissions. Who can hope to guess?

And then suddenly, like a cry in the night, like a cry that is followed by a stillness, came the last message. It is the briefest fragment, the broken beginnings of two sentences.

The first was: "I was mad to let the Grand Lunar know—"

There was an interval of perhaps a minute. One imagines some interruption from without. A departure from the instrument—a dreadful hesitation among the looming masses of apparatus in that dim, blue-lit cavern—a sudden rush back to it, full of a resolve that came too late. Then, as if it were hastily transmitted came: "Cavorite made as follows: take—"

There followed one word, a quite unmeaning word as it stands: "uless."

And that is all.

It may be he made a hasty attempt to spell "useless" when his fate was close upon him. Whatever it was that was happening about that apparatus we cannot tell. Whatever it was we shall never, I know, receive another message from the

moon. For my own part a vivid dream has come to my help, and I see, almost as plainly as though I had seen it in actual fact, a blue-lit shadowy dishevelled Cavor struggling in the grip of these insect Selenites, struggling ever more desperately and hopelessly as they press upon him, shouting, expostulating, perhaps even at last fighting, and being forced backwards step by step out of all speech or sign of his fellows, for evermore into the Unknown —into the dark, into that silence that has no end...

THE FOOD OF THE GODS AND HOW IT CAME TO EARTH

Pearson's Magazine, Dec 1903 - Jun 1904
(7 installments)
First book edition: Macmillan & Co., London, 1904

BOOK I - THE DAWN OF THE FOOD

CHAPTER THE FIRST - THE DISCOVERY OF THE FOOD

I

In the middle years of the nineteenth century there first became abundant in this strange world of ours a class of men, men tending for the most part to become elderly, who are called, and who are very properly called, but who dislike extremely to be called—"Scientists." They dislike that word so much that from the columns of *Nature*, which was from the first their distinctive and characteristic paper, it is as carefully excluded as if it were —that other word which is the basis of all really bad language in this country. But the Great Public and its Press know better, and "Scientists" they are, and when they emerge to any sort of publicity, "distinguished scientists" and "eminent scientists" and "well-known scientists" is the very least we call them.

Certainly both Mr. Bensington and Professor Redwood quite merited any of these terms long before they came upon the marvellous discovery of which this story tells. Mr. Bensington was a Fellow of the Royal Society and a former president of the Chemical Society, and Professor Redwood was Professor of Physiology in the Bond Street College of the London University, and he had been grossly libelled by the anti-vivisectionists time after time. And they had led lives of academic distinction from their very earliest youth.

They were of course quite undistinguished looking men, as indeed all true Scientists are. There is more personal distinction about the mildest-mannered actor alive than there is about the entire Royal Society. Mr. Bensington was short and very, very bald, and he stooped slightly; he wore gold-rimmed spectacles and cloth boots that were abundantly cut open because of his numerous corns, and Professor Redwood was entirely ordinary in his appearance. Until they happened upon the Food of the Gods (as I must insist upon calling it) they led lives of such eminent and studious obscurity that it is hard to find anything whatever to tell the reader about them.

Mr. Bensington won his spurs (if one may use such an expression of a gentleman in boots of slashed cloth) by his splendid researches upon the More Toxic

Alkaloids, and Professor Redwood rose to eminence—I do not clearly remember how he rose to eminence! I know he was very eminent, and that's all. Things of this sort grow. I fancy it was a voluminous work on Reaction Times with numerous plates of sphygmograph tracings (I write subject to correction) and an admirable new terminology, that did the thing for him.

The general public saw little or nothing of either of these gentlemen. Sometimes at places like the Royal Institution and the Society of Arts it did in a sort of way see Mr. Bensington, or at least his blushing baldness and something of his collar and coat, and hear fragments of a lecture or paper that he imagined himself to be reading audibly; and once I remember—one midday in the vanished past—when the British Association was at Dover, coming on Section C or D, or some such letter, which had taken up its quarters in a public-house, and following two, serious-looking ladies with paper parcels, out of mere curiosity, through a door labelled "Billiards" and "Pool" into a scandalous darkness, broken only by a magic-lantern circle of Redwood's tracings.

I watched the lantern slides come and go, and listened to a voice (I forget what it was saying) which I believe was the voice of Professor Redwood, and there was a sizzling from the lantern and another sound that kept me there, still out of curiosity, until the lights were unexpectedly turned up. And then I perceived that this sound was the sound of the munching of buns and sandwiches and things that the assembled British Associates had come there to eat under cover of the magic-lantern darkness.

And Redwood I remember went on talking all the time the lights were up and dabbing at the place where his diagram ought to have been visible on the screen—and so it was again so soon as the darkness was restored. I remember him then as a most ordinary, slightly nervous-looking dark man, with an air of being preoccupied with something else, and doing what he was doing just then under an unaccountable sense of duty.

I heard Bensington also once—in the old days—at an educational conference in Bloomsbury. Like most eminent chemists and botanists, Mr. Bensington was very authoritative upon teaching—though I am certain he would have been scared out of his wits by an average Board School class in half-an-hour—and so far as I can remember now, he was propounding an improvement of Professor Armstrong's Heuristic method, whereby at the cost of three or four hundred pounds' worth of apparatus, a total neglect of all other studies and the undivided attention of a teacher of exceptional gifts, an average child might with a peculiar sort of thumby thoroughness learn in the course of ten or twelve years almost as much chemistry as one could get in one of those objectionable shilling text-books that were then so common...

Quite ordinary persons you perceive, both of them, outside their science. Or if anything on the unpractical side of ordinary. And that you will find is the case with "scientists" as a class all the world over. What there is great of them is an annoyance to their fellow scientists and a mystery to the general public, and what is not is evident.

There is no doubt about what is not great, no race of men have such obvious littlenesses. They live in a narrow world so far as their human intercourse goes; their researches involve infinite attention and an almost monastic seclusion; and what is left over is not very much. To witness some queer, shy, misshapen, grey-headed, self-important, little discoverer of great discoveries, ridiculously adorned with the wide ribbon of some order of chivalry and holding a reception of his fellow-men, or to read the anguish of *Nature* at the "neglect of science" when the angel of the birthday honours passes the Royal Society by, or to listen to one indefatigable lichenologist commenting on the work of another indefatigable lichenologist, such things force one to realise the unfaltering littleness of men.

And withal the reef of Science that these little "scientists" built and are yet building is so wonderful, so portentous, so full of mysterious half- shapen promises for the mighty future of man! They do not seem to realise the things they are doing! No doubt long ago even Mr. Bensington, when he chose this calling, when he consecrated his life to the alkaloids and their kindred compounds, had some inkling of the vision,—more than an inkling. Without some such inspiration, for such glories and positions only as a "scientist" may expect, what young man would have given his life to such work, as young men do? No, they *must* have seen the glory, they must have had the vision, but so near that it has blinded them. The splendour has blinded them, mercifully, so that for the rest of their lives they can hold the lights of knowledge in comfort—that we may see!

And perhaps it accounts for Redwood's touch of preoccupation, that —there can be no doubt of it now—he among his fellows was different, he was different inasmuch as something of the vision still lingered in his eyes.

II

The Food of the Gods I call it, this substance that Mr. Bensington and Professor Redwood made between them; and having regard now to what it has already done and all that it is certainly going to do, there is surely no exaggeration in the name. So I shall continue to call it therefore throughout my story. But Mr. Bensington would no more have called it that in cold blood than he would have gone out from his flat in Sloane Street clad in regal scarlet and a wreath of laurel. The phrase was a mere first cry of astonishment from him. He called it the Food of the Gods, in his enthusiasm and for an hour or so at the most altogether. After that he decided he was being absurd. When he first thought of the thing he saw, as it were, a vista of enormous possibilities—literally enormous possibilities; but upon this dazzling vista, after one stare of amazement, he resolutely shut his eyes, even as a conscientious "scientist" should. After that, the Food of the Gods sounded blatant to the pitch of indecency. He was surprised he had used the expression. Yet for all that something of that clear-eyed moment hung about him and broke out ever and again...

"Really, you know," he said, rubbing his hands together and laughing nervously, "it has more than a theoretical interest.

"For example," he confided, bringing his face close to the Professor's and dropping to an undertone, "it would perhaps, if suitably handled, *sell*...

"Precisely," he said, walking away,—"as a Food. Or at least a food ingredient.

"Assuming of course that it is palatable. A thing we cannot know till we have prepared it."

He turned upon the hearthrug, and studied the carefully designed slits upon his cloth shoes.

"Name?" he said, looking up in response to an inquiry. "For my part I incline to the good old classical allusion. It—it makes Science res —. Gives it a touch of old-fashioned dignity. I have been thinking ... I don't know if you will think it absurd of me... A little fancy is surely occasionally permissible... Herakleophorbia. Eh? The nutrition of a possible Hercules? You know it *might*...

"Of course if you think *not*—"

Redwood reflected with his eyes on the fire and made no objection.

"You think it would do?"

Redwood moved his head gravely.

"It might be Titanophorbia, you know. Food of Titans... You prefer the former?

"You're quite sure you don't think it a little *too*—"

"No."

"Ah! I'm glad."

And so they called it Herakleophorbia throughout their investigations, and in their report,—the report that was never published, because of the unexpected developments that upset all their arrangements,—it is invariably written in that way. There were three kindred substances prepared before they hit on the one their speculations had foretold and these they spoke of as Herakleophorbia I, Herakleophorbia II, and Herakleophorbia III. It is Herakleophorbia IV. which I—insisting upon Bensington's original name—call here the Food of the Gods.

III

The idea was Mr. Bensington's. But as it was suggested to him by one of Professor Redwood's contributions to the Philosophical Transactions, he very properly consulted that gentleman before he carried it further. Besides which it was, as a research, a physiological, quite as much as a chemical inquiry.

Professor Redwood was one of those scientific men who are addicted to tracings and curves. You are familiar—if you are at all the sort of reader I like—with the sort of scientific paper I mean. It is a paper you cannot make head nor tail of, and at the end come five or six long folded diagrams that open out and show peculiar zigzag tracings, flashes of lightning overdone, or sinuous inexplicable things called "smoothed curves" set up on ordinates and rooting in abscissae—and things like that. You puzzle over the thing for a long time and end with the suspicion that not only do you not understand it but that the author does not understand it either. But really you know many of these scientific people understand the

meaning of their own papers quite well: it is simply a defect of expression that raises the obstacle between us.

I am inclined to think that Redwood thought in tracings and curves. And after his monumental work upon Reaction Times (the unscientific reader is exhorted to stick to it for a little bit longer and everything will be as clear as daylight) Redwood began to turn out smoothed curves and sphygmographeries upon Growth, and it was one of his papers upon Growth that really gave Mr. Bensington his idea.

Redwood, you know, had been measuring growing things of all sorts, kittens, puppies, sunflowers, mushrooms, bean plants, and (until his wife put a stop to it) his baby, and he showed that growth went out not at a regular pace, or, as he put it, so,

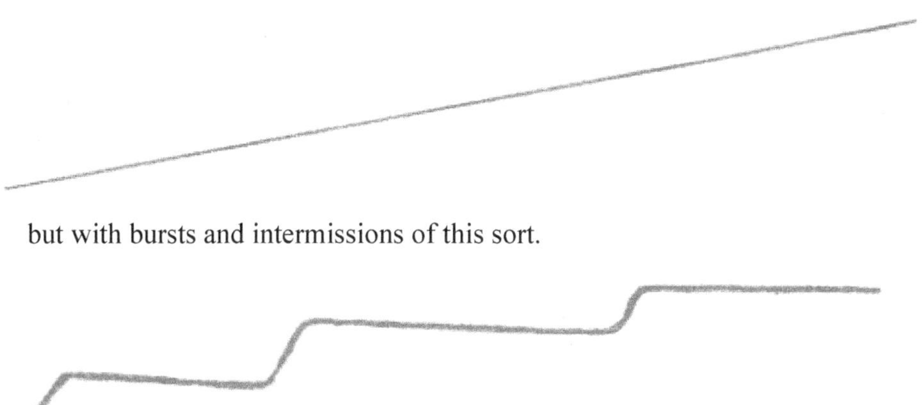

but with bursts and intermissions of this sort.

and that apparently nothing grew regularly and steadily, and so far as he could make out nothing could grow regularly and steadily: it was as if every living thing had just to accumulate force to grow, grew with vigour only for a time, and then had to wait for a space before it could go on growing again. And in the muffled and highly technical language of the really careful "scientist," Redwood suggested that the process of growth probably demanded the presence of a considerable quantity of some necessary substance in the blood that was only formed very slowly, and that when this substance was used up by growth, it was only very slowly replaced, and that meanwhile the organism had to mark time. He compared his unknown substance to oil in machinery. A growing animal was rather like an engine, he suggested, that can move a certain distance and must then be oiled before it can run again. ("But why shouldn't one oil the engine from without?" said Mr. Bensington, when he read the paper.) And all this, said Redwood, with the delightful nervous inconsecutiveness of his class, might very probably be found to throw a light upon the mystery of certain of the ductless glands. As though they had anything to do with it at all!

In a subsequent communication Redwood went further. He gave a perfect Brock's benefit of diagrams—exactly like rocket trajectories they were; and the gist of it—so far as it had any gist—was that the blood of puppies and kittens and

the sap of sunflowers and the juice of mushrooms in what he called the "growing phase" differed in the proportion of certain elements from their blood and sap on the days when they were not particularly growing.

And when Mr. Bensington, after holding the diagrams sideways and upside down, began to see what this difference was, a great amazement came upon him. Because, you see, the difference might probably be due to the presence of just the very substance he had recently been trying to isolate in his researches upon such alkaloids as are most stimulating to the nervous system. He put down Redwood's paper on the patent reading-desk that swung inconveniently from his arm-chair, took off his gold-rimmed spectacles, breathed on them and wiped them very carefully.

"By Jove!" said Mr. Bensington.

Then replacing his spectacles again he turned to the patent reading-desk, which immediately, as his elbow came against its arm, gave a coquettish squeak and deposited the paper, with all its diagrams in a dispersed and crumpled state, on the floor. "By Jove!" said Mr. Bensington, straining his stomach over the arm-chair with a patient disregard of the habits of this convenience, and then, finding the pamphlet still out of reach, he went down on all fours in pursuit. It was on the floor that the idea of calling it the Food of the Gods came to him...

For you see, if he was right and Redwood was right, then by injecting or administering this new substance of his in food, he would do away with the "resting phase," and instead of growth going on in this fashion,

IV

The night after his conversation with Redwood Mr. Bensington could scarcely sleep a wink. He did seem once to get into a sort of doze, but it was only for a moment, and then he dreamt he had dug a deep hole into the earth and poured in tons and tons of the Food of the Gods, and the earth was swelling and swelling, and all the boundaries of the countries were bursting, and the Royal Geographical Society was all at work like one great guild of tailors letting out the equator...

That of course was a ridiculous dream, but it shows the state of mental excitement into which Mr. Bensington got and the real value he attached to his idea, much better than any of the things he said or did when he was awake and on his guard. Or I should not have mentioned it, because as a general rule I do not think it is at all interesting for people to tell each other about their dreams.

By a singular coincidence Redwood also had a dream that night, and his dream was this:—

It was a diagram done in fire upon a long scroll of the abyss. And he (Redwood) was standing on a planet before a sort of black platform lecturing about the new sort of growth that was now possible, to the More than Royal Institution of Primordial Forces—forces which had always previously, even in the growth of races, empires, planetary systems, and worlds, gone so:—

And even in some cases so:—

And he was explaining to them quite lucidly and convincingly that these slow, these even retrogressive methods would be very speedily quite put out of fashion by his discovery.

Ridiculous of course! But that too shows—

That either dream is to be regarded as in any way significant or prophetic beyond what I have categorically said, I do not for one moment suggest.

CHAPTER THE SECOND - THE EXPERIMENTAL FARM

I

Mr. Bensington proposed originally to try this stuff, so soon as he was really able to prepare it, upon tadpoles. One always does try this sort of thing upon tadpoles to begin with; this being what tadpoles are for. And it was agreed that he should conduct the experiments and not Redwood, because Redwood's laboratory was occupied with the ballistic apparatus and animals necessary for an investigation into the Diurnal Variation in the Butting Frequency of the Young Bull Calf, an investigation that was yielding curves of an abnormal and very perplexing sort, and the presence of glass globes of tadpoles was extremely undesirable while this particular research was in progress.

But when Mr. Bensington conveyed to his cousin Jane something of what he had in mind, she put a prompt veto upon the importation of any considerable number of tadpoles, or any such experimental creatures, into their flat. She had no objection whatever to his use of one of the rooms of the flat for the purposes of a non-explosive chemistry that, so far as she was concerned, came to nothing; she let him have a gas furnace and a sink and a dust-tight cupboard of refuge from the weekly storm of cleaning she would not forego. And having known people addicted to drink, she regarded his solicitude for distinction in learned societies as an excellent substitute for the coarser form of depravity. But any sort of living things in quantity, "wriggly" as they were bound to be alive and "smelly" dead, she could not and would not abide. She said these things were certain to be unhealthy, and Bensington was notoriously a delicate man—it was nonsense to say he wasn't. And when Bensington tried to make the enormous importance of this possible discovery clear, she said that it was all very well, but if she consented to his making everything nasty and unwholesome in the place (and that was what it all came to) then she was certain he would be the first to complain.

And Mr. Bensington went up and down the room, regardless of his corns, and spoke to her quite firmly and angrily without the slightest effect. He said that nothing ought to stand in the way of the Advancement of Science, and she said that the Advancement of Science was one thing and having a lot of tadpoles in a flat was another; he said that in Germany it was an ascertained fact that a man with an idea like his would at once have twenty thousand properly-fitted cubic feet of laboratory placed at his disposal, and she said she was glad and always had been glad that she was not a German; he said that it would make him famous for

ever, and she said it was much more likely to make him ill to have a lot of tadpoles in a flat like theirs; he said he was master in his own house, and she said that rather than wait on a lot of tadpoles she'd go as matron to a school; and then he asked her to be reasonable, and she asked *him* to be reasonable then and give up all this about tadpoles; and he said she might respect his ideas, and she said not if they were smelly she wouldn't, and then he gave way completely and said—in spite of the classical remarks of Huxley upon the subject—a bad word. Not a very bad word it was, but bad enough.

And after that she was greatly offended and had to be apologised to, and the prospect of ever trying the Food of the Gods upon tadpoles in their flat at any rate vanished completely in the apology.

So Bensington had to consider some other way of carrying out these experiments in feeding that would be necessary to demonstrate his discovery, so soon as he had his substance isolated and prepared. For some days he meditated upon the possibility of boarding out his tadpoles with some trustworthy person, and then the chance sight of the phrase in a newspaper turned his thoughts to an Experimental Farm.

And chicks. Directly he thought of it, he thought of it as a poultry farm. He was suddenly taken with a vision of wildly growing chicks. He conceived a picture of coops and runs, outsize and still more outsize coops, and runs progressively larger. Chicks are so accessible, so easily fed and observed, so much drier to handle and measure, that for his purpose tadpoles seemed to him now, in comparison with them, quite wild and uncontrollable beasts. He was quite puzzled to understand why he had not thought of chicks instead of tadpoles from the beginning. Among other things it would have saved all this trouble with his cousin Jane. And when he suggested this to Redwood, Redwood quite agreed with him.

Redwood said that in working so much upon needlessly small animals he was convinced experimental physiologists made a great mistake. It is exactly like making experiments in chemistry with an insufficient quantity of material; errors of observation and manipulation become disproportionately large. It was of extreme importance just at present that scientific men should assert their right to have their material *big*. That was why he was doing his present series of experiments at the Bond Street College upon Bull Calves, in spite of a certain amount of inconvenience to the students and professors of other subjects caused by their incidental levity in the corridors. But the curves he was getting were quite exceptionally interesting, and would, when published, amply justify his choice. For his own part, were it not for the inadequate endowment of science in this country, he would never, if he could avoid it, work on anything smaller than a whale. But a Public Vivarium on a sufficient scale to render this possible was, he feared, at present, in this country at any rate, a Utopian demand. In Germany—Etc.

As Redwood's Bull calves needed his daily attention, the selection and equipment of the Experimental Farm fell largely on Bensington. The entire cost also,

was, it was understood, to be defrayed by Bensington, at least until a grant could be obtained. Accordingly he alternated his work in the laboratory of his flat with farm hunting up and down the lines that run southward out of London, and his peering spectacles, his simple baldness, and his lacerated cloth shoes filled the owners of numerous undesirable properties with vain hopes. And he advertised in several daily papers and *Nature* for a responsible couple (married), punctual, active, and used to poultry, to take entire charge of an Experimental Farm of three acres.

He found the place he seemed in need of at Hickleybrow, near Urshot, in Kent. It was a little queer isolated place, in a dell surrounded by old pine woods that were black and forbidding at night. A humped shoulder of down cut it off from the sunset, and a gaunt well with a shattered penthouse dwarfed the dwelling. The little house was creeperless, several windows were broken, and the cart shed had a black shadow at midday. It was a mile and a half from the end house of the village, and its loneliness was very doubtfully relieved by an ambiguous family of echoes.

The place impressed Bensington as being eminently adapted to the requirements of scientific research. He walked over the premises sketching out coops and runs with a sweeping arm, and he found the kitchen capable of accommodating a series of incubators and foster mothers with the very minimum of alteration. He took the place there and then; on his way back to London he stopped at Dunton Green and closed with an eligible couple that had answered his advertisements, and that same evening he succeeded in isolating a sufficient quantity of Herakleophorbia I. to more than justify these engagements.

The eligible couple who were destined under Mr. Bensington to be the first almoners on earth of the Food of the Gods, were not only very perceptibly aged, but also extremely dirty. This latter point Mr. Bensington did not observe, because nothing destroys the powers of general observation quite so much as a life of experimental science. They were named Skinner, Mr. and Mrs. Skinner, and Mr. Bensington interviewed them in a small room with hermetically sealed windows, a spotted overmantel looking-glass, and some ailing calceolarias.

Mrs. Skinner was a very little old woman, capless, with dirty white hair drawn back very very tightly from a face that had begun by being chiefly, and was now, through the loss of teeth and chin, and the wrinkling up of everything else, ending by being almost exclusively—nose. She was dressed in slate colour (so far as her dress had any colour) slashed in one place with red flannel. She let him in and talked to him guardedly and peered at him round and over her nose, while Mr. Skinner she alleged made some alteration in his toilette. She had one tooth that got into her articulations and she held her two long wrinkled hands nervously together. She told Mr. Bensington that she had managed fowls for years; and knew all about incubators; in fact, they themselves had run a Poultry Farm at one time, and it had only failed at last through the want of pupils. "It's the pupils as pay," said Mrs. Skinner.

Mr. Skinner, when he appeared, was a large-faced man, with a lisp and a squint that made him look over the top of your head, slashed slippers that appealed to Mr. Bensington's sympathies, and a manifest shortness of buttons. He held his coat and shirt together with one hand and traced patterns on the black-and-gold tablecloth with the index finger of the other, while his disengaged eye watched Mr. Bensington's sword of Damocles, so to speak, with an expression of sad detachment. "You don't want to run thith Farm for profit. No, Thir. Ith all the thame, Thir. Ekthperimenth! Prethithely."

He said they could go to the farm at once. He was doing nothing at Dunton Green except a little tailoring. "It ithn't the thmart plathe I thought it wath, and what I get ithent thkarthely worth having," he said, "tho that if it ith any convenienth to you for uth to come..."

And in a week Mr. and Mrs. Skinner were installed in the farm, and the jobbing carpenter from Hickleybrow was diversifying the task of erecting runs and henhouses with a systematic discussion of Mr. Bensington.

"I haven't theen much of 'im yet," said Mr. Skinner. "But as far as I can make 'im out 'e theems to be a thtewpid o' fool."

"*I* thought 'e seemed a bit Dotty," said the carpenter from Hickleybrow.

"'E fanthieth 'imself about poultry," said Mr. Skinner. "O my goodneth! You'd think nobody knew nothin' about poultry thept 'im."

"'E *looks* like a 'en," said the carpenter from Hickleybrow; "what with them spectacles of 'is."

Mr. Skinner came closer to the carpenter from Hickleybrow, and spoke in a confidential manner, and one sad eye regarded the distant village, and one was bright and wicked. "Got to be meathured every blethed day—every blethed 'en, 'e thays. Tho as to thee they grow properly. What oh ... eh? Every blethed 'en—every blethed day."

And Mr. Skinner put up his hand to laugh behind it in a refined and contagious manner, and humped his shoulders very much—and only the other eye of him failed to participate in his laughter. Then doubting if the carpenter had quite got the point of it, he repeated in a penetrating whisper; "*Meathured*!"

"'E's worse than our old guvnor; I'm dratted if 'e ain't," said the carpenter from Hickleybrow.

II

Experimental work is the most tedious thing in the world (unless it be the reports of it in the *Philosophical Transactions*), and it seemed a long time to Mr. Bensington before his first dream of enormous possibilities was replaced by a crumb of realisation. He had taken the Experimental Farm in October, and it was May before the first inklings of success began. Herakleophorbia I. and II. and III. had to be tried, and failed; there was trouble with the rats of the Experimental Farm, and there was trouble with the Skinners. The only way to get Skinner to do anything he was told to do was to dismiss him. Then he would nib his unshaven chin—he was always unshaven most miraculously and yet never bearded—with a

flattened hand, and look at Mr. Bensington with one eye, and over him with the other, and say, "Oo, of courthe, Thir—if you're *theriouth*!"

But at last success dawned. And its herald was a letter in the long slender handwriting of Mr. Skinner.

"The new Brood are out," wrote Mr. Skinner, "and don't quite like the look of them. Growing very rank—quite unlike what the similar lot was before your last directions was given. The last, before the cat got them, was a very nice, stocky chick, but these are Growing like thistles. I never saw. They peck so hard, striking above boot top, that am unable to give exact Measures as requested. They are regular Giants, and eating as such. We shall want more corn very soon, for you never saw such chicks to eat. Bigger than Bantams. Going on at this rate, they ought to be a bird for show, rank as they are. Plymouth Rocks won't be in it. Had a scare last night thinking that cat was at them, and when I looked out at the window could have sworn I see her getting in under the wire. The chicks was all awake and pecking about hungry when I went out, but could not see anything of the cat. So gave them a peck of corn, and fastened up safe. Shall be glad to know if the Feeding to be continued as directed. Food you mixed is pretty near all gone, and do not like to mix any more myself on account of the accident with the pudding. With best wishes from us both, and soliciting continuance of esteemed favours,

"Respectfully yours,

"ALFRED NEWTON SKINNER."

The allusion towards the end referred to a milk pudding with which some Herakleophorbia II. had got itself mixed with painful and very nearly fatal results to the Skinners.

But Mr. Bensington, reading between the lines saw in this rankness of growth the attainment of his long sought goal. The next morning he alighted at Urshot station, and in the bag in his hand he carried, sealed in three tins, a supply of the Food of the Gods sufficient for all the chicks in Kent.

It was a bright and beautiful morning late in May, and his corns were so much better that he resolved to walk through Hickleybrow to his farm. It was three miles and a half altogether, through the park and villages and then along the green glades of the Hickleybrow preserves. The trees were all dusted with the green spangles of high spring, the hedges were full of stitchwort and campion and the woods of blue hyacinths and purple orchid; and everywhere there was a great noise of birds—thrushes, blackbirds, robins, finches, and many more—and in one warm corner of the park some bracken was unrolling, and there was a leaping and rushing of fallow deer.

These things brought back to Mr. Bensington his early and forgotten delight in life; before him the promise of his discovery grew bright and joyful, and it seemed to him that indeed he must have come upon the happiest day in his life. And when in the sunlit run by the sandy bank under the shadow of the pine trees he saw the chicks that had eaten the food he had mixed for them, gigantic and gawky, bigger already than many a hen that is married and settleds and still grow-

ing, still in their first soft yellow plumage (just faintly marked with brown along the back), he knew indeed that his happiest day had come.

At Mr. Skinner's urgency he went into the runs but after he had been pecked through the cracks in his shoes once or twice he got out again, and watched these monsters through the wire netting. He peered close to the netting, and followed their movements as though he had never seen a chick before in his life.

"Whath they'll be when they're grown up ith impothible to think," said Mr. Skinner.

"Big as a horse," said Mr. Bensington.

"Pretty near," said Mr. Skinner.

"Several people could dine off a wing!" said Mr. Bensington. "They'd cut up into joints like butcher's meat."

"They won't go on growing at thith pathe though," said Mr. Skinner.

"No?" said Mr. Bensington.

"No," said Mr. Skinner. "I know thith thort. They begin rank, but they don't go on, bleth you! No."

There was a pause.

"Itth management," said Mr. Skinner modestly.

Mr. Bensington turned his glasses on him suddenly.

"We got 'em almoth ath big at the other plathe," said Mr. Skinner, with his better eye piously uplifted and letting himself go a little; "me and the mithith."

Mr. Bensington made his usual general inspection of the premises, but he speedily returned to the new run. It was, you know, in truth ever so much more than he had dared to expect. The course of science is so tortuous and so slow; after the clear promises and before the practical realisation arrives there comes almost always year after year of intricate contrivance, and here—here was the Foods of the Gods arriving after less than a year of testing! It seemed too good—too good. That Hope Deferred which is the daily food of the scientific imagination was to be his no more! So at least it seemed to him then. He came back and stared at these stupendous chicks of his, time after time.

"Let me see," he said. "They're ten days old. And by the side of an ordinary chick I should fancy—about six or seven times as big..."

"Itth about time we artht for a rithe in thkrew," said Mr. Skinner to his wife. "He'th ath pleathed ath Punth about the way we got thothe chickth on in the further run—pleathed ath Punth he ith."

He bent confidentially towards her. "Thinkth it'th that old food of hith," he said behind his hands and made a noise of suppressed laughter in his pharyngeal cavity...

Mr. Bensington was indeed a happy man that day. He was in no mood to find fault with details of management. The bright day certainly brought out the accumulating slovenliness of the Skinner couple more vividly than he had ever seen it before. But his comments were of the gentlest. The fencing of many of the runs was out of order, but he seemed to consider it quite satisfactory when Mr. Skinner

explained that it was a "fokth or a dog or thomething" did it. He pointed out that the incubator had not been cleaned.

"That it *asn't*, Sir," said Mrs. Skinner with her arms folded, smiling coyly behind her nose. "We don't seem to have had time to clean it not since we been 'ere..."

He went upstairs to see some rat-holes that Skinner said would justify a trap—they certainly were enormous—and discovered that the room in which the Food of the Gods was mixed with meal and bran was in a quite disgraceful order. The Skinners were the sort of people who find a use for cracked saucers and old cans and pickle jars and mustard boxes, and the place was littered with these. In one corner a great pile of apples that Skinner had saved was decaying, and from a nail in the sloping part of the ceiling hung several rabbit skins, upon which he proposed to test his gift as a furrier. ("There ithn't mutth about furth and thingth that *I* don't know," said Skinner.)

Mr. Bensington certainly sniffed critically at this disorder, but he made no unnecessary fuss, and even when he found a wasp regaling itself in a gallipot half full of Herakleophorbia IV, he simply remarked mildly that his substance was better sealed from the damp than exposed to the air in that manner.

And he turned from these things at once to remark—what had been for some time in his mind—"I *think*, Skinner—you know, I shall kill one of these chicks—as a specimen. I think we will kill it this afternoon, and I will take it back with me to London."

He pretended to peer into another gallipot and then took off his spectacles to wipe them.

"I should like," he said, "I should like very much, to have some relic —some memento—of this particular brood at this particular day."

"By-the-bye," he said, "you don't give those little chicks meat?"

"Oh! *no*, Thir," said Skinner, "I can athure you, Thir, we know far too much about the management of fowlth of all dethcriptionth to do anything of that thort."

"Quite sure you don't throw your dinner refuse—I thought I noticed the bones of a rabbit scattered about the far corner of the run—"

But when they came to look at them they found they were the larger bones of a cat picked very clean and dry.

III

"*That's* no chick," said Mr. Bensington's cousin Jane.

"Well, I should *think* I knew a chick when I saw it," said Mr. Bensington's cousin Jane hotly.

"It's too big for a chick, for one thing, and besides you can *see* perfectly well it isn't a chick.

"It's more like a bustard than a chick."

"For my part," said Redwood, reluctantly allowing Bensington to drag him into the argument, "I must confess that, considering all the evidence—"

"Oh I if you do *that*," said Mr. Bensington's cousin Jane, "instead of using your eyes like a sensible person—"

"Well, but really, Miss Bensington—!"

"Oh! Go *on!*" said Cousin Jane. "You men are all alike."

"Considering all the evidence, this certainly falls within the definition —no doubt it's abnormal and hypertrophied, but still—especially since it was hatched from the egg of a normal hen—Yes, I think, Miss Bensington, I must admit—this, so far as one can call it anything, is a sort of chick."

"You mean it's a chick?" said cousin Jane.

"I *think* it's a chick," said Redwood.

"What NONSENSE!" said Mr. Bensington's cousin Jane, and "Oh!" directed at Redwood's head, "I haven't patience with you," and then suddenly she turned about and went out of the room with a slam.

"And it's a very great relief for me to see it too, Bensington," said Redwood, when the reverberation of the slam had died away. "In spite of its being so big."

Without any urgency from Mr. Bensington he sat down in the low arm-chair by the fire and confessed to proceedings that even in an unscientific man would have been indiscreet. "You will think it very rash of me, Bensington, I know," he said, "but the fact is I put a little—not very much of it—but some—into Baby's bottle, very nearly a week ago!"

"But suppose—!" cried Mr. Bensington.

"I know," said Redwood, and glanced at the giant chick upon the plate on the table.

"It's turned out all right, thank goodness," and he felt in his pocket for his cigarettes.

He gave fragmentary details. "Poor little chap wasn't putting on weight... desperately anxious.—Winkles, a frightful duffer ... former pupil of mine ... no good... Mrs. Redwood—unmitigated confidence in Winkles... *You* know, man with a manner like a cliff—towering... No confidence in *me*, of course... Taught Winkles... Scarcely allowed in the nursery... Something had to be done... Slipped in while the nurse was at breakfast ... got at the bottle."

"But he'll grow," said Mr. Bensington.

"He's growing. Twenty-seven ounces last week... You should hear Winkles. It's management, he said."

"Dear me! That's what Skinner says!"

Redwood looked at the chick again. "The bother is to keep it up," he said. "They won't trust me in the nursery alone, because I tried to get a growth curve out of Georgina Phyllis—you know—and how I'm to give him a second dose—"

"Need you?"

"He's been crying two days—can't get on with his ordinary food again, anyhow. He wants some more now."

"Tell Winkles."

"Hang Winkles!" said Redwood.

"You might get at Winkles and give him powders to give the child—"

"That's about what I shall have to do," said Redwood, resting his chin on his fist and staring into the fire.

Bensington stood for a space smoothing the down on the breast of the giant chick. "They will be monstrous fowls," he said.

"They will," said Redwood, still with his eyes on the glow.

"Big as horses," said Bensington.

"Bigger," said Redwood. "That's just it!"

Bensington turned away from the specimen. "Redwood," he said, "these fowls are going to create a sensation."

Redwood nodded his head at the fire.

"And by Jove!" said Bensington, coming round suddenly with a flash in his spectacles, "so will your little boy!"

"That's just what I'm thinking of," said Redwood.

He sat back, sighed, threw his unconsumed cigarette into the fire and thrust his hands deep into his trousers pockets. "That's precisely what I'm thinking of. This Herakleophorbia is going to be queer stuff to handle. The pace that chick must have grown at—!"

"A little boy growing at that pace," said Mr. Bensington slowly, and stared at the chick as he spoke.

"I *Say*!" said Bensington, "he'll be Big."

"I shall give him diminishing doses," said Redwood. "Or at any rate Winkles will."

"It's rather too much of an experiment."

"Much."

"Yet still, you know, I must confess—... Some baby will sooner or later have to try it."

"Oh, we'll try it on *some* baby—certainly."

"Exactly so," said Bensington, and came and stood on the hearthrug and took off his spectacles to wipe them.

"Until I saw these chicks, Redwood, I don't think I *began* to realise—anything—of the possibilities of what we were making. It's only beginning to dawn upon me ... the possible consequences..."

And even then, you know, Mr. Bensington was far from any conception of the mine that little train would fire.

IV

That happened early in June. For some weeks Bensington was kept from revisiting the Experimental Farm by a severe imaginary catarrh, and one necessary flying visit was made by Redwood. He returned an even more anxious- looking parent than he had gone. Altogether there were seven weeks of steady, uninterrupted growth...

And then the Wasps began their career.

It was late in July and nearly a week before the hens escaped from Hickleybrow that the first of the big wasps was killed. The report of it appeared in

several papers, but I do not know whether the news reached Mr. Bensington, much less whether he connected it with the general laxity of method that prevailed in the Experimental Farm.

There can be but little doubt now, that while Mr. Skinner was plying Mr. Bensington's chicks with Herakleophorbia IV, a number of wasps were just as industriously—perhaps more industriously—carrying quantities of the same paste to their early summer broods in the sand-banks beyond the adjacent pine-woods. And there can be no dispute whatever that these early broods found just as much growth and benefit in the substance as Mr. Bensington's hens. It is in the nature of the wasp to attain to effective maturity before the domestic fowl—and in fact of all the creatures that were—through the generous carelessness of the Skinners—partaking of the benefits Mr. Bensington heaped upon his hens, the wasps were the first to make any sort of figure in the world.

It was a keeper named Godfrey, on the estate of Lieutenant-Colonel Rupert Hick, near Maidstone, who encountered and had the luck to kill the first of these monsters of whom history has any record. He was walking knee high in bracken across an open space in the beechwoods that diversify Lieutenant- Colonel Hick's park, and he was carrying his gun—very fortunately for him a double-barrelled gun—over his shoulder, when he first caught sight of the thing. It was, he says, coming down against the light, so that he could not see it very distinctly, and as it came it made a drone "like a motor car." He admits he was frightened. It was evidently as big or bigger than a barn owl, and, to his practised eye, its flight and particularly the misty whirl of its wings must have seemed weirdly unbirdlike. The instinct of self- defence, I fancy, mingled with long habit, when, as he says, he "let fly, right away."

The queerness of the experience probably affected his aim; at any rate most of his shot missed, and the thing merely dropped for a moment with an angry "Wuzzzz" that revealed the wasp at once, and then rose again, with all its stripes shining against the light. He says it turned on him. At any rate, he fired his second barrel at less than twenty yards and threw down his gun, ran a pace or so, and ducked to avoid it.

It flew, he is convinced, within a yard of him, struck the ground, rose again, came down again perhaps thirty yards away, and rolled over with its body wriggling and its sting stabbing out and back in its last agony. He emptied both barrels into it again before he ventured to go near.

When he came to measure the thing, he found it was twenty-seven and a half inches across its open wings, and its sting was three inches long. The abdomen was blown clean off from its body, but he estimated the length of the creature from head to sting as eighteen inches—which is very nearly correct. Its compound eyes were the size of penny pieces.

That is the first authenticated appearance of these giant wasps. The day after, a cyclist riding, feet up, down the hill between Sevenoaks and Tonbridge, very narrowly missed running over a second of these giants that was crawling across the roadway. His passage seemed to alarm it, and it rose with a noise like a sawmill.

His bicycle jumped the footpath in the emotion of the moment, and when he could look back, the wasp was soaring away above the woods towards Westerham.

After riding unsteadily for a little time, he put on his brake, dismounted—he was trembling so violently that he fell over his machine in doing so—and sat down by the roadside to recover. He had intended to ride to Ashford, but he did not get beyond Tonbridge that day...

After that, curiously enough, there is no record of any big wasps being seen for three days. I find on consulting the meteorological record of those days that they were overcast and chilly with local showers, which may perhaps account for this intermission. Then on the fourth day came blue sky and brilliant sunshine and such an outburst of wasps as the world had surely never seen before.

How many big wasps came out that day it is impossible to guess. There are at least fifty accounts of their apparition. There was one victim, a grocer, who discovered one of these monsters in a sugar-cask and very rashly attacked it with a spade as it rose. He struck it to the ground for a moment, and it stung him through the boot as he struck at it again and cut its body in half. He was first dead of the two...

The most dramatic of the fifty appearances was certainly that of the wasp that visited the British Museum about midday, dropping out of the blue serene upon one of the innumerable pigeons that feed in the courtyard of that building, and flying up to the cornice to devour its victim at leisure. After that it crawled for a time over the museum roof, entered the dome of the reading-room by a skylight, buzzed about inside it for some little time—there was a stampede among the readers—and at last found another window and vanished again with a sudden silence from human observation.

Most of the other reports were of mere passings or descents. A picnic party was dispersed at Aldington Knoll and all its sweets and jam consumed, and a puppy was killed and torn to pieces near Whitstable under the very eyes of its mistress...

The streets that evening resounded with the cry, the newspaper placards gave themselves up exclusively in the biggest of letters to the "Gigantic Wasps in Kent." Agitated editors and assistant editors ran up and down tortuous staircases bawling things about "wasps." And Professor Redwood, emerging from his college in Bond Street at five, flushed from a heated discussion with his committee about the price of bull calves, bought an evening paper, opened it, changed colour, forgot about bull calves and committee forthwith, and took a hansom headlong for Bensington's flat.

V

The flat was occupied, it seemed to him—to the exclusion of all other sensible objects—by Mr. Skinner and his voice, if indeed you can call either him or it a sensible object!

The voice was up very high slopping about among the notes of anguish. "Itth impothible for uth to thtop, Thir. We've thtopped on hoping thingth would get

better and they've only got worth, Thir. It ithn't on'y the waptheth, Thir —thereth big earwigth, Thir—big ath that, Thir." (He indicated all his hand and about three inches of fat dirty wrist.) "They pretty near give Mithith Thkinner fitth, Thir. And the thtinging nettleth by the runth, Thir, *they're* growing, Thir, and the canary creeper, Thir, what we thowed near the think, Thir—it put itth tendril through the window in the night, Thir, and very nearly caught Mithith Thkinner by the legth, Thir. Itth that food of yourth, Thir. Wherever we thplathed it about, Thir, a bit, it'th thet everything growing ranker, Thir, than I ever thought anything could grow. Itth impothible to thtop a month, Thir. Itth more than our liveth are worth, Thir. Even if the waptheth don't thting uth, we thall be thuffocated by the creeper, Thir. You can't imagine, Thir—unleth you come down to thee, Thir—"

He turned his superior eye to the cornice above Redwood's head. "'Ow do we know the ratth 'aven't got it, Thir! That 'th what I think of motht, Thir. I 'aven't theen any big ratth, Thir, but 'ow do I know, Thir. We been frightened for dayth becauth of the earwigth we've theen—like lobthters they wath —two of 'em, Thir—and the frightful way the canary creeper wath growing, and directly I heard the waptheth—directly I 'eard 'em, Thir, I underthood. I didn't wait for nothing exthept to thow on a button I'd lortht, and then I came on up. Even now, Thir, I'm arf wild with angthiety, Thir. 'Ow do *I* know watth happenin' to Mithith Thkinner, Thir! Thereth the creeper growing all over the plathe like a thnake, Thir—thwelp me but you 'ave to watch it, Thir, and jump out of itth way!—and the earwigth gettin' bigger and bigger, and the waptheth—. She 'athen't even got a Blue Bag, Thir—if anything thould happen, Thir!"

"But the hens," said Mr. Bensington; "how are the hens?"

"We fed 'em up to yethterday, thwelp me," said Mr. Skinner, "But thith morning we didn't *dare*, Thir. The noithe of the waptheth wath—thomething awful, Thir. They wath coming ont—dothenth. Ath big ath 'enth. I thayth, to 'er, I thayth you juth thow me on a button or two, I thayth, for I can't go to London like thith, I thayth, and I'll go up to Mithter Benthington, I thayth, and ekthplain thingth to 'im. And you thtop in thith room till I come back to you, I thayth, and keep the windowth thhut jutht ath tight ath ever you can, I thayth."

"If you hadn't been so confoundedly untidy—" began Redwood.

"Oh! don't thay *that*, Thir," said Skinner. "Not now, Thir. Not with me tho diththrethed, Thir, about Mithith Thkinner, Thir! Oh, *don't,* Thir! I 'aven't the 'eart to argue with you. Thwelp me, Thir, I 'aven't! Itth the ratth I keep a thinking of—'Ow do I know they 'aven't got at Mithith Thkinner while I been up 'ere?"

"And you haven't got a solitary measurement of all these beautiful growth curves!" said Redwood.

"I been too upthet, Thir," said Mr. Skinner. "If you knew what we been through—me and the mithith! All thith latht month. We 'aven't known what to make of it, Thir. What with the henth gettin' tho rank, and the earwigth, and the canary creeper. I dunno if I told you, Thir—the canary creeper ..."

"You've told us all that," said Redwood. "The thing is, Bensington, what are we to do?"

"What are *we* to do?" said Mr. Skinner.

"You'll have to go back to Mrs. Skinner," said Redwood. "You can't leave her there alone all night."

"Not alone, Thir, I don't. Not if there wath a dothen Mithith Thkinnerth. Itth Mithter Benthington—"

"Nonsense," said Redwood. "The wasps will be all right at night. And the earwigs will get out of your way—"

"But about the ratth?"

"There aren't any rats," said Redwood.

VI

Mr. Skinner might have foregone his chief anxiety. Mrs. Skinner did not stop out her day.

About eleven the canary creeper, which had been quietly active all the morning, began to clamber over the window and darken it very greatly, and the darker it got the more and more clearly Mrs. Skinner perceived that her position would speedily become untenable. And also that she had lived many ages since Skinner went. She peered out of the darkling window, through the stirring tendrils, for some time, and then went very cautiously and opened the bedroom door and listened...

Everything seemed quiet, and so, tucking her skirts high about her, Mrs. Skinner made a bolt for the bedroom, and having first looked under the bed and locked herself in, proceeded with the methodical rapidity of an experienced woman to pack for departure. The bed had not been made, and the room was littered with pieces of the creeper that Skinner had hacked off in order to close the window overnight, but these disorders she did not heed. She packed in a decent sheet. She packed all her own wardrobe and a velveteen jacket that Skinner wore in his finer moments, and she packed a jar of pickles that had not been opened, and so far she was justified in her packing. But she also packed two of the hermetically closed tins containing Herakleophorbia IV. that Mr. Bensington had brought on his last visit. (She was honest, good woman—but she was a grandmother, and her heart had burned within her to see such good growth lavished on a lot of dratted chicks.)

And having packed all these things, she put on her bonnet, took off her apron, tied a new boot-lace round her umbrella, and after listening for a long time at door and window, opened the door and sallied out into a perilous world. The umbrella was under her arm and she clutched the bundle with two gnarled and resolute hands. It was her best Sunday bonnet, and the two poppies that reared their heads amidst its splendours of band and bead seemed instinct with the same tremulous courage that possessed her.

The features about the roots of her nose wrinkled with determination. She had had enough of it! All alone there! Skinner might come back there if he liked.

She went out by the front door, going that way not because she wanted to go to Hickleybrow (her goal was Cheasing Eyebright, where her married daughter re-

sided), but because the back door was impassable on account of the canary creeper that had been, growing so furiously ever since she upset the can of food near its roots. She listened for a space and closed the front door very carefully behind her.

At the corner of the house she paused and reconnoitred...

An extensive sandy scar upon the hillside beyond the pine-woods marked the nest of the giant Wasps, and this she studied very earnestly. The coming and going of the morning was over, not a wasp chanced to be in sight then, and except for a sound scarcely more perceptible than a steam wood-saw at work amidst the pines would have been, everything was still. As for earwigs, she could see not one. Down among the cabbage indeed something was stirring, but it might just as probably be a cat stalking birds. She watched this for a time.

She went a few paces past the corner, came in sight of the run containing the giant chicks and stopped again. "Ah!" she said, and shook her head slowly at the sight of them. They were at that time about the height of emus, but of course much thicker in the body—a larger thing altogether. They were all hens and five all told, now that the two cockerels had killed each other. She hesitated at their drooping attitudes. "Poor dears!" she said, and put down her bundle; "they've got no water. And they've 'ad no food these twenty-four hours! And such appetites, too, as they 'ave!" She put a lean finger to her lips and communed with herself.

Then this dirty old woman did what seems to me a quite heroic deed of mercy. She left her bundle and umbrella in the middle of the brick path and went to the well and drew no fewer than three pailfuls of water for the chickens' empty trough, and then while they were all crowding about that, she undid the door of the run very softly. After which she became extremely active, resumed her package, got over the hedge at the bottom of the garden, crossed the rank meadows (in order to avoid the wasps' nest) and toiled up the winding path towards Cheasing Eyebright.

She panted up the hill, and as she went she paused ever and again, to rest her bundle and get her breath and stare back at the little cottage beside the pinewood below. And when at last, when she was near the crest of the hill, she saw afar off three several wasps dropping heavily westward, it helped her greatly on her way.

She soon got out of the open and in the high banked lane beyond (which seemed a safer place to her), and so up by Hicklebrow Coombe to the downs. There at the foot of the downs where a big tree gave an air of shelter she rested for a space on a stile.

Then on again very resolutely...

You figure her, I hope, with her white bundle, a sort of erect black ant, hurrying along the little white path-thread athwart the downland slopes under the hot sun of the summer afternoon. On she struggled after her resolute indefatigable nose, and the poppies in her bonnet quivered perpetually and her spring-side boots grew whiter and whiter with the downland dust. Flip-flap, flip-flap went her footfalls through the still heat of the day, and persistently, incurably, her umbrella sought to slip from under the elbow that retained it. The mouth wrinkle under her nose was pursed to an extreme resolution, and ever and again she told her umbrel-

la to come up or gave her tightly clutched bundle a vindictive jerk. And at times her lips mumbled with fragments of some foreseen argument between herself and Skinner.

And far away, miles and miles away, a steeple and a hanger grew insensibly out of the vague blue to mark more and more distinctly the quiet corner where Cheasing Eyebright sheltered from the tumult of the world, recking little or nothing of the Herakleophorbia concealed in that white bundle that struggled so persistently towards its orderly retirement.

VII

So far as I can gather, the pullets came into Hickleybrow about three o'clock in the afternoon. Their coming must have been a brisk affair, though nobody was out in the street to see it. The violent bellowing of little Skelmersdale seems to have been the first announcement of anything out of the way. Miss Durgan of the Post Office was at the window as usual, and saw the hen that had caught the unhappy child, in violent flight up the street with its victim, closely pursued by two others. You know that swinging stride of the emancipated athletic latter-day pullet! You know the keen insistence of the hungry hen! There was Plymouth Rock in these birds, I am told, and even without Herakleophorbia that is a gaunt and striding strain.

Probably Miss Durgan was not altogether taken by surprise. In spite of Mr. Bensington's insistence upon secrecy, rumours of the great chicken Mr. Skinner was producing had been about the village for some weeks. "Lor!" she cried, "it's what I expected."

She seems to have behaved with great presence of mind. She snatched up the sealed bag of letters that was waiting to go on to Urshot, and rushed out of the door at once. Almost simultaneously Mr. Skelmersdale himself appeared down the village, gripping a watering-pot by the spout, and very white in the face. And, of course, in a moment or so every one in the village was rushing to the door or window.

The spectacle of Miss Durgan all across the road, with the entire day's correspondence of Hickleybrow in her hand, gave pause to the pullet in possession of Master Skelmersdale. She halted through one instant's indecision and then turned for the open gates of Fulcher's yard. That instant was fatal. The second pullet ran in neatly, got possession of the child by a well-directed peck, and went over the wall into the vicarage garden.

"Charawk, chawk, chawk, chawk, chawk, chawk!" shrieked the hindmost hen, hit smartly by the watering-can Mr. Skelmersdale had thrown, and fluttered wildly over Mrs. Glue's cottage and so into the doctor's field, while the rest of those Gargantuan birds pursued the pullet, in possession of the child across the vicarage lawn.

"Good heavens!" cried the Curate, or (as some say) something much more manly, and ran, whirling his croquet mallet and shouting, to head off the chase.

"Stop, you wretch!" cried the curate, as though giant hens were the commonest facts in life.

And then, finding he could not possibly intercept her, he hurled his mallet with all his might and main, and out it shot in a gracious curve within a foot or so of Master Skelmersdale's head and through the glass lantern of the conservatory. Smash! The new conservatory! The Vicar's wife's beautiful new conservatory!

It frightened the hen. It might have frightened any one. She dropped her victim into a Portugal laurel (from which he was presently extracted, disordered but, save for his less delicate garments, uninjured), made a flapping leap for the roof of Fulcher's stables, put her foot through a weak place in the tiles, and descended, so to speak, out of the infinite into the contemplative quiet of Mr. Bumps the paralytic—who, it is now proved beyond all cavil, did, on this one occasion in his life, get down the entire length of his garden and indoors without any assistance whatever, bolt the door after him, and immediately relapse again into Christian resignation and helpless dependence upon his wife...

The rest of the pullets were headed off by the other croquet players, and went through the vicar's kitchen garden into the doctor's field, to which rendezvous the fifth also came at last, clucking disconsolately after an unsuccessful attempt to walk on the cucumber frames in Mr. Witherspoon's place.

They seem to have stood about in a hen-like manner for a time, and scratched a little and chirrawked meditatively, and then one pecked at and pecked over a hive of the doctor's bees, and after that they set off in a gawky, jerky, feathery, fitful sort of way across the fields towards Urshot, and Hickleybrow Street saw them no more. Near Urshot they really came upon commensurate food in a field of swedes; and pecked for a space with gusto, until their fame overtook them.

The chief immediate reaction of this astonishing irruption of gigantic poultry upon the human mind was to arouse an extraordinary passion to whoop and run and throw things, and in quite a little time almost all the available manhood of Hickleybrows and several ladies, were out with a remarkable assortment of flappish and whangable articles in hand—to commence the scooting of the giant hens. They drove them into Urshot, where there was a Rural Fete, and Urshot took them as the crowning glory of a happy day. They began to be shot at near Findon Beeches, but at first only with a rook rifle. Of course birds of that size could absorb an unlimited quantity of small shot without inconvenience. They scattered somewhere near Sevenoaks, and near Tonbridge one of them fled clucking for a time in excessive agitation, somewhat ahead of and parallel with the afternoon boat express—to the great astonishment of every one therein.

And about half-past five two of them were caught very cleverly by a circus proprietor at Tunbridge Wells, who lured them into a cage, rendered vacant through the death of a widowed dromedary, by scattering cakes and bread...

VIII

When the unfortunate Skinner got out of the South-Eastern train at Urshot that evening it was already nearly dusk. The train was late, but not inordinately late—

and Mr. Skinner remarked as much to the station- master. Perhaps he saw a certain pregnancy in the station-master's eye. After the briefest hesitation and with a confidential movement of his hand to the side of his mouth he asked if "anything" had happened that day.

"How d'yer *mean*?" said the station-master, a man with a hard, emphatic voice.

"Thethe 'ere waptheth and thingth."

"We 'aven't 'ad much time to think of *waptheth*," said the station- master agreeably. "We've been too busy with your brasted 'ens," and he broke the news of the pullets to Mr. Skinner as one might break the window of an adverse politician.

"You ain't 'eard anything of Mithith Thkinner?" asked Skinner, amidst that missile shower of pithy information and comment.

"No fear!" said the station-master—as though even he drew the line somewhere in the matter of knowledge.

"I mutht make inquireth bout thith," said Mr. Skinner, edging out of reach of the station-master's concluding generalisations about the responsibility attaching to the excessive nurture of hens...

Going through Urshot Mr. Skinner was hailed by a lime-burner from the pits over by Hankey and asked if he was looking for his hens.

"You ain't 'eard anything of Mithith Thkinner?" he asked.

The lime-burner—his exact phrases need not concern us—expressed his superior interest in hens...

It was already dark—as dark at least as a clear night in the English June can be—when Skinner—or his head at any rate —came into the bar of the Jolly Drovers and said: "Ello! You 'aven't 'eard anything of thith 'ere thtory bout my 'enth, 'ave you?"

"Oh, *'aven't* we!" said Mr. Fulcher. "Why, part of the story's been and bust into my stable roof and one chapter smashed a 'ole in Missis Vicar's green 'ouse—I beg 'er pardon—Conservarratory."

Skinner came in. "I'd like thomething a little comforting," he said, "'ot gin and water'th about my figure," and everybody began to tell him things about the pullets.

"*Grathuth* me!" said Skinner.

"You 'aven't 'eard anything about Mithith Thkinner, 'ave you?" he asked in a pause.

"That we 'aven't!" said Mr. Witherspoon. "We 'aven't thought of 'er. We ain't thought nothing of either of you."

"Ain't you been 'ome to-day?" asked Fulcher over a tankard.

"If one of those brasted birds 'ave pecked 'er," began Mr. Witherspoons and left the full horror to their unaided imaginations...

It appeared to the meeting at the time that it would be an interesting end to an eventful day to go on with Skinner and see if anything *had* happened to Mrs. Skinner. One never knows what luck one may have when accidents are at large. But Skinner, standing at the bar and drinking his hot gin and water, with one eye

roving over the things at the back of the bar and the other fixed on the Absolute, missed the psychological moment.

"I thuppothe there 'athen't been any trouble with any of thethe big waptheth to-day anywhere?" he asked, with an elaborate detachment of manner.

"Been too busy with your 'ens," said Fulcher.

"I thuppothe they've all gone in now anyhow," said Skinner.

"What—the 'ens?"

"I wath thinking of the waptheth more particularly," said Skinner.

And then, with, an air of circumspection that would have awakened suspicion in a week-old baby, and laying the accent heavily on most of the words he chose, he asked, "I *thuppothe nobody* 'athn't *'eard* of any other *big* thingth, about, 'ave they? Big *dogth* or *catth* or anything of *that* thort? Theemth to me if thereth big henth and big waptheth comin' on—"

He laughed with a fine pretence of talking idly.

But a brooding expression came upon the faces of the Hickleybrow men. Fulcher was the first to give their condensing thought the concrete shape of words.

"A cat to match them 'ens—" said Fulcher.

"Ay!" said Witherspoon, "a cat to match they 'ens."

"'Twould be a tiger," said Fulcher.

"More'n a tiger," said Witherspoon...

When at last Skinner followed the lonely footpath over the swelling field that separated Hickleybrow from the sombre pine-shaded hollow in whose black shadows the gigantic canary-creeper grappled silently with the Experimental Farm, he followed it alone.

He was distinctly seen to rise against the sky-line, against the warm clear immensity of the northern sky—for so far public interest followed him—and to descend again into the night, into an obscurity from which it would seem he will nevermore emerge. He passed—into a mystery. No one knows to this day what happened to him after he crossed the brow. When later on the two Fulchers and Witherspoon, moved by their own imaginations, came up the hill and stared after him, the flight had swallowed him up altogether.

The three men stood close. There was not a sound out of the wooded blackness that hid the Farm from their eyes.

"It's all right," said young Fulcher, ending a silence.

"Don't see any lights," said Witherspoon.

"You wouldn't from here."

"It's misty," said the elder Fulcher.

They meditated for a space.

"'E'd 'ave come back if anything was wrong," said young Fulcher, and this seemed so obvious and conclusive that presently old Fulcher said, "Well," and the three went home to bed—thoughtfully I will admit...

A shepherd out by Huckster's Farm heard a squealing in the night that he thought was foxes, and in the morning one of his lambs had been killed, dragged halfway towards Hickleybrow and partially devoured...

The inexplicable part of it all is the absence of any indisputable remains of Skinner!

Many weeks after, amidst the charred ruins of the Experimental Farm, there was found something which may or may not have been a human shoulder-blade and in another part of the ruins a long bone greatly gnawed and equally doubtful. Near the stile going up towards Eyebright there was found a glass eye, and many people discovered thereupon that Skinner owed much of his personal charm to such a possession. It stared out upon the world with that same inevitable effect of detachment, that same severe melancholy that had been the redemption of his else worldly countenance.

And about the ruins industrious research discovered the metal rings and charred coverings of two linen buttons, three shanked buttons entire, and one of that metallic sort which is used in the less conspicuous sutures of the human Oeconomy. These remains have been accepted by persons in authority as conclusive of a destroyed and scattered Skinner, but for my own entire conviction, and in view of his distinctive idiosyncrasy, I must confess I should prefer fewer buttons and more bones.

The glass eye of course has an air of extreme conviction, but if it really *is* Skinner's—and even Mrs. Skinner did not certainly know if that immobile eye of his was glass—something has changed it from a liquid brown to a serene and confident blue. That shoulder-blade is an extremely doubtful document, and I would like to put it side by side with the gnawed scapulae of a few of the commoner domestic animals before I admitted its humanity.

And where were Skinner's boots, for example? Perverted and strange as a rat's appetite must be, is it conceivable that the same creatures that could leave a lamb only half eaten, would finish up Skinner—hair, bones, teeth, and boots?

I have closely questioned as many as I could of those who knew Skinner at all intimately, and they one and all agree that they cannot imagine *anything* eating him. He was the sort of man, as a retired seafaring person living in one of Mr. W.W. Jacobs' cottages at Dunton Green told me, with a guarded significance of manner not uncommon in those parts, who would "get washed up anyhow," and as regards *the* devouring element was "fit to put a fire out." He considered that Skinner would be as safe on a raft as anywhere. The retired seafaring man added that he wished to say nothing whatever against Skinner; facts were facts. And rather than have his clothes made by Skinner, the retired seafaring man remarked he would take his chance of being locked up. These observations certainly do not present Skinner in the light of an appetising object.

To be perfectly frank with the reader, I do not believe he ever went back to the Experimental Farm. I believe he hovered through long hesitations about the fields of the Hickleybrow glebe, and finally, when that squealing began, took the line of least resistance out of his perplexities into the Incognito.

And in the Incognito, whether of this or of some other world unknown to us, he obstinately and quite indisputably has remained to this day...

CHAPTER THE THIRD - THE GIANT RATS

I

It was two nights after the disappearance of Mr. Skinner that the Podbourne doctor was out late near Hankey, driving in his buggy. He had been up all night assisting another undistinguished citizen into this curious world of ours, and his task accomplished, he was driving homeward in a drowsy mood enough. It was about two o'clock in the morning, and the waning moon was rising. The summer night had gone cold, and there was a low-lying whitish mist that made things indistinct. He was quite alone—for his coachman was ill in bed—and there was nothing to be seen on either hand but a drifting mystery of hedge running athwart the yellow glare of his lamps, and nothing to hear but the clitter-clatter of his horses and the gride and hedge echo of his wheels. His horse was as trustworthy as himself, and one does not wonder that he dozed...

You know that intermittent drowsing as one sits, the drooping of the head, the nodding to the rhythm of the wheels then chin upon the breast, and at once the sudden start up again.

Pitter, litter, patter.

"What was that?"

It seemed to the doctor he had heard a thin shrill squeal close at hand. For a moment he was quite awake. He said a word or two of undeserved rebuke to his horse, and looked about him. He tried to persuade himself that he had heard the distant squeal of a fox—or perhaps a young rabbit gripped by a ferret.

Swish, swish, swish, pitter, patter, swish—...

What was that?

He felt he was getting fanciful. He shook his shoulders and told his horse to get on. He listened, and heard nothing.

Or was it nothing?

He had the queerest impression that something had just peeped over the hedge at him, a queer big head. With round ears! He peered hard, but he could see nothing.

"Nonsense," said he.

He sat up with an idea that he had dropped into a nightmare, gave his horse the slightest touch of the whip, spoke to it and peered again over the hedge. The glare of his lamp, however, together with the mist, rendered things indistinct, and he could distinguish nothing. It came into his head, he says, that there could be noth-

ing there, because if there was his horse would have shied at it. Yet for all that his senses remained nervously awake.

Then he heard quite distinctly a soft pattering of feet in pursuit along the road.

He would not believe his ears about that. He could not look round, for the road had a sinuous curve just there. He whipped up his horse and glanced sideways again. And then he saw quite distinctly where a ray from his lamp leapt a low stretch of hedge, the curved back of—some big animal, he couldn't tell what, going along in quick convulsive leaps.

He says he thought of the old tales of witchcraft—the thing was so utterly unlike any animal he knew, and he tightened his hold on the reins for fear of the fear of his horse. Educated man as he was, he admits he asked himself if this could be something that his horse could not see.

Ahead, and drawing near in silhouette against the rising moon, was the outline of the little hamlet of Hankey, comforting, though it showed never a light, and he cracked his whip and spoke again, and then in a flash the rats were at him!

He had passed a gate, and as he did so, the foremost rat came leaping over into the road. The thing sprang upon him out of vagueness into the utmost clearness, the sharp, eager, round-eared face, the long body exaggerated by its movement; and what particularly struck him, the pink, webbed forefeet of the beast. What must have made it more horrible to him at the time was, that he had no idea the thing was any created beast he knew. He did not recognise it as a rat, because of the size. His horse gave a bound as the thing dropped into the road beside it. The little lane woke into tumult at the report of the whip and the doctor's shout. The whole thing suddenly went fast.

Rattle-clatter, clash, clatter.

The doctor, one gathers, stood up, shouted to his horse, and slashed with all his strength. The rat winced and swerved most reassuringly at his blow —in the glare of his lamp he could see the fur furrow under the lash —and he slashed again and again, heedless and unaware of the second pursuer that gained upon his off side.

He let the reins go, and glanced back to discover the third rat in pursuit behind...

His horse bounded forward. The buggy leapt high at a rut. For a frantic minute perhaps everything seemed to be going in leaps and bounds...

It was sheer good luck the horse came down in Hankey, and not either before or after the houses had been passed.

No one knows how the horse came down, whether it stumbled or whether the rat on the off side really got home with one of those slashing down strokes of the teeth (given with the full weight of the body); and the doctor never discovered that he himself was bitten until he was inside the brickmaker's house, much less did he discover when the bite occurred, though bitten he was and badly—a long slash like the slash of a double tomahawk that had cut two parallel ribbons of flesh from his left shoulder.

He was standing up in his buggy at one moment, and in the next he had leapt to the ground, with his ankle, though he did not know it, badly sprained, and he

was cutting furiously at a third rat that was flying directly at him. He scarcely remembers the leap he must have made over the top of the wheel as the buggy came over, so obliteratingly hot and swift did his impressions rush upon him. I think myself the horse reared up with the rat biting again at its throat, and fell sideways, and carried the whole affair over; and that the doctor sprang, as it were, instinctively. As the buggy came down, the receiver of the lamp smashed, and suddenly poured a flare of blazing oil, a thud of white flame, into the struggle.

That was the first thing the brickmaker saw.

He had heard the clatter of the doctor's approach and—though the doctor's memory has nothing of this—wild shouting. He had got out of bed hastily, and as he did so came the terrific smash, and up shot the glare outside the rising blind. "It was brighter than day," he says. He stood, blind cord in hand, and stared out of the window at a nightmare transformation of the familiar road before him. The black figure of the doctor with its whirling whip danced out against the flame. The horse kicked indistinctly, half hidden by the blaze, with a rat at its throat. In the obscurity against the churchyard wall, the eyes of a second monster shone wickedly. Another—a mere dreadful blackness with red-lit eyes and flesh-coloured hands—clutched unsteadily on the wall coping to which it had leapt at the flash of the exploding lamp.

You know the keen face of a rat, those two sharp teeth, those pitiless eyes. Seen magnified to near six times its linear dimensions, and still more magnified by darkness and amazement and the leaping fancies of a fitful blaze, it must have been an ill sight for the brickmaker—still more than half asleep.

Then the doctor had grasped the opportunity, that momentary respite the flare afforded, and was out of the brickmaker's sight below battering the door with the butt of his whip...

The brickmaker would not let him in until he had got a light.

There are those who have blamed the man for that, but until I know my own courage better, I hesitate to join their number.

The doctor yelled and hammered...

The brickmaker says he was weeping with terror when at last the door was opened.

"Bolt," said the doctor, "bolt"—he could not say "bolt the door." He tried to help, and was of no service. The brickmaker fastened the door, and the doctor had to sit on the chair beside the clock for a space before he could go upstairs...

"I don't know what they *are*!" he repeated several times. "I don't know what they *are*"—with a high note on the "are."

The brickmaker would have got him whisky, but the doctor would not be left alone with nothing but a flickering light just then.

It was long before the brickmaker could get him to go upstairs...

And when the fire was out the giant rats came back, took the dead horse, dragged it across the churchyard into the brickfield and ate at it until it was dawn, none even then daring to disturb them...

II

Redwood went round, to Bensington about eleven the next morning with the "second editions" of three evening papers in his hand.

Bensington looked up from a despondent meditation over the forgotten pages of the most distracting novel the Brompton Road librarian had been able to find him. "Anything fresh?" he asked.

"Two men stung near Chartham."

"They ought to let us smoke out that nest. They really did. It's their own fault."

"It's their own fault, certainly," said Redwood.

"Have you heard anything—about buying the farm?"

"The House Agent," said Redwood, "is a thing with a big mouth and made of dense wood. It pretends someone else is after the house—it always does, you know—and won't understand there's a hurry. 'This is a matter of life and death,' I said, 'don't you understand?' It drooped its eyes half shut and said, 'Then why don't you go the other two hundred pounds?' I'd rather live in a world of solid wasps than give in to the stonewalling stupidity of that offensive creature. I—"

He paused, feeling that a sentence like that might very easily be spoiled by its context.

"It's too much to hope," said Bensington, "that one of the wasps—"

"The wasp has no more idea of public utility than a—than a House Agent," said Redwood.

He talked for a little while about house agents and solicitors and people of that sort, in the unjust, unreasonable way that so many people do somehow get to talk of these business calculi ("Of all the cranky things in this cranky world, it is the most cranky to my mind of all, that while we expect honour, courage, efficiency, from a doctor or a soldier as a matter of course, a solicitor or a house agent is not only permitted but expected to display nothing but a sort of greedy, greasy, obstructive, over-reaching imbecility—" etc.)—and then, greatly relieved, he went to the window and stared out at the Sloane Street traffic.

Bensington had put the most exciting novel conceivable on the little table that carried his electric standard. He joined the fingers of his opposed hands very carefully and regarded them. "Redwood," he said. "Do they say much about *Us*?"

"Not so much as I should expect."

"They don't denounce us at all?"

"Not a bit. But, on the other hand, they don't back up what I point out must be done. I've written to the *Times*, you know, explaining the whole thing—"

"We take the *Daily Chronicle*," said Bensington.

"And the *Times* has a long leader on the subject—a very high-class, well-written leader, with three pieces of *Times* Latin —*status quo* is one—and it reads like the voice of Somebody Impersonal of the Greatest Importance suffering from Influenza Headache and talking through sheets and sheets of felt without getting any relief from it whatever. Reading between the lines, you know, it's pretty clear that the *Times* considers that it is useless to mince matters, and that something (indefinite of course) has to be done at once. Otherwise still more undesirable

consequences—*Times* English, you know, for more wasps and stings. Thoroughly statesmanlike article!"

"And meanwhile this Bigness is spreading in all sorts of ugly ways."

"Precisely."

"I wonder if Skinner was right about those big rats—"

"Oh no! That would be too much," said Redwood.

He came and stood by Bensington's chair.

"By-the-bye," he said, with a slightly lowered voice, "how does *she*—?"

He indicated the closed door.

"Cousin Jane? She simply knows nothing about it. Doesn't connect us with it and won't read the articles. 'Gigantic wasps!' she says, 'I haven't patience to read the papers.'"

"That's very fortunate," said Redwood.

"I suppose—Mrs. Redwood—?"

"No," said Redwood, "just at present it happens—she's terribly worried about the child. You know, he keeps on."

"Growing?"

"Yes. Put on forty-one ounces in ten days. Weighs nearly four stone. And only six months old! Naturally rather alarming."

"Healthy?"

"Vigorous. His nurse is leaving because he kicks so forcibly. And everything, of course, shockingly outgrown. Everything, you know, has had to be made fresh, clothes and everything. Perambulator—light affair—broke one wheel, and the youngster had to be brought home on the milkman's hand- truck. Yes. Quite a crowd... And we've put Georgina Phyllis back into his cot and put him into the bed of Georgina Phyllis. His mother—naturally alarmed. Proud at first and inclined to praise Winkles. Not now. Feels the thing *can't* be wholesome. *You* know."

"I imagined you were going to put him on diminishing doses."

"I tried it."

"Didn't it work?"

"Howls. In the ordinary way the cry of a child is loud and distressing; it is for the good of the species that this should be so—but since he has been on the Herakleophorbia treatment—-"

"Mm," said Bensington, regarding his fingers with more resignation than he had hitherto displayed.

"Practically the thing *must* come out. People will hear of this child, connect it up with our hens and things, and the whole thing will come round to my wife... How she will take it I haven't the remotest idea."

"It *is* difficult," said Mr. Bensington, "to form any plan—certainly."

He removed his glasses and wiped them carefully.

"It is another instance," he generalised, "of the thing that is continually happening. We—if indeed I may presume to the adjective —*scientific* men—we work of course always for a theoretical result—a purely theoretical result. But,

incidentally, we do set forces in operation—*new* forces. We mustn't control them —and nobody else *can*. Practically, Redwood, the thing is out of our hands. *We* supply the material—"

"And they," said Redwood, turning to the window, "get the experience."

"So far as this trouble down in Kent goes I am not disposed to worry further."

"Unless they worry us."

"Exactly. And if they like to muddle about with solicitors and pettifoggers and legal obstructions and weighty considerations of the tomfool order, until they have got a number of new gigantic species of vermin well established—Things always *have* been in a muddle, Redwood."

Redwood traced a twisted, tangled line in the air.

"And our real interest lies at present with your boy."

Redwood turned about and came and stared at his collaborator.

"What do you think of him, Bensington? You can look at this business with a greater detachment than I can. What am I to do about him?"

"Go on feeding him."

"On Herakleophorbia?"

"On Herakleophorbia."

"And then he'll grow."

"He'll grow, as far as I can calculate from the hens and the wasps, to the height of about five-and-thirty feet—with everything in proportion —-"

"And then what'll he do?"

"That," said Mr. Bensington, "is just what makes the whole thing so interesting."

"Confound it, man! Think of his clothes."

"And when he's grown up," said Redwood, "he'll only be one solitary Gulliver in a pigmy world."

Mr. Bensington's eye over his gold rim was pregnant.

"Why solitary?" he said, and repeated still more darkly, "*Why* solitary?"

"But you don't propose—-?"

"I said," said Mr. Bensington, with the self-complacency of a man who has produced a good significant saying, "Why solitary?"

"Meaning that one might bring up other children—-?"

"Meaning nothing beyond my inquiry."

Redwood began to walk about the room. "Of course," he said, "one might — But still! What are we coming to?"

Bensington evidently enjoyed his line of high intellectual detachment. "The thing that interests me most, Redwood, of all this, is to think that his brain at the top of him will also, so far as my reasoning goes, be five-and- thirty feet or so above our level... What's the matter?"

Redwood stood at the window and stared at a news placard on a paper-cart that rattled up the street.

"What's the matter?" repeated Bensington, rising.

Redwood exclaimed violently.

"What is it?" said Bensington.

"Get a paper," said Redwood, moving doorward.

"Why?"

"Get a paper. Something—I didn't quite catch—Gigantic rats—!"

"Rats?"

"Yes, rats. Skinner was right after all!"

"What do you mean?"

"How the Deuce am *I* to know till I see a paper? Great Rats! Good Lord! I wonder if he's eaten!"

He glanced for his hat, and decided to go hatless.

As he rushed downstairs two steps at a time, he could hear along the street the mighty howlings, to and fro of the Hooligan paper-sellers making a Boom.

"'Orrible affair in Kent—'orrible affair in Kent. Doctor ... eaten by rats. 'Orrible affair—'orrible affair—rats—eaten by Stchewpendous rats. Full perticulars—'orrible affair."

III

Cossar, the well-known civil engineer, found them in the great doorway of the flat mansions, Redwood holding out the damp pink paper, and Bensington on tiptoe reading over his arm. Cossar was a large-bodied man with gaunt inelegant limbs casually placed at convenient corners of his body, and a face like a carving abandoned at an early stage as altogether too unpromising for completion. His nose had been left square, and his lower jaw projected beyond his upper. He breathed audibly. Few people considered him handsome. His hair was entirely tangential, and his voice, which he used sparingly, was pitched high, and had commonly a quality of bitter protest. He wore a grey cloth jacket suit and a silk hat on all occasions. He plumbed an abysmal trouser pocket with a vast red hand, paid his cabman, and came panting resolutely up the steps, a copy of the pink paper clutched about the middle, like Jove's thunderbolt, in his hand.

"Skinner?" Bensington was saying, regardless of his approach.

"Nothing about him," said Redwood. "Bound to be eaten. Both of them. It's too terrible... Hullo! Cossar!"

"This your stuff?" asked Cossar, waving the paper.

"Well, why don't you stop it?" he demanded.

"*Can't* be jiggered!" said Cossar.

"*Buy the place*?" he cried. "What nonsense! Burn it! I knew you chaps would fumble this. *What are you to do*? Why—what I tell you.

"*You*? Do? Why! Go up the street to the gunsmith's, of course. *Why*? For guns. Yes—there's only one shop. Get eight guns! Rifles. Not elephant guns—no! Too big. Not army rifles—too small. Say it's to kill—kill a bull. Say it's to shoot buffalo! See? Eh? Rats? No! How the deuce are they to understand that? Because we *want* eight. Get a lot of ammunition. Don't get guns without ammunition—No! Take the lot in a cab to—where's the place? *Urshot*? Charing Cross, then. There's a train—-Well, the first train that starts after two. Think you can do it? All right.

License? Get eight at a post-office, of course. Gun licenses, you know. Not game. Why? It's rats, man.

"You—Bensington. Got a telephone? Yes. I'll ring up five of my chaps from Ealing. *Why* five? Because it's the right number!

"Where you going, Redwood? Get a hat! *Nonsense*. Have mine. You want guns, man—not hats. Got money? Enough? All right. So long.

"Where's the telephone, Bensington?"

Bensington wheeled about obediently and led the way.

Cossar used and replaced the instrument. "Then there's the wasps," he said. "Sulphur and nitre'll do that. Obviously. Plaster of Paris. You're a chemist. Where can I get sulphur by the ton in portable sacks? *What* for? Why, Lord *bless* my heart and soul!—to smoke out the nest, of course! I suppose it must be sulphur, eh? You're a chemist. Sulphur best, eh?"

"Yes, I should *think* sulphur."

"Nothing better?"

"Right. That's your job. That's all right. Get as much sulphur as you can — saltpetre to make it burn. Sent? Charing Cross. Right away. See they do it. Follow it up. Anything?"

He thought a moment.

"Plaster of Paris—any sort of plaster—bung up nest —holes—you know. That *I'd* better get."

"How much?"

"How much what?"

"Sulphur."

"Ton. See?"

Bensington tightened his glasses with a hand tremulous with determination. "Right," he said, very curtly.

"Money in your pocket?" asked Cossar.

"Hang cheques. They may not know you. Pay cash. Obviously. Where's your bank? All right. Stop on the way and get forty pounds—notes and gold."

Another meditation. "If we leave this job for public officials we shall have all Kent in tatters," said Cossar. "Now is there—anything? *No! HI*!"

He stretched a vast hand towards a cab that became convulsively eager to serve him ("Cab, Sir?" said the cabman. "Obviously," said Cossar); and Bensington, still hatless, paddled down the steps and prepared to mount.

"I *think*," he said, with his hand on the cab apron, and a sudden glance up at the windows of his flat, "I *ought* to tell my cousin Jane—"

"More time to tell her when you come back," said Cossar, thrusting him in with a vast hand expanded over his back...

"Clever chaps," remarked Cossar, "but no initiative whatever. Cousin Jane indeed! I know her. Rot, these Cousin Janes! Country infested with 'em. I suppose I shall have to spend the whole blessed night, seeing they do what they know perfectly well they ought to do all along. I wonder if it's Research makes 'em like that or Cousin Jane or what?"

He dismissed this obscure problem, meditated for a space upon his watch, and decided there would be just time to drop into a restaurant and get some lunch before he hunted up the plaster of Paris and took it to Charing Cross.

The train started at five minutes past three, and he arrived at Charing Cross at a quarter to three, to find Bensington in heated argument between two policemen and his van-driver outside, and Redwood in the luggage office involved in some technical obscurity about this ammunition. Everybody was pretending not to know anything or to have any authority, in the way dear to South-Eastern officials when they catch you in a hurry.

"Pity they can't shoot all these officials and get a new lot," remarked Cossar with a sigh. But the time was too limited for anything fundamental, and so he swept through these minor controversies, disinterred what may or may not have been the station-master from some obscure hiding-place, walked about the premises holding him and giving orders in his name, and was out of the station with everybody and everything aboard before that official was fully awake to the breaches in the most sacred routines and regulations that were being committed.

"Who *was* he?" said the high official, caressing the arm Cossar had gripped, and smiling with knit brows.

"'E was a gentleman, Sir," said a porter, "anyhow. 'Im and all 'is party travelled first class."

"Well, we got him and his stuff off pretty sharp—whoever he was," said the high official, rubbing his arm with something approaching satisfaction.

And as he walked slowly back, blinking in the unaccustomed daylight, towards that dignified retirement in which the higher officials at Charing Cross shelter from the importunity of the vulgar, he smiled still at his unaccustomed energy. It was a very gratifying revelation of his own possibilities, in spite of the stiffness of his arm. He wished some of those confounded armchair critics of railway management could have seen it.

IV

By five o'clock that evening this amazing Cossar, with no appearance of hurry at all, had got all the stuff for his fight with insurgent Bigness out of Urshot and on the road to Hickleybrow. Two barrels of paraffin and a load of dry brushwood he had bought in Urshot; plentiful sacks of sulphur, eight big game guns and ammunition, three light breechloaders, with small-shot ammunition for the wasps, a hatchet, two billhooks, a pick and three spades, two coils of rope, some bottled beer, soda and whisky, one gross of packets of rat poison, and cold provisions for three days, had come down from London. All these things he had sent on in a coal trolley and a hay waggon in the most business-like way, except the guns and ammunition, which were stuck under the seat of the Red Lion waggonette appointed to bring on Redwood and the five picked men who had come up from Ealing at Cossar's summons.

Cossar conducted all these transactions with an invincible air of commonplace, in spite of the fact that Urshot was in a panic about the rats, and all the drivers had

to be specially paid. All the shops were shut in the place, and scarcely a soul abroad in the street, and when he banged at a door a window was apt to open. He seemed to consider that the conduct of business from open windows was an entirely legitimate and obvious method. Finally he and Bensington got the Red Lion dogcart and set off with the waggonette, to overtake the baggage. They did this a little beyond the cross-roads, and so reached Hickleybrow first.

Bensington, with a gun between his knees, sitting beside Cossar in the dog-cart, developed a long germinated amazement. All they were doing was, no doubt, as Cossar insisted, quite the obvious thing to do, only—! In England one so rarely does the obvious thing. He glanced from his neighbour's feet to the boldly sketched hands upon the reins. Cossar had apparently never driven before, and he was keeping the line of least resistance down the middle of the road by some no doubt quite obvious but certainly unusual light of his own.

"Why don't we all do the obvious?" thought Bensington. "How the world would travel if one did! I wonder for instance why I don't do such a lot of things I know would be all right to do—things I *want* to do. Is everybody like that, or is it peculiar to me!" He plunged into obscure speculation about the Will. He thought of the complex organised futilities of the daily life, and in contrast with them the plain and manifest things to do, the sweet and splendid things to do, that some incredible influences will never permit us to do. Cousin Jane? Cousin Jane he perceived was important in the question, in some subtle and difficult way. Why should we after all eat, drink, and sleep, remain unmarried, go here, abstain from going there, all out of deference to Cousin Jane? She became symbolical without ceasing to be incomprehensible!

A stile and a path across the fields caught his eye and reminded him of that other bright day, so recent in time, so remote in its emotions, when he had walked from Urshot to the Experimental Farm to see the giant chicks.

Fate plays with us.

"Tcheck, tcheck," said Cossar. "Get up."

It was a hot midday afternoon, not a breath of wind, and the dust was thick in the roads. Few people were about, but the deer beyond the park palings browsed in profound tranquillity. They saw a couple of big wasps stripping a gooseberry bush just outside Hickleybrow, and another was crawling up and down the front of the little grocer's shop in the village street trying to find an entry. The grocer was dimly visible within, with an ancient fowling-piece in hand, watching its endeavours. The driver of the waggonette pulled up outside the Jolly Drovers and informed Redwood that his part of the bargain was done. In this contention he was presently joined by the drivers of the waggon and the trolley. Not only did they maintain this, but they refused to let the horses be taken further.

"Them big rats is nuts on 'orses," the trolley driver kept on repeating.

Cossar surveyed the controversy for a moment.

"Get the things out of that waggonette," he said, and one of his men, a tall, fair, dirty engineer, obeyed.

"Gimme that shot gun," said Cossar.

He placed himself between the drivers. "We don't want *you* to drive," he said.

"You can say what you like," he conceded, "but we want these horses."

They began to argue, but he continued speaking.

"If you try and assault us I shall, in self-defence, let fly at your legs. The horses are going on."

He treated the incident as closed. "Get up on that waggon, Flack," he said to a thickset, wiry little man. "Boon, take the trolley."

The two drivers blustered to Redwood.

"You've done your duty to your employers," said Redwood. "You stop in this village until we come back. No one will blame you, seeing we've got guns. We've no wish to do anything unjust or violent, but this occasion is pressing. I'll pay if anything happens to the horses, never fear."

"*That's* all right," said Cossar, who rarely promised.

They left the waggonette behind, and the men who were not driving went afoot. Over each shoulder sloped a gun. It was the oddest little expedition for an English country road, more like a Yankee party, trekking west in the good old Indian days.

They went up the road, until at the crest by the stile they came into sight of the Experimental Farm. They found a little group of men there with a gun or so—the two Fulchers were among them—and one man, a stranger from Maidstone, stood out before the others and watched the place through an opera-glass.

These men turned about and stared at Redwood's party.

"Anything fresh?" said Cossar.

"The waspses keeps a comin' and a goin'," said old Fulcher. "Can't see as they bring anything."

"The canary creeper's got in among the pine trees now," said the man with the lorgnette. "It wasn't there this morning. You can see it grow while you watch it."

He took out a handkerchief and wiped his object-glasses with careful deliberation.

"I reckon you're going down there," ventured Skelmersdale.

"Will you come?" said Cossar.

Skelmersdale seemed to hesitate.

"It's an all-night job."

Skelmersdale decided that he wouldn't.

"Rats about?" asked Cossar.

"One was up in the pines this morning—rabbiting, we reckon."

Cossar slouched on to overtake his party.

Bensington, regarding the Experimental Farm under his hand, was able to gauge now the vigour of the Food. His first impression was that the house was smaller than he had thought—very much smaller; his second was to perceive that all the vegetation between the house and the pine-wood had become extremely large. The roof over the well peeped amidst tussocks of grass a good eight feet high, and the canary creeper wrapped about the chimney stack and gesticulated with stiff tendrils towards the heavens. Its flowers were vivid yellow splashes,

distinctly visible as separate specks this mile away. A great green cable had writhed across the big wire inclosures of the giant hens' run, and flung twining leaf stems about two outstanding pines. Fully half as tall as these was the grove of nettles running round behind the cart-shed. The whole prospect, as they drew nearer, became more and more suggestive of a raid of pigmies upon a dolls' house that has been left in a neglected corner of some great garden.

There was a busy coming and going from the wasps' nest, they saw. A swarm of black shapes interlaced in the air, above the rusty hill-front beyond the pine cluster, and ever and again one of these would dart up into the sky with incredible swiftness and soar off upon some distant quest. Their humming became audible at more than half a mile's distance from the Experimental Farm. Once a yellow-striped monster dropped towards them and hung for a space watching them with its great compound eyes, but at an ineffectual shot from Cossar it darted off again. Down in a corner of the field, away to the right, several were crawling about over some ragged bones that were probably the remains of the lamb the rats had brought from Huxter's Farm. The horses became very restless as they drew near these creatures. None of the party was an expert driver, and they had to put a man to lead each horse and encourage it with the voice.

They could see nothing of the rats as they came up to the house, and everything seemed perfectly still except for the rising and falling "whoozzzzzzZZZ, whoooo-zoo-oo" of the wasps' nest.

They led the horses into the yard, and one of Cossar's men, seeing the door open—the whole of the middle portion of the door had been gnawed out—walked into the house. Nobody missed him for the time, the rest being occupied with the barrels of paraffin, and the first intimation they had of his separation from them was the report of his gun and the whizz of his bullet. "Bang, bang," both barrels, and his first bullet it seems went through the cask of sulphur, smashed out a stave from the further side, and filled the air with yellow dust. Redwood had kept his gun in hand and let fly at something grey that leapt past him. He had a vision of the broad hind-quarters, the long scaly tail and long soles of the hind-feet of a rat, and fired his second barrel. He saw Bensington drop as the beast vanished round the corner.

Then for a time everybody was busy with a gun. For three minutes lives were cheap at the Experimental Farm, and the banging of guns filled the air. Redwood, careless of Bensington in his excitement, rushed in pursuit, and was knocked headlong by a mass of brick fragments, mortar, plaster, and rotten lath splinters that came flying out at him as a bullet whacked through the wall.

He found himself sitting on the ground with blood on his hands and lips, and a great stillness brooded over all about him.

Then a flattish voice from within the house remarked: "Gee-whizz!"

"Hullo!" said Redwood.

"Hullo there!" answered the voice.

And then: "Did you chaps get 'im?"

A sense of the duties of friendship returned to Redwood. "Is Mr. Bensington hurt?" he said.

The man inside heard imperfectly. "No one ain't to blame if I ain't," said the voice inside.

It became clearer to Redwood that he must have shot Bensington. He forgot the cuts upon his face, arose and came back to find Bensington seated on the ground and rubbing his shoulder. Bensington looked over his glasses. "We peppered him, Redwood," he said, and then: "He tried to jump over me, and knocked me down. But I let him have it with both barrels, and my! how it has hurt my shoulder, to be sure."

A man appeared in the doorway. "I got him once in the chest and once in the side," he said.

"Where's the waggons?" said Cossar, appearing amidst a thicket of gigantic canary-creeper leaves.

It became evident, to Redwood's amazement, first, that no one had been shot, and, secondly, that the trolley and waggon had shifted fifty yards, and were now standing with interlocked wheels amidst the tangled distortions of Skinner's kitchen garden. The horses had stopped their plunging. Half-way towards them, the burst barrel of sulphur lay in the path with a cloud of sulphur dust above it. He indicated this to Cossar and walked towards it. "Has any one seen that rat?" shouted Cossar, following. "I got him in between the ribs once, and once in the face as he turned on me."

They were joined by two men, as they worried at the locked wheels.

"I killed that rat," said one of the men.

"Have they got him?" asked Cossar.

"Jim Bates has found him, beyond the hedge. I got him jest as he came round the corner... Whack behind the shoulder..."

When things were a little ship-shape again Redwood went and stared at the huge misshapen corpse. The brute lay on its side, with its body slightly bent. Its rodent teeth overhanging its receding lower jaw gave its face a look of colossal feebleness, of weak avidity. It seemed not in the least ferocious or terrible. Its fore-paws reminded him of lank emaciated hands. Except for one neat round hole with a scorched rim on either side of its neck, the creature was absolutely intact. He meditated over this fact for some time. "There must have been two rats," he said at last, turning away.

"Yes. And the one that everybody hit—got away."

"I am certain that my own shot—"

A canary-creeper leaf tendril, engaged in that mysterious search for a holdfast which constitutes a tendril's career, bent itself engagingly towards his neck and made him step aside hastily.

"Whoo-z-z z-z-z-z-Z-Z-Z," from the distant wasps' nest, "whoo oo zoo- oo."

V

This incident left the party alert but not unstrung.

They got their stores into the house, which had evidently been ransacked by the rats after the flight of Mrs. Skinner, and four of the men took the two horses back to Hickleybrow. They dragged the dead rat through the hedge and into a position commanded by the windows of the house, and incidentally came upon a cluster of giant earwigs in the ditch. These creatures dispersed hastily, but Cossar reached out incalculable limbs and managed to kill several with his boots and gun-butt. Then two of the men hacked through several of the main stems of the canary creeper—huge cylinders they were, a couple of feet in diameter, that came out by the sink at the back; and while Cossar set the house in order for the night, Bensington, Redwood, and one of the assistant electricians went cautiously round by the fowl runs in search of the rat- holes.

They skirted the giant nettles widely, for these huge weeds threatened them with poison-thorns a good inch long. Then round beyond the gnawed, dismantled stile they came abruptly on the huge cavernous throat of the most westerly of the giant rat-holes, an evil-smelling profundity, that drew them up into a line together.

"I *hope* they'll come out," said Redwood, with a glance at the pent- house of the well.

"If they don't—" reflected Bensington.

"They will," said Redwood.

They meditated.

"We shall have to rig up some sort of flare if we *do* go in," said Redwood.

They went up a little path of white sand through the pine-wood and halted presently within sight of the wasp-holes.

The sun was setting now, and the wasps were coming home for good; their wings in the golden light made twirling haloes about them. The three men peered out from under the trees—they did not care to go right to the edge of the wood—and watched these tremendous insects drop and crawl for a little and enter and disappear. "They will be still in a couple of hours from now," said Redwood... "This is like being a boy again."

"We can't miss those holes," said Bensington, "even if the night is dark. By-the-bye—about the light—"

"Full moon," said the electrician. "I looked it up."

They went back and consulted with Cossar.

He said that "obviously" they must get the sulphur, nitre, and plaster of Paris through the wood before twilight, and for that they broke bulk and carried the sacks. After the necessary shouting of the preliminary directions, never a word was spoken, and as the buzzing of the wasps' nest died away there was scarcely a sound in the world but the noise of footsteps, the heavy breathing of burthened men, and the thud of the sacks. They all took turns at that labour except Mr. Bensington, who was manifestly unfit. He took post in the Skinners' bedroom with a rifle, to watch the carcase of the dead rat, and of the others, they took turns to rest from sack-carrying and to keep watch two at a time upon the rat-holes behind the nettle grove. The pollen sacs of the nettles were ripe, and every now and then the vigil would be enlivened by the dehiscence of these, the bursting of the

sacs sounding exactly like the crack of a pistol, and the pollen grains as big as buckshot pattered all about them.

Mr. Bensington sat at his window on a hard horse-hair-stuffed arm-chair, covered by a grubby antimacassar that had given a touch of social distinction to the Skinners' sitting-room for many years. His unaccustomed rifle rested on the sill, and his spectacles anon watched the dark bulk of the dead rat in the thickening twilight, anon wandered about him in curious meditation. There was a faint smell of paraffin without, for one of the casks leaked, and it mingled with a less unpleasant odour arising from the hacked and crushed creeper.

Within, when he turned his head, a blend of faint domestic scents, beer, cheese, rotten apples, and old boots as the leading *motifs*, was full of reminiscences of the vanished Skinners. He regarded the dim room for a space. The furniture had been greatly disordered—perhaps by some inquisitive rat—but a coat upon a clothes-peg on the door, a razor and some dirty scraps of paper, and a piece of soap that had hardened through years of disuse into a horny cube, were redolent of Skinner's distinctive personality. It came to Bensington's mind with a complete novelty of realisation that in all probability the man had been killed and eaten, at least in part, by the monster that now lay dead there in the darkling.

To think of all that a harmless-looking discovery in chemistry may lead to!

Here he was in homely England and yet in infinite danger, sitting out alone with a gun in a twilit, ruined house, remote from every comfort, his shoulder dreadfully bruised from a gun-kick, and—by Jove!

He grasped now how profoundly the order of the universe had changed for him. He had come right away to this amazing experience, *without even saying a word to his cousin Jane*!

What must she be thinking of him?

He tried to imagine it and he could not. He had an extraordinary feeling that she and he were parted for ever and would never meet again. He felt he had taken a step and come into a world of new immensities. What other monsters might not those deepening shadows hide? The tips of the giant nettles came out sharp and black against the pale green and amber of the western sky. Everything was very still—very still indeed. He wondered why he could not hear the others away there round the corner of the house. The shadow in the cart-shed was now an abysmal black.

* * * * *

Bang ... Bang ... Bang.

A sequence of echoes and a shout.

A long silence.

Bang and a *diminuendo* of echoes.

Stillness.

Then, thank goodness! Redwood and Cossar were coming out of the inaudible darknesses, and Redwood was calling "Bensington!"

"Bensington! We've bagged another of the rats!"

"Cossar's bagged another of the rats!"

VI

When the Expedition had finished refreshment, the night had fully come. The stars were at their brightest, and a growing pallor towards Hankey heralded the moon. The watch on the rat-holes had been maintained, but the watchers had shifted to the hill slope above the holes, feeling this a safer firing-point. They squatted there in a rather abundant dew, fighting the damp with whisky. The others rested in the house, and the three leaders discussed the night's work with the men. The moon rose towards midnight, and as soon as it was clear of the downs, every one except the rat-hole sentinels started off in single file, led by Cossar, towards the wasps' nest.

So far as the wasps' nest went, they found their task exceptionally easy — astonishingly easy. Except that it was a longer labour, it was no graver affair than any common wasps' nest might have been. Danger there was, no doubt, danger to life, but it never so much as thrust its head out of that portentous hillside. They stuffed in the sulphur and nitre, they bunged the holes soundly, and fired their trains. Then with a common impulse all the party but Cossar turned and ran athwart the long shadows of the pines, and, finding Cossar had stayed behind, came to a halt together in a knot, a hundred yards away, convenient to a ditch that offered cover. Just for a minute or two the moonlit night, all black and white, was heavy with a suffocated buzz, that rose and mingled to a roar, a deep abundant note, and culminated and died, and then almost incredibly the night was still.

"By Jove!" said Bensington, almost in a whisper, "*it's done!*"

All stood intent. The hillside above the black point-lace of the pine shadows seemed as bright as day and as colourless as snow. The setting plaster in the holes positively shone. Cossar's loose framework moved towards them.

"So far—" said Cossar.

Crack—*bang*!

A shot from near the house and then—stillness.

"What's *that*?" said Bensington.

"One of the rats put its head out," suggested one of the men.

"By-the-bye, we left our guns up there," said Redwood.

"By the sacks."

Every one began to walk towards the hill again.

"That must be the rats," said Bensington.

"Obviously," said Cossar, gnawing his finger nails.

Bang!

"Hullo?" said one of the men.

Then abruptly came a shout, two shots, a loud shout that was almost a scream, three shots in rapid succession and a splintering of wood. All these sounds were very clear and very small in the immense stillness of the night. Then for some moments nothing but a minute muffled confusion from the direction of the rat-holes, and then again a wild yell ... Each man found himself running hard for the guns.

Two shots.

Bensington found himself, gun in hand, going hard through the pine trees after a number of receding backs. It is curious that the thought uppermost in his mind at that moment was the wish that his cousin Jane could see him. His bulbous slashed boots flew out in wild strides, and his face was distorted into a permanent grin, because that wrinkled his nose and kept his glasses in place. Also he held the muzzle of his gun projecting straight before him as he flew through the chequered moonlight. The man who had run away met them full tilt —he had dropped his gun.

"Hullo," said Cossar, and caught him in his arms. "What's this?"

"They came out together," said the man.

"The rats?"

"Yes, six of them."

"Where's Flack?"

"Down."

"What's he say?" panted Bensington, coming up, unheeded.

"Flack's down?"

"He fell down."

"They came out one after the other."

"What?"

"Made a rush. I fired both barrels first."

"You left Flack?"

"They were on to us." "Come on," said Cossar. "You come with us. Where's Flack? Show us."

The whole party moved forward. Further details of the engagement dropped from the man who had run away. The others clustered about him, except Cossar, who led.

"Where are they?"

"Back in their holes, perhaps. I cleared. They made a rush for their holes."

"What do you mean? Did you get behind them?"

"We got down by their holes. Saw 'em come out, you know, and tried to cut 'em off. They lolloped out—like rabbits. We ran down and let fly. They ran about wild after our first shot and suddenly came at us. *Went* for us."

"How many?"

"Six or seven."

Cossar led the way to the edge of the pine-wood and halted.

"D'yer mean they *got* Flack?" asked some one.

"One of 'em was on to him."

"Didn't you shoot?"

"Now *could* I?"

"Every one loaded?" said Cossar over his shoulder.

There was a confirmatory movement.

"But Flack—" said one.

"D'yer mean—Flack—" said another.

"There's no time to lose," said Cossar, and shouted "Flack!" as he led the way. The whole force advanced towards the rat-holes, the man who had run away a little to the rear. They went forward through the rank exaggerated weeds and skirted the body of the second dead rat. They were extended in a bunchy line, each man with his gun pointing forward, and they peered about them in the clear moonlight for some crumpled, ominous shape, some crouching form. They found the gun of the man who had run away very speedily.

"Flack!" cried Cossar. "Flack!"

"He ran past the nettles and fell down," volunteered the man who ran away.

"Where?"

"Round about there."

"Where did he fall?"

He hesitated and led them athwart the long black shadows for a space and turned judicially. "About here, I think."

"Well, he's not here now."

"But his gun—-?"

"Confound it!" swore Cossar, "where's everything got to?" He strode a step towards the black shadows on the hillside that masked the holes and stood staring. Then he swore again. "If they *have* dragged him in—- !"

So they hung for a space tossing each other the fragments of thoughts. Bensington's glasses flashed like diamonds as he looked from one to the other. The men's faces changed from cold clearness to mysterious obscurity as they turned them to or from the moon. Every one spoke, no one completed a sentence. Then abruptly Cossar chose his line. He flapped limbs this way and that and expelled orders in pellets. It was obvious he wanted lamps. Every one except Cossar was moving towards the house.

"You're going into the holes?" asked Redwood.

"Obviously," said Cossar.

He made it clear once more that the lamps of the cart and trolley were to be got and brought to him.

Bensington, grasping this, started off along the path by the well. He glanced over his shoulder, and saw Cossar's gigantic figure standing out as if he were regarding the holes pensively. At the sight Bensington halted for a moment and half turned. They were all leaving Cossar—-!

Cossar was able to take care of himself, of course!

Suddenly Bensington saw something that made him shout a windless "HI!" In a second three rats had projected themselves from the dark tangle of the creeper towards Cossar. For three seconds Cossar stood unaware of them, and then he had become the most active thing in the world. He didn't fire his gun. Apparently he had no time to aim, or to think of aiming; he ducked a leaping rat, Bensington saw, and then smashed at the back of its head with the butt of his gun. The monster gave one leap and fell over itself.

Cossar's form went right down out of sight among the reedy grass, and then he rose again, running towards another of the rats and whirling his gun overhead. A

faint shout came to Bensington's ears, and then he perceived the remaining two rats bolting divergently, and Cossar in pursuit towards the holes.

The whole thing was an affair of misty shadows; all three fighting monsters were exaggerated and made unreal by the delusive clearness of the light. At moments Cossar was colossal, at moments invisible. The rats flashed athwart the eye in sudden unexpected leaps, or ran with a movement of the feet so swift, they seemed to run on wheels. It was all over in half a minute. No one saw it but Bensington. He could hear the others behind him still receding towards the house. He shouted something inarticulate and then ran back towards Cossar, while the rats vanished. He came up to him outside the holes. In the moonlight the distribution of shadows that constituted Cossar's visage intimated calm. "Hullo," said Cossar, "back already? Where's the lamps? They're all back now in their holes. One I broke the neck of as it ran past me ... See? There!" And he pointed a gaunt finger.

Bensington was too astonished for conversation...

The lamps seemed an interminable time in coming. At last they appeared, first one unwinking luminous eye, preceded by a swaying yellow glare, and then, winking now and then, and then shining out again, two others. About them came little figures with little voices, and then enormous shadows. This group made as it were a spot of inflammation upon the gigantic dreamland of moonshine.

"Flack," said the voices. "Flack."

An illuminating sentence floated up. "Locked himself in the attic."

Cossar was continually more wonderful. He produced great handfuls of cotton wool and stuffed them in his ears—Bensington wondered why. Then he loaded his gun with a quarter charge of powder. Who else could have thought of that? Wonderland culminated with the disappearance of Cossar's twin realms of boot sole up the central hole.

Cossar was on all fours with two guns, one trailing on each side from a string under his chin, and his most trusted assistant, a little dark man with a grave face, was to go in stooping behind him, holding a lantern over his head. Everything had been made as sane and obvious and proper as a lunatic's dream. The wool, it seems, was on account of the concussion of the rifle; the man had some too. Obviously! So long as the rats turned tail on Cossar no harm could come to him, and directly they headed for him he would see their eyes and fire between them. Since they would have to come down the cylinder of the hole, Cossar could hardly fail to hit them. It was, Cossar insisted, the obvious method, a little tedious perhaps, but absolutely certain. As the assistant stooped to enter, Bensington saw that the end of a ball of twine had been tied to the tail of his coat. By this he was to draw in the rope if it should be needed to drag out the bodies of the rats.

Bensington perceived that the object he held in his hand was Cossar's silk hat.

How had it got there?

It would be something to remember him by, anyhow.

At each of the adjacent holes stood a little group with a lantern on the ground shining up the hole, and with one man kneeling and aiming at the round void before him, waiting for anything that might emerge.

There was an interminable suspense.

Then they heard Cossar's first shot, like an explosion in a mine...

Every one's nerves and muscles tightened at that, and bang! bang! bang! the rats had tried a bolt, and two more were dead. Then the man who held the ball of twine reported a twitching. "He's killed one in there," said Bensington, "and he wants the rope."

He watched the rope creep into the hole, and it seemed as though it had become animated by a serpentine intelligence—for the darkness made the twine invisible. At last it stopped crawling, and there was a long pause. Then what seemed to Bensington the queerest monster of all crept slowly from the hole, and resolved itself into the little engineer emerging backwards. After him, and ploughing deep furrows, Cossar's boots thrust out, and then came his lantern-illuminated back...

Only one rat was left alive now, and this poor, doomed wretch cowered in the inmost recesses until Cossar and the lantern went in again and slew it, and finally Cossar, that human ferret, went through all the runs to make sure.

"We got 'em," he said to his nearly awe-stricken company at last. "And if I hadn't been a mud-headed mucker I should have stripped to the waist. Obviously. Feel my sleeves, Bensington! I'm wet through with perspiration. Jolly hard to think of everything. Only a half way-up of whisky can save me from a cold."

VII

There were moments during that wonderful night when it seemed to Bensington that he was planned by nature for a life of fantastic adventure. This was particularly the case for an hour or so after he had taken a stiff whisky. "Shan't go back to Sloane Street," he confided to the tall, fair, dirty engineer.

"You won't, eh?"

"No fear," said Bensington, nodding darkly.

The exertion of dragging the seven dead rats to the funeral pyre by the nettle grove left him bathed in perspiration, and Cossar pointed out the obvious physical reaction of whisky to save him from the otherwise inevitable chill. There was a sort of brigand's supper in the old bricked kitchen, with the row of dead rats lying in the moonlight against the hen-runs outside, and after thirty minutes or so of rest, Cossar roused them all to the labours that were still to do. "Obviously," as he said, they had to "wipe the place out. No litter—no scandal. See?" He stirred them up to the idea of making destruction complete. They smashed and splintered every fragment of wood in the house; they built trails of chopped wood wherever big vegetation was springing; they made a pyre for the rat bodies and soaked them in paraffin.

Bensington worked like a conscientious navvy. He had a sort of climax of exhilaration and energy towards two o'clock. When in the work of destruction he

wielded an axe the bravest fled his neighbourhood. Afterwards he was a little sobered by the temporary loss of his spectacles, which were found for him at last in his side coat-pocket.

Men went to and fro about him—grimy, energetic men. Cossar moved amongst them like a god.

Bensington drank that delight of human fellowship that comes to happy armies, to sturdy expeditions—never to those who live the life of the sober citizen in cities. After Cossar had taken his axe away and set him to carry wood he went to and fro, saying they were all "good fellows." He kept on —long after he was aware of fatigue.

At last all was ready, and the broaching of the paraffin began. The moon, robbed now of all its meagre night retinue of stars, shone high above the dawn.

"Burn everything," said Cossar, going to and fro—"burn the ground and make a clean sweep of it. See?"

Bensington became aware of him, looking now very gaunt and horrible in the pale beginnings of the daylight, hurrying past with his lower jaw projected and a flaring torch of touchwood in his hand.

"Come away!" said some one, pulling Bensington's arm.

The still dawn—no birds were singing there—was suddenly full of a tumultuous crackling; a little dull red flame ran about the base of the pyre, changed to blue upon the ground, and set out to clamber, leaf by leaf, up the stem of a giant nettle. A singing sound mingled with the crackling...

They snatched their guns from the corner of the Skinners' living-room, and then every one was running. Cossar came after them with heavy strides...

Then they were standing looking back at the Experimental Farm. It was boiling up; the smoke and flames poured out like a crowd in a panic, from doors and windows and from a thousand cracks and crevices in the roof. Trust Cossar to build a fire! A great column of smoke, shot with blood-red tongues and darting flashes, rushed up into the sky. It was like some huge giant suddenly standing up, straining upward and abruptly spreading his great arms out across the sky. It cast the night back upon them, utterly hiding and obliterating the incandescence of the sun that rose behind it. All Hickleybrow was soon aware of that stupendous pillar of smoke, and came out upon the crest, in various *deshabille*, to watch them coming.

Behind, like some fantastic fungus, this smoke pillar swayed and fluctuated, up, up, into the sky—making the Downs seem low and all other objects petty, and in the foreground, led by Cossar, the makers of this mischief followed the path, eight little black figures coming wearily, guns shouldered, across the meadow.

As Bensington looked back there came into his jaded brain, and echoed there, a familiar formula. What was it? "You have lit to-day—? You have lit today—?" Then he remembered Latimer's words: "We have lit this day such a candle in England as no man may ever put out again—"

What a man Cossar was, to be sure! He admired his back view for a space, and was proud to have held that hat. Proud! Although he was an eminent investigator and Cossar only engaged in applied science.

Suddenly he fell shivering and yawning enormously and wishing he was warmly tucked away in bed in his little flat that looked out upon Sloane Street. (It didn't do even to think of Cousin Jane.) His legs became cotton strands, his feet lead. He wondered if any one would get them coffee in Hickleybrow. He had never been up all night for three-and-thirty years.

VIII

And while these eight adventurers fought with rats about the Experimental Farm, nine miles away, in the village of Cheasing Eyebright, an old lady with an excessive nose struggled with great difficulties by the light of a flickering candle. She gripped a sardine tin opener in one gnarled hand, and in the other she held a tin of Herakleophorbia, which she had resolved to open or die. She struggled indefatigably, grunting at each fresh effort, while through the flimsy partition the voice of the Caddles infant wailed.

"Bless 'is poor 'art," said Mrs. Skinner; and then, with her solitary tooth biting her lip in an ecstasy of determination, "Come *up*!"

And presently, "*Jab*!" a fresh supply of the Food of the Gods was let loose to wreak its powers of giantry upon the world.

CHAPTER THE FOURTH - THE GIANT CHILDREN

I

For a time at least the spreading circle of residual consequences about the Experimental Farm must pass out of the focus of our narrative—how for a long time a power of bigness, in fungus and toadstool, in grass and weed, radiated from that charred but not absolutely obliterated centre. Nor can we tell here at any length how these mournful spinsters, the two surviving hens, made a wonder of and a show, spent their remaining years in eggless celebrity. The reader who is hungry for fuller details in these matters is referred to the newspapers of the period—to the voluminous, indiscriminate files of the modern Recording Angel. Our business lies with Mr. Bensington at the focus of the disturbance.

He had come back to London to find himself a quite terribly famous man. In a night the whole world had changed with respect to him. Everybody understood. Cousin Jane, it seemed, knew all about it; the people in the streets knew all about it; the newspapers all and more. To meet Cousin Jane was terrible, of course, but when it was over not so terrible after all. The good woman had limits even to her power over facts; it was clear that she had communed with herself and accepted the Food as something in the nature of things.

She took the line of huffy dutifulness. She disapproved highly, it was evident, but she did not prohibit. The flight of Bensington, as she must have considered it, may have shaken her, and her worst was to treat him with bitter persistence for a cold he had not caught and fatigue he had long since forgotten, and to buy him a new sort of hygienic all-wool combination underwear that was apt to get involved and turned partially inside out and partially not, and as difficult to get into for an absent-minded man, as—Society. And so for a space, and as far as this convenience left him leisure, he still continued to participate in the development of this new element in human history, the Food of the Gods.

The public mind, following its own mysterious laws of selection, had chosen him as the one and only responsible Inventor and Promoter of this new wonder; it would hear nothing of Redwood, and without a protest it allowed Cossar to follow his natural impulse into a terribly prolific obscurity. Before he was aware of the drift of these things, Mr. Bensington was, so to speak, stark and dissected upon the hoardings. His baldness, his curious general pinkness, and his golden spectacles had become a national possession. Resolute young men with large expensive-looking cameras and a general air of complete authorisation took possession of the flat for brief but fruitful periods, let off flash lights in it that filled it for days

with dense, intolerable vapour, and retired to fill the pages of the syndicated magazines with their admirable photographs of Mr. Bensington complete and at home in his second-best jacket and his slashed shoes. Other resolute-mannered persons of various ages and sexes dropped in and told him things about Boomfood—it was *Punch* first called the stuff "Boomfood"—and afterwards reproduced what they had said as his own original contribution to the Interview. The thing became quite an obsession with Broadbeam, the Popular Humourist. He scented another confounded thing he could not understand, and he fretted dreadfully in his efforts to "laugh the thing down." One saw him in clubs, a great clumsy presence with the evidences of his midnight oil burning manifest upon his large unwholesome face, explaining to every one he could buttonhole: "These Scientific chaps, you know, haven't a Sense of Humour, you know. That's what it is. This Science—kills it." His jests at Bensington became malignant libels...

An enterprising press-cutting agency sent Bensington a long article about himself from a sixpenny weekly, entitled "A New Terror," and offered to supply one hundred such disturbances for a guinea, and two extremely charming young ladies, totally unknown to him, called, and, to the speechless indignation of Cousin Jane, had tea with him and afterwards sent him their birthday books for his signature. He was speedily quite hardened to seeing his name associated with the most incongruous ideas in the public press, and to discover in the reviews articles written about Boomfood and himself in a tone of the utmost intimacy by people he had never heard of. And whatever delusions he may have cherished in the days of his obscurity about the pleasantness of Fame were dispelled utterly and for ever.

At first—except for Broadbeam—the tone of the public mind was quite free from any touch of hostility. It did not seem to occur to the public mind as anything but a mere playful supposition that any more Herakleophorbia was going to escape again. And it did not seem to occur to the public mind that the growing little band of babies now being fed on the food would presently be growing more "up" than most of us ever grow. The sort of thing that pleased the public mind was caricatures of eminent politicians after a course of Boom-feeding, uses of the idea on hoardings, and such edifying exhibitions as the dead wasps that had escaped the fire and the remaining hens.

Beyond that the public did not care to look, until very strenuous efforts were made to turn its eyes to the remoter consequences, and even then for a while its enthusiasm for action was partial. "There's always somethin' New," said the public—a public so glutted with novelty that it would hear of the earth being split as one splits an apple without surprise, and, "I wonder what they'll do next."

But there were one or two people outside the public, as it were, who did already take that further glance, and some it seems were frightened by what they saw there. There was young Caterham, for example, cousin of the Earl of Pewterstone, and one of the most promising of English politicians, who, taking the risk of being thought a faddist, wrote a long article in the *Nineteenth Century and After* to suggest its total suppression. And—in certain of his moods, there was Bensington.

"They don't seem to realise—" he said to Cossar.

"No, they don't."

"And do we? Sometimes, when I think of what it means—This poor child of Redwood's—And, of course, your three... Forty feet high, perhaps! After all, *ought* we to go on with it?"

"Go on with it!" cried Cossar, convulsed with inelegant astonishment and pitching his note higher than ever. "Of *course* you'll go on with it! What d'you think you were made for? Just to loaf about between meal-times?

"Serious consequences," he screamed, "of course! Enormous. Obviously. Obviously. Why, man, it's the only chance you'll ever get of a serious consequence! And you want to shirk it!" For a moment his indignation was speechless, "It's downright Wicked!" he said at last, and repeated explosively, "Wicked!"

But Bensington worked in his laboratory now with more emotion than zest. He couldn't, tell whether he wanted serious consequences to his life or not; he was a man of quiet tastes. It was a marvellous discovery, of course, quite marvellous—but—He had already become the proprietor of several acres of scorched, discredited property near Hickleybrow, at a price of nearly £90 an acre, and at times he was disposed to think this as serious a consequence of speculative chemistry as any unambitious man, could wish. Of course he was Famous—terribly Famous. More than satisfying, altogether more than satisfying, was the Fame he had attained.

But the habit of Research was strong in him...

And at moments, rare moments in the laboratory chiefly, he would find something else than habit and Cossar's arguments to urge him to his work. This little spectacled man, poised perhaps with his slashed shoes wrapped about the legs of his high stool and his hand upon the tweezer of his balance weights, would have again a flash of that adolescent vision, would have a momentary perception of the eternal unfolding of the seed that had been sown in his brain, would see as it were in the sky, behind the grotesque shapes and accidents of the present, the coming world of giants and all the mighty things the future has in store—vague and splendid, like some glittering palace seen suddenly in the passing of a sunbeam far away... And presently it would be with him as though that distant splendour had never shone upon his brain, and he would perceive nothing ahead but sinister shadows, vast declivities and darknesses, inhospitable immensities, cold, wild, and terrible things.

II

Amidst the complex and confused happenings, the impacts from the great outer world that constituted Mr. Bensington's fame, a shining and active figure presently became conspicuous—became almost, as it were, a leader and marshal of these externalities in Mr. Bensington's eyes. This was Dr. Winkles, that convincing young practitioner, who has already appeared in this story as the means whereby Redwood was able to convey the Food to his son. Even before the great outbreak, it was evident that the mysterious powders Redwood had given him had

awakened this gentleman's interest immensely, and so soon as the first wasps came he was putting two and two together.

He was the sort of doctor that is in manners, in morals, in methods and appearance, most succinctly and finally expressed by the word "rising." He was large and fair, with a hard, alert, superficial, aluminium-coloured eye, and hair like chalk mud, even-featured and muscular about the clean-shaven mouth, erect in figure and energetic in movement, quick and spinning on the heel, and he wore long frock coats, black silk ties and plain gold studs and chains and his silk hats had a special shape and brim that made him look wiser and better than anybody. He looked as young or old as anybody grown up. And after that first wonderful outbreak he took to Bensington and Redwood and the Food of the Gods with such a convincing air of proprietorship, that at times, in spite of the testimony of the Press to the contrary, Bensington was disposed to regard him as the original inventor of the whole affair.

"These accidents," said Winkles, when Bensington hinted at the dangers of further escapes, "are nothing. Nothing. The discovery is everything. Properly developed, suitably handled, sanely controlled, we have—we have something very portentous indeed in this food of ours... We must keep our eye on it ... We mustn't let it out of control again, and—we mustn't let it rest."

He certainly did not mean to do that. He was at Bensington's now almost every day. Bensington, glancing from the window, would see the faultless equipage come spanking up Sloane Street and after an incredibly brief interval Winkles would enter the room with a light, strong motion, and pervade it, and protrude some newspaper and supply information and make remarks.

"Well," he would say, rubbing his hands, "how are we getting on?" and so pass to the current discussion about it.

"Do you see," he would say, for example, "that Caterham has been talking about our stuff at the Church Association?"

"Dear me!" said Bensington, "that's a cousin of the Prime Minister, isn't it?"

"Yes," said Winkles, "a very able young man—very able. Quite wrong-headed; you know, violently reactionary—but thoroughly able. And he's evidently disposed to make capital out of this stuff of ours. Takes a very emphatic line. Talks of our proposal to use it in the elementary schools —-"

"Our proposal to use it in the elementary schools!"

"*I* said something about that the other day—quite in passing—little affair at a Polytechnic. Trying to make it clear the stuff was really highly beneficial. Not in the slightest degree dangerous, in spite of those first little accidents. Which cannot possibly occur again... You know it *would* be rather good stuff—But he's taken it up."

"What did you say?"

"Mere obvious nothings. But as you see—-! Takes it up with perfect gravity. Treats the thing as an attack. Says there is already a sufficient waste of public money in elementary schools without this. Tells the old stories about piano lessons again—*you* know. No one; he says, wishes to prevent the children of the

lower classes obtaining an education suited to their condition, but to give them a food of this sort will be to destroy their sense of proportion utterly. Expands the topic. What Good will it do, he asks, to make poor people six-and-thirty feet high? He really believes, you know, that they *will* be thirty-six feet high."

"So they would *be*," said Bensington, "if you gave them our food at all regularly. But nobody said anything—-"

"*I* said something." "But, my dear Winkles—!"

"They'll be Bigger, of course," interrupted Winkles, with an air of knowing all about it, and discouraging the crude ideas of Bensington. "Bigger indisputably. But listen to what he says! Will it make them happier? That's his point. Curious, isn't it? Will it make them better? Will they be more respectful to properly constituted authority? Is it fair to the children themselves?? Curious how anxious his sort are for justice—so far as any future arrangements go. Even nowadays, he says, the cost, of feeding and clothing children is more than many of their parents can contrive, and if this sort of thing is to be permitted—! Eh?

"You see he makes my mere passing suggestion into a positive proposal. And then he calculates how much a pair of breeches for a growing lad of twenty feet high or so will cost. Just as though he really believed—Ten pounds, he reckons, for the merest decency. Curious this Caterham! So concrete! The honest, and struggling ratepayer will have to contribute to that, he says. He says we have to consider the Rights of the Parent. It's all here. Two columns. Every Parent has a right to have, his children brought up in his own Size...

"Then comes the question of school accommodation, cost of enlarged desks and forms for our already too greatly burthened National Schools. And to get what?—a proletariat of hungry giants. Winds up with a very serious passage, says even if this wild suggestion—mere passing fancy of mine, you know, and misinterpreted at that—this wild suggestion about the schools comes to nothing, that doesn't end the matter. This is a strange food, so strange as to seem to him almost wicked. It has been scattered recklessly —so he says—and it may be scattered again. Once you've taken it, it's poison unless you go on with it. 'So it is,' said Bensington. And in short he proposes the formation of a National Society for the Preservation of the Proper Proportions of Things. Odd? Eh? People are hanging on to the idea like anything."

"But what do they propose to do?"

Winkles shrugged his shoulders and threw out his hands. "Form a Society," he said, "and fuss. They want to make it illegal to manufacture this Herakleophorbia—or at any rate to circulate the knowledge of it. I've written about a bit to show that Caterham's idea of the stuff is very much exaggerated—very much exaggerated indeed, but that doesn't seem to check it. Curious how people are turning against it. And the National Temperance Association, by-the-bye, has founded a branch for Temperance in Growth."

"Mm," said Bensington and stroked his nose.

"After all that has happened there's bound to be this uproar. On the face of it the thing's—*startling*."

Winkles walked about the room for a time, hesitated, and departed.

It became evident there was something at the back of his mind, some aspect of crucial importance to him, that he waited to display. One days when Redwood and Bensington were at the flat together he gave them a glimpse of this something in reserve.

"How's it all going?" he said; rubbing his hands together.

"We're getting together a sort of report."

"For the Royal Society?"

"Yes."

"Hm," said. Winkles, very profoundly, and walked to the hearth-rug. "Hm. But—Here's the point. *Ought* you?"

"Ought we—what?"

"Ought you to publish?"

"We're not in the Middle Ages," said Redwood.

"I know."

"As Cossar says, swapping wisdom—that's the true scientific method."

"In most cases, certainly. But—This is exceptional."

"We shall put the whole thing before the Royal Society in the proper way," said Redwood.

Winkles returned to that on a later occasion.

"It's in many ways an Exceptional discovery."

"That doesn't matter," said Redwood.

"It's the sort of knowledge that could easily be subject to grave abuse —grave dangers, as Caterham puts it."

Redwood said nothing.

"Even carelessness, you know—"

"If we were to form a committee of trustworthy people to control the manufacture of Boomfood—Herakleophorbia, I *should* say—we might—"

He paused, and Redwood, with a certain private discomfort, pretended that he did not see any sort of interrogation...

Outside the apartments of Redwood and Bensington, Winkle, in spite of the incompleteness of his instructions, became a leading authority upon Boomfood. He wrote letters defending its use; he made notes and articles explaining its possibilities; he jumped up irrelevantly at the meetings of the scientific and medical associations to talk about it; he identified himself with it. He published a pamphlet called "The Truth about Boomfood," in which he minimised the whole of the Hickleybrow affair almost to nothing. He said that it was absurd to say Boomfood would make people thirty-seven feet high. That was "obviously exaggerated." It would make them Bigger, of course, but that was all...

Within that intimate circle of two it was chiefly evident that Winkles was extremely anxious to help in the making of Herakleophorbia, help in correcting any proofs there might be of any paper there might be in preparation upon the subject—do anything indeed that might lead up to his participation in the details of the making of Herakleophorbia. He was continually telling them both that he felt

it was a Big Thing, that it had big possibilities. If only they were—"safeguarded in some way." And at last one day he asked outright to be told just how it was made.

"I've been thinking over what you said," said Redwood.

"Well?" said Winkles brightly.

"It's the sort of knowledge that could easily be subject to grave abuse," said Redwood.

"But I don't see how that applies," said Winkles.

"It does," said Redwood.

Winkles thought it over for a day or so. Then he came to Redwood and said that he doubted if he ought to give powders about which he knew nothing to Redwood's little boy; it seemed to him it was uncommonly like taking responsibility in the dark. That made Redwood thoughtful.

"You've seen that the Society for the Total Suppression of Boomfood claims to have several thousand members," said Winkles, changing the subject. "They've drafted a Bill," said Winkles. "They've got young Caterham to take it up—readily enough. They're in earnest. They're forming local committees to influence candidates. They want to make it penal to prepare and store Herakleophorbia without special license, and felony—matter of imprisonment without option—to administer Boomfood—that's what they call it, you know—to any person under one-and-twenty. But there's collateral societies, you know. All sorts of people. The Society for the Preservation of Ancient Statures is going to have Mr. Frederic Harrison on the council, they say. You know he's written an essay about it; says it is vulgar, and entirely inharmonious with that Revelation of Humanity that is found in the teachings of Comte. It is the sort of thing the Eighteenth Century *couldn't* have produced even in its worst moments. The idea of the Food never entered the head of Comte—which shows how wicked it really is. No one, he says, who really understood Comte..."

"But you don't mean to say—" said Redwood, alarmed out of his disdain for Winkles.

"They'll not do all that," said Winkles. "But public opinion is public opinion, and votes are votes. Everybody can see you are up to a disturbing thing. And the human instinct is all against disturbance, you know. Nobody seems to believe Caterham's idea of people thirty-seven feet high, who won't be able to get inside a church, or a meeting-house, or any social or human institution. But for all that they're not so easy in their minds about it. They see there's something—something more than a common discovery—"

"There is," said Redwood, "in every discovery."

"Anyhow, they're getting—restive. Caterham keeps harping on what may happen if it gets loose again. I say over and over again, it won't, and it can't. But—there it is!"

And he bounced about the room for a little while as if he meant to reopen the topic of the secret, and then thought better of it and went.

The two scientific men looked at one another. For a space only their eyes spoke.

"If the worst comes to the worst," said Redwood at last, in a strenuously calm voice, "I shall give the Food to my little Teddy with my own hands."

III

It was only a few days after this that Redwood opened his paper to find that the Prime Minister had promised a Royal Commission on Boomfood. This sent him, newspaper in hand, round to Bensington's flat.

"Winkles, I believe, is making mischief for the stuff. He plays into the hands of Caterham. He keeps on talking about it, and what it is going to do, and alarming people. If he goes on, I really believe he'll hamper our inquiries. Even as it is—with this trouble about my little boy—"

Bensington wished Winkles wouldn't.

"Do you notice how he has dropped into the way of calling it Boomfood?"

"I don't like that name," said Bensington, with a glance over his glasses.

"It is just so exactly what it is—to Winkles."

"Why does he keep on about it? It isn't his!"

"It's something called Booming," said Redwood. "*I* don't understand. If it isn't his, everybody is getting to think it is. Not that *that* matters." "In the event of this ignorant, this ridiculous agitation becoming—Serious," began Bensington.

"My little boy can't get on without the stuff," said Redwood. "I don't see how I can help myself now. If the worst comes to the worst—"

A slight bouncing noise proclaimed the presence of Winkles. He became visible in the middle of the room rubbing his hands together.

"I wish you'd knock," said Bensington, looking vicious over the gold rims.

Winkles was apologetic. Then he turned to Redwood. "I'm glad to find you here," he began; "the fact is—"

"Have you seen about this Royal Commission?" interrupted Redwood.

"Yes," said Winkles, thrown out. "Yes."

"What do you think of it?"

"Excellent thing," said Winkles. "Bound to stop most of this clamour. Ventilate the whole affair. Shut up Caterham. But that's not what I came round for, Redwood. The fact is—"

"I don't like this Royal Commission," said Bensington.

"I can assure you it will be all right. I may say—I don't think it's a breach of confidence—that very possibly *I* may have a place on the Commission—"

"Oom," said Redwood, looking into the fire.

"I can put the whole thing right. I can make it perfectly clear, first, that the stuff is controllable, and, secondly, that nothing short of a miracle is needed before anything like that catastrophe at Hickleybrow can possibly happen again. That is just what is wanted, an authoritative assurance. Of course, I could speak with more confidence if I knew—But that's quite by the way. And just at present there's something else, another little matter, upon which I'm wanting to consult

you. Ahem. The fact is—Well—I happen to be in a slight difficulty, and you can help me out."

Redwood raised his eyebrows, and was secretly glad.

"The matter is—highly confidential."

"Go on," said Redwood. "Don't worry about that."

"I have recently been entrusted with a child—the child of—of an Exalted Personage."

Winkles coughed.

"You're getting on," said Redwood.

"I must confess it's largely your powders—and the reputation of my success with your little boy—There is, I cannot disguise, a strong feeling against its use. And yet I find that among the more intelligent—One must go quietly in these things, you know—little by little. Still, in the case of Her Serene High—I mean this new little patient of mine. As a matter of fact—the suggestion came from the parent. Or I should never—"

He struck Redwood as being embarrassed.

"I thought you had a doubt of the advisability of using these powders," said Redwood.

"Merely a passing doubt."

"You don't propose to discontinue—"

"In the case of your little boy? Certainly not!"

"So far as I can see, it would be murder."

"I wouldn't do it for the world."

"You shall have the powders," said Redwood.

"I suppose you couldn't—"

"No fear," said Redwood. "There isn't a recipe. It's no good, Winkles, if you'll pardon my frankness. I'll make you the powders myself."

"Just as well, perhaps," said Winkles, after a momentary hard stare at Redwood—"just as well." And then: "I can assure you I really don't mind in the least."

IV

When Winkles had gone Bensington came and stood on the hearth-rug and looked down at Redwood.

"Her Serene Highness!" he remarked.

"Her Serene Highness!" said Redwood.

"It's the Princess of Weser Dreiburg!"

"No further than a third cousin."

"Redwood," said Bensington; "it's a curious thing to say, I know, but —do you think Winkles understands?"

"What?"

"Just what it is we have made.

"Does he really understand," said Bensington, dropping his voice and keeping his eye doorward, "that in the Family—the Family of his new patient—"

"Go on," said Redwood.

"Who have always been if anything a little *under—under—*"

"The Average?"

"Yes. And so *very* tactfully undistinguished in *any* way, he is going to produce a royal personage—an outsize royal personage —of *that* size. You know, Redwood, I'm not sure whether there is not something almost—*treasonable* ..."

He transferred his eyes from the door to Redwood.

Redwood flung a momentary gesture—index finger erect—at the fire. "By Jove!" he said, "he *doesn't* know!"

"That man," said Redwood, "doesn't know anything. That was his most exasperating quality as a student. Nothing. He passed all his examinations, he had all his facts—and he had just as much knowledge—as a rotating bookshelf containing the *Times Encyclopedia*. And he doesn't know anything *now*. He's Winkles, and incapable of really assimilating anything not immediately and directly related to his superficial self. He is utterly void of imagination and, as a consequence, incapable of knowledge. No one could possibly pass so many examinations and be so well dressed, so well done, and so successful as a doctor without that precise incapacity. That's it. And in spite of all he's seen and heard and been told, there he is—he has no idea whatever of what he has set going. He has got a Boom on, he's working it well on Boomfood, and some one has let him in to this new Royal Baby —and that's Boomier than ever! And the fact that Weser Dreiburg will presently have to face the gigantic problem of a thirty-odd-foot Princess not only hasn't entered his head, but couldn't—it couldn't!"

"There'll be a fearful row," said Bensington.

"In a year or so."

"So soon as they really see she is going on growing."

"Unless after their fashion—they hush it up."

"It's a lot to hush up."

"Rather!"

"I wonder what they'll do?"

"They never do anything—Royal tact."

"They're bound to do something."

"Perhaps *she* will." "O Lord! Yes."

"They'll suppress her. Such things have been known."

Redwood burst into desperate laughter. "The redundant royalty—the bouncing babe in the Iron Mask!" he said. "They'll have to put her in the tallest tower of the old Weser Dreiburg castle and make holes in the ceilings as she grows from floor to floor! Well, I'm in the very same pickle. And Cossar and his three boys. And—Well, well."

"There'll be a fearful row," Bensington repeated, not joining in the laughter. "A *fearful* row."

"I suppose," he argued, "you've really thought it out thoroughly, Redwood. You're quite sure it wouldn't be wiser to warn Winkles, wean your little boy gradually, and—and rely upon the Theoretical Triumph?"

"I wish to goodness you'd spend half an hour in my nursery when the Food's a little late," said Redwood, with a note of exasperation in his voice; "then you wouldn't talk like that, Bensington. Besides—Fancy warning Winkles... No! The tide of this thing has caught us unawares, and whether we're frightened or whether we're not—*we've got to swim!*"

"I suppose we have," said Bensington, staring at his toes. "Yes. We've got to swim. And your boy will have to swim, and Cossar's boys—he's given it to all three of them. Nothing partial about Cossar—all or nothing! And Her Serene Highness. And everything. We are going on making the Food. Cossar also. We're only just in the dawn of the beginning, Redwood. It's evident all sorts of things are to follow. Monstrous great things. But I can't imagine them, Redwood. Except—"

He scanned his finger nails. He looked up at Redwood with eyes bland through his glasses.

"I've half a mind," he adventured, "that Caterham is right. At times. It's going to destroy the Proportions of Things. It's going to dislocate —What isn't it going to dislocate?"

"Whatever it dislocates," said Redwood, "my little boy must have the Food."

They heard some one falling rapidly upstairs. Then Cossar put his head into the fiat. "Hullo!" he said at their expressions, and entering, "Well?"

They told him about the Princess.

"*Difficult question!*" he remarked. "Not a bit of it. *She'll* grow. Your boy'll grow. All the others you give it to 'll grow. Everything. Like anything. What's difficult about that? That's all right. A child could tell you that. Where's the bother?"

They tried to make it clear to him.

"*Not go on with it!*" he shrieked. "But—! You can't help yourselves now. It's what you're for. It's what Winkles is for. It's all right. Often wondered what Winkles was for. *Now* it's obvious. What's the trouble?

"*Disturbance*? Obviously. *Upset things*? Upset everything. Finally—upset every human concern. Plain as a pikestaff. They're going to try and stop it, but they're too late. It's their way to be too late. You go on and start as much of it as you can. Thank God He has a use for you!"

"But the conflict!" said Bensington, "the stress! I don't know if you have imagined—"

"You ought to have been some sort of little vegetable, Bensington," said Cossar—"that's what you ought to have been. Something growing over a rockery. Here you are, fearfully and wonderfully made, and all you think you're made for is just to sit about and take your vittles. D'you think this world was made for old women to mop about in? Well, anyhow, you can't help yourselves now —you've *got* to go on."

"I suppose we must," said Redwood. "Slowly—"

"No!" said Cossar, in a huge shout. "No! Make as much as you can and as soon as you can. Spread it about!"

He was inspired to a stroke of wit. He parodied one of Redwood's curves with a vast upward sweep of his arm.

"Redwood!" he said, to point the allusion, "make it SO!"

V

There is, it seems, an upward limit to the pride of maternity, and this in the case of Mrs. Redwood was reached when her offspring completed his sixth month of terrestrial existence, broke down his high-class bassinet- perambulator, and was brought home, bawling, in the milk-truck. Young Redwood at that time weighed fifty-nine and a half pounds, measured forty-eight inches in height, and gripped about sixty pounds. He was carried upstairs to the nursery by the cook and housemaid. After that, discovery was only a question of days. One afternoon Redwood came home from his laboratory to find his unfortunate wife deep in the fascinating pages of *The Mighty Atom*, and at the sight of him she put the book aside and ran violently forward and burst into tears on his shoulder.

"Tell me what you have *done* to him," she wailed. "Tell me what you have done." Redwood took her hand and led her to the sofa, while he tried to think of a satisfactory line of defence.

"It's all right, my dear," he said; "it's all right. You're only a little overwrought. It's that cheap perambulator. I've arranged for a bath-chair man to come round with something stouter to-morrow—"

Mrs. Redwood looked at him tearfully over the top of her handkerchief.

"A baby in a bath-chair?" she sobbed.

"Well, why not?"

"It's like a cripple."

"It's like a young giant, my dear, and you've no cause to be ashamed of him."

"You've done something to him, Dandy," she said. "I can see it in your face."

"Well, it hasn't stopped his growth, anyhow," said Redwood heartlessly.

"I *knew*," said Mrs. Redwood, and clenched her pocket-handkerchief ball fashion in one hand. She looked at him with a sudden change to severity. "What have you done to our child, Dandy?"

"What's wrong with him?"

"He's so big. He's a monster."

"Nonsense. He's as straight and clean a baby as ever a woman had. What's wrong with him?"

"Look at his size."

"That's all right. Look at the puny little brutes about us! He's the finest baby—"

"He's *too* fine," said Mrs. Redwood.

"It won't go on," said Redwood reassuringly; "it's just a start he's taken."

But he knew perfectly well it would go on. And it did. By the time this baby was twelve months old he tottered just one inch under five feet high and scaled eight stone three; he was as big in fact as a St. Peter's *in Vaticano* cherub, and his affectionate clutch at the hair and features of visitors became the talk of West

Kensington. They had an invalid's chair to carry him up and down to his nursery, and his special nurse, a muscular young person just out of training, used to take him for his airings in a Panhard 8 h.p. hill-climbing perambulator specially made to meet his requirement? It was lucky in every way that Redwood had his expert witness connection in addition to his professorship.

When one got over the shock of little Redwood's enormous size, he was, I am told by people who used to see him almost daily teufteufing slowly about Hyde Park, a singularly bright and pretty baby. He rarely cried or needed a comforter. Commonly he clutched a big rattle, and sometimes he went along hailing the bus-drivers and policemen along the road outside the railings as "Dadda!" and "Babba!" in a sociable, democratic way.

"There goes that there great Boomfood baby," the bus-driver used to say.

"Looks 'ealthy," the forward passenger would remark.

"Bottle fed," the bus-driver would explain. "They say it 'olds a gallon and 'ad to be specially made for 'im."

"Very 'ealthy child any'ow," the forward passenger would conclude.

When Mrs. Redwood realized that his growth was indeed going on indefinitely and logically—and this she really did for the first time when the motor-perambulator arrived—she gave way to a passion of grief. She declared she never wished to enter her nursery again, wished she was dead, wished the child was dead, wished everybody was dead, wished she had never married Redwood, wished no one ever married anybody, Ajaxed a little, and retired to her own room, where she lived almost exclusively on chicken broth for three days. When Redwood came to remonstrate with her, she banged pillows about and wept and tangled her hair.

"*He's* all right," said Redwood. "He's all the better for being big. You wouldn't like him smaller than other people's children."

"I want him to be *like* other children, neither smaller nor bigger. I wanted him to be a nice little boy, just as Georgina Phyllis is a nice little girl, and I wanted to bring him up nicely in a nice way, and here he is" —and the unfortunate woman's voice broke—"wearing number four grown-up shoes and being wheeled about by—booboo!—Petroleum!

"I can never love him," she wailed, "never! He's too much for me! I can never be a mother to him, such as I meant to be!"

But at last, they contrived to get her into the nursery, and there was Edward Monson Redwood ("Pantagruel" was only a later nickname) swinging in a specially strengthened rocking-chair and smiling and talking "goo" and "wow." And the heart of Mrs. Redwood warmed again to her child, and she went and held him in her arms and wept.

"They've done something to you," she sobbed, "and you'll grow and grow, dear; but whatever I can do to bring you up nice I'll do for you, whatever your father may say."

And Redwood, who had helped to bring her to the door, went down the passage much relieved. (Eh! but it's a base job this being a man—with women as they are!)

VI

Before the year was out there were, in addition to Redwood's pioneer vehicle, quite a number of motor-perambulators to be seen in the west of London. I am told there were as many as eleven; but the most careful inquiries yield trustworthy evidence of only six within the Metropolitan area at that time. It would seem the stuff acted differently upon different types of constitution. At first Herakleophorbia was not adapted to injection, and there can be no doubt that quite a considerable proportion of human beings are incapable of absorbing this substance in the normal course of digestion. It was given, for example, to Winkles' youngest boy; but he seems to have been as incapable of growth as, if Redwood was right, his father was incapable of knowledge. Others again, according to the Society for the Total Suppression of Boomfood, became in some inexplicable way corrupted by it, and perished at the onset of infantile disorders. The Cossar boys took to it with amazing avidity.

Of course a thing of this kind never comes with absolute simplicity of application into the life of man; growth in particular is a complex thing, and all generalisations must needs be a little inaccurate. But the general law of the Food would seem to be this, that when it could be taken into the system in any way it stimulated it in very nearly the same degree in all cases. It increased the amount of growth from six to seven times, and it did not go beyond that, whatever amount of the Food in excess was taken. Excess of Herakleophorbia indeed beyond the necessary minimum led, it was found, to morbid disturbances of nutrition, to cancer and tumours, ossifications, and the like. And once growth upon the large scale had begun, it was soon evident that it could only continue upon that scale, and that the continuous administration of Herakleophorbia in small but sufficient doses was imperative.

If it was discontinued while growth was still going on, there was first a vague restlessness and distress, then a period of voracity—as in the case of the young rats at Hankey—and then the growing creature had a sort of exaggerated anaemia and sickened and died. Plants suffered in a similar way. This, however, applied only to the growth period. So soon as adolescence was attained—in plants this was represented by the formation of the first flower-buds—the need and appetite for Herakleophorbia diminished, and so soon as the plant or animal was fully adult, it became altogether independent of any further supply of the food. It was, as it were, completely established on the new scale. It was so completely established on the new scale that, as the thistles about Hickleybrow and the grass of the down side already demonstrated, its seed produced giant offspring after its kind.

And presently little Redwood, pioneer of the new race, first child of all who ate the food, was crawling about his nursery, smashing furniture, biting like a horse, pinching like a vice, and bawling gigantic baby talk at his "Nanny" and

"Mammy" and the rather scared and awe-stricken "Daddy," who had set this mischief going.

The child was born with good intentions. "Padda be good, be good," he used to say as the breakables flew before him. "Padda" was his rendering of Pantagruel, the nickname Redwood imposed on him. And Cossar, disregarding certain Ancient Lights that presently led to trouble, did, after a conflict with the local building regulations, get building on a vacant piece of ground adjacent to Redwood's home, a comfortable well-lit playroom, schoolroom, and nursery for their four boys—sixty feet square about this room was, and forty feet high.

Redwood fell in love with that great nursery as he and Cossar built it, and his interest in curves faded, as he had never dreamt it could fade, before the pressing needs of his son. "There is much," he said, "in fitting a nursery. Much.

"The walls, the things in it, they will all speak to this new mind of ours, a little more, a little less eloquently, and teach it, or fail to teach it a thousand things."

"Obviously," said Cossar, reaching hastily for his hat.

They worked together harmoniously, but Redwood supplied most of the educational theory required...

They had the walls and woodwork painted with a cheerful vigour; for the most part a slightly warmed white prevailed, but there were bands of bright clean colour to enforce the simple lines of construction. "Clean colours we *must* have," said Redwood, and in one place had a neat horizontal band of squares, in which crimson and purple, orange and lemon, blues and greens, in many hues and many shades, did themselves honour. These squares the giant children should arrange and rearrange to their pleasure. "Decorations must follow," said Redwood; "let them first get the range of all the tints, and then this may go away. There is no reason why one should bias them in favour of any particular colour or design."

Then, "The place must be full of interest," said Redwood. "Interest is food for a child, and blankness torture and starvation. He must have pictures galore." There were no pictures hung about the room for any permanent service, however, but blank frames were provided into which new pictures would come and pass thence into a portfolio so soon as their fresh interest had passed. There was one window that looked down the length of a street, and in addition, for an added interest, Redwood had contrived above the roof of the nursery a camera obscura that watched the Kensington High Street and not a little of the Gardens.

In one corner that most worthy implement, an Abacus, four feet square, a specially strengthened piece of ironmongery with rounded corners, awaited the young giants' incipient computations. There were few woolly lambs and such-like idols, but instead Cossar, without explanation, had brought one day in three four-wheelers a great number of toys (all just too big for the coming children to swallow) that could be piled up, arranged in rows, rolled about, bitten, made to flap and rattle, smacked together, felt over, pulled out, opened, closed, and mauled and experimented with to an interminable extent. There were many bricks of wood in diverse colours, oblong and cuboid, bricks of polished china, bricks of transparent glass and bricks of india-rubber; there were slabs and slates; there were cones,

truncated cones, and cylinders; there were oblate and prolate spheroids, balls of varied substances, solid and hollow, many boxes of diverse size and shape, with hinged lids and screw lids and fitting lids, and one or two to catch and lock; there were bands of elastic and leather, and a number of rough and sturdy little objects of a size together that could stand up steadily and suggest the shape of a man. "Give 'em these," said Cossar. "One at a time."

These things Redwood arranged in a locker in one corner. Along one side of the room, at a convenient height for a six-or eight-foot child, there was a blackboard, on which the youngsters might flourish in white and coloured chalk, and near by a sort of drawing block, from which sheet after sheet might be torn, and on which they could draw in charcoal, and a little desk there was, furnished with great carpenter's pencils of varying hardness and a copious supply of paper, on which the boys might first scribble and then draw more neatly. And moreover Redwood gave orders, so far ahead did his imagination go, for specially large tubes of liquid paint and boxes of pastels against the time when they should be needed. He laid in a cask or so of plasticine and modelling clay. "At first he and his tutor shall model together," he said, "and when he is more skilful he shall copy casts and perhaps animals. And that reminds me, I must also have made for him a box of tools!

"Then books. I shall have to look out a lot of books to put in his way, and they'll have to be big type. Now what sort of books will he need? There is his imagination to be fed. That, after all, is the crown of every education. The crown—as sound habits of mind and conduct are the throne. No imagination at all is brutality; a base imagination is lust and cowardice; but a noble imagination is God walking the earth again. He must dream too of a dainty fairy-land and of all the quaint little things of life, in due time. But he must feed chiefly on the splendid real; he shall have stories of travel through all the world, travels and adventures and how the world was won; he shall have stories of beasts, great books splendidly and clearly done of animals and birds and plants and creeping things, great books about the deeps of the sky and the mystery of the sea; he shall have histories and maps of all the empires the world has seen, pictures and stories of all the tribes and habits and customs of men. And he must have books and pictures to quicken his sense of beauty, subtle Japanese pictures to make him love the subtler beauties of bird and tendril and falling flower, and western pictures too, pictures of gracious men and women, sweet groupings, and broad views of land and sea. He shall have books on the building of houses and palaces; he shall plan rooms and invent cities—

"I think I must give him a little theatre.

"Then there is music!"

Redwood thought that over, and decided that his son might best begin with a very pure-sounding harmonicon of one octave, to which afterwards there could be an extension. "He shall play with this first, sing to it and give names to the notes," said Redwood, "and afterwards—?"

He stared up at the window-sill overhead and measured the size of the room with his eye.

"They'll have to build his piano in here," he said. "Bring it in in pieces."

He hovered about amidst his preparations, a pensive, dark, little figure. If you could have seen him there he would have looked to you like a ten-inch man amidst common nursery things. A great rug—indeed it was a Turkey carpet—four hundred square feet of it, upon which young Redwood was soon to crawl—stretched to the grill-guarded electric radiator that was to warm the whole place. A man from Cossar's hung amidst scaffolding overhead, fixing the great frame that was to hold the transitory pictures. A blotting- paper book for plant specimens as big as a house door leant against the wall, and from it projected a gigantic stalk, a leaf edge or so and one flower of chickweed, all of that gigantic size that was soon to make Urshot famous throughout the botanical world...

A sort of incredulity came to Redwood as he stood among these things.

"If it really *is* going on—" said Redwood, staring up at the remote ceiling.

From far away came a sound like the bellowing of a Mafficking bull, almost as if in answer.

"It's going on all right," said Redwood. "Evidently."

There followed resounding blows upon a table, followed by a vast crowing shout, "Gooloo! Boozoo! Bzz ..."

"The best thing I can do," said Redwood, following out some divergent line of thought, "is to teach him myself."

That beating became more insistent. For a moment it seemed to Redwood that it caught the rhythm of an engine's throbbing—the engine he could have imagined of some great train of events that bore down upon him. Then a descendant flight of sharper beats broke up that effect, and were repeated.

"Come in," he cried, perceiving that some one rapped, and the door that was big enough for a cathedral opened slowly a little way. The new winch ceased to creak, and Bensington appeared in the crack, gleaming benevolently under his protruded baldness and over his glasses.

"I've ventured round to *see*," he whispered in a confidentially furtive manner.

"Come in," said Redwood, and he did, shutting the door behind him.

He walked forward, hands behind his back, advanced a few steps, and peered up with a bird-like movement at the dimensions about him. He rubbed his chin thoughtfully.

"Every time I come in," he said, with a subdued note in his voice, "it strikes me as—'*Big*.'"

"Yes," said Redwood, surveying it all again also, as if in an endeavour to keep hold of the visible impression. "Yes. They're going to be big too, you know."

"I know," said Bensington, with a note that was nearly awe. "*Very* big."

They looked at one another, almost, as it were, apprehensively.

"Very big indeed," said Bensington, stroking the bridge of his nose, and with one eye that watched Redwood doubtfully for a confirmatory expression. "All of

them, you know—fearfully big. I don't seem able to imagine —even with this—just how big they're all going to be."

CHAPTER THE FIFTH - THE MINIMIFICENCE OF MR. BENSINGTON

I

It was while the Royal Commission on Boomfood was preparing its report that Herakleophorbia really began to demonstrate its capacity for leakage. And the earliness of this second outbreak was the more unfortunate, from the point of view of Cossar at any rate, since the draft report still in existence shows that the Commission had, under the tutelage of that most able member, Doctor Stephen Winkles (F.R.S. M.D. F.R.C.P. D. Sc. J.P. D.L. etc.), already quite made up its mind that accidental leakages were impossible, and was prepared to recommend that to entrust the preparation of Boomfood to a qualified committee (Winkles chiefly), with an entire control over its sale, was quite enough to satisfy all reasonable objections to its free diffusion. This committee was to have an absolute monopoly. And it is, no doubt, to be considered as a part of the irony of life that the first and most alarming of this second series of leakages occurred within fifty yards of a little cottage at Keston occupied during the summer months by Doctor Winkles.

There can be little doubt now that Redwood's refusal to acquaint Winkles with the composition of Herakleophorbia IV. had aroused in that gentleman a novel and intense desire towards analytical chemistry. He was not a very expert manipulator, and for that reason probably he saw fit to do his work not in the excellently equipped laboratories that were at his disposal in London, but without consulting any one, and almost with an air of secrecy, in a rough little garden laboratory at the Keston establishment. He does not seem to have shown either very great energy or very great ability in this quest; indeed one gathers he dropped the inquiry after working at it intermittently for about a month.

This garden laboratory, in which the work was done, was very roughly equipped, supplied by a standpipe tap with water, and draining into a pipe that ran down into a swampy rush-bordered pool under an alder tree in a secluded corner of the common just outside the garden hedge. The pipe was cracked, and the residuum of the Food of the Gods escaped through the crack into a little puddle amidst clumps of rushes, just in time for the spring awakening.

Everything was astir with life in that scummy little corner. There was frog spawn adrift, tremulous with tadpoles just bursting their gelatinous envelopes; there were little pond snails creeping out into life, and under the green skin of the rush stems the larvae of a big Water Beetle were struggling out of their egg cases.

I doubt if the reader knows the larva of the beetle called (I know not why) Dytiscus. It is a jointed, queer-looking thing, very muscular and sudden in its movements, and given to swimming head downward with its tail out of water; the length of a man's top thumb joint it is, and more —two inches, that is for those who have not eaten the Food—and it has two sharp jaws that meet in front of its head—tubular jaws with sharp points—through which its habit is to suck its victim's blood...

The first things to get at the drifting grains of the Food were the little tadpoles and the little water snails; the little wriggling tadpoles in particular, once they had the taste of it, took to it with zest. But scarcely did one of them begin to grow into a conspicuous position in that little tadpole world and try a smaller brother or so as an aid to a vegetarian dietary, when nip! one of the Beetle larva had its curved bloodsucking prongs gripping into his heart, and with that red stream went Herakleophorbia IV, in a state of solution, into the being of a new client. The only thing that had a chance with these monsters to get any share of the Food were the rushes and slimy green scum in the water and the seedling weeds in the mud at the bottom. A clean up of the study presently washed a fresh spate of the Food into the puddle, and overflowed it, and carried all this sinister expansion of the struggle for life into the adjacent pool under the roots of the alder...

The first person to discover what was going on was a Mr. Lukey Carrington, a special science teacher under the London Education Board, and, in his leisure, a specialist in fresh-water algae, and he is certainly not to be envied his discovery. He had come down to Keston Common for the day to fill a number of specimen tubes for subsequent examination, and he came, with a dozen or so of corked tubes clanking faintly in his pocket, over the sandy crest and down towards the pool, spiked walking stick in hand. A garden lad standing on the top of the kitchen steps clipping Doctor Winkles' hedge saw him in this unfrequented corner, and found him and his occupation sufficiently inexplicable and interesting to watch him pretty closely.

He saw Mr. Carrington stoop down by the side of the pool, with his hand against the old alder stem, and peer into the water, but of course he could not appreciate the surprise and pleasure with which Mr. Carrington beheld the big unfamiliar-looking blobs and threads of the algal scum at the bottom. There were no tadpoles visible—they had all been killed by that time—and it would seem Mr. Carrington saw nothing at all unusual except the excessive vegetation. He bared his arm to the elbow, leant forward, and dipped deep in pursuit of a specimen. His seeking hand went down. Instantly there flashed out of the cool shadow under the tree roots something—

Flash! It had buried its fangs deep into his arm—a bizarre shape it was, a foot long and more, brown and jointed like a scorpion.

Its ugly apparition and the sharp amazing painfulness of its bite were too much for Mr. Carrington's equilibrium. He felt himself going, and yelled aloud. Over he toppled, face foremost, splash! into the pool.

The boy saw him vanish, and heard the splashing of his struggle in the water. The unfortunate man emerged again into the boy's field of vision, hatless and streaming with water, and screaming!

Never before had the boy heard screams from a man.

This astonishing stranger appeared to be tearing at something on the side of his face. There appeared streaks of blood there. He flung out his arms as if in despair, leapt in the air like a frantic creature, ran violently ten or twelve yards, and then fell and rolled on the ground and over and out of sight of the boy. The lad was down the steps and through the hedge in a trice—happily with the garden shears still in hand. As he came crashing through the gorse bushes, he says he was half minded to turn back, fearing he had to deal with a lunatic, but the possession of the shears reassured him. "I could 'ave jabbed his eyes," he explained, "anyhow." Directly Mr. Carrington caught sight of him, his demeanour became at once that of a sane but desperate man. He struggled to his feet, stumbled, stood up, and came to meet the boy.

"Look!" he cried, "I can't get 'em off!"

And with a qualm of horror the boy saw that, attached to Mr. Carrington's cheek, to his bare arm, and to his thigh, and lashing furiously with their lithe brown muscular bodies, were three of these horrible larvae, their great jaws buried deep in his flesh and sucking for dear life. They had the grip of bulldogs, and Mr. Carrington's efforts to detach the monsters from his face had only served to lacerate the flesh to which it had attached itself, and streak face and neck and coat with living scarlet.

"I'll cut 'im," cried the boy; "'old on, Sir."

And with the zest of his age in such proceedings, he severed one by one the heads from the bodies of Mr. Carrington's assailants. "Yup," said the boy with a wincing face as each one fell before him. Even then, so tough and determined was their grip that the severed heads remained for a space, still fiercely biting home and still sucking, with the blood streaming out of their necks behind. But the boy stopped that with a few more slashes of his scissors —in one of which Mr. Carrington was implicated.

"I couldn't get 'em off!" repeated Carrington, and stood for a space, swaying and bleeding profusely. He dabbed feeble hands at his injuries and examined the result upon his palms. Then he gave way at the knees and fell headlong in a dead faint at the boy's feet, between the still leaping bodies of his defeated foes. Very luckily it didn't occur to the boy to splash water on his face—for there were still more of these horrors under the alder roots—and instead he passed back by the pond and went into the garden with the intention of calling assistance. And there he met the gardener coachman and told him of the whole affair.

When they got back to Mr. Carrington he was sitting up, dazed and weak, but able to warn them against the danger in the pool.

II

Such were the circumstances by which the world had its first notification that the Food was loose again. In another week Keston Common was in full operation as what naturalists call a centre of distribution. This time there were no wasps or rats, no earwigs and no nettles, but there were at least three water-spiders, several dragon-fly larvae which presently became dragon-flies, dazzling all Kent with their hovering sapphire bodies, and a nasty gelatinous, scummy growth that swelled over the pond margin, and sent its slimy green masses surging halfway up the garden path to Doctor Winkles's house. And there began a growth of rushes and equisetum and potamogeton that ended only with the drying of the pond.

It speedily became evident to the public mind that this time there was not simply one centre of distribution, but quite a number of centres. There was one at Ealing—there can be no doubt now—and from that came the plague of flies and red spider; there was one at Sunbury, productive of ferocious great eels, that could come ashore and kill sheep; and there was one in Bloomsbury that gave the world a new strain of cockroaches of a quite terrible sort—an old house it was in Bloomsbury, and much inhabited by undesirable things. Abruptly the world found itself confronted with the Hickleybrow experiences all over again, with all sorts of queer exaggerations of familiar monsters in the place of the giant hens and rats and wasps. Each centre burst out with its own characteristic local fauna and flora...

We know now that every one of these centres corresponded to one of the patients of Doctor Winkles, but that was by no means apparent at the time. Doctor Winkles was the last person to incur any odium in the matter. There was a panic quite naturally, a passionate indignation, but it was indignation not against Doctor Winkles but against the Food, and not so much against the Food as against the unfortunate Bensington, whom from the very first the popular imagination had insisted upon regarding as the sole and only person responsible for this new thing.

The attempt to lynch him that followed is just one of those explosive events that bulk largely in history and are in reality the least significant of occurrences.

The history of the outbreak is a mystery. The nucleus of the crowd certainly came from an Anti-Boomfood meeting in Hyde Park organised by extremists of the Caterham party, but there seems no one in the world who actually first proposed, no one who ever first hinted a suggestion of the outrage at which so many people assisted. It is a problem for M. Gustave le Bon —a mystery in the psychology of crowds. The fact emerges that about three o'clock on Sunday afternoon a remarkably big and ugly London crowd, entirely out of hand, came rolling down Thursday Street intent on Bensington's exemplary death as a warning to all scientific investigators, and that it came nearer accomplishing its object than any London crowd has ever come since the Hyde Park railings came down in remote middle Victorian times. This crowd came so close to its object indeed, that for the space of an hour or more a word would have settled the unfortunate gentleman's fate.

The first intimation he had of the thing was the noise of the people outside. He went to the window and peered, realising nothing of what impended. For a minute perhaps he watched them seething about the entrance, disposing of an ineffectual dozen of policemen who barred their way, before he fully realised his own importance in the affair. It came upon him in a flash—that that roaring, swaying multitude was after him. He was all alone in the flat—fortunately perhaps—his cousin Jane having gone down to Ealing to have tea with a relation on her mother's side, and he had no more idea of how to behave under such circumstances than he had of the etiquette of the Day of Judgment. He was still dashing about the flat asking his furniture what he should do, turning keys in locks and then unlocking them again, making darts at door and window and bedroom—when the floor clerk came to him.

"There isn't a moment, Sir," he said. "They've got your number from the board in the hall! They're coming straight up!"

He ran Mr. Bensington out into the passage, already echoing with the approaching tumult from the great staircase, locked the door behind them, and led the way into the opposite flat by means of his duplicate key.

"It's our only chance now," he said.

He flung up a window which opened on a ventilating shaft, and showed that the wall was set with iron staples that made the rudest and most perilous of wall ladders to serve as a fire escape from the upper flats. He shoved Mr. Bensington out of the window, showed him how to cling on, and pursued him up the ladder, goading and jabbing his legs with a bunch of keys whenever he desisted from climbing. It seemed to Bensington at times that he must climb that vertical ladder for evermore. Above, the parapet was inaccessibly remote, a mile perhaps, below—He did not care to think of things below.

"Steady on!" cried the clerk, and gripped his ankle. It was quite horrible having his ankle gripped like that, and Mr. Bensington tightened his hold on the iron staple above to a drowning clutch, and gave a faint squeal of terror.

It became evident the clerk had broken a window, and then it seemed he had leapt a vast distance sideways, and there came the noise of a window-frame sliding in its sash. He was bawling things.

Mr. Bensington moved his head round cautiously until he could see the clerk. "Come down six steps," the clerk commanded.

All this moving about seemed very foolish, but very, very cautiously Mr. Bensington lowered a foot.

"Don't pull me!" he cried, as the clerk made to help him from the open window.

It seemed to him that to reach the window from the ladder would be a very respectable feat for a flying fox, and it was rather with the idea of a decent suicide than in any hope of accomplishing it that he made the step at last, and quite ruthlessly the clerk pulled him in. "You'll have to stop here," said the clerk; "my keys are no good here. It's an American lock. I'll get out and slam the door behind me and see if I can find the man of this floor. You'll be locked in. Don't go to the

window, that's all. It's the ugliest crowd I've ever seen. If only they think you're out they'll probably content themselves by breaking up your stuff—"

"The indicator said In," said Bensington.

"The devil it did! Well, anyhow, I'd better not be found—"

He vanished with a slam of the door.

Bensington was left to his own initiative again.

It took him under the bed.

There presently he was found by Cossar.

Bensington was almost comatose with terror when he was found, for Cossar had burst the door in with his shoulder by jumping at it across the breadth of the passage.

"Come out of it, Bensington," he said. "It's all right. It's me. We've got to get out of this. They're setting the place on fire. The porters are all clearing out. The servants are gone. It's lucky I caught the man who knew.

"Look here!"

Bensington, peering from under the bed, became aware of some unaccountable garments on Cossar's arm, and, of all things, a black bonnet in his hand!

"They're having a clear out," said Cossar, "If they don't set the place on fire they'll come here. Troops may not be here for an hour yet. Fifty per cent. Hooligans in the crowd, and the more furnished flats they go into the better they'll like it. Obviously... They mean a clear out. You put this skirt and bonnet on, Bensington, and clear out with me."

"D'you *mean*—?" began Bensington, protruding a head, tortoise fashion.

"I mean, put 'em on and come! Obviously," And with a sudden vehemence he dragged Bensington from under the bed, and began to dress him for his new impersonation of an elderly woman of the people.

He rolled up his trousers and made him kick off his slippers, took off his collar and tie and coat and vest, slipped a black skirt over his head, and put on a red flannel bodice and a body over the same. He made him take off his all too characteristic spectacles, and clapped the bonnet on his head. "You might have been born an old woman," he said as he tied the strings. Then came the spring-side boots—a terrible wrench for corns—and the shawl, and the disguise was complete. "Up and down," said Cossar, and Bensington obeyed.

"You'll do," said Cossar.

And in this guise it was, stumbling awkwardly over his unaccustomed skirts, shouting womanly imprecations upon his own head in a weird falsetto to sustain his part, and to the roaring note of a crowd bent upon lynching him, that the original discoverer of Herakleophorbia IV. proceeded down the corridor of Chesterfield Mansions, mingled with that inflamed disorderly multitude, and passed out altogether from the thread of events that constitutes our story.

Never once after that escape did he meddle again with the stupendous development of the Food of the Gods he of all men had done most to begin.

III

This little man who started the whole thing passes out of the story, and after a time he passed altogether out of the world of things, visible and tellable. But because he started the whole thing it is seemly to give his exit an intercalary page of attention. One may picture him in his later days as Tunbridge Wells came to know him. For it was at Tunbridge Wells he reappeared after a temporary obscurity, so soon as he fully realised how transitory, how quite exceptional and unmeaning that fury of rioting was. He reappeared under the wing of Cousin Jane, treating himself for nervous shock to the exclusion of all other interests, and totally indifferent, as it seemed, to the battles that were raging then about those new centres of distribution, and about the baby Children of the Food.

He took up his quarters at the Mount Glory Hydrotherapeutic Hotel, where there are quite extraordinary facilities for baths, Carbonated Baths, Creosote Baths, Galvanic and Faradic Treatment, Massage, Pine Baths, Starch and Hemlock Baths, Radium Baths, Light Baths, Heat Baths, Bran and Needle Baths, Tar and Birdsdown Baths,—all sorts of baths; and he devoted his mind to the development of that system of curative treatment that was still imperfect when he died. And sometimes he would go down in a hired vehicle and a sealskin trimmed coat, and sometimes, when his feet permitted, he would walk to the Pantiles, and there he would sip chalybeate water under the eye of his cousin Jane.

His stooping shoulders, his pink appearance, his beaming glasses, became a "feature" of Tunbridge Wells. No one was the least bit unkind to him, and indeed the place and the Hotel seemed very glad to have the distinction of his presence. Nothing could rob him of that distinction now. And though he preferred not to follow the development of his great invention in the daily papers, yet when he crossed the Lounge of the Hotel or walked down the Pantiles and heard the whisper, "There he is! That's him!" it was not dissatisfaction that softened his mouth and gleamed for a moment in his eye.

This little figure, this minute little figure, launched the Food of the Gods upon the world! One does not know which is the most amazing, the greatness or the littleness of these scientific and philosophical men. You figure him there on the Pantiles, in the overcoat trimmed with fur. He stands under that chinaware window where the spring spouts, and holds and sips the glass of chalybeate water in his hand. One bright eye over the gilt rim is fixed, with an expression of inscrutable severity, on Cousin Jane, "Mm," he says, and sips.

So we make our souvenir, so we focus and photograph this discoverer of ours for the last time, and leave him, a mere dot in our foreground, and pass to the greater picture that, has developed about him, to the story of his Food, how the scattered Giant Children grew up day by day into a world that was all too small for them, and how the net of Boomfood Laws and Boomfood Conventions, which the Boomfood Commission was weaving even then, drew closer and closer upon them with every year of their growth, Until—

BOOK II - THE FOOD IN THE VILLAGE

CHAPTER THE FIRST - THE COMING OF THE FOOD

I

Our theme, which began so compactly in Mr. Bensington's study, has already spread and branched, until it points this way and that, and henceforth our whole story is one of dissemination. To follow the Food of the Gods further is to trace the ramifications of a perpetually branching tree; in a little while, in the quarter of a lifetime, the Food had trickled and increased from its first spring in the little farm near Hickleybrow until it had spread, —it and the report and shadow of its power,—throughout the world. It spread beyond England very speedily. Soon in America, all over the continent of Europe, in Japan, in Australia, at last all over the world, the thing was working towards its appointed end. Always it worked slowly, by indirect courses and against resistance. It was bigness insurgent. In spite of prejudice, in spite of law and regulation, in spite of all that obstinate conservatism that lies at the base of the formal order of mankind, the Food of the Gods, once it had been set going, pursued its subtle and invincible progress.

The children of the Food grew steadily through all these years; that was the cardinal fact of the time. But it is the leakages make history. The children who had eaten grew, and soon there were other children growing; and all the best intentions in the world could not stop further leakages and still further leakages. The Food insisted on escaping with the pertinacity of a thing alive. Flour treated with the stuff crumbled in dry weather almost as if by intention into an impalpable powder, and would lift and travel before the lightest breeze. Now it would be some fresh insect won its way to a temporary fatal new development, now some fresh outbreak from the sewers of rats and such- like vermin. For some days the village of Pangbourne in Berkshire fought with giant ants. Three men were bitten and died. There would be a panic, there would be a struggle, and the salient evil would be fought down again, leaving always something behind, in the obscurer things of life—changed for ever. Then again another acute and startling outbreak, a swift upgrowth of monstrous weedy thickets, a drifting dissemination about the world of inhumanly growing thistles, of cockroaches men fought with shot guns, or a plague of mighty flies.

There were some strange and desperate struggles in obscure places. The Food begot heroes in the cause of littleness...

And men took such happenings into their lives, and met them by the expedients of the moment, and told one another there was "no change in the essential order of things." After the first great panic, Caterham, in spite of his power of eloquence, became a secondary figure in the political world, remained in men's minds as the exponent of an extreme view.

Only slowly did he win a way towards a central position in affairs." There was no change in the essential order of things,"—that eminent leader of modern thought, Doctor Winkles, was very clear upon this,—and the exponents of what was called in those days Progressive Liberalism grew quite sentimental upon the essential insincerity of their progress. Their dreams, it would appear, ran wholly on little nations, little languages, little households, each self-supported on its little farm. A fashion for the small and neat set in. To be big was to be "vulgar," and dainty, neat, mignon, miniature, "minutely perfect," became the key-words of critical approval...

Meanwhile, quietly, taking their time as children must, the children of the Food, growing into a world that changed to receive them, gathered strength and stature and knowledge, became individual and purposeful, rose slowly towards the dimensions of their destiny. Presently they seemed a natural part of the world; all these stirrings of bigness seemed a natural part of the world, and men wondered how things had been before their time. There came to men's ears stories of things the giant boys could do, and they said "Wonderful!"—without a spark of wonder. The popular papers would tell of the three sons of Cossar, and how these amazing children would lift great cannons, hurl masses of iron for hundreds of yards, and leap two hundred feet. They were said to be digging a well, deeper than any well or mine that man had ever made, seeking, it was said, for treasures hidden in the earth since ever the earth began.

These Children, said the popular magazines, will level mountains, bridge seas, tunnel your earth to a honeycomb. "Wonderful!" said the little folks, "isn't it? What a lot of conveniences we shall have!" and went about their business as though there was no such thing as the Food of the Gods on earth. And indeed these things were no more than the first hints and promises of the powers of the Children of the Food. It was still no more than child's play with them, no more than the first use of a strength in which no purpose had arisen. They did not know themselves for what they were. They were children—slow- growing children of a new race. The giant strength grew day by day—the giant will had still to grow into purpose and an aim.

Looking at it in a shortened perspective of time, those years of transition have the quality of a single consecutive occurrence; but indeed no one saw the coming of Bigness in the world, as no one in all the world till centuries had passed saw, as one happening, the Decline and Fall of Rome. They who lived in those days were too much among these developments to see them together as a single thing. It seemed even to wise men that the Food was giving the world nothing but a crop

of unmanageable, disconnected irrelevancies, that might shake and trouble indeed, but could do no more to the established order and fabric of mankind.

To one observer at least the most wonderful thing throughout that period of accumulating stress is the invincible inertia of the great mass of people, their quiet persistence in all that ignored the enormous presences, the promise of still more enormous things, that grew among them. Just as many a stream will be at its smoothest, will look most tranquil, running deep and strong, at the very verge of a cataract, so all that is most conservative in man seemed settling quietly into a serene ascendency during these latter days. Reaction became popular: there was talk of the bankruptcy of science, of the dying of Progress, of the advent of the Mandarins,—talk of such things amidst the echoing footsteps of the Children of the Food. The fussy pointless Revolutions of the old time, a vast crowd of silly little people chasing some silly little monarch and the like, had indeed died out and passed away; but Change had not died out. It was only Change that had changed. The New was coming in its own fashion and beyond the common understanding of the world.

To tell fully of its coming would be to write a great history, but everywhere there was a parallel chain of happenings. To tell therefore of the manner of its coming in one place is to tell something of the whole. It chanced one stray seed of Immensity fell into the pretty, petty village of Cheasing Eyebright in Kent, and from the story of its queer germination there and of the tragic futility that ensued, one may attempt—following one thread, as it were—to show the direction in which the whole great interwoven fabric of the thing rolled off the loom of Time.

II

Cheasing Eyebright had of course a Vicar. There are vicars and vicars, and of all sorts I love an innovating vicar—a piebald progressive professional reactionary—the least. But the Vicar of Cheasing Eyebright was one of the least innovating of vicars, a most worthy, plump, ripe, and conservative-minded little man. It is becoming to go back a little in our story to tell of him. He matched his village, and one may figure them best together as they used to be, on the sunset evening when Mrs. Skinner—you will remember her flight!—brought the Food with her all unsuspected into these rustic serenities.

The village was looking its very best just then, under that western light. It lay down along the valley beneath the beechwoods of the Hanger, a beading of thatched and red-tiled cottages—cottages with trellised porches and pyracanthus-lined faces, that clustered closer and closer as the road dropped from the yew trees by the church towards the bridge. The vicarage peeped not too ostentatiously between the trees beyond the inn, an early Georgian front ripened by time, and the spire of the church rose happily in the depression made by the valley in the outline of the hills. A winding stream, a thin intermittency of sky blue and foam, glittered amidst a thick margin of reeds and loosestrife and overhanging willows, along the centre of a sinuous pennant of meadow. The whole prospect had that

curiously English quality of ripened cultivation—that look of still completeness—that apes perfection, under the sunset warmth.

And the Vicar too looked mellow. He looked habitually and essentially mellow, as though he had been a mellow baby born into a mellow class, a ripe and juicy little boy. One could see, even before he mentioned it, that he had gone to an ivy-clad public school in its anecdotage, with magnificent traditions, aristocratic associations, and no chemical laboratories, and proceeded thence to a venerable college in the very ripest Gothic. Few books he had younger than a thousand years; of these, Yarrow and Ellis and good pre- Methodist sermons made the bulk. He was a man of moderate height, a little shortened in appearance by his equatorial dimensions, and a face that had been mellow from the first was now climacterically ripe. The beard of a David hid his redundancy of chin; he wore no watch chain out of refinements and his modest clerical garments were made by a West End tailor... And he sat with a hand on either shin, blinking at his village in beatific approval. He waved a plump palm towards it. His burthen sang out again. What more could any one desire?

"We are fortunately situated," he said, putting the thing tamely.

"We are in a fastness of the hills," he expanded.

He explained himself at length. "We are out of it all."

For they had been talking, he and his friend, of the Horrors of the Age, of Democracy, and Secular Education, and Sky Scrapers, and Motor Cars, and the American Invasion, the Scrappy Reading of the Public, and the disappearance of any Taste at all.

"We are out of it all," he repeated, and even as he spoke the footsteps of some one coming smote upon his ear, and he rolled over and regarded her.

You figure the old woman's steadfastly tremulous advance, the bundle clutched in her gnarled lank hand, her nose (which was her countenance) wrinkled with breathless resolution. You see the poppies nodding fatefully on her bonnet, and the dust-white spring-sided boots beneath her skimpy skirts, pointing with an irrevocable slow alternation east and west. Beneath her arm, a restive captive, waggled and slipped a scarcely valuable umbrella. What was there to tell the Vicar that this grotesque old figure was—so far as his village was concerned at any rate—no less than Fruitful Chance and the Unforeseen, the Hag weak men call Fate. But for us, you understand, no more than Mrs. Skinner.

As she was too much encumbered for a curtsey, she pretended not to see him and his friend at all, and so passed, flip-flop, within three yards of them, onward down towards the village. The Vicar watched her slow transit in silence, and ripened a remark the while...

The incident seemed to him of no importance whatever. Old womankind, *aere perennius*, has carried bundles since the world began. What difference has it made?

"We are out of it all," said the Vicar. "We live in an atmosphere of simple and permanent things, Birth and Toil, simple seed-time and simple harvest. The Up-

roar passes us by." He was always very great upon what he called the permanent things. "Things change," he would say, "but Humanity—*aere perennius*."

Thus the Vicar. He loved a classical quotation subtly misapplied. Below, Mrs. Skinner, inelegant but resolute, had involved herself curiously with Wilmerding's stile.

III

No one knows what the Vicar made of the Giant Puff-Balls.

No doubt he was among the first to discover them. They were scattered at intervals up and down the path between the near down and the village end —a path he frequented daily in his constitutional round. Altogether, of these abnormal fungi there were, from first to last, quite thirty. The Vicar seems to have stared at each severally, and to have prodded most of them with his stick once or twice. One he attempted to measure with his arms, but it burst at his Ixion embrace.

He spoke to several people about them, and said they were "marvellous!" and he related to at least seven different persons the well-known story of the flagstone that was lifted from the cellar floor by a growth of fungi beneath. He looked up his Sowerby to see if it was *Lycoperdon coelatum* or *giganteum*—like all his kind since Gilbert White became famous, he Gilbert-Whited. He cherished a theory that *giganteum* is unfairly named.

'One does not know if he observed that those white spheres lay in the very track that old woman of yesterday had followed, or if he noted that the last of the series swelled not a score of yards from the gate of the Caddles' cottage. If he observed these things, he made no attempt to place his observation on record. His observation in matters botanical was what the inferior sort of scientific people call a "trained observation"—you look for certain definite things and neglect everything else. And he did nothing to link this phenomenon with the remarkable expansion of the Caddles' baby that had been going on now for some weeks, indeed ever since Caddles walked over one Sunday afternoon a month or more ago to see his mother-in-law and hear Mr. Skinner (since defunct) brag about his management of hens.

IV

The growth of the puff-balls following on the expansion of the Caddles' baby really ought to have opened the Vicar's eyes. The latter fact had already come right into his arms at the christening—almost over- poweringly...

The youngster bawled with deafening violence when the cold water that sealed its divine inheritance and its right to the name of "Albert Edward Caddles" fell upon its brow. It was already beyond maternal porterage, and Caddles, staggering indeed, but grinning triumphantly at quantitatively inferior parents, bore it back to the free-sitting occupied by his party.

"I never saw such a child!" said the Vicar. This was the first public intimation that the Caddles' baby, which had begun its earthly career a little under seven pounds, did after all intend to be a credit to its parents. Very soon it was clear it

meant to be not only a credit but a glory. And within a month their glory shone so brightly as to be, in connection with people in the Caddles' position, improper.

The butcher weighed the infant eleven times. He was a man of few words, and he soon got through with them. The first time he said, "E's a good un;" the next time he said, "My word!" the third time he said, "*Well*, mum," and after that he simply blew enormously each time, scratched his head, and looked at his scales with an unprecedented mistrust. Every one came to see the Big Baby—so it was called by universal consent—and most of them said, "E's a Bouncer," and almost all remarked to him, "*Did* they?" Miss Fletcher came and said she "never *did*," which was perfectly true.

Lady Wondershoot, the village tyrant, arrived the day after the third weighing, and inspected the phenomenon narrowly through glasses that filled it with howling terror. "It's an unusually Big child," she told its mother, in a loud instructive voice. "You ought to take unusual care of it, Caddles. Of course it won't go on like this, being bottle fed, but we must do what we can for it. I'll send you down some more flannel."

The doctor came and measured the child with a tape, and put the figures in a notebook, and old Mr. Drift-hassock, who fanned by Up Marden, brought a manure traveller two miles out of their way to look at it. The traveller asked the child's age three times over, and said finally that he was blowed. He left it to be inferred how and why he was blowed; apparently it was the child's size blowed him. He also said it ought to be put into a baby show. And all day long, out of school hours, little children kept coming and saying, "Please, Mrs. Caddles, mum, may we have a look at your baby, please, mum?" until Mrs. Caddles had to put a stop to it. And amidst all these scenes of amazement came Mrs. Skinner, and stood and smiled, standing somewhat in the background, with each sharp elbow in a lank gnarled hand, and smiling, smiling under and about her nose, with a smile of infinite profundity.

"It makes even that old wretch of a grandmother look quite pleasant," said Lady Wondershoot. "Though I'm sorry she's come back to the village."

Of course, as with almost all cottagers' babies, the eleemosynary element had already come in, but the child soon made it clear by colossal bawling, that so far as the filling of its bottle went, it hadn't come in yet nearly enough.

The baby was entitled to a nine days' wonder, and every one wondered happily over its amazing growth for twice that time and more. And then you know, instead of its dropping into the background and giving place to other marvels, it went on growing more than ever!

Lady Wondershoot heard Mrs. Greenfield, her housekeeper, with infinite amazement.

"Caddles downstairs again. No food for the child! My dear Greenfield, it's impossible. The creature eats like a hippopotamus! I'm sure it can't be true."

"I'm sure I hope you're not being imposed upon, my lady," said Mrs. Greenfield.

"It's so difficult to tell with these people," said Lady Wondershoot. "Now I do wish, my good Greenfield, that you'd just go down there yourself this afternoon and *see*—see it have its bottle. Big as it is, I cannot imagine that it needs more than six pints a day."

"It hasn't no business to, my lady," said Mrs. Greenfield.

The hand of Lady Wondershoot quivered, with that C.O.S. sort of emotion, that suspicious rage that stirs in all true aristocrats, at the thought that possibly the meaner classes are after all—as mean as their betters, and —where the sting lies—scoring points in the game.

But Mrs. Greenfield could observe no evidence of peculation, and the order for an increasing daily supply to the Caddles' nursery was issued. Scarcely had the first instalment gone, when Caddles was back again at the great house in a state abjectly apologetic.

"We took the greates' care of 'em, Mrs. Greenfield, I do assure you, mum, but he's regular bust 'em! They flew with such vilence, mum, that one button broke a pane of the window, mum, and one hit me a regular stinger jest 'ere, mum."

Lady Wondershoot, when she heard that this amazing child had positively burst out of its beautiful charity clothes, decided that she must speak to Caddles herself. He appeared in her presence with his hair hastily wetted and smoothed by hand, breathless, and clinging to his hat brim as though it was a life-belt, and he stumbled at the carpet edge out of sheer distress of mind.

Lady Wondershoot liked bullying Caddles. Caddles was her ideal lower- class person, dishonest, faithful, abject, industrious, and inconceivably incapable or responsibility. She told him it was a serious matter, the way his child was going on. "It's 'is appetite, my ladyship," said Caddles, with a rising note.

"Check 'im, my ladyship, you can't," said Caddles. "There 'e lies, my ladyship, and kicks out 'e does, and 'owls, that distressin'. We 'aven't the 'eart, my ladyship. If we 'ad—the neighbours would interfere..."

Lady Wondershoot consulted the parish doctor.

"What I want to know," said Lady Wondershoot, "is it *right* this child should have such an extraordinary quantity of milk?"

"The proper allowance for a child of that age," said the parish doctor, "is a pint and a half to two pints in the twenty-four hours. I don't see that you are called upon to provide more. If you do, it is your own generosity. Of course we might try the legitimate quantity for a few days. But the child, I must admit, seems for some reason to be physiologically different. Possibly what is called a Sport. A case of General Hypertrophy."

"It isn't fair to the other parish children," said Lady Wondershoot. "I am certain we shall have complaints if this goes on."

"I don't see that any one can be expected to give more than the recognised allowance. We might insist on its doing with that, or if it wouldn't, send it as a case into the Infirmary."

"I suppose," said Lady Wondershoot, reflecting, "that apart from the size and the appetite, you don't find anything else abnormal—nothing monstrous?"

"No. No, I don't. But no doubt if this growth goes on, we shall find grave moral and intellectual deficiencies. One might almost prophesy that from Max Nordau's law. A most gifted and celebrated philosopher, Lady Wondershoot. He discovered that the abnormal is—abnormal, a most valuable discovery, and well worth bearing in mind. I find it of the utmost help in practice. When I come upon anything abnormal, I say at once, This is abnormal." His eyes became profound, his voice dropped, his manner verged upon the intimately confidential. He raised one hand stiffly. "And I treat it in that spirit," he said.

V

"Tut, tut!" said the Vicar to his breakfast things—the day after the coming of Mrs. Skinner. "Tut, tut! what's this?" and poised his glasses at his paper with a general air of remonstrance.

"Giant wasps! What's the world coming to? American journalists, I suppose! Hang these Novelties! Giant gooseberries are good enough for me.

"Nonsense!" said the Vicar, and drank off his coffee at a gulp, eyes steadfast on the paper, and smacked his lips incredulously.

"Bosh!" said the Vicar, rejecting the hint altogether.

But the next day there was more of it, and the light came.

Not all at once, however. When he went for his constitutional that day he was still chuckling at the absurd story his paper would have had him believe. Wasps indeed—killing a dog! Incidentally as he passed by the site of that first crop of puff-balls he remarked that the grass was growing very rank there, but he did not connect that in any way with the matter of his amusement. "We should certainly have heard something of it," he said; "Whitstable can't be twenty miles from here."

Beyond he found another puff-ball, one of the second crop, rising like a roc's egg out of the abnormally coarsened turf.

The thing came upon him in a flash.

He did not take his usual round that morning. Instead he turned aside by the second stile and came round to the Caddles' cottage. "Where's that baby?" he demanded, and at the sight of it, "Goodness me!"

He went up the village blessing his heart, and met the doctor full tilt coming down. He grasped his arm. "What does this *mean*?" he said. "Have you seen the paper these last few days?"

The doctor said he had.

"Well, what's the matter with that child? What's the matter with everything—wasps, puff-balls, babies, eh? What's making them grow so big? This is most unexpected. In Kent too! If it was America now—"

"It's a little difficult to say just what it is," said the doctor. "So far as I can grasp the symptoms—"

"Yes?"

"It's Hypertrophy—General Hypertrophy."

"Hypertrophy?"

"Yes. General—affecting all the bodily structures—all the organism. I may say that in my own mind, between ourselves, I'm very nearly convinced it's that... But one has to be careful."

"Ah," said the Vicar, a good deal relieved to find the doctor equal to the situation. "But how is it it's breaking out in this fashion, all over the place?"

"That again," said the doctor, "is difficult to say."

"Urshot. Here. It's a pretty clear case of spreading."

"Yes," said the doctor. "Yes. I think so. It has a strong resemblance at any rate to some sort of epidemic. Probably Epidemic Hypertrophy will meet the case."

"Epidemic!" said the Vicar. "You don't mean it's contagious?"

The doctor smiled gently and rubbed one hand against the other. "That I couldn't say," he said.

"But—-!" cried the Vicar, round-eyed. "If it's *catching* —it—it affects *us!*"

He made a stride up the road and turned about.

"I've just been there," he cried. "Hadn't I better—-? I'll go home at once and have a bath and fumigate my clothes."

The doctor regarded his retreating back for a moment, and then turned about and went towards his own house...

But on the way he reflected that one case had been in the village a month without any one catching the disease, and after a pause of hesitation decided to be as brave as a doctor should be and take the risks like a man.

And indeed he was well advised by his second thoughts. Growth was the last thing that could ever happen to him again. He could have eaten—and the Vicar could have eaten—Herakleophorbia by the truckful. For growth had done with them. Growth had done with these two gentlemen for evermore.

VI

It was a day or so after this conversation—a day or so, that is, after the burning of the Experimental Farm—that Winkles came to Redwood and showed him an insulting letter. It was an anonymous letter, and an author should respect his character's secrets. "You are only taking credit for a natural phenomenon," said the letter, "and trying to advertise yourself by your letter to the *Times*. You and your Boomfood! Let me tell you, this absurdly named food of yours has only the most accidental connection with those big wasps and rats. The plain fact is there is an epidemic of Hypertrophy —Contagious Hypertrophy—which you have about as much claim to control as you have to control the solar system. The thing is as old as the hills. There was Hypertrophy in the family of Anak. Quite outside your range, at Cheasing Eyebright, at the present time there is a baby—"

"Shaky up and down writing. Old gentleman apparently," said Redwood. "But it's odd a baby—"

He read a few lines further, and had an inspiration.

"By Jove!" said he. "That's my missing Mrs. Skinner!"

He descended upon her suddenly in the afternoon of the following day.

She was engaged in pulling onions in the little garden before her daughter's cottage when she saw him coming through the garden gate. She stood for a moment "consternated," as the country folks say, and then folded her arms, and with the little bunch of onions held defensively under her left elbow, awaited his approach. Her mouth opened and shut several times; she mumbled her remaining tooth, and once quite suddenly she curtsied, like the blink of an arc-light.

"I thought I should find you," said Redwood.

"I thought you might, sir," she said, without joy.

"Where's Skinner?"

"'E ain't never written to me, Sir, not once, nor come nigh of me since I came here. Sir." "Don't you know what's become of him?"

"Him not having written, no, Sir," and she edged a step towards the left with an imperfect idea of cutting off Redwood from the barn door.

"No one knows what has become of him," said Redwood.

"I dessay '*e* knows," said Mrs. Skinner.

"He doesn't tell."

"He was always a great one for looking after 'imself and leaving them that was near and dear to 'im in trouble, was Skinner. Though clever as could be," said Mrs. Skinner...

"Where's this child?" asked Redwood abruptly.

She begged his pardon.

"This child I hear about, the child you've been giving our stuff to —the child that weighs two stone."

Mrs. Skinner's hands worked, and she dropped the onions. "Reely, Sir," she protested, "I don't hardly know, Sir, what you mean. My daughter, Sir, Mrs. Caddles, '*as* a baby, Sir." And she made an agitated curtsey and tried to look innocently inquiring by tilting her nose to one side.

"You'd better let me see that baby, Mrs. Skinner," said Redwood.

Mrs. Skinner unmasked an eye at him as she led the way towards the barn. "Of course, Sir, there may 'ave been a *little*, in a little can of Nicey I give his father to bring over from the farm, or a little perhaps what I happened to bring about with me, so to speak. Me packing in a hurry and all ..."

"Um!" said Redwood, after he had cluckered to the infant for a space. "Oom!"

He told Mrs. Caddles the baby was a very fine child indeed, a thing that was getting well home to her intelligence—and he ignored her altogether after that. Presently she left the barn—through sheer insignificance.

"Now you've started him, you'll have to keep on with him, you know," he said to Mrs. Skinner.

He turned on her abruptly. "Don't splash it about *this* time," he said.

"Splash it about, Sir?"

"Oh! *you* know."

She indicated knowledge by convulsive gestures.

"You haven't told these people here? The parents, the squire and so on at the big house, the doctor, no one?"

Mrs. Skinner shook her head.

"I wouldn't," said Redwood...

He went to the door of the barn and surveyed the world about him. The door of the barn looked between the end of the cottage and some disused piggeries through a five-barred gate upon the highroad. Beyond was a high, red brick-wall rich with ivy and wallflower and pennywort, and set along the top with broken glass. Beyond the corner of the wall, a sunlit notice-board amidst green and yellow branches reared itself above the rich tones of the first fallen leaves and announced that "Trespassers in these Woods will be Prosecuted." The dark shadow of a gap in the hedge threw a stretch of barbed wire into relief.

"Um," said Redwood, then in a deeper note, "Oom!"

There came a clatter of horses and the sound of wheels, and Lady Wondershoot's greys came into view. He marked the faces of coachman and footman as the equipage approached. The coachman was a very fine specimen, full and fruity, and he drove with a sort of sacramental dignity. Others might doubt their calling and position in the world, he at any rate was sure—he drove her ladyship. The footman sat beside him with folded arms and a face of inflexible certainties. Then the great lady herself became visible, in a hat and mantle disdainfully inelegant, peering through her glasses. Two young ladies protruded necks and peered also.

The Vicar passing on the other side swept off the hat from his David's brow unheeded...

Redwood remained standing in the doorway for a long time after the carriage had passed, his hands folded behind him. His eyes went to the green, grey upland of down, and into the cloud-curdled sky, and came back to the glass- set wall. He turned upon the cool shadows within, and amidst spots and blurs of colour regarded the giant child amidst that Rembrandtesque gloom, naked except for a swathing of flannel, seated upon a huge truss of straw and playing with its toes.

"I begin to see what we have done," he said.

He mused, and young Caddles and his own child and Cossar's brood mingled in his musing.

He laughed abruptly. "Good Lord!" he said at some passing thought.

He roused himself presently and addressed Mrs. Skinner. "Anyhow he mustn't be tortured by a break in his food. That at least we can prevent. I shall send you a can every six months. That ought to do for him all right."

Mrs. Skinner mumbled something about "if you think so, Sir," and "probably got packed by mistake... Thought no harm in giving him a little," and so by the aid of various aspen gestures indicated that she understood.

So the child went on growing.

And growing.

"Practically," said Lady Wondershoot, "he's eaten up every calf in the place. If I have any more of this sort of thing from that man Caddies—"

VII

But even so secluded a place as Cheasing Eyebright could not rest for long in the theory of Hypertrophy—Contagious or not—in view of the growing hubbub about the Food. In a little while there were painful explanations for Mrs. Skinner—explanations that reduced her to speechless mumblings of her remaining tooth—explanations that probed her and ransacked her and exposed her—until at last she was driven to take refuge from a universal convergence of blame in the dignity of inconsolable widowhood. She turned her eye—which she constrained to be watery—upon the angry Lady of the Manor, and wiped suds from her hands.

"You forget, my lady, what I'm bearing up under."

And she followed up this warning note with a slightly defiant:

"It's 'IM I think of, my lady, night *and* day."

She compressed her lips, and her voice flattened and faltered: "Bein' et, my lady."

And having established herself on these grounds, she repeated the affirmation her ladyship had refused before. "I 'ad no more idea what I was giving the child, my lady, than any one *could* 'ave..."

Her ladyship turned her mind in more hopeful directions, wigging Caddles of course tremendously by the way. Emissaries, full of diplomatic threatenings, entered the whirling lives of Bensington and Redwood. They presented themselves as Parish Councillors, stolid and clinging phonographically to prearranged statements. "We hold you responsible, Mister Bensington, for the injury inflicted upon our parish, Sir. We hold you responsible."

A firm of solicitors, with a snake of a style—Banghurst, Brown, Flapp, Codlin, Brown, Tedder, and Snoxton, they called themselves, and appeared invariably in the form of a small rufous cunning-looking gentleman with a pointed nose—said vague things about damages, and there was a polished personage, her ladyship's agent, who came in suddenly upon Redwood one day and asked, "Well, Sir, and what do you propose to do?"

To which Redwood answered that he proposed to discontinue supplying the food for the child, if he or Bensington were bothered any further about the matter. "I give it for nothing as it is," he said, "and the child will yell your village to ruins before it dies if you don't let it have the stuff. The child's on your hands, and you have to keep it. Lady Wondershoot can't always be Lady Bountiful and Earthly Providence of her parish without sometimes meeting a responsibility, you know."

"The mischief's done," Lady Wondershoot decided when they told her —with expurgations—what Redwood had said.

"The mischief's done," echoed the Vicar.

Though indeed as a matter of fact the mischief was only beginning.

CHAPTER THE SECOND - THE BRAT GIGANTIC

I

The giant child was ugly—the Vicar would insist. "He always had been ugly—as all excessive things must be." The Vicar's views had carried him out of sight of just judgment in this matter. The child was much subjected to snapshots even in that rustic retirement, and their net testimony is against the Vicar, testifying that the young monster was at first almost pretty, with a copious curl of hair reaching to his brow and a great readiness to smile. Usually Caddles, who was slightly built, stands smiling behind the baby, perspective emphasising his relative smallness.

After the second year the good looks of the child became more subtle and more contestable. He began to grow, as his unfortunate grandfather would no doubt have put it, "rank." He lost colour and developed an increasing effect of being somehow, albeit colossal, yet slight. He was vastly delicate. His eyes and something about his face grew finer—grew, as people say, "interesting." His hair, after one cutting, began to tangle into a mat. "It's the degenerate strain coming out in him," said the parish doctor, marking these things, but just how far he was right in that, and just how far the youngster's lapse from ideal healthfulness was the result of living entirely in a whitewashed barn upon Lady Wondershoot's sense of charity tempered by justice, is open to question.

The photographs of him that present him from three to six show him developing into a round-eyed, flaxen-haired youngster with a truncated nose and a friendly stare. There lurks about his lips that never very remote promise of a smile that all the photographs of the early giant children display. In summer he wears loose garments of ticking tacked together with string; there is usually one of those straw baskets upon his head that workmen use for their tools, and he is barefooted. In one picture he grins broadly and holds a bitten melon in his hand.

The winter pictures are less numerous and satisfactory. He wears huge sabots—no doubt of beechwoods and (as fragments of the inscription "John Stickells, Iping," show) sacks for socks, and his trousers and jacket are unmistakably cut from the remains of a gaily patterned carpet. Underneath that there were rude swathings of flannel; five or six yards of flannel are tied comforter-fashion about his neck. The thing on his head is probably another sack. He stares, sometimes smiling, sometimes a little ruefully, at the camera. Even when he was only five years old, one sees that half whimsical wrinkling over his soft brown eyes that characterised his face.

He was from the first, the Vicar always declared, a terrible nuisance about the village. He seems to have had a proportionate impulse to play, much curiosity and sociability, and in addition there was a certain craving within him—I grieve to say—for more to eat. In spite of what Mrs. Greenfield called an "*excessively* generous" allowance of food from Lady Wondershoot, he displayed what the doctor perceived at once was the "Criminal Appetite." It carries out only too completely Lady Wondershoot's worst experiences of the lower classes—that in spite of an allowance of nourishment inordinately beyond what is known to be the maximum necessity even of an adult human being, the creature was found to steal. And what he stole he ate with an inelegant voracity. His great hand would come over garden walls; he would covet the very bread in the bakers' carts. Cheeses went from Marlow's store loft, and never a pig trough was safe from him. Some farmer walking over his field of swedes would find the great spoor of his feet and the evidence of his nibbling hunger—a root picked here, a root picked there, and the holes, with childish cunning, heavily erased. He ate a swede as one devours a radish. He would stand and eat apples from a tree, if no one was about, as normal children eat blackberries from a bush. In one way at any rate this shortness of provisions was good for the peace of Cheasing Eyebright—for many years he ate up every grain very nearly of the Food of the Gods that was given him...

Indisputably the child was troublesome and out of place, "He was always about," the Vicar used to say. He could not go to school; he could not go to church by virtue of the obvious limitations of its cubical content. There was some attempt to satisfy the spirit of that "most foolish and destructive law" —I quote the Vicar—the Elementary Education Act of 1870, by getting him to sit outside the open window while instruction was going on within. But his presence there destroyed the discipline of the other children. They were always popping up and peering at him, and every time he spoke they laughed together. His voice was so odd! So they let him stay away.

Nor did they persist in pressing him to come to church, for his vast proportions were of little help to devotion. Yet there they might have had an easier task; there are good reasons for guessing there were the germs of religious feeling somewhere in that big carcase. The music perhaps drew him. He was often in the churchyard on a Sunday morning, picking his way softly among the graves after the congregation had gone in, and he would sit the whole service out beside the porch, listening as one listens outside a hive of bees.

At first he showed a certain want of tact; the people inside would hear his great feet crunch restlessly round their place of worship, or become aware of his dim face peering in through the stained glass, half curious, half envious, and at times some simple hymn would catch him unawares, and he would howl lugubriously in a gigantic attempt at unison. Whereupon little Sloppet, who was organ-blower and verger and beadle and sexton and bell-ringer on Sundays, besides being postman and chimney-sweep all the week, would go out very briskly and valiantly and send him mournfully away. Sloppet, I am glad to say, felt it—in his more thought-

ful moments at any rate. It was like sending a dog home when you start out for a walk, he told me.

But the intellectual and moral training of young Caddles, though fragmentary, was explicit. From the first, Vicar, mother, and all the world, combined to make it clear to him that his giant strength was not for use. It was a misfortune that he had to make the best of. He had to mind what was told him, do what was set him, be careful never to break anything nor hurt anything. Particularly he must not go treading on things or jostling against things or jumping about. He had to salute the gentlefolks respectful and be grateful for the food and clothing they spared him out of their riches. And he learnt all these things submissively, being by nature and habit a teachable creature and only by food and accident gigantic.

For Lady Wondershoot, in these early days, he displayed the profoundest awe. She found she could talk to him best when she was in short skirts and had her dog-whip, and she gesticulated with that and was always a little contemptuous and shrill. But sometimes the Vicar played master—a minute, middle-aged, rather breathless David pelting a childish Goliath with reproof and reproach and dictatorial command. The monster was now so big that it seems it was impossible for any one to remember he was after all only a child of seven, with all a child's desire for notice and amusement and fresh experience, with all a child's craving for response, attention and affection, and all a child's capacity for dependence and unrestricted dulness and misery.

The Vicar, walking down the village road some sunlit morning, would encounter an ungainly eighteen feet of the Inexplicable, as fantastic and unpleasant to him as some new form of Dissent, as it padded fitfully along with craning neck, seeking, always seeking the two primary needs of childhood —something to eat and something with which to play.

There would come a look of furtive respect into the creature's eyes and an attempt to touch the matted forelock.

In a limited way the Vicar had an imagination—at any rate, the remains of one—and with young Caddles it took the line of developing the huge possibilities of personal injury such vast muscles must possess. Suppose a sudden madness—! Suppose a mere lapse into disrespect—! However, the truly brave man is not the man who does not feel fear but the man who overcomes it. Every time and always the Vicar got his imagination under. And he used always to address young Caddles stoutly in a good clear service tenor.

"Being a good boy, Albert Edward?"

And the young giant, edging closer to the wall and blushing deeply, would answer, "Yessir—trying."

"Mind you do," said the Vicar, and would go past him with at most a slight acceleration of his breathing. And out of respect for his manhood he made it a rule, whatever he might fancy, never to look back at the danger, when once it was passed.

In a fitful manner the Vicar would give young Caddles private tuition. He never taught the monster to read—it was not needed; but he taught him the more

important points of the Catechism—his duty to his neighbour for example, and of that Deity who would punish Caddles with extreme vindictiveness if ever he ventured to disobey the Vicar and Lady Wondershoot. The lessons would go on in the Vicar's yard, and passers-by would hear that great cranky childish voice droning out the essential teachings of the Established Church.

"To onner 'n 'bey the King and allooer put 'nthority under 'im. To s'bmit meself t'all my gov'ners, teachers, spir'shall pastors an' masters. To order myself lowly 'n rev'rently t'all my betters—"

Presently it became evident that the effect of the growing giant on unaccustomed horses was like that of a camel, and he was told to keep off the highroad, not only near the shrubbery (where the oafish smile over the wall had exasperated her ladyship extremely), but altogether. That law he never completely obeyed, because of the vast interest the highroad had for him. But it turned what had been his constant resort into a stolen pleasure. He was limited at last almost entirely to old pasture and the Downs.

I do not know what he would have done if it had not been for the Downs. There there were spaces where he might wander for miles, and over these spaces he wandered. He would pick branches from trees and make insane vast nosegays there until he was forbidden, take up sheep and put them in neat rows, from which they immediately wandered (at this he invariably laughed very heartily), until he was forbidden, dig away the turf, great wanton holes, until he was forbidden...

He would wander over the Downs as far as the hill above Wreckstone, but not farther, because there he came upon cultivated land, and the people, by reason of his depredations upon their root-crops, and inspired moreover by a sort of hostile timidity his big unkempt appearance frequently evoked, always came out against him with yapping dogs to drive him away. They would threaten him and lash at him with cart whips. I have heard that they would sometimes fire at him with shot guns. And in the other direction he ranged within sight of Hickleybrow. From above Thursley Hanger he could get a glimpse of the London, Chatham, and Dover railway, but ploughed fields and a suspicious hamlet prevented his nearer access.

And after a time there came boards—great boards with red letters that barred him in every direction. He could not read what the letters said: "Out of Bounds," but in a little while he understood. He was often to be seen in those days, by the railway passengers, sitting, chin on knees, perched up on the Down hard by the Thursley chalk pits, where afterwards he was set working. The train seemed to inspire a dim emotion of friendliness in him, and sometimes he would wave an enormous hand at it, and sometimes give it a rustic incoherent hail.

"Big," the peering passenger would say. "One of these Boom children. They say, Sir, quite unable to do anything for itself—little better than an idiot in fact, and a great burden on the locality."

"Parents quite poor, I'm told."

"Lives on the charity of the local gentry."

Every one would stare intelligently at that distant squatting monstrous figure for a space.

"Good thing that was put a stop to," some spacious thinking mind would suggest. "Nice to 'ave a few thousand of *them* on the rates, eh?"

And usually there was some one wise enough to tell this philosopher: "You're about Right there, Sir," in hearty tones.

II

He had his bad days.

There was, for example, that trouble with the river.

He made little boats out of whole newspapers, an art he learnt by watching the Spender boy, and he set them sailing down the stream—great paper cocked-hats. When they vanished under the bridge which marks the boundary of the strictly private grounds about Eyebright House, he would give a great shout and run round and across Tormat's new field—Lord! how Tormat's pigs did scamper, to be sure, and turn their good fat into lean muscle!—and so to meet his boats by the ford. Right across the nearer lawns these paper boats of his used to go, right in front of Eyebright House, right under Lady Wondershoot's eyes! Disorganising folded newspapers! A pretty thing!

Gathering enterprise from impunity, he began babyish hydraulic engineering. He delved a huge port for his paper fleets with an old shed door that served him as a spade, and, no one chancing to observe his operations just then, he devised an ingenious canal that incidentally flooded Lady Wondershoot's ice-house, and finally he dammed the river. He dammed it right across with a few vigorous doorfuls of earth—he must have worked like an avalanche—and down came a most amazing spate through the shrubbery and washed away Miss Spinks and her easel and the most promising water-colour sketch she had ever begun, or, at any rate, it washed away her easel and left her wet to the knees and dismally tucked up in flight to the house, and thence the waters rushed through the kitchen garden, and so by the green door into the lane and down into the riverbed again by Short's ditch.

Meanwhile, the Vicar, interrupted in conversation with the blacksmith, was amazed to see distressful stranded fish leaping out of a few residual pools, and heaped green weed in the bed of the stream, where ten minutes before there had been eight feet and more of clear cool water.

After that, horrified at his own consequences, young Caddles fled his home for two days and nights. He returned only at the insistent call of hunger, to bear with stoical calm an amount of violent scolding that was more in proportion to his size than anything else that had ever before fallen to his lot in the Happy Village.

III

Immediately after that affair Lady Wondershoot, casting about for exemplary additions to the abuse and fastings she had inflicted, issued a Ukase. She issued it first to her butler, and very suddenly, so that she made him jump. He was clearing

away the breakfast things, and she was staring out of the tall window on the terrace where the fawns would come to be fed. "Jobbet," she said, in her most imperial voice—"Jobbet, this Thing must work for its living."

And she made it quite clear not only to Jobbet (which was easy), but to every one else in the village, including young Caddles, that in this matter, as in all things, she meant what she said.

"Keep him employed," said Lady Wondershoot. "That's the tip for Master Caddles."

"It's the Tip, I fancy, for all Humanity," said the Vicar. "The simple duties, the modest round, seedtime and harvest—"

"Exactly," said Lady Wondershoot. "What *I* always say. Satan finds some mischief still for idle hands to do. At any rate among the labouring classes. We bring up our under-housemaids on that principle, always. What shall we set him to do?"

That was a little difficult. They thought of many things, and meanwhile they broke him in to labour a bit by using him instead of a horse messenger to carry telegrams and notes when extra speed was needed, and he also carried luggage and packing-cases and things of that sort very conveniently in a big net they found for him. He seemed to like employment, regarding it as a sort of game, and Kinkle, Lady Wondershoot's agent, seeing him shift a rockery for her one day, was struck by the brilliant idea of putting him into her chalk quarry at Thursley Hanger, hard by Hickleybrow. This idea was carried out, and it seemed they had settled his problem.

He worked in the chalk pit, at first with the zest of a playing child, and afterwards with an effect of habit—delving, loading, doing all the haulage of the trucks, running the full ones down the lines towards the siding, and hauling the empty ones up by the wire of a great windlass—working the entire quarry at last single-handed.

I am told that Kinkle made a very good thing indeed out of him for Lady Wondershoot, consuming as he did scarcely anything but his food, though that never restrained her denunciation of "the Creature" as a gigantic parasite upon her charity...

At that time he used to wear a sort of smock of sacking, trousers of patched leather, and iron-shod sabots. Over his head was sometimes a queer thing—a worn-out beehive straw chair it was, but usually he went bareheaded. He would be moving about the pit with a powerful deliberation, and the Vicar on his constitutional round would get there about midday to find him shamefully eating his vast need of food with his back to all the world.

His food was brought to him every day, a mess of grain in the husk, in a truck—a small railway truck, like one of the trucks he was perpetually filling with chalk, and this load he used to char in an old limekiln and then devour. Sometimes he would mix with it a bag of sugar. Sometimes he would sit licking a lump of such salt as is given to cows, or eating a huge lump of dates, stones and all, such as one sees in London on barrows. For drink he walked to the rivulet beyond the burnt-out site of the Experimental Farm at Hickleybrow and put down his face

to the stream. It was from his drinking in that way after eating that the Food of the Gods did at last get loose, spreading first of all in huge weeds from the river-side, then in big frogs, bigger trout and stranding carp, and at last in a fantastic exuberance of vegetation all over the little valley.

And after a year or so the queer monstrous grub things in the field before the blacksmith's grew so big and developed into such frightful skipjacks and cockchafers—motor cockchafers the boys called them—that they drove Lady Wondershoot abroad.

IV

But soon the Food was to enter upon a new phase of its work in him. In spite of the simple instructions of the Vicar—instructions intended to round off the modest natural life befitting a giant peasant, in the most complete and final manner—he began to ask questions, to inquire into things, to *think*. As he grew from boyhood to adolescence it became increasingly evident that his mind had processes of its own—out of the Vicar's control. The Vicar did his best to ignore this distressing phenomenon, but still—he could feel it there.

The young giant's material for thought lay about him. Quite involuntarily, with his spacious views, his constant overlooking of things, he must have seen a good deal of human life, and as it grew clearer to him that he too, save for this clumsy greatness of his, was also human, he must have come to realise more and more just how much was shut against him by his melancholy distinction. The sociable hum of the school, the mystery of religion that was partaken in such finery, and which exhaled so sweet a strain of melody, the jovial chorusing from the Inn, the warmly glowing rooms, candle-lit and fire- lit, into which he peered out of the darkness, or again the shouting excitement, the vigour of flannelled exercise upon some imperfectly understood issue that centred about the cricket-field—all these things must have cried aloud to his companionable heart. It would seem that as his adolescence crept upon him, he began to take a very considerable interest in the proceedings of lovers, in those preferences and pairings, those close intimacies that are so cardinal in life.

One Sunday, just about that hour when the stars and the bats and the passions of rural life come out, there chanced to be a young couple "kissing each other a bit" in Love Lane, the deep hedged lane that runs out back towards the Upper Lodge. They were giving their little emotions play, as secure in the warm still twilight as any lovers could be. The only conceivable interruption they thought possible must come pacing visibly up the lane; the twelve-foot hedge towards the silent Downs seemed to them an absolute guarantee.

Then suddenly—incredibly—they were lifted and drawn apart.

They discovered themselves held up, each with a finger and thumb under the armpits, and with the perplexed brown eyes of young Caddles scanning their warm flushed faces. They were naturally dumb with the emotions of their situation.

"*Why* do you like doing that?" asked young Caddies.

I gather the embarrassment continued until the swain remembering his manhood, vehemently, with loud shouts, threats, and virile blasphemies, such as became the occasion, bade young Caddies under penalties put them down. Whereupon young Caddies, remembering his manners, did put them down politely and very carefully, and conveniently near for a resumption of their embraces, and having hesitated above them for a while, vanished again into the twilight...

"But I felt precious silly," the swain confided to me. "We couldn't 'ardly look at one another—bein' caught like that.

"Kissing we was—*you* know.

"And the cur'ous thing is, she blamed it all on to me," said the swain.

"Flew out something outrageous, and wouldn't 'ardly speak to me all the way 'ome..."

The giant was embarking upon investigations, there could be no doubt. His mind, it became manifest, was throwing up questions. He put them to few people as yet, but they troubled him. His mother, one gathers, sometimes came in for cross-examination.

He used to come into the yard behind his mother's cottage, and, after a careful inspection of the ground for hens and chicks, he would sit down slowly with his back against the barn. In a minute the chicks, who liked him, would be pecking all over him at the mossy chalk-mud in the seams of his clothing, and if it was blowing up for wet, Mrs. Caddies' kitten, who never lost her confidence in him, would assume a sinuous form and start scampering into the cottage, up to the kitchen fender, round, out, up his leg, up his body, right up to his shoulder, meditative moment, and then scat! back again, and so on. Sometimes she would stick her claws in his face out of sheer gaiety of heart, but he never dared to touch her because of the uncertain weight of his hand upon a creature so frail. Besides, he rather liked to be tickled. And after a time he would put some clumsy questions to his mother.

"Mother," he would say, "if it's good to work, why doesn't every one work?"

His mother would look up at him and answer, "It's good for the likes of us."

He would meditate, "*Why*?"

And going unanswered, "What's work *for*, mother? Why do I cut chalk and you wash clothes, day after day, while Lady Wondershoot goes about in her carriage, mother, and travels off to those beautiful foreign countries you and I mustn't see, mother?"

"She's a lady," said Mrs. Caddles.

"Oh," said young Caddles, and meditated profoundly.

"If there wasn't gentlefolks to make work for us to do," said Mrs. Caddles, "how should we poor people get a living?"

This had to be digested.

"Mother," he tried again; "if there wasn't any gentlefolks, wouldn't things belong to people like me and you, and if they did—"

"Lord sakes and *drat* the Boy!" Mrs. Caddles would say—she had with the help of a good memory become quite a florid and vigorous individuality since

Mrs. Skinner died. "Since your poor dear grandma was took, there's no abiding you. Don't you arst no questions and you won't be told no lies. If once I was to start out answerin' you *serious*, y'r father 'd 'ave to go' and arst some one else for 'is supper—let alone finishing the washin'."

"All right, mother," he would say, after a wondering stare at her. "I didn't mean to worry."

And he would go on thinking.

V

He was thinking too four years after, when the Vicar, now no longer ripe but over-ripe, saw him for the last time of all. You figure the old gentleman visibly a little older now, slacker in his girth, a little coarsened and a little weakened in his thought and speech, with a quivering shakiness in his hand and a quivering shakiness in his convictions, but his eye still bright and merry for all the trouble the Food had caused his village and himself. He had been frightened at times and disturbed, but was he not alive still and the same still? and fifteen long years—a fair sample of eternity—had turned the trouble into use and wont.

"It was a disturbance, I admit," he would say, "and things are different — different in many ways. There was a time when a boy could weed, but now a man must go out with axe and crowbar—in some places down by the thickets at least. And it's a little strange still to us old-fashioned people for all this valley, even what used to be the river bed before they irrigated, to be under wheat—as it is this year—twenty-five feet high. They used the old-fashioned scythe here twenty years ago, and they would bring home the harvest on a wain—rejoicing—in a simple honest fashion. A little simple drunkenness, a little frank love-making, to conclude ... poor dear Lady Wondershoot—she didn't like these Innovations. Very conservative, poor dear lady! A touch of the eighteenth century about her, I always Said. Her language for example ... Bluff vigour...

"She died comparatively poor. These big weeds got into her garden. She was not one of these gardening women, but she liked her garden in order—things growing where they were planted and as they were planted—under control ... The way things grew was unexpected—upset her ideas ... She didn't like the perpetual invasion of this young monster—at last she began to fancy he was always gaping at her over her wall ... She didn't like his being nearly as high as her house ... Jarred with her sense of proportion. Poor dear lady! I had hoped she would last my time. It was the big cockchafers we had for a year or so that decided her. They came from the giant larvae —nasty things as big as rats—in the valley turf...

"And the ants no doubt weighed with her also.

"Since everything was upset and there was no peace and quietness anywhere now, she said she thought she might just as well be at Monte Carlo as anywhere else. And she went.

"She played pretty boldly, I'm told. Died in a hotel there. Very sad end... Exile... Not—not what one considers meet... A natural leader of our English people... Uprooted. So I...

"Yet after all," harped the Vicar, "it comes to very little. A nuisance of course. Children cannot run about so freely as they used to do, what with ant bites and so forth. Perhaps it's as well ... There used to be talk—as though this stuff would revolutionise every-thing ... But there is something that defies all these forces of the New ... I don't know of course. I'm not one of your modern philosophers—explain everything with ether and atoms. Evolution. Rubbish like that. What I mean is something the 'Ologies don't include. Matter of reason—not understanding. Ripe wisdom. Human nature. *Aere perennius.* ... Call it what you will."

And so at last it came to the last time.

The Vicar had no intimation of what lay so close upon him. He did his customary walk, over by Farthing Down, as he had done it for more than a score of years, and so to the place whence he would watch young Caddies. He did the rise over by the chalk-pit crest a little puffily—he had long since lost the Muscular Christian stride of early days; but Caddies was not at his work, and then, as he skirted the thicket of giant bracken that was beginning to obscure and overshadow the Hanger, he came upon the monster's huge form seated on the hill—brooding as it were upon the world. Caddies' knees were drawn up, his cheek was on his hand, his head a little aslant. He sat with his shoulder towards the Vicar, so that those perplexed eyes could not be seen. He must have been thinking very intently—at any rate he was sitting very still...

He never turned round. He never knew that the Vicar, who had played so large a part in shaping his life, looked then at him for the very last of innumerable times—did not know even that he was there. (So it is so many partings happen.) The Vicar was struck at the time by the fact that, after all, no one on earth had the slightest idea of what this great monster thought about when he saw fit to rest from his labours. But he was too indolent to follow up that new theme that day; he fell back from its suggestion into his older grooves of thought.

"*Aere-perennius,*" he whispered, walking slowly homeward by a path that no longer ran straight athwart the turf after its former fashion, but wound circuitously to avoid new sprung tussocks of giant grass. "No! nothing is changed. Dimensions are nothing. The simple round, the common way—"

And that night, quite painlessly, and all unknowing, he himself went the common way—out of this Mystery of Change he had spent his life in denying.

They buried him in the churchyard of Cheasing Eyebright, near to the largest yew, and the modest tombstone bearing his epitaph—it ended with: *Ut in Principio, nunc est et semper*—was almost immediately hidden from the eye of man by a spread of giant, grey tasselled grass too stout for scythe or sheep, that came sweeping like a fog over the village out of the germinating moisture of the valley meadows in which the Food of the Gods had been working.

BOOK III - THE HARVEST OF THE FOOD

CHAPTER THE FIRST - THE ALTERED WORLD

I

Change played in its new fashion with the world for twenty years. To most men the new things came little by little and day by day, remarkably enough, but not so abruptly as to overwhelm. But to one man at least the full accumulation of those two decades of the Food's work was to be revealed suddenly and amazingly in one day. For our purpose it is convenient to take him for that one day and to tell something of the things he saw. This man was a convict, a prisoner for life—his crime is no concern of ours—whom the law saw fit to pardon after twenty years. One summer morning this poor wretch, who had left the world a young man of three-and-twenty, found himself thrust out again from the grey simplicity of toil and discipline, that had become his life, into a dazzling freedom. They had put unaccustomed clothes upon him; his hair had been growing for some weeks, and he had parted it now for some days, and there he stood, in a sort of shabby and clumsy newness of body and mind, blinking with his eyes and blinking indeed with his soul, *outside* again, trying to realise one incredible thing, that after all he was again for a little while in the world of life, and for all other incredible things, totally unprepared. He was so fortunate as to have a brother who cared enough for their distant common memories to come and meet him and clasp his hand—a brother he had left a little lad, and who was now a bearded prosperous man — whose very eyes were unfamiliar. And together he and this stranger from his kindred came down into the town of Dover, saying little to one another and feeling many things.

They sat for a space in a public-house, the one answering the questions of the other about this person and that, reviving queer old points of view, brushing aside endless new aspects and new perspectives, and then it was time to go to the station and take the London train. Their names and the personal things they had to talk of do not matter to our story, but only the changes and all the strangeness that this poor returning soul found in the once familiar world.

In Dover itself he remarked little except the goodness of beer from pewter—never before had there been such a draught of beer, and it brought tears of gratitude to his eyes. "Beer's as good as ever," said he, believing it infinitely better...

It was only as the train rattled them past Folkestone that he could look out beyond his more immediate emotions, to see what had happened to the world. He peered out of the window. "It's sunny," he said for the twelfth time. "I couldn't ha' had better weather." And then for the first time it dawned upon him that there were novel disproportions in the world. "Lord sakes," he cried, sitting up and looking animated for the first time, "but them's mortal great thissels growing out there on the bank by that broom. If so be they *be* thissels? Or 'ave I been forgetting?" But they were thistles, and what he took for tall bushes of broom was the new grass, and amidst these things a company of British soldiers—red-coated as ever—was skirmishing in accordance with the directions of the drill book that had been partially revised after the Boer War. Then whack! into a tunnel, and then into Sandling Junction, which was now embedded and dark—its lamps were all alight —in a great thicket of rhododendron that had crept out of some adjacent gardens and grown enormously up the valley. There was a train of trucks on the Sandgate siding piled high with rhododendron logs, and here it was the returning citizen heard first of Boomfood.

As they sped out into a country again that seemed absolutely unchanged, the two brothers were hard at their explanations. The one was full of eager, dull questions; the other had never thought, had never troubled to see the thing as a single fact, and he was allusive and difficult to follow. "It's this here Boomfood stuff," he said, touching his bottom rock of knowledge. "Don't you know? 'Aven't they told you—any of 'em? Boomfood! You know—Boomfood. What all the election's about. Scientific sort of stuff. 'Asn't no one ever told you?"

He thought prison had made his brother a fearful duffer not to know that.

They made wide shots at each other by way of question and answer. Between these scraps of talk were intervals of window-gazing. At first the man's interest in things was vague and general. His imagination had been busy with what old so-and-so would say, how so-and-so would look, how he would say to all and sundry certain things that would present his "putting away" in a mitigated light. This Boomfood came in at first as it were a thing in an odd paragraph of the newspapers, then as a source of intellectual difficulty with his brother. But it came to him presently that Boomfood was persistently coming in upon any topic he began.

In those days the world was a patchwork of transition, so that this great new fact came to him in a series of shocks of contrast. The process of change had not been uniform; it had spread from one centre of distribution here and another centre there. The country was in patches: great areas where the Food was still to come, and areas where it was already in the soil and in the air, sporadic and contagious. It was a bold new motif creeping in among ancient and venerable airs.

The contrast was very vivid indeed along the line from Dover to London at that time. For a space they traversed just such a country-side as he had known since his childhood, the small oblongs of field, hedge-lined, of a size for pigmy

horses to plough, the little roads three cart-widths wide, the elms and oaks and poplars dotting these fields about, little thickets of willow beside the streams; ricks of hay no higher than a giant's knees, dolls' cottages with diamond panes, brickfields, and straggling village streets, the larger houses of the petty great, flower-grown railway banks, garden-set stations, and all the little things of the vanished nineteenth century still holding out against Immensity. Here and there would be a patch of wind-sown, wind-tattered giant thistle defying the axe; here and there a ten-foot puff-ball or the ashen stems of some burnt-out patch of monster grass; but that was all there was to hint at the coming of the Food.

For a couple of score of miles there was nothing else to foreshadow in any way the strange bigness of the wheat and of the weeds that were hidden from him not a dozen miles from his route just over the hills in the Cheasing Eyebright valley. And then presently the traces of the Food would begin. The first striking thing was the great new viaduct at Tonbridge, where the swamp of the choked Medway (due to a giant variety of *Chara*) began in those days. Then again the little country, and then, as the petty multitudinous immensity of London spread out under its haze, the traces of man's fight to keep out greatness became abundant and incessant.

In that south-eastern region of London at that time, and all about where Cossar and his children lived, the Food had become mysteriously insurgent at a hundred points; the little life went on amidst daily portents that only the deliberation of their increase, the slow parallel growth of usage to their presence, had robbed of their warning. But this returning citizen peered out to see for the first time the facts of the Food strange and predominant, scarred and blackened areas, big unsightly defences and preparations, barracks and arsenals that this subtle, persistent influence had forced into the life of men.

Here, on an ampler scale, the experience of the first Experimental Farm had been repeated time and again. It had been in the inferior and accidental things of life—under foot and in waste places, irregularly and irrelevantly—that the coming of a new force and new issues had first declared itself. There were great evil-smelling yards and enclosures where some invincible jungle of weed furnished fuel for gigantic machinery (little cockneys came to stare at its clangorous oiliness and tip the men a sixpence); there were roads and tracks for big motors and vehicles—roads made of the interwoven fibres of hypertrophied hemp; there were towers containing steam sirens that could yell at once and warn the world against any new insurgence of vermin, or, what was queerer, venerable church towers conspicuously fitted with a mechanical scream. There were little red-painted refuge huts and garrison shelters, each with its 300-yard rifle range, where the riflemen practised daily with soft-nosed ammunition at targets in the shape of monstrous rats.

Six times since the day of the Skinners there had been outbreaks of giant rats—each time from the southwest London sewers, and now they were as much an accepted fact there as tigers in the delta by Calcutta...

The man's brother had bought a paper in a heedless sort of way at Sandling, and at last this chanced to catch the eye of the released man. He opened the unfamiliar sheets—they seemed to him to be smaller, more numerous, and different in type from the papers of the times before—and he found himself confronted with innumerable pictures about things so strange as to be uninteresting, and with tall columns of printed matter whose headings, for the most part, were as unmeaning as though they had been written in a foreign tongue—"Great Speech by Mr. Caterham"; "The Boomfood Laws."

"Who's this here Caterham?" he asked, in an attempt to make conversation.

"*He's* all right," said his brother.

"Ah! Sort of politician, eh?"

"Goin' to turn out the Government. Jolly well time he did."

"Ah!" He reflected. "I suppose all the lot *I* used to know—Chamberlain, Rosebery—all that lot—*What*?"

His brother had grasped his wrist and pointed out of the window.

"That's the Cossars!" The eyes of the released prisoner followed the finger's direction and saw—

"My Gawd!" he cried, for the first time really overcome with amazement. The paper dropped into final forgottenness between his feet. Through the trees he could see very distinctly, standing in an easy attitude, the legs wide apart and the hand grasping a ball as if about to throw it, a gigantic human figure a good forty feet high. The figure glittered in the sunlight, clad in a suit of woven white metal and belted with a broad belt of steel. For a moment it focussed all attention, and then the eye was wrested to another more distant Giant who stood prepared to catch, and it became apparent that the whole area of that great bay in the hills just north of Sevenoaks had been scarred to gigantic ends.

A hugely banked entrenchment overhung the chalk pit, in which stood the house, a monstrous squat Egyptian shape that Cossar had built for his sons when the Giant Nursery had served its turn, and behind was a great dark shed that might have covered a cathedral, in which a spluttering incandescence came and went, and from out of which came a Titanic hammering to beat upon the ear. Then the attention leapt back to the giant as the great ball of iron-bound timber soared up out of his hand.

The two men stood up and stared. The ball seemed as big as a cask.

"Caught!" cried the man from prison, as a tree blotted out the thrower.

The train looked on these things only for the fraction of a minute and then passed behind trees into the Chislehurst tunnel. "My Gawd!" said the man from prison again, as the darkness closed about them. "Why! that chap was as 'igh as a 'ouse."

"That's them young Cossars," said his brother, jerking his head allusively—"what all this trouble's about..."

They emerged again to discover more siren-surmounted towers, more red huts, and then the clustering villas of the outer suburbs. The art of bill- sticking had lost nothing in the interval, and from countless tall hoardings, from house ends, from

palings, and a hundred such points of vantage came the polychromatic appeals of the great Boomfood election. "Caterham," "Boomfood," and "Jack the Giant-killer" again and again and again, and monstrous caricatures and distortions—a hundred varieties of misrepresentations of those great and shining figures they had passed so nearly only a few minutes before...

II

It had been the purpose of the younger brother to do a very magnificent thing, to celebrate this return to life by a dinner at some restaurant of indisputable quality, a dinner that should be followed by all that glittering succession of impressions the Music Halls of those days were so capable of giving. It was a worthy plan to wipe off the more superficial stains of the prison house by this display of free indulgence; but so far as the second item went the plan was changed. The dinner stood, but there was a desire already more powerful than the appetite for shows, already more efficient in turning the man's mind away from his grim prepossession with his past than any theatre could be, and that was an enormous curiosity and perplexity about this Boomfood and these Boom children—this new portentous giantry that seemed to dominate the world. "I 'aven't the 'ang of 'em," he said. "They disturve me."

His brother had that fineness of mind that can even set aside a contemplated hospitality. "It's *your* evening, dear old boy," he said. "We'll try to get into the mass meeting at the People's Palace."

And at last the man from prison had the luck to find himself wedged into a packed multitude and staring from afar at a little brightly lit platform under an organ and a gallery. The organist had been playing something that had set boots tramping as the people swarmed in; but that was over now.

Hardly had the man from prison settled into place and done his quarrel with an importunate stranger who elbowed, before Caterham came. He walked out of a shadow towards the middle of the platform, the most insignificant little pigmy, away there in the distance, a little black figure with a pink dab for a face,—in profile one saw his quite distinctive aquiline nose—a little figure that trailed after it most inexplicably—a cheer. A cheer it was that began away there and grew and spread. A little spluttering of voices about the platform at first that suddenly leapt up into a flame of sound and swept athwart the whole mass of humanity within the building and without. How they cheered! Hooray! Hooray!

No one in all those myriads cheered like the man from prison. The tears poured down his face, and he only stopped cheering at last because the thing had choked him. You must have been in prison as long as he before you can understand, or even begin to understand, what it means to a man to let his lungs go in a crowd. (But for all that he did not even pretend to himself that he knew what all this emotion was about.) Hooray! O God!—Hoo-ray!

And then a sort of silence. Caterham had subsided to a conspicuous patience, and subordinate and inaudible persons were saying and doing formal and insignificant things. It was like hearing voices through the noise of leaves in spring.

"Wawawawa—-" What did it matter? People in the audience talked to one another. "Wawawawawa—-" the thing went on. Would that grey-headed duffer never have done? Interrupting? Of course they were interrupting. "Wa, wa, wa, wa—-" But shall we hear Caterham any better?

Meanwhile at any rate there was Caterham to stare at, and one could stand and study the distant prospect of the great man's features. He was easy to draw was this man, and already the world had him to study at leisure on lamp chimneys and children's plates, on Anti-Boomfood medals and Anti-Boomfood flags, on the selvedges of Caterham silks and cottons and in the linings of Good Old English Caterham hats. He pervades all the caricature of that time. One sees him as a sailor standing to an old-fashioned gun, a port-fire labelled "New Boomfood Laws" in his hand; while in the sea wallows that huge, ugly, threatening monster, "Boomfood;" or he is *cap-a-pie* in armour, St. George's cross on shield and helm, and a cowardly titanic Caliban sitting amidst desecrations at the mouth of a horrid cave declines his gauntlet of the "New Boomfood Regulations;" or he comes flying down as Perseus and rescues a chained and beautiful Andromeda (labelled distinctly about her belt as "Civilisation") from a wallowing waste of sea monster bearing upon its various necks and claws "Irreligion," "Trampling Egotism," "Mechanism," "Monstrosity," and the like. But it was as "Jack the Giant-killer" that the popular imagination considered Caterham most correctly cast, and it was in the vein of a Jack the Giant-killer poster that the man from prison, enlarged that distant miniature.

The "Wawawawa" came abruptly to an end.

He's done. He's sitting down. Yes! No! Yes! It's Caterham! "Caterham!" "Caterham!" And then came the cheers.

It takes a multitude to make such a stillness as followed that disorder of cheering. A man alone in a wilderness;—it's stillness of a sort no doubt, but he hears himself breathe, he hears himself move, he hears all sorts of things. Here the voice of Caterham was the one single thing heard, a thing very bright and clear, like a little light burning in a black velvet recess. Hear indeed! One heard him as though he spoke at one's elbow.

It was stupendously effective to the man from prison, that gesticulating little figure in a halo of light, in a halo of rich and swaying sounds; behind it, partially effaced as it were, sat its supporters on the platform, and in the foreground was a wide perspective of innumerable backs and profiles, a vast multitudinous attention. That little figure seemed to have absorbed the substance from them all.

Caterham spoke of our ancient institutions. "Earearear," roared the crowd. "Ear! ear!" said the man from prison. He spoke of our ancient spirit of order and justice. "Earearear!" roared the crowd. "Ear! Ear!" cried the man from prison, deeply moved. He spoke of the wisdom of our forefathers, of the slow growth of venerable institutions, of moral and social traditions, that fitted our English national characteristics as the skin fits the hand. "Ear! Ear!" groaned the man from prison, with tears of excitement on his cheeks. And now all these things were to go into the melting pot. Yes, into the melting pot! Because three men in London

twenty years ago had seen fit to mix something indescribable in a bottle, all the order and sanctity of things—Cries of "No! No!"—Well, if it was not to be so, they must exert themselves, they must say good-bye to hesitation—Here there came a gust of cheering. They must say good-bye to hesitation and half measures.

"We have heard, gentlemen," cried Caterham, "of nettles that become giant nettles. At first they are no more than other nettles—little plants that a firm hand may grasp and wrench away; but if you leave them—if you leave them, they grow with such a power of poisonous expansion that at last you must needs have axe and rope, you must needs have danger to life and limb, you must needs have toil and distress—men may be killed in their felling, men may be killed in their felling—"

There came a stir and interruption, and then the man from prison heard Caterham's voice again, ringing clear and strong: "Learn about Boomfood from Boomfood itself and—" He paused—"*Grasp your nettle before it is too late!*"

He stopped and stood wiping his lips. "A crystal," cried some one, "a crystal," and then came that same strange swift growth to thunderous tumult, until the whole world seemed cheering...

The man from prison came out of the hall at last, marvellously stirred, and with that in his face that marks those who have seen a vision. He knew, every one knew; his ideas were no longer vague. He had come back to a world in crisis, to the immediate decision of a stupendous issue. He must play his part in the great conflict like a man—like a free, responsible man. The antagonism presented itself as a picture. On the one hand those easy gigantic mail-clad figures of the morning—one saw them now in a different light —on the other this little black-clad gesticulating creature under the limelight, that pigmy thing with its ordered flow of melodious persuasion, its little, marvellously penetrating voice, John Caterham—"Jack the Giant- killer." They must all unite to "grasp the nettle" before it was "too late."

III

The tallest and strongest and most regarded of all the children of the Food were the three sons of Cossar. The mile or so of land near Sevenoaks in which their boyhood passed became so trenched, so dug out and twisted about, so covered with sheds and huge working models and all the play of their developing powers, it was like no other place on earth. And long since it had become too little for the things they sought to do. The eldest son was a mighty schemer of wheeled engines; he had made himself a sort of giant bicycle that no road in the world had room for, no bridge could bear. There it stood, a great thing of wheels and engines, capable of two hundred and fifty miles an hour, useless save that now and then he would mount it and fling himself backwards and forwards across that cumbered work-yard. He had meant to go around the little world with it; he had made it with that intention, while he was still no more than a dreaming boy. Now its spokes were rusted deep red like wounds, wherever the enamel had been chipped away.

"You must make a road for it first, Sonnie," Cossar had said, "before you can do that."

So one morning about dawn the young giant and his brothers had set to work to make a road about the world. They seem to have had an inkling of opposition impending, and they had worked with remarkable vigour. The world had discovered them soon enough, driving that road as straight as a flight of a bullet towards the English Channel, already some miles of it levelled and made and stamped hard. They had been stopped before midday by a vast crowd of excited people, owners of land, land agents, local authorities, lawyers, policemen, soldiers even.

"We're making a road," the biggest boy had explained.

"Make a road by all means," said the leading lawyer on the ground, "but please respect the rights of other people. You have already infringed the private rights of twenty-seven private proprietors; let alone the special privileges and property of an urban district board, nine parish councils, a county council, two gasworks, and a railway company..."

"Goodney!" said the elder boy Cossar.

"You will have to stop it."

"But don't you want a nice straight road in the place of all these rotten rutty little lanes?" "I won't say it wouldn't be advantageous, but—"

"It isn't to be done," said the eldest Cossar boy, picking up his tools.

"Not in this way," said the lawyer, "certainly."

"How is it to be done?"

The leading lawyer's answer had been complicated and vague.

Cossar had come down to see the mischief his children had done, and reproved them severely and laughed enormously and seemed to be extremely happy over the affair. "You boys must wait a bit," he shouted up to them, "before you can do things like that."

"The lawyer told us we must begin by preparing a scheme, and getting special powers and all sorts of rot. Said it would take us years."

"*We'll* have a scheme before long, little boy," cried Cossar, hands to his mouth as he shouted, "never fear. For a bit you'd better play about and make models of the things you want to do."

They did as he told them like obedient sons.

But for all that the Cossar lads brooded a little.

"It's all very well," said the second to the first, "but I don't always want just to play about and plan, I want to do something *real*, you know. We didn't come into this world so strong as we are, just to play about in this messy little bit of ground, you know, and take little walks and keep out of the towns"—for by that time they were forbidden all boroughs and urban districts, "Doing nothing's just wicked. Can't we find out something the little people *want* done and do it for them—just for the fun of doing it?

"Lots of them haven't houses fit to live in," said the second boy, "Let's go and build 'em a house close up to London, that will hold heaps and heaps of them and be ever so comfortable and nice, and let's make 'em a nice little road to where they

all go and do business—nice straight little road, and make it all as nice as nice. We'll make it all so clean and pretty that they won't any of them be able to live grubby and beastly like most of them do now. Water enough for them to wash with, we'll have—you know they're so dirty now that nine out of ten of their houses haven't even baths in them, the filthy little skunks! You know, the ones that have baths spit insults at the ones that haven't, instead of helping them to get them—and call 'em the Great Unwashed—*You* know. We'll alter all that. And we'll make electricity light and cook and clean up for them, and all. Fancy! They make their women—women who are going to be mothers—crawl about and scrub floors!

"We could make it all beautifully. We could bank up a valley in that range of hills over there and make a nice reservoir, and we could make a big place here to generate our electricity and have it all simply lovely. Couldn't we, brother? And then perhaps they'd let us do some other things."

"Yes," said the elder brother, "we could do it *very* nice for them."

"Then *let's,"* said the second brother.

"*I* don't mind," said the elder brother, and looked about for a handy tool.

And that led to another dreadful bother.

Agitated multitudes were at them in no time, telling them for a thousand reasons to stop, telling them to stop for no reason at all—babbling, confused, and varied multitudes. The place they were building was too high —it couldn't possibly be safe. It was ugly; it interfered with the letting of proper-sized houses in the neighbourhood; it ruined the tone of the neighbourhood; it was unneighbourly; it was contrary to the Local Building Regulations; it infringed the right of the local authority to muddle about with a minute expensive electric supply of its own; it interfered with the concerns of the local water company.

Local Government Board clerks roused themselves to judicial obstruction. The little lawyer turned up again to represent about a dozen threatened interests; local landowners appeared in opposition; people with mysterious claims claimed to be bought off at exorbitant rates; the Trades Unions of all the building trades lifted up collective voices; and a ring of dealers in all sorts of building material became a bar. Extraordinary associations of people with prophetic visions of aesthetic horrors rallied to protect the scenery of the place where they would build the great house, of the valley where they would bank up the water. These last people were absolutely the worst asses of the lot, the Cossar boys considered. That beautiful house of the Cossar boys was just like a walking-stick thrust into a wasps' nest, in no time.

"I never did!" said the elder boy.

"We can't go on," said the second brother.

"Rotten little beasts they are," said the third of the brothers; "we can't do *anything!"*

"Even when it's for their own comfort. Such a *nice* place we'd have made for them too."

"They seem to spend their silly little lives getting in each other's way," said the eldest boy, "Rights and laws and regulations and rascalities; it's like a game of spellicans... Well, anyhow, they'll have to live in their grubby, dirty, silly little houses for a bit longer. It's very evident *we* can't go on with this."

And the Cossar children left that great house unfinished, a mere hole of foundations and the beginning of a wall, and sulked back to their big enclosure. After a time the hole was filled with water and with stagnation and weeds, and vermin, and the Food, either dropped there by the sons of Cossar or blowing thither as dust, set growth going in its usual fashion. Water voles came out over the country and did infinite havoc, and one day a farmer caught his pigs drinking there, and instantly and with great presence of mind—for he knew: of the great hog of Oakham—slew them all. And from that deep pool it was the mosquitoes came, quite terrible mosquitoes, whose only virtue was that the sons of Cossar, after being bitten for a little, could stand the thing no longer, but chose a moonlight night when law and order were abed and drained the water clean away into the river by Brook.

But they left the big weeds and the big water voles and all sorts of big undesirable things still living and breeding on the site they had chosen —the site on which the fair great house of the little people might have towered to heaven...

IV

That had been in the boyhood of the Sons, but now they were nearly men, And the chains had been tightening upon them and tightening with every year of growth. Each year they grew, and the Food spread and great things multiplied, each year the stress and tension rose. The Food had been at first for the great mass of mankind a distant marvel, and now It was coming home to every threshold, and threatening, pressing against and distorting the whole order of life. It blocked this, it overturned that; it changed natural products, and by changing natural products it stopped employments and threw men out of work by the hundred thousands; it swept over boundaries and turned the world of trade into a world of cataclysms: no wonder mankind hated it.

And since it is easier to hate animate than inanimate things, animals more than plants, and one's fellow-men more completely than any animals, the fear and trouble engendered by giant nettles and six-foot grass blades, awful insects and tiger-like vermin, grew all into one great power of detestation that aimed itself with a simple directness at that scattered band of great human beings, the Children of the Food. That hatred had become the central force in political affairs. The old party lines had been traversed and effaced altogether under the insistence of these newer issues, and the conflict lay now with the party of the temporisers, who were for putting little political men to control and regulate the Food, and the party of reaction for whom Caterham spoke, speaking always with a more sinister ambiguity, crystallising his intention first in one threatening phrase and then another, now that men must "prune the bramble growths," now that they must find a

"cure for elephantiasis," and at last upon the eve of the election that they must "Grasp the nettle."

One day the three sons of Cossar, who were now no longer boys but men, sat among the masses of their futile work and talked together after their fashion of all these things. They had been working all day at one of a series of great and complicated trenches their father had bid them make, and now it was sunset, and they sat in the little garden space before the great house and looked at the world and rested, until the little servants within should say their food was ready.

You must figure these mighty forms, forty feet high the least of them was, reclining on a patch of turf that would have seemed a stubble of reeds to a common man. One sat up and chipped earth from his huge boots with an iron girder he grasped in his hand; the second rested on his elbow; the third whittled a pine tree into shape and made a smell of resin in the air. They were clothed not in cloth but in under-garments of woven, rope and outer clothes of felted aluminium wire; they were shod with timber and iron, and the links and buttons and belts of their clothing were all of plated steel. The great single- storeyed house they lived in, Egyptian in its massiveness, half built of monstrous blocks of chalk and half excavated from the living rock of the hill, had a front a full hundred feet in height, and beyond, the chimneys and wheels, the cranes and covers of their work sheds rose marvellously against the sky. Through a circular window in the house there was visible a spout from which some white-hot metal dripped and dripped in measured drops into a receptacle out of sight. The place was enclosed and rudely fortified by monstrous banks of earth, backed with steel both over the crests of the Downs above and across the dip of the valley. It needed something of common size to mark the nature of the scale. The train that came rattling from Sevenoaks athwart their vision, and presently plunged into the tunnel out of their sight, looked by contrast with them like some small-sized automatic toy.

"They have made all the woods this side of Ightham out of bounds," said one, "and moved the board that was out by Knockholt two miles and more this way."

"It is the least they could do," said the youngest, after a pause. "They are trying to take the wind out of Caterham's sails."

"It's not enough for that, and—it is almost too much for us," said the third.

"They are cutting us off from Brother Redwood. Last time I went to him the red notices had crept a mile in, either way. The road to him along the Downs is no more than a narrow lane."

The speaker thought. "What has come to our brother Redwood?"

"Why?" said the eldest brother.

The speaker backed a bough from his pine. "He was like—as though he wasn't awake. He didn't seem to listen to what I had to say. And he said something of—love."

The youngest tapped his girder on the edge of his iron sole and laughed. "Brother Redwood," he said, "has dreams."

Neither spoke for a space. Then the eldest brother said, "This cooping up and cooping up grows more than I can bear. At last, I believe, they will draw a line round our boots and tell us to live on that."

The middle brother swept aside a heap of pine boughs with one hand and shifted his attitude. "What they do now is nothing to what they will do when Caterham has power."

"If he gets power," said the youngest brother, smiting the ground with his girder.

"As he will," said the eldest, staring at his feet.

The middle brother ceased his lopping, and his eye went to the great banks that sheltered them about. "Then, brothers," he said, "our youth will be over, and, as Father Redwood said to us long ago, we must quit ourselves like men."

"Yes," said the eldest brother; "but what exactly does that mean? Just what does it mean—when that day of trouble comes?"

He too glanced at those rude vast suggestions of entrenchment about them, looking not so much at them as through them and over the hills to the innumerable multitudes beyond. Something of the same sort came into all their minds—a vision of little people coming out to war, in a flood, the little people, inexhaustible, incessant, malignant...

"They are little," said the youngest brother; "but they have numbers beyond counting, like the sands of the sea."

"They have arms—they have weapons even, that our brothers in Sunderland have made."

"Besides, Brothers, except for vermin, except for little accidents with evil things, what have we seen of killing?"

"I know," said the eldest brother. "For all that—we are what we are. When the day of trouble comes we must do the thing we have to do."

He closed his knife with a snap—the blade was the length of a man —and used his new pine staff to help himself rise. He stood up and turned towards the squat grey immensity of the house. The crimson of the sunset caught him as he rose, caught the mail and clasps about his neck and the woven metal of his arms, and to the eyes of his brother it seemed as though he was suddenly suffused with blood...

As the young giant rose a little black figure became visible to him against that western incandescence on the top of the embankment that towered above the summit of the down. The black limbs waved in ungainly gestures. Something in the fling of the limbs suggested haste to the young giant's mind. He waved his pine mast in reply, filled the whole valley with his vast Hullo! threw a "Something's up" to his brothers, and set off in twenty-foot strides to meet and help his father.

V

It chanced too that a young man who was not a giant was delivering his soul about these sons of Cossar just at that same time. He had come over the hills beyond Sevenoaks, he and his friend, and he it was did the talking. In the hedge as

they came along they had heard a pitiful squealing, and had intervened to rescue three nestling tits from the attack of a couple of giant ants. That adventure it was had set him talking.

"Reactionary!" he was saying, as they came within sight of the Cossar encampment. "Who wouldn't be reactionary? Look at that square of ground, that space of God's earth that was once sweet and fair, torn, desecrated, disembowelled! Those sheds! That great wind-wheel! That monstrous wheeled machine! Those dykes! Look at those three monsters squatting there, plotting some ugly devilment or other! Look—look at all the land!"

His friend glanced at his face. "You have been listening to Caterham," he said.

"Using my eyes. Looking a little into the peace and order of the past we leave behind. This foul Food is the last shape of the Devil, still set as ever upon the ruin of our world. Think what the world must have been before our days, what it was still when our mothers bore us, and see it now! Think how these slopes once smiled under the golden harvest, how the hedges, full of sweet little flowers, parted the modest portion of this man from that, how the ruddy farmhouses dotted the land, and the voice of the church bells from yonder tower stilled the whole world each Sabbath into Sabbath prayer. And now, every year, still more and more of monstrous weeds, of monstrous vermin, and these giants growing all about us, straddling over us, blundering against all that is subtle and sacred in our world. Why here—Look!"

He pointed, and his friend's eyes followed the line of his white finger.

"One of their footmarks. See! It has smashed itself three feet deep and more, a pitfall for horse and rider, a trap to the unwary. There is a briar rose smashed to death; there is grass uprooted and a teazle crushed aside, a farmer's drain pipe snapped and the edge of the pathway broken down. Destruction! So they are doing all over the world, all over the order and decency the world of men has made. Trampling on all things. Reaction! What else?"

"But—reaction. What do you hope to do?"

"Stop it!" cried the young man from Oxford. "Before it is too late."

"But—-"

"It's *not* impossible," cried the young man from Oxford, with a jump in his voice. "We want the firm hand; we want the subtle plan, the resolute mind. We have been mealy-mouthed and weak-handed; we have trifled and temporised and the Food has grown and grown. Yet even now—"

He stopped for a moment. "This is the echo of Caterham," said his friend.

"Even now. Even now there is hope—abundant hope, if only we make sure of what we want and what we mean to destroy. The mass of people are with us, much more with us than they were a few years ago; the law is with us, the constitution and order of society, the spirit of the established religions, the customs and habits of mankind are with us—and against the Food. Why should we temporise? Why should we lie? We hate it, we don't want it; why then should we have it? Do you mean to just grizzle and obstruct passively and do nothing—till the sands are out?"

He stopped short and turned about. "Look at that grove of nettles there. In the midst of them are homes—deserted—where once clean families of simple men played out their honest lives!

"And there!" he swung round to where the young Cossars muttered to one another of their wrongs.

"Look at them! And I know their father, a brute, a sort of brute beast with an intolerant loud voice, a creature who has ran amuck in our all too merciful world for the last thirty years and more. An engineer! To him all that we hold dear and sacred is nothing. Nothing! The splendid traditions of our race and land, the noble institutions, the venerable order, the broad slow march from precedent to precedent that has made our English people great and this sunny island free—it is all an idle tale, told and done with. Some claptrap about the Future is worth all these sacred things... The sort of man who would run a tramway over his mother's grave if he thought that was the cheapest line the tramway could take... And you think to temporise, to make some scheme of compromise, that will enable you to live in your way while that —that machinery—lives in its. I tell you it is hopeless—hopeless. As well make treaties with a tiger! They want things monstrous —we want them sane and sweet. It is one thing or the other."

"But what can you do?"

"Much! All! Stop the Food! They are still scattered, these giants; still immature and disunited. Chain them, gag them, muzzle them. At any cost stop them. It is their world or ours! Stop the Food. Shut up these men who make it. Do anything to stop Cossar! You don't seem to remember—one generation —only one generation needs holding down, and then—Then we could level those mounds there, fill up their footsteps, take the ugly sirens from our church towers, smash all our elephant guns, and turn our faces again to the old order, the ripe old civilisation for which the soul of man is fitted."

"It's a mighty effort."

"For a mighty end. And if we don't? Don't you see the prospect before us clear as day? Everywhere the giants will increase and multiply; everywhere they will make and scatter the Food. The grass will grow gigantic in our fields, the weeds in our hedges, the vermin in the thickets, the rats in the drains. More and more and more. This is only a beginning. The insect world will rise on us, the plant world, the very fishes in the sea, will swamp and drown our ships. Tremendous growths will obscure and hide our houses, smother our churches, smash and destroy all the order of our cities, and we shall become no more than a feeble vermin under the heels of the new race. Mankind will be swamped and drowned in things of its own begetting! And all for nothing! Size! Mere size! Enlargement and *da capo*. Already we go picking our way among the first beginnings of the coming time. And all we do is to say 'How inconvenient!' To grumble and do nothing. *No*!"

He raised his hand.

"Let them do the thing they have to do! So also will I. I am for Reaction —unstinted and fearless Reaction. Unless you mean to take this Food also, what else

is there to do in all the world? We have trifled in the middle ways too long. You! Trifling in the middle ways is your habit, your circle of existence, your space and time. So, not I! I am against the Food, with all my strength and purpose against the Food."

He turned on his companion's grunt of dissent. "Where are you?"

"It's a complicated business—-"

"Oh!—Driftwood!" said the young man from Oxford, very bitterly, with a fling of all his limbs. "The middle way is nothingness. It is one thing or the other. Eat or destroy. Eat or destroy! What else is there to do?"

CHAPTER THE SECOND - THE GIANT LOVERS

I

Now it chanced in the days when Caterham was campaigning against the Boom- children before the General Election that was—amidst the most tragic and terrible circumstances—to bring him into power, that the giant Princess, that Serene Highness whose early nutrition had played so great a part in the brilliant career of Doctor Winkles, had come from the kingdom of her father to England, on an occasion that was deemed important. She was affianced for reasons of state to a certain Prince—and the wedding was to be made an event of international significance. There had arisen mysterious delays. Rumour and Imagination collaborated in the story and many things were said. There were suggestions of a recalcitrant Prince who declared he would not be made to look like a fool—at least to this extent. People sympathised with him. That is the most significant aspect of the affair.

Now it may seem a strange thing, but it is a fact that the giant Princess, when she came to England, knew of no other giants whatever. She had lived in a world where tact is almost a passion and reservations the air of one's life. They had kept the thing from her; they had hedged her about from sight or suspicion of any gigantic form, until her appointed coming to England was due. Until she met young Redwood she had no inkling that there was such a thing as another giant in the world.

In the kingdom of the father of the Princess there were wild wastes of upland and mountains where she had been accustomed to roam freely. She loved the sunrise and the sunset and all the great drama of the open heavens more than anything else in the world, but among a people at once so democratic and so vehemently loyal as the English her freedom was much restricted. People came in brakes, in excursion trains, in organised multitudes to see her; they would cycle long distances to stare at her, and it was necessary to rise betimes if she would walk in peace. It was still near the dawn that morning when young Redwood came upon her.

The Great Park near the Palace where she lodged stretched, for a score of miles and more, west and south of the western palace gates. The chestnut trees of its avenues reached high above her head. Each one as she passed it seemed to proffer a more abundant wealth of blossom. For a time she was content with sight and scent, but at last she was won over by these offers, and set herself so busily to

choose and pick that she did not perceive young Redwood until he was close upon her.

She moved among the chestnut trees, with the destined lover drawing near to her, unanticipated, unsuspected. She thrust her hands in among the branches, breaking them and gathering them. She was alone in the world. Then—-

She looked up, and in that moment she was mated.

We must needs put our imaginations to his stature to see the beauty he saw. That unapproachable greatness that prevents our immediate sympathy with her did not exist for him. There she stood, a gracious girl, the first created being that had ever seemed a mate for him, light and slender, lightly clad, the fresh breeze of the dawn moulding the subtly folding robe upon her against the soft strong lines of her form, and with a great mass of blossoming chestnut branches in her hands. The collar of her robe opened to show the whiteness of her neck and a soft shadowed roundness that passed out of sight towards her shoulders. The breeze had stolen a strand or so of her hair too, and strained its red-tipped brown across her cheek. Her eyes were open blue, and her lips rested always in the promise of a smile as she reached among the branches.

She turned upon him with a start, saw him, and for a space they regarded one another. For her, the sight of him was so amazing, so incredible, as to be, for some moments at least, terrible. He came to her with the shock of a supernatural apparition; he broke all the established law of her world. He was a youth of one-and-twenty then, slenderly built, with his father's darkness and his father's gravity. He was clad in a sober soft brown leather, close-fitting easy garments, and in brown hose, that shaped him bravely. His head went uncovered in all weathers. They stood regarding one another—she incredulously amazed, and he with his heart beating fast. It was a moment without a prelude, the cardinal meeting of their lives.

For him there was less surprise. He had been seeking her, and yet his heart beat fast. He came towards her, slowly, with his eyes upon her face.

"You are the Princess," he said. "My father has told me. You are the Princess who was given the Food of the Gods."

"I am the Princess—yes," she said, with eyes of wonder. "But —what are you?"

"I am the son of the man who made the Food of the Gods."

"The Food of the Gods!"

"Yes, the Food of the Gods."

"But—"

Her face expressed infinite perplexity.

"What? I don't understand. The Food of the Gods?"

"You have not heard?"

"The Food of the Gods! *No*!"

She found herself trembling violently. The colour left her face. "I did not know," she said. "Do you mean—?"

He waited for her.

"Do you mean there are other—giants?"

He repeated, "Did you not know?"

And she answered, with the growing amazement of realisation, "*No!*"

The whole world and all the meaning of the world was changing for her. A branch of chestnut slipped from her hand. "Do you mean to say," she repeated stupidly, "that there are other giants in the world? That some food—?"

He caught her amazement.

"You know nothing?" he cried. "You have never heard of us? You, whom the Food has made akin to us!"

There was terror still in the eyes that stared at him. Her hand rose towards her throat and fell again. She whispered, "*No*."

It seemed to her that she must weep or faint. Then in a moment she had rule over herself and she was speaking and thinking clearly. "All this has been kept from me," she said. "It is like a dream. I have dreamt—have dreamt such things. But waking—No. Tell me! Tell me! What are you? What is this Food of the Gods? Tell me slowly—and clearly. Why have they kept it from me, that I am not alone?"

II

"Tell me," she said, and young Redwood, tremulous and excited, set himself to tell her—it was poor and broken telling for a time—of the Food of the Gods and the giant children who were scattered over the world.

You must figure them both, flushed and startled in their bearing; getting at one another's meaning through endless half-heard, half-spoken phrases, repeating, making perplexing breaks and new departures—a wonderful talk, in which she awakened from the ignorance of all her life. And very slowly it became clear to her that she was no exception to the order of mankind, but one of a scattered brotherhood, who had all eaten the Food and grown for ever out of the little limits of the folk beneath their feet. Young Redwood spoke of his father, of Cossar, of the Brothers scattered throughout the country, of the great dawn of wider meaning that had come at last into the history of the world. "We are in the beginning of a beginning," he said; "this world of theirs is only the prelude to the world the Food will make.

"My father believes—and I also believe—that a time will come when littleness will have passed altogether out of the world of man, —when giants shall go freely about this earth—their earth —doing continually greater and more splendid things. But that—that is to come. We are not even the first generation of that—we are the first experiments."

"And of these things," she said, "I knew nothing!"

"There are times when it seems to me almost as if we had come too soon. Some one, I suppose, had to come first. But the world was all unprepared for our coming and for the coming of all the lesser great things that drew their greatness from the Food. There have been blunders; there have been conflicts. The little people hate our kind...

"They are hard towards us because they are so little... And because our feet are heavy on the things that make their lives. But at any rate they hate us now; they will have none of us—only if we could shrink back to the common size of them would they begin to forgive...

"They are happy in houses that are prison cells to us; their cities are too small for us; we go in misery along their narrow ways; we cannot worship in their churches...

"We see over their walls and over their protections; we look inadvertently into their upper windows; we look over their customs; their laws are no more than a net about our feet...

"Every time we stumble we hear them shouting; every time we blunder against their limits or stretch out to any spacious act...

"Our easy paces are wild flights to them, and all they deem great and wonderful no more than dolls' pyramids to us. Their pettiness of method and appliance and imagination hampers and defeats our powers. There are no machines to the power of our hands, no helps to fit our needs. They hold our greatness in servitude by a thousand invisible bands. We are stronger, man for man, a hundred times, but we are disarmed; our very greatness makes us debtors; they claim the land we stand upon; they tax our ampler need of food and shelter, and for all these things we must toil with the tools these dwarfs can make us —and to satisfy their dwarfish fancies...

"They pen us in, in every way. Even to live one must cross their boundaries. Even to meet you here to-day I have passed a limit. All that is reasonable and desirable in life they make out of bounds for us. We may not go into the towns; we may not cross the bridges; we may not step on their ploughed fields or into the harbours of the game they kill. I am cut off now from all our Brethren except the three sons of Cossar, and even that way the passage narrows day by day. One could think they sought occasion against us to do some more evil thing ..."

"But we are strong," she said.

"We should be strong—yes. We feel, all of us—you too I know must feel—that we have power, power to do great things, power insurgent in us. But before we can do anything—"

He flung out a hand that seemed to sweep away a world.

"Though I thought I was alone in the world," she said, after a pause, "I have thought of these things. They have taught me always that strength was almost a sin, that it was better to be little than great, that all true religion was to shelter the weak and little, encourage the weak and little, help them to multiply and multiply until at last they crawled over one another, to sacrifice all our strength in their cause. But ... always I have doubted the thing they taught."

"This life," he said, "these bodies of ours, are not for dying."

"No."

"Nor to live in futility. But if we would not do that, it is already plain to all our Brethren a conflict must come. I know not what bitterness of conflict must presently come, before the little folks will suffer us to live as we need to live. All the

Brethren have thought of that. Cossar, of whom I told you: he too has thought of that."

"They are very little and weak."

"In their way. But you know all the means of death are in their hands, and made for their hands. For hundreds of thousands of years these little people, whose world we invade, have been learning how to kill one another. They are very able at that. They are able in many ways. And besides, they can deceive and change suddenly... I do not know... There comes a conflict. You —you perhaps are different from us. For us, assuredly, the conflict comes... The thing they call War. We know it. In a way we prepare for it. But you know—those little people!—we do not know how to kill, at least we do not want to kill—"

"Look," she interrupted, and he heard a yelping horn.

He turned at the direction of her eyes, and found a bright yellow motor car, with dark goggled driver and fur-clad passengers, whooping, throbbing, and buzzing resentfully at his heel. He moved his foot, and the mechanism, with three angry snorts, resumed its fussy way towards the town. "Filling up the roadway!" floated up to him.

Then some one said, "Look! Did you see? There is the monster Princess over beyond the trees!" and all their goggled faces came round to stare.

"I say," said another. "*That* won't do ..."

"All this," she said, "is more amazing than I can tell."

"That they should not have told you," he said, and left his sentence incomplete.

"Until you came upon me, I had lived in a world where I was great—alone. I had made myself a life—for that. I had thought I was the victim of some strange freak of nature. And now my world has crumbled down, in half an hour, and I see another world, other conditions, wider possibilities —fellowship—"

"Fellowship," he answered.

"I want you to tell me more yet, and much more," she said. "You know this passes through my mind like a tale that is told. You even ... In a day perhaps, or after several days, I shall believe in you. Now—Now I am dreaming... Listen!"

The first stroke of a clock above the palace offices far away had penetrated to them. Each counted mechanically "Seven."

"This," she said, "should be the hour of my return. They will be taking the bowl of my coffee into the hall where I sleep. The little officials and servants—you cannot dream how grave they are—will be stirring about their little duties."

"They will wonder ... But I want to talk to you."

She thought. "But I want to think too. I want now to think alone, and think out this change in things, think away the old solitude, and think you and those others into my world... I shall go. I shall go back to-day to my place in the castle, and to-morrow, as the dawn comes, I shall come again—here."

"I shall be here waiting for you."

"All day I shall dream and dream of this new world you have given me. Even now, I can scarcely believe—"

She took a step back and surveyed him from the feet to the face. Their eyes met and locked for a moment.

"Yes," she said, with a little laugh that was half a sob. "You are real. But it is very wonderful! Do you think—indeed—? Suppose to- morrow I come and find you—a pigmy like the others... Yes, I must think. And so for to-day—as the little people do—"

She held out her hand, and for the first time they touched one another. Their hands clasped firmly and their eyes met again.

"Good-bye," she said, "for to-day. Good-bye! Good-bye, Brother Giant!"

He hesitated with some unspoken thing, and at last he answered her simply, "Good-bye."

For a space they held each other's hands, studying each the other's face. And many times after they had parted, she looked back half doubtfully at him, standing still in the place where they had met...

She walked into her apartments across the great yard of the Palace like one who walks in a dream, with a vast branch of chestnut trailing from her hand.

III

These two met altogether fourteen times before the beginning of the end. They met in the Great Park or on the heights and among the gorges of the rusty- roaded, heathery moorland, set with dusky pine-woods, that stretched to the south-west. Twice they met in the great avenue of chestnuts, and five times near the broad ornamental water the king, her great-grandfather, had made. There was a place where a great trim lawn, set with tall conifers, sloped graciously to the water's edge, and there she would sit, and he would lie at her knees and look up in her face and talk, telling of all the things that had been, and of the work his father had set before him, and of the great and spacious dream of what the giant people should one day be. Commonly they met in the early dawn, but once they met there in the afternoon, and found presently a multitude of peering eavesdroppers about them, cyclists, pedestrians, peeping from the bushes, rustling (as sparrows will rustle about one in the London parks) amidst the dead leaves in the woods behind, gliding down the lake in boats towards a point of view, trying to get nearer to them and hear.

It was the first hint that offered of the enormous interest the countryside was taking in their meetings. And once—it was the seventh time, and it precipitated the scandal—they met out upon the breezy moorland under a clear moonlight, and talked in whispers there, for the night was warm and still.

Very soon they had passed from the realisation that in them and through them a new world of giantry shaped itself in the earth, from the contemplation of the great struggle between big and little, in which they were clearly destined to participate, to interests at once more personal and more spacious. Each time they met and talked and looked on one another, it crept a little more out of their subconscious being towards recognition, that something more dear and wonderful than friendship was between them, and walked between them and drew their hands

together. And in a little while they came to the word itself and found themselves lovers, the Adam and Eve of a new race in the world.

They set foot side by side into the wonderful valley of love, with its deep and quiet places. The world changed about them with their changing mood, until presently it had become, as it were, a tabernacular beauty about their meetings, and the stars were no more than flowers of light beneath the feet of their love, and the dawn and sunset the coloured hangings by the way. They ceased to be beings of flesh and blood to one another and themselves; they passed into a bodily texture of tenderness and desire. They gave it first whispers and then silence, and drew close and looked into one another's moonlit and shadowy faces under the infinite arch of the sky. And the still black pine- trees stood about them like sentinels.

The beating steps of time were hushed into silence, and it seemed to them the universe hung still. Only their hearts were audible, beating. They seemed to be living together in a world where there is no death, and indeed so it was with them then. It seemed to them that they sounded, and indeed they sounded, such hidden splendours in the very heart of things as none have ever reached before. Even for mean and little souls, love is the revelation of splendours. And these were giant lovers who had eaten the Food of the Gods...

* * * * *

You may imagine the spreading consternation in this ordered world when it became known that the Princess who was affianced to the Prince, the Princess, Her Serene Highness! with royal blood in her veins! met,—frequently met,—the hypertrophied offspring of a common professor of chemistry, a creature of no rank, no position, no wealth, and talked to him as though there were no Kings and Princes, no order, no reverence—nothing but Giants and Pigmies in the world, talked to him and, it was only too certain, held him as her lover.

"If those newspaper fellows get hold of it!" gasped Sir Arthur Poodle Bootlick...

"I am told—" whispered the old Bishop of Frumps.

"New story upstairs," said the first footman, as he nibbled among the dessert things. "So far as I can make out this here giant Princess—"

"They say—" said the lady who kept the stationer's shop by the main entrance to the Palace, where the little Americans get their tickets for the State Apartments...

And then:

"We are authorised to deny—" said "Picaroon" in *Gossip*.

And so the whole trouble came out.

IV

"They say that we must part," the Princess said to her lover.

"But why?" he cried. "What new folly have these people got into their heads?"

"Do you know," she asked, "that to love me—is high treason?"

"My dear," he cried; "but does it matter? What is their right—right without a shadow of reason—and their treason and their loyalty to us?" "You shall hear," she said, and told him of the things that had been told to her.

"It was the queerest little man who came to me with a soft, beautifully modulated voice, a softly moving little gentleman who sidled into the room like a cat and put his pretty white hand up so, whenever he had anything significant to say. He is bald, but not of course nakedly bald, and his nose and face are chubby rosy little things, and his beard is trimmed to a point in quite the loveliest way. He pretended to have emotions several times and made his eyes shine. You know he is quite a friend of the real royal family here, and he called me his dear young lady and was perfectly sympathetic even from the beginning. 'My dear young lady,' he said, 'you know—*you mustn't,'* several times, and then, 'You owe a duty.'"

"Where do they make such men?"

"He likes it," she said.

"But I don't see—"

"He told me serious things."

"You don't think," he said, turning on her abruptly, "that there's anything in the sort of thing he said?"

"There's something in it quite certainly," said she.

"You mean—?"

"I mean that without knowing it we have been trampling on the most sacred conceptions of the little folks. We who are royal are a class apart. We are worshipped prisoners, processional toys. We pay for worship by losing—our elementary freedom. And I was to have married that Prince—You know nothing of him though. Well, a pigmy Prince. He doesn't matter... It seems it would have strengthened the bonds between my country and another. And this country also was to profit. Imagine it!—strengthening the bonds!"

"And now?"

"They want me to go on with it—as though there was nothing between us two."

"Nothing!"

"Yes. But that isn't all. He said—"

"Your specialist in Tact?"

"Yes. He said it would be better for you, better for all the giants, if we two—abstained from conversation. That was how he put it."

"But what can they do if we don't?"

"He said you might have your freedom."

"*I!*"

"He said, with a stress, 'My dear young lady, it would be better, it would be more dignified, if you parted, willingly.' That was all he said. With a stress on willingly."

"But—! What business is it of these little wretches, where we love, how we love? What have they and their world to do with us?"

"They do not think that."

"Of course," he said, "you disregard all this."

"It seems utterly foolish to me."

"That their laws should fetter us! That we, at the first spring of life, should be tripped by their old engagements, their aimless institutions I Oh —! We disregard it."

"I am yours. So far—yes."

"So far? Isn't that all?"

"But they—If they want to part us—"

"What can they do?"

"I don't know. What *can* they do?" "Who cares what they can do, or what they will do? I am yours and you are mine. What is there more than that? I am yours and you are mine—for ever. Do you think I will stop for their little rules, for their little prohibitions, their scarlet boards indeed! —and keep from *you*?"

"Yes. But still, what can they do?"

"You mean," he said, "what are we to do?"

"Yes."

"We? We can go on."

"But if they seek to prevent us?"

He clenched his hands. He looked round as if the little people were already coming to prevent them. Then turned away from her and looked about the world. "Yes," he said. "Your question was the right one. What can they do?"

"Here la this little land," she said, and stopped.

He seemed to survey it all. "They are everywhere."

"But we might—"

"Whither?"

"We could go. We could swim the seas together. Beyond the seas—"

"I have never been beyond the seas."

"There are great and desolate mountains amidst which we should seem no more than little people, there are remote and deserted valleys, there are hidden lakes and snow-girdled uplands untrodden by the feet of men. *There*—"

"But to get there we must fight our way day after day through millions and millions of mankind."

"It is our only hope. In this crowded land there is no fastness, no shelter. What place is there for us among these multitudes? They who are little can hide from one another, but where are we to hide? There is no place where we could eat, no place where we could sleep. If we fled—night and day they would pursue our footsteps."

A thought came to him.

"There is one place," he said, "even in this island."

"Where?"

"The place our Brothers have made over beyond there. They have made great banks about their house, north and south and east and west; they have made deep pits and hidden places, and even now—one came over to me quite recently. He

said—I did not altogether heed what he said then. But he spoke of arms. It may be—there—we should find shelter...

"For many days," he said, after a pause, "I have not seen our Brothers... Dear! I have been dreaming, I have been forgetting! The days have passed, and I have done nothing but look to see you again ... I must go to them and talk to them, and tell them of you and of all the things that hang over us. If they will help us, they can help us. Then indeed we might hope. I do not know how strong their place is, but certainly Cossar will have made it strong. Before all this—before you came to me, I remember now—there was trouble brewing. There was an election—when all the little people settle things, by counting heads. It must be over now. There were threats against all our race—against all our race, that is, but you. I must see our Brothers. I must tell them all that has happened between us, and all that threatens now."

V

He did not come to their next meeting until she had waited some time. They were to meet that day about midday in a great space of park that fitted into a bend of the river, and as she waited, looking ever southward under her hand, it came to her that the world was very still, that indeed it was broodingly still. And then she perceived that, spite of the lateness of the hour, her customary retinue of voluntary spies had failed her. Left and right, when she came to look, there was no one in sight, and there was never a boat upon the silver curve of the Thames. She tried to find a reason for this strange stillness in the world...

Then, a grateful sight for her, she saw young Redwood far away over a gap in the tree masses that bounded her view.

Immediately the trees hid him, and presently he was thrusting through them and in sight again. She could see there was something different, and then she saw that he was hurrying unusually and then that he limped. He gestured to her, and she walked towards him. His face became clearer, and she saw with infinite concern that he winced at every stride.

She ran towards him, her mind full of questions and vague fear. He drew near to her and spoke without a greeting.

"Are we to part?" he panted.

"No," she answered. "Why? What is the matter?"

"But if we do not part—! It is *now*."

"What is the matter?"

"I do not want to part," he said. "Only—" He broke off abruptly to ask, "You will not part from me?"

She met his eyes with a steadfast look. "What has happened?" she pressed.

"Not for a time?"

"What time?"

"Years perhaps."

"Part! No!"

"You have thought?" he insisted.

"I will not part." She took his hand. "If this meant death, *now*, I would not let you go."

"If it meant death," he said, and she felt his grip upon her fingers.

He looked about him as if he feared to see the little people coming as he spoke. And then: "It may mean death."

"Now tell me," she said.

"They tried to stop my coming."

"How?"

"And as I came out of my workshop where I make the Food of the Gods for the Cossars to store in their camp, I found a little officer of police—a man in blue with white clean gloves—who beckoned me to stop. 'This way is closed!' said he. I thought little of that; I went round my workshop to where another road runs west, and there was another officer. 'This road is closed!' he said, and added: 'All the roads are closed!'"

"And then?"

"I argued with him a little. 'They are public roads!' I said.

"'That's it,' said he. 'You spoil them for the public.'

"'Very well,' said I, 'I'll take the fields,' and then, up leapt others from behind a hedge and said, 'These fields are private.'

"'Curse your public and private,' I said, 'I'm going to my Princess,' and I stooped down and picked him up very gently—kicking and shouting —and put him out of my way. In a minute all the fields about me seemed alive with running men. I saw one on horseback galloping beside me and reading something as he rode—shouting it. He finished and turned and galloped away from me—head down. I couldn't make it out. And then behind me I heard the crack of guns."

"Guns!"

"Guns—just as they shoot at the rats. The bullets came through the air with a sound like things tearing: one stung me in the leg."

"And you?"

"Came on to you here and left them shouting and running and shooting behind me. And now—"

"Now?"

"It is only the beginning. They mean that we shall part. Even now they are coming after me."

"We will not."

"No. But if we will not part—then you must come with me to our Brothers."

"Which way?" she said.

"To the east. Yonder is the way my pursuers will be coming. This then is the way we must go. Along this avenue of trees. Let me go first, so that if they are waiting—"

He made a stride, but she had seized his arm.

"No," cried she. "I come close to you, holding you. Perhaps I am royal, perhaps I am sacred. If I hold you—Would God we could fly with my arms about you!—it may be, they will not shoot at you—"

She clasped his shoulder and seized his hand as she spoke; she pressed herself nearer to him. "It may be they will not shoot you," she repeated, and with a sudden passion of tenderness he took her into his arms and kissed her cheek. For a space he held her.

"Even if it is death," she whispered.

She put her hands about his neck and lifted her face to his.

"Dearest, kiss me once more."

He drew her to him. Silently they kissed one another on the lips, and for another moment clung to one another. Then hand in hand, and she striving always to keep her body near to his, they set forward if haply they might reach the camp of refuge the sons of Cossar had made, before the pursuit of the little people overtook them.

And as they crossed the great spaces of the park behind the castle there came horsemen galloping out from among the trees and vainly seeking to keep pace with their giant strides. And presently ahead of them were houses, and men with guns running out of the houses. At the sight of that, though he sought to go on and was even disposed to fight and push through, she made him turn aside towards the south.

As they fled a bullet whipped by them overhead.

CHAPTER THE THIRD - YOUNG CADDIES IN LONDON

I

All unaware of the trend of events, unaware of the laws that were closing in upon all the Brethren, unaware indeed that there lived a Brother for him on the earth, young Caddies chose this time to come out of his chalk pit and see the world. His brooding came at last to that. There was no answer to all his questions in Cheasing Eyebright; the new Vicar was less luminous even than the old, and the riddle of his pointless labour grew at last to the dimensions of exasperation. "Why should I work in this pit day after day?" he asked. "Why should I walk within bounds and be refused all the wonders of the world beyond there? What have I done, to be condemned to this?"

And one day he stood up, straightened his back, and said in a loud voice, "No!

"I won't," he said, and then with great vigour cursed the pit.

Then, having few words, he sought to express his thought in acts. He took a track half filled with chalk, lifted it, and flung it, smash, against another. Then he grasped a whole row of empty trucks and spun them down a bank. He sent a huge boulder of chalk bursting among them, and then ripped up a dozen yards of rail with a mighty plunge of his foot. So he commenced the conscientious wrecking of the pit.

"Work all my days," he said, "at this!"

It was an astonishing five minutes for the little geologist he had, in his preoccupation, overlooked. This poor little creature having dodged two boulders by a hairbreadth, got out by the westward corner and fled athwart the hill, with flapping rucksack and twinkling knicker-bockered legs, leaving a trail of Cretaceous echinoderms behind him; while young Caddies, satisfied with the destruction he had achieved, came striding out to fulfil his purpose in the world.

"Work in that old pit, until I die and rot and stink I ... What worm did they think was living in my giant body? Dig chalk for God knows what foolish purpose I Not *I!*"

The trend of road and railway perhaps, or mere chance it was, turned his face to London, and thither he came striding; over the Downs and athwart the meadows through the hot afternoon, to the infinite amazement of the world. It signified nothing to him that torn posters in red and white bearing various names flapped from every wall and barn; he knew nothing of the electoral revolution that had flung Caterham, "Jack the Giant-killer," into power. It signified nothing to him

that every police station along his route had what was known as Caterham's ukase upon its notice board that afternoon, proclaiming that no giant, no person whatever over eight feet in height, should go more than five miles from his "place of location" without a special permission. It signified nothing to him that on his wake belated police officers, not a little relieved to find themselves belated, shook warning handbills at his retreating back. He was going to see what the world had to show him, poor incredulous blockhead, and he did not mean that occasional spirited persons shouting "Hi!" at him should stay his course. He came on down by Rochester and Greenwich towards an ever-thickening aggregation of houses, walking rather slowly now, staring about him and swinging his huge chopper.

People in London had heard something of him before, how that he was idiotic but gentle, and wonderfully managed by Lady Wondershoot's agent and the Vicar; how in his dull way he revered these authorities and was grateful to them for their care of him, and so forth. So that when they learnt from the newspaper placards that afternoon that he also was "on strike," the thing appeared to many of them as a deliberate, concerted act.

"They mean to try our strength," said the men in the trains going home from business.

"Lucky we have Caterham."

"It's in answer to his proclamation."

The men in the clubs were better informed. They clustered round the tape or talked in groups in their smoking-rooms.

"He has no weapons. He would have gone to Sevenoaks if he had been put up to it."

"Caterham will handle him..."

The shopmen told their customers. The waiters in restaurants snatched a moment for an evening paper between the courses. The cabmen read it immediately after the betting news...

The placards of the chief government evening paper were conspicuous with "Grasping the Nettle." Others relied for effect on: "Giant Redwood continues to meet the Princess." The *Echo* struck a line of its own with: "Rumoured Revolt of Giants in the North of England. The Sunderland Giants start for Scotland." The, *Westminster Gazette* sounded its usual warning note. "Giants Beware," said the *Westminster Gazette*, and tried to make a point out of it that might perhaps serve towards uniting the Liberal party—at that time greatly torn between seven intensely egotistical leaders. The later newspapers dropped into uniformity. "The Giant in the New Kent Road," they proclaimed.

"What I want to know," said the pale young man in the tea shop, "is why we aren't getting any news of the young Cossars. You'd think they'd be in it most of all ..."

"They tell me there's another of them young giants got loose," said the barmaid, wiping out a glass. "I've always said they was dangerous things to 'ave about. Right away from the beginning ... It ought to be put a stop to. Any'ow, I 'ope 'e won't come along 'ere."

"I'd like to 'ave a look at 'im," said the young man at the bar recklessly, and added, "I *seen* the Princess."

"D'you think they'll 'urt 'im?" said the barmaid.

"May 'ave to," said the young man at the bar, finishing his glass.

Amidst a hum of ten million such sayings young Caddies came to London...

II

I think of young Caddies always as he was seen in the New Kent Road, the sunset warm upon his perplexed and staring face. The Road was thick with its varied traffic, omnibuses, trams, vans, carts, trolleys, cyclists, motors, and a marvelling crowd—loafers, women, nurse-maids, shopping women, children, venturesome hobble-dehoys—gathered behind his gingerly moving feet. The hoardings were untidy everywhere with the tattered election paper. A babblement of voices surged about him. One sees the customers and shopmen crowding in the doorways of the shops, the faces that came and went at the windows, the little street boys running and shouting, the policemen taking it all quite stiffly and calmly, the workmen knocking off upon scaffoldings, the seething miscellany of the little folks. They shouted to him, vague encouragement, vague insults, the imbecile catchwords of the day, and he stared down at them, at such a multitude of living creatures as he had never before imagined in the world.

Now that he had fairly entered London he had had to slacken his pace more and more, the little folks crowded so mightily upon him. The crowd grew denser at every step, and at last, at a corner where two great ways converged, he came to a stop, and the multitude flowed about him and closed him in.

There he stood, with his feet a little apart, his back to a big corner gin palace that towered twice his height and ended In a sky sign, staring down at the pigmies and wondering—trying, I doubt not, to collate it all with the other things of his life, with the valley among the downlands, the nocturnal lovers, the singing in the church, the chalk he hammered daily, and with instinct and death and the sky, trying to see it all together coherent and significant. His brows were knit. He put up his huge paw to scratch his coarse hair, and groaned aloud.

"I don't see It," he said.

His accent was unfamiliar. A great babblement went across the open space —a babblement amidst which the gongs of the trams, ploughing their obstinate way through the mass, rose like red poppies amidst corn. "What did he say?" "Said he didn't see." "Said, where is the sea?" "Said, where is a seat?" "He wants a seat." "Can't the brasted fool sit on a 'ouse or somethin'?"

"What are ye for, ye swarming little people? What are ye all doing, what are ye all for?

"What are ye doing up here, ye swarming little people, while I'm a- cuttin' chalk for ye, down in the chalk pits there?"

His queer voice, the voice that had been so bad for school discipline at Cheasing Eyebright, smote the multitude to silence while it sounded and splashed them all to tumult at the end. Some wit was audible screaming "Speech, speech!"

"What's he saying?" was the burthen of the public mind, and an opinion was abroad that he was drunk. "Hi, hi, hi," bawled the omnibus-drivers, threading a dangerous way. A drunken American sailor wandered about tearfully inquiring, "What's he want anyhow?" A leathery-faced rag-dealer upon a little pony-drawn cart soared up over the tumult by virtue of his voice. "Garn 'ome, you Brasted Giant!" he brawled, "Garn 'Ome! You Brasted Great Dangerous Thing! Can't you see you're a-frightening the 'orses? Go *'ome* with you! 'Asn't any one 'ad the sense to tell you the law?" And over all this uproar young Caddies stared, perplexed, expectant, saying no more.

Down a side road came a little string of solemn policemen, and threaded itself ingeniously into the traffic. "Stand back," said the little voices; "keep moving, please."

Young Caddles became aware of a little dark blue figure thumping at his shin. He looked down, and perceived two white hands gesticulating. "*What*?" he said, bending forward.

"Can't stand about here," shouted the inspector.

"No! You can't stand about here," he repeated.

"But where am I to go?"

"Back to your village. Place of location. Anyhow, now—you've got to move on. You're obstructing the traffic."

"What traffic?"

"Along the road."

"But where is it going? Where does it come from? What does it mean? They're all round me. What do they want? What are they doin'? I want to understand. I'm tired of cuttin' chalk and bein' all alone. What are they doin' for me while I'm a-cuttin' chalk? I may just as well understand here and now as anywhere."

"Sorry. But we aren't here to explain things of that sort. I must arst you to move on."

"Don't you know?"

"I must arst you to move on—*if* you please ... I'd strongly advise you to get off 'ome. We've 'ad no special instructions yet—but it's against the law ... Clear away there. Clear away."

The pavement to his left became invitingly bare, and young Caddles went slowly on his way. But now his tongue was loosened.

"I don't understand," he muttered. "I don't understand." He would appeal brokenly to the changing crowd that ever trailed beside him and behind. "I didn't know there were such places as this. What are all you people doing with yourselves? What's it Jail for? What is it all for, and where do I come in?"

He had already begotten a new catchword. Young men of wit and spirit addressed each other in this manner, "Ullo 'Arry O'Cock. Wot's it all *for*? Eh? Wot's it all bloomin' well *for*?"

To which there sprang up a competing variety of repartees, for the most part impolite. The most popular and best adapted for general use appears to have been "*Shut* it," or, in a voice of scornful detachment—"*Gam I*"

There were others almost equally popular.

III

What was he seeking? He wanted something the pigmy world did not give, some end which the pigmy world prevented his attaining, prevented even his seeing clearly, which he was never to see clearly. It was the whole gigantic social side of this lonely dumb monster crying out for his race, for the things akin to him, for something he might love and something he might serve, for a purpose he might comprehend and a command he could obey. And, you know, all this was *dumb*, raged dumbly within him, could not even, had he met a fellow giant, have found outlet and expression in speech. All the life he knew was the dull round of the village, all the speech he knew was the talk of the cottage, that failed and collapsed at the bare outline of his least gigantic need. He knew nothing of money, this monstrous simpleton, nothing of trade, nothing of the complex pretences upon which the social fabric of the little folks was built. He needed, he needed—Whatever he needed, he never found his need.

All through the day and the summer night he wandered, growing hungry but as yet untired, marking the varied traffic of the different streets, the inexplicable businesses of all these infinitesimal beings. In the aggregate it had no other colour than confusion for him...

He is said to have plucked a lady from her carriage in Kensington, a lady in evening dress of the smartest sort, to have scrutinised her closely, train and shoulder blades, and to have replaced her—a little carelessly —with the profoundest sigh. For that I cannot vouch. For an hour or so he watched people fighting for places in the omnibuses at the end of Piccadilly. He was seen looming over Kennington Oval for some moments in the afternoon, but when he saw these dense thousands were engaged with the mystery of cricket and quite regardless of him he went his way with a groan.

He came back to Piccadilly Circus between eleven and twelve at nights and found a new sort of multitude. Clearly they were very intent: full of things they, for inconceivable reasons, might do, and of others they might not do. They stared at him and jeered at him and went their way. The cabmen, vulture- eyed, followed one another continually along the edge of the swarming pavement. People emerged from the restaurants or entered them, grave, intent, dignified, or gently and agreeably excited or keen and vigilant—beyond the cheating of the sharpest waiter born. The great giant, standing at his corner, peered at them all. "What is it all for?" he murmured in a mournful vast undertone, "What is it all for? They are all so earnest. What is it I do not understand?"

And none of them seemed to see, as he could do, the drink-sodden wretchedness of the painted women at the corner, the ragged misery that sneaked along the gutters, the infinite futility of all this employment. The infinite futility! None of them seemed to feel the shadow of that giant's need, that shadow of the future, that lay athwart their paths...

Across the road high up mysterious letters flamed and went, that might, could he have read them, have measured for him the dimensions of human interest, have told him of the fundamental needs and features of life as the little folks conceived it. First would come a flaming

T;

Then U would follow,

TU;

Then P,

TUP;

Until at last there stood complete, across the sky, this cheerful message to all who felt the burthen of life's earnestness:

TUPPER'S TONIC WINE FOR VIGOUR.

Snap! and it had vanished into night, to be followed in the same slow development by a second universal solicitude:

BEAUTY SOAP.

Not, you remark, mere cleansing chemicals, but something, as they say, "ideal;" and then, completing the tripod of the little life:

TANKER'S YELLOW PILLS.

After that there was nothing for it but Tupper again, in naming crimson letters, snap, snap, across the void.

T U P P...

Early in the small hours it would seem that young Caddies came to the shadowy quiet of Regent's Park, stepped over the railings and lay down on a grassy slope near where the people skate in winter time, and there he slept an hour or so. And about six o'clock in the morning, he was talking to a draggled woman he had found sleeping in a ditch near Hampstead Heath, asking her very earnestly what she thought she was for...

IV

The wandering of Caddies about London came to a head on the second day in the morning. For then his hunger overcame him. He hesitated where the hot-smelling loaves were being tossed into a cart, and then very quietly knelt down and commenced robbery. He emptied the cart while the baker's man fled for the police, and then his great hand came into the shop and cleared counter and cases. Then with an armful, still eating, he went his way looking for another shop to go on with his meal. It happened to be one of those seasons when work is scarce and food dear, and the crowd in that quarter was sympathetic even with a giant who took the food they all desired. They applauded the second phase of his meal, and laughed at his stupid grimace at the policeman.

"I woff hungry," he said, with his mouth full.

"Brayvo!" cried the crowd. "Brayvo!"

Then when he was beginning his third baker's shop, he was stopped by half a dozen policemen hammering with truncheons at his shins. "Look here, my fine giant, you come along o' me," said the officer in charge. "You ain't allowed away

from home like this. You come off home with me." They did their best to arrest him. There was a trolley, I am told, chasing up and down streets at that time, bearing rolls of chain and ship's cable to play the part of handcuffs in that great arrest. There was no intention then of killing him. "He is no party to the plot," Caterham had said. "I will not have innocent blood upon my hands." And added: "—until everything else has been tried."

At first Caddies did not understand the import of these attentions. When he did, he told the policemen not to be fools, and set off in great strides that left them all behind. The bakers' shops had been in the Harrow Road, and he went through canal London to St. John's Wood, and sat down in a private garden there to pick his teeth and be speedily assailed by another posse of constables.

"You lea' me alone," he growled, and slouched through the gardens—spoiling several lawns and kicking down a fence or so, while the energetic little policemen followed him up, some through the gardens, some along the road in front of the houses. Here there were one or two with guns, but they made no use of them. When he came out into the Edgware Road there was a new note and a new movement in the crowd, and a mounted policeman rode over his foot and got upset for his pains.

"You lea' me alone," said Caddies, facing the breathless crowd. "I ain't done anything to you." At that time he was unarmed, for he had left his chalk chopper in Regent's Park. But now, poor wretch, he seems to have felt the need of some weapon. He turned back towards the goods yard of the Great Western Railway, wrenched up the standard of a tall arc light, a formidable mace for him, and flung it over his shoulder. And finding the police still turning up to pester him, he went back along the Edgware Road, towards Cricklewood, and struck off sullenly to the north.

He wandered as far as Waltham, and then turned back westward and then again towards London, and came by the cemeteries and over the crest of Highgate about midday into view of the greatness of the city again. He turned aside and sat down in a garden, with his back to a house that overlooked all London. He was breathless, and his face was lowering, and now the people no longer crowded upon him as they had done when first he came to London, but lurked in the adjacent garden, and peeped from cautious securities. They knew by now the thing was grimmer than they had thought. "Why can't they lea' me alone?" growled young Caddies. "I *mus'* eat. Why can't they lea' me alone?"

He sat with a darkling face, gnawing at his knuckles and looking down over London. All the fatigue, worry, perplexity, and impotent wath of his wanderings was coming to a head in him. "They mean nothing," he whispered. "They mean nothing. And they *won't* let me alone, and they *will* get in my way." And again, over and over to himself, "Meanin' nothing.

"Ugh! the little people!"

He bit harder at his knuckles and his scowl deepened. "Cuttin' chalk for 'em," he whispered. "And all the world is theirs! *I* don't come in —nowhere."

Presently with a spasm of sick anger he saw the now familiar form of a policeman astride the garden wall.

"Lea' me alone," grunted the giant. "Lea' me alone."

"I got to do my duty," said the little policeman, with a face that was white and resolute.

"You lea' me alone. I got to live as well as you. I got to think. I got to eat. You lea' me alone."

"It's the Law," said the little policeman, coming no further. "We never made the Law."

"Nor me," said young Caddies. "You little people made all that before I was born. You and your Law! What I must and what I mustn't! No food for me to eat unless I work a slave, no rest, no shelter, nothin', and you tell me—"

"I ain't got no business with that," said the policeman. "I'm not one to argue. All I got to do is to carry out the Law." And he brought his second leg over the wall and seemed disposed to get down. Other policemen appeared behind him.

"I got no quarrel with *you*—mind," said young Caddies, with his grip tight upon his huge mace of iron, his face pale, and a lank explanatory great finger to the policeman. "I got no quarrel with you. But *—You lea' me alone."*

The policeman tried to be calm and commonplace, with a monstrous tragedy clear before his eyes. "Give me the proclamation," he said to some unseen follower, and a little white paper was handed to him.

"Lea' me alone," said Caddies, scowling, tense, and drawn together.

"This means," said the policeman before he read, "go 'ome. Go 'ome to your chalk pit. If not, you'll be hurt."

Caddies gave an inarticulate growl.

Then when the proclamation had been read, the officer made a sign. Four men with rifles came into view and took up positions of affected ease along the wall. They wore the uniform of the rat police. At the sight of the guns, young Caddies blazed into anger. He remembered the sting of the Wreckstone farmers' shot guns. "You going to shoot off those at me?" he said, pointing, and it seemed to the officer he must be afraid.

"If you don't march back to your pit—"

Then in an instant the officer had slung himself back over the wall, and sixty feet above him the great electric standard whirled down to his death. Bang, bang, bang, went the heavy guns, and smash! the shattered wall, the soil and subsoil of the garden flew. Something flew with it, that left red drops on one of the shooter's hands. The riflemen dodged this way and that and turned valiantly to fire again. But young Caddies, already shot twice through the body, had spun about to find who it was had hit him so heavily in the back. Bang! Bang! He had a vision of houses and greenhouses and gardens, of people dodging at windows, the whole swaying fearfully and mysteriously. He seems to have made three stumbling strides, to have raised and dropped his huge mace, and to have clutched his chest. He was stung and wrenched by pain.

What was this, warm and wet, on his hand?

One man peering from a bedroom window saw his face, saw him staring, with a grimace of weeping dismay, at the blood upon his hand, and then his knees bent under him, and he came crashing to the earth, the first of the giant nettles to fall to Caterham's resolute clutch, the very last that he had reckoned would come into his hand.

CHAPTER THE FOURTH - REDWOOD'S TWO DAYS

I

So soon as Caterham knew the moment for grasping his nettle had come, he took the law into his own hands and sent to arrest Cossar and Redwood.

Redwood was there for the taking. He had been undergoing an operation in the side, and the doctors had kept all disturbing things from him until his convalescence was assured. Now they had released him. He was just out of bed, sitting in a fire-warmed room, with a heap of newspapers about him, reading for the first time of the agitation that had swept the country into the hands of Caterham, and of the trouble that was darkening over the Princess and his son. It was in the morning of the day when young Caddies died, and when the policeman tried to stop young Redwood on his way to the Princess. The latest newspapers Redwood had did but vaguely prefigure these imminent things. He was re-reading these first adumbrations of disaster with a sinking heart, reading the shadow of death more and more perceptibly into them, reading to occupy his mind until further news should come. When the officers followed the servant into his room, he looked up eagerly.

"I thought it was an early evening paper," he said. Then standing up, and with a swift change of manner: "What's this?"

After that Redwood had no news of anything for two days.

They had come with a vehicle to take him away, but when it became evident that he was ill, it was decided to leave him for a day or so until he could be safely removed, and his house was taken over by the police and converted into a temporary prison. It was the same house in winch Giant Redwood had been born and in which Herakleophorbia had for the first time been given to a human being, and Redwood had now been a widower and had lived alone in it eight years.

He had become an iron-grey man, with a little pointed grey beard and still active brown eyes. He was slender and soft-voiced, as he had ever been, but his features had now that indefinable quality that comes of brooding over mighty things. To the arresting officer his appearance was in impressive contrast to the enormity of his offences. "Here's this feller," said the officer in command, to his next subordinate, "has done his level best to bust up everything, and 'e's got a face like a quiet country gentleman; and here's Judge Hangbrow keepin' everything nice and in order for every one, and 'e's got a 'ead like a 'og. Then their manners! One all consideration and the other snort and grunt. Which just shows you, doesn't it, that appearances aren't to be gone upon, whatever else you do."

But his praise of Redwood's consideration was presently dashed. The officers found him troublesome at first until they had made it clear that it was useless for him to ask questions or beg for papers. They made a sort of inspection of his study indeed, and cleared away even the papers he had. Redwood's voice was high and expostulatory. "But don't you see," he said over and over again, it's my Son, my only Son, that is in this trouble. It isn't the Food I care for, but my Son."

"I wish indeed I could tell you, Sir," said the officer. "But our orders are strict."

"Who gave the orders?" cried Redwood.

"Ah! *that*, Sir—-" said the officer, and moved towards the door...

"'E's going up and down 'is room," said the second officer, when his superior came down. "That's all right. He'll walk it off a bit."

"I hope 'e will," said the chief officer. "The fact is I didn't see it in that light before, but this here Giant what's been going on with the Princess, you know, is this man's son."

The two regarded one another and the third policeman for a space.

"Then it is a bit rough on him," the third policeman said.

It became evident that Redwood had still imperfectly apprehended the fact that an iron curtain had dropped between him and the outer world. They heard him go to the door, try the handle and rattle the lock, and then the voice of the officer who was stationed on the landing telling him it was no good to do that. Then afterwards they heard him at the windows and saw the men outside looking up. "It's no good that way," said the second officer. Then Redwood began upon the bell. The senior officer went up and explained very patiently that it could do no good to ring the bell like that, and if it was rung for nothing now it might have to be disregarded presently when he had need of something. "Any reasonable attendance, Sir," the officer said. "But if you ring it just by way of protest we shall be obliged, Sir, to disconnect."

The last word the officer heard was Redwood's high-pitched, "But at least you might tell me if my Son—"

II

After that Redwood spent, most of his time at the windows.

But the windows offered him little of the march of events outside. It was a quiet street at all times, and that day it was unusually quiet: scarcely a cab, scarcely a tradesman's cart passed all that morning. Now and then men went by—without any distinctive air of events—now and then a little group of children, a nursemaid and a woman going shopping, and so forth. They came on to the stage right or left, up or down the street, with an exasperating suggestion of indifference to any concerns more spacious than their own; they would discover the police-guarded house with amazement and exit in the opposite direction, where the great trusses of a giant hydrangea hung across the pavement, staring back or pointing. Now and then a man would come and ask one of the policemen a question and get a curt reply...

Opposite the houses seemed dead. A housemaid appeared once at a bedroom window and stared for a space, and it occurred to Redwood to signal to her. For a time she watched his gestures as if with interest and made a vague response to them, then looked over her shoulder suddenly and turned and went away. An old man hobbled out of Number 37 and came down the steps and went off to the right, altogether without looking up. For ten minutes the only occupant of the road was a cat...

With such events that interminable momentous morning lengthened out.

About twelve there came a bawling of newsvendors from the adjacent road; but it passed. Contrary to their wont they left Redwood's street alone, and a suspicion dawned upon him that the police were guarding the end of the street. He tried to open the window, but this brought a policeman into the room forthwith...

The clock of the parish church struck twelve, and after an abyss of time —one.

They mocked him with lunch.

He ate a mouthful and tumbled the food about a little in order to get it taken away, drank freely of whisky, and then took a chair and went back to the window. The minutes expanded into grey immensities, and for a time perhaps he slept...

He woke with a vague impression of remote concussions. He perceived a rattling of the windows like the quiver of an earthquake, that lasted for a minute or so and died away. Then after a silence it returned... Then it died away again. He fancied it might be merely the passage of some heavy vehicle along the main road. What else could it be?

After a time he began to doubt whether he had heard this sound.

He began to reason interminably with himself. Why, after all, was he seized? Caterham had been in office two days—just long enough—to grasp his Nettle! Grasp his Nettle! Grasp his Giant Nettle! The refrain once started, sang through his mind, and would not be dismissed.

What, after all, could Caterham do? He was a religious man. He was bound in a sort of way by that not to do violence without a cause.

Grasp his Nettle I Perhaps, for example, the Princess was to be seized and sent abroad. There might be trouble with his son. In which case—! But why had he been arrested? Why was it necessary to keep him in ignorance of a thing like that? The thing suggested—something more extensive.

Perhaps, for example—they meant to lay all the giants by the heels I They were all to be arrested together. There had been hints of that In the election speeches. And then?

No doubt they had got Cossar also?

Caterham was a religious man. Redwood clung to that. The back of his mind was a black curtain, and on that curtain there came and went a word—a word written in letters of fixe. He struggled perpetually against that word. It was always as it were beginning to get written on the curtain and never getting completed.

He faced it at last. "Massacre!" There was the word in its full brutality.

No! No! No! It was impossible! Caterham was a religious man, a civilised man. And besides after all these years, after all these hopes!

Redwood sprang up; he paced the room. He spoke to himself; he shouted.

"*No!*"

Mankind was surely not so mad as that—surely not! It was impossible, it was incredible, it could not be. What good would it do to kill the giant human when the gigantic in all the lower things had now inevitably come? They could not be so mad as that! "I must dismiss such an idea," he said aloud; "dismiss such an idea! Absolutely!"

He pulled up short. What was that?

Certainly the windows had rattled. He went to look out into the street. Opposite he saw the instant confirmation of his ears. At a bedroom at Number 35 was a woman, towel in hand, and at the dining-room of Number 37 a man was visible behind a great vase of hypertrophied maidenhair fern, both staring out and up, both disquieted and curious. He could see now too, quite clearly, that the policeman on the pavement had heard it also. The thing was not his imagination.

He turned to the darkling room.

"Guns," he said.

He brooded.

"Guns?"

They brought him in strong tea, such as he was accustomed to have. It was evident his housekeeper had been taken into consultation. After drinking it, he was too restless to sit any longer at the window, and he paced the room. His mind became more capable of consecutive thought.

The room had been his study for four-and-twenty years. It had been furnished at his marriage, and all the essential equipment dated from then, the large complex writing-desk, the rotating chair, the easy chair at the fire, the rotating bookcase, the fixture of indexed pigeon-holes that filled the further recess. The vivid Turkey carpet, the later Victorian rugs and curtains had mellowed now to a rich dignity of effect, and copper and brass shone warm about the open fire. Electric lights had replaced the lamp of former days; that was the chief alteration in the original equipment. But among these things his connection with the Food had left abundant traces. Along one wall, above the dado, ran a crowded array of black-framed photographs and photogravures, showing his son and Cossar's sons and others of the Boom-children at various ages and amidst various surroundings. Even young Caddles' vacant visage had its place in that collection. In the corner stood a sheaf of the tassels of gigantic meadow grass from Cheasing Eyebright, and on the desk there lay three empty poppy heads as big as hats. The curtain rods were grass stems. And the tremendous skull of the great hog of Oakham hung, a portentous ivory overmantel, with a Chinese jar in either eye socket, snout down above the fire...

It was to the photographs that Redwood went, and in particular to the photographs of his son.

They brought back countless memories of things that had passed out of his mind, of the early days of the Food, of Bensington's timid presence, of his cousin Jane, of Cossar and the night work at the Experimental Farm. These things came

to him now very little and bright and distinct, like things seen through a telescope on a sunny day. And then there was the giant nursery, the giant childhood, the young giant's first efforts to speak, his first clear signs of affection.

Guns?

It flowed in on him, irresistibly, overwhelmingly, that outside there, outside this accursed silence and mystery, his son and Cossar's sons, and all these glorious first-fruits of a greater age were even now—fighting. Fighting for life! Even now his son might be in some dismal quandary, cornered, wounded, overcome...

He swung away from the pictures and went up and down the room gesticulating. "It cannot be," he cried, "it cannot be. It cannot end like that!"

"What was that?"

He stopped, stricken rigid.

The trembling of the windows had begun again, and then had come a thud —a vast concussion that shook the house. The concussion seemed to last for an age. It must have been very near. For a moment it seemed that something had struck the house above him—an enormous impact that broke into a tinkle of falling glass, and then a stillness that ended at last with a minute clear sound of running feet in the street below.

Those feet released him from his rigor. He turned towards the window, and saw it starred and broken.

His heart beat high with a sense of crisis, of conclusive occurrence, of release. And then again, his realisation of impotent confinement fell about him like a curtain!

He could see nothing outside except that the small electric lamp opposite was not lighted; he could hear nothing after the first suggestion of a wide alarm. He could add nothing to interpret or enlarge that mystery except that presently there came a reddish fluctuating brightness in the sky towards the south-east.

This light waxed and waned. When it waned he doubted if it had ever waxed. It had crept upon him very gradually with the darkling. It became the predominant fact in his long night of suspense. Sometimes it seemed to him it had the quiver one associates with dancing flames, at others he fancied it was no more than the normal reflection of the evening lights. It waxed and waned through the long hours, and only vanished at last when it was submerged altogether under the rising tide of dawn. Did it mean—? What could it mean? Almost certainly it was some sort of fire, near or remote, but he could not even tell whether it was smoke or cloud drift that streamed across the sky. But about one o'clock there began a flickering of searchlights athwart that ruddy tumult, a nickering that continued for the rest of the night. That too might mean many things? What could it mean? What did it mean? Just this stained unrestful sky he had and the suggestion of a huge explosion to occupy his mind. There came no further sounds, no further running, nothing but a shouting that might have been only the distant efforts of drunken men...

He did not turn up his lights; he stood at his draughty broken window, a distressful, slight black outline to the officer who looked ever and again into the room and exhorted him to rest.

All night Redwood remained at his window peering up at the ambiguous drift of the sky, and only with the coming of the dawn did he obey his fatigue and lie down upon the little bed they had prepared for him between his writing- desk and the sinking fire in the fireplace under the great hog's skull.

III

For thirty-six long hours did Redwood remain imprisoned, closed in and shut off from the great drama of the Two Days, while the little people in the dawn of greatness fought against the Children of the Food. Then abruptly the iron curtain rose again, and he found himself near the very centre of the struggle. That curtain rose as unexpectedly as it fell. In the late afternoon he was called to the window by the clatter of a cab, that stopped without. A young man descended, and in another minute stood before him in the room, a slightly built young man of thirty perhaps, clean shaven, well dressed, well mannered.

"Mr. Redwood, Sir," he began, "would you be willing to come to Mr. Caterham? He needs your presence very urgently."

"Needs my presence!" There leapt a question into Redwood's mind, that for a moment he could not put. He hesitated. Then in a voice that broke he asked: "What has he done to my Son?" and stood breathless for the reply.

"Your Son, Sir? Your Son is doing well. So at least we gather."

"Doing well?"

"He was wounded, Sir, yesterday. Have you not heard?"

Redwood smote these pretences aside. His voice was no longer coloured by fear, but by anger. "You know I have not heard. You know I have heard nothing."

"Mr. Caterham feared, Sir—It was a time of upheaval. Every one —taken by surprise. He arrested you to save you, Sir, from any misadventure—"

"He arrested me to prevent my giving any warning or advice to my son. Go on. Tell me what has happened. Have you succeeded? Have you killed them all?"

The young man made a pace or so towards the window, and turned.

"No, Sir," he said concisely.

"What have you to tell me?"

"It's our proof, Sir, that this fighting was not planned by us. They found us ... totally unprepared." "You mean?"

"I mean, Sir, the Giants have—to a certain extent—held their own."

The world changed, for Redwood. For a moment something like hysteria had the muscles of his face and throat. Then he gave vent to a profound "Ah!" His heart bounded towards exultation. "The Giants have held their own!"

"There has been terrible fighting—terrible destruction. It is all a most hideous misunderstanding ... In the north and midlands Giants have been killed ... Everywhere."

"They are fighting now?"

"No, Sir. There was a flag of truce."

"From them?"

"No, Sir. Mr. Caterham sent a flag of truce. The whole thing is a hideous misunderstanding. That is why he wants to talk to you, and put his case before you. They insist, Sir, that you should intervene—"

Redwood interrupted. "Do you know what happened to my Son?" he asked.

"He was wounded."

"Tell me! Tell me!"

"He and the Princess came—before the—the movement to surround the Cossar camp was complete—the Cossar pit at Chislehurst. They came suddenly, Sir, crashing through a dense thicket of giant oats, near River, upon a column of infantry ... Soldiers had been very nervous all day, and this produced a panic."

"They shot him?"

"No, Sir. They ran away. Some shot at him—wildly—against orders."

Redwood gave a note of denial. "It's true, Sir. Not on account of your son, I won't pretend, but on account of the Princess."

"Yes. That's true."

"The two Giants ran shouting towards the encampment. The soldiers ran this way and that, and then some began firing. They say they saw him stagger—"

"Ugh!"

"Yes, Sir. But we know he is not badly hurt."

"How?"

"He sent the message, Sir, that he was doing well!"

"To me?"

"Who else, Sir?"

Redwood stood for nearly a minute with his arms tightly folded, taking this in. Then his indignation found a voice.

"Because you were fools in doing the thing, because you miscalculated and blundered, you would like me to think you are not murderers in intention. And besides—The rest?"

The young man looked interrogation.

"The other Giants?"

The young man made no further pretence of misunderstanding. His tone fell. "Thirteen, Sir, are dead."

"And others wounded?"

"Yes, Sir."

"And Caterham," he gasped, "wants to meet me! Where are the others?"

"Some got to the encampment during the fighting, Sir ... They seem to have known—"

"Well, of course they did. If it hadn't been for Cossar—Cossar is there?"

"Yes, Sir. And all the surviving Giants are there—the ones who didn't get to the camp in the fighting have gone, or are going now under the flag of trace."

"That means," said Redwood, "that you are beaten."

"We are not beaten. No, Sir. You cannot say we are beaten. But your sons have broken the rules of war. Once last night, and now again. After our attack had been withdrawn. This afternoon they began to bombard London—"

"That's legitimate!"

"They have been firing shells filled with—poison."

"Poison?"

"Yes. Poison. The Food—"

"Herakleophorbia?"

"Yes, Sir. Mr. Caterham, Sir—"

"You are beaten! Of course that beats you. It's Cossar I What can you hope to do now? What good is it to do anything now? You will breathe it in the dust of every street. What is there to fight for more? Rules of war, indeed! And now Caterham wants to humbug me to help him bargain. Good heavens, man! Why should I come to your exploded windbag? He has played his game ... murdered and muddled. Why should I?"

The young man stood with an air of vigilant respect.

"It is a fact, Sir," he interrupted, "that the Giants insist that they shall see you. They will have no ambassador but you. Unless you come to them, I am afraid, Sir, there will be more bloodshed."

"On *your* side, perhaps."

"No, Sir—on both sides. The world is resolved the thing must end."

Redwood looked about the study. His eyes rested for a moment on the photograph of his boy. He turned and met the expectation of the young man. "Yes," he said at last, "I will come."

IV

His encounter with Caterham was entirely different from his anticipation. He had seen the man only twice in his life, once at dinner and once in the lobby of the House, and his imagination had been active not with the man but with the creation of the newspapers and caricaturists, the legendary Caterham, Jack the Giant-killer, Perseus, and all the rest of it. The element of a human personality came in to disorder all that.

Here was not the face of the caricatures and portraits, but the face of a worn and sleepless man, lined and drawn, yellow in the whites of the eyes, a little weakened about the mouth. Here, indeed, were the red-brown eyes, the black hair, the distinctive aquiline profile of the great demagogue, but here was also something else that smote any premeditated scorn and rhetoric aside. This man was suffering; he was suffering acutely; he was under enormous stress. From the beginning he had an air of impersonating himself. Presently, with a single gesture, the slightest movement, he revealed to Redwood that he was keeping himself up with drags. He moved a thumb to his waistcoat pocket, and then, after a few sentences more, threw concealment aside, and slipped the little tabloid to his lips.

Moreover, in spite of the stresses upon him, in spite of the fact that he was in the wrong, and Redwood's junior by a dozen years, that strange quality in him, the

something—personal magnetism one may call it for want of a better name—that had won his way for him to this eminence of disaster was with him still. On that also Redwood had failed to reckon. From the first, so far as the course and conduct of their speech went, Caterham prevailed over Redwood. All the quality of the first phase of their meeting was determined by him, all the tone and procedure were his. That happened as if it was a matter of course. All Redwood's expectations vanished at his presence. He shook hands before Redwood remembered that he meant to parry that familiarity; he pitched the note of their conference from the outset, sure and clear, as a search for expedients under a common catastrophe.

If he made any mistake it was when ever and again his fatigue got the better of his immediate attention, and the habit of the public meeting carried him away. Then he drew himself up—through all their interview both men stood—and looked away from Redwood, and began to fence and justify. Once even he said "Gentlemen!"

Quietly, expandingly, he began to talk...

There were moments when Redwood ceased even to feel himself an interlocutor, when he became the mere auditor of a monologue. He became the privileged spectator of an extraordinary phenomenon. He perceived something almost like a specific difference between himself and this being whose beautiful voice enveloped him, who was talking, talking. This mind before him was so powerful and so limited. From its driving energy, its personal weight, its invincible oblivion to certain things, there sprang up in Redwood's mind the most grotesque and strange of images. Instead of an antagonist who was a fellow-creature, a man one could hold morally responsible, and to whom one could address reasonable appeals, he saw Caterham as something, something like a monstrous rhinoceros, as it were, a civilised rhinoceros begotten of the jungle of democratic affairs, a monster of irresistible onset and invincible resistance. In all the crashing conflicts of that tangle he was supreme. And beyond? This man was a being supremely adapted to make his way through multitudes of men. For him there was no fault so important as self- contradiction, no science so significant as the reconciliation of "interests." Economic realities, topographical necessities, the barely touched mines of scientific expedients, existed for him no more than railways or rifled guns or geographical literature exist for his animal prototype. What did exist were gatherings, and caucuses, and votes—above all, votes. He was votes incarnate—millions of votes.

And now in the great crisis, with the Giants broken but not beaten, this vote-monster talked.

It was so evident that even now he had everything to learn. He did not know there were physical laws and economic laws, quantities and reactions that all humanity voting *nemine contradicente* cannot vote away, and that are disobeyed only at the price of destruction. He did not know there are moral laws that cannot be bent by any force of glamour, or are bent only to fly back with vindictive violence. In the face of shrapnel or the Judgment Day, it was evident to Redwood

that this man would have sheltered behind some curiously dodged vote of the House of Commons.

What most concerned his mind now was not the powers that held the fastness away there to the south, not defeat and death, but the effect of these things upon his Majority, the cardinal reality in his life. He had to defeat the Giants or go under. He was by no means absolutely despairful. In this hour of his utmost failure, with blood and disaster upon his hands, and the rich promise of still more horrible disaster, with the gigantic destinies of the world towering and toppling over him, he was capable of a belief that by sheer exertion of his voice, by explaining and qualifying and restating, he might yet reconstitute his power. He was puzzled and distressed no doubt, fatigued and suffering, but if only he could keep up, if only he could keep talking —

As he talked he seemed to Redwood to advance and recede, to dilate and contract. Redwood's share of the talk was of the most subsidiary sort, wedges as it were suddenly thrust in. "That's all nonsense." "No." "It's no use suggesting that." "Then why did you begin?"

It is doubtful if Caterham really heard him at all. Round such interpolations Caterham's speech flowed indeed like some swift stream about a rock. There this incredible man stood, on his official hearthrug, talking, talking with enormous power and skill, talking as though a pause in his talk, his explanations, his presentation of standpoints and lights, of considerations and expedients, would permit some antagonistic influence to leap into being —into vocal being, the only being he could comprehend. There he stood amidst the slightly faded splendours of that official room in which one man after another had succumbed to the belief that a certain power of intervention was the creative control of an empire...

The more he talked the more certain Redwood's sense of stupendous futility grew. Did this man realise that while he stood and talked there, the whole great world was moving, that the invincible tide of growth flowed and flowed, that there were any hours but parliamentary hours, or any weapons in the hands of the Avengers of Blood? Outside, darkling the whole room, a single leaf of giant Virginian creeper tapped unheeded on the pane.

Redwood became anxious to end this amazing monologue, to escape to sanity and judgment, to that beleaguered camp, the fastness of the future, where, at the very nucleus of greatness, the Sons were gathered together. For that this talking was endured. He had a curious impression that unless this monologue ended he would presently find himself carried away by it, that he must fight against Caterham's voice as one fights against a drug. Facts had altered and were altering beneath that spell.

What was the man saying?

Since Redwood had to report it to the Children of the Food, in a sort of way he perceived it did matter. He would have to listen and guard his sense of realities as well as he could.

Much about bloodguiltiness. That was eloquence. That didn't matter. Next?

He was suggesting a convention!

He was suggesting that the surviving Children of the Food should capitulate and go apart and form a community of their own. There were precedents, he said, for this. "We would assign them territory—"

"Where?" interjected Redwood, stooping to argue.

Caterham snatched at that concession. He turned his face to Redwood's, and his voice fell to a persuasive reasonableness. That could be determined. That, he contended, was a quite subsidiary question. Then he went on to stipulate: "And except for them and where they are we must have absolute control, the Food and all the Fruits of the Food must be stamped out—"

Redwood found himself bargaining: "The Princess?"

"She stands apart."

"No," said Redwood, struggling to get back to the old footing. "That's absurd."

"That afterwards. At any rate we are agreed that the making of the Food must stop—"

"I have agreed to nothing. I have said nothing—"

"But on one planet, to have two races of men, one great, one small! Consider what has happened! Consider that is but a little foretaste of what might presently happen if this Food has its way! Consider all you have already brought upon this world! If there is to be a race of Giants, increasing and multiplying—"

"It is not for me to argue," said Redwood. "I must go to our sons. I want to go to my son. That is why I have come to you. Tell me exactly what you offer."

Caterham made a speech upon his terms.

The Children of the Food were to be given a great reservation—in North America perhaps or Africa—in which they might live out their lives in their own fashion.

"But it's nonsense," said Redwood. "There are other Giants now abroad. All over Europe—here and there!"

"There could be an international convention. It's *not* impossible. Something of the sort indeed has already been spoken of ... But in this reservation they can live out their own lives in their own way. They may do what they like; they may make what they like. We shall be glad if they will make us things. They may be happy. Think!"

"Provided there are no more Children." "Precisely. The Children are for us. And so, Sir, we shall save the world, we shall save it absolutely from the fruits of your terrible discovery. It is not too late for us. Only we are eager to temper expediency with mercy. Even now we are burning and searing the places their shells hit yesterday. We can get it under. Trust me we shall get it under. But in that way, without cruelty, without injustice—"

"And suppose the Children do not agree?"

For the first time Caterham looked Redwood fully in the face.

"They must!"

"I don't think they will."

"Why should they not agree?" he asked, in richly toned amazement.

"Suppose they don't?"

"What can it be but war? We cannot have the thing go on. We cannot. Sir. Have you scientific men *no* imagination? Have you no mercy? We cannot have our world trampled under a growing herd of such monsters and monstrous growths as your Food has made. We cannot and we cannot! I ask you, Sir, what can it be but war? And remember—this that has happened is only a beginning I *This* was a skirmish. A mere affair of police. Believe me, a mere affair of police. Do not be cheated by perspective, by the immediate bigness of these newer things. Behind us is the nation—is humanity. Behind the thousands who have died there are millions. Were it not for the fear of bloodshed, Sir, behind our first attacks there would be forming other attacks, even now. Whether we can kill this Food or not, most assuredly we can kill your sons! You reckon too much on the things of yesterday, on the happenings of a mere score of years, on one battle. You have no sense of the slow course of history. I offer this convention for the sake of lives, not because it can change the inevitable end. If you think that your poor two dozen of Giants can resist all the forces of our people and of all the alien peoples who will come to our aid; if you think you can change Humanity at a blow, in a single generation, and alter the nature and stature of Man—"

He flung out an arm. "Go to them now, Sir. I see them, for all the evil they have done, crouching among their wounded—"

He stopped, as though he had glanced at Redwood's son by chance. There came a pause. "Go to them," he said. "That is what I want to do." "Then go now..."

He turned and pressed the button of a bell; without, in immediate response, came a sound of opening doors and hastening feet.

The talk was at an end. The display was over. Abruptly Caterham seemed to contract, to shrivel up into a yellow-faced, fagged-out, middle-sized, middle- aged man. He stepped forward, as if he were stepping out of a picture, and with a complete assumption of that, friendliness that lies behind all the public conflicts of our race, he held out his hand to Redwood.

As if it were a matter of course, Redwood shook hands with him for the second time.

CHAPTER THE FIFTH - THE GIANT LEAGUER

I

Presently Redwood found himself in a train going south over the Thames. He had a brief vision of the river shining under its lights, and of the smoke still going up from the place where the shell had fallen on the north bank, and where a vast multitude of men had been organised to burn the Herakleophorbia out of the ground. The southern bank was dark, for some reason even the streets were not lit, all that was clearly visible was the outlines of the tall alarm- towers and the dark bulks of flats and schools, and after a minute of peering scrutiny he turned his back on the window and sank into thought. There was nothing more to see or do until he saw the Sons...

He was fatigued by the stresses of the last two days; it seemed to him that his emotions must needs be exhausted, but he had fortified himself with strong coffee before starting, and his thoughts ran thin and clear. His mind touched many things. He reviewed again, but now in the enlightenment of accomplished events, the manner in which the Food had entered and unfolded itself in the world.

"Bensington thought it might be an excellent food for infants," he whispered to himself, with a faint smile. Then there came into his mind as vivid as if they were still unsettled his own horrible doubts after he had committed himself by giving it to his own son. From that, with a steady unfaltering expansion, in spite of every effort of men to help and hinder, the Food had spread through the whole world of man. And now?

"Even if they kill them all," Redwood whispered, "the thing is done."

The secret of its making was known far and wide. That had been his own work. Plants, animals, a multitude of distressful growing children would conspire irresistibly to force the world to revert again to the Food, whatever happened in the present struggle. "The thing is done," he said, with his mind swinging round beyond all his controlling to rest upon the present fate of the Children and his son. Would he find them exhausted by the efforts of the battle, wounded, starving, on the verge of defeat, or would he find them still stout and hopeful, ready for the still grimmer conflict of the morrow? His son was wounded! But he had sent a message!

His mind came back to his interview with Caterham.

He was roused from his thoughts by the stopping of his train in Chislehurst station. He recognised the place by the huge rat alarm-tower that crested Camden Hill, and the row of blossoming giant hemlocks that lined the road...

Caterham's private secretary came to him from the other carriage and told him that half a mile farther the line had been wrecked, and that the rest of the journey was to be made in a motor car. Redwood descended upon a platform lit only by a hand lantern and swept by the cool night breeze. The quiet of that derelict, wood-set, weed-embedded suburb—for all the inhabitants had taken refuge in London at the outbreak of yesterday's conflict—became instantly impressive. His conductor took him down the steps to where a motor car was waiting with blazing lights—the only lights to be seen —handed him over to the care of the driver and bade him farewell.

"You will do your best for us," he said, with an imitation of his master's manner, as he held Redwood's hand.

So soon as Redwood could be wrapped about they started out into the night. At one moment they stood still, and then the motor car was rushing softly and swiftly down the station incline. They turned one corner and another, followed the windings of a lane of villas, and then before them stretched the road. The motor droned up to its topmost speed, and the black night swept past them. Everything was very dark under the starlight, and the whole world crouched mysteriously and was gone without a sound. Not a breath stirred the flying things by the wayside; the deserted, pallid white villas on either hand, with their black unlit windows, reminded him of a noiseless procession of skulls. The driver beside him was a silent man, or stricken into silence by the conditions of his journey. He answered Redwood's brief questions in monosyllables, and gruffly. Athwart the southern sky the beams of searchlights waved noiseless passes; the sole strange evidences of life they seemed in all that derelict world about the hurrying machine.

The road was presently bordered on either side by gigantic blackthorn shoots that made it very dark, and by tail grass and big campions, huge giant dead-nettles as high as trees, flickering past darkly in silhouette overhead. Beyond Keston they came to a rising hill, and the driver went slow. At the crest he stopped. The engine throbbed and became still. "There," he said, and his big gloved finger pointed, a black misshapen thing before Redwood's eyes.

Far away as it seemed, the great embankment, crested by the blaze from which the searchlights sprang, rose up against the sky. Those beams went and came among the clouds and the hilly land about them as if they traced mysterious incantations.

"I don't know," said the driver at last, and it was clear he was afraid to go on.

Presently a searchlight swept down the sky to them, stopped as it were with a start, scrutinised them, a blinding stare confused rather than mitigated by an intervening monstrous weed stem or so. They sat with their gloves held over their eyes, trying to look under them and meet that light.

"Go on," said Redwood after a while.

The driver still had his doubts; he tried to express them, and died down to "I don't know" again.

At last he ventured on. "Here goes," he said, and roused his machinery to motion again, followed intently by that great white eye.

To Redwood it seemed for a long time they were no longer on earth, but in a state of palpitating hurry through a luminous cloud. Teuf, teuf, teuf, teuf, went the machine, and ever and again—obeying I know not what nervous impulse—the driver sounded his horn.

They passed into the welcome darkness of a high-fenced lane, and down into a hollow and past some houses into that blinding stare again. Then for a space the road ran naked across a down, and they seemed to hang throbbing in immensity. Once more giant weeds rose about them and whirled past. Then quite abruptly close upon them loomed the figure of a giant, shining brightly where the search-light caught him below, and black against the sky above. "Hullo there!" he cried, and "stop! There's no more road beyond ... Is that Father Redwood?"

Redwood stood up and gave a vague shout by way of answer, and then Cossar was in the road beside him, gripping both hands with both of his and pulling him out of the car.

"What of my son?" asked Redwood.

"He's all right," said Cossar. "They've hurt nothing serious in *him*."

"And your lads?"

"Well. All of them, well. But we've had to make a fight for it."

The Giant was saying something to the motor driver. Redwood stood aside as the machine wheeled round, and then suddenly Cossar vanished, everything vanished, and he was in absolute darkness for a space. The glare was following the motor back to the crest of the Keston hill. He watched the little conveyance receding in that white halo. It had a curious effect, as though it was not moving at all and the halo was. A group of war-blasted Giant elders flashed into gaunt scarred gesticulations and were swallowed again by the night ... Redwood turned to Cossar's dim outline again and clasped his hand. "I have been shut up and kept in ignorance," he said, "for two whole days."

"We fired the Food at them," said Cossar. "Obviously! Thirty shots. Eh!" "I come from Caterham."

"I know you do." He laughed with a note of bitterness. "I suppose he's wiping it up."

II

"Where is my son?" said Redwood.

"He is all right. The Giants are waiting for your message."

"Yes, but my son—..."

He passed with Cossar down a long slanting tunnel that was lit red for a moment and then became dark again, and came out presently into the great pit of shelter the Giants had made.

Redwood's first impression was of an enormous arena bounded by very high cliffs and with its floor greatly encumbered. It was in darkness save for the passing reflections of the watchman's searchlights that whirled perpetually high overhead, and for a red glow that came and went from a distant corner where two Giants worked together amidst a metallic clangour. Against the sky, as the glare

came about, his eye caught the familiar outlines of the old workhseds and playsheds that were made for the Cossar boys. They were hanging now, as it were, at a cliff brow, and strangely twisted and distorted with the guns of Caterham's bombardment. There were suggestions of huge gun emplacements above there, and nearer were piles of mighty cylinders that were perhaps ammunition. All about the wide space below, the forms of great engines and incomprehensible bulks were scattered in vague disorder. The Giants appeared and vanished among these masses and in the uncertain light; great shapes they were, not disproportionate to the things amidst which they moved. Some were actively employed, some sitting and lying as if they courted sleep, and one near at hand, whose body was bandaged, lay on a rough litter of pine boughs and was certainly asleep. Redwood peered at these dim forms; his eyes went from one stirring outline to another.

"Where is my son, Cossar?"

Then he saw him.

His son was sitting under the shadow of a great wall of steel. He presented himself as a black shape recognisable only by his pose,—his features were invisible. He sat chin upon hand, as though weary or lost in thought. Beside him Redwood discovered the figure of the Princess, the dark suggestion of her merely, and then, as the glow from the distant iron returned, he saw for an instant, red lit and tender, the infinite kindliness of her shadowed face. She stood looking down upon her lover with her hand resting against the steel. It seemed that she whispered to him.

Redwood would have gone towards them.

"Presently," said Cossar. "First there is your message."

"Yes," said Redwood, "but—"

He stopped. His son was now looking up and speaking to the Princess, but in too low a tone for them to hear. Young Redwood raised his face, and she bent down towards him, and glanced aside before she spoke.

"But if we are beaten," they heard the whispered voice of young Redwood.

She paused, and the red blaze showed her eyes bright with unshed tears. She bent nearer him and spoke still lower. There was something so intimate and private in their bearing, in their soft tones, that Redwood—Redwood who had thought for two whole days of nothing but his son—felt himself intrusive there. Abruptly he was checked. For the first time in his life perhaps he realised how much more a son may be to his father than a father can ever be to a son; he realised the full predominance of the future over the past. Here between these two he had no part. His part was played. He turned to Cossar, in the instant realisation. Their eyes met. His voice was changed to the tone of a grey resolve.

"I will deliver my message now," he said. "Afterwards—... It will be soon enough then."

The pit was so enormous and so encumbered that it was a long and tortuous route to the place from which Redwood could speak to them all.

He and Cossar followed a steeply descending way that passed beneath an arch of interlocking machinery, and so came into a vast deep gangway that ran athwart

the bottom of the pit. This gangway, wide and vacant, and yet relatively narrow, conspired with everything about it to enhance Redwood's sense of his own littleness. It became, as it were, an excavated gorge. High overhead, separated from him by cliffs of darkness, the searchlights wheeled and blazed, and the shining shapes went to and fro. Giant voices called to one another above there, calling the Giants together to the Council of War, to hear the terms that Caterham had sent. The gangway still inclined downward towards black vastnesses, towards shadows and mysteries and inconceivable things, into which Redwood went slowly with reluctant footsteps and Cossar with a confident stride...

Redwood's thoughts were busy. The two men passed into the completest darkness, and Cossar took his companion's wrist. They went now slowly perforce.

Redwood was moved to speak. "All this," he said, "is strange."

"Big," said Cossar.

"Strange. And strange that it should be strange to me—I, who am, in a sense, the beginning of it all. It's—"

He stopped, wrestling with his elusive meaning, and threw an unseen gesture at the cliff.

"I have not thought of it before. I have been busy, and the years have passed. But here I see—It is a new generation, Cossar, and new emotions and new needs. All this, Cossar—"

Cossar saw now his dim gesture to the things about them.

"All this is Youth."

Cossar made no answers and his irregular footfalls went striding on.

"It isn't *our* youth, Cossar. They are taking things over. They are beginning upon their own emotions, their own experiences, their own way. We have made a new world, and it isn't ours. It isn't even—sympathetic. This great place—"

"I planned it," said Cossar, his face close.

"But now?"

"Ah! I have given it to my sons."

Redwood could feel the loose wave of the arm that he could not see.

"That is it. We are over—or almost over."

"Your message!"

"Yes. And then—"

"We're over"

"Well—?"

"Of course we are out of it, we two old men," said Cossar, with his familiar note of sudden anger. "Of course we are. Obviously. Each man for his own time. And now—it's *their* time beginning. That's all right. Excavator's gang. We do our job and go. See? That is what death is for. We work out all our little brains and all our little emotions, and then this lot begins afresh. Fresh and fresh! Perfectly simple. What's the trouble?"

He paused to guide Redwood to some steps.

"Yes," said Redwood. "but one feels—"

He left his sentence incomplete.

"That is what Death is for." He heard Cossar below him insisting, "How else could the thing be done? That is what Death is for."

III

After devious windings and ascents they came out upon a projecting ledge from which it was possible to see over the greater extent of the Giants' pit, and from which Redwood might make himself heard by the whole of their assembly. The Giants were already gathered below and about him at different levels, to hear the message he had to deliver. The eldest son of Cossar stood on the bank overhead watching the revelations of the searchlights, for they feared a breach of the truce. The workers at the great apparatus in the corner stood out clear in their own light; they were near stripped; they turned their faces towards Redwood, but with a watchful reference ever and again to the castings that they could not leave. He saw these nearer figures with a fluctuating indistinctness, by lights that came and went, and the remoter ones still less distinctly. They came from and vanished again into the depths of great obscurities. For these Giants had no more light than they could help in the pit, that their eyes might be ready to see effectually any attacking force that might spring upon them out of the darknesses around.

Ever and again some chance glare would pick out and display this group or that of tall and powerful forms, the Giants from Sunderland clothed in overlapping metal plates, and the others clad in leather, in woven rope or in woven metal, as their conditions had determined. They sat amidst or rested their hands upon, or stood erect among machines and weapons as mighty as themselves, and all their faces, as they came and went from visible to invisible, had steadfast eyes.

He made an effort to begin and did not do so. Then for a moment his son's face glowed out in a hot insurgence of the fire, his son's face looking up to him, tender as well as strong; and at that he found a voice to reach them all, speaking across a gulf, as it were, to his son.

"I come from Caterham," he said. "He sent me to you, to tell you the terms he offers."

He paused. "They are impossible terms, I know, now that I see you here all together; they are impossible terms, but I brought them to you, because I wanted to see you all—and my son. Once more ... I wanted to see my son..."

"Tell them the terms," said Cossar.

"This is what Caterham offers. He wants you to go apart and leave his world!"
"Where?"

"He does not know. Vaguely somewhere in the world a great region is to be set apart... And you are to make no more of the Food, to have no children of your own, to live in your own way for your own time, and then to end for ever."

He stopped.

"And that is all?"

"That is all."

There followed a great stillness. The darkness that veiled the Giants seemed to look thoughtfully at him.

He felt a touch at his elbow, and Cossar was holding a chair for him —a queer fragment of doll's furniture amidst these piled immensities. He sat down and crossed his legs, and then put one across the knee of the other, and clutched his boot nervously, and felt small and self-conscious and acutely visible and absurdly placed.

Then at the sound of a voice he forgot himself again.

"You have heard, Brothers," said this voice out of the shadows.

And another answered, "We have heard."

"And the answer, Brothers?"

"To Caterham?"

"Is No!"

"And then?"

There was a silence for the space of some seconds.

Then a voice said: "These people are right. After their lights, that is. They have been right in killing all that grew larger than its kind—beast and plant and all manner of great things that arose. They were right in trying to massacre us. They are right now in saying we must not marry our kind. According to their lights they are right. They know—it is time that we also knew—that you cannot have pigmies and giants in one world together. Caterham has said that again and again—clearly—their world or ours."

"We are not half a hundred now," said another, "and they are endless millions."

"So it may be. But the thing is as I have said."

Then another long silence.

"And are we to die then?"

"God forbid!"

"Are they?"

"No."

"But that is what Caterham says! He would have us live out our lives, die one by one, till only one remains, and that one at last would die also, and they would cut down all the giant plants and weeds, kill all the giant under- life, burn out the traces of the Food—make an end to us and to the Food for ever. Then the little pigmy world would be safe. They would go on—safe for ever, living their little pigmy lives, doing pigmy kindnesses and pigmy cruelties each to the other; they might even perhaps attain a sort of pigmy millennium, make an end to war, make an end to over-population, sit down in a world-wide city to practise pigmy arts, worshipping one another till the world begins to freeze..."

In the corner a sheet of iron fell in thunder to the ground.

"Brothers, we know what we mean to do."

In a spluttering of light from the searchlights Redwood saw earnest youthful faces turning to his son.

"It is easy now to make the Food. It would be easy for us to make Food for all the world." "You mean, Brother Redwood," said a voice out of the darkness, "that it is for the little people to eat the Food."

"What else is there to do?"

"We are not half a hundred and they are many millions."

"But we held our own."

"So far."

"If it is God's will, we may still hold our own."

"Yes. But think of the dead!"

Another voice took up the strain. "The dead," it said. "Think of the unborn..."

"Brothers," came the voice of young Redwood, "what can we do but fight them, and if we beat them, make them take the Food? They cannot help but take the Food now. Suppose we were to resign our heritage and do this folly that Caterham suggests! Suppose we could! Suppose we give up this great thing that stirs within us, repudiate this thing our fathers did for us—that *you*, Father, did for us—and pass, when our time has come, into decay and nothingness! What then? Will this little world of theirs be as it was before? They may fight against greatness in us who are the children of men, but can they conquer? Even if they should destroy us every one, what then? Would it save them? No! For greatness is abroad, not only in us, not only in the Food, but in the purpose of all things! It is in the nature of all things; it is part of space and time. To grow and still to grow: from first to last that is Being —that is the law of life. What other law can there be?"

"To help others?"

"To grow. It is still, to grow. Unless we help them to fail..."

"They will fight hard to overcome us," said a voice.

And another, "What of that?"

"They will fight," said young Redwood. "If we refuse these terms, I doubt not they will fight. Indeed I hope they will be open and fight. If after all they offer peace, it will be only the better to catch us unawares. Make no mistake, Brothers; in some way or other they will fight. The war has begun, and we must fight, to the end. Unless we are wise, we may find presently we have lived only to make them better weapons against our children and our kind. This, so far, has been only the dawn of battle. All our lives will be a battle. Some of us will be killed in battle, some of us will be waylaid. There is no easy victory—no victory whatever that is not more than half defeat for us. Be sure of that. What of that? If only we keep a foothold, if only we leave behind us a growing host to fight when we are gone!"

"And to-morrow?"

"We will scatter the Food; we will saturate the world with the Food."

"Suppose they come to terms?"

"Our terms are the Food. It is not as though little and great could live together in any perfection of compromise. It is one thing or the other. What right have parents to say, My child shall have no light but the light I have had, shall grow no greater than the greatness to which I have grown? Do I speak for you, Brothers?"

Assenting murmurs answered him.

"And to the children who will be women as well as to the children who will be men," said a voice from the darkness.

"Even more so—to be mothers of a new race ..." "But for the next generation there must be great and little," said Redwood, with his eyes on his son's face.

"For many generations. And the little will hamper the great and the great press upon the little. So it must needs be, father."

"There will be conflict."

"Endless conflict. Endless misunderstanding. All life is that. Great and little cannot understand one another. But in every child born of man, Father Redwood, lurks some seed of greatness—waiting for the Food."

"Then I am to go to Caterham again and tell him—"

"You will stay with us, Father Redwood. Our answer goes to Caterham at dawn."

"He says that he will fight..."

"So be it," said young Redwood, and his brethren murmured assent.

"*The iron waits*," cried a voice, and the two giants who were working in the corner began a rhythmic hammering that made a mighty music to the scene. The metal glowed out far more brightly than it had done before, and gave Redwood a clearer view of the encampment than had yet come to him. He saw the oblong space to its full extent, with the great engines of warfare ranged ready to hand. Beyond, and at a higher level, the house of the Cossars stood. About him were the young giants, huge and beautiful, glittering in their mail, amidst the preparations for the morrow. The sight of them lifted his heart. They were so easily powerful! They were so tall and gracious! They were so steadfast in their movements! There was his son amongst them, and the first of all giant women, the Princess...

There leapt into his mind the oddest contrast, a memory of Bensington, very bright and little—Bensington with his hand amidst the soft breast feathers of that first great chick, standing in that conventionally furnished room of his, peering over his spectacles dubiously as cousin Jane banged the door...

It had all happened in a yesterday of one-and-twenty years.

Then suddenly a strange doubt took hold of him: that this place and present greatness were but the texture of a dream; that he was dreaming, and would in an instant wake to find himself in his study again, the Giants slaughtered, the Food suppressed, and himself a prisoner locked in. What else indeed was life but that—always to be a prisoner locked in! This was the culmination and end of his dream. He would wake through bloodshed and battle, to find his Food the most foolish of fancies, and his hopes and faith of a greater world to come no more than the coloured film upon a pool of bottomless decay. Littleness invincible!

So strong and deep was this wave of despondency, this suggestion of impending disillusionment, that he started to his feet. He stood and pressed his clenched fists into his eyes, and so for a moment remained, fearing to open them again and see, lest the dream should already have passed away...

The voice of the giant children spoke to one another, an undertone to that clangorous melody of the smiths. His tide of doubt ebbed. He heard the giant voices; he heard their movements about him still. It was real, surely it was real—as real as spiteful acts! More real, for these great things, it may be, are the coming

things, and the littleness, bestiality, and infirmity of men are the things that go. He opened his eyes. "Done," cried one of the two ironworkers, and they flung their hammers down.

A voice sounded above. The son of Cossar, standing on the great embankment, had turned and was now speaking to them all.

"It is not that we would oust the little people from the world," he said, "in order that we, who are no more than one step upwards from their littleness, may hold their world for ever. It is the step we fight for and not ourselves... We are here, Brothers, to what end? To serve the spirit and the purpose that has been breathed into our lives. We fight not for ourselves—for we are but the momentary hands and eyes of the Life of the World. So you, Father Redwood, taught us. Through us and through the little folk the Spirit looks and learns. From us by word and birth and act it must pass—to still greater lives. This earth is no resting place; this earth is no playing place, else indeed we might put our throats to the little people's knife, having no greater right to live than they. And they in their turn might yield to the ants and vermin. We fight not for ourselves but for growth—growth that goes on for ever. To-morrow, whether we live or die, growth will conquer through us. That is the law of the spirit for ever more. To grow according to the will of God! To grow out of these cracks and crannies, out of these shadows and darknesses, into greatness and the light! Greater," he said, speaking with slow deliberation, "greater, my Brothers! And then—still greater. To grow, and again—to grow. To grow at last into the fellowship and understanding of God. Growing... Till the earth is no more than a footstool... Till the spirit shall have driven fear into nothingness, and spread..." He swung his arm heavenward:—"*There!*" His voice ceased. The white glare of one of tho searchlights wheeled about, and for a moment fell upon him, standing out gigantic with hand upraised against the sky.

For one instant he shone, looking up fearlessly into the starry deeps, mail-clad, young and strong, resolute and still. Then the light had passed, and he was no more than a great black outline against the starry sky—a great black outline that threatened with one mighty gesture the firmament of heaven and all its multitude of stars.

IN THE DAYS OF THE COMET

Serialised in *The Daily Chronicle*, 1905-1906
First book edition: Macmillan & Co., Ltd., London, 1906

"The World's Great Age begins anew,
The Golden Years return,
The Earth doth like a Snake renew
Her Winter Skin outworn:
Heaven smiles, and Faiths and Empires gleam
Like Wrecks of a Dissolving Dream."

PROLOGUE - THE MAN WHO WROTE IN THE TOWER

I saw a gray-haired man, a figure of hale age, sitting at a desk and writing.

He seemed to be in a room in a tower, very high, so that through the tall window on his left one perceived only distances, a remote horizon of sea, a headland and that vague haze and glitter in the sunset that many miles away marks a city. All the appointments of this room were orderly and beautiful, and in some subtle quality, in this small difference and that, new to me and strange. They were in no fashion I could name, and the simple costume the man wore suggested neither period nor country. It might, I thought, be the Happy Future, or Utopia, or the Land of Simple Dreams; an errant mote of memory, Henry James's phrase and story of "The Great Good Place," twinkled across my mind, and passed and left no light.

The man I saw wrote with a thing like a fountain pen, a modern touch that prohibited any historical retrospection, and as he finished each sheet, writing in an easy flowing hand, he added it to a growing pile upon a graceful little table under the window. His last done sheets lay loose, partly covering others that were clipped together into fascicles.

Clearly he was unaware of my presence, and I stood waiting until his pen should come to a pause. Old as he certainly was he wrote with a steady hand...

I discovered that a concave speculum hung slantingly high over his head; a movement in this caught my attention sharply, and I looked up to see, distorted and made fantastic but bright and beautifully colored, the magnified, reflected, evasive rendering of a palace, of a terrace, of the vista of a great roadway with many people, people exaggerated, impossible-looking because of the curvature of the mirror, going to and fro. I turned my head quickly that I might see more clearly through the window behind me, but it was too high for me to survey this nearer scene directly, and after a momentary pause I came back to that distorting mirror again.

But now the writer was leaning back in his chair. He put down his pen and sighed the half resentful sigh—"ah! you, work, you! how you gratify and tire me!"—of a man who has been writing to his satisfaction.

"What is this place," I asked, "and who are you?"

He looked around with the quick movement of surprise.

"What is this place?" I repeated, "and where am I?"

He regarded me steadfastly for a moment under his wrinkled brows, and then his expression softened to a smile. He pointed to a chair beside the table. "I am writing," he said.

"About this?"

"About the change."

I sat down. It was a very comfortable chair, and well placed under the light.

"If you would like to read—" he said.

I indicated the manuscript. "This explains?" I asked.

"That explains," he answered.

He drew a fresh sheet of paper toward him as he looked at me.

I glanced from him about his apartment and back to the little table. A fascicle marked very distinctly "1" caught my attention, and I took it up. I smiled in his friendly eyes. "Very well," said I, suddenly at my ease, and he nodded and went on writing. And in a mood between confidence and curiosity, I began to read.

This is the story that happy, active-looking old man in that pleasant place had written.

BOOK THE FIRST - THE COMET

CHAPTER THE FIRST - DUST IN THE SHADOWS

§ 1

I have set myself to write the story of the Great Change, so far as it has affected my own life and the lives of one or two people closely connected with me, primarily to please myself.

Long ago in my crude unhappy youth, I conceived the desire of writing a book. To scribble secretly and dream of authorship was one of my chief alleviations, and I read with a sympathetic envy every scrap I could get about the world of literature and the lives of literary people. It is something, even amidst this present happiness, to find leisure and opportunity to take up and partially realize these old and hopeless dreams. But that alone, in a world where so much of vivid and increasing interest presents itself to be done, even by an old man, would not, I think, suffice to set me at this desk. I find some such recapitulation of my past as this will involve, is becoming necessary to my own secure mental continuity. The passage of years brings a man at last to retrospection; at seventy-two one's youth is far more important than it was at forty. And I am out of touch with my youth. The old life seems so cut off from the new, so alien and so unreasonable, that at times I find it bordering upon the incredible. The data have gone, the buildings and places. I stopped dead the other afternoon in my walk across the moor, where once the dismal outskirts of Swathinglea straggled toward Leet, and asked, "Was it here indeed that I crouched among the weeds and refuse and broken crockery and loaded my revolver ready for murder? Did ever such a thing happen in my life? Was such a mood and thought and intention ever possible to me? Rather, has not some queer nightmare spirit out of dreamland slipped a pseudo-memory into the records of my vanished life?" There must be many alive still who have the same perplexities. And I think too that those who are now growing up to take our places in the great enterprise of mankind, will need many such narratives as mine for even the most partial conception of the old world of shadows that came before our day. It chances too that my case is fairly typical of the Change; I was caught midway in a gust of passion; and a curious accident put me for a time in the very nucleus of the new order.

My memory takes me back across the interval of fifty years to a little ill-lit room with a sash window open to a starry sky, and instantly there returns to me the characteristic smell of that room, the penetrating odor of an ill-trimmed lamp, burning cheap paraffin. Lighting by electricity had then been perfected for fifteen years, but still the larger portion of the world used these lamps. All this first scene will go, in my mind at least, to that olfactory accompaniment. That was the evening smell of the room. By day it had a more subtle aroma, a closeness, a peculiar sort of faint pungency that I associate—I know not why—with dust.

Let me describe this room to you in detail. It was perhaps eight feet by seven in area and rather higher than either of these dimensions; the ceiling was of plaster, cracked and bulging in places, gray with the soot of the lamp, and in one place discolored by a system of yellow and olive-green stains caused by the percolation of damp from above. The walls were covered with dun-colored paper, upon which had been printed in oblique reiteration a crimson shape, something of the nature of a curly ostrich feather, or an acanthus flower, that had in its less faded moments a sort of dingy gaiety. There were several big plaster-rimmed wounds in this, caused by Parload's ineffectual attempts to get nails into the wall, whereby there might hang pictures. One nail had hit between two bricks and got home, and from this depended, sustained a little insecurely by frayed and knotted blind-cord, Parload's hanging bookshelves, planks painted over with a treacly blue enamel and further decorated by a fringe of pinked American cloth insecurely fixed by tacks. Below this was a little table that behaved with a mulish vindictiveness to any knee that was thrust beneath it suddenly; it was covered with a cloth whose pattern of red and black had been rendered less monotonous by the accidents of Parload's versatile ink bottle, and on it, leit motif of the whole, stood and stank the lamp. This lamp, you must understand, was of some whitish translucent substance that was neither china nor glass, it had a shade of the same substance, a shade that did not protect the eyes of a reader in any measure, and it seemed admirably adapted to bring into pitiless prominence the fact that, after the lamp's trimming, dust and paraffin had been smeared over its exterior with a reckless generosity.

The uneven floor boards of this apartment were covered with scratched enamel of chocolate hue, on which a small island of frayed carpet dimly blossomed in the dust and shadows.

There was a very small grate, made of cast-iron in one piece and painted buff, and a still smaller misfit of a cast-iron fender that confessed the gray stone of the hearth. No fire was laid, only a few scraps of torn paper and the bowl of a broken corn-cob pipe were visible behind the bars, and in the corner and rather thrust away was an angular japanned coal-box with a damaged hinge. It was the custom in those days to warm every room separately from a separate fireplace, more prolific of dirt than heat, and the rickety sash window, the small chimney, and the loose-fitting door were expected to organize the ventilation of the room among themselves without any further direction.

Parload's truckle bed hid its gray sheets beneath an old patchwork counterpane on one side of the room, and veiled his boxes and suchlike oddments, and invad-

ing the two corners of the window were an old whatnot and the washhandstand, on which were distributed the simple appliances of his toilet.

This washhandstand had been made of deal by some one with an excess of turnery appliances in a hurry, who had tried to distract attention from the rough economies of his workmanship by an arresting ornamentation of blobs and bulbs upon the joints and legs. Apparently the piece had then been placed in the hands of some person of infinite leisure equipped with a pot of ocherous paint, varnish, and a set of flexible combs. This person had first painted the article, then, I fancy, smeared it with varnish, and then sat down to work with the combs to streak and comb the varnish into a weird imitation of the grain of some nightmare timber. The washhandstand so made had evidently had a prolonged career of violent use, had been chipped, kicked, splintered, punched, stained, scorched, hammered, dessicated, damped, and defiled, had met indeed with almost every possible adventure except a conflagration or a scrubbing, until at last it had come to this high refuge of Parload's attic to sustain the simple requirements of Parload's personal cleanliness. There were, in chief, a basin and a jug of water and a slop-pail of tin, and, further, a piece of yellow soap in a tray, a tooth-brush, a rat-tailed shaving brush, one huckaback towel, and one or two other minor articles. In those days only very prosperous people had more than such an equipage, and it is to be remarked that every drop of water Parload used had to be carried by an unfortunate servant girl,—the "slavey," Parload called her—up from the basement to the top of the house and subsequently down again. Already we begin to forget how modern an invention is personal cleanliness. It is a fact that Parload had never stripped for a swim in his life; never had a simultaneous bath all over his body since his childhood. Not one in fifty of us did in the days of which I am telling you.

A chest, also singularly grained and streaked, of two large and two small drawers, held Parload's reserve of garments, and pegs on the door carried his two hats and completed this inventory of a "bed-sitting-room" as I knew it before the Change. But I had forgotten—there was also a chair with a "squab" that apologized inadequately for the defects of its cane seat. I forgot that for the moment because I was sitting on the chair on the occasion that best begins this story.

I have described Parload's room with such particularity because it will help you to understand the key in which my earlier chapters are written, but you must not imagine that this singular equipment or the smell of the lamp engaged my attention at that time to the slightest degree. I took all this grimy unpleasantness as if it were the most natural and proper setting for existence imaginable. It was the world as I knew it. My mind was entirely occupied then by graver and intenser matters, and it is only now in the distant retrospect that I see these details of environment as being remarkable, as significant, as indeed obviously the outward visible manifestations of the old world disorder in our hearts.

§ 2

Parload stood at the open window, opera-glass in hand, and sought and found and was uncertain about and lost again, the new comet.

I thought the comet no more than a nuisance then because I wanted to talk of other matters. But Parload was full of it. My head was hot, I was feverish with interlacing annoyances and bitterness, I wanted to open my heart to him —at least I wanted to relieve my heart by some romantic rendering of my troubles—and I gave but little heed to the things he told me. It was the first time I had heard of this new speck among the countless specks of heaven, and I did not care if I never heard of the thing again.

We were two youths much of an age together, Parload was two and twenty, and eight months older than I. He was—I think his proper definition was "engrossing clerk" to a little solicitor in Overcastle, while I was third in the office staff of Rawdon's pot-bank in Clayton. We had met first in the "Parliament" of the Young Men's Christian Association of Swathinglea; we had found we attended simultaneous classes in Overcastle, he in science and I in shorthand, and had started a practice of walking home together, and so our friendship came into being. (Swathinglea, Clayton, and Overcastle were contiguous towns, I should mention, in the great industrial area of the Midlands.) We had shared each other's secret of religious doubt, we had confided to one another a common interest in Socialism, he had come twice to supper at my mother's on a Sunday night, and I was free of his apartment. He was then a tall, flaxen-haired, gawky youth, with a disproportionate development of neck and wrist, and capable of vast enthusiasm; he gave two evenings a week to the evening classes of the organized science school in Overcastle, physiography was his favorite "subject," and through this insidious opening of his mind the wonder of outer space had come to take possession of his soul. He had commandeered an old opera-glass from his uncle who farmed at Leet over the moors, he had bought a cheap paper planisphere and Whitaker's Almanac, and for a time day and moonlight were mere blank interruptions to the one satisfactory reality in his life—star-gazing. It was the deeps that had seized him, the immensities, and the mysterious possibilities that might float unlit in that unplumbed abyss. With infinite labor and the help of a very precise article in The Heavens, a little monthly magazine that catered for those who were under this obsession, he had at last got his opera-glass upon the new visitor to our system from outer space. He gazed in a sort of rapture upon that quivering little smudge of light among the shining pin- points—and gazed. My troubles had to wait for him.

"Wonderful," he sighed, and then as though his first emphasis did not satisfy him, "wonderful!"

He turned to me. "Wouldn't you like to see?"

I had to look, and then I had to listen, how that this scarce-visible intruder was to be, was presently to be, one of the largest comets this world has ever seen, how that its course must bring it within at most—so many score of millions of miles from the earth, a mere step, Parload seemed to think that; how that the spectro-

scope was already sounding its chemical secrets, perplexed by the unprecedented band in the green, how it was even now being photographed in the very act of unwinding—in an unusual direction —a sunward tail (which presently it wound up again), and all the while in a sort of undertow I was thinking first of Nettie Stuart and the letter she had just written me, and then of old Rawdon's detestable face as I had seen it that afternoon. Now I planned answers to Nettie and now belated repartees to my employer, and then again "Nettie" was blazing all across the background of my thoughts...

Nettie Stuart was daughter of the head gardener of the rich Mr. Verrall's widow, and she and I had kissed and become sweethearts before we were eighteen years old. My mother and hers were second cousins and old schoolfellows, and though my mother had been widowed untimely by a train accident, and had been reduced to letting lodgings (she was the Clayton curate's landlady), a position esteemed much lower than that of Mrs. Stuart, a kindly custom of occasional visits to the gardener's cottage at Checkshill Towers still kept the friends in touch. Commonly I went with her. And I remember it was in the dusk of one bright evening in July, one of those long golden evenings that do not so much give way to night as admit at last, upon courtesy, the moon and a choice retinue of stars, that Nettie and I, at the pond of goldfish where the yew- bordered walks converged, made our shy beginners' vow. I remember still—something will always stir in me at that memory—the tremulous emotion of that adventure. Nettie was dressed in white, her hair went off in waves of soft darkness from above her dark shining eyes; there was a little necklace of pearls about her sweetly modeled neck, and a little coin of gold that nestled in her throat. I kissed her half-reluctant lips, and for three years of my life thereafter—nay! I almost think for all the rest of her life and mine —I could have died for her sake.

You must understand—and every year it becomes increasingly difficult to understand—how entirely different the world was then from what it is now. It was a dark world; it was full of preventable disorder, preventable diseases, and preventable pain, of harshness and stupid unpremeditated cruelties; but yet, it may be even by virtue of the general darkness, there were moments of a rare and evanescent beauty that seem no longer possible in my experience. The great Change has come for ever more, happiness and beauty are our atmosphere, there is peace on earth and good will to all men. None would dare to dream of returning to the sorrows of the former time, and yet that misery was pierced, ever and again its gray curtain was stabbed through and through by joys of an intensity, by perceptions of a keenness that it seems to me are now altogether gone out of life. Is it the Change, I wonder, that has robbed life of its extremes, or is it perhaps only this, that youth has left me—even the strength of middle years leaves me now—and taken its despairs and raptures, leaving me judgment, perhaps, sympathy, memories?

I cannot tell. One would need to be young now and to have been young then as well, to decide that impossible problem.

Perhaps a cool observer even in the old days would have found little beauty in our grouping. I have our two photographs at hand in this bureau as I write, and they show me a gawky youth in ill-fitting ready-made clothing, and Nettie— Indeed Nettie is badly dressed, and her attitude is more than a little stiff; but I can see her through the picture, and her living brightness and something of that mystery of charm she had for me, comes back again to my mind. Her face has triumphed over the photographer—or I would long ago have cast this picture away.

The reality of beauty yields itself to no words. I wish that I had the sister art and could draw in my margin something that escapes description. There was a sort of gravity in her eyes. There was something, a matter of the minutest difference, about her upper lip so that her mouth closed sweetly and broke very sweetly to a smile. That grave, sweet smile!

After we had kissed and decided not to tell our parents for awhile of the irrevocable choice we had made, the time came for us to part, shyly and before others, and I and my mother went off back across the moonlit park—the bracken thickets rustling with startled deer—to the railway station at Checkshill and so to our dingy basement in Clayton, and I saw no more of Nettie —except that I saw her in my thoughts—for nearly a year. But at our next meeting it was decided that we must correspond, and this we did with much elaboration of secrecy, for Nettie would have no one at home, not even her only sister, know of her attachment. So I had to send my precious documents sealed and under cover by way of a confidential schoolfellow of hers who lived near London... I could write that address down now, though house and street and suburb have gone beyond any man's tracing.

Our correspondence began our estrangement, because for the first time we came into more than sensuous contact and our minds sought expression.

Now you must understand that the world of thought in those days was in the strangest condition, it was choked with obsolete inadequate formulae, it was tortuous to a maze-like degree with secondary contrivances and adaptations, suppressions, conventions, and subterfuges. Base immediacies fouled the truth on every man's lips. I was brought up by my mother in a quaint old-fashioned narrow faith in certain religious formulae, certain rules of conduct, certain conceptions of social and political order, that had no more relevance to the realities and needs of everyday contemporary life than if they were clean linen that had been put away with lavender in a drawer. Indeed, her religion did actually smell of lavender; on Sundays she put away all the things of reality, the garments and even the furnishings of everyday, hid her hands, that were gnarled and sometimes chapped with scrubbing, in black, carefully mended gloves, assumed her old black silk dress and bonnet and took me, unnaturally clean and sweet also, to church. There we sang and bowed and heard sonorous prayers and joined in sonorous responses, and rose with a congregational sigh refreshed and relieved when the doxology, with its opening "Now to God the Father, God the Son," bowed out the tame, brief sermon. There was a hell in that religion of my mother's, a red-haired hell of curly flames that had once been very terrible; there was a devil, who was also ex officio

the British King's enemy, and much denunciation of the wicked lusts of the flesh; we were expected to believe that most of our poor unhappy world was to atone for its muddle and trouble here by suffering exquisite torments for ever after, world without end, Amen. But indeed those curly flames looked rather jolly. The whole thing had been mellowed and faded into a gentle unreality long before my time; if it had much terror even in my childhood I have forgotten it, it was not so terrible as the giant who was killed by the Beanstalk, and I see it all now as a setting for my poor old mother's worn and grimy face, and almost lovingly as a part of her. And Mr. Gabbitas, our plump little lodger, strangely transformed in his vestments and lifting his voice manfully to the quality of those Elizabethan prayers, seemed, I think, to give her a special and peculiar interest with God. She radiated her own tremulous gentleness upon Him, and redeemed Him from all the implications of vindictive theologians; she was in truth, had I but perceived it, the effectual answer to all she would have taught me.

So I see it now, but there is something harsh in the earnest intensity of youth, and having at first taken all these things quite seriously, the fiery hell and God's vindictiveness at any neglect, as though they were as much a matter of fact as Bladden's iron-works and Rawdon's pot-bank, I presently with an equal seriousness flung them out of my mind again.

Mr. Gabbitas, you see, did sometimes, as the phrase went, "take notice" of me, he had induced me to go on reading after I left school, and with the best intentions in the world and to anticipate the poison of the times, he had lent me Burble's "Scepticism Answered," and drawn my attention to the library of the Institute in Clayton.

The excellent Burble was a great shock to me. It seemed clear from his answers to the sceptic that the case for doctrinal orthodoxy and all that faded and by no means awful hereafter, which I had hitherto accepted as I accepted the sun, was an extremely poor one, and to hammer home that idea the first book I got from the Institute happened to be an American edition of the collected works of Shelley, his gassy prose as well as his atmospheric verse. I was soon ripe for blatant unbelief. And at the Young Men's Christian Association I presently made the acquaintance of Parload, who told me, under promises of the most sinister secrecy, that he was "a Socialist out and out." He lent me several copies of a periodical with the clamant title of The Clarion, which was just taking up a crusade against the accepted religion. The adolescent years of any fairly intelligent youth lie open, and will always lie healthily open, to the contagion of philosophical doubts, of scorns and new ideas, and I will confess I had the fever of that phase badly. Doubt, I say, but it was not so much doubt—which is a complex thing—as startled emphatic denial. "Have I believed THIS!" And I was also, you must remember, just beginning love-letters to Nettie.

We live now in these days, when the Great Change has been in most things accomplished, in a time when every one is being educated to a sort of intellectual gentleness, a gentleness that abates nothing from our vigor, and it is hard to understand the stifled and struggling manner in which my generation of common

young men did its thinking. To think at all about certain questions was an act of rebellion that set one oscillating between the furtive and the defiant. People begin to find Shelley—for all his melody —noisy and ill conditioned now because his Anarchs have vanished, yet there was a time when novel thought HAD to go to that tune of breaking glass. It becomes a little difficult to imagine the yeasty state of mind, the disposition to shout and say, "Yah!" at constituted authority, to sustain a persistent note of provocation such as we raw youngsters displayed. I began to read with avidity such writing as Carlyle, Browning, and Heine have left for the perplexity of posterity, and not only to read and admire but to imitate. My letters to Nettie, after one or two genuinely intended displays of perfervid tenderness, broke out toward theology, sociology, and the cosmos in turgid and startling expressions. No doubt they puzzled her extremely.

I retain the keenest sympathy and something inexplicably near to envy for my own departed youth, but I should find it difficult to maintain my case against any one who would condemn me altogether as having been a very silly, posturing, emotional hobbledehoy indeed and quite like my faded photograph. And when I try to recall what exactly must have been the quality and tenor of my more sustained efforts to write memorably to my sweetheart, I confess I shiver... Yet I wish they were not all destroyed.

Her letters to me were simple enough, written in a roundish, unformed hand and badly phrased. Her first two or three showed a shy pleasure in the use of the word "dear," and I remember being first puzzled and then, when I understood, delighted, because she had written "Willie ASTHORE" under my name. "Asthore," I gathered, meant "darling." But when the evidences of my fermentation began, her answers were less happy.

I will not weary you with the story of how we quarreled in our silly youthful way, and how I went the next Sunday, all uninvited, to Checkshill, and made it worse, and how afterward I wrote a letter that she thought was "lovely," and mended the matter. Nor will I tell of all our subsequent fluctuations of misunderstanding. Always I was the offender and the final penitent until this last trouble that was now beginning; and in between we had some tender near moments, and I loved her very greatly. There was this misfortune in the business, that in the darkness, and alone, I thought with great intensity of her, of her eyes, of her touch, of her sweet and delightful presence, but when I sat down to write I thought of Shelley and Burns and myself, and other such irrelevant matters. When one is in love, in this fermenting way, it is harder to make love than it is when one does not love at all. And as for Nettie, she loved, I know, not me but those gentle mysteries. It was not my voice should rouse her dreams to passion... So our letters continued to jar. Then suddenly she wrote me one doubting whether she could ever care for any one who was a Socialist and did not believe in Church, and then hard upon it came another note with unexpected novelties of phrasing. She thought we were not suited to each other, we differed so in tastes and ideas, she had long thought of releasing me from our engagement. In fact, though I really did not apprehend it fully at the first shock, I was dismissed. Her letter had reached me when I came

home after old Rawdon's none too civil refusal to raise my wages. On this particular evening of which I write, therefore, I was in a state of feverish adjustment to two new and amazing, two nearly overwhelming facts, that I was neither indispensable to Nettie nor at Rawdon's. And to talk of comets!

Where did I stand?

I had grown so accustomed to think of Nettie as inseparably mine—the whole tradition of "true love" pointed me to that—that for her to face about with these precise small phrases toward abandonment, after we had kissed and whispered and come so close in the little adventurous familiarities of the young, shocked me profoundly. I! I! And Rawdon didn't find me indispensable either. I felt I was suddenly repudiated by the universe and threatened with effacement, that in some positive and emphatic way I must at once assert myself. There was no balm in the religion I had learnt, or in the irreligion I had adopted, for wounded self-love.

Should I fling up Rawdon's place at once and then in some extraordinary, swift manner make the fortune of Frobisher's adjacent and closely competitive pot-bank?

The first part of that program, at any rate, would be easy of accomplishment, to go to Rawdon and say, "You will hear from me again," but for the rest, Frobisher might fail me. That, however, was a secondary issue. The predominant affair was with Nettie. I found my mind thick-shot with flying fragments of rhetoric that might be of service in the letter I would write her. Scorn, irony, tenderness—what was it to be?

"Brother!" said Parload, suddenly.

"What?" said I.

"They're firing up at Bladden's iron-works, and the smoke comes right across my bit of sky."

The interruption came just as I was ripe to discharge my thoughts upon him.

"Parload," said I, "very likely I shall have to leave all this. Old Rawdon won't give me a rise in my wages, and after having asked I don't think I can stand going on upon the old terms anymore. See? So I may have to clear out of Clayton for good and all."

§ 3

That made Parload put down the opera-glass and look at me.

"It's a bad time to change just now," he said after a little pause.

Rawdon had said as much, in a less agreeable tone.

But with Parload I felt always a disposition to the heroic note. "I'm tired," I said, "of humdrum drudgery for other men. One may as well starve one's body out of a place as to starve one's soul in one."

"I don't know about that altogether," began Parload, slowly...

And with that we began one of our interminable conversations, one of those long, wandering, intensely generalizing, diffusely personal talks that will be dear to the hearts of intelligent youths until the world comes to an end. The Change has not abolished that, anyhow.

It would be an incredible feat of memory for me now to recall all that meandering haze of words, indeed I recall scarcely any of it, though its circumstances and atmosphere stand out, a sharp, clear picture in my mind. I posed after my manner and behaved very foolishly no doubt, a wounded, smarting egotist, and Parload played his part of the philosopher preoccupied with the deeps.

We were presently abroad, walking through the warm summer's night and talking all the more freely for that. But one thing that I said I can remember. "I wish at times," said I, with a gesture at the heavens, "that comet of yours or some such thing would indeed strike this world—and wipe us all away, strikes, wars, tumults, loves, jealousies, and all the wretchedness of life!"

"Ah!" said Parload, and the thought seemed to hang about him.

"It could only add to the miseries of life," he said irrelevantly, when presently I was discoursing of other things.

"What would?"

"Collision with a comet. It would only throw things back. It would only make what was left of life more savage than it is at present."

"But why should ANYTHING be left of life?" said I...

That was our style, you know, and meanwhile we walked together up the narrow street outside his lodging, up the stepway and the lanes toward Clayton Crest and the high road.

But my memories carry me back so effectually to those days before the Change that I forget that now all these places have been altered beyond recognition, that the narrow street and the stepway and the view from Clayton Crest, and indeed all the world in which I was born and bred and made, has vanished clean away, out of space and out of time, and wellnigh out of the imagination of all those who are younger by a generation than I. You cannot see, as I can see, the dark empty way between the mean houses, the dark empty way lit by a bleary gas-lamp at the corner, you cannot feel the hard checkered pavement under your boots, you cannot mark the dimly lit windows here and there, and the shadows upon the ugly and often patched and crooked blinds of the people cooped within. Nor can you presently pass the beerhouse with its brighter gas and its queer, screening windows, nor get a whiff of foul air and foul language from its door, nor see the crumpled furtive figure—some rascal child—that slinks past us down the steps.

We crossed the longer street, up which a clumsy steam tram, vomiting smoke and sparks, made its clangorous way, and adown which one saw the greasy brilliance of shop fronts and the naphtha flares of hawkers' barrows dripping fire into the night. A hazy movement of people swayed along that road, and we heard the voice of an itinerant preacher from a waste place between the houses. You cannot see these things as I can see them, nor can you figure—unless you know the pictures that great artist Hyde has left the world—the effect of the great hoarding by which we passed, lit below by a gas-lamp and towering up to a sudden sharp black edge against the pallid sky.

Those hoardings! They were the brightest colored things in all that vanished world. Upon them, in successive layers of paste and paper, all the rough enterprises of that time joined in chromatic discord; pill vendors and preachers, theaters and charities, marvelous soaps and astonishing pickles, typewriting machines and sewing machines, mingled in a sort of visualized clamor. And passing that there was a muddy lane of cinders, a lane without a light, that used its many puddles to borrow a star or so from the sky. We splashed along unheeding as we talked.

Then across the allotments, a wilderness of cabbages and evil-looking sheds, past a gaunt abandoned factory, and so to the high road. The high road ascended in a curve past a few houses and a beerhouse or so, and round until all the valley in which four industrial towns lay crowded and confluent was overlooked.

I will admit that with the twilight there came a spell of weird magnificence over all that land and brooded on it until dawn. The horrible meanness of its details was veiled, the hutches that were homes, the bristling multitudes of chimneys, the ugly patches of unwilling vegetation amidst the makeshift fences of barrel-stave and wire. The rusty scars that framed the opposite ridges where the iron ore was taken and the barren mountains of slag from the blast furnaces were veiled; the reek and boiling smoke and dust from foundry, pot-bank, and furnace, transfigured and assimilated by the night. The dust-laden atmosphere that was gray oppression through the day became at sundown a mystery of deep translucent colors, of blues and purples, of somber and vivid reds, of strange bright clearnesses of green and yellow athwart the darkling sky. Each upstart furnace, when its monarch sun had gone, crowned itself with flames, the dark cinder heaps began to glow with quivering fires, and each pot-bank squatted rebellious in a volcanic coronet of light. The empire of the day broke into a thousand feudal baronies of burning coal. The minor streets across the valley picked themselves out with gas-lamps of faint yellow, that brightened and mingled at all the principal squares and crossings with the greenish pallor of incandescent mantles and the high cold glare of the electric arc. The interlacing railways lifted bright signal-boxes over their intersections, and signal stars of red and green in rectangular constellations. The trains became articulated black serpents breathing fire.

Moreover, high overhead, like a thing put out of reach and near forgotten, Parload had rediscovered a realm that was ruled by neither sun nor furnace, the universe of stars.

This was the scene of many a talk we two had held together. And if in the daytime we went right over the crest and looked westward there was farmland, there were parks and great mansions, the spire of a distant cathedral, and sometimes when the weather was near raining, the crests of remote mountains hung clearly in the sky. Beyond the range of sight indeed, out beyond, there was Checkshill; I felt it there always, and in the darkness more than I did by day. Checkshill, and Nettie!

And to us two youngsters as we walked along the cinder path beside the rutted road and argued out our perplexities, it seemed that this ridge gave us compendiously a view of our whole world.

There on the one hand in a crowded darkness, about the ugly factories and work-places, the workers herded together, ill clothed, ill nourished, ill taught, badly and expensively served at every occasion in life, uncertain even of their insufficient livelihood from day to day, the chapels and churches and public-houses swelling up amidst their wretched homes like saprophytes amidst a general corruption, and on the other, in space, freedom, and dignity, scarce heeding the few cottages, as overcrowded as they were picturesque, in which the laborers festered, lived the landlords and masters who owned pot-banks and forge and farm and mine. Far away, distant, beautiful, irrelevant, from out of a little cluster of secondhand bookshops, ecclesiastical residences, and the inns and incidentals of a decaying market town, the cathedral of Lowchester pointed a beautiful, unemphatic spire to vague incredible skies. So it seemed to us that the whole world was planned in those youthful first impressions.

We saw everything simple, as young men will. We had our angry, confident solutions, and whosoever would criticize them was a friend of the robbers. It was a clear case of robbery, we held, visibly so; there in those great houses lurked the Landlord and the Capitalist, with his scoundrel the Lawyer, with his cheat the Priest, and we others were all the victims of their deliberate villainies. No doubt they winked and chuckled over their rare wines, amidst their dazzling, wickedly dressed women, and plotted further grinding for the faces of the poor. And amidst all the squalor on the other hand, amidst brutalities, ignorance, and drunkenness, suffered multitudinously their blameless victim, the Working Man. And we, almost at the first glance, had found all this out, it had merely to be asserted now with sufficient rhetoric and vehemence to change the face of the whole world. The Working Man would arise—in the form of a Labor Party, and with young men like Parload and myself to represent him—and come to his own, and then—?

Then the robbers would get it hot, and everything would be extremely satisfactory.

Unless my memory plays me strange tricks that does no injustice to the creed of thought and action that Parload and I held as the final result of human wisdom. We believed it with heat, and rejected with heat the most obvious qualification of its harshness. At times in our great talks we were full of heady hopes for the near triumph of our doctrine, more often our mood was hot resentment at the wickedness and stupidity that delayed so plain and simple a reconstruction of the order of the world. Then we grew malignant, and thought of barricades and significant violence. I was very bitter, I know, upon this night of which I am now particularly telling, and the only face upon the hydra of Capitalism and Monopoly that I could see at all clearly, smiled exactly as old Rawdon had smiled when he refused to give me more than a paltry twenty shillings a week.

I wanted intensely to salve my self-respect by some revenge upon him, and I felt that if that could be done by slaying the hydra, I might drag its carcass to the

feet of Nettie, and settle my other trouble as well. "What do you think of me NOW, Nettie?"

That at any rate comes near enough to the quality of my thinking, then, for you to imagine how I gesticulated and spouted to Parload that night. You figure us as little black figures, unprepossessing in the outline, set in the midst of that desolating night of flaming industrialism, and my little voice with a rhetorical twang protesting, denouncing...

You will consider those notions of my youth poor silly violent stuff; particularly if you are of the younger generation born since the Change you will be of that opinion. Nowadays the whole world thinks clearly, thinks with deliberation, pellucid certainties, you find it impossible to imagine how any other thinking could have been possible. Let me tell you then how you can bring yourself to something like the condition of our former state. In the first place you must get yourself out of health by unwise drinking and eating, and out of condition by neglecting your exercise, then you must contrive to be worried very much and made very anxious and uncomfortable, and then you must work very hard for four or five days and for long hours every day at something too petty to be interesting, too complex to be mechanical, and without any personal significance to you whatever. This done, get straightway into a room that is not ventilated at all, and that is already full of foul air, and there set yourself to think out some very complicated problem. In a very little while you will find yourself in a state of intellectual muddle, annoyed, impatient, snatching at the obvious presently in choosing and rejecting conclusions haphazard. Try to play chess under such conditions and you will play stupidly and lose your temper. Try to do anything that taxes the brain or temper and you will fail.

Now, the whole world before the Change was as sick and feverish as that, it was worried and overworked and perplexed by problems that would not get stated simply, that changed and evaded solution, it was in an atmosphere that had corrupted and thickened past breathing; there was no thorough cool thinking in the world at all. There was nothing in the mind of the world anywhere but half-truths, hasty assumptions, hallucinations, and emotions. Nothing...

I know it seems incredible, that already some of the younger men are beginning to doubt the greatness of the Change our world has undergone, but read—read the newspapers of that time. Every age becomes mitigated and a little ennobled in our minds as it recedes into the past. It is the part of those who like myself have stories of that time to tell, to supply, by a scrupulous spiritual realism, some antidote to that glamour.

§ 4

Always with Parload I was chief talker.

I can look back upon myself with, I believe, an almost perfect detachment, things have so changed that indeed now I am another being, with scarce anything in common with that boastful foolish youngster whose troubles I recall. I see him vulgarly theatrical, egotistical, insincere, indeed I do not like him save with that

instinctive material sympathy that is the fruit of incessant intimacy. Because he was myself I may be able to feel and write understandingly about motives that will put him out of sympathy with nearly every reader, but why should I palliate or defend his quality?

Always, I say, I did the talking, and it would have amazed me beyond measure if any one had told me that mine was not the greater intelligence in these wordy encounters. Parload was a quiet youth, and stiff and restrained in all things, while I had that supreme gift for young men and democracies, the gift of copious expression. Parload I diagnosed in my secret heart as a trifle dull; he posed as pregnant quiet, I thought, and was obsessed by the congenial notion of "scientific caution." I did not remark that while my hands were chiefly useful for gesticulation or holding a pen Parload's hands could do all sorts of things, and I did not think therefore that fibers must run from those fingers to something in his brain. Nor, though I bragged perpetually of my shorthand, of my literature, of my indispensable share in Rawdon's business, did Parload lay stress on the conics and calculus he "mugged" in the organized science school. Parload is a famous man now, a great figure in a great time, his work upon intersecting radiations has broadened the intellectual horizon of mankind for ever, and I, who am at best a hewer of intellectual wood, a drawer of living water, can smile, and he can smile, to think how I patronized and posed and jabbered over him in the darkness of those early days.

That night I was shrill and eloquent beyond measure. Rawdon was, of course, the hub upon which I went round—Rawdon and the Rawdonesque employer and the injustice of "wages slavery" and all the immediate conditions of that industrial blind alley up which it seemed our lives were thrust. But ever and again I glanced at other things. Nettie was always there in the background of my mind, regarding me enigmatically. It was part of my pose to Parload that I had a romantic love-affair somewhere away beyond the sphere of our intercourse, and that note gave a Byronic resonance to many of the nonsensical things I produced for his astonishment.

I will not weary you with too detailed an account of the talk of a foolish youth who was also distressed and unhappy, and whose voice was balm for the humiliations that smarted in his eyes. Indeed, now in many particulars I cannot disentangle this harangue of which I tell from many of the things I may have said in other talks to Parload. For example, I forget if it was then or before or afterwards that, as it were by accident, I let out what might be taken as an admission that I was addicted to drugs.

"You shouldn't do that," said Parload, suddenly. "It won't do to poison your brains with that."

My brains, my eloquence, were to be very important assets to our party in the coming revolution...

But one thing does clearly belong to this particular conversation I am recalling. When I started out it was quite settled in the back of my mind that I must not leave Rawdon's. I simply wanted to abuse my employer to Parload. But I talked

myself quite out of touch with all the cogent reasons there were for sticking to my place, and I got home that night irrevocably committed to a spirited—not to say a defiant—policy with my employer.

"I can't stand Rawdon's much longer," I said to Parload by way of a flourish.

"There's hard times coming," said Parload.

"Next winter."

"Sooner. The Americans have been overproducing, and they mean to dump. The iron trade is going to have convulsions."

"I don't care. Pot-banks are steady."

"With a corner in borax? No. I've heard—"

"What have you heard?"

"Office secrets. But it's no secret there's trouble coming to potters. There's been borrowing and speculation. The masters don't stick to one business as they used to do. I can tell that much. Half the valley may be 'playing' before two months are out." Parload delivered himself of this unusually long speech in his most pithy and weighty manner.

"Playing" was our local euphemism for a time when there was no work and no money for a man, a time of stagnation and dreary hungry loafing day after day. Such interludes seemed in those days a necessary consequence of industrial organization.

"You'd better stick to Rawdon's," said Parload.

"Ugh," said I, affecting a noble disgust.

"There'll be trouble," said Parload.

"Who cares?" said I. "Let there be trouble—the more the better. This system has got to end, sooner or later. These capitalists with their speculation and corners and trusts make things go from bad to worse. Why should I cower in Rawdon's office, like a frightened dog, while hunger walks the streets? Hunger is the master revolutionary. When he comes we ought to turn out and salute him. Anyway, I'M going to do so now."

"That's all very well," began Parload.

"I'm tired of it," I said. "I want to come to grips with all these Rawdons. I think perhaps if I was hungry and savage I could talk to hungry men—"

"There's your mother," said Parload, in his slow judicial way.

That WAS a difficulty.

I got over it by a rhetorical turn. "Why should one sacrifice the future of the world—why should one even sacrifice one's own future—because one's mother is totally destitute of imagination?"

§ 5

It was late when I parted from Parload and came back to my own home.

Our house stood in a highly respectable little square near the Clayton parish church. Mr. Gabbitas, the curate of all work, lodged on our ground floor, and upstairs there was an old lady, Miss Holroyd, who painted flowers on china and maintained her blind sister in an adjacent room; my mother and I lived in the

basement and slept in the attics. The front of the house was veiled by a Virginian creeper that defied the Clayton air and clustered in untidy dependent masses over the wooden porch.

As I came up the steps I had a glimpse of Mr. Gabbitas printing photographs by candle light in his room. It was the chief delight of his little life to spend his holiday abroad in the company of a queer little snap-shot camera, and to return with a great multitude of foggy and sinister negatives that he had made in beautiful and interesting places. These the camera company would develop for him on advantageous terms, and he would spend his evenings the year through in printing from them in order to inflict copies upon his undeserving friends. There was a long frameful of his work in the Clayton National School, for example, inscribed in old English lettering, "Italian Travel Pictures, by the Rev. E. B. Gabbitas." For this it seemed he lived and traveled and had his being. It was his only real joy. By his shaded light I could see his sharp little nose, his little pale eyes behind his glasses, his mouth pursed up with the endeavor of his employment.

"Hireling Liar," I muttered, for was not he also part of the system, part of the scheme of robbery that made wages serfs of Parload and me?—though his share in the proceedings was certainly small.

"Hireling Liar," said I, standing in the darkness, outside even his faint glow of traveled culture...

My mother let me in.

She looked at me, mutely, because she knew there was something wrong and that it was no use for her to ask what.

"Good night, mummy," said I, and kissed her a little roughly, and lit and took my candle and went off at once up the staircase to bed, not looking back at her.

"I've kept some supper for you, dear."

"Don't want any supper."

"But, dearie—"

"Good night, mother," and I went up and slammed my door upon her, blew out my candle, and lay down at once upon my bed, lay there a long time before I got up to undress.

There were times when that dumb beseeching of my mother's face irritated me unspeakably. It did so that night. I felt I had to struggle against it, that I could not exist if I gave way to its pleadings, and it hurt me and divided me to resist it, almost beyond endurance. It was clear to me that I had to think out for myself religious problems, social problems, questions of conduct, questions of expediency, that her poor dear simple beliefs could not help me at all—and she did not understand! Hers was the accepted religion, her only social ideas were blind submissions to the accepted order—to laws, to doctors, to clergymen, lawyers, masters, and all respectable persons in authority over us, and with her to believe was to fear. She knew from a thousand little signs—though still at times I went to church with her —that I was passing out of touch of all these things that ruled her life, into some terrible unknown. From things I said she could infer such clumsy concealments as I made. She felt my socialism, felt my spirit in revolt against the

accepted order, felt the impotent resentments that filled me with bitterness against all she held sacred. Yet, you know, it was not her dear gods she sought to defend so much as me! She seemed always to be wanting to say to me, "Dear, I know it's hard—but revolt is harder. Don't make war on it, dear—don't! Don't do anything to offend it. I'm sure it will hurt you if you do—it will hurt you if you do."

She had been cowed into submission, as so many women of that time had been, by the sheer brutality of the accepted thing. The existing order dominated her into a worship of abject observances. It had bent her, aged her, robbed her of eyesight so that at fifty-five she peered through cheap spectacles at my face, and saw it only dimly, filled her with a habit of anxiety, made her hands—Her poor dear hands! Not in the whole world now could you find a woman with hands so grimy, so needle-worn, so misshapen by toil, so chapped and coarsened, so evilly entreated... At any rate, there is this I can say for myself, that my bitterness against the world and fortune was for her sake as well as for my own.

Yet that night I pushed by her harshly. I answered her curtly, left her concerned and perplexed in the passage, and slammed my door upon her.

And for a long time I lay raging at the hardship and evil of life, at the contempt of Rawdon, and the loveless coolness of Nettie's letter, at my weakness and insignificance, at the things I found intolerable, and the things I could not mend. Over and over went my poor little brain, tired out and unable to stop on my treadmill of troubles. Nettie. Rawdon. My mother. Gabbitas. Nettie...

Suddenly I came upon emotional exhaustion. Some clock was striking midnight. After all, I was young; I had these quick transitions. I remember quite distinctly, I stood up abruptly, undressed very quickly in the dark, and had hardly touched my pillow again before I was asleep.

But how my mother slept that night I do not know.

Oddly enough, I do not blame myself for behaving like this to my mother, though my conscience blames me acutely for my arrogance to Parload. I regret my behavior to my mother before the days of the Change, it is a scar among my memories that will always be a little painful to the end of my days, but I do not see how something of the sort was to be escaped under those former conditions. In that time of muddle and obscurity people were overtaken by needs and toil and hot passions before they had the chance of even a year or so of clear thinking; they settled down to an intense and strenuous application to some partial but immediate duty, and the growth of thought ceased in them. They set and hardened into narrow ways. Few women remained capable of a new idea after five and twenty, few men after thirty-one or two. Discontent with the thing that existed was regarded as immoral, it was certainly an annoyance, and the only protest against it, the only effort against that universal tendency in all human institutions to thicken and clog, to work loosely and badly, to rust and weaken towards catastrophes, came from the young—the crude unmerciful young. It seemed in those days to thoughtful men the harsh law of being—that either we must submit to our elders and be stifled, or disregard them, disobey them, thrust them aside, and

make our little step of progress before we too ossified and became obstructive in our turn.

My pushing past my mother, my irresponsive departure to my own silent meditations, was, I now perceive, a figure of the whole hard relationship between parents and son in those days. There appeared no other way; that perpetually recurring tragedy was, it seemed, part of the very nature of the progress of the world. We did not think then that minds might grow ripe without growing rigid, or children honor their parents and still think for themselves. We were angry and hasty because we stifled in the darkness, in a poisoned and vitiated air. That deliberate animation of the intelligence which is now the universal quality, that vigor with consideration, that judgment with confident enterprise which shine through all our world, were things disintegrated and unknown in the corrupting atmosphere of our former state.

(So the first fascicle ended. I put it aside and looked for the second.

"Well?" said the man who wrote.

"This is fiction?"

"It's my story."

"But you—Amidst this beauty—You are not this ill- conditioned, squalidly bred lad of whom I have been reading?"

He smiled. "There intervenes a certain Change," he said. "Have I not hinted at that?"

I hesitated upon a question, then saw the second fascicle at hand, and picked it up.)

CHAPTER THE SECOND - NETTIE

§ 1

I cannot now remember (the story resumed), what interval separated that evening on which Parload first showed me the comet—I think I only pretended to see it then—and the Sunday afternoon I spent at Checkshill.

Between the two there was time enough for me to give notice and leave Rawdon's, to seek for some other situation very strenuously in vain, to think and say many hard and violent things to my mother and to Parload, and to pass through some phases of very profound wretchedness. There must have been a passionate correspondence with Nettie, but all the froth and fury of that has faded now out of my memory. All I have clear now is that I wrote one magnificent farewell to her, casting her off forever, and that I got in reply a prim little note to say, that even if there was to be an end to everything, that was no excuse for writing such things as I had done, and then I think I wrote again in a vein I considered satirical. To that she did not reply. That interval was at least three weeks, and probably four, because the comet which had been on the first occasion only a dubious speck in the sky, certainly visible only when it was magnified, was now a great white presence, brighter than Jupiter, and casting a shadow on its own account. It was now actively present in the world of human thought, every one was talking about it, every one was looking for its waxing splendor as the sun went down—the papers, the music-halls, the hoardings, echoed it.

Yes; the comet was already dominant before I went over to make everything clear to Nettie. And Parload had spent two hoarded pounds in buying himself a spectroscope, so that he could see for himself, night after night, that mysterious, that stimulating line—the unknown line in the green. How many times I wonder did I look at the smudgy, quivering symbol of the unknown things that were rushing upon us out of the inhuman void, before I rebelled? But at last I could stand it no longer, and I reproached Parload very bitterly for wasting his time in "astronomical dilettantism."

"Here," said I. "We're on the verge of the biggest lock-out in the history of this countryside; here's distress and hunger coming, here's all the capitalistic competitive system like a wound inflamed, and you spend your time gaping at that damned silly streak of nothing in the sky!"

Parload stared at me. "Yes, I do," he said slowly, as though it was a new idea. "Don't I? ... I wonder why."

"*I* want to start meetings of an evening on Howden's Waste."

"You think they'd listen?"

"They'd listen fast enough now."

"They didn't before," said Parload, looking at his pet instrument.

"There was a demonstration of unemployed at Swathinglea on Sunday. They got to stone throwing."

Parload said nothing for a little while and I said several things. He seemed to be considering something.

"But, after all," he said at last, with an awkward movement towards his spectroscope, "that does signify something."

"The comet?"

"Yes."

"What can it signify? You don't want me to believe in astrology. What does it matter what flames in the heavens—when men are starving on earth?"

"It's—it's science."

"Science! What we want now is socialism—not science."

He still seemed reluctant to give up his comet.

"Socialism's all right," he said, "but if that thing up there WAS to hit the earth it might matter."

"Nothing matters but human beings."

"Suppose it killed them all."

"Oh," said I, "that's Rot,"

"I wonder," said Parload, dreadfully divided in his allegiance.

He looked at the comet. He seemed on the verge of repeating his growing information about the nearness of the paths of the earth and comet, and all that might ensue from that. So I cut in with something I had got out of a now forgotten writer called Ruskin, a volcano of beautiful language and nonsensical suggestions, who prevailed very greatly with eloquent excitable young men in those days. Something it was about the insignificance of science and the supreme importance of Life. Parload stood listening, half turned towards the sky with the tips of his fingers on his spectroscope. He seemed to come to a sudden decision.

"No. I don't agree with you, Leadford," he said. "You don't understand about science."

Parload rarely argued with that bluntness of opposition. I was so used to entire possession of our talk that his brief contradiction struck me like a blow. "Don't agree with me!" I repeated.

"No," said Parload

"But how?"

"I believe science is of more importance than socialism," he said. "Socialism's a theory. Science—science is something more."

And that was really all he seemed to be able to say.

We embarked upon one of those queer arguments illiterate young men used always to find so heating. Science or Socialism? It was, of course, like arguing which is right, left handedness or a taste for onions, it was altogether impossible opposition. But the range of my rhetoric enabled me at last to exasperate Parload,

and his mere repudiation of my conclusions sufficed to exasperate me, and we ended in the key of a positive quarrel. "Oh, very well!" said I. "So long as I know where we are!"

I slammed his door as though I dynamited his house, and went raging down the street, but I felt that he was already back at the window worshiping his blessed line in the green, before I got round the corner.

I had to walk for an hour or so, before I was cool enough to go home.

And it was Parload who had first introduced me to socialism!

Recreant!

The most extraordinary things used to run through my head in those days. I will confess that my mind ran persistently that evening upon revolutions after the best French pattern, and I sat on a Committee of Safety and tried backsliders. Parload was there, among the prisoners, backsliderissimus, aware too late of the error of his ways. His hands were tied behind his back ready for the shambles; through the open door one heard the voice of justice, the rude justice of the people. I was sorry, but I had to do my duty.

"If we punish those who would betray us to Kings," said I, with a sorrowful deliberation, "how much the more must we punish those who would give over the State to the pursuit of useless knowledge"; and so with a gloomy satisfaction sent him off to the guillotine.

"Ah, Parload! Parload! If only you'd listened to me earlier, Parload..."

None the less that quarrel made me extremely unhappy. Parload was my only gossip, and it cost me much to keep away from him and think evil of him with no one to listen to me, evening after evening.

That was a very miserable time for me, even before my last visit to Checkshill. My long unemployed hours hung heavily on my hands. I kept away from home all day, partly to support a fiction that I was sedulously seeking another situation, and partly to escape the persistent question in my mother's eyes. "Why did you quarrel with Mr. Rawdon? Why DID you? Why do you keep on going about with a sullen face and risk offending IT more?" I spent most of the morning in the newspaper-room of the public library, writing impossible applications for impossible posts—I remember that among other things of the sort I offered my services to a firm of private detectives, a sinister breed of traders upon base jealousies now happily vanished from the world, and wrote apropos of an advertisement for "stevedores" that I did not know what the duties of a stevedore might be, but that I was apt and willing to learn—and in the afternoons and evenings I wandered through the strange lights and shadows of my native valley and hated all created things. Until my wanderings were checked by the discovery that I was wearing out my boots.

The stagnant inconclusive malaria of that time!

I perceive that I was an evil-tempered, ill-disposed youth with a great capacity for hatred, BUT—

There was an excuse for hate.

It was wrong of me to hate individuals, to be rude, harsh, and vindictive to this person or that, but indeed it would have been equally wrong to have taken the

manifest offer life made me, without resentment. I see now clearly and calmly, what I then felt obscurely and with an unbalanced intensity, that my conditions were intolerable. My work was tedious and laborious and it took up an unreasonable proportion of my time, I was ill clothed, ill fed, ill housed, ill educated and ill trained, my will was suppressed and cramped to the pitch of torture, I had no reasonable pride in myself and no reasonable chance of putting anything right. It was a life hardly worth living. That a large proportion of the people about me had no better a lot, that many had a worse, does not affect these facts. It was a life in which contentment would have been disgraceful. If some of them were contented or resigned, so much the worse for every one. No doubt it was hasty and foolish of me to throw up my situation, but everything was so obviously aimless and foolish in our social organization that I do not feel disposed to blame myself even for that, except in so far as it pained my mother and caused her anxiety.

Think of the one comprehensive fact of the lock-out!

That year was a bad year, a year of world-wide economic disorganization. Through their want of intelligent direction the great "Trust" of American ironmasters, a gang of energetic, narrow-minded furnace owners, had smelted far more iron than the whole world had any demand for. (In those days there existed no means of estimating any need of that sort beforehand.) They had done this without even consulting the ironmasters of any other country. During their period of activity they had drawn into their employment a great number of workers, and had erected a huge productive plant. It is manifestly just that people who do headlong stupid things of this sort should suffer, but in the old days it was quite possible, it was customary for the real blunderers in such disasters, to shift nearly all the consequences of their incapacity. No one thought it wrong for a light-witted "captain of industry" who had led his workpeople into overproduction, into the disproportionate manufacture, that is to say, of some particular article, to abandon and dismiss them, nor was there anything to prevent the sudden frantic underselling of some trade rival in order to surprise and destroy his trade, secure his customers for one's own destined needs, and shift a portion of one's punishment upon him. This operation of spasmodic underselling was known as "dumping." The American ironmasters were now dumping on the British market. The British employers were, of course, taking their loss out of their workpeople as much as possible, but in addition they were agitating for some legislation that would prevent—not stupid relative excess in production, but "dumping"—not the disease, but the consequences of the disease. The necessary knowledge to prevent either dumping or its causes, the uncorrelated production of commodities, did not exist, but this hardly weighed with them at all, and in answer to their demands there had arisen a curious party of retaliatory- protectionists who combined vague proposals for spasmodic responses to these convulsive attacks from foreign manufacturers, with the very evident intention of achieving financial adventures. The dishonest and reckless elements were indeed so evident in this movement as to add very greatly to the general atmosphere of distrust and insecurity, and in the recoil from the prospect of fiscal power in the hands of the class of men known as

the "New Financiers," one heard frightened old-fashioned statesmen asserting with passion that "dumping" didn't occur, or that it was a very charming sort of thing to happen. Nobody would face and handle the rather intricate truth of the business. The whole effect upon the mind of a cool observer was of a covey of unsubstantial jabbering minds drifting over a series of irrational economic cataclysms, prices and employment tumbled about like towers in an earthquake, and amidst the shifting masses were the common work-people going on with their lives as well as they could, suffering, perplexed, unorganized, and for anything but violent, fruitless protests, impotent. You cannot hope now to understand the infinite want of adjustment in the old order of things. At one time there were people dying of actual starvation in India, while men were burning unsalable wheat in America. It sounds like the account of a particularly mad dream, does it not? It was a dream, a dream from which no one on earth expected an awakening.

To us youngsters with the positiveness, the rationalism of youth, it seemed that the strikes and lockouts, the overproduction and misery could not possibly result simply from ignorance and want of thought and feeling. We needed more dramatic factors than these mental fogs, these mere atmospheric devils. We fled therefore to that common refuge of the unhappy ignorant, a belief in callous insensate plots—we called them "plots"—against the poor.

You can still see how we figured it in any museum by looking up the caricatures of capital and labor that adorned the German and American socialistic papers of the old time.

§ 2

I had cast Nettie off in an eloquent epistle, had really imagined the affair was over forever—"I've done with women," I said to Parload —and then there was silence for more than a week.

Before that week was over I was wondering with a growing emotion what next would happen between us.

I found myself thinking constantly of Nettie, picturing her—sometimes with stern satisfaction, sometimes with sympathetic remorse—mourning, regretting, realizing the absolute end that had come between us. At the bottom of my heart I no more believed that there was an end between us, than that an end would come to the world. Had we not kissed one another, had we not achieved an atmosphere of whispering nearness, breached our virgin shyness with one another? Of course she was mine, of course I was hers, and separations and final quarrels and harshness and distance were no more than flourishes upon that eternal fact. So at least I felt the thing, however I shaped my thoughts.

Whenever my imagination got to work as that week drew to its close, she came in as a matter of course, I thought of her recurrently all day and dreamt of her at night. On Saturday night I dreamt of her very vividly. Her face was flushed and wet with tears, her hair a little disordered, and when I spoke to her she turned away. In some manner this dream left in my mind a feeling of distress and anxiety. In the morning I had a raging thirst to see her.

That Sunday my mother wanted me to go to church very particularly. She had a double reason for that; she thought that it would certainly exercise a favorable influence upon my search for a situation throughout the next week, and in addition Mr. Gabbitas, with a certain mystery behind his glasses, had promised to see what he could do for me, and she wanted to keep him up to that promise. I half consented, and then my desire for Nettie took hold of me. I told my mother I wasn't going to church, and set off about eleven to walk the seventeen miles to Checkshill.

It greatly intensified the fatigue of that long tramp that the sole of my boot presently split at the toe, and after I had cut the flapping portion off, a nail worked through and began to torment me. However, the boot looked all right after that operation and gave no audible hint of my discomfort. I got some bread and cheese at a little inn on the way, and was in Checkshill park about four. I did not go by the road past the house and so round to the gardens, but cut over the crest beyond the second keeper's cottage, along a path Nettie used to call her own. It was a mere deer track. It led up a miniature valley and through a pretty dell in which we had been accustomed to meet, and so through the hollies and along a narrow path close by the wall of the shrubbery to the gardens.

In my memory that walk through the park before I came upon Nettie stands out very vividly. The long tramp before it is foreshortened to a mere effect of dusty road and painful boot, but the bracken valley and sudden tumult of doubts and unwonted expectations that came to me, stands out now as something significant, as something unforgettable, something essential to the meaning of all that followed. Where should I meet her? What would she say? I had asked these questions before and found an answer. Now they came again with a trail of fresh implications and I had no answer for them at all. As I approached Nettie she ceased to be the mere butt of my egotistical self-projection, the custodian of my sexual pride, and drew together and became over and above this a personality of her own, a personality and a mystery, a sphinx I had evaded only to meet again.

I find a little difficulty in describing the quality of the old-world love-making so that it may be understandable now.

We young people had practically no preparation at all for the stir and emotions of adolescence. Towards the young the world maintained a conspiracy of stimulating silences. There came no initiation. There were books, stories of a curiously conventional kind that insisted on certain qualities in every love affair and greatly intensified one's natural desire for them, perfect trust, perfect loyalty, lifelong devotion. Much of the complex essentials of love were altogether hidden. One read these things, got accidental glimpses of this and that, wondered and forgot, and so one grew. Then strange emotions, novel alarming desires, dreams strangely charged with feeling; an inexplicable impulse of self-abandonment began to tickle queerly amongst the familiar purely egotistical and materialistic things of boyhood and girlhood. We were like misguided travelers who had camped in the dry bed of a tropical river. Presently we were knee deep and neck deep in the flood. Our beings were suddenly going out from ourselves seeking other beings—we

knew not why. This novel craving for abandonment to some one of the other sex, bore us away. We were ashamed and full of desire. We kept the thing a guilty secret, and were resolved to satisfy it against all the world. In this state it was we drifted in the most accidental way against some other blindly seeking creature, and linked like nascent atoms.

We were obsessed by the books we read, by all the talk about us that once we had linked ourselves we were linked for life. Then afterwards we discovered that other was also an egotism, a thing of ideas and impulses, that failed to correspond with ours.

So it was, I say, with the young of my class and most of the young people in our world. So it came about that I sought Nettie on the Sunday afternoon and suddenly came upon her, light bodied, slenderly feminine, hazel eyed, with her soft sweet young face under the shady brim of her hat of straw, the pretty Venus I had resolved should be wholly and exclusively mine.

There, all unaware of me still, she stood, my essential feminine, the embodiment of the inner thing in life for me—and moreover an unknown other, a person like myself.

She held a little book in her hand, open as if she were walking along and reading it. That chanced to be her pose, but indeed she was standing quite still, looking away towards the gray and lichenous shrubbery wall and, as I think now, listening. Her lips were a little apart, curved to that faint, sweet shadow of a smile.

§ 3

I recall with a vivid precision her queer start when she heard the rustle of my approaching feet, her surprise, her eyes almost of dismay for me. I could recollect, I believe, every significant word she spoke during our meeting, and most of what I said to her. At least, it seems I could, though indeed I may deceive myself. But I will not make the attempt. We were both too ill-educated to speak our full meanings, we stamped out our feelings with clumsy stereotyped phrases; you who are better taught would fail to catch our intention. The effect would be inanity. But our first words I may give you, because though they conveyed nothing to me at the time, afterwards they meant much.

"YOU, Willie!" she said.

"I have come," I said—forgetting in the instant all the elaborate things I had intended to say. "I thought I would surprise you—"

"Surprise me?"

"Yes."

She stared at me for a moment. I can see her pretty face now as it looked at me—her impenetrable dear face. She laughed a queer little laugh and her color went for a moment, and then so soon as she had spoken, came back again.

"Surprise me at what?" she said with a rising note.

I was too intent to explain myself to think of what might lie in that.

"I wanted to tell you," I said, "that I didn't mean quite ... the things I put in my letter."

§ 4

When I and Nettie had been sixteen we had been just of an age and contemporaries altogether. Now we were a year and three-quarters older, and she —her metamorphosis was almost complete, and I was still only at the beginning of a man's long adolescence.

In an instant she grasped the situation. The hidden motives of her quick ripened little mind flashed out their intuitive scheme of action. She treated me with that neat perfection of understanding a young woman has for a boy.

"But how did you come?" she asked.

I told her I had walked.

"Walked!" In an instant she was leading me towards the gardens. I MUST be tired. I must come home with her at once and sit down. Indeed it was near teatime (the Stuarts had tea at the old-fashioned hour of five). Every one would be SO surprised to see me. Fancy walking! Fancy! But she supposed a man thought nothing of seventeen miles. When COULD I have started!

All the while, keeping me at a distance, without even the touch of her hand.

"But, Nettie! I came over to talk to you?"

"My dear boy! Tea first, if you please! And besides—aren't we talking?"

The "dear boy" was a new note, that sounded oddly to me.

She quickened her pace a little.

"I wanted to explain—" I began.

Whatever I wanted to explain I had no chance to do so. I said a few discrepant things that she answered rather by her intonation than her words.

When we were well past the shrubbery, she slackened a little in her urgency, and so we came along the slope under the beeches to the garden. She kept her bright, straightforward-looking girlish eyes on me as we went; it seemed she did so all the time, but now I know, better than I did then, that every now and then she glanced over me and behind me towards the shrubbery. And all the while, behind her quick breathless inconsecutive talk she was thinking.

Her dress marked the end of her transition.

Can I recall it?

Not, I am afraid, in the terms a woman would use. But her bright brown hair, which had once flowed down her back in a jolly pig-tail tied with a bit of scarlet ribbon, was now caught up into an intricacy of pretty curves above her little ear and cheek, and the soft long lines of her neck; her white dress had descended to her feet; her slender waist, which had once been a mere geographical expression, an imaginary line like the equator, was now a thing of flexible beauty. A year ago she had been a pretty girl's face sticking out from a little unimportant frock that was carried upon an extremely active and efficient pair of brown-stockinged legs. Now there was coming a strange new body that flowed beneath her clothes with a sinuous insistence. Every movement, and particularly the novel droop of her hand and arm to the unaccustomed skirts she gathered about her, and a graceful forward inclination that had come to her, called softly to my eyes. A very fine scarf—I suppose you would call it a scarf—of green gossamer, that some new

wakened instinct had told her to fling about her shoulders, clung now closely to the young undulations of her body, and now streamed fluttering out for a moment in a breath of wind, and like some shy independent tentacle with a secret to impart, came into momentary contact with my arm.

She caught it back and reproved it.

We went through the green gate in the high garden wall. I held it open for her to pass through, for this was one of my restricted stock of stiff politenesses, and then for a second she was near touching me. So we came to the trim array of flower-beds near the head gardener's cottage and the vistas of "glass" on our left. We walked between the box edgings and beds of begonias and into the shadow of a yew hedge within twenty yards of that very pond with the gold-fish, at whose brim we had plighted our vows, and so we came to the wistaria-smothered porch.

The door was wide open, and she walked in before me. "Guess who has come to see us!" she cried.

Her father answered indistinctly from the parlor, and a chair creaked. I judged he was disturbed in his nap.

"Mother!" she called in her clear young voice. "Puss!"

Puss was her sister.

She told them in a marveling key that I had walked all the way from Clayton, and they gathered about me and echoed her notes of surprise.

"You'd better sit down, Willie," said her father; "now you have got here. How's your mother?"

He looked at me curiously as he spoke.

He was dressed in his Sunday clothes, a sort of brownish tweeds, but the waistcoat was unbuttoned for greater comfort in his slumbers. He was a brown-eyed ruddy man, and I still have now in my mind the bright effect of the red-golden hairs that started out from his cheek to flow down into his beard. He was short but strongly built, and his beard and mustache were the biggest things about him. She had taken all the possibility of beauty he possessed, his clear skin, his bright hazel-brown eyes, and wedded them to a certain quickness she got from her mother. Her mother I remember as a sharp-eyed woman of great activity; she seems to me now to have been perpetually bringing in or taking out meals or doing some such service, and to me—for my mother's sake and my own—she was always welcoming and kind. Puss was a youngster of fourteen perhaps, of whom a hard bright stare, and a pale skin like her mother's, are the chief traces on my memory. All these people were very kind to me, and among them there was a common recognition, sometimes very agreeably finding expression, that I was—"clever." They all stood about me as if they were a little at a loss.

"Sit down!" said her father. "Give him a chair, Puss."

We talked a little stiffly—they were evidently surprised by my sudden apparition, dusty, fatigued, and white faced; but Nettie did not remain to keep the conversation going.

"There!" she cried suddenly, as if she were vexed. "I declare!" and she darted out of the room.

"Lord! what a girl it is!" said Mrs. Stuart. "I don't know what's come to her."

It was half an hour before Nettie came back. It seemed a long time to me, and yet she had been running, for when she came in again she was out of breath. In the meantime, I had thrown out casually that I had given up my place at Rawdon's. "I can do better than that," I said.

"I left my book in the dell," she said, panting. "Is tea ready?" and that was her apology...

We didn't shake down into comfort even with the coming of the tea-things. Tea at the gardener's cottage was a serious meal, with a big cake and little cakes, and preserves and fruit, a fine spread upon a table. You must imagine me, sullen, awkward, and preoccupied, perplexed by the something that was inexplicably unexpected in Nettie, saying little, and glowering across the cake at her, and all the eloquence I had been concentrating for the previous twenty- four hours, miserably lost somewhere in the back of my mind. Nettie's father tried to set me talking; he had a liking for my gift of ready speech, for his own ideas came with difficulty, and it pleased and astonished him to hear me pouring out my views. Indeed, over there I was, I think, even more talkative than with Parload, though to the world at large I was a shy young lout. "You ought to write it out for the newspapers," he used to say. "That's what you ought to do. I never heard such nonsense."

Or, "You've got the gift of the gab, young man. We ought to ha' made a lawyer of you."

But that afternoon, even in his eyes, I didn't shine. Failing any other stimulus, he reverted to my search for a situation, but even that did not engage me.

§ 5

For a long time I feared I should have to go back to Clayton without another word to Nettie, she seemed insensible to the need I felt for a talk with her, and I was thinking even of a sudden demand for that before them all. It was a transparent manoeuver of her mother's who had been watching my face, that sent us out at last together to do something—I forget now what —in one of the greenhouses. Whatever that little mission may have been it was the merest, most barefaced excuse, a door to shut, or a window to close, and I don't think it got done.

Nettie hesitated and obeyed. She led the way through one of the hot- houses. It was a low, steamy, brick-floored alley between staging that bore a close crowd of pots and ferns, and behind big branching plants that were spread and nailed overhead so as to make an impervious cover of leaves, and in that close green privacy she stopped and turned on me suddenly like a creature at bay.

"Isn't the maidenhair fern lovely?" she said, and looked at me with eyes that said, "NOW."

"Nettie," I began, "I was a fool to write to you as I did."

She startled me by the assent that flashed out upon her face. But she said nothing, and stood waiting.

"Nettie," I plunged, "I can't do without you. I—I love you."

"If you loved me," she said trimly, watching the white fingers she plunged among the green branches of a selaginella, "could you write the things you do to me?"

"I don't mean them," I said. "At least not always."

I thought really they were very good letters, and that Nettie was stupid to think otherwise, but I was for the moment clearly aware of the impossibility of conveying that to her.

"You wrote them."

"But then I tramp seventeen miles to say I don't mean them."

"Yes. But perhaps you do."

I think I was at a loss; then I said, not very clearly, "I don't."

"You think you—you love me, Willie. But you don't."

"I do. Nettie! You know I do."

For answer she shook her head.

I made what I thought was a most heroic plunge. "Nettie," I said, "I'd rather have you than—than my own opinions."

The selaginella still engaged her. "You think so now," she said.

I broke out into protestations.

"No," she said shortly. "It's different now."

"But why should two letters make so much difference?" I said.

"It isn't only the letters. But it is different. It's different for good."

She halted a little with that sentence, seeking her expression. She looked up abruptly into my eyes and moved, indeed slightly, but with the intimation that she thought our talk might end.

But I did not mean it to end like that.

"For good?" said I. "No! .. Nettie! Nettie! You don't mean that!"

"I do," she said deliberately, still looking at me, and with all her pose conveying her finality. She seemed to brace herself for the outbreak that must follow.

Of course I became wordy. But I did not submerge her. She stood entrenched, firing her contradictions like guns into my scattered discursive attack. I remember that our talk took the absurd form of disputing whether I could be in love with her or not. And there was I, present in evidence, in a deepening and widening distress of soul because she could stand there, defensive, brighter and prettier than ever, and in some inexplicable way cut off from me and inaccessible.

You know, we had never been together before without little enterprises of endearment, without a faintly guilty, quite delightful excitement.

I pleaded, I argued. I tried to show that even my harsh and difficult letters came from my desire to come wholly into contact with her. I made exaggerated fine statements of the longing I felt for her when I was away, of the shock and misery of finding her estranged and cool. She looked at me, feeling the emotion of my speech and impervious to its ideas. I had no doubt —whatever poverty in my words, coolly written down now—that I was eloquent then. I meant most intensely what I said, indeed I was wholly concentrated upon it. I was set upon conveying to her with absolute sincerity my sense of distance, and the greatness

of my desire. I toiled toward her painfully and obstinately through a jungle of words.

Her face changed very slowly—by such imperceptible degrees as when at dawn light comes into a clear sky. I could feel that I touched her, that her hardness was in some manner melting, her determination softening toward hesitations. The habit of an old familiarity lurked somewhere within her. But she would not let me reach her.

"No," she cried abruptly, starting into motion.

She laid a hand on my arm. A wonderful new friendliness came into her voice. "It's impossible, Willie. Everything is different now—everything. We made a mistake. We two young sillies made a mistake and everything is different for ever. Yes, yes."

She turned about.

"Nettie!" cried I, and still protesting, pursued her along the narrow alley between the staging toward the hot-house door. I pursued her like an accusation, and she went before me like one who is guilty and ashamed. So I recall it now.

She would not let me talk to her again.

Yet I could see that my talk to her had altogether abolished the clear- cut distance of our meeting in the park. Ever and again I found her hazel eyes upon me. They expressed something novel—a surprise, as though she realized an unwonted relationship, and a sympathetic pity. And still—something defensive.

When we got back to the cottage, I fell talking rather more freely with her father about the nationalization of railways, and my spirits and temper had so far mended at the realization that I could still produce an effect upon Nettie, that I was even playful with Puss. Mrs. Stuart judged from that that things were better with me than they were, and began to beam mightily.

But Nettie remained thoughtful and said very little. She was lost in perplexities I could not fathom, and presently she slipped away from us and went upstairs.

§ 6

I was, of course, too footsore to walk back to Clayton, but I had a shilling and a penny in my pocket for the train between Checkshill and Two-Mile Stone, and that much of the distance I proposed to do in the train. And when I got ready to go, Nettie amazed me by waking up to the most remarkable solicitude for me. I must, she said, go by the road. It was altogether too dark for the short way to the lodge gates.

I pointed out that it was moonlight. "With the comet thrown in," said old Stuart.

"No," she insisted, "you MUST go by the road."

I still disputed.

She was standing near me. "To please ME," she urged, in a quick undertone, and with a persuasive look that puzzled me. Even in the moment I asked myself why should this please her?

I might have agreed had she not followed that up with, "The hollies by the shrubbery are as dark as pitch. And there's the deer-hounds."

"I'm not afraid of the dark," said I. "Nor of the deer-hounds, either."

"But those dogs! Supposing one was loose!"

That was a girl's argument, a girl who still had to understand that fear is an overt argument only for her own sex. I thought too of those grisly lank brutes straining at their chains and the chorus they could make of a night when they heard belated footsteps along the edge of the Killing Wood, and the thought banished my wish to please her. Like most imaginative natures I was acutely capable of dreads and retreats, and constantly occupied with their suppression and concealment, and to refuse the short cut when it might appear that I did it on account of half a dozen almost certainly chained dogs was impossible.

So I set off in spite of her, feeling valiant and glad to be so easily brave, but a little sorry that she should think herself crossed by me.

A thin cloud veiled the moon, and the way under the beeches was dark and indistinct. I was not so preoccupied with my love-affairs as to neglect what I will confess was always my custom at night across that wild and lonely park. I made myself a club by fastening a big flint to one end of my twisted handkerchief and tying the other about my wrist, and with this in my pocket, went on comforted.

And it chanced that as I emerged from the hollies by the corner of the shrubbery I was startled to come unexpectedly upon a young man in evening dress smoking a cigar.

I was walking on turf, so that the sound I made was slight. He stood clear in the moonlight, his cigar glowed like a blood-red star, and it did not occur to me at the time that I advanced towards him almost invisibly in an impenetrable shadow.

"Hullo," he cried, with a sort of amiable challenge. "I'm here first!"

I came out into the light. "Who cares if you are?" said I.

I had jumped at once to an interpretation of his words. I knew that there was an intermittent dispute between the House people and the villager public about the use of this track, and it is needless to say where my sympathies fell in that dispute.

"Eh?" he cried in surprise.

"Thought I would run away, I suppose," said I, and came close up to him.

All my enormous hatred of his class had flared up at the sight of his costume, at the fancied challenge of his words. I knew him. He was Edward Verrall, son of the man who owned not only this great estate but more than half of Rawdon's pot-bank, and who had interests and possessions, collieries and rents, all over the district of the Four Towns. He was a gallant youngster, people said, and very clever. Young as he was there was talk of parliament for him; he had been a great success at the university, and he was being sedulously popularized among us. He took with a light confidence, as a matter of course, advantages that I would have faced the rack to get, and I firmly believed myself a better man than he. He was, as he stood there, a concentrated figure of all that filled me with bitterness. One day he had stopped in a motor outside our house, and I remember the thrill of rage with

which I had noted the dutiful admiration in my mother's eyes as she peered through her blind at him. "That's young Mr. Verrall," she said. "They say he's very clever."

"They would," I answered. "Damn them and him!"

But that is by the way.

He was clearly astonished to find himself face to face with a man. His note changed.

"Who the devil are YOU?" he asked.

My retort was the cheap expedient of re-echoing, "Who the devil are you?"

"WELL," he said.

"I'm coming along this path if I like," I said. "See? It's a public path —just as this used to be public land. You've stolen the land—you and yours, and now you want to steal the right of way. You'll ask us to get off the face of the earth next. I sha'n't oblige. See?"

I was shorter and I suppose a couple of years younger than he, but I had the improvised club in my pocket gripped ready, and I would have fought with him very cheerfully. But he fell a step backward as I came toward him.

"Socialist, I presume?" he said, alert and quiet and with the faintest note of badinage.

"One of many."

"We're all socialists nowadays," he remarked philosophically, "and I haven't the faintest intention of disputing your right of way."

"You'd better not," I said.

"No!"

"No."

He replaced his cigar, and there was a brief pause. "Catching a train?" he threw out.

It seemed absurd not to answer. "Yes," I said shortly.

He said it was a pleasant evening for a walk.

I hovered for a moment and there was my path before me, and he stood aside. There seemed nothing to do but go on. "Good night," said he, as that intention took effect.

I growled a surly good-night.

I felt like a bombshell of swearing that must presently burst with some violence as I went on my silent way. He had so completely got the best of our encounter.

§ 7

There comes a memory, an odd intermixture of two entirely divergent things, that stands out with the intensest vividness.

As I went across the last open meadow, following the short cut to Checkshill station, I perceived I had two shadows.

The thing jumped into my mind and stopped its tumid flow for a moment. I remember the intelligent detachment of my sudden interest. I turned sharply, and

stood looking at the moon and the great white comet, that the drift of the clouds had now rather suddenly unveiled.

The comet was perhaps twenty degrees from the moon. What a wonderful thing it looked floating there, a greenish-white apparition in the dark blue deeps! It looked brighter than the moon because it was smaller, but the shadow it cast, though clearer cut, was much fainter than the moon's shadow... I went on noting these facts, watching my two shadows precede me.

I am totally unable to account for the sequence of my thoughts on this occasion. But suddenly, as if I had come on this new fact round a corner, the comet was out of my mind again, and I was face to face with an absolutely new idea. I wonder sometimes if the two shadows I cast, one with a sort of feminine faintness with regard to the other and not quite so tall, may not have suggested the word or the thought of an assignation to my mind. All that I have clear is that with the certitude of intuition I knew what it was that had brought the youth in evening dress outside the shrubbery. Of course! He had come to meet Nettie!

Once the mental process was started it took no time at all. The day which had been full of perplexities for me, the mysterious invisible thing that had held Nettie and myself apart, the unaccountable strange something in her manner, was revealed and explained.

I knew now why she had looked guilty at my appearance, what had brought her out that afternoon, why she had hurried me in, the nature of the "book" she had run back to fetch, the reason why she had wanted me to go back by the high-road, and why she had pitied me. It was all in the instant clear to me.

You must imagine me a black little creature, suddenly stricken still —for a moment standing rigid—and then again suddenly becoming active with an impotent gesture, becoming audible with an inarticulate cry, with two little shadows mocking my dismay, and about this figure you must conceive a great wide space of moonlit grass, rimmed by the looming suggestion of distant trees—trees very low and faint and dim, and over it all the domed serenity of that wonderful luminous night.

For a little while this realization stunned my mind. My thoughts came to a pause, staring at my discovery. Meanwhile my feet and my previous direction carried me through the warm darkness to Checkshill station with its little lights, to the ticket-office window, and so to the train.

I remember myself as it were waking up to the thing—I was alone in one of the dingy "third-class" compartments of that time—and the sudden nearly frantic insurgence of my rage. I stood up with the cry of an angry animal, and smote my fist with all my strength against the panel of wood before me...

Curiously enough I have completely forgotten my mood after that for a little while, but I know that later, for a minute perhaps, I hung for a time out of the carriage with the door open, contemplating a leap from the train. It was to be a dramatic leap, and then I would go storming back to her, denounce her, overwhelm her; and I hung, urging myself to do it. I don't remember how it was I decided not to do this, at last, but in the end I didn't.

When the train stopped at the next station I had given up all thoughts of going back. I was sitting in the corner of the carriage with my bruised and wounded hand pressed under my arm, and still insensible to its pain, trying to think out clearly a scheme of action—action that should express the monstrous indignation that possessed me.

CHAPTER THE THIRD - THE REVOLVER

§ 1

"That comet is going to hit the earth!"

So said one of the two men who got into the train and settled down.

"Ah!" said the other man.

"They do say that it is made of gas, that comet. We sha'n't blow up, shall us?"...

What did it matter to me?

I was thinking of revenge—revenge against the primary conditions of my being. I was thinking of Nettie and her lover. I was firmly resolved he should not have her—though I had to kill them both to prevent it. I did not care what else might happen, if only that end was ensured. All my thwarted passions had turned to rage. I would have accepted eternal torment that night without a second thought, to be certain of revenge. A hundred possibilities of action, a hundred stormy situations, a whirl of violent schemes, chased one another through my shamed, exasperated mind. The sole prospect I could endure was of some gigantic, inexorably cruel vindication of my humiliated self.

And Nettie? I loved Nettie still, but now with the intensest jealousy, with the keen, unmeasuring hatred of wounded pride, and baffled, passionate desire.

§ 2

As I came down the hill from Clayton Crest—for my shilling and a penny only permitted my traveling by train as far as Two-Mile Stone, and thence I had to walk over the hill—I remember very vividly a little man with a shrill voice who was preaching under a gas-lamp against a hoarding to a thin crowd of Sunday evening loafers. He was a short man, bald, with a little fair curly beard and hair and watery blue eyes, and he was preaching that the end of the world drew near.

I think that is the first time I heard any one link the comet with the end of the world. He had got that jumbled up with international politics and prophecies from the Book of Daniel.

I stopped to hear him only for a moment or so. I do not think I should have halted at all but his crowd blocked my path, and the sight of his queer wild expression, the gesture of his upward-pointing finger, held me.

"There is the end of all your Sins and Follies," he bawled. "There! There is the Star of Judgments, the Judgments of the most High God! It is appointed unto all

men to die—unto all men to die"—his voice changed to a curious flat chant—"and after death, the Judgment! The Judgment!"

I pushed and threaded my way through the bystanders and went on, and his curious harsh flat voice pursued me. I went on with the thoughts that had occupied me before—where I could buy a revolver, and how I might master its use—and probably I should have forgotten all about him had he not taken a part in the hideous dream that ended the little sleep I had that night. For the most part I lay awake thinking of Nettie and her lover.

Then came three strange days—three days that seem now to have been wholly concentrated upon one business.

This dominant business was the purchase of my revolver. I held myself resolutely to the idea that I must either restore myself by some extraordinary act of vigor and violence in Nettie's eyes or I must kill her. I would not let myself fall away from that. I felt that if I let this matter pass, my last shred of pride and honor would pass with it, that for the rest of my life I should never deserve the slightest respect or any woman's love. Pride kept me to my purpose between my gusts of passion.

Yet it was not easy to buy that revolver.

I had a kind of shyness of the moment when I should have to face the shopman, and I was particularly anxious to have a story ready if he should see fit to ask questions why I bought such a thing. I determined to say I was going to Texas, and I thought it might prove useful there. Texas in those days had the reputation of a wild lawless land. As I knew nothing of caliber or impact, I wanted also to be able to ask with a steady face at what distance a man or woman could be killed by the weapon that might be offered me. I was pretty cool- headed in relation to such practical aspects of my affair. I had some little difficulty in finding a gunsmith. In Clayton there were some rook-rifles and so forth in a cycle shop, but the only revolvers these people had impressed me as being too small and toylike for my purpose. It was in a pawnshop window in the narrow High Street of Swathinglea that I found my choice, a reasonably clumsy and serious-looking implement ticketed "As used in the American army."

I had drawn out my balance from the savings bank, matter of two pounds and more, to make this purchase, and I found it at last a very easy transaction. The pawnbroker told me where I could get ammunition, and I went home that night with bulging pockets, an armed man.

The purchase of my revolver was, I say, the chief business of those days, but you must not think I was so intent upon it as to be insensible to the stirring things that were happening in the streets through which I went seeking the means to effect my purpose. They were full of murmurings: the whole region of the Four Towns scowled lowering from its narrow doors. The ordinary healthy flow of people going to work, people going about their business, was chilled and checked. Numbers of men stood about the streets in knots and groups, as corpuscles gather and catch in the blood-vessels in the opening stages of inflammation. The woman looked haggard and worried. The ironworkers had refused the proposed reduction

of their wages, and the lockout had begun. They were already at "play." The Conciliation Board was doing its best to keep the coal- miners and masters from a breach, but young Lord Redcar, the greatest of our coal owners and landlord of all Swathinglea and half Clayton, was taking a fine upstanding attitude that made the breach inevitable. He was a handsome young man, a gallant young man; his pride revolted at the idea of being dictated to by a "lot of bally miners," and he meant, he said, to make a fight for it. The world had treated him sumptuously from his earliest years; the shares in the common stock of five thousand people had gone to pay for his handsome upbringing, and large, romantic, expensive ambitions filled his generously nurtured mind. He had early distinguished himself at Oxford by his scornful attitude towards democracy. There was something that appealed to the imagination in his fine antagonism to the crowd—on the one hand, was the brilliant young nobleman, picturesquely alone; on the other, the ugly, inexpressive multitude, dressed inelegantly in shop-clothes, under-educated, under-fed, envious, base, and with a wicked disinclination for work and a wicked appetite for the good things it could so rarely get. For common imaginative purposes one left out the policeman from the design, the stalwart policeman protecting his lordship, and ignored the fact that while Lord Redcar had his hands immediately and legally on the workman's shelter and bread, they could touch him to the skin only by some violent breach of the law.

He lived at Lowchester House, five miles or so beyond Checkshill; but partly to show how little he cared for his antagonists, and partly no doubt to keep himself in touch with the negotiations that were still going on, he was visible almost every day in and about the Four Towns, driving that big motor car of his that could take him sixty miles an hour. The English passion for fair play one might have thought sufficient to rob this bold procedure of any dangerous possibilities, but he did not go altogether free from insult, and on one occasion at least an intoxicated Irish woman shook her fist at him...

A dark, quiet crowd, that was greater each day, a crowd more than half women, brooded as a cloud will sometimes brood permanently upon a mountain crest, in the market-place outside the Clayton Town Hall, where the conference was held...

I consider myself justified in regarding Lord Redcar's passing automobile with a special animosity because of the leaks in our roof.

We held our little house on lease; the owner was a mean, saving old man named Pettigrew, who lived in a villa adorned with plaster images of dogs and goats, at Overcastle, and in spite of our specific agreement, he would do no repairs for us at all. He rested secure in my mother's timidity. Once, long ago, she had been behind-hand with her rent, with half of her quarter's rent, and he had extended the days of grace a month; her sense that some day she might need the same mercy again made her his abject slave. She was afraid even to ask that he should cause the roof to be mended for fear he might take offence. But one night the rain poured in on her bed and gave her a cold, and stained and soaked her poor old patchwork counterpane. Then she got me to compose an excessively polite

letter to old Pettigrew, begging him as a favor to perform his legal obligations. It is part of the general imbecility of those days that such one-sided law as existed was a profound mystery to the common people, its provisions impossible to ascertain, its machinery impossible to set in motion. Instead of the clearly written code, the lucid statements of rules and principles that are now at the service of every one, the law was the muddle secret of the legal profession. Poor people, overworked people, had constantly to submit to petty wrongs because of the intolerable uncertainty not only of law but of cost, and of the demands upon time and energy, proceedings might make. There was indeed no justice for any one too poor to command a good solicitor's deference and loyalty; there was nothing but rough police protection and the magistrate's grudging or eccentric advice for the mass of the population. The civil law, in particular, was a mysterious upper-class weapon, and I can imagine no injustice that would have been sufficient to induce my poor old mother to appeal to it.

All this begins to sound incredible. I can only assure you that it was so.

But I, when I learned that old Pettigrew had been down to tell my mother all about his rheumatism, to inspect the roof, and to allege that nothing was needed, gave way to my most frequent emotion in those days, a burning indignation, and took the matter into my own hands. I wrote and asked him, with a withering air of technicality, to have the roof repaired "as per agreement," and added, "if not done in one week from now we shall be obliged to take proceedings." I had not mentioned this high line of conduct to my mother at first, and so when old Pettigrew came down in a state of great agitation with my letter in his hand, she was almost equally agitated.

"How could you write to old Mr. Pettigrew like that?" she asked me.

I said that old Pettigrew was a shameful old rascal, or words to that effect, and I am afraid I behaved in a very undutiful way to her when she said that she had settled everything with him—she wouldn't say how, but I could guess well enough—and that I was to promise her, promise her faithfully, to do nothing more in the matter. I wouldn't promise her.

And—having nothing better to employ me then—I presently went raging to old Pettigrew in order to put the whole thing before him in what I considered the proper light. Old Pettigrew evaded my illumination; he saw me coming up his front steps—I can still see his queer old nose and the crinkled brow over his eye and the little wisp of gray hair that showed over the corner of his window-blind—and he instructed his servant to put up the chain when she answered the door, and to tell me that he would not see me. So I had to fall back upon my pen.

Then it was, as I had no idea what were the proper "proceedings" to take, the brilliant idea occurred to me of appealing to Lord Redcar as the ground landlord, and, as it were, our feudal chief, and pointing out to him that his security for his rent was depreciating in old Pettigrew's hands. I added some general observations on leaseholds, the taxation of ground rents, and the private ownership of the soil. And Lord Redcar, whose spirit revolted at democracy, and who cultivated a pert humiliating manner with his inferiors to show as much, earned my distinguished

hatred for ever by causing his secretary to present his compliments to me, and his request that I would mind my own business and leave him to manage his. At which I was so greatly enraged that I first tore this note into minute innumerable pieces, and then dashed it dramatically all over the floor of my room—from which, to keep my mother from the job, I afterward had to pick it up laboriously on all-fours.

I was still meditating a tremendous retort, an indictment of all Lord Redcar's class, their manners, morals, economic and political crimes, when my trouble with Nettie arose to swamp all minor troubles. Yet, not so completely but that I snarled aloud when his lordship's motor-car whizzed by me, as I went about upon my long meandering quest for a weapon. And I discovered after a time that my mother had bruised her knee and was lame. Fearing to irritate me by bringing the thing before me again, she had set herself to move her bed out of the way of the drip without my help, and she had knocked her knee. All her poor furnishings, I discovered, were cowering now close to the peeling bedroom walls; there had come a vast discoloration of the ceiling, and a washing-tub was in occupation of the middle of her chamber...

It is necessary that I should set these things before you, should give the key of inconvenience and uneasiness in which all things were arranged, should suggest the breath of trouble that stirred along the hot summer streets, the anxiety about the strike, the rumors and indignations, the gatherings and meetings, the increasing gravity of the policemen's faces, the combative headlines of the local papers, the knots of picketers who scrutinized any one who passed near the silent, smokeless forges, but in my mind, you must understand, such impressions came and went irregularly; they made a moving background, changing undertones, to my preoccupation by that darkly shaping purpose to which a revolver was so imperative an essential.

Along the darkling streets, amidst the sullen crowds, the thought of Nettie, my Nettie, and her gentleman lover made ever a vivid inflammatory spot of purpose in my brain.

§ 3

It was three days after this—on Wednesday, that is to say—that the first of those sinister outbreaks occurred that ended in the bloody affair of Peacock Grove and the flooding out of the entire line of the Swathinglea collieries. It was the only one of these disturbances I was destined to see, and at most a mere trivial preliminary of that struggle.

The accounts that have been written of this affair vary very widely. To read them is to realize the extraordinary carelessness of truth that dishonored the press of those latter days. In my bureau I have several files of the daily papers of the old time—I collected them, as a matter of fact—and three or four of about that date I have just this moment taken out and looked through to refresh my impression of what I saw. They lie before me —queer, shriveled, incredible things; the cheap paper has already become brittle and brown and split along the creases, the ink

faded or smeared, and I have to handle them with the utmost care when I glance among their raging headlines. As I sit here in this serene place, their quality throughout, their arrangement, their tone, their arguments and exhortations, read as though they came from drugged and drunken men. They give one the effect of faded bawling, of screams and shouts heard faintly in a little gramophone... It is only on Monday I find, and buried deep below the war news, that these publications contain any intimation that unusual happenings were forward in Clayton and Swathinglea.

What I saw was towards evening. I had been learning to shoot with my new possession. I had walked out with it four or five miles across a patch of moorland and down to a secluded little coppice full of blue-bells, halfway along the high-road between Leet and Stafford. Here I had spent the afternoon, experimenting and practising with careful deliberation and grim persistence. I had brought an old kite-frame of cane with me, that folded and unfolded, and each shot-hole I made I marked and numbered to compare with my other endeavors. At last I was satisfied that I could hit a playing-card at thirty paces nine times out of ten; the light was getting too bad for me to see my penciled bull's-eye, and in that state of quiet moodiness that sometimes comes with hunger to passionate men, I returned by the way of Swathinglea towards my home.

The road I followed came down between banks of wretched-looking working-men's houses, in close-packed rows on either side, and took upon itself the role of Swathinglea High Street, where, at a lamp and a pillar-box, the steam- trams began. So far that dirty hot way had been unusually quiet and empty, but beyond the corner, where the first group of beershops clustered, it became populous. It was very quiet still, even the children were a little inactive, but there were a lot of people standing dispersedly in little groups, and with a general direction towards the gates of the Bantock Burden coalpit.

The place was being picketed, although at that time the miners were still nominally at work, and the conferences between masters and men still in session at Clayton Town Hall. But one of the men employed at the Bantock Burden pit, Jack Briscoe, was a socialist, and he had distinguished himself by a violent letter upon the crisis to the leading socialistic paper in England, The Clarion, in which he had adventured among the motives of Lord Redcar. The publication of this had been followed by instant dismissal. As Lord Redcar wrote a day or so later to the Times—I have that Times, I have all the London papers of the last month before the Change—

"The man was paid off and kicked out. Any self-respecting employer would do the same." The thing had happened overnight, and the men did not at once take a clear line upon what was, after all, a very intricate and debatable occasion. But they came out in a sort of semiofficial strike from all Lord Redcar's collieries beyond the canal that besets Swathinglea. They did so without formal notice, committing a breach of contract by this sudden cessation. But in the long labor struggles of the old days the workers were constantly putting themselves in the

wrong and committing illegalities through that overpowering craving for dramatic promptness natural to uneducated minds.

All the men had not come out of the Bantock Burden pit. Something was wrong there, an indecision if nothing else; the mine was still working, and there was a rumor that men from Durham had been held in readiness by Lord Redcar, and were already in the mine. Now, it is absolutely impossible to ascertain certainly how things stood at that time. The newspapers say this and that, but nothing trustworthy remains.

I believe I should have gone striding athwart the dark stage of that stagnant industrial drama without asking a question, if Lord Redcar had not chanced to come upon the scene about the same time as myself and incontinently end its stagnation.

He had promised that if the men wanted a struggle he would put up the best fight they had ever had, and he had been active all that afternoon in meeting the quarrel half way, and preparing as conspicuously as possible for the scratch force of "blacklegs"—as we called them—who were, he said and we believed, to replace the strikers in his pits.

I was an eye-witness of the whole of the affair outside the Bantock Burden pit, and—I do not know what happened.

Picture to yourself how the thing came to me.

I was descending a steep, cobbled, excavated road between banked-up footways, perhaps six feet high, upon which, in a monotonous series, opened the living room doors of rows of dark, low cottages. The perspective of squat blue slate roofs and clustering chimneys drifted downward towards the irregular open space before the colliery—a space covered with coaly, wheel-scarred mud, with a patch of weedy dump to the left and the colliery gates to the right. Beyond, the High Street with shops resumed again in good earnest and went on, and the lines of the steam-tramway that started out from before my feet, and were here shining and acutely visible with reflected skylight and here lost in a shadow, took up for one acute moment the greasy yellow irradiation of a newly lit gaslamp as they vanished round the bend. Beyond, spread a darkling marsh of homes, an infinitude of little smoking hovels, and emergent, meager churches, public-houses, board schools, and other buildings amidst the prevailing chimneys of Swathinglea. To the right, very clear and relatively high, the Bantock Burden pitmouth was marked by a gaunt lattice bearing a great black wheel, very sharp and distinct in the twilight, and beyond, in an irregular perspective, were others following the lie of the seams. The general effect, as one came down the hill, was of a dark compressed life beneath a very high and wide and luminous evening sky, against which these pit-wheels rose. And ruling the calm spaciousness of that heaven was the great comet, now green-white, and wonderful for all who had eyes to see.

The fading afterglow of the sunset threw up all the contours and skyline to the west, and the comet rose eastward out of the pouring tumult of smoke from Bladden's forges. The moon had still to rise.

By this time the comet had begun to assume the cloudlike form still familiar through the medium of a thousand photographs and sketches. At first it had been an almost telescopic speck; it had brightened to the dimensions of the greatest star in the heavens; it had still grown, hour by hour, in its incredibly swift, its noiseless and inevitable rush upon our earth, until it had equaled and surpassed the moon. Now it was the most splendid thing this sky of earth has ever held. I have never seen a photograph that gave a proper idea of it. Never at any time did it assume the conventional tailed outline, comets are supposed to have. Astronomers talked of its double tail, one preceding it and one trailing behind it, but these were foreshortened to nothing, so that it had rather the form of a bellying puff of luminous smoke with an intenser, brighter heart. It rose a hot yellow color, and only began to show its distinctive greenness when it was clear of the mists of the evening.

It compelled attention for a space. For all my earthly concentration of mind, I could but stare at it for a moment with a vague anticipation that, after all, in some way so strange and glorious an object must have significance, could not possibly be a matter of absolute indifference to the scheme and values of my life.

But how?

I thought of Parload. I thought of the panic and uneasiness that was spreading in this very matter, and the assurances of scientific men that the thing weighed so little—at the utmost a few hundred tons of thinly diffused gas and dust—that even were it to smite this earth fully, nothing could possibly ensue. And, after all, said I, what earthly significance has any one found in the stars?

Then, as one still descended, the houses and buildings rose up, the presence of those watching groups of people, the tension of the situation; and one forgot the sky.

Preoccupied with myself and with my dark dream about Nettie and my honor, I threaded my course through the stagnating threat of this gathering, and was caught unawares, when suddenly the whole scene flashed into drama...

The attention of every one swung round with an irresistible magnetism towards the High Street, and caught me as a rush of waters might catch a wisp of hay. Abruptly the whole crowd was sounding one note. It was not a word, it was a sound that mingled threat and protest, something between a prolonged "Ah!" and "Ugh!" Then with a hoarse intensity of anger came a low heavy booing, "Boo! boo—oo!" a note stupidly expressive of animal savagery. "Toot, toot!" said Lord Redcar's automobile in ridiculous repartee. "Toot, toot!" One heard it whizzing and throbbing as the crowd obliged it to slow down.

Everybody seemed in motion towards the colliery gates, I, too, with the others.

I heard a shout. Through the dark figures about me I saw the motor-car stop and move forward again, and had a glimpse of something writhing on the ground.

It was alleged afterwards that Lord Redcar was driving, and that he quite deliberately knocked down a little boy who would not get out of his way. It is asserted with equal confidence that the boy was a man who tried to pass across the front of the motor-car as it came slowly through the crowd, who escaped by a

hair's breadth, and then slipped on the tram-rail and fell down. I have both accounts set forth, under screaming headlines, in two of these sere newspapers upon my desk. No one could ever ascertain the truth. Indeed, in such a blind tumult of passion, could there be any truth?

There was a rush forward, the horn of the car sounded, everything swayed violently to the right for perhaps ten yards or so, and there was a report like a pistol-shot.

For a moment every one seemed running away. A woman, carrying a shawl-wrapped child, blundered into me, and sent me reeling back. Every one thought of firearms, but, as a matter of fact, something had gone wrong with the motor, what in those old-fashioned contrivances was called a backfire. A thin puff of bluish smoke hung in the air behind the thing. The majority of the people scattered back in a disorderly fashion, and left a clear space about the struggle that centered upon the motor-car.

The man or boy who had fallen was lying on the ground with no one near him, a black lump, an extended arm and two sprawling feet. The motor-car had stopped, and its three occupants were standing up. Six or seven black figures surrounded the car, and appeared to be holding on to it as if to prevent it from starting again; one—it was Mitchell, a well-known labor leader —argued in fierce low tones with Lord Redcar. I could not hear anything they said, I was not near enough. Behind me the colliery gates were open, and there was a sense of help coming to the motor-car from that direction. There was an unoccupied muddy space for fifty yards, perhaps, between car and gate, and then the wheels and head of the pit rose black against the sky. I was one of a rude semicircle of people that hung as yet indeterminate in action about this dispute.

It was natural, I suppose, that my fingers should close upon the revolver in my pocket.

I advanced with the vaguest intentions in the world, and not so quickly but that several men hurried past me to join the little knot holding up the car.

Lord Redcar, in his big furry overcoat, towered up over the group about him; his gestures were free and threatening, and his voice loud. He made a fine figure there, I must admit; he was a big, fair, handsome young man with a fine tenor voice and an instinct for gallant effect. My eyes were drawn to him at first wholly. He seemed a symbol, a triumphant symbol, of all that the theory of aristocracy claims, of all that filled my soul with resentment. His chauffeur sat crouched together, peering at the crowd under his lordship's arm. But Mitchell showed as a sturdy figure also, and his voice was firm and loud.

"You've hurt that lad," said Mitchell, over and over again. "You'll wait here till you see if he's hurt."

"I'll wait here or not as I please," said Redcar; and to the chauffeur, "Here! get down and look at it!"

"You'd better not get down," said Mitchell; and the chauffeur stood bent and hesitating on the step.

The man on the back seat stood up, leant forward, and spoke to Lord Redcar, and for the first time my attention was drawn to him. It was young Verrall! His handsome face shone clear and fine in the green pallor of the comet.

I ceased to hear the quarrel that was raising the voice of Mitchell and Lord Redcar. This new fact sent them spinning into the background. Young Verrall!

It was my own purpose coming to meet me half way.

There was to be a fight here, it seemed certain to come to a scuffle, and here we were—

What was I to do? I thought very swiftly. Unless my memory cheats me, I acted with swift decision. My hand tightened on my revolver, and then I remembered it was unloaded. I had thought my course out in an instant. I turned round and pushed my way out of the angry crowd that was now surging back towards the motor-car.

It would be quiet and out of sight, I thought, among the dump heaps across the road, and there I might load unobserved...

A big young man striding forward with his fists clenched, halted for one second at the sight of me.

"What!" said he. "Ain't afraid of them, are you?"

I glanced over my shoulder and back at him, was near showing him my pistol, and the expression changed in his eyes. He hung perplexed at me. Then with a grunt he went on.

I heard the voices growing loud and sharp behind me.

I hesitated, half turned towards the dispute, then set off running towards the heaps. Some instinct told me not to be detected loading. I was cool enough therefore to think of the aftermath of the thing I meant to do.

I looked back once again towards the swaying discussion—or was it a fight now? and then I dropped into the hollow, knelt among the weeds, and loaded with eager trembling fingers. I loaded one chamber, got up and went back a dozen paces, thought of possibilities, vacillated, returned and loaded all the others. I did it slowly because I felt a little clumsy, and at the end came a moment of inspection—had I forgotten any thing? And then for a few seconds I crouched before I rose, resisting the first gust of reaction against my impulse. I took thought, and for a moment that great green-white meteor overhead swam back into my conscious mind. For the first time then I linked it clearly with all the fierce violence that had crept into human life. I joined up that with what I meant to do. I was going to shoot young Verrall as it were under the benediction of that green glare.

But about Nettie?

I found it impossible to think out that obvious complication.

I came up over the heap again, and walked slowly back towards the wrangle.

Of course I had to kill him...

Now I would have you believe I did not want to murder young Verrall at all at that particular time. I had not pictured such circumstances as these, I had never thought of him in connection with Lord Redcar and our black industrial world. He was in that distant other world of Checkshill, the world of parks and gardens, the

world of sunlit emotions and Nettie. His appearance here was disconcerting. I was taken by surprise. I was too tired and hungry to think clearly, and the hard implication of our antagonism prevailed with me. In the tumult of my passed emotions I had thought constantly of conflicts, confrontations, deeds of violence, and now the memory of these things took possession of me as though they were irrevocable resolutions.

There was a sharp exclamation, the shriek of a woman, and the crowd came surging back. The fight had begun.

Lord Redcar, I believe, had jumped down from his car and felled Mitchell, and men were already running out to his assistance from the colliery gates.

I had some difficulty in shoving through the crowd; I can still remember very vividly being jammed at one time between two big men so that my arms were pinned to my sides, but all the other details are gone out of my mind until I found myself almost violently projected forward into the "scrap."

I blundered against the corner of the motor-car, and came round it face to face with young Verrall, who was descending from the back compartment. His face was touched with orange from the automobile's big lamps, which conflicted with the shadows of the comet light, and distorted him oddly. That effect lasted but an instant, but it put me out. Then he came a step forward, and the ruddy lights and queerness vanished.

I don't think he recognized me, but he perceived immediately I meant attacking. He struck out at once at me a haphazard blow, and touched me on the cheek.

Instinctively I let go of the pistol, snatched my right hand out of my pocket and brought it up in a belated parry, and then let out with my left full in his chest.

It sent him staggering, and as he went back I saw recognition mingle with astonishment in his face.

"You know me, you swine," I cried and hit again.

Then I was spinning sideways, half-stunned, with a huge lump of a fist under my jaw. I had an impression of Lord Redcar as a great furry bulk, towering like some Homeric hero above the fray. I went down before him—it made him seem to rush up—and he ignored me further. His big flat voice counseled young Verrall—

"Cut, Teddy! It won't do. The picketa's got i'on bahs..."

Feet swayed about me, and some hobnailed miner kicked my ankle and went stumbling. There were shouts and curses, and then everything had swept past me. I rolled over on my face and beheld the chauffeur, young Verrall, and Lord Redcar—the latter holding up his long skirts of fur, and making a grotesque figure—one behind the other, in full bolt across a coldly comet-lit interval, towards the open gates of the colliery.

I raised myself up on my hands.

Young Verrall!

I had not even drawn my revolver—I had forgotten it. I was covered with coaly mud—knees, elbows, shoulders, back. I had not even drawn my revolver!...

A feeling of ridiculous impotence overwhelmed me. I struggled painfully to my feet.

I hesitated for a moment towards the gates of the colliery, and then went limping homeward, thwarted, painful, confused, and ashamed. I had not the heart nor desire to help in the wrecking and burning of Lord Redcar's motor.

§ 4

In the night, fever, pain, fatigue—it may be the indigestion of my supper of bread and cheese—roused me at last out of a hag-rid sleep to face despair. I was a soul lost amidst desolations and shame, dishonored, evilly treated, hopeless. I raged against the God I denied, and cursed him as I lay.

And it was in the nature of my fever, which was indeed only half fatigue and illness, and the rest the disorder of passionate youth, that Nettie, a strangely distorted Nettie, should come through the brief dreams that marked the exhaustions of that vigil, to dominate my misery. I was sensible, with an exaggerated distinctness, of the intensity of her physical charm for me, of her every grace and beauty; she took to herself the whole gamut of desire in me and the whole gamut of pride. She, bodily, was my lost honor. It was not only loss but disgrace to lose her. She stood for life and all that was denied; she mocked me as a creature of failure and defeat. My spirit raised itself towards her, and then the bruise upon my jaw glowed with a dull heat, and I rolled in the mud again before my rivals.

There were times when something near madness took me, and I gnashed my teeth and dug my nails into my hands and ceased to curse and cry out only by reason of the insufficiency of words. And once towards dawn I got out of bed, and sat by my looking-glass with my revolver loaded in my hand. I stood up at last and put it carefully in my drawer and locked it—out of reach of any gusty impulse. After that I slept for a little while.

Such nights were nothing rare and strange in that old order of the world. Never a city, never a night the whole year round, but amidst those who slept were those who waked, plumbing the deeps of wrath and misery. Countless thousands there were so ill, so troubled, they agonize near to the very border- line of madness, each one the center of a universe darkened and lost...

The next day I spent in gloomy lethargy.

I had intended to go to Checkshill that day, but my bruised ankle was too swollen for that to be possible. I sat indoors in the ill-lit downstairs kitchen, with my foot bandaged, and mused darkly and read. My dear old mother waited on me, and her brown eyes watched me and wondered at my black silences, my frowning preoccupations. I had not told her how it was my ankle came to be bruised and my clothes muddy. She had brushed my clothes in the morning before I got up.

Ah well! Mothers are not treated in that way now. That I suppose must console me. I wonder how far you will be able to picture that dark, grimy, untidy room, with its bare deal table, its tattered wall paper, the saucepans and kettle on the narrow, cheap, but by no means economical range, the ashes under the fireplace, the rust-spotted steel fender on which my bandaged feet rested; I wonder how near

you can come to seeing the scowling pale-faced hobbledehoy I was, unshaven and collarless, in the Windsor chair, and the little timid, dirty, devoted old woman who hovered about me with love peering out from her puckered eyelids...

When she went out to buy some vegetables in the middle of the morning she got me a half-penny journal. It was just such a one as these upon my desk, only that the copy I read was damp from the press, and these are so dry and brittle, they crack if I touch them. I have a copy of the actual issue I read that morning; it was a paper called emphatically the New Paper, but everybody bought it and everybody called it the "yell." It was full that morning of stupendous news and still more stupendous headlines, so stupendous that for a little while I was roused from my egotistical broodings to wider interests. For it seemed that Germany and England were on the brink of war.

Of all the monstrous irrational phenomena of the former time, war was certainly the most strikingly insane. In reality it was probably far less mischievous than such quieter evil as, for example, the general acquiescence in the private ownership of land, but its evil consequences showed so plainly that even in those days of stifling confusion one marveled at it. On no conceivable grounds was there any sense in modern war. Save for the slaughter and mangling of a multitude of people, the destruction of vast quantities of material, and the waste of innumerable units of energy, it effected nothing. The old war of savage and barbaric nations did at least change humanity, you assumed yourselves to be a superior tribe in physique and discipline, you demonstrated this upon your neighbors, and if successful you took their land and their women and perpetuated and enlarged your superiority. The new war changed nothing but the color of maps, the design of postage stamps, and the relationship of a few accidentally conspicuous individuals. In one of the last of these international epileptic fits, for example, the English, with much dysentery and bad poetry, and a few hundred deaths in battle, conquered the South African Boers at a gross cost of about three thousand pounds per head—they could have bought the whole of that preposterous imitation of a nation for a tenth of that sum—and except for a few substitutions of personalities, this group of partially corrupt officials in the place of that, and so forth, the permanent change was altogether insignificant. (But an excitable young man in Austria committed suicide when at length the Transvaal ceased to be a "nation.") Men went through the seat of that war after it was all over, and found humanity unchanged, except for a general impoverishment, and the convenience of an unlimited supply of empty ration tins and barbed wire and cartridge cases — unchanged and resuming with a slight perplexity all its old habits and misunderstandings, the nigger still in his slum-like kraal, the white in his ugly ill-managed shanty...

But we in England saw all these things, or did not see them, through the mirage of the New Paper, in a light of mania. All my adolescence from fourteen to seventeen went to the music of that monstrous resonating futility, the cheering, the anxieties, the songs and the waving of flags, the wrongs of generous Buller and the glorious heroism of De Wet—who ALWAYS got away; that was the

great point about the heroic De Wet—and it never occurred to us that the total population we fought against was less than half the number of those who lived cramped ignoble lives within the compass of the Four Towns.

But before and after that stupid conflict of stupidities, a greater antagonism was coming into being, was slowly and quietly defining itself as a thing inevitable, sinking now a little out of attention only to resume more emphatically, now flashing into some acute definitive expression and now percolating and pervading some new region of thought, and that was the antagonism of Germany and Great Britain.

When I think of that growing proportion of readers who belong entirely to the new order, who are growing up with only the vaguest early memories of the old world, I find the greatest difficulty in writing down the unintelligible confusions that were matter of fact to their fathers.

Here were we British, forty-one millions of people, in a state of almost indescribably aimless, economic, and moral muddle that we had neither the courage, the energy, nor the intelligence to improve, that most of us had hardly the courage to think about, and with our affairs hopelessly entangled with the entirely different confusions of three hundred and fifty million other persons scattered about the globe, and here were the Germans over against us, fifty-six millions, in a state of confusion no whit better than our own, and the noisy little creatures who directed papers and wrote books and gave lectures, and generally in that time of world-dementia pretended to be the national mind, were busy in both countries, with a sort of infernal unanimity, exhorting—and not only exhorting but successfully persuading—the two peoples to divert such small common store of material, moral and intellectual energy as either possessed, into the purely destructive and wasteful business of war. And—I have to tell you these things even if you do not believe them, because they are vital to my story—there was not a man alive who could have told you of any real permanent benefit, of anything whatever to counterbalance the obvious waste and evil, that would result from a war between England and Germany, whether England shattered Germany or was smashed and overwhelmed, or whatever the end might be.

The thing was, in fact, an enormous irrational obsession, it was, in the microcosm of our nation, curiously parallel to the egotistical wrath and jealousy that swayed my individual microcosm. It measured the excess of common emotion over the common intelligence, the legacy of inordinate passion we have received from the brute from which we came. Just as I had become the slave of my own surprise and anger and went hither and thither with a loaded revolver, seeking and intending vague fluctuating crimes, so these two nations went about the earth, hot eared and muddle headed, with loaded navies and armies terribly ready at hand. Only there was not even a Nettie to justify their stupidity. There was nothing but quiet imaginary thwarting on either side.

And the press was the chief instrument that kept these two huge multitudes of people directed against one another.

The press—those newspapers that are now so strange to us—like the "Empires," the "Nations," the Trusts, and all the other great monstrous shapes of that extraordinary time—was in the nature of an unanticipated accident. It had happened, as weeds happen in abandoned gardens, just as all our world has happened,—because there was no clear Will in the world to bring about anything better. Towards the end this "press" was almost entirely under the direction of youngish men of that eager, rather unintelligent type, that is never able to detect itself aimless, that pursues nothing with incredible pride and zeal, and if you would really understand this mad era the comet brought to an end, you must keep in mind that every phase in the production of these queer old things was pervaded by a strong aimless energy and happened in a concentrated rush.

Let me describe to you, very briefly, a newspaper day.

Figure first, then, a hastily erected and still more hastily designed building in a dirty, paper-littered back street of old London, and a number of shabbily dressed men coming and going in this with projectile swiftness, and within this factory companies of printers, tensely active with nimble fingers —they were always speeding up the printers—ply their type- setting machines, and cast and arrange masses of metal in a sort of kitchen inferno, above which, in a beehive of little brightly lit rooms, disheveled men sit and scribble. There is a throbbing of telephones and a clicking of telegraph needles, a rushing of messengers, a running to and fro of heated men, clutching proofs and copy. Then begins a clatter roar of machinery catching the infection, going faster and faster, and whizzing and banging,—engineers, who have never had time to wash since their birth, flying about with oil-cans, while paper runs off its rolls with a shudder of haste. The proprietor you must suppose arriving explosively on a swift motor-car, leaping out before the thing is at a standstill, with letters and documents clutched in his hand, rushing in, resolute to "hustle," getting wonderfully in everybody's way. At the sight of him even the messenger boys who are waiting, get up and scamper to and fro. Sprinkle your vision with collisions, curses, incoherencies. You imagine all the parts of this complex lunatic machine working hysterically toward a crescendo of haste and excitement as the night wears on. At last the only things that seem to travel slowly in all those tearing vibrating premises are the hands of the clock.

Slowly things draw on toward publication, the consummation of all those stresses. Then in the small hours, into the now dark and deserted streets comes a wild whirl of carts and men, the place spurts paper at every door, bales, heaps, torrents of papers, that are snatched and flung about in what looks like a free fight, and off with a rush and clatter east, west, north, and south. The interest passes outwardly; the men from the little rooms are going homeward, the printers disperse yawning, the roaring presses slacken. The paper exists. Distribution follows manufacture, and we follow the bundles.

Our vision becomes a vision of dispersal. You see those bundles hurling into stations, catching trains by a hair's breadth, speeding on their way, breaking up, smaller bundles of them hurled with a fierce accuracy out upon the platforms that rush by, and then everywhere a division of these smaller bundles into still smaller

bundles, into dispersing parcels, into separate papers, and the dawn happens unnoticed amidst a great running and shouting of boys, a shoving through letter slots, openings of windows, spreading out upon book- stalls. For the space of a few hours you must figure the whole country dotted white with rustling papers—placards everywhere vociferating the hurried lie for the day; men and women in trains, men and women eating and reading, men by study-fenders, people sitting up in bed, mothers and sons and daughters waiting for father to finish—a million scattered people reading—reading headlong—or feverishly ready to read. It is just as if some vehement jet had sprayed that white foam of papers over the surface of the land...

And then you know, wonderfully gone—gone utterly, vanished as foam might vanish upon the sand.

Nonsense! The whole affair a noisy paroxysm of nonsense, unreasonable excitement, witless mischief, and waste of strength—signifying nothing...

And one of those white parcels was the paper I held in my hands, as I sat with a bandaged foot on the steel fender in that dark underground kitchen of my mother's, clean roused from my personal troubles by the yelp of the headlines. She sat, sleeves tucked up from her ropy arms, peeling potatoes as I read.

It was like one of a flood of disease germs that have invaded a body, that paper. There I was, one corpuscle in the big amorphous body of the English community, one of forty-one million such corpuscles and, for all my preoccupations, these potent headlines, this paper ferment, caught me and swung me about. And all over the country that day, millions read as I read, and came round into line with me, under the same magnetic spell, came round—how did we say it?—Ah!—"to face the foe."

The comet had been driven into obscurity overleaf. The column headed "Distinguished Scientist says Comet will Strike our Earth. Does it Matter?" went unread. "Germany"—I usually figured this mythical malignant creature as a corseted stiff-mustached Emperor enhanced by heraldic black wings and a large sword—had insulted our flag. That was the message of the New Paper, and the monster towered over me, threatening fresh outrages, visibly spitting upon my faultless country's colors. Somebody had hoisted a British flag on the right bank of some tropical river I had never heard of before, and a drunken German officer under ambiguous instructions had torn it down. Then one of the convenient abundant natives of the country, a British subject indisputably, had been shot in the leg. But the facts were by no means clear. Nothing was clear except that we were not going to stand any nonsense from Germany. Whatever had or had not happened we meant to have an apology for, and apparently they did not mean apologizing.

HAS WAR COME AT LAST?

That was the headline. One's heart leapt to assent...

There were hours that day when I clean forgot Nettie, in dreaming of battles and victories by land and sea, of shell fire, and entrenchments, and the heaped slaughter of many thousands of men.

But the next morning I started for Checkshill, started, I remember, in a curiously hopeful state of mind, oblivious of comets, strikes, and wars.

§ 5

You must understand that I had no set plan of murder when I walked over to Checkshill. I had no set plan of any sort. There was a great confusion of dramatically conceived intentions in my head, scenes of threatening and denunciation and terror, but I did not mean to kill. The revolver was to turn upon my rival my disadvantage in age and physique...

But that was not it really! The revolver!—I took the revolver because I had the revolver and was a foolish young lout. It was a dramatic sort of thing to take. I had, I say, no plan at all.

Ever and again during that second trudge to Checkshill I was irradiated with a novel unreasonable hope. I had awakened in the morning with the hope, it may have been the last unfaded trail of some obliterated dream, that after all Nettie might relent toward me, that her heart was kind toward me in spite of all that I imagined had happened. I even thought it possible that I might have misinterpreted what I had seen. Perhaps she would explain everything. My revolver was in my pocket for all that.

I limped at the outset, but after the second mile my ankle warmed to forgetfulness, and the rest of the way I walked well. Suppose, after all, I was wrong?

I was still debating that, as I came through the park. By the corner of the paddock near the keeper's cottage, I was reminded by some belated blue hyacinths of a time when I and Nettie had gathered them together. It seemed impossible that we could really have parted ourselves for good and all. A wave of tenderness flowed over me, and still flooded me as I came through the little dell and drew towards the hollies. But there the sweet Nettie of my boy's love faded, and I thought of the new Nettie of desire and the man I had come upon in the moonlight, I thought of the narrow, hot purpose that had grown so strongly out of my springtime freshness, and my mood darkened to night.

I crossed the beech wood and came towards the gardens with a resolute and sorrowful heart. When I reached the green door in the garden wall I was seized for a space with so violent a trembling that I could not grip the latch to lift it, for I no longer had any doubt how this would end. That trembling was succeeded by a feeling of cold, and whiteness, and self-pity. I was astonished to find myself grimacing, to feel my cheeks wet, and thereupon I gave way completely to a wild passion of weeping. I must take just a little time before the thing was done... I turned away from the door and stumbled for a little distance, sobbing loudly, and lay down out of sight among the bracken, and so presently became calm again. I lay there some time. I had half a mind to desist, and then my emotion passed like the shadow of a cloud, and I walked very coolly into the gardens.

Through the open door of one of the glass houses I saw old Stuart. He was leaning against the staging, his hands in his pockets, and so deep in thought he gave no heed to me.

I hesitated and went on towards the cottage, slowly.

Something struck me as unusual about the place, but I could not tell at first what it was. One of the bedroom windows was open, and the customary short blind, with its brass upper rail partly unfastened, drooped obliquely across the vacant space. It looked negligent and odd, for usually everything about the cottage was conspicuously trim.

The door was standing wide open, and everything was still. But giving that usually orderly hall an odd look—it was about half-past two in the afternoon—was a pile of three dirty plates, with used knives and forks upon them, on one of the hall chairs.

I went into the hall, looked into either room, and hesitated.

Then I fell to upon the door-knocker and gave a loud rat-tat-too, and followed this up with an amiable "Hel-lo!"

For a time no one answered me, and I stood listening and expectant, with my fingers about my weapon. Some one moved about upstairs presently, and was still again. The tension of waiting seemed to brace my nerves.

I had my hand on the knocker for the second time, when Puss appeared in the doorway.

For a moment we remained staring at one another without speaking. Her hair was disheveled, her face dirty, tear-stained, and irregularly red. Her expression at the sight of me was pure astonishment. I thought she was about to say something, and then she had darted away out of the house again.

"I say, Puss!" I said. "Puss!"

I followed her out of the door. "Puss! What's the matter? Where's Nettie?"

She vanished round the corner of the house.

I hesitated, perplexed whether I should pursue her. What did it all mean? Then I heard some one upstairs.

"Willie!" cried the voice of Mrs. Stuart. "Is that you?"

"Yes," I answered. "Where's every one? Where's Nettie? I want to have a talk with her."

She did not answer, but I heard her dress rustle as she moved. I Judged she was upon the landing overhead.

I paused at the foot of the stairs, expecting her to appear and come down.

Suddenly came a strange sound, a rush of sounds, words jumbled and hurrying, confused and shapeless, borne along upon a note of throaty distress that at last submerged the words altogether and ended in a wail. Except that it came from a woman's throat it was exactly the babbling sound of a weeping child with a grievance. "I can't," she said, "I can't," and that was all I could distinguish. It was to my young ears the strangest sound conceivable from a kindly motherly little woman, whom I had always thought of chiefly as an unparalleled maker of cakes. It frightened me. I went upstairs at once in a state of infinite alarm, and there she was upon the landing, leaning forward over the top of the chest of drawers beside her open bedroom door, and weeping. I never saw such weeping. One thick strand

of black hair had escaped, and hung with a spiral twist down her back; never before had I noticed that she had gray hairs.

As I came up upon the landing her voice rose again. "Oh that I should have to tell you, Willie! Oh that I should have to tell you!" She dropped her head again, and a fresh gust of tears swept all further words away.

I said nothing, I was too astonished; but I drew nearer to her, and waited...

I never saw such weeping; the extraordinary wetness of her dripping handkerchief abides with me to this day.

"That I should have lived to see this day!" she wailed. "I had rather a thousand times she was struck dead at my feet."

I began to understand.

"Mrs. Stuart," I said, clearing my throat; "what has become of Nettie?"

"That I should have lived to see this day!" she said by way of reply.

I waited till her passion abated.

There came a lull. I forgot the weapon in my pocket. I said nothing, and suddenly she stood erect before me, wiping her swollen eyes. "Willie," she gulped, "she's gone!"

"Nettie?"

"Gone! ... Run away... Run away from her home. Oh, Willie, Willie! The shame of it! The sin and shame of it!"

She flung herself upon my shoulder, and clung to me, and began again to wish her daughter lying dead at our feet.

"There, there," said I, and all my being was a-tremble. "Where has she gone?" I said as softly as I could.

But for the time she was preoccupied with her own sorrow, and I had to hold her there, and comfort her with the blackness of finality spreading over my soul.

"Where has she gone?" I asked for the fourth time.

"I don't know—we don't know. And oh, Willie, she went out yesterday morning! I said to her, 'Nettie,' I said to her, 'you're mighty fine for a morning call.' 'Fine clo's for a fine day,' she said, and that was her last words to me!—Willie!—the child I suckled at my breast!"

"Yes, yes. But where has she gone?" I said.

She went on with sobs, and now telling her story with a sort of fragmentary hurry: "She went out bright and shining, out of this house for ever. She was smiling, Willie—as if she was glad to be going. ("Glad to be going," I echoed with soundless lips.) 'You're mighty fine for the morning,' I says; 'mighty fine.' 'Let the girl be pretty,' says her father, 'while she's young!' And somewhere she'd got a parcel of her things hidden to pick up, and she was going off—out of this house for ever!"

She became quiet.

"Let the girl be pretty," she repeated; "let the girl be pretty while she's young... Oh! how can we go on LIVING, Willie? He doesn't show it, but he's like a stricken beast. He's wounded to the heart. She was always his favorite. He never seemed to care for Puss like he did for her. And she's wounded him—"

"Where has she gone?" I reverted at last to that.

"We don't know. She leaves her own blood, she trusts herself—Oh, Willie, it'll kill me! I wish she and me together were lying in our graves."

"But"—I moistened my lips and spoke slowly—"she may have gone to marry."

"If that was so! I've prayed to God it might be so, Willie. I've prayed that he'd take pity on her—him, I mean, she's with."

I jerked out: "Who's that?"

"In her letter, she said he was a gentleman. She did say he was a gentleman."

"In her letter. Has she written? Can I see her letter?"

"Her father took it."

"But if she writes—When did she write?"

"It came this morning."

"But where did it come from? You can tell—"

"She didn't say. She said she was happy. She said love took one like a storm—"

"Curse that! Where is her letter? Let me see it. And as for this gentleman—"

She stared at me.

"You know who it is."

"Willie!" she protested.

"You know who it is, whether she said or not?" Her eyes made a mute unconfident denial.

"Young Verrall?"

She made no answer. "All I could do for you, Willie," she began presently.

"Was it young Verrall?" I insisted.

For a second, perhaps, we faced one another in stark understanding.... Then she plumped back to the chest of drawers, and her wet pocket-handkerchief, and I knew she sought refuge from my relentless eyes.

My pity for her vanished. She knew it was her mistress's son as well as I! And for some time she had known, she had felt.

I hovered over her for a moment, sick with amazed disgust. I suddenly bethought me of old Stuart, out in the greenhouse, and turned and went downstairs. As I did so, I looked up to see Mrs. Stuart moving droopingly and lamely back into her own room.

§ 6

Old Stuart was pitiful.

I found him still inert in the greenhouse where I had first seen him. He did not move as I drew near him; he glanced at me, and then stared hard again at the flowerpots before him.

"Eh, Willie," he said, "this is a black day for all of us."

"What are you going to do?" I asked.

"The missus takes on so," he said. "I came out here."

"What do you mean to do?"

"What IS a man to do in such a case?"

"Do!" I cried, "why—Do!"

"He ought to marry her," he said.

"By God, yes!" I cried. "He must do that anyhow."

"He ought to. It's—it's cruel. But what am I to do? Suppose he won't? Likely he won't. What then?"

He drooped with an intensified despair.

"Here's this cottage," he said, pursuing some contracted argument. "We've lived here all our lives, you might say... Clear out. At my age... One can't die in a slum."

I stood before him for a space, speculating what thoughts might fill the gaps between these broken words. I found his lethargy, and the dimly shaped mental attitudes his words indicated, abominable. I said abruptly, "You have her letter?"

He dived into his breast-pocket, became motionless for ten seconds, then woke up again and produced her letter. He drew it clumsily from its envelope, and handed it to me silently.

"Why!" he cried, looking at me for the first time, "What's come to your chin, Willie?"

"It's nothing," I said. "It's a bruise;" and I opened the letter.

It was written on greenish tinted fancy note-paper, and with all and more than Nettie's usual triteness and inadequacy of expression. Her handwriting bore no traces of emotion; it was round and upright and clear as though it had been done in a writing lesson. Always her letters were like masks upon her image; they fell like curtains before the changing charm of her face; one altogether forgot the sound of her light clear voice, confronted by a perplexing stereotyped thing that had mysteriously got a hold upon one's heart and pride. How did that letter run?—

"MY DEAR MOTHER,

"Do not be distressed at my going away. I have gone somewhere safe, and with some one who cares for me very much. I am sorry for your sakes, but it seems that it had to be. Love is a very difficult thing, and takes hold of one in ways one does not expect. Do not think I am ashamed about this, I glory in my love, and you must not trouble too much about me. I am very, very happy (deeply underlined).

"Fondest love to Father and Puss.

"Your loving

"Nettie."

That queer little document! I can see it now for the childish simple thing it was, but at the time I read it in a suppressed anguish of rage. It plunged me into a pit of hopeless shame; there seemed to remain no pride for me in life until I had revenge. I stood staring at those rounded upstanding letters, not trusting myself to speak or move. At last I stole a glance at Stuart.

He held the envelope in his hand, and stared down at the postmark between his horny thumbnails.

"You can't even tell where she is," he said, turning the thing round in a hopeless manner, and then desisting. "It's hard on us, Willie. Here she is; she hadn't anything to complain of; a sort of pet for all of us. Not even made to do her share of the 'ousework. And she goes off and leaves us like a bird that's learnt to fly. Can't TRUST us, that's what takes me. Puts 'erself —But there! What's to happen to her?"

"What's to happen to him?"

He shook his head to show that problem was beyond him.

"You'll go after her," I said in an even voice; "you'll make him marry her?"

"Where am I to go?" he asked helplessly, and held out the envelope with a gesture; "and what could I do? Even if I knew—How could I leave the gardens?"

"Great God!" I cried, "not leave these gardens! It's your Honor, man! If she was my daughter—if she was my daughter—I'd tear the world to pieces!" .. I choked. "You mean to stand it?"

"What can I do?"

"Make him marry her! Horsewhip him! Horsewhip him, I say!—I'd strangle him!"

He scratched slowly at his hairy cheek, opened his mouth, and shook his head. Then, with an intolerable note of sluggish gentle wisdom, he said, "People of our sort, Willie, can't do things like that."

I came near to raving. I had a wild impulse to strike him in the face. Once in my boyhood I happened upon a bird terribly mangled by some cat, and killed it in a frenzy of horror and pity. I had a gust of that same emotion now, as this shameful mutilated soul fluttered in the dust, before me. Then, you know, I dismissed him from the case.

"May I look?" I asked.

He held out the envelope reluctantly.

"There it is," he said, and pointing with his garden-rough forefinger. "I.A.P.A.M.P. What can you make of that?"

I took the thing in my hands. The adhesive stamp customary in those days was defaced by a circular postmark, which bore the name of the office of departure and the date. The impact in this particular case had been light or made without sufficient ink, and half the letters of the name had left no impression. I could distinguish—

I A P A M P

and very faintly below D.S.O.

I guessed the name in an instant flash of intuition. It was Shaphambury. The very gaps shaped that to my mind. Perhaps in a sort of semi-visibility other letters were there, at least hinting themselves. It was a place somewhere on the east coast, I knew, either in Norfolk or Suffolk.

"Why!" cried I—and stopped.

What was the good of telling him?

Old Stuart had glanced up sharply, I am inclined to think almost fearfully, into my face. "You—you haven't got it?" he said.

Shaphambury—I should remember that.

"You don't think you got it?" he said.

I handed the envelope back to him.

"For a moment I thought it might be Hampton," I said.

"Hampton," he repeated. "Hampton. How could you make Hampton?" He turned the envelope about. "H.A.M.—why, Willie, you're a worse hand at the job than me!"

He replaced the letter in the envelope and stood erect to put this back in his breast pocket.

I did not mean to take any risks in this affair. I drew a stump of pencil from my waistcoat pocket, turned a little away from him and wrote "Shaphambury" very quickly on my frayed and rather grimy shirt cuff.

"Well," said I, with an air of having done nothing remarkable.

I turned to him with some unimportant observation—I have forgotten what.

I never finished whatever vague remark I commenced.

I looked up to see a third person waiting at the greenhouse door.

§ 7

It was old Mrs. Verrall.

I wonder if I can convey the effect of her to you. She was a little old lady with extraordinarily flaxen hair, her weak aquiline features were pursed up into an assumption of dignity, and she was richly dressed. I would like to underline that "richly dressed," or have the words printed in florid old English or Gothic lettering. No one on earth is now quite so richly dressed as she was, no one old or young indulges in so quiet and yet so profound a sumptuosity. But you must not imagine any extravagance of outline or any beauty or richness of color. The predominant colors were black and fur browns, and the effect of richness was due entirely to the extreme costliness of the materials employed. She affected silk brocades with rich and elaborate patterns, priceless black lace over creamy or purple satin, intricate trimmings through which threads and bands of velvet wriggled, and in the winter rare furs. Her gloves fitted exquisitely, and ostentatiously simple chains of fine gold and pearls, and a great number of bracelets, laced about her little person. One was forced to feel that the slightest article she wore cost more than all the wardrobe of a dozen girls like Nettie; her bonnet affected the simplicity that is beyond rubies. Richness, that is the first quality about this old lady that I would like to convey to you, and the second was cleanliness. You felt that old Mrs. Verrall was exquisitely clean. If you had boiled my poor dear old mother in soda for a month you couldn't have got her so clean as Mrs. Verrall constantly and manifestly was. And pervading all her presence shone her third great quality, her manifest confidence in the respectful subordination of the world.

She was pale and a little out of breath that day, but without any loss of her ultimate confidence, and it was clear to me that she had come to interview Stuart upon the outbreak of passion that had bridged the gulf between their families.

And here again I find myself writing in an unknown language, so far as my younger readers are concerned. You who know only the world that followed the Great Change will find much that I am telling inconceivable. Upon these points I cannot appeal, as I have appealed for other confirmations, to the old newspapers; these were the things that no one wrote about because every one understood and every one had taken up an attitude. There were in England and America, and indeed throughout the world, two great informal divisions of human beings—the Secure and the Insecure. There was not and never had been in either country a nobility—it was and remains a common error that the British peers were noble—neither in law nor custom were there noble families, and we altogether lacked the edification one found in Russia, for example, of a poor nobility. A peerage was an hereditary possession that, like the family land, concerned only the eldest sons of the house; it radiated no luster of noblesse oblige. The rest of the world were in law and practice common—and all America was common. But through the private ownership of land that had resulted from the neglect of feudal obligations in Britain and the utter want of political foresight in the Americas, large masses of property had become artificially stable in the hands of a small minority, to whom it was necessary to mortgage all new public and private enterprises, and who were held together not by any tradition of service and nobility but by the natural sympathy of common interests and a common large scale of living. It was a class without any very definite boundaries; vigorous individualities, by methods for the most part violent and questionable, were constantly thrusting themselves from insecurity to security, and the sons and daughters of secure people, by marrying insecurity or by wild extravagance or flagrant vice, would sink into the life of anxiety and insufficiency which was the ordinary life of man. The rest of the population was landless and, except by working directly or indirectly for the Secure, had no legal right to exist. And such was the shallowness and insufficiency of our thought, such the stifled egotism of all our feelings before the Last Days, that very few indeed of the Secure could be found to doubt that this was the natural and only conceivable order of the world.

It is the life of the Insecure under the old order that I am displaying, and I hope that I am conveying something of its hopeless bitterness to you, but you must not imagine that the Secure lived lives of paradisiacal happiness. The pit of insecurity below them made itself felt, even though it was not comprehended. Life about them was ugly; the sight of ugly and mean houses, of ill-dressed people, the vulgar appeals of the dealers in popular commodities, were not to be escaped. There was below the threshold of their minds an uneasiness; they not only did not think clearly about social economy but they displayed an instinctive disinclination to think. Their security was not so perfect that they had not a dread of falling towards the pit, they were always lashing themselves by new ropes, their cultivation of "connexions," of interests, their desire to confirm and improve their positions, was a constant ignoble preoccupation. You must read Thackeray to get the full flavor of their lives. Then the bacterium was apt to disregard class distinctions, and they were never really happy in their servants. Read their surviving books.

Each generation bewails the decay of that "fidelity" of servants, no generation ever saw. A world that is squalid in one corner is squalid altogether, but that they never understood. They believed there was not enough of anything to go round, they believed that this was the intention of God and an incurable condition of life, and they held passionately and with a sense of right to their disproportionate share. They maintained a common intercourse as "Society" of all who were practically secure, and their choice of that word is exhaustively eloquent of the quality of their philosophy. But, if you can master these alien ideas upon which the old system rested, just in the same measure will you understand the horror these people had for marriages with the Insecure. In the case of their girls and women it was extraordinarily rare, and in the case of either sex it was regarded as a disastrous social crime. Anything was better than that.

You are probably aware of the hideous fate that was only too probably the lot, during those last dark days, of every girl of the insecure classes who loved and gave way to the impulse of self-abandonment without marriage, and so you will understand the peculiar situation of Nettie with young Verrall. One or other had to suffer. And as they were both in a state of great emotional exaltation and capable of strange generosities toward each other, it was an open question and naturally a source of great anxiety to a mother in Mrs. Verrall's position, whether the sufferer might not be her son—whether as the outcome of that glowing irresponsible commerce Nettie might not return prospective mistress of Checkshill Towers. The chances were greatly against that conclusion, but such things did occur.

These laws and customs sound, I know, like a record of some nasty-minded lunatic's inventions. They were invincible facts in that vanished world into which, by some accident, I had been born, and it was the dream of any better state of things that was scouted as lunacy. Just think of it! This girl I loved with all my soul, for whom I was ready to sacrifice my life, was not good enough to marry young Verrall. And I had only to look at his even, handsome, characterless face to perceive a creature weaker and no better than myself. She was to be his pleasure until he chose to cast her aside, and the poison of our social system had so saturated her nature—his evening dress, his freedom and his money had seemed so fine to her and I so clothed in squalor —that to that prospect she had consented. And to resent the social conventions that created their situation, was called "class envy," and gently born preachers reproached us for the mildest resentment against an injustice no living man would now either endure or consent to profit by.

What was the sense of saying "peace" when there was no peace? If there was one hope in the disorders of that old world it lay in revolt and conflict to the death.

But if you can really grasp the shameful grotesqueness of the old life, you will begin to appreciate the interpretation of old Mrs. Verrall's appearance that leapt up at once in my mind.

She had come to compromise the disaster!

And the Stuarts WOULD compromise! I saw that only too well.

An enormous disgust at the prospect of the imminent encounter between Stuart and his mistress made me behave in a violent and irrational way. I wanted to escape seeing that, seeing even Stuart's first gesture in that, at any cost.

"I'm off," said I, and turned my back on him without any further farewell.

My line of retreat lay by the old lady, and so I advanced toward her.

I saw her expression change, her mouth fell a little way open, her forehead wrinkled, and her eyes grew round. She found me a queer customer even at the first sight, and there was something in the manner of my advance that took away her breath.

She stood at the top of the three or four steps that descended to the level of the hothouse floor. She receded a pace or two, with a certain offended dignity at the determination of my rush.

I gave her no sort of salutation.

Well, as a matter of fact, I did give her a sort of salutation. There is no occasion for me to begin apologizing now for the thing I said to her—I strip these things before you—if only I can get them stark enough you will understand and forgive. I was filled with a brutal and overpowering desire to insult her.

And so I addressed this poor little expensive old woman in the following terms, converting her by a violent metonymy into a comprehensive plural. "You infernal land thieves!" I said point-blank into her face. "HAVE YOU COME TO OFFER THEM MONEY?"

And without waiting to test her powers of repartee I passed rudely beyond her and vanished, striding with my fists clenched, out of her world again...

I have tried since to imagine how the thing must have looked to her. So far as her particular universe went I had not existed at all, or I had existed only as a dim black thing, an insignificant speck, far away across her park in irrelevant, unimportant transit, until this moment when she came, sedately troubled, into her own secure gardens and sought for Stuart among the greenhouses. Then abruptly I flashed into being down that green-walled, brick- floored vista as a black-avised, ill-clad young man, who first stared and then advanced scowling toward her. Once in existence I developed rapidly. I grew larger in perspective and became more and more important and sinister every moment. I came up the steps with inconceivable hostility and disrespect in my bearing, towered over her, becoming for an instant at least a sort of second French Revolution, and delivered myself with the intensest concentration of those wicked and incomprehensible words. Just for a second I threatened annihilation. Happily that was my climax.

And then I had gone by, and the Universe was very much as it had always been except for the wild swirl in it, and the faint sense of insecurity my episode left in its wake.

The thing that never entered my head in those days was that a large proportion of the rich were rich in absolute good faith. I thought they saw things exactly as I saw them, and wickedly denied. But indeed old Mrs. Verrall was no more capable of doubting the perfection of her family's right to dominate a wide country side,

than she was of examining the Thirty-nine Articles or dealing with any other of the adamantine pillars upon which her universe rested in security.

No doubt I startled and frightened her tremendously. But she could not understand.

None of her sort of people ever did seem to understand such livid flashes of hate, as ever and again lit the crowded darkness below their feet. The thing leapt out of the black for a moment and vanished, like a threatening figure by a desolate roadside lit for a moment by one's belated carriage-lamp and then swallowed up by the night. They counted it with nightmares, and did their best to forget what was evidently as insignificant as it was disturbing.

CHAPTER THE FOURTH - WAR

§ 1

From that moment when I insulted old Mrs. Verrall I became representative, I was a man who stood for all the disinherited of the world. I had no hope of pride or pleasure left in me, I was raging rebellion against God and mankind. There were no more vague intentions swaying me this way and that; I was perfectly clear now upon what I meant to do. I would make my protest and die.

I would make my protest and die. I was going to kill Nettie—Nettie who had smiled and promised and given herself to another, and who stood now for all the conceivable delightfulnesses, the lost imaginations of the youthful heart, the unattainable joys in life; and Verrall who stood for all who profited by the incurable injustice of our social order. I would kill them both. And that being done I would blow my brains out and see what vengeance followed my blank refusal to live.

So indeed I was resolved. I raged monstrously. And above me, abolishing the stars, triumphant over the yellow waning moon that followed it below, the giant meteor towered up towards the zenith.

"Let me only kill!" I cried. "Let me only kill!"

So I shouted in my frenzy. I was in a fever that defied hunger and fatigue; for a long time I had prowled over the heath towards Lowchester talking to myself, and now that night had fully come I was tramping homeward, walking the long seventeen miles without a thought of rest. And I had eaten nothing since the morning.

I suppose I must count myself mad, but I can recall my ravings.

There were times when I walked weeping through that brightness that was neither night nor day. There were times when I reasoned in a topsy-turvy fashion with what I called the Spirit of All Things. But always I spoke to that white glory in the sky.

"Why am I here only to suffer ignominies?" I asked. "Why have you made me with pride that cannot be satisfied, with desires that turn and rend me? Is it a jest, this world—a joke you play on your guests? I—even I —have a better humor than that!"

"Why not learn from me a certain decency of mercy? Why not undo? Have I ever tormented—day by day, some wretched worm—making filth for it to trail through, filth that disgusts it, starving it, bruising it, mocking it? Why should you? Your jokes are clumsy. Try—try some milder fun up there; do you hear? Something that doesn't hurt so infernally."

"You say this is your purpose—your purpose with me. You are making something with me—birth pangs of a soul. Ah! How can I believe you? You forget I have eyes for other things. Let my own case go, but what of that frog beneath the cart-wheel, God?—and the bird the cat had torn?"

And after such blasphemies I would fling out a ridiculous little debating society hand. "Answer me that!"

A week ago it had been moonlight, white and black and hard across the spaces of the park, but now the light was livid and full of the quality of haze. An extraordinarily low white mist, not three feet above the ground, drifted broodingly across the grass, and the trees rose ghostly out of that phantom sea. Great and shadowy and strange was the world that night, no one seemed abroad; I and my little cracked voice drifted solitary through the silent mysteries. Sometimes I argued as I have told, sometimes I tumbled along in moody vacuity, sometimes my torment was vivid and acute.

Abruptly out of apathy would come a boiling paroxysm of fury, when I thought of Nettie mocking me and laughing, and of her and Verrall clasped in one another's arms.

"I will not have it so!" I screamed. "I will not have it so!"

And in one of these raving fits I drew my revolver from my pocket and fired into the quiet night. Three times I fired it.

The bullets tore through the air, the startled trees told one another in diminishing echoes the thing I had done, and then, with a slow finality, the vast and patient night healed again to calm. My shots, my curses and blasphemies, my prayers—for anon I prayed—that Silence took them all.

It was—how can I express it?—a stifled outcry tranquilized, lost, amid the serene assumptions, the overwhelming empire of that brightness. The noise of my shots, the impact upon things, had for the instant been enormous, then it had passed away. I found myself standing with the revolver held up, astonished, my emotions penetrated by something I could not understand. Then I looked up over my shoulder at the great star, and remained staring at it.

"Who are YOU?" I said at last.

I was like a man in a solitary desert who has suddenly heard a voice...

That, too, passed.

As I came over Clayton Crest I recalled that I missed the multitude that now night after night walked out to stare at the comet, and the little preacher in the waste beyond the hoardings, who warned sinners to repent before the Judgment, was not in his usual place.

It was long past midnight, and every one had gone home. But I did not think of this at first, and the solitude perplexed me and left a memory behind. The gas-lamps were all extinguished because of the brightness of the comet, and that too was unfamiliar. The little newsagent in the still High Street had shut up and gone to bed, but one belated board had been put out late and forgotten, and it still bore its placard.

The word upon it—there was but one word upon it in staring letters—was:

WAR!

You figure that empty mean street, emptily echoing to my footsteps —no soul awake and audible but me. Then my halt at the placard. And amidst that sleeping stillness, smeared hastily upon the board, a little askew and crumpled, but quite distinct beneath that cool meteoric glare, preposterous and appalling, the measureless evil of that word—

WAR!

§ 2

I awoke in that state of equanimity that so often follows an emotional drenching.

It was late, and my mother was beside my bed. She had some breakfast for me on a battered tray.

"Don't get up yet, dear," she said. "You've been sleeping. It was three o'clock when you got home last night. You must have been tired out."

"Your poor face," she went on, "was as white as a sheet and your eyes shining... It frightened me to let you in. And you stumbled on the stairs."

My eyes went quietly to my coat pocket, where something still bulged. She probably had not noticed. "I went to Checkshill," I said. "You know—perhaps—?"

"I got a letter last evening, dear," and as she bent near me to put the tray upon my knees, she kissed my hair softly. For a moment we both remained still, resting on that, her cheek just touching my head.

I took the tray from her to end the pause.

"Don't touch my clothes, mummy," I said sharply, as she moved towards them. "I'm still equal to a clothes-brush."

And then, as she turned away, I astonished her by saying, "You dear mother, you! A little—I understand. Only—now—dear mother; oh! let me be! Let me be!"

And, with the docility of a good servant, she went from me. Dear heart of submission that the world and I had used so ill!

It seemed to me that morning that I could never give way to a gust of passion again. A sorrowful firmness of the mind possessed me. My purpose seemed now as inflexible as iron; there was neither love nor hate nor fear left in me —only I pitied my mother greatly for all that was still to come. I ate my breakfast slowly, and thought where I could find out about Shaphambury, and how I might hope to get there. I had not five shillings in the world.

I dressed methodically, choosing the least frayed of my collars, and shaving much more carefully than was my wont; then I went down to the Public Library to consult a map.

Shaphambury was on the coast of Essex, a long and complicated journey from Clayton. I went to the railway-station and made some memoranda from the time-tables. The porters I asked were not very clear about Shaphambury, but the book-

ing-office clerk was helpful, and we puzzled out all I wanted to know. Then I came out into the coaly street again. At the least I ought to have two pounds.

I went back to the Public Library and into the newspaper room to think over this problem.

A fact intruded itself upon me. People seemed in an altogether exceptional stir about the morning journals, there was something unusual in the air of the room, more people and more talking than usual, and for a moment I was puzzled. Then I bethought me: "This war with Germany, of course!" A naval battle was supposed to be in progress in the North Sea. Let them! I returned to the consideration of my own affairs.

Parload?

Could I go and make it up with him, and then borrow? I weighed the chances of that. Then I thought of selling or pawning something, but that seemed difficult. My winter overcoat had not cost a pound when it was new, my watch was not likely to fetch many shillings. Still, both these things might be factors. I thought with a certain repugnance of the little store my mother was probably making for the rent. She was very secretive about that, and it was locked in an old tea-caddy in her bedroom. I knew it would be almost impossible to get any of that money from her willingly, and though I told myself that in this issue of passion and death no detail mattered, I could not get rid of tormenting scruples whenever I thought of that tea-caddy. Was there no other course? Perhaps after every other source had been tapped I might supplement with a few shillings frankly begged from her. "These others," I said to myself, thinking without passion for once of the sons of the Secure, "would find it difficult to run their romances on a pawnshop basis. However, we must manage it."

I felt the day was passing on, but I did not get excited about that. "Slow is swiftest," Parload used to say, and I meant to get everything thought out completely, to take a long aim and then to act as a bullet flies.

I hesitated at a pawnshop on my way home to my midday meal, but I determined not to pledge my watch until I could bring my overcoat also.

I ate silently, revolving plans.

§ 3

After our midday dinner—it was a potato-pie, mostly potato with some scraps of cabbage and bacon—I put on my overcoat and got it out of the house while my mother was in the scullery at the back.

A scullery in the old world was, in the case of such houses as ours, a damp, unsavory, mainly subterranean region behind the dark living-room kitchen, that was rendered more than typically dirty in our case by the fact that into it the coal-cellar, a yawning pit of black uncleanness, opened, and diffused small crunchable particles about the uneven brick floor. It was the region of "washing-up," that greasy, damp function that followed every meal; its atmosphere had ever a cooling steaminess and the memory of boiled cabbage, and the sooty black stains where saucepan or kettle had been put down for a minute, scraps of potato-peel

caught by the strainer of the escape-pipe, and rags of a quite indescribable horribleness of acquisition, called "dish-clouts," rise in my memory at the name. The altar of this place was the "sink," a tank of stone, revolting to a refined touch, grease-filmed and unpleasant to see, and above this was a tap for cold water, so arranged that when the water descended it splashed and wetted whoever had turned it on. This tap was our water supply. And in such a place you must fancy a little old woman, rather incompetent and very gentle, a soul of unselfishness and sacrifice, in dirty clothes, all come from their original colors to a common dusty dark gray, in worn, ill-fitting boots, with hands distorted by ill use, and untidy graying hair—my mother. In the winter her hands would be "chapped," and she would have a cough. And while she washes up I go out, to sell my overcoat and watch in order that I may desert her.

I gave way to queer hesitations in pawning my two negotiable articles. A weakly indisposition to pawn in Clayton, where the pawnbroker knew me, carried me to the door of the place in Lynch Street, Swathinglea, where I had bought my revolver. Then came an idea that I was giving too many facts about myself to one man, and I came back to Clayton after all. I forget how much money I got, but I remember that it was rather less than the sum I had made out to be the single fare to Shaphambury. Still deliberate, I went back to the Public Library to find out whether it was possible, by walking for ten or twelve miles anywhere, to shorten the journey. My boots were in a dreadful state, the sole of the left one also was now peeling off, and I could not help perceiving that all my plans might be wrecked if at this crisis I went on shoe leather in which I could only shuffle. So long as I went softly they would serve, but not for hard walking. I went to the shoemaker in Hacker Street, but he would not promise any repairs for me under forty-eight hours.

I got back home about five minutes to three, resolved to start by the five train for Birmingham in any case, but still dissatisfied about my money. I thought of pawning a book or something of that sort, but I could think of nothing of obvious value in the house. My mother's silver—two gravy- spoons and a salt-cellar—had been pawned for some weeks, since, in fact, the June quarter day. But my mind was full of hypothetical opportunities.

As I came up the steps to our door, I remarked that Mr. Gabbitas looked at me suddenly round his dull red curtains with a sort of alarmed resolution in his eye and vanished, and as I walked along the passage he opened his door upon me suddenly and intercepted me.

You are figuring me, I hope, as a dark and sullen lout in shabby, cheap, old-world clothes that are shiny at all the wearing surfaces, and with a discolored red tie and frayed linen. My left hand keeps in my pocket as though there is something it prefers to keep a grip upon there. Mr. Gabbitas was shorter than I, and the first note he struck in the impression he made upon any one was of something bright and birdlike. I think he wanted to be birdlike, he possessed the possibility of an avian charm, but, as a matter of fact, there was nothing of the glowing vitality of the bird in his being. And a bird is never out of breath and with an open

mouth. He was in the clerical dress of that time, that costume that seems now almost the strangest of all our old- world clothing, and he presented it in its cheapest form—black of a poor texture, ill-fitting, strangely cut. Its long skirts accentuated the tubbiness of his body, the shortness of his legs. The white tie below his all- round collar, beneath his innocent large-spectacled face, was a little grubby, and between his not very clean teeth he held a briar pipe. His complexion was whitish, and although he was only thirty-three or four perhaps, his sandy hair was already thinning from the top of his head.

To your eye, now, he would seem the strangest figure, in the utter disregard of all physical beauty or dignity about him. You would find him extraordinarily odd, but in the old days he met not only with acceptance but respect. He was alive until within a year or so ago, but his later appearance changed. As I saw him that afternoon he was a very slovenly, ungainly little human being indeed, not only was his clothing altogether ugly and queer, but had you stripped the man stark, you would certainly have seen in the bulging paunch that comes from flabby muscles and flabbily controlled appetites, and in the rounded shoulders and flawed and yellowish skin, the same failure of any effort toward clean beauty. You had an instinctive sense that so he had been from the beginning. You felt he was not only drifting through life, eating what came in his way, believing what came in his way, doing without any vigor what came in his way, but that into life also he had drifted. You could not believe him the child of pride and high resolve, or of any splendid passion of love. He had just HAPPENED... But we all happened then. Why am I taking this tone over this poor little curate in particular?

"Hello!" he said, with an assumption of friendly ease. "Haven't seen you for weeks! Come in and have a gossip."

An invitation from the drawing-room lodger was in the nature of a command. I would have liked very greatly to have refused it, never was invitation more inopportune, but I had not the wit to think of an excuse. "All right," I said awkwardly, and he held the door open for me.

"I'd be very glad if you would," he amplified. "One doesn't get much opportunity of intelligent talk in this parish."

What the devil was he up to, was my secret preoccupation. He fussed about me with a nervous hospitality, talking in jumpy fragments, rubbing his hands together, and taking peeps at me over and round his glasses. As I sat down in his leather-covered armchair, I had an odd memory of the one in the Clayton dentist's operating-room—I know not why.

"They're going to give us trouble in the North Sea, it seems," he remarked with a sort of innocent zest. "I'm glad they mean fighting."

There was an air of culture about his room that always cowed me, and that made me constrained even on this occasion. The table under the window was littered with photographic material and the later albums of his continental souvenirs, and on the American cloth trimmed shelves that filled the recesses on either side of the fireplace were what I used to think in those days a quite incredible number of books—perhaps eight hundred altogether, including the reverend gentleman's

photograph albums and college and school text-books. This suggestion of learning was enforced by the little wooden shield bearing a college coat-of-arms that hung over the looking-glass, and by a photograph of Mr. Gabbitas in cap and gown in an Oxford frame that adorned the opposite wall. And in the middle of that wall stood his writing-desk, which I knew to have pigeon-holes when it was open, and which made him seem not merely cultured but literary. At that he wrote sermons, composing them himself!

"Yes," he said, taking possession of the hearthrug, "the war had to come sooner or later. If we smash their fleet for them now; well, there's an end to the matter!"

He stood on his toes and then bumped down on his heels, and looked blandly through his spectacles at a water-color by his sister—the subject was a bunch of violets—above the sideboard which was his pantry and tea-chest and cellar. "Yes," he said as he did so.

I coughed, and wondered how I might presently get away.

He invited me to smoke—that queer old practice!—and then when I declined, began talking in a confidential tone of this "dreadful business" of the strikes. "The war won't improve THAT outlook," he said, and was very grave for a moment.

He spoke of the want of thought for their wives and children shown by the colliers in striking merely for the sake of the union, and this stirred me to controversy, and distracted me a little from my resolution to escape.

"I don't quite agree with that," I said, clearing my throat. "If the men didn't strike for the union now, if they let that be broken up, where would they be when the pinch of reductions did come?"

To which he replied that they couldn't expect to get top-price wages when the masters were selling bottom-price coal. I replied, "That isn't it. The masters don't treat them fairly. They have to protect themselves."

To which Mr. Gabbitas answered, "Well, I don't know. I've been in the Four Towns some time, and I must say I don't think the balance of injustice falls on the masters' side."

"It falls on the men," I agreed, wilfully misunderstanding him.

And so we worked our way toward an argument. "Confound this argument!" I thought; but I had no skill in self-extraction, and my irritation crept into my voice. Three little spots of color came into the cheeks and nose of Mr. Gabbitas, but his voice showed nothing of his ruffled temper.

"You see," I said, "I'm a socialist. I don't think this world was made for a small minority to dance on the faces of every one else."

"My dear fellow," said the Rev. Gabbitas, "I'M a socialist too. Who isn't. But that doesn't lead me to class hatred."

"You haven't felt the heel of this confounded system. I have."

"Ah!" said he; and catching him on that note came a rap at the front door, and, as he hung suspended, the sound of my mother letting some one in and a timid rap.

"NOW," thought I, and stood up, resolutely, but he would not let me. "No, no, no!" said he. "It's only for the Dorcas money."

He put his hand against my chest with an effect of physical compulsion, and cried, "Come in!"

"Our talk's just getting interesting," he protested; and there entered Miss Ramell, an elderly little young lady who was mighty in Church help in Clayton.

He greeted her—she took no notice of me—and went to his bureau, and I remained standing by my chair but unable to get out of the room. "I'm not interrupting?" asked Miss Ramell.

"Not in the least," he said; drew out the carriers and opened his desk. I could not help seeing what he did.

I was so fretted by my impotence to leave him that at the moment it did not connect at all with the research of the morning that he was taking out money. I listened sullenly to his talk with Miss Ramell, and saw only, as they say in Wales, with the front of my eyes, the small flat drawer that had, it seemed, quite a number of sovereigns scattered over its floor. "They're so unreasonable," complained Miss Ramell. Who could be otherwise in a social organization that bordered on insanity?

I turned away from them, put my foot on the fender, stuck my elbow on the plush-fringed mantelboard, and studied the photographs, pipes, and ash-trays that adorned it. What was it I had to think out before I went to the station?

Of course! My mind made a queer little reluctant leap—it felt like being forced to leap over a bottomless chasm—and alighted upon the sovereigns that were just disappearing again as Mr. Gabbitas shut his drawer.

"I won't interrupt your talk further," said Miss Ramell, receding doorward.

Mr. Gabbitas played round her politely, and opened the door for her and conducted her into the passage, and for a moment or so I had the fullest sense of proximity to those—it seemed to me there must be ten or twelve —sovereigns...

The front door closed and he returned. My chance of escape had gone.

§ 4

"I MUST be going," I said, with a curiously reinforced desire to get away out of that room.

"My dear chap!" he insisted, "I can't think of it. Surely—there's nothing to call you away." Then with an evident desire to shift the venue of our talk, he asked, "You never told me what you thought of Burble's little book."

I was now, beneath my dull display of submission, furiously angry with him. It occurred to me to ask myself why I should defer and qualify my opinions to him. Why should I pretend a feeling of intellectual and social inferiority toward him. He asked what I thought of Burble. I resolved to tell him—if necessary with arrogance. Then perhaps he would release me. I did not sit down again, but stood by the corner of the fireplace.

"That was the little book you lent me last summer?" I said.

"He reasons closely, eh?" he said, and indicated the armchair with a flat hand, and beamed persuasively.

I remained standing. "I didn't think much of his reasoning powers," I said.

"He was one of the cleverest bishops London ever had."

"That may be. But he was dodging about in a jolly feeble case," said I.

"You mean?"

"That he's wrong. I don't think he proves his case. I don't think Christianity is true. He knows himself for the pretender he is. His reasoning's —Rot."

Mr. Gabbitas went, I think, a shade paler than his wont, and propitiation vanished from his manner. His eyes and mouth were round, his face seemed to get round, his eyebrows curved at my remarks.

"I'm sorry you think that," he said at last, with a catch in his breath.

He did not repeat his suggestion that I should sit. He made a step or two toward the window and turned. "I suppose you will admit—" he began, with a faintly irritating note of intellectual condescension....

I will not tell you of his arguments or mine. You will find if you care to look for them, in out-of-the-way corners of our book museums, the shriveled cheap publications—the publications of the Rationalist Press Association, for example—on which my arguments were based. Lying in that curious limbo with them, mixed up with them and indistinguishable, are the endless "Replies" of orthodoxy, like the mixed dead in some hard-fought trench. All those disputes of our fathers, and they were sometimes furious disputes, have gone now beyond the range of comprehension. You younger people, I know, read them with impatient perplexity. You cannot understand how sane creatures could imagine they had joined issue at all in most of these controversies. All the old methods of systematic thinking, the queer absurdities of the Aristotelian logic, have followed magic numbers and mystical numbers, and the Rumpelstiltskin magic of names now into the blackness of the unthinkable. You can no more understand our theological passions than you can understand the fancies that made all ancient peoples speak of their gods only by circumlocutions, that made savages pine away and die because they had been photographed, or an Elizabethan farmer turn back from a day's expedition because he had met three crows. Even I, who have been through it all, recall our controversies now with something near incredulity.

Faith we can understand to-day, all men live by faith, but in the old time every one confused quite hopelessly Faith and a forced, incredible Belief in certain pseudo-concrete statements. I am inclined to say that neither believers nor unbelievers had faith as we understand it—they had insufficient intellectual power. They could not trust unless they had something to see and touch and say, like their barbarous ancestors who could not make a bargain without exchange of tokens. If they no longer worshipped stocks and stones, or eked out their needs with pilgrimages and images, they still held fiercely to audible images, to printed words and formulae.

But why revive the echoes of the ancient logomachies?

Suffice it that we lost our tempers very readily in pursuit of God and Truth, and said exquisitely foolish things on either side. And on the whole —from the impartial perspective of my three and seventy years—I adjudicate that if my dialectic was bad, that of the Rev. Gabbitas was altogether worse.

Little pink spots came into his cheeks, a squealing note into his voice. We interrupted each other more and more rudely. We invented facts and appealed to authorities whose names I mispronounced; and, finding Gabbitas shy of the higher criticism and the Germans, I used the names of Karl Marx and Engels as Bible exegetes with no little effect. A silly wrangle! a preposterous wrangle! —you must imagine our talk becoming louder, with a developing quarrelsome note—my mother no doubt hovering on the staircase and listening in alarm as who should say, "My dear, don't offend it! Oh, don't offend it! Mr. Gabbitas enjoys its friendship. Try to think whatever Mr. Gabbitas says"—though we still kept in touch with a pretence of mutual deference. The ethical superiority of Christianity to all other religions came to the fore—I know not how. We dealt with the matter in bold, imaginative generalizations, because of the insufficiency of our historical knowledge. I was moved to denounce Christianity as the ethic of slaves, and declare myself a disciple of a German writer of no little vogue in those days, named Nietzsche.

For a disciple I must confess I was particularly ill acquainted with the works of the master. Indeed, all I knew of him had come to me through a two- column article in The Clarion for the previous week... But the Rev. Gabbitas did not read The Clarion.

I am, I know, putting a strain upon your credulity when I tell you that I now have little doubt that the Rev. Gabbitas was absolutely ignorant even of the name of Nietzsche, although that writer presented a separate and distinct attitude of attack upon the faith that was in the reverend gentleman's keeping.

"I'm a disciple of Nietzsche," said I, with an air of extensive explanation.

He shied away so awkwardly at the name that I repeated it at once.

"But do you know what Nietzsche says?" I pressed him viciously.

"He has certainly been adequately answered," said he, still trying to carry it off.

"Who by?" I rapped out hotly. "Tell me that!" and became mercilessly expectant.

§ 5

A happy accident relieved Mr. Gabbitas from the embarrassment of that challenge, and carried me another step along my course of personal disaster.

It came on the heels of my question in the form of a clatter of horses without, and the gride and cessation of wheels. I glimpsed a straw-hatted coachman and a pair of grays. It seemed an incredibly magnificent carriage for Clayton.

"Eh!" said the Rev. Gabbitas, going to the window. "Why, it's old Mrs. Verrall! It's old Mrs. Verrall. Really! What CAN she want with me?"

He turned to me, and the flush of controversy had passed and his face shone like the sun. It was not every day, I perceived, that Mrs. Verrall came to see him.

"I get so many interruptions," he said, almost grinning. "You must excuse me a minute! Then—then I'll tell you about that fellow. But don't go. I pray you don't go. I can assure you... MOST interesting."

He went out of the room waving vague prohibitory gestures.

"I MUST go," I cried after him.

"No, no, no!" in the passage. "I've got your answer," I think it was he added, and "quite mistaken;" and I saw him running down the steps to talk to the old lady.

I swore. I made three steps to the window, and this brought me within a yard of that accursed drawer.

I glanced at it, and then at that old woman who was so absolutely powerful, and instantly her son and Nettie's face were flaming in my brain. The Stuarts had, no doubt, already accepted accomplished facts. And I too —

What was I doing here?

What was I doing here while judgment escaped me?

I woke up. I was injected with energy. I took one reassuring look at the curate's obsequious back, at the old lady's projected nose and quivering hand, and then with swift, clean movements I had the little drawer open, four sovereigns in my pocket, and the drawer shut again. Then again at the window —they were still talking.

That was all right. He might not look in that drawer for hours. I glanced at his clock. Twenty minutes still before the Birmingham train. Time to buy a pair of boots and get away. But how I was to get to the station?

I went out boldly into the passage, and took my hat and stick... Walk past him?

Yes. That was all right! He could not argue with me while so important a person engaged him... I came boldly down the steps.

"I want a list made, Mr. Gabbitas, of all the really DESERVING cases," old Mrs. Verrall was saying.

It is curious, but it did not occur to me that here was a mother whose son I was going to kill. I did not see her in that aspect at all. Instead, I was possessed by a realization of the blazing imbecility of a social system that gave this palsied old woman the power to give or withhold the urgent necessities of life from hundreds of her fellow-creatures just according to her poor, foolish old fancies of desert.

"We could make a PROVISIONAL list of that sort," he was saying, and glanced round with a preoccupied expression at me.

"I MUST go," I said at his flash of inquiry, and added, "I'll be back in twenty minutes," and went on my way. He turned again to his patroness as though he forgot me on the instant. Perhaps after all he was not sorry.

I felt extraordinarily cool and capable, exhilarated, if anything, by this prompt, effectual theft. After all, my great determination would achieve itself. I was no longer oppressed by a sense of obstacles, I felt I could grasp accidents and turn them to my advantage. I would go now down Hacker Street to the little shoemak-

er's—get a sound, good pair of boots—ten minutes—and then to the railway-station—five minutes more —and off! I felt as efficient and non-moral as if I was Nietzsche's Over- man already come. It did not occur to me that the curate's clock might have a considerable margin of error.

§ 6

I missed the train.

Partly that was because the curate's clock was slow, and partly it was due to the commercial obstinacy of the shoemaker, who would try on another pair after I had declared my time was up. I bought the final pair however, gave him a wrong address for the return of the old ones, and only ceased to feel like the Nietzschean Over-man, when I saw the train running out of the station.

Even then I did not lose my head. It occurred to me almost at once that, in the event of a prompt pursuit, there would be a great advantage in not taking a train from Clayton; that, indeed, to have done so would have been an error from which only luck had saved me. As it was, I had already been very indiscreet in my inquiries about Shaphambury; for once on the scent the clerk could not fail to remember me. Now the chances were against his coming into the case. I did not go into the station therefore at all, I made no demonstration of having missed the train, but walked quietly past, down the road, crossed the iron footbridge, and took the way back circuitously by White's brickfields and the allotments to the way over Clayton Crest to Two-Mile Stone, where I calculated I should have an ample margin for the 6.13 train.

I was not very greatly excited or alarmed then. Suppose, I reasoned, that by some accident the curate goes to that drawer at once: will he be certain to miss four out of ten or eleven sovereigns? If he does, will he at once think I have taken them? If he does, will he act at once or wait for my return? If he acts at once, will he talk to my mother or call in the police? Then there are a dozen roads and even railways out of the Clayton region, how is he to know which I have taken? Suppose he goes straight at once to the right station, they will not remember my departure for the simple reason that I didn't depart. But they may remember about Shaphambury? It was unlikely.

I resolved not to go directly to Shaphambury from Birmingham, but to go thence to Monkshampton, thence to Wyvern, and then come down on Shaphambury from the north. That might involve a night at some intermediate stopping-place but it would effectually conceal me from any but the most persistent pursuit. And this was not a case of murder yet, but only the theft of four sovereigns.

I had argued away all anxiety before I reached Clayton Crest.

At the Crest I looked back. What a world it was! And suddenly it came to me that I was looking at this world for the last time. If I overtook the fugitives and succeeded, I should die with them—or hang. I stopped and looked back more attentively at that wide ugly valley.

It was my native valley, and I was going out of it, I thought never to return, and yet in that last prospect, the group of towns that had borne me and dwarfed

and crippled and made me, seemed, in some indefinable manner, strange. I was, perhaps, more used to seeing it from this comprehensive view-point when it was veiled and softened by night; now it came out in all its weekday reek, under a clear afternoon sun. That may account a little for its unfamiliarity. And perhaps, too, there was something in the emotions through which I had been passing for a week and more, to intensify my insight, to enable me to pierce the unusual, to question the accepted. But it came to me then, I am sure, for the first time, how promiscuous, how higgledy-piggledy was the whole of that jumble of mines and homes, collieries and potbanks, railway yards, canals, schools, forges and blast furnaces, churches, chapels, allotment hovels, a vast irregular agglomeration of ugly smoking accidents in which men lived as happy as frogs in a dustbin. Each thing jostled and damaged the other things about it, each thing ignored the other things about it; the smoke of the furnace defiled the potbank clay, the clatter of the railway deafened the worshipers in church, the public-house thrust corruption at the school doors, the dismal homes squeezed miserably amidst the monstrosities of industrialism, with an effect of groping imbecility. Humanity choked amidst its products, and all its energy went in increasing its disorder, like a blind stricken thing that struggles and sinks in a morass.

I did not think these things clearly that afternoon. Much less did I ask how I, with my murderous purpose, stood to them all. I write down that realization of disorder and suffocation here and now as though I had thought it, but indeed then I only felt it, felt it transitorily as I looked back, and then stood with the thing escaping from my mind.

I should never see that country-side again.

I came back to that. At any rate I wasn't sorry. The chances were I should die in sweet air, under a clean sky.

From distant Swathinglea came a little sound, the minute undulation of a remote crowd, and then rapidly three shots.

That held me perplexed for a space... Well, anyhow I was leaving it all! Thank God I was leaving it all! Then, as I turned to go on, I thought of my mother.

It seemed an evil world in which to leave one's mother. My thoughts focused upon her very vividly for a moment. Down there, under that afternoon light, she was going to and fro, unaware as yet that she had lost me, bent and poking about in the darkling underground kitchen, perhaps carrying a lamp into the scullery to trim, or sitting patiently, staring into the fire, waiting tea for me. A great pity for her, a great remorse at the blacker troubles that lowered over her innocent head, came to me. Why, after all, was I doing this thing?

Why?

I stopped again dead, with the hill crest rising between me and home. I had more than half a mind to return to her.

Then I thought of the curate's sovereigns. If he has missed them already, what should I return to? And, even if I returned, how could I put them back?

And what of the night after I renounced my revenge? What of the time when young Verrall came back? And Nettie?

No! The thing had to be done.

But at least I might have kissed my mother before I came away, left her some message, reassured her at least for a little while. All night she would listen and wait for me...

Should I send her a telegram from Two-Mile Stone?

It was no good now; too late, too late. To do that would be to tell the course I had taken, to bring pursuit upon me, swift and sure, if pursuit there was to be. No. My mother must suffer!

I went on grimly toward Two-Mile Stone, but now as if some greater will than mine directed my footsteps thither.

I reached Birmingham before darkness came, and just caught the last train for Monkshampton, where I had planned to pass the night.

CHAPTER THE FIFTH - THE PURSUIT OF THE TWO LOVERS

§ 1

As the train carried me on from Birmingham to Monkshampton, it carried me not only into a country where I had never been before, but out of the commonplace daylight and the touch and quality of ordinary things, into the strange unprecedented night that was ruled by the giant meteor of the last days.

There was at that time a curious accentuation of the common alternation of night and day. They became separated with a widening difference of value in regard to all mundane affairs. During the day, the comet was an item in the newspapers, it was jostled by a thousand more living interests, it was as nothing in the skirts of the war storm that was now upon us. It was an astronomical phenomenon, somewhere away over China, millions of miles away in the deeps. We forgot it. But directly the sun sank one turned ever and again toward the east, and the meteor resumed its sway over us.

One waited for its rising, and yet each night it came as a surprise. Always it rose brighter than one had dared to think, always larger and with some wonderful change in its outline, and now with a strange, less luminous, greener disk upon it that grew with its growth, the umbra of the earth. It shone also with its own light, so that this shadow was not hard or black, but it shone phosphorescently and with a diminishing intensity where the stimulus of the sun's rays was withdrawn. As it ascended toward the zenith, as the last trailing daylight went after the abdicating sun, its greenish white illumination banished the realities of day, diffused a bright ghostliness over all things. It changed the starless sky about it to an extraordinary deep blue, the profoundest color in the world, such as I have never seen before or since. I remember, too, that as I peered from the train that was rattling me along to Monkshampton, I perceived and was puzzled by a coppery red light that mingled with all the shadows that were cast by it.

It turned our ugly English industrial towns to phantom cities. Everywhere the local authorities discontinued street lighting—one could read small print in the glare,—and so at Monkshampton I went about through pale, white, unfamiliar streets, whose electric globes had shadows on the path. Lit windows here and there burnt ruddy orange, like holes cut in some dream curtain that hung before a furnace. A policeman with noiseless feet showed me an inn woven of moonshine, a green-faced man opened to us, and there I abode the night. And the next morning it opened with a mighty clatter, and was a dirty little beerhouse that stank of

beer, and there was a fat and grimy landlord with red spots upon his neck, and much noisy traffic going by on the cobbles outside.

I came out, after I had paid my bill, into a street that echoed to the bawlings of two newsvendors and to the noisy yappings of a dog they had raised to emulation. They were shouting: "Great British disaster in the North Sea. A battleship lost with all hands!"

I bought a paper, went on to the railway station reading such details as were given of this triumph of the old civilization, of the blowing up of this great iron ship, full of guns and explosives and the most costly and beautiful machinery of which that time was capable, together with nine hundred able- bodied men, all of them above the average, by a contact mine towed by a German submarine. I read myself into a fever of warlike emotions. Not only did I forget the meteor, but for a time I forgot even the purpose that took me on to the railway station, bought my ticket, and was now carrying me onward to Shaphambury.

So the hot day came to its own again, and people forgot the night.

Each night, there shone upon us more and more insistently, beauty, wonder, the promise of the deeps, and we were hushed, and marveled for a space. And at the first gray sounds of dawn again, at the shooting of bolts and the noise of milk-carts, we forgot, and the dusty habitual day came yawning and stretching back again. The stains of coal smoke crept across the heavens, and we rose to the soiled disorderly routine of life.

"Thus life has always been," we said; "thus it will always be."

The glory of those nights was almost universally regarded as spectacular merely. It signified nothing to us. So far as western Europe went, it was only a small and ignorant section of the lower classes who regarded the comet as a portent of the end of the world. Abroad, where there were peasantries, it was different, but in England the peasantry had already disappeared. Every one read. The newspaper, in the quiet days before our swift quarrel with Germany rushed to its climax, had absolutely dispelled all possibilities of a panic in this matter. The very tramps upon the high-roads, the children in the nursery, had learnt that at the utmost the whole of that shining cloud could weigh but a few score tons. This fact had been shown quite conclusively by the enormous deflections that had at last swung it round squarely at our world. It had passed near three of the smallest asteroids without producing the minutest perceptible deflection in their course; while, on its own part, it had described a course through nearly three degrees. When it struck our earth there was to be a magnificent spectacle, no doubt, for those who were on the right side of our planet to see, but beyond that nothing. It was doubtful whether we were on the right side. The meteor would loom larger and larger in the sky, but with the umbra of our earth eating its heart of brightness out, and at last it would be the whole sky, a sky of luminous green clouds, with a white brightness about the horizon, west and east. Then a pause—a pause of not very exactly definite duration—and then, no doubt, a great blaze of shooting stars. They might be of some unwonted color because of the unknown element that line in the green

revealed. For a little while the zenith would spout shooting stars. Some, it was hoped, would reach the earth and be available for analysis.

That, science said, would be all. The green clouds would whirl and vanish, and there might be thunderstorms. But through the attenuated wisps of comet shine, the old sky, the old stars, would reappear, and all would be as it had been before. And since this was to happen between one and eleven in the morning of the approaching Tuesday—I slept at Monkshampton on Saturday night,—it would be only partially visible, if visible at all, on our side of the earth. Perhaps, if it came late, one would see no more than a shooting star low down in the sky. All this we had with the utmost assurances of science. Still it did not prevent the last nights being the most beautiful and memorable of human experiences.

The nights had become very warm, and when next day I had ranged Shaphambury in vain, I was greatly tormented, as that unparalleled glory of the night returned, to think that under its splendid benediction young Verrall and Nettie made love to one another.

I walked backward and forward, backward and forward, along the sea front, peering into the faces of the young couples who promenaded, with my hand in my pocket ready, and a curious ache in my heart that had no kindred with rage. Until at last all the promenaders had gone home to bed, and I was alone with the star.

My train from Wyvern to Shaphambury that morning was a whole hour late; they said it was on account of the movement of troops to meet a possible raid from the Elbe.

§ 2

Shaphambury seemed an odd place to me even then. But something was quickening in me at that time to feel the oddness of many accepted things. Now in the retrospect I see it as intensely queer. The whole place was strange to my untraveled eyes; the sea even was strange. Only twice in my life had I been at the seaside before, and then I had gone by excursion to places on the Welsh coast whose great cliffs of rock and mountain backgrounds made the effect of the horizon very different from what it is upon the East Anglian seaboard. Here what they call a cliff was a crumbling bank of whitey-brown earth not fifty feet high.

So soon as I arrived I made a systematic exploration of Shaphambury. To this day I retain the clearest memories of the plan I shaped out then, and how my inquiries were incommoded by the overpowering desire of every one to talk of the chances of a German raid, before the Channel Fleet got round to us. I slept at a small public-house in a Shaphambury back street on Sunday night. I did not get on to Shaphambury from Wyvern until two in the afternoon, because of the infrequency of Sunday trains, and I got no clue whatever until late in the afternoon of Monday. As the little local train bumped into sight of the place round the curve of a swelling hill, one saw a series of undulating grassy spaces, amidst which a number of conspicuous notice-boards appealed to the eye and cut up the distant sea horizon. Most of these referred to comestibles or to remedies to follow the comestibles; and they were colored with a view to be memorable rather than

beautiful, to "stand out" amidst the gentle grayish tones of the east coast scenery. The greater number, I may remark, of the advertisements that were so conspicuous a factor in the life of those days, and which rendered our vast tree-pulp newspapers possible, referred to foods, drinks, tobacco, and the drugs that promised a restoration of the equanimity these other articles had destroyed. Wherever one went one was reminded in glaring letters that, after all, man was little better than a worm, that eyeless, earless thing that burrows and lives uncomplainingly amidst nutritious dirt, "an alimentary canal with the subservient appendages thereto." But in addition to such boards there were also the big black and white boards of various grandiloquently named "estates." The individualistic enterprise of that time had led to the plotting out of nearly all the country round the seaside towns into roads and building-plots—all but a small portion of the south and east coast was in this condition, and had the promises of those schemes been realized the entire population of the island might have been accommodated upon the sea frontiers. Nothing of the sort happened, of course; the whole of this uglification of the coast-line was done to stimulate a little foolish gambling in plots, and one saw everywhere agents' boards in every state of freshness and decay, ill-made exploitation roads overgrown with grass, and here and there, at a corner, a label, "Trafalgar Avenue," or "Sea View Road." Here and there, too, some small investor, some shopman with "savings," had delivered his soul to the local builders and built himself a house, and there it stood, ill-designed, mean-looking, isolated, ill-placed on a cheaply fenced plot, athwart which his domestic washing fluttered in the breeze amidst a bleak desolation of enterprise. Then presently our railway crossed a high road, and a row of mean yellow brick houses—workmen's cottages, and the filthy black sheds that made the "allotments" of that time a universal eyesore, marked our approach to the more central areas of—I quote the local guidebook —"one of the most delightful resorts in the East Anglian poppy-land." Then more mean houses, the gaunt ungainliness of the electric force station —it had a huge chimney, because no one understood how to make combustion of coal complete—and then we were in the railway station, and barely three-quarters of a mile from the center of this haunt of health and pleasure.

I inspected the town thoroughly before I made my inquiries. The road began badly with a row of cheap, pretentious, insolvent-looking shops, a public- house, and a cab-stand, but, after an interval of little red villas that were partly hidden amidst shrubbery gardens, broke into a confusedly bright but not unpleasing High Street, shuttered that afternoon and sabbatically still. Somewhere in the background a church bell jangled, and children in bright, new- looking clothes were going to Sunday-school. Thence through a square of stuccoed lodging-houses, that seemed a finer and cleaner version of my native square, I came to a garden of asphalt and euonymus—the Sea Front. I sat down on a cast-iron seat, and surveyed first of all the broad stretches of muddy, sandy beach, with its queer wheeled bathing machines, painted with the advertisements of somebody's pills—and then at the house fronts that stared out upon these visceral counsels. Boarding-houses, private hotels, and lodging-houses in terraces clustered closely right

and left of me, and then came to an end; in one direction scaffolding marked a building enterprise in progress, in the other, after a waste interval, rose a monstrous bulging red shape, a huge hotel, that dwarfed all other things. Northward were low pale cliffs with white denticulations of tents, where the local volunteers, all under arms, lay encamped, and southward, a spreading waste of sandy dunes, with occasional bushes and clumps of stunted pine and an advertisement board or so. A hard blue sky hung over all this prospect, the sunshine cast inky shadows, and eastward was a whitish sea. It was Sunday, and the midday meal still held people indoors.

A queer world! thought I even then—to you now it must seem impossibly queer,—and after an interval I forced myself back to my own affair.

How was I to ask? What was I to ask for? I puzzled for a long time over that—at first I was a little tired and indolent—and then presently I had a flow of ideas.

My solution was fairly ingenious. I invented the following story. I happened to be taking a holiday in Shaphambury, and I was making use of the opportunity to seek the owner of a valuable feather boa, which had been left behind in the hotel of my uncle at Wyvern by a young lady, traveling with a young gentleman—no doubt a youthful married couple. They had reached Shaphambury somewhen on Thursday. I went over the story many times, and gave my imaginary uncle and his hotel plausible names. At any rate this yarn would serve as a complete justification for all the questions I might wish to ask.

I settled that, but I still sat for a time, wanting the energy to begin. Then I turned toward the big hotel. Its gorgeous magnificence seemed to my inexpert judgment to indicate the very place a rich young man of good family would select.

Huge draught-proof doors were swung round for me by an ironically polite under-porter in a magnificent green uniform, who looked at my clothes as he listened to my question and then with a German accent referred me to a gorgeous head porter, who directed me to a princely young man behind a counter of brass and polish, like a bank—like several banks. This young man, while he answered me, kept his eye on my collar and tie—and I knew that they were abominable.

"I want to find a lady and gentleman who came to Shaphambury on Tuesday," I said.

"Friends of yours?" he asked with a terrible fineness of irony.

I made out at last that here at any rate the young people had not been. They might have lunched there, but they had had no room. But I went out—door opened again for me obsequiously—in a state of social discomfiture, and did not attack any other establishment that afternoon.

My resolution had come to a sort of ebb. More people were promenading, and their Sunday smartness abashed me. I forgot my purpose in an acute sense of myself. I felt that the bulge of my pocket caused by the revolver was conspicuous, and I was ashamed. I went along the sea front away from the town, and presently lay down among pebbles and sea poppies. This mood of reaction prevailed with me all that afternoon. In the evening, about sundown, I went to the station and

asked questions of the outporters there. But outporters, I found, were a class of men who remembered luggage rather than people, and I had no sort of idea what luggage young Verrall and Nettie were likely to have with them.

Then I fell into conversation with a salacious wooden-legged old man with a silver ring, who swept the steps that went down to the beach from the parade. He knew much about young couples, but only in general terms, and nothing of the particular young couple I sought. He reminded me in the most disagreeable way of the sensuous aspects of life, and I was not sorry when presently a gunboat appeared in the offing signalling the coastguard and the camp, and cut short his observations upon holidays, beaches, and morals.

I went, and now I was past my ebb, and sat in a seat upon the parade, and watched the brightening of those rising clouds of chilly fire that made the ruddy west seem tame. My midday lassitude was going, my blood was running warmer again. And as the twilight and that filmy brightness replaced the dusty sunlight and robbed this unfamiliar place of all its matter-of-fact queerness, its sense of aimless materialism, romance returned to me, and passion, and my thoughts of honor and revenge. I remember that change of mood as occurring very vividly on this occasion, but I fancy that less distinctly I had felt this before many times. In the old times, night and the starlight had an effect of intimate reality the daytime did not possess. The daytime—as one saw it in towns and populous places—had hold of one, no doubt, but only as an uproar might, it was distracting, conflicting, insistent. Darkness veiled the more salient aspects of those agglomerations of human absurdity, and one could exist—one could imagine.

I had a queer illusion that night, that Nettie and her lover were close at hand, that suddenly I should come on them. I have already told how I went through the dusk seeking them in every couple that drew near. And I dropped asleep at last in an unfamiliar bedroom hung with gaudily decorated texts, cursing myself for having wasted a day.

§ 3

I sought them in vain the next morning, but after midday I came in quick succession on a perplexing multitude of clues. After failing to find any young couple that corresponded to young Verrall and Nettie, I presently discovered an unsatisfactory quartette of couples.

Any of these four couples might have been the one I sought; with regard to none of them was there conviction. They had all arrived either on Wednesday or Thursday. Two couples were still in occupation of their rooms, but neither of these were at home. Late in the afternoon I reduced my list by eliminating a young man in drab, with side whiskers and long cuffs, accompanied by a lady, of thirty or more, of consciously ladylike type. I was disgusted at the sight of them; the other two young people had gone for a long walk, and though I watched their boarding-house until the fiery cloud shone out above, sharing and mingling in an unusually splendid sunset, I missed them. Then I discovered them dining at a separate table in the bow window, with red-shaded candles between them, peering

out ever and again at this splendor that was neither night nor day. The girl in her pink evening dress looked very light and pretty to me —pretty enough to enrage me,—she had well shaped arms and white, well-modeled shoulders, and the turn of her cheek and the fair hair about her ears was full of subtle delights; but she was not Nettie, and the happy man with her was that odd degenerate type our old aristocracy produced with such odd frequency, chinless, large bony nose, small fair head, languid expression, and a neck that had demanded and received a veritable sleeve of collar. I stood outside in the meteor's livid light, hating them and cursing them for having delayed me so long. I stood until it was evident they remarked me, a black shape of envy, silhouetted against the glare.

That finished Shaphambury. The question I now had to debate was which of the remaining couples I had to pursue.

I walked back to the parade trying to reason my next step out, and muttering to myself, because there was something in that luminous wonderfulness that touched one's brain, and made one feel a little light-headed.

One couple had gone to London; the other had gone to the Bungalow village at Bone Cliff. Where, I wondered, was Bone Cliff?

I came upon my wooden-legged man at the top of his steps.

"Hullo," said I.

He pointed seaward with his pipe, his silver ring shone in the sky light.

"Rum," he said.

"What is?" I asked.

"Search-lights! Smoke! Ships going north! If it wasn't for this blasted Milky Way gone green up there, we might see."

He was too intent to heed my questions for a time. Then he vouchsafed over his shoulder—

"Know Bungalow village?—rather. Artis' and such. Nice goings on! Mixed bathing—something scandalous. Yes."

"But where is it?" I said, suddenly exasperated.

"There!" he said. "What's that flicker? A gunflash—or I'm a lost soul!"

"You'd hear," I said, "long before it was near enough to see a flash."

He didn't answer. Only by making it clear I would distract him until he told me what I wanted to know could I get him to turn from his absorbed contemplation of that phantom dance between the sea rim and the shine. Indeed I gripped his arm and shook him. Then he turned upon me cursing.

"Seven miles," he said, "along this road. And now go to 'ell with yer!"

I answered with some foul insult by way of thanks, and so we parted, and I set off towards the bungalow village.

I found a policeman, standing star-gazing, a little way beyond the end of the parade, and verified the wooden-legged man's directions.

"It's a lonely road, you know," he called after me...

I had an odd intuition that now at last I was on the right track. I left the dark masses of Shaphambury behind me, and pushed out into the dim pallor of that night, with the quiet assurance of a traveler who nears his end.

The incidents of that long tramp I do not recall in any orderly succession, the one progressive thing is my memory of a growing fatigue. The sea was for the most part smooth and shining like a mirror, a great expanse of reflecting silver, barred by slow broad undulations, but at one time a little breeze breathed like a faint sigh and ruffled their long bodies into faint scaly ripples that never completely died out again. The way was sometimes sandy, thick with silvery colorless sand, and sometimes chalky and lumpy, with lumps that had shining facets; a black scrub was scattered, sometimes in thickets, sometimes in single bunches, among the somnolent hummocks of sand. At one place came grass, and ghostly great sheep looming up among the gray. After a time black pinewoods intervened, and made sustained darknesses along the road, woods that frayed out at the edges to weirdly warped and stunted trees. Then isolated pine witches would appear, and make their rigid gestures at me as I passed. Grotesquely incongruous amidst these forms, I presently came on estate boards, appealing, "Houses can be built to suit purchaser," to the silence, to the shadows, and the glare.

Once I remember the persistent barking of a dog from somewhere inland of me, and several times I took out and examined my revolver very carefully. I must, of course, have been full of my intention when I did that, I must have been thinking of Nettie and revenge, but I cannot now recall those emotions at all. Only I see again very distinctly the greenish gleams that ran over lock and barrel as I turned the weapon in my hand.

Then there was the sky, the wonderful, luminous, starless, moonless sky, and the empty blue deeps of the edge of it, between the meteor and the sea. And once—strange phantoms!—I saw far out upon the shine, and very small and distant, three long black warships, without masts, or sails, or smoke, or any lights, dark, deadly, furtive things, traveling very swiftly and keeping an equal distance. And when I looked again they were very small, and then the shine had swallowed them up.

Then once a flash and what I thought was a gun, until I looked up and saw a fading trail of greenish light still hanging in the sky. And after that there was a shiver and whispering in the air, a stronger throbbing in one's arteries, a sense of refreshment, a renewal of purpose...

Somewhere upon my way the road forked, but I do not remember whether that was near Shaphambury or near the end of my walk. The hesitation between two rutted unmade roads alone remains clear in my mind.

At last I grew weary. I came to piled heaps of decaying seaweed and cart tracks running this way and that, and then I had missed the road and was stumbling among sand hummocks quite close to the sea. I came out on the edge of the dimly glittering sandy beach, and something phosphorescent drew me to the water's edge. I bent down and peered at the little luminous specks that floated in the ripples.

Presently with a sigh I stood erect, and contemplated the lonely peace of that last wonderful night. The meteor had now trailed its shining nets across the whole space of the sky and was beginning to set; in the east the blue was coming to its

own again; the sea was an intense edge of blackness, and now, escaped from that great shine, and faint and still tremulously valiant, one weak elusive star could just be seen, hovering on the verge of the invisible.

How beautiful it was! how still and beautiful! Peace! peace!—the peace that passeth understanding, robed in light descending!...

My heart swelled, and suddenly I was weeping.

There was something new and strange in my blood. It came to me that indeed I did not want to kill.

I did not want to kill. I did not want to be the servant of my passions any more. A great desire had come to me to escape from life, from the daylight which is heat and conflict and desire, into that cool night of eternity—and rest. I had played—I had done.

I stood upon the edge of the great ocean, and I was filled with an inarticulate spirit of prayer, and I desired greatly—peace from myself.

And presently, there in the east, would come again the red discoloring curtain over these mysteries, the finite world again, the gray and growing harsh certainties of dawn. My resolve I knew would take up with me again. This was a rest for me, an interlude, but to-morrow I should be William Leadford once more, ill-nourished, ill-dressed, ill-equipped and clumsy, a thief and shamed, a wound upon the face of life, a source of trouble and sorrow even to the mother I loved; no hope in life left for me now but revenge before my death.

Why this paltry thing, revenge? It entered into my thoughts that I might end the matter now and let these others go.

To wade out into the sea, into this warm lapping that mingled the natures of water and light, to stand there breast-high, to thrust my revolver barrel into my mouth—?

Why not?

I swung about with an effort. I walked slowly up the beach thinking...

I turned and looked back at the sea. No! Something within me said, "No!"

I must think.

It was troublesome to go further because the hummocks and the tangled bushes began. I sat down amidst a black cluster of shrubs, and rested, chin on hand. I drew my revolver from my pocket and looked at it, and held it in my hand. Life? Or Death?...

I seemed to be probing the very deeps of being, but indeed imperceptibly I fell asleep, and sat dreaming.

§ 4

Two people were bathing in the sea.

I had awakened. It was still that white and wonderful night, and the blue band of clear sky was no wider than before. These people must have come into sight as I fell asleep, and awakened me almost at once. They waded breast-deep in the water, emerging, coming shoreward, a woman, with her hair coiled about her head, and in pursuit of her a man, graceful figures of black and silver, with a

bright green surge flowing off from them, a pattering of flashing wavelets about them. He smote the water and splashed it toward her, she retaliated, and then they were knee-deep, and then for an instant their feet broke the long silver margin of the sea.

Each wore a tightly fitting bathing dress that hid nothing of the shining, dripping beauty of their youthful forms.

She glanced over her shoulder and found him nearer than she thought, started, gesticulated, gave a little cry that pierced me to the heart, and fled up the beach obliquely toward me, running like the wind, and passed me, vanished amidst the black distorted bushes, and was gone—she and her pursuer, in a moment, over the ridge of sand.

I heard him shout between exhaustion and laughter...

And suddenly I was a thing of bestial fury, standing up with hands held up and clenched, rigid in gesture of impotent threatening, against the sky...

For this striving, swift thing of light and beauty was Nettie—and this was the man for whom I had been betrayed!

And, it blazed upon me, I might have died there by the sheer ebbing of my will—unavenged!

In another moment I was running and stumbling, revolver in hand, in quiet unsuspected pursuit of them, through the soft and noiseless sand.

§ 5

I came up over the little ridge and discovered the bungalow village I had been seeking, nestling in a crescent lap of dunes. A door slammed, the two runners had vanished, and I halted staring.

There was a group of three bungalows nearer to me than the others. Into one of these three they had gone, and I was too late to see which. All had doors and windows carelessly open, and none showed a light.

This place, upon which I had at last happened, was a fruit of the reaction of artistic-minded and carelessly living people against the costly and uncomfortable social stiffness of the more formal seaside resorts of that time. It was, you must understand, the custom of the steam-railway companies to sell their carriages after they had been obsolete for a sufficient length of years, and some genius had hit upon the possibility of turning these into little habitable cabins for the summer holiday. The thing had become a fashion with a certain Bohemian-spirited class; they added cabin to cabin, and these little improvised homes, gaily painted and with broad verandas and supplementary leantos added to their accommodation, made the brightest contrast conceivable to the dull rigidities of the decorous resorts. Of course there were many discomforts in such camping that had to be faced cheerfully, and so this broad sandy beach was sacred to high spirits and the young. Art muslin and banjoes, Chinese lanterns and frying, are leading "notes," I find, in the impression of those who once knew such places well. But so far as I was concerned this odd settlement of pleasure-squatters was a mystery as well as a surprise, enhanced rather than mitigated by an imaginative suggestion or so I

had received from the wooden-legged man at Shaphambury. I saw the thing as no gathering of light hearts and gay idleness, but grimly—after the manner of poor men poisoned by the suppression of all their cravings after joy. To the poor man, to the grimy workers, beauty and cleanness were absolutely denied; out of a life of greasy dirt, of muddied desires, they watched their happier fellows with a bitter envy and foul, tormenting suspicions. Fancy a world in which the common people held love to be a sort of beastliness, own sister to being drunk!...

There was in the old time always something cruel at the bottom of this business of sexual love. At least that is the impression I have brought with me across the gulf of the great Change. To succeed in love seemed such triumph as no other success could give, but to fail was as if one was tainted...

I felt no sense of singularity that this thread of savagery should run through these emotions of mine and become now the whole strand of these emotions. I believed, and I think I was right in believing, that the love of all true lovers was a sort of defiance then, that they closed a system in each other's arms and mocked the world without. You loved against the world, and these two loved AT me. They had their business with one another, under the threat of a watchful fierceness. A sword, a sharp sword, the keenest edge in life, lay among their roses.

Whatever may be true of this for others, for me and my imagination, at any rate, it was altogether true. I was never for dalliance, I was never a jesting lover. I wanted fiercely; I made love impatiently. Perhaps I had written irrelevant love-letters for that very reason; because with this stark theme I could not play...

The thought of Nettie's shining form, of her shrinking bold abandon to her easy conqueror, gave me now a body of rage that was nearly too strong for my heart and nerves and the tense powers of my merely physical being. I came down among the pale sand-heaps slowly toward that queer village of careless sensuality, and now within my puny body I was coldly sharpset for pain and death, a darkly gleaming hate, a sword of evil, drawn.

§ 6

I halted, and stood planning what I had to do.

Should I go to bungalow after bungalow until one of the two I sought answered to my rap? But suppose some servant intervened!

Should I wait where I was—perhaps until morning—watching? And meanwhile—

All the nearer bungalows were very still now. If I walked softly to them, from open windows, from something seen or overheard, I might get a clue to guide me. Should I advance circuitously, creeping upon them, or should I walk straight to the door? It was bright enough for her to recognize me clearly at a distance of many paces.

The difficulty to my mind lay in this, that if I involved other people by questions, I might at last confront my betrayers with these others close about me, ready to snatch my weapon and seize my hands. Besides, what names might they bear here?

"Boom!" the sound crept upon my senses, and then again it came.

I turned impatiently as one turns upon an impertinence, and beheld a great ironclad not four miles out, steaming fast across the dappled silver, and from its funnels sparks, intensely red, poured out into the night. As I turned, came the hot flash of its guns, firing seaward, and answering this, red flashes and a streaming smoke in the line between sea and sky. So I remembered it, and I remember myself staring at it—in a state of stupid arrest. It was an irrelevance. What had these things to do with me?

With a shuddering hiss, a rocket from a headland beyond the village leapt up and burst hot gold against the glare, and the sound of the third and fourth guns reached me.

The windows of the dark bungalows, one after another, leapt out, squares of ruddy brightness that flared and flickered and became steadily bright. Dark heads appeared looking seaward, a door opened, and sent out a brief lane of yellow to mingle and be lost in the comet's brightness. That brought me back to the business in hand.

"Boom! boom!" and when I looked again at the great ironclad, a little torchlike spurt of flame wavered behind her funnels. I could hear the throb and clangor of her straining engines...

I became aware of the voices of people calling to one another in the village. A white-robed, hooded figure, some man in a bathing wrap, absurdly suggestive of an Arab in his burnous, came out from one of the nearer bungalows, and stood clear and still and shadowless in the glare.

He put his hands to shade his seaward eyes, and shouted to people within.

The people within—MY people! My fingers tightened on my revolver. What was this war nonsense to me? I would go round among the hummocks with the idea of approaching the three bungalows inconspicuously from the flank. This fight at sea might serve my purpose—except for that, it had no interest for me at all. Boom! boom! The huge voluminous concussions rushed past me, beat at my heart and passed. In a moment Nettie would come out to see.

First one and then two other wrappered figures came out of the bungalows to join the first. His arm pointed seaward, and his voice, a full tenor, rose in explanation. I could hear some of the words. "It's a German!" he said. "She's caught."

Some one disputed that, and there followed a little indistinct babble of argument. I went on slowly in the circuit I had marked out, watching these people as I went.

They shouted together with such a common intensity of direction that I halted and looked seaward. I saw the tall fountain flung by a shot that had just missed the great warship. A second rose still nearer us, a third, and a fourth, and then a great uprush of dust, a whirling cloud, leapt out of the headland whence the rocket had come, and spread with a slow deliberation right and left. Hard on that an enormous crash, and the man with the full voice leapt and cried, "Hit!"

Let me see! Of course, I had to go round beyond the bungalows, and then come up towards the group from behind.

A high-pitched woman's voice called, "Honeymooners! honeymooners! Come out and see!"

Something gleamed in the shadow of the nearer bungalow, and a man's voice answered from within. What he said I did not catch, but suddenly I heard Nettie calling very distinctly, "We've been bathing."

The man who had first come out shouted, "Don't you hear the guns? They're fighting—not five miles from shore."

"Eh?" answered the bungalow, and a window opened.

"Out there!"

I did not hear the reply, because of the faint rustle of my own movements. Clearly these people were all too much occupied by the battle to look in my direction, and so I walked now straight toward the darkness that held Nettie and the black desire of my heart.

"Look!" cried some one, and pointed skyward.

I glanced up, and behold! The sky was streaked with bright green trails. They radiated from a point halfway between the western horizon and the zenith, and within the shining clouds of the meteor a streaming movement had begun, so that it seemed to be pouring both westwardly and back toward the east, with a crackling sound, as though the whole heaven was stippled over with phantom pistol-shots. It seemed to me then as if the meteor was coming to help me, descending with those thousand pistols like a curtain to fend off this unmeaning foolishness of the sea.

"Boom!" went a gun on the big ironclad, and "boom!" and the guns of the pursuing cruisers flashed in reply.

To glance up at that streaky, stirring light scum of the sky made one's head swim. I stood for a moment dazed, and more than a little giddy. I had a curious instant of purely speculative thought. Suppose, after all, the fanatics were right, and the world WAS coming to an end! What a score that would be for Parload!

Then it came into my head that all these things were happening to consecrate my revenge! The war below, the heavens above, were the thunderous garment of my deed. I heard Nettie's voice cry out not fifty yards away, and my passion surged again. I was to return to her amid these terrors bearing unanticipated death. I was to possess her, with a bullet, amidst thunderings and fear. At the thought I lifted up my voice to a shout that went unheard, and advanced now recklessly, revolver displayed in my hand.

It was fifty yards, forty yards, thirty yards—the little group of people, still heedless of me, was larger and more important now, the green-shot sky and the fighting ships remoter. Some one darted out from the bungalow, with an interrupted question, and stopped, suddenly aware of me. It was Nettie, with some coquettish dark wrap about her, and the green glare shining on her sweet face and white throat. I could see her expression, stricken with dismay and terror, at my advance, as though something had seized her by the heart and held her still—a target for my shots.

"Boom!" came the ironclad's gunshot like a command. "Bang!" the bullet leapt from my hand. Do you know, I did not want to shoot her then. Indeed I did not want to shoot her then! Bang! and I had fired again, still striding on, and —each time it seemed I had missed.

She moved a step or so toward me, still staring, and then someone intervened, and near beside her I saw young Verrall.

A heavy stranger, the man in the hooded bath-gown, a fat, foreign-looking man, came out of nowhere like a shield before them. He seemed a preposterous interruption. His face was full of astonishment and terror. He rushed across my path with arms extended and open hands, as one might try to stop a runaway horse. He shouted some nonsense. He seemed to want to dissuade me, as though dissuasion had anything to do with it now.

"Not you, you fool!" I said hoarsely. "Not you!" But he hid Nettie nevertheless.

By an enormous effort I resisted a mechanical impulse to shoot through his fat body. Anyhow, I knew I mustn't shoot him. For a moment I was in doubt, then I became very active, turned aside abruptly and dodged his pawing arm to the left, and so found two others irresolutely in my way. I fired a third shot in the air, just over their heads, and ran at them. They hastened left and right; I pulled up and faced about within a yard of a foxy-faced young man coming sideways, who seemed about to grapple me. At my resolute halt he fell back a pace, ducked, and threw up a defensive arm, and then I perceived the course was clear, and ahead of me, young Verrall and Nettie—he was holding her arm to help her—running away. "Of course!" said I.

I fired a fourth ineffectual shot, and then in an access of fury at my misses, started out to run them down and shoot them barrel to backbone. "These people!" I said, dismissing all these interferences.... "A yard," I panted, speaking aloud to myself, "a yard! Till then, take care, you mustn't—mustn't shoot again."

Some one pursued me, perhaps several people—I do not know, we left them all behind...

We ran. For a space I was altogether intent upon the swift monotony of flight and pursuit. The sands were changed to a whirl of green moonshine, the air was thunder. A luminous green haze rolled about us. What did such things matter? We ran. Did I gain or lose? that was the question. They ran through a gap in a broken fence that sprang up abruptly out of nothingness and turned to the right. I noted we were in a road. But this green mist! One seemed to plough through it. They were fading into it, and at that thought I made a spurt that won a dozen feet or more.

She staggered. He gripped her arm, and dragged her forward. They doubled to the left. We were off the road again and on turf. It felt like turf. I tripped and fell at a ditch that was somehow full of smoke, and was up again, but now they were phantoms half gone into the livid swirls about me...

Still I ran.

On, on! I groaned with the violence of my effort. I staggered again and swore. I felt the concussions of great guns tear past me through the murk.

They were gone! Everything was going, but I kept on running. Once more I stumbled. There was something about my feet that impeded me, tall grass or heather, but I could not see what it was, only this smoke that eddied about my knees. There was a noise and spinning in my brain, a vain resistance to a dark green curtain that was falling, falling, falling, fold upon fold. Everything grew darker and darker.

I made one last frantic effort, and raised my revolver, fired my penultimate shot at a venture, and fell headlong to the ground. And behold! the green curtain was a black one, and the earth and I and all things ceased to be.

BOOK THE SECOND - THE GREEN VAPORS

CHAPTER THE FIRST - THE CHANGE

§ 1

I seemed to awaken out of a refreshing sleep.

I did not awaken with a start, but opened my eyes, and lay very comfortably looking at a line of extraordinarily scarlet poppies that glowed against a glowing sky. It was the sky of a magnificent sunrise, and an archipelago of gold-beached purple islands floated in a sea of golden green. The poppies too, swan-necked buds, blazing corollas, translucent stout seed- vessels, stoutly upheld, had a luminous quality, seemed wrought only from some more solid kind of light.

I stared unwonderingly at these things for a time, and then there rose upon my consciousness, intermingling with these, the bristling golden green heads of growing barley.

A remote faint question, where I might be, drifted and vanished again in my mind. Everything was very still.

Everything was as still as death.

I felt very light, full of the sense of physical well-being. I perceived I was lying on my side in a little trampled space in a weedy, flowering barley field, that was in some inexplicable way saturated with light and beauty. I sat up, and remained for a long time filled with the delight and charm of the delicate little convolvulus that twined among the barley stems, the pimpernel that laced the ground below.

Then that question returned. What was this place? How had I come to be sleeping here?

I could not remember.

It perplexed me that somehow my body felt strange to me. It was unfamiliar—I could not tell how—and the barley, and the beautiful weeds, and the slowly developing glory of the dawn behind; all those things partook of the same unfamiliarity. I felt as though I was a thing in some very luminous painted window, as though this dawn broke through me. I felt I was part of some exquisite picture painted in light and joy.

A faint breeze bent and rustled the barley-heads, and jogged my mind forward.

Who was I? That was a good way of beginning.

I held up my left hand and arm before me, a grubby hand, a frayed cuff; but with a quality of painted unreality, transfigured as a beggar might have been by Botticelli. I looked for a time steadfastly at a beautiful pearl sleeve- link.

I remembered Willie Leadford, who had owned that arm and hand, as though he had been some one else.

Of course! My history—its rough outline rather than the immediate past—began to shape itself in my memory, very small, very bright and inaccessible, like a thing watched through a microscope. Clayton and Swathinglea returned to my mind; the slums and darkness, Dureresque, minute and in their rich dark colors pleasing, and through them I went towards my destiny. I sat hands on knees recalling that queer passionate career that had ended with my futile shot into the growing darkness of the End. The thought of that shot awoke my emotions again.

There was something in it now, something absurd, that made me smile pityingly.

Poor little angry, miserable creature! Poor little angry, miserable world!

I sighed for pity, not only pity for myself, but for all the hot hearts, the tormented brains, the straining, striving things of hope and pain, who had found their peace at last beneath the pouring mist and suffocation of the comet. Because certainly that world was over and done. They were all so weak and unhappy, and I was now so strong and so serene. For I felt sure I was dead; no one living could have this perfect assurance of good, this strong and confident peace. I had made an end of the fever called living. I was dead, and it was all right, and these—?

I felt an inconsistency.

These, then, must be the barley fields of God!—the still and silent barley fields of God, full of unfading poppy flowers whose seeds bear peace.

§ 2

It was queer to find barley fields in heaven, but no doubt there were many surprises in store for me.

How still everything was! Peace! The peace that passeth understanding. After all it had come to me! But, indeed, everything was very still! No bird sang. Surely I was alone in the world! No birds sang. Yes, and all the distant sounds of life had ceased, the lowing of cattle, the barking of dogs...

Something that was like fear beatified came into my heart. It was all right, I knew; but to be alone! I stood up and met the hot summons of the rising sun, hurrying towards me, as it were, with glad tidings, over the spikes of the barley...

Blinded, I made a step. My foot struck something hard, and I looked down to discover my revolver, a blue-black thing, like a dead snake at my feet.

For a moment that puzzled me.

Then I clean forgot about it. The wonder of the quiet took possession of my soul. Dawn, and no birds singing!

How beautiful was the world! How beautiful, but how still! I walked slowly through the barley towards a line of elder bushes, wayfaring tree and bramble that

made the hedge of the field. I noted as I passed along a dead shrew mouse, as it seemed to me, among the halms; then a still toad. I was surprised that this did not leap aside from my footfalls, and I stooped and picked it up. Its body was limp like life, but it made no struggle, the brightness of its eye was veiled, it did not move in my hand.

It seems to me now that I stood holding that lifeless little creature for some time. Then very softly I stooped down and replaced it. I was trembling — trembling with a nameless emotion. I looked with quickened eyes closely among the barley stems, and behold, now everywhere I saw beetles, flies, and little creatures that did not move, lying as they fell when the vapors overcame them; they seemed no more than painted things. Some were novel creatures to me. I was very unfamiliar with natural things. "My God!" I cried; "but is it only I—?"

And then at my next movement something squealed sharply. I turned about, but I could not see it, only I saw a little stir in a rut and heard the diminishing rustle of the unseen creature's flight. And at that I turned to my toad again, and its eye moved and it stirred. And presently, with infirm and hesitating gestures, it stretched its limbs and began to crawl away from me.

But wonder, that gentle sister of fear, had me now. I saw a little way ahead a brown and crimson butterfly perched upon a cornflower. I thought at first it was the breeze that stirred it, and then I saw its wings were quivering. And even as I watched it, it started into life, and spread itself, and fluttered into the air.

I watched it fly, a turn this way, a turn that, until suddenly it seemed to vanish. And now, life was returning to this thing and that on every side of me, with slow stretchings and bendings, with twitterings, with a little start and stir...

I came slowly, stepping very carefully because of these drugged, feebly awakening things, through the barley to the hedge. It was a very glorious hedge, so that it held my eyes. It flowed along and interlaced like splendid music. It was rich with lupin, honeysuckle, campions, and ragged robin; bed straw, hops, and wild clematis twined and hung among its branches, and all along its ditch border the starry stitchwort lifted its childish faces, and chorused in lines and masses. Never had I seen such a symphony of note-like flowers and tendrils and leaves. And suddenly in its depths, I heard a chirrup and the whirr of startled wings.

Nothing was dead, but everything had changed to beauty! And I stood for a time with clean and happy eyes looking at the intricate delicacy before me and marveling how richly God has made his worlds...

"Tweedle-Tweezle," a lark had shot the stillness with his shining thread of song; one lark, and then presently another, invisibly in the air, making out of that blue quiet a woven cloth of gold...

The earth recreated—only by the reiteration of such phrases may I hope to give the intense freshness of that dawn. For a time I was altogether taken up with the beautiful details of being, as regardless of my old life of jealous passion and impatient sorrow as though I was Adam new made. I could tell you now with infinite particularity of the shut flowers that opened as I looked, of tendrils and grass blades, of a blue-tit I picked up very tenderly —never before had I remarked

the great delicacy of feathers—that presently disclosed its bright black eye and judged me, and perched, swaying fearlessly, upon my finger, and spread unhurried wings and flew away, and of a great ebullition of tadpoles in the ditch; like all the things that lived beneath the water, they had passed unaltered through the Change. Amid such incidents, I lived those first great moments, losing for a time in the wonder of each little part the mighty wonder of the whole.

A little path ran between hedge and barley, and along this, leisurely and content and glad, looking at this beautiful thing and that, moving a step and stopping, then moving on again, I came presently to a stile, and deep below it, and overgrown, was a lane.

And on the worn oak of the stile was a round label, and on the label these words, "Swindells' G 90 Pills."

I sat myself astraddle on the stile, not fully grasping all the implications of these words. But they perplexed me even more than the revolver and my dirty cuff.

About me now the birds lifted up their little hearts and sang, ever more birds and more.

I read the label over and over again, and joined it to the fact that I still wore my former clothes, and that my revolver had been lying at my feet. One conclusion stared out at me. This was no new planet, no glorious hereafter such as I had supposed. This beautiful wonderland was the world, the same old world of my rage and death! But at least it was like meeting a familiar house- slut, washed and dignified, dressed in a queen's robes, worshipful and fine...

It might be the old world indeed, but something new lay upon all things, a glowing certitude of health and happiness. It might be the old world, but the dust and fury of the old life was certainly done. At least I had no doubt of that.

I recalled the last phases of my former life, that darkling climax of pursuit and anger and universal darkness and the whirling green vapors of extinction. The comet had struck the earth and made an end to all things; of that too I was assured.

But afterward?...

And now?

The imaginations of my boyhood came back as speculative possibilities. In those days I had believed firmly in the necessary advent of a last day, a great coming out of the sky, trumpetings and fear, the Resurrection, and the Judgment. My roving fancy now suggested to me that this Judgment must have come and passed. That it had passed and in some manner missed me. I was left alone here, in a swept and garnished world (except, of course, for this label of Swindells') to begin again perhaps...

No doubt Swindells has got his deserts.

My mind ran for a time on Swindells, on the imbecile pushfulness of that extinct creature, dealing in rubbish, covering the country-side with lies in order to get—what had he sought?—a silly, ugly, great house, a temper-destroying motor-car, a number of disrespectful, abject servants; thwarted intrigues for a party-fund

baronetcy as the crest of his life, perhaps. You cannot imagine the littleness of those former times; their naive, queer absurdities! And for the first time in my existence I thought of these things without bitterness. In the former days I had seen wickedness, I had seen tragedy, but now I saw only the extraordinary foolishness of the old life. The ludicrous side of human wealth and importance turned itself upon me, a shining novelty, poured down upon me like the sunrise, and engulfed me in laughter. Swindells! Swindells, damned! My vision of Judgment became a delightful burlesque. I saw the chuckling Angel sayer with his face veiled, and the corporeal presence of Swindells upheld amidst the laughter of the spheres. "Here's a thing, and a very pretty thing, and what's to be done with this very pretty thing?" I saw a soul being drawn from a rotund, substantial-looking body like a whelk from its shell...

I laughed loudly and long. And behold! even as I laughed the keen point of things accomplished stabbed my mirth, and I was weeping, weeping aloud, convulsed with weeping, and the tears were pouring down my face.

§ 3

Everywhere the awakening came with the sunrise. We awakened to the gladness of the morning; we walked dazzled in a light that was joy. Everywhere that was so. It was always morning. It was morning because, until the direct rays of the sun touched it, the changing nitrogen of our atmosphere did not pass into its permanent phase, and the sleepers lay as they had fallen. In its intermediate state the air hung inert, incapable of producing either revival or stupefaction, no longer green, but not yet changed to the gas that now lives in us...

To every one, I think, came some parallel to the mental states I have already sought to describe—a wonder, an impression of joyful novelty. There was also very commonly a certain confusion of the intelligence, a difficulty in self-recognition. I remember clearly as I sat on my stile that presently I had the clearest doubts of my own identity and fell into the oddest metaphysical questionings. "If this be I," I said, "then how is it I am no longer madly seeking Nettie? Nettie is now the remotest thing—and all my wrongs. Why have I suddenly passed out of all that passion? Why does not the thought of Verrall quicken my pulses?"...

I was only one of many millions who that morning had the same doubts. I suppose one knows one's self for one's self when one returns from sleep or insensibility by the familiarity of one's bodily sensations, and that morning all our most intimate bodily sensations were changed. The intimate chemical processes of life were changed, its nervous metaboly. For the fluctuating, uncertain, passion-darkened thought and feeling of the old time came steady, full-bodied, wholesome processes. Touch was different, sight was different, sound and all the senses were subtler; had it not been that our thought was steadier and fuller, I believe great multitudes of men would have gone mad. But, as it was, we understood. The dominant impression I would convey in this account of the Change is one of enormous release, of a vast substantial exaltation. There was an effect, as it were, of light-headedness that was also clear-headedness, and the al-

teration in one's bodily sensations, instead of producing the mental obfuscation, the loss of identity that was a common mental trouble under former conditions, gave simply a new detachment from the tumid passions and entanglements of the personal life.

In this story of my bitter, restricted youth that I have been telling you, I have sought constantly to convey the narrowness, the intensity, the confusion, muddle, and dusty heat of the old world. It was quite clear to me, within an hour of my awakening, that all that was, in some mysterious way, over and done. That, too, was the common experience. Men stood up; they took the new air into their lungs—a deep long breath, and the past fell from them; they could forgive, they could disregard, they could attempt... And it was no new thing, no miracle that sets aside the former order of the world. It was a change in material conditions, a change in the atmosphere, that at one bound had released them. Some of them it had released to death... Indeed, man himself had changed not at all. We knew before the Change, the meanest knew, by glowing moments in ourselves and others, by histories and music and beautiful things, by heroic instances and splendid stories, how fine mankind could be, how fine almost any human being could upon occasion be; but the poison in the air, its poverty in all the nobler elements which made such moments rare and remarkable —all that has changed. The air was changed, and the Spirit of Man that had drowsed and slumbered and dreamt dull and evil things, awakened, and stood with wonder-clean eyes, refreshed, looking again on life.

§ 4

The miracle of the awakening came to me in solitude, the laughter, and then the tears. Only after some time did I come upon another man. Until I heard his voice calling I did not seem to feel there were any other people in the world. All that seemed past, with all the stresses that were past. I had come out of the individual pit in which my shy egotism had lurked, I had overflowed to all humanity, I had seemed to be all humanity; I had laughed at Swindells as I could have laughed at myself, and this shout that came to me seemed like the coming of an unexpected thought in my own mind. But when it was repeated I answered.

"I am hurt," said the voice, and I descended into the lane forthwith, and so came upon Melmount sitting near the ditch with his back to me.

Some of the incidental sensory impressions of that morning bit so deeply into my mind that I verily believe, when at last I face the greater mysteries that lie beyond this life, when the things of this life fade from me as the mists of the morning fade before the sun, these irrelevant petty details will be the last to leave me, will be the last wisps visible of that attenuating veil. I believe, for instance, I could match the fur upon the collar of his great motoring coat now, could paint the dull red tinge of his big cheek with his fair eyelashes just catching the light and showing beyond. His hat was off, his dome-shaped head, with its smooth hair between red and extreme fairness, was bent forward in scrutiny of his twisted

foot. His back seemed enormous. And there was something about the mere massive sight of him that filled me with liking.

"What's wrong?" said I.

"I say," he said, in his full deliberate tones, straining round to see me and showing a profile, a well-modeled nose, a sensitive, clumsy, big lip, known to every caricaturist in the world, "I'm in a fix. I fell and wrenched my ankle. Where are you?"

I walked round him and stood looking at his face. I perceived he had his gaiter and sock and boot off, the motor gauntlets had been cast aside, and he was kneading the injured part in an exploratory manner with his thick thumbs.

"By Jove!" I said, "you're Melmount!"

"Melmount!" He thought. "That's my name," he said, without looking up... "But it doesn't affect my ankle."

We remained silent for few moments except for a grunt of pain from him.

"Do you know?" I asked, "what has happened to things?"

He seemed to complete his diagnosis. "It's not broken," he said.

"Do you know," I repeated, "what has happened to everything?"

"No," he said, looking up at me incuriously for the first time.

"There's some difference—"

"There's a difference." He smiled, a smile of unexpected pleasantness, and an interest was coming into his eyes. "I've been a little preoccupied with my own internal sensations. I remark an extraordinary brightness about things. Is that it?"

"That's part of it. And a queer feeling, a clear-headedness—"

He surveyed me and meditated gravely. "I woke up," he said, feeling his way in his memory.

"And I."

"I lost my way—I forget quite how. There was a curious green fog." He stared at his foot, remembering. "Something to do with a comet. I was by a hedge in the darkness. Tried to run... Then I must have pitched into this lane. Look!" He pointed with his head. "There's a wooden rail new broken there. I must have stumbled over that out of the field above." He scrutinized this and concluded. "Yes..."

"It was dark," I said, "and a sort of green gas came out of nothing everywhere. That is the last I remember."

"And then you woke up? So did I... In a state of great bewilderment. Certainly there's something odd in the air. I was—I was rushing along a road in a motor-car, very much excited and preoccupied. I got down—" He held out a triumphant finger. "Ironclads!"

"NOW I've got it! We'd strung our fleet from here to Texel. We'd got right across them and the Elbe mined. We'd lost the Lord Warden. By Jove, yes. The Lord Warden! A battleship that cost two million pounds—and that fool Rigby said it didn't matter! Eleven hundred men went down... I remember now. We were sweeping up the North Sea like a net, with the North Atlantic fleet waiting at the Faroes for 'em—and not one of 'em had three days' coal! Now, was that a dream? No! I told a lot of people as much—a meeting was it?—to reassure them. They

were warlike but extremely frightened. Queer people—paunchy and bald like gnomes, most of them. Where? Of course! We had it all over—a big dinner—oysters! —Colchester. I'd been there, just to show all this raid scare was nonsense. And I was coming back here... But it doesn't seem as though that was —recent. I suppose it was. Yes, of course!—it was. I got out of my car at the bottom of the rise with the idea of walking along the cliff path, because every one said one of their battleships was being chased along the shore. That's clear! I heard their guns—"

He reflected. "Queer I should have forgotten! Did YOU hear any guns?"

I said I had heard them.

"Was it last night?"

"Late last night. One or two in the morning."

He leant back on his hand and looked at me, smiling frankly. "Even now," he said, "it's odd, but the whole of that seems like a silly dream. Do you think there WAS a Lord Warden? Do you really believe we sank all that machinery —for fun? It was a dream. And yet—it happened."

By all the standards of the former time it would have been remarkable that I talked quite easily and freely with so great a man. "Yes," I said; "that's it. One feels one has awakened—from something more than that green gas. As though the other things also—weren't quite real."

He knitted his brows and felt the calf of his leg thoughtfully. "I made a speech at Colchester," he said.

I thought he was going to add something more about that, but there lingered a habit of reticence in the man that held him for the moment. "It is a very curious thing," he broke away; "that this pain should be, on the whole, more interesting than disagreeable."

"You are in pain?"

"My ankle is! It's either broken or badly sprained—I think sprained; it's very painful to move, but personally I'm not in pain. That sort of general sickness that comes with local injury—not a trace of it! ..." He mused and remarked, "I was speaking at Colchester, and saying things about the war. I begin to see it better. The reporters—scribble, scribble. Max Sutaine, 1885. Hubbub. Compliments about the oysters. Mm—mm... What was it? About the war? A war that must needs be long and bloody, taking toll from castle and cottage, taking toll! ... Rhetorical gusto! Was I drunk last night?"

His eyebrows puckered. He had drawn up his right knee, his elbow rested thereon and his chin on his fist. The deep-set gray eyes beneath his thatch of eyebrow stared at unknown things. "My God!" he murmured, "My God!" with a note of disgust. He made a big brooding figure in the sunlight, he had an effect of more than physical largeness; he made me feel that it became me to wait upon his thinking. I had never met a man of this sort before; I did not know such men existed...

It is a curious thing, that I cannot now recall any ideas whatever that I had before the Change about the personalities of statesmen, but I doubt if ever in those

days I thought of them at all as tangible individual human beings, conceivably of some intellectual complexity. I believe that my impression was a straightforward blend of caricature and newspaper leader. I certainly had no respect for them. And now without servility or any insincerity whatever, as if it were a first-fruit of the Change, I found myself in the presence of a human being towards whom I perceived myself inferior and subordinate, before whom I stood without servility or any insincerity whatever, in an attitude of respect and attention. My inflamed, my rancid egotism—or was it after all only the chances of life?—had never once permitted that before the Change.

He emerged from his thoughts, still with a faint perplexity in his manner. "That speech I made last night," he said, "was damned mischievous nonsense, you know. Nothing can alter that. Nothing... No! ... Little fat gnomes in evening dress—gobbling oysters. Gulp!"

It was a most natural part of the wonder of that morning that he should adopt this incredible note of frankness, and that it should abate nothing from my respect for him.

"Yes," he said, "you are right. It's all indisputable fact, and I can't believe it was anything but a dream."

§ 5

That memory stands out against the dark past of the world with extraordinary clearness and brightness. The air, I remember, was full of the calling and piping and singing of birds. I have a curious persuasion too that there was a distant happy clamor of pealing bells, but that I am half convinced is a mistake. Nevertheless, there was something in the fresh bite of things, in the dewy newness of sensation that set bells rejoicing in one's brain. And that big, fair, pensive man sitting on the ground had beauty even in his clumsy pose, as though indeed some Great Master of strength and humor had made him.

And—it is so hard now to convey these things—he spoke to me, a stranger, without reservations, carelessly, as men now speak to men. Before those days, not only did we think badly, but what we thought, a thousand short-sighted considerations, dignity, objective discipline, discretion, a hundred kindred aspects of shabbiness of soul, made us muffle before we told it to our fellow-men.

"It's all returning now," he said, and told me half soliloquizingly what was in his mind.

I wish I could give every word he said to me; he struck out image after image to my nascent intelligence, with swift broken fragments of speech. If I had a precise full memory of that morning I should give it you, verbatim, minutely. But here, save for the little sharp things that stand out, I find only blurred general impressions. Throughout I have to make up again his half- forgotten sentences and speeches, and be content with giving you the general effect. But I can see and hear him now as he said, "The dream got worst at the end. The war—a perfectly horrible business! Horrible! And it was just like a nightmare, you couldn't do anything to escape from it—every one was driven!"

His sense of indiscretion was gone.

He opened the war out to me—as every one sees it now. Only that morning it was astonishing. He sat there on the ground, absurdly forgetful of his bare and swollen foot, treating me as the humblest accessory and as altogether an equal, talking out to himself the great obsessions of his mind. "We could have prevented it! Any of us who chose to speak out could have prevented it. A little decent frankness. What was there to prevent us being frank with one another? Their emperor—his position was a pile of ridiculous assumptions, no doubt, but at bottom—he was a sane man." He touched off the emperor in a few pithy words, the German press, the German people, and our own. He put it as we should put it all now, but with a certain heat as of a man half guilty and wholly resentful. "Their damned little buttoned-up professors!" he cried, incidentally. "Were there ever such men? And ours! Some of us might have taken a firmer line... If a lot of us had taken a firmer line and squashed that nonsense early..."

He lapsed into inaudible whisperings, into silence...

I stood regarding him, understanding him, learning marvelously from him. It is a fact that for the best part of the morning of the Change I forgot Nettie and Verrall as completely as though they were no more than characters in some novel that I had put aside to finish at my leisure, in order that I might talk to this man.

"Eh, well," he said, waking startlingly from his thoughts. "Here we are awakened! The thing can't go on now; all this must end. How it ever began—! My dear boy, how did all those things ever begin? I feel like a new Adam... Do you think this has happened—generally? Or shall we find all these gnomes and things? ... Who cares?"

He made as if to rise, and remembered his ankle. He suggested I should help him as far as his bungalow. There seemed nothing strange to either of us that he should requisition my services or that I should cheerfully obey. I helped him bandage his ankle, and we set out, I his crutch, the two of us making up a sort of limping quadruped, along the winding lane toward the cliffs and the sea.

§ 6

His bungalow beyond the golf links was, perhaps, a mile and a quarter from the lane. We went down to the beach margin and along the pallid wave- smoothed sands, and we got along by making a swaying, hopping, tripod dance forward until I began to give under him, and then, as soon as we could, sitting down. His ankle was, in fact, broken, and he could not put it to the ground without exquisite pain. So that it took us nearly two hours to get to the house, and it would have taken longer if his butler-valet had not come out to assist me. They had found motor-car and chauffeur smashed and still at the bend of the road near the house, and had been on that side looking for Melmount, or they would have seen us before.

For most of that time we were sitting now on turf, now on a chalk boulder, now on a timber groin, and talking one to the other, with the frankness proper to the intercourse of men of good intent, without reservations or aggressions, in the common, open fashion of contemporary intercourse to-day, but which then, nev-

ertheless, was the rarest and strangest thing in the world. He for the most part talked, but at some shape of a question I told him—as plainly as I could tell of passions that had for a time become incomprehensible to me—of my murderous pursuit of Nettie and her lover, and how the green vapors overcame me. He watched me with grave eyes and nodded understandingly, and afterwards he asked me brief penetrating questions about my education, my upbringing, my work. There was a deliberation in his manner, brief full pauses, that had in them no element of delay.

"Yes," he said, "yes—of course. What a fool I have been!" and said no more until we had made another of our tripod struggles along the beach. At first I did not see the connection of my story with that self-accusation.

"Suppose," he said, panting on the groin, "there had been such a thing as a statesman! ..."

He turned to me. "If one had decided all this muddle shall end! If one had taken it, as an artist takes his clay, as a man who builds takes site and stone, and made—" He flung out his big broad hand at the glories of sky and sea, and drew a deep breath, "something to fit that setting."

He added in explanation, "Then there wouldn't have been such stories as yours at all, you know..."

"Tell me more about it," he said, "tell me all about yourself. I feel all these things have passed away, all these things are to be changed for ever... You won't be what you have been from this time forth. All the things you have done—don't matter now. To us, at any rate, they don't matter at all. We have met, who were separated in that darkness behind us. Tell me.

"Yes," he said; and I told my story straight and as frankly as I have told it to you. "And there, where those little skerries of weed rock run out to the ebb, beyond the headland, is Bungalow village. What did you do with your pistol?"

"I left it lying there—among the barley."

He glanced at me from under his light eyelashes. "If others feel like you and I," he said, "there'll be a lot of pistols left among the barley to- day..."

So we talked, I and that great, strong man, with the love of brothers so plain between us it needed not a word. Our souls went out to one another in stark good faith; never before had I had anything but a guarded watchfulness for any fellow-man. Still I see him, upon that wild desolate beach of the ebb tide, I see him leaning against the shelly buttress of a groin, looking down at the poor drowned sailor whose body we presently found. For we found a newly drowned man who had just chanced to miss this great dawn in which we rejoiced. We found him lying in a pool of water, among brown weeds in the dark shadow of the timberings. You must not overrate the horrors of the former days; in those days it was scarcely more common to see death in England than it would be to- day. This dead man was a sailor from the Rother Adler, the great German battleship that—had we but known it—lay not four miles away along the coast amidst ploughed-up mountains of chalk ooze, a torn and battered mass of machinery, wholly submerged at high

water, and holding in its interstices nine hundred drowned brave men, all strong and skilful, all once capable of doing fine things...

I remember that poor boy very vividly. He had been drowned during the anaesthesia of the green gas, his fair young face was quiet and calm, but the skin of his chest had been crinkled by scalding water and his right arm was bent queerly back. Even to this needless death and all its tale of cruelty, beauty and dignity had come. Everything flowed together to significance as we stood there, I, the ill-clad, cheaply equipped proletarian, and Melmount in his great fur-trimmed coat—he was hot with walking but he had not thought to remove it—leaning upon the clumsy groins and pitying this poor victim of the war he had helped to make. "Poor lad!" he said, "poor lad! A child we blunderers sent to death! Do look at the quiet beauty of that face, that body—to be flung aside like this!"

(I remember that near this dead man's hand a stranded star-fish writhed its slowly feeling limbs, struggling back toward the sea. It left grooved traces in the sand.)

"There must be no more of this," panted Melmount, leaning on my shoulder, "no more of this..."

But most I recall Melmount as he talked a little later, sitting upon a great chalk boulder with the sunlight on his big, perspiration-dewed face. He made his resolves. "We must end war," he said, in that full whisper of his; "it is stupidity. With so many people able to read and think—even as it is —there is no need of anything of the sort. Gods! What have we rulers been at? ... Drowsing like people in a stifling room, too dull and sleepy and too base toward each other for any one to get up and open the window. What haven't we been at?"

A great powerful figure he sits there still in my memory, perplexed and astonished at himself and all things. "We must change all this," he repeated, and threw out his broad hands in a powerful gesture against the sea and sky. "We have done so weakly—Heaven alone knows why!" I can see him now, queer giant that he looked on that dawnlit beach of splendor, the sea birds flying about us and that crumpled death hard by, no bad symbol in his clumsiness and needless heat of the unawakened powers of the former time. I remember it as an integral part of that picture that far away across the sandy stretches one of those white estate boards I have described, stuck up a little askew amidst the yellow-green turf upon the crest of the low cliffs.

He talked with a sort of wonder of the former things. "Has it ever dawned upon you to imagine the pettiness—the pettiness!—of every soul concerned in a declaration of war?" he asked. He went on, as though speech was necessary to make it credible, to describe Laycock, who first gave the horror words at the cabinet council, "an undersized Oxford prig with a tenoring voice and a garbage of Greek—the sort of little fool who is brought up on the admiration of his elder sisters...

"All the time almost," he said, "I was watching him—thinking what an ass he was to be trusted with men's lives... I might have done better to have thought that of myself. I was doing nothing to prevent it all! The damned little imbecile was

up to his neck in the drama of the thing, he liked to trumpet it out, he goggled round at us. 'Then it is war!' he said. Richover shrugged his shoulders. I made some slight protest and gave in... Afterward I dreamt of him.

"What a lot we were! All a little scared at ourselves—all, as it were, instrumental...

"And it's fools like that lead to things like this!" He jerked his head at that dead man near by us.

"It will be interesting to know what has happened to the world... This green vapor—queer stuff. But I know what has happened to me. It's Conversion. I've always known... But this is being a fool. Talk! I'm going to stop it."

He motioned to rise with his clumsy outstretched hands.

"Stop what?" said I, stepping forward instinctively to help him.

"War," he said in his great whisper, putting his big hand on my shoulder but making no further attempt to arise, "I'm going to put an end to war—to any sort of war! And all these things that must end. The world is beautiful, life is great and splendid, we had only to lift up our eyes and see. Think of the glories through which we have been driving, like a herd of swine in a garden place. The color in life—the sounds—the shapes! We have had our jealousies, our quarrels, our ticklish rights, our invincible prejudices, our vulgar enterprise and sluggish timidities, we have chattered and pecked one another and fouled the world—like daws in the temple, like unclean birds in the holy place of God. All my life has been foolishness and pettiness, gross pleasures and mean discretions—all. I am a meagre dark thing in this morning's glow, a penitence, a shame! And, but for God's mercy, I might have died this night—like that poor lad there—amidst the squalor of my sins! No more of this! No more of this!—whether the whole world has changed or no, matters nothing. WE TWO HAVE SEEN THIS DAWN! ..."

He paused.

"I will arise and go unto my Father," he began presently, "and will say unto Him—"

His voice died away in an inaudible whisper. His hand tightened painfully on my shoulder and he rose...

CHAPTER THE SECOND - THE AWAKENING

SECTION 1

So the great Day came to me.

And even as I had awakened so in that same dawn the whole world awoke.

For the whole world of living things had been overtaken by the same tide of insensibility; in an hour, at the touch of this new gas in the comet, the shiver of catalytic change had passed about the globe. They say it was the nitrogen of the air, the old AZOTE, that in the twinkling of an eye was changed out of itself, and in an hour or so became a respirable gas, differing indeed from oxygen, but helping and sustaining its action, a bath of strength and healing for nerve and brain. I do not know the precise changes that occurred, nor the names our chemists give them, my work has carried me away from such things, only this I know—I and all men were renewed.

I picture to myself this thing happening in space, a planetary moment, the faint smudge, the slender whirl of meteor, drawing nearer to this planet, —this planet like a ball, like a shaded rounded ball, floating in the void, with its little, nearly impalpable coat of cloud and air, with its dark pools of ocean, its gleaming ridges of land. And as that midge from the void touches it, the transparent gaseous outer shell clouds in an instant green and then slowly clears again...

Thereafter, for three hours or more,—we know the minimum time for the Change was almost exactly three hours because all the clocks and watches kept going—everywhere, no man nor beast nor bird nor any living thing that breathes the air stirred at all but lay still...

Everywhere on earth that day, in the ears of every one who breathed, there had been the same humming in the air, the same rush of green vapors, the crepitation, the streaming down of shooting stars. The Hindoo had stayed his morning's work in the fields to stare and marvel and fall, the blue-clothed Chinaman fell head foremost athwart his midday bowl of rice, the Japanese merchant came out from some chaffering in his office amazed and presently lay there before his door, the evening gazers by the Golden Gates were overtaken as they waited for the rising of the great star. This had happened in every city of the world, in every lonely valley, in every home and house and shelter and every open place. On the high seas, the crowding steamship passengers, eager for any wonder, gaped and marveled, and were suddenly terror-stricken, and struggled for the gangways and were overcome, the captain staggered on the bridge and fell, the stoker fell head-

long among his coals, the engines throbbed upon their way untended, the fishing craft drove by without a hail, with swaying rudder, heeling and dipping...

The great voice of material Fate cried Halt! And in the midst of the play the actors staggered, dropped, and were still. The figure runs from my pen. In New York that very thing occurred. Most of the theatrical audiences dispersed, but in two crowded houses the company, fearing a panic, went on playing amidst the gloom, and the people, trained by many a previous disaster, stuck to their seats. There they sat, the back rows only moving a little, and there, in disciplined lines, they drooped and failed, nodded, and fell forward or slid down upon the floor. I am told by Parload—though indeed I know nothing of the reasoning on which his confidence rests—-that within an hour of the great moment of impact the first green modification of nitrogen had dissolved and passed away, leaving the air as translucent as ever. The rest of that wonderful interlude was clear, had any had eyes to see its clearness. In London it was night, but in New York, for example, people were in the full bustle of the evening's enjoyment, in Chicago they were sitting down to dinner, the whole world was abroad. The moonlight must have illuminated streets and squares littered with crumpled figures, through which such electric cars as had no automatic brakes had ploughed on their way until they were stopped by the fallen bodies. People lay in their dress clothes, in dining-rooms, restaurants, on staircases, in halls, everywhere just as they had been over-come. Men gambling, men drinking, thieves lurking in hidden places, sinful couples, were caught, to arise with awakened mind and conscience amidst the disorder of their sin. America the comet reached in the full tide of evening life, but Britain lay asleep. But as I have told, Britain did not slumber so deeply but that she was in the full tide of what may have been battle and a great victory. Up and down the North Sea her warships swept together like a net about their foes. On land, too, that night was to have decided great issues. The German camps were under arms from Redingen to Markirch, their infantry columns were lying in swathes like mown hay, in arrested night march on every track between Longuy-on and Thiancourt, and between Avricourt and Donen. The hills beyond Spincourt were dusted thick with hidden French riflemen; the thin lash of the French skir-mishers sprawled out amidst spades and unfinished rifle-pits in coils that wrapped about the heads of the German columns, thence along the Vosges watershed and out across the frontier near Belfort nearly to the Rhine...

The Hungarian, the Italian peasant, yawned and thought the morning dark, and turned over to fall into a dreamless sleep; the Mahometan world spread its carpet and was taken in prayer. And in Sydney, in Melbourne, in New Zealand, the thing was a fog in the afternoon, that scattered the crowd on race-courses and cricket-fields, and stopped the unloading of shipping and brought men out from their af-ternoon rest to stagger and litter the streets...

§ 2

My thoughts go into the woods and wildernesses and jungles of the world, to the wild life that shared man's suspension, and I think of a thousand feral acts in-

terrupted and truncated—as it were frozen, like the frozen words Pantagruel met at sea. Not only men it was that were quieted, all living creatures that breathe the air became insensible, impassive things. Motionless brutes and birds lay amidst the drooping trees and herbage in the universal twilight, the tiger sprawled beside his fresh-struck victim, who bled to death in a dreamless sleep. The very flies came sailing down the air with wings outspread; the spider hung crumpled in his loaded net; like some gaily painted snowflake the butterfly drifted to earth and grounded, and was still. And as a queer contrast one gathers that the fishes in the sea suffered not at all...

Speaking of the fishes reminds me of a queer little inset upon that great world-dreaming. The odd fate of the crew of the submarine vessel B 94 has always seemed memorable to me. So far as I know, they were the only men alive who never saw that veil of green drawn across the world. All the while that the stillness held above, they were working into the mouth of the Elbe, past the booms and the mines, very slowly and carefully, a sinister crustacean of steel, explosive crammed, along the muddy bottom. They trailed a long clue that was to guide their fellows from the mother ship floating awash outside. Then in the long channel beyond the forts they came up at last to mark down their victims and get air. That must have been before the twilight of dawn, for they tell of the brightness of the stars. They were amazed to find themselves not three hundred yards from an ironclad that had run ashore in the mud, and heeled over with the falling tide. It was afire amidships, but no one heeded that—no one in all that strange clear silence heeded that—and not only this wrecked vessel, but all the dark ships lying about them, it seemed to their perplexed and startled minds must be full of dead men!

Theirs I think must have been one of the strangest of all experiences; they were never insensible; at once, and, I am told, with a sudden catch of laughter, they began to breathe the new air. None of them has proved a writer; we have no picture of their wonder, no description of what was said. But we know these men were active and awake for an hour and a half at least before the general awakening came, and when at last the Germans stirred and sat up they found these strangers in possession of their battleship, the submarine carelessly adrift, and the Englishmen, begrimed and weary, but with a sort of furious exultation, still busy, in the bright dawn, rescuing insensible enemies from the sinking conflagration...

But the thought of certain stokers the sailors of the submarine failed altogether to save brings me back to the thread of grotesque horror that runs through all this event, the thread I cannot overlook for all the splendors of human well-being that have come from it. I cannot forget the unguided ships that drove ashore, that went down in disaster with all their sleeping hands, nor how, inland, motor-cars rushed to destruction upon the roads, and trains upon the railways kept on in spite of signals, to be found at last by their amazed, reviving drivers standing on unfamiliar lines, their fires exhausted, or, less lucky, to be discovered by astonished peasants or awakening porters smashed and crumpled up into heaps of smoking, crackling

ruin. The foundry fires of the Four Towns still blazed, the smoke of our burning still denied the sky. Fires burnt indeed the brighter for the Change—and spread...

§ 3

Picture to yourself what happened between the printing and composing of the copy of the New Paper that lies before me now. It was the first newspaper that was printed upon earth after the Great Change. It was pocket-worn and browned, made of a paper no man ever intended for preservation. I found it on the arbor table in the inn garden while I was waiting for Nettie and Verrall, before that last conversation of which I have presently to tell. As I look at it all that scene comes back to me, and Nettie stands in her white raiment against a blue-green background of sunlit garden, scrutinizing my face as I read...

It is so frayed that the sheet cracks along the folds and comes to pieces in my hands. It lies upon my desk, a dead souvenir of the dead ages of the world, of the ancient passions of my heart. I know we discussed its news, but for the life of me I cannot recall what we said, only I remember that Nettie said very little, and that Verrall for a time read it over my shoulder. And I did not like him to read over my shoulder...

The document before me must have helped us through the first awkwardness of that meeting.

But of all that we said and did then I must tell in a later chapter...

It is easy to see the New Paper had been set up overnight, and then large pieces of the stereo plates replaced subsequently. I do not know enough of the old methods of printing to know precisely what happened. The thing gives one an impression of large pieces of type having been cut away and replaced by fresh blocks. There is something very rough and ready about it all, and the new portions print darker and more smudgily than the old, except toward the left, where they have missed ink and indented. A friend of mine, who knows something of the old typography, has suggested to me that the machinery actually in use for the New Paper was damaged that night, and that on the morning of the Change Banghurst borrowed a neighboring office—perhaps in financial dependence upon him—to print in.

The outer pages belong entirely to the old period, the only parts of the paper that had undergone alteration are the two middle leaves. Here we found set forth in a curious little four-column oblong of print, WHAT HAS HAPPENED. This cut across a column with scare headings beginning, "Great Naval Battle Now in Progress. The Fate of Two Empires in the Balance. Reported Loss of Two More—"

These things, one gathered, were beneath notice now. Probably it was guesswork, and fabricated news in the first instance.

It is curious to piece together the worn and frayed fragments, and reread this discolored first intelligence of the new epoch.

The simple clear statements in the replaced portion of the paper impressed me at the time, I remember, as bald and strange, in that framework of shouting bad

English. Now they seem like the voice of a sane man amidst a vast faded violence. But they witness to the prompt recovery of London from the gas; the new, swift energy of rebound in that huge population. I am surprised now, as I reread, to note how much research, experiment, and induction must have been accomplished in the day that elapsed before the paper was printed.... But that is by the way. As I sit and muse over this partly carbonized sheet, that same curious remote vision comes again to me that quickened in my mind that morning, a vision of those newspaper offices I have already described to you going through the crisis.

The catalytic wave must have caught the place in full swing, in its nocturnal high fever, indeed in a quite exceptional state of fever, what with the comet and the war, and more particularly with the war. Very probably the Change crept into the office imperceptibly, amidst the noise and shouting, and the glare of electric light that made the night atmosphere in that place; even the green flashes may have passed unobserved there, the preliminary descending trails of green vapor seemed no more than unseasonable drifting wisps of London fog. (In those days London even in summer was not safe against dark fogs.) And then at the last the Change poured in and overtook them.

If there was any warning at all for them, it must have been a sudden universal tumult in the street, and then a much more universal quiet. They could have had no other intimation.

There was no time to stop the presses before the main development of green vapor had overwhelmed every one. It must have folded about them, tumbled them to the earth, masked and stilled them. My imagination is always curiously stirred by the thought of that, because I suppose it is the first picture I succeeded in making for myself of what had happened in the towns. It has never quite lost its strangeness for me that when the Change came, machinery went on working. I don't precisely know why that should have seemed so strange to me, but it did, and still to a certain extent does. One is so accustomed, I suppose, to regard machinery as an extension of human personality that the extent of its autonomy the Change displayed came as a shock to me. The electric lights, for example, hazy green-haloed nebulas, must have gone on burning at least for a time; amidst the thickening darkness the huge presses must have roared on, printing, folding, throwing aside copy after copy of that fabricated battle report with its quarter column of scare headlines, and all the place must have still quivered and throbbed with the familiar roar of the engines. And this though no men ruled there at all any more! Here and there beneath that thickening fog the crumpled or outstretched forms of men lay still.

A wonderful thing that must have seemed, had any man had by chance the power of resistance to the vapor, and could he have walked amidst it.

And soon the machines must have exhausted their feed of ink and paper, and thumped and banged and rattled emptily amidst the general quiet. Then I suppose the furnaces failed for want of stoking, the steam pressure fell in the pistons, the machinery slackened, the lights burnt dim, and came and went with the ebb of

energy from the power-station. Who can tell precisely the sequence of these things now?

And then, you know, amidst the weakening and terminating noises of men, the green vapor cleared and vanished, in an hour indeed it had gone, and it may be a breeze stirred and blew and went about the earth.

The noises of life were all dying away, but some there were that abated nothing, that sounded triumphantly amidst the universal ebb. To a heedless world the church towers tolled out two and then three. Clocks ticked and chimed everywhere about the earth to deafened ears...

And then came the first flush of morning, the first rustlings of the revival. Perhaps in that office the filaments of the lamps were still glowing, the machinery was still pulsing weakly, when the crumpled, booted heaps of cloth became men again and began to stir and stare. The chapel of the printers was, no doubt, shocked to find itself asleep. Amidst that dazzling dawn the New Paper woke to wonder, stood up and blinked at its amazing self...

The clocks of the city churches, one pursuing another, struck four. The staffs, crumpled and disheveled, but with a strange refreshment in their veins, stood about the damaged machinery, marveling and questioning; the editor read his overnight headlines with incredulous laughter. There was much involuntary laughter that morning. Outside, the mail men patted the necks and rubbed the knees of their awakening horses...

Then, you know, slowly and with much conversation and doubt, they set about to produce the paper.

Imagine those bemused, perplexed people, carried on by the inertia of their old occupations and doing their best with an enterprise that had suddenly become altogether extraordinary and irrational. They worked amidst questionings, and yet light-heartedly. At every stage there must have been interruptions for discussion. The paper only got down to Menton five days late.

§ 4

Then let me give you a vivid little impression I received of a certain prosaic person, a grocer, named Wiggins, and how he passed through the Change. I heard this man's story in the post-office at Menton, when, in the afternoon of the First Day, I bethought me to telegraph to my mother. The place was also a grocer's shop, and I found him and the proprietor talking as I went in. They were trade competitors, and Wiggins had just come across the street to break the hostile silence of a score of years. The sparkle of the Change was in their eyes, their slightly flushed cheeks, their more elastic gestures, spoke of new physical influences that had invaded their beings.

"It did us no good, all our hatred," Mr. Wiggins said to me, explaining the emotion of their encounter; "it did our customers no good. I've come to tell him that. You bear that in mind, young man, if ever you come to have a shop of your own. It was a sort of stupid bitterness possessed us, and I can't make out we didn't see it before in that light. Not so much downright wickedness it wasn't as stupidi-

ty. A stupid jealousy! Think of it!—two human beings within a stone's throw, who have not spoken for twenty years, hardening our hearts against each other!"

"I can't think how we came to such a state, Mr. Wiggins," said the other, packing tea into pound packets out of mere habit as he spoke. "It was wicked pride and obstinacy. We KNEW it was foolish all the time."

I stood affixing the adhesive stamp to my telegram.

"Only the other morning," he went on to me, "I was cutting French eggs. Selling at a loss to do it. He'd marked down with a great staring ticket to ninepence a dozen—I saw it as I went past. Here's my answer!" He indicated a ticket. "'Eightpence a dozen—same as sold elsewhere for ninepence.' A whole penny down, bang off! Just a touch above cost—if that—and even then—" He leant over the counter to say impressively, "NOT THE SAME EGGS!"

"Now, what people in their senses would do things like that?" said Mr. Wiggins.

I sent my telegram—the proprietor dispatched it for me, and while he did so I fell exchanging experiences with Mr. Wiggins. He knew no more than I did then the nature of the change that had come over things. He had been alarmed by the green flashes, he said, so much so that after watching for a time from behind his bedroom window blind, he had got up and hastily dressed and made his family get up also, so that they might be ready for the end. He made them put on their Sunday clothes. They all went out into the garden together, their minds divided between admiration at the gloriousness of the spectacle and a great and growing awe. They were Dissenters, and very religious people out of business hours, and it seemed to them in those last magnificent moments that, after all, science must be wrong and the fanatics right. With the green vapors came conviction, and they prepared to meet their God...

This man, you must understand, was a common-looking man, in his shirt-sleeves and with an apron about his paunch, and he told his story in an Anglian accent that sounded mean and clipped to my Staffordshire ears; he told his story without a thought of pride, and as it were incidentally, and yet he gave me a vision of something heroic.

These people did not run hither and thither as many people did. These four simple, common people stood beyond their back door in their garden pathway between the gooseberry bushes, with the terrors of their God and His Judgments closing in upon them, swiftly and wonderfully—and there they began to sing. There they stood, father and mother and two daughters, chanting out stoutly, but no doubt a little flatly after the manner of their kind—

"In Zion's Hope abiding, My soul in Triumph sings—"

until one by one they fell, and lay still.

The postmaster had heard them in the gathering darkness, "In Zion's Hope abiding."...

It was the most extraordinary thing in the world to hear this flushed and happy-eyed man telling that story of his recent death. It did not seem at all possible to have happened in the last twelve hours. It was minute and remote, these people

who went singing through the darkling to their God. It was like a scene shown to me, very small and very distinctly painted, in a locket.

But that effect was not confined to this particular thing. A vast number of things that had happened before the coming of the comet had undergone the same transfiguring reduction. Other people, too, I have learnt since, had the same illusion, a sense of enlargement. It seems to me even now that the little dark creature who had stormed across England in pursuit of Nettie and her lover must have been about an inch high, that all that previous life of ours had been an ill-lit marionette show, acted in the twilight...

§ 5

The figure of my mother comes always into my conception of the Change.

I remember how one day she confessed herself.

She had been very sleepless that night, she said, and took the reports of the falling stars for shooting; there had been rioting in Clayton and all through Swathinglea all day, and so she got out of bed to look. She had a dim sense that I was in all such troubles.

But she was not looking when the Change came.

"When I saw the stars a-raining down, dear," she said, "and thought of you out in it, I thought there'd be no harm in saying a prayer for you, dear? I thought you wouldn't mind that."

And so I got another of my pictures—the green vapors come and go, and there by her patched coverlet that dear old woman kneels and droops, still clasping her poor gnarled hands in the attitude of prayer—prayer to IT —for me!

Through the meagre curtains and blinds of the flawed refracting window I see the stars above the chimneys fade, the pale light of dawn creeps into the sky, and her candle flares and dies...

That also went with me through the stillness—that silent kneeling figure, that frozen prayer to God to shield me, silent in a silent world, rushing through the emptiness of space...

§ 6

With the dawn that awakening went about the earth. I have told how it came to me, and how I walked in wonder through the transfigured cornfields of Shaphambury. It came to every one. Near me, and for the time, clear forgotten by me, Verrall and Nettie woke—woke near one another, each heard before all other sounds the other's voice amidst the stillness, and the light. And the scattered people who had run to and fro, and fallen on the beach of Bungalow village, awoke; the sleeping villagers of Menton started, and sat up in that unwonted freshness and newness; the contorted figures in the garden, with the hymn still upon their lips, stirred amidst the flowers, and touched each other timidly, and thought of Paradise. My mother found herself crouched against the bed, and rose—rose with a glad invincible conviction of accepted prayer...

Already, when it came to us, the soldiers, crowded between the lines of dusty poplars along the road to Allarmont, were chatting and sharing coffee with the French riflemen, who had hailed them from their carefully hidden pits among the vineyards up the slopes of Beauville. A certain perplexity had come to these marksmen, who had dropped asleep tensely ready for the rocket that should wake the whirr and rattle of their magazines. At the sight and sound of the stir and human confusion in the roadway below, it had come to each man individually that he could not shoot. One conscript, at least, has told his story of his awakening, and how curious he thought the rifle there beside him in his pit, how he took it on his knees to examine. Then, as his memory of its purpose grew clearer, he dropped the thing, and stood up with a kind of joyful horror at the crime escaped, to look more closely at the men he was to have assassinated. "Brave types," he thought, they looked for such a fate. The summoning rocket never flew. Below, the men did not fall into ranks again, but sat by the roadside, or stood in groups talking, discussing with a novel incredulity the ostensible causes of the war. "The Emperor!" said they; and "Oh, nonsense! We're civilized men. Get some one else for this job! ... Where's the coffee?"

The officers held their own horses, and talked to the men frankly, regardless of discipline. Some Frenchmen out of the rifle-pits came sauntering down the hill. Others stood doubtfully, rifles still in hand. Curious faces scanned these latter. Little arguments sprang as: "Shoot at us! Nonsense! They're respectable French citizens." There is a picture of it all, very bright and detailed in the morning light, in the battle gallery amidst the ruins at old Nancy, and one sees the old-world uniform of the "soldier," the odd caps and belts and boots, the ammunition-belt, the water-bottle, the sort of tourist's pack the men carried, a queer elaborate equipment. The soldiers had awakened one by one, first one and then another. I wonder sometimes whether, perhaps, if the two armies had come awake in an instant, the battle, by mere habit and inertia, might not have begun. But the men who waked first, sat up, looked about them in astonishment, had time to think a little...

§ 7

Everywhere there was laughter, everywhere tears.

Men and women in the common life, finding themselves suddenly lit and exalted, capable of doing what had hitherto been impossible, incapable of doing what had hitherto been irresistible, happy, hopeful, unselfishly energetic, rejected altogether the supposition that this was merely a change in the blood and material texture of life. They denied the bodies God had given them, as once the Upper Nile savages struck out their canine teeth, because these made them like the beasts. They declared that this was the coming of a spirit, and nothing else would satisfy their need for explanations. And in a sense the Spirit came. The Great Revival sprang directly from the Change—the last, the deepest, widest, and most enduring of all the vast inundations of religious emotion that go by that name.

But indeed it differed essentially from its innumerable predecessors. The former revivals were a phase of fever, this was the first movement of health, it was

altogether quieter, more intellectual, more private, more religious than any of those others. In the old time, and more especially in the Protestant countries where the things of religion were outspoken, and the absence of confession and well-trained priests made religious states of emotion explosive and contagious, revivalism upon various scales was a normal phase in the religious life, revivals were always going on—now a little disturbance of consciences in a village, now an evening of emotion in a Mission Room, now a great storm that swept a continent, and now an organized effort that came to town with bands and banners and handbills and motor-cars for the saving of souls. Never at any time did I take part in nor was I attracted by any of these movements. My nature, although passionate, was too critical (or sceptical if you like, for it amounts to the same thing) and shy to be drawn into these whirls; but on several occasions Parload and I sat, scoffing, but nevertheless disturbed, in the back seats of revivalist meetings.

I saw enough of them to understand their nature, and I am not surprised to learn now that before the comet came, all about the world, even among savages, even among cannibals, these same, or at any rate closely similar, periodic upheavals went on. The world was stifling; it was in a fever, and these phenomena were neither more nor less than the instinctive struggle of the organism against the ebb of its powers, the clogging of its veins, the limitation of its life. Invariably these revivals followed periods of sordid and restricted living. Men obeyed their base immediate motives until the world grew unendurably bitter. Some disappointment, some thwarting, lit up for them —darkly indeed, but yet enough for indistinct vision—the crowded squalor, the dark inclosure of life. A sudden disgust with the insensate smallness of the old-world way of living, a realization of sin, a sense of the unworthiness of all individual things, a desire for something comprehensive, sustaining, something greater, for wider communions and less habitual things, filled them. Their souls, which were shaped for wider issues, cried out suddenly amidst the petty interests, the narrow prohibitions, of life, "Not this! not this!" A great passion to escape from the jealous prison of themselves, an inarticulate, stammering, weeping passion shook them...

I have seen—I remember how once in Clayton Calvinistic Methodist chapel I saw—his spotty fat face strangely distorted under the flickering gas-flares—old Pallet the ironmonger repent. He went to the form of repentance, a bench reserved for such exhibitions, and slobbered out his sorrow and disgust for some sexual indelicacy—he was a widower —and I can see now how his loose fat body quivered and swayed with his grief. He poured it out to five hundred people, from whom in common times he hid his every thought and purpose. And it is a fact, it shows where reality lay, that we two youngsters laughed not at all at that blubbering grotesque, we did not even think the distant shadow of a smile. We two sat grave and intent —perhaps wondering.

Only afterward and with an effort did we scoff...

Those old-time revivals were, I say, the convulsive movements of a body that suffocates. They are the clearest manifestations from before the Change of a sense in all men that things were not right. But they were too often but momentary illu-

minations. Their force spent itself in inco-ordinated shouting, gesticulations, tears. They were but flashes of outlook. Disgust of the narrow life, of all baseness, took shape in narrowness and baseness. The quickened soul ended the night a hypocrite; prophets disputed for precedence; seductions, it is altogether indisputable, were frequent among penitents! and Ananias went home converted and returned with a falsified gift. And it was almost universal that the converted should be impatient and immoderate, scornful of reason and a choice of expedients, opposed to balance, skill, and knowledge. Incontinently full of grace, like thin old wine-skins overfilled, they felt they must burst if once they came into contact with hard fact and sane direction.

So the former revivals spent themselves, but the Great Revival did not spend itself, but grew to be, for the majority of Christendom at least, the permanent expression of the Change. For many it has taken the shape of an outright declaration that this was the Second Advent—it is not for me to discuss the validity of that suggestion, for nearly all it has amounted to an enduring broadening of all the issues of life...

§ 8

One irrelevant memory comes back to me, irrelevant, and yet by some subtle trick of quality it summarizes the Change for me. It is the memory of a woman's very beautiful face, a woman with a flushed face and tear-bright eyes who went by me without speaking, rapt in some secret purpose. I passed her when in the afternoon of the first day, struck by a sudden remorse, I went down to Menton to send a telegram to my mother telling her all was well with me. Whither this woman went I do not know, nor whence she came; I never saw her again, and only her face, glowing with that new and luminous resolve, stands out for me...

But that expression was the world's.

CHAPTER THE THIRD - THE CABINET COUNCIL

§ 1

AND what a strange unprecedented thing was that cabinet council at which I was present, the council that was held two days later in Melmount's bungalow, and which convened the conference to frame the constitution of the World State. I was there because it was convenient for me to stay with Melmount. I had nowhere to go particularly, and there was no one at his bungalow, to which his broken ankle confined him, but a secretary and a valet to help him to begin his share of the enormous labors that evidently lay before the rulers of the world. I wrote shorthand, and as there was not even a phonograph available, I went in so soon as his ankle had been dressed, and sat at his desk to write at his dictation. It is characteristic of the odd slackness that went with the spasmodic violence of the old epoch, that the secretary could not use shorthand and that there was no telephone whatever in the place. Every message had to be taken to the village post-office in that grocer's shop at Menton, half a mile away... So I sat in the back of Melmount's room, his desk had been thrust aside, and made such memoranda as were needed. At that time his room seemed to me the most beautifully furnished in the world, and I could identify now the vivid cheerfulness of the chintz of the sofa on which the great statesman lay just in front of me, the fine rich paper, the red sealing-wax, the silver equipage of the desk I used. I know now that my presence in that room was a strange and remarkable thing, the open door, even the coming and going of Parker the secretary, innovations. In the old days a cabinet council was a secret conclave, secrecy and furtiveness were in the texture of all public life. In the old days everybody was always keeping something back from somebody, being wary and cunning, prevaricating, misleading—for the most part for no reason at all. Almost unnoticed, that secrecy had dropped out of life.

I close my eyes and see those men again, hear their deliberating voices. First I see them a little diffusely in the cold explicitness of daylight, and then concentrated and drawn together amidst the shadow and mystery about shaded lamps. Integral to this and very clear is the memory of biscuit crumbs and a drop of spilt water, that at first stood shining upon and then sank into the green table-cloth...

I remember particularly the figure of Lord Adisham. He came to the bungalow a day before the others, because he was Melmount's personal friend. Let me describe this statesman to you, this one of the fifteen men who made the last war. He was the youngest member of the Government, and an altogether pleasant and sunny man of forty. He had a clear profile to his clean gray face, a smiling eye, a

friendly, careful voice upon his thin, clean-shaven lips, an easy disabusing manner. He had the perfect quality of a man who had fallen easily into a place prepared for him. He had the temperament of what we used to call a philosopher—an indifferent, that is to say. The Change had caught him at his week-end recreation, fly-fishing; and, indeed, he said, I remember, that he recovered to find himself with his head within a yard of the water's brim. In times of crisis Lord Adisham invariably went fly-fishing at the week-end to keep his mind in tone, and when there was no crisis then there was nothing he liked so much to do as fly-fishing, and so, of course, as there was nothing to prevent it, he fished. He came resolved, among other things, to give up fly-fishing altogether. I was present when he came to Melmount, and heard him say as much; and by a more naive route it was evident that he had arrived at the same scheme of intention as my master. I left them to talk, but afterward I came back to take down their long telegrams to their coming colleagues. He was, no doubt, as profoundly affected as Melmount by the Change, but his tricks of civility and irony and acceptable humor had survived the Change, and he expressed his altered attitude, his expanded emotions, in a quaint modification of the old-time man-of-the-world style, with excessive moderation, with a trained horror of the enthusiasm that swayed him.

These fifteen men who ruled the British Empire were curiously unlike anything I had expected, and I watched them intently whenever my services were not in request. They made a peculiar class at that time, these English politicians and statesmen, a class that has now completely passed away. In some respects they were unlike the statesmen of any other region of the world, and I do not find that any really adequate account remains of them... Perhaps you are a reader of the old books. If so, you will find them rendered with a note of hostile exaggeration by Dickens in "Bleak House," with a mingling of gross flattery and keen ridicule by Disraeli, who ruled among them accidentally by misunderstanding them and pleasing the court, and all their assumptions are set forth, portentously, perhaps, but truthfully, so far as people of the "permanent official" class saw them, in the novels of Mrs. Humphry Ward. All these books are still in this world and at the disposal of the curious, and in addition the philosopher Bagehot and the picturesque historian Macaulay give something of their method of thinking, the novelist Thackeray skirts the seamy side of their social life, and there are some good passages of irony, personal descriptions, and reminiscence to be found in the "Twentieth Century Garner" from the pens of such writers, for example, as Sidney Low. But a picture of them as a whole is wanting. Then they were too near and too great; now, very rapidly, they have become incomprehensible.

We common people of the old time based our conception of our statesmen almost entirely on the caricatures that formed the most powerful weapon in political controversy. Like almost every main feature of the old condition of things these caricatures were an unanticipated development, they were a sort of parasitic outgrowth from, which had finally altogether replaced, the thin and vague aspirations of the original democratic ideals. They presented not only the personalities who led our public life, but the most sacred structural conceptions of that life, in ludi-

crous, vulgar, and dishonorable aspects that in the end came near to destroying entirely all grave and honorable emotion or motive toward the State. The state of Britain was represented nearly always by a red-faced, purse-proud farmer with an enormous belly, that fine dream of freedom, the United States, by a cunning, lean-faced rascal in striped trousers and a blue coat. The chief ministers of state were pickpockets, washerwomen, clowns, whales, asses, elephants, and what not, and issues that affected the welfare of millions of men were dressed and judged like a rally in some idiotic pantomime. A tragic war in South Africa, that wrecked many thousand homes, impoverished two whole lands, and brought death and disablement to fifty thousand men, was presented as a quite comical quarrel between a violent queer being named Chamberlain, with an eyeglass, an orchid, and a short temper, and "old Kroojer," an obstinate and very cunning old man in a shocking bad hat. The conflict was carried through in a mood sometimes of brutish irritability and sometimes of lax slovenliness, the merry peculator plied his trade congenially in that asinine squabble, and behind these fooleries and masked by them, marched Fate—until at last the clowning of the booth opened and revealed—hunger and suffering, brands burning and swords and shame... These men had come to fame and power in that atmosphere, and to me that day there was the oddest suggestion in them of actors who have suddenly laid aside grotesque and foolish parts; the paint was washed from their faces, the posing put aside.

Even when the presentation was not frankly grotesque and degrading it was entirely misleading. When I read of Laycock, for example, there arises a picture of a large, active, if a little wrong-headed, intelligence in a compact heroic body, emitting that "Goliath" speech of his that did so much to precipitate hostilities, it tallies not at all with the stammering, high- pitched, slightly bald, and very conscience-stricken personage I saw, nor with Melmount's contemptuous first description of him. I doubt if the world at large will ever get a proper vision of those men as they were before the Change. Each year they pass more and more incredibly beyond our intellectual sympathy. Our estrangement cannot, indeed, rob them of their portion in the past, but it will rob them of any effect of reality. The whole of their history becomes more and more foreign, more and more like some queer barbaric drama played in a forgotten tongue. There they strut through their weird metamorphoses of caricature, those premiers and presidents, their height preposterously exaggerated by political buskins, their faces covered by great resonant inhuman masks, their voices couched in the foolish idiom of public utterance, disguised beyond any semblance to sane humanity, roaring and squeaking through the public press. There it stands, this incomprehensible faded show, a thing left on one side, and now still and deserted by any interest, its many emptinesses as inexplicable now as the cruelties of medieval Venice, the theology of old Byzantium. And they ruled and influenced the lives of nearly a quarter of mankind, these politicians, their clownish conflicts swayed the world, made mirth perhaps, made excitement, and permitted—infinite misery.

I saw these men quickened indeed by the Change, but still wearing the queer clothing of the old time, the manners and conventions of the old time; if they had disengaged themselves from the outlook of the old time they still had to refer back to it constantly as a common starting-point. My refreshed intelligence was equal to that, so that I think I did indeed see them. There was Gorrell-Browning, the Chancellor of the Duchy; I remember him as a big round-faced man, the essential vanity and foolishness of whose expression, whose habit of voluminous platitudinous speech, triumphed absurdly once or twice over the roused spirit within. He struggled with it, he burlesqued himself, and laughed. Suddenly he said simply, intensely—it was a moment for every one of clean, clear pain, "I have been a vain and self- indulgent and presumptuous old man. I am of little use here. I have given myself to politics and intrigues, and life is gone from me." Then for a long time he sat still. There was Carton, the Lord Chancellor, a white-faced man with understanding, he had a heavy, shaven face that might have stood among the busts of the Caesars, a slow, elaborating voice, with self-indulgent, slightly oblique, and triumphant lips, and a momentary, voluntary, humorous twinkle. "We have to forgive," he said. "We have to forgive—even ourselves."

These two were at the top corner of the table, so that I saw their faces well. Madgett, the Home Secretary, a smaller man with wrinkled eyebrows and a frozen smile on his thin wry mouth, came next to Carton; he contributed little to the discussion save intelligent comments, and when the electric lights above glowed out, the shadows deepened queerly in his eye-sockets and gave him the quizzical expression of an ironical goblin. Next him was that great peer, the Earl of Richover, whose self-indulgent indolence had accepted the role of a twentieth-century British Roman patrician of culture, who had divided his time almost equally between his jockeys, politics, and the composition of literary studies in the key of his role. "We have done nothing worth doing," he said. "As for me, I have cut a figure!" He reflected—no doubt on his ample patrician years, on the fine great houses that had been his setting, the teeming race-courses that had roared his name, the enthusiastic meetings he had fed with fine hopes, the futile Olympian beginnings.... "I have been a fool," he said compactly. They heard him in a sympathetic and respectful silence.

Gurker, the Chancellor of the Exchequer, was partially occulted, so far as I was concerned, by the back of Lord Adisham. Ever and again Gurker protruded into the discussion, swaying forward, a deep throaty voice, a big nose, a coarse mouth with a drooping everted lower lip, eyes peering amidst folds and wrinkles. He made his confession for his race. "We Jews," he said, "have gone through the system of this world, creating nothing, consolidating many things, destroying much. Our racial self-conceit has been monstrous. We seem to have used our ample coarse intellectuality for no other purpose than to develop and master and maintain the convention of property, to turn life into a sort of mercantile chess and spend our winnings grossly... We have had no sense of service to mankind. Beauty which is godhead—we made it a possession."

These men and these sayings particularly remain in my memory. Perhaps, indeed, I wrote them down at the time, but that I do not now remember. How Sir Digby Privet, Revel, Markheimer, and the others sat I do not now recall; they came in as voices, interruptions, imperfectly assigned comments...

One got a queer impression that except perhaps for Gurker or Revel these men had not particularly wanted the power they held; had desired to do nothing very much in the positions they had secured. They had found themselves in the cabinet, and until this moment of illumination they had not been ashamed; but they had made no ungentlemanly fuss about the matter. Eight of that fifteen came from the same school, had gone through an entirely parallel education; some Greek linguistics, some elementary mathematics, some emasculated "science," a little history, a little reading in the silent or timidly orthodox English literature of the seventeenth, eighteenth, and nineteenth centuries, all eight had imbibed the same dull gentlemanly tradition of behavior; essentially boyish, unimaginative—with neither keen swords nor art in it, a tradition apt to slobber into sentiment at a crisis and make a great virtue of a simple duty rather clumsily done. None of these eight had made any real experiments with life, they had lived in blinkers, they had been passed from nurse to governess, from governess to preparatory school, from Eton to Oxford, from Oxford to the politico-social routine. Even their vices and lapses had been according to certain conceptions of good form. They had all gone to the races surreptitiously from Eton, had all cut up to town from Oxford to see life—music-hall life—had all come to heel again. Now suddenly they discovered their limitations...

"What are we to do?" asked Melmount. "We have awakened; this empire in our hands..." I know this will seem the most fabulous of all the things I have to tell of the old order, but, indeed, I saw it with my eyes, I heard it with my ears. It is a fact that this group of men who constituted the Government of one-fifth of the habitable land of the earth, who ruled over a million of armed men, who had such navies as mankind had never seen before, whose empire of nations, tongues, peoples still dazzles in these greater days, had no common idea whatever of what they meant to do with the world. They had been a Government for three long years, and before the Change came to them it had never even occurred to them that it was necessary to have no common idea. There was no common idea at all. That great empire was no more than a thing adrift, an aimless thing that ate and drank and slept and bore arms, and was inordinately proud of itself because it had chanced to happen. It had no plan, no intention; it meant nothing at all. And the other great empires adrift, perilously adrift like marine mines, were in the selfsame case. Absurd as a British cabinet council must seem to you now, it was no whit more absurd than the controlling ganglion, autocratic council, president's committee, or what not, of each of its blind rivals...

§ 2

I remember as one thing that struck me very forcibly at the time, the absence of any discussion, any difference of opinion, about the broad principles of our

present state. These men had lived hitherto in a system of conventions and acquired motives, loyalty to a party, loyalty to various secret agreements and understandings, loyalty to the Crown; they had all been capable of the keenest attention to precedence, all capable of the most complete suppression of subversive doubts and inquiries, all had their religious emotions under perfect control. They had seemed protected by invisible but impenetrable barriers from all the heady and destructive speculations, the socialistic, republican, and communistic theories that one may still trace through the literature of the last days of the comet. But now it was as if the very moment of the awakening those barriers and defences had vanished, as if the green vapors had washed through their minds and dissolved and swept away a hundred once rigid boundaries and obstacles. They had admitted and assimilated at once all that was good in the ill-dressed propagandas that had clamored so vehemently and vainly at the doors of their minds in the former days. It was exactly like the awakening from an absurd and limiting dream. They had come out together naturally and inevitably upon the broad daylight platform of obvious and reasonable agreement upon which we and all the order of our world now stand.

Let me try to give the chief things that had vanished from their minds. There was, first, the ancient system of "ownership" that made such an extraordinary tangle of our administration of the land upon which we lived. In the old time no one believed in that as either just or ideally convenient, but every one accepted it. The community which lived upon the land was supposed to have waived its necessary connection with the land, except in certain limited instances of highway and common. All the rest of the land was cut up in the maddest way into patches and oblongs and triangles of various sizes between a hundred square miles and a few acres, and placed under the nearly absolute government of a series of administrators called landowners. They owned the land almost as a man now owns his hat; they bought it and sold it, and cut it up like cheese or ham; they were free to ruin it, or leave it waste, or erect upon it horrible and devastating eyesores. If the community needed a road or a tramway, if it wanted a town or a village in any position, nay, even if it wanted to go to and fro, it had to do so by exorbitant treaties with each of the monarchs whose territory was involved. No man could find foothold on the face of the earth until he had paid toll and homage to one of them. They had practically no relations and no duties to the nominal, municipal, or national Government amidst whose larger areas their own dominions lay... This sounds, I know, like a lunatic's dream, but mankind was that lunatic; and not only in the old countries of Europe and Asia, where this system had arisen out of the rational delegation of local control to territorial magnates, who had in the universal baseness of those times at last altogether evaded and escaped their duties, did it obtain, but the "new countries," as we called them then—the United States of America, the Cape Colony, Australia, and New Zealand —spent much of the nineteenth century in the frantic giving away of land for ever to any casual person who would take it. Was there coal, was there petroleum or gold, was there rich soil or harborage, or the site for a fine city, these obsessed and witless Govern-

ments cried out for scramblers, and a stream of shabby, tricky, and violent adventurers set out to found a new section of the landed aristocracy of the world. After a brief century of hope and pride, the great republic of the United States of America, the hope as it was deemed of mankind, became for the most part a drifting crowd of landless men; landlords and railway lords, food lords (for the land is food) and mineral lords ruled its life, gave it Universities as one gave coins to a mendicant, and spent its resources upon such vain, tawdry, and foolish luxuries as the world had never seen before. Here was a thing none of these statesmen before the Change would have regarded as anything but the natural order of the world, which not one of them now regarded as anything but the mad and vanished illusion of a period of dementia.

And as it was with the question of the land, so was it also with a hundred other systems and institutions and complicated and disingenuous factors in the life of man. They spoke of trade, and I realized for the first time there could be buying and selling that was no loss to any man; they spoke of industrial organization, and one saw it under captains who sought no base advantages. The haze of old associations, of personal entanglements and habitual recognitions had been dispelled from every stage and process of the social training of men. Things long hidden appeared discovered with an amazing clearness and nakedness. These men who had awakened, laughed dissolvent laughs, and the old muddle of schools and colleges, books and traditions, the old fumbling, half-figurative, half-formal teaching of the Churches, the complex of weakening and confusing suggestions and hints, amidst which the pride and honor of adolescence doubted and stumbled and fell, became nothing but a curious and pleasantly faded memory. "There must be a common training of the young," said Richover; "a frank initiation. We have not so much educated them as hidden things from them, and set traps. And it might have been so easy—it can all be done so easily."

That hangs in my memory as the refrain of that council, "It can all be done so easily," but when they said it then, it came to my ears with a quality of enormous refreshment and power. It can all be done so easily, given frankness, given courage. Time was when these platitudes had the freshness and wonder of a gospel.

In this enlarged outlook the war with the Germans—that mythical, heroic, armed female, Germany, had vanished from men's imaginations—was a mere exhausted episode. A truce had already been arranged by Melmount, and these ministers, after some marveling reminiscences, set aside the matter of peace as a mere question of particular arrangements... The whole scheme of the world's government had become fluid and provisional in their minds, in small details as in great, the unanalyzable tangle of wards and vestries, districts and municipalities, counties, states, boards, and nations, the interlacing, overlapping, and conflicting authorities, the felt of little interests and claims, in which an innumerable and insatiable multitude of lawyers, agents, managers, bosses, organizers lived like fleas in a dirty old coat, the web of the conflicts, jealousies, heated patchings up and jobbings apart, of the old order—they flung it all on one side.

"What are the new needs?" said Melmount. "This muddle is too rotten to handle. We're beginning again. Well, let us begin afresh."

§ 3

"Let us begin afresh!" This piece of obvious common sense seemed then to me instinct with courage, the noblest of words. My heart went out to him as he spoke. It was, indeed, that day as vague as it was valiant; we did not at all see the forms of what we were thus beginning. All that we saw was the clear inevitableness that the old order should end...

And then in a little space of time mankind in halting but effectual brotherhood was moving out to make its world anew. Those early years, those first and second decades of the new epoch, were in their daily detail a time of rejoicing toil; one saw chiefly one's own share in that, and little of the whole. It is only now that I look back at it all from these ripe years, from this high tower, that I see the dramatic sequence of its changes, see the cruel old confusions of the ancient time become clarified, simplified, and dissolve and vanish away. Where is that old world now? Where is London, that somber city of smoke and drifting darkness, full of the deep roar and haunting music of disorder, with its oily, shining, mud-rimmed, barge-crowded river, its black pinnacles and blackened dome, its sad wildernesses of smut-grayed houses, its myriads of draggled prostitutes, its millions of hurrying clerks? The very leaves upon its trees were foul with greasy black defilements. Where is lime- white Paris, with its green and disciplined foliage, its hard unflinching tastefulness, its smartly organized viciousness, and the myriads of workers, noisily shod, streaming over the bridges in the gray cold light of dawn. Where is New York, the high city of clangor and infuriated energy, wind swept and competition swept, its huge buildings jostling one another and straining ever upward for a place in the sky, the fallen pitilessly overshadowed. Where are its lurking corners of heavy and costly luxury, the shameful bludgeoning bribing vice of its ill ruled underways, and all the gaunt extravagant ugliness of its strenuous life? And where now is Philadelphia, with its innumerable small and isolated homes, and Chicago with its interminable blood-stained stockyards, its polyglot underworld of furious discontent.

All these vast cities have given way and gone, even as my native Potteries and the Black Country have gone, and the lives that were caught, crippled, starved, and maimed amidst their labyrinths, their forgotten and neglected maladjustments, and their vast, inhuman, ill-conceived industrial machinery have escaped—to life. Those cities of growth and accident are altogether gone, never a chimney smokes about our world to-day, and the sound of the weeping of children who toiled and hungered, the dull despair of overburdened women, the noise of brute quarrels in alleys, all shameful pleasures and all the ugly grossness of wealthy pride have gone with them, with the utter change in our lives. As I look back into the past I see a vast exultant dust of house-breaking and removal rise up into the clear air that followed the hour of the green vapors, I live again the Year of Tents, the Year of Scaffolding, and like the triumph of a new theme in a piece of music—the

great cities of our new days arise. Come Caerlyon and Armedon, the twin cities of lower England, with the winding summer city of the Thames between, and I see the gaunt dirt of old Edinburgh die to rise again white and tall beneath the shadow of her ancient hill; and Dublin too, reshaped, returning enriched, fair, spacious, the city of rich laughter and warm hearts, gleaming gaily in a shaft of sunlight through the soft warm rain. I see the great cities America has planned and made; the Golden City, with ever-ripening fruit along its broad warm ways, and the bell-glad City of a Thousand Spires. I see again as I have seen, the city of theaters and meeting-places, the City of the Sunlight Bight, and the new city that is still called Utah; and dominated by its observatory dome and the plain and dignified lines of the university facade upon the cliff, Martenabar the great white winter city of the upland snows. And the lesser places, too, the townships, the quiet resting-places, villages half forest with a brawl of streams down their streets, villages laced with avenues of cedar, villages of garden, of roses and wonderful flowers and the perpetual humming of bees. And through all the world go our children, our sons the old world would have made into servile clerks and shopmen, plough drudges and servants; our daughters who were erst anaemic drudges, prostitutes, sluts, anxiety-racked mothers or sere, repining failures; they go about this world glad and brave, learning, living, doing, happy and rejoicing, brave and free. I think of them wandering in the clear quiet of the ruins of Rome, among the tombs of Egypt or the temples of Athens, of their coming to Mainington and its strange happiness, to Orba and the wonder of its white and slender tower... But who can tell of the fullness and pleasure of life, who can number all our new cities in the world?—cities made by the loving hands of men for living men, cities men weep to enter, so fair they are, so gracious and so kind...

Some vision surely of these things must have been vouchsafed me as I sat there behind Melmount's couch, but now my knowledge of accomplished things has mingled with and effaced my expectations. Something indeed I must have foreseen —or else why was my heart so glad?

BOOK THE THIRD - THE NEW WORLD

CHAPTER THE FIRST - LOVE AFTER THE CHANGE

§ 1

So far I have said nothing of Nettie. I have departed widely from my individual story. I have tried to give you the effect of the change in relation to the general framework of human life, its effect of swift, magnificent dawn, of an overpowering letting in and inundation of light, and the spirit of living. In my memory all my life before the Change has the quality of a dark passage, with the dimmest side gleams of beauty that come and go. The rest is dull pain and darkness. Then suddenly the walls, the bitter confines, are smitten and vanish, and I walk, blinded, perplexed, and yet rejoicing, in this sweet, beautiful world, in its fair incessant variety, its satisfaction, its opportunities, exultant in this glorious gift of life. Had I the power of music I would make a world-wide motif swell and amplify, gather to itself this theme and that, and rise at last to sheer ecstasy of triumph and rejoicing. It should be all sound, all pride, all the hope of outsetting in the morning brightness, all the glee of unexpected happenings, all the gladness of painful effort suddenly come to its reward; it should be like blossoms new opened and the happy play of children, like tearful, happy mothers holding their first-born, like cities building to the sound of music, and great ships, all hung with flags and wine bespattered, gliding down through cheering multitudes to their first meeting with the sea. Through it all should march Hope, confident Hope, radiant and invincible, until at last it would be the triumph march of Hope the conqueror, coming with trumpetings and banners through the wide-flung gates of the world.

And then out of that luminous haze of gladness comes Nettie, transfigured.

So she came again to me—amazing, a thing incredibly forgotten.

She comes back, and Verrall is in her company. She comes back into my memories now, just as she came back then, rather quaintly at first—at first not seen very clearly, a little distorted by intervening things, seen with a doubt, as I saw her through the slightly discolored panes of crinkled glass in the window of the Menton post-office and grocer's shop. It was on the second day after the Change, and I had been sending telegrams for Melmount, who was making arrangements for his departure for Downing Street. I saw the two of them at first as

small, flawed figures. The glass made them seem curved, and it enhanced and altered their gestures and paces. I felt it became me to say "Peace" to them, and I went out, to the jangling of the door-bell. At the sight of me they stopped short, and Verrall cried with the note of one who has sought, "Here he is!" And Nettie cried, "Willie!"

I went toward them, and all the perspectives of my reconstructed universe altered as I did so.

I seemed to see these two for the first time; how fine they were, how graceful and human. It was as though I had never really looked at them before, and, indeed, always before I had beheld them through a mist of selfish passion. They had shared the universal darkness and dwarfing of the former time; they shared the universal exaltation of the new. Now suddenly Nettie, and the love of Nettie, a great passion for Nettie, lived again in me. This change which had enlarged men's hearts had made no end to love. Indeed, it had enormously enlarged and glorified love. She stepped into the center of that dream of world reconstruction that filled my mind and took possession of it all. A little wisp of hair had blown across her cheek, her lips fell apart in that sweet smile of hers; her eyes were full of wonder, of a welcoming scrutiny, of an infinitely courageous friendliness.

I took her outstretched hand, and wonder overwhelmed me. "I wanted to kill you," I said simply, trying to grasp that idea. It seemed now like stabbing the stars, or murdering the sunlight.

"Afterward we looked for you," said Verrall; "and we could not find you... We heard another shot."

I turned my eyes to him, and Nettie's hand fell from me. It was then I thought of how they had fallen together, and what it must have been to have awakened in that dawn with Nettie by one's side. I had a vision of them as I had glimpsed them last amidst the thickening vapors, close together, hand in hand. The green hawks of the Change spread their darkling wings above their last stumbling paces. So they fell. And awoke—lovers together in a morning of Paradise. Who can tell how bright the sunshine was to them, how fair the flowers, how sweet the singing of the birds?...

This was the thought of my heart. But my lips were saying, "When I awoke I threw my pistol away." Sheer blankness kept my thoughts silent for a little while; I said empty things. "I am very glad I did not kill you—that you are here, so fair and well..."

"I am going away back to Clayton on the day after to-morrow," I said, breaking away to explanations. "I have been writing shorthand here for Melmount, but that is almost over now..."

Neither of them said a word, and though all facts had suddenly ceased to matter anything, I went on informatively, "He is to be taken to Downing Street where there is a proper staff, so that there will be no need of me... Of course, you're a little perplexed at my being with Melmount. You see I met him —by accident— directly I recovered. I found him with a broken ankle—in that lane... I am to go now to the Four Towns to help prepare a report. So that I am glad to see you both

again"—I found a catch in my voice—"to say good-bye to you, and wish you well."

This was after the quality of what had come into my mind when first I saw them through the grocer's window, but it was not what I felt and thought as I said it. I went on saying it because otherwise there would have been a gap. It had come to me that it was going to be hard to part from Nettie. My words sounded with an effect of unreality. I stopped, and we stood for a moment in silence looking at one another.

It was I, I think, who was discovering most. I was realizing for the first time how little the Change had altered in my essential nature. I had forgotten this business of love for a time in a world of wonder. That was all. Nothing was lost from my nature, nothing had gone, only the power of thought and restraint had been wonderfully increased and new interests had been forced upon me. The Green Vapors had passed, our minds were swept and garnished, but we were ourselves still, though living in a new and finer air. My affinities were unchanged; Nettie's personal charm for me was only quickened by the enhancement of my perceptions. In her presence, meeting her eyes, instantly my desire, no longer frantic but sane, was awake again.

It was just like going to Checkshill in the old time, after writing about socialism...

I relinquished her hand. It was absurd to part in these terms.

So we all felt it. We hung awkwardly over our sense of that. It was Verrall, I think, who shaped the thought for me, and said that to-morrow then we must meet and say good-bye, and so turned our encounter into a transitory making of arrangements. We settled we would come to the inn at Menton, all three of us, and take our midday meal together...

Yes, it was clear that was all we had to say now...

We parted a little awkwardly. I went on down the village street, not looking back, surprised at myself, and infinitely perplexed. It was as if I had discovered something overlooked that disarranged all my plans, something entirely disconcerting. For the first time I went back preoccupied and without eagerness to Melmount's work. I wanted to go on thinking about Nettie; my mind had suddenly become voluminously productive concerning her and Verrall.

§ 2

The talk we three had together in the dawn of the new time is very strongly impressed upon my memory. There was something fresh and simple about it, something young and flushed and exalted. We took up, we handled with a certain naive timidity, the most difficult questions the Change had raised for men to solve. I recall we made little of them. All the old scheme of human life had dissolved and passed away, the narrow competitiveness, the greed and base aggression, the jealous aloofness of soul from soul. Where had it left us? That was what we and a thousand million others were discussing...

It chances that this last meeting with Nettie is inseparably associated —I don't know why—with the landlady of the Menton inn.

The Menton inn was one of the rare pleasant corners of the old order; it was an inn of an unusual prosperity, much frequented by visitors from Shaphambury, and given to the serving of lunches and teas. It had a broad mossy bowling-green, and round about it were creeper-covered arbors amidst beds of snap-dragon, and hollyhock, and blue delphinium, and many such tall familiar summer flowers. These stood out against a background of laurels and holly, and above these again rose the gables of the inn and its signpost—a white- horsed George slaying the dragon—against copper beeches under the sky.

While I waited for Nettie and Verrall in this agreeable trysting place, I talked to the landlady—a broad-shouldered, smiling, freckled woman —about the morning of the Change. That motherly, abundant, red-haired figure of health was buoyantly sure that everything in the world was now to be changed for the better. That confidence, and something in her voice, made me love her as I talked to her. "Now we're awake," she said, "all sorts of things will be put right that hadn't any sense in them. Why? Oh! I'm sure of it."

Her kind blue eyes met mine in an infinitude of friendliness. Her lips in her pauses shaped in a pretty faint smile.

Old tradition was strong in us; all English inns in those days charged the unexpected, and I asked what our lunch was to cost.

"Pay or not," she said, "and what you like. It's holiday these days. I suppose we'll still have paying and charging, however we manage it, but it won't be the worry it has been—that I feel sure. It's the part I never had no fancy for. Many a time I peeped through the bushes worrying to think what was just and right to me and mine, and what would send 'em away satisfied. It isn't the money I care for. There'll be mighty changes, be sure of that; but here I'll stay, and make people happy—them that go by on the roads. It's a pleasant place here when people are merry; it's only when they're jealous, or mean, or tired, or eat up beyond any stomach's digesting, or when they got the drink in 'em that Satan comes into this garden. Many's the happy face I've seen here, and many that come again like friends, but nothing to equal what's going to be, now things are being set right."

She smiled, that bounteous woman, with the joy of life and hope. "You shall have an omelet," she said, "you and your friends; such an omelet—like they'll have 'em in heaven! I feel there's cooking in me these days like I've never cooked before. I'm rejoiced to have it to do..."

It was just then that Nettie and Verrall appeared under a rustic archway of crimson roses that led out from the inn. Nettie wore white and a sun-hat, and Verrall was a figure of gray. "Here are my friends," I said; but for all the magic of the Change, something passed athwart the sunlight in my soul like the passing of the shadow of a cloud. "A pretty couple," said the landlady, as they crossed the velvet green toward us...

They were indeed a pretty couple, but that did not greatly gladden me. No —I winced a little at that.

§ 3

This old newspaper, this first reissue of the New Paper, dessicated last relic of a vanished age, is like the little piece of identification the superstitious of the old days—those queer religionists who brought a certain black-clad Mrs. Piper to the help of Christ—used to put into the hand of a clairvoyant. At the crisp touch of it I look across a gulf of fifty years and see again the three of us sitting about that table in the arbor, and I smell again the smell of the sweet-briar that filled the air about us, and hear in our long pauses the abundant murmuring of bees among the heliotrope of the borders.

It is the dawn of the new time, but we bear, all three of us, the marks and liveries of the old.

I see myself, a dark, ill-dressed youth, with the bruise Lord Redcar gave me still blue and yellow beneath my jaw; and young Verrall sits cornerwise to me, better grown, better dressed, fair and quiet, two years my senior indeed, but looking no older than I because of his light complexion; and opposite me is Nettie, with dark eyes upon my face, graver and more beautiful than I had ever seen her in the former time. Her dress is still that white one she had worn when I came upon her in the park, and still about her dainty neck she wears her string of pearls and that little coin of gold. She is so much the same, she is so changed; a girl then and now a woman—and all my agony and all the marvel of the Change between! Over the end of the green table about which we sit, a spotless cloth is spread, it bears a pleasant lunch spread out with a simple equipage. Behind me is the liberal sunshine of the green and various garden. I see it all. Again I sit there, eating awkwardly, this paper lies upon the table and Verrall talks of the Change.

"You can't imagine," he says in his sure, fine accents, "how much the Change has destroyed of me. I still don't feel awake. Men of my sort are so tremendously MADE; I never suspected it before."

He leans over the table toward me with an evident desire to make himself perfectly understood. "I find myself like some creature that is taken out of its shell—soft and new. I was trained to dress in a certain way, to behave in a certain way, to think in a certain way; I see now it's all wrong and narrow—most of it anyhow—a system of class shibboleths. We were decent to each other in order to be a gang to the rest of the world. Gentlemen indeed! But it's perplexing—"

I can hear his voice saying that now, and see the lift of his eyebrows and his pleasant smile.

He paused. He had wanted to say that, but it was not the thing we had to say.

I leant forward a little and took hold of my glass very tightly. "You two," I said, "will marry?"

They looked at one another.

Nettie spoke very softly. "I did not mean to marry when I came away," she said.

"I know," I answered. I looked up with a sense of effort and met Verrall's eyes.

He answered me. "I think we two have joined our lives... But the thing that took us was a sort of madness."

I nodded. "All passion," I said, "is madness." Then I fell into a doubting of those words.

"Why did we do these things?" he said, turning to her suddenly.

Her hands were clasped under her chin, her eyes downcast.

"We HAD to," she said, with her old trick of inadequate expression.

Then she seemed to open out suddenly.

"Willie," she cried with a sudden directness, with her eyes appealing to me, "I didn't mean to treat you badly—indeed I didn't. I kept thinking of you—and of father and mother, all the time. Only it didn't seem to move me. It didn't move me not one bit from the way I had chosen."

"Chosen!" I said.

"Something seemed to have hold of me," she admitted. "It's all so unaccountable..."

She gave a little gesture of despair.

Verrall's fingers played on the cloth for a space. Then he turned his face to me again.

"Something said 'Take her.' Everything. It was a raging desire—for her. I don't know. Everything contributed to that—or counted for nothing. You—"

"Go on," said I.

"When I knew of you—"

I looked at Nettie. "You never told him about me?" I said, feeling, as it were, a sting out of the old time.

Verrall answered for her. "No. But things dropped; I saw you that night, my instincts were all awake. I knew it was you."

"You triumphed over me? ... If I could I would have triumphed over you," I said. "But go on!"

"Everything conspired to make it the finest thing in life. It had an air of generous recklessness. It meant mischief, it might mean failure in that life of politics and affairs, for which I was trained, which it was my honor to follow. That made it all the finer. It meant ruin or misery for Nettie. That made it all the finer. No sane or decent man would have approved of what we did. That made it more splendid than ever. I had all the advantages of position and used them basely. That mattered not at all."

"Yes," I said; "it is true. And the same dark wave that lifted you, swept me on to follow. With that revolver—and blubbering with hate. And the word to you, Nettie, what was it? 'Give?' Hurl yourself down the steep?"

Nettie's hands fell upon the table. "I can't tell what it was," she said, speaking bare-hearted straight to me. "Girls aren't trained as men are trained to look into their minds. I can't see it yet. All sorts of mean little motives were there—over and above the 'must.' Mean motives. I kept thinking of his clothes." She smiled—a flash of brightness at Verrall. "I kept thinking of being like a lady and sitting in an hotel—with men like butlers waiting. It's the dreadful truth, Willie. Things as mean as that! Things meaner than that!"

I can see her now pleading with me, speaking with a frankness as bright and amazing as the dawn of the first great morning.

"It wasn't all mean," I said slowly, after a pause.

"No!" They spoke together.

"But a woman chooses more than a man does," Nettie added. "I saw it all in little bright pictures. Do you know—that jacket—there's something—You won't mind my telling you? But you won't now!"

I nodded, "No."

She spoke as if she spoke to my soul, very quietly and very earnestly, seeking to give the truth. "Something cottony in that cloth of yours," she said. "I know there's something horrible in being swung round by things like that, but they did swing me round. In the old time—to have confessed that! And I hated Clayton—and the grime of it. That kitchen! Your mother's dreadful kitchen! And besides, Willie, I was afraid of you. I didn't understand you and I did him. It's different now—but then I knew what he meant. And there was his voice."

"Yes," I said to Verrall, making these discoveries quietly, "yes, Verrall, you have a good voice. Queer I never thought of that before!"

We sat silently for a time before our vivisected passions.

"Gods!" I cried, "and there was our poor little top-hamper of intelligence on all these waves of instinct and wordless desire, these foaming things of touch and sight and feeling, like—like a coop of hens washed overboard and clucking amidst the seas."

Verrall laughed approval of the image I had struck out. "A week ago," he said, trying it further, "we were clinging to our chicken coops and going with the heave and pour. That was true enough a week ago. But to-day—?"

"To-day," I said, "the wind has fallen. The world storm is over. And each chicken coop has changed by a miracle to a vessel that makes head against the sea."

§ 4

"What are we to do?" asked Verrall.

Nettie drew a deep crimson carnation from the bowl before us, and began very neatly and deliberately to turn down the sepals of its calyx and remove, one by one, its petals. I remember that went on through all our talk. She put those ragged crimson shreds in a long row and adjusted them and readjusted them. When at last I was alone with these vestiges the pattern was still incomplete.

"Well," said I, "the matter seems fairly simple. You two"—I swallowed it—"love one another."

I paused. They answered me by silence, by a thoughtful silence.

"You belong to each other. I have thought it over and looked at it from many points of view. I happened to want—impossible things.... I behaved badly. I had no right to pursue you." I turned to Verrall. "You hold yourself bound to her?"

He nodded assent.

"No social influence, no fading out of all this generous clearness in the air—for that might happen—will change you back ...?"

He answered me with honest eyes meeting mine, "No, Leadford, no!"

"I did not know you," I said. "I thought of you as something very different from this."

"I was," he interpolated.

"Now," I said, "it is all changed."

Then I halted—for my thread had slipped away from me.

"As for me," I went on, and glanced at Nettie's downcast face, and then sat forward with my eyes upon the flowers between us, "since I am swayed and shall be swayed by an affection for Nettie, since that affection is rich with the seeds of desire, since to see her yours and wholly yours is not to be endured by me—I must turn about and go from you; you must avoid me and I you... We must divide the world like Jacob and Esau... I must direct myself with all the will I have to other things. After all—this passion is not life! It is perhaps for brutes and savages, but for men. No! We must part and I must forget. What else is there but that?"

I did not look up, I sat very tense with the red petals printing an indelible memory in my brain, but I felt the assent of Verrall's pose. There were some moments of silence. Then Nettie spoke. "But—" she said, and ceased.

I waited for a little while. I sighed and leant back in my chair. "It is perfectly simple," I smiled, "now that we have cool heads."

"But IS it simple?" asked Nettie, and slashed my discourse out of being.

I looked up and found her with her eyes on Verrall. "You see," she said, "I like Willie. It's hard to say what one feels—but I don't want him to go away like that."

"But then," objected Verrall, "how—?"

"No," said Nettie, and swept her half-arranged carnation petals back into a heap of confusion. She began to arrange them very quickly into one long straight line.

"It's so difficult—I've never before in all my life tried to get to the bottom of my mind. For one thing, I've not treated Willie properly. He —he counted on me. I know he did. I was his hope. I was a promised delight—something, something to crown life—better than anything he had ever had. And a secret pride... He lived upon me. I knew—when we two began to meet together, you and I—It was a sort of treachery to him—"

"Treachery!" I said. "You were only feeling your way through all these perplexities."

"You thought it treachery."

"I don't now."

"I did. In a sense I think so still. For you had need of me."

I made a slight protest at this doctrine and fell thinking.

"And even when he was trying to kill us," she said to her lover, "I felt for him down in the bottom of my mind. I can understand all the horrible things, the humiliation—the humiliation! he went through."

"Yes," I said, "but I don't see—"

"I don't see. I'm only trying to see. But you know, Willie, you are a part of my life. I have known you longer than I have known Edward. I know you better. Indeed I know you with all my heart. You think all your talk was thrown away upon me, that I never understood that side of you, or your ambitions or anything. I did. More than I thought at the time. Now—now it is all clear to me. What I had to understand in you was something deeper than Edward brought me. I have it now... You are a part of my life, and I don't want to cut all that off from me now I have comprehended it, and throw it away."

"But you love Verrall."

"Love is such a queer thing! ... Is there one love? I mean, only one love?" She turned to Verrall. "I know I love you. I can speak out about that now. Before this morning I couldn't have done. It's just as though my mind had got out of a scented prison. But what is it, this love for you? It's a mass of fancies—things about you—ways you look, ways you have. It's the senses—and the senses of certain beauties. Flattery too, things you said, hopes and deceptions for myself. And all that had rolled up together and taken to itself the wild help of those deep emotions that slumbered in my body; it seemed everything. But it wasn't. How can I describe it? It was like having a very bright lamp with a thick shade—everything else in the room was hidden. But you take the shade off and there they are—it is the same light—still there! Only it lights every one!"

Her voice ceased. For awhile no one spoke, and Nettie, with a quick movement, swept the petals into the shape of a pyramid.

Figures of speech always distract me, and it ran through my mind like some puzzling refrain, "It is still the same light..."

"No woman believes these things," she asserted abruptly.

"What things?"

"No woman ever has believed them."

"You have to choose a man," said Verrall, apprehending her before I did.

"We're brought up to that. We're told—it's in books, in stories, in the way people look, in the way they behave—one day there will come a man. He will be everything, no one else will be anything. Leave everything else; live in him."

"And a man, too, is taught that of some woman," said Verrall.

"Only men don't believe it! They have more obstinate minds... Men have never behaved as though they believed it. One need not be old to know that. By nature they don't believe it. But a woman believes nothing by nature. She goes into a mold hiding her secret thoughts almost from herself."

"She used to," I said.

"You haven't," said Verrall, "anyhow."

"I've come out. It's this comet. And Willie. And because I never really believed in the mold at all—even if I thought I did. It's stupid to send Willie off—shamed, cast out, never to see him again—when I like him as much as I do. It is cruel, it is wicked and ugly, to prance over him as if he was a defeated enemy, and pretend I'm going to be happy just the same. There's no sense in a rule of life

that prescribes that. It's selfish. It's brutish. It's like something that has no sense. I—" there was a sob in her voice: "Willie! I WON'T."

I sat lowering, I mused with my eyes upon her quick fingers.

"It IS brutish," I said at last, with a careful unemotional deliberation. "Nevertheless—it is in the nature of things... No! ... You see, after all, we are still half brutes, Nettie. And men, as you say, are more obstinate than women. The comet hasn't altered that; it's only made it clearer. We have come into being through a tumult of blind forces... I come back to what I said just now; we have found our poor reasonable minds, our wills to live well, ourselves, adrift on a wash of instincts, passions, instinctive prejudices, half animal stupidities... Here we are like people clinging to something —like people awakening—upon a raft."

"We come back at last to my question," said Verrall, softly; "what are we to do?"

"Part," I said. "You see, Nettie, these bodies of ours are not the bodies of angels. They are the same bodies—I have read somewhere that in our bodies you can find evidence of the lowliest ancestry; that about our inward ears—I think it is—and about our teeth, there remains still something of the fish, that there are bones that recall little—what is it?—marsupial forebears—and a hundred traces of the ape. Even your beautiful body, Nettie, carries this taint. No! Hear me out." I leant forward earnestly. "Our emotions, our passions, our desires, the substance of them, like the substance of our bodies, is an animal, a competing thing, as well as a desiring thing. You speak to us now a mind to minds—one can do that when one has had exercise and when one has eaten, when one is not doing anything—but when one turns to live, one turns again to matter."

"Yes," said Nettie, slowly following me, "but you control it."

"Only through a measure of obedience. There is no magic in the business —to conquer matter, we must divide the enemy, and take matter as an ally. Nowadays it is indeed true, by faith a man can remove mountains; he can say to a mountain, Be thou removed and be thou cast into the sea; but he does it because he helps and trusts his brother men, because he has the wit and patience and courage to win over to his side iron, steel, obedience, dynamite, cranes, trucks, the money of other people... To conquer my desire for you, I must not perpetually thwart it by your presence; I must go away so that I may not see you, I must take up other interests, thrust myself into struggles and discussions—"

"And forget?" said Nettie.

"Not forget," I said; "but anyhow—cease to brood upon you."

She hung on that for some moments.

"No," she said, demolished her last pattern and looked up at Verrall as he stirred.

Verrall leant forward on the table, elbows upon it, and the fingers of his two hands intertwined.

"You know," he said, "I haven't thought much of these things. At school and the university, one doesn't... It was part of the system to prevent it. They'll alter all that, no doubt. We seem"—he thought—"to be skating about over questions that

one came to at last in Greek—with variorum readings—in Plato, but which it never occurred to any one to translate out of a dead language into living realities..." He halted and answered some unspoken question from his own mind with, "No. I think with Leadford, Nettie, that, as he put it, it is in the nature of things for men to be exclusive.... Minds are free things and go about the world, but only one man can possess a woman. You must dismiss rivals. We are made for the struggle for existence—we ARE the struggle for existence; the things that live are the struggle for existence incarnate—and that works out that the men struggle for their mates; for each woman one prevails. The others go away."

"Like animals," said Nettie.

"Yes..."

"There are many things in life," I said, "but that is the rough universal truth."

"But," said Nettie, "you don't struggle. That has been altered because men have minds."

"You choose," I said.

"If I don't choose to choose?"

"You have chosen."

She gave a little impatient "Oh! Why are women always the slaves of sex? Is this great age of Reason and Light that has come to alter nothing of that? And men too! I think it is all—stupid. I do not believe this is the right solution of the thing, or anything but the bad habits of the time that was... Instinct! You don't let your instincts rule you in a lot of other things. Here am I between you. Here is Edward. I—love him because he is gay and pleasant, and because—because I LIKE him! Here is Willie —a part of me—my first secret, my oldest friend! Why must I not have both? Am I not a mind that you must think of me as nothing but a woman? imagine me always as a thing to struggle for?" She paused; then she made her distressful proposition to me. "Let us three keep together," she said. "Let us not part. To part is hate, Willie. Why should we not anyhow keep friends? Meet and talk?"

"Talk?" I said. "About this sort of thing?"

I looked across at Verrall and met his eyes, and we studied one another. It was the clean, straight scrutiny of honest antagonism. "No," I decided. "Between us, nothing of that sort can be."

"Ever?" said Nettie.

"Never," I said, convinced.

I made an effort within myself. "We cannot tamper with the law and customs of these things," I said; "these passions are too close to one's essential self. Better surgery than a lingering disease! From Nettie my love —asks all. A man's love is not devotion—it is a demand, a challenge. And besides"—and here I forced my theme—"I have given myself now to a new mistress—and it is I, Nettie, who am unfaithful. Behind you and above you rises the coming City of the World, and I am in that building. Dear heart! you are only happiness—and that— Indeed that calls! If it is only that my life blood shall christen the foundation stones—I could almost hope that should be my part, Nettie —I will join myself in that." I threw all

the conviction I could into these words... "No conflict of passion." I added a little lamely, "must distract me."

There was a pause.

"Then we must part," said Nettie, with the eyes of a woman one strikes in the face.

I nodded assent...

There was a little pause, and then I stood up. We stood up, all three. We parted almost sullenly, with no more memorable words, and I was left presently in the arbor alone.

I do not think I watched them go. I only remember myself left there somehow—horribly empty and alone. I sat down again and fell into a deep shapeless musing.

§ 5

Suddenly I looked up. Nettie had come back and stood looking down at me.

"Since we talked I have been thinking," she said. "Edward has let me come to you alone. And I feel perhaps I can talk better to you alone."

I said nothing and that embarrassed her.

"I don't think we ought to part," she said.

"No—I don't think we ought to part," she repeated.

"One lives," she said, "in different ways. I wonder if you will understand what I am saying, Willie. It is hard to say what I feel. But I want it said. If we are to part for ever I want it said—very plainly. Always before I have had the woman's instinct and the woman's training which makes one hide. But—Edward is not all of me. Think of what I am saying—Edward is not all of me... I wish I could tell you better how I see it. I am not all of myself. You, at any rate, are a part of me and I cannot bear to leave you. And I cannot see why I should leave you. There is a sort of blood link between us, Willie. We grew together. We are in one another's bones. I understand you. Now indeed I understand. In some way I have come to an understanding at a stride. Indeed I understand you and your dream. I want to help you. Edward—Edward has no dreams.... It is dreadful to me, Willie, to think we two are to part."

"But we have settled that—part we must."

"But WHY?"

"I love you."

"Well, and why should I hide it Willie?—I love you..." Our eyes met. She flushed, she went on resolutely: "You are stupid. The whole thing is stupid. I love you both."

I said, "You do not understand what you say. No!"

"You mean that I must go."

"Yes, yes. Go!"

For a moment we looked at one another, mute, as though deep down in the unfathomable darkness below the surface and present reality of things dumb meanings strove to be. She made to speak and desisted.

"But MUST I go?" she said at last, with quivering lips, and the tears in her eyes were stars. Then she began, "Willie—"

"Go!" I interrupted her... "Yes."

Then again we were still.

She stood there, a tearful figure of pity, longing for me, pitying me. Something of that wider love, that will carry our descendants at last out of all the limits, the hard, clear obligations of our personal life, moved us, like the first breath of a coming wind out of heaven that stirs and passes away. I had an impulse to take her hand and kiss it, and then a trembling came to me, and I knew that if I touched her, my strength would all pass from me...

And so, standing at a distance one from the other, we parted, and Nettie went, reluctant and looking back, with the man she had chosen, to the lot she had chosen, out of my life—like the sunlight out of my life...

Then, you know, I suppose I folded up this newspaper and put it in my pocket. But my memory of that meeting ends with the face of Nettie turning to go.

§ 6

I remember all that very distinctly to this day. I could almost vouch for the words I have put into our several mouths. Then comes a blank. I have a dim memory of being back in the house near the Links and the bustle of Melmount's departure, of finding Parker's energy distasteful, and of going away down the road with a strong desire to say good-bye to Melmount alone.

Perhaps I was already doubting my decision to part for ever from Nettie, for I think I had it in mind to tell him all that had been said and done...

I don't think I had a word with him or anything but a hurried hand clasp. I am not sure. It has gone out of my mind. But I have a very clear and certain memory of my phase of bleak desolation as I watched his car recede and climb and vanish over Mapleborough Hill, and that I got there my first full and definite intimation that, after all, this great Change and my new wide aims in life, were not to mean indiscriminate happiness for me. I had a sense of protest, as against extreme unfairness, as I saw him go. "It is too soon," I said to myself, "to leave me alone."

I felt I had sacrificed too much, that after I had said good-bye to the hot immediate life of passion, to Nettie and desire, to physical and personal rivalry, to all that was most intensely myself, it was wrong to leave me alone and sore hearted, to go on at once with these steely cold duties of the wider life. I felt new born, and naked, and at a loss.

"Work!" I said with an effort at the heroic, and turned about with a sigh, and I was glad that the way I had to go would at least take me to my mother...

But, curiously enough, I remember myself as being fairly cheerful in the town of Birmingham that night, I recall an active and interested mood. I spent the night in Birmingham because the train service on was disarranged, and I could not get on. I went to listen to a band that was playing its brassy old- world music in the public park, and I fell into conversation with a man who said he had been a reporter upon one of their minor local papers. He was full and keen upon all the

plans of reconstruction that were now shaping over the lives of humanity, and I know that something of that noble dream came back to me with his words and phrases. We walked up to a place called Bourneville by moonlight, and talked of the new social groupings that must replace the old isolated homes, and how the people would be housed.

This Bourneville was germane to that matter. It had been an attempt on the part of a private firm of manufacturers to improve the housing of their workers. To our ideas to-day it would seem the feeblest of benevolent efforts, but at the time it was extraordinary and famous, and people came long journeys to see its trim cottages with baths sunk under the kitchen floors (of all conceivable places), and other brilliant inventions. No one seemed to see the danger to liberty in that aggressive age, that might arise through making workpeople tenants and debtors of their employer, though an Act called the Truck Act had long ago intervened to prevent minor developments in the same direction... But I and my chance acquaintance seemed that night always to have been aware of that possibility, and we had no doubt in our minds of the public nature of the housing duty. Our interest lay rather in the possibility of common nurseries and kitchens and public rooms that should economize toil and give people space and freedom.

It was very interesting, but still a little cheerless, and when I lay in bed that night I thought of Nettie and the queer modifications of preference she had made, and among other things and in a way, I prayed. I prayed that night, let me confess it, to an image I had set up in my heart, an image that still serves with me as a symbol for things inconceivable, to a Master Artificer, the unseen captain of all who go about the building of the world, the making of mankind.

But before and after I prayed I imagined I was talking and reasoning and meeting again with Nettie... She never came into the temple of that worshiping with me.

CHAPTER THE SECOND - MY MOTHER'S LAST DAYS

§ 1

Next day I came home to Clayton.

The new strange brightness of the world was all the brighter there, for the host of dark distressful memories, of darkened childhood, toilsome youth, embittered adolescence that wove about the place for me. It seemed to me that I saw morning there for the first time. No chimneys smoked that day, no furnaces were burning, the people were busy with other things. The clear strong sun, the sparkle in the dustless air, made a strange gaiety in the narrow streets. I passed a number of smiling people coming home from the public breakfasts that were given in the Town Hall until better things could be arranged, and happened on Parload among them. "You were right about that comet," I sang out at the sight of him; and he came toward me and clasped my hand.

"What are people doing here?" said I.

"They're sending us food from outside," he said, "and we're going to level all these slums—and shift into tents on to the moors;" and he began to tell me of many things that were being arranged, the Midland land committees had got to work with remarkable celerity and directness of purpose, and the redistribution of population was already in its broad outlines planned. He was working at an improvised college of engineering. Until schemes of work were made out, almost every one was going to school again to get as much technical training as they could against the demands of the huge enterprise of reconstruction that was now beginning.

He walked with me to my door, and there I met old Pettigrew coming down the steps. He looked dusty and tired, but his eye was brighter than it used to be, and he carried in a rather unaccustomed manner, a workman's tool basket.

"How's the rheumatism, Mr. Pettigrew?" I asked.

"Dietary," said old Pettigrew, "can work wonders..." He looked me in the eye. "These houses," he said, "will have to come down, I suppose, and our notions of property must undergo very considerable revision—in the light of reason; but meanwhile I've been doing something to patch that disgraceful roof of mine! To think that I could have dodged and evaded—"

He raised a deprecatory hand, drew down the loose corners of his ample mouth, and shook his old head.

"The past is past, Mr. Pettigrew."

"Your poor dear mother! So good and honest a woman! So simple and kind and forgiving! To think of it! My dear young man!"—he said it manfully —"I'm ashamed."

"The whole world blushed at dawn the other day, Mr. Pettigrew," I said, "and did it very prettily. That's over now. God knows, who is NOT ashamed of all that came before last Tuesday."

I held out a forgiving hand, naively forgetful that in this place I was a thief, and he took it and went his way, shaking his head and repeating he was ashamed, but I think a little comforted.

The door opened and my poor old mother's face, marvelously cleaned, appeared. "Ah, Willie, boy! YOU. You!"

I ran up the steps to her, for I feared she might fall.

How she clung to me in the passage, the dear woman!...

But first she shut the front door. The old habit of respect for my unaccountable temper still swayed her. "Ah deary!" she said, "ah deary! But you were sorely tried," and kept her face close to my shoulder, lest she should offend me by the sight of the tears that welled within her.

She made a sort of gulping noise and was quiet for a while, holding me very tightly to her heart with her worn, long hands...

She thanked me presently for my telegram, and I put my arm about her and drew her into the living room.

"It's all well with me, mother dear," I said, "and the dark times are over—are done with for ever, mother."

Whereupon she had courage and gave way and sobbed aloud, none chiding her.

She had not let me know she could still weep for five grimy years...

§ 2

Dear heart! There remained for her but a very brief while in this world that had been renewed. I did not know how short that time would be, but the little I could do—perhaps after all it was not little to her—to atone for the harshness of my days of wrath and rebellion, I did. I took care to be constantly with her, for I perceived now her curious need of me. It was not that we had ideas to exchange or pleasures to share, but she liked to see me at table, to watch me working, to have me go to and fro. There was no toil for her any more in the world, but only such light services as are easy and pleasant for a worn and weary old woman to do, and I think she was happy even at her end.

She kept to her queer old eighteenth century version of religion, too, without a change. She had worn this particular amulet so long it was a part of her. Yet the Change was evident even in that persistence. I said to her one day, "But do you still believe in that hell of flame, dear mother? You—with your tender heart!"

She vowed she did.

Some theological intricacy made it necessary to her, but still— —

She looked thoughtfully at a bank of primulas before her for a time, and then laid her tremulous hand impressively on my arm. "You know, Willie, dear," she said, as though she was clearing up a childish misunderstanding of mine, "I don't think any one will GO there. I never DID think that..."

§ 3

That talk stands out in my memory because of that agreeable theological decision of hers, but it was only one of a great number of talks. It used to be pleasant in the afternoon, after the day's work was done and before one went on with the evening's study—how odd it would have seemed in the old time for a young man of the industrial class to be doing post-graduate work in sociology, and how much a matter of course it seems now!—to walk out into the gardens of Lowchester House, and smoke a cigarette or so and let her talk ramblingly of the things that interested her... Physically the Great Change did not do so very much to reinvigorate her—she had lived in that dismal underground kitchen in Clayton too long for any material rejuvenescence—she glowed out indeed as a dying spark among the ashes might glow under a draught of fresh air—and assuredly it hastened her end. But those closing days were very tranquil, full of an effortless contentment. With her, life was like a rainy, windy day that clears only to show the sunset afterglow. The light has passed. She acquired no new habits amid the comforts of the new life, did no new things, but only found a happier light upon the old.

She lived with a number of other old ladies belonging to our commune in the upper rooms of Lowchester House. Those upper apartments were simple and ample, fine and well done in the Georgian style, and they had been organized to give the maximum of comfort and conveniences and to economize the need of skilled attendance. We had taken over the various "great houses," as they used to be called, to make communal dining-rooms and so forth—their kitchens were conveniently large—and pleasant places for the old people of over sixty whose time of ease had come, and for suchlike public uses. We had done this not only with Lord Redcar's house, but also with Checkshill House—where old Mrs. Verrall made a dignified and capable hostess,—and indeed with most of the fine residences in the beautiful wide country between the Four Towns district and the Welsh mountains. About these great houses there had usually been good outbuildings, laundries, married servants' quarters, stabling, dairies, and the like, suitably masked by trees, we turned these into homes, and to them we added first tents and wood chalets and afterward quadrangular residential buildings. In order to be near my mother I had two small rooms in the new collegiate buildings which our commune was almost the first to possess, and they were very convenient for the station of the high- speed electric railway that took me down to our daily conferences and my secretarial and statistical work in Clayton.

Ours had been one of the first modern communes to get in order; we were greatly helped by the energy of Lord Redcar, who had a fine feeling for the picturesque associations of his ancestral home—the detour that took our line through the beeches and bracken and bluebells of the West Wood and saved the pleasant

open wildness of the park was one of his suggestions; and we had many reasons to be proud of our surroundings. Nearly all the other communes that sprang up all over the pleasant parkland round the industrial valley of the Four Towns, as the workers moved out, came to us to study the architecture of the residential squares and quadrangles with which we had replaced the back streets between the great houses and the ecclesiastical residences about the cathedral, and the way in which we had adapted all these buildings to our new social needs. Some claimed to have improved on us. But they could not emulate the rhododendron garden out beyond our shrubberies; that was a thing altogether our own in our part of England, because of its ripeness and of the rarity of good peat free from lime.

These gardens had been planned under the third Lord Redcar, fifty years ago and more; they abounded in rhododendra and azaleas, and were in places so well sheltered and sunny that great magnolias flourished and flowered. There were tall trees smothered in crimson and yellow climbing roses, and an endless variety of flowering shrubs and fine conifers, and such pampas grass as no other garden can show. And barred by the broad shadows of these, were glades and broad spaces of emerald turf, and here and there banks of pegged roses, and flower-beds, and banks given over some to spring bulbs, and some to primroses and primulas and polyanthuses. My mother loved these latter banks and the little round staring eyes of their innumerable yellow, ruddy brown, and purple corollas, more than anything else the gardens could show, and in the spring of the Year of Scaffolding she would go with me day after day to the seat that showed them in the greatest multitude.

It gave her, I think, among other agreeable impressions, a sense of gentle opulence. In the old time she had never known what it was to have more than enough of anything agreeable in the world at all.

We would sit and think, or talk—there was a curious effect of complete understanding between us whether we talked or were still.

"Heaven," she said to me one day, "Heaven is a garden."

I was moved to tease her a little. "There's jewels, you know, walls and gates of jewels—and singing."

"For such as like them," said my mother firmly, and thought for a while. "There'll be things for all of us, o' course. But for me it couldn't be Heaven, dear, unless it was a garden—a nice sunny garden... And feeling such as we're fond of, are close and handy by"

You of your happier generation cannot realize the wonderfulness of those early days in the new epoch, the sense of security, the extraordinary effects of contrast. In the morning, except in high summer, I was up before dawn, and breakfasted upon the swift, smooth train, and perhaps saw the sunrise as I rushed out of the little tunnel that pierced Clayton Crest, and so to work like a man. Now that we had got all the homes and schools and all the softness of life away from our coal and iron ore and clay, now that a thousand obstructive "rights" and timidities had been swept aside, we could let ourselves go, we merged this enterprise with that, cut across this or that anciently obstructive piece of private land, joined and sepa-

rated, effected gigantic consolidations and gigantic economies, and the valley, no longer a pit of squalid human tragedies and meanly conflicting industries, grew into a sort of beauty of its own, a savage inhuman beauty of force and machinery and flames. One was a Titan in that Etna. Then back one came at midday to bath and change in the train, and so to the leisurely gossiping lunch in the club dining-room in Lowchester House, and the refreshment of these green and sunlit afternoon tranquillities.

Sometimes in her profounder moments my mother doubted whether all this last phase of her life was not a dream.

"A dream," I used to say, "a dream indeed—but a dream that is one step nearer awakening than that nightmare of the former days."

She found great comfort and assurance in my altered clothes—she liked the new fashions of dress, she alleged. It was not simply altered clothes. I did grow two inches, broaden some inches round my chest, and increase in weight three stones before I was twenty-three. I wore a soft brown cloth and she would caress my sleeve and admire it greatly—she had the woman's sense of texture very strong in her.

Sometimes she would muse upon the past, rubbing together her poor rough hands—they never got softened—one over the other. She told me much I had not heard before about my father, and her own early life. It was like finding flat and faded flowers in a book still faintly sweet, to realize that once my mother had been loved with passion; that my remote father had once shed hot tears of tenderness in her arms. And she would sometimes even speak tentatively in those narrow, old-world phrases that her lips could rob of all their bitter narrowness, of Nettie.

"She wasn't worthy of you, dear," she would say abruptly, leaving me to guess the person she intended.

"No man is worthy of a woman's love," I answered. "No woman is worthy of a man's. I love her, dear mother, and that you cannot alter."

"There's others," she would muse.

"Not for me," I said. "No! I didn't fire a shot that time; I burnt my magazine. I can't begin again, mother, not from the beginning."

She sighed and said no more then.

At another time she said—I think her words were: "You'll be lonely when I'm gone dear."

"You'll not think of going, then," I said.

"Eh, dear! but man and maid should come together."

I said nothing to that.

"You brood overmuch on Nettie, dear. If I could see you married to some sweet girl of a woman, some good, KIND girl—"

"Dear mother, I'm married enough. Perhaps some day—Who knows? I can wait."

"But to have nothing to do with women!"

"I have my friends. Don't you trouble, mother. There's plentiful work for a man in this world though the heart of love is cast out from him. Nettie was life and beauty for me—is—will be. Don't think I've lost too much, mother."

(Because in my heart I told myself the end had still to come.)

And once she sprang a question on me suddenly that surprised me.

"Where are they now?" she asked.

"Who?"

"Nettie and—him."

She had pierced to the marrow of my thoughts. "I don't know," I said shortly.

Her shriveled hand just fluttered into touch of mine.

"It's better so," she said, as if pleading. "Indeed ... it is better so."

There was something in her quivering old voice that for a moment took me back across an epoch, to the protests of the former time, to those counsels of submission, those appeals not to offend It, that had always stirred an angry spirit of rebellion within me.

"That is the thing I doubt," I said, and abruptly I felt I could talk no more to her of Nettie. I got up and walked away from her, and came back after a while, to speak of other things, with a bunch of daffodils for her in my hand.

But I did not always spend my afternoons with her. There were days when my crushed hunger for Nettie rose again, and then I had to be alone; I walked, or bicycled, and presently I found a new interest and relief in learning to ride. For the horse was already very swiftly reaping the benefit to the Change. Hardly anywhere was the inhumanity of horse traction to be found after the first year of the new epoch, everywhere lugging and dragging and straining was done by machines, and the horse had become a beautiful instrument for the pleasure and carriage of youth. I rode both in the saddle and, what is finer, naked and barebacked. I found violent exercises were good for the states of enormous melancholy that came upon me, and when at last horse riding palled, I went and joined the aviators who practised soaring upon aeroplanes beyond Horsemarden Hill... But at least every alternate day I spent with my mother, and altogether I think I gave her two-thirds of my afternoons.

§ 4

When presently that illness, that fading weakness that made an euthanasia for so many of the older people in the beginning of the new time, took hold upon my mother, there came Anna Reeves to daughter her—after our new custom. She chose to come. She was already known to us a little from chance meetings and chance services she had done my mother in the garden; she sought to give her help. She seemed then just one of those plainly good girls the world at its worst has never failed to produce, who were indeed in the dark old times the hidden antiseptic of all our hustling, hating, faithless lives. They made their secret voiceless worship, they did their steadfast, uninspired, unthanked, unselfish work as helpful daughters, as nurses, as faithful servants, as the humble providences of homes. She was almost exactly three years older than I. At first I found no beauty in her,

she was short but rather sturdy and ruddy, with red-tinged hair, and fair hairy brows and red-brown eyes. But her freckled hands I found, were full of apt help, her voice carried good cheer...

At first she was no more than a blue-clad, white-aproned benevolence, that moved in the shadows behind the bed on which my old mother lay and sank restfully to death. She would come forward to anticipate some little need, to proffer some simple comfort, and always then my mother smiled on her. In a little while I discovered the beauty of that helpful poise of her woman's body, I discovered the grace of untiring goodness, the sweetness of a tender pity, and the great riches of her voice, of her few reassuring words and phrases. I noted and remembered very clearly how once my mother's lean old hand patted the firm gold-flecked strength of hers, as it went by upon its duties with the coverlet.

"She is a good girl to me," said my mother one day. "A good girl. Like a daughter should be... I never had a daughter—really." She mused peacefully for a space. "Your little sister died," she said.

I had never heard of that little sister.

"November the tenth," said my mother. "Twenty-nine months and three days... I cried. I cried. That was before you came, dear. So long ago—and I can see it now. I was a young wife then, and your father was very kind. But I can see its hands, its dear little quiet hands... Dear, they say that now —now they will not let the little children die."

"No, dear mother," I said. "We shall do better now."

"The club doctor could not come. Your father went twice. There was some one else, some one who paid. So your father went on into Swathinglea, and that man wouldn't come unless he had his fee. And your father had changed his clothes to look more respectful and he hadn't any money, not even his tram fare home. It seemed cruel to be waiting there with my baby thing in pain... And I can't help thinking perhaps we might have saved her... But it was like that with the poor always in the bad old times—always. When the doctor came at last he was angry. 'Why wasn't I called before?' he said, and he took no pains. He was angry because some one hadn't explained. I begged him—but it was too late."

She said these things very quietly with drooping eyelids, like one who describes a dream. "We are going to manage all these things better now," I said, feeling a strange resentment at this pitiful little story her faded, matter-of-fact voice was telling me.

"She talked," my mother went on. "She talked for her age wonderfully.... Hippopotamus."

"Eh?" I said.

"Hippopotamus, dear—quite plainly one day, when her father was showing her pictures... And her little prayers. 'Now I lay me.... down to sleep.' ... I made her little socks. Knitted they was, dear, and the heel most difficult."

Her eyes were closed now. She spoke no longer to me but to herself. She whispered other vague things, little sentences, ghosts of long dead moments... Her words grew less distinct.

Presently she was asleep and I got up and went out of the room, but my mind was queerly obsessed by the thought of that little life that had been glad and hopeful only to pass so inexplicably out of hope again into nonentity, this sister of whom I had never heard before...

And presently I was in a black rage at all the irrecoverable sorrows of the past, of that great ocean of avoidable suffering of which this was but one luminous and quivering red drop. I walked in the garden and the garden was too small for me; I went out to wander on the moors. "The past is past," I cried, and all the while across the gulf of five and twenty years I could hear my poor mother's heart-wrung weeping for that daughter baby who had suffered and died. Indeed that old spirit of rebellion has not altogether died in me, for all the transformation of the new time... I quieted down at last to a thin and austere comfort in thinking that the whole is not told to us, that it cannot perhaps be told to such minds as ours; and anyhow, and what was far more sustaining, that now we have strength and courage and this new gift of wise love, whatever cruel and sad things marred the past, none of these sorrowful things that made the very warp and woof of the old life, need now go on happening. We could foresee, we could prevent and save. "The past is past," I said, between sighing and resolve, as I came into view again on my homeward way of the hundred sunset-lit windows of old Lowchester House. "Those sorrows are sorrows no more."

But I could not altogether cheat that common sadness of the new time, that memory, and insoluble riddle of the countless lives that had stumbled and failed in pain and darkness before our air grew clear.

CHAPTER THE THIRD - BELTANE AND NEW YEAR'S EVE

§ 1

In the end my mother died rather suddenly, and her death came as a shock to me. Diagnosis was still very inadequate at that time. The doctors were, of course, fully alive to the incredible defects of their common training and were doing all they could to supply its deficiencies, but they were still extraordinarily ignorant. Some unintelligently observed factor of her illness came into play with her, and she became feverish and sank and died very quickly. I do not know what remedial measures were attempted. I hardly knew what was happening until the whole thing was over.

At that time my attention was much engaged by the stir of the great Beltane festival that was held on May-day in the Year of Scaffolding. It was the first of the ten great rubbish burnings that opened the new age. Young people nowadays can scarcely hope to imagine the enormous quantities of pure litter and useless accumulation with which we had to deal; had we not set aside a special day and season, the whole world would have been an incessant reek of small fires; and it was, I think, a happy idea to revive this ancient festival of the May and November burnings. It was inevitable that the old idea of purification should revive with the name, it was felt to be a burning of other than material encumbrances, innumerable quasi-spiritual things, deeds, documents, debts, vindictive records, went up on those great flares. People passed praying between the fires, and it was a fine symbol of the new and wiser tolerance that had come to men, that those who still found their comfort in the orthodox faiths came hither unpersuaded, to pray that all hate might be burnt out of their professions. For even in the fires of Baal, now that men have done with base hatred, one may find the living God.

Endless were the things we had to destroy in those great purgings. First, there were nearly all the houses and buildings of the old time. In the end we did not save in England one building in five thousand that was standing when the comet came. Year by year, as we made our homes afresh in accordance with the saner needs of our new social families, we swept away more and more of those horrible structures, the ancient residential houses, hastily built, without imagination, without beauty, without common honesty, without even comfort or convenience, in which the early twentieth century had sheltered until scarcely one remained; we saved nothing but what was beautiful or interesting out of all their gaunt and melancholy abundance. The actual houses, of course, we could not drag to our fires,

but we brought all their ill-fitting deal doors, their dreadful window sashes, their servant-tormenting staircases, their dank, dark cupboards, the verminous papers from their scaly walls, their dust and dirt-sodden carpets, their ill-designed and yet pretentious tables and chairs, sideboards and chests of drawers, the old dirt-saturated books, their ornaments—their dirty, decayed, and altogether painful ornaments —amidst which I remember there were sometimes even STUFFED DEAD BIRDS! —we burnt them all. The paint-plastered woodwork, with coat above coat of nasty paint, that in particular blazed finely. I have already tried to give you an impression of old-world furniture, of Parload's bedroom, my mother's room, Mr. Gabbitas's sitting-room, but, thank Heaven! there is nothing in life now to convey the peculiar dinginess of it all. For one thing, there is no more imperfect combustion of coal going on everywhere, and no roadways like grassless open scars along the earth from which dust pours out perpetually. We burnt and destroyed most of our private buildings and all the woodwork, all our furniture, except a few score thousand pieces of distinct and intentional beauty, from which our present forms have developed, nearly all our hangings and carpets, and also we destroyed almost every scrap of old-world clothing. Only a few carefully disinfected types and vestiges of that remain now in our museums.

One writes now with a peculiar horror of the dress of the old world. The men's clothes were worn without any cleansing process at all, except an occasional superficial brushing, for periods of a year or so; they were made of dark obscurely mixed patterns to conceal the stage of defilement they had reached, and they were of a felted and porous texture admirably calculated to accumulate drifting matter. Many women wore skirts of similar substances, and of so long and inconvenient a form that they inevitably trailed among all the abomination of our horse-frequented roads. It was our boast in England that the whole of our population was booted—their feet were for the most part ugly enough to need it,—but it becomes now inconceivable how they could have imprisoned their feet in the amazing cases of leather and imitations of leather they used. I have heard it said that a large part of the physical decline that was apparent in our people during the closing years of the nineteenth century, though no doubt due in part to the miscellaneous badness of the food they ate, was in the main attributable to the vileness of the common footwear. They shirked open-air exercise altogether because their boots wore out ruinously and pinched and hurt them if they took it. I have mentioned, I think, the part my own boots played in the squalid drama of my adolescence. I had a sense of unholy triumph over a fallen enemy when at last I found myself steering truck after truck of cheap boots and shoes (unsold stock from Swathinglea) to the run-off by the top of the Glanville blast furnaces.

"Plup!" they would drop into the cone when Beltane came, and the roar of their burning would fill the air. Never a cold would come from the saturation of their brown paper soles, never a corn from their foolish shapes, never a nail in them get home at last in suffering flesh...

Most of our public buildings we destroyed and burnt as we reshaped our plan of habitation, our theater sheds, our banks, and inconvenient business warrens,

our factories (these in the first year of all), and all the "unmeaning repetition" of silly little sham Gothic churches and meeting-houses, mean looking shells of stone and mortar without love, invention, or any beauty at all in them, that men had thrust into the face of their sweated God, even as they thrust cheap food into the mouths of their sweated workers; all these we also swept away in the course of that first decade. Then we had the whole of the superseded steam-railway system to scrap and get rid of, stations, signals, fences, rolling stock; a plant of ill-planned, smoke-distributing nuisance apparatus, that would, under former conditions, have maintained an offensive dwindling obstructive life for perhaps half a century. Then also there was a great harvest of fences, notice boards, hoardings, ugly sheds, all the corrugated iron in the world, and everything that was smeared with tar, all our gas works and petroleum stores, all our horse vehicles and vans and lorries had to be erased... But I have said enough now perhaps to give some idea of the bulk and quality of our great bonfires, our burnings up, our meltings down, our toil of sheer wreckage, over and above the constructive effort, in those early years.

But these were the coarse material bases of the Phoenix fires of the world. These were but the outward and visible signs of the innumerable claims, rights, adhesions, debts, bills, deeds, and charters that were cast upon the fires; a vast accumulation of insignia and uniforms neither curious enough nor beautiful enough to preserve, went to swell the blaze, and all (saving a few truly glorious trophies and memories) of our symbols, our apparatus and material of war. Then innumerable triumphs of our old, bastard, half- commercial, fine-art were presently condemned, great oil paintings, done to please the half-educated middle-class, glared for a moment and were gone, Academy marbles crumbled to useful lime, a gross multitude of silly statuettes and decorative crockery, and hangings, and embroideries, and bad music, and musical instruments shared this fate. And books, countless books, too, and bales of newspapers went also to these pyres. From the private houses in Swathinglea alone—which I had deemed, perhaps not unjustly, altogether illiterate—we gathered a whole dust-cart full of cheap ill-printed editions of the minor English classics—for the most part very dull stuff indeed and still clean—and about a truckload of thumbed and dog- eared penny fiction, watery base stuff, the dropsy of our nation's mind... And it seemed to me that when we gathered those books and papers together, we gathered together something more than print and paper, we gathered warped and crippled ideas and contagious base suggestions, the formulae of dull tolerances and stupid impatiences, the mean defensive ingenuities of sluggish habits of thinking and timid and indolent evasions. There was more than a touch of malignant satisfaction for me in helping gather it all together.

I was so busy, I say, with my share in this dustman's work that I did not notice, as I should otherwise have done, the little indications of change in my mother's state. Indeed, I thought her a little stronger; she was slightly flushed, slightly more talkative...

On Beltane Eve, and our Lowchester rummage being finished, I went along the valley to the far end of Swathinglea to help sort the stock of the detached group of potbanks there—their chief output had been mantel ornaments in imitation of marble, and there was very little sorting, I found, to be done —and there it was nurse Anna found me at last by telephone, and told me my mother had died in the morning suddenly and very shortly after my departure.

For a while I did not seem to believe it; this obviously imminent event stunned me when it came, as though I had never had an anticipatory moment. For a while I went on working, and then almost apathetically, in a mood of half- reluctant curiosity, I started for Lowchester.

When I got there the last offices were over, and I was shown my old mother's peaceful white face, very still, but a little cold and stern to me, a little unfamiliar, lying among white flowers.

I went in alone to her, into that quiet room, and stood for a long time by her bedside. I sat down then and thought...

Then at last, strangely hushed, and with the deeps of my loneliness opening beneath me, I came out of that room and down into the world again, a bright-eyed, active world, very noisy, happy, and busy with its last preparations for the mighty cremation of past and superseded things.

§ 2

I remember that first Beltane festival as the most terribly lonely night in my life. It stands in my mind in fragments, fragments of intense feeling with forgotten gaps between.

I recall very distinctly being upon the great staircase of Lowchester House (though I don't remember getting there from the room in which my mother lay), and how upon the landing I met Anna ascending as I came down. She had but just heard of my return, and she was hurrying upstairs to me. She stopped and so did I, and we stood and clasped hands, and she scrutinized my face in the way women sometimes do. So we remained for a second or so. I could say nothing to her at all, but I could feel the wave of her emotion. I halted, answered the earnest pressure of her hand, relinquished it, and after a queer second of hesitation went on down, returning to my own preoccupations. It did not occur to me at all then to ask myself what she might be thinking or feeling.

I remember the corridor full of mellow evening light, and how I went mechanically some paces toward the dining-room. Then at the sight of the little tables, and a gusty outburst of talking voices as some one in front of me swung the door open and to, I remembered that I did not want to eat... After that comes an impression of myself walking across the open grass in front of the house, and the purpose I had of getting alone upon the moors, and how somebody passing me said something about a hat. I had come out without my hat.

A fragment of thought has linked itself with an effect of long shadows upon turf golden with the light of the sinking sun. The world was singularly empty, I

thought, without either Nettie or my mother. There wasn't any sense in it any more. Nettie was already back in my mind then...

Then I am out on the moors. I avoided the crests where the bonfires were being piled, and sought the lonely places...

I remember very clearly sitting on a gate beyond the park, in a fold just below the crest, that hid the Beacon Hill bonfire and its crowd, and I was looking at and admiring the sunset. The golden earth and sky seemed like a little bubble that floated in the globe of human futility... Then in the twilight I walked along an unknown, bat-haunted road between high hedges.

I did not sleep under a roof that night. But I hungered and ate. I ate near midnight at a little inn over toward Birmingham, and miles away from my home. Instinctively I had avoided the crests where the bonfire crowds gathered, but here there were many people, and I had to share a table with a man who had some useless mortgage deeds to burn. I talked to him about them—but my soul stood at a great distance behind my lips...

Soon each hilltop bore a little tulip-shaped flame flower. Little black figures clustered round and dotted the base of its petals, and as for the rest of the multitude abroad, the kindly night swallowed them up. By leaving the roads and clear paths and wandering in the fields I contrived to keep alone, though the confused noise of voices and the roaring and crackling of great fires was always near me.

I wandered into a lonely meadow, and presently in a hollow of deep shadows I lay down to stare at the stars. I lay hidden in the darkness, and ever and again the sough and uproar of the Beltane fires that were burning up the sere follies of a vanished age, and the shouting of the people passing through the fires and praying to be delivered from the prison of themselves, reached my ears...

And I thought of my mother, and then of my new loneliness and the hunger of my heart for Nettie.

I thought of many things that night, but chiefly of the overflowing personal love and tenderness that had come to me in the wake of the Change, of the greater need, the unsatisfied need in which I stood, for this one person who could fulfil all my desires. So long as my mother had lived, she had in a measure held my heart, given me a food these emotions could live upon, and mitigated that emptiness of spirit, but now suddenly that one possible comfort had left me. There had been many at the season of the Change who had thought that this great enlargement of mankind would abolish personal love; but indeed it had only made it finer, fuller, more vitally necessary. They had thought that, seeing men now were all full of the joyful passion to make and do, and glad and loving and of willing service to all their fellows, there would be no need of the one intimate trusting communion that had been the finest thing of the former life. And indeed, so far as this was a matter of advantage and the struggle for existence, they were right. But so far as it was a matter of the spirit and the fine perceptions of life, it was altogether wrong.

We had indeed not eliminated personal love, we had but stripped it of its base wrappings, of its pride, its suspicions, its mercenary and competitive elements, until at last it stood up in our minds stark, shining and invincible. Through all the

fine, divaricating ways of the new life, it grew ever more evident, there were for every one certain persons, mysteriously and indescribably in the key of one's self, whose mere presence gave pleasure, whose mere existence was interest, whose idiosyncrasy blended with accident to make a completing and predominant harmony for their predestined lovers. They were the essential thing in life. Without them the fine brave show of the rejuvenated world was a caparisoned steed without a rider, a bowl without a flower, a theater without a play.... And to me that night of Beltane, it was as clear as white flames that Nettie, and Nettie alone, roused those harmonies in me. And she had gone! I had sent her from me; I knew not whither she had gone. I had in my first virtuous foolishness cut her out of my life for ever!

So I saw it then, and I lay unseen in the darkness and called upon Nettie, and wept for her, lay upon my face and wept for her, while the glad people went to and fro, and the smoke streamed thick across the distant stars, and the red reflections, the shadows and the fluctuating glares, danced over the face of the world.

No! the Change had freed us from our baser passions indeed, from habitual and mechanical concupiscence and mean issues and coarse imaginings, but from the passions of love it had not freed us. It had but brought the lord of life, Eros, to his own. All through the long sorrow of that night I, who had rejected him, confessed his sway with tears and inappeasable regrets...

I cannot give the remotest guess of when I rose up, nor of my tortuous wanderings in the valleys between the midnight fires, nor how I evaded the laughing and rejoicing multitudes who went streaming home between three and four, to resume their lives, swept and garnished, stripped and clean. But at dawn, when the ashes of the world's gladness were ceasing to glow—it was a bleak dawn that made me shiver in my thin summer clothes—I came across a field to a little copse full of dim blue hyacinths. A queer sense of familiarity arrested my steps, and I stood puzzled. Then I was moved to go a dozen paces from the path, and at once a singularly misshapen tree hitched itself into a notch in my memory. This was the place! Here I had stood, there I had placed my old kite, and shot with my revolver, learning to use it, against the day when I should encounter Verrall.

Kite and revolver had gone now, and all my hot and narrow past, its last vestiges had shriveled and vanished in the whirling gusts of the Beltane fires. So I walked through a world of gray ashes at last, back to the great house in which the dead, deserted image of my dear lost mother lay.

§ 3

I came back to Lowchester House very tired, very wretched; exhausted by my fruitless longing for Nettie. I had no thought of what lay before me.

A miserable attraction drew me into the great house to look again on the stillness that had been my mother's face, and as I came into that room, Anna, who had been sitting by the open window, rose to meet me. She had the air of one who waits. She, too, was pale with watching; all night she had watched between the

dead within and the Beltane fires abroad, and longed for my coming. I stood mute between her and the bedside...

"Willie," she whispered, and eyes and body seemed incarnate pity.

An unseen presence drew us together. My mother's face became resolute, commanding. I turned to Anna as a child may turn to its nurse. I put my hands about her strong shoulders, she folded me to her, and my heart gave way. I buried my face in her breast and clung to her weakly, and burst into a passion of weeping...

She held me with hungry arms. She whispered to me, "There, there!" as one whispers comfort to a child... Suddenly she was kissing me. She kissed me with a hungry intensity of passion, on my cheeks, on my lips. She kissed me on my lips with lips that were salt with tears. And I returned her kisses...

Then abruptly we desisted and stood apart—looking at one another.

§ 4

It seems to me as if the intense memory of Nettie vanished utterly out of my mind at the touch of Anna's lips. I loved Anna.

We went to the council of our group—commune it was then called —and she was given me in marriage, and within a year she had borne me a son. We saw much of one another, and talked ourselves very close together. My faithful friend she became and has been always, and for a time we were passionate lovers. Always she has loved me and kept my soul full of tender gratitude and love for her; always when we met our hands and eyes clasped in friendly greeting, all through our lives from that hour we have been each other's secure help and refuge, each other's ungrudging fastness of help and sweetly frank and open speech... And after a little while my love and desire for Nettie returned as though it had never faded away.

No one will have a difficulty now in understanding how that could be, but in the evil days of the world malaria, that would have been held to be the most impossible thing. I should have had to crush that second love out of my thoughts, to have kept it secret from Anna, to have lied about it to all the world. The old-world theory was there was only one love—we who float upon a sea of love find that hard to understand. The whole nature of a man was supposed to go out to the one girl or woman who possessed him, her whole nature to go out to him. Nothing was left over—it was a discreditable thing to have any overplus at all. They formed a secret secluded system of two, two and such children as she bore him. All other women he was held bound to find no beauty in, no sweetness, no interest; and she likewise, in no other man. The old-time men and women went apart in couples, into defensive little houses, like beasts into little pits, and in these "homes" they sat down purposing to love, but really coming very soon to jealous watching of this extravagant mutual proprietorship. All freshness passed very speedily out of their love, out of their conversation, all pride out of their common life. To permit each other freedom was blank dishonor. That I and Anna should love, and after our love-journey together, go about our separate lives and dine at

the public tables, until the advent of her motherhood, would have seemed a terrible strain upon our unmitigable loyalty. And that I should have it in me to go on loving Nettie—who loved in different manner both Verrall and me—would have outraged the very quintessence of the old convention.

In the old days love was a cruel proprietary thing. But now Anna could let Nettie live in the world of my mind, as freely as a rose will suffer the presence of white lilies. If I could hear notes that were not in her compass, she was glad, because she loved me, that I should listen to other music than hers. And she, too, could see the beauty of Nettie. Life is so rich and generous now, giving friendship, and a thousand tender interests and helps and comforts, that no one stints another of the full realization of all possibilities of beauty. For me from the beginning Nettie was the figure of beauty, the shape and color of the divine principle that lights the world. For every one there are certain types, certain faces and forms, gestures, voices and intonations that have that inexplicable unanalyzable quality. These come through the crowd of kindly friendly fellow-men and women—one's own. These touch one mysteriously, stir deeps that must otherwise slumber, pierce and interpret the world. To refuse this interpretation is to refuse the sun, to darken and deaden all life... I loved Nettie, I loved all who were like her, in the measure that they were like her, in voice, or eyes, or form, or smile. And between my wife and me there was no bitterness that the great goddess, the life- giver, Aphrodite, Queen of the living Seas, came to my imagination so. It qualified our mutual love not at all, since now in our changed world love is unstinted; it is a golden net about our globe that nets all humanity together.

I thought of Nettie much, and always movingly beautiful things restored me to her, all fine music, all pure deep color, all tender and solemn things. The stars were hers, and the mystery of moonlight; the sun she wore in her hair, powdered finely, beaten into gleams and threads of sunlight in the wisps and strands of her hair... Then suddenly one day a letter came to me from her, in her unaltered clear handwriting, but in a new language of expression, telling me many things. She had learnt of my mother's death, and the thought of me had grown so strong as to pierce the silence I had imposed on her. We wrote to one another—like common friends with a certain restraint between us at first, and with a great longing to see her once more arising in my heart. For a time I left that hunger unexpressed, and then I was moved to tell it to her. And so on New Year's Day in the Year Four, she came to Lowchester and me. How I remember that coming, across the gulf of fifty years! I went out across the park to meet her, so that we should meet alone. The windless morning was clear and cold, the ground new carpeted with snow, and all the trees motionless lace and glitter of frosty crystals. The rising sun had touched the white with a spirit of gold, and my heart beat and sang within me. I remember now the snowy shoulder of the down, sunlit against the bright blue sky. And presently I saw the woman I loved coming through the white still trees...

I had made a goddess of Nettie, and behold she was a fellow-creature! She came, warm-wrapped and tremulous, to me, with the tender promise of tears in her eyes, with her hands outstretched and that dear smile quivering upon her lips.

She stepped out of the dream I had made of her, a thing of needs and regrets and human kindliness. Her hands as I took them were a little cold. The goddess shone through her indeed, glowed in all her body, she was a worshipful temple of love for me—yes. But I could feel, like a thing new discovered, the texture and sinews of her living, her dear personal and mortal hands...

EPILOGUE - THE WINDOW OF THE TOWER

This was as much as this pleasant-looking, gray-haired man had written. I had been lost in his story throughout the earlier portions of it, forgetful of the writer and his gracious room, and the high tower in which he was sitting. But gradually, as I drew near the end, the sense of strangeness returned to me. It was more and more evident to me that this was a different humanity from any I had known, unreal, having different customs, different beliefs, different interpretations, different emotions. It was no mere change in conditions and institutions the comet had wrought. It had made a change of heart and mind. In a manner it had dehumanized the world, robbed it of its spites, its little intense jealousies, its inconsistencies, its humor. At the end, and particularly after the death of his mother, I felt his story had slipped away from my sympathies altogether. Those Beltane fires had burnt something in him that worked living still and unsubdued in me, that rebelled in particular at that return of Nettie. I became a little inattentive. I no longer felt with him, nor gathered a sense of complete understanding from his phrases. His Lord Eros indeed! He and these transfigured people—they were beautiful and noble people, like the people one sees in great pictures, like the gods of noble sculpture, but they had no nearer fellowship than these to men. As the change was realized, with every stage of realization the gulf widened and it was harder to follow his words.

I put down the last fascicle of all, and met his friendly eyes. It was hard to dislike him.

I felt a subtle embarrassment in putting the question that perplexed me. And yet it seemed so material to me I had to put it. "And did you—?" I asked. "Were you—lovers?"

His eyebrows rose. "Of course."

"But your wife—?"

It was manifest he did not understand me.

I hesitated still more. I was perplexed by a conviction of baseness. "But—" I began. "You remained lovers?"

"Yes." I had grave doubts if I understood him. Or he me.

I made a still more courageous attempt. "And had Nettie no other lovers?"

"A beautiful woman like that! I know not how many loved beauty in her, nor what she found in others. But we four from that time were very close, you understand, we were friends, helpers, personal lovers in a world of lovers."

"Four?"

"There was Verrall."

Then suddenly it came to me that the thoughts that stirred in my mind were sinister and base, that the queer suspicions, the coarseness and coarse jealousies of my old world were over and done for these more finely living souls. "You made," I said, trying to be liberal minded, "a home together."

"A home!" He looked at me, and, I know not why, I glanced down at my feet. What a clumsy, ill-made thing a boot is, and how hard and colorless seemed my clothing! How harshly I stood out amidst these fine, perfected things. I had a moment of rebellious detestation. I wanted to get out of all this. After all, it wasn't my style. I wanted intensely to say something that would bring him down a peg, make sure, as it were, of my suspicions by launching an offensive accusation. I looked up and he was standing.

"I forgot," he said. "You are pretending the old world is still going on. A home!"

He put out his hand, and quite noiselessly the great window widened down to us, and the splendid nearer prospect of that dreamland city was before me. There for one clear moment I saw it; its galleries and open spaces, its trees of golden fruit and crystal waters, its music and rejoicing, love and beauty without ceasing flowing through its varied and intricate streets. And the nearer people I saw now directly and plainly, and no longer in the distorted mirror that hung overhead. They really did not justify my suspicions, and yet —! They were such people as one sees on earth—save that they were changed. How can I express that change? As a woman is changed in the eyes of her lover, as a woman is changed by the love of a lover. They were exalted...

I stood up beside him and looked out. I was a little flushed, my ears a little reddened, by the inconvenience of my curiosities, and by my uneasy sense of profound moral differences. He was taller than I...

"This is our home," he said smiling, and with thoughtful eyes on me.

THE END

www.ingramcontent.com/pod-product-compliance
Lightning Source LLC
Chambersburg PA
CBHW080811020826
48982CB00017B/915

* 9 7 8 1 7 8 1 3 9 2 9 6 6 *